"*A Clearing in the Wild* is Jane Kirkpatrick at her finest. The story is quickly paced and engaging from the first to the last. One of the most difficult tasks for a writer—and Kirkpatrick's specialty—is to contemplate the lives of real people and to re-create a believable episode in those lives that is accurate yet interesting, to both inform and entertain. The dialog sings masterfully with perfect tone, building characters and pushing the story line in succinct phrasing that never overstates. Emma Wagner Giesy's story feels as genuine as if she herself were telling it."

> —NANCY E. TURNER, author of *Sarah's Quilt* and *The Water and the Blood*

"Through her careful research, Jane Kirkpatrick has captured the trials of those who are determined to settle a land that does not easily yield to civilization. She has brought to life another woman in our history whose faith, strength, and commitment is a testament to not only the pioneer spirit but the human spirit as well. Thank you, Ms. Kirkpatrick, for not allowing Emma Wagner Giesy to languish in obscurity."

> —KARLA K. NELSON, owner of Time Enough Books in Ilwaco, . Washington

"Emma Wagner Giesy is brave, willful, and beautiful, and *A Clearing in the Wild* brings her to life without for a moment sacrificing her complexity. Kirkpatrick compels us to think again, and deeply, about the needs of the body, soul, and mind; and in these pages she proves once again that she is a gifted chronicler of the lives of women in the West."

> —MOLLY GLOSS, author of *The Jump-Off Creek* and *Wild Life*

"Jane Kirkpatrick again proves herself to be one of the finest writers working in historical fiction today. With *A Tendering in the Storm*, Kirkpatrick applies her usual meticulous research and rich period detail to give readers a wonderful story with strong, unforgettable characters. Beautifully and thoughtfully written as always, this novel will capture your attention, your imagination, and your heart."

—B. J. HOFF, author of the *Mountain Song Legacy*
and *An Emerald Ballad*

"*A Tendering in the Storm* is one of Jane Kirkpatrick's most compelling novels yet—and that's saying something! With her skilled and lyrical writing, Kirkpatrick brings to vivid life the beauty and severity of pioneer living, a complex provocative villain, and a story that grabs the reader and won't let go. But most of all, Emma Giesy emerges as a remarkable heroine: appealing and vulnerable, but possessing tenacious courage and true strength. This book kept me turning pages far into the night!"

—CINDY SWANSON, online reviewer and radio host

"The title *A Tendering in the Storm* keenly expresses the continuing story of the intrepid Emma Wagner Giesy as she struggles between the comfort and security of her religious community and self-reliance in the midst of tumult. Jane Kirkpatrick's impressive research on this true character reveals many realities of one woman's efforts to carve out a life for herself and her children on the burgeoning frontier of Washington Territory. In her engaging style rich with metaphor and imagery, the author explores issues still relevant in today's world: women's rights, child custody, property rights, domestic violence, and religious freedom. Bravo!"

—SUSAN G. BUTRUILLE, author of *Women's Voices from the Oregon Trail* and *Women's Voices from the Western Frontier*

"I love when a book illuminates a small slice of history that has relevance to our lives today—even better when it does so with interesting characters and a compelling story. Emma Giesy is a woman with flaws and attributes we all can relate to and whose journey is one that easily could have taken place today."

—JUDITH PELLA, best-selling author of the Daughters
of Fortune series

"Jane has a gift for breathing simple beauty into the lives of remarkable historical women characters. In *A Mending at the Edge,* Emma comes off the page and shows readers an unforgettable picture of a very unique Oregon community."

—ROBIN JONES GUNN, author of the best-selling Glenbrooke
series and the Christy Award–winning Sisterchicks novels

"In *A Mending at the Edge,* Jane Kirkpatrick completes the literary quilt of the Emma Wagner Giesy trilogy, piecing together the historical fabric of Emma's personal story with that of the Aurora Colony. Based on a solid historical framework of the Aurora Colony and the broader social, political, and cultural landscape of the 1860s, Kirkpatrick offers a story of hope and achievement that captures the spirit of giving, sharing, and receiving central to 'mending' within a communal settlement."

—JAMES J. KOPP, communal historian and board member
of the Aurora Colony Historical Society

"Jane Kirkpatrick artfully weaves this story for us, rather like Emma and the women of Oregon's Aurora Colony weave together their quilted existence as well as their personal quilting projects. Her masterful placement of the fresh-turned phrase and the graceful metaphor enriches this captivating and yet disquieting story of mid-nineteenth-century pioneer women whose lives are so very different from ours—or are they?"

—SARAH BYRN RICKMAN, author of *Nancy Love and the WASP
Ferry Pilots of World War II, The Originals,* and *Flight from Fear*

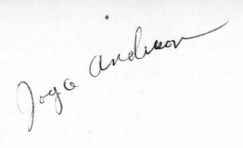

Emma of Aurora

JANE KIRKPATRICK

Emma of Aurora

THE COMPLETE
Change ❖ Cherish
TRILOGY

WATERBROOK
PRESS

EMMA OF AURORA
PUBLISHED BY WATERBROOK PRESS
12265 Oracle Boulevard, Suite 200
Colorado Springs, Colorado 80921

For *A Clearing in the Wild*, Scripture quotations are taken from The Holy Bible, containing the Old and New Testaments, translated out of The Original Tongues, and with the former translations diligently compared and revised. New York: American Bible Society, 1858. For *A Tendering in the Storm* and *A Mending at the Edge*, all Scripture quotations, unless otherwise indicated, are taken from the King James Version. Scripture quotations marked (RSV) are taken from the Revised Standard Version of the Bible, copyright © 1952 [2nd edition, 1971] by the Division of Christian Education of the National Council of the Churches of Christ in the USA. Used by Permission. All rights reserved.

This book is a work of historical fiction based closely on real people and real events. Details that cannot be historically verified are purely products of the author's imagination.

Grateful acknowledgment is made for the use of the Paul Johannes Tillich quote in *A Tendering in the Storm* on page 379.

Trade Paperback ISBN 978-0-307-73215-6
eBook ISBN 978-0-307-73216-3

The books included in this compilation are *A Clearing in the Wind* copyright © 2006 by Jane Kirkpatrick, *A Tendering in the Storm* copyright © 2007 by Jane Kirkpatrick, and *A Mending at the Edge* copyright © 2008 by Jane Kirkpatrick, all published by WaterBrook Press.

Cover design by Kristopher K. Orr; cover photography by Scott Weber (landscape) and Philip Lee Harvey (Emma), Getty Images

Published in the United States by WaterBrook Multnomah, an imprint of the Crown Publishing Group, a division of Random House LLC, New York, a Penguin Random House Company.

WATERBROOK and its deer colophon are registered trademarks of Random House LLC.

Library of Congress Cataloging-in-Publication Data

Kirkpatrick, Jane, 1946–
    A clearing in the wind / Jane Kirkpatrick.— 1st ed.
        p. com. — (Change and cherish series ; bk. 1)
    ISBN 1-57856-734-3
    1. Women pioneers—Fiction. 2. Social isolation—Fiction. I. Title.
    PS3561.I712C57 2006
    813'.54—dc22

                              2005035370

Kirkpatrick, Jane, 1946–
    A tendering in the storm / Jane Kirkpatrick.— 1st ed.
        p. com. — (Change and cherish historical series)
    ISBN 978-1-57856-735-5
    1. Women pioneers—Fiction. 2. Domestic fiction.. I. Title.
    PS3561.I712T46 2007
    813'.54—dc22

                              2007007052

Kirkpatrick, Jane, 1946–
    A mending at the edge / Jane Kirkpatrick.— 1st ed.
        p. com. — (Change and cherish historical series)
    ISBN 978-1-57856-979-3
    1. Giesy, Emma Wagner—Fiction 2. Women pioneers—Fiction. 3. Washington (State)—Fiction. I. Title.
    PS3561.I712M46 2008
    813'.54—dc22

                              2007041707

Printed in the United States of America
2013—First Edition

10 9 8 7 6 5 4 3 2 1

BOOK ONE

A Clearing
in the
Wild

a novel

To Jerry

Cast of Characters

Emma Wagner	young German girl living in Bethel Colony
David and Catherina Zundel Wagner	Emma's parents
Jonathan, age 18	Emma's siblings
David Jr., age 11	
Catherine, age 9	
Johanna, age 7	
Louisa, age 5	
William, age 3	
Christian Giesy	appointed leader of the scouts; Emma's husband
Andrew	his son
Catherina	his daughter
Wilhelm Keil	leader of Bethel, Missouri colony
Louisa Keil	Wilhelm's wife
Willie	his son
Aurora	his daughter
Gloriunda	his daughter
Several other Keil children	
Andreas and Barbara Giesy	Christian's parents
Helena Giesy	one of Christian's sisters
Mary Giesy	sister-in-law to Emma and Helena
Sebastian Giesy	Mary's husband; Christian's brother
Karl Ruge	German teacher in colony
John "Hans" Stauffer	scouts sent west
John Stauffer	

Michael Schaefer Sr.
Joseph Knight
Adam Knight
John Genger
George Link
Adam Schuele
Christian and Emma Giesy

John Stauffer   returning scouts
Michael Schaefer Sr.
Joseph Knight
Adam Knight
John Genger
George Link

Ezra Meeker   Washington Territory settler
*Nora and the gut *doctor*   couple at Fort Steilacoom
   *Simmons and Marie   their children
*Frau Flint and Frau Madeleine   women at Fort Steilacoom
*An-gie   Chehalis maid
   *Pap   her daughter
   *N'chi   her grandson
Captain Maurice Maloney   commander at Fort Steilacoom

Sam and Sarah Woodard   settlers at Woodard's Landing
James Swan   early resident/writer of Willapa
   region

Opal   the mule
Opal   the goat
Charlie   the seagulls

*fictional characters

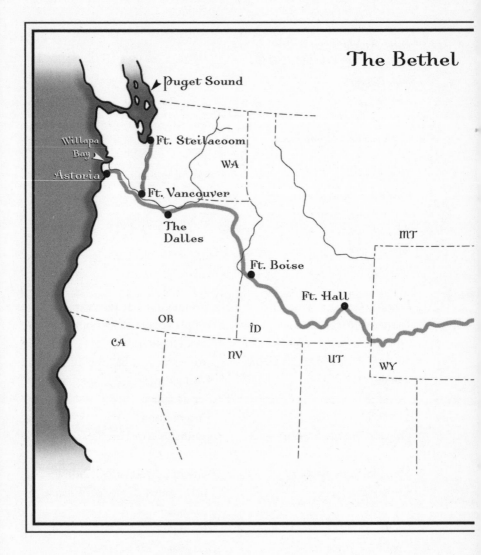

The Bethel

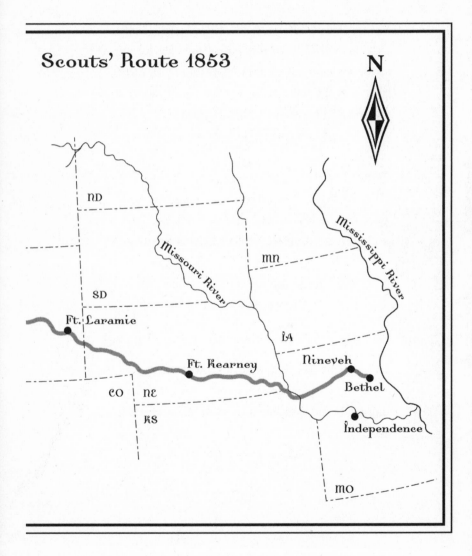

You can tell they're all related even though they're each unique. They resist exposing their tender innards. Something hard must happen to break them open; a foreign source invades. Then a knife slice and they unveil their treasures deep within.

ANONYMOUS, "On Oysters"

And the LORD God called unto Adam, and said unto him, Where art thou?...And the LORD God said unto the woman, What is this that thou hast done?...Unto Adam also and to his wife did the LORD God make coats of skins, and clothed them.

GENESIS 3:9, 13, 21

And all who believed were together and had all things in common; and they sold their possessions and goods and distributed them to all, as any had need.

ACTS 2:44–45, RSV

Part 1

1

The Thread of Love

Some say that love's enough to stave off suffering and loss, but I would disagree. Quietly, of course. Words of dissent aren't welcome in our colony, especially words from women. I should have learned these lessons—about dissent and love—early on before I turned eighteen. But teachings about spirit and kinship require repetition before becoming threads strong enough to weave into life's fabric, strong enough to overcome the weaker strains of human nature. It was a strength I found I'd need one day to face what love could not stave off.

But on that Christmas morning in Bethel, Missouri, 1851, celebrating as we had for a decade or more with the festivities beginning at 4:00 a.m., a time set by our leader, love seemed enough; love was the thread that held the pearls of present joy. It was young love, a first love, and it warmed. Never mind that the warmth came from the fireplace heat lifting against my crinoline, so for a moment I could pretend I wore the wire hoop of fashion. Instead of something stylish, I wore a dress so simple it could have been a flannel sheet, so common it might belong to any of the other dozen girls my age whose voices I could hear rising in the distance, the women's choir already echoing their joy within our Bethel church. Winter snows and the drafts that plagued my parents' loft often chilled me and my sisters. But here, on this occasion, love and light and music and my family bound me into warmth.

Candle heat shimmered against the tiny bells of the *Schellenbaum*, the symbol of allegiance my father carried in the church on such special occasions. The musical instrument's origin was Turkish, my father told me, and militaristic, too, a strange thing I always thought for us German immigrants to carry forth at times of celebration. The musical instrument reminded me of an iron weather vane on top of one of the colony's grain barns, rising with an eagle at the peak, its talons grasping an iron ball. Beneath, a crescent held fourteen bells, alternating large and small, dangling over yet another black orb with a single row of bells circling beneath it. A final ring of tiny bells hovered above the stand my father carried this early morning. As a longtime colonist, he walked worshipfully toward the *Tannenbaum* sparkling with star candles placed there by the parade of the youngest colony girls.

My father's usual smiling face wore solemn as his heavy boots took him forward like a funeral dirge, easing along the wide aisle that divided men from women, fathers from daughters, and mothers from sons even while we faced one another, men looking at women and we gazing back. All one thousand members of the Bethel Colony attended. The women's chorus ended, and I heard the rustle of their skirts like the quiet turning of pages of a book as they nestled down onto the benches with the other seated women.

Later, the band would play festive tunes, and we'd sing and dance and give the younger children gifts of nuts and apples, and the men might taste the distillery's nectar of whiskey or wine, though nothing to excess, before heading home to open gifts with family.

We began the Christmas celebration assembled in the church built of bricks we colonists made ourselves. We gathered in the dark, the tree candles and the fire glow and our own virgin lanterns lighting up the walnut-paneled room as we prepared to hear Father Keil—as my father called him—preach of love, of shared blessings, of living both the Golden and the Diamond Rules. He'd speak of loyalty to our Lord, to one another, and ultimately to him, symbolized on this day by the carrying of the *Schellenbaum* and the music of its bells across the red-tiled floor.

As my father passed in front of me, I spied my older brother, Jonathan, my brother who resembles me. He, too, is small and slender with eyes like walnuts framed by thick brown eyebrows set inside a heart-shaped face. I used to tease my brother about his chipmunk cheeks until the day I overheard Helena Giesy say, "Emma Wagner and her brother look like twins, though Jonathan is two years older. Such puffed up cheeks they share," she said. Our rosy cheeks bind us.

Jonathan held his lower lip with his teeth, then raised his eyebrows, letting his eyes move with deliberateness toward the front and the tall, dark-haired man standing next to Father Keil. Now my heart skipped. Jonathan lifted his chin, grinned. My face grew warm.

I never should have told him.

At least I kept the secret from the little ones, though Catherine at nine, wise beyond her years, would claim she was adult enough to know, but she'd have clucked her tongue at me for even thinking in the way I did. David, Johanna, Louisa, and William, well, they'd have blabbed and babbled without knowing what they really said.

The bells tinkled and the band struck up notes. Later, if the weather held, the band would move out onto the platform around the church steeple and play *Hark! the Herald Angels Sing* so loudly that perhaps the ears of those in Shelbina thirteen miles south would be awakened and our colony would intrude on them, but in a glorious way. We were meant to be set apart by our commitment to the common fund, Father Keil told us, and yet to serve. Lately, Shelbina and its railroad threatened us. My father said Father Keil grew worried that Shelbina's life might lure young men away. Father Keil would do his best to keep Bethel's sons loyal, separated, even though he said our passion should be to bring others to our fold, save others from God's planned destruction of our world, give to those in need, especially to widows and their children. We were to bring to the colony, through our acts of love, the women who wore white globes called pearls around their necks, the fine ladies who sought after jewels and gems that marked false loyalties to luxury over faith.

Neighbors. The people of Shelbina were good neighbors, I always thought. They bought our gloves, our wine, and our corn whiskey. But few of us really knew them. We had no way of knowing if they'd heard about the coming destruction or if they suffered from worries and woes. Our religious colony cherished lives of simplicity, sharing frugal wealth in common, all needs of colonists met, silencing desire for unnecessary passions. Whatever cash we earned went to the common purse. If we needed cash for some outside purchase, we went to that same coffer. Whatever we needed from the colony's yield, we simply walked to the storehouse to secure it. My mother said it eased all worry about the future; I saw it as one more person to have to convince to let loose the purse strings.

We colonists were different from those around us in Missouri; we were an island of our own. We worked to stay unsullied by the larger distractions of the world that Shelbina symbolized even while we attempted to bring others into the joys of our colony's ways.

Only the strongest of us could reach outside and yet stay faithful, Father Keil said. I smoothed my skirt and felt the ruffle.

The brass horns pierced the room, announcing Father Keil's beginning words. Angels' trumpets. Music is the perfect way to celebrate a glorious occasion, I've always thought. Jonathan played in the men's band. Not me. Not girls, not young women. Our music came from our voices raised in the choir or while beating rugs or dyeing wool or serving meals to men. I couldn't carry a tune in a candlestick holder, something else that made me different.

But separation from the women's choir or the brass instruments of music did not keep me from the joy of this day especially.

My father set the *Schellenbaum* on its stand, then took his place across from us, sliding next to my brothers, who then wiggled on down the bench, a place they always sat. We'd been a part of this colony for as long as I could remember. My father had been one of three scouts sent out from Pennsylvania by our leader to find a "place of separation" in the unknown territories, far from the larger world. I was five years old when we moved with other German families discouraged by the changes in George Rapp's colony at Harmony, Pennsylvania. We seceded first to Phillipsburg, then into Indiana, then into Shelby County, Missouri, where our leader imagined Bethel into being. It is a joyous place, Bethel, even though my father says many will be summoned in the morning to discuss reasons we might have to leave again.

Change never troubled me. I welcome change, newness, though I work to keep my pride in check about it. Pride is an evil thing, our leader tells us. We must not envy, must not lust, must not covet. So no one knows I've stitched a ruffle to my crinoline. It is a harmless vanity easily removed but one that warms my spirit knowing it is there, unique on this winter morning as crisp as a hot-ironed crease. I gaze without envy along the row of plain and simple wool dresses of Bethel's sisters on the benches.

Change has its richness in a colony where everything seems the same. At seventeen, I am of marriageable age, so change sticking its head inside my door will be patted like a welcomed dog on its happy head.

Before we left our brick home this morning, my mother cautioned me when I noted that this might be my last Christmas as Emma Wagner.

Next year, next Christmas, I might carry a new name and enter the festivities not as a child, but as a woman.

"He preaches of late, Father Keil does, that one should be devoted to the colony, not marry so young," my mother said as we readied to leave for the service. She combed Johanna's hair into a braid, brushed a crumb from little Louisa's face. "He says perhaps women should marry not at all. Tink of Saint Paul who advised, 'I say therefore to the unmarried and widows, It is good for them if they abide even as I.'"

"But he also said it's 'better to marry than to burn,'" I challenged. I could see my breath through the cold of our large house. I licked my fingers and flattened three-year-old William's cowlick as he sped out the door, then pulled on gloves made by Bethel factory workers.

"Paul says that, too," my mother continued, "but then tells, 'He that is unmarried careth for the things that belong to the Lord, how he may please the Lord: But he that is married careth for the things that are of the world, how he may please his wife.'"

"*Ja,* a good husband should please his wife," I said. "Besides, Father Keil married." I pulled on my woolen hood and tied the bows beneath my chin. "His nine children might say he either burned much or none at all."

"*Ach,* Emma!" my mother chastened. "How you talk. Young Father Keil married before he came to know the Lord as he knows Him now." Her hands shooed me out the door toward the rest of the family.

"He's been a colony leader for many years, and his wife Louisa still has diapers to change," I said, walking backward to keep chatting with my mother. My father held a lantern so we could see to walk to the church on the crunching snow, and he used it to signal me to turn about, gather up my younger brothers and sisters.

"Wiser now he is, so he shares his wisdom with us, and we must listen," my mother finished.

"Who is wiser?" my father said as we joined him beneath the stars.

"You," my mother offered, taking his arm.

I didn't pursue the subject, but my disagreement with her and with our leader's view gave me yet another reason to be joyful about my unseen ruffle. After all, isn't part of wisdom thinking on one's own, doing not what everyone else does but making distinctive marks, as distinctive as…as a Turkish instrument carried by a German man?

Now we sat and listened to the bells of the *Schellenbaum* tinkle at this early hour service. Surely our leader didn't think young men and women would forgo marriage or families for the sake of the colony? How would it grow? Would he rely on new conversions of men going with courage into the outside world, men too strong to be lured into the world's ways?

The tall man standing next to our leader moved to center the *Schellenbaum* on its stand beside the altar. My heart pounded with anticipation. He was my father's good friend, our leader's emissary most recently into Kentucky and the Carolinas. His name was Christian Giesy, and it was him I hoped to marry, though I wasn't sure if he even knew my name.

Christian Giesy. I prayed I'd aged enough that he might see me this Christmas morning as a young woman and not just a snippet of thread tethered to the weaving of my parents.

He did not look my way but instead stared off as though he saw a glorious place somewhere far beyond this room, his eyes as shining as the lantern light flashed against the *Schellenbaum.* I swallowed. Perhaps he too believed as our leader did, that the finest way to honor God meant remaining celibate and unmarried.

I pitched away that disappointing thought.

Our leader raised his voice, large before us. Even errant thoughts of mine were pulled into the cymbal clang of his call to worship. His eyes were deep pools of churning water that nearly frothed with intensity and yet a kind of joy. We young women stopped shuffling our slippers. Men muffled their coughs. Mothers whispered quietly to their children, "Be silent, now." His oldest son, Willie, gazed up at his father as though he were a saint. Only the sizzle of candle wax and the fire's roar and the occasional tinkle of the *Schellenbaum* bells moved by the fire's draft interrupted our leader's words as he drew our faces toward him, toward the words my parents first heard in Pennsylvania, words that took us all in and changed our very lives. The fire waned in the brick church. I felt a chill. We remained awake in the cold and with *his* words. When he raised his voice, a mesmerizing sound echoed words I'd heard so often as a child from him and then from my own father, too, who preached, though without the fervor of our leader. I didn't need to pay attention now. But I willed myself to keep staring at him, to not let my eyes wander onto Christian Giesy.

A tinsmith, Christian, who also served as one of the missionaries our leader sent south to bring in new communal members, was a man one year younger than our leader but wiser and more handsome than our leader had ever been, though Christian's build was leaner, a sturdy pine beside Father Keil's squat oak. The recruits, whom we hoped would eventually convert, were usually people who could advance the colony: wagon makers, farmers, coopers. I wondered if we were contributing to their souls by making them colonists as much as they contributed to our coffers. *Sacrilege, such thoughts.*

My eyes ached from staying open. I refused to blink for fear the lids would overtake me and embarrass me with sleep. Maybe just for a second I could close them.

My head dropped onto my mother's shoulder. "Emma," she whispered. "Sit straight!"

Catherine pursed her lips as I wiped my drooling mouth with the back of my hand, hoping no one else had seen my lapse. Catherine was "too good" and would never sleep in church. Some unseen force moved my eyes to Christian's. I willed my face to heat no crimson blotches on my cheeks as I looked boldly at him. He stared, his dark hair as silky as a beaver pelt, no part, combed back. Long sideburns rolled up into a mustache thick and trimmed. Dark hair acted as a picture frame for a strong face, straight nose, and eyes as blue as the feathers of a blue-winged teal and just as soft. I sighed despite myself and my mother elbowed me. Had he seen me fall asleep? I hiccupped. My mother frowned. When I saw that Christian let his eyes rest on mine before he eased them toward our leader, I couldn't control the racing of my heart.

———

"Ve never neglect the children," our leader said when his sermon about Christmas joy ended and the children swarmed around him. My father said we American children were spoiled now, no longer having to fear the arrival of *Peltz Nickel,* the frightening, chain-dragging, bell-ringing companion of *Belsnickel* and *Christkind.* The former frequented the old country, prepared to punish us for wrongdoing through the year while we waited for presents from the Christmas hosts. Instead, we German-American children of the Bethel Colony witnessed our leader in the form of *Belsnickel,* who brought us goodies and who celebrated with tiny *Schellenbaum* bells instead of ugly chains. Still, I wondered whether even in this colony, because of our German history, joyous things came with the threat of later punishment and chains.

As children gathered around *Belsnickel,* I held back. But then the childhood lure drew me, and I rushed in to reach for the candies and raisins along with the little ones. Peppermints are my favorite, and our leader's wife, Louisa, had placed several inside little strips of cloth tied with hemp. Her youngest daughters, three-year-old Aurora and five-year-old Gloriunda, pushed on either side of me, and I helped them forward, lifting Aurora to my hip, stepping in so my five-year-old sister, Louisa, could reach more easily too. The rest squealed in delight. Their voices sounded like tinkling bells and I loved it.

"Not so much with the little ones," my mother said as I pranced back to her, my young charges now on their own and my hands filled with little cloth bags of sweets I handed out to William, barely three, and to mother and others too embarrassed to reach in with the children. Wool swirled around my legs. She shook her head. "Spending time with the children is easier, I tink, than acting of your age."

"I might be unmarried forever, you tell me, so let my childhood fingers dip into *Belsnickel's* bag, please?"

"*Ach,*" she said, brushing her hand at me dismissively, but she smiled and accepted the peppermint piece I gave her. "We help serve food now," she told me, and I gave Louisa and Aurora a candy. Both scampered to our leader, who lifted them high and nuzzled their necks with his beard, a dozen other children still clamoring at his feet.

Arm in arm, my mother and I walked to where the women uncovered tins of sausages and scrambled eggs kept heated in their tubs. Breads of all kinds and *Strudels* and moist cakes with nuts quickly covered the table. Steins of wine set like sentries along the white cloth overlooked the bounty. Our leader said these common meals following his sermons were celebrations of the Last Supper, served as though the Lord Himself were present, and it did seem as though our community was blessed this day with love in abundance and the spirit of grace.

Dawn seeped in through the tall windows, but outside the ground lay comforted by snow that didn't appear warm enough to melt. We'd have fine ice-skating later. I wondered what Christian would be doing. Enjoying his sisters and brothers and parents, I imagined, since he'd been gone so long. I sensed where he stood in the room. His presence filled a space, and I could see glimpses of him towering above many of the other men as I set tubs of *Sauerkraut* on the table.

The band played now, and Jonathan and Willie—our leader's oldest, my age—tapped their feet while marching notes rang out. Our leader didn't play in the band but sometimes brought out his harmonica. Now he clapped his hands as the children gathered around him for new treats he gave each one. The Christmas celebration proved almost as glorious as when we celebrated our leader's birthday on March 6. His wife's birthday and year were exactly the same, but it was *his* years we all cheered over. Louisa cheered too and said on more than one occasion that her husband was nearly as blessed as our Savior. I wondered if all wives see their husbands as such. She didn't even want us mentioning the day of her birth. My mother said she was a saint, Louisa was, and such a model of a wife and mother.

Perhaps.

The table now looked complete, and Louisa signaled to our leader the readiness.

"Christian will ask the blessing," he said. This surprised me that our leader would permit another to speak on such a spirited occasion.

Christian stepped forward and clasped his hands in prayer, holding them before his straight, strong chest. People in our colony did not kneel to pray. We stood tall, our heads raised, our loyalty and worship given freely, not because it was required as it had been in the old country, in the old religion, but because we believed in our Lord and our leader and stood ready to move to follow both as required.

Christian closed his eyes, and yes, I know I should have too, as did other Bethelites gathered in the church, but the opportunity to watch him, without any others noticing or later chastising me for my boldness, was a gift as precious as the peppermints and twice as sweet.

Christian's words came first in German, to make us feel at home, as one, though we are set apart. Then he spoke them all in English, for it was the language of our adopted nation, a language I'd just begun to learn. "The Lord bless this bounty prepared by grateful hands whose duty is set to minister to others. We thank the Lord for this provision, as for all provision. May we follow Your directives always to worship You and live in Christian love and not false luxury."

He paused then. I thought to add more of what our leader might have said about our colony. Instead, I watched as he turned slightly and searched the crowd. He found my eyes. He smiled, winked, nodded once, and then he said, "Amen."

———

The meal filled our stomachs. I watched as Helena, Christian's sister, laughed with her brother. I hungered as Christian clicked his heels in recognition of one of Helena's friends, closer to Christian's age than I. The Giesys were of Swiss descent, prudent, hard-working, and wise. I served meals and talked with friends, always aware of where my soul was anchored: to Christian, to his dark eyes, his promise of adventure taking him places far from Bethel.

I never once spoke to him. He was the favorite of so many. He never looked my way again, and so the wink became a question for me. Perhaps it hadn't happened.

Just before we'd set to leave, with Jonathan and David Jr. carrying out the *Strudel* pans, my mother and Catherine and Johanna bustling about making sure we left the church without a crumb beneath a table, and Louisa still skipping with Aurora, I noticed Christian Giesy stood beside my father. I straightened my shoulders, hoping it made me look older. I walked to the men then, bold as a bull calf, and heard my father say "trouble." I wondered if they spoke of Shelbina, but then Papa said, "move one more time," and I knew they must be talking of a new colony somewhere. Michael Forstner, a friend of my father's and a carpenter, had built up four colonies already following our leader, most in Pennsylvania: Harmony and Phillipsburg and New Harmony in Indiana, and then Bethel in Missouri. My father spoke often of the intricacies of keeping our colonists separated from the world's influences while still allowing commercial interaction that sustained us all. Our grain and gloves and whiskey were sold to outsiders. We sometimes even talked of mulberry trees and silk production just as those at Harmony did. Harmony was the colony where discord reigned, and my father seceded from it along with all the Giesys, eventually finding our leader to follow to Missouri.

Then I heard my father say to Christian something about "asking for trouble," and before I could lick the peppermint from my lips, that handsome friend of my father's turned to me. He clicked his heels as though a Swiss soldier and bowed at his waist. "Your father consents to my walking you home, should you concur," he said. "Though he warns me of the trouble."

"Trouble is the needle God uses to stitch us into finer quilts," I said before I could censure the spicy words as they rose through the tightness in my throat.

"I warn you," my father told Christian with raised eyebrows, but also with a smile.

We started off walking past the houses that inside were filled with celebrating Bethelites. I hardly heard a word Christian said, aware more of how close he stood, how the backs of our hands barely brushed, yet I could feel the heat of them like hot rocks my mother placed at the foot of our bed to warm the sheets of my sisters and me. Once I nearly stumbled in the snow, and Christian caught my elbow but in an instant released it, keeping chaste as required. He spoke a little of his journeys into Kentucky. I merely listened, hoping he'd not ask questions of me. What in my life was worthy of sharing with so important and so fine a man twenty years my senior? My feelings bounced like bells in a strong wind.

We sauntered toward the sawmill, past brick houses. Up the incline stood Elim, the large three-story home of our leader set up like a castle on a hill. We would walk to it later, and on the second floor, everyone would gather. Suddenly, our leader rushed out of the Latimer *Haus* toward us, his white napkin still tugging at his throat as he strode to where we stood.

"Chris, it is *gut* you have passed by. Ve have much to talk about. I'm finished eating here, so come, ve go to Elim."

Christian smiled at him. "Wilhelm, can it not wait until—"

"You rush along now, Emma Wagner," our leader said, shooing his hands at me as though I were his chicken. "Catch up with your father and brothers and stop bothering Mr. Giesy. He has little time to look after girls who fall behind their families." He tugged at the tuft of hair below his chin kept separated from his beard. "Go, then. See, your father waits now."

I wondered what Christian would do to correct our leader's understanding of my annoying him. *Annoying him.* I pushed my shoulders back straight as a knitting needle.

"Wilhelm," Christian began, but our leader already headed up the hill toward his home. He rolled his arm as though inviting Christian to hurry along, refusing to look or listen to what anyone else had to say. He left his wife and children at Latimers' to fend their own way home.

Christian smiled at me, eyes sparkling and wistful as a boy's. But he shrugged his shoulders, lifted his palms, then pointed with his chin to my father. "Hurry along then, Emma Wagner. There must be trouble I need to tend to."

"*Ja,* there's trouble," I said as I turned my back to him before I had to watch him do the same.

I reasoned something as I stomped away: Keil, our leader, pronounced his own name in the English as *keel,* the word that means the backbone of a vessel. He saw himself as a keel, that portion of a boat's structure which runs from bow to stern and to which all else must attach to form the ship. It is what keeps the ship afloat. But in German the word does not mean "keel," but "wedge" instead, something that splits, heavy like an anchor piercing the sea to hold the ship or keep it from moving forward. As I turned to see the back of Christian walking from me, I began that day to wonder if Father Keil would form a wedge in what I wanted for my future.

2

Dancing Over

"Remember the old German proverb," my mother said later as I sniffled about my budding romance so early thwarted by Father Keil. "Begin to weave / God provides the thread."

I nodded, though unsure of what that meant. Should I spend my time weaving and hope something good would come of my creations when I gave them away? Or did it mean that I should just begin, take my stand, and God would provide whatever was needed to serve His purpose? I let my mother wipe at my tears and cheer me as she said, "There's always the New Year's dance."

Waltzing is allowed by our leader, as are the colony's many festive days, though I suspect Father Keil didn't expect Christian to dance with the likes of me. I know that now. Following the wedge he placed between us on Christmas Day, I neither saw nor heard about Christian's activities for an entire week. I'd said nothing when my father raised his eyebrows as I caught up with my parents Christmas morning, and my mother merely handed me a handkerchief when I failed to hold back tears. But later, gaining rhythm, I threw off my brother's teasing that I'd been left behind like an old potato. "*Ja,* little you know about making stew," I said. "Potatoes, even old ones, give stew substance."

He wrinkled his brows. "What does—"

"Never mind," I said and hurried up the stairs to the loft room I shared with my three sisters, where if I was lucky and the girls played downstairs, I could smooth my rebuff in private.

But midweek, my mother's word of weaving brought hope. So on New Year's Day, with the Missouri winter pining for spring, I thought of dancing. We'd have a celebration later that evening with the brass band playing full force in Elim, the largest house in the colony, where our leader lived and where we often gathered for dances next to his octagonal music room. I had hoped, prayed too, that Christian might ask me to dance at least once, assuming he attended and hadn't been sent off again by our leader to some faraway place to gain additional converts. I revisited each thing he'd said, remembered the tingling of my skin as I recalled the closeness of our hands. Words formed into music as I beat our rugs beneath the opaque sky, then brought the handwoven carpets inside.

To touch the face / Of one so dear / Is like music / Falling on one's ear.

I knew the words were not at all like the elegant music of Papa's second cousin—mine too—Richard Wagner, who couldn't even hear his opera *Lohengrin* performed the year before because he displeased the German government. Franz Liszt conducted instead. Maybe music and dissent mixed in my ancestral blood, though it didn't help me carry a tune. But so mixed passion, too, as Cousin Wagner was a romantic man and so was my father. Even my uncle was an American ambassador to France, that most romantic of lands. My mother still wore beneath her dark high-collared dress a tiny strand of pearls my father must have given her. I'd glimpsed it once before she discreetly tucked it away, blushing as she did.

Later, after New Year's, I'd help my mother store the few Christmas decorations we kept up until Epiphany. I most loved the tiered carving of the Christmas story, each layer a circle, with wooden shepherds on the bottom, then on the shelf above them, wise men, and finally Joseph and Mary with the Christ child on top. The whole structure stood on the floor, and each level spun in circles by the heat of candles moving wooden flaps. My mother had brought it from Germany with her. I'd never seen one in any other colony home, and we were only allowed to display it during this season. Putting it away always marked the end of a celebrating time and then the beginning of the long wait for spring.

Sheppie barked, and I went to the window expecting to see a squirrel scampering. I instead delighted in watching Christian make his way through the melting snow to my father's house. I'd begun to think his little invitation to venture into "trouble" with me on Christmas Day was nothing but a *Peltz Nickel* treat with a twig attached: a promise of a treasure but with a punishment, too. But now, here he appeared, and me with dust fluffs hanging from my dress!

Seeing him stride up the steps onto the porch, his head almost touching the corner filigree, made me forget the punishment part. I pitched aside disappointment brought on by our leader's interruption on Christmas Day. The dust fluffs were forgotten too.

Christian struck the porch post, knocking mud from his half-boot ankle jacks, then he bent to unlace them. Sheppie barked a happy bark, his gray tail wagging like a metronome, his nails scraping across the pine floor, meeting my father approaching the door. The shepherd dog acted as though he knew the man when he surely didn't. But the dog's delight pleased me, and I felt myself emboldened enough to pull back the simple curtain covering our windows and stare out at Christian, willing him to look at me.

He didn't.

"Your beau's here," Jonathan said from behind me.

I turned and shushed him with my chin stuck out and a grit of my teeth. "He's here to see Papa, no doubt," I said, though I hoped I told a lie.

My father answered the door when Christian knocked, and for a moment I wondered if Christian would take offense at the lavish garlands of greens I'd woven dried berries into and hung around the room. I'd set candles in such a way that they, too, looked inviting and shimmered against the wooden cabinet in which my mother kept her good dishes that even today she had not pulled out. It was far from a simple great room, with the festive boughs acting like necklaces, candles flickering, and the fire crackling at the end of the house. Both Catherine and Johanna worked with thread and needles in their laps while Louisa napped. Books spread across the table and on the divan, and I wondered if that would upset him, since our leader didn't care much for books unless they offered practical advice for making better whiskey or gaining higher yields from fields. A colorful purple and green Wandering Foot quilt almost shouted its lavish comfort. Would Christian think us too worldly?

I stepped in front of the wooden Christmas tier to keep him from seeing its fine carving, just in case. My little ruffle, still stitched to my crinoline, seemed heavier. I had yet to remove it.

The smell of my mother's baked cinnamon buns permeated the air. At least good scents were not forbidden in a German colony.

Christian seemed not to notice any of his surroundings. He entered in stocking feet against my father's protest that the floor easily cleaned and he could keep his boots on. Instead, he set the boots with heels precise against the wall, then accepted my father's offer of ale. He didn't even acknowledge me as he bent to pet Sheppie.

My father ushered him into the dining room. "Come along, Jonathan," he told my brother, acting as though I were nothing but a candle stand.

Apparently, if I was to hear the conversation or even share Christian's presence, it would be as a serving woman unless I did something about it.

"I'd be interested in hearing what Mr. Giesy has to say about his travels," I said.

My father turned, frowned. "In the kitchen, your mother needs you."

"*Ja,* I'm sure," I said, "but—"

"Emma…"

Jonathan grinned as he marched by me and motioned to David and even little William to join him with the men.

I couldn't overhear them in the kitchen. When I brought in trays of tea to offer, they looked serious as I slowly served them, my brothers included, sitting stiff as bedposts. None of them even acknowledged my presence with a simple nod of thanks. All this men's talk apparently meant Christian truly had come only to see my father.

"They'll pass laws against communal living," Christian said. "And this will not be good for us."

"We're not like those…others," my father said. "We don't share our wives or husbands. We don't all live in one huge house. We're happy, giving to each other in a Christian way. Why should the government care?"

"Sometimes we do, though, live in one house. The bachelors who come with no family to stay with. And until we build them homes, new recruits and whole families do live with others."

"*Ach,* that is just family," my father said. "You have generations living in the Giesy house. It is nothing wrong."

"All we earn we put into one place, communally. All of Bethel's land is in Wilhelm's name, no one else's. This bothers some officials who see such commonness as…against the nation. They wonder if our loyalty is to our leader rather than to the country, and with the rumblings of war…*ja*, well, they might think we long to become our own country inside this new American state of Missouri."

"Wilhelm would change that in a moment if asked," my father said. "He does not keep the land for himself, only for the good of us all." My father's voice rose.

"I know this, David," Christian countered. He reached for my father's hand and patted it with assurance. Christian had fine, high cuticles, and his nails were white as piano ivory. "But outsiders, they don't understand. It seems strange to them, how we do things here. We are foreign to them, more German than American."

"When you recruit, are you able to win hearts for our Lord?" my father asked.

Christian nodded yes. "But it is harder to describe the necessity for all of us to live in one colony with one storehouse to fill and only one to take from. People wonder why our Lord asks us to live so… communally—"

"When all around us yearn for things, for new dresses, big horses, more fields to call their own," I said and continued before they could stop me. "We prosper by meeting those very needs we say we don't believe in. We sell whiskey and gloves and lumber to those who do not live as we do. I don't understand that either."

Even Jonathan's eyes grew wide. My father frowned. "Emma…"

"What she says I have thought too," Christian said. He sat straighter in the high chair and stared at me, elbows out as his palms rested on his thighs. "It seems a contradiction to separate ourselves and then to take gain from the sales to the fallen world."

He considered something I said important?

"But we do not get rich from it," my father protested. "Only enough to serve one another comes into the storehouse. We tend widows, orphans, no matter if they are colonists or not. That is our mission."

"But perhaps it's tainted," I said, pushing my good fortune. "How do we look to those we seek to convert? Maybe it appears as though we recruit to *our* way rather than to God's."

"Wilhelm's way has led us to our Lord well these years," my father said. He snapped the words out. He pointed toward the kitchen door. "Emma. Your mother has need of you."

"But, Papa—"

"Go."

I threw a glance at Christian, but he looked lost in thought, and once again he seemed unwilling or unable to challenge orders given me by other men. Never mind that one was my father, a respected elder, and the other our spiritual leader. Christian needed to stand firm, I thought, as the door to the kitchen swung shut behind me, bumping the ruffle beneath my skirt.

"I'll bake bread," I told my mother, slamming down the tea tray.

"Now?"

"It will give me something to push around and pound," I said, gathering flour into the doughboy and reaching for salt from the box.

"Well, a house can always use bread."

The fluff of the flour and the saleratus with melted lard seeped into the flour hole I'd made and kept me occupied, if not pleased. I tried not to think of Christian Giesy as being someone weak, easily overpowered by my father. He stood so tall, had brought in too many new recruits to be a weak man. It was even rumored that every day he lifted himself seventy-five times from the floor by his hands without letting his knees even touch. It took strength for such pushing up, strength that must reflect a man of character, too. Even Karl Ruge, the teacher, a highly educated man and a Lutheran still, chose to live in the colony because of Christian's enthusiasm and ability to express our views of love and service to one another. And everyone adored Karl—many admired his fine mind and his long clay pipe.

And yet, and yet, what is a man if he cannot put other men's wishes aside to tend to those of his beloved?

I imagined myself as Christian's beloved. *Ach,* I thought. *You are a Dummkopf.* That's what my father would say. I shook my head and knuckled the dough, imagining the conversation going on without me, imagining life going on without me, farther away, in Shelbina or maybe even Independence.

We Bethel colonists were asked to be in service, to treat others as we wished to be treated, and to go beyond, to help others live even better than we did. The Diamond Rule our leader called it, better even than the Golden Rule. And yet while women served, our voices were rarely heard except in music. Did not our Lord wash the feet of His disciples? Did not our Lord comfort those who grieved? Is that not what women do? And yet we are not invited into the halls of discussion, we are not asked to sit around the tables and talk with men making sense of a family's future. No, we are asked to influence *through* our fathers and our brothers and our sons but never *with* them.

"I hope that's not my head you're thinking of. You knead that dough with such vigor." Christian had stepped into the kitchen, his body dwarfing the doughboy table.

I wiped my forehead with the back of my palm. His height seemed out of place, but his voice fit here, low and calm and smooth as melted butter. "Or if it is, perhaps you'll exchange it for a chance at my feet this evening. Your father consents to my squiring you to the dance, should you be willing."

"And will something more come between us?" I asked, my hands on my hips now.

"Emma," my mother gasped. "Rude you must not be."

"She gives it fairly," Christian said. "I'll do my best to see I give her little more reason to express it."

How could I refuse?

———

This dance held a special tone as it announced the New Year, new beginnings. The year 1852 held prosperity, as Father Keil had already received orders for special wagons made for traveling overland to the Oregon Territory. Whole towns in the Ohio Valley and farther east had signed up to go west, and, hearing of our furniture factory and wagon-building and our colony being so close to Independence and even closer to St. Joseph, many commissioned us to build them sturdy wagons. Even colony women would assist with the construction in order to meet the demand.

It was our practice that as colony work required more effort, each set aside plowing or candle-making and put all hands toward the greatest need, men and women working side by side. "Ve build many vagons this year," our leader told us, and so we would.

Future prosperity lent a festive air to this occasion, and our leader charmed the crowd chattering and eating, paying scant attention to Christian and me. The band played and I watched Willie, our leader's oldest son, step forward and execute a solo on his horn. He twirled himself around so dancers stopped to watch him, including his father, including us. People applauded, clapped Willie on his back as he finished, and shouted out hurrahs from across the large room. A few men drank small glasses of our colony's Golden Rule Whiskey, and women not dancing or serving or watching after children sat in groups, their dark flannels reminding me of clusters of grapes waiting to be plucked.

Christian and I completed a *Schottische,* a pleasant dance with hops and easy twirls, but one that required a man place his hands across a woman's shoulders as they skipped side by side. Christian's hands felt smooth as river stones. The warmth that spread all through me as his palm squeezed mine surprised. He pulled me to him and smiled. I could have spent the entire night this way.

But after the fourth dance, we moved toward the door, where people coming in and out admitted a coolness. I couldn't help but notice the envy in the eyes of girls my age, as I'd spent my whole time with an important man just a year younger than my father. Even when men came by to talk to him, he allowed me to remain, didn't shoo me off, though most of the talk was of Christian's journeys and when he might leave again or about his tin shop and what work he could complete before he left. I never offered a single word, careful not to embarrass him. In our colony, listening was a valued skill, at least for women.

Willie played another solo, this one with even more gusto.

"People say one day Willie will be our leader," Christian said, leaning in to me as we stood still later with our backs against the wall.

"I doubt that," I told him. "He's too fun-loving, wants attention for himself."

"Possibly," Christian said. "But a leader needs to demonstrate enthusiasm in order to have followers. No one wants to be a disciple of a somber soul."

"Father Keil is far from…merry," I said. "Yet here we all are." I spread my arms wide.

"Wilhelm is joyous and kind, Emma. That's how we see him. He has the music, the band. He reminds us that we find abundance in living simply."

"Living simply," I said, disgust in my voice. I still had the ruffle attached, and I decided at that moment I would simply leave it there.

I'd wash it at home, not at the communal washhouse. No one would ever discover my interest in uniqueness.

"What else about Bethel distresses you?" Christian asked. He'd cocked his head to the side and had a wry smile on his face.

"You want my opinion?"

His eyes held mine and he sobered. I noticed that the color of his mustache bore tints of red. "I should know the things that cause unrest in you," he said, his voice as smooth as hot cider, "if you're to be my wife."

I felt my stomach fall into my knees.

Catching my breath I said, "The word *if* looms large."

"Indeed, *if* is larger. As with my dancing, I can step over that word rather than on it," Christian said, "and make the request without venturing further into what brings you happiness or strife. It surprises—"

"No, no," I said. "I want to be asked my thoughts. *Ja,* I do. Will my answers make a difference to the offer? It was an offer, *ja?* Or do I misunderstand?" My words twirled around, caught up now with my feelings like a kite string swirling upward in the wind. "Have you asked our leader? my father?" I didn't want to get my hopes up. I already knew Christian could be easily dissuaded by either of these two men.

"Your father has concurred. Wilhelm has not." I looked away. "Indeed, he knows nothing of it," Christian said, his hand patting mine in reassurance. "I did not wish to begin that…dance until I knew you would step with me. Your father's agreed first. Then if you say to proceed, I will approach Wilhelm. He is a kindly man despite what you may think, Emma. So I believe by his birthday celebration, we will be allowed to announce to all our marital intentions. God willing. You, being willing. You have yet to say if I can step over the *if.*"

"*Ja,*" I said. "I agree to be your wife, no ifs. But when the engagement is complete and we have answered our leader's probing, I hope you'll still be pleased with your offer."

"He doesn't interrogate, Emma. He asks to be sure that husbands and wives will be happy to be together for life. It is his duty as a leader to inquire."

"*Ja*, sure," I said, knowing it wouldn't be the last time Christian Giesy and his future wife would see the world through very different eyes.

We completed the evening with not another word about our future. It was hardly a romantic declaration, all wrapped up in talk of civics and ascendancy. And yet wasn't that what I'd been aching for, to have conversations between men and women, express words that did more than tease the mind? No, I'd been aching to be truly seen by Christian, to be known not as "one of the colony women wearing faded flannel and her hair parted in the center," but as someone another might pick out from a crowd.

Now that he had, I felt lightheaded: I might actually receive what I wanted. I'd begun to weave, and God had just handed me the finest yet most foreign of threads.

3

A Ring
Around the Fire

Youth claims perfect pitch and often fails to note disharmony. When I told my mother of Christian's intentions, she smiled and held me, her apron comforting with *Sauerkraut* smells. "I know," she said. "Your father forewarned me, though he didn't tink what you might say."

"You never saw my interest?" I asked my father later as he drank strong tea at the head of the table.

My father merely raised an eyebrow, his "well, well," look, the same he gave me when as a child I asked some question about why sheep's wool held heavy oils or when I urged him to tell me something I didn't already know. I suppose he welcomed my inquisitive nature, knew in advance the challenge Christian's life would have for me, both encouraging it and tempering it.

Jonathan sounded the only sour note I heard. "What's Christian Giesy see in you?"

"*Ach,* Jonathan," my mother cautioned. "Be happy for your sister, *ja?*"

Jonathan grunted as he cut his sausage, popped a section in his mouth. "He's a tinsmith with the gift of gab," he said. "Think of how many girls he's been exposed to. Why would he settle for you?" I don't think he meant to hurt my feelings, and in truth, he said out loud what would have eventually made its way into my consciousness. But until then, I saw Christian's interest as an answer to my prayers, as a tapestry God saw fit to stitch together: two hearts, two hands, two souls hemmed by faith.

"Do you think Father Keil will forbid it?" David Jr. said. He held his fork midair above his egg. "There is something noble in being a bachelor, I think."

"Why should he?" I asked. "Papa's approved. And Christian is beloved by Father Keil. He wants him to be happy."

"He didn't think of it himself, though," Jonathan said. "Father Keil likes to be in charge of all things. A good leader is, sister. Willie told me that."

My father corrected. "It's a leader's duty to have authority, but this does not mean power used for personal views. He doesn't think he must order everything, Jonathan. Maybe Willie chomps at the reins the way young men do. Willie's time will come."

"It will be a strange marriage with Christian leaving again soon," Jonathan said. "That's his way, his work."

"I'll not hear any more contrary thoughts." I put hands over my ears. "Not from you or anyone else." I left the room.

Christian and I agreed not to say anything outside our families until receiving our leader's blessings. I didn't know what the Giesy family thought of me, though it seemed that Helena was more distant in the classroom, where we helped Karl Ruge, than she'd been before. She acted more formal, but I might have been imagining that. I have an active imaginary life, which led me to wonder if Christian's absence after New Year's was planned or happenstance. Either way, Jonathan proved himself clairvoyant. Christian and I had had no time together since he stated his intentions. But then, he was a busy man, had always been.

He met with our leader and the men's council, a group of twelve who advised about the happenings at Nineveh, an offshoot colony near Hannibal, where we ran a ferry and a steam mill that powered huge textile looms. The men advised about work at Bethel too. Christian was often gone, but I felt sure he'd return for our leader's birthday. It was always a grand affair. I prayed for patience.

Two days before our leader's birthday, Christian again knocked on our door, Sheppie's happy wagging tail expressing my thoughts completely. That day, I asked Christian about what my brother and sister said. We sat at my parents' house on a hard bench set before the fireplace while my family discreetly kept us within sight but out of hearing, my mother spinning and my father polishing a bridle to keep the leather soft. The boys stayed outside, and my sisters whispered in the rooms above us. I could almost imagine them hovering over the opening that allowed heat and sound to rise up through the ceiling. Christian had first spent an hour with my father, telling news that he'd gathered on his travels, leaving me to eavesdrop.

Outside our great-room windows, tiny buds of crocus pushed their way up through the soil, and already robins sat on the porch rails, watching for early worms. The dog slept at my feet. Then at last I had him to myself, after a fashion.

"What did I see in you to make me want you for my wife?" Christian repeated my question. "Your kind spirit, indeed. And your willingness to question even when there might be…consequences. These are good qualities. Necessary for learning, my friend Karl says, necessary for change."

I hadn't thought of myself as unusually kind and said so.

"Remember New Year's Day?" Christian told me.

How could I forget? "It was the day you asked me to be your wife."

"Yes, yes. But more," Christian said. "In the corner of Elim where we gathered sat a woman with three children huddled around her. She was not of us."

I thought back. Yes, there'd been a woman who piled her hair on top of her head in an Apollo knot, the false hairpiece standing up behind the center part instead of in a chignon at the back as we colony woman wore ours. She wore fancy clothes, cloth with new dye, something else that made her different. The rest of us dressed in flannels or woolen dresses, clean but well-faded. New cloth was seen as a luxury we made and sold, unless one had worn out a dress and had already turned it into strips for rugs or repatterned it for a child's gown.

Louisa Keil, our leader's wife, pulled her dark woolen shawl tighter around her as she knelt at that woman's feet. She patted the woman's knee, talking quietly to her. The woman nodded, wiping at her eyes with a handkerchief. Louisa looked up, and spying Christian and me—had I detected a frown?—she motioned us over.

"You're good with *Kinder*," she said to me, nodding to the children. "Help them join in with the others, give their mother a bit of rest."

I remembered that the children's mother wore bruises on her cheek and lip, and I assumed she was one of many women whom the colonists took in to help as they made their escapes from harsh men. Some remained and joined us; others recovered and moved on, often returning to the men who'd harmed them, a choice I never could fathom. I'd taken her children and we'd played Ring-around-the-Rosy, with all of us falling down in heaps, serenaded by their peals of cautious laughter.

"I remember the woman's bruises," I said. Sheppie's tail thumped the floor at the sound of my voice. "I wonder at times if our offering help to such people makes us suspect to other Missourians. We colonists step into the middle of a fray, act as servants to those in need, but such work can cause resentments."

Christian nodded. Missouri was a slave state, but on the border with freer territories, and many people didn't own slaves here. There'd been talk of repealing that compromise that allowed Maine to enter as a free state and Missouri as a slave. Perhaps Missourians feared our colony would harbor escaped slaves, since we rescued broken women. I wasn't sure that we wouldn't. Maybe that was why there'd been discussion about the colony moving again. We danced around issues, and sometimes we stepped on someone else's toes.

"The children, they were so frightened; so many changes."

"You answered Louisa's call without hesitation. You were selfless. This is good. It tells me you can see beyond your own needs to those of others. I had seen this before in you."

His praise warmed me to my toes, and I vowed to give him more reason for such words, though vows among the young are often soon forgotten. "And what else?"

"Those questions," he said. "You ask…pointed questions, a sign your mind keeps working. Just as now, about slave and free. And you're persistent when you want a thing."

"Stubborn, my father says." I felt my cheeks grow warm.

"Indeed." Christian smiled and lifted my hand, placing it in his. I waited for him to give me an example that I could cherish ever after, but instead he said, "And you are beautiful," the words a whisper. "Beautiful as God has made you without adornment. So my admiration for your form, my filling up by looking at you, watching you float across the room as graceful as a swan, causes no challenge to our need to set aside all but simplicity and what is useful. You cannot help how you've been formed." With his other hand he drew his finger around the outline of my lips, an act so surprising that his touch sent shivers through me, past the chignon that gathered at my neck. I swallowed and thought of Saint Paul's words about marriage being better than to burn, about the rocks that must surround such fire or it would flame across a field, taking everything in its path.

My mother coughed, and he dropped his hand from my face as though he'd been stung.

Some days later I told Jonathan that my intended saw the good in me, a loving heart. "Ha," Jonathan said. "The man is blinded then," but the sparkle in his eyes told me he teased.

"By my beauty," I told him, flipping my fingers at my ears. It was an idea still settling in my mind.

My brother softened then. "That you are, sister. That you are."

My only regret from my conversation with Christian was that I wanted to share what in him appealed to me, but he never asked.

———

Fireworks marked March 6, as always, it being Father Keil's birthday. Our leader chose it as the time for our discussion of our marriage.

It was to be a simple declaration of our intentions so that we might begin to tell others of our plans. I saw myself as a person seeking the sonata rather than the dirge. I held on to those notes now.

I knew the rules, of course, about unions among the colonists or outsiders. Father Keil raised few objections, however, if a man became engaged to marry an outsider, as it was believed she would eventually join the colony, accept the colony's ways, and consent would be freely given to their nuptials. She would move in with his family until a home could be built, but at least the couple could begin or continue to work without the colony having to take time out to build a house for them. The man almost always had a meaningful job within the colony already, or he wouldn't be a Bethelite. His intended bride would soon find her place in worthy work.

Women finding men outside created a different problem: even if Father Keil approved their marriage with the man's intention to join us, the building of their house would take labor from other valued work: farming, the furniture factory, our Bethel Plow manufacturing, and this year, building wagons. And should the couple later choose to leave, this new man who had not contributed all his life nor had a family do so before him would require compensation, something our leader offered anyone who later settled out. Men received money for each year of service to the colony whether or not they'd brought wealth in to the common fund; married women received half of what men received for each year of service.

Christian assured me that since we were both of longstanding families, Father Keil would have little objection to our marrying.

We arrived separately to put off wagging tongues. I spoke with Louisa on the main, or family, floor as she mended little Aurora's torn skirt. She didn't ask me about my appointment. Neither did she raise her eyes when, with the arrival of Christian, I stood and climbed the center staircase to Elim's third story.

Once there, Christian and I sat on tall hardback chairs and faced our leader in his office. The large room served as his laboratory, too, where he grew and experimented with healing herbs. People were healthy in Bethel; few had even a sniffle. When they did, our leader offered relief with his blends of teas or things to swallow or rub to bring about cures. Many in the surrounding community even asked for his slippery elm brew or peach tree bark concoctions. They all called him "Dr. Keil," a name that always brought a smile to his lips. It was rumored he'd once had a magical book that held healing potions, written in his own blood. But that was earlier, before he led us as a Christian colony.

Light streamed down through the clerestory windows that from the outside reminded me of an Indian's eyes, narrow. Those third-story openings were barely a third of the size of those on the first and second floors, and they were high above so we couldn't look out through them to the spring beyond.

Father Keil's chair, on a platform behind a heavy walnut desk, would have resembled a throne if the desk hadn't been there. Leaders in Germany lived in castles, had thrones…it was expected of a colony leader, not something meant to be ostentatious.

Or so I told myself.

His forearms rested on the desk, hands folded as in prayer.

It was my first visit to this room. A single bookshelf held titles about medicines and plants. Wooden bowls and pestles perched neatly on a long table off to the side. The room felt almost steamy on this warm March morning, what with all the plants and earth readied to be set out as soon as any threat of a freeze had ceased.

Our leader's eyes looked tired as we waited for him to begin. I thought perhaps as this was his fortieth year, he might be weary of the celebrations of his birth and the fireworks that crackled every now and then. Men seem generally less interested in fusses made over birthdays, or so my father always said when my mother tried to do something special on his day.

"So," Father Keil began when the last singing hiss of a firecracker faded. "You wish to marry."

I knew enough to remain silent until after Christian spoke, though it surprised me that our leader already knew. Christian must have told him. Or rumors spread despite our trying to keep it quiet. Christian told him about conferring with my father and then with me and now with him, how he had prayed about this union and felt God answered after all this time his desire for a workmate by raising me before his eyes.

"You might have talked to me first, Chris," Keil told Christian. "It would have saved this…disharmony now, as you will surely see it." He looked at me for the first time.

My heart began to pound. Fear like a startled cat pounced on my chest. I hoped I didn't whimper out loud. Our leader sighed deeply, turned back to Christian. "I see no good thing to come of this union, Chris."

I nearly bit my tongue through to hold my words in my mouth. I hiccupped. Both men looked at me, then Christian went on as though he hadn't heard what our leader had said.

"She has a loving spirit. I've seen her kindness. Indeed, I've watched her grow into a young woman of substance. Even my sister Helena comments on Emma's good way with the children. She helps with the *Kinder,* so my sister sees firsthand this woman's strengths. 'Suffer the little children to come unto me,' our Lord said. Children know a person's heart, Wilhelm."

"But they lack judgment, *ja?* Until they've grown. Emma is not grown, and she will bring your work down as you must pause to raise her."

Could smoke come from one's ears? Could a heart explode like the firecrackers outside?

"She will be a good mother to my children," Christian said, his eyes lowered now.

"But this is exactly my concern, Chris. You are nearly my age, and to begin now with a family will take you from the work you're called to just when we need you most." He said the word *just* as though it were *yust,* and for the first time I wished we were speaking in German instead of English and wondered why that was so on such an austere occasion. Maybe he knew I had trouble understanding English, even more to speak well in it. Did he intend to demean me before my beloved's eyes? "You will have a woman to worry over, a family. There'll be the need to build a house for you when you should be off recruiting."

He actually thought I would interfere, that I would not support my husband's work? He didn't know me or know my heart. I started to speak, but he held his hand up to stop me as though I were a mule pushing too close to the one in front of it.

"Chris, you are a good man whose strength lies in your compassionate spirit toward our people and a fire that burns for God." He switched to German now. "That fire brings new people to His way. Your life tells the story again and again to people seeking to live according to the Golden Rule, to give one's all to God, and through that, to each other. Look whom you have brought to this colony. Karl Ruge, among others, a man of great wisdom whose practical teachings enhance our youth. He nurtures ideas of invention, just like how we solved problems when we lacked a way to bring water to the fields. Remember? You helped design the special drills to bore holes through the center of the logs to act as pipes. As inventive as the Romans and their aqueducts. But this takes a singular mind of care for others. I know this. I must keep my own family's needs as well as the entire colony, and it is a trial, *ja,* a trial. One our Lord has given me, and only a strong man so anointed can endure. Now, more than ever, with the words of Daniel coming closer, telling us how human conditions will end, we need you and only you to continue as a singular flame for God, Chris, not as a man burdened with family."

I hated that he called him Chris, as though he did not deserve the full use of his own name, as though our leader could ignore a name given at his birth that spoke of who he was and would ever be, Christian. The scent of green plants growing in this warm third-story floor seemed suddenly overpowering. The smell of earth, while usually so inviting, smelled of decay to me now. Our leader stood, revealing his long black coat hanging funereally to his knees.

"She may be good with the *Kinder,* but it's because she is one." He acted as though I were one of his plants that could neither hear nor feel. "In the glove factory, she makes games and distracts. I have seen her toss turnips in the fields as though they were balls for the dogs to retrieve. She is too interested in those who travel to Shelbina, too interested in what is not here at home. These are signs too, Chris, signs I cannot ignore. I tell them to you out of love. For you both. Your union would be wrought with fractures no glue could repair. At the first sign of a trial, you would seek to separate, and this would not be a good witness to the colony."

I wanted to tell my part, defend myself, and reassure Father Keil that I could be in service to my husband and this colony. Disagreement wasn't a sign of rebellion, only wisdom. Were not we Germans known for seeking knowledge? And what of joy? We held dances, our band played for entertainment, so what was wrong with my donning gloves like a rooster top to hop around the factory floor? People laughed, and what was un-Christian about that in the midst of work?

Christian leaned forward, his hands folded together, his forearms resting on his thighs. My heart pounded. He remained silent, and it took all I could not to stand up, say what I wanted him to say. But I had agreed and would show my discipline was as good as...our leader's.

A clock ticked in the silence. Then Christian stood, eye to eye with our leader. He turned to me. I saw a pain there I hadn't seen before. I felt my heart pound, sure that he would say now that he agreed with our leader and dash my hopes for a long and abiding love.

But Christian addressed our leader, though he held my eyes. "I believe you are in error, Wilhelm. I believe your error comes from a good heart, one that honors me with your confidence that I do good things. But I do so with God's help. Indeed, I did not bring in Karl Ruge to teach our children English. God did. I did not bring in new Scots-Irish recruits from Kentucky and Tennessee. God did this. And I believe that God has given me a future wife in Emma Wagner, whose father you so entrusted with our colony that you sent him out to find this Bethel, this "place of God," this "place of worship," as the Hebrew word translates. She's been raised in our ways and knows them—"

"She challenges them," our leader said.

"But she will keep the vows and understands what I am called to do," Christian countered.

Our leader puffed up his chest then. "You will defy me, Chris, over this...this trivial thing?"

"Wilhelm, please. I have no wish to drive a wedge between us. There is a compromise. Emma turns eighteen on the twenty-seventh of this month. We would set the date for then and pray you will be the one to officiate. We will discuss this again when you've had time to pray and consider. Come, Emma. Let's go, give Wilhelm time to prepare for his celebration."

How I wanted to have my say, but for once I chose to be right in silence. And my intended had stood firm and had even named a date, though I would have preferred to have some say in that. To witness a birthday and a wedding anniversary on the same occasion robbed a woman of one celebration. And in a world where there were few, I meant to have as many as I could.

I followed Christian out, feeling the eyes of our leader boring a hole into my back. "We can announce our wedding, then?" I said when we reached the empty second-floor gathering room.

"No," he said. "I want Wilhelm's blessing. It will be better if he comes around, if he sees that we have chosen and he cannot stop us. The colony will be the better if he too is in agreement."

"And if he doesn't ever give his consent?"

On the stair landing, he pulled me to him and kissed the top of my forehead. It was the first touch of his lips upon my skin. "We will marry, Emma. But we'll keep this quiet for now. Agreed?"

"*Ja*," I said, not wanting to be the first to pull away from the firmness of his embrace.

I'd remain silent, but I went home and sewed another ruffle on my crinoline.

4

Choose Life

Right after our meeting, our leader sent Christian on a mission that took him away on my birthday and on the supposed wedding day. But he encouraged Christian before he left by telling him that when he returned in April, we could discuss our marriage possibility again. I suspected he would use the interim time to watch me, so I wore my best behavior. In the glove factory in the afternoons, I stayed to myself, working hard to finish off the deerskin gloves with the finest stitches. Our colony's gloves had won awards in competitions at exhibitions back East, and I liked to think my work contributed. Father Keil made a fine time of hunting the many herds of deer in this part of Missouri, having the meat for our common meals and the hides for the factory. I thought again how blessed men were to do the things they loved yet name their acts as practical and thus always permitted.

Secretly, I didn't mind not having the wedding on my birthday. I could be open about the date as long as the event would happen. Being flexible about accomplishing a thing was always optional, I felt, as long as everyone could agree upon the outcome. Half the time people argued over how to do a thing more than whether it should be done at all. I thought the latter to be the topic of greater importance. If only people would take the time to voice their desires, others could assist them in achieving them; that was my motto.

Christian's absence made me think of him all the more. During the noon break at school, I prompted Helena to talk of her older brother, but she spoke instead of her own choice long years before, to give up the love of her life, the son of the man who would later design the Brooklyn Bridge and who later built his own suspension bridges.

"He was a good man, but we were not well matched."

"But you loved him, *ja?* Isn't that match enough?"

"He chose not to join the colony," Helena said. She swept the tile floor as we talked.

"Christian and I have no such barriers," I said. I wiped the face of a small child whose berry jam smeared across her face, then sent her on her way.

"True, you both share the faith," she said.

"Couldn't you have married Mr. Roebling anyway?" Her story was a legend in the colony, that she had chosen service to the colony over love. My sister Catherine especially admired Helena.

"Yes, but if two people do not share the same hopes, then discord will reign. They will be unequally yoked, as Scripture says."

"Nothing will rain on Christian and me," I chirped.

In silence she stacked the slate boards the children used, making a pile at the edge of the desk. She turned to me then, and I could see Christian's thoughtful eyes reflected in her face, his high forehead and strong jaw. "It does cause concern, your youth compared to his…experience. He's gained so much and given much, not being…hampered by a wife and children. He's important to the colony, Emma. Almost as much as Father Keil. If he marries you, Christian will have little time for…peevishness. We have been successful all these years because our leader knows how to put self aside in order to serve. I hope you consider this." She walked stiffly from the room.

I tried to remember when I had been peevish or irritable with Helena or any of her large family; or when I'd done something to suggest I didn't put others before myself. Nothing came to mind...except the ruffles that she knew nothing of and were of so little import, I couldn't imagine them being any real barrier to the safety of my soul.

I decided not to be peevish and argue after her. There'd be time enough to change her mind when I lived with the Giesys after we were married, while our home was being built.

———

At the second meeting with our leader, silence again became my first task, while our leader spoke a long prayer, seeking guidance and wisdom in this matter. Then while Christian and our leader quoted Scripture to each other, I bit my lip and stayed stiff as a boot hook. Our leader liked certain Old Testament words, and very few chapters from the New, except those that supported the common fund such as in Acts. He used them repeatedly in his sermons but always emphasized neighborly love, self-sacrifice, and prayer, and apparently he believed our marriage would do nothing to enhance those colony virtues.

Self-sacrifice. I knew that was what he wanted from Christian and from me. He wanted us to be like Helena, married to the values of the colony rather than each other. Sitting there, seeing those fiery eyes that made people believe whatever he said, I realized what he expected most of all: obedience. That we'd come a second time to even talk of our marriage must have challenged him. Few ever did. In that instant, I knew he'd never approve this union no matter how we felt. Convincing Christian to marry against our leader's wishes would be the greater task before me. He was second in command. Would he dare defy his spiritual leader?

This second inquisition without my being asked my opinion nor allowed to speak told me all I needed to know about what course I'd take next.

But then our leader turned to me. "Emma Wagner," he said, "I must speak to you of something you know nothing about but is important should you ever wish to marry." *Should I cajole him? Should I defy him? He holds more than authority here; he holds power.* "Do you understand the trials of childbirth, the pain of laboring, and the demand that follows?" He drew a hand up to silence Christian, who began to intervene. I sat like a rabbit with an owl above it.

"Of course," I said, gaining my voice. "I've helped at birthings."

"But not to watch the child agonize into the world," our leader said. "You were too young to see or to assist as your brothers and sisters arrived, too young to gain experience except to comfort little *Kinder* in the household. So let me advise." He made a tent of his fingers, leaned back in his high chair. "The infant presses against the smallest of bony places, where blood pours to weaken the woman as she writhes in pain. She pushes to bring forth this child, rising above the arc of searing torment." He lifted his eyes to the heavens as he spoke, raising his long arms to sweep over the arc he described. "I have witnessed nine such trying times with my own beloved Louisa. All this pain is created to remind women—even devout women like my Louisa—of their early sin. Sometimes," he almost whispered now, "small women do not live through this. Even with poultices to stop the bleeding, they die. Sometimes the infants die. The sins of the father are meted out onto their offspring and death results. You have not witnessed this, Emma Wagner. You are not prepared for this. I cannot have Chris marry a woman whose needs will overpower his work, a woman who could not endure the trials of Eve's first sin."

My face grew warm. I had no choice but to let my tongue speak out. All would be lost if I didn't; it was probably lost before I started. "Perhaps this childbirth pain suggests some flaw in God's design if the birth canal is so much smaller than an infant's head."

He gasped. "You blaspheme," he hissed, his eyes like black coal burning.

There was no going back. "I've heard that your herbs help relieve a woman in her time," I said, holding his stare. "Are you interfering then with God's design for the capture of each woman's soul?"

"Not now," Christian interrupted.

"You're quick with your words, Emma Wagner. But quick wit does not prepare you for life's tragedies. And these will come, mark my word. Mark God's words from Deuteronomy: 'I call heaven and earth to record this day against you, that I have set before you life and death, blessing and cursing—' "

" '—therefore choose life, that both thou and thy seed may live.' Deuteronomy 30:19." I finished the quote, ever grateful the words had not escaped my reading just that morning.

He actually stepped back. I didn't know what Christian might think of my quoting Scripture to our leader; I hesitated to take my eyes from those black accusing coals.

We heard shouts of children playing below us. Our leader's little bottles of tinctures rattled as he stepped from around his desk.

Christian cleared his throat. "You see, Wilhelm, she is called to be my wife and to bring forth my seed. She will look to the good of things and choose life. Is that not what we need? Is that not how the colony will truly grow, not just by new people coming to see our ways but by raising children up in the 'way that they should go'? This too is scriptural."

" 'Be fruitful, and multiply,' " I added.

Christian gave me a look, and I dropped my eyes. To our leader, I said, "I only meant to say that just because one has not experienced something doesn't mean one can't rise to meet the challenge when called to. I am up to the challenges of being a good wife within this colony."

Our leader's eyes focused on something high and behind us. "We may not have long life in this colony," he said finally. "I've told you, Chris, of my concerns, of the work we must do to ready our people. This woman will distract you."

"This woman will renew me."

Our leader clapped his hands then, startling both of us. At least I jerked in my seat. "You vill do vhat you vill do," he said. "I do not give my blessing. It will go against my belief about the rightness of this, but I vill not stand in your way. Marry in Shelby County if you are so inclined to set aside my visdom on this matter. But you may have the party here, at Elim, and have the marriage recorded in the membership book. On April 22. So be it. I have spoken."

"*Danke,* Wilhelm," Christian said, standing. "Thank you, so much. Come, Emma, we have taken up enough of Wilhelm's time."

I rose, confused. Father Keil withheld his blessing and would not marry us here in Bethel, yet he'd let a worldly judge pronounce the vows and then offer us a celebration later in his own home? The last surely marked some form of consent. Did it save face for him, show that he stood firm by refusing to officiate at a marriage he felt was doomed, yet allow him to be generous and showy through a party in his home?

My intended husband acted satisfied with this configuration, as twisted as a pig's tail.

I would not complain. The outcome would be as I wished it: I'd be Mrs. Christian Giesy and show our leader that one young and inexperienced woman could withstand the pangs of bringing forth new babies into life.

———

We married in the Shelby County courthouse. I had long imagined myself walking down the red-tile aisle of Bethel's church, Christian at my side, the colony as witness to our union'. But the courthouse served us well, one of those adjustments to the stepping stones along a trail, if not the final destination. My family came with us, as did some of Christian's fourteen brothers and sisters—but not Helena. Even Karl Ruge stood there for Christian. Good friends and family then witnessed our vows and the new dress my mother sewed for me. She even allowed blinker curls to coil on either side of my rosy cheeks. A short muslin veil covered my face, and I wore gray so as not to appear too worldly.

Because my father had preached and helped found the Bethel Colony, he asked the blessing on our marriage and spoke the prayers when the justice of the peace finished our short vows. And later, at the dance on Elim's second floor, our friends and the rest of Christian's family, too, gathered for the meal—including a goose—that made it almost as festive as Christmas. At Elim, where our leader ruled, Father Keil even clapped Christian on the back and nodded politely as he became, he announced, "the first to call her *Frau* Giesy." He wasn't, but I didn't correct him, grateful he'd chosen to acknowledge my married state.

I looked for Barbara Giesy, Christian's mother, and when my eyes found hers, she smiled. She and I were both *Frau* Giesy now, along with another Barbara and a Mary, already her daughters-in-law. I'd reserve the term *Frau* just for his mother, though. She served food behind the long table, her gray curls brushed tight against her head, as though to hide the flair of their waywardness. Secretly, I hoped our daughters would have such curly hair rather than take after me with my straight strands.

Christian and I hadn't talked of living arrangements, but I assumed we would have Christian's room at the Giesy house until the colony could be freed up to build a house for us. Those worldly people heading west and needing wagons had yet to taper off, even though most pilgrims tried to be at Kanesville, Iowa, some miles west, by May 15 in order to cross the mountains before any early snows. But soon we could set about to make bricks enough, and meanwhile I could learn about the Giesy family and his many other brothers. Helena was his only unmarried sister. Living with them would be my next step as a married woman, one I welcomed.

On my way to *Frau* Giesy's side to help serve, people stopped me for good wishes, admiring the tiny stitches my mother put into my dress. Willie Keil wished me well, as did Louisa Keil, of course. She held my hand extra long and nodded silently. Several of the Nineveh families had come for the celebration too. I trusted the joy each expressed in their words and on their faces. These were good people in this colony who had chosen to follow our leader, to express their faith through actions and works. I belonged among them. Having won my objective to be Christian's wife, I could even allow a softening for our leader. After all, this was his home, and he remained at this gathering for us, which offered a blessing of a kind. Perhaps all would turn out well as Christian insisted.

Then *Frau* Giesy put her arms around me, an embrace of warmth and grace. "Christian has chosen a lovely bride," she said, patting my back as she pulled away.

"Nothing I take credit for."

"Well said," she answered. "I will thank your parents, then."

"As I thank you, for giving me this good man. And for welcoming me into your fold."

"That we do." She brushed at the blinker curls at the side of my face. "We're not so fancy, though."

"Just for special occasions," I said, pulling the curl back behind my ear.

"I hope you aren't too disappointed that you'll be remaining in your parents' home for a time. Until a house can be built for Christian.

And for you. Here, Edna, take this last piece of raisin cake. It's so good. Luella made it, brought it all the way from Nineveh." She so easily wove in words of hospitality to women across the table that I wasn't sure I really heard her other words.

"Excuse me?"

"We thought it best. For so long Christian has served the colony, and I have tended him as his mother and as a colony member when he returned home. That will all change in time, but for now, I'm pleased you found no objection to this plan of you remaining with your parents."

Christian and me living with my parents? Where? Perhaps the boys would move out into the woodshed so my sisters could take their places. It could be arranged. It wasn't what I wanted, but I could adjust. It was one of my strengths, I decided, this ability to move across the trail, back and forth, crawling over rocks laid in the way. No one could set me off the path, at least, and I chose not to let *Frau* Giesy know her news came as some surprise.

"*Ja*, it'll be strange to share my room with him," I said. My sisters would be in the room next door, my parents below us. "But my girlish things I need to put away."

"*Ach*, you have time," she said. "There is *Strudel* at the table's end," she told Willie when he approached, raising his empty plate. "Let me get it for you." He followed her along like a puppy. She served him, then returned.

"He'll stay at home until your house is built. Then you can join him. That way he can continue his work while you'll be with what's familiar and none of your family is inconvenienced."

I kept my face without reaction, pretended that this wasn't something new to me, that my husband and I reached this conclusion together, not that he'd talked of it to everyone but me.

"We all thought that was best, especially since he still must travel."

We all thought? My parents, too? Was everyone in league to keep us separated even after we'd been wed? Or was it yet another test composed by our leader to see how willing I was to support my husband's work?

Well, he would discover—they all would discover—when something truly mattered, I could conform.

————

We did spend our wedding night at my parents' home, and I chose not to bring up the larger issues of our living apart. I didn't want to spoil that night. We'd planned no bridal tour, and if what *Frau* Giesy said was true, then this would be our only evening together for a time until I could convince my husband otherwise. We settled beneath the goose feather comforter, our bodies barely touching as we lay, eyes wide open staring at the board ceiling. He clasped my hand in his, and it felt sweaty, or perhaps it was merely mine. "Emma," he began. *Will he tell me now what I already know?*

I noticed a strange smell in the room, something from Christian's boots, perhaps. I heard scratching at the door. Whining followed, then yipping barks until I rose, and when I opened the door, Sheppie ran in. The dog sniffed wildly beneath the bed. I couldn't imagine what was under it, but the dog squeezed himself under the slats as Christian, standing in his nightshirt, held the lantern high. "A mouse?" Christian ventured as the dog's tail thumped the floor, waking my parents, I was certain.

The dog backed out with a deer leg bone, fresh meat still attached, the pungent scent now filling the room.

"Indeed."

"Jonathan! David Jr.!"

I heard my brothers laugh from beyond the wall. My sisters giggled. I opened the door and shooed Sheppie out, bone and all.

We settled back. "Emma," Christian began again. He lay on his hip, his arm up over my forehead, twirling a lock of my hair.

"What was that?" I heard something swish against the window. Could it be raining? The weather had been fine. Then what sounded like hail hit the panes, followed by the rapping of a snare drum, and then the tubas and the french horns and trumpets woke up the neighborhood. The colony band stood outside our window. A charivari they called it. It was a French event that we Swiss and Germans adopted, meant to celebrate newlyweds on their bridal night. I sighed. Nothing would do now but that we invite all the musicians in and anyone else who made their way through the moonlight to our door, where they would be served wine and cakes and would chatter until they had their fill and went home. Hopefully before dawn.

"At least your mother has cakes to give them," Christian said as he pulled on his britches. "Or who knows what pranks they'd play on us. In some places they kidnap the bride and ask for a ransom of sausage on the bridal night."

"I'd make them pay you to take me back," I said. Christian laughed. He walked to the window and waved at them, but the music didn't stop. "Maybe they'll make us both go with them like on New Year's, *Belsnickel*ing until dawn."

"*Ach*, no," he moaned, but I could tell by the smile on his face as he turned from the window that he was pleased to be chosen for this silliness by his friends and brothers. Most men married younger than he was now, and I think it made him feel welcomed to the fold to have been chosen this, regardless of his age.

"I hope they don't make us go from house to house playing and eating with them," I said. "Or we'll never get to sleep."

"*Ja,* sleep. Or whatever else, *Liebchen,*" Christian said. He'd never used a lover's name for me before. *Liebchen. Sweetheart.* He kissed me then, and I wished this silly charivari could be waylaid until another time. He released me, letting me go first, patting me on the back the way his mother did. I vowed then to make him love me as one who would hold me tight forever, and that one day, I'd be that lover filled up enough to step away first but not far or for long.

"We may as well get this over with," he said to Jonathan's pounding on our door, the younger ones laughing and the dog yipping beyond. Even my father was thumping something on the floor. A broom handle perhaps, thrust against the ceiling.

"Let me help you finish dressing."

Such a wedding night, I thought. Such adjustments I was asked to make!

Christian set the lantern down to help me put my crinoline on. "What's this?" he asked.

Only then did I remember the double row of ruffles he now held, the pale cloth cascading over his wide hands.

"Just a little luxury," I said. "No harm meant." He grunted. I kissed him on the end of his nose. "I choose life," I added. "Remember?"

5

Sent Out

We separated the next day. Oh, not over the ruffles. Christian laughed at those when I told him when they'd been sewn on. "That's a good thing to do when you feel overcome by rules," he said. No, we separated because our leader knocked on our door early in the morning, reminding Christian of a meeting scheduled. My husband leaped from his bed, performed not seventy-five pushing-ups but seventy-six, then dressed and left. When my husband returned, he told me he was being sent out and would be gone some weeks.

"But what of our home? What of our plans? Can I go with you?"

"Now, *Liebchen,* you knew this was a part of who I am."

"But we haven't even talked of where I'm to stay while you're gone or even considered that I might go with you."

"Out of the question," he said, though he kissed the top of my head. "Be restful, *Liebchen.* My going tells Wilhelm that our marriage will not interfere with what needs doing here. Or wherever he sends me."

He assured me he would not be far away and that he'd post letters. "South," he said. "I'm going back to the hills of Kentucky. The government leaves people alone there. Or maybe the hollows of old Virginia." He stopped, thoughtful for a moment in the midst of pulling on his boots with the jack. "Did you know that when Virginia colonized, only the Anglican Church was recognized there? But when the Scots-Irish Presbyterians and Calvinists came south from Pennsylvania, the Virginians let them have their preachers so long as they settled in the hills and acted as a buffer between them and the Indians the aristocrats feared. Isolation served them well, and it will us too. They're hard-working, these potential converts, and not interested in gaining wealth through owning land. They just want to lead faithful lives and hunt and fish and worship as they please and do what is right for their families. They are whom we wish to bring to Bethel."

"How long will you seek them?"

"I don't know. But you're in safe hands here," he said. "Taking care of each other while one is gone is another gift our colony gives to one another." Then he kissed me soundly, picked up his valise, and left.

Perhaps I was naive and inexperienced, as Helena suggested, but I had a sense that Christian's leaving had been purposeful, meant to separate us. But it would not be a wedge between us unless I let it. We'd married. Our leader would one day have to come to terms with that fact.

In the weeks that followed, I began to pay more attention to those married in our colony, how they tended their families. *Frau* Giesy and I often met at the storehouse, where we would pick up flour as we needed. I took more time to listen to young wives expecting a child, knowing one day I'd be there, cherishing this precious gift of life. Mary Giesy, Sebastian's wife, wore a loose dress, but I could still see that she was pregnant. She never stopped her working, and it seemed to keep her healthy, unlike stories I'd heard of women in Shelbina who stayed in bed while their babies grew.

I watched my parents more closely to see the tender ways my father expressed affection with a touch to my mother's waist as she stood at the tin-lined sink washing potatoes. At night, when their soft laughter rose up through the floorboards from their bedroom, I let it comfort me, to soothe the ache of missing Christian and the humiliation of a married woman still sharing her bed with two sisters. One day, I told myself, my husband and I will laugh beneath the comforter again, just us. *It will be my husband's warmth I feel against my back and not my younger sister's knees.*

Summer came and with it the outdoor work we all contributed to. We hoed and weeded the large cornfields that surrounded Bethel town. My father said Bethel was arranged, as in the old country, where people lived next door to one another, farmers and butchers and tailors. They knew their neighbors' business and could also help in time of need. Even though farmers rode their carts out to their fields each day, they weren't separated from other families by miles and miles, each living on isolated farmsteads, making their ways alone for weeks at a time. It was that way in many frontier settlements, with farmers not aware of town concerns and town people thinking they had little interest in the ways of laborers far away. They didn't come to help when a man was injured by a bullock or when a wife had trouble giving birth because they didn't know of the need. In Bethel, farmers rode out together to their fields and returned back each night. We helped one another. And like disciples of old, we went out to transform the world around us.

Christian had been "sent out." The other Bethelites who recruited in the South were all single men. I saw advantage to that now as I ached to start my life with Christian but couldn't.

Autumn pushed in through the steaming summer, bringing with it flocks of geese migrating south that sometimes settled in our cornfields before we could hurry them on with our shouts. Once the corn shocks were in our barns, we let the geese waddle over stubble. For me, everything seemed more vivid that autumn: the sounds of the geese calling, the scent of pork being smoked, the taste of apple cider on my tongue after a day helping with the harvest. My mother said this happened when a woman fell in love; the world seemed brighter, more intense. "Maybe I fell in love after I married," I told her.

"*Ja*, it would be like you to find a contrary way."

The colder nights and river fog in early morning brought bursts of color change to Bethel. Near the gristmill's pond, the maple trees turned red and yellow and all shades in between, and reflected like a mirror in the water. I held my breath one day walking past, and Mary, Sebastian's wife, bumped right into me as I stopped to stare. "Such beauty in this place! I wish that I could paint it," I told her. "So I could hang it on my wall one day. The white walls of the mill a mate to the blue water—"

"*Ach*," Mary said. "You shouldn't covet such things to hang on your walls. Only portraits should hang there or maybe your stitching."

I wondered if I blasphemed to think that man's creations could enhance what God designed. Or if wanting to remember such beauty could truly be a sin.

We Bethelites heard much about sin that fall, and our leader referenced "coming troubles at the end" that stirred his words to such frenzy at times that when I left the church I felt beaten as an egg. He'd give no date, unlike some communal leaders, my father said, who would tell their followers to prepare for Christ's coming on a certain day and then find they had to retract and explain when the date arrived without incident. Our leader spoke of ends, but he always finished with what I suppose he thought were hopeful words, saying God would provide a way out for us, a way for His followers to begin again. I could never tell if he forecast a heavenly change or if he referred to possible political disasters right here in Missouri.

How I wished that Christian sat beside me on the porch so we could discuss our leader's words. I had to write instead. When Christian wrote back, I took his missives to my room, pushed the little ones out the door, and savored them, alone.

He wrote with precise characters marching along the pages, his words providing details of what he saw and heard and even of the weather. He honored me with political talk, of how men in Carolina spoke less of slave and free than the idea that there might be aggression from the North, that one state could somehow impose its will upon another. *Even men who own no slaves will take up arms against the North should they invade,* Christian wrote. *Most living here are as poor as slaves, but they resist ideas imposed by aristocrats, Bostonians, New Yorkers. Yankees. Indeed, for them this disagreement isn't about slaves at all but independence, life without intrusion, something we at Bethel understand.*

But what I treasured most in Christian's letters was that he told me how he felt, how the sound of the Ohio River gurgling in the morning while he fixed coffee over a campfire made him think of my laughter. He described the elegant elms soaring up to blue sky and that the sight of them as he rode through their cool shade reminded him of my compassionate embracing arms and the strength I would give our children one day. He wrote of picking up a walnut, saying it was the color of my eyes. He wrote of missing me. *For so long I missed no one while I traveled, or so I thought. You often came to mind as I watched you grow up, Emma Giesy, and I imagined you as a loving niece who would one day find joy with a husband like Willie Keil or one of a dozen other young men smart enough to see the strength in you.*

Willie Keil? Surely Christian suffered a fever to ever imagine such a union as that.

That you should choose me, Liebchen, *and that I should at last see you as the woman you are instead of only the daughter of my friend, is truly one of God's great gifts. An old man I am and yet not too old. But I might have passed you by if not for your eyes meeting mine on Christmas Day and the prayer I saw in them that only God could answer.*

We became closer by this separation, something I suspect our leader hadn't planned for, and I wondered if I didn't get to know Christian better this way than if I'd moved into his parents' home and heard their stories about him. This way, I learned to tell my own.

I loved the way his words flowed across the page, and I read them again before I slept at night, hearing the low tones of his voice, feeling the quiver of my skin as I imagined his hands upon my body. I could hardly wait for his return, for then I imagined my life would truly begin.

———

I prepared for another Christmas without Christian. I worked hard not to hold resentment toward our leader. It would do no good to blame another for what was, only keep me filled with irritations that would grate at my soul like a file. In his letters, Christian gave no indication of when he'd return, but I hoped he'd come north as the geese flew south. I'd memorized a poem in English called "The Night Before Christmas" that I planned to recite to him, but I'd settle for brothers and sisters and my parents as my audience if no one else. I'd stitched a special pair of gloves for Christian, helped tan the hide myself, and they were wrapped in brown paper tied with ribbon. We called the Christmas Eve gift bearer Kris Kringle now, who'd leave his gifts snuggled within the branches of the tree. Our leader said it was more American to do it this way, and he wanted anyone who might ask or wonder to know that we Germans were loyal to the country.

It was Christmas Eve, and my father called to me to hurry down, to bring a candle so he could restart the fire. I mumbled something about letting it go out and Jonathan or David being capable of such, but I did as I was bid, only to be swung into the arms of my husband, who nearly smothered me with kisses.

"You're back!"

"Rode all last night," he said. "And through this day, which the Lord blessed with sunshine instead of snow. It is good to be home."

Christian brought me fruit and raisins, and when we opened gifts, he took from the branches of our tree a wooden box that had my name on it. It was a pair of woolen mittens like every other pair available at the colony store. I hid my disappointment at wanting something just for me, something purchased on his travels to reassure me that I'd been on his mind. But I soon pitched that thought, grateful he was home for this holiday. *That* would be his gift to me, that he'd arrived. He unwrapped his gloves and admired the special stitching. "I could have used these," he said. "The days are cold alone in Carolina."

Upstairs, as we prepared to bed, he pulled out another package from his pack. He removed the twine covering it.

I held up a new crinoline, one with rows of ruffles circling the skirt.

———

I never wanted to stay in bed so much as I did on Christmas morning. We lingered in each other's arms. "It's our bridal tour we never had," I told Christian as I ran my fingers through his now-full beard, tinted auburn. "Taken in my own bedroom where I grew up." He squeezed my hand, kissed the palm. Then I asked, "Did you come back on your own, or did he call you back?"

"Both. I said I thought it time to return and brought several families with me. He did not protest and so I'm here, to stay now for a time. To go back to tinsmithing and begin my life with you."

My family had already left for worship, and because we'd found it difficult to leave the comfort of each other's arms, it was nearly 4:00 a.m. before we'd crunched over the snow and reached the church. Like schoolchildren caught after the bell, we separated and slipped onto the benches, facing each other across the aisle. The service had already begun, with Willie carrying the *Schellenbaum* this time and standing beside his father, though a step below.

Christian looked toward me often. At first I wondered if he minded that last year he'd been standing beside our leader, and now he sat across from me. But then my face grew warm as I read into his eyes not the envy of a man replaced by our leader's son, but the memories of our sweetest holdings from the night before.

Father Keil's sermon soon stripped away our dreamlike reverie. He talked of change, of needed change. He spoke first of literature, not biblical verses, telling us that *Uncle Tom's Cabin* was a book that caused consternation and would swirl the world as we knew it and this was as Daniel said and John wrote and there would be a terrible war between good and evil and it was our duty to prepare and to protect our families.

It seemed a convulsive text to preach on Christmas Day, harsh words disgorged to pit against tender skin prepared to dwell on charity and love, on God's gift of grace and precious treasures already opened on Christmas Eve, and the peppermints and fruits that would follow with *Belsnickel's* good cheer. I hoped that Christian wasn't taking our leader's dark words too much to heart. I wanted nothing to intrude on this sweet new beginning promised earlier that morning in my husband's arms.

The dance later brought friends to talk with Christian, and I was included in the Giesy gathering of sisters-in-law and their chatter. No one raised the issue of Christian staying with them until we built a house, so I assumed our time apart had erased that plan. I served with *Frau* Giesy and smiled quietly at jokes made about my one day bringing forth a baby as Mary soon would. For me it marked a recognition of my married state, a recognition I felt I'd never truly had.

We heard the pounding on the front door early the following

morning. My father answered, but it was my mother whose "Oh, no!" sent chills through me. Christian slept, and I eased myself from beneath his arm, pulled a quilt around me, and slipped downstairs.

"What is it, Papa?" I asked.

"It's Mary Giesy. Her baby comes too soon," my mother answered as she grabbed for her cape.

"Should I come with you?"

"*Ach,* no. Your father takes me. You tend to your husband and your brothers and sisters should they wake."

But before I could fix potato pancakes for the household, my parents returned. My mother yanked at her bonnet and tossed it in a heap on the table, something I'd never seen her do before. Jonathan looked up in surprise. Catherine's eyes brimmed with tears. I shushed the little ones. My father took her cape and shook his head at us. She pulled at her soiled apron, couldn't get the bow undone, and when my father attempted to help, she slapped at his hands, and then he turned her to him and held her as she sank against his chest and wept.

"I could do no ting," she said. "No ting at all."

"You did what you could, Catherina. It is all we are asked to do."

"But his words, *Herr* Keil's words. I have never heard such a ting, to say that the baby died because of some sin of the parent. Why does he say such tings?"

"The words are biblical," my sister said, her voice soft.

"But are the words meant to bring Mary relief when she lies with her body having given all that it can? Those words have no comfort, and they cannot change what is. The baby has died. Now the parents are asked to bear guilt as well as grief?" My father stroked my mother's back. She pulled away from him, looked at his face, tears wet upon her cheeks. "I don't understand this, David. I don't. Biblical words like these...out of all he could choose...no. These are not the words our

Lord would say, not when He so loved children. He would grieve with Mary and Sebastian, not prolong their pain."

She left us then, but I could hear her quiet cries from behind their bedroom door.

By mid-January, our leader called us all together for a major decision. Women were told to gather too. "There is free land in Oregon Territory," our leader told us. "If we claim the land and live there before the end of 1855, we can each have 160 acres that could start our new colony. Married couples can claim twice the amount. Scouts I send, as Joshua did, send them into this foreign land. They will spy for us and bring back the word, and then we will all go, those who wish to leave here and be in a new protected place where the trials of the larger world will not intrude. No one will be forced to leave, but many will wish to. I wish to," he said, "when the right place is found. These spies—nine I send—will leave with no wagon, only their horses and pack animals. As soon as it is spring here, no later than April. They will do for us what we cannot do for ourselves, be good servants who will save us in the end."

"Is this necessary?" Karl Ruge, the teacher, dared to ask. "You've moved so often, and this is Bethel, a place of worship. We have been here not yet ten years. Are we in such danger?"

"Our young people fall from our ways," our leader told him. "Parents have been letting them grow up in a blasphemous and unspiritual life. It is time we found a new place where government does not wish to interfere with us and where the rules are not yet so bogged down in political mud that we can still make paths through to homes of our liking. No one will care if we have communal coffers from which we draw to take care of ourselves. No one will question how we conduct our business. No one will be lured into sinful ways."

I wondered how the new recruits that Christian had brought back with him would take this. They'd uprooted their families, and while they had no homes of their own yet, they were settling in, finding out about the charity of this colony. Most stayed at Elim's second floor. None wanted for food or clothing or shelter, and each found work to fill their days, even through these winter times, and so had already begun to feel a part of who we were at Bethel.

I wondered what Christian thought with his efforts to find new land south suddenly set aside. Would he see his efforts as failures? It might be a high price to pay as I saw it. But if he had failed, then he'd be unlikely to be sent out so soon again.

Our leader narrowed his eyes at Karl. "We will miss the coming storm if we go to Oregon Territory, while those here in Missouri will be in the center of it, mark my words."

Silence filled the church, a place I now thought our leader had chosen for special reasons. Usually our gatherings were at Elim, not in this sacred space. To defy him here, to disagree with the way he saw the world he'd define as blasphemous, would take strong courage.

"Who do you send, Wilhelm?" my father asked. "There are many willing to follow you and to trust in your vision as we have before."

Our leader nodded appreciatively at my father as he began. "Joseph and Adam Knight. Good brothers. They will go. Stand, please," he said. "Adam Schuele. John Stauffer and John Hans Stauffer, father and son. John Genger." I looked at John Genger's wife. She sat straight as a knife. Each man stood slowly, and I wondered if this was the first they'd known of our leader's choices. I looked down the aisle at the women in their lives. Stunned looks crossed their faces. The weight of future separation formed lines to their eyes. I felt my own heart begin to pound. "Michael Schaefer Sr., George Link." I counted. *One more to name.*

My father hadn't known who would be called to go; at least I didn't think he'd been planted to ask the question of our leader. But now I looked at him, and he chewed his lower lip, perhaps in disappointment that his name had not been called, perhaps in hopes it wouldn't be.

"And one last," our leader said. My father looked up, expectant. "Christian Giesy."

I jerked my head toward Christian. He bent over as he stood. He would not look at me, but I knew he heard the silent *"No!"* screaming from my speechless throat.

6

A Woman's Lot

I should have known, and I suppose my heart did know before my head, and that was why it chose to pound as I watched those men stand. Did their women feel as I did? A blend of pride and pout, a disappointment for us while carrying honor reflected from our husbands and sons.

Adam Schuele had located the Bethel property with my father; he'd been sent out before but never quite so far and to such a wilderness. None of them had ever been gone so long. It would be at least a year, more likely two, before they returned. My father's mouth drooped; my mother patted his arm. She looked relieved.

"You've given enough," I told Christian later in our room, my voice a whisper so as not to let my parents hear. "Doesn't our leader see that these separations are not good for families? Why does he insist we find a new colony now?"

"We've grown closer with our separations. You said this yourself."

"Do you want to leave Bethel? You bring people to it and then you leave? What must they think?"

"They didn't follow me, *Liebchen*. They followed their hearts. Their belief in God brought them to this place. They won't harbor anything against me. Why do you?"

I tried pouting, but he pressed my lower lip with his finger and smiled.

"I'll go to him," I said, "and tell him you must stay home now and that we will start our family."

"*Ach*, you talk like a *Dummkopf*," he said, throwing up his hands. "You can't change this, so you must accept it."

"*Nicht jetzt.*"

"Yes, now," he said. He raised that one eyebrow that I'd come to see as a warning for me not to press too far.

I flopped on the edge of the bed, arms crossed. "He wants me to endure the pangs of childbirth as my wage of sin. So he should let me have time with my husband…so I can later suffer."

A sad smile crossed his face. "How you talk," he said. "A mix of stubbornness and spirit. May it one day be converted into faithfulness and strength when you grow up." He turned away from me and didn't see my mouth open in protest. "It is an honor to be selected. We won't be gone long. Only a few months out, and then we find the land, and then we come back."

"But when you find the perfect spot, won't someone need to remain there to hold the land until the rest of us can arrive? Who'll stay?"

"The leader will stay, I would guess," Christian said, but he wrinkled his brow as though he hadn't thought of that before.

"And who leads?"

"Wilhelm hasn't settled on this yet. We all meet and make plans, all the men and those chosen to go. We know what we look for. Isolation. Good timber for homes. A mild climate without hard snows. Fertile soil for our farms. Maybe a few settlers there so we will have others using the gristmill but not so many people that they poke into our business. We'll find such a place. Already people coming back from the gold fields say Oregon Territory is where the real treasure is, all that free land."

"All that is claimed goes into the colony, *ja?*"

"As at Bethel and Nineveh. It is our way."

"My father would go in your place if you asked him," I said. "He looked so disappointed when our leader failed to call his name."

"Emma." He turned to me as he sat at the side of the bed. "This is not something you can control now. I will go and I will come back, and you will continue as you have until we travel out together with the colony. Then we'll begin our life."

"I want to start our life together now," I wailed. "People don't always come back. Something could happen to you."

"Last year more families traveled there on wagons than ever before. They have new lives there, new chances."

"We have no need of new lives. This is a good life here in Bethel if I could ever begin it with you. If there is something wrong, we can make it better. Our leader can solve the problem that sends us on our way. I'll tell him so."

"Not one word of your protests to Wilhelm. Not one word. Your interference in this might cause him to prevent my going, my doing the work I'm called to do."

It occurred to me only then that perhaps Christian had the wanderlust, that quality of some men who never settle in one place, who are always seeking other hills to climb. His preaching and recruiting gave him reason to roam. He might never stay at home even if we had a child of our own. I felt a chill go through me.

That momentary insight changed the way I looked at him, altered how I thought he saw our marriage too. Like a woman riding on a pillion behind her husband, we traveled the same road but arrived at our destination with very different views. We had different hopes, it seemed, save that we each said out loud we wished a family.

That's what I'd have to focus on, then, making sure we were together no matter where he chose to go, so we could begin this holy work of raising children. I'd either have to convince him to remain here while others headed west, or that he should take me with him.

———

Routine laboring in the colony continued without change through spring. Only the chosen men spent extra time with our leader making plans; only the wives and daughters and mothers of these men moved between pride at their men having been chosen and their own trepidations at being left behind. At least Christian remained with me in my parents' crowded home. At least I could watch his morning ritual of pushing-ups, even if the rest of the day I felt more like a sister and daughter than a wife.

The colony would provide for all the families while the men were gone, that was not a concern. But seeing them go, not being sure if they'd come back or when, that's what troubled, I suppose, as it had women who watched their whaling husbands set to sea or waved a last good-bye to the backs of soldiers as they marched away. We'd memorize their profiles, the outlines of their backs, and cling to these fading memories long after the taste of their last kiss had dried upon our lips.

We'd also dream of a home in the new land, one that would be more glorious and grand than the ones we had in Bethel. That wouldn't be hard for me, not having a home of our own. I'd be left to help my mother with the children and share my bed again with sisters.

I sought a plan. I could show myself as someone needing reining in. If our leader thought I couldn't be left alone here, without a husband to control me, he might then require that Christian stay in Bethel with me.

But when I thought of what I might do—talk overly loud at Elim gatherings or slack off at the glove factory or act peevish with Helena—

the efforts appeared so childish that our leader and maybe even Christian would just laugh and tell my father to keep his thumb on me while Christian headed west. Or worse, my parents would be shamed, and Christian, too.

I considered raising dissent among the newcomers. It might not be difficult, as a couple of the Kentucky families newly recruited had already left us by February. Christian said they'd found nothing wrong in Bethel but that they realized they wanted to claim ownership of land, be able to plant what they wished when they wished, hunt when they wanted. The process at Bethel told them well that this would not be the case as a part of the colony. Our leader decided such things, and most of the men went along with him. Those who didn't, left.

I could be vocal about not understanding why people left. We lived in America, after all, where we ought to be free to make choices. I hoped my words would find their way to our leader and perhaps he'd suggest to Christian that he best stay here to keep my tongue in check.

"You've been encouraging dissent," Christian told me in our room that March evening not long before my birthday. We were readying ourselves for bed. "I hear of it."

"Nothing others aren't saying out loud," I said. "We're free to have our say, even us women. I'm surprised anyone listened."

"You don't know the hardships of women who alone with their husbands and children try to claim a land. *Ja,* they end up with their names on a document. But they alone must do the work, as there are no others invested in their success. If their crops fail, they have no storehouse to deliver grain for their families. It is not all roses, *Liebchen.* You do a disservice when you tell people only of the difficulties of the colony and only the joys of settlement on property alone."

"Many of the newer recruits came from small farms," I said. "They know the trials." I picked up my hairbrush.

He sighed. "You are destined to cause me pain."

"I only want people to know what we're about, and that we are not all perfection, as our leader would have us believe. We do have tragedies here, too. Look at Mary. And our leader blamed her for her baby's death. Do you think he was right?"

Christian shook his head no. "But there is a time to disagree, Emma, and a time to keep silent."

"I'm not well-versed in keeping silent," I said. I pulled my brush through the long strands, rolling the loose hair from the brush into a tiny ball that I could later weave into a wall hanging. Maybe I'd tie a ribbon around it and slip it into Christian's saddlebag so he'd remember me after he'd gone. I forced myself to stop thinking that way. He just had to stay here with me.

"Your words bring suspicion and discord where it need not be, Emma. Will you stop it, for me?"

"Stop talking about the virtues of owning one's own land?" I said.

"About your view of life here. It…unsettles people to hear you speak such things while I'm away."

"Perhaps you shouldn't go, then," I said. "Or maybe in my own house, I'd find a better way to see things."

"Any new home must go to the new recruits, Emma. You have a fine place to reside. It would be selfish to live in your own home alone, a waste of colony labor to build for us when we are leaving."

"That's the point, though. *I'm* not leaving. You are."

His galluses hung loose at his side, exposing his shirt, his wide chest. He took in a deep breath and clamped his jaw shut. His fists rolled up tight, then released. He exhaled a long, slow breath. I stepped back from the force of him. "You will stop talking in the way I've asked, Emma." He'd never given me a direct order before.

"Or?"

"Or face consequences I do not wish to name."

"Because?"

"Because you are the wife of the leader of the Oregon Territory scouts. And you must act accordingly."

———

As leader, he'd remain behind in the Oregon Territory once they found the new land. That meant more than a year before I'd see him again, more likely two. Here's where I'd stay, beneath my father's roof, never in a home of my own.

Pray? I suppose I might have tried that route. But our leader always led our prayers during worship; at home, my father did. We read the Scriptures and did discuss them, but most of Bethel lived content to let our leader set our spiritual tone and be the intercessor for our needs. Our leader would hardly offer prayers for my contentment. I was on my own and beginning to wonder whether my prayers, like my voice in the colony, were ever heard.

I'd have to make Christian want to take me with him. I imagined what miracle would make him do this, what intervention would cause him to set aside the dangers or demands of such a journey so he'd include a woman in the undertaking, one woman, his own wife.

I'd have to press the shared goal we had to begin our family. He'd turn forty this year, 1853. It was time he had a son. I needed to remind him of his mortality and his duty to his wife. Ruth's words from Scripture came to mind: "Whither thou goest, I will go." Perhaps he'd listen to that.

I packed a basket of food. We'd taken a horse cart to the center of town, which offered a kind of park. Keil had laid out Bethel beautifully, with wide streets and trees planted on either side. At the park, a bandstand offered a sheltered place for concerts in the summer. It was deserted in March except for an early crocus poking up through the earth and a wild goose or two. Sheppie trotted on behind us, chased at the geese. Then he panted, waiting for Christian to finish chewing on the chicken leg, sure my husband would toss the skin to him.

Christian wiped his beard with a napkin. "No women on this journey," he said when I raised the issue.

"But you said yourself that more families headed west last year than ever before. Whole families. Including women and children."

"They took wagons, Bethel wagons, sturdy and well built so they had plenty of supplies. And there were others in the party, other women. Ours will be a fast journey of all men, horseback. We've had special saddlebags made to carry what we need. It's not a trip for a woman."

"Those missionary women, that Narcissa Whitman and Eliza Spalding, they rode sidesaddle all the way to Oregon," I said, "years ago. They had no wagons."

"They hooked up with a fur trading group from Hudson's Bay for protection. We'll travel as light as we can to move quickly, act as our own protection. Indeed, God as our protector." He chewed again. "No, Emma," he said to my open mouth. "No women."

"But that will mean another year or more before I bear a child for you. Another year of my dawdling as though I'm married without any of the accoutrements of marriage: no home, no child, no husband at my side. What am I to do?"

He took pity on me and held me. "You're young," he said. "You have plenty of time to have things go your way. There are many who need your help while I'm gone. You can serve them; prepare yourself for when the whole community crosses the plains. Let your kindness rise like cream."

"Cream sours," I said. "I don't just want things to go my way. I want you to have what you said held meaning for you. A wife and family, both."

"*Ja*," he said. "I have a wife. A generous one. I'll settle for one out of two."

———

By early April, having made no progress with Christian, I took my case to a higher authority, asking for an audience with our leader. I was visiting Mary Giesy when Willie stopped by and said his father would see me then.

"We'll talk later, Mary," I said. Her face blotched from the tears she still shed daily over the loss of her son. Just a few more weeks and he might have lived. So small, so tiny, smaller than the palm of her husband's hand. Being with her reminded me of my mother's outrage at our leader's condemnation of this woman. She'd done nothing wrong that I could see. While I believed that our leader had God-inspired visions that led him to the faith and the way we practiced it in Bethel, I also thought his humanity clawed through sometimes, tearing up what God intended. Finding Mary and Sebastian Giesy responsible for their infant's death tore at my sense of fairness and the image I had of God. The God my parents shared with me offered hope rather than the picture of One who stunned His followers with tears over unknown sins so powerful they could cause their child's death.

They would try again, Mary told me, but she worried. "If I can't name what I did wrong to cause the early birth and neither can Sebastian, it will happen again to us."

I wanted words to comfort her. "All we can do is ask forgiveness for whatever sins we commit, even the ones we can't name," I told her.

Mary's purest desire was to live her life so her children would be healthy and well and grow up strong. In my years of knowing her, she'd been close to that perfection, much closer than I'd ever be. She worked hard, lived cleanly, always sat attentively at the sermons, unlike me. She was even more generous than my mother, and my mother gave her all. She actually believed it important not only to give to others so they'd have what *they* needed, but also that in sharing into the common purse, what we gave became not just someone else's, but *ours.*

Unfortunately, considering Mary's virtues highlighted my less-than-angelic ways and our leader's dire warnings about childbirth. I might well be storing up some trouble of my own, when that day came, with my headstrong ways.

I pitched those thoughts aside while Willie walked with me to his father's home. He'd brought Gloriunda with him, and we held the child's hands between us, lifting her every now and then into a swing. My arms ached, and I felt tired from all the nights of sleepless turning, trying to find a way for Christian to stay at home.

"My father said he only had a moment," Willie told his sister as we walked. "So not much time for swinging."

His sister giggled and leaned back, knowing we would catch her, knowing we'd both lift her up. "There's no sense in fighting it," I told him. "When a girl sets her mind to something…"

"*Ja,*" he said. "Especially a German girl."

———

I had one chance, I knew, one opportunity to convince our leader that I should be allowed to go along. I was certain such a request had not occurred to him. He'd be expecting me to beg him to let Christian remain behind. My husband would never raise the issue of my going west. He'd only do so if our leader thought it wise or if he ordered

Christian to do it. Christian would not directly disobey an order. If our leader had forbidden our marriage, I'd still be Emma Wagner with Christian a husband lost to me forever.

"So. We talk again, *Frau* Giesy," our leader said. He wore his long coat for the occasion, but he bent to work at his plants, mortar and pestle in hand. He hadn't motioned me to sit, so I came to stand across from him at the high table. Dried plants lay like corpses between us. "You have news to share with me?" he said. "I hear you share news with many."

I swallowed. "No, no news."

"*Ja,* you tell our new families it would be better to live elsewhere than at Bethel."

"I only discussed what people already spoke of," I defended, "after one of the Kentucky families left. I didn't know them and had nothing to do with their leaving."

"You want to leave yourself, *Frau* Giesy?" He raised both bushy eyebrows at me. He reminded me of a horned toad.

"I go where my husband goes," I said. " 'Whither thou goest, I will go.' I'm a faithful wife."

His voice softened. "Ruth of the Scriptures went with her mother-in-law, not her husband, Emma. Those are a widow's words you speak."

"I fear I might become a widow," I said, "should something happen to Christian on this journey west."

"Ah. You are fearful. This is why you ask to speak to me." He motioned for me to take a chair, and then he put away his plant musings and pulled a chair up before me. Not the inquisition format, but one of a father to a child. He acted the kindly *Belsnickel* who granted gifts at Christmas. He was the "Father Keil" my own father referred to, someone loving who cared for each of us as though we were his own. So many loved this man. Why was I so suspicious? "Tell me what is on your mind."

"I…I think it would be good for Christian, my husband, if I went with him on this journey west."

He raised his eyebrows again, assessing me as though I were an object in the distance he wasn't sure was friend or foe. "This is not even worth considering," he said then and started to rise.

"No, wait. Please, just entertain the possibility," I said. "You always tell us to think creatively, to use our God-given abilities to solve a problem. Remember when you came up with the plan to make a drill to go through the pine logs so they could act as pipes with seams tarred tight? No one had ever done such a thing before."

"It was ingenious, that plan for the fields."

"Yes. So just consider my going along. Please."

He took it as a puzzle, I think, a small challenge from a mosquito buzzing at his ear. "Vell, then. You'd slow them down, I think. This is one reason you cannot go."

"I'd cook their meals. It would free them to make better time."

"You'd tire and they would have to stop for you. You're tiny, Emma. Now your sister Catherine is a big girl—"

"I've never been ill, not once. I know remedies, too, so if one of them became ill, I could minister to them. Perhaps even help others we meet along the trail. Wouldn't this extend our Christian love, our Golden Rule, to serve strangers we find in need? We could even tell them of our mission. They might wish to join us. A woman's presence would suggest family, safety."

"*Our* mission," he said. "You assume much, *Frau* Giesy."

"Only that we are all communal here, so it is our mission whether we go or stay."

He stared at me. "The separation will make you grow fonder of each other, you and Christian, so your hearts will be fuller when you meet again."

"As it did this past year," I said. I paused. "You may be right. Our love just grows stronger as we're apart. Perhaps we should be separated and never discover each other's faults. We will always be on a bridal trip."

He considered that, tapped his finger against his thigh. "Where there are women, there is dissension. How would you explain away this fact, should you go with the scouts?"

"There'd be only one woman."

"And what of the others? What if all the spies wish to bring their wives or sisters or mothers, someone to take care of them, because you are going?"

"Have they brought this to you? No? Then it is safe to say they have no interest in traveling with their men. I do. My husband has been taken from me—sent out in service, I mean—for more months of our marriage than not. I miss him, Father Keil."

"What does Christian say of this?"

"He thinks you would not approve." I ignored the fact that Christian also thought it wasn't wise and that I was not to bring the subject up, ever. "But you know he wants a family and while he is your age, Father Keil, he is well behind you with your nine loving sons and daughters. How will we populate the new colony if not with the children of your loyal followers?"

He adjusted his glasses. "We will populate it by taking more than two hundred people from Bethel with us when the site is found out west and by gathering new followers to our way."

He had that finality to his tone, and I could feel myself losing him to some prepared text. I'd have to put my last ladle into the dutch oven.

"How am I ever to experience what God wants of my womanhood if my husband is never with me?" I wailed it almost. "It's what you said God required of a woman, to conceive so she can know such pain as to be reminded of her sins and save her soul."

"You remember our discussion, then, that you were meant to bear the turmoil as penance for Eve's sin?"

"Yes," I said. "You are wise, Father Keil." I bit my lip against the bile I felt rising in my stomach for my demure demeanor when what I wanted to do was shout.

"Perhaps you have learned something in these past months. I'll think about this," he said. "Then let Christian know."

"No, no!" I grabbed at his arm as he stood. "If your answer is no, please don't tell him I've come to you. Please. He'll be distressed that I've disobeyed him."

"He told you not to come here?"

"He told me not to even think about going with him. He never dreamed that I'd bother you with my concerns."

He pursed his lips, pressed his palms against his thighs, elbows out, and held them that way.

"Perhaps I erred in preventing you from knowing all that a woman's lot entails. Perhaps Christian needs to understand why I could not bless your marriage." He stood, paced back and forth, hands clasped behind his back. I sat still as one of his discarded stems. Then he said, "I *will* send you out with them. You will have the chance to bear him a child, though such a hard journey might cause you to…but both of you believed you were meant to be together. Now you will have the chance to know for certain."

Would Christian blame me for my manipulation? Or would he celebrate that we now had what we both wanted with the direction, if not blessing, of our leader?

"I wouldn't consider it if Wilhelm hadn't suggested it himself,"

Christian said when we lay in bed that night. Our leader had called him into Elim, he told me, and with the others scouts gathered he'd affirmed Christian's leadership of the journey. "Then he said that you would be going with us. It's as though he read your mind, *Liebchen*. His kindness and his vision know no end."

"You don't object, then?" I asked.

"It's an answer to my prayer. He said we'd waited long enough to begin our family. This is a double blessing."

"The first being?"

"That Wilhelm thought of this on his own, that he understood then that ours is a marriage ordained by God." He kissed me. "Still, if you were already with child, I'd make you stay behind even with Wilhelm's suggestion that you could prepare meals for us and minister to any ills we have." He stroked my face. "The trial of the journey might make it difficult for you to conceive, but it will be good to travel with you, to share what we'll discover there together."

"Once in Oregon, we'll find shelter and the promised land our leader says is there, and all will be well," I said.

So Wilhelm had let a lie stand, or at least had let Christian think my going with them was our leader's idea. I wasn't sure I liked conspiring with our leader against my husband, nor discovering that our leader and I had something like a deception in common.

"All will be well, *Liebchen*," Christian said and snuggled close to me.

Within minutes I heard his breathing change to a man in restful sleep, but I lay awake for hours and wondered how far along the trail we should be before I told him we could expect an infant in October.

new Schooling

I enjoyed the attention offered me by this journey's twist. Some of the looks came with clicking tongues, as from Helena and *Frau* Giesy, though neither dared protest too much, since our leader had proposed this idea of my "being sent" as one of the scouts.

"Even ordered that you go, I heard," Helena said. "What strangeness. No woman has ever been told to go with scouts. Men have much to do to carry the message of our religion. Women will be in the way."

Her words reminded me of a time when I was thirteen and Christian Giesy had just returned from one of his journeys south. Perhaps I fell in love with him that hot September day, now that I think of it. We were all in the vineyard harvesting grapes, as the nights had been cool. Our baskets were full of the purple fruit, and several children swatted at bees to keep them from devouring our harvest. That was my task, too, to swat at bees.

Christian rode by on his big horse, and as people recognized him, they stopped working and shouted hellos, welcoming him back. He shook hands with the men, and I remember their grips left purple stains on his wide, soft palms. He dismounted and wiped his wide forehead with the back of his arm, adjusted his hat and pushed it back on his head. His teeth were naturally white, not yellowed as my father's, and his big smile seemed just for me when I handed him a tin cup of fresh water. "It's pleasant to be served on a hot day, *Fräulein* Wagner," he told

me, treating me as though I was someone. "A traveler misses such tending when he has to look after things for himself day after day."

"It's a cup you made," I told him.

"So it is," he said, turning the tin in his large hands. His long fingers wrapped around the cup gently, as though he held an instrument.
He started to put the cup to his lips, then stopped as a wide-eyed boy
stepped up beside me. Christian said his name, squatted to his height,
then offered the cup to him. The boy drank, handed the cup back to
Christian, then scampered off. "His mother's a widow," he said, as
though I didn't know. "Will you refill me?" He handed me his empty
cup. I didn't correct him; no one can fill up another. But I did replen-
ish the liquid. "We both do the Lord's work," he said after he finished
drinking. He turned to talk with the men, then I eased to the sidelines,
watching until Mary called me back to my task.

When I asked my father later what Christian meant by both of us
doing the Lord's work, my father quoted Scripture to me, James 1:27:
" 'Pure religion and undefiled before God and the Father is this, To visit
the fatherless and widows in their affliction, and to keep himself un-
spotted from the world.' That's Christian Giesy for you, always serving.
And you did too, offering cool water for that boy. Christian put the
boy's needs first. That's what Father Keil wants for each of us, to serve
in such ways."

I considered how I could serve on this trip despite the reservations
some might have about my going along. Certainly, there wasn't a rule
against having fun while being a servant, was there?

"You'll take herbs with you," *Frau* Giesy said. She became practical,
accepting things without protest. She might have even enjoyed the challenge of preparing a woman for a scouting journey. She wore her hair
braided three times like a crown on her head, unlike most of the women
with chignons. But then her hair might have been quite curly, and such

gaudiness she would want to hide behind braids. "Herbs offer a service you can provide, and will keep my son and the other scouts well." She patted a loose hair into the braid ring. "I suppose he will worry less with you along."

"My thoughts exactly," I agreed. "I'll make his long days light."

"*Ja,* I'm sure," she said.

"Let me show you about cold camps," Louisa Keil told me at the storehouse one day, where I picked up flour for my mother. "You must make meals quickly for them, often without a campfire. We will prepare pemmican and jerky before you go. Many dried peaches, too. Willie I'll send to listen carefully when men arrive to pick up their wagons. He can tell what overlanders claim as critical to take with them and what they think they can purchase in the West. Whatever else is needed, we'll bring with us when we follow in a year or two." She looked away, distracted. "Perhaps God wishes us to go around the Horn, travel by ship to California, then north?" She put her fingers over her mouth to silence herself. "What am I saying here? *Herr* Keil will decide such things. He always tells me, 'You women stick to your *Strudels,* and let us men deal with travel and theology.'" She dropped her eyes, touched her fingers lightly to the part separating her hair, and slipped away.

A part of me admired Louisa's devotion and acceptance. But another part of me wondered if one day as a leader's wife I'd need to be so docile. I pitched the thought.

"Oh my, oh my," Mary repeated, when we carried the milk bucket together. She'd pulled her hair back so tight it made her eyes look like almonds. "This is wise, you think? How can it be good? You with those men, those spies?"

I wondered why some thought of us as spies, while others considered us scouts. Maybe it had to do with whether we were colonists seeking asylum in a hostile land, or whether we went ahead as foot soldiers, pioneers, making a way for our friends. I preferred the latter.

"Our leader would not have suggested I go if it wasn't a good plan," I told her, already believing he had, in fact, presented the idea. *How quickly our minds tell the story we prefer to remember.*

"My husband says you've angered Father Keil, that he sends you along…as punishment."

I blinked. "Maybe your husband underestimates his brother. Christian approves of my going. Our leader must trust Christian's judgment and Christian trusts his. It's going to be fine, Mary." I took the heavy bucket from her to carry it on alone. "I'll have lots to tell you when we return."

She followed along behind. "Once you find a site, Christian will have to stay to start clearing the wilderness, that's what Sebastian says. I won't see you for a year or more, not until we come west and find you."

"Sebastian doesn't know everything about the future," I told her. "Christian is the spiritual leader, and he'll do what's best for us all. That might mean coming back so he can safely lead all of you from Bethel."

"*Ja,* maybe," Mary said.

My mother shook her head when I told her about my going and my joy in it, but she wiped the worry from her face. "I hoped you would outgrow your need to be…headstrong."

"You and Papa joined our leader when you were older than I am now. You followed him into a wilderness, and see what it gained you. A good home in Bethel."

"We followed our hearts, believing God called us to come here," she said. "Is God calling you to do this thing?"

I asked a question back, something I noticed men did when they wanted to avoid giving answers. "Papa's grandmother joined the Inspirationalists at the colony at Amana, isn't that so? Didn't she raise her voice and say what she thought best? She was accepted and respected. Men followed her inspirations. Maybe this desire to go with my husband into a wilderness is in my blood. Besides," I said, picking at a loose thread on my plain wool dress, "our leader did suggest that I go along."

The more one said a thing the more it turned to truth.

She smoothed my hair back into its chignon. "And did you protest to him, 'Don't send me west with my husband, I beg you'?"

I shook my head.

She sighed. "I suppose he did think of this himself. No woman has ever gone on any of the outreach missions before. Ever. Why *now* is the question. Unless Christian asked for it, but this I doubt based on his reservations."

"My husband spoke with you about this?"

She blushed then. "*Ach,* the walls are too tin in this house."

She turned her back to me, resumed rolling the pie dough I'd interrupted her from finishing. When she spoke again I could barely hear her. "I will miss you, Emma. I will miss you terribly, my daughter who wishes to be known."

"But you'll come when the others come in a year or so, after we send scouts back. You and Papa and Jonathan and David and everyone else. We'll find a place that suits you. We'll be a family again."

Her shoulders sank as she kneaded the dough. "Your father has moved enough, he says. And I am tired too. Too tired to start anew in a wild place." When she looked at me again, I saw that floured fingers had left white streaks on her cheeks when she wiped at her tears.

She wouldn't see her grandchild unless I came back with the scouts. Well, that would be my task then, to ensure that my child would know what it was like to be held by a loving grandmother's hands. Christian would have to assign someone else to stay in the Oregon Territory to begin building. He'd have to bring the news back himself, and me and his child with him.

I considered telling my mother about the baby, but if anyone knew that I expected a child, especially Christian, then everything would change. It wasn't enough that I wanted to begin our family for Christian's sake. I cherished something more.

"I'll have to be the adventurous one for us all," I told my mother. "And hope that Grandmother's spirit travels with me."

———

We would leave on April 23, the day after our wedding anniversary. Our plan included arriving at Independence Rock by the Fourth of July so we would miss any of the heavy mountain snowfalls. That was all I knew from my husband about the arrangements. I learned little more from the women. The scouts shared few tidbits with their wives, mothers, or sisters.

Louisa Keil, Mary Giesy, and I prepared beef pemmican we wrapped in canvas bags that could hang over a horse's neck just in front of the saddle.

"Will you ride sidesaddle all that way?" Mary asked.

"Of course she will," Louisa answered for me. "She wouldn't want to disgrace us by riding like a man would. What would people think?"

"Why would we care what strangers thought?" I asked. "We'll ride through groups of wagons and never see them again."

"Oh, but you might," Louisa said. "As a spiritual leader, Christian must be always at his best. He might recruit new members. You'll want to put your best foot forward, Emma."

"You think that would be the foot that hangs over that uncomfort-able hook on the saddle all the way to the Oregon Territory?" I said but laughed. Louisa smiled like an indulgent mother at a challenging child.

We wrapped cheese in chunks and made hardtack, heavy biscuits that would go into tack boxes especially designed for packhorses the scouts would lead behind them. I wondered if I'd have one, too, but Louisa said she didn't know about that. She'd only been given instruc-tions about the food. I thought she might know more, but Louisa sup-ported our leader without question. She always had a response if someone raised a tiny question. He must confide in her to make her uphold his every word, but she shared little with me.

Frau Giesy wrapped dried herbs inside flat tins with tight covers. "Remember," she told me as I worked beside her, "ashes are a good way to stop blood flow from a cut."

My own mother gave me a sewing kit with several leather laces. "They can mend most anything," she told me. We sewed pockets into my skirt hems and placed in them soap cakes the women of the colony had made together the previous fall, following the rendering of hogs. "I see your crinoline has ruffles stitched to it," she said, raising an eyebrow. I started to explain, but she shushed me with her hand. "They'll make good bandages should you need them, as they're already cut in narrow strips."

"The underslip was a gift from Christian," I told her.

She patted my hand. "Even frills and needless adventures can be turned into something useful, Emma. If a person is willing to adapt and let the Lord lead."

Christian rose on Easter morning, then left without waking me up. I slept more soundly than I had before, and I wondered if dreamless rest helped me push away the little "strand of fear," as I called it, sinking in to sleep whenever I thought of telling Christian he'd soon be a father.

I dressed and met my parents downstairs, and with my arm wrapped through my brother's, we all left together in the dawn for the Easter service. Crows lifted against the pink sunrise as we walked toward the church, and the smell of wet earth and freshly turned soil rose to my nose, a comforting scent. My parents moved on ahead as a slight breeze blew, and I stopped to tighten my dark bonnet.

"Our last walk together for a while," Jonathan said, "and you make us late." He scolded, but when I looked up at him, he brushed at his eye. "Something blew in it," he said, turning away.

"I'll be back," I told him, catching up to him and grabbing at his elbow. I skipped out in front of him, all of them, and walked backward. "Next summer. After we find a place and return to get everyone here ready to come, we'll walk again then."

Jonathan shook his head, no. "Something will happen. It always does."

"You might marry by then," I said. "That would be a good something. We can write in between."

"The letters will take forever," Catherine piped in. "It won't be the same without you here, Emma. It just won't be."

I couldn't disagree with that.

"You have Willie and Jack Giesy and Rudy and each other. The boys are full of fun, Jonathan, and those terrible rhymes. You can make them up too. You'll be in the men's band before long and—"

He pushed past me, rushing ahead, leaving me behind to cover a distance that suddenly loomed desperately far and lonely.

Our leader chose texts for his sermon that told the Resurrection story, of the new life that each of us has and how Christ's ancient followers did not believe at first in the sighting of Him, or that He was no longer dead. Our leader even mentioned that a woman took the message first to the men, a fact of Scripture I had read but an admission that surprised me coming from our leader's lips. *"Ve* must always look for Him, alive," our leader concluded, "as Mary did."

It was a joyous sermon, one that reminded us that the Lord went before us and made our way, even when we sometimes had difficulty seeing His work within our lives.

Then he spoke of Joshua being sent out to discover what kind of land awaited the Israelites and urged those he sent into the wild to trust in Providence to guide and protect us. " 'As I was with Moses, so I will be with thee: I will not fail thee, nor forsake thee,' " quoted our leader.

Then he invited each of the scouts to stand before him. I started to stand, but my mother held me back and shook her head. *"Nein,"* she whispered. My face felt hot. I hiccupped once.

I wasn't really a scout; I understood that then. I was merely a guest on this journey, not one who had anything to offer, not one whose journey needed a blessing.

Our leader invited elders of the church to come forward. The men, my father included, placed their hands on the shoulders of the scouts while our leader prayed for their safety and safe return, referring to them all as spies going into the wilderness. I thought Christian would turn toward me, invite me up, but he didn't. I felt my shoulders droop. My mother put her arm around me and whispered the same words directly into my ear after our leader said them. When I looked across, Jonathan stared at me, but I couldn't read the message on his face.

Following the Easter sermon and prayers, the children looked for baskets of hardboiled eggs several of us had hidden in the churchyard the day before. The women baked ten-inch-long rabbit cookies, and I heard Louisa's youngest and my sister Louisa laugh in delight when they located the sweet treats. My mother said it reminded her of Easter celebrations in the old country: rabbit cookies and eggs, the laughter of family and friends. I'd miss this next spring, but I would plan an Easter hunt of my own for our child.

At the community meal held later, some outsiders came by. Having heard about our large meals on special days, people from Shelbina often rode in and were invited to stay. We welcomed curiosity seekers—or at least we had. We always made guests feel welcome. Our leader said they were all potential recruits, though when they later declined involvement, he often blamed outsiders for bringing into our midst moral decay and the longing for lavish ways. This day, the two young men ate well and talked with the colony men about horseflesh and tack. No one spoke about our impending journey with outsiders present, so it was not until late that evening, after Christian's final meeting with the spies, that I was alone with my husband.

Christian hardly spoke a word as he undressed in our room.

"Which horse will I ride?" I asked as we lay beside each other on the feather bed.

I received no answer. Instead, I heard the soft breathing of a man taken in sleep.

Is he angry with me? Will he be like our leader and share little with his wife? I told myself his silence grew from the journey's weight, but it occurred to me that I had much to learn about my husband's moods. Discovering them in the presence of eight other men on a cross-country journey might not be the place most young wives would choose to learn of their husbands' dispositions. Well, so be it. It was not my fault I knew so little of him; our leader had kept us separated from the start. At last, we'd be together, I the only woman on the journey west.

I pulled the quilt over my shoulder. I'd wanted to be singular and here I was. My husband snored softly, and I thought then as I drifted off to sleep that the schooling I'd just signed onto might be more than I had bargained for.

8

So Many Questions

We prepared to leave early, to the melody of songbirds and crows. That morning, I learned I'd ride sidesaddle on a sturdy chestnut-colored gelding named Fred. My father thought mules might be wise for the pack animals. Christian agreed and thanked my father for the suggestion, one we had no way of knowing would later serve us well.

I savored the flushed faces of friends there to see us off, knowing our leader approved of their delaying the start of their workday in order to celebrate this adventure. Well, he didn't call it an adventure. To our leader and his spies we performed the Lord's work, undertook a serious and purposeful activity. I tried to remember that, but the sweet scent of spring and the profusion of faces there to see us off kept bringing me back to joy.

Christian's somber face reminded me of the concern expressed by our elders about why we were making this journey. The evils of the outside world pushed us into it. Outsiders lured Bethelites away. The railroad threatened to steam through our town, bringing strangers from even farther off to wash away the established colony routines. Our leader worried that we young people were losing our piety and ability to follow God. Hadn't there been rumors of an unplanned infant born into the fold? Hadn't that young girl and her family moved away? These intrusions brought us to this day, not the adventure of a journey into the unknown. Yet that uncertain unknown called to me.

I took deep breaths, tried to soak up every sight and sound and smell of this stepping-off place. I would see things and hear things and know news no one here would learn of unless we told them. I coughed into my handkerchief to veil the grin that would not leave my face.

I learned then of more details worked out in advance by the many meetings Christian held with the others. Fred, my horse, would walk in front of Opal, a white mule I had sometimes walked behind when spelling my brother in the fields. Opal's packs carried a dutch oven and ten tin plates and cups that Christian, one of the colony's finest tinsmiths, had made himself. We scouts—as I preferred to think of us— packed pemmican made not of buffalo meat, but of beef cut into thin flakes and hung to dry before a smoking fire. Papa pounded it into a powder, then packed it into skin bags and poured grease in it to make it solid and sound. We could eat it raw or boil it with a little flour and have a nutritious meal quickly prepared. Flour, tea, sugar, biscuits, Edward's Preserved Potatoes, and cooking grease were packed in canvas bags, enough to take us all across, we hoped, knowing that as we moved west, the prices for products would go up.

Papa also suggested a mixture of cornmeal, cinnamon, and sugar, which he said I should stir into water for a good drink along the trail. His eyes teared up as he told me, a tenderness I'd savor as the miles between us grew.

My mother packed the mixture in an oversized oiled bag and patted it as she pulled the flap over the side of the pack. "When it's empty, you can use it for so many tings," she told me.

Other items needed we planned to barter from better-stocked wagon trains or buy at the forts along the way; we expected to shoot deer or elk as the occasion arose. We'd need to be careful with ammunition, but being frugal and orderly were a Bethel colonist's middle name. Anything we couldn't get for a "good deal," we'd do without, though Christian said we had money enough to look prosperous to appeal to potential recruits, but not so wealthy we invited the attention of thieves.

Christian announced these arrangements to the entire crowd, as a way of engaging each of them in this journey and so they'd know how to pray for us in the days ahead.

We hoped for a wet spring in the prairies so by the time we rode through, the grass would be high and lush and our horses and mules able to feed. Michael Schaefer Sr. silenced anyone who aired concern about Indian troubles or disease we might encounter on the way. "We do the Lord's work," he said. "Worrying is not part of our labor."

"*Ja,*" John Stauffer said. "If I thought it so, I would not have brought my son with me." Hans Stauffer was stockier and taller than his father, the son a security for his father and each of us.

My youngest sisters and littlest brother played and patted Sheppie. They didn't understand that I'd not be seeing them for months, though when the girls sprawled their elbows out at night, they might remember me with fondness by my absence. Catherine actually cried as she said good-bye, then pressed a small German Bible into my hands. "You'll need this," she said.

"Christian will have his along," I told her, attempting to hand it back. "We can only take so much."

"Take it," my mother said. "Each of us needs our own bowl of wisdom from which to draw without having to ask another."

Later I'd be more than grateful for both my mother's words and the book Catherine gave me.

Mother fussed at the cape she wore against the morning chill. My father shook young Joe Knight's hand, then turned to his old friend, Adam Schuele. "I remember when we were sent out those years ago." Adam nodded. "Your good judgment kept us from trouble more than once. This time you have my daughter to look after."

"*Ja,*" Joseph Knight interjected. "For better or worse." He looked at me but didn't smile.

"The prayers of the community, David," Adam Schuele said. "This is what will keep her safe. And us, too."

I tried not to think of the sadness in my father's eyes, focused instead on his hand gently resting on my mother's shoulder as she tried to untie her cape and keep William in check. Successful, she threw the dark green wool around my shoulders and pulled me to her. I felt the bones in her back, tried not to notice how she quivered in my arms. "When you need a mother's holding," she said, "you put this on and think of me, Emma." The cape hung longer than my own, since she stood taller than I.

"I will, Mama," I whispered, "I will."

Finally, it was time. I held each of my sisters and brothers in turn, told Mary I would write. Christian mounted without offering me assistance, so I led Fred to the riding stump and stepped onto the stirrup, swinging my leg high enough to hook my knee over the saddle hook. I had never felt secure on a sidesaddle and more than once had ventured through a field bareback on a nag, just to see what it would be like to ride with greater confidence. But this day I took it as a small sacrifice made to join my husband on this journey.

I adjusted my wrapper over my legs. The wrappers we women wore when we left the colony to go to Shelbina or Hannibal or other outside places served me well now. Made of wool the color of a wet ash, it folded in at a woman's waist and tied with a sash but had room for growth. The overfold prevented anyone from seeing a woman's curves or their absence when she lost them to a growing infant. Like a chrysalis, my wrapper kept the secret of my butterfly beneath its gray.

I laid Mama's cape out over the back of Fred, who pranced a bit, and I nearly dropped Catherine's Bible. I placed it in the saddle pack, then tied the front of the cape at my neck. My mother's hug wrapped me up in her lavender scent.

Adam Schuele's family waved good-bye. All the Giesy clan came out to say farewell to us, or at least to Christian, who steadied his horse next to mine now. Helena did pat my knee as it hung over the sidesaddle. She said she hoped I chose well and that it wasn't too late to change my mind.

"*Herr* Keil will understand if you decided to stay behind," she said quietly as she looked up at me. "He has a gentle heart and would listen to the pleas of a young woman."

"*Herr* Keil is the one who told me I should go. I wouldn't want to upset him," I said. "It's for the good of the colony," I added. "What a woman sees and sends back will reassure the rest of you when you follow. Besides"—I leaned over to her to keep my voice low—"I wouldn't want to challenge Father Keil."

Helena stepped back, her lips pursed. She folded her hands before her as though in prayer. Our leader stood in the center of the half circle we scouts formed around him. He draped his arm around Willie's shoulder. "Willie vill ride in the lead vagon when we leave Bethel to go to the place you choose for us. All of us depend on you now, each of you, to listen to God's Vord and His voice to lead you to the very best place for us to continue His vork. Pay attention to each other," our leader said. "Send back vord of vhat you've found and we vill follow. Be salt and light in this new vorld."

Following this he offered us a blessing general enough to include even me, and the brass band played a German marching song that made my eyes water, knowing it'd be months, maybe years, before I'd hear those horns again.

We started out, and then my brother Jonathan ran along beside us, as did several other young men, Sheppie, and a few other dogs, until we rode around the bend that marked the outskirts of Bethel. There Jonathan grabbed at Sheppie's collar, and the men stood and waved until my brother was nothing more than a tiny dark thread in the quilt that had been the comfort of the only home I'd known. I felt an awful chill.

———

The first day, Christian told me, would be our "rhythm day," finding the preferences of the animals, which horse needed to be in the lead, which could follow easily behind another without wanting to rush ahead, which pack mules would likely tangle us up if we didn't attend to their wishes. None of us owned the mules or the horses we rode, as they belonged to the colony, but Christian at least sat astride a horse familiar to him, unlike the rest of the men and me. The pack animals, too, needed time to adjust to their loads and the hitch of the ropes keeping everything even.

When the road toward St. Joseph narrowed, I brought up the rear, usually with Christian and his pack animal riding beside me. Opal, the mule, pulled against Fred at times, twisting the horse, but with occasional words from me to the mule, Fred was able to move along easily again. "Opal likes attention," I told Christian, who responded with something that sounded like, "She's in good company." But when I asked him to repeat it, he said, "She's in a good place in this company then. You can talk to her back here and keep her in line."

I'd vowed to be as quiet a scout as I could be, not to question what Christian did or directed, and to treat the men with deference and respect. They did know much more than I about being out in the world, and I vowed to watch them as I did my husband. Silence was my word for the day. Silence and listening and seeing so much I'd never seen before.

We rode on dusty trails northwest and passed small acreages with men and women already working their fields in the early spring. Cowbells joined the music of the lambs' bleating, and I could almost taste the feast of new life that always came with the melting of snow. We rested the animals ten minutes of each hour, allowing them to rip at grass while the men checked packs and took drinks of water. The other fifty minutes, we rode steady with little chatter.

It's what I wrote in my journal that evening: *silence,* the whisper of wind while I slept beneath the stars for the first time in my life, the quiet warmth rising as I lay next to my husband in a bedroll, the comforting noise of fingers scraping on tin plates and the smack of lips with our first meal of beef jerky and hard biscuits washed down with spring water. The men said nothing while we shared the meal that Adam Schuele prepared, not me. I wondered if it would be this way all the way to Oregon Territory, and if the meal was an offering of servanthood by Adam or a statement of no confidence in my abilities. When I tried to help he said, with gentle words, "I'm accustomed to this, Sister Giesy. Let me."

Following the meal, Christian offered a Scripture and words of prayer and encouragement—at least that was how I took them. The men nodded and kept their heads bowed as my husband spoke, rising as one to his "Amen," then moving in silence toward their bedrolls.

In the notepad I packed, I wrote of being away from the sounds of the shoe factory, the mill, church bells, the cackling of geese, the thump-thump of my mother kneading dough in the morning, my father sharpening a knife against a big strap of leather, Jonathan riding a horse down the streets of Bethel followed by yips from the dog, William's little snores that sounded like kitten whimpers. I wrote of hearing my husband preach for the first time—at least it seemed like a sermon—and how humble he acted, how willing he appeared to be molded by what the Lord should provide, and his trust in the mission our leader had set us all on.

The other men laid their bedrolls some distance from us, but I could hear an occasional cough and a mumble; a moment of laughter, too, and I wondered if Christian missed being with them, felt stuck here with me. He would have been lying next to them; perhaps they'd share ideas about the route, about the day, about life.

Yet here he was with me. I hoped he wouldn't come to resent my presence.

"I wish we'd brought a dog along," I told Christian in a whisper as I put my notepad away and crawled in beside him.

"*Ja*, Adam Knight said that too. A dog would let us know when trouble comes. We should have thought of it."

"There'll be dogs along the way," I said. "Maybe we could find one that would suit us."

"Unless he was a pup, he'd be loyal to another and eventually leave us anyway," he said. "And a pup would give us headaches getting into the packs at night, chewing the saddle strings."

"I'd watch him," I said.

He didn't respond.

"I would. It'd give me something to do while the rest of you are all working together so hard." He stayed silent, and then I realized by his slow breathing that he slept.

I wondered if our days would be like this: hard, silent rides with shared meals and prayers but few moments to truly be with my husband. And when I was, would not his mind be on the challenges of the mission or on seeking exhausted sleep?

His responsibility in this journey struck me for the first time as I watched the stars, and I hoped, even prayed before I slept, that I would do nothing to trouble him, nothing that would get in the way of my husband's success; though when I, warm beneath my sleeper, prayed those words, I felt a twinge of regret.

I turned over and decided then not to tell Christian anything about my carrying his child. Why worry him when he had so many other worries, and perhaps this one might never come to pass. It was possible I'd lose the child, a thought that sent more than threads of fear through me, threatening to knot up in tangles. That sort of thing happened even in our colony with good care and midwives to assist. *Look at Mary and Sebastian,* I told myself. Better to keep this all silent, wait and see what each day might bring. Besides, this day had already cracked me open, watching my brothers and sisters and parents disappear from my life; I couldn't afford to split my heart further.

I tossed and turned, trying to get comfortable. I slipped my hand up under the quilt rolled beneath my neck. I felt something cool there, hard. I pawed beneath it and pulled out a tin chatelaine. Slender as a finger, it had tiny designs on the side, a flower, a small bird. I removed the cap and inside were four sewing needles, the finest Shelbina had to offer.

Christian must have made it! But why didn't he give it to me? Why let me find it beneath my quilt? I held the gift in my hand. It had a ring so I could wear it around my neck. My husband gave me a gift both pragmatic and beautiful, and I, I kept secrets from him.

Our leader's words from Genesis of a woman's punishment came to me. But oddly, so did the words God said to Adam and Eve first: *Where art thou?*

Where was I, indeed, leaving the safety of my family, carrying secrets, hiding a possible harm from my husband whom I barely knew, who had dimensions and depth I was only now uncovering? What else was I hiding from, and what price would I eventually pay for my wanting to be known, to stand out in this monotony of colony I'd grown up in?

I'd have to eventually tell Christian about the baby. Would he forgive me for not telling him or our leader, who would surely not have sent me along if he had known? At least Christian would believe that of *Herr* Kiel.

I was not so sure. It might have made our leader more likely to have banished me to a wild place, to show me the power of God's words in Genesis that promised I'd bring forth children in sorrow. I tried to remember the rest of that verse: *Thy desire shall be to thy husband, and he shall rule over thee.*

But there'd been earlier words, spoken to Eve as she came out of the Garden, naked and ashamed, words that now spoke to me, a woman who had the will to choose her way. They were words not about the present, nor the future, or what my pushing to be here would eventually mean. They were words about my past. How had I gotten here? What price had I paid? What had I feared would happen if Christian had left me behind?

I prayed for sleep then and that I'd accept the answers to so many questions all begun with God's words to Eve: *What is this that thou hast done?*

9

As Singular
as Sunrise

I counted days by sunrises, noting their distinctive spread of dark to light, the way the pink gave way to ivory clouds against the morning blue. Each noon, Christian read from Lansford Hastings's *The Emigrants' Guide to Oregon and California* until we'd all heard every word written by this man through Christian's booming voice. He halted on occasion, translating from the author's English into the German we all spoke. Adam suggested we should hear the words in English to accustom ourselves to the language of the land we now lived in. The others nodded agreement. No one looked to me.

The writer of this guide blended his enthusiasm with details about river crossings and camping suggestions. But listening, even in the English I still struggled with, it gave me a sense of belonging, of hearing what they all heard at the same time even if some of the subject matter prickled. I hoped I'd find some small piece of information that I could later draw on that might save the day, that would please Christian, make him grateful I'd come along for more than someone to warm his bed. I didn't want to be a burden; truly I didn't. I wanted to belong and not stand out because of trouble, but from what I could offer. I wanted to be as reliable as sunrise, yet as singular.

Christian finished reading the Hastings book the day before we

reached St. Joseph, where we hoped to catch a ferry. Hastings had recommended this Missouri River crossing and the road that would take
us west, following the Platte River. He related details of what each
wagon should contain and what routes were wise and what to be wary
of at various watering places.

More than once in the few days we'd been on our way, I wished we
had a wagon hauling items such as kegs of water and stores of food and
extra clothing more easily reached than that tied up in the bedroll knots.
I had only one change of clothes—a woolen dress, another wrapper, and
my ruffled petticoat—and before the second day passed, as I watched
women doing laundry along the way, I realized I'd probably adjust to the
smell of my own perspiration rather than endure the effort of scrubbing
and pounding at rocks near streams along the trail. Doing my wash and
Christian's would be work enough. For a moment I longed for the large
group of women who scrubbed their laundry together at Bethel. I
pitched that thought. *No sense hanging on to what will not be.*

Most of all, I wished a wagon for the privacy it would have provided when I tended to my hygiene; in the shade of it, if not inside.
But a wagon would have slowed us, the men agreed, so during our ten-
minute respites for the animals, I found a tree or shrub and hoped such
sentinels of sanitation would continue to dot the landscape as we
crossed the continent. I imagined discovering shrubs with new kinds of
berries I could squat behind, increasing my understanding of botany
while managing bloat.

Hastings's book for emigrants did not promise such extensive trees
or shrubs once we reached the prairie country. His little book ignored
most of a woman's needs, so I hoped he might have misunderstood the
importance of mentioning such facts. Instead, Hastings wrote words
that encouraged early starts with longer rests at noon to manage the
daytime heat, or identifying prudent encampments and explaining how

to avoid "noxious airs" found near muddy waters. The author of Christian's noontime read spoke little of diseases and had written his book back in 1845, after the first cholera epidemic, but before this most recent scare that still plagued travelers' westward journeys. After reading the section about "muddy waters" and "noxious airs," Christian urged greater caution at watering sites. "We'll boil all drinking water not from springs," he said, so that we might all arrive healthy and well.

"We'll ask about illness on the wagons we encounter," he told John Stauffer, who patted his horse's neck as they spoke. "They'll have sent scouts ahead and may know of places we should avoid."

"Scouts sending out scouts," Hans Stauffer said. He removed his hat to scratch at his head where an early receding hairline made his hair look like a brown peninsula with white sandy beaches on either side. He scratched that spot so often that a callus formed on the right side.

"How I felt about you sometimes," Adam Knight told his brother, Joe. "When you'd run off as a *Dummkopf* and I'd have to catch you before Mama found out you'd left the yard or were so lost you whizzed your pants in fear."

"At least I explored a place or two over the years," Joe Knight said. A pink flush formed on his cheeks. "While you were busy chasing skirts."

"Joe!" Adam chastised. He nodded toward me.

"Oh, sorry, *Frau* Giesy. I forget you were here."

"I suppose that should be a compliment," I told him, curtsying as I handed him a refilled cup of corn juice. "I don't want to be a bother."

"No bother," Joe replied. He raised a single finger to the air, one of his habits when he spoke.

"I didn't wish you along, *Frau* Giesy," Adam said. "But you weren't no trouble this past week, and you even helped some."

"That might make a fine epitaph," I said. *"She weren't no trouble and she even helped some."*

"Let's not think morbid thoughts," Christian said. "Indeed, you'll help even more before long, become a true member of this scouting party." His words lifted my spirits.

"*Ja?* How will I do this?" Were they going to let me cook then at last?

"You'll be in charge of washing our clothes," Christian told me.

Unintended, my lower lip pouted out.

———

I confess, the excitement of wagons and horses and mules and oxen and people with accents closer to mine—*are they Swiss or maybe from Bavaria?*—intrigued me when we reached St. Joseph, Missouri, where Christian had said we would cross the great river. I heard French and what I assumed to be Spanish intermixed with English, and within an hour my ears hurt with the barrage, and my head ached from deciphering. What were all these people doing here? Where were they going? How would they know when they got there? I began to appreciate that we scouts had criteria, we knew what we needed to find and why we were seeking. Wilhelm held all of us together even in his absence, his words of life and death reminding us of the little time we had in the former and the encroaching hot breath of the latter. Did these others traveling west trust only Hastings's words? Or perhaps the leaders of their wagon groupings? I began to think about leadership and what it meant to the success of our task.

We had all we needed for our survival, were secure in our journey west.

We staked the horses above the ferry, awaiting passage while Christian and Adam Schuele, who understood English the best, prepared to venture forth to find out how long the wait for the ferry crossing would be. Adam headed south.

Christian asked, "Would you like to come along?" I beamed. "You'll need to watch where you walk to avoid horse apples and garbage plaguing the streets," he told me. I didn't mind. I could enter a world I'd never known. I'd love the confusion of people.

"I thank you for the gift," I said. "You were asleep when I found it. I didn't want to wake you."

Christian nodded. "You'll have need of it, mending our clothes."

"My mother sent her sewing kit with me. But this"—I patted the chatelaine hanging beneath my bodice—"the designs on the chatelaine make it more than just a tool. It's…art. Beauty for its own sake."

Christian's ear turned the color of tomatoes, and he seemed relieved when tent store hawkers offered meat on sticks and wild-eyed mountain men announced "essentials" for sale for the journey west. Christian's height caused people to step aside for us, though he never pushed or shoved his way. He tipped his hat to women and children, and I wondered what it would be like to understand all their English phrases as easily as Christian did.

A buxom woman with a painted face must have heard me talking to him in German, for she stepped out from the shade of her tent and smiled, boldly placing painted fingernails on his forearm. She said to me in German as she gazed up at Christian, "Your papa here is a handsome man, maybe in need of someone to look after his *kind*."

I frowned. "I'm not his *kind*." I added in English, "I'm his wife, not his child." Were these the kind of women that Willie and my brother spoke about in whispers after they'd come back from Hannibal?

She stepped closer to Christian and patted the lapel of his jacket as she inhaled his scent. The drift of her perfume rose over the garbage smells from piles around her. "*Ach,* my foul luck," she said, slapping Christian's lapel now in good humor.

I put my arm through Christian's, something I'd never have done in a crowd back in Bethel, where I'd have walked a pace or two behind.

She stepped away but kept eyeing him as though he were a good horse. "I always have an eye for the unavailable."

"Do you have an eye for the time of the crossing?" Christian asked her. "I suspect you've seen these lines before and know how long it'll take."

She stretched her neck to look at the rows of wagons and cattle, people and dogs, that crowded toward the narrow docking area. "Days, I'd say. By wagon?" she asked. "You go west by wagon?" Christian shook his head no. "Moving fast then. Someone on your tail." She leered at me.

I gripped Christian's arm. "*Ach,* you are a—"

"Our marriage is blessed," Christian said, "and our journey, too." She lowered her eyes just a moment, and Christian spoke into that interlude. "You could have such assurances too, *Fräulein.* There is someone always available, someone who would care for you as a parent loves a child. A whole community exists of people who love each other, who serve and demonstrate God's grace on this earth. No needs go unmet. It is a place of Eden."

"An Eden on earth," she snorted, then looked down, stuffed a handkerchief into the cleavage exposed at her breast. "There are always snakes in gardens."

"All the better then to enter all gardens with others."

"One day, perhaps." Her words softened. "If it were me, I'd go north to Harney's Landing. Takes you sooner to the Platte. It's about thirty miles south of Nebraska City, what they're calling it now. Used to be Old Fort Kearny. Ferry's good there, I'm told. Not so long a wait."

"I thank you for your help, *Fräulein.*" He tipped his hat to her again, as though she were a regal lady. "In a year or so, a larger colony will come this way, and you'd be welcome to join us. We're Bethelites. Mostly German, in service to each other as we're commanded."

"If they're as handsome as you, I might join up," she laughed.

"Not the best reason to come along, but God can use even that," he said.

"Danke," she said. "I'll consider it if my fortunes don't pick up." Then she ducked back under her tent awning.

So this was how Christian won people over, not only with his smile and dazzling eyes but with his tenderness, his ability to see through the thick perfume, look past the sagging cleavage. He listened to what she didn't say and treated her with a dignity I hadn't thought she deserved, not with her suggestion that I was too young for Christian or that our marriage couldn't be real. He stepped over those things.

"What did you think of that woman?" I asked as we walked away.

"It doesn't matter what I thought," Christian said. "Like you, she is a child of God and therefore my sister. So I love her just the same."

The same as me? I felt a rush of some emotion I couldn't even name.

———

Christian and Adam Schuele compared notes upon our return to where the horses grazed. We'd made camp a good two miles out of town, as already the grass had been ripped clean by earlier wagons passing through with their stock. We agreed we'd head north, but Adam suggested we take the steamer *Mandan* up the Missouri River instead of going by land.

"We can afford this?" Hans asked John Genger.

John Genger frowned. I'd become aware of the separation of duties of the men. Hans Stauffer handled the stock. The Knights did the packing and cooking and determined when we needed to stop to check packs and ropes and seek supplies. The Stauffers were skilled at finding agreeable sites for our stock and for us to camp and seemed to have a unique understanding of landscape and weather. Adam Schuele and Christian did the negotiating with people along the way and brought into the open any issues needing decisions. George Link hunted and handled the weapons and ammunition. John Genger, the quiet one, kept the money and the records of expenditures.

Back in Bethel, I'd never even heard John Genger talk, and Mary Giesy once told me she thought he might be Jewish. At least one Jewish family lived within the colony, my father had told me, but he never would say who they were.

The unsavory task of laundry became my expertise, but fortunately, these were tidy men more interested in speed than in sanitizing often. Like me, they were anxious to enter land they'd never encountered before, land beyond the Missouri.

"I think we should not spend the money this way," John Genger answered.

"It'll save us time to go by steamer," John Stauffer said. "Our goal is to get west as fast as we can, find the site, and send some of us back to bring the main colony forward. The sooner we do this, the better, *ja?*"

"The steamer would rest the stock," Adam Knight said, nodding in agreement.

"We must save all the money we can in case we need to buy our land rather than get free Oregon Territory land," John Genger said. "This is not wise to spend so freely when we are only out a few weeks." He wore a small-brimmed hat that couldn't possibly shade his eyes from the sun, and he squinted as he spoke.

"You're the banker, John, and we value your advice," Christian said. "We'll pray about this tonight, and we will all decide in the morning."

We will all decide. I wondered if that meant my view would also be considered. If so, I'd vote with John, not because of the cost but because of the steamer. It was worrisome enough to think of crossing a swollen river, but to be on a larger body of water, well, the thought of that made my mouth dry. I hated the lurch of boats and their uncertainty, the need to place trust in the captains and pilots. I had to watch the weather more whenever we went somewhere by boat. I had to grip the sides and never rested, not once. I secretly thanked my parents, who preferred carriages over canoes.

But no one asked my opinion, and so I didn't have to disagree with my husband in front of the others.

In the morning, it was decided. Each man awoke to some assurance that taking the steamer north would be the wisest course. Even John Genger concurred. This surprised me. I hoped for a rousing debate with John taking my side, since my voice wasn't invited into the fray. But no, it appeared all were satisfied with the choice to spend the money and rest the stock. This consensus Christian labeled "God's will."

"Why are so many heading westward?" I asked Christian as we waited to board the steamer, my heart pounding, seeking diversions. The line for the steamer wasn't nearly so long as that of the ferry. "Were they all so unhappy where they were?"

"We didn't leave from unhappiness," he said. "We left because we were sent, for the good of those left behind. We have a privilege to pre-pare for the decisions that matter most in life, not just how to live, but where we go when we die. We listen to our leader and follow his advice. He leads us by his passion for keeping us from eternal damnation. I don't know whose advice all these other people follow."

"Aren't you frightened, even a little?" I asked.

He frowned. "Fear does not come from the Lord, *Liebchen*. I am cautious. We must be careful, *ja*, but not fearful." I rubbed my thumb and forefingers together. He held my hands in his. "Something bothers you? Your fingers tell me their story,"

I rolled my fingers into my palms, and shook my head no. "I feel a little ill. The water makes me dizzy, that's all. It will pass."

He pulled me to him, tucked me under his arm as a mother hen does her chicks. He patted my shoulder. I looked around to see if others frowned at this public display of affection. No one appeared to care. Worldly ways had merit.

"Perfect love casteth out fear," he said. "Perfect, as in complete. We have nothing to worry about."

Now was not the time to tell Christian that his wife objected to watercraft. I'd probably never be forced to take a steamer ever again. The prayers of the men had been answered, not mine. They had a more direct voice, I imagined, than a woman. That was a thought Helena Giesy might have. So this must be God's will, that they all agreed. Mine was a singular fear, one I'd have to swallow.

We were told to come back in the morning.

As we led our animals through the dust back to our camp, I decided it would be difficult to be a part of this jumble of wagons and horses and people and cows without knowing why we were leaving, or if we weren't well led. I had assurance to both of those questions, or so I thought. *Such assurance should help me overcome my fears.*

That's what I told myself as I took a deep breath and boarded the steamer the next morning.

10

Willing Things Well

My mouth watered, my fingernails burrowed into my palms, I felt ill and thought I'd lose my breakfast. I could barely keep my balance with the swirl and sway. But an hour or so out, I apparently got my sea legs, as George Link called it, his chipped tooth giving his words a kind of whooshing sound. I could walk along the deck without a wobble. The water pooling in my throat stayed swallowed, and I breathed in spring air. As the shore sped by, the wind dried my watery eyes. I could hear the steady swish of water rising up over the wheel, pushing us north. When I tired, I leaned up against our stack of packs and saddles piled on deck and pulled my notepad out to write in. I'd decided to describe the fearful parts, but list what went well, too.

I prepared a letter for Jonathan, and later, Hans loaned me a book he'd finished reading and said he wouldn't start it over for a time. I read, and the leather dropped into my apron when I slept as the afternoon heat warmed my face. I could still sleep.

When I awoke, I looked for Christian and found him engaged in animated conversation with a man. And another woman.

That feeling rose again, and I could name it now. Envy, what our leader once described as the greatest sin, for it announced awareness of the self; vanity—desiring more than God provided.

God had given me a good husband when we lived in the cocoon of the colony where each member understood our commitment to each other, would never think to flirt or interfere. Here, amidst the world where people spoke a different language than what I could understand, here the rules were different. Perhaps Christian might regret his vows spoken to a young girl. Perhaps he resented having to translate for me, felt embarrassed by a woman who could not speak English well or gather information that would ease our journey west. The buxom *fräulein* came to mind.

I jotted my worries into my journal and wrote to Mary then to take my mind from my sinful state. She would be working in the school in my place, I supposed, laughing with the children, suffering Helena, assisting Karl Ruge. I hoped we could post the letter somewhere along the way.

It would have been a placid journey if not for the weight of my worry. Not just about the river and how it could claim whole wagons, horses, and lives, but about my deception, for that was what it was. Christian loved Truth, changed his life for Truth, and here he was, unaware of a truth that would affect his life.

That evening, as Christian stood with his arm wrapped protectively around me, I considered again when to tell him. We curled up near our packs. John Genger had booked passage for us but no berth, no privacy. It saved money, and our exposure to the elements would be only for the night. Others, too, slept on the deck. I tried to imagine the best time to tell Christian so together we could enjoy the arrival of this child. But something told me I should wait. We were too close to Bethel here. I could too easily be sent back.

Nothing dreadful happened on the steamer north. It seemed sometimes the bad things I thought would happen didn't. Maybe by imagining the worst, I was able to keep them at bay. Helena said once, we should always think on worthy things, that Scripture encourages us toward joy not sorrow. But joy arrived to welcoming arms; sorrow needed reining in.

———

Instead of being bounced around and tussled, we eased through floating logs and flotsam, landing on the west side of the Missouri the next morning. At last we stood in "the West." We'd sleep this night in Indian Territory, as the scouts called it.

Maybe we were all regaining our land legs, but once on shore with the horses gathered together by the Stauffers and Knights, and Opal whinnying notice, we all stood silent for a time. The breeze played with my hair braids wrapped in swirls around my head now. I hoped the style made me look older. My bonnet hung loose at my back. I could say truthfully that I enjoyed this watery journey and wondered at such a change.

Around us, people bustled away, called out to friends and family, but we stayed silent, staring east. Maybe the men prayed.

Christian looked back across the water toward Nebraska City— what little there was of the town. I touched the sleeve of his coat. "What are you thinking of, husband?"

"Hmm?" He turned to me. The startling, longing look disappeared. "Just saying good-bye," he said. "Foolish. Not to worry, *Liebchen.*" He patted my hand.

"We'll be going back next year, and you'll see it all again," I told him cheerfully.

"Indeed," he said.

His absent-minded agreement made me wonder if he thought we might not return. "We thank God for our safe journey, ask Him to bless the remainder, and then we head west," he said to the group more than to me, his strong arms spread out wide as though he could take us all in, keep us all safe.

It must have worked—this plan of mine—to think of all that could go wrong to prevent its occurrence because little troubled us those first days. We rode our horses on the south side of the Platte and only had to hear about the rugged crossings of those who took the north side of the river. The men talked horseflesh with other travelers, and Hans even made a trade at a farmer's plot, turning over a tiring horse for a sturdier mount, a more willful mule who became a mate of Opal. We found good grass for them to graze on, and at least three times each week, we had wood to fire a hot meal in the evening.

Our camps were efficiently made, the beans cooked easily without sticking to the pan. Joseph Knight pulled out our Golden Rule Whiskey just once those first weeks to settle Michael Sr.'s stomach. We stopped on Sundays for a full day of rest, and Christian even helped me with the laundry on Saturday evenings if we were near water then.

Even the weather cooperated, though sometimes rain poured so hard we could barely see one another as we staked the tents. But my mother's wool cape kept me warm and nearly dry. Thunder boomed and lightning crackled and lifted the hair at the back of my neck, but the stock stayed together, and in the mornings, we repeated our routine of readying with minimal adjustment. Inconveniences, yes. Finding a private shrub when needed, biting my tongue when I'd rather have talked, sleeping without a down pillow at my head. But I held out the image of what we'd have one day when we arrived at wherever we were going: a roof over our heads, a permanent place to stay, sunshine to make the garden grow with just enough rain to keep it watered. Everything we heard of Oregon Territory made it sound like Eden. I could put up with temporary inconveniences knowing they'd be gone at the end of the trail. I vowed to share that with the Bethelites, to prepare them for the joys that would follow the trials of the journey.

As we could, we paralleled larger lines of wagons, camped at night close enough to hear their music and the mooing of their cows. We met a woman named Elliot traveling with her children to join her husband, and a young couple named Bond, all heading to the Willamette Valley in the southern part of the Territory. They eagerly looked forward to their new lives. They spoke slowly when I asked so I could understand them and smiled when my English broke through the German in an understandable way.

Most of the time, though, because we traveled faster than wagons could, we rode alone on the vast prairies, tiny pencil dashes against a slate of prairie green. A band of people so insignificant that even the Sioux took little notice of us, leaving us alone to contemplate the monotony of our days, the certainty of our future.

At one stop, Christian spoke with travelers who said they'd go north of the Columbia River once they arrived in the Oregon Territory, for the land there stood timbered and the Californians bought the logs as quick as they were cut. He shared this news with the scouts. "Timbered ground offers a ready market for logs. It leaves land remaining to farm. This has potential," John Genger said.

Dogs often barked in the distance when we nooned. No lost pups wandered in seeking scraps, though. Our stock became accustomed to the rhythm of our ways. I kept silent, trying to be that woman who "weren't no trouble and even helped some."

Just before Chimney Rock, some days out from Fort Laramie, George Link killed an antelope and brought it in to jerk. The rock pillar could be seen for miles before we reached it, and there we stayed a day beside a trickling spring that offered not enough water to wash clothes in, but ran fresh and not dirtied, unlike the rain-swollen Platte we'd been riding beside. We'd made good time, Joe Knight noted, his finger pointed to the air like the spire of Chimney Rock. "It's just June," he said.

"We are being tenderly led," Christian noted.

At Fort Laramie, we restocked beans and traded some of George Link's good jerked meat for sugar and tea and then left messages to be taken back by those heading east, most returning from the California gold fields or Oregonians bent on bringing the rest of their families out.

———

We were a day out of Laramie, whipped by late June winds that flapped at our tent in the night, when Christian let me know that he knew.

The intensity of his gaze must have awakened me as he leaned up on one elbow, gazing down at me when I opened my eyes. Moonbeams split the tent opening, giving a shadowed hue to his handsome face. "Can't you sleep?" I asked.

He remained silent for a time, then spoke. "I've lived around women all my life. Watched the moods of my mother and sisters and my sisters-in-law wax and wane with the moon." He combed hair from my face with the back of his fingers. He smelled of lye and vinegar from the soap we'd used to pound at the men's jeans.

I swallowed and beneath the blanket, my thumb and forefinger began their nervous rub.

"So I note," he said, "that something is amiss with you."

"I'm fine, husband. This clear air does me well. I may have lost a little weight with our spare servings, but I'm healthy. Soon we'll be in the mountains and—"

"Your face has gained fullness." He hesitated, then added, "And you've had no flow since we've left Bethel. None before that for a month or more, now that I pay attention. I've been remiss. But you, you have deceived me." I heard my heart pound in my ears. "Indeed. It's not a wife's place to keep secrets."

"I haven't *kept* it from you," I said. "I wasn't sure until recently. I didn't want to worry you. My mother lost two children. I might not have the stamina to carry this infant, and I didn't want you to—"

"All the more reason to tell me, Emma," he said. He'd stopped stroking my face. He sat up, lit the lamp, and then returned, his legs folded over, his hands clasped in his lap. He squeezed his hands together, open and closed, steady as a beating heart. "You should not be doing heavy work. The laundry." He shook his head. "Perhaps not even riding as you do, though how else we can do this now I don't know. Maybe you will need to walk more, but this will slow us. I will have to confer with the others."

"Why?" I whispered to him. "It's our baby, our family. It's none of their business. I can do the washing. You help me."

"What happens to them happens to us, and the same is true for them. We are on this journey together. It is not possible to survive it alone. This is our colony here, small as it is, and we must work as one."

"We don't share children," I hissed.

"Your needs and that of this baby now could compromise our task. Father Keil did not know of this or he would never have sent you with us."

I kept my expression unchanged. Our leader didn't know, but he sent me knowing that having a family was my intent. He knew there might be a child born in the Oregon Territory before the main colony came out. He knew I might have a difficult childbirth. He knew and sent me anyway, sent me *because* of the likelihood that I would at last know the results of Eve's sin in Eden and perhaps accept my place.

"Haven't I been helpful?" I put my cold hands over his clasped ones. "You didn't even know because I've been no trouble."

"It brings an issue we have not prepared for. I should have noticed before we left."

"You were busy, preparing. Even I wasn't sure."

"You should have told me." Christian looked lost in thought. He nodded his head as though in agreement, just once. "*Ja,* I'll send you back with Hans."

"No!" I withdrew my hands from his. "That would be wrong."

He was quiet, then, "*Ja,* you're right." I exhaled. "I should take you back. The hardest part of the trip is yet to come. It is my error. I should make the correction."

"No, no. This is your mission." My heart pounded, my mouth felt like fur. "Didn't you say we were tenderly led? This must be a part of it, a sign to show that even with an infant we can prepare for a new colony."

"The devil makes life easy, woos us to his ways so we forget that we are birthed in turmoil. We should not have welcomed such smoothness. I should have seen it as a distraction. So now I pay the price. You and our baby, too, unless we do the right thing now."

He attributes this easy journey to the devil's work; this infant, too?

"What is good comes from God. You told me this, Christian."

"Only when we are obedient, *Liebchen.* Only then."

If he took me back to Bethel, he'd blame me forever for depriving him of this response to his call. "Please listen, Christian." I knelt in front of him, pleading. "I'm healthy and strong. I'm young. There were other women with children traveling west. I saw them at the camps. The Elliots. That young couple, she could be carrying a child even now. Some even held newborns."

"Delivered with the help of midwives or other women, which we have none of."

"We'll be in Oregon Territory before the baby comes. There'll be people, neighbors."

"We seek isolation, Emma. We must prepare houses for ourselves and the others for when they come out. We have much to do before winter comes. A baby…in such wilderness…"

"It will break up the scouts and the success of the journey to go back now. We don't even need to share this with the others. We'll be in the Territory before it matters. Please, Christian. Don't send me back, and don't think of taking me back. I'll help make this work, I will. You'll be proud of me, as proud as any husband of a wife."

"You put yourself before the others in keeping this a secret. It is not a quality I noticed in you before we married. This is a difficult thing, Emma. Something I must pray about further." He unfolded his hands, pressed against his thighs as though to stand. "This is not your fault, Emma. It is mine. I must pay the price."

I'd expected his anger, prepared for it, delayed telling him in fear of it. I imagined it so it might not happen. I didn't expect self-reproach. He couldn't have found words to trouble me more than that he would bear the blame. Now I blamed myself, not for keeping the secret, but for not imagining the worst, and so it came to be.

He stood up then, pulled on his jeans and boots.

"Where are you going?"

"To decide, Emma."

"Can't we decide together?"

"Apparently not."

He stepped out through the tent flap. The whip of the wind blew out the light. When the flap closed behind him, the moonbeam no longer pierced the crack. Darkness hovered in the tent.

11

Open Places

In the morning, we gathered. A hawk of some kind soared above us, yet low enough I could see his yellow eye just before he dipped, then rose to catch a breeze. Even the bird accused. I'd spent the night in remorse, wishing I'd told Christian earlier, wanting to have shared this good godly gift with him, to let there be joy in the child's coming rather than discord. Some events never offer a second chance.

I vowed I wouldn't do this ever again. I'd be a wife who shared everything, a true helpmate instead of one looking out for her own...pleasure. My ears burned, thinking of what my father would say if he knew I'd kept such a secret only because I didn't want to be left behind. My mother's German proverb came to mind: I'd begun to weave, all right, with God's thread; but my tapestry had tears in it already.

The men gathered at the fire. I kept my red and puffy eyes lowered beneath my bonnet, raising them only to locate Christian finishing the tent packing. He would not look at me.

"What is it?" Adam Knight asked Christian. "We should be off now. We can talk at the evening camp, *ja?*"

"Something has...come up, something we need to discuss," Christian said. He motioned me forward then, and when I stopped behind him, he stepped back so I stood beside him, and I thus was ushered into the circle. At the oddest of times, I'd become one of them.

"My wife is with child," he said.

"*Ach!*" Adam Schuele said. He frowned.

"Oh, ho!" Joe Knight said, but he at least grinned.

I felt my face grow hot. I wanted to go back inside the tent, but Christian had already taken it down and rolled the pack onto Opal.

"It's nothing to cheer over," Christian said. "Not here. Not now. We have time to return, Emma and I. So she will be safe with family."

"You're my family," I said, biting my tongue as soon as I said it.

"*Ja.* We're all family," George said.

"Someone else can take her back," John Genger said. "This would be more practical. Not you. We need you. You've been anointed as leader."

"Anyone going back will compromise the mission," John Stauffer said. He pulled at a tobacco strip, then chewed. "We need all of us to build, all of us to decide the site. If one returns now, we'll have fewer to work and even less when we send men back to bring the rest out."

"Pa's right, Christian," Hans said.

"You knew?" Adam Knight asked me. "You didn't tell your husband?"

"I—"

"She told me when she was certain, but I should have known this," Christian said.

"She will slow us down," John Genger said.

"It hasn't—"

"If we are not here, there will be fewer to prepare for each day," Christian said. "You can make better time without us."

"You were chosen by Father Keil." This from Joe Knight's brother.

"We can make adjustments, brother," Joe Knight said. "All will work out well. Change doesn't mean we've erred."

"When? When can we expect this infant to join the scouts?" Hans asked as he scratched at his callus.

Christian turned to me, a puzzled look on his face.

"Am I allowed to speak at last?" Christian narrowed his eyes at me. "October," I told him, then said to the group, "Late in October."

We heard the oxen from a nearby camp being yoked. A child's cry rose and then silenced.

"Nine were chosen for a reason," Adam Schuele said at last. "Nine were commissioned by our leader. Nine plus this woman. She is one of us. She is here to discover her own part in God's plan for us. Her presence offers an opportunity to show the spirit of our colony, that we look after one another, that all needs are provided for with enough left to give away. We will look after you, too, Christian. It is how we do this. As community."

Adam Schuele had scouted for Bethel with my father, and his words now brought my father to mind. My father committed me to Adam's care in addition to my husband's; it had been my father's last request before we left.

The men remained silent after Adam spoke. I didn't know now if they'd take a vote or what would happen. Did Christian's word as leader carry more weight in this instance? Did his status as my husband matter? Was it a greater sin that I kept a secret from the scouts and the will of the colony, or from my husband?

The silence lasted a long time. I thought of words to fill the empty space, but something kept my mouth closed. Instead, I listened to the distant sounds of wagons coming forward, the stomps of impatience and snorts from our stock all packed up and ready to start out. The breeze dried the perspiration above my lip. I kicked at the edge of the fire and watched the sparks light up. The worst that could happen had been said out loud: sending me back.

No, the worst would be if Christian left to *take* me back. It would be years, if ever, before he'd forgive me for that. I poked in the dust with my boot, sending up dust puffs between Christian and me.

"By October we'll be well into Oregon Territory." Michael Sr. spoke at last. "You can winter in Portland or Dalles City if need be while the rest of us find the site and begin the work. This would be better than losing anyone to a return trip."

"Keeping her through the winter apart from us will cost," John Genger said. Then he shrugged. "But maybe some settler will take pity on us and sell out cheaper if they see we have a woman and babe to tend to."

"Oh, ho," Joe cleared his throat. "I say she stays. Who else says this?"

All the men concurred. Only Christian withheld his agreement nod.

"Can you live with this, Christian?" Adam Schuele asked. "Can you accept the consensus of the scouts and trust that what you have is what God wants for you?"

"*Ja,* I can," he said at last. "Though I will wonder always why He chose to let me lead this scouting party but not my own household."

———

The next days were silent ones between my husband and me. We did the work together that we needed, carried messages back and forth between the others and one another about how far we'd travel before nooning. We even washed clothes together in a dirty stream, and he answered me when I asked for the name of the land formation in the distance. We were civil to each other but spoke less than if we'd just recently met. At night, we slept side by side with his arm often draped over me as he snored. He would quickly remove it in the morning.

I wanted to talk with him about this infant. I wanted to ask how he might have rejoiced if we had been back in Bethel or already in Oregon sharing this news. It was this in-between state that bothered him, I told myself. He worried over our safety, about the journey between where we'd been and where we headed.

———

The snake rose up twisting and turning into itself, slithering like a thick rope through the landscape canvas of mountains and trees and rushing rivers until it hissed, "Traitor," its mouth wide and fangs wet.

"Traitor!" I shouted the word loud enough inside my dream that I woke Christian up.

"What is it? What's wrong?" he said, shaking my shoulder. When I couldn't stop the tears and frightened breathing from my nightmare, he folded me into his arms. "Rest now, *Liebchen*. You're all right, now. Shh. You'll wake the others."

"I'm sorry, so sorry, Christian. I should have told you. I feared you'd send me back. It was selfish. I'm so sorry."

"Shh, shh. I have my part in this, *Liebchen*. A man so busy with his work, he fails to notice when God has allowed him to co-create with Him, this is a man who needs forgiveness too."

"But you at least were doing good work. I...looked after my own."

He patted my back. "You're young, Emma. Let this be the only time you deceive me so you needn't have bad dreams."

I thought of staying silent about my other secret...but this might be my chance to truly wash away the deceptive stains I hid within my heart, the chance to change the fabric of my marriage. I took a deep breath. "Father Keil would not have sent me along if I hadn't begged him to," I whispered. I felt Christian's arms stiffen in their hold around me. "I went to him. I told him it wasn't fair that you and I were separated so much within our marriage and that you would want to start a family soon and how could you, with you gone for a year, maybe two or three before I'd see you again. And all because he sent you away each time."

"You went to him after I told you not to."

"Yes, but as Adam said and the scouts all agreed, he wouldn't have sent me along if he hadn't chosen to. No one can badger our leader into doing something he doesn't want to. No one ever has. And you prayed for this, you said that yourself."

"Indeed. He's human and can fall to deception too. Did he know you carried a child already? Did you tell him this?"

I shook my head. "He didn't know. But, Christian, I believe that if he had, he'd still have sent me with you. He told me that women will always be punished in childbirth, that it will be a hard state for us no matter where we are because of what Eve did. I think he hopes I'll find understanding within a difficult childbirth, my cries of pain to tell me of all I share with women through the ages, to remind us of our sins and that we are not unique at all, just one of many who need forgiveness."

Christian rested his chin on the top of my head. "You have a severe view of Wilhelm. I've known him many years. He doesn't dwell on sinfulness, Emma. He dwells on love, on sharing with others all we have, and holding us together so we will find that final respite in heaven. It's Christ's love displayed in his leadership that draws others to the colony. Not all of us could be so deceived to miss a man who harbors such harsh thoughts."

He leaned me away from him, then kissed me on the forehead, my eyes, my cheeks, and finally my lips. "We will start over," Christian said. "This will be a new time for us now." I nodded. *"Gut, gut."* He lay down and motioned to let my head rest on his chest. "We have both erred and been forgiven, *ja?* And we learn from this to talk when there are problems, lest the snake wake us in the night."

I climbed Independence Rock along with the rest of the scouts. We arrived there before the Fourth of July and celebrated the halfway mark of our journey west. Christian thought the rocks too smooth for me, that going up would be fine, but coming down would challenge and I might slip and fall. But I pleaded. I wanted to see the views from above, and finally he gave in.

Standing on top the hill as rounded as brown bread, a person could see forever. For the first time, I realized how the Missouri landscape had restricted my view, the eye, seeking distant vistas, always interrupted by trees and shrubbery and rolling hills. Atop Independence Rock, looking east, I felt as though I could see the bricks of Bethel. Previous travelers had carved names into the stone, witnesses to those pursuing wider horizons. The landscape west looked as still as a lake and twice as wide. The colony had restricted my vision, but perhaps that proved purposeful. They liked dips and valleys where people nestled apart from others, where they could believe they were the only ones in the world; intruders were kept out by clear boundaries and woods. Finding a site in the Oregon Territory with such isolation could prove challenging. I hoped a more open space in the wilderness would be where the Lord would lead.

"Careful now, *Liebchen*," Christian told me. He held my hand and caught me once when my smooth leather soles did slide on the rounded rock.

"The rest of the way looks…easy," I said. "Nothing in our way now. We can almost see the ocean from here."

"These western landscapes are like a woman's wrapper: deceiving," Christian said. He smiled.

He was right, of course, because not a few days later came Devil's Gate, a slice in a granite mountain that looked like a nasty wound. The

Sweetwater River ran through it. We would take the trail south, as the wagons did, even though Michael Sr. thought the animals could make it through the cut without a problem.

How the decisions were made in this community of scouts remained a mystery to me. I would have agreed with Michael Sr. True, the cut was narrow, but it would save time, something the scouts said must be a deciding factor if we found a good campsite and thought to lay over an extra day to rest the animals. "Got to make good time" was the motto, and so we'd head on out whether we were rested or not.

Yet here we could have saved time but didn't.

"Who decides whether we take a certain trail or not?" I asked Christian at noon while we ate jerked beef. "This road around the Devil's Gate took more time. We could have ridden through that cut in the rock."

"Our animals aren't so surefooted, though. If we had a problem in the narrow place, we'd have no help coming along behind us, as no wagons come that way."

"That's reasonable," I said. The breeze lifted my own scent to my nose. I needed to lay out my wrapper to air this night. "But who decided that? Hans makes some decisions about the stock. Wouldn't it have been his call about the ability of the animals?"

"We decide together."

But I hadn't seen it.

Neither did I see the discussion that led to my now riding Opal instead of my horse, Fred. One morning Fred stood packed and Opal saddled while Christian helped me up. Christian rode the traded-for-mule and had for several days.

"The mule's gait is better," he said. "It'll be an easier ride for you."

When we came to a gradual uphill slope some days later that Christian said must be South Pass, I didn't know how he knew that, either, until we reached the top, and I could see streams flowing west now instead of east. We'd arrived at the Continental Divide.

———

I noted graves along the trail, and further into the mountains, large granite boulders shaded a portion of our journey. I longed for the vista offered a few weeks back by Independence Rock. These rocks closed in. I had the fleeting thought that it might be a grand place for an ambush by Indians, something we were told to be wary of at each wagon stop, where we encountered the outside world. I preferred it when we camped away from that sort of thinking. Maybe, like me, travelers thought the worst in order to keep it from happening.

A few days later, we entered a narrow opening through the mountains. The horses and mules pulled back, sidestepped or tried to. They whinnied and strained against the reins. Hans's horse shied first and stumbled sideways, though it kept its footing. That abrupt action appeared to startle the horse behind him and then the one behind it, causing the pack animals to yank their lead ropes. Even steady Opal pranced and swished her tail. "*Ach,* be good now," I chastened her.

Hans Stauffer shouted to move the animals on out faster, if possible, to get into the wider opening where we could find out what troubled them. Perhaps a burr worked its way under a saddle, or maybe a pack slipped. Maybe they smelled an Indian ambush. I looked up. Bare, pinkish rocks rounded over us. I could see a patch of sky, but nothing out of the ordinary on the rock ledges.

Then Opal bolted, pushing her way along the narrow path occupied by the horses ahead. She attempted passage to the right of John Genger's horse directly ahead of me, so both my legs pushed against his horse rather than the rock wall that Opal grazed. I pushed back with my knees and my hands, but the sidesaddle pitched me forward, out of balance, and I let loose the pack animal and hung with both hands onto the pommel.

Unable to squeeze forward, Opal bolted back, making odd sounds of distress, attempting to rear up. Then she bucked, and before I knew what had happened, I'd landed on my back in the dust left behind by Opal, the packhorse running loose behind her. The world swam around as the packhorse's hooves threw pebbles at me as it tried to avoid me. I couldn't catch my breath. It felt like drowning, I imagined, with no way to take air.

Christian's mule barely avoided stepping on me as Christian raced up behind. He jumped off in an instant. "Emma!"

I waved at him, unable to get my breath.

"Stay calm. The air will return," he assured me. At last air filled my lungs, never more sweet, though it was laced with dust. He brushed the dirt from my wrapper as he helped me stand.

Christian's mule bolted past both of us now, the packhorse running loose behind it. "What's wrong with them? What's happening?"

We heard shouts and wailing animal screams coming from the area in front of us. Clouds of dust billowed like fog. Adam Knight shouted. Christian held my elbow and we stumbled forward.

Through the dust, the men had drawn their weapons, but I couldn't see the enemy. One of the packhorses lay on its side, breathing hard, blood in long scratches oozing from its neck.

Through the haze I spied Opal in erratic motions. She stomped with her front feet, pummeling something beige on the ground. Braying sounds pierced the air. "Oh, ho!" Joe Knight shouted.

The creature that lay before Opal attempted to get up, and she bit at its neck, then lifted it, and like a mother cat shaking a mouse to its death to provide lunch for her *Kinder,* she shook the animal back and forth until it hung limp. Then she dropped it.

A young mountain cat lay in the dust. Opal had stomped and bitten and shaken it to death.

I'd never seen a mountain lion before, let alone watched a mule kill one. The wind moved the fine hair of the lion. It had paws as big as my palm.

There were dangers in this landscape I had no knowledge of, dangers in confined spaces, in narrow places without vistas. I knew then that the Lord must lead us scouts to a landscape where we could see for miles, so we could always see ahead to dangers lurking.

12

The Wild of the
Outside World

We made adjustments with one fewer pack animal, the cat's last prey.
We dried the meat. It was my first taste of mule meat, but George Link
said we must never waste what God provided. Piecing together what
had happened, the men decided that the mountain lion must have lain
in wait, hunkered down above us as we moved through the narrow
place. The horses and the mules soon got its scent, and it was Opal who
proved the most indignant at this interruption. Opal stood out.

The feast we held that night brought out harmonicas, and Hans
and George Link and the Knight brothers danced jigs arm in arm to
the sizzle of meat at the fire. Other scouts not dancing or playing
clapped. We rejoiced in our safe keeping and our "guard mule," as we
now called Opal. "Didn't need a dog to tree that cat," Joe Knight said,
his finger held up to the wind.

"But a dog might have forewarned us," I said. "I still hope we can
find a lost pup somewhere."

"At least we were spared," John Genger said. He sat with his ankles
crossed, a cup of coffee in his hands and his Pennsylvania Long Rifle
lying beside him. He didn't play the harmonica. I didn't disagree with
him, though I had a bruise the size of Missouri—and still growing—on

my backside, and the infant hadn't let me have more than a taste of the meat before it began its kicking again.

"We've been looked after," Christian said. And I agreed, even knowing he hadn't seen the bruise yet.

We headed north toward Fort Hall, where we hoped to restock our meager supply of cornmeal, among other things. At one point along the trail, a man with vegetables, onions and carrots and tomatoes, sat beneath a shaded tent. He smiled as he took our money, said something back to Christian, and they laughed. "He's Mormon, up from their place at the Salt Lake," Christian interpreted for us. Later Christian said they'd laughed because the Mormon said his vegetables were so good and so long-lasting that our baby would probably be holding a carrot in his hand when he arrived in this world.

"You told him about—"

"He can see, *Liebchen.* Your round face, the gap in your wrapper." He tugged at the gusset I'd had to sew in to ease the tightness across my breast. The infant had six months by my calculations and would be good size if these past weeks of his kicking and growing foretold it. "He's a man with a good eye." Christian winked, the first sign since I'd disclosed my deception that he found pleasure having with him a wife who would one day bear his child. He handed me many carrots, using one to shake his finger at me, the carrot as limp as resting reins.

After Fort Hall, we heard more rumors of Indian unrest, more than we'd heard on the plains during all the previous weeks. We could take no action, such a powerless state. I made myself think of more pleasant things—part of my new effort to control the future—and posted a letter back to my parents and to Mary and Sebastian Giesy, telling them about our child.

We headed on to Fort Boise, following the Snake River with its deep chasms and frothy, uncontrollable currents. All new things to see.

I tried not to think about crossing that wild stream, something Christian said we'd have to do, and we did when the time came. Here, too, rumors of drowning abounded, but we crossed without trial.

The number of rivers and streams needing fording increased as we headed west. We learned their names, later trying to match up Alder Springs and Burnt River, Mud Springs and the Powder, with stories told by other travelers we encountered.

Even the Blue Mountains gave us little to remember except for their beauty—a lovely spring at the summit, where other emigrants spent the night, and that hazy color people told us came from the Indians burning trees and shrubs to make way for spring grass for their horses. The Nez Perce were said to have many horses.

The terrain changed again after we crossed those mountains, winding down a long hill almost devoid of trees. At the base, it opened to expansive high plains. We encountered round, wide-faced Indians there who watched as we silently rode by. Sometimes in the mornings we'd see their camp smoke not far behind us. Christian said we'd double the evening guards, but they never shortened the distance between us, probably deciding wisely that we had little they might need for barter or theft. They never knew we carried medicinal whiskey, or that Opal was a guard mule of exceptional skill.

For several days we paralleled the river they called the Columbia, crossing the John Day River at Leonard's Ferry. I kept my eyes straight toward the willows fanned out on the far shore, my cheek tight against Opal's. I held my breath as the rickety craft pulled into the current and down to the landing, exhaling as I stepped on the muddy shore. We rode up another bare hill, rested at springs near the top, then headed west, spending the next night at the Des Chutes River, where the rolling water poured into the Columbia. Here we'd either need to swim or pay the ferryman. Fortunately, John Genger agreed we could pay. I was always so grateful when we could pay.

In late September, a snowcapped mountain became our beacon. After crossing Fifteen Mile Creek and then Eight Mile Creek, riding up to the top of a bluff that overlooked the Columbia, we reached Dalles City, right on the river, where the water spilled among huge rocks like strands of a woman's white hair draped in a man's knuckles. They called it Celilo Falls.

Dalles City, or Fort Dalles Landing as some called the town, grew around an army fort, as far as I could tell. Over the post office door a sign read Wascopam, and the postmaster told us in no uncertain terms that we should tell our friends to post letters to that name and no other. Since we didn't plan to stay, I let his invigorated opinion waft by along with his tobacco smoke. Apparently, there were arguments about what the town should be called. Later someone said it had endured ten different names already. At least our colonists never wasted time in such decisions; our leader decided the names.

Dozens of Indian people of various shapes and sizes wandered near the post office and in the town itself. A baker stepped out of a shop with the name *W. L. DeMoss* over the door and offered me a warm piece of soft saleratus bread, the first I'd had since we left Missouri. I took it as a gift divine, the dough as soft as angel's wings against my tongue. *What is it about fresh bread that brings peace to a woman's soul?* "*Danke,*" I said, taking my husband's arm as we moved on.

Dogs sniffed from around various corners of framed buildings; their slender tails rose as they moved in small packs. I wondered out loud if we might rescue one to call our own, but Christian said, "We have enough to worry about just getting ourselves settled in with a babe without a pup in tow."

We passed a marketplace with Indians and others bartering baskets and dried fish, perhaps for canoe rides down the river. Some of the natives had foreheads pitched as steep as a cow's face, while many round-faced Indians stood heads down on a platform as men in the audience appeared to be shouting out bids. *Slavery, here? Wouldn't it be ironic if we colonists left Missouri to avoid a battle involving slaves only to step into another war right here?* I couldn't be sure what transpired, and I vowed to learn more English before the winter turned to spring. So much went on in this "outside world" that I couldn't decipher. To understand this new land and live well here, I needed to interpret for myself the words being said. I couldn't always rely on the interpretations of my husband.

The Indian bartering went on well into the night, along with drums and singing. We slept on the ground a little distance from the town, and Joe Knight suggested we all go down to where the music seemed to rise from. I thought that a grand idea, but this time the scouts reached the consensus that we remain safe where we were. I still didn't know how these things got decided, but Joe looked a little down as he pushed his night pack up against his saddle, punching it more than once for good measure.

Major Rains, the commander of the fort, had a doctor at his disposal. A family doctor also served the town, and in the morning, Christian insisted that I let myself be examined by Dr. C. W. Shaug, though I felt fine. The bruise that had spread like spilled ink across my back from when Opal upended me lingered. I still ached some at my lower back, but I decided it might be the baby protesting the long hours of riding even on a soft-gaited mule.

Dr. Shaug proved to be a big man, kindly, and he did all his examinations with a nurse present and with my wrapper on. Christian stayed to translate.

"I would say late November," he said. "Judging from the infant's size. Is this your calculation too?"

"No," I said, understanding the English name for the month. "October."

"The infant is small if it's to arrive a month away. Have you eaten well?"

"I've been in good health," I said. "Just one mishap on the trail, but otherwise enough to eat to fill me and not even sickness in the mornings, as I've heard can happen."

"Indeed," he said. "Well"—he put the end of his stethoscope into the pocket of his vest—"I'd suggest a physician be present. It could be your baby will need quick, professional decision-making when he arrives. Where do you intend to be in October? That's what you said, October?"

"We've yet to decide," Christian told him. "In the Willamette area. From what we've heard there is still good land available there."

"You're farmers? Yes? Well, that is rich soil country. How many sections are you hoping to file on?"

"Many," Christian told him. "We're the foot soldiers who make way for a large colony that will come out as soon as we get word back to them."

"Foot soldiers. Pioneers. From the Latin *pedant*. Well, then, God-speed to you. There are good physicians there. Some in the French Prairie country, though little land's available there to claim. But make sure you winter near a doctor."

It was an unpleasant thought. I decided to pitch it.

———

We took a steamer downriver to Fort Vancouver. John Genger again said we could pay. It pushed its way along through pouring rain. Misty fog hugged the shoreline, forcing us to imagine the scenery, but I knew there must be high rocks and trees. I felt cold to the bone, my teeth chattering from the elements more than from the dizzying water. By the time we reached the landing at the former Hudson's Bay Company fort, my throat felt scratchy and I sneezed. I could see the buildings up a grassy slope. Here the men hoped they'd get good information about whether to go north or south to form the new colony. I hoped I'd find dryness and warmth.

Ulysses S. Grant, the senior officer who managed the well-laid-out fort, complained that high water would keep them from harvesting the potatoes that year. "But then, everyone appears to be raising potatoes around here to send to the California gold fields."

"At least the floodwaters have kept you from the labor of digging the potatoes up," Christian said. "Otherwise, you'd have watched them rot for lack of sales."

Grant laughed. "Good one," he said. "The silver lining in the darkest of clouds. You'll stay for supper," he ordered more than invited, clicking his heels and bending at his waist toward me. "I'll ask the fort physician to give you something for that cough."

Christian said the invitation would likely not have come without a woman present. I was pleased I could bring some respite to the scouts, who sat at the long table along with senior officers stationed at the fort. The conversation proved lively, and I could understand the hospitableness, if not all of the words.

I loved the lavishly painted dishes, the candelabra, and long-stemmed glassware that looked fit for a queen. Grant commented on the crystal goblets he said he always carried with him from fort to fort. "Something of my own to make a place like home," he told us. The food steamed with freshness, and my mouth watered just watching the platter of corn beef and cabbage move slowly toward my place, served by men with military precision. I wondered where the officers' wives might be, then heard women's chatter from an adjoining room. This would be what our life would be like if we were not bound to the colony. A life filled with worldly things, singular treasures, abundance, men perhaps waiting on women, and sometimes women sitting down beside men. Hadn't the Lord promised us such abundance?

I wondered if Christian might not entertain that idea too as he ran his finger around the lip of the crystal before bringing it to his mouth.

"Perhaps you should winter near here," Grant suggested. "Make your journey to mark land in the spring when the floodwaters recede and you can better see what you'll be getting."

"Indeed. Your suggestion bears some consideration," my husband said, then politely changed the subject. He told me later he didn't want to disagree with the commander, but he wanted to secure our site yet this fall so at the first sign of weather breaking, scouts could return to prepare the main party to come out.

"This might be a good place to winter, though," I offered.

"It would be easier for you and for the child."

"You could stay here too, make forays out north and south but come back here. The colony doesn't expect you to live in hardship. You were never asked to do so when you traveled into Kentucky, *ja?*" He nodded agreement. "You stayed as a guest, the way the disciples were told to receive what others offered, to take nothing with them. The commander offers us a place to winter. Is it not divine intervention?"

"*Nein.* Any area close to here will be too populated." He pulled on his reddish beard. "But you could stay, and in the spring, when the scouts head back, I could come to get you and bring you to wherever we have found a site."

A winter with a bed and roof did invite. But if I remained, Christian would miss the birth of his child. "I'm not staying here without you. I'm one of the scouts. I'll go where you go, as Ruth did." I wiped at my nose. "In sickness and in health," I reminded him.

That night as we slept on a feather bed at the fort, I wondered if I shouldn't urge us all to remain through the winter. Christian might come to see the merits of living closer to the real world of people finely dressed, eating at well-apportioned tables, learning to use English all the time. Maybe he'd see that we could live safely *in* the world while not being *of* it, as Scripture ordained us to be.

Here were many people who could be brought into our fold. Maybe we were being led to *this* place. Maybe we scouts needed to pay more attention to populated sites. *Perhaps isolation shouldn't be the most important factor to consider.* I'd find a way to mention that to Christian.

I watched the light flickering against the pewter and crystal, washing over the gray steins on the table. Our leader back in Missouri saw the heaviness of the world able to snuff out one's light, leaving people lost and alone in the darkness, and so we were advised to look to the colony, return to the colony, trust only in the colony. Our leader would have us isolate ourselves as the true way to resist the world.

But how could we light the world if we were so far from it? There were goodly people populating this country. The commander. The doctors we'd met. Even German women of negotiable affections provided assistance to us on our journey. What we needed had been provided. God was in the world. Surely God could look after us if we lived among others. Meanwhile, we scouts could offer another way to bring light to the wilderness, though it did require risk.

That was the challenge, I supposed, as I watched my husband talk with those worldly men in their uniforms: to be willing to enter the darkness of the unknown wilderness, the outside world, hoping the light one brought would be bright enough and warm enough that it would overcome darkness, and more, encourage others to light a candle there too.

13

Into the Wilderness

I woke up singing, as I understood Christian's mission better than I ever had before. With a little effort on my part, I thought he'd accept my observations about lack of merits within isolation. How could we expand the colony without more people around? If we lived here or near this Columbia River, Christian wouldn't have to travel as he had before to bring people in, as we'd be in the midst of people. All sorts of *Volk*, free and slaves, made their way here, and surely acts of charity toward them formed a part of our mission, to break the holds of bondage of all kinds while serving as the hands and feet of God within the world.

As in St. Joseph, Missouri, I'd already heard French and Spanish, and even some German spoken, and a tongue with clicks and rolls that crusty old mountain men used to converse with natives. Hadn't our Lord walked within the midst of common people? Didn't He appear to His disciples after His death in everyday places where His friends ate together or where they worked beside their fishing boats? This was the goal, then, to be among people, even buxom women attracted to my husband, but to not allow them to lead us astray. *Ja,* I'd have to learn to live with the monster of envy, but isolation would make that lesson more difficult to learn and wouldn't be any protection at all.

Even I could see that this Fort Vancouver and the town of Portland across the river would be where emigrants would come and want to stay. Vistas of green slopes and oats growing high rolled up onto craggy rocks with waterfalls. The weather felt mild, almost warm, even last evening. Timber soared into the skyline in this Columbia country, so all the other criteria except isolation were met. Surely isolation shouldn't be our chief desire. That's what I'd have to convince Christian of, and I intended to begin that morning.

But Christian had dressed early, and I never even heard his steady breathing as he did his pushing-ups. He left so quietly that I slept on. When he returned he expressed enthusiasm about a chance meeting that sealed our fate. Or perhaps where God's concerned, there is no chance at all.

"Get dressed," Christian said. He brushed at his hat, tossing rain-drops on the wood floor of the room we'd been given to sleep in at the fort. "We've found what we've been seeking."

"Near here? I'm so pleased," I said, pulling on my wrapper against the morning dampness. I sent a prayer of thanksgiving upward.

"No, not here. But not far away."

My husband had met an emigrant who'd come out from Iowa the year before, and the man, Ezra Meeker, said we should go north, farther north to a place of such mild weather, such beautiful meadows and prairies, that no one who ever saw it would ever choose to leave.

The walk across the wet grass brought a fresh scent to my nose. Christian and Adam Schuele and Ezra Meeker himself now shared this news with all of us as we stood inside the sutler's store, watching a driz-zling rain fall across the door opening. The sharp scent of salted hides waiting transport lifted from the bales around us.

"Emigrants from the Puget Sound Agricultural Company cleared land there and planted trees, had sheep and cattle, and did quite well. Some have been there since '48. They'd have done better if they could have kept the increase of their herds, but they were indentured, almost, to the Hudson's Bay Company. Now that they've sold out, those farms are available. The lands there are rich and fertile."

"Are there portions there for donation land claims?" asked Michael Schaefer Sr.

"That and to buy," Ezra Meeker told him. Christian raised his eyebrows. "Well, some are fixing to leave, so they'll sell; but more will come, you mark my words. The best part of the Oregon Territory is north of the Columbia."

Meeker looked not much older than I, and he told us he'd come south this past week to stock up on things from the fort's supply and to talk with emigrants recently arrived. He said he knew how hard it had been for him when his group reached Portland last November, trying to find the best place to settle. Meeker planned to head back, and we could travel with him if we wished. Or he'd give us good directions. He said he had intentions of returning east in the spring to guide other wagons out. "Puget Sound, part of the newly formed Washington Territory, that's where I hope they'll all settle."

"What do you think?" Christian asked the scouts as we stood inside the sutler's store. "This Meeker is a kindly sort. Youngish." He spoke in German in front of the man, and Meeker smiled as though accustomed to waiting through translations. Or perhaps he understood German. I couldn't tell.

"What's in it for him?" John Genger asked. "What does he get for guiding us north?"

"Nothing. Or at least he hasn't asked for a guide fee," Christian said. "He has a wife and baby girl, so he knows what a family would need."

"How do you know this about him?" Hans asked.

"He told me so. I trust him."

"How do we travel?" John asked.

"We could head on out to the mouth of the Columbia, catch a ship north that would drop us at Puget Sound. But it would be expensive."

The idea of an ocean voyage caused my stomach to flip. I swallowed and wrapped my mother's cape around me closer. Her lavender scent on the wool had nearly vanished into the wisp of her memory. I rubbed my cheek against the cloth, taking in its comfort, then said, "The ocean voyage would be more expensive than following him back north."

"We'd have to sell the stock to do it," Joe Knight said.

"We might have to sell them anyway, from what Meeker says," Christian told him.

"What sense does that make? We need the mules for farming, the other stock, too. Why did we hang on to pack animals at the Dalles Landing when so many offered to buy if we're only going to sell them now?" This from George Link, and I thoroughly agreed. I nodded my head.

"Meeker says the land is good there, that it's already been farmed in places," Adam Schuele affirmed. "He's introduced hops, so you know the soil is good. We can buy stock from those already there." As the other fluent English speaker, he alone could verify Christian's enthusiasm and assessment of Meeker's words.

I imagined having to part with Opal and didn't like that thought at all.

"Indeed," said Christian. "If we can buy some of those established farms and lay claim to adjoining land, we can have all we need for the colony."

"There are neighbors near?" I asked.

"Most of the travel is by walking or by boat," Christian continued, as though I hadn't spoken. "The woods are too tangled for wagons, but the rivers are perfect for bringing in supplies and for sending sold products out. We'd farm beside the rivers." A gleam formed in Christian's eyes.

There'd be few families there if wagons couldn't make it through the rough.

"Timber everywhere and a ready market for it in California in the gold fields. Indeed. I believe the Lord has led this Meeker into our midst as a beacon, the directional light we need."

Travel by boat? Rivers? Timber without wide open spaces and not even the comfort of the mount my father picked for me? Where were the women? I felt my stomach lurch.

"Wilhelm wanted separation," Adam Schuele reminded. "But there's a fort at Nisqually and another at a place called Steilacoom, so should there be Indian trouble we'd have a secure place to go to."

"Could we talk more about the need for separation?" I said. "Perhaps the way the colony is to grow isn't through new recruiting from far away, but by living closer to people, where they can see the caring in our lives and want that for themselves. Maybe the Lord has led us here to this Vancouver to do things differently than before, and this Meeker is a...distraction."

Only the steady thumping of the rain on the log roof filled the silence. Men moved their eyes to Christian, then to the floor. I might have fine ideas, but today I appeared to be invisible and my words as silent as a preacher's sin.

———

Against my better judgment (not that anyone asked), we sold the stock. How I hated parting with Opal, who'd become more of a pet than a work animal, a confidante for my unspeakable woes. Her new owner, a

Portland farmer, took Fred, too, but I spent most of my time with the man singing Opal's virtues, including her guardian tendencies. He smiled indulgently. At least he spoke German and so could communicate with the horses and mules.

Within two days, we took a scow north on the Columbia River to a landing at Monticello, where once Hudson's Bay people had a fur storage place. There, we were met by tall, somber men and their long cedar canoes. "Cowlitz Indians," Meeker said. "Friendly. They speak some English. Their name means 'seekers,' I'm told. As in a spiritual sense."

"We have that in common," Christian said, and he clicked his boots together and bent at his waist in recognition of their virtue.

They had that curious sloped forehead I'd seen at the Dalles Landing, and I wondered what could cause this but didn't know how to ask. Besides, I didn't want to be rude.

Meeker said we'd pay the Cowlitz in trade goods to take us all north, and I wondered what of our meager goods might appeal to these stately men or to the women who I noticed now sat in the bows of the crafts.

We moved by canoe up the Cowlitz River into the new Washington Territory.

Once again I watched the shoreline glide by, this time while seated with packs of our personal belongings like gray mushrooms at my feet. A Cowlitz woman and child were in our canoe, which held Christian and five other men besides the Cowlitz paddlers. A wooden cradle wrapped around one infant. A brace pressed against the infant's head, answering my question about what made the sharp angle to the forehead. I wondered if it hurt and wished again that I could speak another language. The baby cooed and his mother smiled.

Every now and then a woman reached into rectangular, oval-bottomed coiled baskets to give their babies something to chew. The honey-colored baskets were beautiful as well as practical. Whatever they held comforted the infants. It looked like thicknesses of fat.

The paddlers urged us past sand bars that speared the water, often poling and using ropes to pull us against the current. Occasionally, we got out so they could take their heavy canoes around fallen trees that blocked the waterway. Back in the canoe, I tried not to look at the water rushing by, grabbed the side of the canoe when a swift current caught the craft and might have sent it spinning but for the skill of our handlers. I noted how thin the sides of the boat were. I could find no seams, so the boat was formed of one continuous, long, red, fragrant cedar log.

I caught a glimpse of a huge bird with scarlet feathers that Ezra Meeker named a pileated woodpecker. "A shy bird," he told me through Christian. "One that doesn't like to be seen very often."

"That wouldn't be hard in those thickets," I said.

"Still, you've seen one, so that is something to remember," Christian said. "Meeker says that sightings are rare. A unique experience in this wilderness. You like unique things, if I remember." He patted my hand, stopped my thumb and finger from rubbing themselves raw.

The men spoke constantly of the timber, its size and girth, how dense and how abundant. The river meandered through lush prairies while I forced myself to think not of the possible problems with the water but to watch for dots of color, to let myself be taken in and comforted by the presence of flowers whose names I didn't know. We all marveled at the high, timbered ridges, much taller than the bluffs of Missouri; more foreboding, too. We swatted at mosquitoes, buzzing.

Wide prairies eased out from the water's edge, and we watched deer and sometimes elk tear at grasses. Despite the promise of lush soil for kitchen gardens, I noticed few clearings in this wild.

When we reached Toledo, another small landing with a few log homes and fenced gardens, we stepped out of the canoes and Meeker left us.

"His farm is near Puyallup, quite a bit farther northeast," Christian said. "But he thinks we should go on up to the Sound and see if we can winter at one of the forts there. They'll have doctors."

"But I thought we took this route because Meeker had neighbors that he knew of who had land we could acquire." I knew I sounded irritated, but when they included me in discussions, it was to eavesdrop more than participate. Issues weren't decided within my earshot. Within my presence they merely affirmed decisions already made.

"He's done what we asked of him," Christian told me. It seemed to me he bristled. "His advice has been good. We've seen abundance. We'll explore yet this fall and finalize our location, then send scouts back to Bethel. You have to agree, this is beautiful country."

Beautiful, ja, but empty of all but tall trees.

I assumed we'd walk the rest of the way to Puget Sound, to the promised "bustling" town of Olympia, but instead the Cowlitz paddlers had relatives who met us, and for another trade of red cloth bought just for this purpose back in Vancouver, we could ride their big horses behind them. We agreed, and for the first time since I was very young (when there'd been no one around to see), I sat astride a horse, my left knee no longer steadied by the lower hook. I put my arms around a perfect stranger. We were on solid ground, off of the water.

I could have stayed at Olympia forever. We spent our first night there at Edmund Sylvester's Olympia House Hotel. I heard even more strange languages spoken, including a high-pitched staccato chatter from the kitchen, where I caught a glimpse of an Asian man, his thin long braid swinging like a metronome as he bustled about. For dinner that evening we were served an appetizer Christian understood to be pickled blackberries. "A Chinese delicacy," he told me.

A newspaper lay on the hotel desk counter, and I read its name in English, the same as the river: *Columbia.*

Puget Sound lapped up to Olympia, a body of water as smooth as fine tin. Christian said, "It's the ocean," but it had none of the white-caps I expected from having seen paintings made by those who'd traveled west. The town stepped down from a timbered bluff toward the sea. Houses sat on flattened spots between sawed-off trunks still being pulled by horses and chains. It was a growing place. I loved seeing stumps with steps cut into them for ease in mounting a horse and the window boxes that dotted the few frame houses. Such sights promised the presence of women.

But we were not to stay here. We headed east the next day, merely checked in at Fort Nisqually, a former Hudson's Bay site. There we received directions to the place where Christian (or at least someone) had decided we would spend the winter.

Fort Steilacoom became my home. Located about four miles from the little town of Steilacoom, and some distance from Olympia, it boasted a few log buildings, fenced-in gardens, and an orchard with chickens pecking about. A man named Heath had farmed it for the Agricultural Company, then left when the Company sold it to the U.S. Army.

Most importantly, Christian told me, a doctor remained quartered at the fort. At least I believed he'd chosen for my benefit this little clearing in the timber separated from the town. I suppose he thought that having the doctor would give me peace about this birthing, or give him peace, as he had plans he just now decided to tell me about, plans that offered me no peace at all.

14

Accommodations

A three-story gristmill in Steilacoom promised wheat and population. A sawmill on a place called Chambers Creek meant frame houses rose here in a place named for a group of sturdy-looking Indians known as Steilacooms. The Indians lived in cedar houses nestled back from the shoreline like quiet beneath trees. I noticed their presence first from the smoke rising as if from blackberry brush, then looking closer, I could see the outlines of the houses. When I encountered one or two of the Steilacooms on the paths, they kept their eyes lowered and always stepped aside. They didn't look cowed as those at the auction in The Dalles or Wascopam or whatever they called that town that week. Neither did they look frightening or fierce. Polite. They were simply polite.

Fruit trees grew here—propagated they'd have to be because they couldn't be so large grown from seed. People hadn't been here all that long, at least not white people. The trees promised apples and pears, and I could taste the *Strudels* I'd bake. This would indeed be a good landscape for all of us. Not unlike Olympia, it boasted storefronts and a wagon maker and a church, and women with children walked on the board streets while white birds, seagulls Christian called them, dipped and cried overhead. Christian said there were two settlements here: a Port Steilacoom near the bottom of the bluff and a Chapman's Steilacoom farther up, though I couldn't tell where one began and the other ended. It was how I'd begun to think of our journey here, too. Had it ended? Or were we just beginning the next phase?

The scouts remained at Chapman's Steilacoom, talking to locals, I assumed, gathering new information with Adam Schuele to translate.

But Christian said that he and I needed to walk on through the cedars and blackberry bushes along a narrow trail to reach the fort before dark. We found it clearly defined not by fortlike walls, but by the split-rail fences surrounding large cultivated fields. This garrison didn't match what one might expect at an eastern fort. It consisted of a few log structures, one frame building under construction, barns, small outer buildings, and clothes hanging limply on a line.

Captain Bennett Hill once served as commanding officer, having taken over the land after the death some years earlier of the man who cleared these fields, 106 fenced acres planted in wheat, peas, and potatoes. That commander had been recently replaced by an Irishman, Captain Maurice Maloney. It seemed no one stayed at Fort Steilacoom for long.

Captain Maloney knew not a word of German. His dark blue uniform, frayed at the cuffs, merely heightened the red of his hair and the verdant green of his eyes.

"The accommodations aren't much for ladies," he told Christian. "But you're welcome." He said this with his eyes on me while Christian translated.

"It's the physician we're interested in most," Christian said.

The captain pulled at the sleeves of his military jacket, straightened his shoulders as he responded to my husband's words. "Aye, we have one. Frame building will be completed before long, and he'll have a surgery. Meantime, he's housed in that log one, along with his wife." He pointed to a structure that looked sturdy and stable, with moss growing on its wooden shakes.

"There are women posted here?" Christian asked.

"Aye. A few of the officers have their wives here. Even a child or two."

The captain led us to what I assumed would be our new home. We passed small log houses, and I could see easily that this had once been a farm, though someone's vision of a fort in the future rose too. Soldiers cleaned the barns while others carried buckets that frothed white with milk. Chickens scattered like seeds as we walked.

"What about the rest of the scouts?" I asked Christian. "Are they coming later? Will there be places for them to stay?"

Christian didn't answer. Instead, he took my arm in his and patted the back of my hand. I thought he might be pleased that I thought of someone other than myself.

We met the *gut* doctor, as I came to call him, at his office that was also his home. Christian explained our "circumstance," and I once again suffered an examination—with my clothes on, thank goodness. "November," the *gut* doctor said when he stepped from beneath my wrapper and I stepped down from his stool.

"Indeed. November," Christian said. He pointed his finger at me to remind me of his rightness.

"It should be sooner," I said. "Tell him it will be in October."

"Twice now these men of experience have said November, *Liebchen*. I think we can trust this. And it's good. You will have time now to rest, to settle in before the baby comes."

"I don't want to settle in. I want the baby to come and for us to stay the winter in a civilized place."

"Father Keil often said it is not wise to want or desire, Emma, but to accept what we're given."

"As if he ever did," I mumbled. If he had, we would still be in Bethel instead of here.

At the third log house, we were introduced to Nora, the *gut* doctor's wife, a tiny woman with dark curls peaking beneath a cap that otherwise covered her head. She had small eyes that sparkled like a kid goat's, with the same quick movements as she opened the door, invited us in. She wore a skirt full as a bell, and I wondered how many petticoats the material covered to make it sway so as she walked. Beside her, a child stood with hands akimbo; another, Nora balanced on her hip. I wished I'd known what all she said as she talked with quick, crisp words spoken through a mouth with all of her teeth. I deciphered only *baby* and *room*.

Nora led us to a windowless enclosure at the back of the cabin. A bed and bed stand marked the space. Still with the toddler on her hip, she picked up a ball and a small wooden horse from the floor, and I realized this must have been her son's playroom we'd now taken over. The baby leaned out as she knelt, then pulled in at her mother's neck when she stood up.

"Danke," I said. When she motioned for me to sit, I nearly collapsed onto the bed as Christian removed the pack from my back. We'd left Fort Nisqually early that morning, walked through the two towns of Steilacoom and the final four miles uphill to this fort, encountered Indians, met the commander and doctor and now his family. It was late afternoon. My limbs felt shaky and weak. The pillows, filled with feathers, were soft as lamb's wool on my cheeks.

"This will be a comfort while I'm gone, *Liebchen,*" Christian said, looking around the room.

I yawned. "Are you going somewhere?"

"To arrange things," he said. He kissed my forehead and left, closing the door behind him.

I was too tired to ask for details and must have known by intuition that I wouldn't really like his answers.

The "perfect arrangement" is what Christian called it. A physician nearby; a woman to be with if trouble arose; a military fort safe and secure, set within timbered land in a climate so mild I almost felt as though I'd taken a fresh bath when I hadn't had one in weeks. I would have one this day, though, and that made the day seem blessed.

Then I learned what Christian was really up to, and no amount of my wailing or disagreeing budged him an inch. "You have miscalculated, Emma. I will make every effort to be back by the middle of November. That is your time. The captain says that the weather is rainy but mild well into December, so you are not to worry. All will be well."

"But why you? Can't Adam and the others find the place?"

He shook his head as at a recalcitrant child. His words were sing-song, a repetition. "We are a team sent out, Emma. Finding a place for the colony, that is what matters most. You must remember this. I'll be back in due time."

I'd been a part of that team too, though he said nothing about that.

"I can't even make them understand me," I said. "How will I ever tell them what I need?"

"A good opportunity for you to learn English." He sat beside me on the narrow bed we'd slept one night in. *One night!* He hadn't even chosen to stay a week here, so anxious was he to complete his precious mission. "You said you could adapt, Emma, could make do, so we wouldn't have to turn back, wouldn't have to send someone chosen for this work on a detour. This is what you wanted, *ja*? You get what you want, now."

"You'd leave me? With strangers? In this...fallen world? What about my possible corruption? Aren't you worried about my becoming envious of the luxury here, unable to give it up when the time comes?"

He frowned. I realized I'd never mocked one of the reasons given for our needing to find a new site.

"Are you worried about people here making you do something you shouldn't? I don't believe this of them. They are soldiers. They'll protect you. You're safe here, from all kinds of harm. Even families are here."

I wept then. "I have nothing for the baby when he comes, no swaddling cloths. My own dresses are thin as spider webs."

"*Ach,*" he said, patting my shoulder as we sat side by side on the bed. "I'll ask John Genger to leave an account with the captain. So you can purchase cloth to make a new dress and clothes for the baby. Purchase food for yourself, too, though the captain has said you can eat at his table. It will give you something to do while you wait for this one to arrive." He rubbed my belly with the palm of his hand. "You will contribute now to the Lord's work by waiting."

"I don't want to wait without you. It's why I came in the first place, so I wouldn't need to be alone when the baby came."

He leaned back. "You said you didn't know—"

"I meant when we talked about sending me back," I corrected. "Does the Lord call you to leave your wife behind like this? Isn't there a proverb about an unloved married woman being one of the three things no one can abide?"

"*Liebchen,* you are loved. You must learn not to rely on others to make you happy. Happiness comes from knowing what God calls us to and doing that. All else is false."

"So that's part of your, your…theology, deserting your wife in her hour of need? I thought our leader taught us to treat our neighbors as ourselves. This is not how to treat neighbors, Christian, deserting them when they need you most."

He stroked my hair as I leaned into his chest. "What one comes to believe, one's theology, is in large part what gets written on one's own heart in ways that are hard to describe to another. Like poetry it becomes. Like a beautiful dream that loses its depth in the daylight. Think of Martin Luther. Of John Calvin. Their everyday lives changed who they became and changed what they came to believe. And what others came to believe as well. Ask them about their theology, and they would talk to you of the struggles they had and the choices they had to make in their everyday lives, *ja?* Indeed. It's how they came to know that each of us can speak for ourselves to God." I nodded and sniffled. "I'm not called to abandon you and I don't. I'm called to do what is asked of me, to take care of you and to continue with the other scouts to accomplish what others are counting on us to do. It is why we are here, Emma. Because others are counting on us. You must do your part now."

"But what's wrong with all the scouts staying right here in Steilacoom? Why can't we find donation land claims near here? It's perfect, as you said Ezra Meeker described it. There are already people here and towns and the climate..." I breathed in deep. "It is perfect."

"Well, it may be, but we will not know until we survey more, look beyond what has already been carved out. We look for our own clearing in the wild, Emma. As each of us must do in our own hearts. Perhaps this time without me right at your side, where you are asked to do new things that might frighten you unless you lean onto the Lord, perhaps this is how you will begin to clear your wild."

"The baby really will come in October," I whispered.

"The doctors all say November, and I will be back in November. I always keep my promises to you, *Liebchen.* You can count on this."

My tears did not stop him. My prayers were rarely answered of late, so when he walked through the door away from me, I didn't bother to pray he would stay. Instead, I turned my back on him on the seventh day of October and buried my head in the feather pillow. I didn't know when I'd see my husband again.

The day darkened with rain that fell from a pewter sky. No one knocked on my door to see if I was alive or dead. I lay on my bed, staring up at the peeled logs, watching a spider weave its web. I tried to imagine what the scouts would be doing, how Christian would get along without his wife at his side as I'd been these last months. They'd see, those scouts, how much harder it would be to search for the right site without me along. They'd see. I pulled the wool blanket up around me, feeling suddenly chilled.

Who would fix Christian's corn drink on the trail?

The Knight brothers would.

Who would wash their heavy jeans and shirts?

Christian would, as he'd helped me perform that labor each time. He always acted as a servant, even though he was the chosen leader.

Who would encourage them?

It wouldn't be me even if I had been along. Hans made us all laugh. George kept us fed with fresh game. John Genger kept us solvent. The Stauffers read the landscapes. What had I contributed?

I'd given little with my presence. They'd had to accommodate me on the journey west. My absence offered more to the success of their venture. What kind of uniqueness was that? What kind of theology was I inventing?

"Challenges defined belief," he'd said. I looked back to see what evidence existed for that in my life. When I thought I'd be left behind in Bethel, I'd met that challenge by discounting the virtue of my childhood and lying my way onto this journey. At least, I'd omitted some truths and in that way betrayed those I said I loved most. What would it have hurt me to remain with my parents and travel out with Christian's family in a year or two when they'd found a site? What would I have lost in staying behind?

I felt my stomach knot. To be excluded from this, to be asked to continue on in the colony routine, to never question what our leader asked of us, was that a woman's lot? Was that the belief I couldn't accept? Tears dribbled down my cheeks and into my ears.

In German, the word *to believe* meant to feel deeply about a thing. I did believe in my husband and the work he was called to. I did feel deeply about the success of the journey and the ultimate goal of bringing the colony to a new and different place. But I felt deeply about my own needs, too, my own rights to pursue what I might be called to do. Helena Giesy would say wives were called to support their husbands. Our leader would say we are to shun the ways of the world and serve our Lord on the road our leader chose—the road of obedience to him, service to one another, and lives without envy.

My mother would likely concur with those virtues. I missed her this night. Though I did wonder, as I fell asleep, how that strand of pearls she wore hidden by her collar fit with her living a simple, devoted, colony life.

15

To Need Another

I'd have to ask for help for everything: where to empty my chamber pot, where to get water so I could heat it to bathe. He'd left me helpless as an infant, me who wished to be independent, to do things on my own. I'd become a bummer lamb, that smallest offspring sent for special handling because it couldn't survive on its own.

Worse was that I couldn't even ask without appearing like a *Dummkopf.* I'd have to fumble and mumble along like a toddler just learning to talk. My parents had never encouraged my learning English. They'd never stopped speaking German, even though they'd lived in America for years. Papa said it would make them too much like everyone else, that they'd just meld into the world around them if they spoke as the outside world did. Our leader never encouraged outside learning either, unless it offered practical advice about animals or grain, woolens or wagons. The Bible met our educational needs, he always said, and that book was written in German. Bethel didn't even have a library. Still, my father learned English in order to reach out to those beyond the colony, to recruit people, to buy land for the colony owned by "the world." He'd entered the world without becoming contaminated.

Christian learned English too, and I surmised that our teacher, Karl Ruge, owned a variety of books on more subjects than German or mathematics. I remembered seeing him read a book of plays once, written by someone named Shakespeare. The very tools that would let me survive in the world outside were seeds in my father's garden. I would become fluent in English, that would be my new vow.

Right now, I needed to meld into that outside place, watch and learn as I could, become someone who didn't stand out, at least not for what I lacked.

I slept off and on during that day that Christian left me. I'd awaken, startled by the unfamiliar setting, then think of his leaving me behind. My stomach felt as heavy as a rock plopped into water. *"Tschuess, Liebchen,"* he'd whispered before he left. "Good-bye, sweetheart," he'd repeated in English. I'd turned my back to him.

Hours later, though I needed a bath, I simply could not bring myself to ask where I could heat water or even to bother trying to explain myself. I'd just suffer for a time, scratch where the wool wrapper chafed at my neck and across my belly. I wrote a letter to Mary but couldn't begin to tell her of the awful thing Christian had done, leaving me here alone, putting his precious mission before anything else. Isolation. He'd certainly found that for me, and he didn't need colony wilderness to do it.

Sometime in the late afternoon, a loud thump hit my door, once, twice, three times. It wasn't a knock exactly, coming low on the door as it did. With a push of energy I got up from my bed and lifted the latch.

"Simmons," Nora said to her son, holding a hard leather ball. She shook her head at him, smiled at me with apologetic eyes. Nora motioned me out then and offered me a chair in an open room that housed Japanese prints on the whitewashed log wall. I'd spent the day alone, and now she had a tea service set up in the open room. I could hardly turn her invitation down.

After she poured me tea, she tended her youngest, whose name I didn't yet know, while I sat on an embroidered stool. My fingernails needed attention. My wrapper, all speckled with spots, looked like it had measles. Simmons now bounced the ball against the wall, watching me watching his mother.

Nora used the word *mess* when she changed the napkin of her youngest, a girl with just a fuzz of blond hair. *Could that be the child's name?* "Mess," Nora said with a bit of disgust in her voice, but she grinned at her daughter. I knew it couldn't be a name. But when she proposed we go to the "mess," I wasn't sure I wanted any part of it.

She motioned eating with her hands, and I nodded, though I did wonder if eating would end up in a "mess." My stomach growled with hunger. I'd spent most of my last twenty-four hours in my windowless room, since late afternoon of the day before. A charcoal dusk brushed the sky. I'd brooded and pouted with no one even seeing how I struggled. No wonder I felt hungry.

I should have bathed, should have combed my hair or at least rebraided it. But what did I care? It would serve Christian well if others judged his wife to be a "mess."

A knock on the door revealed a tidy-looking Indian woman, who took the towheaded child from Nora. She said something to Simmons and he laughed, but he put down the ball that he'd been bouncing in a steady rhythm against the wall, and instead from the Indian woman he accepted what looked like skin stretched across a narrow circle. It now assumed his attention as he struck it with his hand. *A drum.* The child played a drum. He made me think of my little brother William, who would have loved such a toy.

Nora motioned to me, then pulled me up from the stool. Her hands felt warm and smooth. She said something and with her eyes asked permission to do something to my face. I nodded, and she brushed the loose curls from around my ears, then led me to the wash basin in the room she and her husband must have shared. *"Danke,"* I said. I'd just do my face. I didn't care about the aroma of me at that moment.

The *gut* doctor came out from the other side of the cabin and bowed slightly to each of us. He pulled his wife's arm through one of his own, then offered me the other. I took it. It must be the custom in these parts, I decided as we walked to the next log cabin. Apparently, the officers and wives were served their evening meals, all taken together like a family.

Walking in to a room full of faces, five men and two other women besides Nora, was not my idea of pleasant. I wished now I had changed my clothes and asked for a garlic compress to reduce the puffiness in my eyes.

I hiccupped. One of the women giggled. My face felt hot. I had to find some way of turning this discomfort into grit. It would be my…theology. If Martin Luther and my husband found meaning in life by facing challenges they'd have preferred not to, then I would do so as well. I'd ask for no special attention, not that I could ask for anything with clarity. I'd listen carefully to what everyone said but watch what people did more. Maybe each day, I'd choose one word that I'd try to remember and write down, making it sound in a way that Nora could read it and say it out loud, and then I'd know I had written it well. I'd know I pronounced it correctly. *Superior.* I knew it as a word that meant someone above me, someone higher up. Why it came to me just then I do not know, but as I looked into the eyes of those women, I felt low and small, making them my superiors I was certain.

For this meal, I'd be lowly, quiet, not bring attention. I'd behave as a deaf woman, using my eyes to interpret whatever I could.

The *gut* doctor stood beside his wife while she made introductions. I heard my name spoken. A blond woman with a long, narrow face raised her eyebrows at my introduction, and I curtsied and repeated her name, as I understood it, with the title, "*Frau* Flint." She waved her hand as though dismissing me, and then whatever she said next made everyone laugh. My face felt as though I'd been sitting beside the fire all day. I caught the English words "emigrant" and "beefy." I knew what emigrant meant, but *beefy?* We'd jerked beef before we left Missouri to feed us along the way. Were they serving beef? I wished Christian were here to help me translate, though with that thought came outrage masquerading as an unexpected hiccup.

Nora patted my hand, then shook her finger at *Frau* Flint the way my mother often did at William when he was younger and avoiding his bath. It was done in jest, and I supposed someone had offered a tease spoken at my expense. I was glad I couldn't understand their comments about my uncontrollable stomach acids.

My brother teased me often at the table, his sign of affection, my mother said. Maybe it was *Frau* Flint's way of being friendly, too. I smiled at her, hoping to win her over.

Captain Maloney sat at the head of the table, and he jumped up to pull out my chair. His quick movement attracted the attention of the other table mates, so I sat while their eyes looked at him instead of at me.

Someone must have prayed a grace, as each one bowed their heads. I did as well, taking in a deep breath and praying for strength to survive this...mess.

I survived the mess—my word for the day—without spilling the juice from the venison onto the apron I'd pulled from my pack, still clean from its last washing the day we arrived at Toledo, the day we left the Cowlitz River behind. I ate the pink-fleshed fish they called salmon and let the white sauce swirl into the inside of my mouth. Butter, sweet butter, something I hadn't tasted for months. I savored it slowly. I listened to the barrage of sounds, knowing that my mother had been insulated from English by living within the colony. Her choice made it easier to remain as a German speaker only. This would not be the case if the colony moved here. We'd all have to learn English unless we settled in a place so remote no one lived there but us. We couldn't rely on just a few like my father or Christian or Adam Schuele to be the salt that seasoned the outside world.

I ate the fluffy white vegetables Nora called *wapato*. Words swirled around me like music sung in a language I didn't know. Eventually, the *gut* doctor stood and broke my reverie. He pulled Nora's chair out so she could stand. I lowered my napkin and started to stand too, but Nora waved me to remain. "Finish," she said, the meaning clear.

Captain Maloney then said something, and Nora spoke in a reassuring tone to me, pointing to the captain and adding the English word *home.* I watched *Frau* Flint elbow the woman seated next to her, and the two patted napkins to their lips but not before I saw the looks they exchanged.

Then my guardians left me.

I dropped my eyes, poked at the pudding a soldier now placed before me as he took my plate away. It wasn't supposed to be this way—me, alone, making a fool of myself with total strangers while my husband explored for new worlds. "Home," Nora had said. I missed being home. Even a windowless room with my husband in it would have been "home." I wanted to go home, but I had none, at least not here.

I had no strength for this.

Indigestion left a foul taste in my mouth. My food no longer appealed, and I could feel that prickle at my nose that told me tears threatened like a summer storm. There appeared to be no reason to continue to endure this. I stood abruptly, nodded at *Frau* Flint and the others and stepped behind my chair, my lumbering body pushing it up against the table. I turned to go unescorted back to my room, but the captain reached my side in seconds. I had no idea what he said, but his hand felt firm at my elbow, and I heard more laughter as we walked out the door, him straightening Nora's loaned shawl over my shoulders.

I said nothing. What could I say? He chattered, using words all foreign to me. He pulled me closer, maneuvered me past a rock in the path that he bent to pick up and toss. He patted my hand, smiled, pulled my arm through his. His voice came low and lilting. He leaned over me to pull my shawl tighter around me. "Chilly," I understood him to say, but his breath felt too warm at my cheek. I was a lamb alone in the wolves' quarters.

I pulled my arm free and set a faster pace, stepping ahead of him. He talked, using a tone like the petting of a frightened pup, as he hurried to catch up with me. My fury at my husband grew. I should not have been left in this kind of setting. I did not deserve to be treated as though I were some trollop free for the taking. What must the captain think of a man who would leave his wife behind?

I couldn't depend on Christian—or anyone else, for that matter.

The lamp in the window flickered as I opened Nora's door. I turned to curtsy to the captain, and before he could say anything either to me or to the *gut* doctor as he had answered my knock, I closed the door in the captain's astonished face.

If Christian wouldn't help me, I'd have to help myself.

————

Tending the children was something I could do. There were only Nora's, I discovered in the days that followed. All the other couples here either had grown families as the tiny drawings in their lockets showed, or they'd left their youngsters behind with relatives while their husbands served in this faraway place.

Simmons, the boy, had decided I could stay when I played ball with him one afternoon, never stopping, never tiring. I'd done such things with William and David Jr., and I found it a soothing thing to do. Nora kept saying, "Thank you, *danke*," and I realized that occupying Simmons allowed her to accomplish necessary tasks when Marie, her toddler, took her nap or when An-Gie, the Steilacoom woman, came to help. Simmons apparently did not nap.

Nora also taught her son and allowed me to sit in on the sessions. I picked up new words that way and found I could recognize some words in the Germanic language of English that sounded much like the German words. This made memorizing the words written down on Simmon's slate next to simple drawings much easier to learn. It also meant I could add to the list of English words I kept in a book I'd acquired on account at the sutler's store.

A few Indian words came into my vocabulary too, words An-Gie said more than once that I thought I understood. She called Simmons *tolo* when she nodded her chin toward the boy. I assumed it meant "boy." She'd call, *"Muck-a-muck!"* and he'd come running, so I guessed that word meant either "eat" or "the stew's getting cold" or something to do with food. She used the word *klose* often, too, and Nora even used it. I guessed that must mean *"gut"* or "fine" or "great," a word one should know in many languages, I decided.

In the afternoon when the women gathered together to stitch, Simmons and I played ball. I knew I should have been working on clothing for the baby, but I devoted my evenings to this task, stitching the flannel into a long dress that I could knot at his or her feet to keep the child warm. In the evenings, I took out my chatelaine and sewing kit to mend my own wrapper and let the pretty tin needle holder hang openly at my neck. The work served as backdrop to the evening time when I talked to the baby as though it could hear me. Listening to the chatter of all the women at the fort fatigued me. I learned better with just Nora or An-Gie to listen to.

So during the day, I played with Simmons. My afternoons with him were much more invigorating than listening to *Frau* Flint and *Frau* Madeleine—the other wife at the fort—gossip about me with words I couldn't understand.

Besides, I contributed more to their conversations by being gone.

I wondered if I contributed to the conversations of the scouts. I missed the men. I wondered where they were, how far away, whether they'd found that perfect place they sought. I missed being with them, all of them.

I missed Christian most of all, especially at night when I could hear the muffled laughter of the *gut* doctor and Nora rising and falling as I sought sweet sleep.

Before long, the anger I carried at Christian's leaving me behind turned into aching and, I decided, a theology of unrequited longing.

———

It was while playing ball with Simmons on October 19 that I stumbled and fell. As An-Gie would say, this was not *klose*, not *gut* at all. I was careful how I fell, aware of my baby even while in slow motion I watched the spruce trees' branches sway above me as I reached for Simmon's ball and lost my footing.

I felt a single sharp thrust beneath my breast that made me gasp for air when I hit on my bottom, hard. Then a jolt at my wrist, where I tried to keep from falling backward. I felt dizzy sitting, holding my wrist. I must have cried out, because Simmons came running.

"Missis, Missis," he said, his small hand patting my shoulder.

"Danke," I told him. I'd ripped the hem of my skirt and would now need to acquire more thread at the store. I smiled to reassure him but swallowed instead as water gathered at the back of my throat. I thought I might be sick. My face must have paled. I felt clammy, lightheaded.

"Mommy! Mommy!" he shouted as he ran to the cabin where the women stitched.

"No, no," I called to him. The last thing I needed was *Frau* Flint making some comment about my clumsiness or my beefy nature. I tried to stand, couldn't. My bulky body rolled on the dirt and spruce boughs I'd slipped on when I went to catch Simmons's tossed ball. I panted now, looked around for something to use to pull myself up with, but we'd been in a field and the tree that gave its boughs up kept its trunk beyond the fence, too far away for me to reach or lean against.

"*Ach,* Christian," I said, wanting to curse him for not being there. I supposed that even if he'd stayed with me, he could have been in Steilacoom for the day or back at Fort Nisqually and not been able to help me now, but I wouldn't let him off that uncomfortable hook when I saw him. I suppose I shouldn't have been playing ball, but it seemed a harmless-enough occupation.

Nora rushed out of the house then, followed by *Frau* Flint and *Frau* Madeleine. An-Gie rushed too, carrying Marie.

"*Ach,* I'm such a bother," I said. They each took an arm, and one got behind me to ease me up. "*Ja.* Good. *Klose,*" I said, nodding. I was still panting and lowered my head to keep the world from spinning. My mother said such behaviors often worked.

Nora on my right put her arm around my waist, *Frau* Flint did likewise on the other side, and with slow steps they took me to the side of the house, where Nora's husband worked in the infirmary. She shouted something to Simmons, and he dashed from the porch, where he'd been staring, and ran through the door to his father.

The *gut* doctor held a towel in his hands, sleeves rolled up, and he frowned as the women led me closer. "I'm good," I said. "*gut.*"

"Here," he said and motioned the women to help me inside.

I tried to pay attention, listen to what he might try to tell me I should do to ease the motion sickness. His kind face and gentle hands helped lay me on the cot. "Good," he said. "Very good."

At last something was *klose,* and I hadn't had to ask for help after all; it had been offered. It was the last thing I remembered before I fainted away.

16

Original Sin

I saw Christian's face in dreamlike motions leaning over me with gentle eyes, caring globes of sky above me that I fell deeply into. I wondered how they'd found him, told him of my need to have him near me, sighed with relief that he'd returned.

But his voice had changed, and when I focused, these were not Christian's azure eyes at all. The *gut* doctor stared at me instead. I pressed my eyelids closed against the disappointment.

Distant sounds of wind through trees rushed against my ears, so I heard little of whatever chatter there might have been within that room. The scent of Nora's lavender soap drifted past me as she placed a cool cloth on my head. Someone brushed glycerin on my lips, a woman's soft finger easing like a skater across my flesh.

I hadn't fallen on my stomach, I knew this. I had protected my baby even in my reaching for Simmons's throw. That was why my wrist hurt so. I'd turned it nearly backward to break my fall. I lifted my hands, opened my eyes to peek. Tiny bits of stone and dirt ground into the flesh of my palms, proof of how I'd kept my child free from harm.

Dirt on my hands.

My wrist throbbed. Nora washed my palms and then my fingers, massaging them, one by one. I flinched at the pain in my left hand, wondering why her touching my fingers should bring such pain to my wrist.

She replaced the cool cloth grown hot from my fevered head. The *gut* doctor left then, and Nora sat beside me, sometimes reading from her Bible words I couldn't understand; sometimes sewing tiny stitches on a quilt square. Simmons came in once and leaned against her, asked a question. His mother gave an answer. He sighed and left. I so wondered what they said.

The day went on in dreamy states and, except for my wrist, I felt no piercing pains, but my body felt as though it carried a rock dropped inside my pelvis. My child kicked once, and my back ached as it never had before. I breathed words of gentleness to him, and he rested for a time.

But in early evening a kind of motion sickness interrupted what had felt like troubled sleep. I sat up, must have cried out, that rock sinking in my pelvis pushing to get out, stretching flesh and searing through my body in an effort to be free. An ache rolled over me more frightening than painful in its change. I was alone, though Nora must have lit the lamp beside my bed. "*Frau* Nora!" I shouted. What was this? It couldn't be labor, could it? I remembered then our leader's admonition that women experience pain in childbirth as a universal act of remembering our Garden sins. Perhaps Fort Steilacoom was too far from Eve's Garden for God to care about my pain, this unusual pain. It was not as our leader foretold. I didn't feel cut in two. I didn't feel as though sin lay on me. I felt discomforted, yes. But it was pain hard to describe... distinctive. Unique. I panted.

I felt wetness beneath me, and then, as though I'd swallowed a horse, a burning pushed through my abdomen, but I swore I wouldn't cry out again. My husband abandoned me. My mother lived months away. No stranger offered comfort.

But then Nora scurried inside the room, took one look at me and left, returned in minutes behind her husband, her skirts swaying. I motioned with my hand to my abdomen, wondering how I might ask for soda for the burning there. A sting of pain rose over me then, followed by a climbing pain that arched above me and made me want to push my insides out. My eyes throbbed like a heartbeat. "Is this it?" I panted. "Does my baby come?"

Before the *gut* doctor could answer, he threw my skirt onto my abdomen. The pain crested. I shouted loud, a wail almost, and then this aching stretching as though I'd ridden through a rock cleft to the wide clearing on the other side.

"Boy, Mrs. Giesy. *Junge*," the doctor said.

"Es ist Junge?" I asked in German. "It's a boy?"

In response, I heard a baby's cry as he held the infant up for me to see. A twisting cord of flesh tied us together, and then I saw toes, then chubby legs and all the parts and hands and head that spoke of his completeness and perfection: our son. The doctor continued speaking, but all I really understood was *Junge*. Boy.

Heartburn. Stretching flesh. Not much to complain about. I lay stunned by the arrival of an infant with so little trouble. My wrist from the fall I took hurt more.

Our leader might say I'd slipped past sin.

As Nora laid the infant on my breast I sighed, so grateful, so amazed that I had given birth with so little fanfare. I felt no guilt at all, but rather joy that I had co-created with our Lord and brought new life into the colony!

The child's dark fuzz brushed against my face. Nora rolled a quilt behind me so I could sit up a bit, then I nestled the boy in the crook of my arm. The size of a watermelon, he promised as much sweetness. I gazed into his face. He'd be tall one day like his father. His hands were large, his fingers long. He was full term, arrived when he should have.

I'd tell them if I could. He wasn't a month early, as the two medical men predicted. I'd love to tell them they were wrong, but it would have to wait for Christian's arrival for that translation.

I wished my husband had been here. He'd missed his son's arrival. Otherwise, this child appeared on time, in October, just as I predicted, without tragedy or unbearable pain.

I named him Andrew Jackson Giesy for the president that Christian loved so much. Christian's grandfather carried the name too, but it was for the president I'd call our son. "A man of the people," my husband called Andrew Jackson, "who fought the banking institutions and other powered men in order to bring better lives to those who worked so hard." It didn't matter that the Senate later censured him. That act was led by his former rival, Henry Clay. Jackson said the banks monopolized and therefore hurt each small farmer. Being censured for seeking truth, my husband told me, was a badge of courage. Experiencing challenge and distress in the name of virtue was a virtue itself.

The year of my birth, Jackson was nearly assassinated for his views. He became even more worthy in Christian's eyes when he died ten years later, having never given up on his beliefs. I hadn't followed politics all that much until I married Christian, but he'd said if our child was a boy, we should call him Andrew Jackson.

As a dutiful wife, when the child opened his eyes to me, I did just that.

I stayed in a daze of wonder throughout that evening, considering our leader's predilections for my disaster. Except for my aching wrist, this childbearing had been an easy venture. Perhaps it was man's duty to imagine the worst and woman's duty to prove them wrong.

I slept with my son beside me, though I woke often to be sure he still breathed, those tiny lips like pumpkin seeds barely moving as air as soft as sunrise moved between them. I so wanted to share these moments with Christian, to have him see that I could do what he hoped: give birth without bother, tend to our child, and as Scripture advised, bring the baby up in the way that he should go so he would never depart from it. I'd begun that very morning saying prayers for Andrew—Andy, as I thought of him—someone firm and sweet and not needing the power of the former president, an infant basking in the love of his mother.

Andrew was the name of a disciple, too, the one who pointed out the boy with the basket of fish when our Lord gave His sermon on the hillside. An observer, that Andrew, and a good and loving man who noticed children and all they could contribute.

I showed my Andrew to Nora in the morning while he wore the long gown I'd made for him. *Frau* Madeleine tucked the blanket under his chest with her bony fingers, speaking in her high-pitched voice. Her words sounded joyous, and I heard her say "bright," a word I'd thought referred mostly to a bold dye or the sun.

I kept him tightly wrapped when I met *Frau* Flint at the sewing time, not certain what her English words might say. She didn't seem the least interested, merely lifted her glasses on her beaked nose to stare at him, grunted once, and returned to her stitching.

Nora brought An-Gie in. She looked at my child and smiled. "*Tolo,*" she said. "*Junge,*" Nora told me in German. An infant boy. Nora motioned for An-Gie to comb my hair. I'd purchased new combs, abalone shells that the sutler kindly said he would order in for the commissary store. I showed them to her, and An-Gie turned them over in her wide brown hands, then began the gentle tugging and pulling on my hair. I felt tended and closed my eyes and hummed as she worked.

Even Captain Maloney's somber face at dinner could not dissuade the joy I felt, showing the seated group my son, who by now had begun to share his own voice with this company. I suppose every new mother thinks her child is the loveliest and best, but I was sure of this. I set aside the ache of knowing others saw his son before Christian did.

The second morning my body felt sore in places I'd never known it to be before. Worse, my child wailed and couldn't be comforted for long, neither by my stroking his face nor planting tulip kisses on his brow, tiny smooches opening to larger ones if only he responded. Did children normally fall asleep even when they hadn't sucked nearly long enough? He cried until he slept, then woke to cry again. I couldn't comfort my son, though I walked him and patted him and changed him. I couldn't help him find nourishment at my breast.

Instead of looking plumper as I thought babies did after a day or so of living, his face narrowed. His skin felt loose around his jerking, slender legs.

I winced when Andy tugged at me and at first Nora smiled, as though this sort of behavior from an infant could be expected. But by the end of the third day when he seemed to sleep more than even attempt to eat, I somehow conveyed my breast pain to Nora. She nodded, then offered poultices of grain. She made motions that I should pump my breast, and I felt my face grow warm. This was the work of milkmaids, with goats or cows, not healthy young mothers wanting nothing more than to nourish their child.

A pale liquid, nearly clear, left my body, but even I knew it wasn't enough to nurture a life. I longed for my mother's wisdom of what to do and chastised Christian beneath my breath for his absence, his missing words that would bring help. Then I cursed myself for not knowing what I should have known, what all mothers surely knew.

It was *Frau* Flint who, with gestures firm and clear, her hands cupped beneath her own ample breasts, brought out bristling behavior from Nora. Nora shook her head. *Frau* Flint pointed to Nora's toddler and spoke. Nora dropped her eyes. They argued, at least the snapping of words, and the pursed lips in between them suggested an argument to me. Nora said, "No," and I knew somehow that *Frau* Flint wanted Nora to nurse my baby. For some reason, this kind woman resisted, but she left and returned with a cup of milk.

Cow's milk would rescue Andy, wouldn't it? *Frau* Flint scowled, as though to say "a waste of time," but Nora soaked a rag in the milk, then brought it to Andy's mouth.

He licked, then spit up over and over again until he fell into an exhausted sleep.

Would my child starve? Could that happen? Surely not with a healthy mother and a doctor right there to advise.

Simmons brought me a book to look at while I rocked my limp child. I hoped the pictures would engage my mind on something bright and pleasant. Instead, the book had strange line drawings of an organ grinder and a monkey, a scrawny, narrow-faced primate that made me gasp instead. It looked too much like Andy.

I pushed back tears and vowed to stay alone, enclosed in my room, dipping into the cow's milk to drip into Andy's mouth, even though he spit it up; even though he slept now most all of the time. Some small nourishment had to reach him. Surely, my milk would drop soon. I'd hold him in my private, windowless room to protect him from what others might say while I was forced to watch my child die; I couldn't begin to imagine what I'd tell Christian when he came back, if he came back.

Nora knocked quietly at the door and then entered. Her words were soft, and I could see she cried. She motioned that she'd take Andy, gestured she'd hold him to her breast. I'd seen Marie eat table foods, so perhaps Nora felt her toddler could survive and her milk was better given to Andy. But then I could see the tears in her eyes and somehow knew what *Frau* Flint didn't: Nora had not enough milk even for Marie anymore. She'd been weaning the child. She had nothing to offer. That was the cause of her tears, not her resistance to share what she had.

I would always remember that moment when I knew my child would die. Nothing stirred the air. My mouth felt dry. I understood then what our leader forewarned: not the physical pain of childbirth; not the agony of sore breasts or healing from the infant's passage from his watery world into our own; none of that was worthy pain to redeem the sin that Eve committed. But the searing wrench of powerlessness, of being unable to tend to one's child, to keep those we love from suffering, such was the curse of a woman's original sin. And I'd committed it.

17

Trees of Knowledge

How I longed for Christian's presence, to shatter all my fears, make them unfounded, reassure me that God would intervene and save Andy's life. Could God create a woman able to give birth without bother, but who then couldn't keep her child alive? What kind of God was that? What kind of mother was that?

I tried to remember the verses my father read about children, of God's love for them. Our leader adored children, gave them sweet treats when he met them on the street. He didn't talk about them much, and I wondered sometimes if he thought little ones kept their parents' eyes from him and he was envious of their interest going elsewhere. I chastened my thoughts. I couldn't afford to offend God by decrying one of his chosen servants.

Andy stopped smacking his lips when I brushed water against them. He looked wizened as an old squash sinking into itself.

I could not stand this, I could not!

I raged into the front parlor, paced before the window, where I watched a light falling snow. Were there no goats here? We hadn't tried goat milk. I pawed through the books on the shelves looking for a drawing of a goat so I could show them. What was the word in English? Might the sutler know of a goat? He'd been so helpful with all of my purchases; surely I could tell him what I needed.

I grabbed my mother's cape and wrapped it around me, leaving

Andy lying so still I leaned over him to make sure he breathed. "I'll bring back what you need, I promise," I whispered, then stepped outside, feeling the wet snow cold against my thin slippers.

The commissary stood at right angles to the officers' housing and the doctor's surgery. With my head down against the sleet, the mix of rain and snow, I nearly knocked over An-Gie. With her, a young woman carried an infant in a board. They appeared headed to the commissary. This plump and round-faced child with large liquid eyes blew satisfied bubbles from its lips. I knew what I had to do—if only I could make her understand.

———

The girl carried her baby wrapped in a board decorated with shells and colorful beads. I could smell the cedar wood. She never looked at me, and it was torture staring at this plump baby, smiling while my child lay motionless. Could she tell that my heart split open at the sight of a healthy, fat child?

I tugged on An-Gie's arm, motioned toward the young girl who might have been a granddaughter perhaps or a niece. I pulled her toward Nora's house. The girl held back, but I urged both her and An-Gie into my room where Andy lay.

I picked him up, held his face to mine to feel the small intake of his breath. Then I motioned to the girl to take him.

"No, no!" An-Gie said, standing between us. "No *omtz*. No *ho-ey-ho-ey*. No trade."

Trade? I knew that English word. I held Andy to my breast. *Does she think I would give my son away in exchange for hers?* I held the back of Andy's head with my hand. He still moved, shuddered almost. "No *ho-ey-ho-ey*," I said. "*Muck-a-muck*. Eat." I made the motion with my hand and lips. *"Cum'tux?"* I'd heard Nora use this word to verify that An-Gie understood. She had to understand.

What kind of mother was I to ask a total stranger to bare her breast to my infant and keep him alive? A desperate mother. A strong mother, that's what I was, doing something I had never imagined I would do.

An-Gie spoke to the girl, who at first shook her head. An-Gie clucked her words, repeated *muck-a-muck,* and eventually, the girl laid her baby down on the bed beside the shallow impression Andy's feathery body had left on the quilt. She opened her skin jacket and untied the strings across her chest. Then An-Gie took Andrew from me and placed the baby in this girl's arms.

My child suckled for the first time in three days.

"Klose," An-Gie said. She patted my arm.

He was weak, very weak. The girl kept touching his cheek, as though to remind him of what he needed to do to live. I heard a soft wail in between, a good sign I thought, that he could protest the delay in his eating.

Finally, both fatigued and satisfied, he calmed, his tiny fingers no longer lifting and bending like a waiting praying mantis's, but instead resting in serenity on the smoothness of his savior's breast.

I wept. *"Klose, klose,"* I repeated over and over, hoping that *good* also meant "thank you." Because of these native women, we both would live, for surely I'd have died along with Andy if he'd left this world.

———

From the parlor window in December, I saw the scouts ride through the cedars, ducking beneath the feathery boughs, stirring up thin layers of snow that turned brown grasses into white. I counted the scouts. There were only seven.

I grabbed a shawl against the cool dusk and raced outside, Andy in my arms. He'd gained weight and felt like the watermelon he'd arrived as. My eyes scanned, seeking my husband's. I didn't find him.

"Where's Christian?" I asked Adam Schuele as he tied up his mount to the hitching post. "What's happened?" The horses' breaths puffed into the cold air.

"Nothing happened, Emma. All goes well, though we still do not find the perfect place for our brothers and sisters in Missouri. We come back so Christian can be with you…at your time." He looked down. "I see we arrive too late."

"So he's safe?"

"Christian stops at the commissary to attend to your bills, and ours. John Genger goes with him to ensure the accounting."

I would deal with the dis-ease of those bills later. Instead, I let my rage rise. Christian might have come here first; he might have seen his son before worrying over obligations of the "mission." Hadn't our separation been sacrifice enough for his success?

"What do you bring us?" Adam nodded toward the bundle in my arms.

"A boy," I said. "Andrew Jackson Giesy. The first new member of the Bethel Colony in the West."

I held Andy up for Adam and the other scouts to see, then pulled him back into the warmth of my chest. Andy cried, and I patted his back while the men stood at a distance, nodding their heads in that way that men do with newborns, that mix of hesitancy wrapped in awe, humbled that women bring forth such lusty life and that they too had a part in it.

George Link made the only specific comment. "He has big hands. He'll carry the *Schellenbaum* well." The rest of the men mumbled agreement before they headed to the soldiers' barracks where they would spend their nights. They walked as though they carried extra weight, though their faces had all thinned since I'd seen them.

All the lamps were lit, and Pap, An-Gie's daughter, held Andy while I swayed her boy in his board by moving my knees as I sang. These two were brothers fed from the same breast. I'd decided not to run after Christian; the sutler would tell him of Andrew soon enough.

The abalone shell combs held my hair in the low knot at my neck. I'd embroidered a tiny white shell onto the otherwise plain woolen dress that I'd made while Christian was gone. I hoped Christian would like it. The wool had been expensive, but it would last a long time. I had never sewn an item from cloth made by someone I didn't personally know. I even knew the sheep back in Missouri and carded the wool with my own hands to tug at the sticks and burrs hidden there. I spun the wool into thread and finally into fiber. I thought of that now, the memory of spinning arriving as a soothing thought for the anxious waiting of my mind.

Like bursts of bubbles from Andrew's lips, little worries popped up. Would Christian be happy with this son? He was a bit thinner than I would have liked. Would he be pleased to see me? Had he missed me at all?

I stood up holding Pap's son, went to the window, sat back down. Where was Christian? Why didn't he come?

Nora's children played on the floor while she and An-Gie fixed their meals. In no time, the *muck-a-muck* call would come. I hoped Christian would be back here in time to walk me to the meal.

The clock ticked steadily, and I decided to give him five more minutes, and if he hadn't arrived, I'd find him even though my interrupting him at the commissary would annoy. I went into my room, patted fresh-scented water onto my neck and throat. It had been nearly two months since I'd seen him. Did I have new wrinkles? I returned, lifted

Pap's baby again, and sat back down. I unlaced Pap's child from his board. Soft moss served as both a pillow for his head and ballast beneath his knees, and as a diaper to keep him dry. I held this chubby child on my knees. Across from me, Andrew continued to suckle at Pap's breast.

I heard footsteps, and when Christian stepped onto the porch, night had already fallen. He wore an expression of dismay, almost irritation, as he eased through the door, head ducked to miss the top of the opening. He stomped muddy snow from his boots and caught my eyes. He moved to the child on my knees, bent down and smiled, a gesture that turned to confusion. "This is our boy? The sutler tells me he arrives ready to play music."

The German words fell across me like music, words I could understand after so much time in the darkness, so much time as though I were deaf. "Pap tends our child," I told him and nodded toward the girl breast-feeding. "She feeds our son, Andrew Jackson."

Christian startled, then took his eyes from the baby I swayed on my knees. He rested his eyes on the baby Pap fed. His cheeks burned red. *Because of the cold,* I thought. He cleared his throat and turned, offering his profile to the girl and our son. "I'll let her finish," he said, coughing, "while you tell me why you let another feed our son."

"Ho-ey-ho-ey," I said, and Pap exchanged my baby for her own. A tiny drop of milk still lingered on Andrew's pink lip as I held him, slender arms akimbo like a spider's. He smelled of fresh milk. "I had no choice," I said. "I…couldn't make the milk he needed." I kissed his tiny mouth of the last drop of white.

Christian looked confused. "He comes too soon," he announced then. He stood, hands straight at his side. "You did something to make him arrive before he was ready." He stiffened his back as straight as a rifle, and I could almost see his finger shaking at me as though I were a wayward schoolgirl, though he held his hands into stiff fists.

"He arrived healthy, a chubby baby," I said. "He came when I expected him to. October 19. It was when I couldn't feed him that he wizened. Pap saved him."

"You fell, the doctor tells me."

I showed him my palms, the tiny pebbles now blue dots beneath my skin. "Yes, but I caught myself when I fell—"

"And injured our son."

"No, he—"

"*Ach*," he said, pushing his hand against the air, both silencing and dismissing me. "I had such hopes for you, Emma. But now you see the consequence of not behaving as a young wife should."

"Christian, please."

But he'd already stomped out the door.

Why was he so upset? Why didn't he give me time to explain?

———

I'd decided to go after him when Christian returned with the *gut* doctor. It seemed like hours but wasn't. Nora still stood patting my back; An-Gie now served stew to Simmons and Marie. Pap held her son, wrapping him back into his baby board.

"We go to eat now," Christian said. "Come."

I handed Andy back to Pap. I didn't look to my husband to see if I had permission for such an act. It was my duty to tend to my child, and I'd done it without him and still would. How dare he judge me while he was off with his precious mission that had once included me and now did not.

I shivered as we walked to the meal together, the silence murky and heavy as mud. Weeks of missing him and this is what returned? I tried to keep up with him, but I faltered, my slipper stuck in the snow-crusted mud. A cry escaped my lips. The sound slowed Christian. He turned. "*Ach, Liebchen,* how does this happen always to you?" He held his hand to mine and pulled me to him. He motioned for Nora and the *gut* doctor to continue on.

"My slipper stuck," I defended when the others disappeared inside the mess hall. But Christian shook his head.

"What trouble you bring upon yourself and others too, it appears."

"I behaved as any wife left behind with total strangers would have," I defended. "I made myself useful to Nora and her husband. I tended to their children to help pay my way."

"Indeed. But not completely, or so the sutler's account tells me."

"Oh," I said. Perhaps this is why he was so angry.

"*Ja,* oh. That's something else we must discuss."

"I was as frugal as I could be," I told him. "I even learned to find cedar bark that can be woven into hats that repel the rain. I let An-Gie introduce me to this landscape. I learned some Indian words that might be useful one day. I dealt with being alone where no one spoke my language, and you dare say I bring trouble on myself?" I crossed my arms. I would have tapped my foot in outrage except that the slipper would sink back into mud.

He picked me up to carry me over the mud then, his motion swift and sure. His arms wrapped warm and welcoming around me. He set me down at the steps, then held my slipper, wiping the mud off with the palm of his big hand.

"I took care of it," I continued my defense. "I found Pap to feed our son, told her what I desperately needed. Even without knowing her language. I did what I had to do, left here alone. I did it, and I'll not let you make me feel less for having done it."

I saw the clench of his jaw relax, though his next words were spoken with annoyance. "*Ach, ja,* I am the *Dummkopf,*" he said, "spending long days trying to find our new home while you are here…spending." He pushed the slipper back onto my foot.

"I needed things," I said.

"Hair combs. Fine wool. A silver spoon?"

"He is our first child. All firstborn sons need something special to announce their arrival. He didn't even have his father here to hold him to the stars and introduce him to God." I lowered my eyes. "I'll find a way to pay for it," I said, though the how of that was far from certain.

He pulled me to him then, snuggling the cape close to my neck. Tingles of connection quivered through me to my knees. "You're cold," he said, quiet. "We should go in to the meal."

"I'm sorry for the purchases. Was John Genger terribly angry with me?"

"More with me, that I left no good instructions for you." He sighed then. "But I am angry more at myself. I carried that into our argument earlier. That was a mistake. You did well to keep Andrew healthy and alive, and I am grateful to have a son. *Ach*," he said. "We scouts, we spend good time and money and don't even find what will work, and then I come home and argue with my wife. An unloved married woman I do not want you to be."

I could see the upturn of his lips in the moonlight.

"Then let's stay here in Steilacoom," I said. "Let's see if we can buy up land here in this good place." I faced him, my hands on his chest. "Our grain could be shipped out by sea from here, and the weather, it isn't so cold. See?" I lifted my ungloved hands up as though to catch snowflakes, though none fell.

He shook his head. "We will talk of this later, *Liebchen*. For now, let me tell you of my sorrow that you were left alone to decide what was best for our child. This is not the way a man should treat his wife. I hoped to get back in time. This was my goal."

"I know. Adam told me. But Andy really did arrive at the right time."

"Everyone says November," he repeated, and I could hear an argument rising that could never be solved. I decided not to add to the fuel of that fire, one better put out. "It will not happen again," Christian continued. "Our next child and the next after that will be born with me at your side."

I should have said then that making such plans simply challenges the devil to interfere, but I wanted to hear those comforting words. With them, Christian lifted my chin and kissed me, stealing my breath and repairing my broken heart all in one act of forgiveness and love.

———

We spent three more months at the fort resisting the rains. A happier time in marriage I'd never had. Christian did explore land sites near Steilacoom. He walked to Olympia and looked at maps with coastlines and dots of towns, but few marks of trails and no roads to speak of. He returned, usually within a few days, telling me tales of what he saw and what he heard. The other scouts too fanned out, returning with crestfallen eyes, drenched to the bone from the rain.

Christian watched our son grow and came to accept Pap's presence in our days and her son, whom she called Nch'I-Wana for the name of the big river, the Columbia, where he'd been born. My husband was a loving father. He watched how Nch'I eased into sleep inside his board, then asked how he might make one. An-Gie giggled when she understood. "No men do," she said, but she showed him, and he cut the board while we women cut the hide that would wrap around Andy, gathered moss to serve as a pillow and to place behind his knees. I stitched tiny squares to make a covering for the boughs that arched out over his head to keep the sun from shining in come spring; to keep the rain out when we went outside. He rode on my back, looking out at the world while my hands were free to help Nora with the laundry or to sew, remaking my overland dress into a shirt and skirt for my son.

While Andrew slept, Christian taught me more English words, and I shared what I knew of the Chinook and Chehalis words Nora and An-Gie and Pap often used. Eventually, I could talk to Nora of places and people. It was she who told me Captain Maloney had merely wished to offer me safety when he'd walked me home after Christian left. My face burned with the memory. Nora and I also talked of something that truly mattered: her offer those months ago to feed my child even at the risk of not having enough for her own, and my wish to thank her for that gift of willingness she gave. She practiced the Diamond Rule, wanting my life to be better than her own.

Rain fell steadily with rarely a break those first months of 1854. The paths between the houses and the mess hall ran like streams despite the wagonloads of woodchips, brought from the mill in Lower Steilacoom, that the soldiers put on them. This land was made of mud. Rain and mud. And trees, trees so large that four men holding hands could not reach around the trunks. Sometimes my eyes traveled one hundred feet up the trunk before I saw branches spreading out.

Sometimes, while Christian traveled to the surrounding towns and while Andrew slept, I'd make my way into the stand of trees, grand fir and Sitka spruce and red cedar. I learned their names. Beneath them, I found the ground soft, but not as muddy as along the meadow trails. I could hear the rain drip on leaves, push through needles, falling soft as teardrops on the forest floor. I'd find a place to sit beneath tree-falls, what Christian said the men called the large trunks pushed over by winds or age against another, or caught up in tangled branches, sometimes crisscrossing narrow trails like sticks set to build a giant fire. I found respite in the cluster of these trees, in knowing I had a warm, dry place to return to. I prayed that Christian would find his mission here, close to Steilacoom.

A couple of the scouts went south into Oregon Territory seeking sites, but in early spring they returned, and at a meeting I was allowed to attend, they shared their news. Christian told them he'd talked to men from the Pacific coastlands who knew of a place with wide river bottoms rich for planting. Nearby, timber waited to be harvested for buildings. The logs offered pilings for shipment to San Francisco, and with the Bethel Colony bringing grist stones, there'd be water for a mill.

"Isolation, too," he told them.

"When do we go then, to see this land?" Hans asked.

"April. When the rain stops and the trails are not so bogged down in mud and the fallen trees are more easily crossed."

"We take axes then," John said.

Christian nodded. "And saws. Ropes. Those are our tools."

"When I look at these trees," Michael Sr. said, "I wonder how many days it will take us to cut one down or try to split it."

"When we find the right place," Christian said, "all will fall into place."

"We've looked at lots of land," Adam Knight said. I heard annoyance in his voice.

"We must all agree on the place," Christian said. "So far, each of us finds some fault with what we see."

"These coastlands you hear about, are they like Ezra Meeker's lands?"

"More isolated," Christian said. "Unlike Steilacoom." He looked at me. "We must not let the demands of the world encroach upon us. Here things are too easily purchased, life made too simple so we forget what we're about."

"Are you sure enough of the coastal site's potential that we could send men back now?" Adam Schuele said. "We've seen the terrain. Those south have too. Could we return to help prepare the rest? We'll be three, four months getting back. That would make it July when we arrive in Missouri."

"It's too late for them to come out this year, and the longer you stay, the more houses we can build. If you go back in August, there will be time to prepare the Bethel Colony for departure next spring."

"We could agree to meet here, then, in Steilacoom, and send word for you to come and get us." This from Joe Knight. I liked this plan. Perhaps I could remain here, too, until the larger colony arrived.

"You think you'd be one to go back?" his brother said with just a hint of teasing.

"No," Christian said, his words cutting off any jesting. "We must find the place together and all feel it is worthy before any return to Bethel. That way we'll know that God has chosen the site, not any of us."

"But not this place?" I interjected.

"No." All the scouts nodded agreement with my husband. "This is not the place we're called to."

I wondered why I felt such a calling here, and yet I was obviously the only one. Why did what I see differ from these men?

"You will have to enjoy your stay here, Emma, for a few more weeks, and then we will all load up, pack what we can carry on our backs and our new mules we've purchased. We'll make a new Bethel."

I nodded agreement. What more could I do?

When the men left in early June, I took a long walk into the cedar trees, Andrew on my back. I prided myself entering the dense trees and finding my way back. I remembered the tree with the moss patch on it that looked like a long, open wound, or the thick bark that had a design in it that resembled a face. My feet made no sounds in the wet woodland. Pap had made a pair of moccasins for me, much more practical than slippers, though I could still feel small cones when I stepped on them at the arch of my foot. I crawled under a new blow-down, careful to push Andrew in his board before me, located the game trail again, and this time walked farther than I ever had before. I made sure of my bearings, then continued on, not sure what I was looking for or how I'd know when I found it.

But I did. Deep into the trees I saw a shaft of sunlight making its way through the denseness. I walked toward it, chattering to Andy as I did, until there it was, taking my breath away.

A meadow. A wide, lush prairie filled with white flowers and pink dots of color. Deer nibbled at the tree line, and overhead large birds called out. It smelled earthy and fresh. I turned around and around, arms outstretched. "This is beautiful," I told Andy. I'd thought this whole country was nothing but trees where rivers cut through them on their way to the sea. All the small towns lick Puget Sound's shoreline. In all our traveling up the Cowlitz, I hadn't seen such wide meadows, such vast prairies. I took this discovery as a sign. There were clearings already prepared for us. We needed to pick one of those and not a place where we'd have to bring down tall, massive trees.

"This could be the land we farm and settle on," I told Andy. It would be the best of both worlds: dark earth easily plowed but isolated and yet close to the sea. And it was right here in a climate we'd already been introduced to, the land that Andy inhaled first. My heart pounded and I sat in the tall grasses, chewed on one long strand that smelled of onion.

I'd been led here, I was sure of it. No matter what the challenge, one just had to keep pushing through dark timbered places, trusting there'd be clearings in the light beyond.

I began my trek back, buoyed by my seeking and discovery, as hopeful as...as *Eve when she first ate of her fruit.*

18

The Winding Willapa

Something isn't right. It is hailing inside our tent. White rocks the size of Andy's fists pelt us. Christian scrambles to repair the torn canvas first, shoving me and Andy toward the back of the lean-to. I lay with my body arched over my son, oddly able to see Christian working frantically as the ice begins to melt and turns to torrents of water filling up our little place, and yet I can see my son beneath me, smiling up. The rain pours down now, and my baby is lifted by the torrent, torn away from me while I grasp, shouting for Christian to stop worrying about the holes in the tent and see what's happening to his family instead. "Christian, help!" I scream, but my words fall on deaf ears while my son floats beyond my reach. I grope! We've camped too close to a river, and now we are a part of. The landscape's chosen us, picked us out to die. Now we're in a craft, a small troubling craft taking on water. I know we have to go under the water to get where we need to be. "Christian, do you know how to get there safely?" He shouts back, "No! I don't have a compass." Andrew cries, and I feel pain in my shoulders.

"No compass? No compass?"

"Emma, you will wake the others."

I opened my eyes, gasping. My husband is arched over me. "You have bad dreams, *ja?*"

My body shook while I reached for Andy, held him close to my chest, slowing my breathing. Then I came fully awake to a storm wailing around us. Wind mostly, not rain. What sounded like hail on top of our canvas tent must've been branches and needles torn loose. Puffs of wind pushed the walls of the tent out like a bloated frog, then sucked them back in. We heard roars like the steam engine at Shelbina. "The trees…?"

"This is an odd storm for August," Christian told me. "The man, Swan, said the weather stayed mild through the summer. High winds didn't come before October maybe. I think we'll be all right." I couldn't stop shaking from the dream. I kept kissing Andy's forehead, and then I remembered Opal, the goat. "Is the goat still tethered?" I asked. Maybe that's what the dream meant, that I'd lose my son because the food he needed had torn loose in the night. Or maybe it meant we didn't really know where we were going, and the weight of this journey would sink us in the end.

The goat bleated then, and Christian lit a lantern, though the wind blew out the light as soon as he opened the flap. *"Verdammt!"* he said, the first curse I'd ever heard from my husband's mouth.

"I find her, Emma. Don't worry," and with that he stepped out into the darkness.

I rocked my son, back and forth. Christian had discounted my grand prairie plan; instead, he and the scouts went west and found what they said was the perfect place. We'd said our good-byes to Steilacoom ten days before, now here we were, in the densest of forests.

Opal's bleating came closer, and then as though the Lord Himself acted as shepherd that night, the goat nearly ran Christian over, pushing back into the tent. It shook its tail of the wet and the wind, its little bell tinkling.

Christian relit the lantern. "I need to make a casing for this light," he said. "To keep the wind from having its way with the oil."

"We need a shelter," I said. "A casing for us. A real home with walls." I stroked the goat with one hand, rocking Andy on my knees. He slept now, and I marveled at his comfort in the midst of chaos. "We'll need a root cellar to hide in if these kinds of storms happen often."

"I tell you, they won't. This is a freak storm, Emma. Don't worry now. Where we go, this will not be so bad. Swan's been here three years. He says the climate is mild not hostile. We'll be all right, and see, the goat finds its own way to safety."

I gripped the goat's rope collar with its tiny bell still dangling from it. "We'll have to hold his collar as his rope's been torn," I said.

"Ja," Christian said. "I'll hold him until daylight, when we can salvage the tether and then move on. "It will be well. You'll see. The place we chose is perfect."

I felt powerless to calm the rush of wind which, as I listened to it, probably wasn't any worse than a rainstorm in Missouri. The dream had heightened my fright.

I held tight to Christian's words. The scouts' unanimity of choice gave me comfort. How could every last scout—save one, me—favor the landscape unless God Himself had spoken to their hearts?

"You rest now, *Liebchen.* With sunlight, the day will be better. We are almost home."

He patted my knee and lay back down under the tarp. He fell instantly asleep, leaving me to grab for the gray goat's collar before it bolted out of the tent opening. It bleated until I spoke to it of the home I imagined in my mind, the words like prayers taking me through the darkness and residue of dreams into a morning calm.

My husband was right. Sunlight made life better.

I stepped outside to see little had changed in the landscape. I saw timbers split and felled months before like some giant hand had flicked its fingers against the forest. Tall firs leaned against others still standing;

more crashed to the ground, their root balls like crones' hands struggling out of forest graves. I squinted. The root balls looked old. The trees that leaned against each other already had moss growing where they met. These trees hadn't blown down in the past night's storm. They'd been down a long time; I just hadn't noticed them when we'd made our evening camp.

"See how the Lord looked over us," my husband said, standing behind me. "Everyone slept well." We watched as the Knights and Michael Sr. and the Stauffers moved from their tents. The only real damage was a tarp with a tear that John Genger set about repairing with the paraffin he carried with him, but I remembered that tear had been there before, too.

I filled Andy's tin cup, fortunately only partway as he batted my hand and whined, letting me know he wanted to do it himself. We spilled less when I'd fed him through the fingertip of a leather glove. I'd poked a hole in the glove to manage the flow. He slapped at my wrist as he reached for it. It had been nearly a year since I'd fallen on that wrist, and still at times it shot pains through my arm. Our son, however, didn't notice. I wondered if every mother experienced pain as we stretched to learn new things, to do things by ourselves. Maybe pain rode before a lesson.

We set out again carrying large packs on our backs as well as on our mules. I carried Andy on my back and walked, draping a bag of items hung by a rope over my shoulders and around my neck. I tugged at the goat, too, as we followed what Christian said was the trail the scouts had cut through this land earlier that spring. I did see evidence of their chopping, but even in the short time since they'd been through here, young shrubs and vines won back the trail. Trees newly fallen across it made us have to choose to either take a day to chop and saw the trees to make an opening or try to go around and make a different trail.

Would we find such signs of effort where we headed? Would one log consume a day to get it where we needed? We'd built brick houses in Bethel. I saw no evidence of material for such here. I couldn't imagine how the wagons coming out from Bethel would make it through here, but I didn't say a word. The scouts chose this. Even practical John Genger and the wise Adam Schuele claimed that God had chosen this site for them all. They could see through these tree-falls and a landscape so big we were all ants in a field of grasses pushing our way through.

Ferns shot up from the forest soil, their fronds edged with tiny dots that looked like perfect black knots of thread. They reminded me of stitching, and I wondered if I'd ever have time for such pleasant needlework again.

This landscape was such a contrast to the meadow outside of Steilacoom that was so open, so easily plowed. But Christian had not even walked there with me, saying he'd been all around, and nothing in that area appealed until this place we were heading to.

Rustling sounds in the distance made the goat pull back on her tether. "Bears," Christian said over his shoulder.

I looked around for bears as I followed him. *A new danger.*

"We're making good noise, so I don't think they bother. I can hardly wait for you to see this new land, *Liebchen.*"

As we walked, I wondered if Moses felt this way leading his people through the desert, sure of the destination but uncertain of the people's readiness for what goodness and trials lay beyond. I thought to mention this perspective to Christian but abstained. He seemed so happy even as the sweat dripped from him and tiny gnats pushed at his face.

"This is a land worthy of God's work," he said as we chewed on hard biscuits when we nooned.

What was one woman's cautious voice against such enthusiasms? I had nothing to say. The scouts' confidence carried me along on this craft without a compass.

———

Twelve days after leaving Steilacoom, we reached the Willapa River. We approached the stream from the east near a bend, so at first it looked tame enough and not particularly swift. A flat spread out from the water's edge, and with sweeping arms, Christian told me, "Here's where we'll make our mark then."

"Right on this bend? This river?"

Narrow meadows, what was once the river's bed, no doubt, lined the river, bearing tall grass and purple flowers. The land we could cultivate at least. The soil looked black when I kicked at a clump of the grass to smell and taste the earth.

"And see, there are plenty of trees to log, for building houses. All we need is here," Christian said.

I looked up at the tops of the trees, nearly stumbling backward. Some stood more than two hundred feet high, making my neck ache as I gazed at their tops. Our tiny saws and axes would be but mosquito bites to the tough, long arms of the trunks that rose before us.

"And this river goes right to the sea, maybe fifteen or twenty miles west at most. We can float logs down, dig for clams at the ocean, have plenty of seafood to add to game. This river lures fish in during the season, Swan tells us. The bounty God has led us to…" Christian stood teary-eyed.

He's in love with this landscape, this formidable, dark, dense landscape.

Christian had no doubts, and the man Swan was spoken of as someone wiser than Moses had been. When we made our way toward a small clearing cut back into timber around the bend, my doubts lessened a little as well. For there rose a sturdy log house almost as large as the surgeon's quarters at the fort. Best of all, a woman holding a bucket in her hand stood before it.

———

Her name was Sarah Woodard. She was but a child, maybe fifteen, with hair the color of pale butter and eyes such a deep blue they looked black at times. Her muscled arms reflected hard work. Sarah and her husband invited us to stay with them at this river crossing for the night. Christian hesitated. In German he said, "We should not get too close to those around here." But Adam said accepting generosity was a kindness in return. I rejoiced. Here lay a feather tick to lie on. We herded the goat in with the Woodard cow and its calf. *They own a cow!*

"We brought it up from California, put onto a ship, and here it is," Sarah's husband said when I commented about the animal. "A brute bred her back so we have another increase next year. We get to keep what we raise, not like those folks who worked for Hudson's Bay Company."

I vowed to have Christian order a cow from California for us. If he intended to send products out on the tide, then south by ship, then we could get them north to ease our lives too. I never thought I'd say it, but travel by ship would be so much easier than what we'd been through overland on what Christian called our "Dutch Trail."

"Why didn't you propose to have the Bethel Colony come out by ship?" I asked Christian. We leaned against a tree at Woodard's Landing, as the place was known. Andy played with the Woodards' dog. The pup brought sticks to him that Andy threw, the makeshift toy landing not far beyond his toes. I shooed the dog back when it started to lick Andy's hair as he sat. "It would be so much easier than to come overland with wagons and stock." I hesitated, then said, "I wonder how the wagons will come through that trail we made. At the first windstorm, you'll have to go back and reopen it."

"You worry over much," he told me. "We'll bring them up the Cowlitz River, as we came in canoes, but only as far north as the Chehalis River. Then it's a short portage onto the Willapa, and they'll be right here, just as we need them to be." I still didn't see how the wagons would come up that Cowlitz trail, but Christian's tone suggested little patience for my questions.

I changed my son's diaper. At least the area offered an abundance of moss for his diaper. I walked to the river and rinsed the cloth, then laid it over a blackberry bramble to dry, checking the ripeness of the berries as I did. It was August. They were ripe enough for pies.

"They'll have no need for wagons here," Christian said when I came back. He'd been thinking of our conversation. He used his preacher voice. "Indeed. All produce and people will go by water to market. Wilhelm's group can sell their wagons in Portland. It will mean more money to purchase grain and other things needed to tide us through the winter."

"But if we've no need for wagons, why not tell the colony to come by ship?"

"Too expensive. Besides, we can use the plows and other personal items they bring. The returning scouts will tell them what we need. Axes, saws, hammers, plows, scythes, seeds."

I wondered if someone would bring out trunks of clothing for us and the other scouts who remained here. *Or perhaps we will return.* That thought proved fleeting as I watched my husband scan this landscape, take some measure of contentment that he had found what he considered the perfect place for the colony.

Whichever scouts returned would have to start back soon in order to be in Missouri before the snow fell. I wanted to talk about that but instead I asked, "And what will the wagon makers do here when they arrive?"

I thought of my brother Jonathan apprenticing as a wagon maker. That had been his plan, to make wagons and sell them to those coming west, his contribution to the colony an important one.

"Maybe they'll build boats," Christian said, his annoyance obvious in his tone. "Or furniture. Each house will need furniture. We adapt in the colony, *Liebchen.*"

Would wintering with the Woodards be an adaptation? We surely couldn't work through the wind and rains of winter to build. But if I said that now, he'd think I coveted comfort. I didn't want any suggestion of weakness, or Christian might consider sending Andy and me back with the scouts—without him.

———

Living in Bethel I knew most everyone. Maybe due to my father's influence, or perhaps because I paid attention to new babies born and did what I could to help at the harvests, adapted, and went where I was told. They were like a family, each willing to help the other no matter what. We were asked to be in service to others, to be ready on Judgment Day to face our Maker and say we had tended to widows and orphans and brought in new sheep to the flock.

Since we'd left Bethel, I'd met dozens of people, some with names I now couldn't remember and some on the wagon trains we briefly joined. We might have nooned with them, listened to their stories and then moved on. The names and faces ran together for me like birds along a rock fence. Maybe our journey intrigued them; maybe they found sojourners in the Lord's vineyard to be of interest. I didn't feel a part of any community with them because we didn't stay in one place together, we didn't share both hardships and joys. A community, even a colony, needed those shared times to bind it together.

I hoped there would be a kind of town when we finally settled. One family named Woodard, a woman plus nine scouts, and a child hardly seemed enough to make up a town. Christian would say our community would arrive full force with the Bethelites and that I must be patient and wait.

But then one morning in late August 1854, even this small fragile community changed.

"Reasonably, it must be George Link," Adam Schuele said in response to the question Christian posed that morning about who would return. "George has a hunter's eye and can repair anything, wagon wheels especially. He can bring the others here safely."

John Genger was chosen along with George, or at least his name came next and he nodded. "We've spent what we must to secure the land, and we will depend on the bounty here for the rest. Essentials you can purchase from Woodards' store, but keep it minimal. There'll be little accounting needed for a time. We need to be sure to have money to bring the first group out while the rest remain at their posts, working."

"Perhaps you should go back with them," Christian said.

Andy rode on my knee, and I bounced him before looking to see who the third person chosen would be. When I lifted my eyes I saw that that the scouts looked at me.

"You'd consider returning?" I asked my husband. He shook his head, no, and in an instant I realized I'd become complacent with my plans. I remembered my earlier vow to do what I could to get Christian to be one of the scouts to go back to Bethel, but the months across the trail and the month here at this Willapa site told me my husband's devotion went to the success of the western colony and that required his effort here. This was his mission, his passion. He'd never desert it, not even for a season. I hadn't imagined that he'd try to send me away.

I took a risk. "Will the scouts return by ship?" I asked. I swallowed hard.

"Maybe we should reconsider returning by sea," Joe Knight said. "It would be less dangerous, perhaps even quicker." He raised his pointing finger to emphasize his point.

"There, you see?" I said. "A sea voyage would shorten time."

"*Nein,*" Christian said. "The expense is too great. Indeed, I'm surprised you'd suggest an ocean voyage knowing how you feel about water."

"I only want to be…cooperative."

"You raise unnecessary issues."

Adam Knight, his eyes cast down, waited to speak. These men were not accustomed to overhearing disagreements between husbands and wives. "Overland is best," Adam said then. "So the Bethelites will have the latest information about the travel. Some may come back to Willapa by ship, and this is good. But to return, the expense is less to go back the way we came."

"It would be better if you returned, Emma," Christian said. "This will be a harsh winter here, everything unsettled. We may need to live in tent houses. Perhaps we could find the resources, John, for fare back by ship?"

The mere thought of me riding those ocean waves without my husband at my side churned my stomach.

"We could consider—"

"No, please," I said. My husband prepared to send me back, get me out of his way so he could stay devoted to his first love and, worse, would take the idea of a trip around the Horn as suddenly legitimate.

"It wouldn't be good. I can help here, I can, Christian. Wasn't I strong along the plains?" I imagined more river crossings and rickety ferries on any return trip; I imagined a long journey back in silence with men perhaps resentful that a woman and child rode with them. I imagined a ship in a windstorm with me and my son all alone. "I could stay with the Woodards. That way I wouldn't be a worry to you."

"No," Christian said, his voice nonnegotiable. "We will not impose."

"We'll have to hunt for ourselves now without George's fine eye," Hans Stauffer said, changing the subject as he scratched that place on his head.

"You've been itching to try," Adam Knight told him.

"*Ja,* now I'll be the hunter," Hans said.

"We'll all have to hunt, and we'll all have to fell trees," Christian said. "You see how much work there is." He stared at me. Did he think that I would agree so he could devote his entire life to this mission, so he'd have no guilt about the conditions he asked me to live in?

"I'll not go, Christian," I said. " 'Whither thou goest, I will go', remember? I can be of use here. I can prepare meals. You will simply have to let me do my share." Andy cried now. He did this at the worst times. "A child needs both his parents," I said. "Surely this is God's order of things. How could you even suggest separating a father from his son, a wife from her husband, when it is not necessary?"

"I believe it is," he said.

The men kept their eyes from us, and finally Adam Schuele said, "Her return could be dangerous, Christian. For her and the boy. I made a vow to her father, to keep her safe. I can't do that if she is on a horse riding sidesaddle back to the States."

"It's not good for a married woman to travel without her husband, not even on board ship, not without at least another woman. These men who stay know their wives and sisters will travel with many others. What would our leader think if you sent me back among men whom I'm not related to?"

Christian might have heard my heart pound, considering how it filled my ears as I waited, my fingers and thumbs making circles on the pads as I wrapped my arms around my son. He fussed and pushed to be set down.

"I decide," Christian said. "Hans and Adam and me, we remain. Then you Knights, you stay too. But in a few months, you go back around the Horn. That way we have both kinds of trips covered. Michael Sr., George, John Genger, John Stauffer, you return now. You'll need safety in numbers; we'll be in this isolated place, which will be our protection. A woman and child would hold you back. We will miss you men, but God goes with you. You bring our families to a good place, the place God chose for our colony."

"We'll build here," Adam Schuele added. "Our colony will keep us spiritually prepared for the end yet allow us to prepare others we come in contact with."

He looked at Christian, whose set jaw locked tight as a closed fist. "Indeed," he said at last. "You're our return scouts. You have special rewards waiting in heaven for your obedient service." It seemed to me he emphasized *obedient* before he turned his back on me.

"Do you agree that I should remain here?" I asked.

"Obedience," he said, "applies even to me."

———

We had a rousing send-off in the morning with prayers and a little music from Hans's harmonica playing. *"Auf Wiedersehen,"* we shouted our good-byes. Christian acted not unlike our leader when he sent the scouts from Bethel, offering up wisdom and guidance, and at that moment, I was as proud of my husband as I had ever been. He forgave my challenging him in front of others. He would perhaps allow me to assist as I could. "We will all sacrifice here as you are sacrificing to return back," he said. "Remember us in your prayers as we remember you in ours."

"Remember our empty stomachs," Hans said. We all laughed, but there was truth to what Hans said. Who knew if we'd have enough ammunition to take the meat we needed? Who knew if we could build three dozen structures within a year so there would be houses for the Bethelites? Who knew if I had just made the best choice for my son and my husband?

I slipped a letter to my parents into John Genger's hand. He tipped his hat as we waved good-bye. Watching their hats disappear through the timber, I thought how a year from now, this would be a new place. What seemed a strange and foreign land would be familiar, and when it was filled with friends and family, it would be the delight of my husband's heart, and I would have played a part in it. I'd been chosen to be here just as the other scouts had been chosen to return.

My heart sang as I turned to begin my new work beside the winding Willapa River.

19

The Giesy Place

We began building on the "Giesy place" about a mile south of Wood-ard's Landing. I picked berries, dried the meat that Hans brought in, shooed away seagulls who pecked at the deer entrails, milked the goat, and while Andy slept, I chopped at slender willow branches—*withes* Christian called them—that could be braided into rope or used for binding while the men felled with their saws.

The timber, both tall and stately, took days to chop through the trunks. I stood in awe of the size of the red cedar they selected first. Smaller than the towering firs and spruce, its long flat needles sagged toward the earth. The tree did not easily succumb. Both its wide girth and the sweat off Christian's brow surprised me. I listened to the chink, chink sound of the axes making their wedge around the base of the trunk. And when the sun set, only small indentations of the axe marked their day's work. Standing inside that forest felt as peaceful as being in the church at Bethel when our leader was absent. Light filtered through the branches. Echoes of bird calls trembled in the silence when the men rested their tools. The air smelled moist, and the forest floor acted spongy against my moccasins, the cedar liking damp, it seemed. I set Andy down and brushed away the needles and picked up a handful of soil to inhale it. Later when a squall moved through, dropping rain on us, we stood with Andy beneath weepy boughs, barely getting wet. I leaned against that dark grain of a thousand years of growing undisturbed until we came and wondered how it was we had found this Eden of our own.

It took the men three days to chop that first tree down.

When at last it cracked and sounds of falling splintered through the forest, Adam shouted to get back. The tree's heaviness lingered in the woods as it sighed against another taller tree and hung there, unwilling to lie down. Sam Woodard called such trees "widow-makers" when Christian rode to get him, seeking advice. Sam offered suggestions to get it down without a death. It required skill and God's blessing, but they accomplished the task.

"Maybe it would be good if you looked for downfalls," Sam suggested. "Find some not rotted. It might be easier."

I thought that good advice, but the men still looked for trees they felled themselves.

By the end of the first week since the scouts had left, they'd felled two huge cedar trees and prepared to cut them into ten-foot lengths for walls. The bark stripped off easily, and Sarah Woodard said she'd seen the Indians pound the bark until it was almost like a cloth. The bark looked fuzzy with fibers floating from it. I pulled some free and found they might work as thread to repair Christian's socks.

The men harnessed two mules brought from Steilacoom and drove them into the forest, and while it may have seemed a good idea, and would be in time, the mules resisted pulling the logs behind them. They startled and reared and snapped ropes, and I could tell that even getting the logs to a building site could take days of wrestling them over brambles and vines into the small clearing at the edge of these trees.

My stomach ached with the possibilities of injury, the snail's pace of the work.

Sometimes, if the men chopped a tree near the top of a ridge, they would try to roll it down, but the tree often hung on another tree felled by a previous storm. The men did then consider chopping and using downed trees, but many rotted in place. They wanted strong, sturdy logs to house us. Cedar, they said, would last forever.

It took a month for the small squat hut we called the Giesy house to rise up at the forest's edge. It needed caulking, something I could do, but the men decided this could be done later. For now, they would set a ridge pole and some cross rafters for later roofing. In time, they'd draw a canvas across it for a winter's roof.

"As the Israelites lived in tents to remember their harvests and all God provided, so will we live," Christian said. The cost of bringing milled lumber from Olympia, or even from a mill Christian learned was built closer to the ocean, meant an expense so great none of the scouts felt it justified. Secretly, I thought they didn't want to have to explain to John Genger where the money went when he returned.

"It'll be easier now that we know how to do it," Hans said when they prepared to move on to build another hut.

Adam Schuele said, "We must show that we can build in this place and live from it as we are asking our brothers and sisters from Bethel to do."

"The weather's mild," Christian noted. "By the time they arrive here next fall, we will have two dozen log homes for them to winter in. Maybe three dozen." It sounded more like a wish than a promise.

I couldn't see how. It was September and we'd only finished one. At one a month we'd only have a dozen by the time the Bethel group arrived.

"Might we stay with the Woodards when the weather keeps us from building this winter?" I asked Christian one night when we lay in a lean-to with our canvas acting as our roof. I could see the stars like white knots of thread in an indigo cloth appearing in a tiny patch of sky not covered by treetops.

"*Nein*," Christian said. "What would it look like for the leader of the scouts to stay in a soft place with feather ticks while the others make their way beneath a canvas tent? We will all stay at the Giesy place if we are unable to build where we need to, but I don't expect that. Last year was mild, Sam said. We can work in the rain."

"At least we'll be in our own place," I said. He didn't correct me.

———

As the weeks wore on, I wondered how these men convinced themselves that they could build enough houses in time for the arrival of the Bethel group. Weren't they counting the days and weeks and months that one small hut required, and it still needing a roof and caulking? They had to hunt for food, which took time too, and we needed to graze the mules closer to the river and give them more rest time. They looked thin from all their efforts. We'd need to gather firewood, dry more deer meat, and perhaps even fish before winter so we'd have food enough to last us.

Once when the work slowed and I couldn't watch any longer as they swung their axes against so noble a tree, I took Andy and walked to the Woodards'. Andy sat playing with clamshells and a knobby shell Sarah called "an oyster house." Andy was nearly a year old, and Sarah had made a cake for him, which we ate on the porch of her house. I loved her view with a small grassy area surrounded by split cedar rails that eventually disappeared into trees. The house sat in a clearing that felt open and wide even with the darkness of the trees beyond. I could hear the Willapa River swishing its way to the sea, pulled there by the tide.

"How long did it take you to build this house?" I asked Sarah. She brought the churn to turn as we finished up Andy's cake.

"It stood here when Mr. Woodard brought me to it," she said. "We added on a room that took a little time, but I don't know how many days the house took to raise."

"What does your husband say about our efforts?" I asked. I knew men gossiped as much as women, though they claimed to be above such matters.

She smiled. "How do you know we talk of this?"

My English had gotten better every day as I made myself use it with Christian and with the Woodards. "My husband talks with me about the world around; yours, too?"

She lowered those dark blue eyes. "He says you Germans are stubborn, that you should live with us while you build. It is the Christian thing to do to make that offer and Christian to accept. But your husband does not do this."

"He gives," I said. "If ever you have need of something, my Christian will provide it if he can. But receiving is harder for him."

"He is generous to his family," she said.

I nodded agreement, wondering what she'd seen that made her say that.

"He names the Giesy place and says it will be for his parents and brothers and sisters."

I felt an envy pang, or was it disappointment? "He takes care of his own, *ja*," I said. I took Sarah's place at the churn, pounding with vigor though I didn't know why.

"Mr. Woodard says your plan to build right on through the winter is also a...crock full of wish. A dream, my words for it," she said. "Instead, the mud will keep you in one place. Venturing out or chopping trees will be too difficult. My husband says you should be preparing food for winter storage now. Chopping wood and keeping it dry for firewood." She stopped my hand and lifted the plunger. "I think it is churned enough." She finished the butter, and we pasted it into wooden molds. "Do you have candles for the winter?"

"Some." I thought of our lantern and how easily that light blew out.

"Plan to stay with us. We'll read and tell stories and sing and maybe even dance while the rains come down."

It had been a long time since we'd danced.

"My husband is determined to have three dozen structures by next fall for when our friends join us."

Sarah nodded her head. "This is the stubborn part my husband says defines yours. You won't be able to work so hard through the rains, and the trees…the trees demand respect and are not easily changed."

"You make it sound as though trees have a soul," I said.

"The Indians say they do. The trees give them so much—canoes and clothes and houses and tools." She showed me a deep scoop spoon made of wood the color of my sister's chestnut-colored hair. "Smell it," she said, and when I did I knew it was a cedar burl. "Something that gives so much needs to be noticed, witnessed to," Sarah said. "It gives up in its own time, giving itself as a gift rather than a taking."

"People are counting on us to have homes when they arrive," I defended.

"This forest and river land will be their home," she said. "People here just take temporary cover inside their houses."

———

Christian's constant enthusiasm and my commitment to be his helpmate silenced me. Even when we poled upriver in the Woodards' boat so Christian could show me another piece of property he'd claimed for the colony, I kept my tongue about whom he built for and whether we could accomplish all he'd set to do so we could make a life here.

It wasn't that the land near the river wasn't lush and laid out for easy tilling, but that these meanders of river were separated by ghastly tangles of vines and trees and sometimes close-in hills that seemed to suck the air from my throat. We could cut trails along the river through those sections, but most likely living here, we would use the boats often, ride in small crafts that were not nearly as grand nor as sleek or as stable as those used by the Cowlitz people. We'd be dependent on this river, to go from here to there. I'd be on water nearly every day of my life if I wanted to visit someone, or become a hermit connected only to my husband and my children.

"I've purchased these three hundred twenty acres," Christian told me when we'd beached the boat and climbed up a high bank. "It was a donation land claim of a man who is prepared to leave."

"But it's so far from Woodard's Landing and our place," I said. "Won't we all want to be close, the way we were in Bethel?"

"This is maybe seven miles, nothing more." He bristled.

"I only meant that in Bethel we all lived close together. In a town, with streets that—"

"Some stayed in Nineveh, you forget. We can have settlements separated by a few miles and still remain true to our cause. We all agreed to settle along the Willapa, Emma. We will need to do things differently in the West. Around us is free land if a family lives on it for five years and improves it. It's theirs. There is no such thing as this in Bethel. We cannot afford to drain the entire treasury there to buy land for us, *Liebchen*." He patted my shoulder.

"I've seen no buggies, or even people except for the Woodards."

"I told you. Here we walk or go by water. It is the way. There's a post office in Bruceport and warehouses, so there are people closer to the bay. We'll go there one day. You'll see. This will be the route nearest to the Cowlitz, and those from Bethel will come across our trail, and maybe by then we'll have time to clear it further so the stock can be driven across too. The returning scouts will advise that we bring only mules or oxen to drive the wagons. Our farm will be along the way for people heading to the coast."

"Whose name is this property in?" I asked, changing the subject.

"In the Territory's eyes, it is ours," he said. "But it belongs to the colony, all held in common as in Bethel."

"Then who owns the Giesy place with the one nearly finished house?"

He cleared his throat. "I claim that for my parents. This section, distant but not so far away, this one will be ours to farm."

Andy shouted, then pointed at a squirrel and took my attention.

"You let us men attend to these things," he said, following me as I changed Andy's diaper. I grabbed at some cedar duff as an absorbent. "Your job is to make what we will build into a home to raise our sons in. Wait here."

He walked down the riverbank and leaned into the wobbly craft we'd pulled up onto the shoreline. From it he took a pack with a shovel pitched over his back. "I begin," he said.

He lifted the sod from a square, pushing and scraping the tall meadow grasses. Sweat dripped from his forehead, but he whistled as he worked. I gingerly walked through the grasses, felt the sun warm my face and knew it must be warm on Andy's too, though I'd set him in the shade. I took his hand and he waddled upright. He still hadn't taken his first steps alone, but with help he grinned at his success. "We may as well see if there are late-blooming berries, since your father is so occupied in digging."

I'd filled my apron with flowers instead, sticking one behind Andy's ear, tickling him as he sat. I slapped at mosquitoes. They'd be swarming by sunset. Andy pulled against my skirt to raise himself and stay balanced. Finally, Christian whistled his single loud tone and motioned me to return to the square he'd scraped out. Across it, he'd spread the canvas. Come," he said. "Let's christen this land we've been given to turn into service to our Lord."

The look in his eye told me he had more than the Lord's service in mind at that moment. I felt a stirring in my own heart. My face grew warm. I marveled that his hours of intense labor poling upriver, then clearing the sod, hadn't weakened him in the least. If anything, it seemed to fire his desire.

"When do we begin work on our house?" I said as he reached to untie my bonnet.

"Don't worry about that now." He pulled me to him.

I said, "Right here? Won't it tire you for the return trip? And what about Andy?"

Christian smiled as he lifted his son still clinging to my skirt, laced him into the board leaned against the tree. His wide fingers wove the rawhide strings through the buckskin covering, then tied them neatly in a bow. Something about the movement softened me.

"Andrew has perfect timing," he said. "See? He sleeps."

Swaddling did usually put Andy to sleep. His father laid the board propped up against the shovel base, but in a shaded area beneath some arching vines. On his cheeks I wiped the mud paste to counter mosquito attacks. Christian replaced the flower behind Andy's ear, and our son took two quick breaths but didn't awaken.

"As for me being too tired to love my wife and then take her safely back to the landing, you forget." He grinned now and began untying my wrapper at the bodice. "Do you still wear the petticoat with the ruffles?" I nodded. "Then here is another occasion to mark your uniqueness on *our* Giesy place." With Christian, life felt right, even in this place so far upriver from the others. Geese called above us on their way south for the winter.

"Trust me, *Liebchen*," he whispered as he led me onto the canvas he'd unfurled on the ground. "It's an easy ride downriver to wherever you wish to go from here."

He kissed my neck, and I felt like a tall cedar going slowly down.

20

Duty-Bound Steps

Fog, like a faithful scout sent ahead to survey the land, eased into the Willapa Valley. Behind it came the storms.

At first we crunched our necks into our shoulders, doing our best to ignore the rains, my mother's wool cape no longer spotted with water but soaked instead. Our lack of attention to the rain must have angered it, for soon it came down harder, and the lean-to Andy and I huddled in beneath a cedar while the men worked in the trees on another Giesy house, not ours, could not keep out the damp. The fire I kept going at the entrance of the lean-to billowed smoke back into our faces. We coughed but chose that discomfort over being drenched.

One or two seagulls continued to seek us out, which surprised me, as we had little to offer them. I now used the deer bladders—the rounded organ that I learned to pick out quickly from the entrails—to hold dried berries. Sarah said she'd seen Chehalis people dry deer ears and later boil them with roots and little plops of flour. That sounded like a dumpling stew, so I did that too. She told me to save the brains for tanning hides (we'd done that back in Bethel) and that the broth from boiled tongue helped people with a cough. I even kept the sinew away from the seagulls, that stringy part along the deer's back strap that proved as tough as any thread I'd ever used before. One day I boiled the shinbones and found the tallow a palatable fat. Even the antlers became digging tools, not that the seagulls hungered after them. The birds had all looked alike to me, but when Andy and I sat in the lean-to and watched them screech at one another, lifting up and settling back, I did notice one with a chip out of his flattened bill. He returned often enough we named him Charlie. He became a friend for Andy.

Opal, the goat, bleated protests, lifting her right leg up onto my squatting knees as I cooked. I protested too when I had to clean out the area of the shelter where I milked her and where she stood during the night. How she must have resented my cold hands on her bag in the morning, but she never kicked. A docile female indeed—as I was becoming.

I considered building a corral for Opal using abandoned branches from the trees but wasn't sure she'd stay in it. And besides, I'd be leaving that corral for Christian's sisters or brothers. It wasn't as though we were establishing the home we'd be staying on. That was selfish of me, I knew, but I'd endure the weather better, I thought, if I knew that one day soon I'd have a place to call our own.

By December, with every day crying rain and a coldness I didn't remember while I lived at the fort, I risked again urging Christian to reconsider staying with the Woodards at least until March, when the rains tended to come more intermittently—or so I remembered Sarah saying.

"You're soaked all the time. I've given up washing, or have you noticed? The mud clutches at clothes, and they're dirty before I even finish, and they never dry. You've started to cough. We'll all be sick, and when spring comes you won't be able to make up for the time you're losing now."

"We have to keep going, *Liebchen*. They count on us. So many count on us." He coughed a racking cough, bent over, barking like a sea lion. When it stopped he said, "In November next year, if all goes well, they'll arrive. How will they live through the winter if we have no houses for them?"

"They'll do what we've done. Live in lean-tos and under canvas."

"They count on us for better, *Liebchen.*"

"Andy and I count on you too," I said. I saw the pain in his eyes and I softened. "Please. Let's stay with the Woodards. They've offered this to us, and you always say the receiving of gifts is as important in the Christian way as giving is. Why shouldn't we learn to receive? Accepting their generosity would be a good witness, wouldn't it?"

"If we stay at Woodard's Landing when the weather is good, we'll lose precious daylight making our way to the woods. Here, we can get up in the morning, and our work is before us, as the Lord provides."

"He provides more work than necessary," I said under my breath.

"Your being here helps," Christian said. He patted my shoulder, then coughed again.

He'd never said such a thing to me before. "You're pleased I stayed despite my…ways?" I said.

He nodded. Dirt caked the lines in his eyes, and for the first time he looked old, my husband did. Old and tired. And sick. I thought back. He'd stopped doing his pushing-ups.

"Why don't you build more homes on the original Giesy place, then?" I said. "We could stay at the Landing and you'd still be close to your work."

"Each claim needs a house or we will lose the deed."

"There's time," I said. "Isn't it five years to develop the land before the risk of loss?" He took a drink of the hot tea I'd made and pulled a piece of tea leaf from his lower lip. *Is he considering my idea?* "At the least, why not roof one house to make it livable? One house we could all stay in and be dry. The one you're working on now, maybe. It's as though you're putting together puzzles, but you don't stay long enough to finish even one."

He shook his head. "You don't understand. When we are all here, we can more easily do the roofs, Emma. We need to keep building walls as we can." His voice had that final note he gave when he'd bear no more protest. "You talked your way into being here. You must now make being here your way."

———

"Can you talk to him, *Frau* Giesy?" Hans said. I patched the scab on his head with a paste of herbs. A light snow fell outside the lean-to while I tended him. My hands were cold even wearing gloves. I'd wrapped Andy in his board to keep him from wandering off while I helped Hans. I didn't want my child getting wet or colder than he already was—than we all were. Even Hans's teeth chattered as I ministered.

"Emma, Hans. It's all right to call me by my Christian name."

"*Ja*, Emma." Hans had scratched until the place on his head bled nearly every day, but this day he'd scraped that spot as well when he crawled under a tree-fall looking for a deer he thought he'd downed. "It rains so hard a man can hardly see to shoot straight," he said. "We really need two men hunting together, one to help the other."

"That'll mean even fewer to haul the logs," I said, dabbing again at his wound.

"I saw some Indians out there too," he said, his voice a whisper then.

"My husband says we're perfectly safe here. I've seen only friendly Indians willing to show me how to make a spoon from a burl. They're very kind."

"But I hear—"

"They're as cold and hungry as we are, I suspect." I'd been startled myself coming upon what Christian said were Chehalis men at the river when I went to rinse out clothes before I stopped bothering. A man batted with a club at large fish coming up the river while the women with him cut them lengthwise into long filets. They'd arranged a kind of dam that appeared to divert fish into a holding pond where they were easily taken. They'd built a fire beneath a lofty cedar and skewered the filets with long sticks they poked into the ground, holding the fish's pink flesh toward the fire. The men wore reddish-colored capes that looked like woven reeds or even bark and basket hats that shed the rain. They didn't seem the least interested in me. When I approached, the women noticed me and offered that cedar burl spoon.

"Still, *Frau* Giesy—Emma—he would listen to you. We'll all be getting sicker if we don't bring in more meat and get out of this wet. Look at us!" He held up his arm and reached his hands around his wrist. "Thin as a cane and barely as useful." He lowered his voice even more. "We should not have sent so many back to bring the rest out. Two would have been enough."

Should I defend my husband's leadership? I wanted to, but Hans did look thinner. We needed fat; we had all lost weight. My wrapper ties circled twice around me now, but I assumed my weight loss came from doing my best to make sure Andy and the men had sufficient food as they were working the hardest. Opal's milk kept me fit. Or so I thought. But I was hungry more often than not. These men must be too.

"We all think we should finish one house, cover it, and wait out this rain. Then we can start in earnest in the spring."

"You've spoken to Christian about this?"

Hans shook his head. "Bring it up even sideways, and he turns us around with those staring eyes. He is a taskmaster, that one."

"He stares at me, too," I said, the most critical of my husband I preferred to get in the presence of Hans.

"*Ja,* but he pays attention."

"Does he?"

———

Adam Schuele sought me out for his cough next. He needed something more than the boiled deer tongue syrup. I made a pepper and sugar tea, having him sip it slowly as the pepper clustered at the bottom of the mug. "It burns," he said. But the cough lessoned for the moment.

"We don't have much sugar left," I said. "I hope the Knight boys don't get that cough."

Hans caught it, too, and Christian's never did go away, though it wasn't as wracking as it had been. But my husband wouldn't hear of leaving or even roofing the hut they worked on. He'd already planned to move on to another Giesy claim, this one for Sebastian and Mary, and haul logs for that house. "Discomfort is part of our mission," he said. "No disciples ever found following the Lord easy. It is how He works out our character, through these trials."

"But the men—look at them." The men stood inside a rotted tree trunk out of the rain, so Christian and I talked in private. "They're ill. They're tired. They're weary of all this. You're thin as a reed. Surely God did not intend for us to kill ourselves in pursuit of this new colony."

"We all chose this place."

"*Ach, ja,* I know. But things change. We have new information now. The trees aren't easily harnessed. There are too few of us working on the huts, so you push too hard."

"Are you saying I shouldn't have sent so many back?"

"No, I… It's just that there aren't people here for us to recruit or to serve, and we're devoting so much time to housing there's no energy left for…listening to God's Word or bringing it to others. Even those who've lived here three or four years before us in the Territory are leaving. Isn't it true you bought out their claims? Perhaps this isn't the way we were supposed to prepare for the others, perhaps we've lost the heart of this mission, the soul of—"

"I'll not hear any more dissension," he shouted. Andy stopped his playing at my feet and looked up at his father. His eyes filled with tears. The goat scratched with her back leg at her bag. "No more," he said, quieting. "We will do it this way and the Lord will keep us. You must not be like Job's wife who did not support her husband in his hour of trial. You must have faith."

That night I dreamed that my soul woke up. The stretching of my stomach seeking food elbowed it awake. My heart pounded fast, then slow, pushing blood into my head to get my brain to work, feeding it thoughts. My bones ached but exerted strength as they poked at my organs, swimming around inside me until my soul awoke. It had been asleep too long while the other parts of me took over. It was the oddest dream, but when I awoke I knew what I needed to do.

———

The tarp must have weighed fifty pounds or more, and as I dragged it, it began to collect mud, adding to my effort. "We'll find fir boughs to lay it on, and I'll haul that," I told my wide-eyed son, who sat staring back at me from a distant tree. I'd wrapped him in a larger board I'd made, liking the security it afforded me at times, tying him in. With my small axe, I chopped a bough from a fallen tree. I did imagine Christian's look when he returned to our lean-to and found us gone. But he'd roll in with Adam Schuele and the others so he'd not sleep in the wet, though they could all cough together once they consumed the pepper-and-sugar tea I'd left for them. And maybe, just maybe, then he'd follow me, and if nothing else, the men would have a few days' rest while he searched.

My routine involved walking ahead through the mud with Andy on my back while I tugged at the goat. Christian once said the goat would follow me anywhere, but I couldn't take that chance. I would set down the small pack I carried around my neck, lean Andy's board against it, tie the goat, then head back to the tarp that lay like a giant gray slug in the rain some distance behind me.

Back at the tarp, I would roll it onto a flat cedar bough, which seemed to reduce the muddy drag. Cedar needles were softer, not as prickly as the fir, but the bark still chaffed against my hands as I dragged. When I would reach Andy again, I'd rest for a bit, say a prayer, take a breath, then put my son on my back, place the bag around my neck and grab for the goat, leaving the canvas behind. If I began to think about how far I'd have to go like this, I'd make myself concentrate on something else. Reality would strip me bare, and I might simply stop. All I would think about was the next step and conserving energy for my work, wasting no effort on future foes I faced nor past disasters. My soul kept me awake.

Carrying my son ahead helped me find the best path and gave me short respite from the aching of my shoulders and my legs that hauling the tarp induced. I'd settle Andy down while I could still see the slug, as I called the canvas; then when I returned for it, I was never far from Andy should danger work its way toward him. We made enough noise with my grunting and his crying out for me "Mama, Mama" off and on that I couldn't imagine any self-respecting cougar or bear would even be in the region, let alone curious enough to try to find us or do us harm. I did once wonder if the goat might attract them as a perfect noontime meal. And once when Andy cried, I remembered Sarah telling me that Indian children are kept quiet during berry-picking because their cries sound much like bear cubs, and a mother bear might seek out the sounds.

I pitched those thoughts away.

I pitched many thoughts away. Thoughts about what my action might mean to my marriage, thoughts about where I was and what had I done. The trees did offer solace as I made my way through them in the mist and rain. Their stillness and stability made me almost worshipful. We hadn't had a church or any fellowship or any time to even read the Scripture because we all fell wet and tired onto our moss beds. I vowed to change that once I reached my destination.

Near the riverbank, Andy and I fell into a mud hole up to my knees. The goat bleated as he jerked the rope out of my hand. The weight of the mud and its sucking felt like a too-tight cape around me. I thought then that maybe I'd made a mistake. Maybe we were meant to endure hardships, and it didn't matter where we endured them: in a lean-to or in a mud hole. Maybe Christian was right about trials gouging out our character and that avoiding them just made the next carving more grievous.

Would we be stuck here? Would Andy and I sink, then be consumed by bears? That thought gave me new energy, and I grabbed at shrubs and vines at the river's bank, yanking at them until I pulled myself free. I lay on my stomach, panting with effort, the sound of the river rushing behind me.

There had to be more than one way to carry out God's plans. That's all I was doing: finding another way. It had been my way that once set upon a course I found turning back a trouble. I believed Christian and I shared that trait. I was doing this not just for the men but for my husband. I, too, like Job's wife, was duty-bound.

Dusk greeted us as we made our final approach toward the four walls of the first hut of the Giesy place. When I'd left that morning, after the men headed into the woods, I thought I'd go to Woodard's Landing. But once on my way I believed going to the Giesy place would make more sense. It was the same distance from where the men worked, and it offered opportunities to redeem myself once my husband came after us. I hadn't yet entertained the idea that he might not.

I'd come three miles from where the men worked, though I'd walked it twice, pulled myself through knee-deep mud carrying Andy, found a different route back for the tarp. Even the goat stayed close to Andy, and by the last half mile or so, I didn't have to take the time to tether it; it trusted I'd be returning.

"At least they weren't working on our site, Andy, or we'd have had to come seven miles or more through brambles and trees." Opal bleated and butted, jerking both Andy and me to my knees. "We're almost there," I scolded.

When I arrived, I stood in the doorway of the hut, the sound of my own voice an icy slice into silence. It was not the quiet that invigorated, I decided, that tingled one's toes or lightened the spirit. It was heavy and dense, as weighted as an anchor. Dark trees towered over us, filling the sky except for the clearing where the hut stood, its uncaulked walls and open rafters making it look like an animal carcass of ribs more than a possible home.

But we'd made it.

In that heavy silence I unrolled the small canvas that held our personal things as rain dribbled off my cape hood. I found sticks to hold the canvas up enough to keep the rain from our faces through the night. We ate jerky and I milked Opal, and both Andy and I drank our fill of sweet milk. In an odd sort of way, it felt homey here. The accomplishment of a thing, even so simple as milking a goat, could give pleasure.

My mother's face came to me, her standing at the doughboy preparing bread, a fire in the fireplace, my brother bent over his studies awaiting my father's return for the day, my sisters chattering as they tied one another's braids into loops that hung at their backs. It had been a simple life in Bethel but a good one.

A dry life too.

What was the point of our being in this Willapa place so far from those we loved, so engaged in a labor that even when completed would seem primitive to those who led orderly, tidy lives back in Bethel? Our brick homes there seemed luxurious compared to these humble dwellings. And where were the people we hoped to influence with our ways? The Woodards thought we were stubborn, maybe even *Dummkopf*. People lived in Bruceport off the bay, Christian said, but we wouldn't go there much except for supplies now and then. We rarely saw anyone else, rarely took time to know what filled the lives of our distant neighbors. We focused only on "the mission," securing an isolated place where we'd be safe when God brought about the destruction of the world. But what if we destroyed ourselves in the process? What if we only saw one another and never touched the world around us at all? If this was the site chosen for us, then where were the people we were to touch with our lives?

I quickly tossed that disloyal thought. My husband would find a way to make sense of this work—if he didn't die of consumption or exhaustion first. I pushed aside the ache of his absence.

One of the true blessings of physical work is that it presses a body to the point of fatigue, so sleep falls upon one like a brick against the hearth. Andy snored softly, our first night alone inside four walls since we'd left Fort Steilacoom. I laid my head down with images of my family dancing in my dreams and, blessedly, fell asleep.

In the morning, I shoved aside the tarp and looked up through the open rafters of the log house. I wondered if Jonah felt like this inside that whale, the rib cage arching over him, his fate to wait.

To wait was a luxury I didn't have. I lifted my arms above my head to stretch and felt my shoulders protest. My whole body ached in new places, my sides, my forearms, my thighs. All the dragging and hauling told this morning story. Maybe I should rest today, I thought. But no, the muscles would only groan again when I began the work of covering the ridge pole, and I wanted it finished when Christian found me. I knew he would; just not when. I'd left a note to say I'd gone to a drier place and for him not to worry. He'd assume the Woodards' but he'd be wrong. I wouldn't take the feather tick Sarah offered either, but I'd make a home in this wet weald, and in so doing maybe Christian would see that resting until spring made sense.

While Andy slept, I milked the goat who'd bedded down beside us. The elk bladder Hans had given me to hold water and milk held most of what Opal gave, and it would stay fresh until we could drink it later. For now, I needed to see what it would take for me to get the tarp up onto the rib cage of this hut to form a roof.

As I stepped outside the four walls, I pulled my mother's cape around my shoulders, surveying my task. The goat followed me out, butted against the back of my knees, but I kept my balance. At least my physical balance. Imagining the work ahead threatened my emotional one. *Begin to weave / God provides the thread.* I smiled to myself at that thought. Weaving was about balance. I had to find that kind of equilibrium in my life.

21

Just a Woman

The drizzle continued as I worked to find two poles. I wanted them ten to twenty feet long. *Surely it won't keep raining every day until Christmas.* Even angels' tears had to stop sometime. But I couldn't let the climate change my course.

Andy wailed to be set free, but I kept him in his board. He drank his milk, which quieted him. "As soon as I figure out what to do about the roof," I told him, "I'll put dough on a stick and cook it." I thought about trying to bat at one of the big fish, as I'd seen the Indians do, but the river ran high and swift with rains, and I didn't want to go anywhere near it.

A strip of venison jerky quieted Andy as I freed his arms from the board, tying the rawhide across his chest. He chewed. I roped Opal to a tree near some brush she promptly ripped at. "I wish our keep were as easy," I told the goat.

The design of the Indian board with its woven shelf out over Andy's head acted like the brim of a hat and kept rain from his face. His eyes followed my movements, and I could see both my brothers in them and Christian, too. "Mama, look," he'd say, and I'd turn to his pointing. "What's that?" he'd ask, and I'd tell him in English and German, sometimes even using Swiss words. But mostly I told him to wait because I was busy. And I was.

The axe weighed heavily against my legs as I walked. I'd taken the tool with me, though I risked Christian's upset. But I needed it for the windfalls I hoped to find, something slender, maybe a tree pushed over or snapped off by a larger one. I entered the edge of the forest, then heard the rustling, though I couldn't see it. No snorts, just the sounds of something moving through the trees. Maybe Christian had already caught up with us!

I eased my way back, picking up Andy with the goat following as we returned to the inside of the log walls to wait.

When Christian didn't appear, I began to worry about the noise. The activity of the men working each day kept the bears and other would-be predators away. Safety lived inside that colony corral. We were alone here, at my choosing.

I considered praying for our safety. The colony teacher, Karl Ruge, had told us we could pray for anything, that we didn't need a priest, as in times of old, to intercede. But surely God would frown at my putting ourselves in injury's clutches, then asking for reprieve.

"You'll have to stay in here, Andy. You too, Opal," I said. I piled sticks and boughs up against the doorway that lacked any other kind of covering. Building a permanent door would be a new task too, but first, a roof. That's what we needed.

I reentered the forest. To make more noise, hoping to stave off un-wieldy beasts, I sang old German songs and hymns my mother taught me, though all singing stopped when I spotted a fallen tree I thought I could manage.

I chopped at the side branches and then began the work of pulling the log through the woods toward the cabin. I looked for the axe marks on the trees I'd made to note my way in and then back out. It was noon when I dragged the log to the cabin and let it lie. One log, really just a branch. A half a day. I pulled away the branches from the doorway and set my son free from his board. Then I took my flint and burned some cedar duff, establishing a cooking fire.

I took water from the small canvas set to catch the rain. After drinking hot tea, I returned to my work. By the time I got that slender log braced up against the wall of the cabin, I hungered for food. I told time by my stomach rather than any sight of the sun. Andy screamed his protest at being confined for so long, but I had to put him back into the board. I wondered how Pap had taught her child to be so quiet in his. A better mother she was than I. Hearing my son's wails, I knew that wouldn't be hard.

I untied the rawhide strips that kept him secure and lifted him from the board, holding him close to me. His cheeks felt cold, and I realized the fire had died while I'd been dragging in the tree. I may have been successful at one of my tasks, but the second long branch I needed would have to wait until we were warm once again.

———

The work fatigued, reminded me of how weak I had become. I puffed hard as I braced the second log at an angle up against the wall of the cabin, felt my legs wobble as I headed back into the trees to look for a third. This one would be longer, and by the time I found it and dragged it close, dusk had fallen and I collapsed. We'd have to spend another night beneath the small canvas.

I'd never ached so much nor been as tired. Tears squeezed from my eyes, and I hoped as I fell asleep that the branches filling the doorway would be enough to keep us safe. Andy coughed once and I held my breath. *Please don't let him get sick. Please just let him sleep.*

In the morning, it snowed, the flakes falling through the open rafters and covering the muddy floor. I felt defeated until Andy stuck his tongue out to capture them and he giggled. His joy tweaked my own. "It's not often it snows inside a house, is it?" I asked. He laughed again and raised his hands to catch more.

I could see my breath as I puffed to build up the fire that had stayed through the night. Such small blessings gave me joy, and I decided that was how I'd restore my vigor, reminding myself of what God had provided and what I'd already accomplished, and that I did this thing for the good of the colony, for the good of my husband.

My son and the goat settled, I rolled the canvas out full, laid the log at one end, then rolled the wet canvas up around it. It lay as a cross-beam on the ground, against the two logs leaned against the wall of the cabin. Now the work truly began. My goal was to somehow push the rolled tarp up onto the leaning logs, and when it reached the roof edge, to unfurl the tarp which was wrapped around the log, pushing it up over the ridgepole and letting it fall down over the far side, unfurling the canvas with it. It would be my roof. If I could make it work.

Early efforts frustrated. I rolled it halfway up the leaning poles with little trouble. But once it hit a certain pitch, it slid back down, and my weakness prevented me from stopping it. I had to start again. I didn't want it unrolling onto the leaning poles, and that became a problem as well. A Greek myth came to mind, of a god sentenced to push a piece of dung up a hill and having it roll back over him so he had to start again. I even tried to pull the rolled tarp up by wrapping a rope around the cylinder I'd formed, climbing up the leaning poles to the top of the walls, and tossing the rope over the top to pull it from the other side. But it was too short. Some tasks needed more than one person to complete them.

After the fourth try, this time using another short log to push up against the tarp only to have it nearly reach the edge before it fell back against me, I simply sat in the melting snow and cried. Maybe I wasn't large enough to do this; maybe I wasn't strong enough. Every muscle protested. I kept looking in the direction I'd come from, hoping Christian would soon figure out where we'd gone.

"Mama, look!" Andy said, spying something out through the uncaulked walls.

"Your papa?" I said.

But it wasn't Christian.

Two Indian men appeared, dressed well against the weather with bark capes that draped over their shoulders and hung down to their knees. A fur of some kind showed beneath the cape. They wore hats the color of cedar and simply appeared through the mist. I moved away from the hut, hoping they'd follow me and not find my son.

But Andy shouted again. "*Ja,*" I whispered, "I see." I tried to keep my words calm, though my heart pounded.

They stood at the cabin's edge. "How can I help you?" I said in German. "Maybe some biscuits?" I had a little more flour and could mix it with water and bake it in the fire. I'd have to go inside the hut for that, and then they might take Andy or the goat. I looked at my makeshift door. They could dismantle it with a sneeze.

Instead, their eyes moved to the tarp. "Oh, please don't want that, please," I pleaded. If they took my tarp, this would all be for nothing!

One said something to the other. "I need it," I said, wishing I knew Chinook or Chehalis or Shoalwater or whatever language they spoke. Words could be such bridges, but the lack of them built walls.

They moved toward the tarp and I wailed. "*Nein,* please!" They squatted at the tarp, each at one end, and they lifted. *They are taking my tarp!* But instead of walking off with it, they lifted the tarp rolled around the log, and the two of them hoisted it up over the top, then let it finish rolling over the other side. I heard my long branch drop with a thud on the soft ground. One of the men held the tarp near the leaning poles to keep it from being pulled up and over. It was just as I'd imagined it would work.

The taller of the two men said something to the other, who disappeared into the trees for a time, then returned with long strands of some kind of vine that he'd cut with a knife he carried at his waist. I hadn't noticed the knife before. *Sometimes it's good to be blinded by fear.*

Then they did something I wouldn't have thought to do: they lifted one of the leaning logs up onto the roof the length of the tarp. With the vines, they lashed the tarp to the edges of the outside rafters and used the log to secure the length of the tarp. It would prevent the wind from lifting it up, and it hadn't occurred to me to do that—not that I could have by myself. They repeated their effort on the other side, and I stood back when they finished, amazed at this gift in the middle of nowhere. I didn't mind in the least that I hadn't done it all by myself.

"How can I ever thank you?" I said, smiling, bowing, hoping my actions told them how grateful I was, how embarrassed that I'd thought they were thieves. *"Kloss,"* I remembered. "Good. *Danke.* I'll fix tea for you, *ja?"* I motioned with my hands as though to drink, and they looked at each other and the taller one shook his head. They both had round faces, their woven hats arched out to keep rain from their eyes.

I wanted to know how to make those hats. I'd have to ask Sarah Woodard, who knew so much about this landscape and its people.

They wouldn't let me prepare tea or anything else for them. Instead, they grunted as though satisfied with their work and then moved into the trees.

I stepped inside and felt the dryness, the slight darkness with a tarp now over our heads. We were in a cave of our making, and I did a little dance, swirling around, singing to Andy. "We have a roof over our heads, we have a roof over our heads. We entertained angels unaware as Scripture tells us."

"Mama," Andy said when I danced dizzily past him. I was too lightheaded from the lack of strong food to dance for long.

"What?" I said, catching myself before I fell.

"Look."

One of the Indians stood in the doorway; he was naked from his shoulders to his waist.

"Did you want tea after all?"

He stared at me, then stepped aside while his friend hung the coat-like skin cape he'd worn over the door opening, darkening our log cave further. The fur side faced in. Elk hair moved in the breeze that seeped in through the openings between the side logs. The jagged cut of the elk skin was long enough; it nearly reached the bottom of the doorway. I could stitch a piece of hide to it, maybe even take Andy's board apart to completely cover the opening. Once caulked, this house would be snug as a mouse in a wheat barrel.

Then the other Chehalis man stepped inside. The sight of this bare-chested man standing in the cold brought me to my senses. "No," I said. "You will be sick if you give us this." I made a motion of being cold, flapping my arms, then pointing to him. "You take," I said, stepping around him to touch the hide. The fur felt so heavy and soft and smelled of smoked wood.

He struck his hand against his chest and said a word that might have meant "strong" or "a gift, don't reject it" or "we're going." At least I hoped that was what he was saying. He stood close to me. Did he want something in payment for the hide?

Before I could do anything else, he pushed the hide aside and stepped out, letting it flap behind him. I squinted through the logs and watched as the one man pulled his cedar bark cape over his shoulder, and the two men left, moving at a steady trot past the cabin, back toward the river until they disappeared.

Our leader had told us colonists long ago that we must not only live the Golden Rule, of doing unto others as we would have them do unto us, but to go further, to live with the Diamond Rule, where we gave so that another's life wasn't just like ours but was better. To give in this way was the mark of true Christian love. This was the first time I'd really understood.

———

It felt like heaven to be out of the rain and the wind, to have places dry enough to sit without globs of mud attaching themselves like ticks to my skirt and Andy's pants. The ground remained wet, but piles of moss provided a soft carpet. The elk hide deterred wind at the doorway, even though it blew in through the wide cracks of the walls. The hide looked so heavy and warm I considered taking it down and wrapping us up in it, hanging our blanket over the doorway instead. But by the time the fire merely glowed as an ember, I felt warmer than I'd been in weeks, and I trusted it was due to the gift of the roof and the draft-stopping hide.

I used the boughs that had once filled the doorway to make a kind of lean-to for the goat and tethered her outside, at least for part of the day. Eventually, her bleating became so constant I returned her inside. She wasn't a dog, but she served as good company for Andy, I decided, and we'd seen nothing of Charlie, the seagull. Opal's body heat warmed up our house. *Our house.* As I milked her, I felt a twinge of guilt that I'd deprived the men of this white gold, not acting the Diamond Rule at all.

It had been four days since we'd left, and I confess I expected my husband long before this. He could have been at the Woodards' in but a short hike, discovered I wasn't there, then surely he'd know I was here. Where else might I go? *Will he think I tried to make my way back to Fort Steilacoom?* I hadn't thought of that before. He'd be outraged if he arrived back at the fort after several days only to find I wasn't there either to greet him. No, that trip from the Fort had been troubling in summer; he'd know I'd never attempt it in the winter. I circled my fingers and thumbs, trying to rub away some of that uncertainty.

I would do what I could do. I would make a caulking and secure this cabin even tighter.

Finding mud was no problem, but what to mix with it to make it strong and harden, that was a question. I'd known of houses caulked with mud and straw, but we had no straw here.

But we had forest duff, needles and vines and small dead branches and moss, lots of moss, for the taking. I put Andy in the board, though he cried to be set free, and put him on my back. I donned my mother's cape and set out for the woods, returning with an apron full of small twigs and forest discards and moss. I dug a hole, let it fill partway with rain, broke the side walls of dirt into it, adding forest duff, wet grasses, brambles, and branches. Then I stirred, hoping the twigs and such would be enough to thicken it. I had no idea what men used to do this. I kept stirring and adding until my mixture felt thick as cold pea soup and my stirring stick stood upright in the goop. Then I spread the mixture on the lowest log wall, stacking it between the logs, filling in the missing spaces, slapping moss onto the wet glob. I let Andy help with the stirring. We worked the day and rested in the night, warmed by a small fire I made inside, letting the smoke drift out through the top layers of logs. The fire offered small light in the darkness.

In the morning we began again. It would take many days at this rate, but the work filled a hole growing in my heart. It kept me from thinking of what I would do when we ran out of flour and jerky; from imagining Christian's first words when he found me. The effort held at bay the worrisome thoughts of what my life might be like from now on, pushed back the fear that my husband might not seek me at all.

22

Last Times

"Last times" take on new meaning once we admit they exist. I remember the last time I wrapped my arms around my mother. I cherish the memory of the last time my father lifted his eyebrow to wink at me before we headed west; the last time Jonathan ran along the boardwalk chasing a ring with a stick while Sheppie barked behind him; the last night I slept with my sisters; the last warm kisses from my two youngest brothers. They are bittersweet memories claimed as markers of my life.

Last times began to cloud my days. Rain poured down in sheets as I tried to remember the last time I'd slept totally warmed, wrapped up against my husband, not worrying over a small cut in a canvas that unless I repaired it soon would force rain inside this finally dried-out place.

This day was a marker, too, as Andy and I ate the last of the jerky I'd brought with us. "We can live on Opal's milk for quite a long time," I told Andy. "But then I guess I'll have to take the axe to club those fish and hope that I can land one or two." I didn't say out loud that I might have to return to face my husband's wrath. Or lack of it. Perhaps I was so insignificant against the mission of his life that he hadn't noticed yet I'd gone.

Today was the last day I could put off clubbing a fish, the last time I dared tell myself that Christian would find me, that he'd want to find us. By my counting, I'd been here nearly three weeks, listening to the rain, trying to stay out from under the holes in the canvas, bringing the goat in from her grazing, reworking my caulking recipe, adding mosses with the hope they one day would harden to snug these walls into a home.

The last time. I hadn't thought that the last time I'd kissed Christian good-bye that it might truly be the last time.

I had to toss that thought, or I'd fall into a morass of misery more engulfing than the mud.

Instead, I considered my monthly flow. I'd completed it, though it was barely noticeable. *My last flow? No more chance of a child?*

I needed to eat more. I'd have to try hitting those fish if I could see them in the water...if I could get close enough to the river to see. The Indians I'd watched doing this actually stood in the water, the harsh current pushing against them so hard they sometimes lost their balance, though they laughed as they splashed, something I was sure I wouldn't do. The thought of that rush against my legs while I struck a fish in such a way as to throw it onto the bank tired more than frightened me. But I had to eat more to keep Andy alive; Andy had to eat more too. We needed fat from the fish. The Lord had provided a stream and the abundance of fish, but that stream, rolling and swift... I swallowed back nausea just thinking of it.

I entertained the thought of going back. Such a groveling that would be, admitting that I needed help in surviving, though didn't we all? Worse would be telling myself the truth that preparing this colony truly was the most important thing in my husband's life, more important than locating his family, making sure they were safe. He would do anything to serve, but it looked to me that he served the colony over anyone else.

That was sacrilege, I was sure. Fortunately, our leader couldn't see inside my head, and he lived several thousand miles away, so even his dark eyes weren't here to accuse. *The last time he accused me…* I drove away that thought too.

"Mama, look," Andy said.

I wondered what my son saw now, annoyed that he hadn't found any new words to share with me. "Mama, look" greeted my every moment or so it seemed. Or maybe I felt put upon because he'd been waddling behind me poking the caulking with a stick all morning, saying "Mama, look!" showing me a bug or a twisted root or stopping to look and giggle when his slender belly made gurgling sounds.

"I'll look later," I told him.

I'd gone too far this last time with Christian. Perhaps I should have stayed with him longer while I prodded him to be a leader who tended to the needs of his men and still found a way to be a husband aware of his wife. But I had tried. Hans had asked that I try to make Christian see the men's need for rest. And I had. Even coming here had been a part of that effort; that was all it really was. I'd manipulated for the last time when I'd talked my way into coming along, when I'd kept our son a secret for a time. I might not always make the best choices, but they weren't meant to deceive or get my way, only to be of help.

"Trial," I said out loud. "A word with two meanings. Someone being judged and someone being challenged. As you are at this moment, poking at my hard labor and telling me that my caulking is inferior." I patted Andy's head, then returned to my work.

I'd had no more dreams about my soul awaking or going to sleep. Now my dreams were of food, luscious roasts and steamed yams and corn boiled and spread with fresh butter. When was the last time I'd eaten that well?

But in daylight, my soul did sleep. I couldn't find a way to reach within me, to recall the Scripture verses that might have brought me ease, or to concentrate long enough to read from Catherine's Bible. Our leader rarely emphasized hopeful verses; my mother told me of them, words that promised help in times of trial. I tried to remember some of those. Christian would be angry with me if he knew how weak my faith was, how I struggled to find meaning in this effort.

"Mama, look," Andy repeated.

"What is it?" I sounded harsh; I knew it and felt instantly sorry. I turned and squatted to him, apologized. "Mama's a real trial this morning, isn't she? Let me just finish this little dab here, please." He leaned his head into my chest, bunting me just a bit. He pointed behind me. He probably wanted to show me yet another hole he'd poked into the caulking. My temper was frazzled as an old rope. Did the lack of food make me irritable?

"Papa. Papa."

"Papa is a new word for you," I said, standing and lifting him onto my chest. "Good for you!"

As I turned, there stood Christian, the hide door pushed back.

I could see his hair, a mass of wet locks, his jaw squared and set.

"Woman," Christian said, "what have you done?"

I rushed into his arms before he could say another word, handed him his son.

"Your woman," I told him. He grunted, but his arm closed around me while he held Andy with his other.

From behind him I heard coughing, and there stood Adam, Hans, and Joe and Adam Knight.

"Come in, come in," I urged them. They all had longer hair and scratched at their arms.

"We have wasted days looking for you," Christian said gruffly, stepping back from me to let the others pass inside. "Worried days." He sounded cross, but I also heard a catch in his throat.

"We were sure you were at the Woodards', so we didn't even start to look until last week," Joe said.

"Don't ever do this again to me," Christian said, leaning toward me. "You will remain with me to work things out. You won't run off like a wayward child and risk yourself and my son. We will do what must be done together."

I bristled. Did I look like I'd risked his son, whose arms draped around his father's neck? Did I look like a wayward child running off, only hoping to be found? I started to challenge him, but instead I took a deep breath and chose to be happy rather than right.

"I've provided a house with a roof on it," I said. "I've kept me and my son out of the rain, and I didn't mean to—"

"You disobeyed."

Adam coughed then, a hard racking sound. "I brought pepper," he croaked. "Will you make us tea?"

"*Ja,*" I said. "Be dry and warmed by the fire, and I'll fix you some. We have a roof," I said, pointing upward. "You'll not believe how the Lord provided it."

They all crowded inside the hut they'd built, the men squatting on their heels, leaning against the walls, slipping their wet caps off, looking around for pegs. Their rain slickers were soaked, and the room felt humid. "No pegs," I said. "And I haven't gotten the walls all caulked either, but a good start."

"Where'd you get the elk hide?" Hans asked. He fingered the fine fur at the doorway.

"Some Chehalis or Quinaults. They helped me with the tarp and then left me that hide. One took it right off his back. They acted the Diamond Rule."

"They made your life better than their own," Hans said, nodding.

"They're acclimated," Adam said. "They can handle this weather bare chested." He wiped at his mustache that dropped nearly to his jaw line. His beard had filled in over his chin and onto his cheeks. His hand quivered. He coughed. *Maybe I shouldn't have left them; maybe I could have kept them from getting so ill.*

"We'll be accustomed to the rain in time," Christian said.

I watched as Adam glanced at Hans, who shook his head, as though warning not to press the matter further. Christian's tired eyes lifted to the tarp roof and the sound of the steady rain. "But for now, we will rest," he said. "We will hunt together and smoke the meat and gain some strength. We'll repair that split in the canvas before it grows longer." His eyes lifted to the canvas top. "Small fractures should always be fixed before they become too large." He stared at me when he said this. "Indeed. This is good common sense."

Adam's wracking cough interrupted Christian. When he'd stopped, Christian continued. "We will get well. And when the weather lets up, we'll build another hut, *ja?*" He looked at me. "But we'll build it where the land borders this claim, at the corner, so there will be closer neighbors and so we can come back here each night for a dry place to rest." He lifted Andy up into his arms. Andy's head touched the tarp, he sat so high on his father's shoulders.

"We might even finish our next one with a wooden roof before moving on to another. The Lord led us here. He provides. This is what we must remember. He'll make the way for us to prepare for our brothers and sisters. On time."

"You've made a wise choice in coming here now, husband."

Christian grunted. "I have a...creative teacher."

I leaned into him, patting Andy's legs that hung like two sausages on Christian's chest. "And your teacher learned a lesson too," I whispered.

He furrowed his brow but didn't pursue what I'd said.

That night, curled into our bedroll, Christian asked me, "What lesson is it that you learned, *Liebchen?*"

"Sometimes I should act even when my husband thinks I shouldn't, and not wait so long before I do."

He grunted. "You could have told me where you went. I assumed you went to Woodard's Landing and allowed you a few days to come to your senses and return. When you didn't and when you weren't there, then I worried. There was no need for that."

"You'd forbidden it. And would anything less have gotten you to tend to your men, let alone me?" He didn't answer. "You're a good leader, Christian. You've set the task the men can respond to. You decided as you did about resting here, getting strong, that is a good sign."

He grunted, then lay quiet for a time. We could hear the cadence of the men's breathing as they entered into sleep. Andy made little wheezing sounds, and I gently squeezed at his nose that had started to run.

"But you have to notice others, what they need. It can't all be for the colony," I said. "Men work harder and longer when they know the task has meaning and gives to others. We can't just say that's so; we have to act it, even here so far from home."

"You defied me, *Liebchen.* You risked our son and your own life. This is not the way to be heard."

"You risked us, too," I said. Then added quickly, "You're here now. Let's let it end there."

"*Ja,* because the men tell me I'm foolish to give up a bed warmed by my wife."

"That's the reason you came to find me? Because you wanted a convenient bed warmer?"

"Shh. I came because I love you and our son. But I carry with me the knowledge of a failing." It took a strong man to admit a mistake. "I need to believe that God's Spirit speaks not just to me but to you as well, though you are just a woman."

"I am just a woman," I said. "But I'm a dry woman lying beneath a roof. And I'm a woman willing to share her bed with a stubborn husband."

"And I with a stubborn wife."

We celebrated Christmas with a goose Hans brought down, whose feathers I stuffed into a dried elk's bladder that I softened with the animal's own fat. No *Belsnickel* brought gifts by as he did at Bethel, but I had enough sinew thread left to sew the elk bladder into the perfect pillow for Christian's head. I took my precious needles from the chatelaine that hung around my neck. Christian winked as I did.

A couple of the men had whittled toys for Andy, which he played with now, the wooden horse in one hand chasing after the wooden goat of almost the same size in another. I did not expect nor did I receive any tangible gift from my husband. That we were all together with food in our stomachs and aware of the Lord's presence in His provision was present enough. That and our own Christmas service reading from the Bible. Christian ended the day saying we must make more time for prayer and worship. Our lack of such, he said, explained why our efforts moved so slowly and with such turmoil.

The Knight brothers surprised, saying that if they left now they could return to Bethel in time to help bring the larger group out. Joe wanted to go by ship to San Francisco.

"But we need help here," Christian said.

"You'll do little till spring. Then in summer, maybe you could hire the Indians," Joe replied.

I thought, *It must've been hard for boys Jonathan's age to be isolated for so long.*

"Indeed," Christian grunted. "And if I say no?"

The brothers looked at each other.

"Maybe we'd leave anyway," Joe said.

That night, I knew Christian lay awake, his Bible open in his hands. In the morning he gave his consent to the Knights, who headed back after the first of the year, the tide taking them out to sea.

———

Through January the men hunted together, once bringing home a bear whose hide became a welcome blanket on the coldest nights. We had meat we smoked inside a branch-covered lean-to. The smell of meat made my mouth water sometimes, even in the night. Stews were frequent, and all of us regained some strength. We read together, finding Scriptures our leader had never preached on, wondering if we had the right to say what we thought the words meant. We were not learned, after all; we merely lived and hoped our lives reflected what we loved.

One day when I went into the woods to graze the goat, I startled several Indian women gathering cedar root and bark. I motioned to ask what they'd do with their bounty, and one of them made a pounding motion against the bark, then pointed to her cape. I could pound it into a mat to cover the floor or perhaps make a cape for Andy, even for the men. This might be the last winter when we were so wet because we lacked the proper clothing.

I nudged Christian into making a trip to Woodard's Landing.

"We're not asking them for anything," I said. "We're just being good neighbors to visit." He finally agreed, and we spent the day in each other's company, talking and singing. Sarah had an angel's voice, and her singing taught me new English words. I considered her my friend and overlooked her clucking tongue when I told her of my leaving Christian for a time and living in the woods alone.

"The Indians...," she said. "You took a terrible risk."

"Either way," I said, "if I hadn't gone, I'm not sure we'd all still be alive. The men needed rest."

"You are overly dramatic, Emma," Christian said, overhearing us.

"You were all sick. I made a way for us to have a roof over our heads."

"No, *Liebchen.* That was God's work, not yours."

How I hated it when he defined anything good I did as something brought about by intervention. Did I offer nothing? Did I not at least act in concert with God, sometimes? Or was that route only possible through the works of men?

At times, there were slight breaks in the rain, or it drizzled more than poured. After the men began to feel better, on those still days with the weather offering fog rather than rain, they'd work in the woods, bringing out the logs they needed and stacking them. When it drizzled, they'd work on the structures, Christian still bent on having three dozen houses roofed and ready by the time the larger group arrived.

I still didn't see how we could accomplish this. The Bethelites might not understand the primitiveness of this place. What had the Knights and Michael Sr. and John Genger and George and John Stauffer said to them by now? Would they be enthusiastic? What would they say about a place where horses bogged down in mud and people used the river if they wanted to truly go somewhere? Would the promised richness of the soil and the bounty in the woods be enough to overcome the challenges?

I calmed my unease about the arrival of the others by remembering that the more experienced colonists had been through this all before. Helena Giesy, Christian's sister, would likely say this was an easier creation of a colony than when they moved to Missouri, conquering hardwood trees and plowing meadows. Missouri was a wilderness of sorts in the 1840s, and there were Indian scares there, too, with Andrew Jackson's Removal Act forcing the natives onto reservations far from their home lands.

I'd arrived in my parents' home well after those early years. I didn't know the trials they might have lived through. Maybe all new adventures had missteps and trials and, as Christian said, I was merely being dramatic.

Spring arrived, and with it improved health for us all. Even the goat gained weight. I watched my husband lash a log behind a mule to pull it to a clearing. We Germans were accustomed to hard work. It was what defined us. It's what helped carve a Bethelite's faith. Hard work and a hope we walked on God's path.

Now began the work in earnest. The Bethelites would be here in less than six months.

Part II

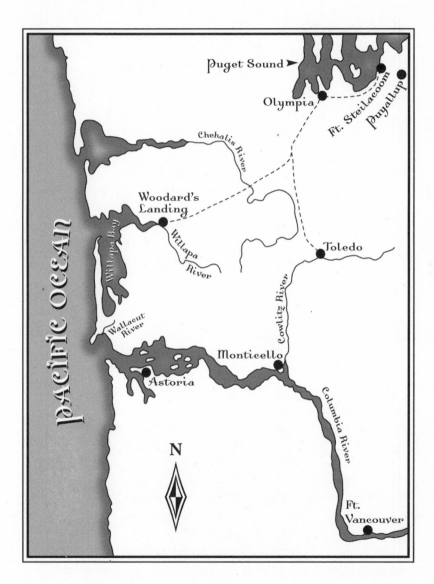

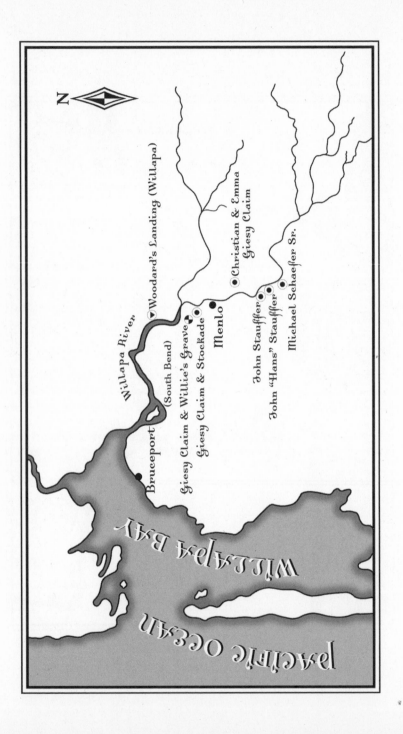

23

Virtue and Vice

"Mama," Andy said, and he handed me a clutch of wildflowers as white as chalk. Spring 1855, and I pitched any worrisome thoughts away. White trillium carpeting the forest floor distracted me. Pink and white orchids grew on tree trunks, or so it appeared; flowers with podlike blooms turned the meadows beside the rivers blue. Moss green as cats' eyes lay curled around tree roots, waiting to be patted. This valley formed a tapestry, a quilt of such richness I wondered that I ever questioned my husband's choice to come here. The air smelled fresh each morning, and the river, raging as it did carrying all that rain to the sea, kept within its banks, and I felt blessed.

I walked the tall grass meadows with Andy running now before me, still falling down sometimes but always picking himself up to carry on. The goat trotted after him like a dog. I could hear the sounds of hammering, the grunts of men raising logs to rafters. They coughed less now, the lingering illness of the winter fading. Still, each night I heard Christian's lament about their lack of progress. "Soon we'll have to send someone out to meet Wilhelm's group," he told me. "That will leave fewer of us to work the logs."

"Maybe, with so few of us here, you could wait and hope that Michael Sr. or George will be coming with them and can lead them here."

"*Nein.* We should have them come a different way, across the bay. We'll need to send someone out to lead them."

While I questioned that wisdom, I kept silent. I could do little to speed the progress except dig roots, pick berries when they were ripe, tan the hides as best I could, boil river water for drinking now that the rains had ceased, and watch after Andy. An-Gie had showed me how to find the *wapato* and a few other roots to dry. Christian called one camass and said we could cook them, which I did. And once, startling me in the woods, two Chehalis women showed me mushrooms they motioned for me to pluck from the forest floor and eat. They were white as beach sand and tasted like sponge, it seemed to me.

This Willapa Valley offered such abundance of cedar and fir and hemlock and yew, and yet we paled against the requirements to rein such bounty in. We had fewer than five huts built, and those would be roofed with tarps from the wagons of the Bethelites once they arrived. Knowing that a large wagon train would soon bring 150 people or more into this clearing pushed at the men, but they could work no harder than they already did. It fell to me to raise their spirits, to force them to look at what they'd done rather than what was left to do. "You've bought the land. You've befriended Indians. You've staked out boundaries. You've met townspeople, you've spent money wisely to keep us fed, you've sent off the scouts on time. You've kept your wife and son close by, and on top of that you've built huts. Houses," I told Christian one dawn. I took a breath.

Christian held a chunk of biscuit out for the seagull to peck at. This new bird still wouldn't take anything from Christian's hand, only mine and Andy's. He didn't have the chip from his bill, but a hole in his webbed foot marked him as unique. We called this one Charlie too.

"And on top of that, you've been as faithful a man as I've ever known, trusting always that you were doing the Lord's work, never putting yourself first in anything. You are a good man, Christian Giesy, and this place will one day reflect all that you have done to take it from the wild into a welcoming place."

He dropped the breadcrumb. "Yet the bird does not trust me."

"What does a bird know anyway?"

He grinned. "Your passion and vision remind me of Wilhelm's."

"I'm nothing like our leader," I retorted. The thought startled. I picked up the crumb and held it out. Charlie waddled over, his beak never touching my finger as he lifted the bread from me as I squatted. "Wilhelm is…visionary, I agree. But he's also…selfish."

Christian frowned. "That's not a word I'd use to describe either of you."

"Don't compare us," I said. My voice shook. I wondered where this trembling came from.

"I only meant that both of you use words that change the minds of people, take them from lowly places onto hilltops where they can see farther than they did before. I see compassion in both of you, too. *Ja,* I know how you feel about Wilhelm." He'd raised his hand to silence my open mouth to protest. "But sometimes when we see only another's faults, we ignore the other side of those flaws. He's driven, yes, but also passionate. He acts boldly when needed, though you'd say arrogant. He's a leader, and sometimes that makes a man single-minded. But that's you, too, Emma." My face felt hot with such words. "You must be careful you don't define our leader with such a narrow view that you become more like those negative qualities you claim he has and ignore the strengths on the opposite sides that each of you share. Virtue and vice, they live together."

I blinked, at least a dozen times. Charlie pecked at my wrist, wanting more food, but I had none in my hand. Food for thought is what Christian gave me, and I found it hard to swallow.

Andy and I often went out with the men, me serving food to them with some hope that it sped their days. It also gave me opportunity to walk what would someday be fields of grain. I imagined our fields with wheat bending in the breeze. I squeezed my eyes shut to picture our house built one day. I visualized my son growing up to work beside his father. Imagining what might be gave me respite.

The colors in this landscape took my breath away. All the fresh green of moss and trees, the still wet, black vines, the reddish bark of cedars, a rushing river, browned by the tumbling banks of mud that tried to define it, a sky a staggering blue, all acted as an admiring audience for the promise of the meadow's performance. *Lavish,* I thought. *This is lavish.* Certainly a God who could create such as this would not protest displays of beauty on a person or a place. I wondered if my mother had come to that conclusion and that was why she kept the strand of pearls about her neck.

For some reason an old sermon of our leader's came to mind, in which he spoke of the prodigal son. He said the word *prodigal* had more than one meaning, and one of its meanings was "lavish, abundant." That wayward son's father lavished him with good things, so surely wishing to have abundance was scriptural, wasn't it? Surely wanting abundance couldn't be prideful. Why would God have created all that lush growth and glorious land if not for us to experience the fullness of it all? *What good is creation if one doesn't find awe and joy in it?*

I thought back to Bethel. Filigrees and fluff had been permitted on our houses. Elim, Wilhelm and Louisa's home, stood recognized from the other homes with its size, its many chimneys, and wide porches framed with gingerbread cutouts. Perhaps lavishness was permitted in places other than on an individual person.

I loosened the tie on my worn wrapper, let the warm breeze flow through to dry the perspiration on my skin. I heard the men shout to one another and direct the mules, who jerked against the straps as they hauled another log out of the woods. Perhaps we could be ready for those coming behind us, ready not with physical things like houses but ready to receive them into an abundant place. Maybe Christian was right about my ability to express myself. I could use words to help them see the bounty here, to trust that this was a place chosen for us. Perhaps this bountiful place would be enough to meet all the needs of these people. A house to live in wasn't nearly as critical as land that could raise grain.

Christian's parents would bring the grist stones, coming by ship around the Horn; they'd make it possible for us to have flour before the year was out. Wheat of our own grinding, if we got some planted. I needed to honor all that we scouts had done surviving in the Oregon Territory for two winters, keeping always focused on meeting the needs of the colony. Well, almost always.

Andy raced ahead of me, running without falling for his longest time yet. He'd grown. I counted his months. Nineteen. I thought back to the time I carried him. Under other circumstances, another brother or sister would be good for him. But here, with such work to do, it would be better to wait until we were settled into our own hut. I thought to the last time I'd had my monthly flow. It had come back with the good food of the hunters. But I had not known it now for three months. *Three months.* This was already May.

I looked down at my abdomen, ran my hands around it in a warm circle of affection. It was already too late to wait: if I counted right, this baby would arrive in...December. The wettest, coldest, and dreariest month, but also the most prodigal time.

———

Mules can be a trouble at times, but they are more reliable than a horse. We scouts had moved ourselves and were back living in lean-tos to be closer to the work sites while the men labored at their tasks. I assured Christian that the exercise of plowing would be good for the baby I carried, since I could do little to help them in the woods.

After a time of cleaning his ear with his finger, his newest sign of being in thought, he consented, saying we'd repay the Woodards for the use of their mule by giving them wheat. We couldn't spare any of our animals; they were needed for dragging logs.

"It would be better to plant oats," Sarah told me. "Wheat doesn't grow well here. We usually order flour in."

"They grew wheat near Steilacoom," I remembered.

"Even in a short distance the climate affects what grows."

"We have wheat seed," I said. "No oats."

She shrugged.

I didn't share the conversation with Christian. But we borrowed the Woodards' plow and mule, and I began the work, pulling the heavy straps over my shoulder, gripping the plow handles while wearing my leather gloves. The Woodards' mule had plowed fields before. I could tell he didn't like it.

A mule being asked to do what he doesn't like consumes one's energy completely, allowing little time to think of anything deeper than how far the wheat field furrows sink. I longed for that distraction as I watched the men begin to question once again their ability to complete their labors in time. Plowing fields kept my mind from disappointing thinking.

I'd seen the men plow fields back in Bethel. And I knew it would take me long hours of being jerked by the single-bottom plow when it might strike a rock or it would pitch over and fall, and I'd have to hoist the handles and blade up, hoping the mule would stand firm. We put blinders on him to avoid distractions from birds swooping overhead or any other skittering thing that might shake an animal's confidence and make it bolt. A dried leaf could do it; a bear would surely cause a stir. Both the mule and I did best when kept from distractions.

I'd tethered Andy with a long vine of cedar root I braided into a sturdy rope so he wouldn't go wandering off too far from the edge of the field I worked on. The rope was another gift of the landscape brought to my attention by the Chehalis women I saw now and then. Maybe when they'd seen my makeshift cedar cape, they'd decided I had potential and shared bits of their experience with me.

Andy explored the ground for ants and salamanders and other insects with names I didn't know. He particularly liked the slugs, the slimy finger-length creatures the color of the scorched flour I used to treat Andy's diaper rash. Their little antenna broke the monotony of their bodies, and Andy loved to touch them. Slugs and his wooden toy horse and goat, Charlie and the live goat kept him company. He even napped in the shade of the tree he was tethered to. At least we'd never found a snake here; only spiders kept us on our toes.

I'd pounded cedar bark with a rock into a kind of mat. He lay on that now as I worked. I found that the best time, his napping time, when I didn't carry this nudging worry over him in the back of my mind. The river flowed close, and while it no longer crested near the banks, it was still wide and hungry and would easily consume an adventurous child. I wondered if my mother had worried like that when I was little and Bethel was being built. I planned to write her when the others arrived, bringing precious paper with them. What paper we had we'd used up, so I couldn't even make the notes I wanted, to remind myself of how I felt with all we did here. I'd have to be like the Indians and memorize the tales. At least that's what An-Gie said they did, and thus she'd found little need to read or write.

The mule's tail swatted at flies and tiny bugs, and the animal occasionally looked back toward me, though I knew he couldn't see me with the blinders on. I'd "gee" and "haw" him to turn right or left, and we'd jerk forward. Sometimes I sprawled in the earth as he'd skip ahead before I was ready; sometimes I'd fall into the furrow and have to shove the plow off of my leg, then sweat and ache to get it upright again. My left wrist still gave me sharp pains when I tried to lift or twist with it too much, a remembrance of our Andy's birth.

The soil beside the river was rich and dark, and the plow turned over deep chunks of dirt within the furrows. I'd sink down nearly to my knees at times. I'd pulled the wrapper up between my legs and tucked it into my apron's belt so I wouldn't trip on the hem. The dress was threadbare, though I washed it only once a week, grateful that the breezes dried it through the night.

By June we'd returned the mule, and I'd broadcast the seed. I convinced my husband we were sending it out the way Christians and Muslims of old must have done it. If all went well, we'd have a crop by fall, and the gristmill stones Christian's parents were bringing would grind our own wheat first.

The men slept out under the stars now as they worked on huts yet farther away from the original Giesy claims. Christian and I slept again in a lean-to so we could see the moon as it slivered through the tree tops. We spoke of our own growing family and how pleased his parents would be when they arrived, knowing that at last their firstborn son had made them grandparents and would soon do so again. It was almost like being in Bethel.

"When will you begin our home?" I asked one noon while I fed Christian hard biscuits and a jerky stew with mushrooms and *wapato* chopped in. The field I'd plowed was on the Giesy claim he'd singled out for his parents and brother. I would have plowed "our" fields, but the seven miles between the sites made that difficult. There were two river crossings needed to reach our claim even riding the mule, something I didn't relish with Andy, the mule, and a plow to manage too.

"Time enough to build ours," he said. "There'll be more hands here by October, and we'll build ours then. Not before."

"Can we go back so I can see where our hut might sit? I like to imagine what it will look like and what the view through the windows might be."

"Women," he snorted. "What does the view matter?"

"Each window offers something special; each woman's home will be different from the others, individual. I like thinking of how we'll place things there. Besides, we take little time for imagining, for doing anything except work. This can't be good, not in a land that is as flashy as a feather cape."

Christian dipped the hard biscuit into the stew, sucked on it. "Why is it so important for you to stand out? Perhaps we should consider building one large house for several families. That way there'll be no argument about who got the best site, whose house is bigger or better. It borders on envy to want such things."

I knew our leader thought envy to be one of the deadliest of sins. Now my husband swirled my opinions into our leader's stream, combining desire with sin rather than with imagination. I wished I'd kept my thoughts to myself. Living in one large family house forever did not seem like a wise idea to me. Envy wouldn't be the only deadly sin that would ripple the surface of that river if that were to be my fate.

"The other side of envy is…compassion," I told him. "Being aware of what others need."

"Ja," he said after a moment's thought.

"I simply wish to be the wife of Proverbs 31," I continued. "She bought fields, burned a late candle on behalf of her family, and was praised for clothing her household with scarlet and having coverings of tapestry and her clothes made of silk and purple. Her children sang her praises and so did her husband."

"Proverbs 31 also says, 'Favor is deceitful, and beauty is vain: but a woman that feareth the LORD, she shall be praised.'" He could always silence me with his better understanding of Scripture. He continued. "I worry that at times you seek favor from the wrong places, Emma. Favor is deceitful."

I felt my face grow warm despite the cooling breeze. *Should I simply suffer in silence or should I speak a piece?* I took a deep breath.

"This place is rich with beautiful flowers, with trees that tower so high I get dizzy looking up at their tops reaching to the sky. Game is plentiful for food and skins, and even the river that I give wide berth to, even it offers up those things we need: fish and a way to get from here to there when the vines tangle our paths. I can't believe such abundance is meant not to be noticed. You sing the praises of the timber and the soil that will grow grain that we'll grind and sell to others, people living on Puget Sound, people coming here because of this land's rich resources. I can't believe I was created to pretend I don't notice that these gifts are wrapped in a landscape of loveliness."

"*Ja*, you notice. But then you start to compare, to put your own mark on the landscape by saying, 'Here is my view. It is prettier than your view.' Or 'Here is my house. Even the pegs are sturdier than yours' or 'My door is wider' or… *Ach*." He brushed the air in disgust. "It is dumb talk you make. We are called to live together, one as the other, no one standing out. We have come here to prepare a way for others. We will be as one, brothers and sisters together."

"Chosen," I said. "Does God not pick us out then, see us as special? How can recognizing what makes us different be sinful?"

"He chooses us to serve Him," Christian said.

I could hear the irritation in his voice and knew I should stay quiet, bite my tongue, pitch the thoughts of what I'd say next and would likely later regret. But it was not my way to remain silent, not my way to be like other community women, and I couldn't help but believe that Christian knew that of me and had "chosen" me because of it.

"So some are not selected. How do we know? How do I know if I'm of the elect if I don't name the things that make me stand apart from…unbelievers, from those not chosen?"

"Those selected for His service have trials," he said. "Remember Moses. Remember Mary and Jacob and Ruth. They all found trouble as a part of their decisions to be obedient."

"But see, they stand out, those men and women of the Bible, and we don't think unkindly of them," I said.

He coughed. "They weren't selected for their talents, nor for the best of anything they made nor for the most exquisite view nor for gathering the most people around themselves. They were and are unique, *Liebchen,* because of what they lived through, because of how their faith deepened by the things they faced and overcame. Our Lord reminds us that we do not choose Him, but He chooses us. He's chosen us to follow Him here to Willapa to be in service to Him. And when the others arrive, they too will see that we are all chosen to be together."

I wanted to believe that this place was specifically meant for us, but I didn't want to be "chosen" for the trials I had to face. We'd had our share of them already, with the weeks of dreary weather, heavy rains, and dark skies that stole our energy like maple sap taken from its tree.

"The Lord uses trials to turn people around, Emma."

"I wonder, then," I ventured, "if He wants us to leave here, since progress has been so slow on the huts. Maybe it's His way of turning us around?"

Christian stared at me.

I remembered what our leader told me, about women needing to support their husbands, that suffering in childbirth was our penance for disobedience and betrayal. "Maybe we've taken a side road and are here in Willapa not to serve God but to serve our leader. Maybe that's why things have gone so slowly." My heart pounded. It was the most direct I'd been with Christian in challenging his thinking.

"We have lessons to learn from this time, Emma. Remember, all the scouts chose this place. All agreed as we have worked: agreed on which huts to build, even when to wait out the weather. We even agreed on who should go back to bring out the other Bethelites and how they should return. We discuss, and then the Lord moves us toward His way."

He swirled the water of our uncertainty now, convincing me where I'd earlier encouraged him. I supposed that is what marriage looks like, that exchange of hope between people who love.

"*Liebchen,* whenever you doubt that we belong in this place, you make yourself think of those early signs of certainty. They are memories that not only comfort but help move us ever forward."

"As when I stumble behind the mule in the field."

"*Ja.*" His voice had softened. "You don't question whether you should be behind that plow. You pick yourself up and keep going. That is what we faithful Germans know to do."

24

Natural Wealth

"Emma, bring the corn drink," Christian shouted to me.

"Can it wait?"

"No," he said. "Bring it now."

I had enough to do at the river, washing the men's shirts. I'd spent the day chopping at weeds in the grain field, a lost cause. Fall approached, and I wondered if we'd even have a crop given the strength of the weeds and the short stems. And I hadn't seen Charlie the seagull all morning, and Andy kept asking, "Charlie? Charlie?"

My husband's words annoyed. Why bother me when I worked, making me pull the rope on the corn drink to bring it to the men? Surely they could get it themselves. I pushed against my knees and stood. That's when I noticed we had company.

The men arrived with furtive eyes, silent as snails. They were Americans, they said. They spoke only English but told us that from now on, we should only speak our German so if the Indians approached they'd think we were French or British, anything but American. They'd come through the eastern part of the Territory and told stories of the Yakima tribe's uprising. "Dozens of other tribes are angry with the wagons pulling across the mountains and taking their lands. Government won't protect us. You'd best use what resources you've got to secure your people. Your strange language. That's a weapon here."

"Is it just in the western territories?" Hans asked. "Not a problem in the prairie places, then?" I knew he thought of the Bethelites making their way from Missouri.

"Everywhere." The American took a swallow, letting the corn drink pour down like streams separating his thick beard. He wiped his face with his palm. "You folks got people coming across?" I nodded. "Worry for 'em," he said. "Unless they act like foreigners, French or Germans or whatevers, they'll arrive without their hair if they arrive at all."

The men quenched their thirsts, then informed us of the failed treaty negotiations in this Washington Territory, as it was called now, and the government's plan to get all the tribes to sign a new treaty that would place all Indians on land set aside for them. Reservations. "Even the Shoalwaters of this country resist. I guess cuz they weren't named specific and given their own place." Only the Nez Perce remained calm, they told us. "But don't worry; they'll war against Americans too. The Cayuse have already joined up. What horrors they heaped on those poor Whitmans. Don't have to wonder what atrocities they're capable of."

I frowned. I hadn't heard of the Whitmans' trouble. I'd have to ask Sarah to see what she knew of them, but for now I could only imagine the trials being experienced by our colony heading west. What if they were attacked? What if they never arrived? Maybe it was good that my parents and brother weren't coming west, but Christian's brothers were, and Mary and Sebastian would be making their way.

The Yakima, the men told us in hurried conversation over a camp-fire, had killed a miner making his way from Puget Sound across the northern part of the Territory into Colville country. "Took all his gold," they said. "Slaughtered him up and down. Then more Ameri-cans were found dead. Never Frenchies or Brits," the men complained. "Watch your backs, you Germans, living out here close to Nisqually and those Hudson's Bay folks. Those Brits don't want others coming here either, messing up their trading. They'll get those Indians riled as they did back in New York years ago." He patted his sidearm. "Be ready to shoot first."

I remembered the Chehalis men who gave us the elk hide door, who'd roofed our very house. I'd seen a few Shoalwater people at Woodards' who seemed friendly enough. In my halting English I suggested as much, but the Americans cut me off. No woman would have sway with them, I guessed, especially one who spoke with any kindness toward the natives. The men sat on mats of cedar bark that Indian women had shown me how to make. Cedar capes made from the pattern of a gift lay stacked ready for winter's use. Surely these were peaceful people, even those charged with warring.

The Americans hitched a ride on the mail boat heading out from Woodard's Landing toward the sea. At the Bay they planned to catch a ship back to the States, and if we were smart we'd do the same, they told us. Those were the last things they said before parting.

"Are you worried?" I asked Christian that night. A spider tickled a slender strand across my arm, and I brushed at it.

"Only about the colony. Here, we're safe enough," he said.

But something in the night must have caused Christian to reconsider the men's words. He told Hans and Adam that he'd head to Woodards' to see if any letters had arrived from the colony. I asked to go along, but he refused. "You'll be safer here," he said, so I knew something troubled him. Signs of autumn appeared in the foliage. Geese already flew south. While my pregnancy had been fine so far, my wrapper had to be extended farther than before, and when I walked, I floated like a boat shifting from side to side. I'd miss seeing Sarah, but today staying behind didn't bother. Christian pushed the small boat with a sail into the water. He'd bought it on account. I didn't mind not being on the Willapa, but I did miss my husband that night.

When he returned in the morning, he came with news that would change our direction. He said an agent named Bolen, sent to investigate the miner's murder, had been killed by Indians too. The Shoalwaters had been left out of the treaty and were using their hatchets and guns to protest. An outraged Governor Stevens called the Indians defiant and ordered the military to shoot to kill. Added to this, several of the plains-area Indians said they'd seen enough of wagons coming across their lands and wanted no part of this proposed federal treaty. That angered the governor even more so that he called for war against all Indians.

My palms grew wet as I wondered how our leader's wagon train fared.

"They'll come this way, too," Christian said. "We're on their land, even though we've gained it fair and square from the government. But it won't be ours if we can't hold it against an uprising."

"Maybe we shouldn't have claimed it," I said.

He ignored me.

I thought about the words our leader said to us, that we would go west to find a place where the world could not encroach upon us, where we could take care of our own without harm to others and be able to give back in return. Give back on our terms. But there was no place like that.

"We'll build a blockhouse to defend ourselves," Christian told us. "We have no one here to protect us except us, except the work of our hands."

"It'll delay the hut-building even further," Adam complained.

"*Ja.* But protection for the larger body will be necessary once they arrive. We must fortify now." Christian put his little finger into his ear, thinking as he scratched it. "Maybe we were meant to do this now, to better prepare for the time when all will end."

He hadn't spoken much about the *last days,* not since we'd arrived.

I didn't like talking about it now, but I did notice that when he did, when Christian asked us to think about our own possible deaths, that the scouts appeared more encouraged rather than fearful. They worked with greater enthusiasm. They questioned his decisions less. I wondered if that was something Wilhelm understood, that we follow a leader more faithfully when we're reminded of encroaching death.

As though to prove me right, we woke with urgency. Christian said we'd build the stockade wall on top of the hill of the Giesy claim, near where we'd first built our completed log house. No one disagreed. Christian and Hans and Adam cut logs fifteen feet long while I dug at the trench as I could. After the others joined me, we dug the trench three feet deep in an area around the house and then wider—to encompass another house Christian said we'd need to build as soon as we finished the stockade.

I rubbed tallow onto my hands to counter the blisters, thinking how nice it would be when the others arrived with amenities we hadn't had for so long. My lanolin and lemon were long used up. My hands were rough as cedar bark and nearly as red. *Ach!* I chided myself for longing for small bits of luxury in the midst of preparing a safe place for others.

Andy found all the activity joyous, climbing down into the trench and walking his way along it, his towhead like a dandelion floating on a sea of dirt.

"Keep him out of there," Christian shouted to me. "The sides could cave in, and we don't know where he is when we bring the logs to stand."

I pulled him up and then found myself accomplishing no work at all until he slept, for he headed for the trench each time I loosed his hand. I wondered why it is we are pulled to that which is dangerous, to places we should best leave alone. As I watched Andy return time after time to the trench, then look back to see if I would catch him before he jumped in, I wondered about this challenging nature we were born with and what kind of God kept calling us back when we were wayward so often.

On September 12, 1855, we heard voices and the sounds of animals crashing through the timber. Christian shouted, "To the stockade!" and ran toward me. I grabbed Andy and scooped him into my arms, lumbering like an old boat. The stockade remained unfinished, but at least there were three sides completed. My heart pounded. The sounds couldn't come from the Bethel group. It was too early. We didn't expect them until late October, maybe even in November. We mustn't panic. Perhaps another group of Americans headed toward the Bay to leave this territory behind. I'd think it was that, hoped only good would soon charge through that brush.

And then I heard German. Was it? *Ja!* And the cries of a child, and then through the openings of the timber and the vines came Peter Klein, a Bethelite, and a dozen others, twenty-five in all, men, women and children weighted down with packs on their backs and driving a few cows before them.

"From what George told us, I knew we couldn't make the trail with wagons," Peter said. He laughed and his eyes sparkled. "But the cows helped thrash it down for us—those we didn't lose."

I named the people who'd come, hugging the women and children, getting their stories of when they'd left, the trials they'd had along the way. Andy clutched my knees as I walked, and I realized he hadn't ever seen children before, had never gazed into the eyes of one his size.

My greatest joy was when I reached Mary Giesy. I held her in my arms with just the hint of guilt that I had a child of my own and would soon produce another, when last I'd seen her, she grieved the loss of her son.

"Did you have trouble? With Indians?"

Mary shook her head. "No. It was almost…boring," she said. "Day after day of walking, sleeping out under the stars. We were just anxious to leave Bethel, and with Willie turning ill, the rest of the party decided to wait for him to improve. We came on ahead. Michael Schaefer Sr. drew maps and told stories until we felt we'd been with you all coming across."

"Willie's ill? Something bad?"

"The malaria. He gets it every year, remember? It's one reason *Herr* Kiel wants to come west, to have his children in a healthy place."

"Except for mosquitoes, spiders, and an occasional bear, this is a heavenly place," I said. I hugged her again. "I'm so glad you came with Peter's group, before all the rest."

"*Ja,* me, too," she whispered in my ear. "I wanted my baby to be born in this Washington Territory and not somewhere along the way."

Her dark eyes danced with her news. She hardly looked pregnant, and when I stood back to gaze at her, she giggled. "We have until next year to prepare," she said. "The baby isn't due until January."

I calculated.

Mary smiled. "*Ja,* the first week away from Bethel I conceived. On the trail."

"Is it sacrilege," I whispered, leaning in to her, "to think we all might do better away from our leader?"

Her eyes grew large and then she laughed. "At least you haven't changed," she said. "That's comforting when everything else surely has."

But I had changed, at least inside. I was stronger and more aware of my husband, more willing to help him succeed. And one way was to celebrate the arrival of this first group. He'd pay attention to the task, but joy fueled the laborers. Oh, how we sang and celebrated in the September air so crisp, with the spruce trees in their prime, of full brush of branches arching out over the forest floor. The hemlock and fir, even a tree Christian called yew, stood in their glory, piercing the perfect blue sky. I loved the looks of the children as they eyed those massive trees, saw the thickness of such timber; ignored the catch in my stomach as the women looked upward, shaking their heads at the treetops. Mary nearly fell over backward trying to see the top. I caught her before she fell.

"It can be tamed," I told Mary when she said she'd never seen anything so dense, so foreboding.

I took in with good cheer the approval of Peter's wife and some young girls as they noted my pregnancy and patted my Andy's head as I held him on my hip.

"*Ja*, it is good to be here," they told me.

"What is the three-sided yard?" one asked.

"Part of a stockade," I said. "Just a precaution. Against Indian trouble."

They looked with judging eyes at the log house with its pitiful canvas roof. They didn't seem pleased at the height of the riverbanks where we'd have to slide down to pull up buckets of water. The amenities they'd left behind loomed larger. I knew those looks. Yes, they were grateful to be at the end of their journey, but alarmed perhaps at what this next step in the journey entailed. I tried not to dwell on their expressions, the looks that said, "Where are we? And what have we done?"

"They left Bethel early," Christian told me that evening. He wasn't telling me anything Mary hadn't already said. As we talked, he walked with me to the river, reached down, and pulled up the bucket with corn juice from where I tied it to keep cool. We didn't purchase much corn, just enough to make the drink that I swirled round with my long burl spoon. I imagined how many new things I'd have once Christian's parents arrived with our trunks. "They came overland," Christian said. "Wilhelm is but a few weeks behind. We'll need to send Hans or Adam out to meet him and bring him on up."

His words held…caution, I suppose, perhaps a wariness that he'd be judged by that man. But no, those would be my thoughts pushing their way through like an unruly toddler. Christian would be worried about their safety, about having enough for them to eat once they arrived, about having shelter and safety from any uprisings.

"Joe Knight never made it back with them," he said then.

"He didn't? What happened?"

Christian shook his head. "He…made his own way, going to California, Peter tells me. Adam returned, said they were but a day out when Joe announced he wanted to work for a while, maybe in California. There were words exchanged and then they separated."

"Maybe he met up with them. Maybe he's with Wilhelm's group now," I said, chirped almost.

"They argued. The scouts separated. They didn't agree once they left here. This is not a good sign."

"But now you'll have help to build the houses," I said. "All those men. You'll have them built in no time."

He hesitated before taking my lead away from the discomforting news about Joe Knight. "*Ja*, we finish the stockade, then build a gun house, high so we can see all around. Peter thinks it necessary, as all they heard along the way were rumors of massacres." He looked away from me.

"But with all this help—"

"Peter says our leader brings thirty-seven wagons, more than I thought for this first journey. I figure six people to a wagon. That's two hundred and twenty people who will arrive here in less than two months."

I swallowed. He didn't need to say more. The rains would come soon. The cool air promised that. And now there was a defection, a hole in the tapestry of the scouts. I had nothing to say to bring comfort.

In the morning, the men finished the stockade wall with the logs stood up on end, side by side like little fishes in those metal tins I'd once seen. The stockade surrounded the house we'd built. Then the men enclosed it with a heavy log gate hung on leather straps and began chopping more logs to build the gun turret area while other men began another hut inside the stockade.

I kept my voice light for the women, to reassure them. I showed them how we would have enough to eat to feed their children. "Food is the servant of the heart," I said. "We can go to the ocean and dig for clams. They try to hide but we find them. We might buy an oyster or two as well."

"You've done this?" Mary asked.

I shook my head, no. "But my friend Sarah digs for clams and she eats the oysters, and there are fish in the river, and elk and deer and even bear in the forest. We won't go hungry," I assured them. I showed them my dried berries. I suggested that we could all sleep under one roof but that we had so little rain in these months that their canvas tarps would protect them against the elements until all had houses. I made sure to call them houses—not huts.

As the men worked on the houses, we dug potatoes I'd planted and roasted them. Hans had help now and brought in good-sized deer. We all had fresh meat, and I showed them how to dry it.

Then later in the week, with the scythes they brought with them, we women cut the skimpy grain and talked as we worked, like women of old who bent to their harvest. It felt good to be in the company of women again. I looked out over the heads wrapped in dark scarves tied at the back of the neck, and for the first time I didn't mind that I wore one too, for it made me one of them again. To be able to answer their questions, to calm their worries, to offer comfort in this wilderness, that was what love was. Noticing another's need and tending it.

The Wolfer girls looked after the younger children as we tied the shocks, then broke the small heads into our aprons. We'd grind the grain on river rocks until the grist stones arrived and we had a mill of our own. The other women followed suit, and it seemed to ease the fears of the uprisings, of all the unknowns that face anyone who enters a wilderness place. Acting together to help others forestalled our deeper fears.

We had grain for our children to eat, enough for ourselves and one another, at least for a time. Our men prepared a safe place for us. We had friends and family together for the first time in more than a year. What more could we ask for?

Karl Ruge, our teacher, had once quoted Socrates, who said contentment was natural wealth; luxury, artificial poverty. I saw natural wealth here. I wanted to believe that everything would be well. We'd been chosen to come here. All had agreed. We had nothing to fear.

25

The Confluence
of Streams

"Emma," Christian shouted. He looked happy. "Michael's here."

Michael Sr. rubbed his chin. Before we could send anyone out, Michael Sr. had left Keil's train to come ahead, letting us know they were close. George Link and John Genger would bring them on in the rest of the way. We gathered around him, breezes swirling our thin dresses. Wilhelm's wagon train was somewhere east of The Dalles along the Columbia River. Instead of telling us how they all fared, he told us rumors of the Indian wars and the soldiers who dotted the river passages with troop transports. I tried not to feel nervous about the possibility of attack. No Indians here had frightened us. Our remoteness probably helped, I decided. They'd have to come looking for us; we wouldn't likely stumble upon trouble. We'd built that stockade. But that was cautionary, something a good leader would do.

"Your brother travels with Keil," Michael Sr. said and nodded to me.

"He and Willie just couldn't be separated now, could they?" I said. "Thank goodness, or my brother would have stayed home." *Jonathan traveled with them.* My brother, soon here holding his nephew, telling me how Mama and Papa were, the girls and little boys, what the journey had *really* been like. I could hardly wait.

"Ah…*ja,*" Michael Sr. said. He cleared his throat, turned back to the others. He changed the subject then, but not without leaving me wondering at the wariness in his voice. "Their journey west has been uneventful," Michael Sr. continued, then said that our leader was primed to love this place because of the ease of the overland passage. "When I left them at The Dalles, they'd had gifts of horses given to them by Cayuse, and they'd been treated like royalty by the Indians coming across, or so Wilhelm tells it. It's only since they reached Oregon Territory that there are Indian worries. On the plains, sometimes whole deer would be killed, dressed, and left for our arrival at an evening camp." Entire Indian families came in more than once and were fed by the colonists. "One night we were joined by thirty braves and their wives and children and their dogs, too." He grinned. "Of course, Wilhelm had invited them, although he never once said anything to Louisa or the others, so we thought we were under attack at first."

I could imagine the fear and then surprise Louisa, Keil's wife, must have felt, taking a deep breath and finding a way to feed those additional people without even the benefit of preparation. "Keil, he is ready to love this place because I tell him of all the possibilities. He is excited, I can tell you that," Michael Sr. told us. His eyes scanned our progress, and I thought I saw a small frown. "At one point on the journey Keil was burdened, but he separated himself and went to a high mound, and there he wrestled with the enemy, and God said He'd walk with him."

"Does he think the game left by the Indians is an example of that?" Peter Klein asked.

"Maybe. And Adam's letters reached home ahead of time to raise their enthusiasm. But more, the Indians were subdued by the…hearse," he said. "I've come ahead to tell so we can send a delegation to the Columbia River to bring them here."

At last they would see what my husband had contended with and how well he'd done despite the trials. The stockade had a blockhouse within it and gun turrets at the top. The fields of grain were harvested, and we had plenty of potatoes. Christian had hoped we'd even sell some and ship them south, our first produce sale. But the Californians apparently planted their own this year and weren't interested in any of ours. Still, anyone could see that love and labor had gone into this clearing to prepare for the community. I loved Michael Sr.'s enthusiasm. The safe trip by the main colony affirmed that the journey west was of divine calling.

But what was this hearse?

Already a light rain dribbled over us as we talked, the drops of water on my husband's hair like light spots of diamonds flashing when sun broke through the clouds. The air smelled sweet, and the contrasts between the dark trunks of trees and the needles of green stood crisp against the mist. I wanted the new arrivals to see what we saw, this beauty and not the challenges still to be faced.

"What is this hearse you speak of?" Sebastian Giesy asked.

Michael Sr. looked around then and nodded toward the stockade. "A sturdy blockhouse. Good. We'll be safe here. When the Indian things calm down, we can move to our houses."

"We didn't expect so many," Christian said. He added, his voice low, "We have fewer houses ready than planned, but not for lack of work. You know of our challenges here. Wilhelm will understand."

Michael Sr. averted his eyes. "He may expect more from us. He's… not always realistic." He pulled at his beard. "When I told him you had a son, he groused and said, 'That's not what I sent him out there to do.' "

The men chuckled low, all except Christian. I felt my cheeks grow warm and was grateful when Peter Klein said, "Why do we send men to the Columbia River to meet them? Won't they sell their wagons in Portland and come the way we did?"

Michael Sr. shook his head and then looked cautiously at me. He took in a deep breath. "They have a hearse. Willie died before they left. Wilhelm's beloved son."

This was news even Peter Klein's early-leaving train had not known. Our leader loved that boy more than anyone—more than Louisa, I thought, though I'd never said as much. I wondered how he'd dealt with the loss of *his* son. Did he blame himself, his own sinful state, as he had with Sebastian and Mary? Or did he blame Louisa? I shivered for her. How hard to leave behind a loved one deep in Missouri soil.

"*Ja,*" Michael Sr. continued. "It was a big loss. Malaria. Your brother grieves, *Frau* Giesy. They delayed starting west because of Willie's death."

"To take time to bury him," I said.

"No." He swallowed. "To bring Willie with them."

"What nonsense is that?" Christian said. "They brought Willie's body across the mountains, the plains, through Indian country?"

"*Ja.* Keil had a lead- and tin-lined casket made. He would have asked you with your skills, but you were here. So it took a little longer to make. Then he placed the body inside. He steeped it in our Golden Rule Whiskey. He composed songs sung each morning by the colonists walking behind the *Schellenbaum. Herr* Keil believes it is that which kept the Indians from harassing them. The Indians saw their journey as a sacred one, that our people tend well to the dead. Adam says Indians came in and looked at the hearse. *Ja, Herr* Keil wanted to bury his son here in this place that calls us all. Well, almost all. He names this place Aurora for his daughter without even seeing it."

He'd brought his dead son all the way across the mountains. I couldn't imagine how hard that must have been for Louisa, and for the colonists, each morning following that hearse carried in an open ambulance with fluttering black fringe around the top. Keil would have made it big and ornamental, I had no doubt about that.

"Hopefully nothing bad has happened to the wagons after you left, Michael," Christian said. "It will be good if all things continue to go well. It will make him more understanding of our…of our progress here."

It was the first indication I had that my husband worried.

"Our leader will see that this is the place we were meant to be, or he wouldn't have had such an untroubled journey here," I said. That became my prayer. "Moving a hearse across the country. *Ja,* that is quite a feat."

While Christian prepared to leave to meet Wilhelm's group, I busied myself quizzing Michael Sr. about who else had come, which families, and who remained behind. Certain families were more easy-going than others, less dependent on sturdy roofs over their head, I imagined, more able to bundle up with another family and make a joy of it rather than a misery. "At least they'll have wagons to spend the winter in," I told Michael Sr. as he looked around the stockade. "We can pull quite a few inside the perimeter."

"Tents. They'll have to live in tents or inside the stockade house," he said. "Most of the wagons were ordered sold in Portland. I told them they can't easily come across the trail where the younger men will push the cows through. You say we're to go farther down the Columbia toward the old Astorian fort and have Keil come up the Wallacut River?"

Christian nodded. "It's closer to the coast. We'll cross the Bay and finish here on the Willapa River. The portage at the Wallacut will challenge them, with that hearse. Moving that wagon will be the worst. It's a heavy thing."

"You bought boats with sails, *ja?*"

"One or two," Christian answered. "And there are larger boats that come in as far as Woodard's Landing."

"*Ja*, then everything will go well."

"I hope," I said. *It must.*

———

"Why can't I go with you to meet them? I haven't seen my brother for nearly two years." I bounced Andy on the side of my hip. He fussed. While I didn't relish the trip across the Shoalwater Bay or down the Wallacut River to the Columbia, I did like the idea of standing beside Christian with our son in my arms when we greeted our leader.

"Because you and Andy will be more people to transport back and portage."

"I could help," I said.

"You would bounce our next child to arrive early?" Christian stopped his packing and patted my stomach. "We'll be on the river and then the bay more than not, and you don't like water travel, if I remember. We may have to wait for transport. Besides, who will feed the goat and that bird?"

"If needed I can take the boat," I said. "I took it with you to look at our land not long ago."

"*Ja*, you did," he said and grinned, his eyebrow lifted with the memory.

We'd gone alone and marked the outline of our house with logs so I could see the view, a prairie view that bled into timber with willows lining the river and a big leafed maple I recognized as similar to trees at Bethel. We'd spread an elk hide and placed it where the rope bed would stand. Andy had stayed with Mary and Sebastian, so we were alone for the first time in years. I lay on my back next to him, looking up at a bird's-egg-blue sky. He'd rolled on his side, his arm draped over my growing belly. My husband then kissed me sweetly. I'd teased him that he lay down on his job, skipping away for an afternoon while there was work yet to do. He'd laughed. "Our leader will know when he sees you and Andy that I lay down more than once." He kissed me again. "I love you, Emma Wagner Giesy. I love you and am grateful you came to this valley with me to begin a new life for us and for the colony."

I cherished the moment, a rare respite for Christian, one I knew wouldn't be repeated once our leader and the remainder of the group arrived. Especially now that Keil had spoken with some disdain about my pregnancy and Andy's arrival. But I held the memory of that languid afternoon in my heart because Christian saw me as doing something worthy despite my willful ways.

I smiled even as Andy pulled on my ear and said, "Down, Mama. Want down."

Christian brushed his beard against my cheek. "Your mind wanders," he said. "Or do you plot?"

"Me?" I said.

He laughed, then sobered. "I'll be back as soon as I can. We have a heavy hearse to bring and many people, and they are tired from their journey and grieving as well. It makes sense that you stay here to prepare to welcome them."

"Imagine, bringing a hearse across those mountains," I said. "What makes that man's mind work? Surely he knows that Willie's soul isn't in that body. Do you suppose he wanted to show everyone that once he says, 'You can ride in the lead wagon, Willie,' that he keeps his promises, no matter what?"

"Indeed. Strong-willed is the other side of stubborn."

"But imagine what that must have been like for Louisa. To watch this hearse that holds your firstborn rumble out every day. To follow it and be reminded every single morning that the child you loved is dead, gone forever. Would she go to it every night and pray over him? Would she listen for the sound of the wind in the *Schellenbaum* or whatever bells he probably put on it? How could you sleep? And Michael said Keil composed funeral dirges, German songs that everyone sang each morning as they set out. For five months! Think of that, Christian. The man…spurs himself."

"Or finds his own way to grieve," Christian said.

"But at what cost? That's a nearly impossible feat, to bring such a heavy thing. His success will only serve to make him think anyone can do anything if they simply set their minds to it." That thought spilling into my words caused a grimace to form on Christian's face. "And he names this place Aurora, for his *daughter*. How must that make Louisa feel?"

"Maybe she suggested it," he said. Then, "You remain. Make those here on the Willapa continue to feel welcome, *ja?* As a good wife should. As the wife of a leader should."

We'd spent so much time being equals here, me doing what I could without regard for whether it was a woman's place to speak or stay silent, whether something was women's work or not. I wondered if that would all change, if what we'd come to cherish in our time together would now be set aside.

"Maybe if I joined you, Keil would see that here we stand side by side to do the work we're called to. There's no need to separate men from women either in the worship house or in our labor."

"That isn't what they'd see, *Liebchen*. They'd see a foolish man who couldn't control his wife and brought her along at the risk of her state. What kind of leader would that make me?"

"You draw out the strengths of all of us," I said. "That's the kind of man you are. Not one who would put an entire colony at risk by bringing the body of his son across the mountains."

He grunted, but I saw the corners of his mouth rise up, and I knew then that he agreed with me, prideful as it might be. He acknowledged that he had led this small colony of scouts well. We claimed him as our leader, and Peter Klein's advance group of colonists deferred to him with respect. With the arrival of *Herr* Keil would come the story of how two strong streams of men came together. I could almost imagine the froth that would rise from that joining, prayed for the settling of it in a hopeful manner.

26

What We Set Aside

Christian insisted I remain, but he couldn't prevent me from meeting him first at his return with our...with Wilhelm. And so with Andy, I made my way to Woodard's Landing to wait. Louisa rode heavy on my thoughts. I knew she'd be critical of the primitive houses here, but she'd stay silent unless her husband spoke. That was her way. But perhaps the pain of her child's death blanketed her, too, with change on this journey west. Maybe she would speak up and influence the others in negative ways.

A west wind tugged at the braids I'd twisted into a crown at the top of my head. My cedar cape kept the drizzle at bay. My eyelashes caught droplets I blinked away. The air held a chill, and I lifted Andy to my widening hip both to rest his weary legs and for the added warmth seeping into my bones.

I'd make a treat of this day with Sarah, I decided, and set aside my worries about Louisa and the rest as I waited for my husband's return. Christian had left spirited, pleased that soon he'd show our leader all we'd accomplished. I wanted their return to be an eventful day, and I calculated that if all went well, they should arrive this afternoon.

Sarah and I spoke of my baby coming, and she smiled wistfully when I teased her that she'd have one before long too.

"I lost a child this spring," she said, her voice as quiet as a pine needle falling to the forest floor. She'd never told me of her loss, nor had

I noticed, always consumed with my own life. My face flushed with regret. "We'll wait now, my husband says, until I'm stronger." *Stronger?* She was one of the strongest women I knew. She shrugged, then added, "All things happen for a reason, don't you know? We don't always see it in our time."

She didn't equate suffering with evil, or pain with sin. The wisdom from someone so young humbled, left me unsure how to comfort her.

"There'll be a midwife for you next time," I said. "Or you must tell me. I think I could midwife. My mother did." Andy played with the Woodard dog that rolled a ball with his nose, back and forth between them.

"Will your mother be here for you?" she said.

I sighed, picked up needlework, and began to stitch on her sampler. Apparently, she didn't have a chatelaine to hold her needles, as she kept her needle stitched onto the cloth. I missed using needle and thread for pretty things, and not just to mend a shirt or draw bear grass through cedar to make a basket, but who had time for such? "My parents already said they wouldn't come. But my brother's with the colonists. So that's almost as good, though not for midwifery."

She smiled. "Things will all change now, Emma." Her doelike eyes dropped to her hands clasped in her lap. "You'll have your German friends to speak with soon, women and children to fill your days. You won't come this way so much."

Would we be pulled into a ball of colony yarn wrapped tightly around one another, never letting our threads roll out toward our neighbors? "I will," I promised. "Once we finish the houses, it will be like a real village. You'll have more neighbors, not fewer; more people coming for the mail boats. We'll travel in for supplies and to ship things out. We'll have big picnics and our band will play again." I was surprised by the joys I could name from my time in Bethel and equally pleased that I hoped they'd be repeated here.

Then in a moment, I wondered if they would. No clearing stood wide enough to make a town here, such as we had in Bethel with room for house-lined streets. Worse, Wilhelm might insist we not associate with our neighbors except in commerce for fear they'd corrupt us the way one bad potato can spoil the lot.

Ach, no. I couldn't let myself worry over such thoughts. With all the people here at last, the building would go more quickly, and each family could work on its own house. We'd be constructing ours, and now I liked the idea of its separation from the others. I could visit Sarah as I wished without colony eyes watching. I wondered why I'd fussed at Christian about the distance. Except for the river passage required at certain times of the year, and the river crossing when we wanted to travel north, we'd be out from under the scrutinizing eyes of our leader, Christian's parents, everyone. It would take more effort to visit friends like Sarah. But if Mary and Sebastian took a claim close to ours rather than on the Giesy site, where the blockade house sat, I'd have friends close. We'd have our own lives and yet have the advantage of giving to and sharing with the colony. It would be better than when we were in Bethel, each looking over the shoulders of another, each feeling guilty when our eyes might move from the pull of our leader to something of our own interest.

"Will the new families be disappointed that they must build their own homes?" Sarah asked.

"Only some," I said. I looked away, poked the needle into the cloth, and set it down. "They'll see that even our home is left for last and that we put the needs of the elders first. They'll understand." I said the last as a hope as much as a promise.

Toward the end of that afternoon, we spied Christian's boat. Tears of hope welled up inside me, though a drizzle welcomed their arrival. I stood on my tiptoes at the wharf, Andy's hand gripped in mine, looking for Christian and my brother. I found my husband's hat bobbing above the others, but it was our leader who stepped off first, his brow furrowed.

His scowl reminded me of Andy when he did not get his way.

———

"Jonathan?" I asked Christian when I caught up with him. I peered behind him.

"Wilhelm sent him back to Portland with most of the wagons," Christian said. "Wilhelm said we needed the money we'd get for them there, and we have little need of so many wagons here." His voice sounded cheerful within the earshot of others; but a caution formed in the lines of his eyes, a pained look that only an attentive wife might notice.

Then Louisa walked down the gangplank, her hands carrying an infant, holding on to a toddler. Next came Aurora. *Aurora.* The child had grown. Kindly, she tended to a younger brother. Louisa nodded to me, then stood to the side while they harnessed the mules and pulled off the hearse carrying their Willie.

The casket was massive. I marveled again that something so large and cumbersome could have come all the way from Missouri. The challenges must have been immense.

"He can rest now," I told Louisa, walking up beside her and patting her arm. She held her brown cape tight around her. "And you, too."

She nodded her head. "It's been a long journey." She looked around. I hoped Woodard's Landing appeared inviting with its tidiness behind the picket fence Sam built. How organized and civilized it all looked to me with the small warehouse, store, and post office all under one roof. Prosperous, I decided. Large sunflowers still bloomed beside the Woodard house, though it was nearly Thanksgiving. Surely Louisa and Wilhelm would see the promise here; surely being thankful for all we'd done would come as easily as the autumn rains. "My husband is tired and weary," Louisa said then. "I must help him find rest."

"Where are our lodgings, Chris?" our leader asked.

I saw in Keil's eyes that engaging intensity that brought people to him. But I also saw the tiredness mentioned by his wife. Something else, too: sadness perhaps, which sloped onto his shoulders and showed in the downturned lines around his mouth. He looked older than when we'd left him, while Christian appeared carved by the elements and stood leaner and more muscular than when we'd left Missouri.

"We'll take advantage of the Woodards' hospitality and spend the night here at their request," Christian said. "In the morning, we'll make our way to the claims I've purchased."

"I'd prefer to go to our own homes now," our leader said.

"A fresh start will be better in the morning," Christian insisted, and to my surprise, after a hesitation, our leader agreed.

"And the others…?" I said.

"In their tents this night," Christian said. "That's how they've slept along the trail. They understand the vigor of building a new community."

I watched as the men moved to set their tents in the potato fields. The women huddled in small groups, some waiting out of the rain on the Woodards' porch, then moving to shelter under their canvases. I counted as I could. It looked like seventy, and with the Klein group, more than one hundred people were here already. But more than twice that number were yet to come.

The women didn't raise their eyes to mine, busying themselves with the solidness of land after their days on the boats. They were tired, I decided. It would be better when we were together tomorrow at the stockade and they met up again with Peter Klein's group, who would tell them of how hard we'd worked and how the land demanded more than we'd imagined. The scouts would all be here again save two, claiming as we had before that this was our promised land. We would have a gathering in worship led by…Christian, perhaps, or our leader. All would be well.

It had to be well.

—————

"Let's walk, then," our leader said to my husband in the morning. "Show me this place you all chose." His words chopped like an axe to a tree trunk. He'd grown stronger with rest under the Woodards' feather tick. Voices echoed in the relentless rain, which I prayed would stop so they could see the grandeur of the trees instead of the misty fog veiling their tops. My teeth chattered, from the cold, I assumed. Our leader acted like a man who had to be convinced instead of a man grateful for what God had provided. I wanted him to see the possibilities here as my husband saw them; not the way I'd first seen it and only later been wooed over to my husband's view.

Our leader impatiently grabbed at his hat while ordering Louisa to bring him a hard biscuit and jerky, as though she was a servant instead of a wife. Christian would have to win him over quickly. Something had changed from the time Michael Schaefer Sr. reported on our leader's optimism over the journey to what I saw now.

Louisa pulled her cape up over her head and rushed out to their wagon to bring back a cold breakfast for her husband. I opened my tied bag and gave Christian jerked meat, a piece of dried fruit, and a biscuit. "I planted and ground the wheat for this myself," I told the new arrivals.

Louisa frowned, and I wondered if she thought me prideful.

"We'll take the mules, Wilhelm," Christian said. "The road is too muddy this time of year to try to walk it."

"Ach," our leader said, striking the air with his hand, but he followed Christian out into the rain to saddle the mules.

I made it my duty to raise my own spirits as well as those of the others while we waited at Woodards'. I told them stories of our time here, making the tales light, about the goat's antics or the delight of watching bobcat kits racing in the spring sun or how moss made the perfect bed matting and it was free for the plucking. The women warmed up more, and I told them that the earthen floors of the houses were nearly as hard as the tile back in Bethel, that in summer, berries literally dropped their fruit at our doors. We'd found a wild honey tree and so had sweetness. I assured them of this land's sweetness.

We were joined by several of the Klein group then, too impatient to wait for us, and so the gathering increased with German words chattering through the forest like chickadees. Soon both men and women were together in the warehouse Sam opened for us so we'd have a drier, though no less crowded, place to wait.

I listened more now and learned of events along the trail, and that's when Karl Ruge told of Keil's strange arrest and trial. The Klein group hadn't heard of it either, and as Karl spoke, I wondered if the arrest and brief trial of our leader in The Dalles had caused the change in his attitude from one of happy assurance to what I saw as discouraged doubt.

"They accused him of disloyalty to the American government in a time of war with the Indians," Karl told us. "He was arrested for treason."

"For treason?" Peter said.

Karl nodded. *"Ja,* but it was all a mistake. Some Americans reported that Wilhelm said such things when it was another, one of the Indians who befriended us, who said Americans were bad."

"They arrested him for disagreeing with the government?" I said.

Karl blinked as he turned to me, surprised I guess that a woman raised her voice in this mixed group.

He hesitated only a moment. "*Ja*, by golly. Wilhelm sent the rest of the group ahead while he and I tried to get to the bottom. We did, though they paid no heed to what either of us reported about our loyalty. Instead, another American came to our rescue, testifying that he'd heard the exact same words spoken by this same Indian. The court took the word of that American over anything Wilhelm or I could say."

"I'll bet Wilhelm hated that," I said, then clasped my hand over my mouth. Wilhelm Keil demanded recognition, acclamation almost; he hadn't had it in this territory so far. But I didn't need to announce it. I looked for Louisa. Her sunken cheeks burned red.

"It…grieved him," Karl said, his eyes resting with kindness on Louisa.

Late in the day, one of the colonists who'd remained at the stockade came through the forest and said we were to bring the hearse and come to the stockade. I saw this as a hopeful sign that our leader had seen our land and approved and now we could move toward home. *Home.*

"No. I don't think my husband would want the hearse hauled by any but our two mules," Louisa said. "And they are being ridden by our…by Wilhelm and Chris." She crossed her arms over her narrow chest. "I'll wait here with the hearse until he brings the mules back." She wrapped her cape around herself, an immovable log.

"We must take people to the stockade area," Peter said. "We will wear out our welcome at the Woodards'. Wilhelm wants this done."

Louisa hesitated, bit her lower lip, but then the lessons ingrained to women, that we must follow our men, overtook her and she nodded. Peter and the other men harnessed two oxen to haul the hearse the last mile or so to the Giesy claim and stockade. The rest of us would form the funeral march that followed.

I helped pull up tents and talked with several of the women, assuring them that there were roofs, at least a few, so we could get in out of the rain once we arrived at the Giesy site.

And we did so, many of us huddling into the log house I'd spent the last winter in, more pitching tents outside.

I'd claimed this hut as my own last winter and noticed anew the hides that I'd helped tan, the sleeping mats that bore our blankets, the moss that I'd cleaned the slugs from. It now belonged to…all of us. My stomach knotted. I wondered if Christian and I would be allowed to take the elk hide gift when we moved, or would that now remain as a part of the house rather than a part of our lives?

Louisa sat down on my blanket, pushed it back behind her so she could lean against it. She patted the soft bedding, looked around. She nodded approval. Her eyes met mine. Once again all that we had would have to be shared with everyone else.

In that moment I knew that the colony had truly arrived.

———

"He's taken Wilhelm to your claim," Adam Schuele told me. "He wanted him to see the widest prairie and where the gristmill could be placed. All our ideas Chris wants to share with him."

"What has our leader said?" I whispered. We stood in a large tree-fall that some of the men had scraped out for a dry place to sleep. "Does he give an indication of his approval from this morning's trip?"

Adam looked away, picked at some pitch stuck on his hand. "He spent a good amount of time on the hill behind the stockade overlooking the valley." Adam shook his head. "I don't know. We were all so sure…"

"Because it is a good place," I said, certain. "I struggled at first, remember? I didn't think this land could support us all. It took so much work just to build, but Christian assured me. You assured me. That all the scouts agreed, that's the true sign that we have chosen well, that it was chosen for us. Surely our leader will not dispute that?"

Adam said nothing, walked over to take the blinders from the horses he said were given as gifts to only Keil's sons. They were chestnuts with white spots spattered across their sides. Adam tied the horses at young trees far enough apart that they didn't entangle each other. The goat ran around trying to decide if all the additional dogs were pets or peril.

Work would set my mind at rest, quell my imaginings of what occurred between Christian and our leader. I helped milk the few cows that Peter's group had driven down the trail. I showed the new women the latrine area, commented on the berries we could eat to supplement our diet. "You can squat and eat," I said, grateful for their chuckles. I urged them not to hunch their shoulders against the rain, as it did no good and only caused later aches. "We can weave capes," I said. "Right from this land. What we know of wefts and warps serves us here." I showed them where I kept food cool in the river, the large drums that we collected rainwater in for drinking and washing. They peered at the meager grain storage. "I know there isn't much, but we can buy flour through the winter from the ships coming in." Potatoes were plentiful. We'd have a little milk now with the few cows here, though not enough for all these people. We could perhaps buy a few more of Sarah's eggs, maybe even some of her chickens. "We have plenty of ammunition, so we can have game to eat. We won't go hungry, that's certain," I told them.

Christian had planned well, considering he never knew how many people would actually come here or the circumstances when they did.

"It'll be a bit squeezed in together, and we'll need the tents still," I told the women. And maybe a few more of these rotted logs carved out for people to stay in. "It doesn't snow much here at all, and by February, the sun comes out more often and flowers begin to bloom. By March, this is an Eden, it truly is. Even I plowed and seeded the grain field, the soil is so easily broken."

"Will we rotate being able to sleep under the roof?" one of the women asked.

"The doctor will need *this* roofed house," Louisa told her. It was the first time she'd engaged in the conversations, and I noted that she referred to Wilhelm as the doctor. "Or had you planned that for yourselves, Emma?"

My faced burned. "We'll live in a tent through this winter as we did most of the last," I said. "All the scouts lived in this house; it wasn't 'ours.' We built it for the colony."

"*Ja*, well, you call it the Giesy place, so I assume," Louisa said.

"Christian claimed the land in his parents' names, as the law requires, but of course it is for the colony."

"The land in Bethel is in my husband's name."

"But here, the free land needs specific people named," I said. I was even more grateful that Christian had made it clear where our claim would be...far down the road, seven miles down the road, and we'd spent no time at all on building it at the expense of building for others. He'd sacrificed a dry home for us to make homes for others. Couldn't they see his generosity?

"I note there is no Keil place," Louisa said. "Or does my husband go there with your husband, and you have saved the best for last?"

She grieved; I needed to remember that, to chalk away the blemish of her words.

"This stockade, this roofed house will house you as it does all of us. It isn't Elim yet, I know. But once we have a mill, we'll have all the timber we could need to build grand houses just as we had in Bethel, just not with brick." Even Christian's parents would not assume they alone would have a roof over their heads. "There are some other structures on adjoining claims, a few, with canvas roofs. With so many of us, now we will be able to finish those."

It flashed through my mind that with so many people here we'd also be spending more time hunting, more time handling food than we had before. I hoped that Christian had put in a large-enough order for wheat to come into Woodards' warehouse, and I wondered if some of the party still to arrive might come up the Cowlitz and take the trail as Peter Klein had and bring sheep. Mutton would taste good, and we could use the wool to spin to replace our threadbare clothes. That reminded me that I hadn't noticed that our leader's group included any trunks marked with our name on them. So it would be Christian's parents I'd have to count on. They carried the grist stones and were coming by ship. Surely they would have our trunks and bring our personal effects.

When Christian and Wilhelm returned, I could tell that something was very wrong. Our leader walked with his shoulders bent, striding well in front of Christian, who slowly unsaddled the mules. Wilhelm walked purposefully. He stopped at the hearse standing beside the log house and gazed around, finally pointing at Louisa that she should follow him, and they disappeared behind the hearse.

"What does he think?" I asked Christian. Andy patted the mule's front leg. "Did he approve of God's choice?"

"Take the boy. He could get hurt." I reached for Andy, lifted him. "Well?"

"He does not," Christian answered me then. "But he says he has no choice but to bury his son here." He wouldn't look at me, just started brushing the mule.

"But that's good. He'll want a home close to where his son is buried."

Christian turned to me, his eyes like my old dog's when I'd refused to give him a bone. "He's telling people to head back south, into Oregon Territory. He's sending Michael to stop the rest from coming here. He wants them to find jobs in Portland through the winter. He says the women can clean and cook, and maybe there is work for the men there. He's sure there is nothing here."

"Jonathan won't even come north, then?" I asked.

"Don't cry over your brother," Christian snapped.

"I…I hadn't meant to. I'm just disappointed."

"*Ja,*" he said, leading the mule away from me. "You and *Herr* Keil have that in common."

27

Drowning in Bounty

In the midst of people deciding who would leave first and who would remain, leaving in the spring instead of this winter, Sam Woodard told us, "The army says we should all move into an area that can be defended well. Sarah and I will come here if that's agreeable. The stockade, it's more isolated. A few others in the valley are being urged to come this way too."

"More outsiders in this small space?" Louisa said. Wilhelm frowned at her. Probably more for having expressed an opinion than for what she said. She stepped back and clasped her hands before her now-bowed head.

"How good we have a place of safety you can come to," I noted. "And that we can share it with others, as good Christians, as we did in Bethel."

"*Ja,* come here," Wilhelm said, speaking to Sam as though Christian weren't even present, as though I hadn't even spoken.

"What we have is always available to you, Sam," Christian said. "Did the army say what the new threat was, or how long it might be, all of us here together?"

Sam shook his head. "Only that the whole region is a prime target. The governor's dislike of all Indians has fired even the friendlier ones. The Shoalwaters feel left out of the negotiations, so they're refusing to go to another tribe's designated reserve. Governor Stevens wants no negotiating with anyone. So the Indians have nothing to lose by attacking whenever they wish."

One of the men who'd traveled with Wilhelm said, "Our leader charms the Indians. We had no trouble coming across, did we, Wilhelm?"

"No," Wilhelm said. "No trouble. But here is different. Ve have trouble here."

So we would all be housed inside the stockade walls with our tents and a few under roof. Christian assigned men to rotate watch at the guardhouse; Wilhelm voiced his opinion about who would follow whom. I noticed that the men took orders given by either Christian or *Herr* Keil.

Inside the house that evening, several of us scrunched together at one end, the smells of wet wool and smoke filling our heads. Adam and Michael Sr. and other scouts who'd been a part of this journey from the beginning stayed close together. I wished that the Knights were here, but Adam had signed up for the military when they'd reached The Dalles with Keil's group and was said to be fighting the Cayuse. How strange that was to me with Wilhelm speaking pacifism, at least before we left Bethel. No one knew where Joe Knight was. I longed to know what had happened and why after all this distance and all we'd done together that the Knights had decided to separate.

I poured hot tea into mugs while Hans spoke with several men about heading out in the morning as a group to bring in meat. John Genger had acted as a hunter on the trip out, and he oiled his gun as Hans spoke.

"Didn't you hear Woodard say we're not to go into the woods?" Wilhelm said. "Too dangerous."

"I think he meant alone and to fell trees," Hans said.

John Genger stopped, his oil rag midair. "We have to eat, Wilhelm."

"I saw a few deer when we brought the hearse here yesterday," Hans told him. "Off by that ravine, where we took out the big root ball, remember?" Michael Sr. nodded.

"We must preserve the ammunition now so ve can defend ourselves," Wilhelm said. "How foolish it would be to use it all up gathering food. Ve must think ahead. We are planners, we Germans."

"The people need food, Wilhelm," Christian said, his hand resting on our leader's forearm. "And we're still quite a distance from the trouble farther east. It's good to be here together and be cautious, but we have hungry children."

"Did I not see fish jumping in that river?" Wilhelm countered. "If this is such a promised land as you have dubbed it, Chris, then let us fish. Let us club them as you say the Indians do."

"To supplement the meat, yes, but to—"

"There will be no using the ammunition except for defense." Wilhelm's voice boomed, silencing even the children whimpering as they tried to fall asleep. Rain pattered on the peeled logs, and the pitch in the cook fire flames hissed like huddled witches.

"Wilhelm, my friend and leader," Christian said, his voice like the stroke of a gentle hand on a skittish cat. "In this clearing there are different ways of doing things. It is not a challenge to you that I tell you that having meat makes sense. We will be frugal with the ammunition. Hans knows this."

Wilhelm's eyes grew large, the white around them reminding me of a buffalo's eyes. Christian dared challenge him in front of all of us, and challenge he must, or we could all die of starvation.

"I have paid the bills," Wilhelm began. "The one thousand dollars you charged for this and that; it has cost us almost eight hundred dollars just to bring these few people from Portland to this godforsaken place. To pay off the claims you've bought will deplete us even more. I need to make these decisions now, Chris. No ammunition for hunting.

I'll not risk the loss of ammunition when we may need it to defend ourselves against those Indians. You have brought us to a hellish place, Chris. Now I must get us out."

———

"Send a letter to Bethel," Keil directed Karl Ruge. It was the third day behind the stockade. At least fifty people remained; the others had risked the river and the bay to return to Portland as Keil directed. The rain fell steadily. Andy hadn't seen the seagull for several days, but he'd stopped asking when I'd snapped at him. I tried to imagine myself alone, in my own home, but Keil's voice took me from my escapist thoughts. "Tell them we will bury Willie here, on the hill just beyond the stockade walls. Then we will all go to Portland and spend the winter in better conditions." I watched the pain in my husband's eyes, moved to stand beside him.

"We will do what Judge John Walker Grimm suggests," he dictated to Karl. He'd apparently met this man in Portland while the judge shipped apples to California. Grimm sold fifty-six apple trees to a man named Adair while Keil watched. Pippins and Winesaps and Northern Spy apples (such detail our leader recalled and had Karl Ruge put into the Bethelites' letter), and the judge told the colonists where the trees were grown, somewhere in an area on the Pudding River in Oregon Territory. Our leader saw hope in such trees for the colony; he didn't see hope in this clearing.

If such a man can ship apples south, why can't we ship our grain south and other products we grow, just as we did in Bethel? I hoped Christian would say such things, but he didn't. He stayed silent as a saw leaned against the wall.

Then Keil began what to me was a tirade against this landscape. He

had Karl write terrible things about this valley, about how long it took
them to ride a mule seven miles, of how he had to cross the Willapa six
or seven times to get from one claim to another, and that the road to
our claim had been the most dangerous trail he'd taken since he'd left
Bethel. "The soil may be rich, but it is covered with three to four feet
of decaying tree trunks," he dictated. "The land grows anything, but
there is no one here to buy it except ourselves. There is no prospect of
more people coming here, as the rain sends everyone away, everyone
with any sense; and everything we need is too far away and too expensive to get. A barrel of flour in Oregon costs three dollars and fifty cents,
while here it costs fifteen to twenty dollars, and it will be impossible
much of the year to even get it here by boat. There is no good farm land
and can never be." He looked up at me. "Little fields cleared beside the
river. A pittance. There is no fodder for cattle or sheep; the land is covered with trees or what is left of them. If we built a distillery, only a few
oystermen would consume our product. In one day I can see the problem of this place, and yet the scouts, they claim this as God's land. They
were not listening to the voice of our Lord, our Savior." He took in a
deep breath. "They listened to one another."

My husband sank into himself. I couldn't bear to look at him.

I stared instead across the room at Louisa. *Does Louisa look proud?*
No, it was another emotion I saw there in the eyes that gazed back at
mine. Pity, perhaps, that emotion that covers fear.

Keil finished with the admonition to any Bethelites still in Missouri to remain there. "You are a poor, unbelieving people without me,"
he dictated so each of us could hear. "Like Moses, I've led my people
through the desert, and no one has sacrificed his firstborn to the Lord
except me, myself." *He left out Louisa's sacrifice.* "But God has called us
to be at peace." His words were full of consuming fire, not a word of
peace except the word itself.

He finished by having Karl tell them that when they wrote, they must send their letters to the Portland post office, Oregon Territory, and a copy to Bruceport post office, as he wasn't sure when the weather would let them bury Willie or when the army would release us from this stockade so we could all leave this hellish Willapa Valley. As a last act of control, he ordered cattle, mules, and oxen to be taken to Portland to be held there or sold. Once Willie was buried, those favorite mules of Wilhelm's would be taken south as well.

Christian got up and left. I wanted him to fight, to send another letter, to see what he had seen before, in the beginning. I followed him out as Mary reached to distract Andy. Outside, I couldn't see him, as he'd walked into the foggy mist. At the brush-covered lean-to where the cows lay, I found the goat tethered near the outside. Even she had been asked to share her space. I put my arms around her neck and felt hot tears pour out onto her musty hair. We'd waited for this day, this time, with such anticipation. All our efforts for nearly two years had been for the benefit of the colony, and it had abandoned us. *Poor Christian.* I didn't know how I could comfort him. I mumbled a prayer for him, not sure if we'd moved away from God or if God had stepped away from us.

How could we not have seen what Wilhelm saw in just a few days here? Maybe because he was a visionary, had always seen more than others. But we'd followed his directions and listened, believing God spoke to us as well. Had our souls slept while our hearts worked long hours?

I had once seen this place as Keil did. I'd seen the troubles he wrote of but told myself, for Christian's sake, that they could be overcome. I hated that I hadn't stood my ground with Christian and the other scouts and insisted that we leave, that we find a landscape more hospitable to clearing, to building, to life.

But more, I hated having anything in common with *Herr* Keil.

———

At dusk on the afternoon of November 26, 1855, we sang the funeral dirge *Herr* Keil composed for his son's burial. We followed Willie's hearse to the gravesite on the hill, the bells of the *Schellenbaum* tinkling in the rain, the majority of us carrying small candles that flickered as we walked. It took the mules and men to push the heavy casket up the hill and roll it over tangled vines and small fallen logs. How they had ever brought this boy's body all that distance, all that way, was a feat few would ever attempt, let alone achieve. Couldn't Keil see that his very act of doing the impossible was but a forerunner for what we could do here in this bountiful place?

With ropes, the men lowered the casket into the ground as we sang our German dirge. Then Keil spoke, our faces shadowed by the candle-light. He reminded us that light would overcome darkness; Christ's light would shine above all. His words heartened me, spoken in German. Everyone spoke in German now. What was American, even English, was being set aside.

But as we filed back down the hill toward the stockade, I knew we'd buried more than this boy. We buried promises, efforts, and our future.

———

The Woodards joined those of us at the stockade, and then began the strangest time in Willapa that I could remember. The first nights were chaotic and close. Children cried, and the smells of their dirtied napkins permeated the air. Thank goodness for abundant moss that all the women soon used. Old men sweating and women perspiring in the damp heat added to the mixture of scents strong enough to make a pregnant woman ill. Rain dribbled in through slits in the canvas roof when we bedded down that first night with townspeople and us Germans together, with growls in our stomachs. A few people had come inland from Bruceport on the Shoalwater Bay, having been told of our isolated encampment.

I pushed back hot tears while my husband snored into my neck, his arm across my chest. I longed for escape in his whispered words of love; I longed to feel hopeful once more. As I lay, eyes resisting sleep, I recalled Christian's return from his walk in the mist. Since then, he'd turned inside himself, his eyes empty as the grain bucket.

By the second night, it was decided the men would risk time in the woods in order to build another house so those staying in tents outside would have better shelter.

I wondered how Sarah felt with this German spoken all around. She'd so often opened her home to us; we had so little to offer back.

Bickering broke out. Hunger takes away one's patience. People moved into tents to have time alone. Smoke from the cooking fires—with little to cook—permeated the entire area.

The Woodards remained but a week, deciding to take their chances back at the wharf. "We can't help you," Sarah told me as I begged her to stay. "We add to your trials. So many of you to feed, and the rule you have about saving ammunition will only keep you hungry while there is game available." She shook her head. "Maybe it isn't so bad with the Indians. Maybe the military exaggerates."

"I'll miss your company," I told her.

She patted my hand. "My husband says we'll send peas to you and a bag of potatoes from the warehouse. We'll pray the ships will come before long and bring the flour you ordered."

After a day of trying to finish another house, Christian said, "Tomorrow, you must club fish." His voice was low, but everything was easily overheard. There was no escaping unless we went outside and stood beneath a cedar tree. Andy cried and I rocked him as we sat our backs against the logs. *Herr* Keil played scales on his harmonica, up and down, like a bad whistler who refuses to stop.

"Just send Hans and John out into the woods," I whispered. "There is plenty of meat. Keil doesn't have to know. Why—"

"*Nein.* We are not to use the ammunition. Wilhelm forbids it."

"Overrule him," I said.

"We'll club fish. All of us, though the more we men can work in the woods, the better. So you must set the tone and get the women to help."

My face grew hot. It was insane, this thought of clubbing fish when we could feed ourselves well with game. What was my husband thinking? What was *Herr* Keil thinking?

I shook my head, too outraged to even argue with words.

In the morning, Christian reached for my hand. "I'll show you how to do it," he said. "Let Andy sleep."

We eased our way past sleeping bodies. Louisa, awake, followed our movements as we made our way out through the door.

The rain had stopped, though a heavy mist sifted around the stockade. I could make out the men in the gun turret area and felt a flash of outrage that they would stand there with ammunition while we would club fish for our food.

"Like this, watch now, Emma," Christian said. He'd picked up an oar for each of us, then he let himself slide down the side of the bank, taking dirt with him. His feet sank into the mud, and the edge of the river filled in around him up to his calves. "Come." He held out his hand to me.

The water mesmerized, swiftly flowing along, carrying branches and leaves. But within its roiling it carried food for the taking. I could see the fish roll, giving up flashes of silver and blood red. I hiked my skirt up between my legs and hooked it into my apron belt, then used my oar to balance myself as I slid down the bank and sank, the wet squishiness against my moccasins, cold on my feet, my ankles. I shivered.

Christian moved a few feet away from me so as not to hit me by accident when he struck at the fish. "See," he pointed. And then with a loud slap and whack, he hit a dog-head salmon swimming upstream. He slammed it into the bank. "One chub," he shouted, then unstuck himself enough to strike the fish before it flailed and tossed itself back into the water. He grabbed it by the gills, and from the effort it took to hold it up, it must have weighed what a wagon hub weighed, several pounds. "Now you."

What did this man think? It took all my effort to maintain my balance, standing, with the pressure of the water against my legs, let alone strike at a fish. My belly threatened to get into the way of my oar swing. Bile rose against my wishes. I spit, took a deep breath, and then whacked but only hit the water, splashing cold onto my chest and face. I struck again and again. What would my baby think, getting baptized early with splashes from the Willapa River?

"Try to reach underneath one," Christian said. "Use the wide end of the oar to lift and then throw the chub out."

I glared at him. "Why don't you just shoot it?" I said. "Why don't you shoot a deer or an elk? Butcher one of the oxen. This is—why are you letting him do this to you, to us?"

"Lift it out. Hit it. Like this," he said, sliding back down into the water. "Can't you do anything I tell you?" He struck at the fish, the river, sliced the oar into the water's rush, and the silvery flesh rose from the river and soared into the air, where he struck it again and again, then tossed it up high on the bank. He returned like a madman, I thought, pushing and clubbing. I pulled away, clawed my way back up to the top of the bank. My heart pounded as I watched this man I didn't know. The curls of his hair were matted with the rain, and bits of mud speckled his face like freckles. He walloped and whacked until he had fifteen of the fish, their tails still swishing and jerking on the bank. He slid back down into the stream, a grunt coming from him with each blow. Sweat poured off him.

"Enough," I shouted. "It's enough, Christian."

He struck the water, even though there were no fish being lifted out. How he must ache. Despite the current and the depth, I slid back down and pushed my way over to him, touched his shoulder. He shivered.

This was what love was then: meeting another's need, not our own.

"Christian," I said. He jerked and stared at me, his eyes vacant and filled with such sadness I thought if I stared longer I'd sink away. "Christian," I whispered to him and opened my arms. He leaned into me then, and we stood in the rush of the water while I felt more than heard my husband's deep sobs.

———

"They'll make good eating," I told the women. "See how we clean them." I stabbed the head with a knife, asked Mary to hold it tight to the wood slab. Then with another knife I filleted them, cutting lengthwise from the head to the tail, then turning them over and slicing another long side, piling the bones with tiny bits of flesh left on them beneath the rough table we used. "We can make fish soup from the heads and bury the bones in the garden. My friend Sarah said not to let the dogs eat the raw flesh. It will kill them. The fish tails and bones will make everything grow better come spring."

"We'll not be here to see that," Louisa said, her arms crossed over her chest.

I ignored her comment, kept helping the women. Mary gouged

out the side of a chub, nearly cutting it in two. "It takes practice," I told her, wiping the slimy film from the fish off my hands in the dirt.

There were no fish left to smoke after that first meal. I tried to make light of it, that wasn't it grand we had bounty from the water for our bellies and bounty from the forest to cover our heads. The thought of going out again in the morning sent chills down my back, but if we women killed the fish, the men would be free to build. And if they built, perhaps Wilhelm would change his mind and want to remain.

I wanted so much for people to see the good in this place, to not question what God had provided for us. How could this not be the chosen place when each of the scouts had concurred?

But one had defected. Now the whole colony planned to leave. I wondered if we would.

"We'll go out tomorrow, and we can bring back enough for two or three meals," I told the women.

"Should you be doing that?" Mary asked. "Might you hurt the baby?"

I shook my head. "Christian showed me how. I'm healthy, though a little weak. But the fish will be good for us. It has fat, and if we can find a dry place to smoke, we can pound some into pemmican like we do dried venison or beef. It'll be good for the men to have when they work so hard."

"It's terribly oily," one of the women noted as she wiped her hands on her apron. "It almost looks like wax. And they stink." She wrinkled her nose.

"Maybe we can burn the oil," I said. I wondered why I hadn't thought of that before. We could put the oil into tin cups and burn it for light. Another bounty.

That's what I told Christian that night when he returned with thirteen other men who had been working to build another house.

"Some bounty," he said.

"But it is, just as you said it was." Even though we'd moved into a tent outside so one of the other families could sleep within walls, we spoke in low whispers. *No need for everyone to hear our business.*

Christian lay silent, but I knew he didn't sleep. "Our leader is right, *Liebchen.* How could I not have seen that what is here is not enough to sustain us all? I should have sent word when I realized how long it took to build one house. Or we should have looked elsewhere, maybe closer to your Steilacoom. I should have diverted them in The Dalles, given them a better choice. A good leader would have. That's what Wilhelm is doing now, giving people a better choice."

"To die of starvation because he's afraid of Indians?" I said.

"The fish will be enough. And the ships will come in, and Sam Woodard will send word that flour is here. We'll count on that. Until spring."

I thought of taking a rifle and trying to bring a deer down myself. I thought of what that act would do to my husband. I decided against it.

———

After three weeks, the men had completed one more house. We did not celebrate, as I thought we should have, marking a good thing, a met goal. We didn't even pray over the safety of the men as they'd worked in the woods and built another house within the stockade. Even the band instruments stayed silent. The children complained about the fish and potatoes, fish and potatoes, all we had to eat. The close quarters railed against our good natures, and people snapped at one another. To find privacy, we might leave one of the two houses within the stockade, but just outside were people in tents to maneuver around; others camped beneath cedar trees outside the stockade but close enough to seek cover if needed. The path to the latrines grew muddy and slick, and even the constant rain did not cleanse the stench.

Then the fish stopped swimming upriver. We were left with potatoes and a few of the Woodards' peas and the small amounts of milk that the cows and goat gave up. We divided all of it among the children.

"Perhaps when the flour arrives," Louisa said when I commented out loud inside one of the houses that it would be nice to celebrate the addition of the house, since we hadn't celebrated much at Christmas. We hadn't broken bread together in any special way; in fact, we had no bread to break.

"The band played in Bethel whenever we completed a new home," I said. "Will we not keep the same customs in our new colony?"

"This will never be our colony," Wilhelm said, in a rare act of speaking directly to a subject I'd raised. His voice silenced even the children. He sighed then. "Please will you write another letter, Karl?"

Dictating letters seemed to be all Wilhelm did now that Willie was buried and several had gone south with the cattle. Now the weather appeared too inclement for Wilhelm to head south to Portland himself.

Karl Ruge brought out paper and lead. He was such a kindly man with his graying beard and no mustache, his cheeks reddened from the wind and rain as he helped with the building. He was of an elder's age and could have simply stayed back with Wilhelm and the women and children, teaching, one might have said. But he chose to participate in my husband's efforts to ease the discomforts of this place. He rolled the lead across his knuckles while he awaited Wilhelm's dictation. He winked at Andy, who watched Karl's hands with careful eyes.

In this latest letter sent to the Bethelites, Keil reported on how long it took us to build the house and then announced that next week he would leave for Portland to see how the rest of the colony fared. "Take your time in coming out," he said. "Until we find the place the Lord has called us to, I wouldn't leave my home in Bethel."

The Lord had called us here. How was it that one man could change that? What about the voice *we* heard? I started to speak, but Christian anticipated and squeezed my arm as he stood behind me. I turned to look at him, and he shook his head. *Silence,* he mouthed. *Silence.* My greatest challenge.

Would it be so sinful to ask for help, maybe from people at the coast town of Bruceport, I wondered. They might have flour we could buy now. Keil wouldn't let us, I supposed. He was the keel, the wedge in this ship.

I dreamed that night of water, of Wilhelm taking me on a small boat across the Shoalwater Bay to the Wallacut River, then upriver on the Columbia and into Portland. At least that had been his plan. I ate from the leg of a deer in my dream but didn't swallow it. My hunger continued. Then the ship capsized in the bay, and I couldn't reach Wilhelm; I was too frightened to throw him a rope, too frightened to help him, and so he had drowned.

I woke up with a start, my heart pounding. What kind of mind did I have, dreaming of the death of Keil? Christian patted my arm. "Water," I said. "I dreamed of swirling water."

I shivered and felt wet. My whole mat was wet. I looked up. No leaks. And then I knew: my water had broken. My second child pressed its way into this chaotic world.

28

It Is Finished

"Get Mary," I told Christian. "My baby comes."

"I'm already here," Louisa said. She'd slipped into the corner of the Giesy House that now belonged to everyone. "Let's not bother Mary or alarm her. In case something goes wrong."

"Something goes wrong?" I croaked. *Why bring in the ghost of suffering at such a time like this?* "I've been through this," I said, firm. "Maybe I don't even need a midwife. Christian will help me."

"*Ach,* it's no job for a man. He has things to do, don't you, Chris?" She shooed her arms at him as though he was the goat. "Don't be selfish and risk your baby," Louisa said, patting my arm. "We women must suffer the pangs of childbirth together. Leave now, Christian."

"I missed Andrew being born," he said.

"Men usually do," she said. "Well, then. If we need you, we'll send someone." She pushed him aside.

I wanted him to stay, to resist the push and pull of others, but he stepped away. Louisa hung a quilt for privacy, which I later appreciated when the waves rose and ebbed through my body, carrying me up and over the pain. I didn't cry out, though, at least not that I remembered. Muffled conversations of others in the house drifted to me as did the smell of the cooking, the crying of a child. I tasted sweat on my upper lip and welcomed the wet cloth Louisa placed on my forehead as I waited for the next cry of my child's journey into life.

Christian didn't go far. I could hear his voice as he spoke to others, commented on the leather hinges he'd made for doors. He waited within earshot. Had I told him that Louisa made me nervous? Knowing he waited just outside the door comforted. I'd tell him that when this was over.

This infant wouldn't come as swiftly as Andy had. The day waned as the baby pushed its way closer to arriving into the world. Then we heard shouts from the gun turrets announcing an alarm.

I struggled to sit up. Louisa helped steady my shoulders. "I'll see what it is. You wait here."

"Did you think I planned to take a walk?" I snapped.

I heard her say in English, "No. She is indisposed," but then she stumbled aside, and Sarah Woodard bent through the opening of the door. I sighed relief. Even if she brought news of Indian attacks it would be good to have her here.

"What news?" I said between pants.

"No attacks," she said. "But the first ship of the New Year arrived."

I leaned back against Louisa. "Good. There'll be bread, then, grain for us all."

With full stomachs and a greater variety of food, tempers would cool. Maybe playing music would be considered acceptable. Karl Ruge could return to reading nightly to us from his books while smoking his long clay pipe. Our hungry stomachs had elbowed our souls, and many of us couldn't listen for long. Music would soothe. Surely any hostile Indians wouldn't mind the sound of trumpets and horns. Maybe we'd begin thanking God again as a group for all He had done. My husband would be vindicated. Flour, as he'd ordered it, well in advance of the arrival of this many people, would mean nourishment and a sign that my husband was a good leader, someone who could anticipate and provide, with God's help. Always with God's help.

Sarah looked down, then wiped my sweaty forehead. Rain dripped from her cape, and steam rose up from the moist wool already warming within the close heat of the house. "Your family arrives," she said. "They say they are Giesys, and they bring grist stones."

"Christian's parents." We'd have more to feed, but we'd also have more support for Christian. They'd see the possibilities here. They'd want to remain where Christian and the scouts had done so much to prepare for their coming. And there'd be flour. Food. Our hunger filled at last.

"We'll have a big meal," I panted. "With bread and cakes maybe. And the band will play."

Sarah's eyes went to Louisa's. She leaned into Louisa and whispered something. Louisa shook her head, no. "What is it?" I asked. "Tell me what's wrong."

"No," Louisa said. "You don't need to know."

"Here we share good news and bad," I panted.

Sarah nodded. "The ship brought only one small bag of flour. Sam and I will ration what we can and share what we have with you."

"One bag of flour? Didn't they understand the order?"

"Maybe a mix-up, my husband tells me. It happens," Sarah said.

"Or maybe your husband did not order as much as needed, thinking you would have grain here to grind," Louisa said.

"He would have done what he thought was right," I defended. The pain began its rise. I gasped.

"Nothing good comes of this place," Louisa announced. "But we will help with this baby. Then you'll travel better to a new place, one my husband picks that will be good for all of us."

"One small bag," I cried, then gripped Sarah's hand as Catherina, my daughter, arrived without further fuss into the promised land of the Willapa Valley.

The first months of 1856 were marked by the cold, icy winds and incessant rains, but with small signs that we were still blessed, still under the shelter of our Father. I found myself clinging more often to the words of faith that Karl Ruge dispensed in nightly prayers for us all. Wilhelm remained distant, aloof; my husband acted faded and fatigued. I hoped that my leaning on faith wasn't temporary, that perhaps I had learned how to trust even in the midst of disaster. The Israelite tents pitched before they crossed into the Promised Land were reminders of where our shelter truly came from. I waited each day to hear Karl Ruge's gentle teaching, his encouraging words of "*Ja,* by golly, that's right!" that followed a positive comment or small success.

The goat kept my babies alive as Andy drank goat milk and ate the lumps of cheese we made, dripping the rich milk through Mary's petticoat, the cloth as close to muslin as we could find. The other colonists allowed our baby and other young children to drink the milk first, but when Mary's baby, Elizabeth, arrived in February, we rationed ourselves even more to ensure that Mary had enough to eat to make milk for her baby. When she offered to nurse Catherina, too, I whispered gratitude and remembered how An-Gie had found help for Andy. My daughter would have the blessing of a friend.

Wilhelm had yet to head south. He stayed and continued his insistence about Indian troubles, so we could not bring in game. I missed the cows and mules. We could have sent men and cattle into the prairies, where they would have had plenty of grass to consume, but Wilhelm didn't trust that the men watching them would be safe. While I rocked my infant to sleep, I imagined the rich prairies south, where one day Christian and I had hoped to build our home. I remembered walking that prairie, sitting in the quiet of the trees, listening to rain patter onto the needles that carpeted the ground. The silence would be broken only by the cry of a pileated woodpecker or a deer stepping on a fallen branch as it made its way past.

At night, I dreamed of food that I just couldn't swallow.

Potatoes baked in the coals soon lost their flavor. The same meal we'd had for weeks lacked both savor and salt. We caught very few fish now.

Barbara, my mother-in-law, busied herself with her grandchildren. She rocked them, and though she was skinny as a bedpost, she never mentioned how hungry she must have been. I hoped she noticed that I never complained about food, either, except in my sleep.

At least my mother-in-law had brought a trunk with our name on it, and at last I had a fresh change of clothes, a dress with a plain petticoat. Tenderly lifting items from the trunk served as a distraction from the ache in my stomach. I could grab a handful at the waistband of my petticoat, I'd lost so much weight. My old under slip with the ruffles had been stripped long ago into bandages for wounds and washed over and over to manage my monthly flow. My mother had made a baby's quilt and a small dress that might have been used for a christening, if we had such things. We would dedicate the baby to the Lord in time, maybe when we had a church or Wilhelm felt the occasion was right. Karl Ruge, who remained a Lutheran, spoke of christenings, and I thought the idea of it a lovely thing and wished we'd do it as a colony. When this time of want had passed, I'd talk to Christian about it, if he'd hear me. More and more he spent time staring, having little to say, carrying the weight of this starvation into a dark solitude.

Starvation. It was the first time I'd thought the word. Even thinking it made me feel disloyal to my husband.

I smelled each item I pulled from the trunk, imagining my mother's hands on each one, my father's eyes looking over them as she wrapped the child's gown in precious paper I'd use to write to them to tell them of Catherina. Inhaling deeply took away the dizziness I assumed came with the hunger. One last quilt made of red and black squares lay folded at the bottom of the chest. I lifted it out and something dropped on the ground beside my foot. My mother's pearl necklace.

Why had she sent it? Was she telling me that a luxury was acceptable, or that as one matured, one no longer needed such things?

"What's that?" Louisa asked. The woman was like the mist, appearing quiet and cold.

"Something my mother sent me." I folded it back into the quilt, liking the feel of the smooth round stones, perfectly strung. I'd look at it later.

"Your mother," Louisa said.

"*Ja?*" I prepared to defend.

"She found a way to be…noticed without taking away from anyone else."

A compliment? "We all need to be noticed," I said, stuffing the quilt into the corner of the trunk.

"*Ja,*" she said, looking at her husband who slept, his head bobbed forward onto his chest, his arm wrapped around Aurora, who slept seated beside him. "There you and me, we agree."

———

Through the drizzle of March, a letter arrived in Bruceport on the coast, and Sam Woodard brought it to us. One of Keil's nieces, Fredricka, had married Benjamin Brown, a man she'd met in The Dalles, in the Skamania country east of where we were. The couple had met again in Portland and married January 3, 1856, beginning their new year in the Washington Territory. They'd decided to live separate from the colony, an act I thought very brave for Fredricka. I'd tell her so whenever I got to see her again. Her father, Keil's brother, had remained in the area with them, but when someone commented on his following in his daughter's footsteps, leaving the fold, Wilhelm announced, "He looks for a place for our colony. He's still engaged in the Lord's work."

The Lord's work. The words sounded empty. It seemed all of us were engaged in Wilhelm Keil's work, trying to find a place to serve him. If it were otherwise, we'd be discussing how to move forward here, how to make what the scouts had chosen *here* into the service we'd set out to perform. We'd be hunting and feeding our people. There were a few other English-speaking people besides the Woodards who might come to join us if we demonstrated strength, showed ourselves to be loving and generous rather than stingy with our hope.

"Do you think this time here might change Wilhelm's mind?" I asked Christian. "Maybe seeing that we survive even with little grain and without using ammunition to hunt will help him think differently. Maybe he would bring everyone from Portland after all in the spring."

Christian said nothing.

"We still have the promise of a spring to win him," I said. "Even I long for the prairie and when we can begin building on our place." I patted Catherina's bottom as I rocked her to sleep.

He turned to me then, my husband, his handsome face marked now by puffy skin beneath his eyes, the bones of his cheeks sharp as elbows, the hollows near his mouth as cavernous as caves. He'd lost teeth. So had I. Many of us had. We'd had a last apple peel sometime in January. I couldn't remember. But what he said then was more frightening than any of the physical fears we'd faced and overcome. "There is no future here, Emma. Father Keil is right."

By mid-March, Wilhelm decided the weather was agreeable enough that he would now act according to the letters he'd had Karl Ruge write. There'd been no more messages of Indian attacks and, in fact, we'd not heard of one person dying in the region due to hostile natives. Wilhelm's coat hung on him like a jacket slipped over a chair, waiting for someone to put it on and give it substance. But his voice still boomed.

"I will leave for Portland and from there onto a new life. A place has been found, according to the Bruceport letter. You are all good people," he said then, giving up a small crumb of praise. "Some of you may wish to stay until you can sell your claims, but the rest should be prepared to go with me before the week is out." He'd gathered everyone into the largest of the houses inside the stockade.

Coughs and muffled cries of children answered him first. Then Hans Stauffer said, "I'm staying here. I never once thought the Lord wasn't in this place, and I think we can still make a go of it. With ammunition—no offense, Wilhelm—we can eat well and have skins to put into service."

Adam Schuele nodded agreement. Michael Sr. and the Stauffers did too. "We all believed it was a good place when we found it. Even a woman could plow the soil here, and that means with more hands, we can have more ground planted. We can sell the grain and—"

"To whom?" Wilhelm asked. "And the grain, it's puny. Besides, you'll eat up your own profits."

"Near the bay, a man named White, who is a former Indian agent, he buys property, and those from San Francisco will come north to live here, for the climate. We'll sell to them," Hans said.

"The climate!" Wilhelm laughed at that, a big deep laugh without joy in it. His bushy eyebrows raised, then lowered into a scowl.

I hoped Christian would stand and speak. Here were two men agreeing that remaining was worthy work.

"It is a fine climate in the spring and summer and fall," I said, finally.

Wilhelm turned to me. "It is a place that encourages women to go beyond their position."

"Our Lord never asked women to take a place behind," I said quietly. Louisa gasped. "I know the apostle Paul had many thoughts of how women should be in the worship, but work is worship, too, and we women always served where we were called to work back in Bethel. We worked side by side with men. We do that here, too. But in deciding things, we were silenced, though not by our Lord."

"There are flowers blooming in the woods already," Mary said. I turned to her and smiled at her gift of support. "I would like to see how this landscape changes when the rain is replaced by more of the sun." Her eyes met mine.

"You, Christian," Wilhelm said. "You have your hands full enough with this woman of yours. I will understand your wish to remain here with her."

If Wilhelm couldn't see the good in this place, then we'd just let him leave. Without him here, Christian's waned confidence could return. We'd have a life again, not one focused on what was good for the colony but for our own families.

"And you make my point, Mary Giesy," Wilhelm said. "This place encourages defiance. The landscape itself commands too much. Ve learn to protest against it and mistakenly believe ve must protest against our leaders."

Louisa's eyes watched the floor, but I noticed that her hands folded in prayer had turned her knuckles white. *Does she wish to speak? She won't, not here, not now.*

"Who leaves with me?" Wilhelm asked. "And who wants to remain?"

Peter Klein and several others said then that they would leave. They looked apologetically at Christian as they spoke. One by one the group expressed their wishes until we got to the part of the circle where Christian and I stood. I waited to hear my husband say that we would stay; we'd build our Giesy place upriver. Wilhelm had even approved of it.

"We do," Christian said. "My family and I go with you."

I turned to him. "We can't abandon all you've done here."

He shook his head at me, signaled silence.

"No," I said. "It'll destroy you."

"We do not need to heed the voices of women," Wilhelm said gently. A man who had won could afford to be gracious. "I believe you have made a good choice, Chris. In some things, at least." He turned away from me. "Who else?"

"You can't, Christian," I pleaded. "You can't turn your back on all this. You did well. It is an Eden, it is. How can you say God acted wrongly?"

Wilhelm turned back to me to answer. "In Eden, God asked, 'Where are you?' and 'What have you done?' He punished Eve for being independent, for pushing beyond. God gave the Garden, *ja,* but then He removed people from it. He changed His mind."

"God is unchanging," I hissed at him.

"So then, you have come to accept your role, that God made woman of man and that you bear the sins of what happened. Your punishment will be always as a mother in peril at childbirth, at the mercy of her husband, never to make her own choices. Never," he said. "A good woman knows her place and stays there. She goes where her husband tells her." He turned to Louisa. She smiled at him, but I thought I saw something besides docility in her eyes, something I couldn't name.

I felt my hands grow wet with sweat. Catherina squirmed. *Not now, not now.* This was not about me being submissive; it was about supporting my husband. "Even when God removed them from Eden," I said, "He provided for them. He made clothes for them from animal skins, from the very bounty of the Garden. He was tender and loving and forgiving."

Mary had her arm crooked, holding her infant. She bore a healthy baby here, even with the trials of coming across the plains. "Don't you want your baby to grow up where she was born?" I asked Sebastian. Mary had expressed her wishes openly, but so far Christian's brothers had not.

I turned to *Frau* Giesy, Christian's mother. Surely she'd know that leaving now would be a final defeat for her son. It would deplete him. I pleaded with my eyes. She said nothing.

"Don't you want to finish what you started?" I asked my husband. "You're the one who convinced me of the merits of this clearing. You told me to put aside our own wishes for what God wants of us. Wasn't this colony to be in service to others? Who's to say that there aren't many in need of His love here? The settlers, though not many, might be soil we can plant seed in. Each other." I whispered that last. "We can be salt and light to the world around us if we open our arms wide. Even to each other."

"We have no need of a world so large around us," Wilhelm said. "Such intrusions only bring trials. Wars."

"You sent us out to find an isolated place, to find one where our faith could take root. But there is no isolated place, not really. And now you abandon your own mission? For…comfort?" I said.

"Emma—," Christian said.

"But you said this place was chosen for us, that we were chosen. When I struggled with the rain and mud, you're the one who reminded me."

"There are no people here, Emma," Christian said. He had tears in his eyes. "Father Keil is right. There are none to buy our products, none to bring into the fold. Only us, and we cannot feed ourselves, let alone those around us. Maybe some oystermen on the coast who are lost, maybe to those few we can bring the message of love and compassion, but not if we cannot survive."

"Perhaps we are the lost." I cried now, the words suffering through sobs. "Maybe we are the ones who need someone to reach out to us. Maybe what Wilhelm preaches isn't all that we're to understand. Perhaps this is the very place we were led to, so we could discover Him for ourselves before we attempt to tell others how He is."

"Stop now," Christian said. "It's no good, Emma. No good. It is finished." Christian took me in his arms and held me. His tears on my cheeks mingled with my own.

29

No Salve, Save Love

Word reached us of the death of Jacob Keil, Wilhelm's brother, and then of Fredricka and Benjamin, in an Indian massacre near Skamania on the Columbia. Not three months of marriage living outside the colony, and Fredricka and Benjamin's lives were over. So there had been Indian attacks in the world around us, but we'd been safe in our Giesy stockade.

I thought of our colony in Bethel, how it had been insulated from the world around it, but not for long. We needed that outside world, too, in order to survive. Nonbelievers bought our furniture and wagons, our whiskey and quilts. It was an intricate task blending isolation with protection, melding worldliness with spiritual calm, and Wilhelm must have done it well in the beginning to have so many remain with him for so long.

Or perhaps it was his talk of our deaths that kept us looking into his eyes, finding solace and obedience in his fold.

Had we spent so much time only with one another that young souls like Fredricka and her husband had no skills to make it in that outside world? These were questions I wanted to talk about with Christian but couldn't. I watched him suffer hopelessness, feeling that he had no meaning now, his inability to forgive himself, and worse, how separated he was from those who loved him. These were wounds as deep as if he'd sliced himself with a butchering knife, and I had no salve—save love—to offer to heal the wound.

Christian said what brought us together in the beginning was our wish to be in service, to treat one another with the Golden and the Diamond Rules. I wanted to make Christian's life better than my own, but I couldn't.

He'd committed to taking Wilhelm back to Portland.

A ship arrived, bringing us many sacks of grain. It was the same ship Christian and Wilhelm would leave for Portland on. We baked bread and packed it into the trunks of those heading into Oregon Territory. Christian suggested we prepare to leave too, but Wilhelm hedged. "You've endured this long. A few months more vill make no difference to you, *ja,* Chris? Until the site is ready, Louisa and I will rent a place in Portland, and when ve find the colony is ready, ve send for you. It's unfortunate, this kind of…separation," he said. "A better site would have prevented these adjustments needed now. *Ja,* that's so, Chris?" My husband nodded his head as Keil patted his back. It didn't look like brotherly love.

I seethed for my husband. Wilhelm didn't even want us with him while we waited. He treated us like children sent to the back of the room for our misbehavior while everyone else played outside. We'd been asked to wait until *Herr* Keil determined the perfect place…when we were already there. I could hardly stand it.

"We won't leave now either, then," Andreas, Christian's father, said. "No reason to find yet another place to wait while Wilhelm seeks out a new site." Sebastian Giesy nodded agreement. So at least I'd have company waiting. I smiled at that wish, when once I'd only wanted to be left alone.

"The rest of us will travel together for safety," Wilhelm said. "It was good we saved ammunition."

I wondered if Christian would decide that protecting Wilhelm would still be reason to go to Portland with him now when his parents said they'd wait in Willapa. Or would he think risking us, Andy and the baby and me, on this trip south might not be wise?

"You stay with my parents, here, Emma. You and the children."

"No. I'm sorry that I am always saying no to you, husband, but we need you here if we're here. Wilhelm does not ask his wife to remain away from him while he waits for their new home to be readied."

"I'll come back for you. I need to do this, Emma. It is the least that I can do for Wilhelm, considering." He gave me the look that said he'd bear no more dissent from me, so I waited until evening and asked him to walk with me to the far corner of the stockade area. Willie's grave overlooked us from the hill beyond. I carried Catherina in the board on my back, and Andy chased field mice before us. Dogs fought over a deer antler shed the previous winter that lay among needles and leaves. They growled and barked in the distance, and I wrapped my shawl around me against the evening chill. We hadn't had rain all day. White trillium bloomed on the forest floor. A spider busied itself with a web against the cedar's bark.

"Don't you see?" I said. "Wilhelm could go alone and let everyone wait here now that we have grain. No one needs to be uprooted while he finds the perfect place. But the truth is, he will take a group with him, and then while he waits in Portland, he'll disrupt them again, send others out as he did the scouts while he waits in luxury until they've built his *gross Haus,* his grand house," I said, repeating it in English.

"I doubt there are many grand houses for rent in Portland," Christian said.

"He isn't thinking about the colony's needs, not now. He's thinking of his own. He talks about his sacrifice with the death of Willie, but it was he who said we should leave Bethel, leave the simple yet contented lives we had there. He bears no responsibility for the hardships we've endured for the sake of the colony. He might accept your protection while he travels south, but he doesn't need to travel at all, and he doesn't seem all that concerned for those of us left here."

"It's a terrible thing to lose a child."

"It is! But Willie died in Bethel, not as a result of his sacrifice to come here. And think of what the colonists endured traveling with that hearse. That journey was made harder because of Wilhelm's...tending. He didn't think anything of the challenges others faced because of his orders. And now he will take us away from what we believed was God's calling for the colony and for us. Can this be right, husband?"

Andy chased a dog and rolled with the puppy belonging to one of the arrivals of Klein's train. Christian dug in his ear, so I knew he was thinking. "I know you didn't come here to please yourself, Christian. You came because of what you believed was good for all of us. That's true leadership, it is. Being faithful to your beliefs for the good of everyone."

"Indeed." He sighed. "I'll be back, and then we'll make our way together to the new colony. My father will look after you until then."

"You see? You think of us, of who remains behind. He doesn't. He thinks only of himself."

Christian shook his head. That pain of helplessness settled in the lines of his eyes. "That's not true, Emma. He's a good man, has always been so. This is...this is an unusual time. New nails have been pounded into his life, and like us, they stand out a little. This is something I can do, to help now. I need to do that." I pouted, I knew. "What we did here, Emma, is done."

My husband was falling into Wilhelm's way. Soon he'd want me to walk behind him on that path again. I could do that, and would, if it kept Christian from seeing himself as a failure, this place only as a sign of lost dreams, just a memory of a clearing he once made in the wild. "If Wilhelm was a true follower of our Lord," I said, "he'd be preparing other leaders now to take his place. He'd begin to trust others and not only his own visions. I thought he'd chosen you, but he won't relinquish control. But you would. You're the better leader, Christian."

"You say this because you want your own way, Emma."

His words stung, but I let them sink in to find their truth before I answered. "We are all entitled to want things to go well with us. That's not un-Christian. But what I want most of all is for you to believe in what you're doing. I confess I don't hold Wilhelm in the esteem you do, so you're right to sift through what I say about him. Nothing he's done since he arrived has made me trust him more. If you go with him, I'll follow you, Christian. But I want to follow the husband who saw the possibilities here, not the man who walks with the slumped shoulders of defeat. You changed my mind, husband; now I want to change yours."

———

What do men do while they wait? They whittle. They plow. They build. They talk of the future. At least that's what Christian's brothers and parents did, working together to finish a roof or push with their adzes to smooth a wooden doorway. They considered gristmill sites as though they might stay on here along the Willapa River. The plow my in-laws brought on their ship turned soil. They planted oats, as Christian's father thought it had a better chance than wheat of maturing in the cool climate. I wondered why they bothered when it was clear Christian accepted Wilhelm's decision that the Willapa Valley was a mistake. He intended to follow *Herr* Keil to wherever it was he might go. Christian even traveled with him, left us here to…wait. There'd be no one to harvest the oats.

At least we had food now, with the shipment of grain and Wilhelm no longer limiting the use of ammunition. Hans stayed with us, and so did his father, who had arrived with Keil and Christian and the hearse. All the scouts were accounted for now except Joseph Knight. For the rest of us, we simply waited for the perfect place to go to, the one Wilhelm would find for us. Except for me.

Louisa's last words before they left stayed with me. "We women are asked to support our husbands," she said. "Even when it may not be the best decisions that they make."

"Are you talking about our living on fish all winter while your husband prevented us from hunting?"

She straightened her shoulders. "That too." She tickled Catherina's chin, and my daughter jerked in my arms, flailing to reach out to Louisa. "She reminds me of Aurora at that age, all eyes and mouth, so ready for living." I nodded. *Louisa talks as though we might be...equals, even friends.* She reached for my daughter, who went willingly to her. "I referred to our coming here and then leaving here," she said. "I can see why your husband chose this place and how you found contentment here."

"You see contentment?" That wasn't a word I would use to describe my current state, but I had found gratitude here. Peacefulness did come floating to me when I walked the prairie, when I huddled in the trees to think, when Mary and her family arrived with the Klein train, when we'd worked together to bring in our meager grain, when Catherina had been born healthy and strong. A double rainbow colored the sky.

She continued. "I would be content to stay here, to walk daily to my son's grave. I'll miss not being able to do that. And here," she looked up at me, paused. "Here, the weight of decisions would not lie only on my husband's shoulders but on all the men's, especially your husband's shoulders. It would relieve my husband of much strain." Her dark coal eyes stared into mine. "When things did not go well here, my husband wouldn't need to bear all the weight. There is something good in that."

Louisa knelt and fussed at the mud caked on Aurora's skirt. All I could see was the white scalp that lined the part in her graying hair. "It is a sadness that either of them bears it," she said. "They follow our Lord, and yet they refuse to let Him carry their burdens."

I'd never heard Louisa express such thoughts, nor any colony woman for that matter. Did she question her husband's choices? Yet she followed him.

It didn't have to be that way for me, for us. Why should Christian bear the responsibility for this failed venture? It was only a failure if we defined it so, not because our Lord did. It was another part of a journey, not something so disastrous nothing good could come from it.

"Maybe we refuse to let Him carry our burdens too," I said. She nodded, and it came to me that if this landscape was truly what we'd been led to, there had to be a way to make our being here successful despite Wilhelm's pronouncement about it. I didn't know how that could be, but for the first time since my husband said we'd be leaving, I felt light as the orange butterfly that landed only for a moment on Louisa's shoulder.

———

Sarah had asked for goat's milk in exchange for eggs, and I carried it to her with Catherina on my back. With Andy in Mary's good hands back at the stockade, I made my way through the spring forest to the landing, walking the nearly dried-up path beside the Willapa. There had to be something we could do here, something that might intrigue Christian enough to make him remain. It had to be a new thought, a new way. I remembered hearing of the Rappist Colony back in Pennsylvania discovering silkworms as a way to contribute to colony funds. Maybe mulberry trees would grow here, and we could become a western silk-growing group. In Bethel, it was furniture-building and wagon-making and Golden Rule Whiskey that brought in money to serve the colony. Those needed people to purchase them, and as Wilhelm noted, we had few people here able to do that.

If the whole colony couldn't be supported in this valley, perhaps a small portion could. That smaller group could contribute to the larger group wherever we ended up. No, wherever *they* might end up. Wilhelm saw our success here as a challenge to him; that's why he twisted my husband into the ground beneath his boots like the remains of old tobacco. I couldn't stand by and let that happen.

If Christian moved us south, if we followed Wilhelm, my husband would forever carry the stigma of failure. *A man's heart deviseth his way: but the LORD directeth his steps.* I had to trust that proverb.

I reached Woodard's Landing, and Sarah motioned for us to sit. She lifted Catherina in her cradle board and braced her upward at the corner of her chair. I was tired and not expecting answers to the voiceless prayers lifted while I walked. *Show me the way. Show me the way.*

A warm fire crackled in the fireplace, and beside Sarah on the rough plank table laid an open book. *Shakespeare,* a word I sounded out in English. Karl Ruge had such a set of books that he'd brought with him, and through the waiting months stuffed together in the stockade houses, he often read to us using different voices for all the parts. We'd scoffed when he said all the roles had once been played by men. Wilhelm snubbed books and said there was no book but the Bible with anything to offer. Still, he listened when Karl read.

"*The Merry Wives of Windsor,*" Sarah said when I picked up the book. It smelled musty and damp, but most things did here.

"What makes the wives merry?"

"I'm not sure," Sarah said. "He talks about oysters, so it's fitting for this Willapa place." She laughed, then quoted, " 'Why, then the world's mine oyster / Which I with sword will open.' I think it will have a happy ending."

"Oysters are so hard to open he needs a sword?" I said. I'd eaten one or two oysters at Woodards'. Christian had opened the shell, then dug around and removed the meat. He opened his mouth, and the slimy white strip slipped down his throat. We'd boiled the remainder, as the oysters didn't easily give themselves up from their safe little shells. I found them tasty but not particularly filling.

"I think it means the world is rich and wonderful and can be tasted like a good oyster, and the character in the play plans to do that with his power, his might. The Californians must think a little like that. They order so many oysters and pay so much for them."

"This is part of Shakespeare's writing?"

She shook her head. "Our oysters here are as good as those anywhere in the world—even from the Orient, my husband says. I always thought it amazing that right in the middle of those ugly-looking oysters grow pearls. They grow out of irritations, things that don't belong, and yet they make themselves a part of the oyster. I like those little treasures in a story."

I thought of my mother's pearls. I had no idea they came from the misshapen, craggy shells called oysters, oysters that grew just downstream.

"Our Willapa oysters don't offer up lovely pearls," Sarah told me. "They're dull in color and uneven. Not nice and round. But they're pretty to me." She pulled a slender strand up over her collar. "See? They're not perfect but each is unique. Each one individual. I like that better than the perfect ones that I've seen that all look alike."

Unique. Formed out of irritation. I asked her to tell me more.

"They grow them in beds, like farmers do their wheat," she continued. She unwound Catherina from her board and held her firmly at her shoulder, patting her back as she talked. "Only in ocean water and in the tide flats. It takes a hardy soul to be an oysterman, someone who can work in the wet and up to their knees in mud or out on the skiffs, yanking and raking up clusters of shells, and yet can wait. They have to keep guard against predators, just like farmers have to keep birds from their fields. That's what my husband says."

What kind of predator would harm an oyster? Their shells looked like long tongues with bumps, and if what Sarah said was right, they were impossible to get inside of without a knife or some large rock to break them open. What could harm something so hard and well defended?

"People rob oyster beds," she said. "And there are green things in the ocean that can kill them. Things you'd never expect. They have to be tended. Everything has something wanting to destroy it.

"Only the faithful watchman can prevent it," I said.

Sarah nodded. "In San Francisco restaurants and saloons, raw oysters sell for one dollar apiece on the half shell. Same as what an egg costs there. Gold miners think nothing of celebrating their new wealth with extravagant dinners that always include fresh raw oysters."

Was it really just like farming? We Bethelites knew about farming. Perhaps the Willapa Colony could remain here yet. We could earn our way to repay what Wilhelm had invested in us. Our market didn't need to live close to us; we could ship our wares. Willapa could become the world that was "mine oyster" for those who chose to stay in the place the scouts had staked out. We'd simply have to learn something new from this Edenlike place.

"Should you go alone?" Karl Ruge asked me. He wore a dark suit coat that made his white attachable collar look all the whiter. He folded back a shock of silver hair with his hands as he talked. During all the rains and time of mud, Karl had always looked tidy, and he'd done his own wash, never asking any of the women to do it for him. "Maybe you should wait until Christian comes back. This would be better, by golly?"

"I need to find out about oyster farming. A dollar apiece. Think of that."

"For fresh ones, *ja,* shipped across the Bay and into the ocean. But most go for a penny, boiled on the streets of mining towns, or so I'm told. It is not a gold strike, Emma Giesy. This is not an easy thing you think of."

"It's farming. We know how to do that," I said. "We know about planting and tending and praying over the harvest."

"The oysters must be planted and grown," Karl said. "That means more investment. And learning how to replant, to not overharvest. Investments in ships to send them south. One still needs to find a way to live while the oystermen wait. All that will cost money, Emma."

"But if we were successful, we could pay off what the land has cost us and even contribute to the new colony when Wilhelm decides where that will be. We can still be a part of it but...separate." Oyster farming would make us unique, but I knew that was a word that also meant "extraordinary," a concept perhaps too close to "prideful" for Karl Ruge's simple ways.

"It is still not good that you travel by yourself. Your in-laws would not approve."

Karl was right about that. Barbara and Andreas, Christian's parents, had raised their eyebrows at me on more than one occasion since Christian left with Wilhelm: when I spoke up in a gathering, when I went alone to see Sarah, when I acted like myself.

"Do you have a reason to go to Bruceport?" I asked Karl.

He rubbed his white chin hair. "The post office there is where Wilhelm said for mail to come from Bethel. There and Portland. I should see if he's sent us word of where we are to find him or if there are letters from Bethel that need answering."

Karl hadn't gone with Wilhelm. I was curious about that, though it was none of my affair. He'd begun teaching the children of those who had decided to wait until Keil actually found a new place rather than adjust once again for a few weeks or months and then move to the more permanent site. Maybe Karl felt useful here.

The weather turned balmy, as it usually did in April, and with men able to hunt now, the cries of hungry children no longer pushed at us. Karl instructed out under the trees, using sticks and hard red berries to teach math and the beauty of the landscape to teach English. He said it was the finest schoolhouse he'd ever taught in.

Being in the Willapa Valley may not have been luxurious, but it was familiar, and with the rain ceasing it was gloriously pleasant. Perhaps Karl, too, wanted to move only once more and would take in the bounty of this place before choosing something else.

"*Ja,* by golly. I have reason to go to Bruceport," he said finally. "To get the mail."

"Christian might have sent me a letter. His parents would understand my wish to go there with Sam Woodard and be unconcerned if you came too, Karl. We'll do this together."

The Willapa ran full and wide, but I could see both shorelines, a comfort to me. I took deep breaths and made myself exhale so as not to get dizzy. Sam Woodard and Karl handled the oars and the sails. I could hang on tight to my son and daughter. Oystering would mean more time on water, more time *in* water, I realized. I'd need to have the children stay with their grandparents so I could help with the harvest, or maybe we'd need to move closer to the oyster beds so I could learn to open the shells or prepare them for shipping. *Closer to the water?* In Bruceport, I was told, the tide came in under the boardwalks. What could be closer than that? There'd be water everywhere, seagulls chattering to us every day, and not just Charlie appearing every now and then for scraps.

I took a deep breath. If this would be a way to bring my husband's confidence back, then overcoming my fear of water would be worth it. *Show me the path. Show me the path.*

Long-handled rakes leaned against log sheds as we eased closer toward the bay. Low flat boats, skiffs Sam called them, piled high with oyster shells, moved across the water toward the open sea and a large ship waiting there. Near a cluster of buildings, native women bent over piles of shells, sifting and sorting, their scarves tight around their heads. They stood and stared as we slipped by. I waved. They didn't wave back. Where the tide had gone out, beyond the buildings, I watched more native women stand in the low tidewater beside their baskets. They looked as though they walked on water, the mud slithered with a film that reflected them as they worked. Stacks of discarded oyster shells pocked the shoreline like a chain of small white mountains.

We anchored our boat, and carrying Andy, Sam splashed toward shore. I lifted my skirts and followed. I asked Sam if he could recommend an oysterman that I might talk with.

"You didn't come to get the mail?" he said.

"That, too, but I also want to talk oysters." I sat to put my shoes back on.

"Lots of folks do," he said. "They'll be nearing the end of their harvest soon. Never eat an oyster in a month that doesn't have an *r* in it," he advised. He scanned the wooden fronts of oystering warehouses. "I'd try that last place there, not far from the mouth. Supposed to be an American from San Francisco. He might answer your questions."

———

"Joe Knight! You're here? You've been here all along?"

"Not all the time," he said sheepishly. "Now let me answer your questions. They're middens, those discarded shells," he told Andy, who pointed at the piles of nubby shells. "Middens are what's left after we cull the good ones and then take out the meat to dry. The Indians do it that way mostly, drying the meat for use later. We like them fresh, of course. Earn more money that way." He pointed with that finger in the air and winked. He lived in a small log house set with a walkway to the beach, and he had opened his arms wide to Karl Ruge when we found him. To me he tipped his hat, shook Andy's little hand, and smiled at Catherina. It wasn't until I heard his German-accented English and saw that finger pointing that I knew for sure who he was.

"How long have you been here?" I asked.

"This time? About six months."

"You never went back to Bethel," I said. I bounced the baby on my hip. "You left the Willapa River but never returned. People wonder where you are. You need to let your brother know you're all right."

"I started to," he said. "But the two of us split after we worked on a bridge." His blond hair poked out from under his narrow-brimmed hat. He had a tiny mustache but no beard now at all. He still poked with his fingers when he talked. "I went to San Francisco and then came back. This was as far as I got."

"But why didn't you let us know? Why not return to help us?"

"*Ja*," he said, looking down. "I wasn't sure colonists would understand my journeying into San Francisco. Then once the weather changed and I decided to come back, I thought maybe oystering would be a good thing for me, better than chopping trees so tall you can't see their tops without lying flat on your back. I was going to help you build through the winter. But I stopped here." His face colored. "I'd worked in California, so I had a little money and invested in an oyster claim. Right here," he said, waving his arm. Apparently, right at the mouth of the Willapa River lay a natural bed of oysters. "It has everything I need. Even people to show me how to do it. The Indians, mostly."

"You had no scares of massacres?" I asked.

He shook his head. "They might have been scared at what a bad oysterman I was. The women laughed at a man gathering oysters at first, but I notice lots of white men do it. We float along in the skiffs dragging our tongs until we stumble onto something that feels right. Then we grab with those tongs and, hand over hand, pull up whatever we've caught onto: rocks and broken shells and mud and clusters of oysters. We sort through it until we find just what we're looking for. The pearl, the best oysters. We dry or ship the rest for boiling, then discard the shells."

"The pearls here are not as large or perfect, I hear," Karl Ruge said.

Joe nodded agreement. "Perfection isn't my aim. Never was. Living full, that's what I wanted. I still share," he said. He sounded defensive just a bit. "I give back. Don't have to belong to a colony to do that."

Karl nodded.

"The Indian women say we should put the shells back into the water," Joe said, returning to a safer subject. "As a protected place for the young oysters to grow up in. No one else does it, though. It's hard work but I like it."

I wondered what he'd say when I proposed he needed a partner.

———

On the boat ride back, my mind raced with possibilities. Here, Christian could find meaning and good work; here, he could perhaps forgive himself for being human, for doing the best he could, though all hadn't turned out as he'd once hoped. But how to convince him that such a move could be a statement of faith?

"You are in deep thought, *Frau* Giesy," Karl said.

I nodded. "I want to find a way to help my husband see oystering as a buttress to his faith. And I want to be sure I'm not making my own religion up, as I sometimes think *Herr* Keil has, while I wrangle with how we should be in this western place."

"There is an old Norse word for religion that translates in the English as 'tying again,'" he said. He gazed out across the water, the silence broken only by the swish of the boat cutting through the water. "Somehow I think those Norsemen must have realized that life unravels us at times. It is the way of things. It is our faith, our religion, I believe, that then binds us together."

"'Begin to weave / God provides the thread,'" I said. "My mother gave that German proverb to me." It came to me then what that proverb meant: that life is a weaving with our fine threads being broken and stretched. It's our calling to keep weaving, find ways to tie things together again.

30

A Pearl Unique

"The band played in Portland," Christian said. "March 22, 1856, our first performance in all these years."

"You played?"

He shook his head no, his enthusiasm apparently coming from the association with the players, not anything he did himself. "Jonathan played."

"You saw my brother? Is he well?" I clutched at his arm. "I wish he'd come back with you."

"He seemed content to be with the band and those who wintered in Portland. They played at the request of someone named Grimm, the same one who told Wilhelm about the apples. He sold us 256 bushels of oats at forty cents a bushel and 165 bushels of wheat at seventy cents each. They can begin grinding flour, and best of all, I've brought apples and more flour to tide us over until we leave. They'll take the grain to Aurora Mills; that's what Wilhelm calls the land they purchased. He's named it for Aurora."

Not for Louisa, I thought.

"It's a rolling piece of prairie south of Portland. Many acres. It already has a gristmill on it. Their neighbors are from French Prairie, named for all the retired Frenchies of Hudson's Bay and their Indian wives."

"So we can keep the grist stones your parents brought here, then."

Christian looked puzzled. "We won't be here, so why would we leave them?" He looked around. "In fact, I wonder why they've wasted time plowing up the soil and planting oats here."

"Have they already begun to build Wilhelm's *gross Haus* at Aurora Mills?" I asked.

He looked away.

"I suspect Keil and company wait in Portland in a nice warm house where food is plenty and he can hold court—I mean preach—to many, while my brother and others like him build his house for him. My own brother who doesn't even make a way to see me or his niece and nephew. Well, so be it." I brushed at my apron, though I saw nothing there.

"You can see him when we join them in Oregon, *Liebchen*," Christian said.

"I don't plan to go to Oregon, Christian. And when I tell you what I've found and who agrees with me, you won't want to leave here either."

"Emma…"

———

We took our small boat to our claim, seven miles up the Willapa from Woodard's Landing. I wanted a pleasant place to talk to Christian, and he was willing to take me to the site he'd once picked for us to build on. He was saying good-bye to the landscape, he said; I was beginning to say hello. We stood there now, overlooking the four logs we'd left last fall to outline the house. They'd been pushed and tossed in different directions. Maybe from stout winds. I hoped not from high water or flooding. Andy whined to be carried on his father's shoulders, and he did, riding high while reaching for the leaves of trees. I held Catherina in my arms. We ate biscuits with butter, a luxury, then sat on a quilt my mother had sent in the trunk.

It was now or never. "The scouts were right, husband. The Willapa Valley will provide everything we need if we're patient and are willing to accept not the perfect pearl but one that is distinctive."

"Indeed."

"Karl thinks that oystering can work," I said, after telling him about Joe Knight and our trip to Bruceport. "He's willing to remain here to make it happen and teach any children who stay here too."

"Karl is? He's so…loyal to Wilhelm. Always has been. And Joe…" He shook his head.

"It isn't disloyal to follow your heart," I said. "Karl didn't go with Wilhelm to Portland because he believes there is something here worth staying for. Everything about it here, except the rainy winters, is an Eden. We'd appreciate the blooms and beauty less if we had nothing to contrast it with, and therein lies the joy of the rainy winter months, the dark heavy clouds that shadow our days and promise sunshine in due time. I never thought I'd say such a thing, but I mean it, Christian. I do."

"Wilhelm is right, though. There is still no market here for whatever we might produce."

"But you were right too. We're on rivers and near oceans, so we can ship things to markets." He shook his head, still not convinced. I tried another tactic. "It doesn't mean that Wilhelm was wrong about this place. It just means others can listen and hear something else. Wilhelm has done that. He's decided to go somewhere else. Neither of you made a mistake. Each is free to make other choices. We just have to make a change in what we thought we'd do. Less grain farming and more… oyster farming."

"Emma, I—"

"At least until we get field crops established. We can cherish what we have, still be a part of the colony if you wish, but separated. Maybe the way Nineveh was back in Missouri."

"Nineveh grew just a few miles down the road. We'll be a hundred and thirty miles distant from Aurora Mills. It'll make decision-making difficult."

"Not if we're really…separate." Andy draped his arms around his father's neck as the child stood behind him. "He missed you terribly," I said, then continued. "We can pay off the land claims with what we sell. And maybe, just maybe, living communally isn't what we were called to do. We can still be faithful to our beliefs even if we don't have a common fund."

Christian shook his head. "What beliefs are there except to follow Wilhelm's way of serving? I have trouble seeing anything else."

"But that's it, Christian. Maybe, like Wilhelm, you too are visionary and you can see things differently if you can stop blaming yourself for what happened here. We don't need to separate our hearts from the other colonists nor from our neighbors to be in service. We can look at what our neighbors might need. Your recruitment brought in good people like Karl Ruge, but most were people who just made the colony bigger and produced more work. It didn't bring people in who had needs that we could meet. We tended one another, but isn't giving to those truly hurting what service is all about?"

He dug at his ears. He was thinking.

"Oystering, if we're successful, would allow us to be good neighbors to the colonists and to those here."

I decided to be still. My father said to sell a wagon, one needed to sing its virtues and then be quiet and listen to how the customer would then tell him why he needed that very wagon, how he had a big family and could use a sturdy vehicle, or how his wife was sickly and needed one that handled the ruts well. The rest would be simple.

Christian stayed silent a very long time. I'd probably strained my threads in trying to describe what I meant, in trying to tie things, again. He stayed quiet too long.

"We could share the costs and profits of those at Willapa, maybe send a percentage each year on to Aurora Mills. Tithe our harvest. But there won't need to be *one* leader with all the weight of the success or failure on his shoulders. We can decide as a family what to do, or as a group of families. We don't need to wait for just one ruler."

A seagull, probably not Charlie, flew overhead with several others. "Bread, Papa. I want to throw him bread," Andy said. I overlooked the fact that my son asked his father and not me for bread and handed a biscuit to Christian who gave it to Andy. The child threw up breadcrumbs and squealed in delight when a bird swooped down to catch a crumb in midair.

"Even the seagulls adapt to new opportunities," I said. "You know Wilhelm will never let another lead while he's alive, and he won't prepare another to take his place. So we should listen to our hearts, listen to what we think we're hearing and follow that."

Christian played with a long strand of grass, running it through his wide fingers. He watched Andy's interest in the root of a cedar tree. Catherina had decided to nap.

"We came to serve people, *Liebchen*. Wilhelm was right about that. This place has no people to recruit or bring into the fold, none to help prepare for the last days ahead."

"We don't bring them in, God brings them. Didn't you tell me this once? And we don't have to be so separated from our neighbors. Look at all those oystermen. Look at Joe. I think he feels a bit guilty for having left us. If we join him, you could help relieve that. There are dozens of people suffering in silence. We might hear them if we weren't listening to the chop of trees building the colony for the sake of…the colony. We can't just worry about our little group, Christian. How else can we be salt and light?"

"Father Keil sent us west to protect us from the world."

"Maybe we'll best prepare for the end times by behaving as though we can't control their coming. Because we can't. We can only love one another, trust we're not alone here. We can be good neighbors to people like Sarah and Sam. Remember how the Chehalis offered us hides and house-building help? Perhaps there are things we can do for those people whose lives are changing with these treaties and with us being here. Perhaps living in the world instead of apart from it will make us better servants in the end."

"My parents will want to go with Wilhelm. They've followed him their whole lives. From Pennsylvania to Missouri—"

"If you said you were staying and that you wanted something a little different from what we had at Bethel, I think they'd remain. They've already finished the log house they started for Mary and Sebastian. They're even going to roof it." He raised his eyebrows in surprise. "They trusted your judgment. So does Karl. So do I."

He leaned over Catherina, brushed a spider making its way toward her neck. "You think I can be an oysterman." He shook his head. "I can't believe Joe Knight is. He never seemed the type to branch out on his own."

"We never know what we'll do," I said, "when challenged. We're like oysters sometimes, I think. Trying to stay deep in the mud, out of the way, but then we get selected. But we're not alone, even in the worst of storms."

"I doubt Joe was 'challenged' by some storm to become an oyster-man," he said.

"How can you know?" I asked him. "There he was all that time, and we didn't know it because we never ventured far outside our own little world."

He rose to follow Andy. He lifted the child onto his shoulders once again. He stood above me, and I shaded my eyes with my hand. "We can't know for certain about anything," I continued. "We listen, try to do our best to help our families and our neighbors, that's all we can do. Here, Andy. A little more bread for you to toss." I handed it to him and Christian set him down. I picked up the picnic things, started to carry them to the boat. "I'd like to ask Jonathan to come stay with us. At least make the offer. He might not come, of course."

"*Ja,*" he said. "All we ever wanted to do was to take care of those we loved. It was all we did, we scouts. You included, Emma."

"Love's the thread. Then listen," I said. I put my finger to my lips. We could hear the wind through the treetops, the soft breathing of a baby, the shouts of a child racing a seagull, the rush of the river water behind us.

"I like what I hear," he said.

"We can go with you to the coast, maybe sell the claim," I ventured. "Or we can build our house, and I'll remain with the children while you're oystering."

"I don't like being separated from you."

"Seasons," I said. "There'll be seasons when we're apart, as when we were first married, but I won't long for you so much because I know you'll be doing something you've chosen to do, not something you do because you felt yourself a failure."

"You think we Giesys and Stauffers and Schaefers can survive not as colonists but as friends and family, together? Neighbors, too?"

"It's a path that has meaning, Christian. I truly believe that."

"I listen to you," Christian said. He reached his arm around me, pulled me close.

"Does that mean you'll stay?" I sank into his eyes, as inviting as a warm bath in winter. I was sure I knew the answer.

———

Christian woke me in the morning. "I do my seventy-six pushing-ups, and then we go down to see Joe Knight," he said. "I want to know that this is part of what was to happen here, not just the hardships, but the unexpected turn of events." For the first time since Wilhelm had arrived in November, my husband had a sparkle in his eye. I recalled a psalm where the speaker asked that he not be ashamed in God's sight for what he had done, and God answered. So He'd answered again. I nearly cried watching my husband lift and lower himself on the moss-covered floor. He did seventy-seven. "One for good measure."

We took our boat with the small white sail on it out onto the Willapa River, heading for the bay, and worked our way around the point to where Bruceport thrived. The wind and tide worked with us. Karl Ruge came along. I held my breath as the boat lifted onto a swell, then slapped down hard. Working with oysters would surely take the fear of water from me. Familiarity breeds freedom, I decided.

On this trip, the children stayed with their grandparents so I could concentrate on the details Joe could tell us about this work we were stepping into. I wanted to listen and look and smell what would become the way of our lives.

A Chehalis woman ran the trading post right on the bay. Her husband had died the year Andy was born. "Drowned in the Wallacut River, Captain Russell did," Joe Knight told us. "But in 1851 he introduced the first Shoalwater oysters from here to the San Francisco merchants. We can thank him for that and for what we do because of it."

"I'll thank the Provider of the oysters," Christian said.

Joe dropped his eyes, ran his hands through his thick blond hair. "*Ja*," he said. "Him too."

So on this day at the Willapa Bay, Joe Knight and Christian and Karl discussed how they would work together as oystermen. I watched as oyster boats came alongside schooners out in the bay and men handed up their baskets of oysters. I counted twenty-eight boats, twenty-one scows, and thirteen canoes coming and going out to the huge schooner. "Some of the holds have timber in them too," Joe told us. "It's a lucrative place with gold from the forests and ocean here for the mining."

Christian would stay with Joe and work the oyster beds; Karl's investment came from money he had saved on his own as a teacher before he became a part of the colony. His contribution would pay wages for workers, and one day, the children and I would work in the oyster beds, filling up baskets to be taken out to schooners.

I'd remain on our Giesy place once we finished our log home. I'd be within a few hours' travel downriver to see Mary and Christian's parents, less time than that when the paths were dry and the mule surefooted. I could see Sarah and be there for her when she had need of help to deliver her baby. I'd make quilts again. We'd get sheep and weave when I wasn't plowing or milking or planting oats and peas.

The wind whipped Christian's hair as we made our way back toward the landing. His hair looked thinner, but his thick reddish beard framed his face. We'd spend the night at the stockade and then move the few things we had to the site he'd chosen for us long before, seven miles up the Willapa. We'd live in that tent a few more weeks, until his father, brothers, and nephews helped finish our house at last.

"I hope during the winter months if I have to be gone, that you and the children will stay with my parents or with Sebastian and Mary," Christian said.

"If it will make you feel better, we will," I told him.

Christian helped any of those who'd stayed behind to make their way to Aurora Mills, the site where Wilhelm would soon take up residence. As he talked with his family, his brothers and his parents, he found each wanted to remain in the place Christian had chosen, the place all the scouts had selected. "What is the likelihood that all nine men—and one woman—would be duped by the devil?" Christian's father said. "This must be a good place."

I didn't suggest that he used a poor standard, since hundreds of Bethelites were scattered throughout the Oregon Territory because of *one* man. Had we all been duped? Or was God still in charge of the colony, even our Willapa splinter, no matter what we humans chose to do?

Michael Schaefer Sr. and his son and children did stay. Even John Genger and the Becks, who came out with Wilhelm, presented their decisions at a gathering at the stockade that June. The Stauffers remained too. The tents of those leaving were all rolled up and ready to board the ship that would take them to the Columbia River and the Oregon Territory and Keil.

"We don't do it for you, Christian," his father said. "Though we are glad it is you who found this site first and put your sweat into building us a house. We stay because of the promise here. Yes, it will be hard to clear the ground, but what else do we have to do in this life? Yes, it will be difficult to build more houses, but we have many hands now. And there is something…pleasant about living close but not so close to one another as we did in Bethel. We can build a school and gather for worship. We depend on one another for help. We'll look to the Lord for guidance instead of just Wilhelm."

"We might have baptisms and communion," Karl Ruge said.

"Without Father Keil, we have no leader for those," Mary said.

"We didn't do it when we did have a leader," Sebastian reminded her. He didn't even seem surprised that his wife spoke up in this gathering of women and men.

"*Ja,* by golly. We'll celebrate the sacraments as they did in the early church," Karl Ruge said, clapping his hands. "We'll share the duties and the joys together."

"We can begin with my Elizabeth and your Catherina," Mary said. "We have a christening to look forward to. Maybe we can invite Sarah and Sam."

Christian then brought out a basket of oysters, and the men with their knives cut the membranes to open the shells. "Show me," I asked Christian. "I want to be able to do that."

He stood behind me and placed his warm hands around mine. I could feel the heat of his chest as he leaned against my back. Then with the knife I held, his hand clasped over mine, we sawed back and forth until the oyster shell cracked and I could twist it open with the tip of my knife. Inside was the white flesh of the oyster, moist and lying like a shimmering jewel on the half shell. And in the corner was a surprise: the tiniest gem, a pearl.

It was more the color of earth than ivory.

"Indeed. Did you know that pearls come from irritations, from something like sand gritting its way into the oyster, and it wants to get it out? It forms this shell within a shell," Christian said. "A little protective covering to keep the sand from doing damage to the oyster. In the end, it gets picked up for its singular beauty and becomes more a part of the world than it ever imagined." He was already becoming an expert on his new calling.

I had known. But this first pearl my husband gave me marked a new beginning in our lives, one I'd thought might never come about. My husband leaned on his faith and his family just a little more than he ever had before.

Best of all, when I later placed that little pearl on the thread of the dozen pearls of my mother's and hung it openly at my neck, I knew it would always stand out as unique and singular, though clearly, it belonged.

READERS GUIDE

1. How would you characterize the role of women within the Bethel Colony? What changes occurred in the Willapa Valley that redefined the role of the women there? Who or what brought about those changes?

2. It's said that feeling unique and being acknowledged for that uniqueness is a prerequisite for a healthy sense of self. Do you agree or disagree? Can you identify something that is unique about you? Has that gift/talent/behavior ever been noticed by others? Is receiving appreciation for that recognition an act of vanity? What was unique about Emma?

3. After their marriage, why didn't Emma attempt to go with her husband on his recruiting into Kentucky or other places in the Southwest? If she had, would that have changed her desire to go west with the scouts?

4. Was Emma's decision to travel to the west with the scouts an act of love for her husband or the result of her own wish to be independent of the colony? Was she a scout?

5. What were some of Wilhelm Keil's strengths as a leader? How did he hold so large a colony together for such a long time? What were his flaws as a leader?

6. What did Wilhelm and Emma have in common? Did those qualities tend to help them or get in the way of what they said they wanted for themselves and their families?

7. What were some of Emma's growing pains? Was leaving her husband while they were building that first winter her only

choice? How might she have accomplished the same result with different actions?

8. What do you think the German proverb "Begin to weave / God provides the thread" means?

9. What tied the Bethel Colony together? What held the Willapa scouts together? What threats worked against the success of the Willapa Colony? Are there similar threats to communities of faith today? What helps them continue on?

10. Are there any parallels in our contemporary time to what Emma refers to when she says, "It was an intricate task blending isolation with protection, melding worldliness with spiritual calm"?

11. What was the Diamond Rule practiced by the Bethel Colony? Is such a rule substantiated scripturally for Christians? other world faiths? Did Wilhelm Keil demonstrate the Diamond Rule in his reaction to the scouts at Willapa?

12. Did Emma manipulate Christian to remain in Willapa? Was her interest in staying on after their harsh winter an act of love for her husband, a desire to be free of the colony, or from a new belief that she followed God's direction for her life? Do you think Emma would have remained in Willapa without Christian if he hadn't agreed with the possibilities of her plan?

13. Why did Christian concur with Wilhelm about the need to leave the valley? What made Christian change his mind? Are there likely to be conflicts between Emma and Christian in the years ahead, and if so, what do you think will enable them to accommodate each other in helpful ways?

14. Though we see the other women in this story through the eyes of Emma, what are Mary's strengths? Sarah's? Louisa's? Emma's mother's? her sister Catherine's? Do these women change

throughout the story, or are they static characters acting as backdrops for Emma's choice and change?

15. Toward the end, the author has Emma identify four spiritual pains* that she sees plaguing her husband, keeping him from seeking healing solace and from making the choice that Emma hopes he will: hopelessness, unforgiveness, separation from those who love him, and lack of meaning. What examples of Christian's behavior does the reader have that help define these four areas of Christian's struggle? How does Emma attempt to help him throughout their marriage?

*These four spiritual pains are described in greater detail in Richard Groves and Henriette Anne Klauser, *The American Book of Dying, Lessons in Healing Spiritual Pain* (Berkeley, CA: Celestial Arts, 2005).

ACKNOWLEDGMENTS

While I alone am responsible for this story and its speculations and errors, I could not have come close to authenticity without the help of many. I gratefully acknowledge the help of director Bruce Weilepp and other members of the Pacific County Historical Society in South Bend, Washington, for their assistance in gathering material about the early colony. Bruce's enthusiasm for my fictionalizing this story was of great support in the early collecting of information. It was while visiting the museum in South Bend and touring the old sites—Willie's grave, Old Willapa, and other Territory places—that I also found James G. Swan's book written in 1857, which provided detailed information about life during Emma's time.

I give special thanks to Erhard Gross of Astoria, Oregon, who not only offered specific advice about the flora and fauna of the Pacific Coast country, but walked me through the German language used in this story. He conferred with me about the nature of such a German society in the middle 1800s in America, and his careful reading of an advanced copy and his conversations with me about the role of women and religion and Christianity were always thought-provoking and appreciated, as were the conversations and fine German meals prepared by his wife and my friend, Elfi, at their bed-and-breakfast.

James J. Kopp, PhD, director of Aubrey R. Watzek Library at Lewis and Clark College and a scholar of utopian societies, made himself accessible for a variety of questions about community and specifically the Aurora settlement. He has a special interest in Aurora, is a board member of the Old Aurora Colony Museum and Aurora Historical Society, and lives in Aurora. I am especially grateful for his index of material, his willingness to spend time with me to explore the archives, and for his kind speculation with me about the lives of women at Bethel, Willapa, and Aurora.

I thank as well the Aurora Colony Historical Society for their maintaining of the facility where I've spent many days as a tourist hearing the stories, seeing the quilts, and wondering what life back then was really like, long before Emma's story called my name. I give special thanks to Alan Guggenheim, director of the Old Aurora Colony Museum, and his staff, board, and volunteers, especially Irene Westwood, for allowing me access to archival material and making me feel welcome even while they prepared for their annual quilt show at the museum and for the sesquicentennial celebration of the beginning of the Aurora Colony scheduled for 2006.

David and Pat Wagner opened their family files, and I am deeply indebted to their kindness and their passion for history. Annabell Prantl, author and historian, deserves thanks for locating several articles from the Marion County Historical Society in Salem, Oregon, and providing them to me. As an octogenarian, she is an inspiration and encouragement to my work and has connections to Pacific County.

Karla and Peter Nelson of Time Enough Books in Ilwaco, Washington, offered assistance about Pacific County and life in that landscape, including oystering, as well as reading an advanced copy of *A Clearing in the Wild*. They also obviously love books, something else we hold in common, and they understand the beauty of the landscape despite its demands.

The Fort Steilacoom Historical Society provided important information, as did the Steilacoom Historical Society. I'm especially grateful to Susan and Milt Davidson of Steilacoom for meeting me at the museum on a blustery Sunday afternoon and answering questions and "speculating" with me.

I thank Blair Fredstrom, who used her days to search genealogy connections, and for being willing to explore with me the lives of strong women and their challenges in territorial times. I thank Sandy Maynard for helping me type when I broke my arm early in the writing of this book and her later support during the deaths and illnesses that challenged the telling of this story. Carol Tedder is a prayer partner extraordinaire, and I have "groupies" who appear to help me at the most need- ful times. They are angels each one, and I thank them.

To my writing team in Oregon, Washington, Wisconsin, Pennsylvania, and Florida and at WaterBrook Press, a special thanks for your support and encouragement and prayers, especially during the writing of this book. You all know who you are and why you are appreciated so much.

A special acknowledgment goes to readers everywhere who find these stories and allow them to nurture them. Thank you for sharing with me through your letters, e-mails, and presence at events how these stories have touched your lives. I thank you for carrying me and these stories in your hearts.

Finally, to Jerry for his patience, his love of history, his mapmaking, and his willingness to live for twenty-nine years with a girl of German descent who some might say is both stubborn and strong-willed: Thank you. You are my clearing in this world's wild.

Jane Kirkpatrick

Suggested Additional Resources

Allen, Douglas. *Shoalwater Willapa*. South Bend, WA: Snoose Peak Publishing, 2004.

Arndt, Karl J. R. *George Rapp's Harmony Society 1785–1847,* rev. ed. Cranbury, NJ: Associated University Presses, 1972.

Barthel, Diane L. *Amana, From Pietist Sect to American Community.* Lincoln, Nebraska: University of Nebraska Press, 1982.

Bek, William G. "The Community at Bethel, Missouri, and Its Offspring at Aurora, Oregon" (Part 1). *German-American Annals,* vol. 7, 1909.

———. "A German Communistic Society in Missouri." *Missouri Historical Review.* October, 1908.

Blankenship, Russell. *And There Were Men.* New York: Alfred A. Knopf, 1942.

Buell, Hulda May Giesy. "The Giesy Family." *Pacific County Rural Library District,* memoir. Raymond, WA, 1953.

———. "The Giesy Family Cemetery." *The Sou'wester.* Pacific County Historical Society, vol. 21, no. 2, 1986.

Cross, Mary Bywater. *Treasures in the Trunk: Memories, Dreams, and Accomplishments of the Pioneer Women Who Traveled the Oregon Trail.* Nashville: Rutledge Hill, 1993.

Curtis, Joan, Alice Watson, and Bette Bradley, eds. *Town on the Sound, Stories of Steilacoom.* Steilacoom, WA: Steilacoom Historical Museum Association, 1988.

Dole, Phillip. "Aurora Colony Architecture: Building in a Nineteenth-Century Cooperative Society." *Oregon Historical Quarterly,* vol. 92, no. 4, 1992.

Dietrich, William. *Natural Grace: The Charm, Wonder and Lessons of Pacific Northwest Animals and Plants.* Seattle: University of Washington Press, 2003.

Duke, David Nelson. "A Profile of Religion in the Bethel-Aurora Colonies." *Oregon Historical Quarterly,* vol. 92, no. 4, 1992.

Ficken, Robert E. *Washington Territory.* Pullman, WA: Washington State University Press, 2002.

Gordon, David G., Nancy Blanton, and Terry Nosho. *Heaven on the Half Shell: The Story of the Northwest's Love Affair with the Oyster.* Portland, OR: Washington Sea Grant Program and WestWinds Press, 2001.

Hendricks, Robert J. *Bethel and Aurora: An Experiment in Communism as Practical Christianity.* New York: Press of the Pioneers, 1933.

Keil, William. "The Letters of Dr. William Keil." *The Sou'wester.* Pacific County Historical Society, vol. 28, no. 4, 1993.

Nash, Tom, and Twilo Scofield. *The Well-Traveled Casket.* Eugene, OR: Meadowlark, 1999.

Nordhoff, Charles. *The Communistic Societies of the United States.* New York: Hillary House, 1960.

Olsen, Deborah M. "The *Schellenbaum:* A Communal Society's Symbol of Allegiance." *Oregon Historical Quarterly,* vol. 92, no. 4, 1992.

Simon, John E. "William Keil and Communist Colonies." *Oregon Historical Quarterly,* vol. 36, no. 2, 1935.

Strong, Charles Nelson. *Cathlamet on the Columbia.* Portland, OR: Holly Press, 1906.

Swan, James G. *The Northwest Coast or Three Years' Residence in Washington Territory.* Harper and Brothers, 1857.

Swanson, Kimberly. " 'The Young People Became Restless:' Marriage Patterns Before and After Dissolution of the Aurora Colony." *Oregon Historical Quarterly,* vol. 92, no. 4, 1992.

Synder, Eugene Edmund. *Aurora, Their Last Utopia, Oregon's Christian Commune, 1856–1883.* Portland, OR: Binford and Mort, 1993.

Weathers, Larry, ed. *The Sou'wester.* South Bend, WA: Pacific County Historical Society, 1967, 1970, 1972, 1974, 1979, 1986, 1989, 1993.

Will, Clark Moor. "An Omnivorous Collector Discovers Aurora!" *Marion County History, School Days I, 1971–1982,* vol. 13, Marion County Historical Society, 1979.

———. *The Sou'wester.* Several letters between descendant Will and Ruth Dixon, plus notations, essays, correspondence, and drawings of the Old Aurora Colony Museum, Aurora, Oregon. Raymond, WA: Pacific County Historical Society collection, May 29, 1967.

BOOK TWO

A Tendering in the Storm

a novel

To the descendants
of Emma Wagner Giesy.

CAST OF CHARACTERS

AT WILLAPA BAY

Emma Wagner Giesy	German American living in Willapa Bay area of Washington Territory
Christian Giesy	Emma's husband and former leader of scouts
Andrew "Andy" *Catherina "Kate"* *Christian* *Ida*	Emma's children
Sebastian "Boshie" and Mary Giesy	one of Christian's brothers and his wife
Louisa Giesy	youngest sister of Christian, sixteen years old
Martin Giesy	a future pharmacist and one of Christian's brothers
John and Barbara Giesy	one of Christian's brothers and sister-in-law
Rudy, Henry, and Frederick Giesy	Christian's brothers
Andreas and Barbara Giesy	Christian's parents
Karl Ruge	German teacher, remained a Lutheran
Joe Knight	oysterman and former scout
Sam and Sarah Woodard	settlers at Woodard's landing
Jacob "Jack" or "Big Jack" Giesy	a distant cousin of Christian's
Wagonblast family	German Americans traveling to the Bay with Keil, not members of the colony

AT BETHEL

David and Catherina Zundel Wagner   Emma's parents

David Jr.   Emma's siblings
Catherine "Kitty"
Johanna
Louisa "Lou"
William

Andreas "Andrew" Giesy Jr.   one of Christian's brothers; physician and codirector of Bethel Colony in Keil's absence

August Keil   one of Wilhelm and Louisa Keil's sons, sent to assist with colony business

AT AURORA MILLS

Wilhelm Keil   leader of Aurora Mills, Oregon, Colony

Louisa Keil   Wilhelm's wife
Willie   their deceased son, buried in Willapa
Gloriunda   their daughter
Aurora   their daughter
Amelia   their daughter
five other Keil children

Jonathan Wagner   one of Emma's brothers
Helena Giesy   one of Christian's sisters
*Margaret   a woman of the colony
Nancy Thornton   painter in the Oregon City area

* not based on a historical character

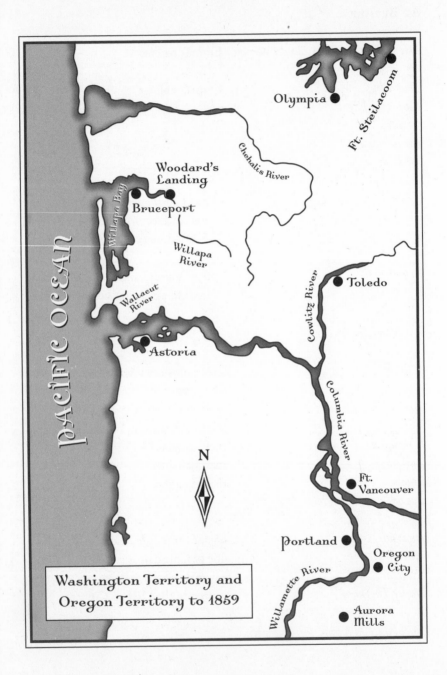

Pacific Ocean

Olympia

Ft. Steilacoom

Chehalis River

Woodard's
Landing

Bruceport

Willapa Bay

Willapa
River

Wallacut
River

Toledo

Cowlitz River

Astoria

Columbia River

N

Ft.
Vancouver

Portland

Oregon
City

Willamette River

Aurora
Mills

Washington Territory and
Oregon Territory to 1859

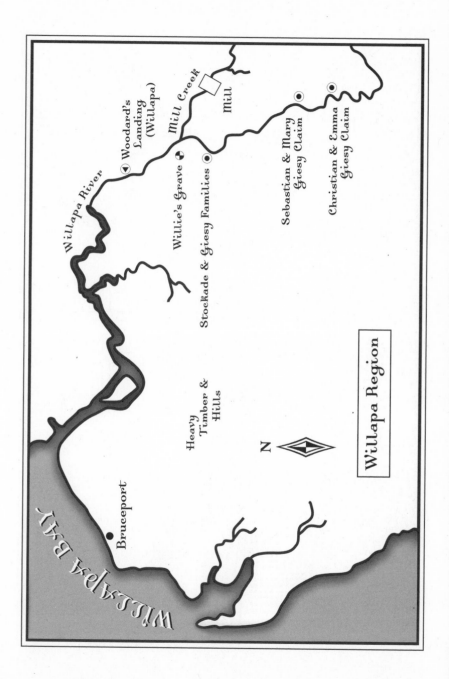

Willapa Region

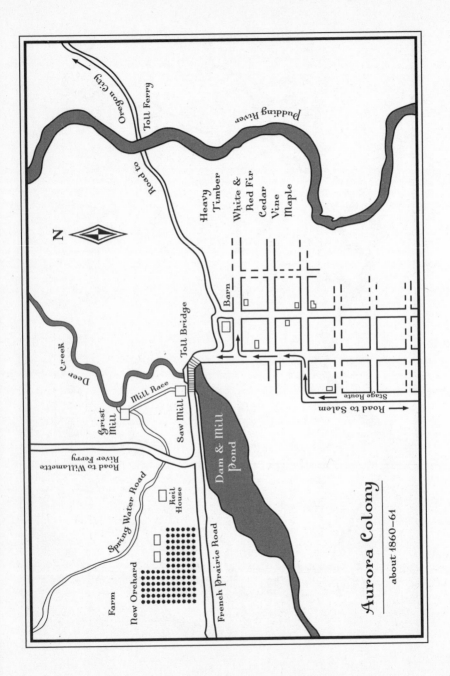

Aurora Colony

about 1860–61

We cannot kindle when we will
The fire that in the heart resides,
The spirit bloweth and is still,
In mystery our soul abides.
MATTHEW ARNOLD

Who is among you that feareth the LORD, that
obeyeth the voice of his servant, that walketh in darkness, and hath no light? let him trust in the name of
the LORD.... Behold, all ye that kindle a fire, that
compass yourselves about with sparks: walk in the
light of your fire, and in the sparks that ye have kindled. This shall ye have of mine hand; ye shall lie
down in sorrow.
ISAIAH 50:10–11

But if we walk in the light, as he is in the light, we
have fellowship one with another.
1 JOHN 1:7

Grace strikes us when we are in great pain and rest-
lessness. It strikes us when we walk through the dark
valley of a meaningless and empty life.
It strikes us when we feel that our separation is deeper
than usual.... Sometimes at that moment a wave of
light breaks into our darkness, and it is as though a
voice were saying: "You are accepted."
PAUL JOHANNES TILLICH
in *The Shaking of the Foundations*

Prologue

The light of the whale-oil lantern I hold above my head fans out across the darkened beach like the tail fins of a dog salmon. I can only see what the arc of light unveils; beyond, all is black. A tiny crab startles at my feet. Tree roots of once noble firs have fallen and been tossed against the shore like the sticks my Andy uses for his sword play. Their roots, like knurled knuckles, reach out to me, then disappear as I pass by them in the night. It's as though they seek me out of darkness. That's an illusion, for I move toward them carrying the lantern Christian made for me, and they lie there still but for the brush of salty breeze lifting sand against their barren roots. It's me who advances and then passes on by, darkness closing in behind me on the scent of loam and sea.

Though I cannot see the gentle waves pushing across the shoals on Willapa Bay, I know the tide line by the sound. I hear the lap of water and watch as some small bird flies through my arc of light. I know the sea is there and in the daylight I will find it once again, but it will look so different. This is the promise of a night walk on the beach, this, and that my light might shine upon some treasure, glass jars blown by hands and mouths a thousand miles away, arrived here whole, despite a shipwreck, glowing green beneath my fleeting light. I look for that. Something to remind me of the treasures of my days. Something to remember that is a joy instead of the times I stumbled in the blackness with no hand to catch me while I fell.

"Let me hold the lantern higher for you," my husband says. "I'm taller, Emma. Let me be Luke, Bearer of Light."

"*Ach,* no," I tell him. "I want to do it by myself, see what my light uncovers from the darkness."

"*Ja,* it's what you do, Emma." He spoke from the blackness behind me. "One day, I pray you won't."

We return to the tent and our sleeping children.

I lie down beside my husband, find comfort in his brackish scent, a blend of oystering and mustache oil and sweat. In our closeness, he gives to me without regard for what I might give him back. He offers without obligation, without debt. That is perhaps the greatest gift of love. In it lies sweet shelter.

1

Emma

The Image of a Hinge

A quiet surf oozed around our wooden shoes as we inhaled the salt and sea of Washington's Willapa Bay. Beyond swirled the Pacific. I pulled my skirt up between my legs and tucked the hem into the waistline of my Sunday apron.

After months of having our days and nights and futures directed by *Herr* Keil, formerly of Bethel, Missouri, and now of...somewhere far away, I found that his departure from Willapa left a tear in our family's fabric. That surprised me. I suppose when one devotes outrage and anger toward a person and then they leave, well, then one has pent-up steam to let off. We must find new things to fill the space, or so I told my husband.

That's what we'd done this spring of 1856 in Washington Territory.

"What do we do first?" I asked our partner, Joe Knight. Joe, a former religious scout, had spent a year already in Bruceport on the Bay finding out about how one nurtured and protected oysters from starfish or drills or human thieves.

"Begin to see with new eyes. There," Joe said. He pointed with his finger. "Those red alder saplings I placed in the water. That marks our bed." He looked down at my clog-clad feet and shook his head. "You need boots," he said. "And you'll need to study the mud and sand. As the tide goes out, the mud can suck a grown man right in if he's not careful. Someone as little as you are, or the children…*ja,* well, they could sink to Beijing." He grinned, and might've been teasing, but I stepped back, putting my feet on solid wet sand.

"*Nein,*" my husband told him. "She has no need of boots. She's going up the Willapa River where she'll be safe."

"I could learn oystering," I defended.

"Emma, you agreed to remain with my parents until we build our house," my husband, Christian Giesy, said. I stared at piles of oysters in the distant sea. They reminded me of cobbled dirt in dark fields back in Missouri. "Indeed, *Liebchen,* that was a primary condition of my considering the possibilities in oystering, that you and the children will be safe."

I pouted, dug at the sand with my toes. I could see Indian women separating oysters in culling beds. The green crown of leaves topping their alder stakes fluttered in the breeze. It was May and no one was allowed to harvest again until September, but clumps of oysters still had to be broken apart so they could grow larger, stronger. "I just thought I could help," I said.

"You want to avoid living with my parents," he told me. *He knows me so well.*

Joe interjected then with oyster talk. The salty air brushed against my face as I listened, still holding my Kate. Our two-year-old Andy slapped at shoalwater pools with his hand and looked so sweet. "His hand is already tan as walnuts," Christian said, when I pointed with my chin toward our son. "Same color as your eyes and your hair. I'll miss seeing those every day."

"*Ja,* me too."

Joe cleared his throat. He spoke mostly English now, having learned it from his time in San Francisco. My husband bent his head to catch Joe's words over the loud calling of the seagulls fighting over clams or waiting for us to throw dried bread up to them.

"Charlie?" Andy pointed. I shook my head.

"During spawning," Joe continued, "the water'll be milky with the eggs and sperm of oyster beds. They're a saucy creature, they are." He looked at me, and I thought he blushed.

I surely didn't. These were necessary discussions of the natural way of things. Why was a woman expected to be protected from the lusts of life?

Herr Keil, our *former* religious leader, came to mind. In spite of his own prolific family-building—he had several children—he advised lives of celibacy for the rest of us. This complicated, I thought, his view that women are saved from damnation only when they bear children and have to endure the pain of Eve's sin. I doubted he'd thought of that contradiction as yet.

Ach, I must not let every thought come back to Keil!

I took a deep breath that pushed against my Kate. I rested my chin lightly on her bonneted head and watched an old woman scrub at the mud of an oyster in her lap. She wore a scarf around her full brown face that marked her as a Chinook or Shoalwater or even a Chehalis native. Something in the way she held herself promised strength if not wisdom too. Both were necessary to survive on this Bay.

Andy squatted at the tide pool, pulled at a starfish. He laughed as he plopped back onto the mud.

"There are four tides a day on this Pacific," Joe said. "Our work is dependent on being out there on the flats when the tide goes out and exposes the oysters. We break up the clusters. If there's an oyster ship awaiting, we pick the larger ones, toss them into baskets or bags and sail them out, and we've earned our wages. There are more oysters out farther, have to reach them by boat and bring them in closer to seed our beds. In the winter, you'll be working in darkness, so you best get that lantern of yours ready."

"Indeed," Christian said. "I've been meaning to make a tin cover for Emma's lamp, one where the wind can't ever blow out the light." He smiled at me, then brushed a wayward hair strand beneath my bonnet. Both the act and the look he gave me told me I was cherished.

I wanted to live with them in Bruceport, though it would mean close quarters along the beachfront, huddled in huts made of driftwood or maybe out on stilts built over the oyster beds. But I could cook for Joe and Christian and the children. Our family would be together. That's what I wanted.

But I had compromised. Anything to avoid going to Oregon with *Herr* Keil. I'd agreed to stay with the children miles away with the remainder of Christian's kin and the scouts. My in-laws would "look after me," as Christian put it. One day on the Willapa River, once we built it, I'd have a home to call our own. This was my desire, a home without a dozen other people in it. A dwelling, safe, filled with my family and only the things I treasured, safe from others telling us what to do or think.

"Best you ready yourself for the boat," Christian told us. Andy began dragging a very long, double fork–like tool, scraping it across the beach as though it were a boat in tow. Christian lifted it from him and the tongs stood on end at least two times the height of my husband, who was over six feet tall. The tool had a hinge to open the two forks.

"Works like a pincher, *ja*?" Joe said, as he reached with his thumb and middle finger to pretend to pinch at Andy's nose. My son giggled. "You'll get skilled enough using those tongs, Christian," Joe said. "As I steer our oyster boat, you'll stand on the bow and with the tongs feel the bottom like you were searching for treasure. When you feel a clump, you close the hinge and pull them up and drop them in the basket in the boat."

Christian tried to open and close the long oyster tongs. "Like fishing in the dark," Christian said. He was awkward on land, and both he and Joe laughed.

"It'll come to you in time," Joe said. "Worst part will be learning to stand on the bow without slipping yourself into the Bay, though a salty bath will wake you up."

"Perhaps I should learn how to swim," Christian said. Joe hesitated but then chuckled, clapping Christian on the back.

"That's a good one," Joe said. "*Ja*, that's a good one."

I'd remember that day later, hold it to me like a hug that time permits to bring one warmth. My husband and I began a new adventure, one not sanctioned by the infamous *Herr* Keil. The tools of our new trade were long tongs and sailboats. It was a new way of tendering through life's storms, and I was hopeful despite my disappointment.

———

"We've weathered the biggest storm of 1856," Christian told me as we walked back toward the shoreline. His arm wrapped around me while tide-water unveiled its treasures. Wet sand clung to our wooden shoes. Our son chased after quick-footed birds. A skiff of wind lifted our son's little flat hat, and Christian took two steps in his brogans to retrieve it. "I'm not a rich oys-terman yet, *Junge*," he told Andy, tapping the hat onto his head. "So hold on to this."

My husband's reference to the storm referred not to the great western winds that blustered in off the Pacific Ocean and toppled trees, leaving them crisscrossed on the forest floor. My Swiss-born husband wasn't even talking about the martial law imposed in the Territory by Governor Stevens, meant to protect us from the Indians. No, my husband referred to the turbulence that brewed and bubbled then settled after it tore our colony of Christian believers in two and nearly splintered our marriage as well. It was the "bread of adversity" and "the water of affliction" as Scripture notes it that Christian and I, Emma Wagner Giesy, his wife, had weathered.

My husband, a tall man (I barely reached his chest) with a compassionate heart, once shared in the leadership of our colony of one thousand Missouri Bethelites who planned to move the settlement to the Washington Territory. Instead, earlier this spring we severed our relationship with the mostly Ger-man members of the Bethel colony who ventured west. The former scouts and many of my husband's fourteen brothers and sisters and their families stayed here. After our terrible winter when Keil refused us the use of ammu-nition to hunt, wanting it saved for "protection," Keil ordered many of the colonists not to come north from Portland. So I never even saw my brother, though he rode in Keil's wagon train. Keil barked his orders and the colony split. It was like chopping willows at the root base.

A few noncolonists chose to settle in our Willapa Hills and Valley. A family named Wagonblast had joined up with Keil at St. Joseph, Missouri, and remained at the Willapa, their young children right now probably playing jack stones, oblivious to the anxieties of their elders. Karl Ruge, an old teacher who'd been faithful to *Herr* Keil though he remained a Lutheran, stayed. I was glad for it. I found comfort watching Karl smoke his three-foot-long clay pipe with its wide bowl that curved up like an elbow. The smoke swirled around his stringy beard, lifting like mist to the cedars above. Karl loved words and read books without apologizing, so at the very least, our children would have an education beyond *Herr* Keil's Bible or teaching of practical things, "useful reading" Keil called it. Karl's presence gave me reason to hope such education would include my daughter Kate one day, and not only my son. Without the colony rules to shape us, everything would be new. Or so I hoped.

One other Giesy named Big Jack, a distant cousin of my husband's, traveled around the Isthmus of Panama to settle here too, where the timber towers and the blackberry brush tangles. Big Jack chose the Giesy name, I'm told, to start anew. His arrival in Willapa caused a storm. But that's a story better left for later.

I loaded the children onto the mail boat going upriver with the incoming tide. We'd been apart before in our marriage, when my husband recruited for new colony members. But I'd grown accustomed to his snores, his pushing-ups each morning, his mustache-covered kisses smelling of earth and onion every day, and I would miss him. *Keil is the fault of all this separation.* Ach! *My life must not always come back to Keil.*

But perhaps once one has given their all, foolishly even, as *Herr* Keil would put it, to a grand dream, then abandoning what we'd done here and turning back would be…a violation of that pioneering spirit. To "listen to reason," as our colony leader said, and follow him to Oregon would remind us always of the months and years we put into readying this place for others, believing we were in the palm of God's hand. To leave would make us ever regretful. Or so we told ourselves that spring.

It takes time for the mind to swing upon a different hinge.

We're a hopeful people, we Swiss and Germans, and faithful and perhaps dreamers too, or we never would have journeyed west at all. We heeded the *Sehnsucht,* that great yearning, rather than remain in the warmth of our brick Bethel houses with readied fireplaces and streets with sturdy names like King and Elm. We gave up living close to bustling cities like Hannibal and Independence. Instead, we live isolated—fifteen river miles from the vast Pacific Ocean.

It was my plan that convinced my husband to try oystering. It was a kind of farming, though of the sea instead of land. Farming was something we knew about. Christian had been a tinsmith and recruiter, but in the colony we all set aside our various tasks to help with planting or weeding or harvest. We knew that farming required focus and effort. Risk pervaded farming, too, but with many hands helping, we could bring in a good harvest if the locusts or hailstorms didn't get it first. But in Bethel, even if we lost the harvest or it was poor, we would still be fed. For whatever anyone earned making gloves or wagons or cloth or preserves went into a common fund. Then whatever we needed we were allowed to take out. We cared for others, served up the Diamond Rule, making others' lives better than our own. But we owned not a thing in our names. It was all in Keil's name. I think that's one of the things that turned Keil off of Willapa: he wanted all land to be his.

Here, because of donation land claims, Christian and I had land in our names, as did his parents and brothers. But we didn't have the security that if a crop failed we might still eat, unless we leaned on our neighbors or found some other way to live.

Our leader said we'd made him broke almost, buying up land claims when we could have gotten free land in a more forgiving landscape. Worse, he claimed we'd been unfaithful, hadn't listened to the calling of our God, and that was why we'd had such a trial here attempting to build our homes, clear ground, survive the wailing winters.

I think that hurt my husband most, the suggestion that his faith wasn't strong enough to stave off suffering and loss. I remembered once Keil saying Brother John Will back in Bethel lacked faith enough for Keil to heal his tailor's arm. In the church, Keil upbraided him for this weakness. That very day, Brother Will hanged himself for failing Keil, and our leader chastised him even then, saying his arm could not sew but it could work well enough to bring on his death. I feared such might happen to my husband if we had stayed in the shadow of Keil.

We'd been sent to find a place of isolation so that our children would not be influenced by the outside un-Christian world; to find timber and a place where one could sell our produce, our furniture, our milk and cheese, and our wagons to others as we had in Bethel. Our choices required a delicate balance, weighing safety and isolation with survival and success through commerce with the outside world.

I'd found my place in this Willapa country. I recognized wild celery now and knew how to prepare it. I located *wapato,* Indian potatoes, and knew how to cook them. While at the beach, I watched as the Shoalwater people collected clams, raking at the sandy dimples that signaled a clam's presence. They dug pits and heated stones until the rocks glowed, then laid the clams on top of the stones, covered them with mats of weeds and grass, and watched the steam as the clam juice filtered down onto the hot rocks, the sizzle offering up a scent like the blacksmith's cooling of hot iron.

My friend Sarah Woodard, who lived with her husband at the landing, showed me how to strip wild raspberry roots to find that center as tender and tasty as a cucumber. We learned much from those outsiders, if we listened, watched. Keil didn't see this. He let the light of insight illuminate few of his dark thoughts.

Perhaps that's why in the end my husband agreed to try oystering. We hoped to prove that challenges are not necessarily God's punishment for disobedience. They do not mean one has erred. If we forge ahead, we'll still find blessings and new paths. That's what I told myself as I waved good-bye to him that day.

———

As I write this, years later, my youngest daughter, Ida, works at her school books. She asks me to explain the word *hinge,* using English. I'm not sure when she decided to speak just English, but it pleases me as a mark of her independence. I press my hand upon the circle of braids she wears at the top of her head and inhale the sweetness of her. I tell her first that a hinge is the thing that keeps the two sides of the oyster shell together, so what is inside may stay alive. She frowns. "It's the little piece of flesh that opens and closes, allowing the two sides to be a whole." Then I show her the top of Christian's lantern, how the hinge lets it open and close. She nods, returns to her writing, leaving me to ponder still.

A hinge is so much more. It divides two sides of a story. It is what separates mourning from joy, belief from aimlessness, surrender from independence. It's what holds those halves together. "A hinge is a circumstance upon which later events depend," I add, more for me than for Ida. Who could have known that day on the river how I'd soon long for the hinge of faith, and with it the hope that I'd once again find home.

2

Louisa

Before my husband received the call to prepare him to sit at the right hand of Jesus, he was a tailor.

It's fitting he was such, for tailors create and re-create. They stitch and mend and realign, ever mindful of the cloth, the thread, and the person who will wear the mantle on the body God prepared. Oh, I know my husband, Wilhelm Keil, does not truly create as God does. But God works through him, and he comes as close to our brother Jesus as any man can and still have his feet upon this earth. He chose me as his wife, kissed the part in my dark hair, never mentioned the tiny mole at the side of my face that I saw as imperfection. He chose me to be the mother of his children, and I am blessed to be his handmaiden. Well, hand*matron* I suppose I should say, though not to Dr. Keil, who might object to such musings on my use of words. It's why I write in this private little book the thoughts I'd not share with him.

Dr. Keil must not be distracted. We need his wisdom and his visionary sight. Our journey west from Bethel was a quilt requiring many stitches to hold it all together, and we're still sewing. He'll use whatever he must to be successful and to carry out his belief in what he is called to do.

Some years back, when he dabbled in the mystical, he wrote his formulas for healing in a book. He used his blood for ink. I did not know of this when I met him. A wife is not privy to a saint's workings, nor should she be.

Emma Giesy might take note of that. She's one who wants to know her husband's thoughts, and while her husband is not the leader that mine is, she will be challenged in how to be a good wife to one who is a lieutenant in God's army. What such leaders share with their wives are gifts we cannot ask for, nor do we deserve them when they arrive. We're to treat such secrets as fragile porcelain easily crushed. But my husband told me of that blood-lined book when he burned it and found his true calling in gathering disciples to him to live communally, each according to his need, each according to his gifts so all are loved and served as the book of Acts advises.

I write these words not in blood but blackberry-juice ink.

He receives no pay, my husband. In Pennsylvania, he once led a group of followers away from the American Methodist Evangelical Church when he learned they intended to pay their pastor four hundred dollars in annual wages. "Four hundred dollars!" he raged, and rightly so. No one should receive a salary for doing the Lord's work. God provides, for heaven's sake. The products of our hands and fields will fill the common purse, but this is the outcome of doing the Lord's work, and pay enough.

That's why we sell whiskey.

Yet he works so hard, has such responsibility for this flock now spread across two thousand miles from that desolate Willapa Valley to here in Portland, Oregon, and back to Bethel. We still have friends in Pennsylvania—Phillipsburg and Harmony—though my husband is no longer considered the head of those colonies, just the one in Bethel. Nearly one thousand people rely on his leadership and guidance. Only a quarter of us headed west last year. This was wise in retrospect as what awaited us was troublesome indeed. Still, the lack of full compliment worried my husband, I could tell. He mentioned often those left behind. Everyone wanted to come, he told me, but some had to be left behind to run the businesses until we are established here in the West. Andrew Giesy, Christian's brother, is a trustworthy man. He stayed behind to lead at Dr. Keil's request.

Others have waited to leave Bethel only because they want to come to a settled place. "Such little faith," my husband says. But I tell him, "It is evidence that we have too long been influenced by the world." We do need to find an isolated place where we can live without so many worldly things to compare ourselves with. To some, even among the Bethelites, we appear to lack, and yet we had sturdy homes, food enough for all, help when needed, and opportunity to work at many tasks, all in service to each other and our Lord.

But I've spied magazines with drawings of women wearing huge hats, the cost of which could feed a family for a week. I see them now on women who ride past in primitive carriages on the muddy streets of Portland. I watched when men rode into our old Bethel to buy up wagons, smoking their cigars. I do not mind the smoking. Tobacco comes from the land, so it is a gift from God. But their vests were draped with gold chains and watches they look at just for show as they stayed overlong, bothering the workers with their many questions, filling their heads with thoughts of fine horses and money for themselves. They don't watch the time. They take our men and women from their labors, so they do not seem to need their watches.

Yes, going west was good. The discussions before leaving energized the old and encouraged the young. I only wished we had all come. I miss David and Catherina Wagner and others whom I've served meals with at the *gross Haus*, our Elim. Such a lovely house. The Wagners sent their oldest son, and this was good. And they sent their daughter Emma, though I suspect that was a relief. She has such a willful way about her. She never would wear her hair with the part down the middle as I do, as most matrons of the colony who understand their place do.

What happened there in Willapa did nothing to change my mind about that woman's passion to be different. Christian Giesy is a good man, though I worried about his possible distraction with a young and spirited wife so close. My worries were well founded. They remain at Willapa, for now, which presents new challenges for my husband, all because the scouts did not do proper work. Or perhaps were all distracted by that Emma.

We sold colony property to raise funds for the journey west. My Willie and Jonathan Wagner prattled on at length about this grand adventure. Eighteen our Willie was when he died, and we carried him across the continent to bury him in Willapa, kept inside our Golden Rule Whiskey and lead-lined coffin. Friends suggested we make a barrel to place him in, but my husband insisted on the proper coffin.

To lose a child, well, what can be said to help a grieving mother? Willie longed for newness and change and so he has it now. I do not think this is anti-scriptural. After all, we went west at my husband's insistence, so it must be scriptural to make change.

I suppose Dr. Keil is not really the Lord's true brother, or else he'd be able to read my thoughts and know that I worry for our children's safety as we huddle in this thin wooden house in Portland in the Oregon Territory. I worry for my own safety too, and most of all for my husband. It is what a wife should do.

I miss Bethel but this is something I would never tell my husband. He has enough to worry over. Each day consists of his tending. His secretary, Karl Ruge, decided to remain at Willapa, an ache in my husband's side, of this I'm certain. There'll be few letters going back east now, at least until we have something more hopeful to say.

I must not let him think I feel hopeless, but I do. My son is dead. I live in someone else's house in a strange city where the smell of horse dung overpowers that of spring flowers. My children are hungry and must wait until the end of the day to see if someone in this West Coast Portland will pay me for my washing of their clothes, and then pay me correctly since I speak no English and wouldn't know. Or we wait to see if an ill person will feel well enough to pay Dr. Keil in grain or rubbery vegetables for his herbal treatments. He is such a wise and loving man and feels great weight that he could not rescue our son Willie from malaria. Now, I have little hope of even visiting his grave since we have separated from those at Willapa. I can only hope that maybe Christian's mother or John's wife will keep the grave up. I doubt Emma would even think of such a kindness.

Oh, I mustn't malign her. That's un-Christian of me. She has her own cross to bear with that willfulness of hers.

While I scrub on the washboard, I remember Willie. He was to ride in an ambulance on a small cot for comfort, and thus we planned to walk beside him. That's what *comfort* means in Greek, my husband tells me, "to come along beside."

Willie begged us not to leave him behind. He could have stayed with the Wagners or a dozen other families and come with the group Dr. Keil hopes will come next year, when we are ready for them. Much depended on Christian's successes at Willapa and the returning scouts were all hopeful. So much timber, they said. We could have a mill in no time and sell the lumber easily.

I directed my daughter Amelia about which quilts to take, how to wrap some of our precious things like dishes in the flour barrels. They weren't fancy dishes. We kept a separate barrel for Dr. Keil's glass cups in which he mixes herbs. Gloriunda and Louisa, my namesake—well, a portion of my namesake—brought clothes to show me and I'd nod, leave or take. My parents named me Dorothea Elizabeth Louisa Ritter, but Dr. Keil preferred Louisa and so that's what I'm called, my daughter too, for the Prussian queen, our beloved queen.

There was so much to sort through. It's all still packed in barrels. We're still not home.

"God heals," Dr. Keil says. I know that is so. Didn't my husband heal me of a weak leg? I limp some, but the leg is healed. My faith was enough to heal. I didn't want to remember Brother Will's death.

One never knows how another will respond to such deep and separating grief even when one has lived with the other for more than twenty years. My husband believes that deaths of children are a mark of sinfulness of the parent. My heart pounded at Willie's deathbed while I waited for Dr. Keil to turn to me and ask, "What have you done?"

Those were God's very words to Eve.

I'd heard my husband ask a grieving mother this; listened while a father wept in search of what sins he'd committed that had fallen onto his own flesh and blood. My husband would take those parents in his wide arms, both pulled into his woolen vest, and beg God's forgiveness for what neither of them could name. And they would go away, those parents, adding guilt to grief. They never heard a sermon letting them believe that God's lap was large enough to take them in, sin and all, and give them rest. My husband never failed those parents, exactly. He didn't continue to rail against their sinful ways, but he did agitate them, I believe, especially when they could never find the cause, or when they had trouble imagining a God who would punish an innocent over the foul acts of the innocent's elders.

I'd done nothing wrong, nothing I could remember. My husband was perfect, called so by God to lead us all. So where did that leave us with this gaping hole of pain that had once been a mother's heart meant to love a son? Dr. Keil says there can be no pain without sin, no suffering without evil.

With Willie's death, I prayed that Dr. Keil would find another way to hear the Word, some other understanding than that if a child dies it is because a parent sinned. I wanted my grief and Willie's death to lessen another mother's pain, not add to it.

I waited for his charge, but none came. He shook his head as though he couldn't understand it. I could. Life and death are tethered together. That I understood didn't mean I wished it wasn't so.

———

All that was one year past. I spent the anniversary of my son's death scrubbing clothes of people I didn't know. I wanted someone to talk to, to share my grieving with, but Dr. Keil did not speak of Willie once we buried him at

Willapa. It's not good for a mother to weigh her daughters down with her grief. And so I held it to myself, wondering if the time would come when we'd be living closely again with other colony members, close enough that we shared our meals, and expressions of grief could be shown in between the slicing of potatoes and the serving of our men.

"Ah, Emma," I said out loud, "I hope you're strong."

The thought surprised.

It is time I stopped my writing in this diary and look instead to the comfort of my children and their father. Tending to each other is how we'll all survive. Dr. Keil has found a site not far from Portland where he says we will eventually move, all of us, even those in Willapa. He calls it Aurora Mills, for our daughter. I want to celebrate my lovely, patient, faithful daughter's having a town named for her, such a sign of fatherly affection. But I feel a mother's regret for her too. There is much weight carried in a name. If things do not succeed, well, she will bear that weight.

Ah, these are unfaithful thoughts. Of course Aurora Mills will succeed. It is my husband's following of God's plan. It must succeed: my daughter's name is attached to it.

Still, if it does not, I'll tell my child that perhaps the town was named "Aurora" not so much for her but for the Latin word for *dawn*. There is always dawn even after the darkest nights.

3

Emma

No Sin to Stand Out

Christian's brothers, my brothers-in-law, were known to be good thinkers, hard workers, men who contributed well to the coffers of the common fund. Martin, with a penchant for healing herbs (not unlike our *Herr* Keil), lived with his parents along with Christian's sister, another Louisa, so my children and I got to know them best as that's where we boarded. The Wagonblasts without relatives here felt a bit lost. They left in the summer. I didn't know where they went.

Rudy and Henry came up from Portland next, staying with Mary and Sebastian (whom my son called Uncle Boshie) though the bachelors intended on building their own house. The brothers might have stayed with Christian's parents, but I was there. Associating with me, I suspected, was like spitting on the spider when it was still hot: people wanted to avoid the spray.

I hoped they'd work on our home but instead they began to build the mill along a little creek that flowed into the Willapa not far from the claim Christian and I had purchased.

Building the mill was quite an event. They split spruce for the walls and floors but ordered lumber for the second story and bins from a kind of tree called redwood that came all the way from California. John Giesy said the redwood formed ships' ballasts and would last forever and resist insects. My in-laws had brought the grist stones from Missouri and left them in San

Francisco, so a contingent sailed south in the summer to bring them north to install them in the mill. Boshie named the tributary Mill Creek, of course, though I was always partial to wondering what the natives might have called it. Names of places are important, I always thought, and *Mill Creek* lacks the particularity of a stream like the *Cowlitz*. Christian couldn't help much as he was busy oystering, but even Karl Ruge, the old teacher, augured holes for the pegs to keep the floor notched in place.

The mill rose up out of the blackberries and willows, topped the trees near the river, then formed a peaked roof with a window at the top. What a view there'd be from the mill. While I chomped at my bit so our house could be built, I knew that the community needed the mill, and I was pleased at least to be a part of the venture, offering my *Strudels* and *wapato* dishes to keep the men fed.

My brother Jonathan did not come to help with the mill, not even for a visit. Nor did Christian's distant relation Jack, who'd headed for Portland within days after his arrival. I'd have nothing to tell my sister Catherine about him the next time I wrote. I was not sure where her curiosity about this Giesy cousin grew from, but each letter from her asked if I had seen him. He was much too old for Catherine. The Giesy brothers said Jonathan and Big Jack were busy helping to build at Aurora and making cider vinegar. *Herr* Keil already had an industry going from those bushels of apples he'd purchased. He turned the skins into cider to sell back to the Willamette Valley settlers for twice what he'd paid them for the apples. *Shrewd* would be a word for him. Christian would say *inventive*.

Martin brought a comfort, though. My own supply of herbs had been used up the past two winters, and Martin shared his with me. I was grateful for the tansy that we hung near the food to keep the flies away. We spread some on the floor, too, and I think it kept out spiders, at least a bit. Martin didn't speak much to me, but he had Christian's gentle ways. He'd step aside if I came through the small room carrying Kate and even picked up the tin plates after a meal, washing them in the bucket—what they call pails here in the west—as though it wasn't a woman's task at all.

Karl Ruge and Mary Giesy and some of the others met on a clear Sunday morning at the stockade after the mill was finished. John Giesy said we'd use the stockade for a school too, but this day Karl read from Scripture mentioning the word *Andrew,* and my little Andy perked up at the sound of his name. It was a good gathering time of worship and expressions of gratitude. I missed Christian most during these times. I could always stare at him on the men's side if the messages bored. His absence made me impatient for his presence.

Afterward, we sat in the shade watching while the men took turns splitting cedar bark into shingles we'd use to roof our houses and replace those leaking canvas tarps.

"Keil's not building his house yet in Aurora," Rudy told us. "He sent a dozen men and one woman to cook for them out to Aurora Mills, but that *gross Haus* will be temporary. It'll be big and the bachelors and some of the families can come out and start laying up houses on the property. Get a store going so we can bring neighbors in to sell to them and meet our own needs too."

One woman. I wondered who she was and whether, like me, Keil had sent her out as punishment for being independent, though I turned that into triumph.

"Doesn't he fear people will want to stay in Portland, maybe not follow him to Aurora?" I asked.

"Nein," Rudy said. He stopped to wipe his brow of sweat. Karl Ruge motioned for the frow, offering to give Rudy a break, but John Stauffer, one of the scouts, stepped in to spell him. I handed Rudy a tin of water. He drank his fill.

"Ja, he waits until he has his usual comforts, I suppose," I said under my breath. Then louder, "He wouldn't want to be there to encourage the flock or

gain an understanding of the time and effort that such building of a community takes. It might change his mind about building a colony from scratch."

"*Ach,* don't talk so dumb," my father-in-law told me. His words stung. "He knows about building up colonies from Pennsylvania to Missouri and now here."

"Not here," I said.

"He went to Aurora Mills for the Fourth of July celebration," Rudy noted. "Most everyone from Bethel traveled out from Portland to see where one day soon they'd be living. Our band played." He said "our band" as though we were still a part of it. "They had good food and dancing. A hearty time."

I felt a pang of something. Regret?

"Next year we'll have such a celebration here," I said. "With steaming *wapato* mixed with herbs."

"There were speeches, too," Frederick told us, "about the candidates for the presidential election and the locals, too." I'd forgotten there was to be an election, even one in this Territory too, I supposed, though I didn't know who might challenge whom. I wondered what Christian thought about the candidates. Martin added that the group learned news of a man named John Brown and a war that people called "Bleeding Kansas" and the repeal of our Missouri Compromise, meaning slaves' lives were still in peril.

Martin spoke as though he didn't want to upstage his older brothers. "It was good we left Missouri. Things will get worse there."

"Not so sobering now, Martin. Talk about the good things," Rudy said.

"Like my John being named school superintendent," my sister-in-law cooed. I didn't even realize there'd been an election for that.

"*Ja, ja,*" Henry said. "Or that Christian has been named a territorial marshal. From all that fuss in the stockade, we hear."

"He earned top votes as the territorial representative, too," John said. "Twenty-two votes."

This was news to me too, that Christian had been given some sort of commission, an important job in the Territory, been elected a representative, and I'd known nothing about it. He'd been named a justice of the peace the first months after we were in Willapa and even made Sarah and Sam Woodard's common-law marriage official, but at least he'd told me about that.

"When did—"

"It was a festive time, that Fourth of July." Rudy said, taking the topic elsewhere. He laughed with a high-pitched giggle and began rocking back and forth on the balls of his feet in preparation for a story. "That Big Jack," he shook his head as though indulging a teasing toddler, "he gets himself some fireworks, *ja*? We don't any of us know where he got them, but he sets the fireworks up behind the privy and waits. He might have had a pint or two of our whiskey behind there with him, you know Jack. Well, he peeks around and sees one of the girls go inside. He lets her settle down like a hen on her nest, and then he counts and sets the flame. What an explosion! It nearly caught the grass on fire, and it sent all the blackbirds in the oak tree flying up in a squawking haunt. Such a laugh we got from that: the noise, the birds, the girl squealing." He shook his head, still smiling. "And then her charging like a bull through the door with her drawers lassoed around her ankles so tight she fell on her face." He slapped his knee with glee.

"That doesn't sound very funny to me," I said. I held a yarn ball for Kate to grab for as she sat on my lap.

"Big Jack didn't think it was funny neither, because he got tangled up in some blackberry vines trying to come out and watch what was happening. He ended up stuck behind the privy and never even saw the fuss. He just doesn't always think things through, that Jack. And she wasn't that hurt, Emma." Rudy chuckled, then took the frow back from John. I watched my mother-in-law shake her head with a smile on her face.

"Well I hope she was all right," Mary said.

"Martin gave her some bee balm tea to relieve her nausea—"

"And her flatulence," Rudy joked.

Henry ignored his brother's interruption. "And the borage compress Dr. Kiel made for her relieved the swelling on her chin."

"Lucky she didn't have her tongue between her teeth when she fell," Rudy said. "She'd have ended up as the silent Schwader girl!"

"At least she has teeth. Those apples Keil bought helps with that." Henry wiggled what looked like a loose tooth.

"And Dr. Keil was there to fix things," Martin said. "He's a great, good man whose timing is divinely apportioned."

Divinely apportioned? Martin's declaration of adoration of Keil made me look twice at him. Maybe Big Jack wasn't the only Giesy who just didn't always think things through.

———

That autumn, we harvested the oats we'd planted. We winnowed the grain, then took the heads by mule to the mill, where Boshie ground it. Our first. Our own. We'd have to buy our wheat, though. The climate proved too cool too long to place our hope in raising wheat. Sarah said it rained ninety inches a year here. I couldn't imagine that was true. Still, it was strange to have grown our own sustaining food in Missouri. Not here. Oats might do. Maybe millet.

The men hunted together and we smoked venison and bear meat and salmon filleted on sticks the way we'd seen the Indians do it, but we did it on our own, all of it.

I suppose it's somewhat prideful to be always touting doing things without the help of others, but when one has been under the thumb of a leader strong as an oak but just as unbending, it's difficult to resist the celebration of what we accomplished without him. I couldn't remind Mary and the others enough that here we surrendered to no one.

Sometimes, when I heard the *we* and *us* of the Giesy brothers and his father talking about Keil's colony, I did wonder if they saw the colony as "separated" in the way I did. I kept my tongue quiet. I wished to avoid arguments while I lived under their roof. The Giesys, too, tended to ignore me unless I asked a direct question, even when we were gathered together for family meals. They weren't unkind, really. They treated women and children as grass beside a main trail; sometimes it got stepped on, but it didn't really matter to the journey.

Except where our oystering was concerned. My in-laws had strong opinions about that and expressed them. "Christian would do well to come back here and prepare his house and farm," my father-in-law intoned over gravy and beans, "instead of playing with the oysters. He receives a payment now, for his marshalling. He'll need to know what's happening here to best represent us in the territorial legislature. How can he meet those obligations while he is busy playing at sea farming?"

"Karl Ruge thought it a good idea," I defended. I stitched in the candlelight, kept my eyes to my work. "And this way he'll represent not just us Germans but others, too, when the legislature is in session." My husband was seen as a leader by those outside of the colony. Another reason for *Herr* Keil to want us to come back under his wing, no doubt.

"We Giesys belong to the soil."

"When was Christian named the marshal?" I asked.

"I'm surprised he didn't tell you," my mother-in-law said. "It was during the Indian scare, before we got here."

"Maybe he didn't tell me because he felt embarrassed that he was a marshal with a gun but not allowed to use it, not even for hunting," I said. "*Herr* Keil acted like the marshal."

"Christian has nothing to be ashamed of," my father-in-law said. His tone left no room for my reply that I hadn't said Christian should be ashamed at all, just embarrassed. Maybe to this family these were one and the same.

I looked over at Andy and wondered if as young as he was, he could sense the disapproval in his grandfather's voice.

"Oystering gives my husband a new pearl to seek," I said.

"A pearl he would not be looking for without the influence of his wife, *ja*?"

I knew he meant it as an insult but that isn't how I took it.

———

Even though my children and I stayed in the Giesy Place—what had once been the meager home Christian and I shared—and daily took tea with my in-laws and sewed while Andreas read the Bible each evening, we talked very little toward any topic that satisfied. I'd propose a question, about service for example, and how in the book of Luke, the apostle pointed out that John and Peter, two of the Lord's disciples, performed "women's work" by being sent to prepare the Passover meal and looking for a man carrying water.

"*Ach,*" Andreas scoffed. "He did not call it women's work."

"Well, no, but it must have been. Women usually prepared meals, and they always gathered at the wells getting water. That's where our Lord found them. Or they washed men's feet to be hospitable to guests, so they gathered water for that. Here, Sarah tells me that Indian men serve meals when guests come. And they handle canoes and help gather the food too, even though the women prepare it. I think that's very enlightened."

"Women's work is defined biblically," my father-in-law replied. He took a draw on his pipe. "Women are less able to perform heavier tasks or ones that require a weighty mind."

"Those water jugs must have been heavy. I certainly feel it in my shoulders when I carry the bucket from the river. And didn't women work together with the apostle Paul? I'm sure I read where he sends greetings to women who work with him, which couldn't mean just serving food *to* him. They studied with him. And isn't that what Mary and Martha argued about?"

"They serve the men," my mother-in-law cautioned. "That is what women do, and Martha was right to bring our Lord's attention to Mary's wishing to be like the men. Women need to know their place."

"But our Lord didn't chasten Mary. He told Martha not to complain. And then later we read about men helping with the water so—"

"Enough, Emma Giesy," Andreas said. The Swiss men always seemed to shout. He looked over his spectacles. "You don't want to set an argumentative example for your children." He nodded toward Andy, who watched me the way a blue heron studies fish.

Andreas was right about one thing: if Christian wasn't oystering, we'd be living in our own home now, and I'd be out from under the wary eyes of Andreas. Maybe Christian would take me with him to Olympia when the legislature was in session. Maybe that was why he hadn't told me about his election, because he knew I'd want to accompany him if we had no home of our own. Mary and Boshie's home had been finished first, then the mill, followed by harvest and then building a barn on the Giesy Place with stalls. We would milk cows there when someone went to Oregon to retrieve the cows that had been here before Keil himself sent them south. We needed hay storage as well and root cellars for our garden supply. And smokehouses for the meat. None of us wanted to repeat the winter we had just survived. We'd be better prepared and would use our ammunition for game when we needed, too. We weren't a colony but a community able to live separate lives.

———

In August, we women gathered up the mat grasses from the cattail flags. Mary and I loaded the bundles onto the mules and led the animals to Sarah Woodard's house at Woodard's Landing. Sarah knew how to make the mats, though first we'd strip the flags to dry them in the sun. "In the winter, when it's raining, we'll weave these," I told Mary as we walked along. "The Indians wrap belongings in them to keep things smelling fresh and dry, and they line their walls with them to help keep out the wind and rain, and they lay them over soft moss to sleep on. Sarah says they aren't as attractive to bugs as our feather mattresses."

Andy carried his own little bundle, and Kate rode like a veteran in the board I carried on my back. Mary's little one also rode on her back and we both giggled once when I said I wondered if we'd be mistaken for Indians walking single file along the path with babies on our backs. "Not likely," Mary said. "My straw-colored hair will give me away, and you're slender as a cattail. Most of the native women I've seen since we've arrived in this country are built of sturdier stock."

"I'm sturdy," I protested.

"In your mind, maybe." She crossed her eyes and I laughed.

"No, seriously, even if we look fragile, like Sarah does, we're still strong as oxen. You ask Sarah. She'll agree. It's something I've learned about myself since coming here. What we can do on the inside isn't always reflected by what's on the outside."

"Sounds like an oyster shell," Mary said, as we reached Sarah's and laid the bundles near their warehouse.

I laughed. "Women of Scripture were capable, and we can't look much different from them. They were small-bodied too. They must have had good minds to have even decided to follow our Lord in the first place, to take that risk of being ridiculed or even killed. What was on the inside wasn't reflected by what was on the outside." I settled that thought with a nod of my chin.

"You're not saying women were like the men who followed him, are you?"

"Don't you ever wonder that if we were made in God's image, man and woman, how then God must be like us, too, and not just like our men?"

Her eyes were as big as horse apples but I continued.

"I mean there's all that talk of blood in Scripture, and we women know about that, don't we? And we understand water and baptism, feeling like we'll die before we give birth."

Mary stopped in her tracks. "That's…repulsive," she said. "I could never imagine God as being…soft and…sideways, tricking people into things, without saying something outright, the way we women do. Or silly thinking. God's nothing like a woman."

"But that's just it, Mary. We aren't soft all the time or we'd never have survived last winter. You wouldn't have come across the plains pregnant with Elizabeth. And as for being sideways, well, think of scriptural Jacob who tricked his brother and his father. That's sideways thinking not left to women. And we wouldn't do it nearly as much if we could just be ourselves, nice and direct, without having to worry about offending the men. And silly? *Ach,* look at how we have to plan ahead and organize so our children are fed each day, or learn how to dye wool and spin it into clothing, or use the land to gather these very stalks so we can have mats to sleep on. We know how to live in…Eden. We've learned to read, even to speak another language. We're born with those abilities to learn. Don't you want Elizabeth to grow up feeling that she's as capable as any brothers she might have? I want that for Kate. I don't want her thinking she isn't as important as Andy."

"You better not let Andreas hear you spout such things," Mary said. Her voice shook. "Even if Christian lets you."

"Christian's never heard it before," I said. I took a deep breath and quieted my voice. "Sometimes I come to wisdom by saying thoughts out loud and I hear it myself for the first time, just when you're hearing it too."

"Oh, Emma," Mary laughed then. I know she thought I teased but to be certain, she added, "I think I'd keep that kind of talk buried inside your oyster shell." She tapped my head.

"You couldn't have said anything more uplifting to my soul, except for the part about having to keep it all quiet," I told her.

Christian and Joe both came from Bruceport, and along with his brothers, we all worked together to build my house at last. Our house, I knew, but it was difficult for me to think of "ours" knowing I'd be alone there with the children more often than not.

Even with the help, the construction still took two solid weeks.

Ours was a crude building, ten by fourteen feet with a loft and two cutouts for windows and, of course, a door facing east to catch the morning sun. The men pegged the cedar beams so the loft would be sturdy and a safe place for storage, and as our family grew, it could accommodate more feather ticks, mats, and children too. The scent of the beams would fill the house. We built a fireplace and cat-and-clay chimney so the loft would be warm in the winter. This was perhaps a luxury, but one we could build with the availability of more tools like the big auger that Rudy brought, which pegged the beams, and the frow with its slender blade set at a right angle to the handle. Shingles! How I coveted them, especially after the memories of living under a canvas roof.

If the scouts had carried such tools we'd have made better time in building up our colony, but we traveled light and fast and despite *Herr* Keil's belief, we were frugal with the money and didn't pay to buy many tools.

We all worked to make the fireplace, stacking logs over, each other, then mixing mud and riverbank clay with dried grass and boughs. I tried to think of some herb or spice to mix in with the clay so when we heated our supper there'd be an added aroma, but spices were scarce. For now. Andy loved playing with the mud and forming it into little loaves that Christian called cats. My husband helped his son pat the mud dry and both of them nodded approval at each other with smudges of dirt on their faces.

Christian and Martin worked late to build a little cover for Opal, the goat, so I'd have some place out of the wind and rain to milk her. Goats are hardy but can't stand the rain. That first night, I laid on the floor the elk hide we'd been given by a helpful Indian, and there Christian and I whispered. I would have liked to go outside but the mosquitoes raged after sunset. "When they finish the other houses, the men will come back and build a half barn for the mule and cows," Christian said, keeping his voice low so he wouldn't wake the children.

"We're to have a cow?"

"I've worked it out," he said, his eyes sparkling in a tease. Bugs buzzed at the lantern sporting new tin slats Christian had made.

I said, "Maybe from your marshal pay or legislative allotment?"

"Maybe," he said. He dropped his eyes.

"Why didn't you tell me?"

He shrugged. "I wasn't named for doing anything grand," he said. "Indeed. Just recognition of the stockade being built, that we did a good thing to help people. Sam suggested me since we have more Germans here now than other Americans. If someone away from here has a problem, then I can bring about a solution. I don't expect much of that in our colony."

Our colony? "You mean here in Willapa?" He nodded. "Won't you have to make arrests?"

"Indeed. But there's little crime, and the sheriff will handle most things."

"But winning an election as territorial representative. I didn't even know you campaigned."

"I didn't. It was a vote at a meeting same time as John was elected school superintendent and Sam elected sheriff and John Vail as fence viewer."

"I wish you'd told me yourself," I said. "So I could honor you too."

"Ah, Emma," he said. He reached his arms around me. I felt the strength of him. He smelled like a man of the sea, not the earth. I kissed him, tasted salt on my lips. "You honor me by being my wife and staying here through all that has happened. But we're as different as flowers and bees. You bloom vibrant while I, I just want to slip by, have a taste, but never stay long enough to be noticed."

"It's no sin to stand out," I protested. "You do no one a favor by pretending you aren't a worthy man. You're a good leader with a fine mind. A loving husband and father. Responsible to others. Inventive. To deny that means to question your Creator, doesn't it?"

He was thoughtful. "Maybe."

"And besides," I said snuggling beneath his shoulder. "We may be as different as flowers and bees but I believe both are needed to make things grow. And the flower definitely needs to stand out so the bee can find her!"

The fresh scent of peeled logs filled our heads. It was the first night in four years of marriage that we were together, just our family. I wouldn't hear the snoring of a brother or sister, or the sounds of the scouts turning in their tents right beside ours, or the entire community gathering together in the stockade to survive the winter. We were alone at last.

I'd preserved wild strawberries in the spring, dried them, and now added them to goat's cheese to make a kind of fruit pudding that each of us could eat. It tasted sweet and the lumps mixed in our mouths. "This is good, Emma," Christian said. I beamed. "It is good to be with you and the children. Good to be home." He kept spooning the soft food into his mouth, feeding Kate just a taste as she'd wakened, then fell back asleep. His blue green eyes looked darker in the shadows. But they had life, pools fed by the rivers of wrinkles beginning to flow into them.

He finished, wiped his reddish beard with his hand, then set the bowl down on the mats covering the earth floor. "But you should have made enough for all of us," Christian said. "All those who helped with the house. It would have been a godly thing to do."

"I didn't have enough berries," I said. "Besides, I wanted to celebrate with just us, for our family. We don't have to do everything together here, do we?"

"Everyone here is our kin," Christian said. "Even the scouts. Joe. Karl Ruge."

"Well, I know, but I meant—"

"I know what you meant. I just wish you didn't have to enjoy so much being separated from them, Emma. They love you and want to make your life easier. They're generous people. They open their hearts to strangers and friends alike."

"They love Andy. And Kate," I said. "I know." I defended against his eyes raised to disagree.

"You don't know," he said. "You are afraid you'll disappear in this large family, but you will always stand out."

He knew me so well. "They love me like a child of God. But my earthly ways and my ideas, well, those the Giesys could probably do without."

"Not this Giesy," he said and reached for me.

That night we lay on mats and he held me while owls hooted. Treetops split the moonlight that spilled through the open window. Tomorrow I'd tan hides to cover the opening. There were shelves to make, pegs to auger into the walls to hang drying herbs and our few clothes. So much to do.

"Emma," Christian said. "Be here with me now."

"*Ja,*" I said. Staying in one place with another is as difficult sometimes as praying. But I became as whole that night with him as I'd ever been alone. With his caresses I lost the questioning in my mind. My thoughts of things to do were silenced by arms holding me, soft words whispered at the nape of my neck. The busyness of my hands found calm as I pressed my fingers against his bare back and tasted of the sweetness of his mouth. His temple where my lips brushed that soft depression was as sweet as a baby's breath. And when he kissed my face, holding it in the cocoon of his hands, I lost myself in him, my husband. I surrendered, unafraid, as unfurled as an apron string in the wind. I marveled later that I had.

In the morning, I thought I'd tell Christian about the images that washed up before me as he held me close, but I decided I couldn't find the words to speak out loud so I'd hear what I knew. But I wondered if what I'd felt that night with my husband was what a holy relationship should be: safe, attached to someone loving, sinking into mystery, surrendering, receiving, finding meaning in the unexplained, being refreshed from the encounter.

I was in love with Christian Giesy as I'd never been before. Such love was marked by trust, surrendering one's all as though to a watery world without the fear of drowning. He knew me well and loved me still, my husband. I imagined that these were the marks of a spiritual relationship as well.

Just for a short time I imagined that, forgetting that even great tenderness can be a harbinger of change.

4

Louisa

My husband, Dr. Keil, set the rules for constructing *das grosse Haus*. Each team of men—four to a team—must cut one entire tree down before they can eat their breakfast. If meat is scarce, they must shoot a deer, and I imagine Rebecca had quite a time dressing out four deer between breakfast and noon. But then, it was easier to cut the trees on Deer Creek near the Pudding River, where we're building up our colony, because they are not so big as those in Willapa. Not that I excuse what happened there, the poor progress the scouts made. Well, maybe I do excuse it some. They had fewer men and they had Emma. Rebecca was chosen for her skill at doing what she's told without retort.

A dam is already on the creek, so there's a mill race too, Dr. Keil tells the others and I overhear. Twice each month, at first, he took the riverboat from Portland to Oregon City and then, by prearrangement, one of the carpenter teams would come to pick him up in a wagon and drive him from there to Aurora Mills. He often took our little Aurora with him. I would have liked to go along but with so many children to tend to and the laundry I took in, it was best I stayed here in Portland.

We all visited for the Fourth of July. It was a joyous time. How I love the music! I think I could endure most anything in this life as long as there is music to return to. Dr. Keil composed a march the band played and it was a happy tune, not the dirge that we'd listened to all across the continent following Willie's casket.

There I am again, always thinking about Willie. But the rains have begun in Portland, so I think of him more often. It was in this month of November last year that we buried him. I still can find no cause within myself for his death; I know it must be my fault, my error, for my husband is perfection. That he has never accused me openly is a mark of that.

I did not cry, not then, not when he died. Some might have thought me cold. I'm not. I am practical. Death can be hastened by man's action, but death visits everyone. Still I will someday ask why Willie went before me or his father. Somehow this does not seem divine, but then I have no wish to question God. I'm sure there is a reason.

I plan for Christmas here in this Oregon Territory, for the delivery of *Belsnickel's* kind gifts. We'll find fruit perhaps or maybe some small wooden toy for each of the little ones. The band will play. Perhaps we will all go out and stand in the *gross Haus* and sing even if it is not yet completed. It will feel like church. We need to work to finish up the *Haus* so we can move forward and build the church. My husband says we must prepare the farmsteads, plant the orchards in the places where the men have cut the timber. Much to do before we build a church, and even then it will not be so grand as the one we have in Bethel.

I do wonder how they fare in Bethel.

Dr. Keil named Andrew Giesy, Christian's younger brother, to be in charge of Bethel when we left. This surprised me as I expected Andrew to travel west as so many of his brothers did. Maybe my husband had spoken his reasoning and I missed it. I did seem to miss things during those days.

Jack Giesy has been here of late. He makes me laugh and sometimes I forget that he is already thirty years old or more and should have put aside childish pranks like changing sugar in the bowl for salt when I was not looking, or staying up all night "drawing pictures" he tells us. When he doesn't tip his flask too much he is a kind companion for the little ones. He likes to keep them awake late, though, and often misses breaking fast in the morning while he snoozes. Once I heard he tossed a cat against a wall when it ventured near his face as he recovered from his partying. Disturbing. But he has a cheery smile. Willie would have had a smile like that, if he had lived.

Why can't I let him go?

I can't speak to Dr. Keil of such things. They are trivial in the world of import and detail he attends to. A flash of feeling so intense swells up into my face sometimes, making it hot and my breath short all at the same time. I want him to stop being Dr. Keil and *Herr* Keil and our leader and to just be the father of our children, my husband who would hold me through this pain.

But this too is envy, selfishness. "Why do you worry, woman?" he told me one night when I felt the tears coming and asked if he might pray with me for something soothing to fill the gaping hole within my heart. "Why do you worry?" he repeated, adding, "I am doing our Father's work."

These were scriptural words spoken by our Lord to his parents when they had thought him lost but he was instead teaching in the temple.

I am a weak woman. Soft. Thinking only of myself. I am commanded not to worry so long as my husband does the Lord's work.

Despite the routines of my day, there are surprises, small treasures I take as signs that God is with us: enough grass to feed our stock; a child pulled back from a fast wagon racing through the streets of Portland; a leggy yellow flower brought by Jack Giesy and tucked into my apron at the waist.

While we brought no sheep with us—a decision I thought an error as we would need the wool for weaving clothes—I had brought lanolin along, and mutton tallow laced with lemon. Neither ever went rancid and at night I rub the cakes on the feet of the children and our own, soothing the blisters on our feet. Even a good cobbler can't make room for every corn or callus. I give out my healing salve as needed. One night as I fell onto the quilt beside Dr. Keil and spoke my tired prayers, I told him, "I am pleased I brought the mutton salve for our blisters." It was such a little thing to bring me pleasure, this packing something that could serve. "So many say it helps even with wind-chapped hands."

"No need for it," my husband said. "Have them step in their own urine and let the air dry their feet and chapped hands. Each will be clear by morning." He rolled over and I heard him snore within minutes.

I lay awake wondering if there was something sinful in offering up a simple joy. There must be. Otherwise, why would my wise husband find need to offer an alternative to what I'd said? Yes, urine would soften hands, but was it so wrong to be pleased that lanolin could do the same? Hadn't God provided that as well?

I must put these pages away. I'm tired and that's when doubt abounds.

5

Emma

Kindling Your Own Fire

I didn't mind not having anyone around but my children. I liked tending to their everyday needs and preparing for my husband to come home. I could make my own decisions about what to eat or what task to do next without having to please a man's stomach or his clock. In the evening, I lit my candles and burned them for as long as I liked without anyone complaining that I interrupted their sleep with my drawing or reading. All in all, it was the best of both worlds: I had a husband and children to love and care for, and I had time for myself within my own home. I wondered if women married to soldiers carried such thoughts, wanting their men with them but not minding that they could rule their own roost and collect eggs when they wished while their men were gone.

The first week after Christian returned to the Bay, I reveled in that aloneness. It slipped into the late evening after the children slept in their beds. The days were filled with weaving mats or pulling heavy needles through tanned hides to make winter breeches. I ground cornmeal for mush, milked the goat, filled the hollowed log with the grass of last summer. It would have been a pleasure to have a cow through the winter, but Christian said that tending the animal would have been too much for me with the little ones underfoot and the goat to milk as well. On the cold, rainy mornings when I could bring the goat inside to milk her, I agreed with Christian, though good butter would have been a salve against milking in the morning chill.

In this house I felt no fear from the outside world. It was built with love and the door was sturdy with a latch from the inside. During the day I left the latch string out so anyone coming past would know this was a friendly place. Sarah said that was the custom here. If the string was pulled in, it meant no one should knock or stop by. Not that I expected anyone to visit, but I heard that the Shoalwater people sometimes stopped to trade milk for fish or fresh bread for berries.

From my in-laws' house, we'd moved the trunk my parents had sent out with them. Its rounded top stood at the end of the rope-mattress bed that fit in the back corner of the house. The men had made a bed along with a rough table and chairs cut out of smaller tree stumps to add to the table chairs the Giesys brought for us. One finely made rocking chair sat at the hearth. Mary has its mate in her home. It was another bonding of us two women. She and Boshie lived but two miles from us, close enough to call for in time of help; far enough distant we never feared eavesdropping on each other's lives. It was the perfect arrangement, and we had chosen it all ourselves.

At my leisure I could read my sister Catherine's letters and write back, though I did the latter more infrequently than I might have. I wasn't sure why.

Karl Ruge made his way to visit once in a while after the misty rains began in earnest in November. He'd split wood for me. If he saw me dragging out a pail of ashes to my soap pit, he would lift it from me saying, "By golly, I'm not so old I can't lift a bucket. Even if I am so old I'm ready to kick it."

"You're not that old, Karl," I told him. He was but a few years older than Christian. I wished he wouldn't bring up his age. He'd grin and sometimes stay to smoke his pipe while I heated hot tea and he spoke with Andy. I knew he stopped by for Andy's lessons, but sometimes he'd bring me the loan of a book. I preferred the titles in German, for I could read and disappear inside the story. The English ones made difficult reads but Karl said I could keep the books for as long as I liked. Once he brought *Uncle Tom's Cabin* and when I finished reading it, he said we could discuss it together, to see if I had captured the meaning in a book written in English. Imagine, a man willing to discuss a book with a woman! A book about people and lives and change and not just about Scripture! What would my mother-in-law say? *Unseemly* came to mind. Well, just the idea of it spurred me on to test myself against the English words. I stoked the fire later than necessary to keep its reflected light upon my page.

Still, a house without a husband reeks of separation. I thought about Christian often through the winter months and spring and seemed to see him everywhere. Andy had his deep-pool eyes and he held his hands on his hips, elbows out, when I scolded him. Christian often stood that way too when I raised my voice. I had to turn away to keep from smiling when Andy reminded me of his father. I had to be stern at times, for Andy's safety. He played too close to a honey tree, ran without looking into the denser trees and could become lost within them. It is a parent's role to be dour at times. For protection of the ones we love.

Kate's hair was blond at birth but now at a year old, it was coming in with a kind of reddish tint and in the sunshine shone like her father's hair. I often talked to the children about their father, what he might be doing, what he was eating for supper, that he was probably already in bed while my Andy persisted in asking questions just to keep himself from falling asleep. "Does he cook?" Andy asked. I wondered. I'd heard that fur trappers took native wives; maybe Christian had found a Shoalwater woman to cook for him and Joe. I'd have to ask. I didn't know how I felt about that.

The children carried Christian's kindness in them too. On more than one occasion when I hadn't returned to the house from milking the goat as fast as I wished, I'd see Andy bent over his sister, patting her little hand while she cried, hungry, sitting on the floor. He was not the least bit mean or jealous, that boy; he had a naturally giving heart.

Christian was missing these moments, and yet I felt closer to my husband with him gone than I ever had when we'd been separated before. I'd been annoyed when he left me behind after we were married, heading into Kentucky to recruit for *Herr* Keil. If he'd been a bug I'd have smashed him with my slippers when he left me to birth Andy alone at Fort Steilacoom. But now while he was at the Bay, I carried a low flame for him, one that flickered with longing when I thought of him, one that I knew would ignite when he came home and blessed my face with the brush of his mustache. Until then, something in our joined spirits kept us linked though physically we lived apart. How strange a marriage is.

When Christian came home every other week or so, he stayed but a few days, so it was as though we had a honeymoon. I giggled when Christian first used that word. It was December and we'd had a rare respite, a patch of clear sky that revealed a full moon shining on the river outside our home. The children were fast asleep. Avoiding the muddy path, we walked through the timber to the river's edge. The air smelled fresh as new cut flowers and was so full of moisture from the dripping trees that I wiped my face with my shawl, thinking it must be misting. Clouds could roll in and drown the moon in an instant but we wouldn't know until the rains began again, as we couldn't see the arrival of storms or clouds. The hills and trees kept us from anticipating much. I pulled my shawl around me to ward off the chill. Even the insects had flown to their bunks. The river gurgled, carrying its cargo of rain and tree branches and needles and lichen to sea. We could hear splashing, likely where a tree-fall cut the water, forcing the stream surge to go around it. Under the canopy of trees, our voices carried.

"Honeymoon," Christian said as we stood together. "The word means sweetness as in *honey* and the *moon* means the sweetness leaves like the moon fades. It's a part of life. The ebb and flow of things. A good descriptive word."

"I'll pray our marriage will be a harvest moon, then, filling us up with good memories. Then when it threatens to fade, we'll have the return of the honey to look forward to."

"Indeed, you would find the hopeful part of the waning moon," he said. "But it won't just threaten to fade, Emma. It does fade."

"Two honeymoons a month would keep us from noticing the darkness in between," I said.

"The Americans call two full moons in one month a 'blue moon' and say something is as 'rare as a blue moon.' Indeed," Christian continued, "a happily married man, for instance, or so my father says. Little does he know." He kissed my nose.

"Look at us," I said. "Our waning did not last. We are renewed here."

"But it is not our doing, Emma. God controls, not us. Remember the scripture: 'Behold, all ye that kindle a fire, that compass yourselves about with sparks: walk in the light of your fire, and in the sparks that ye have kindled. This shall ye have of mine hand; ye shall lie down in sorrow.' "

"Well that's just...dour. The idea that all we get for kindling our own fires is the hand of God giving us sorrow. What kind of hand is that?"

"One to help us when we're grieving," he said. "To remind us that we cannot do anything on our own. We will grieve. We are not asked to move by our compass, Emma."

"But we have to kindle our own fires. We have to read the compass. We can't wait around for others to do it for us. Look what happened with Keil. We waited for him to fan our flames here, and he doused them with buckets of outrage. We looked to him for our compass and see where it took us! He'd take us south to Portland and Aurora, but we went to the sea and found oystering to rescue us." I pulled away from him, disappointed that he couldn't see how pushing ahead, following the course we had, had rescued us. Oh, God had a place in it, but we made it happen, didn't we?

"No matter what we do, there will be sweetness and there will be bitter. To think differently is to find disappointment in God where none is warranted. I worry over you, Emma, that you try too hard to see all good things as coming from your effort. When tragedies happen—and they will as sure as the moon wanes—then you'll blame yourself. This will not be good."

"*Ja,* like you blamed yourself," I said.

It was an unkindness of me, to poke in my husband's freshest sore. Loving someone was in part knowing their deepest wound but choosing not to poke it or to pick at the scab. But did the man think that his deciding to work on the coast had nothing to do with me? Did he think that every good idea came only from God, or that God couldn't speak through another? Didn't God make us all creative creatures?

Still, I should have countered what I said, apologized. Instead I pitched the thought away.

Worse, he reached for me with tenderness. I shrugged my shoulder.

"Stick to the tenth verse, Emma," he said. "We pay a price if we try to do things ourselves. Indeed, we must kindle God's fire to light our path in darkness, trust in Him, not anyone or anything else. 'Who is among you that feareth the LORD, that obeyeth the voice of his servant, that walketh in darkness, and hath no light? let him trust in the name of the LORD, and stay upon his God.' "

He pointed toward a black form wiggling along the riverbank then. "Otters," he said. "They play even at night. They've not a worry in the world. We can be like that if we but trust."

He'd forgotten how sad he'd been. He'd forgotten how defeated he was before I convinced him to try something different. *Ja*, it was easy for him to trust now. He sounded more like a preacher or maybe a marshal or some legislator to me than my husband.

Rains began then, having slipped past the moonlight while we talked. The drops softly pattered my woolen shawl. When he took my hand to help me as we walked the muddy path back to the house, all I wanted was to pull away.

———

Christian still oystered at the Bay when our little community celebrated *Herr* Keil's birthday (and Louisa's) on March 6, just as we'd done back in Bethel. I confess, I resented the celebration for the Keils' birthdays. The Keils didn't live here, hadn't wanted to live here, and weren't a part of this community, even if they had buried their son Willie on the hill. Equally annoying, the celebration occurred on a Friday, not even a day when we'd otherwise have gathered at the stockade for worship, so I had to make the lengthy trip with the children and stay over, then return the following day to milk the goat.

Living seven miles south of the stockade made it no simple journey. Not that I'm complaining, just explaining.

Before I left, I rose in the dark, carrying the lantern to the lean-to where Opal rested. I wished I could milk her later instead of earlier since I wouldn't be back to milk her until tomorrow. Her little bag would be swollen for sure. I had to have time to skim yesterday's cream and leave today's milk in another tin Christian had made for me. When that was finished, I packed a few items, brought ingredients to make a special dried-berry dessert, then woke the children and they dressed. We ate a simple breakfast of oats with molasses and then I saddled the mule—on loan to us from Andreas—hanging the lantern by a rope over the animal's neck.

We rode the mule, the three of us, with a sack of goodies draped over the saddle horn. Andy hung on behind me, his little legs stuck out on either side; Kate rode in front, tied to me with a sash around her middle. A saddle was a luxury Christian had purchased for us. And no, I did not ride sidesaddle, and I didn't care who knew it.

The path was muddy but the mule surefooted. Little squalls sprayed water on us and of course the branches overhanging the trail wetted us down, but the cedar capes I'd woven worked well to keep us dry. The smells were rich with loam and leaf, and the beginning spring colors stood out against moss and tree bark. A red mushroom shaped like a small tulip caught my eye. Little prince's-pine moss that worked well for diapers spurted up from old logs, and there were leaves that looked like reindeer horns and bore the same color. I wished I knew the name of every single one. Perhaps I'd make that a school lesson with Karl Ruge. These small treasures of the landscape made the day a gift.

When we reached the river ford, I had to put the children in the little boat we kept there, stake the mule, then row the boat and the babies across the stream. Once I'd have lost my breakfast at the mere thought of being on the river at all, but now it was part of who I was, this calculating where to put the boat in and imagining where I'd take it out on the other side. Sometimes we got spun around in the current, but I knew where I was headed and kept my eye on that certain tree or log to keep me ever forward.

Once on the other side, I left Andy to look after Kate, grateful for the moment that she was occupied and sitting while I rowed back to the other side. I unstaked the mule, tied his rope to the boat, then once again made my way across the swift-flowing stream. I docked the boat, untied the mule, loaded him back up and off we went, knowing we'd be repeating the event the next day.

We'd spend the night with my in-laws. We rode along the trail, clopped through one or two little streams that appeared in the spring. Blackberry vines threatened the trail; moss-thickened branches hung from the big cedars, forcing us to keep watch and for me to duck, but still there was time for musing. My in-laws loved seeing the children, and I know they missed them, but my mother-in-law never failed to say things to the children that I knew were meant for me. "We hardly ever see you, Andrew. What's your mother doing that she can't come visit more often, hmm?" Or to Kate, as my daughter sat on her knee, "Why, your little hands feel cold. Didn't your mother put gloves on you when you traveled? *Oma* will warm them up." She'd kiss my daughter's hands and I'd feel the layers of guilt flatten me out like the batter of a cake.

I countered those negative anticipations by remembering that today I'd see my friend Sarah Woodard when I traveled north, and she was the reason I headed out early. She was the pearl in the bottom of this oyster. Sustaining friendships has a cost attached. This one meant managing two children and a mule and a rowboat on a swollen stream and enduring the disappointments of my children's grandparents in order to spend a few moments with Sarah and Sam.

On the Keils' birthday, I rode the mile or so beyond the stockade to invite the Woodards to our event. The foliage was thick enough that my in-laws wouldn't see me riding by. Sometimes Sam and Sarah attended our extended-family events, though usually not on a Friday. *Ach,* such a poor time for a celebration!

At Sarah's, I unloaded the children and Andy scampered toward the Woodards' dog, who lapped his face in happy recognition. I received Sarah's surprised hug, watched as she lifted Kate into her arms while I set a tub of goat cheese on her table. The cheese was tart and aged; the way I knew she liked it. In return, she gave me butter and eggs and we spent a few hours catching up, discovering what news she had about the territory.

After Kate fell asleep I asked Sarah if she knew about Christian being named the territorial marshal and being elected to the legislature.

"Oh yes," she said.

"He never told me," I said.

She pondered for a bit, then said, "Men are like that sometimes. They don't let you notice who they are. They think it's prideful."

"*Ja,* prideful," I said, deciding then that Christian didn't want to set a bad example for me by enjoying his honor. Or maybe he thought I'd dote on him, tell it to others as though it were *my* honor. I didn't think of myself as a woman who always made sure that others knew of her husband's goodness, but maybe Christian thought I was. "I wouldn't have gossiped about him," I said.

"No. You don't gossip. Your mind is too busy thinking." She paused. "He maybe didn't want to worry you. The marshals have to enforce the laws and the legislators make them and, well, with Governor Stevens, it can be unpredictable. That man hates all 'evil-disposed persons' as he calls the Indians and anyone who disagrees with him. At least the martial law's been lifted."

Christian had been carrying this responsibility on his shoulders, too, and never said a word to me.

"Maybe he thought he had told you," Sarah said. She smiled. "Sometimes that happens between Sam and me. He thinks because everyone knows that I must know too."

"These men, so complicated," I sighed.

"While we women are as easy to see through as glass."

We both laughed at that, and I was reminded again that journeying to visit Sarah was worth the river crossing and the little irritations I'd find later with my in-laws.

———

"So, here you are," my father-in-law announced when I arrived just after the midday meal. The table would be filled again as more people joined us so I didn't feel badly that they were just finishing up as we arrived. "We celebrate *Herr* Keil's birthday."

"And Louisa's," I added as I handed Kate to my mother-in-law and stepped down off the mule. Andy had already slipped off the back of the animal and missed the swish of the mule's tail as he jumped aside then ran to his favorite uncle, Boshie.

"You almost missed the festivities, Emma," my mother-in-law said. "Did you have trouble with the mule?"

"*Nein.* I went over to invite the Woodards. I hadn't seen Sarah for so long."

"*Ja,* you don't get up much this way. Not even on New Year's Eve this year. Too bad." She paused as she cleared a pan of cake from the table. "You missed some time with your husband by coming so late."

"What? Christian is here?"

"Was here," Rudy said. "He came very early with the tidewaters but couldn't stay. Still much work to do he said, and so he headed back."

"He said to tell you he'd be home before too many days," Boshie said.

"He missed seeing the children," my mother-in-law noted. She smiled at Andy. "His housekeeper brought fresh clams that we finished right off. So good."

What was wrong with Christian? Why wouldn't he have told me, sent a message at least that he was coming? I suppose he couldn't have. It was an impulsive visit made because he had some moments free and the river agreed with his plan.

"I guess he knew we'd be celebrating Wilhelm's birthday," Martin said.

"And Louisa's," I added, again. *Who was this housekeeper?*

"*Ja,* hers too," Henry acknowledged. "So he assumed you'd be here."

Rudy told me that Christian had almost set out to find us, thinking something might have gone wrong, but the rest of the family assured them I could take care of myself and would be along shortly.

"None of us ever figured you'd pass right by and go visit Sarah first," my mother-in-law said. "That's too bad, isn't it? I know he missed seeing the children."

She's already said that.

I felt sick. I missed my husband and regretted having the chance to see him and hold him if only for a moment. Why hadn't I just stopped by before I went to Sarah's? Well, I hadn't wanted to get caught by the family and maybe not had a chance to see Sarah at all. I should have expected Christian might come since it was a festive day, one we always celebrated back in Bethel. But things were different here. My husband was a law enforcer and I hadn't been told of *that*! I swatted at a spider crawling up my skirt and sent the poor thing skittering past a distant stump.

Some of Christian's brothers got out their instruments and played German marching tunes. They sang later and for a moment I was back in Bethel, swept away with the music. The women sewed awhile, then chattered until it was time to put out bowls of potatoes and deer meat and an array of *Strudels* using the berries of last summer. They invited me into their chatter, talking about their children's antics or their latest success with a recipe or two. Christian's youngest sister, Louisa, played with Kate and I was grateful. The day turned balmy and while clouds scudded across the treetops, it rained in little patches that sent us running for the stockade, our shawls wrapped tight around us. It was a pleasant day.

But I couldn't let go of how I'd missed seeing Christian. The children too, as my mother-in-law reminded me. Why hadn't he stayed just a little longer? I wondered if he often made little side trips that far upriver, but not far enough to reach his own home. The most annoying thing of all: that he had remembered Keil's birthday and took the time to come celebrate it with his family but hadn't waited around long enough to see his wife and children.

"Papa didn't want to see us," Andy said, leaning his head on my lap as I sat.

"*Ja*, he did." I ran my fingers through the silkiness of Andy's hair. "He just had work to do so he had to get back to the sea."

"I wish he lived with us, Mama. I'd like a daddy around."

"He lives with us," I said. "He'll be back before long. Summer is better. He can be home more often. He's taking care of us."

Even my son felt deserted. His father and I had agreed that we could manage the separations. I could kindle the fires alone in the morning; he'd bring home the resources we needed to see us through the winter. But Andy had no say in it. *Ach*, that was the way with children.

We finished the meal and I heard myself sighing more than once as the evening approached and we put the children to sleep. "Don't let it upset you," Mary Giesy told me. She sat down beside me on a stump chair, my oil lamp beside me. A breeze picked up, chilling the hair on my arms. I wouldn't stay out here for long.

"What makes you think I'm upset?" I asked.

"Your hands tell," Mary said. She nodded toward my fingers that had apparently been working on their own, my thumb and forefinger rubbing against each other.

"*Ja,* Andy heard everyone say that Christian was here but didn't stay. He thinks that's his fault."

"I heard him," Mary said. "But you got to see Sarah. That was a nice treat, wasn't it?"

"It cost me seeing my husband. I chose something pleasurable, but had to pay the price. That seems to be my way."

"Maybe not," she said. She looked away.

"What do you mean?"

"Oh, nothing." She picked at a grass stem. The light of the lantern flickered against her face. We heard a swish above us. An owl settled in a tree. She wouldn't look at me. She bit the side of her cheek. The night cast strange shadows. Or no…

"I'm just sorry I missed him."

"I wonder how it was that Christian could have gone downriver without at least seeing your mule tied to the Woodards' post. Surely he'd have stopped by when he saw the mule."

"*Ja,*" I said. "That is a mystery."

She cleared her throat. "You're good at puzzles." She stared at me.

I stared back. "Christian didn't miss me, did he?" I said. "He never even came. You all just told me that to…tease me."

"Don't tell I said." She leaned into me to whisper. "Rudy saw you riding by and he said we should play a trick on you, for wanting to spend more time with your friends than with us."

"But that wasn't it at all," I said. "I had cheese to deliver and eggs to get and—"

"Emma, it's me you're talking to," Mary said. I dropped my eyes. She did know the truth. "I wasn't supposed to tell but you looked so miserable. And then I heard Andy leaning his head on your lap..."

"But why let me think about it all day?" I said. "Couldn't they see too?"

"Not really. You hide your feelings pretty well. I just know you and I knew you'd feel awful about keeping Andy from his dad. So I had to give you a clue. They didn't mean any harm, Emma, really they didn't. And when you tell them you know, they'll laugh and be as happy as anyone that you bested them and figured it out. They might accuse me of telling you, but—"

"But it's cruel, just as they were laughing over Jack's antics with that girl in the outhouse. They let Andy think his father didn't want to see him."

"They think of it as joking. They've been doing it to each other for years. Think of it as a...as a compliment that they involved you in an elaborate plan and each kept the secret. You were the center of it even though you didn't know. Think of it that way and when you tell them, you'll be the center again."

"I won't tell them. Let them feel miserable that they let their grandchild or nephew think his father didn't wait for him. I'll tell Andy but I'll just let them live with their guilt. I'll plan something...I'll stir them up one day and they'll see how it feels."

"Oh, Emma, please. Don't make this a big thing, now. Laugh with us. Don't stand out in this."

"It's not a laughing matter," I said. I stood up, my chin thrust out. "It was hurtful. If a woman can't feel safe with her family, then who can she feel safe with?" I woke the children and we began a night ride home.

6

Louisa

"Food is the servant of the heart, Louisa," Doctor tells me. "Bring them food that their hearts will be warmed."

I hurry to serve. This is how we win new converts to the colony. I know that only men are permitted true recruitment, heading into other territories or states to invite people into our communal society, but we women contribute through our service and especially our food.

People in Portland pay the doctor in food. Wild turkey, venison, chickens, eggs, milk. The latter we don't need so much of since we brought our own neat milk cows across the continent, their little neck bells ringing as they ripped at grass. But several died on the journey west and now we are sending a herd north to Willapa, so perhaps we'll welcome payment in cream.

Chris Giesy made the request. After all, he told my husband in his last letter, the cows had been planned for the Willapa Valley and there is good grazing on the prairies and the Giesys know how to run a dairy. They just need the milk cows that my husband sent to Portland for safekeeping during the winter last. Chris thinks there might be some contracts to be had with the Russians for cheese and butter, sending the produce north by ship. Apparently the British did something like this. They never allowed their people to own cows; they were always working for the British, to be sure they met their contracts. I think Chris added that about the British to make sure we knew this wasn't some wild scheme of his. Or Emma's.

Chris has a cross to bear with his Emma.

So Jack and some of the other young men who like adventure will take the cows north. Jonathan Wagner remains at Aurora Mills. He is helping with the accounting of the new buildings going up there, some using milled boards and not just logs. So responsible, that Jonathan, though I imagine his little nephew Andy would like to meet him. Well, maybe on the Fourth of July they will all come this way to celebrate, though I doubt Emma will ever leave that place, not even for a visit. To do so would be to admit the error of her ways in staying there. She'd have to confess to her part in the separating of our colony. She must come to understand that we women have no real say in the colony life. We are like that Dred Scott, who we learn is not a free man after all. The chief justice has ruled and the Missouri Compromise has been repealed. Slaves, like women, have no voice. It is the way of things.

So I serve meals to people the doctor brings home with him. By their clothing they look important, maybe investors in our colony efforts. The doctor says they are kind men, just ordinary travelers seeking new adventures. But they speak loudly as they tell of Yakima uprisings in bloody detail. They scare the children with their wide-flung hands, and words, like rifle blasts, boom out. I recognize more of their English words each day. Virginians they are and Americans too, who keep telling their stories of the Indians and their trials on the journey across.

As I watch them eat, standing aside to notice when platters need refilling, I think about our crossing. We had no trouble with the Indians, and I think people knew that, so they asked to travel with us. But like these men, I don't think they shared our expression of faith. They used our faith as safety within the confines of our trouble-free journey. I wonder if that is the interest of these American men who see our colony as an easy way to live, not having to work too hard because there will always be food and shelter even if they act lazy. They misunderstand. We Germans are never lazy. And if the war comes, I think our boys will go, if asked, though this is something my husband and I have never spoken of. Might these men I serve have sons they wish to harbor in our colony?

We Germans must always be prepared to be hospitable, not question the motives of others, that's what the doctor says. I pour corn juice into their tins, and they nod, raise the cup as though to toast me as I step back into the shadows.

My husband has a big heart, inviting strangers in. Once, on the journey across, a Sioux brave rode in with his two sons. The doctor invited them to eat at our table too, along with Americans. Because he is so good to communicate even with those of another language, the doctor understood that these Indians were reluctant to eat for fear there would not be enough for all of us. The doctor assured them they were guests and should eat first, that there was plenty for his wife and children. My children did go hungry that night but for a worthy cause.

The Americans traveling under our safe harbor scoffed and left the circle around the fire.

The Indians stayed late into the evening with the rest of us, who watched with empty stomachs as the doctor carried on conversations with his hands. I wondered if they'd ever leave so we could go to our beds. Hunger is easier to manage when asleep. The Americans laid their bedrolls farther from our campfire, and I noticed they slept with their rifles across their chests.

The Indians lingered. With the palm of his hand, one pointed toward me, and later my husband said he spoke of my black hair, as black as his, and that like him, I parted mine in the middle. Something in common. Then Aurora stood up, my sweet little daughter. I would have put her to bed earlier, but the doctor liked her company, and she snuggled beneath his arms as he made signs with the Indians. She gave them her comforter, her little patched quilt I'd made for her with the wool I dyed myself.

"Are you sure you wish to give that away?" I said as she carried it toward them.

She turned to look at me, then back to her father. "Of course she will be generous," the doctor told me. "That is what we do." He beamed at her.

I remembered how the red madder root stained my fingers when I dyed the yarn. I thought of the days I spent stitching the little squares. With each poke of the needle I said a prayer for her. Others in our colony stitched it too. It was a gift of love from all of us, not just from me. I didn't want her to give it away. It was as though I was losing Willie again, a precious thing departing.

I scolded myself as I saw the happiness on the face of the Indian. It was wrong of me to remember an object so fondly and to compare it with the loss of my son.

Then the doctor gave the man an oxbow so he could make for himself a bow of fine Missouri wood. I wondered if the doctor expected each of us to give them something. I had nothing I wanted to part with.

"Bring your friends in the morning," my husband signed. Where he learned such signing I will never know. Neither did I know what we'd feed them except dried peaches.

Just before dawn, twenty-five Indians drove a dozen oxen and neat cows into our camp. They were animals we'd lost, and we were grateful to see them. The natives brought fresh meat, too, and berries. We made ready, my girls and I, to serve the men and their families with them. My girls were eleven years, eight years, and six years old then, but they all knew how food was the servant of the heart. We served them a *Strudel* with dried peaches I baked in our dutch oven, as people called it, rising at four o'clock to do it. The Americans ate heartily though they sat at a distance. The Indians squatted to eat the baked goods and when they had their fill, the women and children ate. We sang for them then, and they grunted agreement with bits of *Strudel* falling on the men's bare chests, catching in the ends of their silky hair.

Then one meandered toward Willie's hearse.

I wanted the hearse left alone, but the doctor stood and as though he showed off a new horse or a new wagon just completed, he spoke in loud words, calling August to help him. They lifted the top of the coffin. My stomach twisted like a snake as I watched them view my Willie.

There was no need of this. I rose to protest, but the Indians all moved toward the hearse now. They lowered their heads as though in prayer and stepped back, seemingly aware of the sanctity of death. The doctor continued to tell them about the whiskey and how it kept Willie pure until we could bury him in the West. The Indians kept their eyes down and then the doctor put the top back on.

The Americans grumbled things I couldn't understand, though they made motions like men who drink too much and pointed to the Indians. But the Indians mounted up then, and waved to us when the trumpet sounded and the *Schellenbaum* tinkled its bells as we headed out once again behind Willie's hearse. Like Lot's wife, I looked back. I did not dissolve into salt. The Indians stayed as silhouettes against the horizon for as long as I could see.

"I have power over the Indians," the doctor told me that afternoon when we rested. "I could get them to do anything I wanted."

"You are worshiped by many, Husband," I told him.

"*Ja, ja,* I know this." He tugged at that tuft of hair beneath his lip. "These Indians, I have a special way with them. Did you see how they looked at Willie?"

I ached. Yes, I saw.

So why he was frightened during our time in Willapa still confounds me. So frightened he would not let the men use guns to hunt for food and our children went hungry at night, again.

I suppose we do things we cannot foresee when trouble drops onto our doorstep. We may try to step over it, go around, but usually we walk through. By God's grace we walk through.

And now, here in Portland nearly a year since we left Willapa, the doctor is happier, at last, as he used to be. His trips out to Aurora Mills excite him, and he returns full of ideas for how the colony will prosper. He carries no ill will toward the Willapa branch that I can see.

I've made a bread pudding with fresh milk. I serve these Portland Americans, and my husband says Jack Giesy will take the cows north. The Americans finish their pudding and leave our Portland home, tipping their hats at me and saying, *"Danke."* My husband gives me no indication of who these Americans are, but he seems happy. So, Jack Giesy is in charge of taking the cows to Willapa. "Big Jack" is what many call him.

"Would it be good to send others with him who have more experience with cows?"

"Jacob needs the challenge, to know that people depend on him. When he has others around who will pick him up, he can act the *Dummkopf.* Sometimes it takes a challenge to help the children think no longer as children but as men."

"Maybe Peter Klein could go," Aurora says. She is now eating the pudding that I held back for the children. "Peter went to Will-pa before anyone else arrived." She is seven and is still troubled by that Willapa word. I smile at her. She can almost read my mind.

The doctor taps her little upturned nose. "Ah, my Aurora, always thinking. But no, you women lack understanding. I will send some of the younger boys along, but Jacob will be in charge and we will see if he can live up to the challenge."

I pack a bag of food for Jack and the boys he takes with him and pray he will not stop by Chris and Emma's or stay for long if he does. Emma has a way of serving ideas into men's heads while their stomachs are filled up with her *Strudels.*

7

Emma

The Waning Moon

On March 26, 1857, I turned age twenty-four. Christian came to spend the day even though I knew it took him from his work, it being a Thursday and during the season when big schooners anchored outside the Bay looking for baskets of oysters to buy for San Francisco.

"Like newlyweds," Martin said, when Christian appeared at noontime still wearing big rubber boots he said were a part of his uniform. Martin said "newlyweds" not with disgust but with a tone of envy, as though he too might like such a marriage arrangement. We met at the stockade, of course. It was our gathering place now. I didn't even mind the journey by mule and boat and mule again, suspecting that Christian might actually come for my birthday.

There were presents for me too. Karl Ruge gave me *Germania Kalender* published by the famous Geo Brumder of Milwaukee. It was filled with stories and cartoon pictures and ads for pharmaceuticals in the back, and Ayer's Sarsaparilla. Martin leaned over my chair as I turned the pages. "New herbals," he noted.

"Very thoughtful," Christian said. "I know Emma likes to write what she's done on the dates, and she hasn't been able to do that with only a calendar from 1855 that Mary brought with her."

The book had a hard cover with a lovely drawing of a lion on the front. It was written in German and I loved it. The stories I could read to Andy and

Kate. It contained advice and information about lots of things, such as when to plant, the tides, days of full moons. How someone figured out all those details and still got them printed in a book in time for use always surprised. This one had recipes in it and a little word trivia. I read that the Italian word for "religion" translated into English as *ambassador.* "An ambassador offers us help in a foreign land," Karl said. "Religion does, too."

"Thank you," I said, holding it to my chest. "I'll treasure it."

"*Ja,* by golly, I thought you might," Karl said. He dropped his eyes. A hint of pink formed on the circle of weathered cheeks framed by his white beard.

Barbara Giesy gave me an embroidered handkerchief, and my mother-in-law said she had something new to eat for the occasion. She called it coconut. It was green and in the middle had a substance that felt smooth but tasted quite fine. "It comes from the Sandwich Islands," she said. "On board a ship. I thought you'd like it. It's…different."

"It is," I said. Andy took a taste and so did Kate, who scrunched her nose at me. "She likes tart things," I said.

Mary's gift was a new needle for my chatelaine and a thimble made of bone.

They were being terribly kind to me, my husband's family. I suspected Mary had told them that I knew of their petty joke and they wanted to win me over so I wouldn't come up with something back in kind. Maybe they felt a little guilt.

I wasn't planning anything, not that I hadn't tried. But every idea that had come into my head seemed silly or cruel, though I believed their joke was too. Still, I wasn't sure I was willing to let their generosity on my birthday buy their way out of guilt.

"And what did you get your wife?" my father-in-law asked Christian.

Christian pulled a tiny misshapen pearl from the knotted bag he wore around his neck. "Just this," he said. "To add to her string of them."

"Pearls," my sisters-in-law cooed.

"Extravagance," my father-in-law scoffed.

"Not when you don't have to purchase it," Christian told him.

"Ah, but you've paid for it. With your time and hard work and being away from home," he was told.

"I have another gift," Christian said. "But of course I don't know for certain when it will arrive."

"That cow," I said, knowing. "Andy, let's look for the cow your papa gave me." I set the presents aside and took my son's hand. We pretended to look for a cow under a leafy fern and inside a rotting cedar trunk.

"Cows don't grow in trees, Mama," Andy said. "Do they, Papa?"

"Indeed they don't. They should have been here by now. Wilhelm said he'd send a dozen from Portland, so we can begin dairying and give the goats a rest."

I hadn't realized he'd contacted Keil. I wondered when he'd done that. I hoped Wilhelm wasn't bringing the cows himself. Well, of course he wouldn't be. He was tied to his precious Aurora Mills.

Before dusk drifted in along with the usual evening March showers, we left the partiers to their music and dancing and began our trek home. Christian planned to stay the night, then take the boat back down to Bruceport in the morning. At the river crossing he said, "Someday we'll have to build a bridge so you don't have to struggle so much to take the trail."

"It's only bad a few weeks out of the year," I said.

"Indeed, but it looks dangerous, so swift as it is."

When we crossed to the other side I helped tie up the little boat, then loaded Andy up on the mule while Christian held Kate. I turned to reach for her and saw instead my husband staring at me. The expression on his face warmed my soul.

"What?" I said.

"You've changed, Emma. Once crossing this river would have made you physically ill. Now, you take the boat without effort and cross even when the river runs high."

"*Ja*. The children need me to know what I'm doing," I said. "I don't want to frighten them."

"So it is true," Christian teased. "Children do raise their parents up."

We slept soundly that evening so I didn't hear the cowbells the next morning until they were nearly upon us. "Yahoy." I heard the shout. A man's voice.

"Christian." I shook my husband's shoulder. "Wake up. Someone's here."

My husband rolled off the rope bed, grabbed his britches, then opened the latch. A drizzle of rain silvered the door opening, but I could still make out yellowish animals moving in the mist. The bells sounded muffled now under the rain.

"Are these Bethel cows?" Christian shouted.

"*Ja*. For the Giesys," a man answered.

"Leave them and come in out of the rain, man. There's plenty enough fodder to keep them content for a time. How many are there of you? Come now," he called to the herders, stepping back to invite them in.

How many men were there? I threw on my shawl around my nightdress and pulled the nightcap down over my ears. The air chilled. I'd have to fix a meal quickly. I'd build a fire, stir up johnnycakes. We had venison sausage I could fry, fruit preserves to spread on the cakes. I gave some of the goat cheese to Kate to keep her happy until I could milk the goat, handed Andy a bite of biscuit, then told him to dress as I set about my work.

While I was busy tending my family, being happy in my home, and while my back was turned, Jack Giesy stepped into my life.

———

Jack looked harmless all wet from the drizzle. He removed his hat when I turned around and swatted the wet of it against his thigh. "*Ach*," he said. "My mother taught me better manners than to baptize a woman's floor first thing in the morning."

"It'll soak in," Christian said, coming in behind him. "No matter. Here, take one of the stools. You too, Gus. What about the others, won't they come in?" Christian asked.

Jack shook his head. "We've got the other along, you know, that 'surprise' you wanted." He grinned at me. "The cows were nothing coming across the Cowlitz Trail," Jack said. "But those…hogs," he said. "Whooee! They'd rather rut in the underbrush than be herded."

Still, they'd had no trouble to speak of, to hear Jack tell the story. They brought the stock from Portland across the Columbia up through the thick brush to our home, the one farthest south of all the Giesy claims.

"It was cold," Jack said. " 'Cept for yesterday when the sun shone on us, when it could penetrate the trees. This is some country you've chosen, Chris. Alluring though, all the ferns and birds and I bet butterflies too, when there's time to let them land on your hand." He put his hat on his knee and motioned to Kate, who sat wide-eyed on her raised mat. She smiled and lowered herself from the mat then waddled, falling but once, to his arms.

"That's Cousin Jack," Christian said to her. "You've just met a distant relative."

I handed Gus, one of the herd boys, a mug of hot black tea and hesitated before Jack, not sure how he'd manage a hot tin and my daughter on his lap. With the ease of a dancer moving his partner from one side to the other, he transferred Kate to his opposite knee, then reached for the cup. *"Danke,"* he said. He obviously knew how to juggle a thing or two. "Two lovely girls you have here, Christian." He sipped, then let a slow grin move across his lips. "This may be a wet boarding house, Christian, but I like the service." He lifted the mug up as though it were a beer stein, nodded to Kate, and drank. I smelled the slightest scent of ale with his movements.

That was all there was to it, that first meeting. Jack joked about the journey, talked of moving through the night as the moonlight held. Gus frowned with Jack's talk of having energy enough to go all night. He told us the whiskey flask had kept them warm and he still had some left. They'd had no difficulty with the cows at all. "I don't know why Wilhelm was so opposed to this valley," he said.

"He was right," Christian said. He kept his eyes from me. "There were too many to prepare for, so taking the others to Portland, that made sense. But with these few hardy souls left, we'll make a go of it."

"Music comes from the river and trees like a symphony playing," Jack said. "I'm anxious to see the Bay, see what this river flows into. Who knows, maybe I'll stay."

Jack set his empty cup down on the earth floor, then responded to Kate's reaching for his mustache. He trimmed it, I could tell, for not a single hair reached down over his full upper lip. Mindlessly I touched my own lips. They were sore from Christian's beard and the kisses he'd left there. The taste of my husband still lingered.

"Don't let her pull your mustache," Christian said. "She has a wicked grip for just a little one."

"I'm used to little women," he said. I don't think the look he gave me was anything more than to enjoy his own joke. Jack took Kate's fingers in his hands, then blew against them, making a funny sound that caused both Andy and Kate to break into laughter. He was a natural with children. It must have been a Giesy trait.

"I'd better get you fed or you'll eat her fingers off," I said.

He popped Kate's fingers into his mouth as I said it, and she squealed, a sound that quickly turned to fear, perhaps as she realized what I'd said. Jack laughed.

"No, no, Kate." I reached for her. "He won't eat your fingers. It's all right. *Ach,* I'm sorry," I said.

"No matter," Jack said, then turned to Christian to begin their talk of cows and hogs. I put Kate back on our bed, then served the men their breakfast.

It was lighter outside now, the sun not showing itself but reflecting against the drizzle. Christian put on his canvas-waxed slicker and boots and stepped outside with Gus to send in the other two young men who'd traveled north with them. These were boys I didn't know, but when I asked as I served them, they did tell me about Jonathan and described Aurora Mills with steadied glumness.

They joked with Jack, though, who sat back from the table to take another cup of tea. He crossed his long legs at the ankles and each time I brought something to that end of the table to serve the boys, I had to step over them, my skirts catching on his brogans.

"Guess I could make your life easier," he said after the third time.

"*Ja.* You could, but then I don't know many men for whom that's a priority," I said.

He laughed.

Christian called to him and he stood, put on his hat and tipped his fingers to it. "My thanks to you, the infamous Emma Giesy," he said, then ducked his head to go out of the door.

Infamous Emma Giesy. Where had that come from?

I stood in the open doorway, shouting directions and pointing at which cows I thought would be good for us to keep. They all looked pretty similar, with wide bony back hips and neat short horns at their heads. Ayershires they were, a sturdy animal known for both meat and milk, though sometimes prone to opinion. They'd fit in well.

Their selection made, Christian, with Andy close behind, led the two cows toward the lean-to, where the goat resided. At least the cows were docile. I'd heard of some of the wild cows with long horns that roamed the Territory, orphans from Spanish herds brought north some years before. At least these with Christian could be led. We'd have to work on the barn soon though a stanchion would have to do for now. The winters were wet but mild and the mules had fared well just standing out under big cedar trees. We'd raise the barn in the summer when oystering wasn't so demanding.

The hogs would be a little different to manage. "I'll ask Boshie and Karl if they can build a moveable corral," Christian said. "I don't want the hogs wandering too far. Bears could get them, or they'll meander away and we'll never get them back."

"I can return later and help," Jack offered. "But wouldn't it be better to just keep all the hogs in one place? You're raising them in common. Separating the cows because it's just easier for a family to handle them two at a time, that I can see, but the hogs, well, why not keep them all together?"

I looked at Christian.

"Maybe it would be better for you to take the hogs on. Rudy might be willing to manage them all."

"I believe you're mistaken, Jack," I said. "We're not a branch of the colony at Aurora."

"Not the way I heard it," Jack said. He stretched. "But whatever way you want to go, Chris, it's fine with us. We're only what six, seven miles from Rudy and the rest?"

"Indeed. Take the hogs," Christian said. "There's too much going on now to ask Martin or Rudy to come here and build while I'm at Bruceport. Rudy'll do well with the hogs."

My husband avoided looking at me. He handed Jack the pack of food I'd prepared for them, then set about arranging a standing place for the cows. I heard him and Andy talking softly to the animals. When I walked out to get Opal, the goat, to milk her, I made sure I didn't look at them. One wrong look back and I knew I'd say something I could only later regret.

———

Christian returned that day to the Bay, and I kept my words to myself, not wanting to start talking to hear what I thought, not wishing to stumble into an argument that couldn't be resolved before he left. I kissed him good-bye and told him to have a safe trip and wondered when I'd see him again. "Next month, for certain," he said. "It's too much time away from you and the children."

I also didn't ask him to explain the present tense of his last words, a sentence that sounded like he was having serious second thoughts about being away, oystering. I decided to keep my own counsel or talk with Mary later to see if I could sort out how I felt about the "common fund colony" that had returned like a counterfeit coin promising riches but taking a toll instead.

Did Mary and Boshie see their work at the mill as contributing to the common fund? Maybe until the redwood was paid for or the time devoted to splitting the spruce wood. Maybe all was just an exchange until people got on their feet, not the return of the common fund. I refused to believe we were somehow just a stepchild of Keil's colony.

In the kitchen later I spoke out loud, though I knew Andy didn't understand. "How will we have something to leave you if your father keeps with the old ways of the common fund?"

I stomped the stick in the washtub, thumping so hard that the pepper mill fell off its shelf. I picked it up and slammed it back onto the shelf, causing the lid on the saltbox to jar open. I took a deep breath. I needed to calm down. *Ach,* even the seedlings I'd nurtured through the winter shivered with my outrage in their potato skins filled with dirt.

This was his family's influence. They saw this community as a branch, just as Nineveh had been a branch to Bethel. We were all to be one happy family here with Keil as the trunk of the big, happy tree. Maybe that was why his family didn't chastise Christian too much for taking risks with the oysters. They assumed he'd bring resources to help them with their needs. Maybe that was why they teased me, knowing that I was the *Dummkopf,* the one kept in the dark, the only one who didn't know anything about it.

But we'd put our own money into oystering. Well, Christian's physical labor was our part. Karl had put money in and so had Joe Knight, money he'd earned laboring in San Francisco.

Maybe I was the only one who assumed that we chose to remain as independent people, not replicas of Keil's vision. That might explain why there was no rush to build a church; any church would be constructed in the main community, now Aurora. Maybe that was why there was so little push toward a school even with a superintendent. The main community would offer that.

Well it was not to be, not here, not under my kneading hands. *Nein*. If I was in the dark, then I would be like a mushroom and grow there, learn what I needed. I'd get Karl to think about offering a regular school schedule as soon as the weather changed. April to September were good months for schooling; Andy was still too young, really, to take the mule on his own to the stockade and back, but John Giesy's children were old enough and the Stauffers and Schaefers had school-age children. John could order the schedule, free children for harvest, then offer school for a few more months until the rains came in earnest. I'd talk to him. And I'd ask Andreas and John to consider regular preaching on Sundays, like a real community. Sarah and the others might come if we acted like people who knew where our bounty came from and took time each week to express our gratitude.

When Christian returned in April, I already had the garden dug up and the small seedlings I'd nurtured through the winter set into the prodigal soil. I'd planted tiny flower seeds, too, totally impractical. He and the mule worked a larger field and we planted potatoes. It was already decided, he told me, that though it was expensive to have wheat brought in from Toledo on the Cowlitz, wheat raised by the Hudson's Bay Company, that's what we'd do. Growing wheat on the Willapa was toil in disaster. The grist mill already handled seventy-five bushels a day. "Sam says oats can make it, but you saw for yourself the small heads of the wheat you grew last year," Christian told me.

But I wanted a harvest to call my own.

"Ah, woman, you are stubborn. You cannot change the seasons to your wishes." But he let me plant wheat. I'm sure his brothers called it "Emma's indulgence."

That spring I had little time for complaining even to myself. The cows needed milking twice a day and the cream skimmed and kept cool in the river. I churned butter, hands on the plunger and my foot rocking Kate as she sat in the rocking chair fighting sleep. I was secretly glad I didn't have the pigs to tend to as well.

When Christian was gone, Henry or Rudy sometimes brought over meat that I smoked, keeping the fire going at just the right flame. I asked after everyone's health and was told all were fine, even Jack, they said, who had gone south to the Columbia to pick up the next load of wheat. "He didn't stop on his way through," I said.

"It would be unseemly," Henry said. "A young man visiting with his cousin's wife while her husband's away."

"I only meant I could have offered him something to eat," I said. "Shown the Diamond Rule." My words must have bristled if the raised eyebrow of Rudy and the way he looked at Henry were any indication. But then they were both safe in my presence, doing nothing unseemly. It just took two of them to deliver a ham.

Weeding took hours, and keeping my eye on the ever-moving Kate and Andy meant I had little time not already devoted to simply surviving. When Christian came home, I sighed with relief, though it meant cooking bigger meals and washing clothes whether I felt like it or not. But by the next morning, his presence was enough to buoy. Just knowing he was there, within the call of my voice, gave me rest. I did raise the common fund issue with him, finally, one day in June.

He sighed. "It is the best way here, Emma. We should have good return on the oysters this year, a good return. Some of what we make must go to *Herr* Keil, as they too struggle to build up the colony and have so many more to worry over. We agreed to pay back what the colony loaned us. You remember."

"*Ja,* but not beyond that. I didn't believe we would simply go back to where we were before," I said. "We set out on a different path by staying here."

"Was it so bad to know the weight was shared by others?" he asked. "To know we can care for widows and children, those in need beyond ourselves, is that so hard? It's the way to live the Diamond Rule, making life better for others."

"We were to care for our own first," I said.

"Emma. That isn't what you told me long months ago. You said we should reach out more to others. How else would the world read the story of our faith, if we just kept it to ourselves, our own little community?"

"Is that why you've taken in a housekeeper?" I asked.

"What? Who said that?"

I shrugged my shoulders.

"They tease you, Emma. I've no housekeeper. If you saw our hut you'd believe."

"Well, good. But this common fund made up of only former Bethelites does keep us as our own little colony. It doesn't reach out to others. People don't even come to the church services because they feel it's all us Germans. Andreas won't use English. How unwelcoming is that for our neighbors? I don't think any of the other settlers are sending their children to the school, either."

"John tells me you had words with him about that."

"*Ja.* I did."

"But because we take care of each other, we *can* give to others. Not just the tithe, but beyond the tithe. John will come around. My father will speak in English if there is someone there to hear him. Don't you see that, Emma? We are a generous people, passing good things on."

"So Joe's investment, his own money, he returns that now to the colony?"

"If he wishes. Karl too. But our share of the earnings, a portion each year, will go to pay Wilhelm. The rest, into a common fund. It is the best way I know how to take care of my family. I could not be away so much, Emma, if it wasn't for the others carrying my weight here."

"I haven't asked them for anything!" I said.

"They tend the hogs. We'll have good bacon and hams through the winter. They grind the grain and bring it. They helped build this very house. They bring you game."

"I could shoot my own game if you'd teach me how. But then how would I get the ammunition if not from your brothers? Or would you provide it for me? If I begged? If I used the proper words, nothing unseemly?"

"Whatever you need you may receive by just asking."

"You will not allow a discussion of this?" I asked.

"Indeed. Discuss all you wish. But the decision is made."

I gathered up willow branches for the mats and took them out to dry in the sun. Nothing had changed. Nearly four years of working side by side with my husband, holding his hand when he thought to drown in disappointment, praying for him, doing all I could think to do and still, he made the decisions. I was still just a woman, a wife, a mother, allowed to have an opinion but, like an unwatered seed, never see it grow into harvest.

The late-afternoon sun soothed my face as I sat with my back to the wall. With a stick, Kate patted at a spider as she sat. The goat followed Andy through the grasses while Christian lifted the bucket and went out to milk the cows. I closed my eyes. There had to be a way. I wanted more for my children than having to beg every time I had a desire. Andy was a smart child. He'd be a good student who might one day want to go far away to school, the way my uncle had, the worldly ambassador. How could I fuel my children's dreams if all we worked for poured into a pool others could take from? And if they could give when we asked, they could also withhold, those Giesy brothers. Just as Keil could. The man still ruled us even though he was miles away!

I started weaving a basket from the fronds left over from last year's mat-making. The baskets I attempted through the winter months were poor results fit only to hold the roots I dug. They made good storage at least but wouldn't be anything I could possibly sell. I lacked talent. I lacked gifts. The weather worked against my wheat. How could I be independent?

I got up and went into the cabin, put the fronds back up in the loft. They'd continue to dry there. When I came down the ladder, a letter lay on the table. Christian must have brought it from Bruceport, though I hadn't seen it that past evening. It was from Catherine. Dear, lovesick Catherine. At least that's how I saw her. Jack was much too charming for Catherine, too old for her as well. He was a bit of a buzzard with a songbird's voice.

But I read the parts about Papa now having property in his name. So not all that he earned had gone into the common fund in Bethel. I tried to remember what he might have sold or where he might have worked to earn his own money. Somehow he had found a way to earn resources that didn't go into the colony. So it was in my Wagner blood to do something innovative. Christian hadn't said that anything *I* might earn had to go into the common fund. And didn't he give me that twinkle in his eye when I teased him about his territorial marshal pay? Maybe he would withhold something for his own. Maybe he wouldn't object if I did as well.

Ach, there is always a way. Begin to weave; God provides the thread. How could I have forgotten?

———

The Fourth of July celebration was the greatest joy of my days in Willapa. Christian came to get us and we all went back with him to Bruceport. I liked the sense of a bustling town, with street vendors serving pork on sticks and hard-boiled eggs for sale right on the street. A band played, though not our German one. We'd heard the Giesys playing when we stopped at the stockade just to say hello as we made our way back to the Bay. His brothers didn't seem to mind that we weren't staying for the Giesy celebration; at least no one said anything to me that suggested that. At Bruceport people made speeches standing on the steps of Coon and Woodard's Store and Public House (Sam Woodard had a branch he owned here). I saw a few women and Andy made eyes with tykes his age. Christian pointed out where the justice held court. I listened to talk of events back East and the obstinacy of Governor Stevens. Posters about the martial law still hung on a board outside the wooden hut that passed as the sheriff's office. One hung upside down.

When Christian bent down to remove a stone from inside Andy's boot, I noticed his thinning hair and a tiny mole I'd never seen before at the back of his head. He needed to wear his hat. I wondered where he'd left it.

It was a slow-paced day with few worries. Karl Ruge would milk the cows and tend the goat and mule. That night, we placed our blankets and mats on the beach, far enough from the incoming tide but not too far to see blasts of fireworks sent out over the water and the long island that separated the Bay from the sea. We set the lantern behind us. Andy pressed his hands to his ears with each loud sound, but he grinned. We heard what we thought were "probably a few happy Americans celebrating," Christian said. "Or gun shots."

"Will you have to keep the peace?" I said. "Take someone to jail or something?"

"Not likely," my husband said, pulling me toward him. "They'll wind down and sleep it off come morning."

The mosquitoes buzzed about our heads, but I'd put a mud paste on the children's faces and hands and at their ankles, making sure they kept their shirts and pants on. We'd pitched netting over us like a tent and kept the fire going. When the children fell asleep and the mosquitoes were carried off by an ocean breeze, I asked Christian if we could walk just a little way along the beach. "To see if we can find a glass jar or some other shipwrecked treasure," I said.

"We'll stumble around like drunkards more likely."

I laughed at him and he indulged me once again, allowing me to hold the lantern as I scanned the driftwood exposed by the light as macabre shapes. What was so clear in the daylight was so easily obscured in the night. Christian sniffed the salty air, then pinched his nose to wipe away the drainage. It was an act of his I detested, but I let it pass without comment. I must do things to annoy him too, I thought. There was no sense in making this pleasant time a misery.

We found no treasures, nothing delivered from a distant sea. We walked past piles of discarded oyster shells. "A settler built a kiln one year and tried to burn the shells into lime," Christian told me. "But he decided the hard-shell clams yielded a better lime. Might be something to consider down the road. Lime makes a fine fertilizer, which we'll need in time as we use up the land."

My husband the innovator, always thinking of the future.

Back at the netting, I recognized that I had found a treasure: my treasure was the companionship of my husband and sleeping family. It seemed the time to give Christian my Fourth of July gift. I pulled the rolled parchment I'd brought with me out of my bag. "What's this?" he asked when I handed it to him. He sat up, hunched over it in the lamplight.

"It's a drawing I made of you," I said. "A likeness."

He didn't say anything as he stared. I thought he might have been disappointed.

"I'll get paint one day and it'll look better," I said. "And the light isn't good here. But Andy recognized it when I showed him. And I made a little tiny sketch of it in my letter home, and Catherine knew exactly who it was though she couldn't read the medal. There." I pointed.

"Who told you about the medal?" he said.

"Your father. It's an artillery service medal, for your marksmanship, he said. You didn't actually ever shoot at any...person, did you?"

"*Nein*. They give medals out just for being ready in a time of war," he said.

"We weren't really at war," I countered.

"Not how Governor Stevens saw it. Anyway, it is a good picture, Emma. You have a talent I didn't know you had. But you ought not waste your time on making a likeness of me. Draw the children instead."

I shrugged but beamed with his praise. I didn't let his alteration of an idea serve as criticism.

That night my husband showed me how he loved me in the quiet while our children slept. He kissed me with a tenderness that brought shivers. I thought I might tell him in the morning of my plan to earn money of my own, but at that moment I didn't want to speak of common funds or independence. I only wanted to be with him, to know him and let him know me. That night we spoke all the words of love we could imagine, tasted of the honey of our full moon.

8

Emma

A Compass Lost

"But why? Can't you just send it to him? Why do you have to go to Aurora?"

"And why must you always question what I do and the way I have to do it, Emma?" Christian said. "Besides, I want to see how the colony there progresses."

We stood at the water's edge. Joe Knight held Andy's hand and the two stood a distance away, being polite. I suppose we did sound as though we'd had this argument before. Soon Christian would be lifting me and then the children, carrying us out to the tender to get into the boat that would sail us up the Willapa.

This argument annoyed more than others, though, because I'd misunderstood, thinking he planned to return to the Willapa with us after this captivating weekend of the Fourth. Instead, his plan sent us home while he headed across the Bay then down the Wallacut River. He'd take a steamer up the Columbia to Portland. To see *Herr* Keil. To make our payment. "It would be too dangerous to put something so precious into the mail," he insisted. "What if it were stolen?"

"You're the marshal. You could catch the culprit," I said. I was being difficult, my back lifting like a frightened cat's.

"I won't stay there, Emma. I'll be back. Maybe I can talk your brother into coming for a visit. Would you like that?"

"Don't wheedle your way through my annoyance by offering up my brother," I snapped. "If he wanted to come he would have. He must be holding some grudge I don't even know about to have stayed away so long."

"Not every act that you don't like has something to do with you, *Liebchen*." I frowned at him. "Indeed. I can bring back things we need. Treasures for the children. Some pigment and resins for that painting you want to make. Maybe I'll look for a ewe."

"Something more to place in the common hold I suppose," I said. Into his silence I blew like old sheets in the wind, knowing soon they'd wear thin. I sighed. "A bred ewe would be nice. To make our own yarn would be good and we could start our own little flock. *Ja, ja,* I know," I said, holding up my hand before he could comment on things held in common. "Maybe you can make me a spinning wheel so I won't have to use Mary's." I wiped Kate's face with my handkerchief. "I do wish your family had thought to bring out more of our household things when they came. Though I realize we had few household things in Bethel, having never had a home of our own before, you always being gone."

"I can see this is the day when everything I say upsets you and reminds you of past indignities. You have an amazing memory, *Frau* Giesy," he said, "and I can tell you are about to share that gift with me if I stay here any longer."

I sighed again, this time motioning for Joe to bring Andy. We'd had such a good weekend together at Bruceport. I wished we could just stay; maybe build ourselves a house on stilts over tide flats. I'd have to mention that to Christian.

But not now. Now it was Monday and a new week and Christian was going to Aurora. I hoisted Kate into my arms, then Christian lifted us both and sloshed across the shoals and shallow water to our waiting boat. Joe Knight followed with Andy.

"I wish they had a dock," I complained, just for something to say. My husband settled us onto the craft. "When will you leave then?" I asked.

"Tomorrow, barring anything going wrong here that needs my attention."

"Is Joe going with you? Maybe we should come along."

"One of the herd boys is heading back with me. He's just arrived. I'll be back in a week or so. Think of me as being here working instead of there at Aurora. Then maybe it won't seem like such a terrible separation."

"*Ja*. Tell a story to my mind."

"Draw another picture," he said. "I'll look at it when I get back." He kissed my nose then, a rare public expression of affection. His hand lingered in mine and he squeezed it, then turned and sloshed his way back toward the shore.

I watched him and remembered a dream I'd had where we'd gone underwater together. I asked him if he knew how to get where we were going and he said no, that he'd lost his compass.

"Do you have your compass?" I shouted. He held his hand to his ear as though he couldn't hear. The wind whipped the sail insistently. At the water's edge, he turned and I waved a last good-bye. The boatman pulled his anchor and we moved out into the stream.

I'd have to think of this separation as just like the others, with him oystering while I tended the children. It's no different. Nothing to worry over. *Tell ourselves stories*, ja. *That is what we must do when we pull up our anchor and have only our compass to trust as we sail away.*

———

Maybe it was the dream. Maybe it was the idea that he was leaving me for Keil, doing Keil's bidding once again. Perhaps it was nothing more than women's intuition. I wasn't sure what compelled me, but about a half hour up the Willapa, with the seagulls crying above us, I shouted to the oarsman, "Turn back, *ja*?"

He frowned and I spoke my English more slowly. "I want to go back."

"The Mister won't be liking it," he said.

"The Mister will understand that you listened to his wife," I said. "Besides, you'll earn twice the fee."

"We'll stay with Papa?" Andy asked.

"*Ja.* We'll stay and if nothing else, see if we can convince him not to go away at all." I imagined Christian's frown when he saw us but I pitched that thought away. I could turn his frowns to laughter.

Kate patted my cheek as the oarsman began rowing the craft back toward the Bay. Now that we headed west, I was in an even greater hurry to arrive. It was silly. I'd just said good-bye but I felt a joy in heading back toward him, in surprising him. I'd change his mind, I would.

A dark bank of clouds formed in the western sky and I told myself it was wise we'd turned back. Why, there might be a squall or something. This storm would blow over tonight and then we could both leave together in the morning—if Christian still insisted on going to Aurora after I tried one more time to convince him otherwise.

I held Kate against my chest and she slept. Andy shouted up at the seagulls. This was what a woman did, try to convince her husband of reasonable acts to take. Christian would forgive me the extra cost of the oarsman having to bring us back.

As we approached Bruceport again, I watched as an old man loaded chairs and a bedstead and barrels onto a raft tethered to a piling at the river's edge. His long white beard caught in the swirl of breeze. Shoalwater women culled oysters. Tiny drifts of smoke from cooking fires reached up to a sky now dotted with a mix of dark clouds. The sun still warmed our faces. I licked my lips. The oarsman clanged a bell and I watched as Sam Woodard stepped out of his warehouse. He put a telescope on us and I waved. Then Christian soon stood beside him and I waved again, my whole arm sweeping across the sky. They walked toward us, both wearing their oystering waders, followed by shadows on the wet sand. The herd boy joined them from off to the side and before the oarsman could say anything I said, "I forgot something."

"What did you forget that was so important?" Christian said. He crossed his arms over his chest. He didn't look angry but wore a small frown of concern. Sam smiled and shook his head.

"We forgot that we had one more day to spend with you," I said. "One more day before you leave for Aurora Mills. A chance to spend it with your family and here we'd sailed away. We can all leave together in the morning. You go your way; we'll go ours. If you still insist on leaving us."

"*Ach*, Emma." Christian said. "You waste this oarsman's time and other people's money in this foolish return."

"Maybe," I said. "But you can't deny you'll like having someone tonight to share your bed."

"She has you there," Sam said and the herd boy laughed with him.

It's the details one remembers. The way the sun slanted through the clouds. The perspiration on my face. The lack of premonition. I stood with the children at my side on the riverbank, where Christian had sent me while he helped the old man at his raft. I don't think Christian would have seen the old man if he hadn't come out to greet us again. I don't think the herd boy or Christian would have been at that place where the river poured into the Bay. But he was. They were. I stood with my children cluck-henned against my hem. Christian said he had to help that man who was going to lose everything on that raft if he didn't get things tied down. The next thing I knew, he was on the rickety craft with the man, tying the pieces of furniture down, the herd boy helping with ropes and a canvas tarp. "I'll just be a minute," Christian had said. "Just wait up there on the bank with the children."

Sam had gone back inside. We stood waiting, watching them work.

Then came the squall.

It was a freakish burst of wind and rain that tore at the tether, then spun the raft and its cargo out toward the Bay. I'm not even sure of how it transpired. I'd turned my face from the blast of rain and wind, then looked back. A cedar dresser shifted against a barrel on the raft and then as though in slow motion, the old man reached to resettle it but instead fell backward into the sea. I heard his shout, an "Oh!" of surprise. I watched as Christian moved swiftly to that side of the raft, his tall body leaning down, then he dropped to one knee to reach his hand out, the black heel of his waders etched against the skyline. The herd boy grasped a bedstead as it shifted with Christian's weight on that side and the wind acting as a swirling agent, pushing then lifting. They were no longer attached to the piling, had become like a leaf in the sea.

"What's Papa doing?" Andy asked.

"He's helping someone who was foolish enough to move furniture out in a squall," I said.

Christian reached for the man. I couldn't see him. He must have slipped under the raft. Christian jumped in then. *He didn't remove his waders.* He held on to the raft, but by then it had swirled out farther and waves washed over it. I lost sight of the herd boy, hoping he stood on the far side reaching for Christian or pulling the old man up.

"His waders. They'll fill," I whispered.

The wind took their shouts from us, if there were any. And then with relief I saw the old man swimming toward the shore, leaving the raft of his furniture. The herd boy wasn't on the raft; I couldn't see Christian gripping it. They must be on the far side. Surely I'd see him and Christian any moment following the old man, swimming to safety.

But I didn't.

The raft drifted away.

The old man stood dripping on shore looking back at it.

"Christian? Christian!" *This can't be happening!* I ran, sweeping Kate up into my arms, screaming. "Christian! For heaven's sake, where are you? Where?" I sloshed toward the water, moved back and forth along the shore-line. "Christian! Please. Where are you?"

The old man stood panting, his hands on his thighs as he breathed heavily. "Where is he? What have you done to my husband?" I wanted to pummel him, but Kate clung to my neck.

"Papa? Where's Papa?" Andy asked.

The old man coughed up seawater. He shouted for Sam, who had already run from the warehouse at my cries, I suppose. "He's out there!" I screamed. "Christian is out there. And the boy. They were with the raft. They went under. Please, please, please. Sam! You have to save him! I don't even know if he can swim!"

Sam signaled the oarsman who had already pushed his craft out to the sea. Together they rowed toward the raft that bounced and jerked toward the long island that separated the Bay from the sea. Wind still whipped at us. Maybe Christian was hanging on and I just couldn't see him.

It was Sunday, July 6, about four in the afternoon. I dropped to my knees in prayer.

"I'm so sorry, Missis." The old man coughed. "So sorry. The furniture was just old stuff."

———

They recovered Christian's body in the dusk, cut him free from the ropes, brought him to me.

I could not believe my eyes. I could not. A swell of outrage surged through me. A waste, that's what it was. A complete and total waste of two lives. Christian, always doing for others, always acting the Diamond Rule, making one's life better than his own. But at what cost? The old man saved himself! He didn't need fixing or helping. He did it on his own! Oh, the irony, the irony. God must be laughing at me, I thought, to take my husband over such a trivial thing as old furniture and to save the man who'd caused it.

But there he lay, on the wet sand, his face the color of gray stone. I threw myself across his chest. Tears did not come. "Oh, Christian, how could you? How could you leave me here?"

Christian lay still as I brushed the sea life from his face and straightened the collar at his neck. "How could you?" I whispered. "We had so much time before us."

The herd boy's body washed ashore the next morning.

———

I don't remember much of what happened next. I know I wanted to take Christian home. I told Sam that and he nodded, said he'd have a casket made up quick as he could and he'd row us up the Willapa himself. I guess we must have stayed in the cabin, but I didn't see Joe Knight until the next morning when he put his arms out to me, his eyes as red as sunset from the tears he'd shed. The children said almost nothing. I think they must have seen my eyes, my constant shaking of my head, my muttering words: "Such a waste. Such a waste."

In the morning, I carried my children and walked by myself to the river. We piled into a wide craft with the caskets at the center and headed home. *Home.* Things would be better if I could just get Christian home. I knew I should grieve the herd boy and his parents but I had only so much room for grief and I gripped it tight in my fist, held it just for my husband. The outrage I held for the nameless old man, for Keil and for God.

How would I tell Christian's parents? How would I tell his friends? Karl Ruge, Martin? His parents would say Christian shouldn't have been at the ocean anyway, "messing with oysters." Karl might say it as well, perhaps blame himself for being our partner. Would they acknowledge that if he hadn't been planning to return money to Keil, he would have been working the oysters that day? Keil had some part in this just as he did in every bad thing that happened to us. If Christian had been working oysters, he might not have seen the old man—that wretched, surviving, old man—and then he'd still be with us, brushing the hair from Andy's eyes, kissing Kate on her nose, telling me I cost him extra money by coming back. *Maybe I'd cost him more than that.*

At Willapa, Sarah came out with a smile on her face. Then she saw the look Sam wore. She stared at me, the children, and the boxes in the center of the tendering craft.

"Oh, Emma," she whispered. "How…"

"Stupid," I said. "It was all such a waste." She held me in her arms then, and at last I could weep.

———

"You will leave the casket here," Barbara said after we arrived at the stockade and Sam told her what had happened. She rubbed her hand along the wood. "We will prepare the body properly."

"I want to take him home," I said. "We can bury him on his own place."

"Nein," Andreas countered. "He will be buried beside Willie, on the hill. Leave him here. Leave your son here as well. Take the girl and go home if you must. Martin will come get you when we are ready."

I bristled. "My children will go home with me," I said. "And my husband."

"You no longer have a husband," Barbara said. "I no longer have a son. You go." She patted my back. We shared a grief. "You will find comfort at your cabin; I find comfort in preparing my son's body, *ja?*" I could let her have this time with Christian, I decided. I nodded. "I will take the children," I said.

"I'll go with you," Martin told me. "Karl too. We'll see you safely there."

The air felt balmy as we rode in silence. How could the weather be perfect on a day dripping such grief? I held myself together until we reached the house. Opal bleated her greeting and I felt tears burn against my eyes. I blinked. "I'll milk the goat," Martin said. "Go on inside."

I carried Kate on my hip. Andy removed the lantern from the mule, the lantern Christian had made for me, the light that had last illuminated our lives as we walked the beach seeking treasures. Had that really just been a few days before? Karl opened the door. Andy ran in with the lantern and just the sight of it there on that table, knowing Christian would never again light that lamp, took my breath away.

Karl reached for Kate before I fell.

———

Darkness already shrouded when I awoke. A pinprick of light glowed from the candle on the table. Strange shadows danced against the walls. The candle shouldn't be lit over there, away from me. My tongue felt thick and my eyes were gooey. I scanned the room stopping at Mary, who sat beside the light. I could hear the scrape of her needle through cloth as she found the hole in the cross-stitch she worked on. Her face held no features. Where were the children? What was she doing here? I tried to sit up.

Then I remembered. My breath came from an empty hollow welled out in my heart. I suppressed a sob, I thought.

"You're awake," Mary said. She set her needlework down on our rough table and came closer.

"Where are the children?"

"Andy went back with Martin for now. Just for a little while, to give you time to come to the understanding of this. Kate's asleep, bless her. She patted your head for the longest time and then finally just dozed off. I carried her to the cradle. I'm so sorry, so very sorry."

"What time is it?"

"Midnight or so."

"You should go home, be with Elizabeth and Boshie. It isn't necessary for you to be here. I'll be all right. I'll get Andrew in the morning. I want him with me."

She patted my shoulder. "You can get him at the service. You need your own rest."

"Is that possible? Do you know what's happened? Of course you do. I just mean—"

"I know what you mean. But please. Let me just stay with you. I want to be here."

I lay back on the pillow but in doing so I smelled my husband, the salt of him, the brush of his mustache on my mouth, the weight of his head on my breast. I jerked up.

"What's wrong?"

"It's him. Here." I shook my head. "I need to get up, work, do something. There's the funeral. His clothes. I need to give them clothes for the burial."

"Yes. John and Henry are taking care of those things, Emma. They all want—we all want to help. We're all just so sorry. They're making the arrangements, digging the…next to Willie's grave. Martin can dress the body. He knows about those things with herbs and whatnot."

"I should wash his body. It's what a wife does."

"His mother will help with that. It will help her grieve."

"Yes. Help her grieve a senseless death."

My mind swirled to capture the image of Christian's last moments alive on this earth. The flailing, the rush of water, going under the raft, getting tangled in the ropes. Maybe he tried to save the boy, but the young man's panic pulled him under. Did the old man try to save Christian or just himself? *Does Christian know how to swim? Did he?* He'd joked about it once. Perhaps it was no joke. What courage it must have taken for him to work the oysters, to be brother to the water if he didn't know how to swim. *Why did I have no foreboding? Were we not as close as I imagined? Surely if we had been as one, I would have heard him crying out to me or been warmed by the presence of a comforting God preparing me for loss. I felt nothing. I, who feared the water, hadn't been worried when he decided to help the old man; just annoyed that he would take the time from us.* "I had every reason to fear water," I told Mary.

"It was an accident from what Sam says. Just an—"

"It's Keil," I said, interrupting. "Christian insisted on taking the certificates to Keil so he could pay our debt. Always it's been Keil, driving our lives and now Christian's death." I stood, paced. "The goat," I said. "Someone needs to milk the goat."

"Boshie did that. And fed the mule. There's nothing you need to do but rest. Build up your strength. It hasn't even hit you yet, Emma. That much I know. When we lost the baby, well…"

Her voice trailed off. I couldn't listen. My mind rolled around thinking that when Christian came home I'd tell him all about this, how strange I felt, how empty, how my husband had squandered his life in a meaningless way. *He's not coming home.*

I resented Mary then. I resented her having already grieved and lived through what I had yet to bear. I resented that she still had a husband she'd go home to. I resented her knowing what to do when I didn't.

I gazed at the door, expectant though I knew that he wouldn't walk through it. Could the human mind hold two opposing thoughts at once? Mary had grief's ritual down. Everyone knew what to do except me.

I wanted Andy with me. I wanted to decide about the casket. I wanted my husband buried here, on our property. Why did it have to be in the place Keil picked for his son? Why was it Keil, always Keil? Didn't I have say in any of this?

I picked up Kate and held her to me, her sweet little face like a full moon, so round, so glowing in the lamplight. I brushed at her nose and the crackled sound she made as she breathed ceased. I watched her chest move in and out. I wanted to hold her tight to me but I didn't want to wake her. My fingers made round motions on her skin. She and Andy were all I had now. All that mattered.

"Emma? Are you all right?"

Who knows how long I'd stood there. My heart felt snowed on, wet, thick, suffocating snow. Mary lifted Kate from my arms, my daughter's little legs hanging over Mary's forearm, relaxed, her head lolling in safe sleep. Mary pressed her onto the bed, pulled a light cover over her legs.

"My mind feels foggy." I inhaled, couldn't get a deep breath. "I'll fix tea. I need tea."

"Let me do it for you," Mary said.

"He's my husband, the father of my children. Five years, Mary. That's all I'm to get? Five years? What kind of God would be so unloving that—"

"Oh, Emma, don't. Don't blame, not now."

I looked at her. I wasn't sure what I was supposed to do, but here was something forbidden, something I *wasn't* supposed to do. My contrary ways, what Emma Wagner Giesy was known for.

My husband understood me. Maybe he was the only one who had ever understood me. And now he was gone.

That thought finally brought the tears I hoped would cleanse my angry soul.

———

They stayed with me three days, the Giesy women. They helped me select clothes for Christian to be buried in and carried them off. I compelled them to bring Andy back despite my mother-in-law's suggestion that Andy stay longer with them, "where he would have male influences to guide him during this trying time."

"He has the memory of his father to guide him," I said. "And me."

Having Andy home gave me strength. I needed that success. Power, after all, is setting a goal and gathering resources to make it happen.

When my mother-in-law brought him back to me, she spent the day. It was her first visit to our home since the house was built. We looked at my garden with a good stand of peas and onions and potatoes. The wheat field looked paltry. "Planting that was a waste when you can get wheat ground at the mill," she said, pointing with her chin toward the field. She looked to the flowers. "And posies." She clucked her tongue. *Waste. A life given for nothing, that was a waste.*

I didn't defend. I had no energy. Christian understood my efforts.

"He loved fishing," she said then. "He'd plop his line into the water, even little puddles of water in the spring. Then he'd come running to tell me he'd seen a fish there. He was always so hopeful." She sighed. "He loved the mountains. I always thought we'd go back one day to Switzerland, just to see them and what we left behind. Did you know that he broke his arm once, running and falling? He didn't even cry but it was so crooked I knew it was broken. His father set it. I nursed him and now…" My arm brushed hers and she reached to grab my hand. She squeezed it firm, and the warmth of it and its strength brought tears. She was perhaps the closest anyone could come to knowing of the emptiness I felt. "A parent isn't supposed to outlive a child," she said, wiping at her eyes. "Especially not a child who has lived to forty-five." She released my hand, fumbled at her sleeve, then blew her nose in the handkerchief she'd kept there.

Andy ran past us, chasing the goat, grabbing for the animal's twitching tail. It bleated in unison with my son's laughter. I could not imagine my life without that child. How would I survive the loss of his laughter or of Kate's? What must it be like for my mother-in-law to have given birth and witnessed a son grow to manhood, and then to watch him be buried? Death was difficult enough, but to lose a part of my own flesh? Such courage it takes to be a mother.

My mother-in-law said, "Such strange events we see in living. I must cherish the years I had with him. You too, Emma. Others, Mary, had only minutes with the child she lost. And you, just five years as a wife." She took my hand again. "But you're young," she added.

I braced myself for the words, "You'll marry again," but they didn't come. I would never do that, not ever marry again, and so I'd never have another child that I would worry would one day be lost to me. These two were enough to worry over.

Christian wasn't supposed to leave a wife and two small children, but I didn't say this to her.

"The service," I said. "I—"

"It is being handled, Emma." She patted my hand. "You have too much to think about now. His brothers and father will take care of those details."

These were details I wanted to take care of, but my tongue fell silent under the weight of her grief.

———

I fought sleep, fearing I'd have to face the loss again each time I woke. The children both slept with me, something my mother-in-law suggested. "It will ease the pain of not sharing a bed," she said. She forgot that my bed stayed empty for weeks at a time when Christian traveled, when he farmed the oysters. In the night, a child's elbow now pressed against my back; a tiny arm draped across my face. I dozed and woke from dreams where Christian fell over a cliff all tangled up with a mule; or where he sank into deep mud and I couldn't pull him out; or, the worst, that dream where we together dived underwater in a craft and I'd asked if he knew how to get where we intended to go and he said, "No, I've forgotten my compass."

I planned to grieve after the service. I'd simmer until then, temper the slow boil I felt brewing that without watching would spill over and sear a hole clear through my heart. When everyone left us alone, my children and I would decide what we would do, not Christian's family, not everyone else who thought they knew best. When we were our own island, then we'd decide when to cross the water to the mainland or whether to stay all alone.

Karl and Boshie came to escort us to the stockade for the service. It was one of those glorious summer days with every sweet scent of wildflower imaginable floating in the air and yet one could not hold on to any particular scent. Birdsong became so loud at times I didn't even hear the clop-clop of the mule crossing the river. A bridge might be there one day, but my husband wouldn't build it. Tiny flashes of memory of trips taken with Christian formed, then darted like dragonflies, away. I'd never hear him call me *Liebchen* again. Never feel his mustache prick my lips. No physical sensations; no recognizing his gait from a distance. Just memories and perhaps not even them if they sifted through my mind forever as they had this week, like seeds scattered in wind.

I didn't want to arrive. I didn't want to see his family's faces, be "Emma" for them, behave as they expected. I wanted this over so I could be alone with my children. Alone with my grief.

Outside, people spoke in low voices and stopped talking when we walked past them. Even my black dress hushed against my legs. I'd put lumps of sugar in the hem pockets, something to soothe the children with later, and the tiny weights tapped my ankles. I stepped inside the stockade where I expected to see the casket and my husband, one last time.

Sarah and Sam stood there, a few others from the area. All the Giesys. The Stauffers. George Link, John Genger, the other scouts. And then as they parted for me, I saw him.

He opened wide his arms to me and I rushed into them trying desperately not to sob, not to bring attention to my wails, but I could not contain the mix of joy and agony his presence represented.

"Ah, Emma," my brother Jonathan said. "It's with great sadness I come now to see you. Great sadness."

"*Ja*, I know, I know. But you are here. I so need you to be here. Thank you. *Danke*." Shared blood comforted as none other.

"Thank Wilhelm, too, Emma. He brought several of us." He said these words as whispers in my ear. Frozen water replaced my blood.

I stepped away from Jonathan, scanned the crowd until I saw him standing with that beard, those eyes that never seemed to blink, eyes that took people in and kept them, that drew people across water they couldn't swim in, just to please him. I felt a buzzing in my head, but my breath came short and I didn't trust myself to speak. I just prayed, yes prayed, that Keil would not approach me, would not attempt to offer sympathy.

"We come today to help our sister, the Widow Giesy, put her husband to rest," Keil said then to the group. "She is among family and friends who know how to serve widows and orphans as our colony has done for years. She is like a daughter to me. We come to say good-bye on this earth to our friend, Chris Giesy, her husband, the father of this fine boy." Andy stood against my hip looking down. Keil touched the top of his head. "We come to light these candles and climb the hill where we will place this man who was like a son to me into the ground next to"—his voice croaked—"my son, my Willie." He cried now and tears rolled down his face. Others comforted him, patted his back.

Singing began, men's voices rising in a German dirge. I saw the *Schellenbaum*. I heard the tiny tinkle of the bells. Keil had brought the staff of honor to be carried before my husband's casket.

When the dirge ended, Keil regained his composure and he continued. "We prepare to lay Chris Giesy's body in the ground, but we know his spirit has already gone before us. It waits for us in heaven where we will all be united one day. All of us, sinners all and yet forgiven by an act of grace."

At least he does not blame me for Christian's death. At least not yet.

He motioned then for the men inside to lift the casket they'd been shielding from my view. It was made of redwood, leftover from the mill, I imagined. A second, smaller casket sat off to the side; the herd boy's casket. "We go now to the burial site," Keil commanded.

This was the service? No talk of what Christian had meant to so many people here? No scriptures I could cling to for their comfort? What about the way he led us here and protected us, couldn't we talk about that? Jonathan had my arm but I pulled back. "I…I want to see him. My husband's body. I need to see him."

"The casket has already been sealed shut, Widow Giesy," Keil said.

Already I've become the Widow Giesy. No longer Frau *Giesy. No longer Emma.*

"But you…you saw your son every day coming across the prairie. You said good-bye to him over time." I heard a gasp from some of the women, but it didn't stop me. "Now you deprive me of one last time to touch his face, to hold him just once more?"

"Emma," Jonathan said. "The lid's already pegged tight."

I wiggled free of his arm. "They wouldn't let me wash his body and dress him. They deliberately didn't want to wait before they pegged it shut."

Keil asked, "What does the Widow Giesy say?"

Jonathan said, "She is distraught. That's all. To be expected."

"I'm not! I only want to see my husband one last time before I never see him ever again." The group, silent, parted when I pushed through them and stopped at the head of the casket.

"Open it," I ordered.

A part of me prayed they'd refuse, begged in my heart they'd deny me so I could place my anger onto all of them instead of where it was.

Joe Knight held one end of the casket and he motioned for the men to put it back down onto the saw horses. His eyes looked swollen from crying.

I stared, as desperate as a prisoner waiting for a pardon. I wanted to see an empty casket. Maybe it was all an elaborate joke. Maybe Christian was alive. Maybe I was mistaken in having witnessed his drowning. Maybe I'd turn and see my husband standing there, strong, tall, healthy, waiting to take me home, the joke elaborate and cruel but one I'd forgive. *Oh, God,* I prayed. *I will forgive them, forgive You; I'll not carry a grudge, I'll not.*

Jonathan said, "She won't believe until she sees."

"Ja," Herr Keil said. "It is like Elijah and his servant, Elisha. The servant

had to see his master's death in order to believe he must put on the mantle of his master and carry on."

But it was my brother whose grief became the face of truth, my brother's orders that lifted the casket lid so at last I could believe.

The women had lined the wooden box with quilt pieces and given him a pillow filled with herbs. My nose filled up with scents of lavender mixed with the unmistakable smell of death. I touched his face then, felt the rubbery wrinkle of his skin, ran my fingers across his cold lips. Was that a bruise on his cheek? I patted the artillery medal he wore on his chest and removed it. No one stopped me.

Andy pulled at my skirt and asked to be lifted up. I held Kate now, not sure when I'd lifted her. "Andy, I can't…," I said. Then Big Jack Giesy stepped in and with ease hoisted my son.

"Daddy's sleeping?" I nodded. "He slept from the water too." How else to explain to one so young? Andy asked to be set down, and then he leaned his head against me, pushing the ruffles of my crinoline and the hard hem sweets against my legs.

I had two children to remember him by, that's all I had. These two children would keep his memory alive while his friends placed his body in the ground.

I turned, my breath a weight stuck in my chest. They pegged the cover shut. Jonathan directed me outside, up the steep hill. Those gathered carried candles and began following us, the bells of the *Schellenbaum* tinkling in the wind.

"Papa's lantern," Andy said pulling back. "We carry his lantern, Mama?"

"It's with the mule," I told him. "We don't have time to—"

"But Papa's lantern has Papa's light. It—"

"Never mind," Jack Giesy told Andy. "There's enough light with the candles."

"But—"

"Go get it," I told him.

"You maybe could indulge your son a little less," Jack said.

I saw Jack raise an eyebrow of warning. His intervention annoyed. "Go," I said.

Andy raced to the mule. He returned with the lantern, and we trudged up the hill behind the casket, my son's small hands gripping the lantern handle as though he gripped his father's hand.

I really don't remember what *Herr* Keil said at the grave. The wind whipped the dirt, reminding me of ash. All the candles blew out. We didn't need them for light; it was still afternoon. The lantern light continued to glow. My mind took in only small tidbits of his words. A raccoon scampered through the graveyard behind Keil.

I wanted this to be over. I wanted to plant the cedar sapling Jonathan carried for me, then saddle the mule and return home, curl up with my children and my memories, uninterrupted by what others thought I should or should not do. I wanted to lie there, maybe until we all died.

Jonathan helped me tap the seedling into the ground at Christian's grave, then we left the cemetery to eat. *How can I die if I eat?* All had brought food. People did tell stories then of Christian, food being appetite for memory. They spoke of his adventuresome spirit even as a child. His teasing on Ash Wednesday, how as a boy he called the last child out of bed the *Aschenpuddel,* the ash puddle; how his brothers and he wrestled; how his older sister Helena taught him; how his younger sisters adored him.

Then *Herr* Keil suggested they replay the funeral dirge he'd composed for Willie. The men agreed and their horns intoned a heaviness. It was too much.

"Here are Christian's papers," Sam told me as I rose, gathered up my children, and walked out to our mount. I retied the lantern, making sure we wouldn't lose it. Sarah and Sam stood on either side of me. He handed me the folded leather satchel. "It was on his person, tucked in a belt."

"We took everything out," Sarah said. "Sam dried them. They're all in German so you mustn't think we pried."

Her words made me smile. "You would never pry," I said. "Thank goodness you were one of the first to be there, Sam." I clutched the papers to my breast. "Thank you for this."

Sam said, remembering, "His last words the day you left were of you, Emma."

"Were they?" I wiped at my eyes with the sleeve of my dress.

"He said if you needed anything, to remind you that the family would always take care of you. Oh, and just before he left, he pocketed his compass and said to let you know he'd found it, hidden under his books. Did he get a chance to tell you himself?" I shook my head, no. "He was quite adamant that I tell you. I suspect you know what it means."

He'd found his direction; I had now to find mine.

9

Emma

Water-Stained Wisdom

Those first weeks after the service were like the water-stained pages I unfolded from Christian's leather wallet. I remember moments of clarity but mostly I couldn't make sense of much at all. Even before I left the service, that arbitrary time I'd given to myself to begin to face the future, even then my thinking had begun to warp.

I felt obsessed about seeing what Christian carried in that wallet. I could have found the certificates to pay off *Herr* Keil and get that out of the way, finish what Christian had started. But I didn't want to open it with everyone around. It was something tangible of my husband that I could hold on to, and I didn't want to share it. Keil could wait. This was his fault anyway. Christian wouldn't have been on the Bay if Keil hadn't insisted that the real colony form south of the Columbia. If he had accepted what the scouts claimed, none of this would have happened. If he'd realized how much Christian contributed to the larger community here by his marshalling, being the justice of the peace, a legislator, he'd see why we could not follow him to Aurora. Christian and I had come to this place so certain of God's guidance, and now this.

I lacked shelter in this storm.

My brother would be returning with Keil in a few days, though he offered to take me back to my home. *Our home. My home. Did it matter what I called it?*

Once again I would have another adult in the house, but this one was my brother, whom I dearly loved, and I trusted it would be a soothing time.

"We're going to go back to Aurora Mills, up the Willapa," Jonathan told me while still at the stockade. "And Wilhelm will come in a day or so with the others, bringing the herd boy's casket. I can join them then. He's brought you apple cider too. For the children's teeth."

I wanted nothing from Keil but the children did need cider. I had no dried apples to give them. "We can take the cider with us now," I said. "That way Keil won't have to stop by. It'll be easier for him to take the casket across the Bay and up the Columbia rather than carrying it overland. That's the way he brought Willie's casket." *It was the route Christian took to his death.*

"He had a hearse then. Now it is just us and the mules. The boy is light. Keil has decided. I'm coming back with you now, Emma," Jonathan said. It wasn't an offer but a directive. He stepped back into the stockade to let Keil know, I supposed. He came out with Jack Giesy.

Jack tipped his hat at me. "I'm sorry for your loss, *Frau* Giesy."

I looked for the tease in his face, but his condolences sounded sincere. Right then hollow platitudes would have angered me.

Jack had been the one to lift my son up for a last look at his father. Jack touched Andy's hat. My son didn't jerk away. The two had twisted a thread together. "Thank you," I said. I nodded my head to him and finished saddling the mule.

Boshie and Mary stood near my brother and Jack when I finished and led the mule to a stump, where I stepped up into the stirrup. Sarah lifted Kate up to me, the child all wide eyes and smiles. Mary wiped at her eyes.

I caught a look in Jack's eyes, a blend of surprise and disapproval, I thought, and so I said, "Sidesaddles aren't much used in these parts. Certainly not when one is holding a child."

Before stepping back Mary whispered, "We could see your crinoline ruffles when you lifted your leg over."

"*Ja*, well, fortunately for me, I don't care," I said.

Jonathan mounted up and we headed south toward my house.

Christian wouldn't see the garden harvest. He wouldn't be there to tell me that my wheat had been a waste. He wouldn't find another perfect small cedar tree to decorate with blown egg shells like the one we had last Christmas. Last Christmas. Christian had seen his last Christday, my last birthday, our last anniversary. How many "lasts" could there be? A last senseless death. I wondered then if I'd ever have another thought that didn't carry with it a reference to my Christian.

———

Jonathan stayed busy those days he shared with me. He milked the cows while I handled the goat. He chopped wood in the late summer dusk when the air cooled. He often knelt to weed with me and surprised me with his love of words, something we shared that I hadn't known of. "The word *therapy* comes from working with decay and decomposition," he said. "As in a garden. Yet in that decay, the soil builds up if we add to it, tend it. It's the way of life."

"I like the gardening but it's just that, work. Not much tenderness in ripping out weeds."

"More though, Emma. Your grief, it must be worked and reworked through your own thinking until you come to a place of resolution. So you can go forward. From dust to dust. We are all built up eventually, again. If we allow it."

He failed to engage me with such talk that Christian's death was somehow related to an act of nurture, soil decaying and being restored. I wasn't ready to be restored. I planned to have a few words with God, once my brother left me alone, about what had happened here, words about the life of a worthy servant being taken in exchange for an old man's insistence and inferior furniture. "Doing for others. Helping our neighbors." Keil and this whole act of servitude had taken us from Bethel to here.

For now, I'd change the subject.

"Christian planned to bring back a bred ewe for me, for wool," I said.

"We will bring several up. *Ja.* Andreas and John talk of sheep too." He looked around. "Lots of twigs and such will get in the wool here unless they're fenced and fed," he said. "Be difficult to clean but the fodder would be good. Christian must have talked with his father about it."

"He was going to bring one just for us," I said.

My brother let that pass without comment.

That evening when I served him bean soup with fresh lettuce from my garden, and biscuits with molasses followed by a cake with berries and freshly whipped cream, he pushed his chair back and stuck his hands in his waistband and said, "That was good, Sister. Good flavors, filling but not heavy. I like that."

"A compliment's a rare thing," I said. "Especially from a brother."

Andy and Kate both licked spoons full of the cream. Jonathan cleared his throat. "I should do it more, then." He picked at his nails as I cleared the table of the tin plates that Christian had made. Andy, wearing a mustache of white, came to sit on his uncle's knee. Jonathan bounced him as though he rode a horse but then said Andy was getting too big for him. "See how I huff and puff?" Jonathan told him.

"Like the wolf and the three pigs," Andy said.

"Like that."

I washed Andy's and Kate's faces, then picked up my stitching and wasn't looking at Jonathan when he said, "Emma, now that you are widowed, it will be foolish for you to hold on to this idea that you can have your own sheep and whatnot, without the others to help you." I looked at him. "Christian understood that communal care is the best care. Each has a gift that can be shared, and together no one has to bear the great weight of doing all, alone. It is the Christian way, Emma."

"Obligations come with gifts," I said. "Accept the cows and then one must meet the obligation of the contract for butter someone else signed. Take on the sheep and then one must shear when others shear, not when I might want to."

"Ah, Emma. When we give something away, our hands are empty then, right in front of the person receiving our gift. We stand exposed, admitting that we're needy too. Then they give back. It puts us all in the same place. We are part of the colony. The community."

"I'm not alone. I have the children. We'll do *gut* here. *Gut*."

He ran his fingers through his hair, a habit he had. "It's for the sake of the children…that you should think about coming back with me. There is room in the *gross Haus*. Louisa would welcome you, I know."

I laughed. "Louisa would take me in, but welcome me? That I doubt." I took a needle out of my chatelaine, changed thread, and continued mending. "Louisa didn't come to Christian's burial."

"Their children, she has them to care for."

"But in a communal place, wouldn't someone else care for them while a woman took time to grieve with her sister?"

He sighed. "You always could find fault."

"Not faulting. I don't complain, just explain. I see things how they are."

"You see things how you want to, unique but not always right," my brother said.

As if being right mattered to me. Only where my children were concerned or my husband, well, then it mattered that the right choice was made, the right decision carried out. "I'm not a welcome member at Aurora. It is foolish not to admit that. Even your offer to bring me there would not remove the stain."

"You're not thinking clearly, Emma. There is no stain. All is forgiven: your rush to join the scouts, your push to keep Christian here, the oystering, all of that is overlooked in the wake of this great loss. We only want to help."

My face felt hot. I had no need of forgiveness. Keil, now he ought to be seeking forgiveness for what he'd caused here, for the suffering and hardships and even Christian's death. But it would do no good to attempt to convince my brother. I stepped over his words and merely told him once again that we'd remain here, in the house Christian had built for us. "We'll be *gut* here," I said. "Just *gut.*"

"We've planted hops at Aurora. Our brew masters will have good work to do," he continued as though I hadn't made my stand. "Oregon has scheduled a constitutional meeting and will become a state before long, long before this Washington Territory with all its arguments over Indians and martial law. Your children would have more chance to find meaningful work one day if you came with me to Aurora."

"There is progress here," I said. "That man Swan who first invited Christian to this region, he supports the building of a canal from Puget Sound to the Columbia River coming right through Willapa Bay. It would mean great economic growth. We have a future. Right here."

My stomach burned at any words of the future. I couldn't imagine my life without Christian. Each morning since his death had been trial enough, to wake up, face the empty pillow beside me, rise and tend to the children as though nothing had changed. At times, I pretended that their father would be coming home any day now in the summer lull of the oyster harvest. I supposed that was a gift of sorts, that the children were accustomed to being without their father for long periods of time. Now, even though Andy had seen him "sleeping" on the beach and in the coffin, Andy might simply be waiting for him to come back. And Kate? Kate would not remember his face at all. She would know him only as a memory. She'd know her mother only as a woman, bitter, widowed.

One evening while Jonathan chopped at logs so I'd have firewood for winter, I finally opened Christian's wallet. I'd been longing to do it, yet dreading it, as once it was done I'd have no more tangible thing of his to anticipate discovering. It would all be memory from then on, nothing unveiled as something new. It was the last of my connection with him as an undiscovered man.

I unfolded the wallet. Inside was the certificate that would pay off our debt. It was smudged, water-soaked but decipherable, its intent clear. Maybe I could invest the money back into oystering with Joe so he could hire the labor that Christian would otherwise have provided. Or I could use the money to purchase the ewe or pay outright for the cows or buy a hog myself. Maybe I'd use it to make my way in this world by traveling to Olympia or Oregon City to paint miniature portraits of prominent people there, people who would pay to have a good likeness made of them. Of course doing so with two young children posed a problem, but I pitched that thought away. The certificates offered a future, though the one I envisioned opposed Christian's hopes.

To pay Keil…I could barely stand the idea of it.

A smaller piece of paper was folded into the leather. I could be grateful that they'd quickly recovered Christian's body, or the sea and salt would have ruined everything inside. I held a piece of paper that looked like a letter. I unfolded the layers.

It was one of my own, sent to him when he traveled in the South that first year we were married. He'd saved it. I read it again, filling in the words smudged by the creases and the water. I'd told him I'd support his work, do what must be done to make him grateful he had come to marriage late in life. One day we would have a family. He wanted that. I'd forced myself along on this journey west because of that. Well, that and other reasons. If I hadn't, he wouldn't have known his son and daughter who were his legacy, nor this place, this valley he'd felt called to and trusted. I'd helped him find a way to be here. Staying here would honor all he'd sacrificed; leaving would mean the work he'd done here had been for nothing. I folded the letter back into the wallet. Those were the only two things he'd carried with him.

At some point, Keil and the herd boy's casket and those who'd come to the funeral would head back by way of our land. I could simply hand Keil the certificates that would pay off our land debt. We had no donation land claim; Christian had purchased our three hundred and twenty acres from a former settler. If I kept this certificate and converted it into cash, I'd have enough to purchase all we'd need to get us through the winter—the grain, cloth, whatever else. I'd be independent of the Giesy clan and Keil too.

Or I could give the certificate to Keil and end the debt, knowing to do so meant I'd be in debt to Christian's family. There was no way out of the obligation, not the way Keil set up the colony, not the way he controlled and mastered everyone to do his bidding, not the way Christian had followed Keil through the years. *Such a senseless death.*

I would ask Keil to forgive the debt. That would be the Christian thing to do for a widow and her children. Indeed, to not do that, I decided, was an unforgivable act.

I prepared meals and offered additional food for their sacks. The latter they rejected, saying they'd been given enough by the Giesys and Schaefers and others to make it back to Oregon well fed.

"You'd reject the Diamond Rule?" I asked. "How can I make your life better than my own if you won't take my offerings?"

"*Ach,* Emma," Keil said. His dark eyes bored into me. "While it is true that it is more blessed to give than to receive, it is also true that all of us must receive. When you accept a gift, you practice accepting forgiveness."

I'd done nothing requiring forgiveness, and I felt the hair at my scalp tighten. Maybe I needed forgiveness for my un-Christian thoughts about Keil. Perhaps for coming back and bringing Christian out to the water where he saw the old man in need. Perhaps I needed forgiveness for that. No. I was doing what a wife did, making time to be with her husband. My thoughts were pure and simple theological explanations of his actions. Considering holding on to the certificates, to not carry out my husband's wishes, that was an act of caring for my children. If I handed over the certificates, we'd be at the mercy of this colony. I'd be dependent. I and my children would be required to accept help from others. Our life would not be better than Keil's; we would never be on the better end of the Diamond Rule, a rule that had taken my husband's life.

But to withhold the payment denied the vow I'd made to further Christian's work, his ministry, his wish to serve the colony and Christ.

Ach, jammer! These men put me in such a whirlwind of confusion.

In the end, I behaved without courage. I gave Keil the certificates. I suppose it was my own letter Christian had carried with him all those years that was the deciding factor. I'd made a vow to support his work. Even being in this valley was a sign of my willingness to support his work. He'd made a vow to Keil and the nurture of the colony. And while I resented that he'd done it, that he'd kept his lifeline to communal living, I wasn't sure I was strong enough to keep the certificates and turn them into independence. I wasn't sure I could live with the consequences of reaching for something that Christian might not have supported had he lived. And if I failed, then I'd have lost Christian's last hope along with my own.

With the payment, the land was free and clearly mine as Christian's widow, the debt to the colony paid off. I had not even a half dime of my own to do anything without the help of others. I read the letter again in the quiet of the night, the light from Christian's lantern reflecting on the smudges.

"Here it is, *Herr* Keil," I'd said. "Christian meant to give this to you."

"Not '*Herr* Keil' but 'Brother Keil' to you, Widow Giesy." He patted my hand like a child's. "Your husband was one of my best friends. You must know that. He was like a brother to me." I said nothing. "As it should be," he said then. "This payment will help all of us at Aurora Mills. We'll remember your husband. He was a true saint in the work of our Lord."

"It's too bad you couldn't have told him that while he lived," I said.

"It was a hard time when we were here. My son...then the Indian wars. No houses ready for us. All the rain. Here today, this, this climate in August is lovely. But the rains will come again and there will still be much work to keep the cows from disappearing into the woods. The rivers will rise and you will struggle to get your crops to market. We have a better site in Aurora Mills." I straightened my shoulders, prepared to defend. "But I honor the effort of the Giesys and the building of the mill and the work of the scouts who stay here. We're friends, all of us. You must see that too, Widow Giesy. You are still a part of the colony. For the sake of your son if for no other reason."

"For the sake of both my children, then," I said, "I give you the payment as Christian wanted." I paused. "Though I am prepared to receive it back, to have you make my life better than yours. The Diamond Rule—"

"Emma," Jonathan said.

"Which way is it then, Brother? If I receive, then I'm a good and noble widow; but if I ask, then I am somehow a sinner?"

"You ask for something that would take away from many, Widow Giesy," Keil said. "I cannot grant such a thing that would rob those in Aurora of their needs."

"My children have needs too. They are robbed of their father's love and care because of his generous willingness to save an old man from drowning."

"You and Christian chose this place. Remember that."

Oh, I'd remember that. But this bitter exchange would mark a new time. I knew this as I watched Keil and Jonathan and others leave to carry the herd boy back to Aurora. I vowed that I would do whatever it took to keep my family together and free of influences I rejected, influences that had taken Christian's life from me.

I vowed it again on the day after Keil left, when I faced the first days of morning sickness.

10

Emma

Holdfast

That day, weeks ago when Christian and I walked along the beach, the day following our nighttime excursion, he pointed to a stringy plant, seaweed that clasped its greenish tendrils tight around a rock. "Holdfast," he told me.

"It does appear to be holding fast, *ja*," I agreed. "Clinging tight."

He corrected me and said that was the very name of that attachment. It was a holdfast, a noun. The seaweed was made in such a way it could not loose its hold on the rock's surface. They were bound together by their very nature.

"As we are," I told him that day.

"It's how we are in God's sight," Christian corrected. "Man and God, a holdfast." He clasped his wide palms together. "Woman and God too," he added and smiled, a deference to his independent-thinking wife.

"But are we not a holdfast, too?" I asked. "You and I?"

"Human beings can separate," he said. "But not each of us from our Creator. We are bound in storms, in trials, even unto death."

He was right, of course, at least about the two of us not being so attached the bond could never be broken. On this first day when I was alone with my children, I dismissed Christian's observation that a holdfast existed between the Creator and all created ones. I didn't feel anything holding on to me, didn't want to even talk to that Being I had once believed would keep us safe.

There were details to tend to. Christian's clothes, for one. His brothers could wear the pants or the shirts. Those nearly worn out could be cut into pieces and crafted into quilts. The boots might be kept for Andy. They were a good pair, heavy. Those waders, they brought on his death, filling as they did. I would burn them one day when I burned out a stump. But I didn't want to give any of it away or cut any of it up. To do so meant saying he would no longer need them and that meant, well, it meant that he wasn't coming back.

As I went about my day heating water for laundry, fixing a meal for the children, wondering if the lettuce looked ripe, I heard myself saying, "I'll ask Christian about that." Other days I knew for certain he was gone, but then I'd set an extra place at the table and not even notice it until Andy started counting.

I feared I'd forget what he looked like and often took out the sketch I'd drawn, just to stare.

Then one day when my bonnet hung drying in the sun, I wore Christian's flat-top hat out into the garden to shade my face. It offered more protection than my bonnet, and I could see if something moved at my side better too. The next day I pulled one of his shirts over my head. I fell to my knees, overtaken by the scent of him. When I stood again, I found comfort, my thin arms lost within the blousy sleeves, the barrel of the shirt covering the new life I carried. I wrapped a cord around me to keep the cloth from billowing out and decided I would wear it daily. Later I pulled on a pair of his pants and rolled the legs up and tacked them with thread. It was easier to milk the cows in the pants, and if people stayed away as I hoped, no one would know that I'd taken to wearing my husband's clothes. I could keep Christian with me, and when they became too worn by wearing, I'd sew a tiny dress for the infant he'd never know, or make a quilt from the scraps.

My initial reaction to the baby I carried was one of disbelief, then anger at the injustice of it all, then resolution. I'd been left to raise not two small children but three. This infant would be a constant reminder of what he could never hold fast to. A father.

I carried that fatherless child through the September harvests and into the mild October breezes. I began to talk to the baby, a sure sign that I accepted it was there. Maybe I could talk to Christian that way too, accept that he was gone but still with me.

Some days, though, talking to my husband felt like praying, and I didn't want to give God that satisfaction.

I wrote letters to my family. I made candles and soap. I dried herbs from my garden. I dug potatoes. I used the handsaw to cut some of the twigs to size for cooking and while I did, found myself annoyed again at Keil. Why hadn't Keil sent handsaws with us when we'd come here? So many things I did each day made me remember my outrage at Keil.

Despite the morning sickness, I dragged myself out of bed to milk the goat. Andy learned to stoke the fire, carefully, but it proved a huge help. I tried peppermint-leaf tea to settle the sickness. I hadn't remembered having morning bouts with either of the other two children, but this one, this one protested its place within me. I thought often of Keil's words spoken long years before about the fate of a woman, how she would suffer for her Eden brashness of seeking knowledge, daring to want more. In return, her punishment was pain in childbirth.

Yet he'd been encouraging young men and women to wait to marry and even seemed to bring to sainthood women like Helena Giesy who chose to never marry at all. How would Helena come to know her place if painful childbirth was the chosen path for women? He never had answered that question for me, saw it as one more challenge to his authority.

I moved through the days as though in a fog, still. Andy could take me from it with his questions, and Kate could sometimes make me smile as I watched her get her legs beneath her now and run without as much falling. She'd plow toward my lap and throw herself at me, sure that I would catch her. I'd swoop her up into my arms and blow air bubbles on her belly. She'd arch her back in laughter and almost flip herself from my arms. Standing, she'd toss me a kiss from her tiny palm just before she lowered her head to run toward me and start the whole routine again. She always began again, even when she stumbled. She was strong, my daughter. And yet fine grained. Like flint.

I saw in Andy more of his father as the days went by. He seemed to know what time I needed to go out to milk the cows. Young as he was, he tended Kate carefully while I milked them, then skimmed the cream. His eyes were Christian's, especially when he couldn't untie a knotted rope or when the goat bunted him when he least expected. Once he said, *"Ach, jammer!"* and I smiled rather than chastised him for his close-to-cursing words.

In the house one day Andy asked me when his father was coming back from the Bay. I finished scrubbing the potatoes, gaining time. I sat him down and pulled up a stool beside him. "Remember when your uncle Jonathan was here? He stayed for a time after the funeral. That was when we said good-bye to your papa because he can't come home anymore. Jonathan can come to visit us again, but not your papa. He's not a living being anymore. He doesn't hurt, but he doesn't breathe or eat. He's gone to heaven." Did I believe this? Was I telling my son a lie? Yes, I believed there was such a place, and surely Christian would be there. It was here, the hellishness of this earth, where I thought God had forsaken us. "To heaven, Andy, where good men go."

"Why didn't he take me with him?"

I pulled him to me. "He didn't mean to leave you behind, or me or Kate or his friends. It just happened, and when it happens like that, he doesn't even get to say the words good-bye or reassure us, though I know he would have wanted to." I made it sound like it was perfectly understandable that death followed life. But I still woke every morning hoping I'd hear his footsteps at the door or smell the salt of him when he turned toward me and kissed my nose. How could I expect a four-year-old boy to understand? "That's hard, isn't it?" He nodded. "We must be like flint," I said. "Hard but firm, and when we think of Papa, it will be as though we struck a spark like we do when we light the cooking fire. We'll remember lovely things about him then. We'll keep him with us that way," I said and patted his chest with my hand. "We'll hold him fast in our hearts."

"Like when we slept at the beach," he said.

"*Ja,* that's a good memory. We had to fight off the mosquitoes, didn't we?"

"Papa put up netting. They went away then. We could only hear buzz-buzz."

"He took good care of us, didn't he?"

Andy stayed quiet a long time and then he said, "He didn't want to go, did he, Mama? He just wanted to help that man, didn't he?"

"I'm sure he didn't wish to leave you, not ever. But one day we will all go, and—"

"Not you!" He startled. He pushed away, then hugged me tight, burying his face in my lap. "Not you!" I could feel his shoulders shake and then the sob.

I patted his back. "Not me, not anytime soon." No one can ever know such things, but it was a lie I thought I'd be forgiven for, as it seemed to comfort my son. He reached up around my neck as though to have me lift him. "I can't right now," I told him. "I'll hold you here, beside me. You'll have another brother or sister before too long, and you're so big that lifting you isn't good for the baby."

He patted my stomach then. I told him to put his ear to my belly, to listen to the heartbeat. I knew he'd hear my heart beating, but in time, if this pregnancy progressed well, he'd be hearing the sounds of his sibling. Kate waddled over then, and she too put her head to my stomach. "We three," I said, caressing their heads. "We three will be all right. We must just hold fast."

———

The work I had to do now lost a certain luster. I no longer milked the cows so we'd one day be independent. I milked them for the milk I would make into butter. It wouldn't be long and I'd have no more milk; the cows would be bred back and they'd need what they made to prepare for their own calves when they came in the spring. I suppose I was grateful in one way that no one had brought a bred ewe up from Aurora and that Rudy had taken the pigs to raise. A ewe would have been one more thing to manage. When the cows dried up, we'd rely on the goat then for our daily milk. I wondered if this next infant would have trouble eating, if I'd have trouble feeding it as I had my others. Time would tell.

For the first time in my whole life, I felt like I had too much time and nothing I cared to do with it.

I had hurts and no one to salve them, and few reasons to treat the wounds myself. I had ideas but nowhere to go with them, no one to listen to them, not even to tell me that what I thought about wasn't worth the trouble. Malaise. That was the emotion that haunted me those first months after Christian died.

"You're a wealthy widow," Mary said one day. She'd brought Elizabeth over to play with Andy and Kate while we churned butter. She'd take the round molds with her when she left, and they'd be transported to the Woodard's, where they'd be shipped north or south. Contracts had to be met, and those of us in Willapa were meeting the needs for butter in faraway places. Soon we'd add pork to our obligations. John and Andreas had found markets for our products just as Christian said they would. But what was earned went to the common fund. Or so I supposed. I didn't see any payment for my labors.

I also hadn't seen much of Mary since Christian's death, and now that she was here there was a strain between us.

"Wealthy?" I asked.

"You own your property. Isn't it what you always wanted, to have your own place?"

"It isn't how I imagined it," I said.

"I know, but still, you have property and value in your own name. Christian left you taken care of."

"All I can do with this land is sell it," I said. "If I stay here, then I have no choice but to depend on all of you to take care of me. To be…communal, again."

"Is it really so bad to share?" she asked.

"I'm adjusting," I said. "I can't contribute much myself except the butter, and before long that'll stop too. So that adds to my…beholding, something I've never liked."

She churned for a time then said, "Maybe you could hire Jack. To do your work."

I laughed. "I don't have any way to pay anyone, let alone a wanderer like Jack."

"You could pay him in shares to the property, for each year worked or something like that. You could keep accounts. You can't chop wood or do the hard labor, not with your baby on the way. And the others can't always get here after their day of work. I mean to be helpful, as we should be to widows and orphans."

I raised an eyebrow, more interested in how she knew I carried a child than in the thought that others might resent having to help me after completing their own day's work.

"How did you know?"

"You're starting to show," she said. "Only a little, but your face, it's rounder already. I noticed at the last gathering at the stockade."

"Do Christian's parents know?"

She shrugged. The children's laughter rose, and Mary motioned for Elizabeth to come to her so she could say a few settling words. She sent her back with a finger of warning. "He's…good, Emma," she said, turning to me.

"Who?"

"Jack. He doesn't complain about my cooking and—"

"Jack's living with you now? You and Sebastian and Karl?"

She shrugged her shoulders. "I don't mind and Boshie likes the conversations with the others. Oh, Jack keeps odd hours sometimes, but usually he helps with chores so Boshie has less to do when he gets home. I think he wants to help, if you let him."

"You mean work without being paid?"

"You have such a difficult time letting anyone help you."

Her avoidance confirmed my hesitance. "There's something about him, Mary. When he first came here, with the cows, there was something…I don't know, he's…cocky."

"Confident," Mary defended. She was a good judge of character, at least I'd always thought that about her. She shared my dislike for Keil. Or had.

"Arrogantly pert," I said. "He…swaggers."

"He's young."

"He's older than me, if I remember correctly."

"Is he? He likes his brew, but it seems to make him happy rather than demanding as with some men. And Boshie doesn't like him to drink and Karl doesn't either, and Jack honors that. He even goes outside to smoke. He's… funny. He does unexpected things, sort of like you do. That's why I thought he might be someone you'd enjoy talking with. It was just a thought, a way to make your days easier," she said.

"My days aren't hard, Mary. They're…lonely."

"Well then, maybe Jack could bring you laughter. Laughter wipes out loneliness like ash to a stain."

———

While my husband was alive but working at the Bay, a man could not visit me alone without some consternation. Karl was sometimes deemed safe enough; he was twenty years my senior and he offered lessons to Andy. But otherwise, the men honored civility and didn't come alone.

But now that I was a widow, men could come by without hesitation, in the name of service, in the name of helping me out. They could sit at my table and be served noodles and *Strudels* and never once feel out of place. I was set apart, as different as I could be from every other woman along the Willapa as I wore the widow's robe. *I am set apart.* That thought brought a wry smile. *Oh, one must be careful what one wishes for. There is a chance it will arrive in peculiar ways.*

Jack Giesy showed himself one day, tipped his hat and said, "Mary Giesy says you maybe could use some help."

"I'm not in a position to hire anyone. I have no cash and—"

"Well, let's just see what we can work out," he said. He didn't push past me as he stood, hat in hand. He stomped his feet in the wet. It was November and the rains were with us. I'd have to invite him in. It would be the neighborly thing to do. "I'm flexible," he said. He blew on his hands to warm them. *Why won't I invite the man in out of the rain?* "About pay, I mean. We maybe could get…creative with the books." He added a grin, one that slid its way from my eyes down over my body to my toes. It made me want to slap his face.

I didn't, but it did confirm my instinct to send him packing, which I did.

"I've no need of wood chopping," I said. "I know how to do it and in my own time. I thank you for the offer. Let me give you some cheese to take back to Mary."

Fortunately, he didn't step inside or follow me while I got the cheese. I held the bag out to him and he put his hat back on and took it from me. *"Danke,"* he said, still wearing that grin.

I watched him saunter down the path with an axe over his shoulder. Something about his swagger told me he'd be back. I just hoped I'd be ready, and able to hold fast to what really mattered.

11

Catherine

My Dearest Emma,

Papa tells us that you have seen Jonathan but for sad reasons, as we learn of Christian's death. Jonathan tells us you saw your husband last on the Fourth of July. While the Aurora Band played in a town called Butteville, you were at the Bay having your last days with Christian. I'm so sad for you, Emma. We celebrate Christmas here and wish that you and your children were with us so we could put our arms around you and warm you in the cold of your suffering. To lose a love, oh, how tragic that is. How do you ever stand it? But we are grateful he was acting the hero in saving another's life. That must bring you comfort.

Herr Keil writes to our teacher, Herr Wolfer, so we learn of his traveling to your remote country for the funeral. How that must have comforted you to have him there to stand beside you, to speak last words over Christian's grave. We miss him here. Papa says the spirit of the colony is missing something without Wilhelm, so the men are talking now of when they'll take the second wave out from Bethel to Aurora Mills. Sometime in 1862 or 1863. That's still five years away! I'll be an old maid by then.

Do you ever see Jack Giesy? I just wonder.

Mama says I should write of everyday things, that talk of thread and harvests bring comfort more than other words. So I will tell you that the hops harvest was

good this year. "Never let September winds blow across your hops," Papa says, and
so the men spent August bringing in the harvest. Mama says the hops poultice is
what saved her bad tooth, so it is good for something besides making beer. I always
think it grand when something can be useful for more than one thing.

Women in Shelbina are wearing puffs and pads under their skirts called bus-
tles! I've seen them. You could hide a child inside one they're so big. Mama says we
girls can't wear them. It would make our sister Lou look less like a chicken leg, all
straight up and down, though. I don't need one. I carry the bustle God gave me,
or so Mama says.

We heard word of a terrible massacre not far from where Tante Mary lives in
the Deseret country. Mama is worried, as Indians killed an entire wagon train of
people heading to California out of Arkansas. She worries about her sister and
wishes Tante had never married a Mormon saint who took her far away, espe-
cially if it means they might be in the middle of an Indian war. Tante Mary says
it was a terrible thing, the people being killed in a beautiful meadow in the
mountains, and that more terrible things may come from the story. She doesn't say
what, but the army is sent to investigate because it was Indians against Ameri-
cans. A few children survived and the Deseret saints who came upon the train and
chased the Indians off found them and took them in. Mary and Uncle John
Willard took one in. A girl. I don't know her name.

Does Uncle Jonathan write to you from France and Germany and England?
Our cousins write too. How different their lives are from mine here in Bethel! But
they learn of wars too. There is a war with other Indians in a country called
India. Uncle Jonathan says they are warring against the British even though both
have lived side by side there many years. Uncle Jonathan has returned to France
and Papa's pleased he is not being sent to that India to negotiate a peace.

There are uprisings everywhere in this wide world. I wonder why. There are
rumblings about slave and free states here, and Papa says a war will come and
Missouri will be the black powder that starts it. Is anyone fighting in your Wash-
ington Territory? I just wonder.

There is not much more to tell you. So I will write you these words even though Mama says everyday mentionings bring more comfort than Scripture when a wound is wide open and needs more time to heal. I try to imagine what it must be like to have had love taken away like a boat drifting out to sea. Oh, I should not use that image. I'm sorry. (I can't erase on this thin paper.) Maybe it is more like having a leaf blown from a tree. A red maple leaf wider than Papa's palm, one that would cling for a long time to the branch, resist the winds and make one think it would stay through the winter and hang on forever. Then in an instant, it waves like a limp hand and is gone. I think if I'd been watching the leaf and loved it and came to expect to see it there every day, well, when it was gone, I'd be very sad. I think I might even be angry at God for having allowed it to happen. God is all-powerful, so why not stop the wind? Why not let a young girl enjoy the beauty of that leaf? It means nothing to hear someone say it is just the way of things, that leaves form, cling for a time, then die and go back to the earth. But why? That's what I ask.

I think I'm not supposed to ask such questions, but I would if it was my husband. I would ask and would grieve for the answers.

Mama says it is a sign of maturity when one can form the questions but not be frustrated by the lack of answers. She says wisdom is when we have gratitude in the midst of all uncertainties.

Since there are so many unanswered questions, every question must not have an answer. I just thought of that. Maybe that's what confuses people, that belief that there must be an explanation for all things. It makes me feel defenseless to not know things, though. I don't like living as though I'm standing in my crinolines with all the world to see. I don't want to fear something happening as it did to those Arkansas travelers who ended up dead. I don't want to have to decide what to do next if I survived that. How would those children understand that all they'd loved had been taken from them? Maybe living with Tante Mary and Uncle John Willard will be their answer on this earth.

Papa says you never should have talked Christian into staying at Willapa and instead should have gone to Aurora with Father Keil. I wouldn't say that to you because if I were you, I'd feel badly for having encouraged Christian to stay. And the others stayed too, so poor Keil doesn't have all the help that he needs now, and he urges us to come from Bethel soon.

Lou and Johanna and David Jr. are helping William with egg scratching for the Tannenbaum. He has a nice eye for detail and holds the blown egg as though it was a young rabbit about to hop out of his hand. We will hang the ones you made as a young girl. William looks at them as though to copy what you've done and Mama says that's good, for you always did make scratching pictures well. We boiled the eggs in onion skins longer than usual and they have a chestnut hue, nearly the color of a tintype picture, Papa says. We will put Christian's name and date of death on one, Emma, as a remembrance that he will be forever in our lives. We'll hang it on the tree.

I found this verse to give you from Isaiah, who says there is light to follow, that your face may be like flint, hard and firm and ready to make a spark when touched by the loving hand of God. Be like flint, Emma, and not like one who makes her own flames. It is best to rely on God for the fires of your life. Father Keil will help you. Please don't be angry if the words are not what you want to hear. I just felt I had to tell you.

Your sister, Catherine

12

Louisa

My husband the doctor preaches today. Every other Sunday as is his way. Whether it will be on simplicity, humility, self-sacrifice, or neighborly love none of us knows. Even I don't know, though some might think I do. The doctor doesn't share his views with me before he expresses them. Like the others whom he serves, I pull out the threads of his weaving that speak to me. I don't mean to suggest that he has anything to say just for me, only that today he preaches and it will be well with us all when he is finished and I will take a tidbit away that will help me learn to live better.

It is February, a month here balanced like a good quilt with warm days of sunshine backed with rain showers and occasionally snow. The snow never lasts. It merely covers things up for a time until light and heat melt it or the clogs and boots of workmen walk the snow into mud.

The men work hard at building yet more houses. They will not be set close to each other as they were in Bethel but instead will have a block of area around each one, giving room to build a barn and a summer kitchen later. Each will have a small garden, a smokehouse, and pens for hogs and our sheep. This is a new concept that my husband adopts. I think he might have seen the merit to the Willapa sites being somewhat separated. Or maybe here in this Oregon Country he could see that we didn't want to make our "community" appear too tight-knit, so that people from surrounding areas fail to come here to buy our goods. All things change in new places. It troubles me at times to know what few things one can expect to remain the same.

This land is an Eden. We'll have fine crops to sell to the hundreds of settlers who arrived last fall, many in poorer shape than when our colony reached Willapa. We may have walked across the country, but we had enough food, thanks to my husband's good planning and the Lord's provision.

Yet as hungry as those settlers looked, they recovered with the help of friends. They plan a dance. Our men practice, for the band will play for the Old Settlers' Ball at Oregon City, which should be a grand affair. We won't attend, of course. But our musical men will get to watch the candles shimmer against the finery of the dresses requiring yards and yards of cloth. One can only hope they've sewn such gowns with easy seams so all that material can be put to good use later making clothes for their men and their children. Imagine leaving such a hoard of cloth sewn up in a dress worn but once a year, and then just to dance!

Still, I do love to dance.

Neighborly love. That is what the doctor spoke of today. It always makes me think of Emma Giesy and her struggle with being a good neighbor. She was such a giving girl back in Bethel. Oh, self-centered as young women are, but kind too. It's been some months now since the doctor traveled north to attend the funeral of Chris Giesy, yet we have heard not a word from Emma, his widow. Oh, I know, one does not always behave as expected when in the swirl of grief, but I did think she might have sent word by way of her brother, perhaps thanking the doctor for his sacrifice, traveling there in the heat of summer. It was a fine service, the doctor told me. The men played a Beethoven piece. Beethoven followed by one of our German family tunes familiar to all of us, lighthearted, the doctor said, for a service commending a body to the grave should be a joyous time. A man's soul has already left and gone on to a better place. We bury but the body.

I know this is a terrible thing to admit, and I would never tell the doctor this, but I am grateful that my Willie will not have to lie alone now on that hilly site so far from us. Chris Giesy lies beside him and that's a comfort to me. His mother will visit the grave and as she does, she'll be there for Willie too. No one wants to be alone, not even in death, though of course we are. For the living, there is a comfort with two graves there. I hope Emma sees it as such. We placed a stone for Willie with a willow tree on it, weeping for him always.

We prosper here in Aurora. We women work side by side to feed the men, who work long hours to build more homes. We're readying our fields to plant, though spring will not find us until all the Easter eggs have been eaten. That was the rule in Missouri. The Pudding River runs full but within its banks, and there is the smell of spring in the air, that scent of a Missouri root cellar sprinkled with birdsong that marks the ending of a long winter of despair.

The almanac says today it will bluster and blow so I should work inside, on my *Fraktur,* perhaps. I'm to make the letters perfect for writing special papers and documents so they look as they did from the old country, when our German printer of renown, Gutenberg, printed the earliest books. It is one of the things the doctor does not object to. The lettering is beautiful when completed by one who works hard to make the *w* just so or the *m* look like a lightning-split hickory tree. It might be that I could earn money by making baptismal certificates with the lovely letters so they might be hung on the walls of our neighbors, who are mostly Methodists and Catholics. Our colonists could hang them as well. Not baptismal certificates, no, we do not celebrate that sacrament. But perhaps a marriage certificate could be written out with the *Fraktur.* I'll ask the doctor if this might not be an act of neighborly love, to commemorate a marriage day. The doctor will likely tell me there's no time for such foolishness. He still does not think marriage is what young people should put their hopes in. "We have too much to do to be ready for our neighbors from Bethel," he'll say.

I have clothes to mend, more to wash, food to prepare, and the young ones who fall in love, well, they are of no good for getting things done.

At least I can sing while I work. There may be foolishness in singing or playing in the band, but at least it can be done while one is being useful. Perhaps that is what the doctor objects to in my suggestions: they do not appear useful, only pleasurable, like enjoying the look of the lettering on a page. Being useful is what the doctor says God calls each of us to be, though I'm not sure how the band is useful. Oh, it raises money.

Rudy Giesy arrived this past week. He has bought a farm in our country from a man named Anderson. It's close to us in Aurora, and Rudy will raise any sheep that the colony wishes to keep. He's also going to take a sheep or two back with him to Willapa, where Henry will now keep the pigs. Rudy says he'll give a ewe to Emma Giesy as she harps on it so.

Forgive me. He did not use the word *harp*. He said she asks for one. I imagine that means repeatedly. She knows what she wants. I must be kinder especially now that we learn she is with child again. This must be a trial for her, long and odious, to grieve her husband's death while tending his children and then to learn another comes. Or perhaps she sees the child as the gift it is, sent by Chris from beyond the grave in a way. Some of us count, but we have not seen her so we don't know when this baby might be due.

Karl Ruge too visits with Rudy. It's been months since I've seen the old teacher. Karl and Rudy brought fence posts of yew wood all the way from Washington Territory. They'll surround the farm that Rudy bought.

I am hopeful Rudy is the first of many who will leave Willapa and come here to stay. It is what my husband prays for.

They brought news of Big Jack Giesy too, that rascal. He's been working at the Bay, helping where Chris Giesy died. Chris made good money there, the doctor tells me, and paid off the Colony loan. Chris left his widow a landholder in her own name now. She should be happy, though I do wonder what makes Emma happy.

When he's not oystering, Jack stays with Mary and Sebastian, along with Karl. It must be the season as he didn't come to help with the yew posts. I don't know why this matters. He's just a young man but he so reminds me of what my Willie might have been if he had lived, though without Jack's lust for liquor. Still, he is a joyful, unpredictable soul, and any sin can be forgiven if one can be made to laugh.

Gloriunda and Aurora are a big help to me and the other women. Rudy brought a big spinning wheel for us to use, almost as big as those we had back in the textile mills in Bethel, where we had to walk the thread to and fro. With this one, we can sit and use one foot to move things forward. It was a gift from the Giesys. Well, what is a gift when one shares everything essential with one's neighbors? Was it theirs to give, or did it belong to all of us?

We've been finding what we need for dyes. That is a gift! God provides even the smallest things. Red from the madder root that flourishes in the garden. We've found black walnut trees, and since it stains the fingers, it stains wool brown too, and when left long enough, black. Peach leaves brought with us from Bethel give us green. And thus we weave the cloth for quilts or clothes.

Some of us are excited that there's to be a harvest fair this fall at a place called Gladstone. We plan to take our woven goods with the colors of the earth and trees to be judged. We can take baked goods as well. They welcome essays and music entries too. Perhaps the men will earn certificates for their baskets. Perhaps we women will.

Maybe I could make up such notifications of award with my improved *Fraktur* letters. *Ja,* this would be a good thing for the Aurora colony women to be working toward. It is good to have a goal to look to. The men have theirs: to build the colony, to plant and prune, to make a way to tend each other through the common fund. Why not the women? Why not let us have a special goal, something to mark our days in some interesting way? So long as our goal includes the tending of others, this should not be troublesome to the doctor.

I can almost see my *Fraktur* lettered certificate hanging there against the logs.

I suggested this to the doctor later in the week. He said nothing for a time, then told me that his next sermon must need be on humility.

———

We hear of difficulties in the Washington Territory. Two Indians have been hanged, though some say they were innocent wretches. Any of us could make mistakes; any of us could falter and fall and once hanged for it, there is no way to earn redemption. Not that redemption is earned, exactly. It is freely given. But any of us can be wretches in need of that gift of forgiveness.

I used the word *wretch* to mean someone exiled, in distress because they are alone and are, as in German, full of *Elend*, of misery. Some days this is how I feel here, as though I travel in a foreign land, exiled from what once gave pleasure. This is not to blame anyone, not my husband or God or anyone else. But I feel wretched just the same.

I worry about our friends on the Willapa with such wretched happenings. We learn too this month that the Indian uprising of last September, which took the lives of one hundred and twenty sojourners in that Deseret country, may not be blamed entirely on the natives. It is now believed that saints also took part in the killings. I find this nearly impossible to believe, but some children remembered. They saw the white flag of truce flown by their parents and uncles and older brothers. When the Deseret saints came in to say they'd negotiate the peace, they instead attacked, killing everyone save those few children they thought would not be old enough to remember. But they were. They do. Poor wretches.

So I fear for those in that country too. We hear they have rebelled against the governor appointed to the territory, and the military has moved in to make the peace there. Emma Wagner's aunt lives there. I pray that she is well.

I pray for us here too. Whenever some bad news comes about a group set apart as the Deseret saints are, the Americans around us get nervous, or so my husband tells me. They wonder if we will attack our neighbors or pretend to be neighborly when we really aren't. They weave us into the same pattern as those they do not understand. Soon, instead of coming to our storehouse to purchase pear butter or to buy up a new bed that one of our men made, they'll stay away. Maybe start rumors about us because they cannot understand our tongue, and then like others who stand out, we'll be asked to move. All of us here in Aurora would be wretches. Yet not alone at least. In the colony we always have that hope, that we will never be truly alone.

I hoped that Rudy's purchasing land near us meant he'd be coming here for good. He's a laughing soul, and my husband needs that to lighten his efforts to keep this colony prospering. I thought Karl, too, would stay but he returned. He purchased school items from the common fund for those Willapa children. But what of ours here? Our children need learning all year long. They should speak English so they won't stand out as different in this land.

My husband says we can teach our children as we go, as we did along the trail. We'll build a school after the church. But first we need more homes, and also more buildings so we can manufacture barrels and chairs and weave our cloth, all things these people of Oregon need. We will win them over by having what they want. "Who needs a church when we have the *gross Haus* in which to meet?" he asks me.

No one needs the church building to worship God, it's true. But back in Bethel, what my husband did not know is that many of us found solace in that building, even when he wasn't there to lead us. We women slipped in, sometimes together, sometimes alone. We sat in a quiet place, the scent of cooled candle wax and brick mortar falling gently on our shoulders. We prayed. We felt less wretched. And when we left, we could resume the work, serve the people, tend our families. It is harder for me to find that place of peace when there are people always around us, living here, needing cooking, mending clothes. A child needs a nose wiped, another a napkin changed. I wonder if I sin by wishing for time alone, by longing to make my letters pretty, to dream of recognition at the harvest fair, or to find a joke to laugh at. Maybe to enjoy a little teasing.

At least I have the choir to sing in. I wonder if Willapa has a choir. Does Emma sing in it? Probably not. She is honoring her husband's death, preparing for a new arrival, tending her children. She must feel wretched indeed. There must be something I can do for her even from this distance. I don't know what that is or why she comes to mind so often. I will listen harder to my husband's next sermon on service. There is always something in what he says for me.

13

Emma

Chipping Flint

That winter wore like a threadbare cloth, covering just enough to keep me breathing but offering little warmth. I struck my flint to start the February fire. I must be like flint. Strong. My young sister's letters urged me to let God lead the way for me so I could avoid more of His harsh lessons. What more could He do to me than make me a widow? My sister wrote of a spiritual world both confining and remote.

I sparked the riven wood with my chipped flint and hung the pot filled with water on the crane, then pushed it back over the flames. I tried to imagine the convenience of starting a fire without having to make the spark from the stone. Maybe if one waited long enough, all things changed for the better.

Karl's visits offered sparks of interest. My threadbare cloak of grief warmed a little more when he stopped by, filling me in on various news items of the day. He took a German newspaper, and while it was rarely current, having to come from Bethel or Milwaukee or beyond, he did still seem to know more about the outside world than any of the rest of us. It was easier to think of events back in Missouri than to face the struggles just down my road.

Mary came less often, and when I attended church, something felt different with the other Giesy women. I blanketed their festivities, I feared. They must not tease a widow, just offer help to her.

Karl was easier to be with. He gave his time without reminding me that I had so little to give in return, save a good meal for him, a little conversation about words. We talked of tending Christian's grave and how even that word *tend* has many meanings: looking after, caring for. Yet it brought images of fragility too. I felt tender, not strong like flint. Karl sat and talked while I rolled out egg noodles. Sometimes he gave Andy guidance on a lesson. I welcomed the sound of his voice, his thoughts about life, and the smell of his tobacco reminded me of my father. We spoke of him.

"Have you written and asked your father to come here?" Karl asked. "To help you now that you are widowed?"

I shook my head. I stuck my arm inside the fireplace, testing the temperature. The hair on my arm singed slightly as I pulled it away. "I doubt they'll ever come west, even when more of the Bethelites do, sometime in 1862 or 1863 my sister tells me. That'll give the colony leaders there more time to sell things, but also time for Aurora to be ready for them, I suppose. Keil doesn't want a repeat of what he found here." I heard the disgust in my voice.

"*Ja,* some of us take to change, and some of us find it troubling because we don't know how things will turn out." He drew on his pipe. This one had a foot-long stem. "We want to live in certainty and there is none save faith."

"It could have been better if Keil had waited before bringing the first group out. We scouts wanted a better welcome instead of what Keil turned it into, a huge mistake and disappointment."

Karl took a long time to respond, the draw of his pipe filling the silence. "It might still have been too much to hope for, Emma Giesy, that this would be a timber place where we could cut and sell the harvest. Sam Woodard tells us that he and his partners logged and hand-hewed timbers square so they would not roll when shipped on the boats. A lot of work that took. Their first shipment went through fine to California and they got paid."

"See," I said. "We just needed time to hand hew." I picked up a pan for the noodles.

He raised a hand to silence me. "The second load was lost at sea. The third load became frozen at the water's edge and was carried away in the spring. The fourth load rotted because they could never find anyone to buy it. Imagine such frustration! The first turned out well so they kept going. But eventually, they had to face what was. That's when Sam built his warehouses and moved inland to farm."

"So you're saying that even if we'd had more time to prepare, the people would still have been better off in Aurora?"

"By golly, I think so."

"Why don't you go there then?" I asked. I slammed the spider down, the three-legged frying pan clanging at the hearth. My children stopped their activities and stared.

Karl looked away. "Willapa helps Aurora now, as does Bethel," Karl said. "It all works out."

"My husband is dead. I don't see how that's 'working out.'"

"*Ja*, I misspoke. I meant that Willapa contributes to Aurora now just as Bethel does. All things do work out as Romans says, 'to them that love God and who are called according to his purpose.'" He set his pipe down to cool the bits of tobacco left. "Though what Bethel contributes could be impaired if war comes. I'm glad to be here, apart from all that. You can be glad too, Emma Giesy. Your children will grow up away from the battles. Maybe your father will want to avoid war too. Then he'll welcome an invitation from his daughter to come west to meet his grandchildren. You could give him a reason to bring his sons west."

"I can't ask him to come just to help me. And he has daughters too."

Karl nodded. "Ask, Emma. A parent does what is necessary for his children."

"Not for grown children," I said. "They should manage on their own once they leave the nest."

"*Ach,* one never stops being a parent. Or so I'm told."

"Unless one loses a child," I said. "Maybe by coming here I am lost to them."

"You think of Christian, *ja*? It was a hard loss for Andreas and Barbara. Even so, Christian's parents, they are still his parents, still with memories of him and with his children alive waddling around before them. If you asked your parents, I think they'd come to help, by golly."

I imagined them all here in this house with me. My mother would midwife my infant, my father and brothers would joke and laugh, and I would hear the sound of a man's voice and perhaps not ache with longing so for Christian's. My young sisters, Lou and Johanna, they could play with their niece, and William would take Andy by the hand and give my son a chance to be a little boy instead of a little man who looks after his mother and sister. And Catherine, well, she'd talk of love, tell me to put my husband's clothes away and read me hopeful scriptures that promised goodness if I just obeyed. Such words made me feel empty, sometimes angry.

It would be good, though, to hold my mother in my arms again. Maybe in giving her comfort I could receive a bit of my own.

———

My mother-in-law and Christian's aunts, the other scouts' wives, brought me food that spring and helped me dye the yarn I'd spun. They brought me eggs to boil at Easter. Their husbands came by to chop more wood, see to the fields, make sure this widow had what she needed. How I wished I could have received their gifts of time and labor without feeling embittered by my need. I remembered a sermon Keil had once given about true Christian community requiring honesty among its members, especially about our weaknesses. Once shared, each could support the other, he said. He quoted something from James about our confessing to each other, then praying for one another so that we might be healed. What courage that would take, I decided, to confess how I felt about God, my life, everything here that kept me in an anxious, often angry state. And praying? I hadn't done that for some time. It would take courage to confess or pray. I didn't feel safe here without Christian, and safety is surely the first requirement for a healing heart.

I'm not sure when I admitted to the growing resentment of the women that their husbands had to tend to me and my children in addition to their own. They said how good it was they got to act on the Diamond Rule by helping me. But I could tell. Mary mentioned more often than needed Jack's willingness to stop by. I'd already told her Jack made me uncomfortable. Christian's sister-in-law, John's wife, noted how busy her husband was with the school and the mill and so many other things, and wouldn't it be nice if someday I found someone else who would take me as his wife. She said it all in the same breath and then asked my forgiveness if she spoke too soon after Christian's death.

"Yes," I said. "It is too soon and will always be."

"You're young," John's wife said. She patted my hand. "A whole life awaits you."

It wasn't a life I looked forward to.

———

My mother-in-law sent shivers through me when she noted that in some parts of the world when a son dies, his oldest son is given as a ward to the father's family, a grandparent or an uncle. "This has happened even among fine Americans," my mother-in-law told me as she calmly stitched her husband's pants. We worked side by side at her table. "Meriwether Lewis, who came across the land with the American Clark over fifty years ago, he was raised by an uncle after his father died, even though his mother was perfectly capable. Of course if she'd remarried right away that might not have been so."

"Are you suggesting I can't bring up my own son?" I asked.

"It was just an observation," she said. "How Americans do things."

I tried to remember if such a custom had occurred in the old country, or even as part of the colony. But of course in Bethel, all lived close to each other, so it wouldn't be difficult to have a fatherless boy influenced by his uncle while still living in his mother's house. Maybe that's all she meant.

Still, I found myself feeling ill after that conversation with my mother-in-law and vowed to do much more of the work here in the cabin myself. The men could stop by to do their duty to the Widow Giesy, but they'd see that I already had chopped wood aplenty, that the goat was already fed, that I'd put bacon grease on her udder to be a healing balm, that I'd kindled my own fires just fine. They'd leave and could tell their wives that their help wasn't needed, that they didn't have to stop by the widow's place this week at all. With the cows dried up, Boshie would put them in with their two animals. John already had the mule.

It was a fantasy, of course. Maybe if I hadn't been carrying this infant, maybe then I could do it all. But I could barely swing the axe. Keil had been right about one thing: my small frame worked against me in this landscape. He expected it to mean I'd have trouble delivering an infant, my punishment for being Eve's daughter, still seeking more. But so far, that punishment hadn't happened. My two babies had arrived with relative ease.

I avoided the men when they came to help, set by the door the packed bags of *Strudels* or dried fruits I'd prepared for them in return for their effort so I would be less indebted. On Sundays, when otherwise we might have made our way to the stockade for Andy and Kate to see their cousins and relatives, I rested at home with my children cluck-henned under my arms, and I read to them from the almanac, or we made cookies and decorated them with dried fruit. If anyone asked, I claimed the weather kept us away.

I did have difficulty putting Karl's suggestion from my mind. Perhaps my parents might come out to help if I asked. My longing for them surprised me. But truth be told, I suspected that within a very few weeks of their arrival

I'd be wishing them gone, as uncertain for the cause of my agitation as I had ever been. *A contrary woman* was my Americanized name.

———

My second son and third child arrived as I expected on April 4, nine months to the day after his conception. I awoke with a familiar ache in my back and milked a bleating Opal that morning, suspecting this might be the day. The day before, I'd brought wood in so we could heat water, and I made a huge pot of beans for the children to eat. I talked to Christian, said things out loud, and reminded him that once all those male doctors had insisted I was wrong about the date of Andy's birth. But I was sure this time, I really was, just as I'd been before.

When my water broke late in the April afternoon, I sent Andy for Mary. But by the time she arrived, I held my baby in my arms. It seemed right that I delivered this child alone. Doing so affirmed my strength. Kate sat off to the side, quiet as a mouse. "You have a new brother," I told her after I'd cut the cord, then washed the child and wrapped him in the gown I'd made from one of Christian's shirts. The scent of my husband was still in it, nearly a year after his death. Kate ran her finger over the baby's forehead, looked up at me and smiled. "Mine," she said.

"All of ours," I told her.

I named the baby Christian. He had a fuzz of reddish hair, not unlike the wisps of red that sometimes showed in his father's beard. "Your father would have loved you dearly," I told my youngest son. That night, with the baby satisfied by Opal's milk, I felt my eyes fill to overflowing. "You're missing all this, Christian," I said. "It isn't fair. You should have lived and not me. You were the better person, the finer parent. But you were so…good, too good, and look at how we're left now?" I kissed the tears from my son's forehead. Andy came to me and pressed his head against my arm. Kate slept.

This was my family now. Christian's life did go on, but not with him in it. With this Christian's presence in my life, I'd have no time for wondering about the meanings of words. I'd have no time for anything but keeping three children alive and showing without doubt that I didn't need an uncle or a grandparent to fill a father's void. I didn't need anyone at all.

———

Renewed purpose filled my days. I dried lovage to sweeten the cabin and ground the root into powder to pepper my venison stews. The cabin smelled fresh; food nourished. Spring meant renewal to me, and with it a change in how Christian's memory filled my days. Christian and I had married in the spring. Baby Christian smoothed the rough edges of the loss. I thought of my husband a little less, not every waking moment as my baby was my first morning thought now. I heard myself laugh out loud once when the baby blew bubbles, again when he greedily consumed the goat's milk fed through the finger of a glove. I didn't blame myself for not being able to produce milk on my own. It was the way of things for me, something I needed to accept. I adapted. That too was a sign of strength.

When the goat took Andy's handkerchief stuffed at his waist and shook it as though it were a flag, running away when Andy tried to grab it, we all laughed.

It was spring, when the unexpected can be more innocent than romantic, when creativity proves delightful rather than calculated.

I could see why people fell in love in spring.

I decided to fall in love too, but with sketching and drawing. I planned to talk with Sarah Woodard about my idea and see if she and Sam could help. They knew everyone in the region, and Olympia would be the logical place to try to find customers. How I'd get there and what I'd do with the children, I pitched those thoughts away, but the germ of the idea was there, that tiny irritant inside the oyster shell that might one day grow into a pearl. I'd begun to think of the future with more than just dread. I didn't know when that actually happened, just that it did.

Big Jack arrived carrying an egg etched with this new infant's birthday on it. It had fancy lettering, almost like the *Fraktur* that marked our German documents. It was beautiful, with the flowing letters scratched onto a kind of chestnut-colored egg, and an intricate border on the top and bottom. I had no idea who'd made it. Jack had knocked on our door, placed the egg in my hand when I opened the latch. His palm was as wide as a butter paddle, dwarfing the delicate egg. He said nothing, just turned on his heel and left.

A present, most likely from Christian's grandparents. I felt a twinge of guilt keeping my children from visiting time with them.

In early May, Sarah brought me a laying hen. It had been a long time since I'd seen her. We put the chicken in the smokehouse and together we made a little roosting nest for her, though Sarah assured me the chickens would roost in the trees at night if left out. "They're like seagulls that way," she said.

Back in the cabin, Sarah held the baby to her and sang softly. I knew she longed for a child of her own, but though she was nearly twenty and had been married to Sam for nearly five years, this had not happened. I wondered if it felt strange for her to see me with three children all without a father while she and Sam, all ready and willing, still had none. She bowed her blond hair to my son whose eyes had closed.

"He takes to your singing," I said. "I can't carry a tune in a candlestick."

Sarah smiled and when she looked up, I saw tears in her eyes. She sat in the rocking chair while I heated tea. It was May but still chilly. I lifted Christian from her arms and placed him in the baby board I'd used for Kate. Sarah lifted her cup, and that's when she noticed the scraped egg on a shelf I'd tacked to the logs. I'd placed the egg on a little stand I'd made of twigs. "That's beautiful," she said. "Did you do that work?"

I shook my head. "I don't know who did it, but Jacob Giesy brought it by."

She laughed then. "I should have recognized it, though this is a little fancier than what I've seen. He makes charcoal drawings on rocks and signs his name." She looked at the egg more closely. "See. Right here is a little *JG*."

I'd thought the lettering was just a part of the decoration, but she was right. I hadn't remembered seeing any such rocks with charcoal drawings on them, but then I hadn't gone very far from my hearth. "He draws well?"

"Oh yes. He made a likeness of our old dog on the side of the warehouse. It would wash off in the rains, so I asked if he'd do one on paper and he obliged. I think at first he thought I'd be upset with him, or Sam would. He hadn't asked if we wanted that picture on the warehouse." She set her cup down and turned the egg around in her hand. "Was it a baptismal gift?"

"No. We don't celebrate baptisms," I said. "Dr. Keil doesn't think it a necessary sacrament for either children or adults." Karl Ruge, who remained a Lutheran, did consider infant baptism important, though. I would ask him about that. "Maybe I should have Christian baptized. If for no other reason than that Keil wouldn't want it," I said.

"Oh, Emma." Sarah laughed. "When we have a child, I'll want him baptized." She stood over my son as he slept. "It means he'll be forever in God's hands." She fluffed Christian's reddish hair, pulled it between her fingers so it stood up like a cock's crown.

I wasn't of the opinion that being in God's hands was always that comforting. I studied the egg. "I didn't know this about Christian's cousin," I said. "I assumed someone else had done the etching."

"Jack's very talented. He speaks good English, or at least I can understand him." I was still trying to imagine the artistic side of Jack when she added, "Sometimes he's a bit…unpredictable, but very generous too, it seems, to have given you this special gift."

I'd thought he'd been merely the delivery person who at last understood that I didn't want him around. Why on earth would Jack give my son such a precious gift?

My fingers fidgeted.

"I wonder if maybe you and Sam might have some ideas about how I could earn money on my own, sketching people or painting portraits or making drawings of their homes that they could send to their families back East. I know there are no printers here, none needing lithographers, but maybe in Olympia?"

"I'll ask Sam. But I think it would mean you'd have to…travel. I'm not sure how you could do that, with the children so young. And you a woman alone."

"You're not going to tell me that it might be 'unseemly,' are you?"

"Never," she said. She lifted an eyebrow. "But I'm certain there are those who would."

"*Ja*," I said. "But maybe, since so many have been telling me they don't mind helping, maybe they'd keep the children for me when I made such trips. They can act the Diamond Rule by doing so and send their husbands over to milk and feed without worry about what the Widow Giesy might do to them." Sarah frowned. "They wouldn't have to be long journeys, a week or so at a time."

"How could you be separated from him for even a day?" Sarah said, nodding toward Christian.

"If it meant I could provide for them on my own it would be worth it in the end."

"You say that now, but I don't know. Don't you remember how it was when Andy stayed with his grandparents after Christian died?"

"That was different. I was confused and frightened. I'm more certain now of what I need to do."

Kate came over then and I made a cat's cradle for her out of string. Andy asked to use the corn mill that Karl Ruge had brought us at Easter. It made grinding corn so much easier, and we could use just enough for the corn drink or the mush we wanted for breakfast. He swung his little arm round and round, dropping corn kernels into the hopper. They clinked like tiny pearls dropped into a tin cup.

It would be difficult to leave my children. Sarah was right about that. But Andy would be old enough to come with me.

"Maybe you could make some drawings that Sam could show to people," Sarah said. "That way you wouldn't have to leave here. You could draw our place or maybe the children's portraits. Or the trees. That might be a place to begin. You wouldn't have to worry then about tongues wagging over your leaving your children behind."

. She was right, of course. This next year must be devoted to my children. But I could make some portraits in between. I'd have to borrow money for the charcoal and paper, but I could pay it back when I sold something. "Would Sam make a loan to me for the supplies?" I asked.

"I'm sure he would. But you might also think of asking Jack. He seems to have a good supply of paper."

I didn't ask Jack Giesy, but I did find another way to take the next step. I wrote to my parents. I told them of Christian's birth and drew a small picture of his face, his eyes like Christian's, his mouth with a wide space between his nose and the top of his slender upper lip. "Room for a fine, bushy mustache one day," I told them. "As his father always had."

Asking for the money was the easy part. I told my father what I planned to do and that I thought I could make a living this way, so I wouldn't be so dependent on the colonists here in Willapa. My father had somehow accumulated independent resources or he couldn't have purchased property in his name. He'd understand that kind of inventive thinking…at least if I'd been a son he would. *I'd have you send the money to me when the other colonists come out,* I wrote. *But that might not be for a long time from what Catherine tells me, so perhaps you could send it to me by ship.*

Then came the hard part, the expressing of my real need. *The children should know all their grandparents, not just Christian's. The future may hold changes for me, travel if I'm to do this work successfully. I could do it more easily if you came to visit and perhaps even stayed. I'd know then that the children were in good hands.*

Would I move across the country to an unknown wilderness in order to help my child? Would I move my family if my father or mother needed me? Would I make such a sacrifice for my children one day? Yet here I was, asking this very thing.

If they agreed to come, I'd be sinking deeper into debt.

14

Emma

Keeping All Together

I marked the first anniversary of my husband's death by going to his grave. I took the children, of course. I decided we'd also spend the day with Christian's parents, as they'd seen little of us through the spring and now into the summer. Maybe with a little time together I could shake the agitation of my mother-in-law's comment of some months ago, about the eldest child being given to the grandparents to raise. Enough time had passed, surely. I could be generous with my children's time.

We made the trek walking, then climbed the bare hill to the cemetery. Someone had built a small fence around the two graves, probably John, since he seemed to be in charge of so many things now that Christian wasn't. A warm breeze brushed against my face and Baby Christian's reddish hair. Andy acted solemn but Kate was a typical *Kinder,* running about and doing somersaults near the cedar sapling I'd planted.

From a distance I could see the stone that marked Willie Keil's grave. I wondered when they'd set the stone and felt an immediate sense of guilt that I had no such marker for Christian. That I'd not known of the occasion when Willie's stone had been set also discomfited. Perhaps the family was protecting me, not wanting to invite me on the occasion of a grave marker while I still carried a child. More likely, they thought I'd be uninterested in anything having to do with Keil.

But then we approached Christian's grave, and it had a marker too. Not a stone one, but wood, laid flat. Someone had cut his name and birth and day of death into it. No one had bothered to tell me of its setting, either.

The whole community probably clucked their tongues even now that it had taken so long for me to comment on this gesture, which could only mean that I hadn't spent much time grieving at my husband's grave. True, I hadn't spent much time at this grave. In fact, this was the first time I'd come since the day he'd been buried, and that only because it was the anniversary date, a time designed to be the end of mourning. I could only hope. Sarah said a husband's family set the time of mourning for an Indian widow, established ways she must behave during those years. It had sounded constricting when she'd told me, but at least the rules were clear and there was an ending time.

I imagined Christian's family thinking ill of me that I'd stayed away. They wouldn't understand the difficulty I'd had in traveling seven miles with the children. I didn't always have the use of their mule. Walking and carrying three young children wasn't an easy task at all. They might think of that.

Still, if I made my way to Olympia to paint or draw, the family would say that I could travel when I wanted to.

After we put dried flowers on Christian's grave, I took the children down the hill and over to where Andreas and Barbara lived. I waited for the inevitable comment about how long it had been since I'd visited them, but instead they opened their arms wide to the children.

Henry continued to work in the fields, but Martin waved when he saw us and moved toward the house. He wiped his hands on his jeans. He had a pleasant face, this brother of Christian's. He was tall, almost too thin, and leaned into his walk as though to resist a wind that might otherwise blow him away. He shook Andy's little hand and smiled into the open face of Baby Christian. He nodded his head to Kate, too, who was sitting on her grandfather's knee.

"Emma's brought the boys to stay for a bit," my mother-in-law said.

"That would be *gut*," Martin said. "For her to stay too."

"Just for the afternoon," I told them. "We need to go back before dark." I gave Barbara some salal-berry cakes I'd carried with us. I'd dried them and stored them through the winter. These were the last that I had, but soon the bushes would be filled with the small berries as purple as a bad bruise, and I'd make more cakes again.

"Oh, *ja*, but it stays light till after ten now," Barbara said, unwrapping the berry cakes from the leaves they were wrapped in.

"So we have time to catch up on news," Martin said.

"I don't have much of that," I said.

"Time or news?" he asked. He smiled.

"You don't come to the Fourth of July celebration," Andreas said. He looked tired and moved a cane I hadn't remembered his using. It must have been a difficult winter for him too, having lost his oldest son to death. Andreas wouldn't have stayed at Willapa without Christian's being here, and I wondered why they remained now. Probably because his brother John was here and his other sons.

Barbara said, "We'll give you news, then. John says the children should go to school from June to harvest and then stop, starting again in October until the rains come too much. Andy should stay here for that. You want him educated, *ja*? The travel would be hard for him and Martin enjoys his company."

"He's never been separated from me," I said, wishing now I hadn't taken the time to come here, wishing I hadn't even considered being generous and sharing my son with this family. It always seemed to end with suggestions for how I could do things better.

"That's not so," Barbara corrected, "when his father—"

"They're planting teasel," Andreas said. "To card the wool. Down at Aurora Mills. That's news."

"It grows wild along the river here," I said. "We just need wool to card. No one ever brought up sheep."

"We have sheep here," Henry said. "Rudy brought them."

"There's talk of building a teasel factory in Aurora," Martin said. "It'll be a good sheep production place. And they're beginning to build furniture to sell to nearby settlers. It's a busy place there."

"I suspect one day some of our young men will head that way if things pick up," Andreas said. "Rudy bought a sheep farm there."

"They have a cemetery," Barbara said. "Can't have a village without a cemetery."

"Speaking of cemeteries, who made the wooden marker for Christian's grave?" I asked. "I'd like to thank them and apologize for taking so long to do it."

"Imagine growing teasel. Stuff is like a weed back home," Andreas said.

"The Shoalwaters use it to brush their hair," I said. "I've seen them once or twice doing that by the river." They sometimes came to trade with me, offering up fish for my bread. I didn't tell my in-laws that. "About that marker," I tried again, but then the conversation took a troubling swing.

"Those Indians will be in trouble for not staying on their reservation," Andreas said, "if they're coming so far south as your place. Could be dangerous. You should live back with us."

"*Ja.* Why don't you leave Andy with us for a few days at least," Barbara said. "We miss seeing him, and you have the baby to look after."

"Andy's a big help to me," I said.

"*Ja,* that's as it should be," Andreas said. He tapped his cane on the floor. "But he must miss having a man around to show him things."

"Karl Ruge comes by," I said. My thumb and forefinger made circles against each other and I bit the inside of my cheek.

"What kind of wood did they use for Christian's marker?" Martin asked. "That might tell us who did it."

"Wood? I don't know. It looked like cedar. It was nicely done."

"It's too bad you're so busy," Barbara said. "Maybe whoever did it would have asked you to be there when they set it. But they know how much work it must be to come this way. We so seldom see you."

"I'll ask around if you'd like," Martin said. I nodded.

"What's the point of living near your family if you don't take advantage of them?" Barbara continued. She handed Andy a cookie and a big glass of milk. He sat on the chair, his legs swinging beneath him. He looked happy and I realized I hadn't seen that smile much since his father had died. Maybe I was selfish in not letting him come here more often.

"I was under the impression that I took too much advantage," I said, "having to have so much help since…Christian's death."

"Well, that's what we do for each other," she said. "We take care of each other. And having a little time for Andy to spend with his *Oma* would just be a nice way to repay."

"I should have made a marker for my brother," Martin said.

"You might think about how you could be generous to others since you want to not be beholden to people." Her words were sharp.

"We really need to be getting back," I said.

"What's your hurry?" Barbara said, softer now.

"Generosity, that's a good thing in our colony," Andreas said. "But why they want to plant teasel, *ach,* that's beyond me."

Surely I was strong enough to resist any real effort by them to lure Andy from me. I'd never heard of anyone in the colony having their child raised by another against their will. But it reinforced my view that showing few signs of needing them was the better course of action for our future.

My fields were plowed and planted into oats, not wheat, as the men suggested. They'd harvest the crop on my land just as they did on their own. Whatever they sold would be brought to the common fund of the family; whatever was milled would be shared with the families both here and probably at Aurora. I had no say in it. I stayed out of their way. When the cows had their calves and they were weaned, Boshie brought them back. He kept the calves, the increase, so the bulls could be sold and the heifers kept to expand the herd. The increase was payment for his tending them through the winter. I could once again have the milk for butter and to supplement the goat's milk for the children, and of course to meet whatever butter contracts we Willapa people had.

Sometime late that fall, people began calling the stockade Fort Willapa, and a post office was even established there with John Giesy as the postmaster. He wore so many hats, that John. Christian wore many hats too. He'd been a legislator for less than year. My brother Jonathan wrote that Oregon had indeed held its first election of state officials. Next year for sure, Oregon would be a state, or so Jonathan said. He didn't invite me to come there in his letter, but it was clear he felt Oregon the better of the two places.

A few of the Willapa women sent some of their weavings down to Oregon for a harvest festival at Gladstone, not far from Aurora. Mary suggested I bake a special *Strudel* for the event. I scoffed. "By the time it arrived it would be either hard as a rock or worse, covered with a hairy mold they'd have a hard time passing off as a frosting."

"Maybe we should hold our own fair," she said.

But there weren't enough people for such an event in Willapa. There probably never would be. That very thought made me feel disloyal to Christian, and I apologized to him out loud.

Mary and Elizabeth and Boshie made plans to go to Aurora, though. It was to be Mary's first visit. "Karl Ruge is going with us, but Jack's staying so he can look after things." Her face was flushed with excitement about the trip. "He'll come by here too. I've asked him to do that, so don't be rude to him."

"I've never been rude," I said.

"You can be...hard," she said.

I wanted to ask why it was that when women said what they wished that they were considered "hard," but when men said what they thought they were just wise and authoritative, a quality to be admired.

"I'd really rather Jack didn't come by," I said.

"What's wrong with him?"

"I just...he looks at me strange. Like I was some sort of exhibit at a fair," I said.

"Maybe you're just not accustomed to having a man show interest. Maybe you're suffering a bit of lovesickness. You pursued Christian. He never really had a chance to woo you."

I turned to her. "Lovesickness? I'm so far from such a thought. And Christian chose me, he did. That you'd—"

"People do marry for things other than love, you know," she said. She looked away, acted as though my table needed dusting, and she did that now.

"Mary, I...I don't know what to say to such strange thinking."

She shrugged. "It's what is, Emma. Most women who are widowed do remarry, and not all of them are so fortunate as to fall in love before they do it. Think of your children."

"They're all I do think of."

———

When Mary returned from her visit to Aurora she was full of stories about plum orchards that had been planted and how a new railroad was running a short distance along the Columbia River in the Washington Territory, and that in Oregon City there was a school that women attended and that she'd seen an advertisement for people making daguerreotype portraits, for a fee.

"Daguerreotype portraits. They must have been lovely," I said.

"Much too expensive for the likes of us. And probably too worldly," she added in a whisper, "though I'd love one made of Elizabeth."

I hadn't shared with her my plans to draw portraits. She might think that was too worldly also. Neither did I tell her about my limited interactions with Jack Giesy while they'd been gone. Jack had come by, tipped his hat, and acted the cocky gentleman.

Andy warmed to him, running right up to Jack as he swaggered into the yard. I kept my face emotionless but I could hardly deprive my son of time with the man who'd helped him say good-bye to his father.

I let them stay outside. It was October and the air smelled fresh as mint. Jack showed him how to make a whistle from a bird carcass Andy handed to him. Then Kate begged to go outside too, as she squatted beneath my legs, pushing my skirts aside. She ran to where Jack and Andy sat beneath a cedar tree, her little face so close to what Jack worked on that her eyes must have crossed.

Jack laughed and patted the cedar boughs on the ground beside him, and she sat. Andy raced toward me when the whistle was finished and the sound he made was that of a hawk flying high overhead. I stopped my butter churning and picked up Baby Christian, the forlornness of the whistle haunting. Kate shouted, "Me too, me too!" and Andy ran back and gave her the whistle, though she couldn't make the song.

Christian watched with careful eyes all this activity while I held him, standing in the doorway of my cabin. I wondered what he could see from that distance. Could he feel the dry air? The vine maple had turned red already, announcing the coming of autumn. I would welcome the rain.

"Come over, Mama," Andy shouted. He motioned with his arm.

There'd be no harm in that, I supposed. The grass was crisp as I walked across it to where Jack sat, to where Kate had returned the whistle to him telling him it was "lame."

"*Lame*," Jack said. "There's a new term for something broken."

"She sees the goat sometimes limping," I explained. "We have to take a stick or stone from his hoof."

"Let's see if we can heal it," Jack said and blew on the whistle to Kate's delight. She studied it and then she grabbed for it. Andy grabbed back and Kate started to cry, a high-pitched wail. "You best stop, little lady, or you'll get yourself in trouble," Jack said in a stern voice. *A little too stern,* I thought. It just made Kate cry louder.

"I'll handle my children," I said, bending to take the whistle. "Andy, go get your sister a drink of water." He hesitated, then accepted that what I recommended must be the correct course of action.

"You spoil the girl," Jack said.

"She's considerably younger than her brother and can't solve problems without bringing attention to herself," I said. "You have no children. It's hardly your place to comment."

"*Ja.* Not my place," Jack said. "But your boy will lack proper respect for himself and your daughter will neglect her role of silence if their mother's words aren't balanced by a good man's words to guide them. Their mother too."

"If you came here to tell me how to behave, I'd say it was time for you to leave."

"Maybe I could chop that stack of wood for you," Jack said. "That's the reason I came. To help a widow out."

Furious, I ignored him. "It's all right, Kate," I said. She'd calmed a bit. "When you're older you'll make the whistle work."

"Andy go."

"I know. For now, you go drink the water your brother's getting for you." She gave in reluctantly and I saw myself in her eagerness to do all things that her older brother could.

"About the wood?" Jack asked. "I maybe could chop you up a winter's supply."

He made offers with a ready escape when he said "maybe could." If I turned him down he could say, "I only maybe offered," and if I accepted, well, then he had the upper hand. If I took something from him, he'd want something in return. He had obligation written all over his high forehead, wrapped into that lazy, almost leering grin. In another time I might have flirted back, just for fun, but not now, not with Jack.

"The work is good for me," I said. "A good change from churning butter."

He cocked his head in that way he had. "They always said you were a stubborn woman," Jack said.

"They?"

He stood up and when he did, he stood too close. I could smell the soap that had scrubbed his skin and see the pores in his chin. I shifted Christian into the crook of my other arm and stepped back.

"You know who 'they' are," he said. He stepped away, leaned against the cedar tree, picked at his cuticles. "The relatives. They say it with some admiration, though," he added.

"I doubt that." Baby Christian squirmed against me. I put him onto my shoulder and patted his back. He burped and the smell of sour milk filled the space between us. "There's little room for the admiration of women in this colony."

"Not true, not true. Look at Helena Giesy. Never married, just gives her life to Bethel. She's coming out to help Keil, did you know that? And we all think Louisa Keil is a saint. She never makes demands or questions. Mary Giesy is a generous woman too, taking me and Karl Ruge in, treating us like family though we're two old bachelors. So you see, women are noticed."

"For what they *do*," I said. "Not for who they are." He squinted at me. "And you are hardly an old bachelor." I wished I hadn't added that last, but his characterizing himself as someone like Karl annoyed.

"I'm not? Well, that's good news. Must mean I'm young enough to chop that wood for you before I go." I shook my head. "You don't want me to go?"

"No. I mean *ja,* I think it's time you left."

"Is there anything else I *can* do while I'm here?" Now he lifted an eyebrow and with it came that half leer, eyes twinkling. His legs crossed at the ankles, arms folded across his chest. So self-assured.

"You've treated my children to a pleasant hour. I'd say that was more than enough. The rest I can take care of myself."

He jerked himself forward off the tree trunk, an act that startled me and caused Christian to begin to cry. The children had returned, Kate carrying a tin cup and Andy now chasing at the goat. Jack moved in a little closer and patted Christian's back. Anyone passing by might think it the perfect family scene.

"It's not easy raising three children on your own, Widow Giesy. It is a man's duty to tend to the widows in his family. You and I've grown up with the colony's wishes about widows. Christian would want that tradition carried on. You know that. A woman is meant to be with a family, with a man to shape her life." He squatted and picked up dirt and rubbed it between his hands. "Pitch," he said by way of explanation. He looked at me then. "I'll return to the oyster beds before long and won't be so available to…help you out. So you might think of tasks you'd like done before the rains come hard. I can oblige. I'm as decent a man as you'll find in these parts with all sorts of hidden talents, lots of time to give. I rarely sleep. Mary will tell you. And I'm a patient man despite what you may think of me."

"I never thought you weren't patient or anything else," I said. "You flatter yourself, Jack Giesy, that I think of you at all."

He laughed. For a moment he looked less like the wolf of the three little pigs' fame and more like Mary's little lamb. *Can he turn on that boyish grin at will?* Apparently so, for he added, "Oh, you think about me, Emma Giesy. I bet you put that little egg I made for you in a nice prominent place in your house. Will you let me see where it sits? Or are you too frightened that once I'm inside your home you might not get me out?"

"It was a gift for Christian. And I should thank you for it. I do now. I hadn't known you made it, just that you delivered it. And nothing about you frightens me," I lied. "I'm just cautious about what sorts of critters come into the house."

I went inside, brought the children in with me, then seethed in silence as I heard him chopping wood that he must have known I'd one day burn.

———

After he left I chided myself for not asking him about his drawings. But to do so invited an intimacy I wasn't prepared for. An artist's work exposes, and one wishes to do it on one's own terms. I might have asked him what he thought about selling portraits, but I didn't want to know his opinion enough to risk his rejection of mine. Maybe with daguerreotypes being sold now even in the streets of a small town like Oregon City, there'd be no need for my making drawings. Maybe photographic likenesses would be preferred.

Once the children were in bed at night, though, I did light Christian's lamp and take out my charcoal and the last of the papers I had to draw on. I ironed the damp paper flat, then filled in the sketches, made the ferns detailed, darkened the bark so it looked almost real enough to pick up. I hadn't heard anything from my parents about sending me money or supplies, or coming to this land. They probably didn't realize what courage it took to make the request.

My days were filled with diaper changing, though Kate had trained herself. The first time she successfully found the privy of her own accord we were at Fort Willapa at the last service I thought we would attend before Christmas and the truly heavy rains came. Kate told Christian's youngest sister what she needed, and Louisa took her out. Kate came roaring back in and announced to everyone that she'd "wee'd all alone." She carried the word "all" out as though it was a long song. John was giving the sermon that day. He stopped short, turned his head toward the women's side of the building. He smiled at her and then the rest all laughed. I loved him for that, for noting that a young girl's early success should be shouted to the world.

Christmas came and then the New Year which brought treasures from my family. The joy I felt with the gifts surprised. They sent wooden toys for the two older children and a silver rattle for Christian. I realized they must have begun gathering up gifts and sending them as soon as they learned of the baby's birth in order to get them here at this special time.

For me, my parents included charcoal and paper as gifts. The latter was crinkled from the damp weather and the days it took for it to reach me. Still, it would be my beginning, and I hadn't had to ask a Giesy or a colony member for this start.

My father wrote nothing about coming either to visit or to stay, though. So, that was the way it would be then. Whatever I could do with the drawing would be my next step toward independence. I would have to do this on my own. I'd keep my children with me, and perhaps we'd travel together to make my sketches. Never mind that my parents weren't going to be able to make the journey or did not wish to meet their grandchildren. There were good reasons for them not coming, I was certain.

I'd always wanted to live on my own, and so I would. I might even sell this property. It was in my name. I could sell it and use the money to begin my newest life. Why not do that? Why not leave this place behind?

The thought of leaving what Christian and I had built together left me breathless.

Here, I was as close to independence as a widow with three children living in a communal colony could come. The money received from any sale would eventually be used up. I couldn't take the risk. I felt like a harlot accepting the work of others on our behalf, but I refused to be like other widows who married someone they didn't care for because they couldn't make it on their own. I would find ways to pay back Christian's family, I would.

And if Andy hadn't gotten ill, I might well have made it work.

15

Emma

The River of Transport and Hurdle

Andy's fever spiked and waned for days. He coughed so hard he seemed to bring his insides out. I kept him cool in baths of agrimony, the water turning yellow from the plant we dyed wool with back in Bethel. Here I used it to make him teas to help the vomiting, but it did little good. I put a mustard plaster on his chest, went through my shelves to see if there was anything I could give him that might help. Catnip tea did nothing but make him sleep. His round face poured into tiny hollows at the cheeks. His lips quivered and cracked. Little ones had no reserve against a storm like this, I decided. His face sank pale with pain.

He must have picked it up at the Christmas gathering with all the others. I remembered now hearing Joe Bullard and the fence viewer, Mr. Vail, coughing. Children played in spite of runny noses, their little hands lifting doughnuts from the table, then putting some back for those more heavily sugared. I tried to keep Andy and Kate from the ailments of others. But it was Kate's birthday celebration, too, and I hadn't wanted to deprive her of what I thought would be worthy attention.

For all the good that did. Her grandparents were kind to her, giving her a cookie and patting her on the head. The aunts commented on her pretty curls, but it was Andy and Christian they doted on that day, commenting on Christian's reddish hair and Andy's stance with his hands on his hips, just the way his father used to stand. My daughter didn't garner much interest.

My present to her of a special covered basket made of tulle pleased her. "For treasure?" I nodded. I could have as easily given it to her at home. A good reason to stay the winter closed up in our cabin, alone.

But my insight came too late. Now the January rains poured themselves out like wretched tears on our cedar-shake roof, leaks forming in places where the shakes were saturated by the constant downpour. Mornings when it didn't rain we could barely see the cows in the half barn for the fog. I hated leaving Andy even for a moment, but the cows had to be milked. I'd come back in, wash his soiled clothes, and hang them at the rafters, but they took days to dry in the dampness, even with the fire burning hot. At least I had plenty of chopped wood, thanks to Jack Giesy. I gave him that grudging thanks.

I brought the goat into the house to stop her mournful bleating and so I could milk her. I cleaned after her, but nothing seemed to stop the stench of the mix of her *Dreck* and Andy's illness.

I knew I should go for help but I couldn't take Kate or Christian into the weather and I couldn't leave Andy alone. With this discouraging rain, they probably took to heart my constant insistence that I needed no help.

Midweek I stopped milking the cows because I didn't want to be away from Andy. Taking all three of the children to Mary's seemed overwhelming and unsafe, but I had to do something. I had to get additional herbs or get him to the doctor. There was only one thing to do.

"Mama!" Kate cried as I pulled on my scarf and Christian's heavy oiled slicker.

"It's fine, *Liebchen*," I said. "I'll be right back. Don't worry." I swung open the door and stepped into the downpour. It chilled but it wasn't icy, wasn't about to become snow. Water ran like spring freshets along the muddy path, so instead I walked beside it. I slipped my way to where the cows mooed in the half barn. They stood, heads up when they saw me. They hadn't been milked since the morning before. They wouldn't like what I was about to do. I untied them, then I picked up a stick and shouted, startling them both. One mooed and switched her tail at me.

"Get out! Go! Go on now!" I swatted again but they merely moved a little and stood looking at me, the rain making their short horns as shiny as the Bay. "Please, you've got to go. Go to Mary's, please." I switched them again. They moved but a foot, the cold evident in the moisture at their nostrils.

If I'd wanted them to stand still and not move despite my shouts, they would have run in all directions.

I put the rope around the neck of one of them, the one with the bell, and began to drag her forward from the comfort of the half barn. They could be so contrary, these animals. We'd tamed them into dogs who didn't want to be in the wet and the cold. Who could blame them? But it was all I could think of to do, to let loose the cows and swat at them and head them in the direction of Mary and Boshie's and hope that when the Giesys saw the animals loose and needing milked they'd know that something was wrong.

Finally I dragged the recalcitrant cow out onto the path. The other followed at a desperately slow pace. *How long have I been gone from Andy?* "Shoo!" I shouted, getting behind them now. "Shoo!" They both turned back toward me. Then, as though they shared a signal, each began running toward me, back into the half barn. "No, please!" I felt the tears come. *"Ach, jammer! What is the matter with you?"* They split around me as though I were an island and they the moving river, their hooves splashing mud onto my dress, my slicker, my face. They stood inside then, chewing their cuds, their bags swollen out between their legs.

I stomped to the house to get Christian's percussion gun. One shot, that's all I needed. Thank goodness Christian hadn't left me a flintlock. In this rain, the powder would have been nothing but mud and I'd not have gotten off a single shot.

Before I left with the gun, I tended to Andy, his face so hot. "Katie, you put this cloth on your brother's forehead. Do it now. I'll be right back. Never mind the gun. It'll be fine, *ja.*" Christian cried now too. He was sitting up by himself and had just started to crawl. I scanned the room to see if he could reach anything that could hurt him. "You watch Baby, too, Kate. Make sure he doesn't get too near the fire."

"You're crying, Mama," Kate said.

I wiped at my eyes. "It's just rain. Go; do as you're told now."

Outside I hit at the cows with the butt of the gun and this time, as though to humor me, they moved out single file down the path. "Go! Go!" I shouted. Instead they stopped. But before they could turn around and race past me again, I aimed the rifle and shot. The recoil forced me flat against the ground. I knew I'd have a bruise the size of the Territory in the morning, but I looked with joy to see them both running down the path toward Mary and Boshie's, their full bags swaying out between their legs as they ran.

"Oh, thank God," I said. "Thank God."

It was the first time I had prayed since Christian died. At least it was a prayer of gratitude and not one of complaint.

Heading back toward the house I thought that I should have tied something in writing to the bell! How could I have not done something so obvious, to tell them what I needed? *Ach.* There was no calling those cows back now. I'd have to hope that the cows arrived and that Boshie would bring them back and not decide to "help me out" by keeping them.

"Please," I said out loud. "Please bring someone back who can help us." I wiped my son's forehead with a cooling cloth. At least the cool rain was good for something.

So when hours later I heard the cows bellow and I opened the door to hold up the lantern and look out, I believed even Jack Giesy could be an answer to prayer.

Jack led with that sly grin, and said something about my not letting him come in "until the cows come home."

"Of course I want you in here. Those cows did their duty bringing me help."

"You? In need of something?" His smile broadened if it was possible, one hand still holding the lead rope of a cow.

"I need you to take care of Kate and Christian while I get Andy to Woodard's Landing and Dr. Cooper."

The smile vanished. "The boy is ill?" His concern seemed genuine.

"You think I'd send my cows out for some silly reason? A fever. He's had it for a week, sometimes a little less, sometimes a little more. He hardly eats. I've done what I could but he needs a doctor. I need to take him to the doctor."

"Don't be troublesome, Emma Giesy," Jack said. He moved with the cows toward the barn and tied them, then walked as quickly as I'd ever seen him back to the cabin. "The boy is ill and must be taken, as you say." He stomped water from his brogans. "But I can do that faster and safer. Your place is here with your other children."

"But Andy needs—"

"To be taken care of quickly. Let's bundle him now. No more about it. I'll look after him."

I stared. It was the best choice. I'd have to trust this man. I found the blanket, wrapped Christian's oil slicker around Andy, then lifted this bundle so light into Jack's arms. "I want to come along, Andy, but I can't. Cousin Jack is taking care of you." He lay still against Jack's chest. "Thank you," I said. "Please. Let me know what's happening. Please."

"As soon as I can," he said.

So I let Jack take Andy to his grandparents, where Martin was and where the doctor could be called from Woodard's Landing. I let him take my son.

———

True to his word, Jack did come back two days later, with news that filled me with relief. Dr. Cooper said Andy rested quietly at Andreas and Barbara's. "It's a kind of bronchitis," Jack said. "Doc Cooper gave him baked onion juice, a little sugar and glycerin. Calmed the cough some. He doesn't look so tired. And he slept they said."

"Is he well enough to travel?"

"Oh, not for a bit yet," Jack said. "Your mother-in-law said not to worry, to just take good care of Kate and Christian. She said she hoped you'd accept their help for once with this."

"I wouldn't have let you take him if I wasn't willing to do what was best for him," I said.

"Something I know," Jack said.

"Did he give you any idea of how much time before I can come to get him?"

"Martin said he'd bring him back when he got better."

"Martin did? Oh, good."

Knowing Martin tended him brought comfort. He'd understand my need to have my son back and could remind my in-laws about whom Andy really belonged to. I sent Jack off with thanks, grateful that he left without resistance or suggesting any future obligation.

———

By February 1859, the rains let up. Sun breaks came occasionally, chasing off the fog, and one morning I bundled up the children and we set off. I stopped at Mary's and asked if she would mind watching Kate and Christian while I went to fetch Andy.

"Is he that much better then?" she asked.

"Jack says he makes steady improvement and he's been there two weeks. It's time for me to bring him home."

"Or at least visit him," Mary said. Her cheeks were rosy as though she'd been out in the sun but it wasn't that warm. "I'd be lost without Elizabeth for that long."

"I have been," I said. She rubbed her belly as I talked. "Are you…will you have a child?"

"*Ja!* We are so happy. I wanted to tell you but it's hard to share a joy when someone is in sorrow in her own life. I thought Jack might have told you."

"I don't like to have him around much," I said. "Except now, to share news about Andy."

"You should talk more to him. He's funny, sometimes, Emma. He could make you laugh. You used to like to laugh."

"That was before my husband died and I had three children to raise. I don't have much time for frolic," I said.

"A little light conversation with Jack wouldn't take much effort," she said.

"When is your baby due?" I asked.

"Summer. It will be a good time for a little one with fresh vegetables from our gardens. Elizabeth will have a new brother or sister." She smiled at her daughter working diligently on a stitching sampler. Kate already had her face in the sampler, looking closely. "I can watch the children for you but you'll come back today, won't you? I don't have goat's milk here."

I'd brought goat's milk along just in case, but I assured her I'd be back, hopefully with Andy, before it got dark.

"It gets dark early," she warned me. "And the river's running high, you know."

"Then I'd better be off."

When I arrived at the crossing, my boat wasn't moored where it was usually left. Other people used the craft; it was a custom, just as it had been back in Bethel. I thought of it as "my boat," since Christian had bought it. I moved up and down the shoreline trying to find where whoever used the boat last might have tied it, muttering beneath my breath about the inconsiderateness of them. I looked across the water to see if someone had already used it to cross and sure enough, I saw it there, tied to a willow, the water pushing against it so it was nearly flush with the opposite bank.

The river was way too high to attempt to wade it.

Letting Jack take Andy had been the right thing to do. I'd have risked all three of my children in that boat with the Willapa so high. I'd have lacked the physical strength to cross it, much as I would have wanted to. Will was sometimes simply not enough. Timing was as much a factor in success as effort.

There was nothing I could do on this shoreline. If I waited for whoever had taken the boat to return, it would likely be too late to make it to Fort Willapa to get Andy and come back. The river ran swift, and managing the boat with Andy on the return trip could be a challenge too. But if I attempted to wade it I could at least see him, at least know that he was doing well.

I couldn't.

The rush of water darkened before me. I'd ridden on boats. I'd taken a mule across a stream. I'd stood in the water and clubbed fish to survive a winter. But I could not imagine myself with water to my chest pushing against the strength of the current and being strong enough when I reached the other side to then bring Andy back.

I told myself this obstacle was nothing out of the ordinary in a place like this where the rivers acted as both transport and barrier. There was nothing strange in having family look after a child, especially a sick child.

Watching the river rush, undercutting the banks while it carried swirls of trees and branches, I came to one conclusion that day: I couldn't leave my children behind while I traveled off to follow a scheme to paint or draw and make money of my own. If I went, they'd have to go with me.

I hoped my in-laws explained what would keep me away. Andy would see Jack or others coming and going and might not understand that a younger brother and sister and a raging river kept his mother from being with him.

I can't even cross a river to visit my son.

My routine continued through that month. I milked the cows. Karl came by once or twice, but without Andy there to teach, he seemed uncomfortable. He didn't even take time to smoke his pipe. Jack picked up the butter, spent a little time talking. He wasn't going back to the oyster beds, he said. Too much work for a laboring man with no potential for ownership, not that Jack wanted that. "I think communal living is the perfect answer for a young man's life. No worries, labor that helps others, never without a roof over one's head."

"Don't you ever want to just have something to call your own?" I asked.

He shrugged. "Owning property doesn't give a man much over one who doesn't. Why, we had neighbors back in Harmony who worked twice as hard just to keep everyone fed because they had land, property, and slaves. If war comes, they'll die for that property, and why? I don't see the point. Not when you can live taking care of your neighbor while your neighbor...takes care of you." That last he added with that grin again telling me he had more than one intent to convey.

"I'm sure Joe Knight's been pleased to be working for himself."

"Maybe could be. But I think he'll tire of the effort before long and head back to San Francisco. Maybe even Bethel. Oystering is a constant job, and the beds are property, so he has to watch them diligently so no one steals the shellfish. He stays awake nights worrying. None of us colony members do. Not worth it if you ask me."

"I thought you said you rarely slept."

He grinned. "True enough. But I'm not awake worrying."

"Christian never felt the need to own things either," I said.

"But you, you're one to believe that if you own a sheep you'll soon have wool and yarn and weavings to sell."

"*Ja,* and if the sheep belongs to the community, then no one cares especially for it. No one calls it by name or worries over it. Instead of it being an animal with wool becoming a weaving, it'll be but a sheep growing old."

"Don't let those who tend sheep in Bethel hear you say that. They looked after the animals as though they were children."

"But they aren't. And if the Bethelites would want to do something different, they don't have the authority to sell those sheep now, do they? They own nothing after all that work. Everything is in Keil's name. *He* has property. What'll happen when he dies? His sons will get all the work you've put in."

He shrugged. "I've had a good life."

"Don't you ever…want something else?"

He smiled then. His dark eyes told me I didn't want any answer he maybe could propose.

———

He was an interesting man, Jack Giesy, I had to say that for him. I could see a few of his virtues. But he presented a caution as well. I wanted to keep on his good side, as I might need his help bringing Andy back so I wouldn't have to wait until the river lowered. Meanwhile, I would treat him like a brother, listening to his news.

One day, when he'd kept his distance, made Kate laugh with the faces he made and so seemed safe and predictable, I asked him if we could plan a time when he could go with me to pick up Andy. "You're asking me for help, again? If I was a betting man, I'd have lost such a wager, that Emma Giesy would ask a man for help more than once in a lifetime."

"Am I really as difficult as that?"

"Maybe could be you are."

"So I am, then. Your answer?"

"*Ja,* sure. I'll go with you. Let's make it for Sunday next."

———

He brought a mule. "We'll need it here to work the fields anyway soon enough, so Boshie said to bring it. I'll leave it here when we get back." We loaded Kate and Christian up on the animal and the two of us walked the mile or so to Mary and Boshie's.

"You'll be back by dark?" Mary asked, as we unloaded the children.

I assured her we would. Karl was there. He drew on his pipe, asked after my health. I told him I missed our visits and he said, "*Ja,* by golly, I'll have a new almanac to bring to you soon. We'll check the best times to plant." Then he nodded to Jack and headed back into the house, taking Kate by the hand while Mary held Christian on her hip.

Jack led the mule to a stump step so I could get astride the animal. He frowned again and I remembered his discomfort with my swinging my leg over the animal. "You don't have a sidesaddle," I said.

"You had one. We should have taken it."

"And made it impossible for the children to ride? No. There's nothing wrong with a woman riding in a way to make her secure."

He grunted but swung up behind me.

"Feeling secure?" he whispered in my ear as he pressed into my back, reached for the reins and clicked his tongue at the mule that started off throwing me into Jack's chest as it fast-trotted toward the river.

Jack didn't want an answer, which was just as well. I felt secure enough that I wouldn't fall off the mule but I resented this man breathing so close to my neck. I resisted the scent of him against me. I bristled at the warmth of his body seeping so close to mine. How could he be upset by the impropriety of my leg swinging over a mule's rump but not have the slightest discomfort with an unmarried man's body heat warming a widow's robe?

Recent rains left the ferns and trees sparkling with raindrops. As the sun hit them, it reminded me of candles on the *Tannenbaum* at Christmastime. Birds twittered and I heard one lone seagull flying upriver and wondered for just a moment if it might be our Charlie. Andy would have been delighted to see a gull. It somehow marked the coming of spring.

Jack's arms held me on either side of my shoulders, like a cow's stanchion, as the mule plunged and pushed against the water, but we crossed the river without incident. On the other side, I suggested that I'd like to walk a ways. Jack complied and the conversation went easily back and forth between us talking of wheat and sheep. Safety. Walking was safer.

At a rock outcropping I noticed what looked like the remains of a drawing of a flower maybe or a dragonfly. "Look," I pointed. "Could that be a natural design of lichen or is it a...drawing? Yes, I believe it is."

"Maybe could be," he said, grinning.

"You did that."

"*Ja*, sure. I have hidden gifts you know nothing about."

"I know the egg you scratched for Christian showed a fine talent," I said.

"As if you'd know how to evaluate such talents, Emma Giesy."

His retort had been said in jest, but it stung just the same. I wasn't going to say anything to him about my own artistic bent. "Don't you worry that it'll soon be washed away?"

"Maybe could be it's all the more precious that way, knowing it's fleeting, not long for this world. If we lived that way, knowing we're on the way to dying, we'd take more time to do the things that bring us a little pleasure, don't you think, Widow Giesy? I bet your Christian wishes he'd spent more time in his marriage bed than with his oyster beds."

He was so brassy. Did Christian have regrets? Could those who died still harbor longing the way those they left behind did? I couldn't imagine that. It was a theological question, one I'd have to explore with Karl, not with this man who sent signals of friendship wrapped up in tempered heat.

As we approached Fort Willapa I could feel my heart start pounding. It would be so good to see Andy! I'd clipped pictures from my almanac and glued the tiny pieces with flour paste to form entirely new designs, ever grateful for my sharp scissors that let me practice the craft of *Scherenschnitte*. I'd made him a tiger and a parrot and wrapped the cuttings in cloth for Jack to deliver to him. I imagined Andy opening them and finding pleasure in the little pieces of paper that were transformed into something new. Little pictures I'd sent so he'd know that he was constantly on my mind. Kate even took some stones from her treasure basket and sent them with me. "So's he'll know I got them for Andy," she told me. "I wants them back."

"He'll be bringing them back," I'd told her as I kissed her forehead good-bye.

Now at last I'd be seeing him and taking him home. I'd ask Martin for as many herbs as he could spare so if the cough came back I'd have a way to stop it before it got so bad he fevered and I had to be separated from him again.

Martin came out of the house as we tied the mule to the post. "Such a long way you've come," he said. He leaned forward, always leaning into things. He looked over at Jack.

"She wanted a visit," Jack said.

"*Ja*, that's good, but there's only me here, don't you know?"

"Where's Andy?" I asked. I looked toward the field. He must be well enough to run and play outside. How wonderful! But then they could have brought him back. I felt a rush of heat to my face but held my tongue.

"They've gone to Aurora Mills," Martin said. "Jack didn't tell you? Just for a visit, don't you know. They'll be back in a week or so."

I turned to Jack. "You knew he wasn't here and yet we came all this way, for nothing?"

"You needed an outing," he said. "Tell me it wasn't a pleasant journey?"

"When will people stop deciding what I need or don't need?" I said. "What I need is my son back. What I need is to be able to take care of things without other people cutting up my life like it was some little piece of paper they could recompose into something else entirely. How dare they just take my son! How dare they!"

"He wanted to go," Martin said softly.

"*Ja*, and if a five-year-old wished to ride a mule across a swollen river you would let him? This is what a grownup does, make good decisions for a child."

"Mama and Papa had never gotten to share their grandchild with their friends at Aurora. It's been nearly two years since they've seen the Bethel folks. They're going to bring back sheep when they return. It'll be fine, Emma." Martin reached out to offer me his hand. "Come inside and have tea."

"No tea. I just want to go home." I swung around swiftly and began walking out ahead of the mule and Jack. My mind burned with the outrageousness of it all. They'd had to come right by our place if they went to Aurora crossing the Cowlitz. Maybe they took a ship, crossing the very bay that had taken Andy's father's life. Without talking to me, his mother, about any of it!

I heard Jack shout something about not being in such a hurry.

"I must get home before dark, remember?" I said. "I have children to attend to." I stopped short. "Don't I?"

"Of course Kate and Christian are there, waiting for you," Jack said as he caught up with me. He moved the mule to stand before me. "Why don't you get up here and ride with me."

"I'll walk," I told him, pushing past the mule. "At least it's some small portion of my life I still control."

16

Louisa

If it weren't for the music I should think we colonists would have taken much longer to find our place of belonging in this West. It soothes us when the day's work shifts from outside to inside and the candlelight becomes our comforter. Through the open windows (where there are blessedly few insects despite our closeness to the river) the men's chorus lifts its melody above the treetops, and even while we women sit and spin we can hear them, sometimes their rhythm a perfect fit for the thump of our wheels. Beethoven's Ninth with its lovely chorus makes me feel as though I am at home in Germany; the words bypass my heart and go directly to my soul. I love the rousing songs they sing too. They practice for the festivals. The settlers here enjoy festivals. There seems to be one scheduled nearly every month somewhere within carriage distance. I suppose it is something to look forward to. It breaks up the monotony of difficult fieldwork, all the adjustments needed to find the way in a new land. We Germans know how to celebrate with our brass horns and dances and wonderful food. It is good we brought those customs with us along with the drums and brass horns.

My husband has actually composed some pieces, though more for the band than for voices. I like "Webfoot Quickstepp" because it makes me tap my feet and I have to stop my spinning! I don't believe he composed that one but it is one of my favorites. Sometimes he lets others think he has composed them all. I notice he says "I made up some strongly medicinal wine from Oregon grape" when in fact someone else did the work but he oversaw it. I think "we" might be a good word to use there instead of "I," but of course I'm not likely to suggest it.

We Bethelites are becoming "webfoot" people. After last winter we started calling ourselves that because of the incessant rains. Andreas and Barbara Giesy, when they visited this spring, said the same was true of the Willapa though they claimed those ocean breezes bring in sunbreaks more often than we saw here through the winter past. I wonder if people back in Missouri would understand a sunbreak.

Then in the summer the ground becomes dry as old coffeecake and we smell smoke sometimes in the morning where a fire to burn brush or stumps has gotten out of hand. It can take over an entire field and lick at trees the farmer hadn't planned to burn at all. Fire is a terrible thing but oh so necessary in these parts, where the stumps must be burned to clear the ground and then dug at with a crowbar so the workers are covered with soot.

Our mill turns out lumber for houses and we are building steadily. The doctor rises early and he has tasks for everyone. It is as though this journey west has given him new vigor. I worry he might decide that we need to expand our family. I pray not, though I know Eve was admonished to submit to her husband's wishes. I wish only to keep my eight living children healthy and well, and to do so I must keep myself healthy and well. Women die in childbirth. I see it. It is almost as dangerous as cooking in the summer kitchen with the fire sparking as we stir; a woman's dress is suddenly aflame. Such morbid thoughts I think! Eve did as she was bid by her husband after she ate of the Tree of Knowledge. The doctor forgets that the man ate of that fruit too. Maybe, just maybe, Eve wasn't tempting him as the serpent had but instead was hoping to feed him, the very thing a woman is called to do and a man will complain about if she doesn't.

I would never say such a thing to the doctor. Never. But I think it. In this diary of sorts, I write it.

So far, the doctor's diligent work, the young people's problems he has to solve, his music pleasure, and the laughter with his children before they go to bed keep him willing to be held in our marriage bed without requesting the fruit that would bring another child into the world.

I still think of Willie every day.

The children are good. They don't speak his name but the grief sneaks up on me like a black cat racing across my path, unexpected and promising to make the day go badly. I wonder if Emma Giesy has that experience too. I don't know why I think of her as often as I do. Perhaps because we share a grief now, having lost someone so dear to us, someone who was the chalice of our lives. It surprised me to see that she'd let her Andy from her sight to come here with his grandparents. It is a side of her I must assess through different eyes.

The boy and his *Oma* and *Opa* remained here several weeks. Andy enjoyed the other children living in this colony, even though it is a hike to the distant farms nestled among the firs. In the town proper there is still just this big house and several smaller dwellings and the colony store, but we keep working. As in the old country, we go out to the fields and orchards, returning back home at night. The doctor says the new arrivals, those not of our colony of course, look for land separated from each other where they can't see the smoke of a neighbor's house. We've adopted this western way somewhat. Hiking is good for children the doctor says. Even little ones like Andy.

He has sad eyes, though, that child of nearly six. He has seen trial in his young life, with his father's death. I asked about his sister and brother and he answered clear and firm, "They're well, *Frau* Keil." Like a little man he is, so like his father, ready to take on responsibility at a young age. Watching the boy makes me think of when his father first came to the doctor and said he wished to be in service to the colony. My husband beamed. He groomed Chris for such a role and my husband is a grand teacher. This is not to malign George Wolfer back in Bethel or Karl Ruge in Willapa. These are both great teachers with university degrees. But my husband, who lacks such schooling, is a true teacher, a true guide, and he helped Chris see what must be seen in order for the colony to be successful.

His death was tragic indeed, as the doctor led Chris to the understanding that taking the Bethelites to Aurora Mills and not staying there in Willapa was the only sane course of action. It was so good that Chris came to accept this before he died. Imagine if he had carried thoughts that my husband betrayed him; imagine if he had died with such beliefs? I wonder now if his wife encouraged him to persist at oystering as a way of helping Chris save face. It would be a grand gesture on her part if she had. But I suspect she liked more the idea of having her own cabin to stay in far from others the way these eastern settlers seem to like their land in the West. That oystering scheme suggests that Emma had no intention of letting her husband come here one day to take his chosen place as the heir to the doctor's work. At least it earned him good money and Chris met his duty and sent the money to repay what the colony had put out for him.

In time, they'll all come here, the doctor says. Every one, and then they'll know this was truly God's plan. He says we can "rest assured we are following God's plan when things go well and in time, all things go well."

I have questioned this in my mind. Not that I would share such thoughts with the doctor. *Nein.* But Willie died. And Chris died, a man meant to lead this colony, perhaps share in the doctor's work so he could rest a bit. I get confused then between what is suffering meant to compensate for our sins and what is suffering that will one day bring God's plans to fruit? Who to ask? There is no one. I know the question alone would be seen as challenging the doctor, and so I won't ask it. I'd not do anything to add to the weight he carries here.

It was good to see Andy Giesy closer to the true activities of the colony. He could learn from the doctor. But I can't imagine Emma letting him go. It amazes me still that the boy has spent such time apart from her at all.

I suppose she is busy just doing woman's work with that new baby. I've set aside my *Fraktur* work. There is too much washing, mending, cooking, planting, harvesting to do. But this fall, the doctor let us take two days to attend the fairs at Linn and Benton counties. We prepared the wagons with food we'd need for the travel and the stay away from our home. The children jabbered in excitement as we took four wagons of people to the events.

Some of our harvest was entered to be judged, including our apple cider vinegar, some hogs, a sheep, our oats, a quilt, a *Strudel* or two. Food. We women put so much of who we are into our food. The doctor said the fair is a way of announcing our wares and thus while we cooked and played and offered venison sausage and spoke about its special flavorings, we invited others to taste. Thus we worked to let others know that we value quality and are easy people to be among. We also bring business to the colony. Sometimes it seems no matter what Dr. Keil chooses to do, he can find a way to turn it into good for the colony.

The children scampered around, and while there were many people we didn't know in attendance, the atmosphere was one of neighborliness, of goodwill. People smiled and the women nodded their bonnets at each other as they walked on the arms of their men, serenaded by distant fiddles and the smells of cooked beef wafting through the air.

There were booths with lovely things a woman might have decorated. Tin pots painted with bright colors. I was reminded of the pottery my mother had in our home in Germany and for the moment felt all wistful. I saw whittled figures made of soft woods that must have been brought from the old countries by settlers in the region. Miniatures. Even a scene meant to be Adam and Eve in the garden. Several people painted landscapes of trees and that mountain they call Hood that has snow on it all year round. We can see it from Aurora Mills. What pleased me most, though I did not tell my husband, was that I peered at the lettering on the bottom of the paintings and read first names like "Nancy" and "Mary." Women's names! Imagine. Here in this wilderness, women painting pictures for display. A woman even sat in one booth and handed out papers in English I could not read. The doctor had turned aside to talk to someone about horses, so I took the leaflet. I will save it and ask Karl Ruge when I see him next. I thought I heard the woman say the English word meaning "school," but I can't imagine there'd be a school here for women to learn to paint.

I saw show towels embroidered with scripture, so there are other Germans here, not just of our colony. My favorite item was a butter mold. A flower was carved with intricate leaves that one would press against the butter. Such butter would sell more quickly at a market than a simple mold or none at all. And it was beautiful, nearly as lovely as my *Fraktur,* which I saw no examples of at the fair. I brought the doctor by and hinted here and there until he said we should make such a mold. "Something unique to the colony," I said, "yet grand enough to be the centerpiece at a fine table."

"I've had a good idea," he said and nodded. I know he meant it was his idea but for just a moment it felt as though he'd paid me a compliment.

We walked the uneven grounds, surrounded by the scents of venison and even a beef being turned at a spit. Chickens and hogs, fruits and flowers; the displays were like music to my eyes. Our band would be playing in the evening.

Then came my husband's finest words to me in weeks: "See all these people, Louisa?" the doctor said to just me. "See them all coming from near and far, leaving their homes in the East, arriving here? They'll need all we have to give them." Soon, the doctor said, we'd begin weaving and tailoring and making shoes and we'd have these items to sell and display at the fairs. "We'll have furniture and blacksmith's work. Helena Giesy will come out, and she'll help weave cloth and piece quilts to replace the ones people had to leave behind or that are so worn out from being room dividers and sick robes and warmth to wrap around a woman's shoulders when she steps out to milk her cows. We'll make new quilts made with the wool we raise and dye and spin right here." His eyes were shiny with the possibilities. "Whatever they have need of, we will sell to them. Helena will come and she'll be followed by others. All will go well here now. It is God's will."

That "will" question again. I wished he hadn't said it, for it took me back to my lost Willie. Instead of feeling as warm as if I'd been wrapped in a quilt, I was chilled, even in the hot October afternoon; even with the band playing the "Webfoot Quickstepp." So quickly grief could transport me. I guess my mind knew before I could remember that as in life, the band would follow the joyous piece with the heaviness of a funeral dirge.

17

Emma

A Prayer Against the Sail

My Kate put a piece of cloth as a sail on a cedar bark boat she'd made, then set it afloat in the barrel of collected rainwater. She'd made a twig mast and somehow drilled a hole through the tough cedar bark, then stuck the stick there so it bravely held the sail. She set it afloat. It twirled around once, twice, then tipped over. She lifted it out, reset the sail and set it afloat again. Her breath pressed against it; it toppled again. She kept picking it back up, setting it on the water. The cloth sail was saturated, the bark too uneven to keep the mast upright. Before long it would be waterlogged and probably the whole thing would sink. But still, time after time, Kate continued, doing the same thing, expecting her sail to stand upright and her craft to move where her breath sent it, to get a different result even while she hadn't yet come to realize that she must change what she was doing. I couldn't stand it.

"It won't work," I told her, swiping the bark, pulling the cloth from its stick mast and squeezing the water from it with my fist. "Why do you keep doing it over and over? Can't you see it's finished? Done. You're defeated."

She stared, those wide blue eyes looking into mine, and then I saw her lower lip quiver.

"You broke it," she accused.

"It was already broken. It won't float. It isn't balanced right for one thing. The sail is saturated; it's too wet. It isn't ever going to do what you want it to."

She blinked. I'd never yelled at the children, not ever. My parents had never shouted at me. They might not talk to me for a time when I upset them; they might raise an eyebrow as an indicator that I'd gone too far, but they never shouted, never grabbed at me the way I'd just grabbed at Kate.

"Andy could make it go," she said. She crossed her little arms over her chest, her lip still shaking.

"*Ach,* he's not here."

"When's he come home, Mama?"

I didn't know. My shoulders sagged. I pulled her toward me and she let me comfort her. "I'm sorry, *Liebchen.* I'm so sorry. I miss him too."

"Did he go away like Papa did?"

"No. Not like Papa. He's with *Oma* and *Opa.*"

I was like that little sailboat tipping in the wind and no amount of setting it back up would take me to where I wanted to be. It wouldn't do any good to try to get Andy returned, I knew that. My son was healthy—at least if I believed Martin—and maybe Andy wouldn't even be alive if I hadn't handed him off to Jack.

Yet I felt betrayed and had since that day.

I walked hard all the way back that day, resisting Jack's cajoling that I should ride. At the river crossing I did let myself be pulled up—behind Jack this time—onto the mule, but as soon as he splashed across the water I slid off over the animal's rump and continued my purposeful stride.

"Did you know that Andy was gone, Mary?" I asked when we reached their homestead.

"Gone where? Didn't he come back with you?"

She was either a marvelous actress or didn't know, for her grief, when she looked behind me and realized Andy wasn't with me, was a gasp that any mother would recognize.

"Andreas and Barbara took Andy to Aurora. They didn't say a word to me, not one. They just rode off with my son, probably putting him on board a ship and sailing across the very sea his father died in. With not a word to me, as though I were nothing more than a heavy anchor hung around their necks."

"Maybe they went to have *Herr* Keil look at him, give him special herbs?"

"No one said anything about his still being ill. They were just 'traveling,' enjoying themselves and stealing *my* son." With the last of the words my fury caught in my throat and I felt the lump there clog and strangle.

"How awful, Emma." Mary patted my arm. "I can't imagine that they did this to harm you. Andreas and Barbara are loving people. It's only for a family visit."

"Why not tell me then?" I swallowed, my breath short. "Because they don't have to. Because I'm just this widow and they can justify anything they want by pointing out to all how much they're helping me. 'She has three little ones at home, you know. A widow, too, and not all that skilled in her needle-work, don't you know. Helping her son is the least we could do.'"

"Emma. They're not like that, they aren't."

"I feel so...useless."

She put her arms around me and that touch of comfort, warmth against my shoulders after so very long, brought the heartache to my eyes. "Just wait," she said. "It will get better."

Jack had put the mule up, and I heard him come up toward the house. He stayed silent, for which I was grateful. No teasing comment about the strong Emma Giesy withering like the last leaves of fall, nothing funny to try to set aside my powerlessness pouring out as tears.

"What you're going to do now is have some tea," Mary said. "Karl and Boshie are at the mill and won't be home for a time. We can just sit and be. Your Kate missed you, and Christian, well he's quite the chunk. You're feed-ing him well, Emma. Come along, now." She urged me toward the door.

"Opal and the cows feed him well, not me," I corrected. One more in-adequacy pointed my way.

Jack opened the door and I let them lead me into the house like a lamb.

"Where's Andy?" Kate asked when she saw me.

"With his *Oma* and *Opa*." I wiped at my eyes. "He'll be home shortly," I said, hoping it wasn't a lie.

"I miss him," she sighed, looked at my tear-stained face. She patted my hand as I sat at the table, then returned to her play with Elizabeth.

Later, after the tea had soothed me and the children's laughter had pierced the afternoon malaise, I lifted Christian from his nap and told Kate we needed to go home.

Jack did not protest when I declined his offer to help me take the children to our cabin. "This is something I can do myself," I said. I had to keep finding those things I could make happen, or like an untethered boat, I'd simply drift away.

———

I did drift during the following weeks. I felt as though I walked while asleep doing just what I must, answering the children without inflection. Later in the week, Jack came by again and startled me out of my lassitude.

He made an offer. He proposed it like that, that he "maybe could have an offer to make," and I thought it probably had something to do with the work around my cabin in return for my sewing up his clothes. Or to maybe go to Aurora and bring Andy back. That thought perked me up. Or at the very least to go there and find out when they planned to return. For a moment I wondered if he'd offer to take us there and I wondered if I'd go. All those thoughts in the span of a few seconds.

Instead Jack asked for my hand in marriage.

I laughed. "Why would I ever consider marriage, especially to you, Jack Giesy, a confirmed bachelor?"

"I wouldn't be such a bad catch," he said. I thought I smelled alcohol on his breath and he had a bit of a glassy look in his eye. Maybe that was why he was being so bold as to "maybe could" make his offer.

I sighed. I had little time for such nonsense. "Are Mary and Boshie moving you out with their family expanding?" I said.

"Maybe could be. But that's not the reason I'm—"

"It's out of the question. Simply not possible," I said. I brushed my hands at him as though shooing flies. "I thought maybe you'd offer to find out when Barbara and Andreas were coming back. That's an offer I'd consider."

"Has it occurred to you that if you were married and Andy had a father that maybe Andreas wouldn't feel the need to have Andy with them? They'd know he had a man to look after him, raise him up correctly."

I stared at him. "That would never be a reason to remarry," I said.

"Haven't heard about wagon-train weddings, I guess. Women do what they gotta do to survive." He walked to the saltbox I kept near the fireplace, lifted the lid. He wet his finger then stuck it into the salt, returned it to his mouth, his eyes holding mine while he sucked on his finger. "There are worse reasons to marry," he said at last. "For money. Now that's not necessary in our little communal lives, is it?" He licked his lips of the salt. "Or for convenience. Maybe could marry because it's easier than courting. Or because your bed's been cold long enough." He reached for the salt lid again but I grabbed his wrist.

"There's no sense in spoiling the salt," I said. "I'll get a spoon and salt dish and you can have your own."

"Will you now?" His look darkened. I still held his wrist. He was close enough I could smell the rye on his breath. I felt my heart pound; my face grew hot. I hadn't touched a man with any kind of emotion for over a year. I was aware of the strong bones of his wrist, how my small hand didn't begin to surround it. Confusion rattled my thoughts.

Christian crawled between us then, and Kate followed him as though Christian was a mule leading a wagon. Kate shouted, "Gee! Haw!" I released Jack's wrist and he stepped back to let the children pass. Then before I could catch my breath he reached for my arm and held it tight, pulling me toward him.

"Why not marry so you can show your saltiness in the way God intended? And have your sons with you?" Jack said. "Seems like a mother would do anything to accomplish that."

"You're hurting me," I said. He wasn't but I couldn't explain what was happening, how uncomfortable I felt yet how…invigorated. *This is insane.* "Let loose. Please."

"Aren't you the salty *Frau* Giesy?" he said. "Can't you break the hold?"

"If you don't release me I'll—"

"There's nothing you can do or say to make me do a thing, Emma Giesy. Time you learned that." He reached his free hand past my ear, flicked the saltbox lid open, then licked his finger. He stuck it into the saltbox, pressed it toward my lips. "We're to be salt and light in the world, *ja?*" I tasted the salt, had all I could do not to bite his finger. "A good wife knows how to be such salt." He released me then, like an animal trap sprung open.

I stumbled back. My hearted pounded like the butter churn. "There has to be another way for a mother to raise her children without having to…to marry for it." I was certain that I could do this without the Jacks of this world. I just hadn't thought how. And now I couldn't think clearly at all because Jack stood before me and he was smiling, head cocked, dark swath of hair angled across his eyes, his face flushed.

"Ah, Emma." He crossed his arms over his chest. "In time you'll cease to resist."

"Never," I said. Oddly, I felt as though a light breeze pushed wind at my sails.

———

I made the trip back to Fort Willapa each week, hoping to see Andy returned. I talked briefly to Martin, hearing his "don't you knows," resisting a retort that no, I didn't. I held no ill will toward him, not really. He spoke quietly and carried on the work that needed doing to manage the farm. I knew it wasn't easy work they tended to. A twinge of guilt came with our having chosen this landscape that made so many demands on everyone. Maybe the thing for me to do was to go back to Bethel, to be with my parents. Go to Aurora, get Andy, and then head back East, though I wasn't sure how I'd finance that. Sell the land, perhaps, but I doubted any of the colonists would purchase it and I might be many years finding someone wanting to move into the region and live in our little cabin. My life had taken on twists as tangled as a tobacco string.

During the school term, Karl stayed at Fort Willapa, so I seldom saw him. He was busy with the students. Andy should have been among them. I did see Sarah. I didn't tell her about Jack's offer. I put that evening in an oyster shell, clasped tight the hinge. I didn't want to find the meaning of my confused emotions by blurting it out without having considered every aspect of it first.

Instead, I heard Sarah's news. She was pregnant. "December," she told me. Her blond hair looked silky and the luster on her skin shone like a fresh peach. "Maybe he'll have the same birthday as your Kate," she said. "We can celebrate birthdays together."

"*Ja*, that would be *gut*."

She knew about my frustration with my in-laws and how they'd taken Andy visiting. I still considered them just "visiting." I had no need to see *Herr* Keil or any of those colonists again, but I'd given Andreas until fall, feeling certain they'd return home to help with the harvest. If they didn't bring Andy back then, I'd go to Aurora Mills and get him. Somehow. Meanwhile, I clung to the thread that said what everyone else did: my in-laws were simply trying to be helpful, and they'd bring Andy home in due time.

I also told Sarah about the day I'd been abrupt with Kate, had taken her toy boat and chastised her for trying to do the same thing over and over with no hope of it ever getting better. "Sometimes I think I do that myself," I said.

"We do what we know to do and hope it will work. It takes great courage to change. Anytime we do something new, it's risky. I'm nervous about this baby," she said. "Sam says I'm so soft that I cry when the chickens squawk. I don't know how I'll be with an infant to watch over."

"You'll be *gut*," I said. "The very best. And you won't have in-laws living close by to make you question yourself."

"I talked with Sam about your drawings," Sarah told me then. She rocked Christian on her lap, his head against her breast, eyes closed in comfort. "He says he could take one or two to Olympia to see if there's interest."

"I'd pay him for his time," I said. "Out of whatever was paid me."

"It would be a gift to you, Emma." She patted my hand. "Sam wonders if you might have someone take your pictures south into Oregon City. There's a teacher there, a woman, who has taught painting now for over ten years. She shows her work at fairs and sells them. There must be enough interest if she's taught a class that long."

I hadn't imagined people could be taught to paint, that it was something more than a natural bent. But even a gift could be made better with practice, wisdom, and time.

"Maybe my work isn't good enough yet," I said, suddenly cautious. "Maybe I should take some classes, if I could afford them, if there was an instructor close by."

"Don't be afraid now, Emma," Sarah said. "You make lovely drawings. Let Sam take them. I'm not sure I can be a mother but I'm going to do it; you have to have confidence that you have natural talent and can do this, even without lessons." She hesitated. "If you feel strongly that you need lessons, maybe Jack would—"

"No. Jack has nothing to teach me."

I wrote again to my parents. I told them about Andy being with the Giesys and how much I missed him and how if they were here, if David lived here or Papa, then there'd be no question about where Andy belonged. I even asked my father if there was some legal means by which I could make sure Andy wasn't kept from me. We seldom used lawyers for anything in the colony. I wasn't sure there were even agreements signed about the land people worked in Bethel. It seemed all was in Keil's name and there hadn't been a lawyer involved in any of it except between Keil and whomever he bought the land from. The sellers never knew that the money they received came from the efforts of many.

But I heard nothing more from my parents. Just school-girl letters from my sister Catherine that reminded me that once I'd been young, with problems no larger than whether to put ruffles on my crinolines and wondering if I'd ever grow up enough to marry.

Finally, in time for the harvest, Andreas and Barbara returned home and this time, when the leaves were turning their vibrant red and the air begged for the rains to begin, this time when I made the trek with Kate, Christian carried in a sack on my back, this time when we arrived, Andy was there to meet us.

I was never more soundly greeted in my life than by my son that day. "Mama," he said, running to me. "Mama."

My heart pounded and I could hear his too. I felt relief in his arms clinging to my neck as I squatted to him. He enclosed Christian too, then Kate threw herself into the bundle of us. "I'm so glad you're here, so glad," I said and kissed his hair, his forehead, his cheeks. Such a reunion! "Look at me. You've grown taller. What do you have to say to that?" I said, not expecting an answer.

"Why didn't you come get me?" he challenged. "Why didn't you ever come back?"

I hadn't planned what I'd say to my son, an amazing lapse on my part, for here he was, asking why I'd abandoned him. How to answer without creating a greater rift between his grandparents and me? Or maybe that was just what I should do; put a distance between us that wouldn't be easily bridged.

I had dreamed of what I'd say when I finally saw Barbara and Andreas eye to eye. No, I did not pray about it despite my sister's insistence that prayers were like kisses sent to the wind. I'd had little time for prayers of late, and when I had in desperation sent one out, Jack had been the answer. One could never be certain with Jack, and that's how I felt about prayer.

The speeches for my in-laws I'd composed in my head would have made the president of the States nod his head in approval for their eloquence and passion. But once these two people stood before me, once Andreas's cane tapped unsteadily and Barbara's eyes filled with tears, once Andy shivered beside me, I said very little at all.

Instead I inhaled and breathed out slowly. "I knew you were safe, Andy," I said. "I knew you were all right, but when I came back—"

"We trust you had a good summer," Barbara said. "People in Aurora send greetings."

"That's good of them." I kept Andy in the crook of my arm, my fingers firmly planted at his elbow. I didn't look at him. I knew there'd be more to say to him but better if I could do that when we were alone, in our home, safe. I could protect him under my wing. I didn't want to let him go. He did look healthy. I was certain they'd been good to him. It was just the separation that confounded and their unwillingness to acknowledge my authority over my son.

"He's had no recurrence of the bronchitis," Barbara said. "And we've returned with extra supplies in case it happens again this winter. We'll be prepared."

"I'll be pleased to take the supplies with me along with Andy's things," I said. I held my breath, waiting for resistance.

"*Ja.* I'll get them for you," she said and turned back into the house. Her compliance surprised. I'd thought I might have to demand that they let me have Andy back. Once again, I appeared to have little intuition.

Andreas tapped with his cane. "We enjoyed the boy very much," he said. "Good boy. Smart. Needs good tutoring. Needs to be in school."

"He missed most of his schooling this summer," I snapped. "John had any number of children enrolled. Karl taught them, but Andy was with you."

"*Ja*. We gave him an education in traveling from here to Aurora. He saw the orchards planted there. He heard the band play. He could play a brass instrument himself before long. They have no school yet in Aurora. Still, you should let him stay here to go to school now, until the rains come, *ja*? Then he comes home to be with you for Christmas."

Here it was: the demand had just been delayed to throw me off my guard. "I've missed my son. His brother and sister have missed him as well, and you heard him ask why I didn't come to get him."

"Young children must not make these decisions. It is up to us, those who know better," Andreas said. He coughed.

"I'll get him into school in a day or so. I'll do whatever it takes. I'll do it," I said. "Me." I tapped my chest. "His mother."

"Maybe we erred," Barbara said, handing me the cloth bag tied with a braided rope that held his things. She didn't let go, so we held it in tension between us. "We meant no harm. We wanted only to help you, Emma. This is all any of us wants to do for you. Yet you seem so unwilling to allow it."

"Asking might be a good way to begin," I said pulling the bag from her grip. "Imagine if I just took your Louisa for months at a time, just whisked her away while you weren't looking?"

"And would you have let us take Andy?" Andreas said. "If we had asked?"

"He belongs with me, his family."

"He needs us in his life too," Barbara said.

"*Ja*, and it is the grandfather who must lead the child now. We let you have your mourning time. Now you must come to your senses. There must be a man in this child's life. It is the right way."

"Karl Ruge, his teacher, is in his life. You lead him. Martin does, don't you know. He has many good men to influence him. Isn't that the very benefit of the colony? He needs one good mother to tend him. He's only five," I pleaded.

"The age of *Kindergarten* in the old country. Some in the States, too, begin school at such an age and the *Kinder* stay where they can be easily schooled."

"*Ja, ja,* I know." I'd stepped back and Andy leaned heavily into me.

"Then we will see him in school," Andreas said. I nodded. "And you will bring the children to visit."

"I always did."

"More often."

"Yes," I agreed. "*Ja.* And in return, you will never take him away from this valley and from me without my agreeing."

"We will never take him away again without you agreeing," Andreas said. "But you must think about the possibility of the benefits for the boy living somewhere besides with you."

"It will never be better for him to live anywhere but with me until he's old enough to be on his own," I said. "Never."

"You speak boldly, Emma Giesy," Barbara said. "Yet one never knows what life holds for us."

"My children come first, that much I can know."

"We'll see," Barbara said. "We'll see."

Andy took the knapsack from me. "Let's go, Mama," he said.

We turned, me carrying Christian at first, then as we moved down the road, I let him walk. Kate skipped beside her Andy, swinging his hand. Andy hadn't spoken after I'd interrupted him except to ask that we leave. As we walked, though I cajoled him, he didn't say a word.

But the farther we got from Fort Willapa, the more he relaxed. He smiled at Kate, who kept hopping beside him, or jumping in front of him. He laughed once at Christian, who attempted a somersault and landed with cedar boughs blanketing his hair. At the river we waded across, it was so shallow in this season before the rains. Since Kate and Andy were barefoot, they splashed on ahead. I took off my leather-soled shoes, tied the laces and swung them over my shoulder, then lifted Christian as we walked across. The mud

felt cool and oozed between our toes. On the other side, I decided to stay
barefoot, to feel the dry grass beneath my feet.

The water splashing freed Andy and he laughed now with Kate and then
came beside me and took my hand in his. It felt cool.

"When you were sick, when I saw you last," I said, "your hands and face
and legs were hot to the touch, you had such a high fever. It's good to feel
how cool you are, even on this warm day."

"You didn't come to get me."

"I did try, Andy. I couldn't bring the babies that far with the weather so
bad and sometimes Auntie Mary couldn't watch them. But I did try. Did you
get the little paper pictures I cut for you? Jack said he'd bring them to you."

"They weren't you."

"I know. Then one day I came to take you home, but they'd already
taken you to Aurora. When I learned you'd gone my heart felt broken, as broken as when Papa went away."

"I thought you'd gone like Papa!" He wiped at his eyes. "They told me you
were home. Then we left and I didn't know why you didn't come with us."

I should have tried harder.

"Did you like Aurora?" I asked.

He shrugged his shoulders. "I liked the orchards. We went to a fair
before we came back."

He'd found good things to like despite his disappointment. This was the
sign of a wise child in the making. Secretly, I was relieved that he hadn't said
he loved Aurora or that he wanted to go back or that he wished he could stay
with Barbara and Andreas forever and ever. He'd forgive me in time, I felt
sure of it.

"I'll make it up to you, Andy. I'll take you to school each day and wait
for you if you want, so you'll know that I'll be there. Would you like that?"
He nodded. It would take a great effort and the younger children would have
to come too, but it would be worth it. "We'll get up early and I'll milk the

goat and we'll pack something to eat and we'll get you to school. We'll make it a festive time."

"What will you do all day?"

"Why, we'll visit Sarah and sometimes we'll stop at Fort Willapa and see your *Oma* and *Opa,* so they'll know that you're where you're meant to be, in school. It'll only be for a month or so before the rains start and then we'll be at home, just you and us. Our family."

We walked a ways farther, passed where Karl and Jack and Mary and Boshie lived. No one came out to greet us and I was grateful. I just wanted for us to be home.

When we rounded the path where our cabin stood in the distance, Andy sped up. He pointed at "his" special cedar tree that shot up beside the barn. He called for Opal, who offered happy recognition bleats and a swinging tail. The cows mooed, more for their need of milking than Andy's call to them. He danced around and then he stopped. We caught up to him. "Is everything all right?" I said.

"It'll be hard for you to take me and Kate and Christian to school every day, Mama."

"We'll do just fine."

"I wouldn't leave you if I didn't have to go to school," he said. "It's all right. I know how to get there and back. I wasn't sure I'd remember."

I squatted to his level and pushed the hair back from his face. Barbara had kept it trimmed well. They'd done all the right things—except let him be with his mother and brother and sister. "You'd remember," I said. "You have a good mind. But we'll take you. That's what we should do."

"Because sometimes we do what's hard, even when we don't want to?"

"Yes," I said.

"Because it's what's good for everyone."

"*Ja.* Exactly that, my little wise one. How did you get to be so wise?"

"It's what *Opa* always says."

18

Emma

Gruel or Guide

I rose in the dark, milked the cows and goat, gathered the eggs and fed the chickens, then woke Andy up to grind the corn for mush. I packed us cheese and venison cakes with berries and a hard-boiled egg for each—good, hearty food for our journey. I even told myself that this was the true calling of a woman, to prepare food for her children and keep the hearth warm and ready, and perhaps that's all Eve had intended in that garden long ago, nothing tempting at all. The thought—and how *Herr* Keil would cringe at it— made me smile.

Next I roused the children, dressed them, checked their road-hardened feet for slivers, then put Christian on my back. We could probably get leather shoes if I asked a Giesy, but it was one more "generosity" I wanted to avoid. Instead we'd save for Sundays the thin-soled shoes, or for when the weather changed. Our clogs we saved for muddy days. Kate walked sleepily beside me, carrying a doll I'd made for her out of one of Christian's socks. I'd wound yarn for curls and painted on the face and given her an ever-present smile. I wished sometimes I could do the same for me.

Dawn lit our river crossing. Sunlight shining through the trees revealed an opaque sky sliced by sharp cedar boughs. At first it looked like giant balls of spider webs hanging as though ornaments in a Christmas tree, but it was bouquets of sky peeking through the branches instead. A small gray bird sang to accompany us and the smell of earthy loam near the river richly marked our way. Christian awoke at the water and then walked partway. But he tired easily and I soon put him on my back. We arrived at Fort Willapa, the schoolhouse, just as other children arrived. Andy walked inside and before we could head to Barbara and Andreas's, Karl Ruge came to stand at the door.

"By golly, you made it," he said. "*Gut* for you."

"*Ja,* it took some effort," I said, "but we are all here for Andy."

"It makes a long day for the *Kinder,*" he said. He nodded at Kate, who leaned against my leg. Christian hadn't stirred so I knew he still slept.

"I keep my commitments," I said.

"*Ja,* by golly, I know that about you. Even when they're tough ones." He smiled and waved me off as he turned to respond to loud voices I heard coming from inside. Andy nodded at me like a little man and turned toward the sounds of children.

I pasted on a smile as we headed for my in-laws. My exchange with Barbara and Andreas was strained, but we passed an hour or two. I helped Barbara spin while she cuddled with Christian, showed Kate how to thread a needle. "Begin to weave," she said. "God provides the thread." It was an old German saying my mother had given me. It once encouraged my days, but I hadn't thought of it much since Christian's death. I wasn't sure God cared much about the weaving of my life.

We had a light dinner and in the early afternoon, I said I needed to talk to Sarah and we spent the rest of that day visiting with her. We picked up Andy midafternoon and began the trek home. I knew once there I'd need to skim the cream from the morning milk and churn. I wanted to grind the corn so Andy wouldn't have to do it at dawn. I'd split some kindling so each day we could have a hot meal at the beginning of our day. Dinner and supper would be cold. It was just the way it was.

I reminded myself that we only needed to keep up this pace for a few weeks. I could do this until the rains began. A person can do most any dreadful thing for a time, as long as one knows there's an end.

The first day was the hardest, as we had not yet made it a routine. It was dusk when we arrived back at the bend that marked our property. Christian bobbed on my back. Kate begged to be carried too, but we were so close to being home I told her I couldn't. She scowled and sat down in the path, arms crossed over her chest. She reminded me of my sister Johanna when she was little, marked by a stubborn pout. "I won't go 'less you carry me," she said.

I sighed. "Don't be difficult."

"Carry me."

"I'm carrying your brother. It isn't much farther until we're home."

"I'm hungry. I want to eat now."

We were all hungry. Tired and hungry and discouraged by effort we knew needed to be repeated. Trying to convince Kate that she wasn't hungry or could keep going would be a useless effort too. Sometimes one just had to face a troubling thing straight on and see if it could be converted into merit.

"*Ja, ja,* I'd like to eat now too," I said. "I'm hungry enough to eat an entire…tree. Maybe that one there." I pointed to a giant fir rising up so high Kate fell over trying to see the top. She looked up at it, lying on her back, then back at me, and little lines formed across her brow. "I'd chew the bark and have toothpicks already in my mouth to clean my teeth." I bared my teeth at her the way a horse does when it's smiling. "After that, I could eat a whole…horse if there was one here."

"I could eat a cow," Andy said. "That's how hungry I am." He'd stopped for us.

"Eat cow?" Christian said, waking.

"Not our cow," I told him. "I could eat…the river," I said.

"You drink a river, Mama," Kate told me as she pushed herself up to sit.

"*Ja,* you're right. Such a smart girl." I reached for her hand and pulled her up. "Come along then, what would you eat?" She offered up the house. Andy laughed at that and I smiled too. "Now that's a hungry *Kind,*" I said.

She went on to describe things inside the house, and Andy added the barn, and before we had eaten the fence rails, we were home, hearing the cows moo, and the goat bleat its discomfort with this new routine.

I fell onto my rope bed that night as tired as I had ever been. My shoulders ached from carrying Christian, from churning late into the night. And yet I could not sleep. The soothing breathing of all my children underneath this roof should have been all the lullaby I needed, but instead I lay awake, the low embers of the fireplace casting the merest hint of pink against the logs. My throat had a scratch to it that I hoped wouldn't go into my chest or worse, be something contagious. That thought forced me to sit up in the bed. What if I got sick? I coughed. Seven miles was simply too far to go twice a day. I lay back down. That could not happen, not now, not after all we'd been through. I turned on my side, the ache of my shoulder causing me to gasp out loud. I listened. The children slumbered on.

Out of my aching came the words of a psalm, the sixty-ninth: "Save me, O God; for the waters are come in unto my soul. I sink in deep mire, where there is no standing: I am come into deep waters, where the floods overflow me. I am weary of my crying: my throat is dried: mine eyes fail while I wait for my God." A psalmist somewhere once felt as disheartened as I felt. Yet if I remembered well, there were psalms of rescue too. What happened in between seemed far removed from me.

I'd never prayed for the rainy season, but I did that night, my words hopelessly self-centered, asking that the rains might come early so I could keep my commitments. I did everything necessary to be the holdfast for my family, but when I imagined expending this much effort for the rest of my life, the floods overflowed.

That night I dreamed of the river. Our small boat was moored for when the water became too deep to walk across. A ship of safety waited. But it was on the other bank, so far from where I needed it to be to help me make a safe crossing.

In the second week of October Andy made his request.

"No," I told him.

"Just until school is out, Mama," he insisted.

"No." I coughed. There was something on the trail that made me sneeze and sniffle. It would pass. "There are only a few more weeks until the rains come, and then Uncle John will declare the school year over until spring. We can do this until then."

"Kate's grumpy," he said. "You stay up late. It would be better if I—"

"*Nein!* It is a mother's job to decide such things. You will not stay with your grandparents. You will not!"

"Karl's there. I could study at night. Now I'm too tired, Mama."

"I'll ask Karl not to give you so much work to do."

"Just let me stay at *Opa's*. I don't want to see Christian all tired and you carrying him so much. You'll get sick. It'll be my fault. Because I have to go to school or I can't live with you anymore."

"Who told you that?"

"That's why you make us go every day and take us all. So you'll know I'm there and no one takes me away again. I know."

He'd come to his own conclusions and however distorted they were, he may have been right about a portion of it.

"I want you not to worry about my leaving you again."

"But sometimes I fall asleep in school and Karl Ruge hits my fingers with a ruler to wake me up."

"He does?" I didn't like hearing that. "Well, it doesn't hurt you very much, does it?" He shook his head.

"I don't like the ruler. I don't like sleeping when I want to stay awake. To do good for you, Mama. To do good for you, that's why I go."

An obedient child, pushing every day, just to take care of me.

"We'll finish this week out and then see if the weekend comes and brings us rain. Then we won't have to make any decision about it at all. All right? We'll let things be and just wait and see."

"If it rains on Sunday can we stay home?"

"Your grandparents will expect us. When the time comes, Andy, I'll make the choice. It's what mamas do. It won't be on your shoulders, I promise."

The weekend was a balmy one, the perfect weather for picnics and harvest festivals, so we made our way to the Sunday meeting. At least we'd had one day without having to leave the cabin. And we didn't have to pack food for each of us for Sunday. Instead I'd gotten up early to make a *Strudel* and we carried it in a pan wrapped in a show towel. I knew there'd be plenty of other food for after the Sunday sermon, meat and harvest vegetables brought by those who lived closer.

After the sermon I tied the strings beneath my bonnet and watched Andy stay away from the other children as they played. He looked tired and listless.

Sarah and I talked, as she and Sam had joined the gathering this day. A few more of the settlers not affiliated with us Germans had begun to share our Sabbath time. If Christian had lived, he would have thought that a good sign. Sarah beamed in her pregnancy, her face flushed and smooth, her eyes sparkled as though they were diamonds. I so hoped that things went well. Mary was due anytime now too. In fact, she hadn't made the trek this Sunday. Neither had Jack, and I found myself surprised that I noticed he was missing. Well before the afternoon waned, my little family headed back. We stopped at Mary's and she was abed but said she was only tired. The baby was still a month away by her calculations. I told Boshie to be sure to come get me when needed. He nodded but had that confused look on his face. "You could stay with my children while I come back and midwife," I clarified. "Or send Karl if he's here, or Jack. They could do the same."

"*Ja, ja.* That would work," he said. "Plenty of time, *ja,*" he said, and I could tell by the tone of his voice that he remembered their first child, who had died at birth.

"Elizabeth was born strong and healthy. This one will be too," I assured him, though of course, who could know?

Upon arriving home I knew instantly that something was different. The cows weren't mooing. The goat barely looked our way. A small stream of smoke rose up through the chimney, though I'd been certain I put the fire out before we left.

"We have visitors," I told Andy.

I guessed that it was Jack, making himself at home. He'd probably told Mary and Boshie he was laboring at the coast when in fact he was hanging around, trying to make himself useful. I felt a mix of irritation and anticipation. I didn't want to have to deal with any of his "maybe could" offers, but fire in the fireplace meant we could have a warm supper for us all. I was certain that was where the anticipation came from.

We approached the house. Of course it might have been a traveler just assuming a welcome, as so many did where settlements were few and far between. I'd left the latch string out, suggesting invitation. I pressed against the door. The inside was dark but for the little window light and the fire. I smelled venison and beans.

"*Gut* evening," the visitor said, and when my eyes adjusted to the inner darkness, I recognized him and his voice. There stood my brother Jonathan, an apron tied around his waist.

———

"Papa wrote you could use some help," he said. "So here I am."

"You're better than early rains," I said as I crushed myself against his chest.

"I've been called many things, Sister, but never better than rain."

I removed my bonnet and Kate's too while Jonathan served us a hot supper that tasted better for the gift of it. Over the meal my brother met Christian for the first time. It was good to hear him and Andy exchange words,
and just the sound of his voice, a gentle man's voice in the house, felt like
music to my ears.

Jonathan took Andy to school in the morning. Work still called my
name, but I could stop in between chores and sit for a moment with my children. I even napped, something I hadn't done since Christian was born. I
prepared a big meal, hot food with fresh biscuits fixed in the dutch oven, for
the "men" when they arrived home at dusk.

They made better time than our little troop had and arrived in higher
style: Jonathan and Andy rode home on one of the colony's mules. "They
made a loan to you," I said. "That makes for an easier day, doesn't it Andy?"

"Would have done it for you too, if you had asked," Jonathan said, stepping off the mule.

"The mules are always in use for the fieldwork," I said. "I didn't want to
be a bother and make someone have to come and get it."

Andy led the mule to the half barn as Jonathan put his arm around my
shoulder and pulled me into his side and kissed my forehead. My brother had
one blue eye and one brown eye. That mix always fascinated me, and when
I looked up at him both those eyes had a twinkle in them. "You make everything so difficult. All I had to do was ask for the mule. People want to be
helpful."

"You're his uncle. They would do things for you."

"Emma…"

"You know they took Andy to Aurora without my knowing it." I shook
myself free of his one-arm hug.

"Maybe they should have said something, but what they did caused no
harm, not really. Except that now you push yourself until your clothes nearly
fall off your bony frame, for what? To make sure they know you are up to

doing the impossible? That's not the way we Wagners do it," he said. "We persevere, *ja,* but we cut our losses before they cut us."

I crossed my arms over my chest. "Meaning?"

"You have choices, Emma. They are not all bad."

"Ach," I said, dismissing him as I walked toward the house.

"For one, your life and that of the children's would be easier if you lived with Barbara and Andreas. They would extend such an invitation, I know this. The community would add a room perhaps, that you and the children could call your own. I know this is important to you to have your own place. But then Andy would not have to travel so far to school; you would not have to drag the children out each day. You would be close to others so your spirit could be filled with friendships. You could stay and work with your mother-in-law, together raise your children."

"And who would keep up my cabin?"

"Maybe Karl would move into it. Or Jack Giesy. They could manage the land. The cabin isn't what matters, Sister. It's the people; they're who matter."

I scowled at him and Kate looked up at that precise moment, her eyes drawn from the wooden blocks that Jonathan had brought her. She scowled then too, mimicking me.

I made my face look calm. "And my other choices?" I said.

"You could come back with me to Aurora Mills." He silenced me with his open palm to the air. "Think of this. You would have all the help you needed with the children. You could have people close to give to you but more, you could help others. This is what your life misses now, Emma. Christian was devoted to making other lives better, and that kept him a good and faithful servant. You've turned…inside yourself, leaving no room to look after others."

"Ach, no," I said. "I only look after my children. Should I sacrifice them in order to help someone *Herr* Keil thinks needs tending? Is this why you came here, to talk me into coming to Aurora? Because I'm not welcome there

and never will be. *Herr* Keil made that clear to me when he said we'd failed him by choosing this place. To leave it would but confirm his view of our error, and I'll not do that to Christian, I won't."

"Christian is dead, Emma. And Aurora would be better for your children."

"They don't even have a school there."

"Ah, Emma. Then we go back to allowing your son to stay with Andreas, to make his life easier. And yours."

I asked him why he didn't take Andy with him if that was what everyone thought my soon-to-be six-year-old son needed, to be living with the guidance of a man rather than his mother.

"I travel too much. I shouldn't even have traveled here as they have need of me at Aurora. But *Herr* Keil suggested I come."

"You said Papa told you to come."

"He did."

It occurred to me then that Jonathan was here not to offer me support, but to do business with the colonists, talk about farming and harvests and contracts for butter or cheese, look into fields that would serve sheep or goats or hogs, all for the good of the colony. The Aurora colony, of course. Helping his sister and his niece and nephews, well that was secondary.

"I'm sorry you had to take time away from your colony duties," I said. "I can take Andy to school tomorrow and I'll ask if the mule can be made available to us until the end of the term. We'll take care of things here."

"Emma. I'm here. I'll stay until the term is over. You'd still have to take the children with you. Andy's not quite old enough to go it on his own."

"Maybe he is. Maybe he just needs to learn young that you have to take care of things yourself. *Ja,* he can ride the mule. Then you won't be inconvenienced and you won't have to feel guilty that your niece and nephew are spending their days walking back and forth and going nowhere, as you suggest."

. He shook his head. "You'd slap a hand rather than grasp its strength."

I pitched his thought away. He didn't know what it was like to live on the outside, to be a woman alone and dependent on the generosity of others. He didn't know how weak and empty it made a person feel to take hold of a strong hand and not know when it might gruel rather than guide.

———

It was my cough that made me relent and let Jonathan continue to take Andy to school. By the end of the week, the rains came and with it congestion that filled my lungs until I sounded like the wild geese that flew overhead, barking with their plaintive cries.

Jonathan described my symptoms to Martin who said the catarrh could be helped with powdered ginger made into a tea. I was to lie beneath as many quilts as we could spare and "sweat the inflammation out," Jonathan told me. I was grateful my brother stayed through this ordeal. I recovered, but the best news was that the term then ended and we had no need to travel anywhere for a time.

We might have enjoyed the remaining days with Jonathan before he headed back to Aurora Mills except that Jack Giesy made himself known again. He arrived to fetch me for Mary's delivery. I felt well enough to go. I still coughed some, but nothing as I had.

As I readied my few things to take, my brother and Jack talked about crops and weather and people they each knew back in Phillipsburg, Bethel, and Harmony. They had an immediate camaraderie even though they'd shared little time together for years. A part of me envied that. We women were always eavesdropping, rarely a part of the sharing. Jack talked of boat building at the coast; Jonathan spoke of the wine-making at Aurora. Then Jack chided Jonathan, telling him he should find himself a good woman and my ears perked up, wondering if my brother had been courting. When Jonathan teased him back, I wished I'd kept my eavesdropping to myself.

"I've got myself a chosen one," Jack said. "She just doesn't want to accept it." He looked over at me. "But she will."

I wished Jack hadn't offered to walk me back to Mary's, but obviously the man lived there. Jonathan assured me he had the children in hand and then he smiled, those two-colored eyes shining. "Don't you two get lost along the way."

"*Ach, jammer!*" I said.

"Methinks the *Fräulein* complains in jest," Jack told him.

"I'm a married woman," I reminded him. "That's *Frau* to you." I stepped out into the rain.

Fortunately, the rains were steady enough to dissuade conversation. The patter against my oil-slicked hood—Christian's old one—served well to keep my head dry and my mouth shut.

Mary's baby, a girl, born without incident, they named Salome. Elizabeth looked on in wonder at this doll whose arms moved with jerks and starts that matched her legs. "She's dancing, Mama," Elizabeth said.

"Like a good German girl should," Boshie told his daughter. He ruffled Elizabeth's hair and gazed with tender eyes upon his newest daughter and his wife.

The love I saw pass between them, the raising of their spirits by this newness in their lives, made my heart ache with its emptiness. I'd had no one to share Baby Christian's new life with, save the children. No one who looked upon me the way Boshie looked at Mary. I supposed I never would again.

19

Emma

Waiting to Be Found

There is something to be said for customs that keep men and women separated unless chaperoned by those who care about their souls. I remember when Christian courted me back in Bethel, my parents walked before us, where they could quickly turn around if I called out. When he came into our home, my parents sat at the far end of the room, working, but with one eye always on the two of us, making sure nothing untoward might happen. They felt responsible. It annoyed me as a young girl but now, at twenty-five years of age, the widowed mother of three, feeling lost and alone in an uncertain world, I longed to know that someone I loved and trusted looked after my interests, that someone else might know what was best for me and cherish my soul in their hands.

Fatigue now framed my future. I was tired of a life promising only the drudgery of every day, of keeping my children alive rather than contented. I failed to even have the energy to paint, to get my drawings to Sam Woodard to see if they might sell. Even the path toward something better took too much from me and I chastened myself for my sloth. If I hadn't had the children to feed, I would have failed to eat, for it didn't seem worth the effort to feed the emptiness. My life was a walk in the deepest beach where if the blowing sand didn't cover me, the pounding surf soon would. It had been only two years without Christian. It seemed like dozens, and the almanac of living loomed before me without a hopeful story in between the calendar of days.

I suppose in part the sight of Mary and Boshie and the comfort of their family proved the crowning blow for my state. The whole time Jack and I walked back the night of Salome's birth, I thought of Mary and Boshie and of Christian, and then about the man walking beside me with no chaperone to even care what we did. I waited for Jack to do something, say something that would strike the flint of his interest, give me a reason to snap at him, at anyone, to relieve this irritated frame of mind.

But he chatted little through the rainfall, and when he did it was to point out a drier place to step along the trail. He whistled a marching tune. Once, when I slipped, he reached his hand out and caught me, but instead of holding it as I thought he might, as I hoped he might so that I could challenge his forwardness, he let me loose, faced forward, and kept whistling.

Maybe because Jack had been the only man to offer interest to me, maybe that was why I half expected him to do so now, while we were alone, no children, no one else to monitor what was said or done. We were two grown adults. What did it matter to anyone else what two grown adults said or did to each other? No chaperones necessary when the woman was a widow, her virtue already molded into wisdom she could carry on alone. I didn't feel wise so I said nothing.

Then just before we reached the bend where the cabin would be in sight, Jack stepped in front of me. He put his hands on my shoulders. "Consider, Emma Giesy. Consider how long you want to work as hard as you have chosen to do these past years. Consider how two are stronger than one, as Ecclesiastes notes, and three strands are best of all. You and I would be those two strong strands, and the third would be our children."

I thought he'd translated that verse with a theological error, that the third strand was meant to be God. It was why marriage was a sacrament for Karl Ruge, a Lutheran, and many other communities of faith. Marriage wasn't such a sacrament for the colonists. Karl had officiated at marriages back in Bethel as though it was just a matter between people and the state. But I suspect that Karl prayed for them and saw his role not just to say the words but to weave people together, forever, in God's sight.

Still, Jack offered his children as a third strand woven together within *our* marriage. He appeared to say that he'd accept Christian's children as his own, as though they were his responsibility too. Maybe he understood their importance to me. It was a side to him I hadn't considered.

He lifted my chin. His fingers were warm despite their being wet from the rain. He had a solid jaw, gentle lips he opened now, just wide enough to slip a pumpkin seed through them, if he'd had one to chew. "Emma," he said, "the time for playing has passed. You're a grown woman. Time to step up to it."

He kissed me then.

His lips were thinner than Christian's but the pressure he placed against my own felt firm. When I moved my head back, uncertain as to what churned within me, the pounding heart one of hope or shuddering with fear, his lips came with me. I pushed him back gently. His face stayed close to mine, so close, but he released my lips. "I know you compare me," he whispered. "This is a natural thing. But in time, I'll make you forget Christian Giesy. I'll replace whatever you cling to about him with something real. Alive. You won't be carrying around the memory of a tired love of an old man. If you admit it, you long for a young man, one meant to meet your challenges. That's me."

He didn't say he wanted to take care of me for the rest of my days. He didn't say he cherished me. He didn't say he loved me. It was as though he'd confessed to wishing to win a competition, a race he ran with a dead man.

I gave no answer, just said we needed to get back. I walked past him, half expected him to grab at me and twirl me around, but he didn't. He was quite the gentleman after that. At the cabin, he came inside, talked with Jonathan, and then nodded his head at me. He slapped his hat against his jeans leaving water like a dog shaking itself of the rain. He smiled.

He seemed harmless there in the presence of my brother and my children. I took in a deep breath. I wasn't ready yet to risk that this Jack who stood before me, gentle as a lamb, was the real Jack who would stay that way forever. I wasn't yet that tired.

———

Jonathan left the following morning to return to Aurora Mills. He made one more encouragement that I consider letting Andreas and Barbara keep Andy, or that all of us move in with them, or perhaps all of us come live with him. But I discouraged him from thinking that any of those options would ever come to pass. I didn't tell him about Jack's vision for my future.

I missed my brother, put the longing into work. I pulled the last of the cabbages and buried them beneath the grass hay in the lean-to beside the half barn. Then, because the flour was a little low, I decided to tend to that myself, not wait for "the men" to take care of it.

On my own, I made my way to the mill. I still had the mule we'd borrowed and decided to use it to bring home a sack of flour that would tide us over for the winter, then return the animal. It had rained in the morning, so I waited until the November mist lifted in the afternoon. Often we had sunbreaks in the late afternoon, and this day proved no exception. Andy said he'd watch the little ones, and though he seemed young to do so, he had an old man's soul and I knew somehow the children would be safe, perhaps behave even better for him than they did for me.

There were many things that caught my eye as I rode. I vowed to come back and draw, then chastened for making commitments I failed to keep, even to myself.

The mill had weathered into gray over the years, and mosses already dotted the shingles of the lower portion of the roof. The oyster schooners carried redwood for ballast as they sailed north from San Francisco, sold it for a profit, and then refilled their cargo holds with baskets of oysters they marketed when they reached that city. Maybe if Christian had lived they'd have branched out and owned their own ships. But likely Christian would have just used the money to pay off Keil and contribute to the colony. Always for Christian, it was the colony that mattered.

Still, seeing the structure in the distance brought a comfort to me. "Oh, Christian," I said out loud as the mule twitched its ears. "How I miss you." Christian would have loved taking his sons to the mill, would have cherished seeing how the lumber weathered to this settled, sturdy gray. He would have scowled at my doing this work, riding the mule, gathering supplies for the winter. He'd have claimed it as his duty, his obligation as a husband and father, and he would have expected his family to have tended me in such a way there was no need of my doing it for myself. Of course for one to give there must be a recipient. "They would have done it," I told the bird that flitted through the air, "if I wasn't so stubborn, if the cost wasn't so great to let them place me into obligation." Repayment was always required of any charity received, of that I was certain.

I arrived to human stillness though I could hear water rushing through the mill race. The mill door stood open. It was late in the day. I should have come earlier. But Boshie would have ground extra bags of flour, and I could load two on the mule to balance the load and leave a note saying that I'd taken them and to make a mark against what I owed.

I tied the mule to the hitching post and when no one answered my calls, I pushed the door and went inside. Dust mites rose in the air toward the shafts of setting sun that came in through the upper windows. It smelled of grain and earth and the powder of flour crunched against my feet. The huge millstones stood quiet. I looked up toward the tower where the windows looked out on each side and wondered what the view from there might be, standing at the ledge, looking out. A ladder reached to it from the main opening. A loft with windows that was the office looked out over the grist stones and there was probably a stairway to the top of the tower from there. The ladder would be a long climb up, a difficult one, but the view would be spectacular.

I was about to decide if I was up to that ladder climb when I felt a breeze behind me and turned.

"I maybe could think this was destiny, my finding you here," Jack said as he pulled the door shut behind him. More dust mites rose up.

"I was just getting some grain loaded."

"You were thinking of climbing that ladder to the window ledge," he said. He smiled and the tension I'd felt with his presence lessened.

"I wasn't sure I had the stamina for the climb."

"Risky thing to do, but then you always did like a little risk." He moved closer to me. I swallowed. "This is your lucky day," he said, reaching past me toward one of the interior posts, his breath just inches from my ear. "I have a key to the office and we can take the stairway from there. It's a much easier route to the view of paradise." He held a key that had hung hidden behind lengths of rope.

Doing it the hard way was my way. But the day ran late. Why not do it the easy way? He had a key.

So we took the steps up to the office loft. Jack opened the door and at the back a stairwell twisted its way up to the window that looked up the creek. I climbed the steep steps. Actual glass was used in this window, and my fingers felt cool against it when I brushed a circle into the grain dust. The perspective was spectacular, with the sunset pouring over the rain-coated trees. The willows sported red and the ferns had just the hint of rust color at some of their edges. I could actually see beyond the treetops to the sky. The world of Olympia lay that way. Fort Steilacoom, where Andy had been born, bustled miles beyond. Another world. A better world. There was something more, something worthy of all this effort to just live.

I lost all sense of where I was for the moment. It seemed that the view promised something greater than what my life had shown so far. Hope rose up in the forest mists, a hope of life filled with moments of joy yet to come.

"You can see the northern lights from there sometimes," Jack said. I turned to look down at him. He stood below me as there was only room for one person at the window ledge. "Dancing colors, late at night. Early morning. Quite a sight."

"You're a poet," I said.

"Makes me want to paint it, but I doubt one could capture the vibrancy of the colors. At least nothing I've ever attempted satisfied."

I almost told him that I shared his love for drawing, for capturing on paper something in the world that could nurture later. Instead I said, "You're here at such hours?"

He shrugged. "It isn't easy for Boshie and Mary always having someone about."

I looked down through the staircase and saw the bed then on the redwood floor. My fingers began making circles on their own. I noticed drawings on the walls I hadn't seen before either, drawings of faces with strange features, heavy lines around eyes, swirls of hair that moved off one sheet of paper and onto another. They were tacked up nearly covering the wall by the bed. Jack's work. Jack's dark and heavy work.

I took one last look at the view, the promising view, then stepped back from the window ledge. He reached up for me and took my hand to help me. He didn't release it but instead pulled me to him. Not in a possessive way as he had in front of the saltbox, but with a gentle firmness, offering security.

The drawings stared at me. The bed reminded me of an animal trap covered with deceitful familiarity and harboring something troubling beneath it. "This isn't a good place for me to be," I said.

"*Good* is a relative word," he said. "I can help you load the mule of the flour. That way it won't be a wasted trip." His breath was sweet as though he chewed mint leaves.

"I wasn't thinking it was wasted," I said. "I loved seeing the view from the window. Thank you for that, for showing me that. I hadn't realized there was a stairwell. Did John design the mill? I can't remember who—"

He put his fingers to my lips. "Quiet, Emma Giesy," he said. I let him pull me to his chest. "Just let yourself be cherished for this moment."

He moved his hands across my back and held me firm. And in that space of safety, I succumbed to comfort.

Not that we did anything untoward. He did not even try to kiss me. He just held me and I felt myself sink into his arms, the first time since Christian's death that I'd felt comforted without an expectation.

I really don't know how long we stood there, my head on his chest, my fingers fanned up toward his collarbone, then pushed together as though in prayer; between us yet, my hands. He stroked my hair, the back of my head, and I blinked back tears. It was all I wanted, just this salve; the reassurance of a man's hand against my head.

I closed my eyes to the pictures on the walls.

"Andy's watching Kate and Christian," I said finally. "I really need to go home."

He nodded, his chin tapping gently on my head. I was aware of his height, his bigness. I felt so small beside him. He inhaled, a deep, long breath, and something in the sound of it or maybe in the way he held me made me acknowledge that the world is full of wounded souls. I pulled away. He preceded me down the winding stairway from the office, locked the office door behind us, and we took the stairwell past the redwood flour bins to the main floor. Outside and in silence, he hefted the sacks of flour into the panniers on either side of the mule's rump, then put his foot out so I could step into the clasp of his palms as a stirrup. I grabbed the reins then swung my foot over the back of the mule, lifting it high to keep my skirt from catching at the packs. I remembered his grimace when I'd done that at Christian's funeral. He did it again now.

"A woman does what she has to," I said. The animal's ears twitched as I settled onto his back.

"Maybe could be," he said.

"Thanks, Jack," I lifted the reins. "For the help with the flour. And the view."

"I thought maybe I startled you when I first came in," he said.

"*Ja,* well, you did. Truth is I'm never quite sure…about you, Jack Giesy."

"I'm an uncomplicated man," he said. He cocked his head to the side. "Maybe could be you're not accustomed to such as that." He stepped back, swatted the mule on his rump, then let me and the mule pass.

The twilight was enough to see by, and the mule made his way along the trail, surefooted. I patted his neck, ducked beneath low-hanging branches. I realized I didn't even know the mule's name. It struck me as odd that I would think of that now. Other questions came too: Had Jack walked to the mill? I'd seen no other mule around. Or maybe he slept there often, to have so many drawings up, and such strange ones. His life carried a bit of emptiness in it too: a man alone, moving from site to site to work, but without a place to call his own. Did men need such things? Many of the Bethel bachelors lived together in Keil's house, and no one seemed to think they'd even want a home of their own. Maybe it was a woman's dream, that desire to make one's nest, fix the quilt on the cot the way she wanted and not have to negotiate with someone else about it.

For just a moment an image flashed of me, sitting on that quilt on Jack's bed in the mill office, sitting beside Jack Giesy, not frightened but desired. Was that the promise the mill view offered? Or something more? I didn't know. I kicked the mule into a faster trot.

———

The winter months wore on with their usual sheets of rain. Andy rigged up a stick marked by inches and kept it standing in a tin set on a stump out near the half barn. "Three, Mama," he shouted. It couldn't be. I'd just emptied it the morning before. But it had rained so hard the whole day that at times I thought the barn was gone because we couldn't see it. Each time I left the house to milk the cows, the path became more mired in mud, so I made new paths. The old ones just didn't work anymore.

In December, Henry and Martin came to take the cows away until spring so I wouldn't have to milk them nor worry about churning the butter. We'd do well with goat's milk, and Martin assured us we could have butter whenever we wished. With fewer chores to do, I'd have time for drawing. But I found time to create new excuses for not doing so too.

There were Christmas presents to make and eggs to scrape, letters to write. I wrote cheery things to Jonathan about how well we were doing, and to my family in Bethel I made it sound like my begging them to rescue me the year before had been a momentary lapse. On Christmas Day we made our way to my in-laws' without incident. The men brought out their instruments and we tapped our feet with pleasure to the music. While there I learned of the arrival of Edwin Woodard, Sarah and Sam's first child. For a few hours, I left all three children with Andreas and Barbara and rode the mule, whose name I learned was Fritz, to Sarah's. She was radiant and her son wailed a healthy cry until she fed him from her breast.

"He's a fine boy," I said. "Look how big his hands and feet are. He'll grow up to be a strong man."

She nodded. "Like your Andy. I wish you'd brought him. All the children."

"Letting them have time with their grandparents is a good thing," I said. "It keeps the lid on the teapot that is our life with them. I never know when the fire will get kindled again and things will boil over."

Sarah understood and despite the changes in her life, like a true friend, she still made room for me. "Did you bring them, your drawings?" she asked as she stroked Edwin's fine hair. I shook my head. "You won't go forward if you don't put your foot out," she said.

"I'm not ready to get that foot stepped on just yet. Maybe this winter, when the rains keep us inside, I'll make more. The mill makes a good subject."

"You already have some you could send with Sam," she said. "What are you afraid of?"

I didn't know.

"I'll bring you one in honor of Edwin," I said.

"We won't sell that one, Emma. You know that."

"I've come to accept that there's no future in the drawings." It was the first I'd admitted that even to myself. "It won't make me independent. I'll still have the obligations of my husband's family. Even if I had the money to hire help so I could make my own way, I wouldn't want to travel without the children, so what would be the point? I just can't see a future with any kind of creativity in it, Sarah. I'm just to raise my children. That's my life now. I'm not complaining, just explaining."

I made it sound beleaguered. Not every life was meant to have peaks of joy scattered throughout it. Or maybe my peaks had all come within the first years, when I was a desired woman, a wife and member of a scouting party that had carried out a worthy task. My peaks had been the births of my children, though even Christian's had been laced with melancholy.

"Your life could be more," Sarah said as I left. "If you'd let it."

"I can't let go of Christian's wasted death," I said.

"You have to forgive yourself," she said.

"Me? I didn't do anything. It was that old man. And Keil."

"It's hard to receive good things when your hand is a fist against the world, Emma."

"Ach," I said. "You just don't understand." But then, neither did I.

———

With the rain and the rise of the river I begged off of the New Year's Eve celebration, even though it promised to be festive with this new decade inviting us out of the old: 1860. We read of rumors of war back in the States. A new president would take office soon. Those changes felt far from our daily lives.

I half expected Jack to knock on our door on New Year's Eve but he didn't. I hadn't talked with him since our encounter at the mill. He'd been at the Christmas gathering but we kept our distance. Perhaps our last encounter proved too intimate for him, too exposed as he simply stood beside me rather than attempted to lead me here or there the way men tend to do. It was pleasant to remember just the safety of that moment when he held me with no demands, nothing to indicate that he needed, wanted, or would take more.

We waited out the rains, watched for the dusting of occasional snows. Andy and Kate played games and we read stories from the almanac. I even read a few stories from the Bible my sister Catherine had pressed into my hands before Christian and I left Bethel. I'd put Christian's away, to be given to Andy one day. Andy liked knowing that Luke was a doctor, "like I want to be one day, Mama," he told me. It was a new admission for him, a wish he'd never expressed before. Maybe his time with Martin had influenced him well. I told him he'd make a good one and I meant it, though I wondered how we'd ever make that happen.

Kate liked the book of Luke too, especially the story of the woman who'd lost her coin and couldn't find it. Kate misplaced everything, it seemed. We were always on a search around the house, the loft, the half barn, or wherever she might have been, seeking her stocking doll. Andy proved the tidy one. And Christian appeared to be in between. I liked the lost coin story too, for it showed a woman at the hearth, looking for something that mattered to her even though she already had other coins. She kept seeking. I wondered how she'd lost that coin. She must have been a good manager to know just how many coins she had. Maybe it had fallen from her purse. It had rolled away, perhaps, was missing through no fault of her own. The woman understood that. Things happened that separate us from what we loved through no fault of our own. But the woman kept searching until she found it, and then she had a festive party with her friends.

"Mama finds me, *ja?*" Christian patted my hand, taking me back from my own losses to this room filled with warm scents of food I'd prepared, of my children freshly bathed in heated rainwater and ready for bed. "Find me, Mama." Christian moved to hide under the bed, sure that the story was something about hide-and-seek.

"*Ja,* I'll find you," I said. "If you ever get lost."

During the days, deer munched outside our window, then startled if we opened the door. Near the river, we found otter slides and sometimes the air was so quiet, the trees so still, that in the distance we could hear the crunch of a large animal, maybe an elk blazing its own trail through the wilderness. Karl Ruge visited once or twice, the pleasant smoke from his pipe staying in the cabin for hours after he left. A few times I bundled up the children and we walked to Mary's to see how Elizabeth and Salome grew. We found Karl there, reading and smoking that pipe, and Boshie when he wasn't at the mill. But no Jack.

I split my own kindling that winter. My arms gained muscle and I began to feel healthy again. The little outrages that flushed my face happened less often. A sheen returned to my skin that had been missing in the months since Christian's death, and I thought it might be the result of my body finally adjusting after my last baby's birth. Or maybe as I made sauerkraut, or added vinegar to the warm potato salad I prepared nearly every day, and watched the children take pleasure in the rolled cakes I made, I'd come to some level of peace in this widowing life. I even wondered if I'd one day not think of myself first as a widow, then a mother, but once again as a woman. Perhaps I too was a missing coin, cherished, waiting to be found.

20

Louisa

MARCH 1860

Many days pass by without my writing in this notebook.

We learn of illness at the Willapa. Not the fever and ague that people suffer from here but of some lung discomfort. Emma has let her sons stay with Andreas and Barbara again, though I understand it is she who is ill and not the children. Little Kate apparently remains with her, and Mary and others stop by to look after them, though I cannot imagine that this suits Emma well. I know I hate being ill almost more than anything for it means others must tend my needs, so while I feel sick I also feel a burden. Well, worse is when the children fall ill. I struggle even more when my husband ails as he has this past winter. I suspect it is his worries that bring him down. He sees what must be done but hasn't been accomplished yet. He wants Aurora ready for those coming from Bethel, and yet he needs them here to build. His need to be ready weighs on him while his need to have more help, to build up the businesses here, presses on him too. His leadership is a balancing, just as the way one pieces a quilt requires measuring this and that in order for things to come out as they should.

I would offer to assist him with his worries, but he would not see of it. And truth is, I am not much able to help with financial things. Jonathan Wagner carried that skill from what I overheard as my husband talked with our son, August, before he and Jonathan headed back to Bethel. My husband hopes these two boys, well, men now, can spur along the sale of homes in Bethel so people will give up the comforts there to serve each other here. Jonathan can perhaps help the Wagners too, as their daughter, Louisa, injured herself at Elim while at a dance. She fell from the second story of our old home and now has trouble standing at times. My husband says bad things happen there because of the delays, but I believe bad things just do happen. They are part of the ebb and flow of life. I do not attach all suffering to sin as does my husband, though these words to him I'd never say. No need to add to his burdens.

Now there are more worries here for my husband, as neither Jonathan nor August are here to help him. But Helena Giesy has come. She traveled by ship up the Columbia and did not even visit with her parents first in Willapa. She didn't even stop to visit her brother's grave before coming here to aid my husband. Well, the colony.

My husband says she is a saint, turning down a marriage proposal so she could devote her life to the work of the colony. He spends long hours with her. She is so helpful and never tires of tending to him.

I can barely manage all the household work with my leg giving me such an ache. I don't tell my husband of it. He healed it after all, and it must be my lack of faith that keeps me limping. I miss August, but my husband ordered him to Bethel so it must be for the best. My Aurora, already eleven, is a help almost more than her sister Gloriunda, two years her senior. Gloriunda has a tendency to laziness while Aurora knows no rest. She's like me in that. While I am honored by the pattern I am also worried for her, as her devotion to family requires the buildup of much steam and the promise of terrible despair when such runs out. One is always seeking fuel. Fuel does run out when one loves others so much. How to fill up again, that is a mother's constant quest.

We will celebrate this March the beginning of my husband's forty-eighth year. All believe that we share a birthday, but his is actually later this month.

It's mine we celebrate on the sixth of March. I'm older than Wilhelm by twelve days, but he honors me by telling all we share a birthday. He does not like a woman being older, I suspect, for he assumes wisdom comes with age. His voice is still strong as he preaches. He stands upright and his eyes burn with an intensity I remember from his youth. But afterward, he pales. I prepare him tea and hover over him as he leans back in his rocking chair, his wide chest taking in deep breaths. Others do not see this; it is a wife's duty to recognize such sinking and to puff up pillions of encouragement to surround her husband's head. I remind him of his birthday and the partying we'll do. Those not yet living here, those still in Portland, will come out to celebrate, I remind him. But he replies that it will sadden him because they cannot stay in Aurora Mills as we have insufficient housing. He wants the next group of Bethelites to come out, and yet where would they stay? More here in our house, I suspect. As Helena is. I asked my husband once if this might not have been the dilemma Christian Giesy and the scouts faced. He sat silent for a long time, his eyes closed, and I thought he might have fallen asleep. Instead he said, "I might have been too hard on those good people. Perhaps I should tell them so. Maybe they might even now come here to help us out if I expressed more sorrow."

An apology? From my husband? I would not have thought of it, but he is so wise! It has good merit. The Giesy family supported him in Bethel. Andrew Giesy Jr. runs the colony in Bethel with David Wagner's help until August arrives. I think my husband longs for such an alliance here and might have had it with Christian if not for Emma's forcing those families to stay in Willapa. I wonder if she carries guilt in that, her husband dying on a bay they had the chance to leave but didn't.

Perhaps that is too harsh. I carry no less a weight wondering if I might have done something different that would have saved our Willie. But no. I have come to believe that death is unrelated to the choices others make. I wouldn't say that to my husband.

Now Emma forces no one to do anything as far as I can tell. So they ought to come here, those Giesys. And Karl Ruge. Why hasn't he joined us, my husband's oldest friend? Karl wrote the letters back to Bethel, dictated by my husband, and I think his good mind added well to my husband's thinking. He should be here. His presence would so help my husband with his trials. And if Martin Giesy came, he could treat the people that my husband has to heal now, in the midst of everything else he's asked to do. He is becoming known for his healing, and even newcomers from Portland make their way here for his herbs and concoctions. So in the midst of business dealings, to serve us all, he stops to heal a small child or offer a salve to a man whose wound weeps. Martin could help immensely in Aurora.

Jack Giesy, too, that man of impractical cheer, he would lighten our days if he lived here. What keeps him in that Willapa country anyway? All the dairy cows, all the farmland, all of that work could be put in place here, near Aurora Mills, and we would join together again as we lived in Bethel. All of us except Willie. And Chris.

Well, I believe I have just uncovered the solution to my husband's strains. If the Bethel people cannot come west sooner as planned, then why not join together those who are already here, who had once planned to be a part of this colony under my husband's leadership? John has leadership abilities. He's the school superintendent there in Willapa. We don't even have a school here as yet. So much would be better if they lived with us. Even with Emma. I must write to John's wife, to Sebastian's wife, to Barbara, to remind them of what they once planned to do and let them know how much we need them, how much Wilhelm needs them. It would be the Diamond Rule if they came to make his life better than theirs. And they could see their daughter too.

Ja, that's what I'll do, write to the women. Paul himself wrote to women who worked beside him in the church. *Ach.* Not that I compare myself to Saint Paul, but women had work then as we do now. Those in Willapa have proven they can endure in difficult times. Now they must prove that they are one of us still. It is time for all God's children to come home. A mother understands that call. "And again, I will put my trust in him. And again, Behold, I, and the children which God hath given me." So says Paul as he writes to the Hebrews. It is a wife's duty to address her husband's needs and to hope those around her will understand how much more they can carry together than alone.

My husband might object.

If he knew.

But I would write as one communal wife to another, a coworker in the service. The women will see the value in our joining up. I will even write to Emma, for all the good it will do. But no one should be left out. All should be called to come home. My husband might even consider me a saint like Helena should I succeed. *Ach,* no. My husband would say that a mother cannot be a saint. She has no time.

21

Emma

Cheers, and Smart You Are!

I shook my head at Andy, wanting him not to approach too close. My throat felt coated by slivers of glass that ground against each other each time I swallowed. My skin ached to the touch. The winter season might have drifted further into hope but it didn't. When I found myself too weak to milk the goat, I sent Andy to Mary's. The child protested, saying he could milk the goat; he could fix our meals and tend me. But he went, returning with Jack and Boshie.

"We'll take the boys to their grandparents and I'll bring Martin back to doctor you," Boshie said. My face flamed from fever. I hadn't considered that suggestion, but fearful as it was, it held merit. I pointed to Kate, but Boshie shook his head. "Kate's of an age she can help bring you water to sip."

"Please," I croaked. "I don't want any of them ill."

"I'll stay to look after Emma," Jack told him. "Take them all. Kate's small. She'll not take up anymore room than the boys."

"She's little. But you here—"

"The widow is ill and in need of care," Jack said. "I'll stay only until the women come to help."

Jack helped the boys find whatever they'd need to take with them. He hurried Kate along as she looked for her stocking doll and nearly had to leave without it, but Andy located it up in the loft. Andy scowled the whole time.

I watched the movements around me as though in a dream, my throat a cave of broken glass, swollen, my eyes throbbing with pain. What might it take for me to get the children to return when I was well? I couldn't begin to imagine. I pitched the thought away.

They left and Jack proved the perfect helpmate, heating tea, helping me sit up and holding the cup to my lips. I knew the women were all busy, had children and families of their own to take care of, but I would have liked to hear the sound of a woman's voice. I would have liked to have a woman help me to the slop jar and settle me on it rather than Jack Giesy just before he turned his back. Oh, he did step behind the curtain. But the sounds one's body makes embarrasses in the presence of others, especially men. A woman would understand.

"Could your sister Louisa come?" I asked Martin when he arrived.

He shook his head. "She looks after the children and is a big help to Mother, don't you know."

He looked at me with sympathetic eyes though, and the next day, when Sarah Woodard arrived, I knew without asking who had suggested she come.

"You should have sent word to me right away," Sarah said.

"Didn't want…to bother," I said.

"Ach," she said and pushed the air with her hand. She grinned. "Now I'm sounding like you!"

Jack came in with an armload of fire logs, and he startled when he saw Sarah. "What are you doing here?" he asked.

"Martin thought I might be able to help," she said. She placed the board Edwin was in onto the rocking chair, then put a stick beneath the rockers to keep it from moving and possibly pitching the baby out. "I'm to let you go, Jack Giesy, though Martin says you've been quite the good doctor for Emma."

"Does he?" He hadn't put the logs down next to the fireplace. "We really don't need any extra help."

"I'm enjoying…Sarah's visit, Jack," I said. My throat pain had lessened, but now I barked like a sea lion. No one could speak while I hacked. "She's my friend."

"She maybe could infect her baby," Jack said.

"As I feed him from myself, he stays healthy. I won't let Emma hold him." Jack scowled. *What is going on with Jack?* "I brought mail for you too," she said digging into her pack. "It came to Woodard's Landing just this morning. I bet it's the fastest mail service you've ever had out here."

I nodded and lifted my hand for the mail, but Jack reached past me, his long arm taking the letters from Sarah's fingers. "She can read them later," he said. "No sense wasting reading time while you have a guest." He pushed the letters into his shirt blouse before I even got to see who they were from.

"Jack—"

"At least one is from someone in Bethel," Sarah said. "And I think the other was from Aurora Mills. Oh, and one from far away in France."

"A cousin," I said.

Jack's proprietary manner bothered me. Maybe he felt I owed him that liberty for the care he'd been providing. Once again I could see how receiving a gift came riding on that horse as obligation. I had no energy to push it off.

Jack fed the fire, and when I motioned to Sarah to help me move to the slop jar, he rose from his squat to assist. "No," I croaked. "Let Sarah, please."

"She's as small as you are," he said.

"I'm small but I'm strong," Sarah chirped. "It's a woman's prerogative to have a sister assist her with her hygiene needs. A gentleman like you should know that."

"*Ja.* Well, I do know that," Jack said, backing off. "But don't come crying to me if she pulls you over." He turned his back to us and poked at the fire.

Sarah winked at me, then put her arm around my shoulder to help lift me up. My head spun with light spots, but I steadied myself on her arm as we took the few steps to the end of the bed, then pulled the curtain that separated the bed and slop jar from the main part of the cabin. The porcelain felt cool against my buttocks. I panted a bit to catch my breath, lowered my head. "Are you all right?" she whispered. I nodded. She rubbed my back in small circles, and when a wracking cough came on me, she squatted and held me with both arms. "I hope Martin's bringing you good teas," she said. I nodded. "He's a little worried that you haven't made the gains he thought you might by now," she added. "Especially when you've been getting such good care."

"A stubborn cough," I said.

"Are you finished?" I nodded but as she went to help me up I put my hand to hers to stop her.

"Let's just sit here for a moment," I said. "A moment...alone." She nodded understanding. "Have you seen the children? Jack tells me so little."

"They are all well. Rosy and happy."

I coughed. "Whatever this is, they might have missed it then."

"You did the right thing."

"How long can you stay?"

"A couple of days. But then one of the Schwader girls will come. And I've arranged for Louisa to help while I look after your children. Barbara, John's wife, will come. Each will spend a night so you won't be alone and before long, you'll be well."

"So Jack can leave."

She nodded. "If you weren't so sick, people would already be talking. But we do what we must, *ja*? See, I speak some German now." She smiled.

"*Ja.*" She helped me stand. "Will you tell him?"

"I will," Sarah said.

I took a deep breath. It exhaled as a sigh of relief.

———

Jack left begrudgingly. I suppose he enjoyed knowing where he'd be each night, and he'd been helpful. But with him gone I did feel as though my strength returned. The women took their turns with me. Each was gracious and gentle, careful not to let me think they didn't want to be there. They had their own families to care for, and who knew how contagious I might be? I was grateful that they stoked the fires, kneaded the dough, gathered eggs. At the lamplight they stitched and we talked as my throat improved and the coughing faded, and time passed as gently as a feather drifting in the breeze. I felt like one of them, as though perhaps Christian's family really was my own. The families were the most gracious when someone was in need, real need, they would have said, not need resulting from one's willful choices. They each showed a charitable spirit that was always there, but I'd never acknowledged it before. I made a point of saying thank you.

When Mary took her turn, Boshie brought Salome to her for nursing, then took the baby back home. I appreciated this extra effort and told them both so.

She shrugged. "We take care of each other, *ja?*"

I nodded. "Have you talked to Jack of late?"

"Ah, a little interest?"

"Not the way you think. When Sarah was here, he received my mail from her and I can't find the letters anywhere. He must have forgotten to leave them. Could you ask him for them? I think one was from my parents and one came from Aurora Mills."

"Perhaps your brother tells you that Dr. Keil struggles with many responsibilities and needs the Bethelites to come out to help, but they're not ready. They're being tardy." She smiled as she stitched. "Like recalcitrant children."

"Things aren't all perfection under *Herr* Keil's direction?"

"No need for sarcasm," she said. "He's sent August back to help your father and Andrew Jr. move things along so everyone can join them soon. Even some of the Portland people haven't gone out to Aurora Mills yet. They like earning wages and having a little spending money for themselves, I guess." She stopped her work to spread butter on a piece of bread that Louisa had made the day before. "I heard that even Joe Knight quit the oyster business and headed back to Bethel."

Hearing that made me sad. One more connection with Christian was broken and Joe hadn't even stopped to say good-bye. "What about Karl's investment?"

She shrugged. "I think Karl lost interest once Christian wasn't involved. He was never drawn to the rough and tumble of keeping the oyster claims guarded or tonging for oysters in the moonlight. Jack liked that pace, at least sometimes. He can stay up all night, that Jack. Karl has the school and that's his first love. He'll get some of his money back if he sells his interest. Who knows, maybe Jack will buy him out."

"Jack has money to invest?" I said.

"He doesn't have much to spend his money on except rum now and then."

"I guess I thought everyone put their earnings into a common fund, so there'd be little room for private investment."

"Not all of it," she said. "Here, we own our land, just like you do, Emma. But we're sharing the increase of the cows, and putting a portion of the butter money into the common fund and keeping some to use as we see fit. This new territory demands that we invest but still work together."

She sounded like Boshie when she said that last.

"I don't recall receiving any money from my work with the butter contracts," I said.

She stood up and busied herself at the pantry, wiping the breadcrumbs into the palm of her hand. "I'll just throw these out to the birds," she said. She stepped to the door. It took her a long time. I guess she watched the seagulls swoop down to get them. Finally, she came back in.

"Mary. Are some people receiving private pay for their labor and able to keep some to invest for themselves and others not?"

"Maybe people thought that because the men tend to your stock and your firewood and look after things as you're a widow, well maybe they thought your share of any increase would be better spread around to those who've been helping you."

I felt my face burn.

"Or maybe they're setting your share aside for your children's needs. For when they might want to go to school. That would meet with your approval, wouldn't it?"

"What difference does my approval make?" I said. "My decisions appear to need filtering by what others think, so I rarely get the chance to make them."

"Oh, Emma. You make it sound so dramatic. We welcome your opinions. Decisions just have to be made whether you're around to hear about them or not. It's not a woman's place to worry over such things anyway. You should be grateful you have so few worries. Think of poor Brother Keil."

———

Decisions. Which ones did I have left to make? I could decide when my children came back home to me and set the date as Christian's April birthday. I'd force myself to be well and able to do for my own family. Though I was still weak, I had the Schwader girl, who was staying with me last, saddle her mule and then asked her to take me to the Willapa stockade and to the Giesys and my children.

Andy ran in from the river when he saw us approach. Kate jumped off a stump she'd been standing on, and even Christian waddled to me. I could not describe the joy I felt at seeing them and having them run toward me, wiping away the fear that separation might make them wish I'd never come.

I slipped from the mule, caught my balance with a lightheadedness. Then I took steps toward them as they threw their arms around me. My children, back in my arms.

"You don't look too well yet," Barbara said when I stood, my knees like *Spätzel.* I used Andy's shoulder for steadying. "Martin, look at her eyes. They're sticky, *ja?*" I sneezed, and instead of the German phrase that meant "God bless you," she said in Swiss-German, "Health to you. Cheers, and smart you are!"

"I don't feel so smart as all that," I said. "It's just the spring foliage making my nose itch."

"Still, you shouldn't push too hard."

"It's Christian's birthday, and I'm here to celebrate and take them home."

"Oh, I don't think that will be a good idea," Andreas said. "School starts just this next week and you don't want to go through what you did last fall, pushing yourself to get Andy here. That might even be why you're so ill now. You're a pretty fragile soul, Emma Giesy."

"I gave birth to that boy in the wilderness, so I'm anything but fragile."

I'd expected resistance, but I hadn't thought about school starting or how I'd counter that. He was right: I couldn't maintain the pace of last fall. At least not for a while yet.

"I think Andy's old enough to ride the mule," I said. "If you'll make the loan of Fritz to me."

Andreas tapped his fingers on his cane. Martin stood beside him in silence. Barbara said, "We'll be in need of the mules for the spring seeding. Andy would have to walk all that way by himself. You wouldn't want that."

"I saw bear tracks this past week, big as washtubs," Andreas said. "Just through the school term. You take Christian and Kate. They'll be handful enough for you while you're healing. Have you even spent a night without help since you took ill?"

They redefined every human foible into weakness. I didn't have a mule to call my own, but that was to help me out so I wouldn't have to winter him. I had no cows, but that was so I wouldn't have to be troubled to milk them nor someone else be forced to come by to do the same. If I became ill, well, it must be because I overworked—but how could that be when I did so little? Everyone else did it all for me. Other people got sick. Andreas needed a cane. Mary caught a cold, though I suppose even that was my fault. Even my effort to meet the butter contracts were considered insufficient compared to what everyone else already provided for me. I wasn't holding my own, and now my son would have to struggle to get back and forth to school because of my self-ishness, my need to be in charge of my own family. That's what they were saying.

A fire roiled inside of me. My fingers moved in their circles, so I hid them in fists.

"Andy," I said. "Your grandfather's right. You'll be better off staying here through the school term."

"But—"

"I'll come back for you. You're not to worry."

"Can I come home when we don't have school?" His eyes pooled with tears. One slid down the side of his face and he brushed at it. "Can I come home on the day before Sabbath? And come back when you come to worship?"

"I don't see why not," I said.

"Such a long way to go for just one day," Barbara said.

"*Ja*, it is. But sometimes being home for even a little while, where he can play with his brother and sister, sometimes that struggle is worth it."

"I'll bring him to you," Martin said. "So you won't have to worry about the bears or whatnot, and you without a mule."

"That's generous of you, Martin," Andreas said. "With my mule and fieldwork time."

"Consider it part of my contribution to tending widows and children," Martin said. He sounded a little testy, something I'd never heard before. "That's what we're doing all this work for, isn't it? To be of help to each other?"

"*Ja*, you're right. I shouldn't have talked so," Andreas said. He patted Martin's arm, seeking forgiveness.

I finished the afternoon holding my children while from time to time they ran to play with the others. They always came back to check on me as though I were part of a game and served as home base. I longed to leave, to take Kate and Christian, but that also meant less time with Andy. I barely heard the conversations going on around me. I was not a part of this community, not a part of the Giesy family, not in the way Christian once imagined we'd be. If he had lived, it would have been different, but he hadn't. It was time that I accepted that.

I sneezed again and Barbara said, "Cheers, and smart you are!" It wasn't a blessing. It was a challenge and a charge.

If I was ever to have control over my children and my life, I needed to get smart.

———

It was July before Andy came back home to stay. Martin had brought him once or twice on the weekends as he'd offered. His father's quick retort to him on Christian's birthday made me think that Martin might be longing for something more in his life too. He was a fine healer and I'd never imagined him as one who would toil the earth to make his living, or should I say his contribution. I hadn't realized until that day that he probably took care of his father, as the elder Giesy had deteriorated with both age and the grinding of his bones. Andreas needed help to stand and sit. Barbara seemed healthy and strong, but who knew what aches and pains she might seek remedy for when others weren't about. Louisa, their youngest, was nineteen now and like my sister Catherine, I assumed she hoped to find a mate. Instead, she too looked after her parents, cooked and cleaned for them and her brothers, and Karl Ruge during the school term, and now my son too. Helena might have assisted had she not chosen Keil over her father.

Louisa was a good girl, though I didn't think she took much interest in the almanacs or books, and that saddened me. I wanted Andy to be enthused by stories and not just focused on the work of learning. If he wanted to one day be a doctor, he'd be filled with science and medicine and studies far beyond anything I could ever help him with. But he'd be a complete man, one able to come up with solutions to problems no one else could if he matched his scientific mind with art and music and stories. The arts were the keys to imagination's door. Louisa didn't have much imagination. She'd been a silent caregiver the nights she spent with me and went to bed before the sun had even set. Perhaps she longed for rest the most: rest was her key to survival.

I knew the fall school term would begin after harvest and Andy'd go back to school, back to Andreas and Barbara's. Andy knew it too. One evening while we sat beneath the cedar tree taking in a cooling breeze before the mosquitoes came to call, he asked, "Isn't there any way I could stay here with you, Mama, and still go to school?"

"You are with me." I hugged him. "Look what a fine artist you're becoming. I believe that's a woodpecker you've drawn."

He tapped the pencil lead against his lip and I saw myself in that behavior. "Couldn't you come live with *Opa* and *Oma* while I'm in school? I miss you so very much."

"There are just too many people there already, Andy. And we have Opal to care for here. I know it's hard, I do. The shape of the bird you've drawn is perfect. Have you been practicing?"

"*Opa* says drawing is a useless thing," he said. He tapped the lead against his lip. "He says Jack wastes his time with pencils. He doesn't want me to draw things when I'm there."

"But music is fine. The men's band, that's fine, but not art?"

Andy looked confused at my outburst. "He says I need to have a man to influence me."

"Oh, does he?" Yet Jack Giesy's influence would be with the arts, and Andreas disapproved of that.

"With Papa gone I don't have that," he said. "That's the real reason *Opa* wants me to stay with them. Because I don't have a papa anymore."

"Smart you are," I said under my breath. They could claim they kept Andy due to my health or the distance or Andy's young age or the lack of a ready mule. They could say whatever they wanted, but my son was right about the cause of their attention. I sneezed and Andy said in Swiss, "Cheers, and smart you are, Mama."

I knew in that instant just what I needed to do.

———

It was three years and one month from the date of my husband's death when I sought out Jack Giesy with a purpose. It took me several days to find out where he was, and I did that searching on my own so as not to start rumors before they were facts. I couldn't ask many questions. I used the pretense that I looked for my letters and wondered if Jack still had them.

A part of me dreaded what I had to do, as Jack would see it as a win. He'd made an offer that sounded like a business proposition and I'd declined, because I didn't want my life to be a business arrangement but more because marriage had not been in my envisioned future. But neither had becoming a widow. Things changed. One had to decide what one cherished and what was subject to transformation.

I'd decided not to kindle my own fire but begin to depend on someone else. And I'd be able to tell my sister Catherine all about Jack Giesy now, so she could stop wondering. I felt a tiny twinge of guilt when I thought of my sister and her interest in Jack Giesy, but hers was a girlish longing and it would pass.

Jack must be staying at the mill. I had the children with me as we pushed a wheeled cart there. I pulled the bar and the children pushed and we stumbled over the tree roots out onto the trail, then picked our way through the forest road. We made a terrible racket, which was good. It would keep the bears and mountain lions away.

When the mill came into view Christian looked up in awe. "So big," he said. He rode inside the cart and tried to stand up. I motioned him to remain seated.

"You haven't been here before, have you? Your papa helped build this mill." It offered a kind of peace as I remembered the vista I'd seen from the upper windows. A new perspective, that's what the mill represented. I noticed unused redwood lumber stacked beside the mill and a thought came to me in seeing them. I'd ask Boshie if I could have a few of the boards to add something new to my home.

"Mama?" Andy asked, touching my hand. I blinked and gave attention back to my children. We went inside and I signaled that the children stay close to me as the big stones ground noisily away. I found Boshie and asked if he could help load our cart with two sacks. He scolded me, saying he would have brought flour by, that it wasn't necessary for me to come all that way and to bring the children too.

"I was looking for Jack," I said. He raised one eyebrow. "He has some letters of mine that he forgot to deliver."

"Ah. Well, he isn't here now. There was talk that he might go back to Bethel. They're having trouble getting things ready to come west, and people are worried about a war there."

This had not occurred to me, that he might go back to Bethel. His offer might not even be an option any longer. I blinked several times in my thinking.

Maybe I should talk with Martin. He was kind and generous, and perhaps he'd like moving into a cabin some distance from the demands of his parents and brother. Or maybe Karl Ruge. Why didn't I consider Karl as a mate? He could meet the criteria that my in-laws might require, perhaps even better than Jack Giesy "maybe could."

So calculating I was. So…pragmatic. *Herr* Keil would be proud of my practical process; it was so much like his own.

"If you see Jack, tell him I'm looking for those letters, will you?"

Only Jack had made an offer. Only Jack demonstrated a willingness to take another step with me. Was it a step into a calm or into a storm? That I didn't know.

I looked at him anew and saw the bigness of him. He must have been working in the forests felling trees, or maybe he'd been building boats again. His neck and arms were well-muscled. He was tan and he walked purposeful as a mule heading back to his barn. I was outside using a drawknife against one of the redwood boards Boshie had given me.

"I hear you're looking for your letters." He removed his hat, then slapped at his thighs with it, leaving dust motes in the air. "When Boshie said you'd asked about them, I checked my pack and there they were. Imagine."

I put the drawknife down and brushed my skirt of the wood curls, then put my hand out. He held the letters just above my reach. "I didn't even open them," he teased. He sniffed them. "Don't smell of perfumes, so they're from men."

"Aside from my family, there are no men who would be writing to me," I said.

"Pity." He continued to keep the letters above my head. I could see that the seals had been opened and then pressed back but not tight. He'd read them all right.

"Jack. Please," I said.

"Oh, look at that lower lip pooch out like your Kate's."

"I like you better when you talk to me without the teasing or jockeying," I said. He kept his hand raised. I sighed. "Fine," I said. "I guess you can carry

them around for another five months. I'm sure it's old news by now anyway."
I turned to go back into the cabin.

"Can't you take a little teasing, always so serious?"

"If you didn't come over here to give me the letters, why did you come?"

"For entertainment," he said. "I haven't had much of that in the woods."

"I hate to disappoint you then," I said. I held his stare. "You're like some
schoolyard bully having his way." I crossed my arms over my chest, feeling
like my mother. She used to do that, cross her arms and tap her fingers when
her children behaved badly. "It occurs to me," I said as I tapped my own fingers at the elbows, "that some men like to be treated as though they were children. Are you one of them, Jack Giesy?"

He took one quick step toward me and slapped the letters against my
shoulder. "Here," he said, holding them like they were a glove and he'd just
challenged me to a duel. "Take 'em, fine lady." He used a deep Missouri
drawl, exaggerating the *a* in *lady*, but he let me take the letters.

"Thank you. That's better. Now, would you like some tea?"

He raised an eyebrow in surprise. "You're not setting me in the corner
with a dunce hat on?"

"Oh, Jack."

"I'll take some tea. Maybe there'll be something entertaining happening
here after all."

———

Oh, I can see now the complications I ought to have seen then, but I held
fast to just one point of view, one perspective, and it wasn't of the divine. I
had one direction I thought that I could take, as I did when I felt compelled
to go west with Christian, when I didn't tell him that I carried his child,
didn't advise him that I'd already met with Keil and pushed my agenda. This
time I'd considered other options, though not a one of them would work.

This was the only real out, this alignment with Jack Giesy, whose marriage to me would grant me a level of independence from the Giesy family of my husband. More, it promised the presence of my sons.

I told Jack that. Looking back, the explanation might have been an error in judgment, but I wanted to be as honest with him as I could be about our arrangement.

"And what would be in this for me?" he asked.

"You'd get the land," I said. "Once married, it would be yours, of course."

"You'd give it up just to have your boys living with you?"

"I'd have no choice. The law would say it was yours, my husband's. And yes. I think that's what Christian would want."

He held a small oyster shell the size of Kate's little palm and just as pale. He plopped it back and forth between the palms of his hands. "Look at this." He motioned Andy to come to him. "See that little tiny hole? That's from a drill, a little snail that attaches itself to the oyster and drills right down through the shell to suck out the meat."

"I know. My papa showed me," Andy said.

"*Ja?* Did he tell you to watch out for them?" Andy shook his head. "They look harmless and they're so small you wouldn't think they could cause any problems to a shell as hard as an oyster's is, but they do. Worse than starfish." He handed the shell to Andy, who took it to Kate and Christian for further study. Jack turned back to me.

"And I'm to assume you want this relationship to be what, like brother and sister then?"

"That would be my preference."

"It isn't mine," he said.

"Unless there's comfort that moves in or lights a spark."

"Such already exists for me," he said. "And it's a woman's duty if she weds."

"I know. But you can understand, can't you? I mean, you did make the offer some time back and were willing then to make a go of it without apparent care if I returned affection for you or not. You've spent a little time in my presence, and though I was ill you were willing to stay with me, to take care of me. It wasn't so bad then, was it, just being in the same place together, making things work?"

"The way this maybe could work is if we try to make it a true marriage."

Oh, I should have prayed then. I should have prayed that if this was my own doing and not God's, that He please get my attention, make me know and tell me whether I was smart here or not, taking some action that I'd later say was wasted. I should have prayed that my sons would be well tended no matter where they lived, that perhaps my being in their lives was not the most important thing for them. I should have begged for God to show me the path so that I might act according to God's plan. That's what I should have prayed.

But I'd stopped praying. And as with the spring rains that forced me to make new paths, that's what I was about. I was a woman of new walkways. A verse from Job drifted into my thoughts: "But He knoweth the way that I take: *when* He hath tried me, I shall come forth as gold." I'd never cared much for the emphasis placed on the word *when*. I'd had enough trials.

"A man has needs," Jack said. "It's a condition of this arrangement."

"If that's the only way this will happen," I told him, "I'll meet them."

22

Emma

On Reflection

I silenced all the cautionary voices that woke me in the nights before I did it. I listed what I'd tried that had not worked and got as smart as I could about what truly mattered in my life.

Drawing could not be my exodus. It was silly to believe a little picture could turn into something grand enough to support me and my children. My parents were not coming to rescue me. I couldn't go to Aurora Mills and be forced to live side-by-side with the man whom I held accountable for all my miseries, even though Jonathan had once invited me there. My efforts to remain on the Willapa and work toward the common fund would never earn me a place among Christian's family; worse, it wouldn't be enough to keep my children with me. Each spring I'd be fighting family just to have time with my son—my *sons*, as soon they'd worry over their youngest grandson's upbringing. As long as I was a widow with male children to raise, my in-laws would seek to "protect" them from unseemly influences. They didn't mind that Kate was under my thumb.

What mattered most to me was *my* influence in my children's lives, *my* presence to nurture them and hand down to them the values of their father and me. Being able to do that required desperate action.

Jack left after we struck our bargain, and I then read the letters that made me ache all the more. A cousin spoke of the good life in France. The one from my sister advised me to confess sins I didn't know about and reminded me of the dreariness that life would hold for me back in Bethel if I returned, once again a daughter living with her parents. Bethelites wouldn't build me a home there, not ever. I learned of my sister Lou's accident and the new worries she brought to my parents' lives. They'd never come west now, that was certain. They had new demands to care for their own family. I could understand that.

From Aurora Mills came a letter from my brother with news that he would head back to Bethel in the spring. He was likely already there. His absence just affirmed my need to do what I did.

———

All three children were to stay with my in-laws for the week of our marriage. "You're going visiting?" Barbara asked.

I took a deep breath. "No, Jack Giesy and I are getting married."

"Well, well," Andreas said. "What does Wilhelm have to say to that?"

"We didn't ask his permission," I said. "There was no need."

"You should marry here then," Barbara said. "Let us have the family around you as you make this change." She smiled. "We can have the band play. A party."

Martin came in while I talked to his parents, and I felt discomfort, as though I was doing something childish and resisted being caught.

"We'll need to transfer the land titles and things in Olympia anyway," I said. "We'll go to Steilacoom too. I have good memories there, of where Andy was born."

"A waste of time lamenting over old memories," Andreas said. "But we always like the boys to visit so they can stay."

He rarely mentions Kate.

"Don't let Big Jack get you into any trouble now," he added. "Get him too close to rum and he becomes another man." He tapped his cane.

"He hasn't done much like that of late now, has he?" Barbara said. "He's a good boy." She clucked her tongue at her husband.

———

"Kate's looking a little bit peaked," Barbara said the day Jack and I left for Olympia. "I wonder if you shouldn't take her with you. Andreas is fragile these days. He just got over a bad cold."

Andreas did look frail with his watery eyes. Dark reddish spots covered his face and the backs of his hands. "Whatever will work best for you. We'll take Kate along."

"Not possible," Jack said. "We can't be hauling a child around all that way. Wouldn't be good for her."

"I'll ask Sarah then," I said, and she was pleased to watch my daughter when I said I was going to Olympia. "Are you going to take the paintings to show around at last?"

"Shh. No," I silenced her. Jack stood talking with Sam outside. "No more talk about paintings or drawings except for fun, for pleasure. I've other issues to tend to there."

"I didn't mean to pry," she said.

"*Ach,* I know. I'm just nervous." She looked quizzically at me. "I'm going to Steilacoom to get married to Jack Giesy."

"When did this all happen?"

"It didn't happen in the way you think. It's an…arrangement. So that I can have my sons with me and the family will see that I have a man to help me. I'll stop being the Widow Giesy, stop being a burden. Most of all, we'll stop these months of separation when Andy isn't living with me. And I'll have a plan for Kate and Christian, too, when he's of school age."

"Oh, Emma, do you think that's the best way? Wouldn't it be better to go back to Bethel with your parents? Maybe go to that Aurora place where people live a little more closely together so the boys could stay with you and still go to school?"

I shook my head. "There'll always be this tension with the Giesys, this idea that without a father I'm not properly raising my sons. And I can't go to Aurora Mills, I just can't. It would be betraying Christian, and worse, I'd have to live with the gloating of Keil if I threw myself on the colony's mercy."

"Marriage is such a drastic step to take without even love in it to help see you through."

"This is my help. I'm taking care of things myself. I'm getting married."

"I'd always seen Jack as a bachelor," she said. "He has his own ways, seems to like to come and go, work at odd jobs here and there. The artistic person who can be flighty, maybe."

"We both love to draw," I said. "We'll be a perfect match then."

"I guess that is a tie... Does he like your work?"

"He doesn't know of my *work*. I've never told him or shown him. But I like you calling it a tie. It reminds me of that verse my mother always said. 'Begin to weave; God provides the thread.' "

"I hope this is God's thread, Emma, and not just a badly tied knot. I really do."

I knew there was a church in Steilacoom and somehow I thought that being married inside it would cover my less-than-sacramental motives for being there. I could have asked Karl Ruge to officiate and wed us in Willapa. Karl was a dear soul, but I guess I knew even then that he held me in a special place in his heart. I hoped that marrying Jack wouldn't tarnish that. I couldn't bear to hear him read the vows to us when this was a loveless marriage I was vowing to uphold forever.

Jack behaved as the perfect companion on the mule-riding journey. The trail across required chopping of overgrowth and he tended to that with ease. He smiled, made light little jokes, and looked like a happy groom-to-be. We met no one on the trail and had to sleep out for three nights in our tent. We talked easily together. He said kind things about the food I'd prepared and brought along. He made no demands. I wondered for just a moment if perhaps this might work out. Two adults looking after children, making decisions to affect the little ones' futures without harming their own.

We reached Olympia and in conversation, mostly Jack's, as his English was still much better than mine, we learned that the church in Steilacoom was Catholic and the priest traveled greatly. Even if he had been there, he wouldn't have married us outside his faith.

"We'll marry here, then," Jack said. "Find a JP."

My heart twinged with the memory of Christian's role as a justice of the peace.

"Can we still go to Steilacoom?" I said.

"What for?"

"Maybe a judge there could marry us. It's where Andy was born. I just want to walk there, to look at Puget Sound again."

"You can see the water right here."

"Please."

He hesitated. "Let's marry now then. Get a judge here. Tomorrow or the next day maybe we'll go to Steilacoom."

"That's a good compromise. See, we can work things out." I said it as much to convince myself as him.

The judge spoke the words to make our marriage legal though certainly not blessed. We moved next door to the land office, wrote the changes to transfer property. My hand shook when I signed the new documents. Christian's home, my home, was no longer mine.

We spent our wedding night in the same hotel Christian and I had stayed in when we'd first come west. Could that have only been seven years previous? A Chinese cook still shouted from the kitchen. In our room, the sheets smelled clean, and fresh water filled the pitcher. Thank goodness it was not the same room. Still, time had skipped across my life like a small stone across the Willapa. It had left its tracks: three children. I was doing this for them.

That night, to meet my wifely obligations, I sent my mind to the salty ocean sands that looked barren but gave birth to green grasses. I imagined the tides flowing in and out, washing away the choices that disappoint, leaving behind reminders of what I would cherish always: my sons, my daughter. All else didn't matter. One did what was necessary for what one cherished. That night in my mind, I was in the oyster beds at Bruceport, looking across to the shiny cobbled flats where the tide unveiled abundant oyster shells. I remembered a lantern light held high that showed me only as much as I needed to see: the oysters, hard shells harboring life inside. Oystermen watched over them to make sure the tiny snails didn't attach themselves and drill inside, sucking out the life from within. I was quite sure there was no one looking out for me. I'd have to do that myself.

———

Reluctantly, two days later, after we'd walked around Olympia, visited a boat-building site, looked at a furniture store but purchased nothing, Jack took me to Steilacoom. He described it as a puny town, but it had a territorial jail built the year after Christian died. There were blacksmith shops and stores and many more houses than when I'd been there before. I was sure I'd seen evidence of a sawmill or two, and a tailor shop opened its doors to the breeze beside a small hotel. A brewery sent smells into the air. It looked like a vigorous town to me. I loved being out in it after all these years. I wished we'd stayed here when we first arrived in the territory. Maybe Christian would still be alive. I pitched the thought aside.

I still marveled at the window boxes of the little houses and the wide-openness of a sea-lapping town. We walked. I carried a parasol and, near Gore Street, I stopped before the orchard that Nathaniel Orr and Phillip Keach had planted beside Orr's furniture store. "I remember this place," I said. Then farther up the hill I saw both the Catholic church and a Methodist Episcopal church. "We could have gotten married here," I said. "In the Methodist church."

"A judge was fine," Jack said. "Maybe could make no difference."

It was in Steilacoom though, in front of that old church, where I asked Jack to halt. The light was perfect, the air balmy. We'd weathered our first few days together with more hope than hassle.

"What now?" Jack removed his hat and brushed at the dust in irritation as I settled onto a stump.

"Just be patient," I said. I drew out some papers carried in my reticule, found the charcoal and began to sketch the town: the way the little houses marched up the sloping hillside away from the water; that wide, square building with its steeple spired into the blue sky. I was going to put us into the picture. I thought Jack would like that.

Jack frowned. "I didn't know you could draw," he said. "Did I know this about you?"

"It's just little sketches. I sometimes draw things in letters, do little portraits. I could draw you sometime if you'd like. I'll sketch you in right here." I smiled up at him. He grunted. "Oh. Well, as I said, they're not very good."

"All this time you never mentioned it."

"Wasn't important." I held the paper on my knees as I sat.

"Maybe could be you don't always know what's important," he said. His voice held a warning that I ignored. "Look at those pelicans," he said then, pointing. As I looked up he lifted the charcoal from my fingers, leaned over me, and began scribbling the birds in flight, making them fly right on top of what I'd sketched. They were morbidlike, his pelicans, as though from a bad dream, all dark with storm clouds around them with lines so heavy I could barely make out what I'd drawn beneath.

"Jack. Don't. Here, I'll give you another paper to draw them on."

"I'll draw where I like." He marked so hard the page tore.

"Jack." I grabbed at the charcoal. It broke. "*Ach.* Look at this now."

"Your pelicans have flown right off the page," he said. He laughed.

"So childish." I threw up my hands.

"Am I? Is that how you treat a husband? You stay here and draw then," he said. "I'll follow those birds toward that brewery we passed a while back."

"Jack, please. What's this about?"

"Jack, please," he mimicked. "I won't stay here to be whipped by a woman." He strode off. *Do I follow?* My fingers made nervous circles at the pads. I should have chosen another time to talk to him about my drawings. I should have never let him see my efforts at all. But I hadn't expected this kind of response. I wasn't in competition with him. I smoothed the paper. The hole was in the very center. Like the drill of a snail damaging the life of the picture. I folded what was left of it, picked up the broken charcoal pieces that had fallen when he'd ripped the paper. My reticule was full again but my heart was empty.

I raised my chin. I wouldn't be cowed by his childish behavior. Let him do what he wished; I'd do likewise.

Jack's behavior shouldn't have surprised me, but it did. He wasn't a man who tolerated equality. He always had to be above another. Frankly, his drawings were better than mine, so I saw no reason for him to be jealous, and that's what the behavior had looked like to me. A bit of jealousy over my simple sketches. I decided to let time do its healing. I walked the few miles out through the trees toward the fort, where Andy had been born. Later I'd reassure Jack that he was the better artist, and that we could put this spat behind us. Until then, I'd enjoy my day.

Like a town itself, the fort was much larger than before, with several more buildings and what looked like officers' quarters. Men hung laundry and others stood guard. The Yakima War of years back would have required greater troops here, which would account for the additional buildings. Or maybe they were readying for the war between the States that my sister Catherine wrote about. I walked along the split rails to where I'd taken the fall that Christian thought had brought on Andy's delivery. I looked for An-Gie, the Indian woman who had been so helpful to me, but I didn't see any other women, not even any officers' wives. I was a woman alone on my honeymoon.

I should return and see if I could find the brewery and Jack. *Honeymoon.* Where the sweetness waned, that's what Christian had said.

I bypassed the brewery and returned to the hotel. The waiter took me to a table without a second thought, which was gratifying indeed, me never being sure of my English. I wasn't sure of much these days. I ordered biscuits and tea and ate it in the dining room alone. People watch, that's what I did, saw how women dressed in this outside world and noted how my plain black dress stood out, my bonnet years out of fashion. The women all wore hoops to keep their skirts billowed out like tulip bulbs. I saw how men and women treated each other in public. I thought about what my next steps would be if my husband just walked away and left me here in Steilacoom. I'd go back and get my children. That would be the first step. I didn't have a second one.

"You're like a cat," Jack said. He startled me, having come into the dining room from a back way, spied me, then sat down across from me, his eyes glaring even as he sat. I slowly sipped my fourth cup of tea, keeping my hand steady. My heart pounded. *Do I bring up his absence or let him?*

"Like a cat...because I enjoy high places?"

"You always land on your feet."

I made myself smile. "Jack, you have your...interests. I have mine." He didn't smell of barley. Maybe he hadn't gone to the brewery after all. "I didn't tell you about my drawing because the pictures are so amateur. I certainly don't think they equal your own in any way."

He grunted. "When you're finished, I've something to show you."

He acted the proper husband in the presence of others. He ordered a coffee and I took my time with the tea. Finished, he pulled back my chair, then put out his arm so that I could take it as we walked. He took me up the street to a gift shop near the Sound. It was almost closing time. "They get imported things in here," he said. "I'll buy you anything you want. A wedding present."

"That's…not necessary, Jack."

"Maybe could be it is."

He urged me to look around, and the shopkeeper talked with him as though this wasn't the first time they'd met. He smiled at me, called me Missis.

Most of the wares looked European. There were German pewter candlesticks, silver bowls, and what looked like Italian pottery. Furniture from England or possibly back East sat nestled in the back of the cluttered store. Nothing practical to speak of, mostly luxury items for people who had others to do their work for them.

"These must be terribly expensive," I told Jack in German.

"Get a keepsake," he said. "It's what a husband does, *ja*, gives his wife something for their wedding?"

I thought of Christian's presents to me months after our marriage, brought back from his journey to the world outside: a ruffled petticoat that we later tore up to use as bandages in Willapa. He'd made a chatelaine for me to hold my sewing needles, and he'd given me a tiny Willapa Bay oyster pearl the year before he died, the most precious gift of all. None of them extravagances like those in this store.

"Look here, for now," Jack said, tapping on my shoulder as I stared. His words brought me back to the present. "Something to remember this occasion."

What was this occasion? Not a honeymoon, not sweetness hoping to return. Seek something practical, something to remind me that I did this for a reason, a good reason, the love of my children. What attracted me first was a plate, made up of six oyster-shaped wells to hold oysters on the half shell. A depression in the center would serve for a sauce. Someone had painted the outside edge and the center piece so it was like a work of art. The shop owner said it was French imported and the thin lip ledge was painted with gold. "This is lovely," I said. It made me think of my cousin in far away Honfleur, France.

"Shall I wrap it for the missis?" the shopkeeper asked.

"Not yet," Jack said, as he saw me set it down and pick up something else. "She's not one to easily make up her mind."

What won me was nothing practical at all. It was a single oyster shell, four or five inches across. I knew it couldn't be a Willapa oyster, as those I could hold in the palm of my hand. This would fill Jack's big paw. On the smooth inside, someone had painted what looked like an old mill beside a sea, using reds and rusts and purples. Mountains marched down to the water alongside the building.

"This is beautiful," I said. "I wonder who…?"

The owner shook his head. "Not signed. But it's a beauty. Wouldn't want to ever serve anything on it but rather hang it on the wall. Or maybe set it on an easel." He pointed to the little stand.

"Completely impractical," I said.

"Would you like it?" Jack asked.

"It must be very expensive."

"That's not the answer to my question."

"*Ja,*" I said. "I would like it." I could sink into that scene.

Jack paid the storekeeper, and I received it as a gift from my husband, though I did wonder what price he might extract for my reception of it. I also wondered where he got the money. Perhaps the Willapa colony, knowing we were marrying, gave him resources. Maybe he did keep some of his earnings to spend as he saw fit just as everyone else appeared to do. When the census taker had come around in June, he'd mumbled something about my own assets being among the highest for the region, but that was the land, of course. I owned the land. *Had* owned the land. Having discretionary currency was a luxury a colony widow did not have, nor, apparently, did a wife.

I held the shell up to the window light to better see it. It might have been a scene from Spain or Portugal, judging from the terrain and the building's shape. Maybe one day I'd go to such a place of promised serenity. It would remind me that peacefulness existed somewhere along with security and calm. The mountains were treeless and the water looked almost transparent. Onto the water, the artist had painted a reflection of the mill and a small boathouse. Inside would be a boat. I could imagine that, a boat to take its owner back and forth to deliver items from the mill. A *tender*, I'd heard such transferring crafts called. I squinted, then gasped.

"What is it?" the shopkeeper asked. "Is it broken?"

"No, nothing," I said. "It's beautiful." I had seen in the reflection something I'd missed in the painting. I looked at it now with new eyes, my keepsake with a deeper meaning. The building wasn't a mill at all, it was a church. A tiny cross had been placed at the top, a cross I would have missed except that I'd seen it reflected in the water.

23

Emma

Flaming Fires

We married on a Sunday, the sixteenth, and returned to Willapa a week and a day later to collect the children and to tell any who didn't already know that we were now husband and wife. We stopped for Kate at Sarah's, who patted Edwin's bottom as she held him on her shoulder. *Does she wear a worried look?* Sam came in and took him from her easily, curling the child in his arms. He was a natural with the boy, as Christian had been. Jack was...fair with my children. He gave distinct orders laced with teaching instruction. Hadn't he explained the drills to Andy well? Gentle words came from him, except for the outburst over the drawing. He'd even made me laugh a time or two. The oyster painting was packed in my valise, a sign of his generosity and that he sought forgiveness with objects rather than words. We were compatible. I stuck tendrils of hope like wispy strands of hair into the braid of my life.

"Looks like Jack's ready to get on home," Sam said. "Declined my invitation to share a meal."

"He's anxious to have some say in the farming of my place. Our place."

"You've married Jack Giesy," Sam said. "Didn't know any courting had gone on. Guess I don't get as much news from you Germans as I thought."

I cleared my throat. "I told him about my drawings," I told Sarah cheerfully. "He wasn't pleased at first. But he adjusted." I picked up Kate's bag, held my daughter's hand in the other.

Sam smiled. "No wonder he's thinking of home."

"For the boys," I said. "That's who I did it for. So my in-laws will stop wondering about their future. Not much courting involved with that."

"A business arrangement, is it?" Sam said.

"*Ja,* I guess."

Sarah squeezed me when I left, whispering in my ear, "You'll have to give me details later."

"Jack'll be fine. A little volatile but that's an artist's prerogative, *ja?*"

I'm not sure what I expected from my in-laws. Were they still my in-laws? I hoped I'd see relief that in their minds at least, I was at last under someone's control. Perhaps joy if they thought our union had been brought about by a romantic inclination. Maybe Barbara would plan a party for us after all. Maybe John would authorize the stockade for such an event.

Andreas tapped his cane as we approached. "You don't even have to change your name, *Frau* Giesy. Very practical." He smiled.

Jack wore a cocky grin. Henry teased him about leaving bachelorhood behind. Barbara offered us something to eat, and Louisa, Christian's youngest sister, ran between her fingers the new bonnet ribbons Jack had let me buy. I did feel as though I'd been brought into a family circle of sorts.

After the pie, Jack said, "Get Christian. We should head home." My son Christian held a wood carving of a horse that I suspected Martin had made for him. I hadn't seen it before.

"*Ja, ja,*" Andreas chided. "You'll want to be home a lot now that you have a bed already warmed up for you. Boshie will get you regular at the mill now too, and he won't need to keep that bed there for you." Andreas's laugh turned into a cough. Louisa patted her father's back and Martin said soft words to his mother. She nodded, looked away.

Andy had come into the room again. He'd welcomed us when we first arrived, then returned to help fill the wood box for his grandparents. He stood before me now, his hands on his hips, elbows out. "Jack says it's time

to go," I told him. "We need to listen. Do you have your things?" He nodded. "Let's go then." He turned to get his bag.

"I said get Christian." Jack reached out to prevent Andy from getting his
bag. "No need to have Andy come with us now."

"*Ja,* he wants time with his wife without big ears around," Andreas joked.
Everyone laughed.

I looked up at him. "You're joking, *ja?*"

"School term is on. I'm sure Andy went to school today. I'll pick him up
at the end of the week." He kept his voice light but I felt a tension there that
none of the others seemed to notice.

"But...that was the point," I said. "Why—"

"Oh, their first argument," Henry joked. "You picked yourself a hot coal
when you fired up Emma Giesy."

"I know how to manage fire," Jack said. To me he said, "I told you to get
Christian. Come along, now. Wife." He patted my hand. "Kate's waiting and
so am I."

"But you said—"

He put his hand behind his ear as though he needed a horn. "I can't hear
you." I saw Andy flinch out of the corner of my eye. "You said we married so
you'd have your boys and Andreas and Barbara here wouldn't have a hold on
your sons."

"Jack!" I felt my face grow hot. "There's no need to—"

"That's why you married?" Barbara said. She set the pie plate back down
at the table, clasped her hands in front of her. "Because you don't want us to
have time with your children?"

"Of course I want you to have time with them. I want Andy to go to
school, of course, but he's old enough to ride the mule each day during the
term, and with Jack at home, he won't have to help with so many chores when
he gets back each night, and if the weather is bad, Jack can take him to school.
Jack and I can do the work there; we won't need to trouble the rest of you."

"I'm the hired hand, am I?" Jack said.

"Jack—"

"The owner of the land but a hired hand."

His voice had gone from snarl to a forced banter. I knew from the fire in his eyes that he fumed.

"I meant Andy'd have you to help influence him. In the evenings of the school term as well as weekends. There'll be less need for everyone else, Boshie and others, to come to help us and they won't have to worry about my son's future influences."

Martin shifted from side to side, glancing at the children. I wished he'd take them outside. Andy frowned and now Kate whined, "I'm hungry, Mama." Into her whining, Christian threw the wooden horse. It landed at my feet.

Quick as a snake, Jack grabbed Christian's hand. "You maybe could hurt someone." Christian's eyes were as big as a bear's paw and his lower lip slipped out. Kate whimpered. "You, young lady," he turned to Kate, hovered over her, "have no need to cry about what to eat. You eat well from the way I see it." Kate backed away from him, sniffed, then buried her head in my skirt. I picked her up.

"Jack, please. She's just a child."

"Jack, please," he mimicked.

Jack had provoked this for the audience, I suspected. He understood our agreement. I'd given him what he wanted. He needed to be reminded. He needed to treat us all with a little more respect, but I couldn't say that to him here. It would only enflame the smoldering rage, and I knew one should never feed a fire one wanted to go out.

"By golly, what do we have here?" Karl said. He must have been out walking or working late at the school. He stepped inside, a blend of welcome then confusion on his face.

"A little family spat," Jack said, his voice light again, joking.

"Let's just go," I said, my heart pounding. "I'll bring Andy back in the morning. We all need to be together now. Come along, boys." I didn't want

Andy wondering if he was to be left behind again. He'd already been through that. I turned Kate to me to wipe the tears from her face.

"Andy stays." Jack's words wore hardness of coal. "I'll collect him at the end of the week. It's been decided." He whisked my youngest son up into his arms, not in a gentle way, not in the way Sam had held his son nor as Christian had once lifted Andy. Christian leaned away from him and fidgeted, pushing against Jack's tight hold. "Stop it," he said. "Listen to me. Just listen to me." He shook him. My son looked like a terrified kitten held in the jaws of a dog. He stopped squirming. "Come, Wife."

"Wife?" Karl said.

"Wife, my old bachelor friend," Jack said. He slapped Karl on the shoulder as he passed.

"By golly." Karl looked at me. I couldn't describe the expression in his eyes.

"*Auf Wiedersehen*," Jack said, all cheery again. He waved to everyone, then meandered out of the room, shifting Christian onto his shoulders. Through the open door, I watched as he plopped Christian on the mule's back, then swung up behind him. "Are you coming, Wife?" He almost sang it.

"You'd better go, dear," Barbara said. "No sense in having a major feud. Andy'll be fine here. You'll see him at the end of the week." She actually sounded sympathetic but I couldn't be sure. I could never be sure.

My hands felt wet. Taking Andy out with me would enflame Jack more and make Andy the target. But to leave him…

I kissed Andy good-bye, held his slender shoulders against me for a moment, then left without my son.

———

We rode back in silence. I slipped Kate a piece of sausage, which offered her comfort. She remained quiet, taking her cue from me as she sat before me on the other mule. At least I wasn't riding sidesaddle. At least Jack had succumbed to that little practice he obviously didn't approve of. That was a sign he could change. This was a temporary outburst, a quirk of his character. He'd calmed after the Olympia drawing fiasco, even became generous afterwards. He'd do so again.

I thought about his tactics. He used an audience to his advantage, getting other people to help affirm his belligerent wishes maybe even *because* he was belligerent. Like a school bully. He hadn't threatened force, really. His abruptness with Christian concerned me; I didn't like how he'd silenced Kate. But if I complained about it to Barbara, for example, she'd probably tell me he was just being an attentive father, getting accustomed to his new role. Still, he threatened in his quick movements, grabbing, moving close to a child's face. It was a violation, though I couldn't describe why. My in-laws would simply say children need to behave and I'd spoiled them. A child wasn't supposed to throw things; that was true, but the fright surely did not fit the crime.

I wondered how Christian fared sitting in front of Jack. I couldn't see him. I kicked the mule to ride beside them, to offer an encouraging smile to my son.

Jack pressed his knees to the mule. They moved ahead. The trail narrowed and I wouldn't have been able to ride beside them for long anyway. Was it the trail or was he excluding me? We crossed the river without incident, rounded the bend.

I'd always found comfort in the sight of my home and breathed a sigh of relief that in my absence it had not gone up in flames. I'd never lost anything to a fire as many had, and yet I always feared it. My home had been my refuge since Christian's death. A warm hearth welcomed, though I knew that if one wasn't diligent about putting sparks out, they could cause destruction instead.

Jack was unpredictable. Self-centered. I'd known that. But I hadn't counted on his perfidiousness, nor had I ever seen it directed at my children before. Being firm had always worked, even when we'd been alone. We were home now, on safe ground. I'd deal directly with him. Such men might pretend strength when underneath they felt weak. His offense at my little drawings back in Olympia supported that. Jealousy was an emotion rooted in insignificance. I needed to weed that out.

"I'll fix us something to eat, Jack," I said, riding up beside him as we came into the yard. The cows munched contentedly and the goat gave a perfunctory bleat, so I knew Boshie had been by and milked them. The chickens cackled from their tree branches, safe from predators for the night. "After the children are in bed we can talk."

"Nothing to talk about, Emma," he said.

"Well *ja*, there is. If this is going to work, we've got to talk things through. Andy's schooling is one of those things."

"Already decided," he said. "You made the right choice in following my directives."

"I wanted to avoid a scene," I said. "I complied though I didn't agree with you."

He laughed. "As if I care about why you did it. Just so you do what I say."

"Jack," I cajoled. "We really can't keep up a lifetime of your giving me orders without my having any say in them. I'll resist every time, and it'll fatigue you if nothing else. Make you old before your time." I gently poked his arm in play.

He grabbed my chin, surprising me. He held me, fingers firm. "I'm not worried about aging quickly," he said. "Though you might be."

He released me, pushed me away. Christian patted the mule's neck and when Jack told him to stop, the action was instantaneous. "Good boy," he said. Then, "That's the response I want from you, Emma, when I tell you something."

"You can't be serious," I told him. At least he was speaking to me in a civil voice. "I'm not ever going to sing every note in the tune you call."

He slipped off the mule, then lifted Christian to the ground. "You've got yourself a challenge, Emma Giesy, learning to sing the tunes I want you to play."

I felt sick to my stomach, even a bit dizzy as he led the mule away. It was the long trip, highs and lows staining each other, the washing of emotions, hope scrubbed now with anxiety and bleached by the uncertainty I'd placed us all in.

He fed the animals while I took the children into the house and started the cooking fire. The room smelled sour from being closed up for a week or more. Even the cedar shelves I'd made needed fresh air around them to renew their fine scent. Spiders flitted across the floor and a new web had been produced in the corner of the only window sill. I opened that window, wiped the stickiness of the web onto my apron. I left the door open to the outside and felt the breeze pull through. My hands shook.

But the children's delight in being home made me forget my discomforts for the moment. They ran around the cabin, bounced on the rope bed. Kate crawled underneath to find a wooden toy she'd been missing. Christian danced a little dance, his bare feet slapping on the floor.

By the time Jack came in, I had a stew going and added fresh vegetables from the garden. The carrots would take a bit to cook, but added to the onions and cabbage and potatoes, we'd soon have a hearty meal. I mixed up cornbread, aware that Jack pulled up a chair and sat at the table. I waited for him to speak, and when he didn't I told him I thought it would be a few minutes before the carrots were tender and the cornbread browned well.

"Take your time," he said. "I'm in no hurry."

"That's good," I said. "While things are finishing perhaps we could—"

"No mood for talking. You'll get used to my moods, but talking won't be a mood I'm in much."

I ladled the cornmeal onto the dutch oven top, slipped the pot close to the fire, then sat. "I'm confused, Jack. I thought we shared a number of interesting conversations over the past months about this and that. We had lovely dinners together in Olympia. We talked about the Pony Express making its first run from St. Joseph to Sacramento, how that would improve communication between us and those back in Bethel. We visited stores. We carried on as though we were two adults. Did I dream that? Did I just imagine that, Jack Giesy?"

"I'm a complicated man," he said, apparently forgetting that he had claimed otherwise not long ago. He leaned back in his chair, crossed his legs at the ankle, his arms over his chest. "Just the sort of challenge I would have thought the independent Emma Giesy would have liked." He grinned. I was heartened.

"I know we both need time to adjust to this…arrangement. But you seem so inflexible suddenly when before you'd been, well, congenial. Surprising, yes, but even your teasing stopped eventually. See, I've already put the painted shell up on the shelf." I pointed to the gift he'd bought me. "But this side of you, this…dare I use the word…this rigidness. Well, that's something I never saw reflected—"

"Don't know how to reign right now do you, *Frau* Giesy?"

"I'm not trying to reign over you at all. I just want to walk beside you and have some say in my own life."

"Christian spoiled you. Everyone talked about that, you want to have words about something. Indulged you. It made you a problem to yourself once he wasn't here to take care of things."

I felt tears burn behind my nose but I wouldn't let him see that, I wouldn't. "I just want a good life for my sons and my daughter, with me in it."

"Your sons. Always it's about your sons."

"And Kate. The children. I'm a mother, Jack."

"You'd better widen your kingdom a bit then, for you have a husband now, in more than just a document. You remember that."

"I'd like to make my home a safe and welcoming place for all of us."

"My home," he said. "And a nice one it is, too." He looked around. "Did Christian make all those lovely shelves with the curlicues at the edge?"

"I did those. It filled my long evenings. Don't change the subject, Jack. You should know this: I'd be a better companion and wife if I knew what I could count on."

"You might at that," he said. He drew close and breathed against my face, then leaned back. "But it wouldn't be nearly as much fun."

Jack refused to let Andy ride the mule back and forth, so he still stayed with his grandparents while in school. Jack's swagger increased after Andreas died in late October.

I knew Andreas had looked frail, but I hadn't imagined him so ill as to die. He'd always recovered. His dying made me grieve Christian anew. I grieved for Barbara, too. Losing a son and a husband. Word was sent to Bethel and to Aurora Mills of Andreas's death, but we couldn't delay the burial. John decided we'd bury him in the cemetery with a small ceremony led by Karl, and when the Giesys from Bethel arrived, then they'd have to come to Willapa with Rudy to mourn their father's death.

If only I had waited to marry Jack, I thought the morning of the burial. My sister would have said I should have let God handle things, not kindled my own fire. She might have been right. Now there was no one voicing the need for Andy to have a father in his life. Martin wouldn't try to take the children from me. Barbara had no more standing than me. Rudy and Henry were too interested in farming to worry over the upbringing of their nephews.

I assessed my present status. Maybe if I hadn't married Jack, I would have faced increasing pressure to keep Andy from me. But with Andreas's death I'd gained nothing by marrying Jack, not one thing. And I'd lost a great deal.

We were all together now, though. Perhaps we'd figure out what made

Jack happy or tense and we could begin to function as a family, though a strange one. I imagined the next school term when my sons would be old enough to ride the mule, Christian behind his brother. They'd return to be with me every evening. I'd be the primary influence in their lives, and that's what this marriage had been all about.

Only Jack's demand for compliance of wifely duties brought me sorrow. I had no love for him and any congeniality we experienced together could be shattered in a moment by his teasing or his brusqueness with the children. Before we married he hadn't shown the intensity of such precarious colors.

So when the children were tucked in the week after Andreas's burial and he said, "Wife. Such is the time," I knew of his intentions. It was my duty. I betrayed Christian by being with Jack, by demeaning a portion of our marriage that had been loving and good, trading all that in for this. My mind soared to those tidal places that had been gentle in my memory. They told me I could do this. I could meet my obligations so long as I did not let Jack intrude on this place that was me. During those intimate moments, I traveled somewhere safe in my history or my dreams, far from Jack's bed.

I'm doing this for my children. Those were the words that moved through my head: *for the children.* That loving choice could surely cause no real long-term harm.

In November, I threw up my supper. I tried to reach the slop jar. I'd woken up sick. My head throbbed as I fell back onto the bed, the back of my hand wiping the scum from my mouth.

"Ach, jammer!" Jack said rolling over, sniffing the air like a dog. "What kind of sickness is this that wakes you up? What did you feed us that was bad?"

"You won't get this," I said. "I can assure you of that."

The rains came, though not steady as they'd be by December. Already my sickness was greater with this child than with the other pregnancies. I thought back. It had been August when I'd had my last flow: I was probably three months along. I must have conceived the first night as Jack's wife. My bones ached and my legs swelled. I thought of *Herr* Keil and his charge that difficult childbearing was the result of Eve's sin. I'd had no difficult deliveries as yet; I'd count on my stubbornness to see me through this childbirthing too.

There were the usual chores to attend to, milking the goat and the cows, and I continued to do this while Jack worked at the mill. He was good with fixing problems there, making things work. I cherished the time with my children while he was gone, all of us relieved by Jack's absences. I found myself wishing he would find a job that would take him away as it had before we were married. But Joe Knight had sold out his oyster operation and headed back to Bethel. And they wouldn't work much in the woods with the heavy rains, so Jack seemed content to be a millwright and a farmer, a grouchy stepfather and demanding husband.

My stomach roiled daily. When the time came for Jack to arrive home, I noticed that all of us became a little noisier. We laughed a little louder at the antics of Christian attempting to do a somersault. Kate needed greater comforting in the late afternoons. Andy grew quiet, almost sullen. Our world of ease and closeness seeped away from us with the waning of the day.

Would I have prepared the venison stew in the way Jack preferred, or would he fly into a rage about my trying to kill him? Would he object to my using millet flour to make him a berry *Strudel,* or would he object if I didn't? He might complain that I'd wasted time with my redwood shelves that lined the walls now. Sometimes he brought the children little gifts, but if they didn't give him proper gratitude, he fumed. His irritations increased rather than lessened after I'd met my wifely obligations.

"You need to bake things," he said one day as he brought word that several from Aurora would be arriving to honor Andreas's death. I hoped I wouldn't have to attend this second service just because I felt so ill and travel made me sicker. I'd already gained more weight than I had with the other children in just these first few months.

"*Ja*," I said. "You can take my *Strudel* with you."

"We'll all go," he said. "Let them all see that we're a family and that I've done my part to carry on the Giesy name."

"Jack, the travel, with the river higher now from the rains, will just be troublesome for us all. Why don't you go alone, Husband? It'll be easier on you. I'll stay here with the children."

He stared at me as though I were an unsolved problem. "You don't want to see Keil, do you? That's it. Don't want to face the consequences of your getting Christian to push him aside."

"Keil is coming? *Ach*, that has no bearing. I'm just tired. Your child is—"

"You bore a baby in this wilderness," he said. "Then two more. Don't tell me you're not sturdy as an ox. This is about you whining your way out of something."

"I'm strong, but sometimes women have difficulties that—"

"What you're owed," he said, "for being a woman. For being one who… drives others away."

"What on earth are you talking about?" I sighed. "No one's left Willapa because of me. They chose on their own to head for Portland and then Aurora Mills. I just wanted us to remain here. Christian wanted to remain." I kneaded dough for cinnamon rolls. Cinnamon was the only spice that quelled my stomach.

"It maybe could be you drove *someone* away long after Keil left, long after Christian died," he said.

"*Ja*, well, it can't be the great Jack Giesy because you're still here, aren't you?"

His hand stopped just short of my face.

"You will go with me to the service," he said. "We'll honor my uncle's death and you'll meet up with Wilhelm Keil. Maybe even apologize to him for your part in the separation of the colony."

He was insane, my husband, all interested in the well-being of the colony. I touched the side of my face where I'd felt the rush of air just before he stopped his hand. "You will not go away from me," he warned.

"I'm standing right in front of you," I said. I used soft words so as not to aggravate him. I was grateful the children were occupied in the half barn, tending the goat.

"You go away when we are as man and wife," he said.

That was a truth, and it was likely to remain. I had to keep something of myself, something he could not control. This new infant had to have a strong mother ready for it. I moved away from him. I was going to be sick.

24

Louisa

We are going north to Willapa this December, such a terrible time with all the rains, but then death does not consult our almanac. It will be a safe time to be away from here with all running smoothly, harvests all in, thanks to the help of those joining us from Portland and beyond, from my prayers being answered. Is it prideful to believe my prayers for assistance were the ones God heard?

So we go to Willapa. We remember Willie's burial. We'll have a ceremony for Andreas, my husband's longtime supporter, and we'll honor my boy's life too. It will be good to comfort Barbara by holding her in my arms and not just sending letters. Even good rag paper is a poor substitute for flesh.

With all disappointments come possibilities. Andreas's death is the perfect occasion to urge the Willapites to come to their true home here in Aurora Mills. Giesys have good heads for business and they could manage a colony store for us. My husband misses John's fine leadership and Boshie's good will, and I miss that Boshie's round red face. He shares a limp with me too, and we encouraged each other in the Bethel days.

My husband misses those he sent back to Bethel, too: Jonathan Wagner and August, but they are needed to urge the Bethelites to proceed with haste to sell the lands there so we can purchase more here. Quit claim deeds have been signed and sent back by Pony Express, a luxury of the outside world that we have not had before this far west. There should be no problem selling the land there. No legal problems, though there is much talk of that war, and perhaps people will not want to invest in farms or businesses when one does not know whether blood will be shed on the soil they've purchased. The old country knew many wars, and people in this place have known few save for the Indian wars. They don't know how long wounds fester even after the last shot's fired.

My husband foretold the future and we are safer here in this Oregon State. I want my sons with me on this soil. Maybe they won't be required to fight if that time comes.

The band plays again at Butteville on the Willamette, and the Old Settlers still plan a ball for January. I saved the invitation from a few years back, printed as though the occasion when our band played was for royalty. We attended another harvest fair this fall. The Oregon Agricultural Society formed, so there is strong interest in farming and markets just as my husband predicted. My husband says we will become a part of this in time, when all of us are here together again at Aurora Mills. I wonder if then it will feel like home and this *Sehnsucht*, this yearning, for home will cease its pull on me. Or with Willie buried elsewhere and with Bethel far away, perhaps it never will.

Jack Giesy took a wife! That it is Emma Giesy made all of us drop our soup spoons at the news. Perhaps that's why she failed to answer my invitation to come here. I asked her to let old disappointments go, to let us all be together to help each other as we once did in Bethel. With three little children she might see now the advantage of friends close by, of sharing worry as well as wealth. I even told her that my husband now acknowledged that he was too harsh on Christian Giesy, that he didn't give sufficient weight to the demands on such a small group asked to build houses for so many. These nearly five years since have told well how many hands it takes to build a colony, and there were too few, just too few for the Willapa colony to adequately prepare for all of us. My husband never spoke those words out loud to me, but I have a sense that it's how he feels now. We have not enough hands to prepare for the next Bethel group, which my husband hopes will come next year, 1861, for sure. The Willapa group needs us too. No community can just give; it must receive as well. But without my husband to rein them in each day, well, they'll stray. I can't imagine why Jack Giesy chose Emma except that somehow, Jack strayed.

Truth? Emma did enliven us. She made us laugh with her unique views that bubbled like good brew. Oh, we looked aghast at things she said but she did make us think a little differently about our work. Sometimes, about ourselves. I didn't tell her all of that, of course. I only told her that forgiveness came with the letter and I even asked her to forgive my husband. I didn't tell him that, of course, but it must go both ways I think. Those two are like two strong rivers coming together where there is bound to be froth.

I thought I'd offended her in my letter but now I understand; it was her marriage that took her time. Jack Giesy. *Ach,* who can know the ways of men? Jack's sense of humor will make her laugh, and this is a good thing for a woman as she grows older. My husband finds little humor in life with me it seems, though he does dance at the Old Settlers' Ball, if not much with me. Well, I have a bad hip. Aurora is his favorite partner; she's young and so light on her feet.

We leave in the morning for Willapa. Karl Ruge was here a week ago buying tobacco and shoes and he reminded us that after harvest, the Hebrews held the Feast of Tabernacles where they celebrated God's bounty in their lives. We have had a good harvest. The hops do well. Grain grows tall. The soil is deep and black and truly could grow anything, I think. We have apples and cider in our Eden.

We will rejoice and, as Scripture says, the Lord God will bless us in our harvest and in all the work of our hands, and our joy will be complete. Joy. Perhaps now in her life again, Emma will have joy. Jack can bring that and maybe she will discover that being a wife among the colonists will not be so constraining as she always seemed to think. Perhaps she will find her *Sehnsucht* satisfied at last too. A woman of faith can hope for such things for her sister.

25

Emma

The Keel of Confusion

The Aurora Mills group came up the Cowlitz Trail. They followed the Willapa so they reached us first. We heard the horses and the dogs they'd brought with them as the afternoon waned. In the rainy months, I told time more by when the children expressed hunger than by any afternoon change in light. Pewter clouds greeted us in the morning and dropped rain on us throughout the day. We kept the fire going inside and listened to the drizzle against the cedar shingles. With the group's arrival I began to prepare a meal for ten or twelve. I heard no children's voices, but then a journey with little ones slowed travelers. This was meant to be a quick trip.

Jack was at home when they arrived, and he greeted *Herr* Keil and several of the others as the men now tended to the horses. Three women came into the cabin led by Helena, her presence a surprise. They took chairs, weary from their journey, their dark dresses and bonnets indicating they'd come to mourn. I hung their capes on the pegs near the fire. I fluttered around them, trying to make them comfortable, knowing that Helena would be judging my efforts and that before long *Herr* Keil would be standing in my home. He'd probably begin with chastising me for my being with child, for my having married without asking his consent.

"Well, Sister Giesy," Louisa said. "I hear you wed again. And to Jack Giesy at that." She sounded happy for me. "Perhaps you've calmed that jokester down some?"

Helena said, "It might have been better to let others help you rather than add to your trials with a marriage."

I dropped my eyes. "Widows do what they must to provide for their children. May I get you something to eat? You must all be hungry." I didn't look at them. I didn't want Louisa or Helena to see the pain in my eyes.

"Did the Willapa colony not provide for you then?" Louisa asked, surprise in her voice. "You married our Jack not for love but to provide for your sons?"

"Of course they did," Helena said. "I heard that my brothers had to come by all the time to milk Emma's cows and tend to other of her chores."

"Not that they were asked to," I said. *They've been corresponding with Barbara.* "Not that I didn't appreciate that they did, though," I hastened to add. "Some sugar cookies and tea? We'll have supper before long, but I wasn't sure what time you might get here or how many there'd be. Or even if you'd come this way rather than coming up the Wallacut River as you did when you brought Willie's hearse." I could have bit my tongue for mentioning that. "I meant, I just wasn't—"

"Well, don't go saying that the colony here didn't take care of things," Helena insisted. She brushed lint from her skirt. She must have bought new traveling clothes. The cloth looked new.

"People don't always do so well after the loss of someone they love," Louisa countered.

"Things needed tending after Christian died," Helena reminded.

Do these women argue?

"And then you had that new baby," the third woman said. She had been introduced to me as Margaret. She kept her bonnet tied so tight around her throat it almost disappeared in the soft flesh of her neck. "So soon too. Was it even nine months?"

My face burned. How could they think any such thing? That the Aurorans talked about me and my affairs shouldn't have surprised me, the gossip and speculating, but I'd learned well that one knew so little, really, of what went on beneath another's roof.

"My son's name is Christian," I said. He looked up at the sound of his name. I smiled, shook my head, and he and Andy and Kate returned to pretending to look at my latest almanac, though I knew they stayed curious about these new arrivals. "He is his father's son."

"Oh, I didn't mean to suggest—"

"I'm sure the Giesys did the best they could for you," Louisa said. "But it is sometimes hard to tend to things when people live spread out as you are here."

"*Ja*, it's much easier to help each other as in Bethel," Helena said.

"And Aurora Mills," Louisa added.

"Well, there too, though we're still spread out more than at Bethel."

"And not so many niceties as back there either," Margaret lamented.

Dissention at Aurora?

I hurried to place a plate of cookies on the table, set before them tin cups Christian had made, and brought out loose tea to strain. The hot water steamed through the fragrant leaves. Then I donned my shawl to fetch eggs.

"The men can handle things, Emma. You don't need to help them," Louisa said. She chuckled.

"Oh, see, she can't be without her Jack," Helena cooed. "You always did like to do what the men did. Heading west alone with all those scouts." She clucked her tongue. Christian's sister had never married yet acted like she knew all about men and women's ways. Louisa hid her giggle behind her fingers.

"I'm getting eggs," I said. "So I can make *Spätzel* later."

"The noodles don't take much time," Louisa said, waving her hand in dismissal. "Wait here with us. Sit. Talk."

"I like to dry the noodles," I said.

"They take a time to dry in this damp weather. I noticed that in Aurora Mills, too," Margaret said.

"We adjust," Louisa said. "That's what we women do. You don't have to go to such lengths for us, Emma. Just boil them like we all do. No reason to be fancy. Anyway, we don't need so much to eat now. You rest."

"You must be tired, too, Emma. I notice you're with child." Helena nodded toward my burgeoning girth. Small-framed women always swelled early.

"Oh?" The soft-fleshed woman adjusted her glasses. "You've a good eye, Helena."

"That's why you didn't respond to any of my letters," Louisa said. She fanned herself with her bonnet as she sat beside the fire. "Just so busy with the children, a marriage, and now a little one. When is the child due?"

I didn't want to talk about my pregnancy nor anything else with these people. I wanted to leave to get the eggs. But I hadn't been aware of any letters sent to me. In fact, no letters had arrived to me since Jack and I had married, which was odd now that I considered it. I didn't want to face *Herr* Keil any sooner than necessary either, so staying to talk might be wise. Keil was the reason my life had become so grim, the reason I'd had to make so many decisions. Maybe those eggs could wait.

"June," I said, turning back to the room. "The baby is due in late June. And I've never received any mail from you, Louisa. Only my brother sent a letter from Aurora Mills telling me he was heading back to Bethel, and that was sent nearly a year ago."

"You were married in September or the summer then?" Helena said, holding her fingers up as she counted. So cheeky!

"He and August left together," Louisa said. "But I sent you more than one letter. I wonder where they might have gone." Louisa rubbed her hip. I'd forgotten she had a limp. The ride must have been difficult for her, and the rain would just make it worse.

I thought of Jack's teasing me with the letters I had gotten before I became ill. No doubt he'd confiscated Louisa's letters, read them, and threw them aside as "women's missives" of little merit. I wondered who else might have written to me, offered me encouragement of sorts. Maybe my parents? Even my sister's letters made me smile. They might not after I told her about Jack.

"What news did you share in them? Do you remember? And yes, Margaret, we married September 16 to be exact, in Olympia."

"I just wrote that we missed you." Louisa sat up straight. "And I told you that my husband realized his error in being so hard on Chris, on all the scouts who stayed to help build homes for us before we came out from Bethel." Her words stopped my hand midair. Louisa brushed her fingers to smooth the hair on either side of the center part.

"The doctor made no error," Helena said.

"He would not call it an error. Those are my words. But he's realized the difficulty involved in building a colony in this vast country. I do believe he shared that with Chris, at least in the way men do that sort of thing, and that Chris forgave him his harsh words. Building up a colony in this landscape takes more hands than just to hold hammers; it takes hands to hold each other up. That's why he so hopes those back in Bethel will come out soon and those of you here will find your way home to Aurora. He's such a good, good man who wants the best for all of us." ·

She made her husband into some sort of saint. It was unlikely that *Herr* Keil would have had any real change of heart. Christian might have forgiven Keil, but Keil would calculate his apologies, especially if he saw some benefit to himself in it. Apparently there was, as Christian had since repaid the land debt. It was what had killed him. I looked at Louisa. She exaggerated her husband's abilities, she so adored him.

"Your parents might come to Aurora soon too, Emma. You could join them," Helena said. She hadn't noticed my absolute amazement at Louisa's words. ·

"I don't think they'll ever come west."

"That's not what your father wrote to my husband," Louisa said. "He said they would come to be of assistance to you, their widowed daughter. Of course they didn't know then that you'd remarry so soon."

"It was almost three years," I defended.

"*Ja*, well, a bed gets lonely after a time with only one in it." Helena said.

"And you'd know of that how?" I asked.

"Well, I just suppose." The other women laughed and nodded their heads. Helena's face took on a rosy hue.

"They've already left to come here?" I changed the subject and knew my voice raised an octave because Andy looked up, a question in his eyes. "Why didn't they tell me?"

"They were going as far as that Deseret place, where the Mormon saints are," Louisa said. "I worry over that because of the skirmishes there. The soldiers were called back to the States, so there's little protection for outsiders."

"My aunt lives near Deseret. They're just visiting, I'm sure."

"*Ja*, I know. They didn't have mail service for quite some time, so it must have been hard for your mother to know how her sister was. They'll be surprised when they get here to find you safely taken care of by Jack Giesy." She sighed. "My Wilhelm will be so pleased that they've come to help him at Aurora Mills."

I'm not sure why this news stunned. Maybe because of the timing. Perhaps my brother had returned to Bethel to handle things and help my parents come out. But they would have written to me if that had been in their plans. I'd not gotten Louisa's letters. I must have missed getting their letters as well.

Their arrival would bless me and my children. Jack wouldn't impose his threatening ways with my father present.

"I suppose they'll go on to San Francisco and then take a ship north. That's what I did," Helena said.

"They could come up here to see you and then of course come up the Columbia later to settle in Aurora Mills," Louisa persisted. "You'll have to come too, Emma. Jack can bring you and we'll be together again."

"Then they'll be here by spring," I said. I didn't want to disagree with Louisa about their ultimate destination. I had no intention of ever coming to Aurora Mills or letting my parents settle there.

"We don't know when they left, you understand," Helena said.

"Just that they plan to. I think my tea is strong enough, *danke*." Louisa put the strained tea on a plate I'd set beside each cup. I wished I had pretty teacups, porcelain, like the ones I'd seen in that shop in Olympia. My mother had lovely tea things. Maybe she'd bring them with her. I'd write to them, tell them of the marriage myself and welcome them to my home. Our home. If they hadn't left yet. Jack would have to build them a cabin. He had to. Lou could heal here. Their presence would bring safety. Maybe with safety I'd let myself become Jack's wife in truth and not just in demand.

Herr Keil and the other men entered then, removing their capes and coats and brushing water from them. They stomped their feet, but the mud was always with us this time of year. I stepped back away from the door; the scent of wet wool mixed with tobacco filled the room. I said to no one in particular that I'd be back in a moment; I was going to get the eggs. My heart felt light as a feather with the idea of my parents on their way west, and I wanted to be alone to savor the thought.

"*Ach,*" Keil said. "Jack. You go do that. We need some tea here for these men."

I didn't look at my husband or Keil. I just stood at the door, sideways to them all, waiting for the explosion.

"Brother Jack, you're already wet." Keil's voice rang out in the small cabin. "You go now. Pick up those eggs and bring them back. *Frau* Giesy and I have much to catch up on." He laughed then. "*Frau* Giesy. I don't even have to remember to call you by a new name."

Why would he call me at all?

I wanted to go outside, but I couldn't let my first encounter with Keil be a defiant act over eggs. "Go," Keil ordered. Jack brushed past me without protest, an act that surprised me almost as much as Keil's interest in having a conversation with me.

"Come." He took the only empty chair, then patted the one next to him that the soft-fleshed woman had vacated as he sat. She heaved onto our bed, using it as a chair, the children scurrying behind her. "Sit down now and tell me how things go with you," Keil said.

I couldn't believe he was speaking to me, asking me to sit while men stood. "I…we're fine," I said. I didn't sit. There was too much to do, too much going on. "Let me get you tea."

"Louisa can do that, *ja*?" Louisa nodded and grabbed the potholder so she could pour water into his cup. "How are your boys?"

"My boys grow strong." I motioned for Andy to come forward. He stood in front of me and he lowered his head in deference to Keil.

"He is well taught. This I can see. And does he do his lessons with diligence? My friend Karl is your teacher, *ja*?" Andy nodded.

"It was good of you to let Andreas and Barbara bring him to Aurora Mills," Louisa said. I bit my lip but decided they didn't need to know that Andy had gone there without my consent.

"And that he had days with his grandfather before he passed," Helena said.

Keil agreed, patted Andy on the head. "And your other son, Christian is it?" I nodded. "Where is he?" He twisted around. "*Ach, ja,* there's the boy with his father's name. That was good to call him for Chris." He patted my clasped hand. His flesh felt clammy. I pulled my hands away.

"And here's my daughter, Kate," I said.

Kate stood, her light curls dropping into her eyes as she skipped between the adults to stand before him.

"*Ja,* your daughter." He reached in his pocket for peppermint sweets, and when she bit into the candy the smell of mint filled my head, taking me back to Christmas and my parents. He handed one each to Andy and Christian too. "I miss my little Aurora even though we will see her again in just a few days when we return home."

Does Louisa fidget?

Louisa sighed. "It was hard to leave them, but the weather…well, the journey is better this way."

"Is it true that my parents are on their way here?" I asked, the words flooding from my mouth. I ignored Helena's frown.

Keil looked surprised, turned to Louisa, then back to me. "They don't come yet, though. I've asked them, but..."

"Oh. I thought—"

"They do consider it, and I think they'll come before too long. They know, as do all the rest there, how we struggle. We would struggle less if people from this Willapa country came to Oregon too. I've asked Jack to consider this and will tell John and Henry and Martin and my good friend Karl the same when I see them tomorrow. They've proven that they can make it here. But the work is hard and there is more commerce available at Aurora Mills and less rain." He laughed. "We should gather all the saints together in one place."

He droned on for a time while my mind wandered to my parents. They hadn't already left then. Louisa was wrong. She hoped for something and created a world that wasn't real, just as she imagined things about Keil's great goodness.

Maybe I did the same thing. There'd been no letters from my parents about coming out to help, and yet I'd grabbed onto that thread as though it were a rope thrown to a drowning woman, and I'd plunged my children into a treacherous pool in the process. The only way out meant giving Jack what he wanted and hoping in time he'd see the children were no threat.

I felt my eyes begin to tear and bit my quivering lip. My parents weren't going to rescue me. No one was. I shook my head without realizing it.

"What? What do you disagree about?"

"Nothing, *Herr* Keil. My mind wanders. I need to prepare supper for us."

"Louisa, you help. You go now." He shooed her with his hands. *He treats her like a child.*

Jack opened the door then and gentled the eggs onto the table.

"Sister Giesy needs to rest, *ja?*" Keil said. "She still grieves the loss of her Chris."

Jack glared at me as though I'd caused him some personal grief. There'd be no rest for me.

———

The evening continued in those hop-skip jumps when I felt lightened by an interest Keil took in our lives and burdened by the uncertainty of how Jack would respond to it. I hadn't remembered Keil being congenial before except on Christmas or his birthday in March, and maybe New Year's Eve. My father had always described him as a compassionate man, a fine leader with the colony interests at heart. My family had followed this man from Pennsylvania to Indiana to Missouri. I'd never understood why they absorbed all he said, acting like a sponge. Christian had too. Did they all see a different person?

I'd missed detecting Jack's darker side, or at least recognizing all the behaviors I thought I could live with or change. Maybe grief and change and babies had impaired my thinking about Jack. Now about Keil too. Was Keil the friend my husband always claimed, or was Jack more of a culprit than I thought?

At least my husband did nothing to challenge me in front of Keil while I prepared the meal. I convinced Louisa to rest, too, while I cooked. Busy chattering with the men, Keil didn't even seem to mind that I contradicted his directive to Louisa. No one would prepare my meals in my house, not even at Keil's command.

Jack made jokes while I worked. He didn't bark at the children. He told tales of life in Willapa that made it sound Edenlike. He said "his place" was one of the finest in the valley. Every time he said "his place," a hot poker seared my side.

"Did you do the woodwork?" Keil asked. "It took a fine hand to make the loops on those plate shelves."

"What? No. That's Emma's plaything," Jack said. "She doesn't have time for such little frivolities now." He reached around me as I bent to check the bread baking at the side of the hearth. He patted my stomach and laughed. Louisa giggled. I felt my face grow hot, but as I leaned over the fire, no one else appeared to notice.

"Ah, another child," Keil said. "It will take you from your work, Jack." He wagged his finger at him. "Now that you know the cause of such things, you should be able to stop at just one."

"Give me more hands to do my work," Jack countered. "That is what children are for, *ja*? To work so as we age we will be taken care of."

"The colony takes care of us in our aging," Keil told him.

I prepared a hearty vegetable stew instead of *Spätzel*. I thickened it with flour, then poured it across freshly baked biscuits. We had slaw kept in a wooden barrel cooled at the river, and without protest when I asked him to, Jack brought that in and I sweetened it with dried berries. The aromas filled the small space and Margaret moaned that the food smelled "divine."

"Let's begin then," I said.

Keil held up his hand. "We will bless the food," he said.

It was a custom I'd ignored after Christian's death. I thought of such blessings then as wasted words, since the food had not blessed us with life or good health or a future without grief. My husband was dead. My son had almost died with illness, me as well. What good did blessing the food bring us? But Keil's prayer included my name and Jack's and my children and everyone else who stood in that room, one by one. He asked that each of us would be remembered and blessed by God and he finished by saying, "especially the hands that have prepared this meal."

My shoulders rose.

We ate our fill, all of us, me sitting next to Margaret on the bed. The men finished off what was left of the stew.

"I didn't remember you as such a cook," Helena said. She picked up the tin plates.

"She lived with her mother always back in Bethel," Louisa reminded her. "And we didn't have much to eat during the winter we were here. How many ways are there to prepare those salmon? Remember, Emma?" Louisa laughed.

She laughs! One of the worst times of my life brought about by her husband's demands that we club fish rather than use ammunition to shoot game, and she laughs.

"She didn't have the chance to show her talents until now," Louisa continued. Little bits of biscuit fell from her mouth as she talked. She put her fingers to her mouth in embarrassment. "*Ja,* this is so *gut.* Our Lord has given you a gift, Emma." Her pleasure in the eating was a compliment I decided to accept by staying silent.

I hadn't thought of my cooking as having any kind of talent behind it. It was what must be done to keep my family living. But Louisa was right: I had developed my own style, mixing cabbage with dried berries; thickening stews into sauces as tasty as *Strudels.* Even more, cooking kept me where the activity was, but I didn't have to talk with people if I didn't want to. I was with them yet still apart, and no one would be critical that I acted haughty because I wasn't gossiping or telling stories. I had good reason to be silent: I was cooking. I was serving. Louisa's words put a festive hat on an otherwise ordinary outfit.

After the meal, as people rolled out their blankets and covered the floor with them, Keil offered up words I'd never heard him say before, about the power of sleep to bring us peace, to help us be better servants in the morning. I wished he'd been so comforting during the harsh winter when I was pregnant with Kate. I wished he'd encouraged the scouts through those months. The old feelings of resentment returned with the memory of how we'd suffered. The men lifted the chairs and turned the seats onto the table to give more room on the floor.

"Ecclesiastes reminds us that 'the sleep of a laboring man is sweet,'" Keil said. The men all murmured in agreement.

"A laboring woman, too," Louisa said, then she gave a little gasp with her fingers to her lips. I looked at her. She'd spoken out loud my very thoughts. I looked at Keil but he said nothing. It was as though he hadn't heard. Helena acted deaf as well. Only Louisa and I shared a glance.

"Children, you sleep in the loft," Jack said then. He didn't need to give such an order. It was where they always slept. "We'll give you our bed," Jack said, as Louisa rolled out *Herr* Keil's blanket and mat. It was the common thing to do when guests came, for the hosts to give their finest, the Diamond Rule, making someone else's life better than our own. It surprised me that Jack would offer it before I could. I nodded agreement even though I would have welcomed the softness of the bed.

"*Nein.* Louisa and I will sleep on the floor. This is not a problem," Keil said.

I caught the look in Louisa's eye. She was tired and that hip of hers must hurt her as she leaned to the side.

"Perhaps the men would consider sleeping on the floor and Louisa and I could share the bed," I said.

Jack scoffed.

"*Ja,*" Keil said. "That is a *gut* idea, a better one."

He's so congenial. He must want something. But what?

"*Nein,*" Louisa said. "It is not good that my husband should sleep on the hard floor while I lie in a soft bed. No. The men need to be well rested. Emma and I will adjust on the floor along with Helena and Margaret, and you two men can sleep well on the bed as men should." The other men had chosen the half barn outside.

Keil didn't protest. It served his purpose.

I wished that if Louisa was going to defy him it wouldn't have resulted in my sleeping on the floor. I thanked Louisa for the blanket roll she handed me that was hers; she would use her husband's. I turned to see Jack staring at me. He had a sly grin on his face. He must have known that wherever I slept, I would welcome a good night's rest lying beside someone other than him. I smiled back at him. My sleep that night was sweet.

In the morning, I prepared a large breakfast of eggs with slices of ham and a cinnamon loaf I'd made two days before. The cabin smelled like a good home should, and as they washed their faces in the cold water, nearly everyone commented about the pleasant aromas and later, how good things tasted. I took time to fry the bread and put some of my jams onto tiny tins that dotted the table. All of it was gone when the meal was finished.

"If only it would stop raining," Margaret complained as she tied her bonnet. She sighed. "I'm full as a tick and wish I could just stay right here."

"The mules are surefooted," her husband reminded her. "You'll be fine."

"It surprises me," I said, "that you would all come in this rainiest of months. It was never a time that you liked, if I remember, *Herr* Keil."

"Brother Keil. You must call me Brother Keil," he said. He patted my shoulder. "We are of one family, *ja*?" He put on his hat. "That was a difficult time for us all. Willie, our Willie…well, we grieved." He shrugged. "But it is good to come now to honor him again as we did with Christian's burial, to stand beside his grave as we will stand beside Andreas's and Christian's. We'll do this together, all of us."

"Emma, are the children ready?" It was Jack speaking.

I took a deep breath. "I won't be going with you all today," I said. I didn't look at Jack. I could use an audience too. "There's no reason to take the children into the weather, and my stomach is still upset. I'll have a good meal ready for when you return. It will save Barbara and her daughter from having to prepare something there for afterward."

"We'll spend the evening with Barbara's or John's family," Keil said.

"*Ja*, that's good," Louisa agreed. "Emma was sick twice in the night. All that good stew, *kaputt*. Such a shame. You should stay home." She rubbed her hip absently.

"It would be a greater shame for you to miss this service of your former father-in-law," Helena said.

"My uncle," Jack said. "They will set a carving today to mark his grave. You will come and bring the children too."

"Jack, I—"

"No, Jack." Keil stopped him. "Tomorrow or the next day we'll return and your meal will give us a good start back home, Sister Giesy. Thank you. Helena will represent you at the funeral," Keil said. His voice held all the authority that I remembered. "Your wife has served us all well here and will do so again," he said to Jack. "No need to come out into the rain with the children. Jack, you can show us the way."

"You know the way," he said. Keil frowned and Jack seemed to reconsider. "*Ja*, well, you maybe could have forgotten."

"*Gut*. We go then." Keil clapped his hands together. The party packed up what they needed. I stayed out of Jack's way. I knew I'd have a large meal to prepare eventually, but I'd also have a day or maybe two alone with my children. And I had been sick in the night. None of that was anything but truth. A bold truth perhaps, knowing that Jack wouldn't like my using it to get my way.

I watched them saddle the mules and noticed none of the women rode sidesaddle. Pragmatics won out here in this western landscape. The rain was steady but not as hard as it had been the day before. Still, they all ducked their heads into their necks to keep the water from dripping down their backs. I waved good-bye until they rounded the bend. They'd stop at Mary and Boshie's before heading on. The gathering would grow as they traveled north. It would grow without me.

I drank a cup of tea to help settle my stomach, then changed clothes, putting on Christian's old pants and a shirt that worked well to milk the cows in. I didn't wear those clothes unless I was alone with just the children. "You stay in here and stay dry," I told them. "Andy, keep an eye on your little brother."

"Yes, Mama," he shouted down from the loft.

I wrapped a scarf around my head, found my gloves, donned my wooden shoes. I'd get eggs and make the egg noodles for this evening, let them dry over the little pegs I'd drilled below the redwood shelves. They'd be ready by tomorrow even with the moist atmosphere. Maybe I'd make some special dessert. I felt almost happy and hummed a little tune.

I opened the door. There stood Jack.

26

Emma

Marrow and Fatness

Jack pushed me back into the house. "Don't you ever defy me in front of others," he said. "Not ever." He had his hand at my throat. He squeezed hard. "I will decide what you'll do, not you. Do you understand that, Wife? No more of this whining about being sick." He smelled of whiskey and wool. His face glared into mine, the whites of his eyes like a raging buffalo's. His nose flared. Spittle soured at the corner of his lips. My throat throbbed. "I will decide what goes on under my roof, not you."

"Mama?" It was Kate. "I'm come down the ladder."

I croaked, "No, stay there!"

He released me, throwing me back into the table. The edge gouged my thigh. "You enjoy this day, your last day of getting your way. I'll be back tonight."

"But they aren't returning until—"

"I couldn't leave my poor, pregnant, sick wife home all alone, now could I? It'll be just us again. You. Me. And your children. I'll try not to do anything to upset *your* children." He scanned the room and I thought he searched for them, but instead he stomped to the shelf that held the oyster painting of the church I'd come to love. His wedding gift. He grabbed it. "I told them I'd forgotten something and had to turn back. It'll make a nice little addition to the marker on Andreas's grave."

———

I lay awake and startled at every sound; every creak in the roof or the floor made me twitch. In between I thought of Helena. Would she urge her relatives to go to Aurora? Would they all go and leave Jack and me here? I felt sick again. Got up. Lost my supper. How odd that after all this time Keil's prophetic charge that I'd suffer in childbirth should come to pass. An old psalm wove its way into my sleepless state: "When I remember thee upon my bed, and meditate on thee in the night watches. Because thou has been my help, therefore in the shadow of thy wings will I rejoice." The sentences didn't seem right, so I rose and lit Christian's lantern and read an earlier verse. "My soul shall be satisfied as with marrow and fatness; and my mouth shall praise thee with joyful lips."

That was what was missing of course: I'd stopped praising, stopped praying, and so I was hungry all the time, never satisfied. Now in my night watch I didn't feel like meditating. I only knew the shadow and not the sun.

Jack didn't come back that night.

The next day, Andy stayed close to me, getting me a damp cloth for my face, brewing me savory tea to help my indigestion. It was an herb I added to beans to prevent stomach winds. "Where did you learn that?" I said.

"Martin showed me. He gave it to *Opa* when his stomach failed him."

"At least there's something to relieve the constant complaining of my bowels," I said.

"*Opa* got sick, like you."

"Not like me," I said and smiled. "But we all get ill sometimes."

"*Opa* died."

"My sickness will pass," I assured him. I hugged him with one arm. "I'll be fine. Remember when you were sick? You got better, *ja*? Why don't you go work on your lettering or whittle with your knife. Do something restful. Before Jack comes back. He'll have duties for you, I'm sure."

He stiffened at the mention of Jack, then nodded his head.

"Jack's never...hurt you, has he?" He shook his head but looked away. "That's good. We'll just try to do what he asks and make him happy, all right?" He didn't agree but continued to sit with me.

Jack and Keil's party would be back anytime. I needed to rest just a moment longer and then would finish preparing the supper meal that I decided would be meatballs. I had day-old biscuits I could soak with the dried venison, which needed plumping, and enough bacon to add flavor to the sauce. It would feed all of us and wouldn't lose flavor if they didn't arrive until late. I should have planned a dessert, something sweet, but we had no liquor to finish off a great cake and besides, fresh berries were always better. Maybe a thin pancake with maple-sugar chunks would suffice. I just didn't feel well enough to care.

"You should go play now. Do something else besides take care of your old mother."

"I like making you feel better."

"*Ja, ja.* Every mother should have such a son as you," I said. I might have had a headstrong child or one demanding or perhaps one injured like my sister Lou, one who had some sort of accident that changed her. I felt a wash of gratitude that I'd been given this kind of child who was healthy and caring and alive.

"I'll read from the almanac," he said and climbed the loft. The other two entertained themselves with Kate acting as a teacher and Christian her patient student. I knew it wouldn't last for long, but for the moment their brother was free of their care.

I worried about Andy. He was seven but he acted much older. I'd done that to him, I knew, depending on him so much. He easily assumed responsibility for his younger brother and sister, and I had to watch that I didn't just expect him to perform tasks that were really mine to do or might have been his father's, had he lived. Before Jack, Andy milked the cows. He still did when Jack failed to come home until late. He made sure the wood box never stood empty. He even heated the water for the laundry. He was a kind soul who showed no interest in hunting or being present when the hogs were rendered or when we had to kill the chicken for dinner. He'd reacted with my mentioning Jack and I wondered if Jack teased him about his not wanting to hunt. Perhaps Jack hadn't physically hurt him, but physical wounds weren't the only kind.

Jack. When he came back, it would be with Keil's crowd, a different kind of audience. Perhaps he'd be congenial, polite, compliant.

I rolled myself off of the bed, donned my day-apron, tying it loosely around my thickening waist. It wasn't even four months. How large would I be when it was time for this child to be delivered? I began the meatballs, got bacon from the smokehouse with Jack ever on my mind. Jack certainly danced to Keil's tune when the man spoke and Jack didn't ask him to repeat any notes. "*Ach*, Emma," I said out loud. "You've managed to make your life miserable with two authoritarian men plaguing your days. Such a waste."

Keil's authority managed Jack, at least. Once Keil was gone, would Jack be his old self? I considered that Keil's influence was not so strong over people who had been his followers for years. Karl Ruge was here in Willapa. So were the Giesys. Yet the Bethel group delayed. I wondered why.

I could ask Keil to talk to Jack about being less…unpredictable. Jack might listen to Keil. But asking Keil for anything would invite a lecture about how I could be comfortable living in Aurora Mills. He might tell me I wouldn't now be struggling with my morning sickness (and evening sickness, too, it seemed) if I lived a more faithful life, was faithful to his colony. Worse, Keil wouldn't believe me that Jack could be like an angry cat, pouncing and hissing and scratching the people he claimed to care for, then purring as though nothing had happened.

I'd have to comply with Jack's wishes and maybe find more reason to bring other people around for added safety. But I also had to be careful about not granting him an audience.

The second night, we waited again and still Jack did not come. Neither did the others. Jack and Helena probably commiserated about my refusal to attend the memorial gathering. I imagined him giving that oyster shell to Barbara and her even thinking he'd painted it himself. I shouldn't have cared about that luxury item with no practical claim, but it was something lovely that gave me comfort. Now the memory of it would chafe.

When the party finally arrived the next afternoon, I had the meal prepared. The men took time tending to the animals, then came inside. The rain had let up and the sky looked like milk with cream spreading through it. The dogs they'd brought along growled over bones.

Jack came in last. He flopped a rabbit on the floor by the door. "And what did Andy do while I was gone?" he charged.

I frowned. "His usual chores. Why?"

"He didn't check the traps," he said. "If he had, you could have prepared this for us. It's been a long time since we've had *Hasenpfeffer.*"

"I prepared a good meal for you," I said. I kept my voice light. "We can fix the rabbit in the morning. It will give everyone a good start." I began immediately to dress the animal.

Jack grabbed my arm to stop me. "Andy can do that. It was his chore he failed to attend to."

"I don't mind," I said. "Please, the rest of you, sit, eat before it gets cold and loses its flavor over our discussions here." I smiled and urged them to fill their bowls with the meatballs and find a place to sit.

"*Ja,* boys will be boys," Keil said. "You missed plenty of your chores as a *Junge,* Jack. Quite inventive in getting out of them, as I remember." He laughed then and failed to see that Jack did not laugh with him. "We will ask the blessing," Keil said, his accent thick as he prepared to pray.

I bowed my head. Once again with Keil's words, a silent comfort washed over me. I felt my shoulders sag with the weight of life I carried and felt warmed by the hope that a special blessing did come to those who prepared the meal with love. Aside from loving my children, I didn't think I loved anything or anyone anymore. Maybe my parents in a distant way, the *Kinder* of my family. But life, or sunrise and sunset, the smell of cedar in the air, the warmth of well-chinked logs, the taste of salt on my lips, even the presence of friends, none of those had warranted the emotion of love or even gratitude. Keil's prayer reminded me that I had prepared food joyfully and that God saw that as love. Perhaps that was enough love for now.

I stood back to make sure all were served, called the children when the adults had finished, and offered seconds to Jack before anyone else. He glowered the whole time. When I'd served all the thin pancakes with the hot maple sugar and butter treats, people made comforting sounds about being satisfied. There were a few scraps for the dogs outside. People yawned, made ready for bed. "We will make the same arrangements as before," Keil announced.

I nodded while Helena, Louisa, Margaret, and I rolled out mats as the men put chairs up on the table so we'd have more floor space. I'd need to boil the water and wash the dishes yet, but having everyone settled down would make that easier.

"Andy will finish the rabbit now," Jack said.

"Please, Jack. It really is easier for me to do it while I clean up. There's no need to have the boy—"

"He must do what he's told," Jack said, his voice loud. "I'll not have you make him into a sniffling rabbit."

"Jack—"

"Get over here, boy," he ordered. "Pull the guts out and skin this animal."

"I don't think he's ever dressed an animal before," I protested. "Let me just show him—"

"Must you insist on defying me, woman?" Jack said. He grabbed my arm, then thinking better of it, he dropped it. The cabin stilled as before a storm.

I watched my son as he made his way through the adults, some already lying down, others still standing or sitting on the floor. He didn't look cowed or defiant either. "I can do it, Mama," he said.

"Your mama is not the one asking," Jack said. "I am. You listen to me, now, you hear?" He boxed at his ear but missed as Andy ducked. "You have a weak stomach, is that it? Can't stand to handle what will feed you?"

I saw just a tiny flash of anger cross my son's eyes, but he held his temper and began the task of gutting the animal. The group went back to their settling in while Andy kept his head low. Tears formed around his nose and he wiped them with his forearm as he worked. He did the work cleanly, using a knife with skill. The odor of intestines and blood was greater than wet wool and old soot. It wasn't that Andy shied from the blood or body juices of the rabbit, I could see that. He didn't have a weak stomach. He grieved the animal's death. Had he gone to the trap and found it still alive, he would have tried to tend it, not bring it home for dinner.

At last he finished and washed up, stepped outside and hung the hare from the rafter, tossed the entrails to the dogs. I'd fry the hare in the morning. I finished washing the tin plates, wiped out the dutch oven and hoped that Jack would be asleep by the time I lay down beside Louisa on the floor.

No one slept yet. Keil had asked a blessing on our sleep, but people chattered as though they were sitting upright on a divan, telling stories in the darkness. The air cooled in the cabin as the fire died. They talked about the service, about Andreas's long and good life. Helena said perhaps she should have stayed with her mother; Keil assured her she was needed at Aurora. Louisa said the oyster shell Jack placed at the grave looked peaceful next to the wooden marker Keil had made himself. Every now and then a person would fail to respond and I knew that, like a star disappearing in the dawn, the person had drifted to sleep. Maybe that's what death was like when one died in their sleep, just a gentle not responding to an earthly voice; listening instead to one from somewhere else. I hoped that was how it had been for Christian when he died…just a change, not so much a challenge. I closed my eyes, hoping for sleep.

Instead, I lay awake remembering Christian. I heard Jack's steady breathing and knew he lay awake as well. Louisa said the oyster shell painting looked good next to a wooden marker Keil had made for Andreas's grave. Then it came to me: *Keil must have made the one for Christian's grave too, all those years ago. How very odd that he should have.*

———

I prepared the *Hasenpfeffer* to kind reviews. "Andy did a fine job in dressing the animal," I said. "A good dressing is half of the flavor." The women nodded. We knew that field dressing made the venison, reduced the gamey taste if a man handled the carcass well, but I appreciated their praising Andy for his effort. The men had saddled the animals and rolled up their slickers to where they could reach them easily. The air felt heavy with rain, but we could see patches of blue sky flirting with the clouds. Jack had gone into the barn to milk the cows, I assumed. I thought it odd that he'd begin that chore before the colonists left, but perhaps he knew we'd be talking for a while. It seemed we Germans were forever talking. Even as our hands were on the latchkeys ready to leave, we'd stop and find some new topic that needed exploring. It had been a while since I'd enjoyed the little gabbing that went on. When it wasn't about me, gossip was intriguing. As when they'd talked themselves to sleep the night before, it was a comfort. Even now I didn't mind Louisa directing her words at me, trying to get me to change and come to Oregon.

"But if my parents are on their way out, they'll come here," I said. "Imagine how disappointed they'd be if we weren't present to greet them. I'd want them to see all that we've accomplished." I spread my arm to take in the half barn and the fields we'd planted, the smokehouse. Our lives these past seven years were written on the landscape. "Besides, Jack won't leave."

"You should come for a visit at least," Louisa said. "You don't even know all the advances we've made at Aurora because you've never been there to see, not once. Come next year for the harvest festivals. Such precious things to look at. Some of the men are weaving baskets in the winter months, and they are highly valued at the fairs."

"I think they'll all come to Aurora," Helena said with authority. She patted her thick braids wrapped tightly around her head. "They'll listen to my urgings." *I wonder how Helena fits into Louisa's life.* I suspected those in Bethel might have been pleased to see Helena go. *Does Louisa welcome her?*

"You could use a basket for your eggs, Emma," Louisa said. "We're back to weaving again. My husband purchased sheep and we're dying the wool as we used to and showing it at the fairs. Maybe you could display some of your woodwork, and Jack could bring his drawings." She got all excited with that idea and clapped her hands. "The band plays as it did back in Bethel, and we are helping our neighbors, just as we did back there. That's why we came. To serve our neighbors, to make their lives better than our own."

She reminded me of…me, five years previous when I'd tried to convince Christian and all the Giesys to remain here in the Willapa country, to see the goodness in the crude huts, the huge timber that took its toll on all of us, when all I wanted was to find freedom for myself, relief for my husband. That's what Louisa wanted too. I could see that.

"You could cook us up a storm at Aurora," Margaret said.

"What's this talk about Aurora Mills?" Jack said. He'd come out of the half barn carrying a bucket of milk. He set it down. "This is my home now. And my wife and children stay with me."

"Well of course they'd stay with you, wherever you went, Jack," Helena said.

"We could all help each other more if we were closer, don't you think?" Louisa said. "That is the Christian way, to help each other. And if all of you were to come to Oregon—we're a state already, not like this Territory—we could better welcome all the Bethelites and be in service to our neighbors too."

Louisa actually meant what she said. Charity was in her heart: charity for her husband, for the colony, even for those of us who had separated ourselves.

She just never saw her husband's faults, the way he ruled over others, the way he set all the tasks before people, then manipulated them into acting whether they wanted to or not. No, Jack and I agreed on that, we could never go to Aurora Mills.

Through all of this Keil said nothing, nodded his head as his wife pleaded his cause. Finally, "Louisa," he cautioned. "Sister Emma and Brother Jack would come if they could, but they are needed here. We are grateful for the hospitality they've shown us. You have Helena to help and others as well. We're fine."

I nodded to him, then hugged each of the women and watched with my shawl wrapped tightly around me in the clear, cold air as the colonists rode off through the trees following the river. Jack waved at them too. It would be at least four, maybe five days before they made it back to the relative comfort of their homes. They'd take respite in the cabins of strangers along the way. Had they accomplished what they'd come for? Had they meant to mourn, or lure us to Aurora? Maybe Karl Ruge or Barbara or the others had agreed to move. I hadn't even asked.

Their leaving left a longing. No more marrow or fatness, just a hunger. I'd liked having the house full of people. Jack hadn't barked as much and because of guests, I'd received two days without Jack here at all.

I turned to go back in when Jack closed the space between us in quick steps. He smelled of rye. *Did he hide it in the half barn?* "Things are going to be different now," he said. "No more of this pampering. You prepare meals for a dozen without complaint, yet with me you are always sick. Always whining. This will cease."

"You wanted me to serve our guests properly, didn't you? I was doing what you wanted. I had to do it in between being sick."

"You loved the little pearls they threw to you about how good things tasted and how skilled you are. You knew exactly what you were doing, winning them over so they'd try to lure you away from me, hide you away in Aurora Mills."

"Oh, Jack," I scoffed.

"It won't happen, Emma Giesy. Your mind may go away from me but you will never leave, at least not alive."

"Don't be melodramatic, Jack," I said.

He stopped me. He gripped with his hand, that wide palm squeezing my arm until if felt like no blood flowed through it. "You're hurting me," I said. My fingers tingled.

"Pain in your arm maybe could be just the beginning of your worries," he said. "It just maybe could be." He pushed me away then, and I stumbled but caught myself as he stormed into the cabin, shouting for Andy.

"You leave him alone," I said. I rushed after him, rubbing my arm. "Whatever you want done, I'll do it."

"Andy!" he shouted. "Get out here."

I tripped over the milk bucket. *"Ach!"*

Jack turned and, in a flash I didn't see coming because I stared at the milk spilled at my feet, he struck me. The back of his hand rocked my chin up through my teeth and into my eyes. I fell. That is all I remember.

27

Emma

You, You, You, Must Go

The voice began inside me when my eyes eased open to my new world. The words whispered over the broken place in my tooth, across my swollen lips. *You, you, you, must go. You, you, you, must go.*

It was nearly dark inside the cabin. I tried to make sense of things. Jack must have carried me to the bed. With the tip of my tongue, I felt the puffiness from the cut my tooth made. Andy sat at the foot of the bed, his back to me. I heard Kate and Christian chattering on the floor beside us, arguing over a toy. Christian stuttered, "That my-my-mine, Katie. My-my-mine." Shame washed over me, shame that I'd let this happen.

When I moved, Andy turned. I forced a smile. I brushed the chestnut strands out of his eyes. "Are you all right?" I asked him. He nodded. "Thank God for that," I said.

You, you, you must go. You, you, you must go.

My eyes closed. I'd been going my whole life, trying to make things happen, trying to push my way into a world I thought needed changing. Once I'd claimed a husband I loved, chose a wilderness to be with him. We'd survived a winter designed by the devil himself and lived to tell of it. We'd remained to build a home, a place I once called my own. Scripture promised "peaceable habitation, sure dwellings, quiet resting-places" and with Christian, I'd had that despite the trials. All was gone now. The song said I should go too.

I stared at the peeled-log ceiling. I wasn't capable of leaving. I had no-where to go.

Jack came in. Andy slipped to the far side of the bed. I almost felt him shiver. I sat up, kept myself from wincing as Jack knelt beside the bed. "I don't know what happened to me," he said. "I never meant to hurt you. I didn't." He pressed his head into my lap like a small boy. I didn't touch him. He lifted his head. "It's like I'm a firecracker that sizzles and snaps and then explodes. I promise to do better." He had tears in his eyes. "It was the whiskey, I think. It must have been. I've never struck a woman before, not ever."

"And the children?"

He shook his head. "*Nein.* I didn't do anything to harm the boy, did I, Andy?" Andy shook his head. "See. It will be better now. There were too many people around; too much going on. We just need to be here alone. It will be all right now." He patted my hand and I flinched. He stood then. "You get up now, Emma. See what I've done for you." He sounded cheery again as though all was forgotten. He helped me stand. The room spun, eventually settled. "I've made you a drawing," he said, nearly gleeful now. "Of us and all the children. You can make a wood frame for it when you feel up to it. Make those curlicues that Keil commented on. We'll be a good team. I draw; you frame. Look at it."

He pushed the paper into my hands. He'd made cartoonlike characters of us, like the drawings that accompanied little stories on the editorial pages of our German newspapers. He'd captured our essence as he saw us with slight exaggerations of a facial feature or behavior. He'd placed us outside with trees looming behind us and storm clouds shadowing. Kate stooped at the outside edge staring under a salal-berry bush. Next to her stood Andy with a lead rope on Opal. He petted it. Christian was drawn clinging to my skirts on the far side of me. Jack sketched me towering over him as he knelt in front, staring out into the wilderness, the rest of us a kind of semicircle around him. He put grotesque smiles on all our faces. He'd drawn a dark fence around us. While he looked vulnerable kneeling, he also blocked the fence opening. We'd have to clamber over him to get out.

It was a hideous drawing, more accurate than I wished. I had to change that picture.

———

After the New Year, we had a hard freeze. This had never happened in Willapa before, or so Sam Woodard reported at a Sunday gathering we attended late in January. Jack insisted we all go to both the New Year's gathering at the stockade and this late January event. I told him how tired I was and he said we could spend the night with Barbara then. When I protested, his nostrils flared and his eyes got that white around them and I said, "I'll go. We'll all go." Which we did. I was learning not to resist.

The men discussed how hard the ground had frozen and whether it would stay cold. The men had had to break the ice off the grass in addition to breaking the ice on the water troughs for the cows and mules to drink. Everything took much longer to do in the freeze, all the chores, and they commented on that. But it hadn't rained as much, and that was a gift, I thought.

I kept what was happening in our household to myself, not that the women questioned, but they might have seen the quick flinching of my children when someone reached out to hand them a cookie or might have wondered at the hollowness of my face. They looked the other way. But then I'd have denied any problems even if they'd asked. I had my stories: I wouldn't complain, not even explain.

We returned home, burned more wood, and still the house felt constantly drafty and cold. We walked as though on ice around the house. February's rains lasted the entire month with few sunbreaks. That's when Jack's temper roused itself again, and I wondered if his disposition might be mixed up with the weather. When it was cold but dry, he was happier; when it rained he found fault. That didn't explain his behavior in dry September, though. He was just an unpredictable man. He'd always been and I thought I could contain it. But I was so much weaker than I'd realized.

In March, my growing size repelled Jack; he blamed me for "eating so much that even affection between a husband and wife was impaired." I still had morning sickness and hardly ate a thing. I tried to explain about pregnancy, but he'd storm out of the cabin and be gone for hours. I savored the time without him, yet his absences scraped at my heart, knowing his return would bring pain of uncertainty.

He made lists of our errors. My list was the longest. My failure to patch up a pair of his pants adequately. My inability to know that he wouldn't want fish for dinner. That I spoiled the children, he said, turning my sons into rabbits scared of their shadows, feeding Kate into a "fat little pig."

I had never seen him hurt the children, physically, the way he'd struck me. And while he did aggress me again that month, it was in the smokehouse. He bent my fingers back getting me to admit fault for changing my mind about what we'd be eating without first getting his permission. He locked the smokehouse door, seeming to make sure the children didn't see him. Perhaps he knew that if the children witnessed his violence against me again, or if they ever tried to intervene and were hurt themselves, that then I would take a different tack through this storm. I would listen to that song: *You, you, you must go.* I wondered if I could.

I'd written to my parents, telling them of Jack's striking me and his sporadic behaviors that frightened us. I'd given the letter to Mary to mail. She'd taken it from my shaking hands, said nothing except she'd send it off. She wouldn't look me in the eye. I urged my parents to please come, that with them here, Jack would remain good, I felt sure of it. His bravado would be heightened and tempered by an audience, but he'd use words instead of fists to hurt us, and words we could endure if they were with us.

I heard nothing from them.

Jack made the trek to the Woodards' to pick up any mail, and he always returned empty-handed. I told myself they were on their way; I just didn't know it yet. It was a thread I hung on to.

The persistent cold weather went all the way to the coast, or so Karl Ruge said when he brought me a new almanac. He hadn't come by much since Jack and I married, and I missed his visits to my farm—our farm. My face had healed of any bruises that day and while my fingers swelled, I didn't think any were broken. There'd been no recent altercations with Jack, so I wasn't sure why Karl asked me if I was all right.

"I'm fine," I lied. His eyes wore concern. I picked up a piece of wood I carved, settled it against my burgeoning girth.

"We don't see you so much, so I just wonder." His wording made me think of Catherine and I smiled. "You smile," he said. "I guess I shouldn't worry. You're a newlywed still, *ja?*"

"I was smiling thinking about my sister. She's always 'wondering' about things. I haven't heard from her or Papa since well before I married Jack. I wonder how Lou is doing. She had a fall. But they don't write. So..." I shrugged. "Tell me what you hear about weather on the coast."

"There was a very high tide in February," he said. "Along with the freeze, the oyster beds... Well, ice formed over the oysters at low tide. Then the rising tide picked them up like sand dollars and floated them on to another's beds. Some even floated out to sea. Joe picked a good time to get us out of the business, by golly." *Another dream, gone. Did I ever think I might carry on the oystering on my own?* The sound of my wood scraping filled the silence. "You don't look well, Emma. Your eyes. That's why I ask."

"Just a woman's lot," I said as cheerily as I could. I wasn't about to discuss this troubling pregnancy with Karl nor mention the uncertainties of living with Jack. I worked with my drawknife, making another shelf to put in the loft, so the children would have a special place for their treasures of rocks and shells and pretty flowers pressed into books. I had yet to make a frame for Jack's drawing. He'd added that to my list of sins, tacked the drawing up along with several others that marred the back of the cabin. My finger stuck out at an odd angle. I stopped, folded my hands together as in prayer, resting them on my stomach. I felt the baby kick. "Do you have news of Missouri?"

"The war begins," he said. "Already Alabama and Georgia and Louisiana have joined those who remove themselves from the Union. They elected Jefferson Davis and Alexander Stephens as their president and vice president. Two presidents we have now! This is not good. There can be only one leader in a country." He took a draw on his long clay pipe. "Poor Lincoln. He has a bigger problem keeping people together than Wilhelm does, by golly."

"Maybe the people from Bethel will come out now. Maybe they'll hurry here to avoid fighting. Has Missouri seceded?"

"No. I hope you're right, Emma. It grieves me to see Wilhelm so tired in his efforts. They still have no church there, no school, either."

"I wonder what keeps you here instead of with your old friends at Aurora Mills," I said. He dropped his eyes. I thought the color on his neck and ears darkened.

"John has need of me here. School starts next month," he said. "I'll look forward to seeing Andy. Pretty soon your Christian will be old enough to come too, *ja?*"

"Kate's old enough now," I said.

"*Ja,* that's right." He hesitated, then said, "Well, we'll look for her then, too."

It would get her away from Jack's scowling. It was the first happy thought I'd had in weeks.

The days turned into themselves, and before I realized it, I was about to turn twenty-eight years old on the twenty-sixth of March. I had three beautiful children who needed me to help them remember that their father was a good, good man. I had another child on the way and a husband who was dangerous to me but appeared quite normal to those around us. He could make people laugh, and did; the contrasts frightened me all the more.

I rolled away from him the morning before my birthday and pulled my shawl on over my shoulders and lifted my belly from my thighs. This boy was larger than any of my other children. At least I assumed it was a he, since I'd gained such weight. I prepared a breakfast, then packed pancakes spread with thick butter and put several slices of smoked ham into a small bag. I thought of the chapter in the book of John where the disciples are fishing and see a fire on the shore, and then a man, who turns out to be Jesus, asks them to "come and dine." How I wished I could begin my day that way, being served and filled up. What a birthday that would be!

Jack expected food ready for him to lift up as he headed for the mill. Things were picking up there, and Jack showed surprising skill at repairing things, supporting his claim at "blacksmithing some" before coming west. I tried complimenting him on his abilities. He'd scoff, saying I couldn't manipulate him so easily.

The men began their spring routines that took them out of their cabins during the day, to the fields or the mill or the forests and away from the skirts and apron strings of their wives and *Kinder*. It was spring. I'd have the day without Jack.

I felt more hopeful in spring.

Jack slept as I waddled toward the half barn to milk the cows. I did the milking again, finding it a soothing thing to do each day. Routine had its way of bringing comfort. The smell of the warm milk made me ill, but I'd relieve my stomach and then return to finish the work, the cows looking bored with me as I pulled on their tails to help myself ease onto the stool again. I buried my head in the warmth of their udders, using their tails again to stand when I finished.

An eerie silence greeted me outside. The cows bellowed for no reason that I could see. I opened the gate so they could graze among the bushes and trees, but instead they ran together around the yard area, twisting their necks and tails up into the wind that had picked up. Swirls of leaves and needles blew about, driven from the east, which was unusual. There'd been no rain that morning yet, and now the sky had an odd greenish cast to it. Through the hole between the trees, I watched as the sky changed color and within seconds appeared black as charcoal. The goat bleated with her mournful cry. She shook her head, her little beard flapping as though she spoke to the wind. "I'll be back to milk you," I said, carrying the bucket to the house. That's when I felt the wind blast against me, pushing me forward as I reached the cabin.

"The wind's up," I told Jack as I came in, slamming the door behind me, which took more effort than it should have. "Listen to it."

We felt the house shake then with the violence. Through the window, I could see that trees leaned closer to the ground than I'd ever seen them, white oak leaves skittering through the air. Thunder rolled across us and then a lightening strike flashed and split Andy's cedar before our eyes.

"Andy. Kate. Christian. Get down here, now," I shouted. In Missouri, such a storm would drive us to the root cellar, but there was none here, nothing deep in the earth to offer protection. I just wanted them all close to me, huddled together. Christian cried and Jack told him to shut up, but I wanted to howl myself. My ears hurt. I held Christian and Kate, watched Andy who stood near the window staring at the storming rage outside.

"We-we be all right, Mama?" Christian asked.

"We will," I told him, sounding as confident as I could. I hoped the goat had taken shelter in the half barn, as the wind would just skitter her aloft.

Jack glowered. I screamed when I heard a loud crack, then saw a cascade of branches fall beside the house, their leaves darkening the window.

"What's wrong with you?" Jack said. "It's only a storm!" He stood up then and pulled open the door and plunged himself into the tempest. The rain and wind thundered through the open doorway sounding like a herd of horses.

"Jack! Get back here!"

But he stood against the elements, drenched within seconds, his arms outstretched, his head back, taking in the downpour, his hair whipping. He stumbled back, catching himself as leaves and boughs and branches brushed past him.

"Jack!" I left the children and made my way to the door. *Do I close it and let him stay out there as he wants, let what happens, happen to him? Or do I go out after him and try to bring him in?* I anchored myself to the door frame, my feet spread to the doorjambs. I reached my hand out. "Jack! Please! Come back in before you get hurt." I didn't dare let go of my hold, for the wind would surely knock me over. I called several more times, but he was a pugilist against the storm. There was nothing I could do to change his mind. I pulled myself back through the door. Andy helped me pull it shut.

"You took a bath with your clothes on, Mama," Kate said. I stood drenched before them.

"Ja," I said. "And Jack's still taking his." I couldn't imagine what mood he'd be in when he came inside...if he came inside.

The storm subsided after a time into a drizzle, minus the blustering winds. A sunbreak followed behind. Jack entered as though he'd done nothing strange in standing out in a raging torrent. He looked almost...rested, the wild gaze gone from his eyes. He offered no explanation for not coming in when I called him, no comfort to the children. Such a contrast to Christian's tendering in a storm.

"Should be the last blow of the season," Jack said. He wiped his hand across his face, shook it of the rain. "School starts in April, right, Andy boy?" My son nodded.

"Kate gets to go too," Andy said. Kate smiled, nodding up and down. They were both quite recovered from the fear of the storm, already looking for the rainbow that followed.

"Something I decided out there in that little shower. Kate'll be needed when the baby comes. Just you," Jack said, pointing his finger at Andy. "Like before. I'll take you to school and leave you there at the Giesys. They'll like that."

"Mama?" Andy asked.

"Your mama agrees with me. She thinks that's just fine, don't you, Mama?" Water dripped off of his forehead. A puddle formed at his feet. *"Ja?"*

Is he crazy or just making me so?

"We'll talk about it later," I said. "I need to get some dry clothes on. You do too, Jack."

"No talking," he said. He grabbed my hand and pushed the wrist back. I saw Andy from the corner of my eye. His look…reflected Jack's, all dark and dangerous.

"I'll change and then head on over to the mill to see how it fared." Jack released my wrist. Behind the curtain, Jack stripped off the wet clothes, dressed, and left, grabbing the food sack as he walked out the door. His leaving was my sunbreak.

"I won't go without Kate and I won't stay there," Andy said. "You need me here."

"I want to go to school too. You said I could go, Mama."

"I'll talk to Jack. Whatever is decided will be the best for you. And I'll be fine."

"He doesn't listen to you. To nobody," Andy said. He kicked at the rocking chair, making it move without anyone in it.

"You don't have to worry. I—"

"I won't stay at *Oma's*," he screamed. "I won't." He opened and closed his fists at his side. It was a movement of his father's at his most frustrated. "I have to take care of you."

I pulled him into my arms. "And sometimes that means doing things you can't imagine can be helpful but in the end turn out to be. You have to trust me, Andy. It's best if we do what Jack says. Best for all of us. You have to stay at your *Oma's* house." Kate started to protest. "No, Kate," I said. "You can't go to school just now. You," I swallowed, pointed at Andy, "must go."

"You-you-you must go, Andy," Christian said. I turned to my youngest son. Had I said those words out loud? Had he heard them before? No.

"I wish Papa was here." Andy sobbed the words into my shoulder.

"*Ja,* I wish it too." I stroked his back, swallowed my own tears. "But it is not to be. He didn't wish to leave us, but he did and so we must be wise, *ja?* We must make good decisions. Mama hasn't always done that, has she? *Ja,* well, she will do better."

Jack would return, but in what mood, who could say? He'd taken another step up that ladder of intensity by hurting me in front of the children. He was growing less cautious. He'd hurt the children next.

"Will you ask God to take care of us, Mama?" Kate asked.

I brushed the curls from her face. "I'll ask," I said. "Perhaps I'll even be heard."

28

Louisa

Even back in Bethel my husband sang her praises, as it was Helena who gave up the love of a good man because he would not join the colony. Wilhelm showed her as an example to the young people, how even without marriage one can be in service to the Lord. Maybe even be more in service without the distraction of a family. I heard him say that once, "without the distraction of a family." I don't think he meant it quite the way it sounds.

I would not ever say this to my husband, but sometimes I wondered about Helena's love affair with that bridge builder. Where had they ever met? Helena never left the colony and the bridge builder had no cause to purchase items from our colony store. His father built a famous bridge in Brooklyn and one wonders how Helena would have encountered such worldly folk. I should not judge.

Once I heard Emma Wagner—she wasn't married yet—say something of that sort too, that perhaps Helena exaggerated her sacrifice; or maybe that Helena was the rejected one and her story was a way of saving face. That Emma. So here we are, she and I thinking the same thing, again.

I was pleased to see how at home Emma made us feel on our journey north. Even Helena found no fault except in Emma's refusal to attend the memorial of Helena's father. But goodness, three little children, another on the way, a husband who was not the funny Jack that I remembered, rather one prone to melancholy and caprice—no wonder she wished a day at home. A wife and mother could understand Emma's wish even if Helena couldn't. She's much too quick to judge, that Helena. *Ach*, but so am I at times, so am I.

My husband raves about Helena's organizing the children and how she spoke to Karl Ruge, urging him to come to Aurora to teach them here. My husband thanked her profusely for her effort. I talked with Brother Karl too, but something holds him there in Willapa. Maybe he likes making his own choices without need to negotiate with my Wilhelm. Lord knows I'd like such an escape at times. To have to justify to my husband's satisfaction each thing I think, even if it's what we should have for dinner, is a tiring task. Warranted of course, as my Wilhelm needs much tending so he can give back to others. Even the slightest inconveniences that I can remedy, I wish to. Still, can there really be great fault between serving wilted lettuce with a vinegar dressing and one made with eggs and oil instead? Can it really matter whether the spoon-fork is lined up perfectly with the plate tin before one begins to eat? Does the food taste any less grand if the serving utensil sits a fingernail's width off from where he thinks it should? And where is it written that his is the card that trumps all others? *Ach*, I use gambling terms to describe my husband's wisdom. There is probably a sin there, and if my husband heard me say such things, he'd tell me to go deep to find it. I have no time. Maybe Helena does. A saint would, I suppose. There is still too much to do here every day and each day finds yet more undone. Surely God will understand if I fail to add one more trespass to my daily list.

Ah, I complain, I judge. I must not. Good things have happened in the midst of trials here. Helena has assumed the task of table preparation at our big house, and now the serving will be perfection. I can concentrate on gardening and helping with his herbs, being with my children, dying wool, writing letters back to Bethel urging others to come west. In any spare time, I can listen to the band rehearse while practicing my *Fraktur*. Is life so difficult that I should complain or use words such as *escape*? *Nein*. Life is good and could only be better if those from Bethel and Willapa would stop their stubborn ways and join us as intended all those years before. Perhaps we're closer to that end now that we've visited Willapa again. Maybe Emma and Big Jack will come. Maybe Barbara Giesy in her widowed state. After all, there's been a change for good: Helena came west, an act my husband says marks the start of the next migration. My husband is so pleased. I must be too. I'm sure that Helena is.

29

Emma

A Reason to Run Off

The unusual April frost along the Willapa felt fitting for the coldness of my life. I was bedridden at the middle of the month and most of May, grateful that Kate hadn't gone off to school with Andy. She was a fine helper for me and somehow knew how to scuttle out of Jack's way when he returned from the mill in a foul mood or when he sauntered in from the half barn whistling a tune. Kate reacted to him either way with caution, her eyes on me to see how to proceed. I hated that she wouldn't remember the love of her father, the safety and reliability that marked a good man. Instead she'd have this ebb and flow of an erratic stepfather to mark her memory. Maybe she'd never marry because of it, and who could blame her? Was that why some women chose the unmarried life? I'd never considered that before.

I knew my being in bed when he arrived home annoyed Jack, but I could not rise except to reach the slop jar. "Chamber pot" he called it, as though changing a name could make the thing different. The baby shifted and kicked and moved well, but it was the swelling I couldn't stand, literally, and so I was abed. My body bloated, my ankles, my fingers. My face puffed and my eyes sometimes stuck together, especially in the morning. I remembered my mother speaking of these things happening to pregnant women, and that bed rest was all that could be done except for drinking chamomile tea and steaming my face with the bouquet of herbs. Kate secured both for me until I ran out of tea and Jack refused to request more. He said I should just drink coffee like everyone else.

On weekends, Andy helped with the laundry and stayed out of Jack's way. During the week, Kate followed my directions carefully to make sure she served the bacon crisp as Jack insisted, the coffee sweet, and the whipped cream stiff enough to support a cinnamon stick. Christian, with his stutter ever increasing, huddled close to me whenever Big Jack stomped around.

I counted the days until the end of June when the baby was due and my life would return to some semblance of normalcy. *Ach!* My life had never been normal, not since I'd headed west with Christian. And I didn't want to return to the norm that was Jack. But I did need to stand, to hold my child, make a new plan and pray I had the power to complete it.

On the twenty-third of June, the baby made motions as though to arrive. Andy worked outside with Jack, cutting branches off the big cedar that had fallen in the March storm. At the first sharp pain in my back, I sent Kate out to tell Jack to send for Mary. I heard her shout as she headed out the door, "Andy, Mama's having that baby. She says to go get Aunt Mary." *Tell Jack,* I thought, but it was too late.

Andy ran inside. Jack followed him. "You women. You can wait until we're done here."

"I'll go," Andy said.

"You're always looking for a reason to run off. You stay and help."

"This isn't exactly running off, Jack," I said. A pain rose up and through me and I panted until it eased. "It might be sooner than you think. Please, just go get Mary."

"Please. Just go get Mary," Jack mocked.

I fell back onto the bed and closed my eyes. "Not now, Jack."

"*Ach,*" he said. "I'll go then. Get this over with."

"Go finish up your work, Andy," I said. "Kate's here. Mary will be soon."

My oldest son moved at a snail's pace toward the door.

"Get out there!" Jack shouted at him. Andy slipped past him so the foot Jack kicked at him struck only air.

I felt the sweat on my brow, the rising of another pain. I pulled myself up onto my elbows. "Don't you hurt my son!"

Jack cursed me then, used words I've never heard a man say to any human being, only to mules or cows or hogs that didn't do what they wished. Kate's eyes were big as eggs and she put her hands to her ears. Jack hit the back of her head with his palm as she sucked her head into her narrow shoulders, moving out of his way as he pushed on by. Christian began to cry now next to me, and I shushed him, hoping to defend what I could.

Jack stomped outside. The goat bleated as she always did at a human's presence whether friend or foe. I heard him shout something to Andy that I couldn't understand. I hoped Andy didn't talk back. Jack's retort came from the direction of the trail to Mary's. Mary would come back with him and Jack would behave with her here. He'd show his cheerful side, the side that Mary expected. Sarah might believe me if I told her about my captivity, but I couldn't imagine any one of the Giesys giving any credit to my charges.

I was grateful when Mary arrived. We spent a long evening together as I panted and squeezed her hand to press against the pain. I heard myself saying as a rhythm to the arch, "You, you, you, you, you," but I silenced the end of it, kept "must go" to myself.

In the early hours while the children slept, I felt as though my insides tore in two. The warmth of my own blood seared like salt rubbed into an open wound. My second daughter arrived in the world.

"She's a big baby," Mary said. "She's torn you. I'll have to sew. It'll be painful."

"Let me see her first."

Mary laid her on my stomach while she tended to the cord. I'd decided to call her Louisa for our Prussian queen, but mostly for my sister. She could have been Kate's twin, the two looked so alike. She was the largest of all my children, and yet she weighed not more than eight pounds. Her heart-shaped face looked wrinkled and stressed from all the pushing and shoving, but she had blue eyes and a fluff of tiny dark curls covered her head like a cap. She didn't look a thing like Jack.

Mary's stitching hurt worse than the delivery, if that was possible. She used the needle from my chatelaine, moved it through a hot flame to sanitize it and then began to sew with a heavy thread. My baby's size and my great weight gain and lack of movement and that puffiness must all have added to the complications.

"Louisa?" Jack said when I introduced him later to his daughter. "No, we're not naming her for your sister. Didn't you say she fell and is strange now? Why would you name a child after someone not whole? No."

His words stung. My sister was whole and so was this child. "After Louisa Keil, then. Think of her name as honoring *Herr* Keil," I said, believing that might move him.

"*Nein.* If it has to be a girl rather than a boy you bear me, then I pick a solid name, a strong one. I pick Ida," he said. "Ida is what we'll call her. After my mother."

It was the first mention of Jack's real family he'd ever made.

Ida did have a good suck, and praises be I had milk to feed her. It seemed a wonder that after three children my fourth could take nourishment from me, a special though ironic gift. All the other children arrived as easy as otters slide the riverbanks but had been challenging to keep alive after that. Ida's pregnancy and delivery carried memories of complications, but in her taking her own breath, she gained weight and was a healthy child who made few demands. And I could fill her up. The smallest of blessings.

Jack paid little attention to Ida, wrinkled his nose at the smell of her soiled napkins. He couldn't use her so he ignored her, I thought.

In early July I told Jack I thought I should see a doctor. I knew from my own scent that I had a serious infection, and the pain grew worse. "Can you go get him for me, or will you help take us all there?" I dreaded riding a mule feeling as I did, but I didn't know if he'd believe me that I needed a doctor. "Maybe you could put me in the cart. I'm not sure I can ride."

"You want my help and then you want to tell me how to give it? You...woman," he said with such disgust in his voice that tears pooled in my eyes. My emotions were like a pot left boiling then cooled, then boiling again as though someone stoked the fire beneath it.

"You just want an excuse to get someone else to come here."

"I think the stitches are infected."

"Use your healing herbs, Emma Giesy. I've no time to run off and bring someone back for you for sympathy."

"Jack. I need someone. Send Andy, then."

"Stop being a burden on me, you and your children."

"Jack—"

"Will these demands never end?" He pressed his head between his hands. "These...these complaints that are in your head?"

"I'll go, Mama," Andy said. He ducked past Jack and headed toward the door, but Jack grabbed him and held him up with his arm. Jack was tall and strong and he lifted my son. While he dangled there, Jack struck him with his fist. My son yelped.

"You will do as you're told," he raged, then threw Andy against the door. I rose, shouted. He turned on me. "I'll break your cussed neck," he said. "Enough of this lying in bed." He began a tirade of cursing. Andy picked himself up and before Jack could reach him, my son shot through the door and ran toward the road.

"See what you've done?" Jack said as he headed out after Andy. "You did this!"

I prayed now.

I prayed that my son would know the little back ways to take through the trees, to be a silent as a mouse as he raced for help. I prayed that Jack would tire and return, be disgusted though his rage simmered. *Why does this have to be so hard?* I leaned back onto the bed. I was a little coin lost in the corner of a kitchen hearth, hoping to be picked up by someone safe and kind and loving. I'd once wanted to be the shiniest coin in the realm. Now, I just wanted to be found.

———

Jack returned, had not chased after my son. He ate, then left, and did not come back to the bed that night. This wasn't the first time he'd spent nights away. I was never sure where he went; I didn't care. The doctor arrived the next day. Andy was not with him. The doctor confirmed my suspicions and gave me packs to place across the stitches to try to pull out the infection.

"The stitching was well done," he said. "But there was infection there. It has gone…inside, *Frau* Giesy. It may affect your being able to conceive again if we aren't successful in treating it."

"I just want to be well enough to look after the four I have," I said.

"You have a good son there in Andy."

"He didn't come back with you."

The doctor didn't look at me, kept working. "He said he wanted to visit his grandmother. Fine lad. Very thoughtful."

And wise, I thought. *Very wise.*

Jack complained the following week about Andy's not being there to do his chores. I didn't try to defend my son, finding that my words only angered Jack more.

Later, I felt well enough to be up churning the milk for the first time in months. The day was hot and I waited until the evening to do it. I sat. Standing still caused pain. Ida slept and Jack stayed away late, a relief for us all. I finished the churning, then went to the half barn to bring in the chickens and check on Opal. I petted her back, ran her silky ears between my fingers as she nudged at my cane. I took short steps and breathed deeply. Kate had helped milk the cows and now played with her doll, convincing her younger brother that he was a dog. They laughed together like normal children. I leaned against the barn wall. If only it could be like this always, the children in peaceful habitations, secure dwelling places. At least Andy was safe. How ironic that I'd married Jack to keep my children with me and now my son's being with his grandmother was the better choice. I walked back into the house.

There sat Andy, Jack's muzzle loader laid across his knees.

My heart pounded. "What are you doing, Andy?"

"I'm waiting for Jack so he won't hurt anyone anymore."

You, you, you must go. You, you, you must go. Seeing my son sit there with a gun in his hands brought the words back. Andy had to go; so did we. If we didn't, Andy would do something that would grieve him for a lifetime. If Jack even knew he considered it, he'd harm the boy. I knew that too. Violence begat violence. I couldn't stay here any longer. I had to take my children and get out. I just didn't know how I'd do it.

"Andy, go back to your *Oma* and your uncle Martin, and stay there until I come to get you, all right?"

He shook his head. "I have to take care of you. He hurts people and he hurts you, and a papa isn't supposed to do that."

"I know. But you can't fix things by hurting Jack back. That isn't the way to do this. Your father would never want you to do it that way."

"Papa would want me to take care of you."

"And you have done such a fine job of it. You will, if you go now, before Jack comes home. Go stay with Martin."

"You won't come. It'll be like that other time."

"That's not true. I will come. See, I'm up using a cane now. Andy, give me Jack's gun. Please. You have to listen to me."

I'd let my son have too much say in our lives, depended on him too much, and now when I needed him to just be a child and listen, he resisted. "I'm still your mama, remember?"

He shook his head. "You're sick still."

Please, please, please. "I'm better. I've churned the milk and fed the chickens. Andy." I grabbed for the gun and had it in my hands before he could hold back. I was still stronger than he was despite my ailing. "Now go. You'll be safe at *Oma*'s. That's what matters. Please." He held his fists at his side, opening and closing them. I leaned into him then and hugged him to me. "You have to go," I whispered. "I'd die if Jack hurt you; you mean so much to me. It doesn't seem right, I know, but doing this, leaving, will be the greatest gift you can give right now. I'll make plans. I'll find a way. But first, you have to be safe."

I felt his shoulders sag, and then he straightened. "Should I take Christian with me?"

I hadn't thought of that. "*Ja,*" I said. "That would be *gut.* Both of you, safe there." Then it would be easier for me to take Kate and Ida away from here while Jack was gone. I could collect the boys and then sail down the Willapa to the coast. Or maybe I could pick them up and go to Olympia or Steilacoom. And what then? I couldn't even stand for longer than ten minutes.

I started to cry but swallowed the tears. "Take Christian. I'll say that Karl came by and took him to visit you at his grandparents. Jack won't question that. You go. Christian," I called him in from outside. He ran with glee to Andy. "You boys be very quiet now. Andy is taking you to visit *Oma,* but you must stay out of Jack's way. He'll be coming back soon and you'll want to miss him on the trail. So you have to be quiet and very careful. It's a game," I told Christian. "No cheating. Just listen to your brother."

"Wh-what do I take?"

"Nothing," I said. "You both go. Now."

"Mama?" Kate asked. "Can I—"

"No." I hated that I put her at risk because she was a girl. "I'll need your help with Ida, and Jack would question why I let you go with Karl. We'll go there later."

My heart pounded as I put Jack's gun back on the pegs, then threw food into a bag for the boys. Andy took the bag over his shoulder, then reached for Christian's hand. Andy would be eight in October; Christian had just turned three. I hugged them both, then said, "Hurry. Stay away from Mary and Boshie's house, don't let them see you. Go straight to *Oma's*. Promise me." Andy nodded and I stifled a sob as I watched them walk bent over like little old men who'd already seen more than they should have.

My mind began to spill with possibilities. I'd wait until tomorrow, after Jack had left for the mill. Then I'd pack what we needed for the baby and forget the rest. I scanned the room. Leave everything here. And go…I still didn't know where, only that we had to leave this place and never return.

Sarah and Sam would take us in, but then Jack would direct his wrath at them, maybe Edwin. They might loan me some cash, though, enough for the ship's fare to…someplace. Maybe San Francisco, where we could get lost in the crowds. Maybe I could head back to Bethel, face my parents and beg their forgiveness. But I was so weak. Such long journeys would be too much, especially with four children in tow. Would it be better to wait for a month or so, until I was stronger? My eye caught Jack's gun. I remembered the look in Andy's eyes. He would kill Jack if given a chance. Jack wouldn't let them stay at Barbara's forever. He'd want Andy to work here. How ironic that having my son close to me could be the worst thing for him.

What would Jack expect when he came home to an empty house? That I'd gone to Sarah and Sam's. *So not there.* Maybe he'd think of Steilacoom, because I loved it there. *Not there.* Where do I go? Where, oh, where?

Aurora Mills.

The words stung like sand against my face. I tried to pitch the thought away but I couldn't. Go to Aurora Mills after all Keil had done to my life? I'd be admitting everything I'd done here was a mistake, was somehow wrong. I'd be failing Christian.

But of course I wasn't failing Christian. He wasn't here to fail. And he'd already forgiven Keil for that harsh winter those years past. Before he died he'd come to see Willapa as a part of Aurora Mills, as a part of the colony's growth here in the West, much as I hated that. Christian would be pleased I was heading there; maybe he was even pushing me in that direction, if a husband's spirit could do such a thing. But I couldn't; I just couldn't go there.

My brother wasn't there anymore. My face burned with the thought of having to ask for help. I could not find a way to live within the constraints of that colony; I could not!

But there was only one I could ask for asylum, one who might be strong enough to hold Jack in check. A rush of emotion heated my face. Should I leave Andy and Christian behind? Just for a time. I'd come back for them. I would. But once I was gone, would Jack take them, use them to compel me to return? We'd all have to go. To Portland. To San Francisco. It didn't matter where, just so long as we were far from here.

30

Emma

Attenuated Anguish

Once decided, my heart pounded with firm direction. Feed the baby. Prepare an evening meal. Act normal. Think. It felt good to be acting, to move past just huddling in fear, coughing up responses.

"Where's Christian?" Jack asked as we sat at the supper table. He'd arrived home, completed his usual chores, then come inside. His eyes looked red as though he hadn't slept well. I tried to remember how long he'd stayed up when he awakened in the night; couldn't remember when he'd come back to bed.

"Karl came by and picked him up," I lied. "He was visiting Martin and Barbara and thought we might want to go as well, to see Andy." Jack grunted. "But of course I told him I wasn't up to anything like that. I was sure Barbara would enjoy seeing both her grandsons and I didn't think you'd mind."

"People just come by and decide what to do with my children?" he said.

"I imagine he thought he was doing me a favor, taking a child off my hands with this little one so demanding."

"Her name is Ida. It means 'work and labor,' things children should learn at a young age," Jack said

"Does it?"

"You maybe could use her name."

"Yes, I could. And do." I served Jack his favorite, a cake with cocoa and honey and some of that coconut we occasionally got from the Sandwich Islands. He ate his fill, went outside, returned, dozed in his chair, then stood up with a start. "I'm going to bed. Keep your cleanup quiet."

He never even held his daughter. Instead, he snored while I stood over the hot water then sat at the table cleaning the dishes and watching him sleep. Later, I held Ida to me, feeding her, rocking her softly. Kate slept in the loft. I planned my future and what I'd take with me. Only eight years previous I'd made a similar sorting of what to take from Bethel to this new land.

The chatelaine Christian made me. I'd leave my drawing pencils. No room for those. The pearl necklace my mother sent me, the one I'd had Christian add the smaller Willapa pearl to. I'd pull it from its wrapping in the trunk after Jack left in the morning. Something of Christian's. His medal for marksmanship and my drawing of him. And the letter he'd carried from me. I pulled it from its hiding place and reread it. I'd once promised faithfully to support his work. Had that meant following Keil, or was Christian's real work about living out the Christian tenets of loving God and loving one another? Of late I'd done little of either. I never had reached out to the Shoal-water or Chehalis people in this region, even when they came by to trade their fish for my bread. I hadn't taught my children to trust in God but rather to look to me for all their needs, and then I'd failed them, kindling my own flames and burning away a path of faithfulness. The food I'd fed them had kept them alive but not living. Would going to Aurora Mills change that? Would going there be what Christian had wanted for us all along?

My mind froze with fatigue. I hoped it would thaw by morning.

That night, I lay down beside Jack for the last time. My movements didn't wake him. Hours later, when the moon was full in the window, I felt him rise from the bed while I pretended sleep. He dressed and went out. I hoped he'd come back, keep some little semblance of routine. Let him eat breakfast, get ready for work, leave. If this was one of his wandering-around nights, he might go straight to the mill and I wouldn't know for certain. I imagined how to adapt my plan, how long to wait before leaving if he never returned in the night. Was I "beginning to weave," hoping God would provide, or had I long ago used up God's thread and now weaved on my own?

I dozed, awoke to Jack shouting, then pulling a chair from the table where he sat. I rushed up to fix his meal, lightheaded. "I'll milk the cows for you," I said, preparing cakes for him. "If you want to get an earlier start to the mill."

"You're up to that now, are you?"

"I'll give a try," I said, making my voice light as a butterfly. I hated knowing those cows would be bellowing before evening, but I couldn't possibly take the time to milk them once Jack left. I couldn't use up what strength I had for that.

He grunted. "I'll see you this evening, then," he said, as he picked up the food bag I'd prepared while he ate.

I nodded agreement. What was one more lie?

As soon as he left I woke Kate, helped her dress, fed her, then told her to watch the trail. "If you see Jack coming back for some reason, you come and tell me. Don't wait to say hi to him, just come let me know." She nodded agreement, then headed out.

I'd taken what food Kate and I might need, one change of clothes, and then I looked for the pearls. They'd been wrapped in soft cloth and buried at the bottom of a trunk brought by Christian's parents for us when they came west. I pushed the latch and lifted the lid. They might be valuable enough to sell. Maybe it would buy our passage to…somewhere. Like taking a walk on a dark beach with a lantern to mark the path, I had just enough light for my next step but not yet a vision of where we'd end up. I folded my letter to Christian and put it in my reticule.

I felt a rush now, placing Ida in Christian's old baby board and wrapping her securely. She slept on the table while I went out to saddle Fritz. Another irony: my husband had access to a mule all the time for farming; now I'd use him to slip away. Kate came running when she saw me. "Nothing, Mama. Just the birds and those scamper rats."

"Ground squirrels," I said. "That's good. Now go inside and pick out your favorite toy. Just one. We're going on a trip."

Her eyes brightened. "To see Andy and Christian?"

"In part," I said.

I scanned the house. Only memories remained to be packed.

The act of saddling up took strength. I stopped to catch my breath. The infection continued to need treatment, but if I could stay well for the next few days, that was all I needed. Maybe we should just head east, follow the Cowlitz, leave the way Louisa and Keil had come and gone. But no, that would mean backtracking with the boys, and we might run into Jack coming home.

I returned to the house, fed Ida, who was crying, then put the baby board on my back and grabbed the food sack, which I placed over Fritz's neck. His tail flicked at flies. Kate carried her favorite soft doll. The cows bellowed and Opal bleated. "Sorry girls," I said, setting the cows and Opal loose. I hugged the goat, inhaled her earthy smell. "Good-bye." She bleated. At least they could graze. I hoped she wouldn't follow us. Then I grabbed Kate, lifted her up, and led the mule to a stump so I could mount. I felt a warm trickle on the inside of my thigh. *Blood.* It would just have to be. I couldn't stop to poultice it.

The mule trotted north along the trail. I looked back once, saw the goat trailing us. I turned the mule around. "Tie Opal back up," I told Kate. "Poor thing," I said. I couldn't afford the attention her presence would bring us.

When I looked back the second time, I saw only what Christian and I had done there together: the cabin, the half barn, the garden, that section of frivolous flowers. We'd made a life believing we followed God's plan. I turned away. I didn't know what would happen next and could only see a few hours in front of me, a small light in the dark, unveiling just what I needed next and no more. I'd have to trust God for the rest.

We approached Mary's house, Kate humming to make this a happy outing. Karl sat on the porch smoking his pipe. I waved but didn't stop the mule from its fast-paced walk.

"*Frau* Giesy," he stood, shouted to us. "Where are you off to this fine morning?"

"I thought I'd visit the children," I yelled back. "Have a good day."

"They're both at the Giesys then?" I waved and nodded. We kept riding. "Well, stop for some tea then. You've plenty of time."

"*Nein.* We need to be back before Jack gets home."

"*Ja,* by golly. You have a nice trip then," he called out. "Tell Henry and Martin hello for me."

"I will," I sang back over my shoulder. I held my arms to my stomach. My body ached all over.

We crossed Mill Creek. Jack worked upstream. There'd be sympathy galore for him once I was gone. Everyone would remind him of my willful ways and how difficult a wife I was and how fortunate he was to be rid of me. I could imagine how I'd add to the conversations at the stockade after I was gone. The mule plodded across the creek. I turned around now and then to see if anyone followed us. No one did. And I began to think I might be able to do this, I just might.

The Willapa ford came next. No need for the rowboat today. The mule splashed us across. Kate giggled at the wet splatter on her legs. On the far bank I slid down so I could nurse a hungry babe. "You stay close by, Kate," I said. I staked the mule so that it could rip at grass while I unwound Ida from her board. "Shh, *Liebchen,*" I said. She was my sweetheart now. I sang softly to her, felt the breeze against my breast. *The last time I'll see these trees,* I thought. I recorded last times, again.

When she was sated, I put Ida back in her board, then tried to stand. I felt dizzy, my knees as weak as *Spätzel.* I needed to eat. "Kate," I said. "Come help Mama walk to the mule." I looked around. "Kate?" Where had she gone? "Kate!"

"Here I am, Mama," she stepped out of the willows.

"Don't get out of my sight. Mama worries. She needs to see you all the time."

Kate's lower lip pooched out, but she came to me, helped steady me while I went to the mule. I opened the sack and gave Kate a biscuit and jerky, chewed a pancake myself. Kate and I drank from the canteen, then put the cork back. I lifted Ida. We were barely three miles from home and already I felt exhausted.

That's when I heard the sound.

"Hush, Kate. Someone's coming."

"Papa Jack?" Her voice quivered.

"I hope not."

There was no sense hiding. If it was Jack, I'd do my best to defend my story: we had chosen the day to visit. He'd take us back home. I'd try another day. Part of me almost wished it would happen that way, I was so tired. But I remembered seeing Andy's eyes as he held Jack's muzzle loader across his bony knees, and I knew there was no turning back even if it was Jack behind us on the trail.

It wasn't Jack, but Karl, who approached fast for an older man. "Karl," I said. I heard relief in my voice. "Did we drop something when we passed by?"

"No, by golly. I decide to take a visit to Martin's myself. You don't mind if I walk with you?"

"Not at all," I said. He'd slow us down but maybe his presence would give me cover if Jack appeared.

"Do you have business with Martin?" I asked Karl as we walked. We kept his slower pace. I tried not to let my fingers fidget.

"Maybe I'll see how the school is readied for the term. Talk to Martin about the latest news and whatnot." He walked in silence for a time. Then, "Maybe I'll take a trip out to the sea. Remember when we did that, you and me and Christian?"

"I do," I said.

"*Ja.* A long time ago that was. Christian's gone."

"Such a waste," I said.

"Joe's back in Bethel."

"It was a very long time ago."

We moved to the rhythm of Kate's humming. Inside my own head I heard the refrain of *You, you, you must go,* less driven now that we were on our way, but still like a drumbeat, like a husband's voice, encouraging. Maybe I should listen to that voice even if I wasn't sure of the outcome.

I took a chance. "I wonder if you might like to take the trip again," I said. "With the children and me."

"Oh, *ja,* that would be a good thing sometime."

"I mean…today," I said.

"Oh? Is that your plan then?"

I bristled. "What do you mean, 'my plan'?"

"You're not planning to come back home tonight, Emma Giesy. I knew you told a lie when you said that."

My mouth went dry.

"Why would you say that?"

"You have Fritz carrying a lot of food along for just an afternoon visit," he said. "A big pack for such a little time away from home."

"And if it were true that I wasn't planning to come home this evening—"

"I'd say it would be better if you went south on the Bay and then down the Wallacut. Jack won't think to look for you that way. He knows you don't like the ocean."

Karl knew! He knew about Jack's sporadic behavior. He knew we were in danger. He even knew about some of my demons.

I swallowed. "Will he know where we're headed?"

"*Ja,* to Aurora Mills. It's the only place left for you to go." He hesitated, then added, "But you don't have to go alone."

———

Aurora Mills. Keil. To go there was an admission of my need and failure, a silencing of my song. Yet it was what everyone else thought best for us. My parents were upset that I hadn't gone there with Keil in the first place. Jonathan thought I should have gone there after Christian died. Louisa Keil and Helena, Christian's sister, thought we should all come there to help relieve Keil's burdens. Maybe I had to lean on the wisdom of others in order to move me through my distorted world.

I can't go there.

"If it's so obvious, I should go to San Francisco, then. Or…" I sighed. I could smell the rot from my stitches. Going anywhere distant was a fantasy.

"Your husband recruited me," Karl reminded me. "I came to the colony as a way to be in service, to live my faith. When he went oystering, I promised your husband that whatever you needed would be provided. I didn't expect you to resist good gifts." He smiled. "You don't have to let Wilhelm Keil decide your life for you, Emma, even if you do accept his help. I am led by a faithful God, by golly. Not by Keil."

Was he suggesting that living in the colony didn't mean one must follow all Keil's teachings? I recalled a man in Bethel who'd operated a store in the middle of the town but never joined up.

"About Jack," I told Karl. "He's—"

"He spent long nights up and down at Boshie's. That's why Boshie provided a bed at the mill. He had a place for his drawings there," Karl said. "Strange drawings." He sped up to get in front as the trail narrowed, then walked beside Fritz again. He cleared his throat. "Jack hurts you. I didn't know how to help. Now I do."

"I...I annoy him, the children and I do. I think he struggles with how to live in a full house after staying alone at the mill."

"You're not leaving him because he's annoyed," Karl said.

I looked away. Shame bled through me. "I'm not a good wife, Karl. I am willful and wanting. But Jack...Andy...I have to get my children someplace safe. Jack, well Andy—"

"Aurora Mills. We'll keep you safe there if you let us."

"I have a pearl necklace. I can sell it, buy our way to San Francisco or Olympia."

"And then? With four little children? You will be like a widow, Emma, all over again but in the outside world, where people are not always friendly."

"They aren't always friendly inside this colony, either."

"Surrender, by golly. You are strong enough to accept the help of others, Emma. It does not mean your demise."

Tears of weariness slid down my cheeks. The visions of an artist's studio in Olympia rose before my eyes and faded. Those things would never be if I went to Aurora Mills. But Karl was right. My sons would be safe. I'd be safe. As much as Keil dominated the colonists, he was more like a band's conductor, using his wand to guide and direct but never to strike us. We women worked harder to express our music there, but we could. *We.* Was I still a colonist at heart?

We moved in silence then until reaching Barbara's home. This would be my last time here, too. I slid from the mule and stood for a time, just leaning against the animal, breathing in his scent of sweat. My whole body throbbed. My legs quivered with weakness. Ida made crying noises and I moved to pull her from my back. Karl assisted me. He grinned at the little wizened face that was my daughter. He would have made a fine father.

Andy ran out of the cabin. "You're here, you're here! I was afraid you wouldn't come. Or that Jack hurt you again."

"Shh, now. I'm fine," I said, holding him into my skirts.

"Let me help you," Barbara said. *Had she not heard Andy's words about Jack?* "You shouldn't be riding on a day like this. The boys do well here. There's no need for you to worry over them."

"She's taking us away," Andy said. He fairly sang the words. "We're going far away aren't we, Mama?"

"We may," I said. "I just need to rest now."

"Where are you going?" Barbara asked. "You surely didn't leave anything in Olympia you have to go back for."

I gave her a weak smile, motioned for the steps and sat down on them.

How can I possibly take these children and leave, moving fast enough to not be caught by Jack?

"I'll fix you something to eat," Barbara said.

Food. It solved everything for us Germans. Just feed the worry or problem and it would make it better. I shook my head. "No. We have to be going." I thought of the tides taking us out and wanting to be on a ship that went with it. I'd have to throw myself on the mercy of these people and ask them for money. Money to get away from them. Money to take my children to a place I could only hope was safer than where they were.

"You need to eat," Barbara insisted. *Is she stalling for time?*

"If you want to help, I need to go to Sarah and Sam's. If you'll watch Kate and the boys for a minute more."

She frowned.

Louisa shuffled outside with Christian following at her heels. He ran to me, patted my back. Maybe Louisa could travel with us.

"You'll be back right away?" Barbara asked.

I nodded. Karl frowned, but when I motioned to him, he assisted with my mounting the mule and handing Ida up to me. "I'll introduce her to Sam and Sarah. They haven't met her yet."

"I'll come too, Mama," Andy said.

"I'll be back," I said. "You wait here with Christian and Kate." I ignored my son's scowl as I pressed the reins to the mule's neck.

I rode the short distance to Sarah's and shouted for her. I didn't dare get off the mule for fear that I wouldn't have the strength to get back on. She opened her door to me, her own child on her hip. "Emma! Come in, come in."

I shook my head. "I've come to ask for money. I need money to buy fares to take me and the children away from here. I know I'm always thinking of myself, never was a good friend to you, and now I'm here being needy again."

"You can stay here, with us," she said. "Tell me what's going on."

"It wouldn't work. Jack would be here constantly demanding. I have to go away, far away. Someplace safe." I pulled the pearls from my reticule.

"Oh. Jack. Well, where will you go? Olympia? Portland?"

"Aurora Mills will keep my children safe," I said. I said it as though it was a truth.

"We'll get the fares for you," Sarah said. "It's a gift. I don't want your pearls and neither would Sam. Go back and get the children. The boat will leave before long. If you miss this one, you'll have to wait until morning."

I loved that she asked no more questions, just accepted my need. I headed back realizing she really hadn't met Ida. The sting of loss pricked my eyes. I couldn't afford to pay attention to it now. We were escaping. I'd deal with the difficulties of Keil when I reached him, but Karl was right: Keil needn't map out my life or my faith. I didn't want Jack to illustrate who I was, either. I needed to do that myself.

We were on our way. It was what I sang to myself as I headed the mule back. I sang it until I saw Jack, hands on his hips, a glare in his eyes, standing in the middle of Barbara's yard.

My heart pounded and the mule must have sensed it. Fritz started to dance around, bouncing Ida's board more. She whimpered. Not even a month old and she was being jousted around like a single egg in a basket.

"Well enough to ride, I see." Jack reached for the bridle and held the mule steady. Fritz sidestepped at Jack's abrupt movement.

"Did they not need you at the mill?" I asked as innocently as I could.

"I thought I should check on my sons, see if they were really here. Now I have the surprise of Ida as well."

Andy's eyes peeked from around the cabin's corner. "They're fine. You can go back to your work."

Martin stood beside his mother on the porch, and Karl had taken out his pipe and smoked as he stood on the other side of Jack. Were they my allies or allied against me? Had Karl gone to tell Jack before he caught up with us?

"*Ja,* everyone is well, Jack," Martin offered. "You go back to work and come later. Spend the night here. A little outing for you all. Emma travels to visit the doctor and stopped here. She'll go home with you tomorrow. Nothing more."

His voice soothed like one of his herbs, and I reasoned that he wasn't against me even though his words could be interpreted to express as much. "Come inside now. Mother will prepare food for you and you can go back to work."

Andy stood off to the side, watching. Jack hesitated, then let loose the bridle. He squeezed the calf of my leg with his wide hands. *A warning.* He walked into the house, and Martin looked at me before stepping in behind him. Was it a signal I should go? Stay? Would they keep him inside? Would he really just eat and go back to work? There wasn't time. The boat would leave. I signaled to Andy to come to me. "Go get Kate and Christian," I whispered to him. "Go. Now."

Karl shook his head at me as he saw Andy scramble around the back of the cabin. "It's too dangerous," he said, approaching me. He didn't look at me as he stroked the mule's neck. "You are too weak to start now and Jack is too close. Wait until morning. Come, I'll help you dismount."

"But—"

Jack came out of the house while Karl assisted me. He held a hunk of bread and cheese. "Be here when I get back later," Jack said. He held my gaze and it seemed to me he willed the opposite of his words; he willed me to go, to take my children and leave him before he did something that couldn't be taken back.

"Don't I always do what's best?" I said.

"*Ja,*" Jack said. "You're an obedient woman." With that he mounted his own mule and trotted off.

"Now," I told Karl when Jack was well out of sight.

"You take Ida and Kate and go," Martin said, coming out on the porch. "Leave the boys here."

"No! He'll come back and when I'm not here he'll blame Andy. Or worse, Andy will—"

"I won't let Jack hurt him or let Andy do anything rash. I promise you, Emma," Martin said. "The boys are my nephews. I only want the best for them. And for you. Go now while you can. You go to Aurora Mills. You trust me with your sons. Their presence here will buy you time."

"*Ja,* by golly, time is what you need, to get to safety and make a way for all your children," Karl said. "But help too. I'll go with you, Emma," Karl said.

"But you said to wait until morning."

"Martin's offer is sound. Leave the boys for him to bring later."

Were they all in this to take my sons away?

"We'll tell Jack you've gone for a visit to Aurora Mills," Martin said. "Maybe that you're hoping your parents are there by now. We'll suggest that you'll be back."

"He'll believe this if the boys are here," Barbara added. "He'll know you wouldn't stay away from them for long." She took my hand, the way she had the day she spent with me after Christian died, the day I'd once felt close to her. "That's what I'll tell him."

They would lie for me? Maybe they lie to me.

Would Andy ever forgive my leaving him again? Still, they were right. Jack wouldn't come after us if he saw the boys there. He'd be outraged and angry, but he'd expect my return and might not follow. Especially if he realized that Karl was along. Jack would expect Karl back for the school term. He'd expect me to come back with him.

The big unknown was whether I could trust Martin to do as he said, to bring the boys as soon as he could. He was a kind man, an uncle, the brother of my husband. Family. But he was a Giesy, as Jack was.

I had to trust them all and hope they were the calm in my storm.

"You'll prevent Jack from hurting the boys? And Andy...you'll keep him from, doing anything...foolish? You can't let Jack take them home with him."

"I promise this," Martin said. "Go now."

Andy rounded the corner with Christian in tow. Kate breathed hard, running to catch up. "We're going now, Mama?" It was Andy.

"*Ja.* But only Kate and the baby and me and Karl. Martin will bring you and Christian soon. He's promised."

"You can't go!"

"I have to, Andy." I reached for him. "Jack won't try to follow us if you're still here. He'll think I'll be back. Please. You can help by staying here with Christian and being quiet about Martin bringing you to Aurora Mills. Which he will."

Andy jerked from me. He stepped back, tears pooling and running down his hot face. He ran from me then, and while I wanted to pursue him, let him know he was not lost, I couldn't. The tide would not wait. Leaving now was our best chance.

"Comfort him, Martin," I said. Martin took Christian's hand. My youngest son twisted to see where Andy ran, turned back to stare at me. "I'll see you soon," I said. "Be good for *Oma* and Uncle Martin." Christian nodded. "When?" I asked Martin. "When will you bring them?"

"When the timing is right," he said.

It was as committal as he would get.

31

Emma

An Offer Tendered

I forced Andy's face from my mind. We rushed now. Martin loaned Karl a mule. We fast-trotted to the Woodards' wharf.

"Where are the boys?" Sarah asked as she helped me dismount, steadied me as I leaned against the mule, breathing hard. Kate rode with Karl and she stayed frozen on his mule.

"Martin's promised to bring them later," I said. "Oh, Sarah, pray that I can trust him. Pray that he won't hand them over to Jack." She held me and the gentle warmth of her arms brought the tears. "Pray. Please."

"I will, but your prayers are heard, too, Emma."

I wasn't so sure. I was returning to the colony I'd wanted most to avoid, leaving my sons behind. All I'd ever wanted to do was protect my children. Instead I'd made choices that put them in peril. That wasn't a path that led to answered prayers.

I pulled at my bonnet strings. "Maybe I should have taken my drawings to Olympia. Maybe I should have let the Willapa people take care of me without complaint, been grateful for what I had."

"If you can't accept the goodness your family offers now, how will you ever accept what God has to give? This is the first sketch," Sarah assured me, "of the new drawing you'll make." She held me by the shoulders, staring into my eyes. "What Karl gives, what Martin offers, those will keep you going for now."

She handed me the tickets. "And your help," I said. "Thank you. I'll pay you back, I will." I owed so many so much. I wondered if this was how Christian felt about repaying Keil. Debts mounted up inside the heart and mind. Maybe repaying Keil for our land was Christian's way of wiping the slate clean rather than an admission that he wanted to return to colony life under Keil's rule. Why hadn't I thought of that before?

Ida stirred in her board and I lifted her from the mule.

"We need to go, by golly," Karl said. He'd lifted Kate, dismounted, then taken the satchel from my mule's neck. All our earthly goods. Karl had brought nothing with him save the clothes on his back. But then, he trusted that he'd get whatever he needed at the Aurora colony store. Maybe one day I'd trust in that too.

Sarah kissed me good-bye and we walked as fast as I could to the mail boat, stepped up and in. We thanked the tide and the boatman's strong arms for oaring us away.

The sky loomed above us like a blue porcelain plate. No storms in the wind. Seagulls dipped and called. The oars sloshed against the Willapa River, and it seemed we ached away from the shore, hesitating, the craft resisting the boatman's efforts. Maybe hesitation marked all important changes, where the heart sensed that newness waited and took a last inspiring breath. The Willapa Hills watched our escape. I wished we could have gone once more to Christian's grave. I would have picked up the oyster shell painting as a reminder of how I didn't always see things at first glance, that I needed reflection to find true meaning. I wish I could have forgiven the old man whose furniture lured my husband to his death. No, it wasn't the furniture at all. Some things just happened to people. Christian had died caring for others. It was how he lived.

"Help me live to be a better, wiser mother," I whispered with a kiss to Ida's head. It was the only prayer now that mattered.

In Bruceport, Karl purchased fares for our journey south. Another debt owed him. The weather had shifted and dark clouds billowed up out over the sea. It was July and just threatened. I kept my eyes from the site where Christian had died. We took a wooden boat out to a waiting ship. Karl called it a tender, as I had heard before. But he explained, "A vessel attendant on another. It ferries supplies back and forth from ship to shore. The coal car behind an engine on a train is called a tender too."

"It serves something larger than itself," I said.

"*Ja*. It's a *gut* word."

"As you tender us to safety." As Martin tendered his offer to bring me my sons. "It's caring for another when we...when I...feel so fragile." I felt the tears press behind my eyes, blinked them away.

———

They put us in a small storeroom with one cot. I wasn't sure this ship took many passengers, but they'd agreed to take us. The room smelled of fish and lumber, ropes, and the sharp scent of pack rats. As soon as the children were tended, Karl said, "You rest now, Emma. I will watch the babies."

I didn't think I could sleep but I did. I dreamed then of a kitchen hearth with ten women dressed in white, their caps tied tight beneath their chins, all looking alike as they stood, five on each side of a long table piled high with food. Wonderful, steaming German food served on plates painted with mills and flowers and flying birds. Show towels hung on slender racks around the room. I wasn't sure how I could see the designs painted on the plates with so much food piled on top of them, but I did. Colorful, beautiful landscapes blessed by *Strudels* and cakes and sugar cookies. At the head of the table stood a man who looked familiar but I couldn't place him. It wasn't Christian or my father. His eyes looked dark, his eyebrows white and flying. *Where are the other men?* I wondered. The man at the head of the table gave a blessing to the food and bid the women to sit down. Chairs scraped against the wood floors. Their skirts swished and in seconds, they were seated, all except me. I couldn't move my chair! I struggled and pulled and felt my heart beating, working so hard. My children stood off to the side, waiting to come to the table, but I couldn't move the heavy chair or invite them to sit!

Then the man at the head of the table stood and called me by name and motioned me forward. How had he recognized me? We all looked alike in our uniforms of white. My heart pounded. I wiped my hands on my apron. I was being called before this dark-eyed man all because I couldn't get the chair to move!

But then this face, once fearful, turned friendly, his eyes warm molasses, not dark eggs of coal. He offered me his hand, reached out to me. "Come closer, Emma." He sounded welcoming. "You have nothing to fear." I wanted to surrender, to let him lead me forward, but I didn't know if I could trust him. I didn't know who he was. My father? Jack? Keil? "Come closer, Emma. Take this chair." He offered me a wooden chair large enough to hold me and my children, all of them. *"Komm und is,"* he said. *Come and dine.* I wrapped my arms around my children and we sat and ate at last, the children crying with joy.

I woke up with a start. "Ida?" I'd heard a soft cry. I looked around the small room.

"The *Kinder* are *gut,*" Karl said. "But I think your little one might be hungry. I can look after Kate but can't do what you can do for Ida." He smiled. He sat on the floor and played a game with strings, keeping Kate entertained. I lifted Ida from her board. So small. So tender. So easily crushed. She breathed deeply and returned to sleep now that I cradled her. Even without food she lay content just being in the comfort of my breast.

"I've asked for the ship's doctor to visit you later," Karl said. I nodded my thanks. Maybe the kindly man in the dream was Karl. But the man had been able to pull me from the others. He knew my name and didn't chastise me for my weakness. He understood that I couldn't make it to the table on my own.

I dozed after that, my baby heavy on my chest. I awoke when the doctor knocked on the door. He stepped over a coil of rope just inside the cabin and offered me a fresh poultice for my still seeping stitches. He and Karl discreetly left me to complete my ministrations. Later I fed Ida, grateful that I had what she needed, that we were not dependent on Opal or the kindness of strangers to keep her alive. We had enough food for the evening supper. Tomorrow would take care of itself.

With Kate in my lap, I asked Karl if the ship headed to the Wallacut River, if we'd have to portage to the Columbia or whether we'd head out to sea.

"I thought the way down the slough to the Wallacut might be too rough for you." It was the way Christian would have gone if he had lived. "We go to the ocean and sail south to Astoria. There we cross the bar and take another boat to Portland, and then ride the stage to Aurora Mills.

"If Jack comes overland could he beat us there?"

Karl looked thoughtful. "*Ja*, that is possible. It will take us a few days. We may need to rest in Portland. For you." *Unlike Jack, Karl doesn't think I pretend to be ill.* "Jack might go night and day and get there first."

"What will I have gained," I said, "if he meets us there?"

"You won't stand alone when you face him. But more, you'll have a safe place to stay when he leaves."

"I couldn't have done this without your help. Just getting in and out of the tender vessel took more effort than I imagined."

Karl shrugged. I thought the color on his face might have darkened, but the candlelight was dim in the small cabin. I wished, then, that I'd brought along Christian's lantern. It grieved me that I'd left it behind.

"*Ja*, by golly, you will be safe there. That will be an answered prayer."

I hadn't known Karl prayed about me or my family. He'd kept a watchful eye through the years and thank goodness it was friendly. "Christian's family never accepted me," I said. "So I tried to stay out of their way, not owe them any debt."

"*Ach*, Emma, you tell yourself a story there," Karl said. "You never waded in to their family. You always swam offshore, by yourself."

"And swam right into a shark named Jack," I said. "But doing things on our own—isn't that what we Germans are about? The strong don't need others."

"We all need tending," Karl said. "We are children in God's sight, and every good parent knows not to let their child stray too far from a father's love."

"Or a mother's," I said, though I'd let my children stray into Jack's life, bringing them harm. Through the closed door I could hear the water push against the ship's sides, a steady swishing rhythm taking us to Aurora Mills. "You're so kind to go with us, Karl," I said. "I am so grateful."

He shrugged. "I'm ready to stay. John will handle the instruction at Willapa and it's time there was a school at Aurora Mills. A church too. Wilhelm may need prodding about building the church." Karl grinned. "He still thinks he is in control of the colony, but I see how his grip slips and by golly, I think that's a good thing for us all."

"It's easy for you to say such things. As a man, Keil listens to you."

"It isn't Keil I'm trying to please," he said.

The words felt like a splash of cold water on my face. Who was I trying to please? Kate came to lie on the cot while I sat, her head in my lap. She snored a child's snore of contentment. The room smelled of fish and the old ropes that felt scratchy when I lifted them out of the way. "When you disagreed with Wilhelm and stayed in Willapa, that didn't change your confidence in the colony?"

"*Nein.* My confidence is in doing the Lord's work. It doesn't matter where I live to do that. Remember, Emma, in the Hebrew, *religion* means 'tying together again.' Sometimes Wilhelm's doctrine tied tight knots, but it's Christian love that binds. I look for God's threads to guide me, not Wilhelm's. You can do this too."

———

The journey gave me rested time to think, to grieve. When the image of Andy's despair at being left behind came to me, I spoke a prayer for him, that one day he'd understand. We sailed into Astoria, my stomach sickened from the rough bar crossing between ocean and river. Two mighty forces pushed against each other and I wondered if that was Keil and me. We stayed a day in the Oregon coastal town so I could rest and see another doctor. Then we took a smaller craft toward Portland. The costs of this journey grew, and I knew Sarah had not loaned us more than the first passage. Karl had provided the rest. I was in debt to him. Maybe I always would be. In debt to his kindness, to Mary's midwifery, to Sarah's understanding. I owed so much. People had kept us alive after Christian's death. I owed them too. Maybe I even owed Jack.

No. All Jack ever gave me was the oyster shell painting, and he'd taken that back. Well, he'd fathered Ida, but I felt nothing was due him for that.

The stage left Portland at eight o'clock on that early August morning, taking us through Oregon City. The stage road hugged black basaltic rocks to the east, followed the river at the west. Though the sky was cloudless, I heard a sound like thunder as we rounded a bend. Then I saw it. Mist rose up from nearly a quarter mile of horseshoe-shaped falls stretching across the Willamette River. Tons of water silvered its way over the ridge of rocks and plunged thirty feet to the depths below, rolling and surging, then cascading out toward the Columbia that separated us from Washington Territory. "It's where the Indians fish for salmon, by golly," Karl shouted above the noise. Docks stacked with wheat ready for shipment jutted out well below the falls. "It will drive industry too," Karl continued. "That chief factor of Hudson's Bay chose this site long ago. He knew. We're but a few miles now from Aurora Mills. It's a good place to settle, Emma." He smiled, and I thought he might take my hand in his and pat it. Instead he lifted Kate's little chin and directed her eyes. "A rainbow," Karl said. *"Ja?"* She nodded at the arc of color and light spinning over the waterfall. I saw her smile. She hadn't done much of that.

Maybe this *was* what I was supposed to do. Maybe when our minds and bodies are frayed, we have to do things that others think best, even when those things seem so contrary. In order to mend we allow others to light our paths back to safety, back to our place of belonging, into the folds of faith.

There were prairies here, more wide-open spaces, not unlike Missouri. The stage stopped and we waited for the tollman to come out and lift the gate. The driver shouted to get the man's attention but he didn't leave the tollhouse. We decided to walk across, as we were the only passengers and none waited on the other side. We carried little luggage, and I managed that while using my cane. For a moment I hesitated again, wondering if the tollman might be held hostage inside by Jack or if Jack would jump out at us partway up the hill. Would it always be thus, fears of the possibilities overtaking joyous potential? Only if I allowed it, I decided. I would force myself to think of the good that could be until such thinking was habit. It was what I controlled now, my thoughts.

The stage rolled through the open gate, and I balanced myself with my cane. Kate squatted to make mud pies along the riverbanks. It was a pleasant enough landscape with fir and white ash and cedar dotting the prairie. The air smelled fresh and sometimes when the wind lay, I thought I heard a band's music. We looked like a typical family of the time, especially during war, when the man of the family soldiered off somewhere and a grandfather became the support that a woman with children needed.

"What this place needs is an alert tollman, by golly," Karl said, as annoyed as I'd ever seen him be. A man came out of the small wood hut that housed him, stretched. He must have fallen asleep in the warmth. "Sorry," he said, putting his pail out for us to drop in our tolls.

"You missed six dollars to collect if you'd been awake for the stage," Karl told him.

"Not mine to earn or keep," he said, smiling. "He'll pay on his return."

The grassy trail followed a natural incline, taking us into the town I'd so dreaded. I knew it in my imagination. My son had been here, the only family member to see this place. Well, Jack had been here. I just hoped he wasn't here now.

"Are we there, Mama?" Kate asked. She slapped dirt from her hands.

"Almost," I said. I stopped to catch my breath and touched her head.

The sun warmed her dark curls. I shifted Ida on my shoulder, the weight of her a comfort.

"Look for the biggest house," Karl said. "That's Elim, or at least what Wilhelm is living in until they build him his big house one day."

Louisa had made it sound so glorious, but Aurora Mills wasn't much more than a few houses. Perhaps what gave someone the joy of home wasn't in the actual features of a place, the structures or even gardens, but in the people. Maybe that was why I'd convinced Christian to stay in the Willapa country with his family, our family. Then he died and all the relationships changed. Who I was as Christian Giesy's wife became the burden of Christian Giesy's widow. Worse, I didn't know who I was without him. Here, Louisa was surrounded by people who loved her and whom she loved back. No wonder she sang the town's praises.

We passed a single log house, then another with cut boards. Flowers grew at a window box. I wondered if the Wagonblast family that had walked their way across the continent with Keil and spent the winter with us had come here or had found lives outside the colony. *Perhaps they'll take me in.* I stopped, the compass needle spinning around toward new options.

"What is it, Emma?"

I started forward again. "I will trust and not be afraid," I said under my breath. "The Lord, the Lord is my song."

"From Isaiah," Karl Ruge said. "Think of this too, Emma Giesy: 'If we walk in the light, as he is in the light, we have fellowship one with another.' Like the disciples, we hold all in common. But we all have something to give; we share even what we fear as we walk in that light." I nodded. *"Ja,* by golly, that's what you must cling to now, sharing what you have and what you fear."

Beyond, hops fields would soon be ready for harvest. Small apple saplings grew amid stumps of trees. "I suppose Wilhelm still requires a tree be cut before breakfast," Karl said. "He's planted hickory trees, did I tell you this? Brought all the way from Bethel." He pointed then. "That's it." We walked up a grassy grade to a two-story house with a wide porch on both levels. My heart started to pound; I held back. Karl spoke: "This is the way. Walk thee in it."

"Knock and it shall be opened," I said, the old scriptures coming back to me like homing pigeons sent by someone I loved.

Before Karl could knock on the door it opened from the inside and there stood Louisa Keil, a smile on her face.

"I told Helena it was you!" she cried. "I said, 'Emma Giesy and Karl Ruge are walking up our path,' and she laughed. See who will laugh now! It's them!" she shouted back over her shoulder. "Come see, Husband. And little Kate too." She tried to squat, but her hip must have hurt. Still, Kate appeared to remember her from when they'd visited last year, because she didn't seem shy with Louisa.

"Can I have a cookie?" she asked. "I'm fairly hungry."

"*Ja*, sure. And who is this?" Louisa asked, as she steadied herself. She leaned over Ida's face.

"Ida," I said. "Jack's child."

"So fragile-looking, yet made such a long trip. You just come inside." She spoke the *j* so it sounded like *yust*. "My goodness, you must be weary. Are Jack and the boys behind?" She looked past me toward the trail.

"Jack isn't coming. I hope," I said.

"Ah," she said. Her words carried no judgment.

"You've left your husband?" Helena Giesy asked. " 'The Lord God of Israel hateth putting away.' " She quoted the Old Testament's Malachi.

"*Ja*, divorce He abhors, but more, He hates violence. It is in the same verse, Helena." I thought I caught Louisa smile as I turned to her. "The boys will come later, when Martin brings them."

"Then you are welcome to stay for as long as you like," she said, inviting us into the cool of the wide entry where a staircase rose to the second floor. She reached for Ida. "Helena, prepare food for our guests. God has led you here," she said to me. "That is all we need to know about the circumstances." She scowled at Helena, who hadn't moved yet. I hadn't noticed before Louisa's flying white eyebrows.

32

Emma

Prayers of Preparation

Within minutes of our untying our caps, Keil entered, filling the room. "Karl," he said, giving him a bear hug, slapping his back. "Always good to see you in Aurora. Look, girls," he motioned for his children, and four of them like stair steps stood beside him. "See who is here now. My old friend, Karl. Your teacher," he said. The children nodded politely, and then he dismissed them to one of the big rooms on either side of the entry. To Aurora he said, "Take Sister Emma's children with you when you go."

I hadn't been here five minutes and Keil, who had not even acknowledged my presence, already directed my children. "Kate can go, but Ida I'll keep with me."

"*Ja*, she's so young. Barely a month old she looks like," Louisa said.

Keil didn't seem to notice that she stood with me in defying him. "Get Kate some milk. And cookies," Louisa said, and Kate happily went with young Aurora, never looking back.

"So. You come to stay this time," Keil said. He spoke to Karl and it wasn't a question. "I cannot get those from Bethel to hurry along." I waited for Karl to reply as Keil motioned him into the side room. "You," Keil continued, turning to me, motioning me to follow. "Emma Giesy. Why are you here without the rest of your family?"

"I've come for…protection," I said. "From my husband. I'm no longer a widow, but I seek a widow's solace."

Those piercing dark eyes stared, ready to intimidate at a moment's notice. "I would not have let you marry Jack Giesy if you had sought permission, which you should have."

"I was never good at permission-seeking," I said.

"*Ja*. This I remember," he said. He raised his finger to the air. He grunted then crossed his arms over his broad chest. "Now you come seeking a widow's solace."

"As the colony protected women back in Bethel whether they were members or not. Whether they'd made wise choices placing them in need or not. Isn't that so? It was the Diamond Rule we tendered there, to make others' lives better than our own."

"Divorce we do not approve of."

"She quotes Malachi to us," Helena said. The tall woman had stepped into the room uninvited. I was pleased to see that Louisa had as well.

"Violence covering like a garment, the Lord does not approve of that either," I said. "Does God ask us simply to endure? Is this the Diamond Rule of the discipleship?"

I teetered at the top of a pyramid and could imagine Keil pushing me either way: to this colony and safety or back to the bed I'd made. I felt my face flush to be in such a precarious place, throwing myself at the mercy of the man I so despised. I decided then that if Keil would not receive us, I would get the boys and we would go to San Francisco, someplace far away, and we would make a path, God willing. But I'd never go back to Jack. I didn't belong with him.

"I won't need your protection for long," I offered. "I have a plan."

"*Ja*, you always did have that," Keil said.

"Women and children in need have always been safe with the colony," Karl said. "It is the Lord's most important directive to us. Is that not right, Wilhelm? Is that different here in Aurora Mills than it was back in Bethel?"

Keil placed his fingertips together in front of him, Karl's words causing him to pause.

"We offer protection for any who need it. Women, children, slaves. Does she need it?" He asked Karl.

He'd accept Karl's assessment but not mine. "I've seen enough of Jack's ways to be worried, by golly. Emma has no reason to come here otherwise. She gives up what she and Christian worked together for. She prays that Martin will bring her sons soon and that you will allow her to stay. Perhaps she can go somewhere else after that."

"Martin thinks about coming? To stay?" Louisa interjected.

"He would be a big help here," Helena said.

"As I've often said," Louisa added. "With your doctoring, my husband. You would have relief."

"Louisa, you mustn't—"

"It's true, Husband. Maybe more will come from Willapa now that Karl and Emma have. If we treat Emma as we should."

Keil sighed. "Oh, the weight of leadership." He looked at me. "Both of you speak truths. I know Jack. Something…happens to him at times." Keil looked away. "We saw it here. I thought it was the whiskey and prayed he would give it up."

"I speak another truth," I said.

"What is that, Sister Emma?" Keil said.

I swallowed hard, and my fingertips, crooked now from Jack's maltreatment, made tiny circles against the pads of my thumb. I had to be willing to accept the colony's help but also to assert my claim. "I ask for asylum then not as any widow but as the widow of the leader of the colony's scouts, as the wife of a man who did God's bidding and yours with a faithful heart. It is my due."

"You are a bold one, Sister Emma," Helena said. "After all that has happened."

"She only asks what a mother needs," Louisa said. "Even our Lord tells us to seek that."

"Christian would want you to do this, Wilhelm," Karl said. "Without asking, she deserves it. She is here asking. That is enough."

Keil clapped his hands. "You're right, Karl. You will stay here with us, in this *gross Haus* where we live and the bachelors live and where you can help Louisa and the girls with the cooking. You will give and receive in return. And our presence will offer the greatest protection for when Jack comes here. And I know he will."

"It will be like before when we all stayed together," Louisa said. Her voice was light, and she sounded like she planned an approved wedding. "Just like when we lived in the stockade together, only without the harsh winter this time."

"And without the husband who loved me," I said.

Louisa leaned in to me and patted my arm. "It has been four years, Sister Emma. Time to turn old griefs into tender stories."

———

In the days that followed, Keil couldn't have been more congenial to me. Maybe because I'd brought Karl with me. Maybe because we all awaited Martin's arrival with my boys, and Keil hoped he would convince Martin to remain, too. Maybe because I worked hard. Perhaps Louisa said good words about me and maybe Helena said nothing. I never complained, not once. Whatever the reason, he treated me as though I was a singular person, and I began to think I did deserve a life without threats, a safe dwelling place. Being here would never replace what Christian and I had built together in Willapa, but it would remind me always that God did provide and with that would come peace.

Helena led prayers in the morning before we began the day's cooking in the bottom floor of the house. I hadn't realized there were four stories when I'd arrived. It was a pleasant act, I found, starting the day with praise for life, thanking the hunters who provided the meat and those who tended the flour mill, hoping that harvest would go well. She asked that the food be prepared with love and then we'd begin, joined by other colony women, Louisa included.

Had the women done this back in Bethel? I couldn't remember. I'd lived in my family's home then, just a daughter helping my mother. We hadn't shared kitchens as we did here. We spoke a table grace but hadn't offered prayers for preparation. *Prayers for preparation.* That's how I began each morning now. I prayed that the boys would arrive soon, asked that Jack might never come. In the evening as we prepared to bed down, Keil spoke words to give us restful sleep. The bachelors and Keil's children all slept on the top floor, to which they'd go after the evening prayers. Keil and his wife slept on the first floor. Kate and I rolled out mats at the far side of the first floor in the kitchen area. I could see the moon rise through the window. I'd be able to hear anyone arriving on the porch. It was a short walk to the privy. How simple my needs were now. I'd be full every day if my sons were just here, if I was sure they were safe and that Andy had not returned to our home to get into Jack's way.

———

The time spent with the Keils gave me a new picture of Louisa. She did what she wanted, though mostly what she wanted was what Keil would approve of. Still, she influenced her husband and she lightened the tone for the workers, made little jokes. I'd always seen her as serious, somber even. Perhaps Helena's presence had rescued Louisa from having to be so stern. She liked words and their sounds and joked that my *Strudel* was as "fine as a frog's hair." When Keil's voice took on a frustrated tone, it was Louisa who calmed him and suggested who could assist, since he must be tired, so very tired, with all the burdens he carried. Once I thought she patronized with those words, but she meant them. She saw how he labored to make the colony operate and wanted to support him. It was how I'd served Christian once; I wished my wants were as generous and simple now.

One day Louisa surprised me by suggesting that I make a few drawings. "Why?" I asked.

"There's a harvest fair in October. Wilhelm says it will be the first-ever Oregon State Fair, and we can enter things that are judged. Paintings and needlework and dried fruits and baskets, even essays, words. And flowers."

"Women enter these things?"

"Last year there were several women who earned recognition. You draw lovely pictures. I've seen you do them for Kate. So then, go to the store and ask for drawing material."

"I doubt they'll have such a thing as pencils and whatnot."

"They'll get what you need. It's the common fund. Don't you remember?"

I remembered. "I'd always resented that practice," I told her. She raised an eyebrow. "It made me feel weak almost, that if I took something, then I'd always owe someone else. Or if I had nothing to give, then I was taking advantage of another. That's how I felt in Willapa after Christian died. It's why I tried so hard to do it on my own. Marrying Jack seemed like a good way to not be dependent on the Giesys."

"*Ach*, Emma," she said. She patted my floured hand as I kneaded the dough. I added a little loaf sugar to sweeten it, something we didn't have in Willapa. I sat to do much of this work, still weak. "We put things into the common basket so it can be taken out. It's what love is. We all have things to give. The work we do that tends to others, that goes into the basket. What we grow for sale. Even our listening hearts, those are all a part of the fellowship of the common fund. It's not only money, Emma. There is always enough for everyone and all contribute. We put things in; we draw things out. Only God is enough."

"Andreas and Barbara wanted to raise my boys. They kept Andy there while he was at school. I didn't feel I could argue much since I was such a burden on everyone. That could happen here too."

"*Ach*, no. Here you are cooking. That is enough. You go now and get some drawing things when we finish here, *ja*? I insist."

I tried to imagine what I'd draw. The fields around Aurora Mills? The little house with the window box? The tollman asleep at his post? Would Keil approve of this frivolousness, a woman drawing pictures when she could otherwise be working?

"Will *Herr* Keil object?"

"He has his music. We have our needlework, show towels. Some men weave baskets and work with the looms, too, or they play in the band. These are practical, but they also lend beauty and lighten another's day. That is a contribution too."

"I suppose I could draw the girls," I said. "Aurora and Gloriunda, my Kate."

"Send one back to your parents. They'd like that. I'd like that. A drawing of my Aurora and Louisa and Amelia and Gloriunda."

"My parents do not write to me."

"Maybe they do but Jack intercepted their letters. They will write now to Aurora Mills and you can know you'll receive the letters. I still think they'll come here, and they won't have to make a detour to Willapa."

"Unless Martin fails to bring the boys."

"Did he say he'd bring them?" I nodded. "Then don't borrow trouble. Practice thinking good thoughts." She cocked her head as though she'd just said something out loud that surprised even herself.

I did go to the store and ask for paper and lead. I sketched eleven-year-old Aurora as she sat with Kate peeling an apple to eat. I drew my daughters, even Ida. I watched the other children as they played and saw the harvest of this colony, this place where people helped one another. There was a cost, yes, the little gripes and disappointments that flared up between people living close together. But the common bond of caring helped put the firebursts out. The heat diminished with familiarity and reminded me that in this living church, which is how I'd come to think of the people if not the colony, there were challenges, but none too big for God to turn around. Had I taken all the children and spent the time with Andreas and Barbara after Christian died, I might have been able to keep my home and my family together in Willapa. Instead I'd spoken vows with another and here I was, separated from the very children I'd hoped to always have with me. But no, I must not dwell on what was past. I had made the best decision I could then with no intention of making a poor choice. I'd done the best I could then; that's what I had to remember.

While I worked, I healed. I thought of that dream I'd had on the ship and decided it was a spiritual feast I'd been missing. I'd been trying so hard to get to the table but always doing it my own way. Someone strong sat at the head of the table. It wasn't Keil or Louisa or Karl. Most importantly, it wasn't me.

———

I hung wash on the line strung between two trees beside the washhouse. I heard a child's voice shouting, "Mama, Mama!" It wasn't Kate.

"Christian?" I turned toward the sound, and there my youngest son came running like a happy dog, his arms out and his legs swinging sideways as he tried to keep his balance with such uneven ground matched against his speed. I knelt as he approached, the cane dropping at my side. He knocked me over with his joy. "Christian, Christian, Christian, how good you look. How good you feel!"

"I took a bath. Martin made us."

"You were reluctant to take that bath. Tell her that," Martin said, as he caught up with Christian in the bundle of my arms.

"What's 'lucktent' mean, Mama?" Christian said, a small frown on his face.

"Unwilling," I said, kissing his sweet-smelling hair. "Mama can get reluctant, too, sometimes, avoiding things she doesn't want to face."

"Thank you, Martin," I continued. "For bringing him. Them." I wanted to ask if Jack had interfered at all, but I didn't want to upset Christian with such talk. I looked around. "Where's Andy?" I stood up. My heart skipped a beat. I couldn't see him.

"At the tollman's house. Karl's there, and Andy recognized him."

"Oh, good," I said. It was a sign that Andy could wait to see me. I felt a twinge of regret. He nursed a wound still open. I'd missed him more and needed to seek him out. "Take Christian inside to Keil's, will you, Martin? Kate's there and Ida. I'll go greet Andy, if I can."

I limped as I walked, thinking of what to say, of how I could explain why I'd left him behind again. Why I'd had to. I imagined Martin had told him some of it, but I wasn't sure how much Andy understood.

I sidestepped down the little knoll to the bridge. The stage already moved on up the road, having just brought Martin and my sons. Andy stood between Karl and the tollman, his hands on his hips as though the men spoke of harvest troubles or the price of wheat.

"Andy," I called to him. I was sure he heard me. Karl looked my way, said something to my son. "Andy." He turned to me then. "Come join me," I shouted. I walked closer, babbling as he stood, a solemn look on his face. "I'm so glad you came. I prayed that Martin would bring you. I missed you so." I knelt down. He looked through me, as though I were a stranger, someone he wasn't sure he'd met before. "Andy, I'm so sorry I had to leave you and had to make you wait. I'm so sorry. But you're here now. We're all together at last."

I don't know if it was the prayers I'd spoken daily since the day we'd arrived or if it was the prayers of preparation spoken by so many, but my oldest son did then walk toward me and put his arms around my neck. I pulled him to me, breathing in the sweetness of him, relishing his soft and tender skin, the clean smell of his neck as I kissed it. "It's a new beginning, Andy. We'll make our way here." He let me hold him and then he pushed away.

"You left us."

"I had to, Andy. It was the only way to trick Jack. I had to trick him so I could get here safely. And now you're here safely, too, so you see, it worked out." He stared. "Forgive me, Andy. Please. I should have done so many things differently and I'm sorry. I truly am."

He turned from me and walked away.

"Where are you going?" I asked. My heart thudded.

"To get something." At the tollman's house he lifted an object from a satchel. I recognized it and my throat caught in tightness. He carried the lantern that Christian had made the holder for; the one he'd held above us the last time we'd walked on the beach.

"Oh, Andy. You risked—"

"I went when I knew Jack wouldn't be home. It was Papa's. I carried it at his funeral, remember? I couldn't let Papa's light stay behind."

———

While I pulled weeds in the herb garden, Martin reported of Jack's return the day we'd left. He'd railed against me for changing my mind and heading off on "some fool trip to Aurora Mills," but he had calmed when he saw Andy and Christian still with my in-laws. I winced as Martin told the story, for it confirmed that I had used my sons to ward off the wrath of their stepfather. "But Henry and John, they both talked to him about how it might be good for you to go to Aurora with the girls. We reminded him that the children annoyed him and he agreed. We might have mentioned that he had the land to keep up; he owned that farm, so why not head home and farm it regardless of how long it took for you to return; we promised to keep the boys with us. Seemed to calm him," Martin said.

"Do you think he'll come here?" I asked. I could smell the woolly applemint when I brushed at its leaves in the late garden.

Martin squatted beside me. "*Ja,* he'll come here." He paused. "We should have spoken up when you said you planned to marry him. Most of us knew of his...ways."

"*Ja,* but I wouldn't have listened," I said. "So you can forgive yourself for that."

"Just let us help you when he comes."

As the grain harvest moved to a rush and the pumpkins were nearly ripe, we had fruit to turn into butter, vinegar to make. In late September when nights turned cooler and the mill race filled with confetti of colorful leaves, Louisa insisted that the portrait I'd drawn with colored pencils of Aurora should be entered in the state fair competition. I blushed.

"I like the one of the tollkeeper," Karl said. "You captured his sleepy look with his head against his chest while people wait for him to collect the toll. We could have the state contract for mail if we kept alert eyes, by golly. I think that man needs looking for another job."

"Well, then, enter both," Louisa said. "*Ja.* Enter them both."

So I did.

It felt like play as we walked around the fair grounds in October, looking at the harvest people brought as examples of their efforts. We ate our lunch, and the aroma of our warm potato salad and herbed sausages brought people our way, asking if we had any for sale. We had none but invited people to join us, and we laughed together over the food and the fair. At one booth I encountered the Wagonblast family. After hugs all around, I learned they'd gone from Willapa to Cathlamet, then down to Oregon City. They were practically neighbors!

In the booths showing crafts and wares, I lingered over the paintings and noted the name of one Nancy M. Thornton on several. One of her paintings already had a ribbon on it from the Benton County Fair, dated 1859. *Women were painting here that early,* I thought. The notation said she now taught in Oregon City at the Female School for Instruction of Young Ladies and Misses. Maybe I could take classes from her. Maybe my daughters could go there one day. And that took me to thoughts of my sons, who ran freely around the grounds, their little flat-top hats like lily pads in the sea of people. They would all go to school here. Andy would have a chance to be a doctor as he said he wished to be. He was still standoffish with me, but I prayed he'd warm again to his mother. Christian's stuttering had ceased since coming to Aurora Mills.

If only I'd done this before. If only I'd let Christian's family help me. No, I would stop such thoughts. I still had control over how I thought, and my meanderings must buoy me up, not hold me hostage.

After sunset, we rode back in a wagon, many of us from the colony gathered together on loose grass hay. Several sang, and the men had their brass instruments and a concertina they played now as we bounced along. The boys sat in a cluster of children. I shifted to find a better way to sit, grateful the stitches had at last healed. I held Ida in my arms. Kate had her head in my lap, already asleep, her fingers wrapped around a pale pink ribbon. The picture of Aurora had won an award. Not the top prize, but recognition just the same. A half dime came with the prize, the first real currency of my own I'd earned. I had it wrapped in the handkerchief that also held my pearls. My life was blessed.

It was dark when we reached Aurora Mills, and we carried sleepy children from the wagon. Aurora walked with Kate in hand and I had Ida in my arms. Both Christian and Andy slept on the grass hay of the wagon. I'd come back and fetch them later. I felt a lightness in my steps despite my fatigue. It almost felt like joy. Hope, that was it. I felt hope in my heart for the future I'd create here.

Helena opened the door, and Karl carried in some jars of vinegar that had also won ribbons and quarters to boot. Keil's "strongly medicinal" Oregon grape wine had won Keil a blue ribbon, which he held as he entered. Ida lay in the crook of my arm. Louisa brushed past me as Kate plopped down on the mat next to the door. "Let me light the lantern," she said. I moved Kate toward her own mat in the room on the other side and planned to return to get Christian when I heard Louisa exclaim, "Oh, you startled me!"

"I maybe could have done more than that," Jack said. "For keeping me from my *Kind.*"

———

It doesn't take much to shatter a silky peace. I should have sensed that he was there, waiting for us. If I'd had any kind of motherly intuitiveness I'd have known, should have felt his glowering in the dark, menacing my children and my life. What a terrible thing I'd attracted into our lives with my willful ways.

"Now Jack," Keil said. "There's no reason to be upsetting."

"My wife and children defy me? That's reason to be more than upsetting. You've no right to harbor them"—he poked at Keil's chest—"as though they needed shelter in a storm."

"Every right in the world, Jack. We are Sister Giesy's family, and she's come to visit us." *Visit. Does he intend to send me back?* "Now just settle down. We are all tired. You bunk up there with the bachelors, and we can talk in the morning. It's been a long day. I imagine for you as well, *ja.*"

We might have staved off the suffering and loss then but for Louisa's meant-for-cheering words: "Emma won a ribbon for her drawings," Louisa said. "See what a fine job she did penciling our Aurora?" She held the drawing up beside the lamp she'd lit.

"A perfect likeness," Helena agreed. She pushed the drawing toward Jack, who stood across from me.

Neither of them could have known how their praise of my work would enrage Jack. But I did.

Fearing he'd punch a hole through the drawing, I stepped in front of it.

"But it's not as fine a job as you might do, Jack," I said. "Jack's quite an artist himself." I turned toward Louisa.

Quick as a slap, Jack lunged across the space between us and swung to strike me with the back of his hand. The back of his hand cracked against the side of my face. I stumbled back, still holding Ida in my arms. "Come here, Wife!" It was just like him to cause pain then wonder why I resisted his commands.

Louisa cried out, *"Ach, nein,"* and I heard Kate scream as she ran toward me. I held Ida close to my chest but ducked my head over her, pushed Kate behind me to protect them both, knowing in a moment he would strike at me again. I hoped the boys remained asleep outside. Cajoling, capitulating, surrendering to such as Jack was not the answer. Neither was defiance. Maybe stating the obvious was.

I faced him. Something in my eyes must have reached him. His arm, midair, stopped. "It's over, Jack," I said. "You were right about our arrangement. Our loveless marriage never worked."

"You made a vow," he hissed.

"Not to let you destroy my life or the lives of my children. I made no vow about that. You go, Jack. You must go. I won't try to make a claim on the property that once belonged to me or ask you for help to raise your child. I've made my way here, and here I'll make my life."

He stepped closer, but I didn't back away. "Take Ida, Louisa," I said. She moved like an angel, whisking in then out of the scene of destruction. With her free arm she moved Kate before her.

Jack towered above me. "You—" He raised his fist again. *Let the blow come; my children are safe.* I closed my eyes. Waited.

"No, no, no, no, no! You will not do this, Jacob Giesy." It was Keil. He was slightly shorter than Jack, but his words held greater force. "This is the widow of a man whom I loved as a son, and you will harm her no more. You will go now. Now. Right now. You will return to Willapa or go wherever you wish, but you will not approach Sister Giesy again. We will protect her as a widow. Leave her be."

"She holds my child."

"Whom you paid no heed to when you struck at the child's mother." This from Karl, who had lit candles and the lamps to tint the room with light. "You might have hurt your daughter too."

"You too, Karl?" Jack said. He stood like a frightened animal now, cornered.

"No sympathy, Jack," Keil said. "The deed is done. Now go."

"Where are my sons?" he shouted then. I was sure Jack would strike Karl, but he didn't. Instead he glared at me, his face grotesque in the flickering light. "What have you done with those boys?"

"Take care of yourself, Jack," Helena told him. "Go now before you do something you will later regret." He acted as though he'd just become aware that Helena was even there. Her voice seemed to soothe him with its firmness.

"Those boys are in good hands," Keil said.

"There'll come a time, Emma Giesy," Jack said, "when you are not pampered by people you've bewitched. You'll not know when you're alone and then we'll see what maybe could happen."

We gave him the last word, and when no one responded, no one added fuel to his fire, his passion died. He lumbered out. I watched him while standing in the doorway, hoping that he wouldn't stop at the wagon where the boys slept. He headed toward the tollhouse and never saw Andy's head pop up from the grass hay, never saw Christian slide down on the opposite side of the wagon and watch their "Papa Jack" walk away before rushing up the steps of Elim and into my arms.

"You're shaking," Louisa said as she helped me to the chair. "Boys, help me get some water for your mama's face."

"Will he come back?" Andy asked.

"Don't borrow trouble," Louisa told them. "We'll see what happens in the morning."

Jack was nowhere around by morning. No one reported seeing him about, not near the furniture building nor at Rudy's sheep farm. The tollman said a big man had crossed in the night, his shoulders hunched up like "a firecracker ready to explode." He'd headed north, away from Aurora Mills. Away from us.

33

Emma

The Found Coin

I hardly slept, still wearing that fogginess of danger past without time to let peace massage my soul.

"We must build the church next," Helena noted in the morning as we cleaned up following the morning meal. "The prophet Haggai warns about building for ourselves before we build for God."

"My husband has been busy," Louisa defended. Then she added, "But if we had a church, I'd take you there, Emma, and we could just sit in the cool and thank God for your good fortune in arriving here, your children being safe. And you've earned recognition for your work, all in one month's time." She looked at the drawing of Aurora she'd hung on the wall.

"I have more than that to be grateful for," I told her. To Helena I posed, "Perhaps Brother Keil is right in having his home serve as a place of worship. It does double the work that way."

Louisa liked this idea. "*Ja,* that's right, Emma. A German efficiency. And maybe it gives the home a needed uplifting into the spiritual realm. A home, a hearth, surely God wants those to be central in our lives." She smiled, pleased with herself.

Helena's lips puckered as if gathered by threads. Like Keil, Helena didn't like to be disagreed with.

"I think I'll find a quiet place away today, though," I said. "That would be an advantage of a church building, finding quietness in the middle of a day."

Louisa smiled. Helena straightened her shoulders and began scrubbing potatoes.

The women gave me room to stretch after the tautness of Jack's visit, but I could see by Helena's rigid back and Louisa's grin that the communal threads that tied us together would also be stretched here. I would try not to break them, give each person room to save face.

I walked with the children across the open grasses just beginning to give up their brown to the greens of autumn rains. I looked back toward Keil's house as we walked, the soft October winds lifting the strings of my bonnet. Keil lived at the highest point of the village, but *he* wasn't the highest point. He had authority, yes, but not over our souls, not over our thoughts, not over our expressions of faith. In truth, he was an aging man who made mistakes too. I didn't need to seek his approval anymore, nor live in defiance of him.

I'd packed a lunch, and I spent the day with the children. When we returned, it was dusk. I lit the oil in Christian's lantern, thanking Andy again for bringing it. Then I knocked on the door of the private room the Keils occupied upstairs. "Emma," Louisa said. "Come in. You had a good afternoon, *ja?*"

"*Ja,*" I answered. "I wish to speak to *Herr* Keil, now. Is this possible?"

"Father Keil," she corrected.

I hesitated. "Brother Keil," I said. "I already have a father."

"*Ja,*" she said. "That makes sense. He works with his herbs." She pointed downstairs toward the room across from the kitchen. As I descended the steps, Andy saw me from the side room and nodded, but he didn't rush to me as he once would have. We had knots yet to tie, that was certain. I moved past him, carried the lantern down another flight, taking the shadows with me to where Keil worked. I was glad to be wearing leather soles instead of my wooden ones.

At the workshop, I waited amid the earthy smell of plants until Keil looked up. "Do you have a moment, Brother Keil?"

"Ah, Sister Emma. I recall occasions when you asked for my time. To seek permission for marriage if I remember well; then to convince me that letting you become a scout would be good for our colony. Of late, to seek refuge." He shook his head. "So many needs a woman has."

Ja. But you also found refuge in my home," I said. "And I served you and yours, as my husband did. We gave what we had to give. My husband gave all he had, his very life, on behalf of another. Is this not the communal way?"

He returned to his mortar and pestle. "So, what is it you wish now?"

"I come to ask that the colony in Aurora Mills build me a house. As the widow of a colony leader, I seek a home for my sons and daughters to grow up in."

He stopped his work, laid the pestle down, brushed his hands against his wool vest and folded his hands over his wide chest. "Our house, where you stay, is insufficient for your many needs, Emma Giesy?"

"It is. This is not to insult your generosity. Not at all. I'll work here, cook and clean and wash and serve others, and those labors and my love in doing them will go into the common fund. But I wish my own home, my own place to teach my children and to raise them as their father would wish it. It's what I reach for from the abundant basket the colony is always speaking of."

"You'll be more vulnerable to Jack's antics should he return, living alone."

"I'll not let my life be only a reflection of what Jack might do to us," I said.

He was quiet a long time. If he refused, I'd already decided that in the spring I would take the children and leave. Maybe go to Oregon City, where they'd still be able to see their uncle Martin and I could still have them attend school with Karl. I could continue to work here and contribute and receive from the common fund, but I would find a way—sell my paintings or my pies—to put a roof over my children's heads.

"Well, I think that could be arranged then," Keil said.

"What?"

"We can arrange to have a house built for you, Emma Giesy. The Diamond Rule prevails. Or do you insist on building it with your own hands?" He chuckled.

"I could," I told him. "But no. I am more interested in what happens afterward, in making it a home."

———

"Here's my half dime," I told the shop tender at the colony store. It was late in the day, and shadows already covered the shelves of cloth and hats and newly cobbled shoes. Garlands of greens draped around the store and holly with red berries decorated harnesses for sale. The long pattern book of our feet lay on the shelf for the cobbler to use when we requested new shoes. Outside, a light snow fell. My shawl fell loose across my shoulders, though it was colder than normal. That's what everyone said, but I felt warmed in this communal store.

The shopkeeper had been the tollman, but Karl had moved into that role. The colony had the state contract for collecting tolls now. Still living in Keil's house with us all, Martin mixed up herbs to help ill people and had plans to go to medical school the following year. We hadn't heard anything from Jack since the day he left nearly two months before. Christmas approached. They hadn't started on my house yet, but Keil had assured me that as the widow of Christian Giesy, I would have a home. When he'd announced it, Helena grimaced and mumbled something again about how not building the church first invited trouble. Keil acted as though he hadn't heard.

I'd picked the house site, close to where the school would be built, not far from the Pudding River, so Andy and Kate wouldn't have to travel far. I knew what my view would be and in the spring, I'd have the home I wanted.

"I earned the money from a picture I drew," I told the shopkeeper as though he might care.

"Did you now? And what would you like in return?"

"Nothing. It's to go into the common fund, as cash against my ledger page. Later I'll need shoes for my sons and hair ribbons for my daughters. But I'm also going to have a home one day, just for me and my family, so I want to contribute."

I planned to make more drawings and to acquaint myself with that woman painter, Nancy Thornton. I had a plan for the next state fair as well, but so far I hadn't had the courage to bring that up with Brother Keil. It's how I thought of him now, like a brother rather than some sort of god who supposedly held all the answers. I'd taken one small step toward seeing Keil through different eyes. One small stitch in time, that's what I told Andy as we two tended our frayed threads too.

The shopkeeper opened the ledger book to my page, *Emma Giesy* written across the top. I took the small coin from my reticule and promptly dropped it. *"Ach, jammer!"* I said, as it rolled across the wooden floor and spun itself against a pickle barrel where it disappeared in the shadows. I heard it stop rolling.

It was all I had to give. I patted beneath the lip it had disappeared under. "It isn't much," I said. "But I earned it myself. Do you have a lantern I could hold to help me see?"

The shopkeeper complied and as he held the lamp high above me, I was reminded both of the woman of Luke searching for her lost coin and the walk along the Willapa beach Christian and I had taken that last night we had together. The lantern lit the way, and all else was darkness. We'd had enough light to take the next step. It was all we needed. Some days and nights, that was all the light there was.

I found the half dime and let out a little shout, then handed it to the shopkeeper. "I must call all my friends," I said. "I've found my lost coin."

He didn't seem to understand the biblical reference. *"Danke,"* he said and simply marked it in the book as *cash*. "That is our way, to have a generous spirit," he said then. "Your offering goes from 'yours' to 'ours' so now it belongs to 'us.'"

"So it does." I turned to go, as satisfied as if I'd just eaten a nourishing meal.

Epilogue

Bethel, December 1861

Dearest Sister Emma,

Herr *Keil writes that you are in Aurora Mills. Jonathan says you should have gone there when he asked you to, and Papa says it's good that you've come to your senses. But I fear it is not enough to bring us there anytime soon. Lou is not well now. She catches every little ailment and looks as frail as an old chicken. The men have trouble settling land issues, and Jonathan says he will not come back west for two or three more years until these things are worked out. I never know what "these things" are. The boys I know here are saying they will go to war and so girls my age will likely never marry. We'll be like Helena, only without even a proposal to decline.*

I have forgiven you for marrying Jack Giesy. It's better if I forgive you than to be angry with you always, for unforgiveness is the greatest sin. After all, we received forgiveness from our Lord, so what right have we to not give it back? Gift giving and receiving is the way of our lives, Papa says.

I'm glad your children are all there and I will be pleased to meet Ida some-day. Mama does remind Papa that she has "family she's never even met." Papa sighs then. She tells him she needs to see her sister in the Deseret country, so maybe we'll come that far before I'm an old woman. Maybe I'll find a husband there. Or maybe we'll just keep coming west to find you. Pray that we do something some-time soon.

Have a blessed Christ Day, Sister. We will hang your etched eggs in your memory. Do you welcome the New Year with gladness? I just wonder.

Your loving sister, Kitty
(It's how I call myself now. There are too many Catherines in our family, don't you think? You're lucky there's only been one Emma. Papa says the rest of us are lucky that's true too.)

READERS GUIDE

1. This is a story about giving and receiving. Who gave up the most in this story? Who knew how to receive? Why are both capabilities important in our lives and in the life of a family?

2. This is also a story about community and individuals within a community having a voice and making choices. Could Emma have found a way to remain at Willapa and experience contentment there? What voice did Louisa have at Aurora Mills? Did either woman pass up opportunities to be heard more clearly?

3. Emma and Louisa both speak of the great longing, the *Sehnsucht,* that is within each of us. In the German language, the word implies something compelling, almost addictive, in the human spirit that drives us forward on a spiritual journey. What was Emma's great longing? Louisa's? Did these women achieve satisfaction in this second book of the series? Is there a relationship between human intimacy and such spiritual longing?

4. Give some examples of when Emma "began to weave" without waiting for God's thread. What were the consequences? Is it wise to "begin to weave" without knowing the outcome? Can we do otherwise? How do we live in ambivalence?

5. The author uses the metaphor of light throughout the book. Is having enough light for the next step really enough? What role does light play in Emma's discovery that finding meaning in life's tragedies requires reflection? Give some examples of Emma's reflective thinking. When might she have been more reflective? Would you describe Louisa as a reflective woman? What prevents us from being more reflective in our everyday lives?

6. How can we receive without feeling obligated? What qualities of obligation sometimes diminish gifts that others might give us? Why does that make it difficult to receive them?

7. Strength is often defined as self-sufficiency. How did Emma's strength reveal itself? What made it possible for her to ultimately accept the gifts of others?

8. Did Emma use her sons in order to get her own way? Discuss your opinion.

9. How much of Emma's feeling of isolation was self-imposed? How much was isolation related to the demands of the landscape? How much was a spiritual isolation or feeling of abandonment? Did you agree with how the author conveyed these qualities of isolation?

10. Did Emma make the correct choice at the close of the book? Have you ever had to make a choice where all options appeared poor? What helped you take the next step?

11. Molly Wolf in her book, *White China: Finding the Divine in the Everyday,* characterizes spirituality as milk and religion as the milk jug. Without the milk, the jug is dry and does not nourish, but without the jug the milk spills all over the table. What does this metaphor have to say about the Willapa community and the Aurora community's expression of religion and their spirituality?

12. Sometimes we stumble in our faith, and because of stress, loss, and challenges too great, we ache, moving away from what might give us strength. How did Emma stumble? Who or what brought her back to the source of her strength? What did she find she could trust? Are there times in your life that are reflected in Emma's journey?

ACKNOWLEDGMENTS

C. S. Lewis once wrote of the German word *Sehnsucht,* referring to the longing or yearning of the human spirit. My German friends tell me the word carries weight, that such longing is almost an addiction, a compulsion. For me, *A Tendering in the Storm* is an interweaving of the *Sehnsucht* of one Emma Wagner Giesy, who lived in the nineteenth and twentieth centuries, and our own contemporary longings—to be known, to be loved, to find meaning despite life's trials. Through exploration of our longings, we are freed to live full, community-integrated lives and to discover how fortunate we are to have gifts enough to give away.

A great many people provided gifts to me in the researching and writing of this second book in the Change and Cherish Historical Series. Dr. David and Pat Wagner, descendants of Emma, provided access to family letters and photographs and artifacts, as well as the generosity of their home and a private tour of relevant Northwest-area sites. As with the first book, they willingly let me speculate about their ancestor and offered ideas of what might have motivated Emma's actions. Their discovery of a letter in Emma's hand was a delight to all of us, and her words turned us in a direction we might otherwise not have gone. David also read an early manuscript, and I am grateful for his suggestions and his encouragement of my telling this story.

The family of Dr. Jerry Giesy, descendants of one of Christian's brothers, shared copies of several colonists' "calling cards." It was a delight to discover Emma's card there, surrounded by pink flowers. The Bruce Giesy family donated a quilt of Emma's to the Society. Seeing her work helped inform her character. The Giesy's enthusiasm for my storytelling is greatly appreciated.

A great-granddaughter of Emma's, Louise Hankeson, and great-grandson M. L. Truman provided information about the circumstances of Christian's death and the impact of that day on Emma throughout her life. I am grateful for their sharing.

Irene Westwood, a volunteer at the Aurora Colony Historical Society (ACHS), in Aurora, Oregon, became a valued ally and exemplarly researcher. The information she located helped explain Emma's comments in her letter, clarified the family story, and set the stage for the decisions Emma later made. Irene is steadfast and asked the kinds of questions that make a novelist smile. There is no way to thank her enough.

Patrick Harris, curator at the ACHS, could not have been more helpful. He answered obscure questions (Did the bridge across the Pudding River wash out in the 1861–62 floods?), went through ledger books with me from the Keil and Company Store, tracked legal and land documents, and even gave me a walking tour of the Aurora National Historic District. He has a wonderful memory for colony names and descendants and like me, I think, finds great joy in discovery of some detail that will turn the story. He always greeted me with enthusiasm, as did all the staff and volunteers throughout the facilities of the colony. I am grateful to Patrick along with board members Norm Bauer and James Kopp, who read advance copies of the book, gave me insights about Aurora, took me on tours, and made helpful suggestions. Alan Guggenheim, former director of the Aurora Society, provided me with copies of architectural information and the news of Emma's interest in having a home of her own with the colony. John Holley, current executive director, continued to set the tone of access to the archives and the support of these stories, for which I'm grateful. The cadre of volunteers at the society is a gift not only to visitors but to my own research as well.

In Pacific County, Karla and Peter Nelson of Time Enough Books put me in touch with Dobby Wiegardt, a longtime oysterman who showed me a native Willapa oyster shell and talked about the oystering life, lending authenticity to this story. They also introduced me to Truman and Donna Rew, who offered their guesthouse (overlooking the Columbia River where it meets the Pacific) while I was in the area researching. Their generosity is greatly appreciated. The

Nelsons also hosted a grand launch at the Ilwaco Heritage Museum in Ilwaco, Washington, for the first book in the series, *A Clearing in the Wild*, and they've welcomed my husband and me and our wirehaired pointing griffon into their store with warmth. Their support, their reading of advance manuscripts, and their good humor could not have been more welcome. I thank them.

Bruce Weilepp, former director of the Pacific County Historical Society, and Sue Pattillo, board member, provided information and thoughtful speculation about how things were accomplished in the 1850–60s of this rain forest–like part of Washington State. Nancy Lloyd of Oysterville gave countless hours of creative research and speculation, offering a variety of suggestions, all of them valued. Board member Ken Karch sent me a CD of all the Pacific County Historical Society's journals, and it was in that search I discovered Christian had been a justice of the peace and a legislator. I am grateful!

Pacific County resident Marlene Martin and her daughter Joni Blake, and a cousin, Cameron Baker, descendants of another Giesy line, offered assistance to visit the Willapa cemetery and their ideas about what happened when. To all of these people I extend appreciation.

The Douthit family of western Oregon provided details about their ancestors (the Wagonblasts), and Oregonian Bernie Blum provided fascinating land-transaction information that provided insights about Emma's life. He included documents that gave me Emma's sister's nickname as well. A number of Keil descendants provided family stories that helped enrich Emma's journey.

The Oregon Historical Society and Oregon State Archives again provided valued documents.

Erhard and Elfi Gross provided valued reference on German words and usage but even more, made us at home with wonderful German cooking that Elfi is known for and that provided authenticity for Emma's interest in preparing fine German dishes.

Several descendants from Bethel contacted me after the release of the first book, including Lucille Bower, who continues to live in Bethel. Along with those from the Aurora colony and Willapa, and descendants from earlier colonies spread throughout the country, their stories became important threads in the weaving of this story.

I am especially grateful to the help of my editors: to Erin Healy and to Dudley Delffs of WaterBrook Press, a division of Random House, and to the team who supports me there in all departments, and to my agent, Joyce Hart, in Pittsburgh. I couldn't do this without them all.

My prayer team of Carol, Judy, Gabby, Susan, and Marilyn (posthumously), as well as many others who I know hold both Jerry and me in their hearts, make this storytelling seem like praying and thus a joy. Thank you. My friends Blair, Sandy, Kay, Barbie, the Carols, Susan, and my writing friends form my "colony," without whom I'd be as isolated as Emma was. Thanks for keeping me in your loop.

My family (extended and selected) and especially Jerry, have come to understand my quirks and timing, offered help in countless ways, and taught me to be a better recipient of God's good gifts. Thank you for knowing me and loving me anyway.

For whatever is authentic about this story, I give credit to the above people and others too numerous to mention; whatever errors exist are mine.

And finally, to readers who continue to honor me with your time, thank you. You make these men and women come alive to me through your letters and visits to my Web site, and through your kind words at signings and events. I hope you'll look for a continuation of Emma's story and the colony's journey in book three.

With gratitude,

Jane Kirkpatrick

SUGGESTED ADDITIONAL RESOURCES

Allen, Douglas. *Shoalwater Willapa*. South Bend, WA: Snoose Peak Publishing, 2004.

Arndt, Karl J. R. *George Rapp's Harmony Society 1785–1847*, rev. ed. Cranbury, NJ: Associated University Presses, 1972.

Aurora Colony Historical Museum. *Oregon Music Project, Publication and Performance of Previously Lost Original Music Written by Members of the Aurora Colony Bands, Ensembles and Choral Groups between 1856 and 1883*. Unpublished manuscript, Aurora, OR: Aurora Colony Historical Museum, 2006.

———. *Emma Wakefield Memorial Herb Garden*. Aurora, OR: Old Aurora Colony Museum, n.d.

Barthel, Diane L. *Amana, From Pietist Sect to American Community*. Lincoln, NE: University of Nebraska Press, 1982.

Bek, William G. "The Community at Bethel, Missouri, and Its Offspring at Aurora, Oregon," pt. 1. *German-American Annals*, vol. 7, 1909.

———. "A German Communistic Society in Missouri." *Missouri Historical Review*. October 1908.

Blankenship, Russell. *And There Were Men*. New York: Alfred A. Knopf, 1942.

Buell, Hulda May Giesy. "The Giesy Family." *Pacific County Rural Library District*, memoir. Raymond, WA, 1953.

———. "The Giesy Family Cemetery." *The Sou'wester*. Pacific County Historical Society, vol. 21, no. 2, 1986.

Bush, L.L. "Oystering on Willapa Bay." *Willapa Harbor Pilot*. South Bend, WA, 1906.

Cross, Mary Bywater. *Treasures in the Trunk: Memories, Dreams, and Accomplishments of the Pioneer Women Who Traveled the Oregon Trail.* Nashville: Rutledge Hill Press, 1993.

Curtis, Joan, Alice Watson, and Bette Bradley, eds. *Town on the Sound, Stories of Steilacoom.* Steilacoom, WA: Steilacoom Historical Museum Association, 1988.

De Lespinasse, Cobie. *Second Eden. A Novel Based upon the Early Settlement of Oregon.* Boston. The Christopher Publishing House, 1951.

Dietrich, William. *Natural Grace: The Charm, Wonder and Lessons of Pacific Northwest Animals and Plants.* Seattle: University of Washington Press, 2003.

Dole, Philip. "Aurora Colony Architecture: Building in a Nineteenth-Century Cooperative Society." *Oregon Historical Quarterly,* vol. 92, no. 4, 1992.

Dole, Philip, and Judith Reese. "Aurora Colony Historic Resources Inventory." Unpublished manuscript funded by Oregon State Historic Preservation Office, in private collection at Aurora Colony Historical Museum.

Duke, David Nelson. "A Profile of Religion in the Bethel-Aurora Colonies." *Oregon Historical Quarterly,* vol. 92, no. 4, 1992.

Ficken, Robert E. *Washington Territory.* Pullman, WA: Washington State University Press, 2002.

Gordon, David G., Nancy Blanton, and Terry Nosho. *Heaven on the Half Shell, The Story of the Northwest's Love Affair with the Oyster.* Portland, OR: Washington Sea Grant Program and WestWinds Press, 2001.

Hendricks, Robert J. *Bethel and Aurora: An Experiment in Communism as Practical Christianity.* New York: The Press of the Pioneers, 1933.

Keil, William. "The Letters of Dr. William Keil." *The Sou'wester.* Pacific County Historical Society, vol. 28, no. 4, 1993.

Knapke, Luke B., ed. *Liwwät Böke: 1807–1882 Pioneer.* Minster, OH: The Minster Historical Society, 1987.

Lloyd, Nancy. *Willapa Bay and the Oysters.* Oysterville, WA: Oysterville Hand Print, 1999.

McDonald, Lucile. *Coast Country: A History of Southwest Washington.* Long View, WA: Midway Printery, 1989.

Nash, Tom, and Twilo Scofield. *The Well-Traveled Casket.* Eugene, OR: Meadowlark, 1999.

Nordhoff, Charles. *The Communistic Societies of the United States.* New York: Hillary House, 1960.

Olsen, Deborah M. "The *Schellenbaum:* A Communal Society's Symbol of Allegiance." *Oregon Historical Quarterly,* vol. 92, no. 4, 1992.

Simon, John E. "William Keil and Communist Colonies," *Oregon Historical Quarterly,* vol. 36, no. 2, 1935.

Snyder, Eugene Edmund. *Aurora, Their Last Utopia, Oregon's Christian Commune, 1856-1883.* Portland, OR: Binford and Mort, 1993.

Staehli, Alfred. *Old Aurora Colony Museum Architectural Conservation Assessment,* pt. 3. Aurora, OR: Kraus House, 2000.

Stanton, Coralie C. "The Aurora Colony Oregon." Thesis, Oregon State University, 1963, in the collection of Aurora Colony Historical Museum.

Strong, Charles Nelson. *Cathlamet on the Columbia.* Portland, OR: Holly Press, 1906.

Swan, James G. *The Northwest Coast or Three Years' Residence in Washington Territory.* New York: Harper and Brothers, 1857.

Swanson, Kimberly. " 'The Young People Became Restless': Marriage Patterns Before and After Dissolution of the Aurora Colony." *Oregon Historical Quarterly,* vol. 92, no. 4, 1992.

Weathers, Larry, ed. *The Sou'wester.* South Bend, WA: Pacific County Historical Society, 1967, 1970, 1972, 1974, 1979, 1986, 1989, 1993.

Will, Clark Moor. "An Omnivorous Collector Discovers Aurora!" *Marion County History, School Days I, 1971–1982,* vol. 13, Marion County Historical Society, 1979.

———. *The Sou'wester.* Several letters between descendant Will and Ruth Dixon. Raymond, WA: Pacific County Historical Society collection, May 29, 1967.

BOOK THREE

A Mending at the Edge

a novel

*This book is dedicated to the volunteers, staff, and board
of the Aurora Colony Historical Society and Museum
for their passion in honoring descendant stories
as they keep history relevant and alive.*

Cast of Characters

At Aurora

Emma Wagner Giesy	German American
Andrew	Emma and Christian's older son
Catherine/Kate/Catie	Emma and Christian's daughter
Christian	Emma and Christian's younger son
Ida	Jack Giesy and Emma's daughter
David and Catherina Wagner	Emma's parents
Jonathan, David Jr., Catherine "Kitty," Christine (the foster child), Johanna, Louisa "Lou," and William	Emma's siblings
Joe Knight	oysterman, former scout, Matilda's brother
Adam Schuele	colonist, former scout with Christian and Emma
Wilhelm Keil	leader of Aurora, Oregon, colony
Louisa Keil	Wilhelm's wife
Willie (deceased; buried in Willapa), August, Frederick, Elias, Louisa, Gloriunda, Aurora, Amelia, Emanuel	Keil children
Martin Giesy	colonist, a future pharmacist and physician, and Christian's brother
John and Barbara (BW) Giesy	colonists, Christian's brother and sister-in-law
Elizabeth	John and Barbara's daughter
Karl Ruge	colonist, teacher, toll keeper, Emma's friend
Barbara Giesy	colonist, Christian's mother, widowed
Helena Giesy	colonist, Christian's sister
Louisa Giesy	colonist, Christian's sister
Martha Miller	colonist, a woman of the colony
Nancy Thornton	painter in the Oregon City area
Almira Raymond	a member of Emma's house church
Matilda Knight	sister of Joe Knight, an original scout

Jacob Stauffer	colonist, son of John Stauffer, an original scout
Henry C. Finck	music teacher
Henry T. Finck	Henry C's son, Andy's friend
Christopher Wolff	colonist, instructor and leader of a Bethel wagon train
John and Lucinda Wolfer	colonists who tended ill people in the community
Catherine and Christina Wolfer	mother and daughter who saved the plate
Mr. Ehlen	colonist, wounded Civil War veteran
Lorenz Ehlen	son of Mr. Ehlen and friend of Andy and Kate's
Brita Engel	a *Zwerg* and a woman in need
Charles, Stanley, and Pearl	Brita's children
Opal, the goat	
Clara, the chicken	
Po, the dog	

At Willapa Bay

Christian Giesy	Emma's deceased husband and former leader of the scouts, buried in Willapa
Sebastian and Mary Giesy	Christian's brother and his wife
Elizabeth	Sebastian and Mary's daughter
Louisa Giesy	Christian's younger sister
Sam and Sarah Woodard	settlers at Woodard's Landing
Jacob "Jack" or "Big Jack" Giesy	Emma's second husband

At Bethel

Andreas "Andrew" Giesy Jr.	colonist, Christian's brother, preacher and co-director of Bethel Colony in Keil's absence
August Keil	colonist, Keil's son sent to assist with colony business

* *not historical characters*

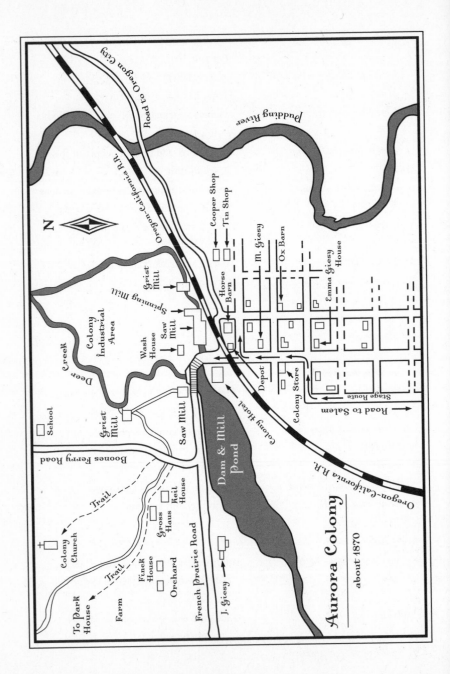

Aurora Colony

about 1870

Women are the brooms of the world—they clean houses and they clean souls. But often they get put back in the corner until the next mess needs to be cleaned up.

ALISON SAAR, artist, *Expanded Visions:*
Four Women Artists Paint the American West,
Women of the West Museum, 2000

Each community has a different rhythm.... We have our own individual rhythms within the community: ...some devote their lives to the daily maintenance of the community while others breathe life into it through their art, music, and poetry. We may find ourselves in a radically altered relationship to the community as we move to its edges or outside it entirely for brief or lengthy periods of time....

Rhythms of community can be both life-giving and stifling, liberating and oppressive.... We listen to and follow the Spirit's own rhythms as it moves with us.... We listen to the stories of other women in other communities.... We better understand what it means to be a creative, spirited community of healing, of hope, of resistance, and of transformation.

JAN RICHARDSON,
Sacred Journeys: A Woman's Book of Daily Prayer

Then they that feared the LORD spake often one to another: and the LORD hearkened, and heard it: and a book of remembrance was written before him for them that feared the LORD, and that thought upon his name.

MALACHI 3:16

1

The Hope Inside

Of all the things I left behind in Willapa, hope was what I missed the most. But memory is a flighty friend, wisping in to warm or warn when one can least expect it. I wanted to remember Christian—my first husband—and the hopefulness that we'd brought with us across the plains from Missouri to the wet Washington Territory in 1853. Remembering him recalled that good part of me, before change had rubbed me raw. After that, much had happened to take hope from life, and I questioned whether expectation was a virtue one could nurture or if once lost would never sprout again. My friend, Karl Ruge, a lover of words as I am, says that in English, *despair* means "to fall back from hope." But for my friends, I would have drowned in despair.

On this dark day, rain pounded like Indian drums on the cedar shakes above us. Through the wavy glass windows I watched raindrops splash out over the full, coopered barrels stationed at the *gross Haus* corners, a collection place for wash water. We needed to do the wash, what with all the people and mud. It was how one belonged to this colony, sharing in work and in the waiting together through storms. Out the window, I could see an east wind whipping the young walnut trees in the yard beyond. The bare branches looked like skeletons instead of as intended, hopeful sentinels standing guard over this small colony in the infant state of Oregon.

A deep roll of thunder rattled the windows in the entryway where I cluck-henned my boys and Kate around me, holding Ida in my arms. We huddled in a corner of the *gross Haus,* the three-story building being built by Brother Keil (I refused to call him *Father* Keil as do most others in our communal society). We shared the house with two dozen others, all longtime members. I'd found safety here. But I never knew when that fragile calm might be shattered. The smell of wet wool filled my head as cloaks and coats draped every railing or chair or blue bench, drying out. Colonists from the low-lying areas drove wagons here when the rivers began to rise early in December, adding still more numbers to an already-crowded house. The *gross Haus* rose up on the highest knoll of the village, like a castle of old, visible from a great distance. Of course. It was Keil's house.

The aroma of sausage and beans bubbling in the large pots in the kitchen reached my soggy senses. Someone lovingly prepared a meal where hunger served as sauce. But just as quickly, the scents reminded me of my family still in Missouri, family where the threads of connection had been strained since I'd come west. I'd received no letters from my parents since my decision to leave Willapa and come here with my four children. Well, we hadn't all come at once. I arrived first with my friend Karl Ruge and my daughters; my sons were brought to me later by their uncle Martin Giesy, a tactic of safety we'd all felt necessary. But my sister Kitty had written from Missouri to say they were coming to Oregon, so things would change. Dared I hope they would change for the better?

My cheeks felt cold, and Kate's six-year-old upturned nose looked red as a summer rose. The children would probably collect sniffles with so many people huddled so closely together. Andy especially had to fight off frequent illnesses. Failing health affected our days—our entire lives, in fact. We'd lived the past years not far from the Pacific Ocean where we'd seen days of downpours, and some said that our part of the wild endured ninety inches or more in a year. Coughs arrived with the weather. I'd thought it would be better here in Oregon, but the past days of January 1862 had yet to reveal that a sun did shine somewhere overhead or that rivers in Oregon really did know how to flow within their banks. Not very hopeful, that thought.

I'd reentered this community for the loving embrace it promised, the kind built on grace and faith, not domination or control. Embraces can constrict. Other members of my husband's family had taught me that.

A few log houses, a stage-stop barn, a grist and lumber mill, and some board homes composed Aurora, the village the colonists had been building since 1856. The structures clustered in a swale, like eggs in a chicken's nest. Deer Creek and Pudding River helped define its tree-lined borders. A quarter mile from the houses ran a deep ravine, and near the top of that hill, Brother Keil had built his house with a view looking out over his domain. Other colonists had been assigned farmland farther away. A few had settled nearer the Willamette River some eight miles west. Most of us this winter were staying in the yet-unfinished Keil house, high above the creeks and flooding waters.

Another crack of thunder. Kate shivered against me. "We don't hear thunder so much here," Helena said. She's the older sister of my deceased husband, Christian, tall and formidable, and her observations usually come out as dogma. But now she fidgeted with the braids formed like a crown on the top of her head, and she startled at the rumble too. It was the first time I'd seen Helena look even the least bit flummoxed.

"I like the sound of it," Louisa told her cheerfully. "It reminds me of Missouri." Louisa is Brother Keil's wife and the mother of their eight living children. "I haven't seen any lightning, so that's a good thing, *ja?*"

"*Ach,* you find cream in even stale milk," Helena told her, brushing her hand in the air as though she brushed away flies. Still, they spoke as old friends, family perhaps, as women accustomed to sharing differences that really didn't matter.

I hadn't found anything wrong with Louisa's tying thunder to a good memory from Missouri. Problems only arose if you stayed wrapped inside the comfort of old thoughts, refused to unbind yourself to move forward.

Rain pounded like hail now, pelting nearly horizontal. I patted Kate's arm with reassurance.

"*Ach, Jammer,*" complained one of the bachelors, as close to cursing as he'd get in this mixed company that included women and children.

"I hope it doesn't break those windows!" another said. Glass was precious here and perhaps not all that practical. Brother Keil had promised that eventually all would have glass windows, though first, we needed houses. A minor detail to him, a throbbing desire to me. I so wished for a safe place, a home of my heart, a place where I truly belonged and was accepted as I was.

Ida began to cry, and I unfolded myself from the cluster of my children. "I must feed your sister," I told them and moved out of the corner, across the pine flooring dotted with colorful rugs, and headed down the stairs to the kitchen, where I could nurse her in the presence of women only. The children began to follow, the boys included. I turned to them, Ida on my hip but clawing at my bodice. "Don't come down those stairs, now. Wait here. I'll be fine and so will you."

Kate and Christian stopped, nodded their heads in agreement. Andy, the oldest, glared at me, his arms crossed over his chest. He didn't turn around as the other two had. "Don't come down these steps," I repeated.

I wished I felt more hopeful about my relationship with him.

Ida squirmed and fussed as I took the narrow steps, then crossed under them into the kitchen area. I looked up to see if the children had moved away, and they had. They were like hinges in the midst of all the changes, swinging toward security by clinging to me, then pushing away for independence.

A row of windows bordered the ceiling and looked out onto the sodden ground, but the room felt gloomy. Rain painted everything dark. Even my quilted petticoat couldn't ignore the chill. Thank goodness a fire glowed in the fireplace. It spit and snapped with raindrops racing down the chimney. I could smell fresh bread nestled against the brick firewall, baking in the bank of warm ash. Women bustled about, so I pulled a chair into the wide hallway and sat in front of the blue cabinet built from floor to ceiling. It had glass doors, of course. We waited for houses, and Keil had our craftsmen build fine furniture for him and order in new glass. I folded back Ida's Nine Patch quilt from around her face, helped her find my breast, and nodded to the other women working at preparing pork and beans. Along with bread and peas, potatoes and what fruits we'd dried, ham and beans were our staple food this winter. The chickens hadn't produced since November.

I silenced the chatter in my head to focus on Ida and give her all she needed to be calm and eat. My younger daughter would be seven months old before long and had spent most of her early life in turmoil. We'd made our escape from her threatening father, leaving nearly all we owned behind. She'd adjusted to living huddled with so many others while I worked, cooking and washing and mending. I also worked at holding my tongue.

I'd come to Aurora in good part because those few I trusted thought it best. Worn down and hopeless, I'd leaned on them. It had been a good decision. Still, I lacked confidence in the choices I'd made since Christian's death. Grief, I've learned, has many siblings—guilt, anger, fear, unworthiness, separation from those who love us, resistance to change. They clamor for attention in times of trial, and sometimes I heard those brothers and sisters of grief speak louder than the call of comfort that can come from family and friends.

Ida suckled eagerly. Of my four children, only Ida could I nurse; wet nurses and the goat's milk had rescued my others. I should have found it hopeful that I could feed this child and that I fed her in a dry, safe place. But too much had happened. Time, like a good chalk, had yet to erase the stains I carried on my heart.

"*Ach*, someone comes in through the root room door," one of the kitchen women said. She had disgust in her voice, as though the intruder should know better than to drag his muddy boots through the food larder instead of stomping and removing his brogans at the covered porch outside, above us. I felt the gush of wind carry the scent of roots, which were hung to dry in the rafters behind the hallway door. Wood slammed against the doorjamb. "I will tell him to go around," she said as she moved past me.

For a moment I had this twinge of premonition. It could be Jack Giesy, my second husband, come back. He had a claim on me, though not on my heart. Brother Keil had sent Jack packing last fall, but I knew Keil could change his mind. At the sound in the root room, I wondered if perhaps he had.

Ida fidgeted, her blue eyes wide, and she stared at me as she let her hands flop away from my breast. My only child of the four to have blue eyes. If I ignored her, she could make me pay, with her new teeth coming in. I smiled nervously at her, brushed her walnut-colored hair, the same color as mine, but with dozens of tight curls instead of my strands pulling loose from my bun. I shushed her as my fingers lifted those ringlets. "It's all right," I said. "You go ahead and suckle now. Mama is with you." I tried to relax as I plotted my escape route up the stairs if Jack came through the door.

"What are you doing in here?" I heard the kitchen woman say, and I swallowed hard, started to stand. "Soaked like a swimming kitten you are. *Ach.*"

I craned my neck to see who followed her in.

"Andy," I said when I saw my almost-nine-year-old son. Irritation followed relief. "Didn't I ask you to stay upstairs? And why on earth would you go outside and get all wet rather than use the stairs anyway?" Water dripped off his chin, puddled at his boots.

"You told me not to come down the steps," he said. "I wanted to do what you said." A raindrop like a tiny pearl hung from his long eyelashes. His dark eyes twinkled with a hint of guile. My head began to pound.

Ida sat up then. Her eyes moved to the popped cornball Andy held in his hand. She reached for it. "And where did you get that?" I asked.

"At Christmas, remember? *Herr* Keil gave them to all the children. I saved mine."

I wondered if some of the cornballs might have been kept back in the root room and if he'd lifted one as he walked through. It didn't look soaked. I didn't like him lying to me or being disobedient. *I must not think these bad thoughts about every little thing that happens. He might have had it in his coat.*

"Someone will need to clean up the mud mess in the hallway," the kitchen woman said. Under her breath as she passed by me she added, "Some people need to keep better control over their children, *ja?*"

"I'll tend to it," I sang out to her. To Andy I spoke firmly, "Go get a broom and sweep up this mud. Now."

"That's women's work," Andy said.

"So is disciplining a wayward boy." He dropped his eyes. I softened. He'd been through so much. "You see we're fine here, nothing to worry about. Get the broom, and then maybe you can go into Brother Keil's workroom to see what medicines he's mixing." I nodded toward the opposing door. "Go on." Then to Ida I said, "Finish up here." I pushed Ida's face back to my breast. "Mama has things to do."

My son moved off, and I heard Brother Keil welcome him in. Relief flooded me. Only later did I remember that Andy had failed to sweep up the dirt. I vowed he'd do it later.

I patted Ida as she ate. How could I not feel hopeful with a baby growing fat at my breast? Oh, I once had wishful thoughts and a profound belief that I could do all things necessary for my children, alone. But belief in one's own strength is not enough. Firm wishes held out like hope are not enough. I'd had high hopes for my second marriage too, but I'd come to that union like the mule who wore blinders when it plowed, unable to see what frightening things could catch me unaware.

Jack Giesy always had his problems and was never a steady man, but I'd failed to see that until he threatened my children's fate and, *ja,* my own, leaving me bruised and broken in more than my bones. Toward the end, I'd had to keep him separated from Andy, most of all, Christian's son who thought he'd have to rescue his family by doing harm to Big Jack.

Now here I was, settled in Oregon, in a tentative embrace of those very German American colonists who had once rejected what my first husband and I—and colony scouts—had been sent out from Bethel, Missouri, to do. We'd found a new site in the west, but it was not to Keil's liking, and so our group had split. I'd once rejected them too, refusing their help after my husband's death. Finding the balance between strict molds and a singular support, that was what I longed to find, and I would. I resolved that I'd remember myself back into a hopeful state, where I saw the possibilities instead of the disappointments. Soon, I prayed, my parents and brothers and sisters would arrive from Missouri and we'd have a grand reunion. I'd have a house of my own. I'd raise my children, keeping them close. My husband would stay away. I'd contribute to the colony and be known for more than being contrary. These were my wishes.

My fingers ached still from Jack's wrenching them the year before. Ida curled her small fist inside mine.

Another whoosh of the root cellar door. *"Ach,"* I shouted to the kitchen women, "it's probably my other *Kinder* following their brother. I'll see to them."

I placed the Nine Patch over my shoulder and open bodice and hiked Ida on my hip. I scrunched the mud on the floor and approached the root room door, rehearsing what I'd say to these urchins and what to do to hold Andy accountable for being a poor model for them.

Root smells and damp earth greeted me. My eyes glanced down to the height of the eyes of my children, or at least where I expected them to be. I saw, not foreheads, but knees.

When I looked up, I stared into the dark, brooding face of Jack Giesy, the husband I'd hoped would let us be.

"Aren't you pleased to see me?" He angled toward me like a snake, as though to put his arms around my shoulders and his daughter, sucking us in. Rain dripped from his felt hat. A half sneer marked his face. I recognized it as a look that formed a prelude to his outbursts of rage. Who knew how long he'd been nursing some perceived injustice that he thought could be remedied by bullying his way in here?

I backed up. My hands grew wet. My heart pounded. Ida fussed. I saw movement behind Jack. Someone short had slipped through the door, slammed it shut with a thud. *How could Andy have gotten behind him?* He'd give fuel to Jack's fire. *Please, may it not be one of my children!*

Jack reached for Ida then, his daughter; but I twisted, holding her head pressed into my chest. "Don't touch her," I hissed. My jerking from him caused me to stumble. Jack stumbled back too, I thought from the force of my words.

Instead, a small stranger pushed her way around Jack. She waddled from side to side to stand between us. The size of a child, she wore the face of a worried woman.

She pulled on my skirt. "I know you can help me," the high, breathy voice said. She grabbed my hand, thumped a startled Jack on his thighs when he tried to move around her to grab at me. He groaned, struggled to catch his balance as she fast-walked out toward the rain, pulling at my skirts. I pushed past Jack, covered Ida's head, and scurried along.

I had no idea who this woman was or what she needed. But in the midst of my dread at seeing Big Jack, she'd sliced through my despair and somehow seen hope inside me.

2

Spinning Straw into Gold

I'd heard of small earth men, as they were called, in German stories such as *Rumpelstiltskin*. They bargained for a child by helping a princess turn straw into gold. They were magical people, part of a fairy tale. I'd never met one, only seen pictures of them as part of circus acts. Karl Ruge said the Indians thought such small-statured people were mystical, with a close attachment to the divine. Some people didn't like them. They claimed the little people made them nervous, judged them solely by appearance. The *Zwerg* I'd read about were short men with long white beards. But here stood a woman, indeed, with a wide forehead and long, thick dark hair chopped at the nape of her neck. I had never been this close to a being so…different…and despite the tightening of my throat for fear of Jack lurking behind me, her presence in that small root room had brought me strange comfort.

My comfort was short lived as Big Jack followed us outside.

"Don't run away from me," he said, grasping my shoulder, spinning Ida and me around.

"Leave me be." I struck at his arm, which he lowered, no longer a threatening fist.

"What do you think, Wife?" he whined, his palms raised in surrender. It was part of his pattern to intimidate, then snivel and cajole when he remembered there was a witness. "I maybe could see my daughter and my sons? That's all I want. To be a good father."

"You were asked by Brother Keil to leave," I said. My heart pounded in my ears, but my voice sounded steady, even loud against the muffle of wet grass and trees. The little woman still tugged on my skirt. "And they are not your sons."

"I was asked to hold my temper, to do no harm, and I plan none," he said. He removed his hat and smoothed back the hair that curled behind his ears and at his neck. He needed it cut, something I used to do for him before all that had happened between us. The drizzle caught in his beard. "There were hard freezes in Willapa," he said. He cleared his throat. "I thought I'd seek warmth here in Aurora. You'd maybe not begrudge a man comfort, would you?"

We will talk of the weather, then, as though we are old friends getting reacquainted.

I pushed Ida's head farther under the quilt. I should get her out of the drizzle, though people in this western country looked more casually for shelter than in Missouri, where one rushed to get out of the weather. Here, rushing and scrunching up your shoulders against the rain offered scant relief, just an aching neck.

"You've no time for aweather chatter," the little woman told me. "I have a sick baby in the cart under the front porch and—"

I turned to her. "Let's bring him in, then."

"Along with two others."

"I'll take Ida back inside while you go and get them," Jack said. "I maybe could help. That is my daughter you're carrying, *ja?*"

I slipped behind Jack, fast-walked back into the root room, and nearly stumbled over Andy, who'd been listening at the door. "Get Brother Keil," I told him. "Go." His eyes got round as a leather ball, and I knew he spied Jack beyond me. "Go now! Do as I say."

Andy came to himself and scooted ahead of me into Brother Keil's workroom while I marched toward the kitchen, grateful to see that Louisa Keil had come down to check on the status of the ham and beans. "Louisa," I said, intercepting her. "Please, take Ida for me. Stay in the kitchen. There's a...problem in the root room."

"Her boy comes in there all full of mud," the kitchen grump told her, hands on her hips, a spoon held out like a bird's broken wing.

"That's not the problem," I said. "And we'll clean it up, I promise. It's Jack."

"*Ja*, sure," Louisa said. Her eyes held concern as she took my child. I buttoned up my bodice. I loved it that Louisa didn't question me further.

Behind me I heard, "What's this?" Keil's voice boomed as Jack came back in. "Oh, Jack Giesy. It's been some time since we've seen a Willapa Giesy."

These men forget so easily.

"He comes to make trouble," I said.

"*Nein.* I make no trouble," Jack protested. "A man needs a dry place and a moment or two with his family. Is this such a bad thing?"

Brother Keil tugged at that tuft of white beard at his chin. "*Nein.* You come inside, then. The draft pushes against the lanterns and scrapes the wall," he said as Jack moved toward the stairwell. I hesitated. *Leave Ida so close to Jack?*

"Remember, Louisa," I warned. She nodded and headed up the stairs. I'd have to trust her.

I slipped past Jack, pulling the quilt tighter around my shoulder like a shawl.

"And where do you go, Sister Giesy?" Keil called out to me.

"She's helping me," the little woman told him. She'd followed me back in. Keil looked down. Her protruding forehead hid her eyes.

"And who might you be?"

"Brita-witha-one-t Engel. Are you coming?" she dismissed him, pulling on my skirt.

"*Ja*, well then, I guess that is all right that you go help another," Keil said to my back, as though I needed his permission for anything at all.

The rain now let up and turned into a soft mist that dribbled through the slats of boards on the porch. Huddled back as close to the house foundation as they could get were Brita's children. Two boys stood by the two-wheeled cart. Their coughs nearly covered the soft murmuring of a baby. Brita lifted the infant, and I scooped up the younger of the two standing children. The older boy was about my Andy's age, though taller than his mother. She told him to bring the cart, and he pulled it after us, coughing all the while, as we headed back into the house through the root cellar. I could see my breath in the air. We'd have snow by morning.

I knew change and challenge waited for me inside the *gross Haus,* but for now I felt grateful to this Brita for giving me a meaningful diversion. Her troubles rose above my own.

Brita spoke to her boys in German mixed with English words, and she interspersed *"danke"* with her English "thank you" to me.

"It's what anyone would do," I told her, holding the door so she could pass in front of me, followed by the tallest child pushing the cart before him.

The baby cried now, a weak wail. "I've no milk for her," Brita said. "The cave we stayed in flooded, and the goat ran off with a thundering, a final brick to bring my chimney down."

"I can wet-nurse her," I heard myself say. "But we have cow's milk and goat's. And this one?" I nodded my chin to the child I held. His cough sounded wet and rattled.

"He throws up cow's milk. It's why we got the goat. He's so tired from acoughing." She pulled at my skirt again, and I realized that Brita couldn't see the face of the child I held unless I squatted down. She wiped spittle from the toddler's mouth. "Poor Stanley," she said. "So sickly."

"Let's see what Brother Keil might have to offer for remedies."

My eyes adjusted from the darker root room to the lantern-lit hall. No Jack in sight. I heard musical notes from the horns coming from the highest level of the house. Band members dealt boredom a blow by practicing a tune or two or took a work break from finishing the upper floors. Andy's head stuck out from Keil's workroom, then slipped back when Keil entered the wide hall. Louisa came back down the steps, patting Ida's back. The red trim of her quilted petticoat swirled a flash of color as she stepped. *A furbelow, from Louisa?* It was a bit of stitching spice I had never noticed before. *Why do I notice such insignificant details when my world is spinning apart?*

Charles, Brita's older boy, left the cart and sat down on the bottom step, holding his head in his hands. Dark circles framed his chipped nails. They disappeared as he clutched his dirty blond hair. He held himself in a wracking cough. Brita placed a handkerchief to his mouth, comforting him. I saw green mucus there.

"Let me see your tongue," Brother Keil said. Charles lifted his head, opened his mouth. I was vaguely aware of people standing near the kitchen, though I didn't see Jack's profile. I cast a glance toward the workroom; it stood empty. *He's upstairs with Christian and Andy and Kate. I should have warned them. I need to protect them.*

"Does your chest hurt? *Ja,* I figure as much," Keil said when Charles nodded, an action that began another round of coughs. The child in my arms, maybe two or three years old, also coughed now. I wondered if the warm room didn't aggravate their symptoms.

Keil opened one of the doors in the large blue cabinet and took out a vial of dark liquid. "Pulsatilla," he said. "It should help the cough. Then we get you some food and a dry place to rest, but no sleeping on the left side, *ja?* You'll be better then, in the morning."

I knew about the juice compressed from that flowering plant. Martin, Christian's brother, used it for a toothache once, and after Christian's death, he'd given it to me and said it would help me be less sad. I don't think it did, but then nothing save grace and time could have helped me. I hadn't known pulsatilla would stop coughs. I'd always treated my son with dulcamara, carefully measured, as it could be dangerous. But he got better in the warmth and worsened in the cold and damp, unlike this child. That Andy hadn't yet contracted some winter's ailment was a gift in itself, which I'd just then thought to be grateful for.

"We should put the family in a separate place," I said. "Maybe keep the coughs from spreading."

"*Nein,*" Keil said. "The boys can go with the other men. The one you hold, he is a *Junge?*"

"They stay together," Brita said, moving in that side-to-side gait to stand before him. Despite her small size, she acted fearless in front of Keil. "With their mother."

My own children and I were clustered together in the evenings in this wide hallway at the behest of the Keils, but during the day my boys were urged to spend time with the older boys and men staying at the upper floors. Now they couldn't, not with Jack there.

A fiddle joined the horns. I heard a concertina.

"Can't they rest here with us, in this corner area?" I said.

"I said to send them to the men now. Go. It will be better. We must have some sort of order in this household. I am still in charge."

"If they remain here, Charles can step into the root room sometimes, where the cool air might make him feel better," I said. "I'll gather up some quilts and they can settle on the floor, not spread the coughing through the rest of the house."

"That's a good idea, Husband," Louisa told him. She nodded to me that we should exchange children, I taking Ida from her while she comforted Brita's middle child. Her willingness to support me against her husband both surprised and comforted me.

"She needs goat's milk," I told Louisa. "It would be best if they are close to their mother."

"It's a strange, new place for them, Husband," Louisa told him.

"*Ach,*" he said, dismissing us. "You women do what you will. I have more important matters to attend to than sick children," and with that he turned back into his room, as unpredictable as a household goat.

Jack bounded down the steps then, and I realized too late that I didn't want Brother Keil to leave. My taking umbrage with him might have upset him, and now that the accommodations for the Engels had been decided, I had my own troubles to contend with.

"I have the right to see my daughter," Jack said.

"You put her in harm's way, so I don't think you're owed anything more than to gaze on her face, which you are now doing. You didn't like the responsibility of me and the children. You have a farm that ought to have gone to my sons, but you have it. I left everything for you."

"Emma," he began, took a step toward me. I backed up, clutching our daughter between us. She stared at him with wide eyes. "A woman is meant to be with her husband. He has the right to discipline his wife. Scripture says she's to surrender to him."

"Surrender to a husband who treats her with love. You have a habit of referring to the portions of Scripture you prefer," I said, "and interpreting them so they support you."

"As do you."

One of Jack's manipulative tools was his ability to hit a target with his piercing darts, making me question myself and thus giving him room to maneuver. But not this time. "We are not a matched team, Jack. I regret that I offered up our marriage bargain at all. Not only for what it did to hurt my family…but you too. It pushed you. Ida is the only good thing to come out of it, *ja*? But let's keep her from being pulled and tugged at like a flighty kite. She needs…a solid place to be, safe. She needs to be here."

"Which is why I've returned."

"You're not staying."

He reached to touch her head. She leaned back into my chest but allowed his caress. I shivered and she fussed.

"I'll build a house for us," he said, removing his hand from her hair. "One without the memories of Christian in it, so we maybe could have our own life, put the pieces back together, Emma." A cunning boy's look came to his face. He smiled and raised his eyebrows, as if he were asking me to put my skates on and join him for a swing around the frozen ponds beside the Pudding River.

For a moment I wondered if we could. Maybe he had changed.

But then I saw Andy on the landing, his arms crossed over his chest. It would never work. "The pieces of our puzzle never did fit, Jack. It was a labyrinth of loss."

Behind me I heard the rustle of Brita and her children, the chatter of women in the kitchen. Louisa giggled at something I hoped had nothing to do with us. Everyone could hear our marital discussion. The safety found with others also robbed me of needed private space.

"We could be together again, and with Brother Keil and others close by, I won't be tempted to let you twist my good nature into something foul." He smiled.

"Take her, would you?" Brita said, at my knees again.

"What?" I said, turning to look down.

"Hold her for a moment, please? The…privy makes an urgent call."

"But—"

Brita was already waddling out through the root room. The weight of the second child in my arms brought me back.

Jack said, "Your Kate is as short and squat as that *Zwerg.*" His insult was the perfect nail to hammer my decision tight. Having Big Jack Giesy back in my life on any terms was nothing short of insane. I'd have to ask Brother Keil for wolfsbane to calm me down, or be sent to an asylum if I even considered moving into a house with Jack Giesy. It wasn't worth the price. I slowed my breathing, grateful for the children that weighed against my chest.

"No, Jack." I looked at Brita's child in the crook of my arm as I talked. "You should do what Brother Keil said weeks ago. Leave us and stay gone." He grunted, and I looked up at him. His face clouded again. Somehow the presence of these children in my arms, the music from above, and the smells from the kitchen all served to remind me that I was not alone. The presence of the others didn't have to be an anchor to hold me down but could be a raft to buoy me up.

"You take in vagabonds and circus imps and their kin but want to send me out into the rains? Not even Doctor Keil would do that. No. A divorce is wrong."

"I haven't said I'd divorce you," I told him. A divorce would be one more thing that might separate my parents from me. In this country, regardless of the circumstances, divorced men always got the care of the children. No, I'd never choose divorce and risk that!

Brita returned and took her infant back into her arms. I didn't know her story yet, but she had a way of intervening at the perfect moment. "You said you could awet-nurse my Pearl," she said.

"*Ja,*" I told her. "As soon as I get Brother Keil."

I entered Keil's workroom without knocking and asked him to step out. Patiently, acting calm, I explained again my plight, my need to be free from Jack's pressuring presence. Getting other people to do what you want takes effort. You'd think after my years with Keil back in Bethel, trying to get him to let me go west with my husband, I'd have learned how fatiguing that is. It's a woman's necessity, to name her desires and then find ways to achieve them by meeting the needs of others. I remembered how my uncle, the vice counselor to France, wrote of having to think in such ways, organizing certain gestures, looks, and words, pulling them together to create a new image, like disparate fabric pieces forming a quilt. It was all such a puzzle, this living.

Keil looked over my shoulder at Jack, then finally spoke. "He's calm, Sister Giesy, despite a justified distress at being separated from his wife. If he lives with the bachelors and stays away from your boys, he can stay." I opened my mouth to protest, but Brother Keil quieted me. "I decide these things, not you, Emma Giesy. All are welcome at my door."

He looked at Brita and her brood, nodded his head as though to assure himself that all really were welcome, and then he returned to his room.

Jack grinned. "So. I have license to convince you, Wife," he said. "In my timing." He tipped his hat at me in a rakish way, then took two steps at a time up to the main floor. I heard his boisterous laugh as he brushed at Andy's hair when my son ducked beneath his hand and descended the steps to me.

What could I do? I'd need to keep the children constantly within my sight, hen-clucked around me, have them stay in the wide hall near the kitchen where Brita had joined us with her coughing sons. I'd need to wear vigilance like a cape.

"I don't like Jack's being here, Mama," Andy told me later, as we settled in for the night. Christian nodded his head in agreement as he slipped into his bedsack.

"I know. I don't either," I whispered. "But Jack won't hurt you as he did before. There are always people around. And you needn't worry over me either. I'll be fine. We have friends."

"We had friends before, but they didn't help," Andy said.

"You forget Karl," I reminded him as I pushed the cloth beneath his chin. "He helped us. And so did Martin."

Andy nodded. "But I can't be with Martin with Jack up there."

"When the weather improves, building will begin again, and maybe Martin will have his own house soon, and you can go stay with him sometimes. Or maybe your *Opa* and *Oma* will arrive from Missouri and we can live together with them. Maybe Big Jack will leave. Maybe Brother Keil will build *our* promised home. Any number of things will happen to change, Andy."

"So far, most of what's changed has been bad."

"That's the way the walnut rolls sometimes," I said. I brushed his straight blond hair from his eyes. "And besides, we're here together. There's nothing bad about that."

———

Sleep did not come easily for those huddled on the floors in the hallway. Outside, the weather turned beastly cold, and the mighty Columbia and the Willamette River froze over. Adam Schuele, one of the original scouts, made his way to th*e gross Haus*, and I heard him and Brother Keil arguing. Such close quarters made privacy a treasure. Adam had given his all, yet Brother Keil kept him now at arm's length. I wondered if Keil held a grudge because Adam hadn't joined the colony in Aurora but had remained instead for a time to help Christian and me and the other scouts still in Willapa. When he left, he'd returned to Bethel, not come here. He'd only recently shown up in Aurora. These acts of independence bothered Brother Keil, though I wasn't sure that's what brought on the intense voices behind the closed door. I closed my ears and thought of pleasant times past.

After the Pudding River went back into its banks, oval pools of water clustered in the low-lying areas and froze into perfect skating ponds. The cold kept us mostly indoors. Men bundled up to feed the animals or to bring in hams from the smokehouses. They couldn't heat the mills up to work, and the logs froze together. The men around Aurora stayed indoors, weaving baskets or using builder's sand to smooth the banisters. They set up a loom in the parlor area. Jack stayed in the house with the rest of them, rarely venturing outside, keeping me and the children stuck in the hall, where I told them stories or made up puzzles to keep their minds clear.

We all bundled up to race to the privy and, shivering, returned.

We did hear of Solomon Durbin in the town of Salem taking a team of sixteen horses with three sleighs attached and driving them across the frozen Willamette River. Someone took a photograph celebrating the winner in a contest to see who could handle the biggest sleigh and team.

"Men," I said, when Helena mentioned the competition and the lengthy sleighing season in the usually temperate valley. "So cold they can't work, but not too cold to compete."

"We women aren't so competitive as that," she agreed.

Through the winter, Brita looked after Ida and Christian, my younger son, while I helped in the kitchen, contributing to the colony as I'd agreed to. A few of the women spoke asides about "extra mouths to feed" or of an "invasion of *Zwerg*," but most of the colonists lived out their belief that it was worthy work to make another's life better than their own: the Diamond Rule, the luster of our Christian faith.

At night, I listened to Brita's stories that made my past and current trials look like puppies playing. She had endured a life of jeers and jokes over things she couldn't control: her small size, her pointed ears, her waddle-walk. One night she quietly told of the death of her husband in a circus fire and her journey to bring her husband's children north from California. They'd lived in a cave for a time, only to have that refuge washed away in the floods. So much loss seemed more than a person could bear, yet she had.

In the *gross Haus*, with the cacophony of coughs from Brita's brood, my own sons soon took ill, and I spent the spring doing what I could to comfort them. Both Martin and Brother Keil drew remedies from the blue cabinet we slept near.

Jack's presence on one of the floors above us cast shadows over my days. I could encounter him on our rushes to the outhouse. I had to serve him meals at the long men's table. At any time his dark looks might turn into actions. I listened for intruding steps in the night, planned activities based on smidgeons of information gleaned at the table to guess where Jack might be. Uncertainty fatigued as much as the hard work of doing the laundry for dozens.

I prayed for my parents' arrival. They'd be the stakes on either side of my family, safe and separate from Jack. I longed for my own home, with locks to restrict unwanted visitors. I hoped that Brother Keil would keep his word and soon build me a house.

"This is such a beautiful day," Brita announced one spring morning. We were bending over, planting beans in plowed fields of black earth.

"It is." I stood and stretched my back. "You're such a hopeful person, Brita, despite all the tragedies you've faced. How do you do it?"

"You can't always get what you want in this life," Brita said. Her smile filled her wide face. "But as any wise *Zwerg* knows, a hopeful soul learns to spin gold from the straw she's been given."

3

A Closer Weave

May 4. I wore Brother Martin's felt hat to keep the sun from my face while dipping water from the barrels to feed the bean plants. Helena clucked her tongue at me, but a hat opens the face while a bonnet is a blinder, and I have enough of those in my life already. I intend to weave a straw hat for myself.

June 10. I wrote to my parents. They've long supported Keil, and I wonder if our staying in Willapa instead of going with him is the reason they do not contact me. I'm trying to find the perfect stitch to hem my need for them while not sounding as though all my edges are frayed.

Dear Parents, Sisters, and Brothers,

Several days ago Brother Keil received some letters saying that none from Bethel will come to Oregon this year. For me, no news, not even an answer about the letter Brother Keil sent to you in the beginning of this year, where he said it would be helpful if Jonathan would come and take over my personal business. I would have written sooner to you, if several of my children had not taken ill, Christian and Kate. Now the little ones, thanks to God's blessings, are healthy and very active again, but it took many months before they recovered from the nasty fever.

Dear Parents, I am willing to obey and respect all orders which you gave me personally and the advice for my children's well-being, but you will forgive me if I ask what *delays you after such a long separation and bitterness for which I have no explanation? I long for a peaceful reunion with my good loving Parents, Brothers, and Sisters. How to arrange that I do not know. But I hope that Brother Jonathan, if not on his way already, will arrive this summer and will give poor Keil relief. He has so many worries, the whole town surrounded, some wondering if our communal ways are a challenge to them, and Jonathan could help relieve him of me and my children at least. Most of all, I am grateful for the daily love and devotion that Keil and his whole family have shown to me. I wish you to come not for my benefit but his, when he has so many continuous responsibilities to carry already. He is hoping my family will give some relief to ease the situation.*

Many hearty greetings to my good Parents and my Brothers and Sisters, to my Friends, and everyone who knows me in Bethel, who remember me lovingly.

Live well and keep on loving. Come soon.

Your obedient Daughter and Truly Devoted Sister.

P.S. I almost forgot, Big Jack has been here since Epiphany. I'm hopeful he'll leave soon as Andy stays with me and goes to school. I am doing what Brother Keil says to do. Greetings to little Louisa. We think of her often. I remain your loving Daughter and Sister,

Emma Giesy

That summer, while waiting for my parents, I churned butter or toted water from the spring, carrying questions about what I'd done to upset my family so that they'd stopped writing to me. I had left Jack, yes, but I hadn't divorced him. There were only one hundred divorces in the whole territory, or so Karl Ruge had told me when I once broached the subject with him—just in passing, of course. I'd explained to my parents why I'd left him. My brother Jonathan had urged me to come to

Aurora long before I even married Jack, and here I was now, so the problem couldn't be that I'd come to Aurora to stay. They'd always supported Keil. I'd thought my being here would please them.

The crops had been late coming on, as we'd had a very cool spring to follow the hard winter. The wheat crop promised to be smaller than normal, and I supposed in some ways Brother Keil might have been glad that the Bethelites would not be coming this year from Missouri. Feeding them—and housing them—once they arrived promised to be a major task. Yet he lamented their delay as I grieved my parents' silence.

Thousands of new settlers had come into the valley the previous winter, but few of them spoke German. They came from the Ohio Valley and farther east, and some from the rebellion states, so Brother Keil said he felt "surrounded" by those who might see the world differently. People seemed threatened by our sharing of resources. I'd thought that was the point and part of why we invited others to learn more about us, why we helped people as we could, to introduce them to our ways. But I suppose we did want to change other people's ways at least a little; we just didn't want their presence to change ours.

I'd listen to railroad talk at the long dining room table where we served the men. More than thirty thousand miles of tracks marked the country now, and Congress had authorized the Union Pacific Railroad to build from Nebraska to the Deseret country of Utah, where my aunt lived. That rail line would meet up with one being laid eastward from California. More people would come...but apparently not my parents.

"We'll get a spur through here one day," Brother Keil said, as he motioned for Louisa to bring him more coffee. "That will bring us work for the men and industry for Aurora." His wife hustled to him, fluttering over his comforts. Her constant deference to him was not a good model for her daughters, in my opinion, or for other colony girls either. But every now and then she resisted him. Perhaps she'd found that balance a marriage requires. I didn't like eavesdropping on other people's lives. Oh, how I longed for that home of my own!

Big Jack took his seat in the middle of the men, and I kept my eyes averted from his. I worried over our crops he'd left behind in Willapa.

Who farmed it now? Why didn't he go back? I'd give him no satisfaction by asking.

The men nodded in agreement that the railroad would be a good thing for Aurora. I shook my head in wonder. Keil had sent us west nearly ten years earlier to find a new colony site, specifically to avoid the bad influences that a railroad would bring. Now here he was championing it. I'd never understand the thinking of men. Sometimes Brother Keil's enthusiasms centered more on economics than on living a faith-filled life. We didn't even have a church building yet and held a service only once a month. I thought that a loss, even though I took issue with a few of his points of view on religion. Well, perhaps I took issue with his views of economics too. After all, he'd belittled Christian's and my plans for farming oysters as a way to survive in the Washington Territory, and yet it had served us well—until Christian's death.

Again my thoughts turned to Christian. How I missed his strength and vision. I understood Louisa better now, since we had both suffered the deaths of loved ones dearer than skin. *Ja,* she hovered over her husband, but she did not judge me that I failed to hover over the husband I'd been left with. Well, the one I'd poorly chosen.

If my parents would come, if my brother Jonathan could help me build the house and use his good business mind here, the entire colony would benefit. I had to press that point to my parents when I wrote next. They believed in generosity and in the work of Keil's communal society. At least they always had.

I think Brother Keil secretly liked to have us under one roof. He puffed up, sitting at the head of the long table, and faked chagrin when he was called out by local people seeking medicinal help. He'd sigh and say, "*Ach,* the demands," as he pushed himself away from the steaming food, while the women scurried to gather up his tailored coat and bag, several vying to go with him to serve as nurse. If Louisa was in the kitchen, Helena answered his every beck and call, bringing him his pipe or tobacco twist.

"Catie," Brother Keil called out to my daughter as she sat stitching. "Ah, you do such fine work, Catie."

"I'm Kate," she corrected him. But she beamed with pride at his recognition of her efforts.

"*Gut*, very *gut*. You'll make a fine seamstress one day. I'll show you special stitches if you'd like. I was trained as a tailor, you know, *ja*?" He patted her hair and didn't look at all chagrined when I frowned at him, though he did take his hand from her head.

To the young girls and those of marriageable age, Keil told stories, tweaking their cheeks and patting their shoulders as though they were recently out of their pinafores, instead of young woman harboring hope in their hearts. Most of his stories were about women being in service to their community and their Lord, about how they found happiness through these means rather than in marriage. It was a theme he'd been increasingly harping on even though it hadn't worked to keep Christian from marrying me. Now he urged celibacy even to married people. I thought it was renewed effort to keep us all available for the work of building the colony rather than our faith.

I watched to see if Louisa noticed his flutterings with the serving women. There might not have been anything untoward occurring between them, but he did sometimes let his hand linger longer than I thought necessary at a woman's waist when he moved through a crowded group to his seat at the table. I watched looks pass between two mothers when one of the daughters ducked and quickly moved away from Keil as he attempted to pat the braids on her head. And once I thought his face turned pink when a mother slapped his hand as he reached across her to pick up an oatmeal cookie from the pan in the kitchen. Her reaction said more about what part of her anatomy his hand had brushed than about his taking the cookie.

Louisa didn't appear to notice these little indiscretions. If I'd have mentioned it, she'd have defended Keil as she always did. They had found a way to be together all these years. She tittered and laughed overly much at his jokes; in return he allowed her to do *Fraktur* lettering. Each evening she put coals in the pan to make the flannel sheets warm before he slipped into them. I hoped she warmed up her own side of the bed, since she had a bad hip that pained her in the cold weather. When I asked her once, she looked surprised and said, "*Ach,* we don't sleep in the same bed. The hard floor works best for me and gives the good doctor fine rest, what he needs to be fresh to serve so many."

"Many of us colony women sleep alone," I said.

"How else do we wives get so much done," Louisa said, "except if we've had a decent night's sleep?" She didn't see the humor in what she'd said.

I never saw Brother Keil do helpful things for her, at least not the way Christian had for me. I don't think he ever made a gift for her, though I saw him tailor a dress for Aurora's doll, the daughter for whom he'd named the town. Christian had given me gifts of his tinwork, a chatelaine to hold my needles, for example, and a real pearl taken from an oyster. And once, when we were both young, he'd given me a ruffled petticoat that said he understood more than anything else my need to be unique in the midst of so many common threads.

Keil scoffed at such frivolities between a husband and his wife, as I recall. But Christian's gifts had fueled me as coal to a fire. They helped me endure our separations and warmed over the chill of words sometimes spoken in haste.

Even now, as I lifted the chatelaine from the chain around my neck, I could almost feel Christian's presence. My throat tightened. I blinked back tears and stepped back into the kitchen, wiping my eyes with the edge of my apron. I thought my grief had spent itself, but I'd cried more since being here than in those first months after Christian's death.

Of course, the greatest gifts Christian gave me to remember him by were our children. They were his legacy, the one I was meant to take care of.

At the close of the evening meals, while we served men desserts piled high with sweetened cream, several of us women washed the heavy dinner plates. Painted with tiny tea leaves, each one was different, though they were clearly a set. As I wiped them dry, I watched Louisa follow Keil to their quarters on the first floor. He said something and she laughed. He laughed too. *I shouldn't judge what happens in any other couple's bedroom,* I decided. It was a fault of communal living that stitched a married couple too close beside others, without a proper sash between them.

I carried the dishwater out to put into the barrel to be used on the floors later. I sometimes wished that I shared Louisa's oblivion and acceptance. Instead, Keil's actions drove me to think of how to get my girls out from under his roof before my Kate became old enough to notice.

I walked a narrow path, though: Keil might be willing to build my house only if Jack moved into it with me.

I began to wonder if moving elsewhere might be a choice, if I should take that train to some faraway place and begin again. Perhaps I could find employment with a family in Portland, cooking while caring for their children and maybe my own. There were wealthy families there who might want a German maid.

"Emma," Jack said, catching me on my way back into the house. Twilight lingered in the August evening. I stood rigid as a churn paddle at the sound of his voice.

"What do you want, Husband?"

"I've discovered a puzzle," he said. He chewed on a toothpick. "I thought you maybe could explain it to me."

"I've no spare time for puzzles, Jack Giesy. They expect me back in the kitchen to work, where you should be off to as well. Earning your keep."

"*Ja,* earning is the puzzle." He tapped at the air with his finger. "I understand you earned a ten-cent piece for one of your paintings at the fair last year." I nodded agreement before the wariness hit. "A wife's earnings belong to her husband. You must remember that, Emma. What did you do with your profit?"

I swallowed. "They were given over to the common fund," I said.

"But against your ledger page, *ja,* Emma? So you can buy against it?"

"I've only gotten things for my children."

"Not women," he said. "They shouldn't have a ledger page."

Haven't I seen other women's names in the store book? Perhaps not. "Helena has her own page," I risked.

"No, she doesn't. But if she did, it would be because she is a single woman, Emma. Brother Keil let your page slip by, because you behave like a widow when you're not. It's my earnings you'll squander if you select a ribbon in exchange for it. I thought I'd let you know that I know." He yawned then. "I encourage your work, but don't assume you are making gains from it. You'll have to see me if you care to spend it from now on. I'll see to the ledger page to make sure it reflects the truth, so you needn't worry over that detail. Have a good evening, Wife," he said as he turned to go into the house.

I had forgotten the laws of this land. I didn't even own the clothes on my back; my husband did, along with my earnings.

I waited until I was sure it was safe, returned to the kitchen, and made my way to the wide hall to be with my children. I envied Brita for a moment, despite her challenges and losses. She at least could work for herself.

"He's a good one, that Martin," Brita said. We sat together and carded wool brought in from one of the Giesy farms. It was a soothing thing to do before we bedded down. "And your Andy likes him well too. Follows him around when he feeds the chickens on the way to the store to work." I'd noticed that too and sometimes felt saddened that my son preferred the company of Martin to me.

"Seems a waste," I said. "Martin should go to school and become that doctor instead of helping to run a store. Then he could really remove the weight from Brother Keil's shoulders. Maybe then we'd get more homes built."

"Perhaps Brother Keil doesn't want help," Brita said. "People often say one thing and may even believe it, but then they do things that make getting what they wish almost impossible. I should know. I've had a habit of such myself."

"How could that be?"

She shrugged. "I didn't want to be stared at for my...size, but then joined the circus where they paid me to endure the insults. I got the very thing I didn't want."

She wasn't alone. I had wanted independence from Christian's family in Willapa after his death but then made a poor marriage that left me even more dependent on others. Our minds moved our bodies into the strangest places.

Brita didn't want to join our colony or be a permanent part of our family. She had other hopes, and someday before long, she'd move on, she said. Until then, she was grateful for the work in return for the shelter. The colony women assigned tasks to her, including caring for the children. While she looked after my Christian and Ida, keeping them out of Jack's way, I helped cook at the new Aurora Hotel, now serving the stage route. We'd located it in the old house that had been the Keils' first home, at the base of the hill. I wasn't working for Jack, I told myself, but for my children. I checked the ledger and saw I still had a page in my name, but Jack had posted *tobacco twists* on the debit side. I didn't notice any other pages with a woman's name on it, not even the single women.

Karl had opened school in the toll hut, and Andy and Charles, Brita's oldest, were there during the day. When I wasn't at the hotel, Brita was still there, scrubbing pans nearly as large as herself or raking white linen tablecloths across washboards, so the guests would feel pampered when they ate with us. Brother Keil proposed that such exquisite care would make customers stop at our business, even though they were but a half day's ride from their destination in Portland. What but fine German food and excellent service could make them forget how tired they were from riding the stage all the way from Sacramento?

So far, the stages stopped at our site, and we sent people off filled to the brim with our biscuits and bratwursts. I made sure the colony goat was milked so Pearl would be fed, since I'd weaned Ida. While we worked, Brita would tell stories of unusual things, such as chickens that laid blue eggs.

"They're from someplace very warm in South America. I saw them with my own eyes. Sailors from ships sailing into San Francisco had them. Prettiest birds, with no tail."

"That can't be true," I said.

"It is. They're acalled"—she hesitated, trying to remember—"Araucana. Brown and reddish with sprinkles of blue in their feathers. But no tail. Shortened. Like me." She grinned, her mouth nearly filling her lower face.

"Ach," I said. "You tease."

"I don't. You look for them. They'll come this way."

Perhaps because she was an outsider, I found it easy to share laughter and my longings with her. I didn't have many women friends. Mary Giesy was a Willapa friend, but there'd been strain there. Jack had lived with them once. I suspected she thought I'd treated him unfairly by leaving.

"My father would stand for me if he were here," I told Brita one day. "He'd tell Jack it was time to go back. Or my brother Jonathan would."

"Family stands for you," she said. "My family what took me from the orphanage couldn't have been better to me. They chose me, even when they could see what they was agetting."

Family stands for you. It hadn't happened that way for me. I wanted to make it so for my own children.

I enjoyed cooking at the stage hotel, away from Keil and Jack. Some of the guests teased me, and while I was a mother and a married woman, I saw nothing wrong with smiling and letting people know I enjoyed making spinach salad the German way or peeling potatoes or serving freshly made blackberry pies. Food prepared with unhappy hearts causes indigestion, so I wanted to be sure such didn't happen to my guests. I thought of them all as *my* guests, and doing so made my frustration with Jack's power over me less draining.

I eavesdropped on guests' conversations when I refilled their coffee cups or brought out the bread puddings for their desserts. They spoke openly of events happening far away. Gold had been discovered in the mountains east of us, and people expected a rush as they'd had in California. Quite a lot of chattering went on when Stonewall Jackson and General Lee defeated the Union forces at Bull Run for a second time. Someone boasted that Colt was producing more than one thousand guns a day for the war effort, and a new kind of gun had been patented that had ten barrels and could fire two hundred fifty shots per minute. Admiration mixed with worry on men's faces at this talk of the Gatling gun, as they shoved my hot potato salad into their mouths. "At least the army abolished flogging last year," one of the men said, to bring a lighter note.

Keil had sent letters back to the Bethelites, telling them to be careful what they spoke about there. He declared that we were Unionists, one and all, and they should be too, though quietly. A part of me wondered what it must be like for the men to be silent about something that mattered. It was a new path for them, a path we women knew well.

One evening, a lone man with a limp stepped off the stage, settled at the table, and said he was from Missouri. I saw the others show new interest. Missouri was a state of widely divided loyalties, which had seen abolitionist battles even before the war began. Keil had urged the Bethelites to send the young men west, where emotions didn't run so hotly, or so he thought. But we'd heard that Oregon had raised the first cavalry of six companies preparing to enter the war. Maybe the boys weren't safe even here.

"I come from Virginia, first," the man said. He needed a shave, or perhaps he planned to grow a beard. At his table, the men moved away ever so slightly at his mention of one of the seceding states. So far, the people we'd encountered from South Carolina or Virginia had been civil, and we'd heard of no altercations resulting in forced duels or, worse, deaths. But we were wary of arguments, even so far from the fighting.

"Where are you heading?" one of our colony men asked him, and he hesitated.

"Is there a welcome here?"

I watched as the men cleared their throats, diverted their eyes. I waited for someone to say something. Didn't we open our doors to everyone in need, isn't that what Brother Keil had always said? *Isn't that why Jack is still here?*

"We're a Christian community," I said. "Everyone in need is welcome."

I heard a woman gasp from the kitchen. Then my name was called.

"It isn't a woman's place to make such statements," Lucinda Wolfer whispered to me. She acted more upset that I'd spoken than that I'd spoken the truth. She'd come out from Bethel with her husband, John, and two daughters, first to Willapa, but then she'd followed Keil to Portland and on to Aurora. I hadn't noticed in Lucinda the gossipy nature that plagued some women, even though she now chastised me for answering that Virginian. At least she hadn't corrected me in front of the others. "Father Keil determines who's in need and who should be offered refuge. Don't let Louisa or Helena know you said such a thing or even spoke up at all."

"But I was only being welcoming."

"Something a woman should not do in our communal ways."

Just one more thing defining what a woman could do in a family by what she wasn't supposed to. I still had much to learn.

4

And It Will Change

September 6. Dried blackberries on the rooftop. Covered them with muslin to keep the birds away. Filled four baskets. Now have fifteen baskets of dried berries, various kinds.

September 8. Made tomato figs. Used brown sugar Louisa said that I could have. Exposed them in the summer sun. Will take some with us to the fair. Still no plans for my house. Still no word from my parents. My dear Kate now wants to be called "Catie," spelled differently and because Brother Keil calls her that. He influences my children too much.

October 1. We learn of Antietam and the twenty thousand killed there, counting both sides, and well we must. The battle moved into the north but without a win or defeat or so the telegraph tells us. Such is the news of warring.

The vine maple asserted itself through the green with its vibrant red, marking a seasonal shift. We finished harvests, dried fruits and vegetables. Colonists spoke then of the produce they'd bring for exhibit at the state fair. Sometimes in the cooling nights when I curled up with my children snuggled around me on their mats, I felt like carded wool, thick and full of tiny seeds that needed constant combing to get the blemishes out, so the wool would be useful one day. This distance between me and my parents stuck like a burr I couldn't card out.

Begin to weave. God provides the thread. Louisa wrote out the German proverb in her *Fraktur* lettering and hung it in the hotel. I read it every day. My mother had shared it with me as a child. Where was the thread of my life? I wasn't weaving a thing.

"The rats have gotten into the butter," Lucinda Wolfer told me. She showed me a butter block from the octagon cool house, where we kept butter immersed in spring water until we took the blocks for trade. The one she showed me had bite marks and tiny scrapes I took to be where the mold had been held by the rodent's claws. I was surprised the rat had gotten into the water, though I supposed they did swim. I wondered if all of the butter might be contaminated.

"When I have my own place," I told Lucinda, "I'm going to build a buttery at the river's edge, with the sides deep enough down that the rats can't penetrate."

"*Ja,* I have plans for when we build a house too," she said. "But it'll be some time, my husband says." She stared at the rat bites. "We could cut it off and take the remainder to Oregon City and trade it across for butter there," Lucinda said. "It won't hurt anyone if they don't know about the rats."

I laughed. "I can see you explaining to the shopkeeper why you're trading butter for butter. He'll go to the storeroom, change the wrappings, and give you back the same rat-butter you'd brought. After all, 'It won't hurt anyone if they don't know about the rats.' "

Lucinda laughed with me. "*Ja,* I could see that happening in Oregon City, all right. Well then, we'll scrape off where they've bitten into it and use it ourselves. But I'll get another today for our sauce. The idea of eating what the rats left…" She shivered.

We finished up, and that night, after the children were in bed, I imagined my house and its buttery. It would be a double house, not like the Missouri "saddle bag" houses, which were two houses built completely separate and joined by a common middle section. They called the hinge section a "dogtrot" used by both households. Keil's house was somewhat similar to that design. Mine would have no dogtrot. It would have two entrances at the front and two fireplaces downstairs, one in the kitchen and one on the other side of a shared stairwell. The stairs would be enclosed, so people could sit in the parlor while others went upstairs or down, no one being the wiser.

Upstairs there'd be bedrooms on either side of the stairwell, and a hall wide enough to allow trundle beds or cribs for toddlers. Two families or maybe more could live in the house and come and go as they needed, without bothering the other. But they'd be close enough that if one called for help, the other would hear it. There'd be front and back covered porches. And I wanted glass windows, to let the light in and to let me see what dangers might be lurking on the porch. Maybe the Wolfers would move in with us. Maybe Brita. My parents and brothers and sisters.

I got up and found paper that had wrapped one of Ida's birthday presents, now carefully folded for reuse. On it, I drew the plans, deciding that even if Jack never left, even if my parents never arrived, I'd push to have my house be the next one the colony constructed. There'd be a buttery, and I'd find a way to keep the rats out.

———

Brother Keil had a number of entries for the state fair. He'd prepared his strongly medicinal Oregon grape wine once again. He entered dried fruits too, including peaches. He'd gotten the peach trees from a French Prairie farmer who'd brought them to Oregon in the late thirties from the California missions. The leaves made fine green dye for our wool. Several of the young men had worked some of the bulls to halter, so they could show them entered under the Aurora Colony's name.

The animals trailed along behind us as we rode in the wagons, shaking their big heads of the flies. Brother Wolfer sat astride one of his finest horses to enter in the race. We Aurorans didn't have much stock to speak of, so I wondered about the likelihood of an Aurora horse winning a race. I liked the calming murmur of a horse as he nuzzled his velvet nose up against mine, and I wondered why we didn't have more of them in Aurora. I guessed that Missouri mules were our choice because they were such good workers. Always it was about work.

Louisa took her *Fraktur* pieces to show. Some of them reminded me of the punch paper kit patterns, models they were called, that we girls were taught to stitch. "Trust God for Every Need." "God Bless This House." Simple words of wisdom that our fathers would show to interested suitors as indications of our proper training. The words were drawn on paper cards with holes for where the threads should go, and we stitched right over them. I thought that Louisa's *Fraktur* with letter flourishes would make a lovely model for my Kate, and she'd be ready soon to do such work. She had already stitched on a quilt with Aurora Keil. I wondered if my parents still had the paper models I'd made, which I'd hung over the main room door. Thinking of my parents saddened me yet again. I pitched the thought away.

Several women had knitted socks with actual heels in them, rather than the plain straight tube. Very inventive, and more comfortable for a man to wear inside those heavy brogans. We entered skeins of hand-dyed wool, all perfectly carded, dyed, and spun. We had well-fed sheep that offered up their wool. *We.* I said that often these days, *we* of the colony.

I'd had no time to draw or paint in these past months, nor the interest, so when Louisa asked, I told her that I didn't plan to go to the fair, that I had nothing to enter. "You need to come with us, Emma," Louisa told me. "As you did before. Didn't you have a fine time at the fair?"

"But when we came back...there were problems, remember? Jack showed up. We argued..."

"*Ach, ja,* but he is already here now. There'll be many of us together when we come back, and he can do you no harm. He's staying behind. Come with us." I must have grimaced, or maybe I rubbed my fingers as I did when anxious. "Emma. You can't allow past things to keep you from possible pleasantries. It won't be the same. It can't be. You're older and wiser, *ja?*" Louisa said. "You make it different this year. Have a pleasant time with your children. Listen to the band play." She drew in her breath. "I can work an entire day of beating rugs, knowing I will hear music at day's end." She clasped her hands and heaved a happy sigh.

The girls were eager to go, and so were my sons. "We can't buy anything," I said, relenting. "We have no money." I didn't add that even if we did have money, Jack would decide how to spend it. They agreed they'd ask for nothing. We took Charles and Stanley and Pearl too, along with my four, and Louisa and I baked and cooked for us all. With other families from the colony we walked or rode the nearly twenty-five miles toward Salem. We'd spend three nights and be there for the entire second day, always said to be the best.

On arrival, we spread quilts on the grass where we ate and would later sleep beneath a canvas tent. I hoped we'd have plenty to feed the hungry Aurorans with some left over to share with others. Our food would attract people to Aurora, more than Keil's medicinal wine or a winning horse. Sharing food would bring us notice. Selling sausages on a stick would bring in cash as well. Being at the fair had purpose for us colonists, more than just fun.

Women walked arm in arm, in and out of the exhibit barns, and I heard the band warming up. It always amazed me that the tiny piccolo could be louder than the large trombone, its piercing tone uplifting while searing through the drums and bass. Being little didn't mean being ineffective or unnoticed. Brita showed me that.

I walked through one of the tents where someone had brought rabbits in a cage to show. I had Ida on my hip. I pushed Pearl in a cart I'd rigged for her, and she slept now beneath the shady basket weave above her head. I'd seen an Indian woman carrying a child in a board with a woven shade and did my best to duplicate it. I talked to Ida about the bunnies, and she leaned into me, excited and frightened at the same time. Next to the rabbit vendor, foiling my idea that there'd be no surprises, stood a man with odd-looking chickens…without tails.

"They lay blue eggs," he said. Several people around him scoffed when he showed us the shell. One man accused him of dyeing it with blackberry juice. "No, no," he insisted. "This is the color she lays."

I tried to remember the name of the bird Brita had said: *Araucana*.

I must have said the name out loud because the man turned to me. "That is the name!" He pointed. "The woman knows this is true! Yes! The bird has blue eggs, sometimes green."

People moved closer then. I did too. The eggshell was sky blue with tints of green. The chickens strutted. They wore their rust and ebony, ivory and turquoise feathers as though they knew they were unique. The vendor had three birds, and just as Brita had said, their tails looked chopped off. The vendor said they came from South America and were for sale.

"How much would one be?" I said.

"Maybe twenty dollars."

Someone said, "You aren't in the gold fields now."

The vendor responded with a sheepish grin. "Maybe fifteen?"

The eggs would be interesting things to show people and to serve at our hotel table. We'd save the shells for Easter etching...

"I'll buy one," I offered. "But for five dollars, no more." I fully expected he'd come back with ten, but he didn't.

"Sold," he said.

I swallowed at my success. I didn't know how I'd pay.

People wandered away. The vendor pulled up a basket of reeds, opened the cage, and put one of the chickens inside it, laid the flat strands on top. I could see the chicken through the separation in the reeds. Her tiny eyes met mine. I decided to call her Clara. She'd fill that empty place in my heart that Opal, our goat, had left when I'd come to Aurora with nothing but my children.

"You have coins?" the vendor said.

"I don't." He frowned. He'd be upset if our transaction had sent a paying customer away when I couldn't come up with what I'd offered. "I intend to pay with...food." The word came into my head. "I'll bring you food for the time you're here, baked myself. Berries I dried myself. Strudels."

"Fresh bread?" I nodded. "Hmm. I don't really need food," he said, moving to put the chicken beneath his vendor bench.

"Everyone does. That's how your chickens work for you, *ja*? Keep

Clara for me. I wouldn't name her if I didn't intend to pay for her, would I? And before the afternoon is over, I'll bring you a basket of food."

"Five dollars' worth," he said.

"Five dollars' worth."

The chicken would be a communal one. Her eggs would only add to the notoriety of the colony. Keil would like that. She'd pay her own way. And since I'd baked the goodies I planned to trade, I'd pay my own way too. I put Jack's claim aside. Such are the ways we tell ourselves stories. I gave this one a happy ending.

———

Louisa and Brother Keil wandered over the fairgrounds, Louisa a step or two behind her husband. She didn't appear to mind. I wished she did. I watched to see if he took special notice of the women in their finery, and he did, tipping his hat at them with a smile. He was always the showman. A few tall, handsome Indians rode fine horses toward the racetrack, followed on foot by women in their regalia. Young girls strutted by, pretending not to notice the boys who stared at them, as if they hadn't come to the fair just to walk by those boys. One of the colony musicians strode past me carrying his *Ophicleide,* a wind instrument that twisted like a snake up into a bell, running from the ground to well up past his dark hat when he sat to play it. The brass finger keys gleamed in the setting sun, like buttons on a uniform, against the smooth wooden horn.

My boys ran with a kite, Charles at their heels; enough breeze lifted the diamond fabric high in the air. While Ida and Pearl slept, I took out my sketchbook to capture the boys' exuberance.

The act of moving lead across the paper soothed me. I'd forgotten that I took joy in capturing what lay before me. In my mind rose my mother's sharp words about my drawings—she said they had no practical value—Jack hadn't liked my drawings either. *Not here, not now. I must think on good things.*

I kept drawing. I smelled stick candy stiff with peppermint that someone carried past me. I wished that I could bring that scent to paper. I listened to the rhythm of voices around me. I heard a Spanish-sounding man—Portuguese, someone said he spoke; French and English. Brits and Scots and Irish, mostly men, and the clicks and swishes of the Chinook language spoken by the natives gave a mix that made me feel as though I belonged in this interesting if not always predictable world. My sons laughed, and my heart caught in my throat with the sheer joy of it. To see them happy, healthy was a gift beyond measure. *I can see God in this.*

"You're smiling," Lucinda Wolfer said as she plopped down beside me, her skirts billowed out enough to make me wonder if she'd reinforced her petticoat with wild rose limbs. We Auroran women didn't wear hoops as did women on the outside, but we weren't averse to being inventive in our effort to be fashionable.

"Jack is more than twenty miles away. That's cause for smiles."

She nodded. "Watching the *Kinder,* that's restful too, *ja?*"

Kate ran over and plunged without asking into the food basket. *"Ach,* no," I said. "You wait until we're all ready to eat."

"But I'm hungry, Mama."

Kate's constant state of hunger probably explained why Jack's comment about her being a "fat little Kate" had so buttressed my resolve against him.

"Come here," I said, placing my drawing things beside me. My days were well-sewn patterns, and we had scant time for impromptu tying of loose though important threads. I opened my arms to her, and she fell into them. I nuzzled her neck, knocking her straw hat from her head, and in her effort to retrieve it, we both fell backward onto the quilt.

"Mama," she laughed. "You bottom-upped me!"

"So I did," I told her. I helped her stand, brushed at the hem of her dark dress. Her stockings had begun to slip, but she didn't seem to mind. Once I'd wondered if she'd ever laugh again, ever feel safe again, and here she giggled like a normal child. If Brita had been able to come, perhaps she could have set aside some of her bad memories of fairs too. There was no bearbaiting here, and with new friends present, perhaps the memories of that devastating circus fire could have healed a bit.

Beyond our quilt, Andy and Charles had their heads together now, looking at something they held in their hands. A frog perhaps, or maybe a grass snake. The kite lay askew, leaned against their knickered knees. Charles's presence had tempered my son, and while I saw less of Andy when he was at school, following Martin, or off rolling hoops with Charles, I enjoyed hearing his laughter. Now they gathered string for another run with their kite.

I was glad I'd come. Hesitation didn't always mean that what followed would be worrisome. Plans could prevent some difficulties. I should have hesitated more before I married Big Jack; I knew that now, but I hadn't. At some point I'd have to forgive myself for that.

Christian called to Kate then, and she grabbed at her hat, bent to kiss my head, and went running, all thoughts of food forgotten.

"If only all our hunger could be assuaged so easily," Lucinda said. She patted my hand.

"I've some biscuits and strudels I need to deliver," I said. "Some of my preserves and a few things like that. Would you care to come with me?"

"Where are you taking them?"

"I've made a trade for us."

"We could use some Buena Vista pottery. Are you trading for a kraut jug?"

"*Nein.* Colony food for a chicken who lays blue eggs." Lucinda raised her eyebrows. "*Ja,* blue eggs. Think how lovely they'll be on Easter."

"Are you trading rat-tasted butter?" she asked, her eyes laughing.

"No butter. Some beans, but mostly our baked goods. Five dollars' worth," I said.

She never asked if Brother Keil had approved such a purchase. She knew no woman would propose such a thing unless she'd been granted our leader's permission.

When the wagon pulled up the grade toward the Keil house, I had a moment's hesitation yet again, remembering our return from the fair last year. Big Jack had been waiting for me. He'd struck at me then, in front of everyone, and Brother Keil had sent him away. As we walked up the steps to the *gross Haus,* I wondered if Jack would be there this time. It'd be like him, to recall the same event and maybe even attempt to reenact it. Maybe take any earnings from me he thought I might have.

I had to set aside these loathsome thoughts. They did nothing to improve my life and kept me from enjoying the new memories from the day.

Martin met us on the steps. "We need to talk," he said.

"What's happened?"

He shook his head, nodded to the children as though they ought not to hear. He helped unload the wagons and carried Ida in while I brought Pearl. Charles and Stanley chattered to their mother about everything they'd seen. Martin returned, lifted Christian, who had fallen into a sleep so soundly that he could be lifted, carried, and laid down without missing a beat of his snoring.

"Did you have a good time?" Martin whispered to Andy. *Martin sounds so calm. He can't have bad news.*

Andy nodded, and Kate began telling him in her boisterous voice about the monkey who sat upon a wooden music box, then started dancing.

"We need to finish unloading," I told her. "Settle down now." I scanned the area, looking for Jack. All I wanted was to know what Martin had to tell me.

"I'll get Clara," Kate whispered. She ran back out to see if she could lift the basket with the chicken in it by herself.

I had to help her. We set the basket next to her, as she cuddled beside Pearl and Ida on the mats that Brita had laid out for us all. I'd have to build a movable pecking cage for Clara in the morning.

When I came back out to the wagon to get the last blanket twisted around the food basket, Martin stopped me. "Jack's gone back to Willapa. He says 'for good.' "

I caught my breath, put my fingers to my throat to keep me from crying out with joy. "Could my life be so blessed?"

"Karl talked with him on the bridge. He said he'd had enough time in Aurora. Said he's going back where having an ale or two isn't considered demonic."

"Truly," I said. I sat on the lowest step, removed my bonnet. It was like him to do the unexpected. I was so pleased I hadn't wasted hours in anticipating how he could mess up our return. "That's it then? I'm…free," I said. *Can it be?*

———

I knew I wasn't totally free. I was still married to Jack Giesy. But as the days went by without Jack around, I realized that ambiguous position provided a certain safety too. I was not a woman who'd be sought after by a man. Even if I were, I could easily put off such an adventurer by saying that I was a married widow. That alone ought to confuse a suitor and send him looking elsewhere. I'd already attempted to blend one family into another without success. I had no wish to try again. I could devote my life to caring for my children. If I wanted to hear a man's voice or smell a pipe, I could visit Karl Ruge or walk up Keil's steps to the main floor, where bachelors congregated in the evening, making music, talking.

Jack had taken up so much space in my life that I could hardly imagine a day without worrying about his next move, without defending my children from him. But maybe life did offer strange twists that turned us around like a top. *Ja,* they did.

———

Late that fall, Henry C. Finck arrived from Bethel, bringing his five children including ten-year-old Henry T (as he was known). The child squinted at the vials in the blue cabinet, reading each label aloud and telling any who would listen what the name would be in Latin. He was precocious, but his love of learning could make him a good pal for Andy.

"We will have the best, most wonderful Christmas this year," Louisa crooned. "*Herr* Finck is a genius with the music. We'll have choirs and a Pie and Beer Band too, not only the Aurora Band. There'll be music for those left behind when the band travels off to dances and such. And he's a widower too, Emma. You think of that."

"Nothing to think of," I said as I stitched. "I'm still a married woman, remember?"

"*Ach,*" she said, waving her hands at me. "I so easily forget."

"If only I could."

A rooster crowed while we served the men their suppers, reminding me that no one had said anything about how I'd paid for my chicken. One of the bachelors said, "He's looking for that Clara of yours, Sister Emma, the one that looks like she was tossed out of the creation oven before there was time to put tail feathers on her."

"She's the way she was intended to be," I defended to the men's laughter.

"She does stand out."

"As Emma likes to," Helena said. She set a plate of ginger cookies on the table and wouldn't meet my eyes.

Everyone liked the blue eggs. They liked the idea of the colony having such a unique chicken. But Helena saw it as yet another way I was being a separate dish in a community that honored blended stews. The colony owned the chicken, this I knew, but I did name her and did build the cage for her. Perhaps Helena was threatened by my having something attached to my name instead of the chicken's belonging to us all.

I thought about that the rest of the evening. The next morning I took Clara out and put her with the other chickens, scratching for worms behind the Keils', and prayed that the hawks would resist the delicacy.

———

As the rains began again that year, Brother Keil arranged for Karl to read Scripture to us twice monthly, but he himself stopped leading worship. Louisa hinted it was his gout that pained him. During worship, we women sat on one side of the big upstairs room, and the men sat on the other. Karl sat at the head, his back to the fireplace. I liked hearing the words but wished we could have sung more hymns as we had back in Bethel. Still, the band sometimes played. Brother Keil liked band music.

After our meetings, I found I wanted to talk, to make the readings relevant for how we lived in Aurora, and not just focusing on way back when the words were first written. When we were in Willapa, Karl and I could have talked like the old friends we are. But here, people clustered around us in the *Haus* and there was no time to speak freely as friends. Karl spent days at the toll hut, but I didn't feel right about visiting him. It wouldn't be "seemly," as Helena was fond of saying. That's what she told me about discussing the readings too.

"It isn't seemly," Helena said, "for us to discuss Scripture, without structure provided by a religious leader."

"My husband will feel better soon," Louisa said. "Then he'll lead us as he has before. Instead, let's use this time together to stitch or card."

In the back of my mind I remembered a scripture about people "hearkening together," but I couldn't name it. I'd look for it in Christian's Bible and then make my case again. If I ever got my own home I'd have a talking time there, or at least invite others to come. I might ask my mother for that verse when I wrote her next. She might respond to a question of faith, if not to my plaintive calls for them to come west. I sat down to do it right then.

———

In November, Brita left us. "It's atime," she said as she folded her children's meager things into the middle of their quilts and blankets. I fidgeted, agitated, maybe envious at her ability to set a goal and meet it. She'd decided some weeks earlier to help a neighbor outside of the colony, in addition to assisting at the hotel. That's where she'd been working the night we'd returned from the fair. The people Brita had gone to assist weren't part of the colony, and so they paid her with currency, even a greenback, said to be in great circulation back in the States. Her new employers worked her hard, and she returned to the *gross Haus* exhausted each night. But she could keep her earnings. She'd make better wages at the Durbin Livery Stable in Salem, once she moved there.

"Aren't you worried about working with such big animals?" I asked.

"I'm just cleaning stalls," she said. "It's warm and inside work, and there's a room my children and I can stay in. I'm close to the ground, so my back doesn't ache as another's might. Besides, there's a soothing to be found around a breathing animal like that. If a dog or chicken or goat is company, why not a horse?"

"But Pearl…" I said.

"The Durbins like to have babies about. The boys can help with feeding and such, and I hope to make enough to send them to school. I'm not a saying it's forever, but for now, we'll be together, and I'll be putting money aside for when the new Homestead Act's set up."

I hadn't heard of this and said so. She told me of the act, which would give one hundred sixty acres to anyone over twenty-one who was willing to farm, build a cabin, and stay for five years.

"I'm saving money so we can buy seed and other things we need," said Brita.

While I had been imagining a house with two sides to share with her (though I'd never expressed it), she had proceeded with dreams of her own.

Andy regretted Charles's leaving. He'd found a real friend in the blond-headed boy. "He was my lookout, Mama," Andy told me. "So we never were surprised by Big Jack."

"His leaving is good timing, then," I said. "Jack is gone. See how God provided for us, all we needed?" Andy nodded, though I could still see the loss in his eyes.

"I'll look out for you," Christian offered. Andy shrugged, but Christian didn't seem to notice. Christian had his big brother back. "Andy's more in-trusting than Stanley or Pearl," my younger son told me.

"The word is 'interesting,'" I said.

"That's what I said," he defended. "In-trusting."

"Well, maybe that's a good word too," I said.

Ida, too, noted the change in our hallway constellation of stars.

"Pearl gone?" she'd ask, her personal doll somehow come up missing. When I explained that yes, Pearl was indeed gone, my youngest child brushed aside the mending I worked on, pulled herself up onto my now-empty lap and demanded in her small but charged voice, "Mama, hold!"

And I'd held her, my chin on her head as she leaned against my breast. "Mama holds," I said. I'd hold my impatience in getting a home, hold my sadness at Brita's departure. Most of all, I'd hold out hope that my parents would join me one day. Until then, holding my children safely was a prayer I lifted up for myself. All families need the glue of someone to hold.

5

Seeking Meaning

December 12. Kona coffee sells in Portland along with crushed sugar. I've no need now for the sugar breaker Christian had the blacksmith make for me. I have happy plans for holiday cooking. Food to heal the sorrowful souls. Clara has stopped laying eggs.

December 13. I let the flour dry on the back of the range all night. My cake rose higher than expected. Perhaps it is a sign of good things to come.

Only Kate appeared oblivious to the departure of Brita's family. The Keil girls pampered Kate the most of all my brood, and they continued after Brita left, playing hiding games with her, letting her go with them to gather eggs or feed the goats. Aurora, who was nearly thirteen and looked more mature than that, showed Kate how to stitch the paper model "In God We Trust," and my daughter insisted they were "wise words" when she showed it to me. A twinge of guilt tweaked me that I'd taught Kate neither how to do the stitches nor nurtured her spiritual life to help her find those wisest of words. The Keil girls were doing it for me.

"It's lovely, Kate," I said. "But why did you sign it 'Catie'?"

"*Ja.* Father Keil says that's my name."

"It's not the one your father and I gave you."

"I like it," she said and pooched her lower lip out in protest.

I loved her independence but resented Keil's latest intrusion into my life. It was probably nothing worth arguing over, I decided. "Well,

I'll still call you Kate," I said with more assurance than I felt. "And that'll be that."

———

When the annual sickness came, I took a deep breath. This was how our winters wore on. But now I was among people who could help me care for my children if they became ill, as they had that first hard winter. I could be hopeful. Everyone had sniffles. It was part of living.

"The people your little *Zwerg* helped out are ill now," Lucinda Wolfer told me.

"She isn't my little person," I said, "any more than anyone else's."

"*Ja, ja.* I meant no offense."

"Besides, they were healthy when Brita left."

I knew that Brita had worked hard steaming the bedclothes because she told me of the demanding work, the tubs so tall she stood on stools to stir the clothes with an oak paddle.

John Wolfer, Lucinda's husband, that kindhearted man, asked Brother Keil if he shouldn't go and help another family across the Pudding who suffered from the illness, even though it might be smallpox. "It's the Christian thing to do," John said.

"*Ja,* it is that." Keil was on his way out the door to help another household, and he had already been by to treat John's friends. Martin, too, had begun visiting the sick, and more than once Andy asked if he could go along to help. I'd refused him that, fearful of what he might contract. Andy'd scowled as he used to, arms crossed over his small chest and his leather shoes kicking at the sideboard. "You're prone to sickness," I told him. "It wouldn't be good."

"They've had what medicine I can give them," Keil told Martin and John as they stood before the blue cabinet. Both healing men were filling their leather medicine bags. Andy glared at me with darkened eyes. "It's mostly tending now. You'll need to wash the linens, John. Use soap but don't breathe in the steam. Keep the windows open to air

things out, and don't get too close to them. You understand? And always wash your hands afterward. We know now that helps. That doctor who came from the States in '52 with wagons to Portland made
everyone wash their hands and boil the water, and they lost not a soul,
though cholera raged around them. You wash your hands." John nodded and left by the root room door.

"I hope this isn't smallpox," Brother Keil said to Martin. "It could
race through Oregon as it did of old." Brother Keil had taken to wearing a frock coat he had tailored himself. It was the fashion now, but it
still surprised me that he'd take the time to be in style. He checked the
stitching on the cuffs.

"We'll do what we can," Martin said. He touched Andy's hair.
"Your mother's right. You stay here and keep those sniffles from getting
worse. When you're better, you can help."

Andy looked up at me. "When the sniffles are gone." His face
relaxed, and the kindness of his heart, wanting to help others, showed
through his eyes.

John Wolfer traveled back and forth to assist the ill family but
finally returned to stay when the man and two of their children died.
The man's wife and another child appeared unaffected.

"You did your best," Brother Keil told him in the workroom. I
could hear them as I tended the children in the wide hall. "And you've
not become ill, so this is good. If the cold weather comes, it'll freeze out
the disease."

"We can hope," John told him.

I wanted us to do something that wasn't weighted with illness and
loss. I'd begun to realize that I grieved Brita's leaving. In the past when
my heart felt broken, I'd slammed the door on it, then opened it later
to a slug in the garden named Jack. This time I wanted to recognize my
sadness and do something thoughtful rather than impulsive. I looked
for a happy task. I decided to begin furnishing the house I didn't have
yet. I found four, empty wide-necked bottles and solicited Louisa and
Lucinda Wolfer's help.

"We really have so many other things to do," Louisa said.

"But music makes you happy, and making these glasses will make me happy."

"Drinking glasses?"

I nodded. "Put the leather thong around here," I directed. "That's where we'll want the top of the glass to be, right at the base of the neck. Now I wrap a good cord twice around the bottle."

"Have you done this before?" Lucinda asked. She looked doubtful.

"I watched the men do it in Bruceport," I said. "And because it takes three, I got to help. I remember the details."

"Let's pray you do," Louisa said. She straightened her apron and set her feet, as though she was readying to catch a pig before it ran between her knees.

"You hold this end of the cord, and, Lucinda, grab the other. When I say so, take turns pulling back and forth on your cords as fast as you can, but keep the bottle straight."

"I don't understand how this will get you a glass," Lucinda said.

"The bottle will heat up where the cords are pulled," I said. "Then when the glass is hot…I'll grab hold of it to know…I'll drop a stream of cold water where the cord is, and when you remove the cord, the bottle will break just above the leather, and I'll hold a glass in one hand and a candlestick holder in the other. It's *gut*!" I sang out.

We set about our tasks, the leather thong marking the top, me with the cold water ready. Louisa pulled first; Lucinda pulled back. They see-sawed and we laughed until the cord smelled hot. "Reminds me of a taffy pull," Louisa said.

"Now?" Lucinda said.

"Let's get it good and hot," I said.

A tiny trail of smoke rose up, and I lifted my apron bottom to hold the bottle. With my free hand I dribbled the cold water, set the ladle down, then took hold of the top.

"*Ach, Jammer!*" I said, shaking my hand of the stinging heat.

"Emma," Lucinda chastened. "Are you burned?"

I shook my head no, reached for a quilted pie pad, and held the top as the glass separated like a yolk from a perfectly tapped shell. "My first furnishings for my new home," I cheered.

"Well, I'll be," Lucinda said. "Who would have thought? I've turned a tin can into an apple corer by sticking it into hot coals to cut off the top, but I've never turned a molasses bottle into a drinking glass."

"You are such a clever woman, Emma," Louisa said, smiling.

"Someone told me once you had to spin into gold the straw you were given," I said. "Let's see how many more we can make. Some for the colony, of course."

———

Two days later, Lucinda became ill. She was followed by Brother Keil's son Elias, a big, strapping boy who helped with the animals. And then Gloriunda Keil's giggling lessened. Aurora lay panting beneath her mother's cooling forehead rag. Louisa, Keil's oldest daughter, complained of headaches, and then the cough came. Amelia took on suffering next, her frame as slender as a spring sapling overwhelmed by quilts. We were tending them all at the *gross Haus,* steaming linens, making sure none of the healthy children were nearby to breathe in the harmful mists. Spoonfuls of laudanum got handed out like candy to help ease their discomfort. I feared that the blue cabinet would soon be empty. I wished again my children were in their own home, away from the spots and the coughs of so many.

Even more, though, I was afraid that the Keil children would die. The Keils had already lost a son, Willie, who they'd carried across the plains in his own casket and buried next to my husband in Willapa. Brother Keil had preached on more than one occasion that a child's death spoke more to the sins of the parents than about the child. I'd never understood such thinking, and to speak it at a child's funeral seemed as cruel as the death itself. I ached for Louisa, who went from bed to bed to comfort them. Five children ill. She took few moments even to eat, spending all her time and energy attempting to get her children to sip beef broth and hold it down. Reddish spots formed on their chests. Their youngest, Emanuel, Louisa relegated to our hallway area, since he showed no signs of illness. Frederick Keil, already a young man in his twenties and not coughing, stayed with the bachelors on the top floor. I thought his mother might have appreciated his assisting her, but it wasn't likely he'd offer and Louisa wouldn't ask. She'd already lost one son to illness.

"Those ugly boils," Louisa said. I'd just come downstairs from the bedroom where Lucinda convalesced.

"Don't they mean that the pox is taking its course?" I asked. "Isn't that a good sign?"

"Oh, I pray they'll get well now," she said. "I do." She said it with a wail. "What could I have done to bring this on? What?"

I reached to touch her hand. We Germans weren't known for demonstrations of affection, and the wartime Sanitary Commission urged people not to touch another's clothing during times of illness, but comfort sometimes required an abandoning of the rules.

"You didn't do anything," I told her, relying on my understanding of the gift of grace. "Illness…happens. It isn't brought on by a parent's behavior or as punishment. How could it be as punishment? We've already been forgiven for our many sins, remember?"

Louisa shook her head. *"Nein, nein.* There is reason for everything. Look at Job."

"But not everything is reasonable," I said. "Christian's death wasn't reasonable, drowning to save another who saved himself. Your Willie was too young to die, too good, and yet he did. That's not reasonable, it just is."

"Ja, that's why I fear this. My husband believes the sins of the father are given to the children."

In this case I thought Brother Keil couldn't place blame on the sins of the *mother.* Surely he wouldn't. But I knew Louisa heard it that way. She'd carry the blame. We all did when someone we loved was in distress, wondering what we might have done differently to prevent it.

I stood beside her, my arm around her waist now. She was taller than I was, but she leaned for comfort into my smaller frame. Her ribs felt as thin as knitting needles. I wanted to say something to encourage her. I tried to remember what Karl Ruge had said after Christian died. I'd trusted that someone who cared for me on this earth could be the hand that reached out to keep me from falling. Then a psalm came to mind. *"Behold, the eye of the LORD is upon them that fear him, upon them that hope in his mercy.... Our soul waiteth for the LORD: he is our help and our shield."* I recited it softly to Louisa.

"Ja," she whispered. "I'll hope that God is merciful to end our suffering." She cried then, against my shoulder.

To end suffering. Theirs and my own. I prayed for an end to the suffering of my friends. Our own healing often came when we prayed for others. Karl had told me that too. After a time, Louisa dabbed at her eyes and put the cloth in the basket where we kept all used linens.

"We can transform things," I told Louisa. "We stitch tiny scraps into comforting quilts, spare and splendid in their beauty. We make glasses out of old bottles. We take sad times and find the threads of wisdom there and weave it into the next generation. We're alchemists, we women," I said. "We change things."

"Ja, but Eve turned a lovely garden into a place of separation," Louisa said.

"We need to think of hopeful things, Louisa." I took a deep breath. "For now," I said, "let's trust that God will change us through our prayers, *ja?* We'll pray the sicknesses of hearts and bodies will pass over and only small scars will be left behind."

On November 27, we learned that Solomon and Isaac Durbin's livery in Salem, where Brita had gone to work, had burned to the ground.

On the same day, my parents arrived.

They stepped out of the ox wagon on a cool day with misty rain beading onto our wool cloaks and dresses. I'd come out of the house through the root room door to bring in a bucket of rainwater, breaking loose the lace of ice around the edge. I looked up, saw the wagon, and recognized my mother. I was speechless. Raindrops tap-tapping on leaves filled the otherwise still air.

My mother walked to me, wrapped her arms around me, and patted my back, not long enough for me to be the first to let go, but firmly enough.

"You look well, Emma," she said, surprise in her voice. Then, "*Gut.* That's *gut.* Where are your children?" She looked around. "Ah. So, this is your Andy." She pointed with her chin, past me to where the children had once again followed me out. They must have seen the wagon through the main floor windows.

I gathered up words. "Say hello to your *Oma,*" I told Andy, pushing him forward to his grandmother. Andy shook her hand. Kate curtsied, without my even telling her. "This is Christian," I told her, introducing my younger son, who had turned four in April. "And Ida, the baby, is inside. We should go in, to get out of this weather."

"Jack's girl," my mother said. Water misted off of her felt bonnet.

"My girl," I corrected.

"Your Christian has his papa's eyes. Kind eyes. Well, all the brothers and sisters have his eyes, don't you think so, Mr. Wagner?" It's what she called my father. "Ida has brown eyes too?"

I shook my head no. My father nodded agreement to my mother's words. He hadn't reached out to hold me, and so I held back too, my fingers making circles against my thumb pads. I couldn't have borne it if I'd reached my arms to him and he'd stood rigid as a backsaw, cutting through my hoped-for warmth. I was glad I held a pail in my hand. Then my brother Jonathan greeted me with a bear hug, around bucket and all. "Sister," he said. "You finally made your way to Aurora."

"You too," I told him. I smiled. "Has it changed much?"

"*Nein,*" he said. He gazed around. "Jack told us where you'd be staying."

"You fooled me with your grand words about Aurora," I told him, ignoring the reference to Jack. "You described an Eden here, but it isn't."

"*Ja, ja,*" Jonathan said. "But Eden is in the mind too, Sister. So it becomes what you make it, *ja*? What your mind's eye brings to it."

" 'I think myself happy.' "

My mother nodded. "From the book of The Acts," she said.

"It can be done, Sister," Jonathan said, "with faith." He held his index finger up to the air like a teacher giving me a good grade. "It can be done."

I was reintroduced to my younger brothers and sisters then. William had been four when I left Bethel; he was nearly fourteen now and towered over me as he asked if they could carry things inside.

"*Ja,*" I said. "Go right in through there. Ask for biscuits in the kitchen. I'm sure you're hungry, *ja*?"

He nodded and moved past me. Louisa, sixteen, stood slender and pale. She held her head at an angle, and one eye drifted off to the side as she smiled at me. Johanna, eighteen, nodded and said with no nonsense, "Sister," then took Lou's arm, following William inside. Kitty, as she called herself, was twenty and had always complained in her letters about the size of her hips, but I envied her robust roundness. Beside her, I felt insignificant as a string beside a rope. She was lovely. Her eyes held adoration, and I felt my face grow warm.

Another woman I didn't recognize stood beside Kitty. She stood back from the crowd. Her dark hair parted in the center, and her skirts billowed out from a waist as thick as a walnut trunk. *How can Kitty think herself big compared to this woman?*

"This is our foster daughter," my mother said. "Christine's her name." She curtsied toward me, her back as straight as a ladle. Her skirts made a hush as she bowed.

"Your...foster daughter?"

"I wondered how you'd look after all this time," Kitty interrupted. She'd closed the gap between us, grabbed my narrow shoulders, and held me at arm's length, then pulled me into a closer hug. "And now I have two older sisters. Isn't that grand? You look young as a twig," she said. "You've been married twice and me not even once." She rolled her lower lip out, the way Ida did when she didn't get her way.

"*Ach,* Kitty," my mother chided her. "How you worry over nothing."

David Jr. was twenty-two and, like my oldest brother, Jonathan, a grown man with a full, dark beard. He stood beside the team, absently rubbing the harness. Both of them began gathering things up out of the wagon, David Jr. saying he'd take the ox team to the barn if I'd direct him.

I pointed toward the ox barn down in the village, then said to my mother, "I didn't know you'd fostered a child. A person. Taken in a child when you haven't even written…

"Christine." I nodded to her, my stomach flummoxed indeed.

"She had a need; we could meet it," my father said at last.

"Yes. Of course," I said. "That's what we Wagners do."

In the midst of my confusion, I still managed to warn them then about the illness. It was everywhere in the country, but at least here we kept precautions in the *Haus*. I thanked Kitty for writing to me and hoped I didn't sound wounded that my parents hadn't. I invited them to sleep inside.

"Oh, we'll stay in the wagon," my father said. "So don't drive it away, David. It surely can't rain like this all the time." To me he said, "We're used to the wagon. Slept in it while visiting your aunt in the Deseret country."

"But there's room here," I insisted. Then thinking that maybe they didn't want to stay where I was, I added, "Or you could stay with the Snyders. Or at Adam's, though he lives a good seven miles out. You boys could bed down with the bachelors on the top floor." I couldn't imagine them spending one more night in that wagon. "I wish I had a home for you to stay in," I said. "But there were more important things happening here than building a house for me." I said it cheerfully. I didn't want them to think I complained. "Then the illnesses…," I said. "No one has had much interest in doing anything except nursing the sick."

"Another reason for us to go elsewhere," my father said.

William had come back out, holding a biscuit. "Oh, let the children spend the night inside," my mother told him. "And I'm going in out of this rain to see Louisa and Helena at the very least."

"And to meet Ida," I told her.

"*Ja.* To meet Jack's Ida." She sighed but patted my arm as she walked by. Christine, my new sister, followed close behind.

Inside there were greetings all around. Even Keil came out of the sickroom where he'd been attending his ailing children. He held my father in a bear hug. Neither man spoke a word, and they cleared their throats and looked at the floor when they released each other. *They hold affection for each other, so it's something I've done that kept my parents from coming here.* Amelia, looking somewhat improved, descended the steps and hesitated. Frederick's face lit up. He'd not taken ill, and neither had Emanuel, but it is a weight, I think, to be healthy while watching those you love suffer.

"She recovers," Keil said, nodding his head toward Amelia.

"You can stay here," I assured my family.

"*Ja,* you must, David. We have much to catch up on," Keil said.

"Well...you boys bunk for the night in with the bachelors, as your sister suggests," my father told them. "Your mother and I will remain in the wagon."

"Just until we build you a house," Brother Keil said. "It is so good to have you here, David. *Ja,* this will be good."

My father grunted in that way he did before he said something he thought might be disagreeable. "We'll stay until we find our own property, Wilhelm."

"You're not going to live in Aurora?" I blurted.

"We'll do better on our own."

Keil took that poorly. Perhaps he was already worn down by the smallpox; or perhaps it had something to do with old memories, like the time when Adam Schuele had returned. He wore a puzzled look when he turned away. He said nothing more, walked back toward his workroom.

"Jonathan will stay. He's prepared to help manage the store," my father called after Wilhelm. "But we are too many to add to your burdens here, with the children ill and all. We'll make our own way. Perhaps find land to homestead."

I didn't think Keil was listening. But I was. "Would you…that is, would you allow me and my children to come with you, then?" I asked. I'd spoken a thought out loud and heard it myself for the first time. It wasn't good timing.

Keil reentered the room, his eyes boring into mine. "We have not made life here good for you, then, Sister Emma?"

"*Ja*. I mean, no, you have been very good to me and my family. But as my father notes, many mouths to feed are burdensome."

"What should we do with these, *Frau* Giesy?" One of the newer girls came down the steps carrying dirty linens, unaware that she was interrupting.

"Steam the linens well. Maybe put some lavender in the water to make it smell pretty for the Keil girls. Don't inhale the steam."

"*Ja, Frau* Giesy," she said as she hurried out to the washroom. Her red and green coverlet offered bright color in an otherwise drizzling day.

"You should think twice about leaving," Keil said to me. "This communal place has served your family well. Or do you so easily forget? Did you not request a home?" He stared at me.

"You promised me a home, but—"

"I've had things on my mind, *ja*? Are you so impatient and self-centered as to begrudge a man that? What more can we do for you!" He turned and closed the door to his workroom.

I wanted to remind him that I'd worked very hard to pay my way here, only to have my husband assume my earnings. I'd waited a long time for a home that didn't appear any closer to being constructed. Now here was my family. How could he object to a family gathering itself together after so long a separation? But of course he was right: I was thinking of myself and my family, and not the suffering of his.

I looked at my father. I felt a hopefulness that even without knowing the why of our separation, my family would stand with me. I was not alone.

"I'd say you were settled in well here," my father said. "You seem to be able to direct people." He nodded toward where the girl had passed by with the linens. "And Keil obviously thinks your being here is of use.

I wouldn't want to interfere with your successful arrangements. We'd best find a place apart. Come, Mrs. Wagner," he told my mother. "We'll get us biscuits and warm up by the fire and then settle in for the night. Christine, Daughter, you're welcome too. You're family."

My *sister* nodded at me, then followed them into the kitchen. I tagged along behind, like a beaten-down puppy.

6

An Elevating Purpose

My friend Lucinda Wolfer died just a few days after my parents arrived. The smallpox from the family John cared for had made its way to his very own bed. Grieving with John and Lucinda's family kept me from pursuing Brita's fate at the burned-out livery in Salem, but it also took my mind from the unease between me and my parents.

I wished we'd had a church where we could hold ourselves together in our grief. I missed the bells and almost told Helena so. She had so much wanted the colony to build a church before we built a single other dwelling. I hated to think it, but she was right. In Bethel, the bells had rung out for glorious occasions, but also for funerals. It was a fitting requiem for lives lost, the bells tolling like the years, a reverberating silence when the last clang had rung. Lucinda had been a good friend, and I felt that somehow the tiny *Schellenbaum* bells tinkling in its standard in the drafty room were not enough to tell the world of our great loss.

"I've found ways to not worry so much over the unexpected," I told Karl one day when I brought hot soup to him at his toll hut. During the winter months, after school, I risked wagging tongues by taking sustenance to him before dusk. Boiling the onions to arouse more flavor from the potatoes, I remembered my mother saying that as people grew older, they longed for intensive tastes. I had to skip over puddles and walk on the spongy grass and balance my hand just so, since my fingers hadn't healed well after one of my bouts with Jack. Still, I kept the soup kettle level.

"All my worrying over what I'd do when Jack came here, or what he'd do while he stayed, came to nothing," I told Karl. "He up and left—

after reminding me that by law, he deserved all my earnings." I took a deep breath to wash the disgust from my voice. "I'm sure John Wolfer followed Martin's and Brother Keil's advice for caring for the ill, but Lucinda died anyway. My parents finally arrive, but there is still this strain between us. It doesn't seem fair, any of it. I told Louisa that not everything had a reason, but I'm having trouble believing that myself today."

Karl nodded. "*Ja,* it is good to come to that place. Death and uncertainty are a part of our lives. We wrap our grief with good memories of what encouraged us; they remind us that we live through such things. In the unpredictability, that's where the Spirit comes to bring us comfort."

"I wish the Spirit wouldn't wait until I'm miserable," I said.

"*Ja,* you hear His voice in the calm too, not just the storms, but we have to learn to listen." I looked at the tin ladle I'd brought with me from the hotel. It had an emblem, a leaf, at the back. I recognized it as one that Christian had made. I'd found it, now among the common drawer utensils. I'd considered keeping it out for myself but didn't.

"What is left to do then is to find meaning, Emma, not a reason. To live a life despite worry or planning against disasters. Things will happen. Worse would be to let fears of death or disappointment frame our days. We are placed here with desires. *Ja,* desires," he affirmed when I lifted my eyebrows. "It is part of our journey to discover what those desires are and then to find a way to live them fully as intended. That's why we listen."

"I only wish suffering weren't so much a part of living," I sighed. "Surely that's not a desire for life."

"That's what family is for," Karl told me.

"Family is for suffering?" I asked. "Well, that explains a few things."

"*Nein, nein.*" He laughed. "Family helps us through our suffering."

I considered that, then replied, "I'm not sure my family understands that's part of their task. I'd hoped that with them here, my life would be easier. But instead..."

He whittled as we spoke, though I noticed he had a Shakespeare book open on his table. Next to it lay a soft journal called *The Atlantic Monthly.* He never said I'd interrupted his reading, but then, he wouldn't.

"Each day events that trouble you can draw you closer to Providence, Emma." Karl always came back to Providence's place, never passing judgment, though, when I failed to recognize it on my own. "Can you see God weaving through your confusion?"

It was a difficult question for me to answer. He'd asked me that before, when Jack arrived and then was sent away. I did think I'd seen protection, with friends who had reached out to me, with my having the courage to risk leaving Willapa to come here. There my husband's family had stepped away from me, drawn a veil over what they didn't want to see. Here the colony had kept us from Jack's harm. The Aurora community had allowed me back, even opened their hearts to me, in that reticent German way of touching with a nodded head more than embracing arms.

"God is there, Emma, present at the end of a thread, pulling us toward Him. And if we ask ourselves in every situation how He is working in that experience or even our worry or disappointment, then we can feel that tug on the thread."

"I suppose I'll know that it's not me, hung up on a twisted twine that will simply break if I pull back too hard?" I said and smiled.

"*Ja*. You'll know. If you let yourself."

"There's grace in that thread, I suppose."

He handed me a wooden doll he'd carved for Ida, then bent to slurp his soup. "*Gut*," he said. "Just the right amount of pepper too."

I left, strangely reassured. Only later did I remember I hadn't asked him what it might mean that my parents had fostered an adult child. I probably couldn't have said it without petulance pouting from my tongue. Maybe God was in my forgetting.

———

The suffering of the Keil children did eventually end; but for those who cared about them, our suffering did not. Nineteen-year-old Elias Keil died first, followed by Louisa. She was eighteen, close to the age of

Kitty. Amelia suffered on, but Gloriunda died the same day as Louisa, just short of her sixteenth birthday. And then Aurora, amiable, adorable, admirable Aurora, passed away on December 14. Aurora, the dawn, was thirteen.

Kate was inconsolable. She was nearly six now and old enough to feel the pain of loss, especially of her friend Aurora.

"She's sleeping, Mama. Wake her up." Kate hiccuped from all her crying. We stood at the doorway of the Keils' large room, on the second floor above his workroom. I had my hand on her slender shoulder, keeping her from entering. Louisa knelt at Aurora's bedside, still as a blue heron. That bird quilt Aurora had stitched now lay across her, the reds and blues splashing in each block like spring birds against a stormy sky. They moved as through the air across Aurora's still form. Soon we women would help wash the body of this latest child to die, and wrap her in the loving folds of quilts, and then place her in the ground. My mother and sisters would work at my side. I'd sent them word.

Though she insisted that Aurora was sleeping, Kate must have known it was more than that. She cried so hard, but still she hoped. I didn't want Kate worrying about going to sleep or fearing she might not wake up when she went to her mat. "No. She's not sleeping, Kate. She's died," I said.

"Is it like when the tomato died because we didn't water it enough?"

"Something like that, only she didn't die because of anything you or I or her mama and papa didn't do."

"Is she with Papa?" To this I concurred, grateful that once again I believed in the words I'd spoken to my daughter about when we'd see the Keil children again.

"What's heaven like, Mama?" Christian asked me later.

"We don't really know," I said, brushing his blond hair from his forehead. Kate sat up, turned her head to me. Her eyes were swollen. "But let's imagine that for our beloved Aurora, it's a place where young girls quilt, all day long, because she loved to stitch, remember?" Kate and Christian both nodded their heads. "And she never has to take any stitches out, and there's always enough material to make the perfect block and border; always another one to piece together, with each one telling Aurora's story."

"Are there people around?" Kate asked.

"Chattering like squirrels. Outside a choir is practicing, and Aurora is healthy and well and happy, surrounded by those who love her, who sit and stitch beside her."

"When I see a quilt, I'll think of Aurora," Kate said.

"When I see birds, that's when I'll think of her," Christian said. "She liked birds and got mad at me when I brought one down with my sling shot. I didn't mean to. Well, maybe I did, but she sure got mad."

"Remember the good things, Christian. She'd like that."

We buried the Keil children in a fresh graveyard on the hillside above the *gross Haus*. Lucinda had been buried in the Aurora Cemetery, in the dip of the valley, but Keil wanted his children closer to "where the church will one day be."

Louisa clasped in her arms the bird quilt Aurora had so beautifully stitched. "She worked so hard on this," she said. "See here, where she poked her finger. There's a little bloodstain on the pink bird. I forgot to tell her that it would have come out with her own spittle on it. No one else's will take blood from wool, only the one who poked herself." Louisa's lips trembled. "Here's where she made a mistake and started over." She fingered tiny white stitches that formed a *V* against the madder red block. "So many things I never got to tell her. Or Elias or Gloriunda or Louisa." She whispered that last name. "Oh, Emma." Her eyes grew large, and I could see that the reality of her own death became clearer too, with the unnatural outliving of her children. As I held her, the rough wool of Aurora's quilt brushed against my cheek.

Brother Keil did not preach his usual sermon about the sins of fathers being passed on to children. He could barely speak at all, his grief so raw, his throat constricted by his tears. Louisa stood beside him in the cold, holding him up as she balanced at his elbow. The cardboard of her black bonnet sagged to hide her face. Twenty-two-year-old Frederick stood on Keil's other side, while nine-year-old Emanuel huddled against Louisa's skirts. Amelia still wasn't completely recovered and remained at home.

The band played a funeral dirge made all the more morose by the accompaniment of drizzling rain. John Wolfer, still reeling from his own great loss, Karl Ruge, and several other men, including my father, carried forth the scriptures for the day. Adam Schuele stood off to the side. Whatever rift had split him and Keil was still continuing, but he'd put it aside to grieve with his old friend. I looked around. We were not alone in our sorrow. So many in the outside community beyond had died of the pox as well, and I wondered if they had such arms of comfort to surround them.

Every death brought Christian's back for me. In mourning him, I'd turned inside, hoping to mend the tears in my heart alone, praying there'd be no more sorrow. But there always is. Loved ones left. Friends departed. I'd have to dare to make new ones. I'd come to see that it was the mark of our character, how we let others be the patch in our lives when we felt the most torn apart. If only I could remember it.

In the weeks that followed, Brother Keil walked the halls at night, came to his workroom, and puttered there until early morning. His face wore a vacant look, and when people requested aid, he sighed heavily and sent them looking for Martin. He didn't come out often to the blue cabinet near where we slept to select vials or healing potions nor put any new concoction inside. Instead he stayed in the room, surrounded by healing herbs that did little for his soul. I wondered if he blamed the herbs for failing to heal his children, or if he blamed himself. Or God, the way I once had. He never said.

He discouraged Louisa from entering his workroom, but did allow Helena to come in once or twice. Louisa would look expectantly at Helena, who shook her head sadly when she came out, often carrying a pot of tea that had cooled without his having tasted of it. In the morning, if he did leave his workroom, Keil's eyes would be rimmed in red.

Helena finally coaxed him to join us at the large plank table for a meal one day in January. He ate but failed to brush breadcrumbs from his beard and the frock coat, now stained. Louisa tried to talk him into changing it, "to brush the soil, Husband." But he resisted, rubbing the frayed edges of the hem. He'd worn that coat when he nursed his children, held their frail bodies to his chest. Perhaps he thought that taking it off would break the bond he still felt with them.

I remembered wearing Christian's clothes after he died, and the comfort of that scented cloth.

Men came to ask Keil about the mill contracts or the purchase of horses or selling a wagon or an order for barrels. They left shaking their heads and talking of his "hollow eyes." If they had some question about finances or land, they found him disinterested. "Do what you will," he said, waving them away with his hands.

Even my father was unable to rouse him. He came out of the office and told my mother it was like "talking to a post."

"Maybe you and Adam Schuele together could get him interested," I said.

"We're in his craw, old Adam and me," my father said.

While Keil grieved, my father, David Jr., and William spent their time scouring the area for the perfect land to purchase. Somehow my family had means to buy, without the colony's help. I wasn't sure how my father had arranged that—he must have sold property back in Bethel or had private contracts we'd never known about—and so far we had yet to be alone so I could ask him. His silence, with his presence so near, was almost worse than when we'd been separated by a thousand miles. At least then I could make up reasons why I hadn't heard from them: the letter had gotten lost, Lou's health took much of their time, they were busy helping manage things at Bethel. Once here, I could see that my wish to bridge our differences was not a bridge he wished to cross. I had thought I'd find a time to sit with my father and chip away at the wedge between us, but his physical presence hadn't opened that door. I'd have to open it myself.

We did not celebrate Christday that year. No sweets or treats, no band playing songs to make our feet tap. Even the boys' and girls' choirs did not practice their singing. The Feast of Epiphany that others in the surrounding community might celebrate in January was a day like any other in Aurora. Our community felt like a backwater—water swirling in one place. Only a flood would wash new water in and remove unwanted debris.

———

In the spring, Henry C. Finck decided to plant an orchard at the far edge of the village, up on a point not far from Keil's house, but on land deeded to the musician rather than the colony. Like my parents, he seemed to have independent funds. He and his children set about planting apple starts he'd purchased from Luelling. He had a dozen varieties, from yellow bellflower to Rhode Island greening and my favorite, rambo. He had plans to sell the apples in California. But every day, he came by to visit Brother Keil, encouraging him with talk of music. He said they ought to order bells for the church that would be built one day. Keil apparently said nothing, and Henry C would come out of the room, and if another man was waiting, they'd talk for a time.

Henry C and Karl Ruge spoke of education, since they were the only university graduates at the Aurora Colony. Keil had hoped Christopher Wolff would come from Bethel and bring his university expertise, but so far, he hadn't. They had camaraderie at least, Henry C and Karl. I served them hot coffee with cinnamon buns swathed in butter and envied their discussions, while most of what we women explored as we sewed or sipped steaming black tea was mundane, the merits of yeast over saleratus or the best cork bluing recipe to use.

Even though Brother Keil and Louisa still had each other, they slipped past each other in the wide halls, sometimes without even nodding their heads in acknowledgment. Once or twice "tailor Keil" entered our sewing room, where we women stitched on quilts or patched and mended. He had a fine eye for design and had always encouraged us to make dresses without such full skirts, so we would not catch our hems on fire at the hearths. He approved our hiking the hems up into our apron waistbands too when we worked. Again, for safety. He sometimes nodded at Louisa's stitching, and I saw her beam at his notice. *Was I ever so needful of recognition from my husband?*

None of us knew what to do to help Brother Keil and, in so doing, comfort Louisa.

Jonathan had already moved into the Keil and Company Store, which was still being run out of one of the log buildings. He'd begun taking over the bookkeeping. There'd been a bit of a tussle with the existing shopkeeper over Jonathan's role. Both men had asked for an audience with Keil, who'd said something like, "Jonathan was here before. He knows what to do," and that had been taken as the proper transition of authority, at least on my brother's part. Jonathan had opened a ledger page with my father's name on it and written, *Brandy, yds. of hickory, tobacco for Jonathan* on the page. My father was taking from the common fund, so he must have planned to contribute to it as well.

I asked to see my page and saw more debits than entries. Few of the former were mine.

"Someone has to do something," Helena said one afternoon. We sat in the Keils' room, where Helena and Louisa spun yarn. My mother and sisters knitted, and even my foster sister, Christine, sat there. Her hands clicked needles as fast as my sister Johanna's. I noticed Johanna's kind smile and how good she was with Lou, quick to respond when my sister had one of her quaking episodes. I could see that Johanna'd been good help to my mother.

I supervised Kate with a sampler and mended Andy's pants. He'd torn them when he and Christian had climbed down the banks of the Pudding to watch logs float by. When I chastised him about the river, he told me they looked for crawfish to serve at the hotel so it wasn't all play. I'd warned them to avoid the rivers, but the Finck boy, with his new ideas and adventurous ways, had set my sons to doing risky things, even when he wasn't with them. He hadn't grown up around Keil and didn't hold the same reverence for him that most young people in

Aurora did. Water had always been a fright for me, one that increased after Christian's drowning, but I wasn't sure the boys listened.

Kate raised her sampler to me, and I leaned over to guide her little hands. Ida played with a wooden duck Martin had carved for her. At least today my boys were with Martin, at a new building finally going up. Martin had suggested a pharmacy be built, more central to the colony, one that he and Brother Keil could stock and distribute from— if Brother Keil ever showed any interest again. Martin and Helena, brother and sister, had argued in their quiet way, as Helena insisted that the church should be next.

Earlier, when I'd gone to the site to watch the latest house going up, I noticed Frederick Keil there, sweat dripping from his brow. He grieved the deaths of his brother and sisters with a hammer in his hand. I'd seen Kitty bring bread and cuts of ham out to Frederick. They were of an age together. Frederick was a good boy and might be a match for my sister. She blushed with the young man's attention.

Together, Kitty and I had walked back to the *gross Haus*. I wanted to talk to her about Frederick but hesitated breaking into her happy spell. Then we'd begun our stitching, spinning, and weaving in the presence of Frederick's mother, and it didn't seem the time.

Brother Keil was in the workroom below us. He'd placed a mat there, and Louisa said he now slept every night on the hard floor, as though "paying penance." I hoped she'd resumed sleeping in their softer bed and had given up the hard floor herself, but I noticed the bed in the room where we worked did not look slept on. The quilt frame was kept by a pulley above the bed and lowered when we began work, double stitching so many of the rows. Perhaps it was too difficult for her to sleep in it, since her girls had died among the quilts.

"If only more Bethelites would come out. Perhaps Henry C will write them and encourage them to come. Or do you let them know of how things are here, Catherina?" Louisa directed her question to my mother.

"Or those from Willapa," Helena said. "They could come here. They're much closer."

"We tell them how it is here," my mother said.

"*Ja.* If people returned to our folds, then Dr. Keil would become interested in living again, I know it." Louisa's eyes pooled with tears.

I worried more about her than Brother Keil. He could lock himself in his workroom, but Louisa still had the daily obligations that never went away: meal preparation, laundry, tending to the children, endless work. We couldn't give Louisa the things she needed most: her children back or her husband able to share in her mourning. Louisa kept on, wearing herself thin. Her arms sticking out at the end of mourning-dark sleeves looked like Clara's legs. Keil was…neutralized in his grief. He was bread without yeast. It didn't need as much watching.

"Jonathan helps with the ledgers, doesn't he?" I asked. "I see him and Brother Keil smoking their pipes together. Maybe that helps him, Louisa."

"And the music, the choral practices, those ease him, wouldn't you say? 'Music washes the soul of the dirt of daily living,' " my mother finished by quoting an old German proverb.

"He needs an…elevating purpose," Helena announced. She placed her needle into the batting. The movement caused the scissors at her waist to clink against the quilting frame. She stared out into the room. "Pipes and music will not do it. Something to engage his mind so he is not thinking of his loss so much, that's what he needs. A task to remind him of God's faithfulness despite the darkness of the days he experiences now." She inhaled as though to orate: "I remember after I made my decision not to marry, I needed such an elevating project."

Her supposed fiancé had been a bridge builder. I thought to say something about a bridge being elevating but bit my tongue instead.

"We should begin the church. That's exactly what we need now. I've thought that for a very long time."

"Perhaps we should telegraph them," Louisa said. "The Bethelites. There's a way to do that now."

"Better we get the Giesys and Stauffers to all come from Willapa," Helena said. "They can help us. My brother John can be here within days from Willapa, instead of the months it would take Missourians to get here. Surely they will listen now to our needs, with Father Keil so mournful and without Emma there to restrain them from doing what should have been done long ago. Oh!" She touched her hand to her mouth, as though suddenly aware that I sat before her. She'd spoken out of habit. She dropped her eyes.

"*Ja,* I was so powerful, I could keep all the Giesys up there against their will," I said. "*Ach!*" I'd poked the needle into my finger. Kate looked up at me, a question in her eyes. "I'm fine," I said. To the others I said, "I didn't keep Adam Schuele there. Or Karl Ruge. Or even Martin. They're all here now."

"*Ja,* we don't talk so much about Adam," Louisa said.

"I didn't mean, well, I guess I did mean it," Helena said. She clasped her hands in her lap. "None of them listened to me or Father Keil when we were there for Christian's burial. That would have been the right time to make the necessary change, and Father Keil was hopeful of that, or he wouldn't have made such a lengthy trip."

"He would have," Louisa said. "He loved Christian like a son."

"But they hung on," Helena continued. "Martin even said it was in part because of you, Emma. They didn't want to abandon what you and Christian had so wanted and worked for. Even my mother stays there in part because of you."

"Not because of me," I protested. "She and Andreas took my son and came here, remember? And Adam Knight left, and so did Adam Schuele. They went all the way back to Bethel. I didn't hold them there against their will."

"Will you never let my mother forget that? My parents meant no harm in bringing Andy here," Helena said. To my mother she said, "Did she tell you that my parents kidnapped her son? Goodness, it was such an affair. They were trying to help, give Emma room to take care of her other children." Back to me, she said, "You were with child again, after all, waiting for young Christian to be born and had your hands full. It would have been a better thing for him to have lived with them."

"Well, your mother has your sister to look after her and your brothers," I said. "There's no reason for her to come here." I felt my fingers begin to rub against each other; I took a breath, felt calmer.

"*Ja, aber,*" Helena protested, "we need to be all together now, as the disciples in the book of The Acts: 'They were all with one accord in one place.' My brother John could handle finances. Just until Father Keil is restored," she hastened to tell Louisa. "The Stauffers would help at the mill—"

"My Jonathan is doing a good job taking care of finances," my mother said.

"Perhaps Emma's being here will make it easier for the Giesys to come now," Louisa said. "You could be right, Helena."

"They haven't come yet," I reminded her. "I've been here more than a year. If I were so busy holding them hostage, why wouldn't they have come if they'd wanted to?"

"People sometimes don't notice that their shackles have been removed," Helena said, "until someone else points it out to them." She picked up her needle. "I'll point out to them how much better we fare here."

I didn't comment. At Willapa everyone had a single-family home, not like here where we crowded together like piglets in a piggery, where maybe that had caused the Keil deaths.

"You should ask them to come, Emma. Now is the time."

"It would be my good fortune that only Jack would listen."

"That wouldn't be good," Louisa agreed.

We worked together in the quiet then, me piecing my red wool blocks into a quilt pattern that put the blocks on edge, as though the squares were diamonds. It was a unique design, one that had come from my imagination as I was thinking of the Diamond Rule. My sister Lou had commented on how pretty it was. Kitty had said it reminded her of a symbol on a deck of cards, at which Helena had gasped. The point took extra doing to get to a sharp edge, but I found that the concentration required to make that perfect edge took away some of the irritation of the conversation.

"Let's invite Sebastian, then," Louisa said. "He and Mary and the girls. Sebastian helped construct the mill there, didn't he? He's a good hand with a hammer, and that's what we need now. Good hammer hands."

I swallowed hard. *No.* Mary and Sebastian were our old neighbors, and I suspected that Jack lived with them once again. Their exodus could spur Jack to come back here with them. I took another stitch at that red square edge. I poked my finger with my needle and sighed. Only my own spittle would get rid of the stain.

7

An Open Door

*March 26, 1863. My birthday! Christian would have brought
me an oyster shell or maybe some small treasure of tin. Instead,
I will bake myself a pudding using carrots in place of eggs,
well boiled and mashed and sent through the sieve. It tasted
good in January when the hens stopped laying. Lighter than
any egg pudding I've made.*

In March, we traveled by wagon to Salem for the reopening of Durbin
Livery Stable. My parents didn't go. They'd been staying with Adam
Schuele, my father's old friend, and attending events far away proved
too much trouble, my mother said. Jonathan took their wagon and my
children. I rode or walked along when my *Hinterviertel,* my backside,
became tired. In the distance, we could see tall poles being set for the
telegraph wires that would come right through Aurora. "We won't have
to go to Portland to communicate with Bethel now," Jonathan noted.
He appeared quite pleased with Aurora's continued entry into the wider
world, with no worry over the prospect of the outside contamination
that had once brought us west.

Andy acted glum during the entire trip. He poked at Christian's
shoulder with his fist, not so hard he hurt him but enough to annoy his
younger brother, who'd whine so I'd turn around. I pointed my first
finger at him and scowled.

"Stop it now! This is a fine outing your uncle is taking us on, and
we don't need to be upsetting his ears with your antics."

"He hits me, Mama," Christian complained.

"Andy…," I warned. "You mustn't hit the boy."

"He took my cap and stuffed it in the straw," Andy charged.

"Christian…?"

"He poked me."

"Andrew Jackson Giesy, you are older. You are wiser. You cease. This instant."

"Or you'll what?" He set his jaw in defiance. I could feel heat come to my face, and my palm opened as though against my will. I swung back to strike his cheek, but then Andy mimicked me: "Mustn't hit the boy."

I stopped myself, my arm in midair, turned around, clasped my hands in my lap. *What have I almost done?*

"They raise your dander, Sister," Kitty said. "Just being boys, *ja*?"

"Naughty boys," I said.

"They're bored. It's a long trip," Jonathan noted. "You don't spend much time with them, I notice. They are always with Martin."

I felt my face burn. "I'm busy doing," I said.

"Some might say you should be doing with your boys," Jonathan said.

"Do you say that?"

"I'm just supposing."

"Today they should appreciate the outing. They have much to be grateful for, and they fail to notice it."

"Children are students of their parents," he said.

"What are you saying?"

Jonathan shrugged his wide shoulders. "I don't hear you saying so much about all your blessings, Sister. Maybe all they hear of is the disappointments. It's what they remember, then."

"I've had my share," I said.

"*Ja*, you can be right about your past, Sister, but hanging your hat back there only lets sun burn your face today. I don't see you tap your feet to the band music here. You don't dance anymore. Have you made little wooden shelves, like you once did? You must be a good steward of your trials, as well as of your gifts."

"I'd never considered the tithing of my trials," I said. "Who would want ten percent of misery given to them?"

"You tithe the lessons learned from suffering," he said.

"My brother the philosopher," I scoffed.

"Happiness doesn't appear to have been invited to Emma Wagner Giesy's house," my sister sang out.

"Emma Wagner Giesy doesn't have a house," I sang back, off-key, of course.

We rode without speaking, my attention now on Ida, sitting quietly beside me. Kate daydreamed out the wagon back. She looked to the past too, it appeared, her eyes always on the distance. The boys still bickered, but I heard no more howls. Kitty began teaching Kate a round. *When was the last time I danced? When was the last time I wanted to sing?* I remembered Sarah Woodard of Willapa talking about her Indian friends, the healing ones. They asked these questions of ill people, to assess how far they had fallen from doing things that pleased them and brought them healing. Singing and dancing, working with wood, and painting brought me comfort, but I wasn't doing them. I quilted, yes, but less because I found solace in the act and more to get the quilt top done. Was that what my sons saw in my life, a working woman, tending her children, avoiding one husband, grieving another, pursuing her parents, but always working? I turned to look at them. The boys and Kate were old enough to witness some of my struggles. Was Jonathan saying I needed to share more of my joys as well?

I couldn't even name a present joy. Perhaps that was the heart of the problem, the place where I needed to begin.

"I love spring," I said to no one in particular. Then to the boys and Kate, I said, "See the buds on the trees? They're different trees from those we had in Willapa. Not such big firs or cedars here. Remember when we used to play that game of how hungry we were, telling each other what we'd eat?" Kate shook her head. "It was when we walked Andy home from school. You, dear Kate, were hungry enough to eat everything in our house," I reminded her. "And, Andy, didn't you want to eat the tree?"

"I don't remember," he said. He'd stopped punching Christian.

"You ate the tree," he said then. "So you'd have toothpicks in your mouth when you were finished."

"That's right. You've such a good memory."

"I ate the cow. And Kate said we could wash everything down with the river."

"See, you remember it all." It pleased me that he recalled a difficult time that we'd converted into something fun. "I like that."

"What did I want to eat?" Christian asked.

"You were so small you did somersaults, or tried to. And by the time we'd eaten everything in sight, we were home."

"That was before Big Jack," Andy said.

"*Ja.* It was before him. Just like now, though. We're going to a new place to have a good time for the day. Your uncle drives the wagon; we have food packed to serve people, so we won't need to eat fence rails," I added. "And we will see Brita and her family again—I'm sure of it. When we come home, you'll have aunties to entertain you. It's a grand day. One to remember."

"And the sun shines," Kate said.

"So it does."

"So we can wash down whatever we eat with spring water instead of a river, right, Mama?"

I smiled at her. She began singing Kitty's round. This happy thinking could be catching.

———

I had never seen the old Durbin Livery Stable in Salem, but the new one was grand. Horses grazed on the short spring greens behind the planed wood building. Two of them stood with their heads over each other's necks, as though chattering. Several more nickered over the half doors of their stalls, which had been newly whitewashed. The horses liked all the activity of men and women arriving, their liquid eyes following the women dressed in their finery. Sometimes one whinnied low when a woman stopped to pat her gloved hand at a soft nose. The parasols didn't frighten these animals, a sign they were trained to be with happy, dancing people.

To celebrate their rebuilding after the fire, the Durbin brothers had organized a cotillion party. Tickets were four dollars for the dinner, but Jonathan had managed to get several gift tickets since the colony band was to play. Brother Keil had come out of his cave to sit at one of the tables. Louisa had remained behind, feeling a bit under the weather, or so she'd said. Sometimes I suspected she liked it when she had time to herself in that big house she had to share with us all.

We colony women had been asked to prepare cold foods—fried chicken, carrot loaves, dandelion salad, and jars of pickled cherries and tomato figs—and baskets of doughnuts and breads made with our hops and potato yeast.

I watched to see if Jonathan danced and which woman he might choose. My brother had shown no interest in any woman that I could see. I wondered if he'd left a sweetheart at Bethel. He kept his nose to the ledger books, as I kept mine to my children and work.

Today I looked forward to seeing Brita. She'd been here to help rebuild after the fire so maybe that gave her a chance to put memories of the circus fire behind her for good. Something about her perseverance inspired, and I'd missed that once she left. I hoped she'd put her homestead plan into action too. My father hadn't said a word about the Homestead Act, and my mother told me he didn't really intend to use it. "He wants to purchase a place with a dwelling already on it," she said. "Most of those places have better land than what's left for the Homestead Act." I wasn't being included in the search. I pitched that loss away. Today, as Jonathan had encouraged me to do, I'd be grateful for what was.

Helena served the table where Brother Keil sat with some dignitaries. People raised happy eyes to me as I brought steaming platters and cold dishes. Here I could eavesdrop without appearing like a gossip. And we didn't need to wear our bonnets here. We'd donned straw hats we'd made ourselves, so our faces were open to receive their kind smiles.

"Oh, you'll like these pickled cherries," I told one frowning man, who said he'd never heard of such a thing. "The cloves and cinnamon and vinegar combined will pucker up your lips so quick, you'll collect a friendly kiss from your sweetheart there, *ja?*" I nodded to the woman seated beside him, who fanned her blushing face at my words, while those at the table laughed with good humor, then dove into the cherries. They nodded assent and pointed with their fingers for more as their mouths puckered.

When we'd finished our serving, we stood at the edges and watched the dancing. People loved to dance in this Oregon State, and the swoosh of their dresses brought back good memories of Missouri, when even young girls learned the *Schottische,* that slow waltz, by standing on their fathers' shoes to be "best girl" for the dance. It was how my father had taught me. How I wished Christian and my father could have been here to teach Kate.

I made sure not to make eye contact with any of the men standing loosely at the edge. They'd be bachelors, and it would not be good for them to think I was available, though I stood with the single women. As I watched the dancers move around the smoothed plank floor, I realized I did miss dancing with a man. But couple dancing was a thing of my past. Maybe after everyone had eaten, Kitty and I could swing around the floor, for the women often coupled up while men smoked their pipes. Fewer men than women attended in any case, a reminder again that our states were at war and young Oregon men were off training for battle.

"Would you care to dance?" It was the voice of a stranger, a man not much taller than I, but well formed.

"I don't much," I said.

"Oh, go," Kitty told me. She pushed at my elbow. "It's only a dance. I'll watch the girls."

Wasn't this what Jonathan urged me to do, participate more, just enjoy?

So I did. He was a jockey, he said, who rode horses in races when he wasn't working on nearby farms. When asked, I told him I was a mother, a cook, and a wife.

"Your husband's at war?" he asked.

"*Nein.*" It was all that I said. He nodded politely at the dance's end, bowed at his waist, then turned to leave. I complimented myself on experiencing a moment of joy, until I met a glare sizzling across the dance floor from the eyes of Brother Keil.

———

I hadn't seen Brita anywhere among the crowd. While others danced, I took Ida by the hand to wander by the stables. Kate and the boys were being watched by Jonathan and my sister. A breeze brought the unmistakable scent of horses to my nose, and Ida said, "Horses?" I nodded yes. Brita had been hired to work the stalls, and it was there, far from the dancing, that I found her.

I crouched to her height, and we held each other for just a moment, our shawls wrapped loosely at our shoulders. Pearl sat playing on a blanket in an empty stall, and Brita took her toddler's hand as we walked and talked. Ida held my hand too and attempted to skip, her dark curls bouncing. Men sauntered outside to smoke their cigars, while in the distance women fanned themselves, warm from their dancing exertions.

"I'd show you our quarters," Brita said, "but they've stacked ice blocks there right now, to have them closer for the party. Once this is over, my life goes back to normal."

I couldn't imagine what normal was for Brita. She was raising children who within a very few years would be bigger than she was. Charles already was. I saw the boys together at a distance. They threw rocks at some sort of target in an open field. I remembered how close I'd come to striking Andy for his sassiness and was grateful that I hadn't. For Brita, there'd be no physical means to keep her children under control. Jack had tried to control me that way. I suppose Brita had learned faster than the rest of us that size wasn't much help in keeping one's children in check. I could still grab Andy's ear, but he hated it, and I didn't like doing it. I needed to find some tender way between us, instead of arm twisting.

Brita acted as though nothing could impede her way, not even a fire in the place where she lived and worked. She hadn't heard that the family she'd served in Aurora had lost their father and two of their four children of smallpox, nor had she heard of Lucinda's death or the Keil children's.

"I'm sorry to hear," she said. "It's good that *Frau* Keil has you there, then, for comfort. It appears Mr. Keil is recovered." She nodded toward him, leaning into some discussion with a well-dressed man, Helena close by his side.

"This is his first outing since the children died," I said. "And I'm not sure I'm much comfort to Louisa, but my mother and sisters bring her nurture."

"Your family came? But that's good. I'm surprised you even remember me, with your whole family with you now."

"You're memorable," I said. I was pleased to see her smile. We walked awhile, and then I said, "Brita, tell me all you know about that Homestead Act."

If it surprised her, my change of subject, she made no mention of it. She sat down on the tongue of an unhitched wagon. I could see that she'd stitched up her skirt hem with tiny, even stitches.

"Go off to the courthouse. Find land that hasn't been aclaimed and claim it. Build a house on it and stay there five years and it's ayours. I've got a spot far south of Salem. It's not open, so I'll have work to do to clear it for planting."

"Even women can do this?"

She nodded. "The land is yours in even shorter time if you're a veteran, if you're coming back from the war. They wanted to give aspecial help to soldiers. But why would you do that, Emma? Didn't they promise to build you a house right there in Aurora? And your family is there now."

"I wonder if that will ever happen. Brother Keil mourns the deaths of his children so deeply he rarely comes out of his workroom cave. When he does it's for something…promotional. Certainly not to build a woman a promised house. Helena wants a church, and that makes good sense. Part of me feels selfish, wanting the colony to build me a home when there are others who need them too. Sometimes I wonder if the trials we've faced have been because we haven't taken time for gratitude and worship, just as Helena says."

"It would be difficult to build a house on your own," she said.

"You're planning to do it."

"But if I had someone close to help me, I'd accept the help."

"I never told you, but the house I want will have room for two families. We could make them totally independent or have one kitchen that we both used. Have a good roof and a place for people to be private, but within a shout should they need help. I'd thought maybe you'd join me there, you and the children, but then you left."

I wanted her to say she'd return. It would give me a reason to push for the house daily. We started walking again, out across the meadow. I slowed my pace, partly for Pearl's shortened steps, but more for Brita, who still moved by shifting her weight from side to side. She finally stopped, picked up Pearl, and bounced her lovingly as she faced her, her daughter's legs around her waist.

"Your double house idea is lovely," Brita said. "But I'm not the one to live on that other side."

"Because you want your own home."

She nodded. "Though when I first came for help, that house you describe would have been a good place to collect myself again and get my children settled down. Not that the hallway by the blue cabinet wasn't a restful place," she hastened to add. "But a house with only one other family around would abeen better. It's a fine idea, Emma."

"But?"

"People like me must be prepared in case someone pulls the rug from beneath our feet. I want to know that I made the rug I stand on and laid it in the house with my name on the door. I want to know that it is my home and that I'll leave when I choose, and not when someone else says I must."

"I'd never ask you to leave, Brita."

"It wouldn't be your home, though, Emma. The colony would have the house, and they could do with it what they pleased. That's the other side of sharing everything."

"One's own place" was a slender thread of the colony life that others could snip off. Still, no one had ever been expelled from Keil's colony. Even back in Bethel the Bauers had built ten businesses right inside Bethel after they'd said they no longer wanted to be a part of Keil's communal ways. Keil had left Bethel, and it might be yet another way Keil kept control over us colonists here, promising things but never delivering. I'd have to get approval from him to use the house, even if he authorized the two-family design. "Maybe Keil will determine who would live on the other side."

"Unless you were strong enough to stand your ground," Brita continued. "That's the only way a woman, even a small woman, can have what she wants. You got to care deep to step over people's open-mouthed gasps that you'd dare something so outrageous or that it could ever succeed."

"How did you ever get so wise, Brita?"

She laughed. "Ah, the fire-eater taught me all that."

———

Spring turned into summer, slow but steady as the milk that dripped into the lumps that formed cottage cheese. Still no word about my house. Still no movement toward the church. My parents kept themselves distant from the village. I began thinking about work I could do to make a living apart from the colony. Maybe Jack wouldn't know where I was, and an employer would assume I was widowed and eligible for my own earnings. I wasn't sure that the colony would want me around, working for them, if I found another place to live. It was acceptable for Henry C, the music master, to live within the village and yet earn money from the outside that he said he would use to send his son to Harvard one day. He never took a dime for lessons given to colony children, and Jonathan said he believed in the communal ways of sharing. But a woman? I doubted they'd pay me for my cooking or sewing. Truth told, I did have much to repay them for. They'd rescued me and my children two years earlier. Still, by the time I found land to build on, what I contributed in work to the colony ought to make things even with what they'd given to me, Clara the chicken included.

Two years I'd been here. It was a year already since Jack left the second time. I decided to ride along one day when the men delivered butter to Oregon City. They'd stop at Solomon Weil's pottery shop there too, to make trades. I asked and they let me off at the Clackamas County courthouse. "I just want to check on something for Jonathan," I told the driver, never quite sure if he'd report to Keil or not. It wasn't a total lie…just a half truth. I'd let Jonathan know of my results of looking at land maps and deeds. I sought unclaimed land that had already been surveyed. Most of it was far from Aurora or any other place where my children could go to school or where I could find employment. Maybe I'd have to do what Brita did, first find a paying job and then save up enough so that all I needed to do was work at proving up my land within those five years.

If I began this fall of 1863, I reasoned, my Andy would be fifteen by the time it was mine. I'd need his help to do it. But Andy needed to be in school. And how would I do that? We'd be as we had been in Willapa: isolated and alone. Still, throughout the summer, I rode to look at various sites. When I rode with my sons, no one asked any questions of where I was going. When I came to the barns alone, the men would frown as I asked for a horse or a mule, as though without children around a woman was somehow up to no good. I gave no explanations to them. Let them wonder.

The search took time, what with fitting it in between the constancy of colony work. And I had to feel strong enough, when I went alone, to endure the disapproving looks of the men.

To gain such strength, I'd begun reading the Scriptures again. Karl had recommended it, and once, before Christian died, I'd found the time of reading full of peace and wisdom. I'd deprived myself of both by ignoring those words. My sister Kitty had preached Scripture to me in her letters. At least that was how I'd seen them. I'd lifted her words and carried them as weights, instead of as the wings she intended. But then that psalm had come to me to comfort Louisa and to remind me that once I'd found nurture in the psalms and other scriptures too.

Kitty loved the psalms and even taught the group of us a psalm to sing while we worked. It was a part of her, Scripture and song, and they weren't meant to make me wear a cloak of guilt just because I didn't experience faith the way she did. One summer morning, I'd been reading in the book of Revelation: "Behold, I have set before thee an open door, and no man can shut it." The words spoke to my heart, and I decided to take my little man, Andy, with me to see if we could find that "open door."

Andy didn't seem all that happy to go with me. I wanted to talk about what I proposed to do and how it might affect him. I asked Kitty to look after my other children, so I could devote this time to my older yet more distant son.

"I promised to help Martin sort out the new shipment," he said.

"Martin will do fine without you for a few hours."

"I don't like that old horse they always pick for me either. He tries to bite me whenever I bend over."

"Don't bend over near him, then."

"Martin teaches me things, Mama. Important things. I should stay and help him." I reminded him that Martin wasn't his father and that I, as his mother, would decide how he spent his time. I too had things to teach him. He said he didn't care to spend his time riding around anyway, and he didn't know why I wanted to live someplace else either. "I like Aurora, Mama."

"*Bitte,* don't make this difficult, Andy."

He crossed his arms over his narrow chest.

"I'll take care of the horse," I said.

"That I'd like to see," he sassed. I didn't reprimand him. Instead, I decided to do him one better.

———

"Is that dinner, Mama?" Andy asked as we walked toward the barns for our afternoon excursion. I'd told him there'd be a delay because I had something special to prepare. He nodded toward the basket I carried. It was a colony basket, made from ash and oak and brought from Bethel.

The cover fit tightly to keep flying bugs out, but the weave let air flow through. Inside I had cold ham slices and bread and several hard-boiled eggs in blue shells. But I also had a very hot baked potato, just taken out of the coals.

"Dinner and a surprise," I said.

When we arrived at the barn, one of the men saddled the mule and then led up Andy's mount, the horse he didn't like. "Mama...," he began.

"That one bites, so be careful," the stableman said.

"*Ja,* so I'm told," I said. "Give me a moment." To Andy I said, "Act like you're having just the best time." I showed them a pocket I'd made, and put the hot potato in it. Then I tied the pocket around my waist, with the hot tuber at my backside, making sure the horse was busy munching and not paying attention. "You watch." I led the horse down the fence line and tied him loosely to the rail. I gave him plenty of rope to move his head. I chattered about the weather as the man placed the saddle on the horse's back. And then I deliberately bent over to check the stirrup, my backside toward the horse's head. The potato was hot enough that I could feel it through my dark calico dress and petticoat.

"*Ach,* be careful," the stableman warned.

I heard the tug of the rope and the horse twisting his head, and I knew he'd be reaching to bite the potato in my pocketed *Hinterviertel.*

"Mama..."

"Shush now," I told him in a singsong voice. "We're just chattering away here."

I felt the pocket move. The horse grabbed and bit into the hot potato.

The animal twisted his head back. I heard the halter rings rattle against the rope, followed by the thump of a half-eaten potato hitting the ground at my side. The stableman chuckled low. "A hot *Kartoffel* never had such a bite."

I straightened, fussed with the leather, and then found a reason to once again bend with my *Hinterviertel* toward the horse's biting end. The horse twisted his head but did nothing. "I doubt he'll ever do that again," I said, standing up. "He'll think he did it to himself too, if we don't make any real notice of it. So, are you ready to ride with your mama?"

The stableman smiled as he walked away, shaking his head. Andy nodded and mounted up. I thought I saw appreciation in his face. "You outsmarted him, Mama," Andy said.

"Yes, I did."

Martin wasn't the only adult my son could learn from. Perhaps I'd opened my very next door.

8

Acting as Though Hopeful

Andy and I had a grand day out riding. I'd made a map, thinking maybe my father would be interested if I found a good piece of property, even if it couldn't be a homestead claim. Being with my son made me grateful: we had a roof over our heads, and we had family around us, though neither fit the image I'd planned. Serenity settled in my mind while we rode. I could accept the present experiences while still pursuing something different and, hopefully, better.

Andy spoke with animation about his time with Martin and his pharmaceutical activities.

I asked, "And do you want to work with apothecary things, be a healer of sorts?" Then thinking I should not just ask questions but state my thoughts if I wanted to influence my children, I added, "Healing would be a good thing to do."

"When someone needs their leg cut off, I want to cut it off," Andy said. I raised my eyebrows. "When someone breaks an arm, I want to set it. And if—"

"You…want to cut off limbs?"

"Only to help people, Mama." I heard the disgust in his voice. "If there's infection. I want to heal and fix things. Make it better."

"That's *gut*," I said. "Very good." This was a change from the time when he'd wanted to hurt Big Jack. "It would take both strength and courage to do such work," I said.

"I have both."

"You say that very firmly for one who is not quite ten years," I said. I shook my head, and he raised his eyes in question. "Your father and I headed west ten years ago. The years slipped past me like an otter sliding down the Willapa River's banks." As we rode, I pondered silently. What did I have to say for them? More important, what did I want the next ten to look like?

"I'm old enough to know what I want to do when I grow up," Andy said. A slight breeze lifted his straight brown hair, and he pushed it away from his eyes. He rode without a hat and squinted into the sun. He had new boots on. I hadn't purchased those for him. Martin must have. Or maybe my father. *Had he needed shoes and I'd failed to see it?*

"You want to be a doctor in ten years then, *ja?*"

"Is there a way that can happen, Mama?"

He lifted those sable eyes that caused my throat to tighten. Oh, how I wanted to be the person he saw, someone who could do anything to make her children's lives better than her own.

"Only Karl Ruge and the music master have university degrees here. But they could prepare you for a university. While you study hard now, I'll try to find a way to send you later." I thought perhaps my father might help pay for his schooling. Or maybe the colony could, but I didn't propose either solution. Better not to lift up hopes that would only be later dashed.

We found ourselves near Adam Schuele's farm and reined our horses down the long lane. Keil had given directions for a road to be built from Aurora to a Giesy farm, a road that bypassed Adam's farm altogether, making it difficult for Adam to bring his goods to Aurora. I hadn't realized the convolutedness of this trail until we'd ridden this less-traveled road.

I hoped we'd see my parents here.

Adam greeted us with a bear hug. He raised hogs, and the pungent scent of the pigs rose to my nose despite the distance of the pens from the house.

"What brings you here, Emma?" Adam asked. He could use my first name because we'd been through so much together that first winter in Willapa.

"I thought maybe I'd see my family," I said. "And we're thinking to find a homestead plot, my son and I, so we're riding and beholding."

"Like father, like daughter, wanting to live somewhere outside of Aurora." Then, "Didn't I hear Keil had agreed to build you a house?"

"Did he, Mama?"

"With his children's deaths, he's been morose and not interested in much of what's going on. I'm afraid our home isn't very high up on his list," I told Andy.

"The Homestead Act is a good thing. I considered it myself."

"You and Keil…quarreled," I said, risking the intimacy.

"He thought we scouts made a mistake." His hands quivered as he pulled a chair out for me. He was aging like my father.

His words burned at my stomach. I'd been a part of that so-called Willapa mistake too.

"*Ja*, well, that is his loss. He's envious of what we had there in Willapa, building a new place different from what Aurora is, everyone with their own home in their own name instead of Keil and Company."

He looked wistful. "Those were good times, *ja*? We took care of you, Emma, as your father asked us to. And you took care of us."

"My parents, they've—"

"They didn't want to come out here at first," Adam said. "But they tangled with August Keil and Andrew Giesy when Wilhelm sent that son back to Bethel and told that Giesy to help your father manage affairs in Bethel. Then leaving seemed wise. But I don't think they wanted to deal with what might greet them here, either." He'd been hulling some berries when we came in, and he handed a few to Andy now. "I told your parents not to come, to stay there where land was in their name and not Keil's only. But they wanted to help family." He smiled at me. "And Jonathan is a big Keil supporter."

"They didn't want to come here—"

"But they did. For you."

"But then why aren't they here for me?" How much could I tell him? And in front of Andy. "My parents are…" I looked at Andy. "We should be going," I said. "Thank you for the spring water and the berries. Will we see you on the Fourth of July? The band will play. Maybe there'll be a horse race."

"Of course," Adam said. "But you ask *Herr* Keil again about your home. Maybe you can get him to sign a statement, Emma. Wilhelm believes in the written words he signs. You remind him that your Christian paid back the money loaned to him by the colony to buy your Willapa land. That's right, *ja?*" I nodded. "Get it in writing, and you can have your colony house without fear of its being given to someone else before you're ready to give it up. *Ja*, that would be better for you and your children than trying to homestead on your own."

Adam was a good man, a calm and faithful man, not unlike my Christian. Perhaps my parents resented that I'd begged them to come, causing them to leave their home in Bethel for this…this distant colony with tangles in the threads that should have joined us together, instead of separating us further.

Adam ruffled Andy's hair, told the boy the story of his birth, and boasted that he'd been one of the first to greet my son in this world. Andy's sparkling eyes told me he enjoyed the attention. We spoke our good-byes. As we rode back, I thought of Adam's words. If I pushed for the house, got it in writing, rather than try to homestead, Andy could continue to go to school and to learn from Martin, and maybe, just maybe, I could convince the colony to send Andy to medical school when that time came.

"Get it in writing" was what I remembered three days later, when we learned of Adam's death. He'd collapsed on his way to attend the Fourth of July picnic in Aurora, 1863. I resolved I'd make my home a memorial to Adam, to the scouts who had been my family, and to Christian too. I'd dedicate my home to making other lives better than my own…if I ever got a home of my own.

———

Keil didn't attend the funeral, so Karl Ruge spoke the blessing. My parents and brothers and sisters were there to mourn Adam, and of course, my brood did too. Few others attended, and I wondered if perhaps it was the hold Keil still had over people, muting even their wish to openly grieve someone who no longer held favor in Keil's eyes. I'd filled two of the glasses we'd made with blooms from the herb garden. I placed one on Adam's fresh grave, then walked over and put the other on Lucinda Wolfer's grave.

I chose the next day to see Jonathan. "Has Keil said anything about my house being built?"

"What brings that up?"

"I spent some time with Adam before he died, and we talked about it."

"I'm surprised Adam would be interested," Jonathan said. I thought he bristled a bit.

"And the answer is?"

"He picked a site. But he hesitates. He wants to be fair."

"Fair? After what I've given? The colony owes me a home. I'm widowed because of the colony."

"*Nein,* Sister. There is another way to see that. You had separated from the colony."

"Separated, yes, but my husband continued to act as though we belonged to Aurora, and he repaid what the colony gave us to make purchases in Willapa."

"Some still stay in Willapa, and Brother Keil knows that is in part because of Christian's decision. Money for all those purchases has not been returned." He shrugged his shoulders. "I wouldn't demand the house, Emma. There are many others who would like a home built for them, and they might resent your receiving one before them."

"*Ach!* Then I'll go homestead," I said.

"*Ja.* I hear you're stopping at the courthouse in Oregon City."

"I meant to tell you. I just forgot," I said.

Jonathan sighed. "You can't homestead, Emma."

"I can find a place. Women alone can do this," I said. "Single women and widows are allowed. My friend Brita is going to do it. She has acreage—"

"If they are heads of households. But you aren't. You can't homestead, because you're married still. Unless you're thinking of getting Jack to homestead with you…or maybe…a divorce."

A fly could have buzzed in and out of my mouth without my noticing, I was so aghast at his words. *How can I keep being surprised at the boulders on my road?* Women bore the brunt, no matter how dangerous it might have been to remain married to some brute. Women were left to fend for themselves and their children, to pay for the rest of their days for the poor choices they once made. Women suffered whether they stayed married, chose to live with the disgrace of divorce, or dangled dangerously in between.

"I don't want a divorce," I wailed. "I want a home."

"You could find someone else to file for you, I suppose," Jonathan said. He'd leaned back in his chair, the front two legs lifting. He now dropped them down with a plop. "But that wouldn't be legal, and there'd be no way to protect yourself if they decided to write you out of it someday in the future."

"Papa…?"

"Papa's looking for land with potential that can support his family. He doesn't want to depend on the colony. He's wrong in that, but that's his way."

"I'm not the head of the household."

"Not in the law's eyes," Jonathan said. "I'm sorry, Emma." He patted my hand, offering comfort. "Without Jack around, your oldest son comes closer to being that."

———

My former mother-in-law, who was still the grandmother of my children, arrived in Aurora in late July. My sister-in-law Louisa Giesy,

Christian's younger sister, held her mother's hand, and they were swinging their arms back and forth in delight. John and his wife, Barbara
White Giesy (I thought of her as BW), came in the wagon with their
girls. Behind them followed Sebastian and Mary with their children.
They'd even brought Opal, our goat.

No Jack Giesy in sight.

Louisa Keil gushed. "So good, so good you are here! Now my husband will have all the help he needs." She clasped her hands, unclasped
them. Her eyes glistened with happy tears.

"John is a good head at business," BW said of her husband. "It was
a good time maybe to come and help Brother Keil out. Sometimes
older men with more experience can do a better job." She looked
straight at me, and I wondered if she knew that my brother had been
the manager and done fine work for the colony.

Everyone gathered at the ox barn. Neither Louisa nor Helena, who
had joined us, acted surprised at their family's arrival, so once again
news had come in and slipped past me like bats in the night. The
women stepped down and shook dust from their skirts. We'd be taking
them to the log hotel for something to eat, then setting yet another
family up in the *gross Haus. There isn't any more room.* "From the looks
of your wagons, you must be planning to stay a long time," I ventured.

"Ach, ja," young Louisa Giesy said. Her face was flushed. "Didn't
you know?" She'd lost that drifting look she'd had while she tended to
her mother and my children, back in Willapa. Something had inspired
a change. Maybe it was the move out of the Willapa Valley.

"Louisa stays for sure," Helena said. She smiled and put her arm
around her sister.

"Goodness, *ja,*" Louisa Keil said. "She's here for her wedding. It's
one marriage my husband has approved."

"Who are you marrying?" I asked. People exchanged looks, so
apparently everyone else knew.

"My son," Louisa Keil said. "Frederick. They've been writing back
and forth for years."

"Some things don't change, *ja,* Emma? You're always a step behind," my mother-in-law chided. "But then you don't always have so much to contribute either."

I felt my face grow hot. A headache threatened. My fingers did their rubbing dance of irritation.

I turned to Mary. "Thanks for bringing our Opal," I said. "At least goats don't keep secrets."

Mary blushed. We'd been neighbors back in Willapa but hadn't communicated at all since I'd left. The goat's knees had dirt spots on them, like dark brown eyes on white legs, and she pushed her way to me, yanking against the tether. She placed her front feet on my shoulders. "Opal missed you," Mary said.

"Emma spoils her goat as she spoils her children," my mother-in-law said. "It's so good that our Jack let you have her."

I scratched behind Opal's ears, no longer ambivalent about their arrival. Except for the goat, I was wishing they'd all stayed at Willapa.

A few days later, I saw Keil swinging his cane with more lift than the day before, so I left my post at the hotel and intercepted him on the path. He headed toward the millpond area. A tiny mist of steam rose from some hot springs in the lowlands across from the mill, and today I could smell the sulfur in the breeze. On winter mornings, the area made me think of fairy tales and dragon mouths blowing hot breath in the air.

"Brother Keil," I said. He turned at my voice. His eyes grew wider. *Wariness?*

"Sister Emma," he said. "Walk with me."

I kept his pace, which was slow, though he had long legs and we could have strode right out if he hadn't been so run down. "To what do I owe the pleasure?"

He is in one of his good moods. Thank You, God!

"I want to begin my house," I said. "It's been nearly two years since you said I could have a place of my own for my family. I've proven myself to be a good worker. I've caused you no trouble and been a help, I hope. You need more room in the *gross Haus*. It seems the time."

He sighed. "It is difficult to think of such things when my mind has been so filled with grief and the business of affairs here. And I've enjoyed seeing you and your children outside my workroom. I've hardly left our Aurora, you know." His voice caught at the name of his lost daughter. I wondered if maybe he'd change the name of the town now, since it grieved him so to speak it.

"The cotillion put a lift to your steps for a few days," I noted. "Helena was a fine encouragement there for you." *Bite your tongue, Emma.*

"What? Helena? *Ach, ja, aber* such joys are fleeting." He paused. "Like a dance at a spring cotillion, *ja?*"

Touché, as my uncle, the vice counselor to France, would say.

I looked up at the crows gathering in the firs. "The Giesys offer you good support, *ja.*"

"Very *gut*. Very *gut*."

"And soon you'll have a new daughter-in-law."

"A Giesy," he said. "She's a good girl for my Fred."

"It's wise to allow marriage," I said. I could have bitten my tongue again for raising a potentially contentious issue. "But the happiness of your children was always paramount. This I know." I cleared my throat. "I have a design for the kind of house I want. It will be for two families, one on each side though a two-story house. It will have two front doors."

"Helena believes we should build the church next," Keil said. I remained silent. A part of me agreed with her, but I so wanted that house! "But such a huge undertaking needs people," Keil continued. "I've had to send our boys out to work in Portland and Oregon City and Salem, because we have not enough sales from products here. So they are not available for building. I pray for people to come from Bethel and all the rest from Willapa. Maybe you could share your home with one of those from Willapa?" He turned to me, smiled.

"Not Jack Giesy," I said.

"Families are best when reconciled," he said.

"This is not negotiable."

"There is always hope within a family, Emma. You must remember this."

"Aurora has become my family," I said. "I've reconciled with it."

He found a tree stump and sat down on it, the cane now between his knees with his hands resting on it. He pushed his hat from his forehead. He motioned me to sit beside him. I don't suppose he liked having a woman look down on him. "Maybe your parents would live in your house. I have failed to understand your father's moving about the country, as though Aurora was insufficient to meet his needs."

"I have no control over my parents," I said.

"I suppose this is true. That Christine they fostered is a sturdy woman. Hard worker in the hotel. She exudes…mystery, that one. Perhaps you could have her share the house with you. It would make her travel easier. Now I understand she rides in from Adam Schuele's place."

"Perhaps. I know that I could make the house be in service to the colony, I could promise that much."

"We could use a house for the unmarried women, such as we had back in Bethel," he said.

"It would have to be twice as large," I said. "We have so many."

He frowned at me. I wondered if he thought I was being critical of his not allowing some to marry. But he moved on. "*Ja,* well, maybe we don't have material for such a big house. Those women can remain at the *gross Haus* or stay with their families."

I wanted to say, "Or you could allow them to marry," but I held my tongue. No sense getting distracted from my present doing.

"And you would commit to working here as we see fit, to giving back what we give by building you a house?" Keil insisted.

"Yes. If you'll allow me to use the house to benefit the colony as I see fit," I said.

He stared at me awhile. The scent of sulfur from the hot springs nearby filled my head.

"But there is this pressure, about the church," he said.

"I'll write letters myself, urging more to come from Bethel," I said. "I'll approach them as the wife of your former lieutenant. My little house will require few people to build it. And you'll have more room in your house for those who come."

"You don't think we are challenging God by building for ourselves first, Sister Emma?" I couldn't tell if he truly wanted my opinion about a theological matter—something so rare it was frightening—or if he was looking for new words to silence Helena.

"The church building is important," I said. "But even in the beginning, the early followers went from house to house to worship and practice their faith. More important than even the structure is that there be a time set aside to worship. As we once did, all together. Even twice a month, Brother Keil. You've let that lapse in your grieving." He raised an eyebrow. *Don't be critical.* "I mourned Christian poorly," I said. "Separated myself from everything, everyone. When I first came here, our twice-monthly gatherings in your home helped bring me back. I miss them."

He stayed silent for a long time. Perhaps I'd gone too far by offering up any personal thoughts about a spiritual matter. He wouldn't think it was my place.

"I will have Jonathan draw up our agreement, and he can begin your house," he said at last. "Or perhaps it should come from John Giesy. Maybe he should sign it."

"You ought not to bother John with such an insignificant matter, him having just arrived. Jonathan can tend to it." I felt my heart pounding. I was so very close. "Should I assist by talking with my brother?"

"I'll see to it. Of course, you'll want to write those letters to Bethel. Get them to come out. Your home will be your reward."

"There is a meadow—"

"*Nein,*" he said. He pounded the ground with his cane. "We will build it not far from the Pudding, but in Aurora proper."

"Not on the site I choose?"

"Nein."

"But is it a site that will flood?" I cautioned. "Water is a fright to me. My husband—"

"I know." He patted my knee, kept his hand there. I moved as though to brush lint from my skirt and stood. "Well, it might be closer to the slough than you'd like, but you will adapt, Emma Giesy. You always adapt, *ja*? And it will make it easier to build there. We don't want you too far out. Isolation is not a good thing for a woman. And besides"—he smiled now—"I wouldn't want Emma Giesy too far from my sight."

9

Diamonds on Edge

August 9, 1863. Louisa and Frederick's wedding day. I baked the wedding cake. Fifteen eggs (three blue), butter, sugar, three pounds of seeded raisins, serviceberries, molasses, cinnamon, cloves, and bolted flour! It rose like a mountaintop in an oven set at dark yellow paper heat. When cooled, the frosting smoothed across it like a dragonfly flitting at the river's edge. There were several other cakes but many commented mine was tastiest. Is this pride, I wonder? Or a gift received?

October 3. We have new arrivals! I fell back on the grass and sent arrow prayers upward for my house.

Brother Keil officiated at his son's wedding, and it did seem to lighten his step. Louisa Giesy's face glowed, framed by white blossoms in her hair. She allowed Helena and the rest to fuss over her. Frederick, too, appeared to have matured, wearing a tailored suit that his mother let everyone know had been sewn by his father. Several of our colony now worked in the tailor shop, and people from Salem and Oregon City came to make purchases at our growing garment industry. Trust Brother Keil to find a way to use even his son's own wedding as a way to promote our products.

Martha Miller attended, along with other single women and men of the colony. Martin was there, and Karl Ruge and my foster sister, Christine. It was as festive as Christday without all the presents.

Jonathan and my sister Kitty came too, despite snatches of malcontent expressed by my sister about the Willapa Giesys' arrival. I mostly saw Kitty at the hotel kitchen, which gave us little time to talk of family or future. But while the Aurora Band played for the wedding festivities, she and I sat on my new red and blue quilt.

"What did you call this?" Kitty asked, running her palm across the blocks. "It still looks like Diamonds on Edge to me."

"I suppose it is, but I wanted a new name, one unique to me. I call it Running Squares, and I added a few different things to make it mine."

"The wide border of squares," she noted, "with double rows of quilted stitches." She pressed her fingers against the red block in the border, then turned it over. "*CG?* For Christian?"

I ran my fingers over the cross-stitched initials. "I started the quilt before he died," I said. "Diamonds on Edge is how I felt after he died. Our Diamond Rule, about making another's life better than our own, seemed to be pushed on edge when Christian died to save another man." I sighed. "So Running Squares it is now, since I seem to be always running somewhere." She sighed.

For the wedding celebration, men placed flat boards into a square beneath the trees, and people danced and danced while we sat and watched. Festivities—weddings—were truly some of the best times at the colony, and I noticed that outsiders made their way here without invitations, knowing there'd be music and good food. Given the smiles and laughter, I wondered if they also came to be rejuvenated among us Germans, as we lived simple yet productive lives, knowing how to celebrate as well as toil, sometimes doing both at once. They didn't know the inner turmoil, the trials that strained our communal threads. We probably looked to them like a serene pastoral scene, painted and hung over a fireplace.

"I didn't even know they knew each other," Kitty said.

"What?"

She nodded toward the glowing wedding couple. Louisa carried a bouquet of blue flowers with long white ribbons hanging down, standing out against her dark wool dress. "Frederick never mentioned Louisa to me." She spoke with a tone of wonder, mixed with betrayal. "I don't know how I could not have known."

"There's no reason to be hard on yourself," I said. "Did you and Frederick talk so much?"

"When I brought the dinner baskets to the field I sometimes shared a word or two. But then this one time, he took me on a boat on the Willamette River, moving up the backwaters. He was a gentleman," she assured me. "We saw lush water plants, and the trees draped over the boat like a green veil, just so pretty with the sun sparkling on the river." She wiped at a tear.

"It sounds lovely," I said. "Though a little risky without a chaperone."

"You could draw it, I suppose. I couldn't, but you could. I'd have it as a memory, then."

"Have you ever tried to draw anything?" I realized I didn't even know what she liked or didn't, what her talents were or weren't, except her love of music. Here she was, my sister who had been so dear to keep writing to me when I'd felt abandoned by everyone else, and I'd paid scant attention to her now that she lived within touch. "Maybe I could teach you to sketch."

"It's not an interest of mine," she said. "Except to remember that day. Maybe I'll put it into a song, though what's the use of that? He's gone off to someone else."

"It's still your memory. You felt...cared for. Nothing wrong with that."

"The day was dreamy." She smoothed the quilt border over and over with her palm. She chewed her nails. I'd never noticed that before.

"Backwaters hold mystery," I said. "There's life in the water's edge, sometimes things there we never see in the faster-moving stream."

Her eyes watered. "I thought I was special." She removed a handkerchief from her basket and dabbed at her nose. "But all the while he courted Louisa. How could I not have known that?"

"Maybe Frederick didn't even know. Maybe he looked for a friend and found that in you. Maybe he didn't realize that Louisa would come into his life as a future wife. Perhaps his mother influenced the Giesys to come here now, and then—"

"But they'd been writing to each other!"

"It doesn't take away the fact that he was there with you that day."

"He did mention marriage." I looked at her. "Oh, not ours, no. He said his father didn't approve of marriage, that he thought it took us from the important work we had to do to live the Christian life."

"He would say that," I muttered.

"I actually agreed with him," Kitty said. "But I thought I could devote my life to the colony in the way you do, Emma, if sometimes I had happy days with Frederick, rowing a boat or sitting at the bandstand and listening with him beside me."

I didn't want to think about her view that *I* was somehow a model "single" woman in her eyes. I nodded for her to continue. "I thought my biggest obstacle to a marriage one day would be Father Keil, but it turned out to be a Giesy."

She leaned against me and cried then. I held her, rubbing her back. "It'll be better in time, it will, Kitty. This is something I know." Wounded by a Giesy; that was something my sister and I had in common.

———

As I'd promised, I wrote letters back to friends in Bethel, everyone I thought might still think kindly of me. I encouraged them to come, to help us build. I smiled to myself; Christian would have been pleased, though he'd have wagged a finger at me. I was encouraging them to come mostly to ease my guilt at wanting a house before a church could be built.

The autumn turned to times of harvest. Sometimes I wondered why I was so happy when the seeds sprouted in spring gardens, as they promised hard labor come fall. In between gathering pumpkins and potatoes, we dried apples, peeling and slicing them, the juice sticky against our fingers. Some we hung to dry, stringing them with big needles onto flax. Kate helped with that, though she ate nearly as many as she threaded. Days we spent making soups of vegetables and meat, to preserve the broth. We made *Kraut* until I could smell the cabbage in my sleep. We dried seeds to be used for next spring's plantings too. Ida carefully turned each one over on the cloth, her tiny fingers barely bigger than the seeds. We dug trenches lined with straw to keep cabbages and watermelons covered for use in the dead of winter. In between we did the usual: laundering, rug beating, daily meal preparations, care of our families.

I was aware, slowly, that our women's work did allow a certain amount of laughter, a bit of pleasantry, as we exchanged stories. Perhaps I was being allowed to become a part of things here. Helena's quick tongue could calm as well as strike, and when she raised some scripture for an occasion, it was often done not with a hammer but on a platter, offering something up to nourish, if someone chose to pluck the morsel. Sometimes in the midst of stirring beans in crocks, I'd look over at the elder Louisa Keil and see her crying, and without even thinking I'd put my arm around her shoulder and just let her, knowing how memories like steam arise to take us somewhere else and how a loving shoulder can be enough to bring us back.

Even Mary Giesy had begun to joke with me as she had in years past, before Jack. She was the only woman besides me who'd spent time around Jack. I wasn't sure how long they intended to stay, for she still called Willapa home. Once she even praised a suggestion I'd made. "Nailing drying strips to the ceiling was a good idea, Emma," she told me. "I wished I'd done that years before. The mosquito netting worked well hanging from there too, with our dried apples and peaches, when I could get them."

"You hung them right in your kitchen?" Martha Miller asked. "Didn't you have a drying shed in Willapa?"

"*Ja,* good and high so we didn't bump them with our heads. It made the room smell nice. It was Emma's idea. At least I saw it at her house."

My life was a river's flow. I'd be an outsider at the edge, then move slowly into the current of influence. Perhaps I wasn't so selfish. I was able to give, to be in service, doing for others. Maybe I had more to give because I spent time at the edge, seeking to nurture myself.

All the while I worked, I prayed that I'd be doing the work of drying food and preparing for winter in my own home before too much longer. But soon after the wedding, Keil ordered construction of John Giesy's house. Frederick and Louisa's, he said, would be next.

Fortunately, Brother Keil began to hold services again, and I hoped that would ease the pressure to construct the church until we had more people to help. "My brother talked sense into Brother Keil," Helena told us as we dried wild grapes in the airing boxes. Apparently Brother Keil wasn't going to get all the grapes for medicinal purposes. "John told him he simply must hold services until such time as we could construct a building."

"John convinced him?" I'd heard it was John Will who had approached him. But I had as well. I wondered if I should tell her about my conversation with Brother Keil. Helena and I were alone at the big red dryer, placing fruit on the flat pads.

"Oh yes," she continued. "My brother said they'd come from Willapa just to follow him and his great relationship to our Lord. He said none of us could afford to lose that connection if our colony was to succeed here as it had in Bethel. It was all about Brother Keil's great faith and how he led us in it."

Those were the very things my brother told me John Will had expressed to Keil. Helena was usurping a bit of influence, it seemed.

"Well," I said, "I'm glad he listened to someone."

At the toll bridge, Karl Ruge let out a shout I heard from the hotel. Several of us stepped outside that cool morning, because it wasn't the usual announcement that someone had attempted to cross without paying. It was the wrong time of day for the mail run or the stage bringing passengers to eat with us. A wailing cry, then a trumpet blast, then another horn or two echoed in the air.

"What do you suppose is going on there?" Helena said, hurrying from the ox barn, her hands shading her eyes.

I watched Michael Rapp and Henry Burkholder, the blacksmith, men in their midthirties, running like boys toward the bridge. Conrad Yost came out from his post to see what the ruckus was. The young Snyder boy who'd come along on Keil's first trip out started to skip. Andy rushed by me as well. "Come, Mama," he shouted. Martin walked slowly toward us, his sleeves still wearing the straw-woven cuffs worn to protect the cloth as he worked. His forehead frowned in question. Henry C's choral class stopped their vocalizing beneath the trees, and the girls clustered together, chattering.

"What is it?" I asked, as Martin got beside us. He shook his head as though he didn't know. And then I could see for myself. I'd truly have to trust in God's timing if I'd ever get my home built.

Conflicted was the word for my feelings as I watched the first of many wagons drawn by big Missouri mules roll across the bridge. I counted twenty, thirty, forty. A light wagon pulled by mules preceded more wagons, each pulled by two teams of oxen. Then the pattern began again with mule-drawn wagons, oxen-led ones carrying cages of chickens at the sides. Behind them, dogs barked and kept a flock of thin sheep bleating forward on the wooden bridge. In the distant dust, I could hear mooing. A few rust and white colored cows with short horns shook the bells around their necks and trundled across the bridge, driven by young men riding on still more stout-looking mules or astride Morgan horses.

"They sound like the three billy goats gruff clumping across the bridge, Mama," Kate said. "Trap, trap, trap. 'Eat me when I'm fatter!'" Kitty had heard the story from Norwegian travelers in a wagon train and shared it with my children, much to their delight.

"Is the troll under our bridge?" Christian asked, his eyes the size of apples.

"*Nein,*" I said. "Trolls are only in stories." I thought of Jack and forgave myself the lie.

Christian and Kate had joined us and Amelia Keil too. She carried Ida from the lawn beside the ox barn, where she'd had the youngest children in tow. Pox scars marked her face, but otherwise she had survived the pox when her siblings had not. She lifted Ida to my arms. My head began to ache. All these people arriving would change things again. *Poor me!* I started to think, then, *Nein. Fear must not be my master.* I would make things change for the better.

I think myself happy, like the apostle Paul. I reached for Kate's hand. "Pick up your skirt," I said. "This is a joyous occasion." And we started to run too.

There were forty-two wagons in all. Jonathan sent one of the boys up to the Keils' to tell them that the Missouri Bethelites had at last arrived. He stopped at the mills along the way, so soon all the Aurorans were there, greeting old friends from Bethel.

Joe Knight touched his fingers to his hat brim in greeting. Joe and Adam Knight were both former scouts, and their grins carried a brother's familiarity.

"Isn't Matilda with you? The women…?"

"We went to Willapa first," Joe said. "The women will come up later on boats. We'll bring them here, but we brought the cattle down overland. Stauffers are coming too. We've scooped up the Willapa contingent, Emma. We're coming here as you did."

"All of them?" I asked, uneasy.

"*Ja,* well." He coughed and looked down. "I was sorry to hear of your troubles with Jack Giesy, Emma." He looked me in the eye then. "But you found safety here." I nodded. "You deserve that."

"Oh, I don't know if any of us deserves anything good," I said.

"You do no one good by not taking up what the Lord provides, though." He leaned toward me so only I could hear and added, "And Jack didn't come with us."

Adam Knight reined in his horse, then, to say how sorry he was about Christian's death.

"*Ja,* that was a long time ago now," I said. It was the first time I'd characterized my loss that way—that it was a long time ago. And suddenly, it had been.

"No one wrote to say you'd be coming. Didn't you get my letters? And with forty-plus wagons? It's like when Keil came out with lots of people and us not really ready with houses for you all."

"But here it's the third of October, *ja*? Didn't Keil tell you? We wrote to say we'd be arriving. Most of us are hoping there'll be houses ready, since there are working mills here. Not like at Willapa at all."

"I imagine the important people knew," I said.

"It doesn't rain so much here as it did in Willapa," Adam Knight added. "This is the truth, *ja*, Emma? Tell me that Keil has not exaggerated in that."

"Brother Keil was right about rain," I laughed.

Professor Christopher Wolff captained this train, and he stepped down now from the first wagon. He was the one who'd read Keil's letters to the Bethelites, sent first from Willapa and later Portland. He shook his head.

"This...this is not what we expected," Christopher said. He scanned the area.

I looked to see what he saw. A few scattered houses with a smokehouse or two. Partially built commercial buildings. The ox barn and our hotel of sorts beside it. Privies like pox marks at the end of scratched paths. Tree stumps, a few corrals, a horse or two ripping at grass, a few Missouri mules.

George Wolfer stood beside him, shaking his head. "When I met an old Bethelite at the bridge, I asked, 'How far to Aurora?' and he said, 'You are right *in* Aurora.' Can this be?"

"I'm afraid this is it," Jonathan told him.

Christopher Wolff had a university degree, was considered brilliant, and had just successfully led more than forty wagons and two hundred fifty people across the plains. But at this moment, he looked as though he'd stepped in a pile of manure and couldn't imagine how he'd get his boots cleaned. I was only one step ahead of him in scrubbing at the uncertainties of Aurora under the direction of Dr. Keil.

The wagons stayed circled in the middle of Aurora for several days as we feasted, listened to music, and put all work aside to welcome the Bethelites and hear their stories. Andy took a liking to Lorenz Ehlen, a boy of about thirteen whose sunset-colored hair waved away from his high forehead. He pushed it that way as he talked about the most exciting part of the trip.

"It was as we left," he said. "The last three wagons caught fire and burned, and we had to leave them and push everybody else into other wagons while we urged the others on. We unhitched the mules and the oxen and pushed them along."

"A fire?" I said. "Did someone not properly care for the fire starter?"

I looked to Mr. Ehlen. He was a widower who had brought along his five children. Without a wife to assist, accidents like that could happen. We sat at their evening campfire, one built the right size. Lorenz's father rubbed at his arm and shook his head.

"Nope," the younger Ehlen said. He popped the end of his lips so the English word sounded different. "The Confederates burned 'em. The antiabolitionist Confederates."

"In Bethel?" I asked.

"Nope." That pop again. "They caught us as we came through St. Joseph."

"That's an amazing story," Andy said.

"Well, Lorenz might be exaggerating a bit," Mr. Ehlen said. "He has a dramatic flair. We did have some trouble with a little fire. And it was hard to hide our Union support. But I'm not sure we can attribute the disaster to the Confederates."

"It could have been," Lorenz protested.

"I was discharged from the army with a wound, just a few weeks before we headed this way. Ought not to have worn my uniform, I'm guessing. They knew we were Unionists."

Andy pressed for more details. Christian wanted him to describe how he got his wound, then Andy asked if he could see the arm that hung useless at Mr. Ehlen's side.

"Andy," I said. "You mustn't pry—"

"It's all right. The boys should know what can happen when you stand for something. I've long lamented the practice of slavery. But when they threatened the Union itself, then I had to go to fight. But it was time for us to come and find a new place to live. Build us up a new home and restore things in the colony the way they used to be. I was tired, I think, not looking forward to the journey out. House building, well, it can trouble a one-armed man." He patted his elbow, setting the limb to swinging slowly. "Sometimes a man's not certain of a thing, but then he gets propelled forward, and he knows he has to act to catch himself or he'll fall flat on his face. Coming here was me, catching myself."

"That's not just a man's discovery, Mr. Ehlen," I said. "Not just a man's."

———

Keil appeared to revive with the arrival of those wagons. He'd given directions for where people should park, pointing with his cane. Over the next few days, he had Jonathan set up ledger pages at the Keil and Company Store, as he called the communal shop, so people could get their supplies. At least we had supplies for them, though the addition of two hundred fifty-two people strained our resources, or so Jonathan said. John Giesy said we'd do fine.

Checking our own kitchen larder, I knew we'd be hard pressed. I wondered why Keil hadn't pushed us to grind more wheat, to make sure we dried more fruits and vegetables, if he knew there'd be this big arrival. Maybe he wasn't sure the Bethelites would really come. Perhaps he planned to purchase supplies from the ships. He must have cash, if that was his plan.

Keil announced with some bravado, "There is plenty of land for you all east of here. You must not worry. This is our Eden, and now we will make it a garden that will become known the world around."

Keil made a big show of assuring the new arrivals that there was enough for everyone in the storehouses: enough thread for the women, enough wheat for bread, enough land to plow. No one said out loud that there weren't enough houses, though once the Knight and Stauffer women arrived from Willapa, the looks on their faces as they gazed around spoke loudly enough.

On the final feast day, my parents came to town, word having reached them at Schuele's. My mother and sisters sat on a quilt beneath the trees, brushing flies away from the baskets of bread and slices of ham and hard-boiled eggs. My children were with them, my Ida enjoying the pampering of her aunts. I'd sat with them all for a time, watching Lou work on her sampler while Johanna hovered. Lou hadn't had a quaking fit for several weeks now, my mother said. Johanna knew what the quaking looked like, and she took it as her mission to be prepared, sometimes anticipating a fit by a certain look in Lou's eyes or the way she held her head.

Christine stood to the side with my father, listening to the new arrivals. I hadn't seen her engaged in much conversation. My father talked with Mr. Ehlen, nodding his head, and I heard "abolitionists" and "war" as words drifted from the trees. *He avoids me.* When he walked over toward the corrals and Christine joined my mother and sisters, I assumed he wanted to smoke his pipe alone. I asked my mother if she'd watch my children.

"I will," Christine offered. She had the sober face of someone accustomed to disappointment, always preparing for more. "I never had any brothers or sisters," she said. "Except you Wagners later in life." It was the most personal information I'd heard about her.

I thanked her, and while the band played in the distance, I followed my father. He tapped at his pipe burl. Mr. Ehlen had apparently given it to him, as it had *Antietam* and a date carved into the outside of the bowl. Perhaps it was where he'd received his wound.

"Have you located any property to homestead?" I thought it an innocent enough question.

"What I do with property should be of no concern to you, Emma Giesy."

"Papa," I said, blinking back the tears that the harshness of his words had sprung, "I wanted only to talk…about…where I could find you and my sisters and brothers and mother, when you settle down. I miss seeing you. I didn't mean to pry."

His eyes softened. "Your brothers work in Oregon City. Your sisters help look after the Schuele fields for now. I suspect we'll winter again with them. Except for Kitty." He scoffed. "Where she picks this new name thing up, I'll never know."

"Kitty distinguishes herself that way. Maybe to be sure you don't confuse her with Christine."

He stiffened his shoulders. "We have room enough for many children, no matter how they disappoint us."

I wanted to ask if I disappointed him, but I didn't have the courage. "It's a wonder that you would have added a child, a woman, into your family. Our family."

"She needed a safe place to be, Emma. It is the Christian way, to offer safety."

"Safe from what?"

"That's Christine's story to tell," he said. The sharpness of his words sliced like paper against a child's tender skin. I was still at the edge of my family.

"Will Christine winter with you?"

"She plans to stay with the Keils. Ask her your questions, Emma. She's a grown woman, like you, on her own."

"I don't understand this…bitterness between us," I said finally, deciding to state my case.

He tapped his pipe against the split rail, sucked on the now dry stem. He sighed. "Christine works well at the hotel, or so they tell me," he said. "I hear talk that Keil will build a real hotel soon. One where many can stay over if they wish. There is railroad talk too." He shook his head. "Imagine. Keil sends people west to avoid the influence of the railroad on our children when the tracks were laid twenty miles away, and now he plans ways to bring the railroad right through his Aurora, right to our doorsteps."

"I've wondered about that too. What is it? What did Brother Keil do to make both of you separate from him?"

"It is no concern of yours, Emma."

"I wonder if whatever separates you from him also separates...us," I said. "I've come to...understand Keil and his motives. Yes, he can bob like an apple in the water, sometimes showing his colors, sometimes making one hold his nose to approach him. But he puts whatever is earned through the hotel or our wheat sales or apples back into the colony. He buys more land so new people will have places to farm. Except for the *gross Haus,* he doesn't live above the rest of us." I spoke the words softly and hadn't thought they'd sounded too complimentary of Keil. But my father, who'd been talking to me as we had of old, now bristled.

"You defend him," he said. "He replaces faith with economics. That was never the intent." Then, "You have made your bed, Emma. You lie down with Giesys..."

"But you loved Christian. Like a son he was to you!"

"*Ja,* Christian. He was a good man. The best of the lot. My good friend. And he died."

My father grieves my husband's passing too. That hadn't occurred to me.

He paused. "And you ended up giving up Christian's land to a ne'er-do-well."

"All the Giesys aren't like that. Just Jack. I was doing the best I could. I hadn't heard from you. I wanted you to come out, to help me, but—"

"Jonathan offered you a way out. You could have come to Aurora after Christian's death, and he would have helped you. You could have sold the land eventually in Willapa, so you could buy your own in your son's name. All the scouts fared well except for Adam, and that was because of Keil. But you had to do it in your way, didn't you? After all I'd taught you about staying close to the land. As long as you have land, no one can ever take it from you, Emma."

"The Indians here would argue with you," I said.

"What? *Ach, ja.* This is true enough, but I'm not obligated to have them listen to me," he added. "If I were, they would probably ignore my advice as my daughter and son do."

It's what I did with the property that upsets him? I've behaved un-wisely about the land and for this I can't be forgiven?

"*Aber* in Bethel, you belonged to the communal ways," I said. "You helped start Bethel. That was your life. That's what you taught me, Papa. I thought you were angry because we remained in Willapa, because we tried oystering as something apart from the colony. Or because I remarried. To be angry because I tried to find safe haven for my children here in Aurora…"

"Because you let a Giesy get your land." He nearly shouted. "*Ach.* Why should I expect a woman to be quick enough to outfox a Giesy? Even now Andrew Giesy, who works with August Keil to *sell* the com-munal land in Bethel, tries to say the property I held as my own there must go into the common fund, while August Keil operates *his* land as though it is his personally. He puts nothing into the communal pot. He hasn't since he returned to help Andrew make the sales. Keil replaced me with his son as co-manager back there, quick as a lynx. He'll replace Jonathan too, you wait and see."

"I didn't know you had trouble back in Bethel," I said. "I'm sorry."

"*Ja.* I held that land in my name from the beginning, and sold it… *Ach,* never mind. It is too easy to get under another's spell, and I sus-pect that's what has happened to you."

"Jonathan trusts Brother Keil," I said.

"Maybe. But we would all be better if we had land in our own names. We could still offer help to others, still be communal in the Christian way. You remember that, Emma."

"I'm a woman. Land can never be in my name."

He shook his head and began to walk away. I couldn't let him. I wasn't finished. I reached for his shirtsleeve. He stopped.

"Papa. We'll talk again, *ja*? I want so for us to enjoy the company of each other again one day. This conversation, it doesn't leave me... satisfied."

The set of his jaw loosened, and I thought the lines to his eyes crinkled as they might before he smiled. "Satisfaction is what comes from a good stew," he said.

"I make an ample one. With many pieces blended into the whole to make an altogether new flavor. You'll come to my house and have it sometime? When I have a house?"

He said nothing for a moment, then he patted my shoulder. "*Ja*, Daughter. I will one day come for your satisfying stew."

In that second week, several Wolff wagons began pulling out, heading east to the land assigned to them. The Knights said they'd look at property in the Oregon City area, and I could tell that like my father, they wanted land of their own. Mrs. Kraus, a widow with three children, said she'd remain in the Aurora area and hope for a house. *Join the wait for the walnut to roll your way,* I thought but didn't say. Triphena Will, holding her six-month-old infant, Leonard, told her husband, "I'd like to go home now." You could tell by her crying-red eyes that she meant back to Bethel.

Then began the meetings to ensure proper posting of what people brought in from Bethel to Aurora—who would get credit for what, who would be building barns and houses, who would go to work in the fields, who would find work outside the colony but bring resources back in return for their assignment of land, which new craftsmen could begin work making the big lathes needed to turn the long pillars for the church. These were experienced builders. Aurora was the sixth colony they'd built up while following Keil. Wolfers and Wagners and Forstners had their names attached to places like Harmony in Pennsylvania and, of course, Bethel. I could feel the swirl of progress in the fall air.

With all the reconsidering, I asked Jonathan to show me my page in the ledger book. The fabric I'd purchased was noted, as was the flour I'd been given for personal use on the distribution days. I noticed Clara was on the page as an acquisition and debits placed against it. A good portion of the debits were Jack's. But my page lacked acknowledgment of what I'd brought into the colony, and after my father's words, such mention seemed important. If the colony ever dissolved, I'd want to have compensation for what I'd contributed and not—heaven forbid—still owed.

"Shouldn't there be a page that says what I've contributed?" I asked my brother.

"It's there," he said. "Your hours of labor against what you've purchased—your shoes, your thread, your coffee. That dime you gave in cash for having won the award for your drawing at the Agricultural Fair."

"But that comes out even for the first year," I said. "I'm not accumulating. And there's nothing to note what I brought in through the Willapa land. That we paid it back. Or the work I've done here at the Keils', the stage stop, the gardens."

"*Ja,* I see what you say now. You really need that in order for there to be no question about our building you a house. We need to reassure that you are a full member of the colony," my brother told me.

"There's no question but that I'm a member of the colony," I said. "Who's challenging that?"

"No one," Jonathan said. "Yet. But we need to be sure in case someone does. Your husband isn't a member, so that's the rub."

"*Ach.* My husband risked his life coming out here for those of Bethel. And he believed he belonged to the colony here, even if I didn't. The Giesys are all here. Have they brought funds into the colony? Did they sell their land in Willapa? Make the certificate say when Christian joined, then, along with his wife."

"But Jack Giesy isn't a member, Emma. I don't think you can join without your current husband."

I stared at him. "We took in runaway women and never asked their husbands about doing it," I said.

"But they did not join up if they were married."

"Brother Keil would never think to stop a Giesy who wants to join up, would he? Louisa knows I'm a member. Helena would vouch for me. I'm a Giesy, for heaven's sake. It's what drives my father from me!"

"I don't know," he cautioned.

"Will you build me a home or not?" I actually stamped my foot. This had gone on long enough.

Jonathan sighed and pulled a sheet of paper from the cubby in his desk. "Keil wants you to sign this," he said. He slid the paper across the oak to me. "I've been…hesitant to show it to you."

I, Emma Giesy, will agree to abide by the rules of the Aurora Colony as directed by Father Keil, offering up what I have to give in service to the colony. In return, the colony will provide care and keeping for me and my family including the building of a home.

"Will he sign this?" I said. Jonathan nodded. "Would you?" He nodded again. "It doesn't say anything about my being a full member of the colony."

"*Ja,* you're right about that." Jonathan looked at the paper again.

"I don't need to be an official member, but I need something else here. It must read, 'care, education, and keeping for all my children and me.' And I want to add these final words." I wrote five more words onto the tail of the agreement and slid it back across the desk to my brother.

Jonathan looked at it and inserted the first suggestions I'd made. He read my final five words. "*Ja.* He will sign, though he might wonder what you mean by 'designed for use by her.'"

"Tell him it will be for service to our Lord," I said. "Then let's get this house underway."

10

Hammers in Hand

*November 15, 1863. Bryonia helps the headaches. Resting
in a chair overlooking the river helps too. At night, I sit
outside in the rocker and wrap myself in the Running
Squares quilt. I stare at the stars and imagine each one
disappearing until there is only a dark sky and I am alone
beneath it but not lonely. My powerlessness disappears; my
headache subsides.*

*November 16. I've left no room to write, having spent myself
on headache notes yesterday. Perhaps it is enough to say this
was a good day despite the rains.*

The sounds of hammers throbbed, but not for my house, in my head.

I dressed Ida, hurried my other children to don their petticoats and
trousers, hating the pain in my head when I bent over to hook up Ida's
buckled shoes. Together we went to Martin, to see if he could give me
some powders. I'd decided not to bother Brother Keil, and besides, I
didn't want to depend on his ministering to me—nor to deal with his
cloying at my asking for assistance.

Tall, slender Martin, always leaning forward, was one of the finest
men I'd known. I'd trusted him and Karl Ruge to help me in my darkest hour, and it affirmed for me that while I'd made some bad decisions
in my life, all of them weren't so. I admired Martin, and sometimes
small movements of his hands or the way he stood reminded me of
Christian, his oldest brother. I ached then in remembering.

"You'll need Bryonia," Martin said, after asking me a few questions about the onset of the headache and any other aches and pains I might have. He gave me a paper cone of crushed roots, told me how to take them, then mixed up a batch in water for me to take half the dosage before I left. My heartbeat throbbed against my eyes, and everything in Martin's apothecary appeared to have halos around it. It was early, before he usually opened his still-unfinished shop, and the lantern cast a soft glow.

"In the old country, don't you know," Martin said, "they called Bryonia 'wild hops,' and it had a way of helping coughs as well." He had me sit down, let Ida waddle around, squat, and touch the white knobs on the many drawers that rose to the high ceiling. Andy took Christian and Kate to show them the back room.

"Maybe it would work for baking instead of yeast," I said.

Martin laughed. "It would add quite a strange sensation to bread dough. I'm not sure I'd recommend it."

I hadn't been in his apothecary shop much, but I could see why Andy liked being here. A big desk sat at one end. Scents and smells pleasantly penetrated my aching head. The vials of bottles and dye packets had been placed in finely measured wooden boxes with dovetailed ends that lined the walls to make a comforting pattern. Martin had stained the wood with blood and milk, giving it a reddish cast instead of our usual colony blue. He must have made the little boxes himself.

Andy led his throng back in, showing me how he swept the floors and how Martin let him unpack the barrels when they were delivered.

"He's good help," Martin said.

"His time with you is good for him too."

I thought I saw color rise on Martin's neck. "We got to know each other in Willapa," he said. "Careful," he cautioned my son, settling some glass bottles onto a shelf. "Those will break." I noticed that Andy didn't sass him back when Martin gave instruction. He carried himself proudly, his younger brother and sister watching with admiring eyes.

"Do you ever wish you were back in Willapa?" I asked Martin.

He pulled at his galluses. "I worried about leaving John to look after my mother. Well, Louisa looked after her too, of course. I didn't mean to leave her out." He looked away. I guess my penchant for reminding people that women were citizens of equal merit had dribbled over onto Martin's plate.

"I know you didn't," I said. A raging romance had blossomed between her and Frederick Keil, so Louisa must have yearned like the rest of us. I wondered if Martin did.

"We Swiss don't intend to exclude girls, Emma," Martin said. "I know you think that," he added, when I opened my mouth to protest. "It's a way to keep you women safe, to make sure you don't have to struggle with the challenges that men have to face. Sometimes sending girls to school to learn more than simple reading and writing exposes them to…unnecessary demands on their thinking. Brain sickness can result," he added.

I looked at him through squinted eyes. "You're teasing me, *ja?*"

He looked ruffled.

"Living gives us those demands, Martin. Then we lack good tools for how to solve the problems, tools the boys get through education." I didn't mention that stretching of a woman's mind could also help to lift the monotony of her days, while she worked beside her husband or brother, plowing fields or digging up potatoes, or while she ran the piles of laundry through the hand wringer. If it weren't for the complicated quilt patterns we constructed that kept us sharp as our needles, our brains would be tied up in knots. Brain sickness, indeed! The men around me found any number of pleasant distractions in their lives. The Pie and Beer Band provided excuses for the bachelors to gather. They tossed balls around and formed elaborate practical jokes that took weeks to implement, while we women worked: cooking, stitching, doing the laundry. Thank goodness for the girls' choir at least, and Kitty's in-structing us in choral psalms.

"Enjoy your time with your sons…and daughters…while they're with you," Martin said.

"Why wouldn't they be with me? Oh, you mean when they're not in school. *Ja,* well, here my girls will be educated now that Christopher

Wolff has arrived." He raised an eyebrow. "Karl's going to be a professor again and work with him. Henry will teach music, and Karl and Christopher the mathematics and science and English. Maybe even offer evening classes in Greek and the classics. He told Jonathan he would and that women could attend too."

"Brother Keil has approved the curriculum?"

"Karl assured me that Kate and all the girls would attend school. How can a people do better than they have if they don't take advantage of teaching all their citizens, *ja*? Teaching them to think and reason. Aren't we supposed to make sure others' lives are better than our own?" I could hear my voice rise. I wasn't sure why I became so bristly by the suggestion that girls weren't as worthy as boys, that women didn't deserve to be stimulated as well as men. *Brain sickness.* I pitched that thought away.

Martin pressed his palm down as though to calm me. "In this new country, that's what we should work for, that all the children go to school. Adults too," he said. "And former slaves too, now that the president signed a proclamation for them to be freed in the rebellious states." He brushed at a smudge on his galluses, then ran his thumb up under one of the two wide straps holding up his trousers. "They aren't citizens yet, but education should be meant for all, don't you know."

"I wonder if that's why the wagons were burned," I said. "When the Wolff train left."

"I think that might be an exaggerated story," Martin said. "The conscription law wasn't in place when they left Missouri, and that's when the trouble arose, at least in New York. Negroes have signed up to join the Union forces now, even though they don't need to. The rest of us, we can get out of going to war, if we have three hundred dollars. I imagine they can too, if they have the money."

I hadn't realized there was such a way out, or what the cost might be. "You're of age," I said. I squinted up at him. My eyes hurt so. I heard Ida pounding with something on the other side of the counter.

Martin leaned over. "Ida," he said. "Play with this." He took a soft leather ball from a shelf and gave it to her to toss. Her pounding ceased.

"*Ja.* John and Wilhelm and I have had discussions," he continued. "I want to go to the Wallamet University, in Salem. I hope to do so this fall, but…there are other expenses the colony undertakes now, with so many new arrivals. And the conscription requirements, well, I have no children, of course, so I am a logical man to go."

I shook my head slightly, wishing immediately that I hadn't.

Martin thought I was disagreeing with him about it being logical that he would go to war as he insisted that the bachelors were the most likely to be called up to serve. "We need you here, Martin."

He ran his thumb up under his galluses again. "Maybe if I were gone, Wilhelm would find new reason to engage with the colony, not be so distant as he's been."

I wondered if Martin was tired. He'd taken on many of Keil's patients, and now there'd be even more to serve. He wouldn't be able to go on to school if his days were taken up with mixing potions and pills, and if Keil stayed locked in his workroom, who would offer healing herbs? Once I'd felt competent using herbs myself, but I hadn't kept my sons from being ill, and no one was interested in having a woman treat them anyway.

"He's come back into his own, what with the Bethelites here," I said. "You help him. Better you should go away to school instead of to war. That would arouse the need for Brother Keil to return to his doctoring, and be a much better use of your time and contribution to all of us."

"Wallamet offers no medical courses as yet," he said. "But they do have art courses." He smiled. "Did you paint something for the Agricultural Fair this year?"

"*Ach,* that's nothing I can find time for now," I said. "I'm getting a house built, did I tell you?"

"That will be good for you, Emma." He said the words, but they lacked enthusiasm, which struck me as odd. "It is a good use of the colony funds."

I reflected that the cost of my house might cost Martin his schooling or maybe even send him to war, or some other man as well. Maybe that's why he hadn't shown much regard for my home. Perhaps I was being selfish in wanting my own house. *"The desire accomplished is sweet to the soul,"* the proverb said. Surely that meant that having a desire lacked sinfulness and that achieving it brought sweetness.

I tried to get Andy to come with me as I left to nurse my headache further. He insisted Martin had more work for him to do. Kate and Christian begged to remain too, and even Ida looked at me, yearning in her eyes. I allowed only Andy and Christian to stay. I needed Kate to help me with Ida. We girls had work to do.

———

All winter long I said, "This is the last": the last Advent season of anticipation that we'd celebrate while living in the hall of the *gross Haus* beside the blue cabinet, the last Christmas when *Belsnickel* would bring us gifts to tuck beneath the evergreens of the *Tannenbaum,* the last time I'd catch my breath when the root room door opened and I smelled that wet earth and remembered the day Jack Giesy returned.

Karl told me once that early Christians imagined there was a golden thread, given its light by the beginning of the world. They believed that it extended to us each Advent season, so we were all linked with those who'd come before, and we carried the thread on to our next generation. So while I celebrated these last times, it was also the next time, and perhaps the first time as well, for my children, that they'd be drawn together by the thread of remembering.

Then while reading one morning, I found the verse I'd been looking for, the one to tell Helena that we women could express ourselves about Scripture without a man's guidance. *"Then they that feared the LORD spake often one to another: and the LORD hearkened, and heard it: and a book of remembrance was written before him for them that feared the LORD, and that thought upon his name."* It was from Malachi 3:16. I'd have to tell her.

On the Twelfth Day, Epiphany, a celebration Karl said the Lutherans observed, when the gifts of the Magi were given, I felt hopeful by remembering all those last times framed by next times. I was looking forward, carrying that golden thread while taking stock of where I was. The thread made me think of Brita and her words that one must turn into gold the straw one is given. I hoped to turn my straw into a house that would serve.

———

I walked to the site of my house's going up. It was March and my birthday. I'd given myself the present of helping dig the basement, though with many hands, I'd not done much. Framing and standing the walls proved a more time-consuming effort with only a few men assigned. The diggers, too, were soon called off to work elsewhere. I loved the smells of earth and loam almost as much as the scent of sea, and I pitched as much dirt as I could before rushing to work at the hotel.

I'd thought that maybe Joseph and Adam Knight would be around to help, as they'd shared in building Willapa. In early December, they'd gone to meet the women coming by boat from Willapa, including Joe's sister, Matilda, a woman nearly my age. She had sad eyes, a fact that surprised me. I remembered her as a young girl with self-assurance, who thought me pushy to want Christian as my husband.

We'd embraced and she said I looked well and I told her likewise. She'd be staying at the Keils', she told me. She and my mother and the sister, Christine, arrived at the same time in the colony store. Matilda said she needed thread and calico. I was there talking to Jonathan. Matilda said something to my brother about a girl back in Bethel, and Jonathan had turned beet red. He must have had a sweetheart that I hadn't known about.

"*Ja, ja,*" my mother said. "That girl you liked so well up and married, just like that, as soon as we left, I guess. You should have brought her with you, Jonathan. I'll have no grandchildren to carry on the Wagner name if you don't get busy."

"Brother Keil discourages marriage, Mother. You know this, *ja?*" Jonathan told her.

"It seems shortsighted," Matilda said wistfully. "How will the colony grow unless our families grow?"

"We'll recruit," Jonathan said. "Bring others into our happy fold. Adopt." He nodded to Christine.

"I'm not sure how happy it is, to have so many bachelors and single women as our community calling cards," Matilda said. I laughed and she smiled.

"Maybe you should come in on Tuesday next," I told my mother, my eyes inviting Matilda and Christine too. "We're going to stitch one of young Louisa Keil's quilts."

"Matilda is a magician with a needle," my mother said.

"We can use that. And then I'll show you the progress on my house. I'm sure there'll be some." I'd looked pointedly at Jonathan.

They'd come then to the quilting time, but Matilda stitched in silence while young Louisa Keil chattered on about her new marriage. Then we'd all walked out to see my lot, which was all there was to see of my house in December.

I hadn't chosen this site. Keil had. He must have plans for more houses to go up nearby so I wouldn't be "isolated." Oak and alder trees, with branches hanging over the construction site, covered the lot. There were no street names yet. But my house would be at the edge of the colony. The Pudding River rushed in the distance, but I tried not to concentrate on the sound. A white frost dressed the trees beneath a clear blue sky. They'd been the first I'd shown my "home" to, claiming it as mine. No one contradicted me that day, and I was grateful.

Now, in March, my brother and Mr. Ehlen, with his one arm, pounded square nails into studs, a structure of wood lying flat, not even resembling a wall. Then together they stood it up, and I could see the outline of a room now. I noted where the stairs would go, that divided my "two houses" on the ground floor. A hole had been cut out for the stairs into the root cellar.

In the next few days, other men would come to build fireplaces with bricks Conrad Yost baked in a kiln across the river. One man was known for his stair building, a special art, and he would be there soon.

On my birthday, boards climbed up the sides to cover the wall studs, and I could imagine the rooms and what I'd see out of my windows. I'd grown up in a brick house with my parents back in Bethel, overlooking a wide community garden. Christian and I had lived in a log house (after the winter under tents). This would be my first framed house, made with the lumber cut from the mill the colony operated.

"It's going to be a dandy house," Mary Giesy said. I was surprised to see her there on this spring day, especially since it was a good twenty-minute walk from the *gross Haus.* She pulled a shawl tight around her shoulders. She'd brought dear Opal back to me. Even now the goat meandered among the workers, being shooed off every now and then, until she found some shrubs along the river's bank to chew on or a pile of wood on which to climb.

"A dandy house. Yes. I can thank Jonathan for that." I'd brought him his basket of food, but he wasn't ready to stop yet. The air smelled fresh, with damp soil and sawdust mixed with honeysuckle. The men chattered as they worked.

"Family is good, *ja*? Sometimes I forget that," Mary said. I wondered what could have caused her to forget, but I wasn't going to ask. "So you will move in here before long."

"I'm counting the days." I leaned into her. "I won't have to hear Brother Keil clearing his throat or making wind when he's in his workroom and forgets my family and I live outside his door."

Mary laughed. It was a twinkling sound. Four-year-old Salome stood to her side, hugging her mother's skirts. Elizabeth would have been in school with my Kate. Mary's skirt swirled out as she set down a basket on the ground beside her. *Is Mary wearing a hoop?* "I hear it is a two-family house you designed. Very practical. Efficient. Communal."

"The German way," I said.

"And inventive. So, your way. Emma's way."

I couldn't tell if she spoke with a sense of appreciation or if something darker loomed behind her words.

"It's come at a cost," I said. "I was separated from my boys, you remember. And Jack—"

"I'm so sorry," she blurted then. "Oh, Emma, I should have been more aware. I should have listened to what we were thinking inside, when I saw you grow scared as a rabbit. We... I have prayed that I would never again remain silent when someone looks at me the way you did those months. If a child jumps when I approach, the way Andy and Christian did when they stayed with us, I will act, Emma. I will not remain silent. I didn't want to see it." Her voice broke. Salome moved away from her, still holding onto her mother's skirt. She looked up at her mother, whose bonnet covered her face so I couldn't see her crying, but I could tell she was. Her shoulders shook. "Can you ever forgive me, Emma?"

Only Christian had ever asked me to forgive him. It wasn't a human being's role, was it? I put my arms around her. "There's nothing to forgive, Mary. We all do the best that we can. If you could have done differently, you would have. As would I. I'm working at forgiving myself for the things I put my children through. Even Jack. That's all the forgiveness I can muster, or should. You have nothing to be ashamed of."

"Oh, I do, Emma." She whispered the words and looked away. Then more firmly she said, "Poor Jack." She wiped at her eyes. "He mopes around, works at the mill some, takes his charcoal and makes drawings."

I bristled at her apparent compassion toward Jack. "I'll not go back with him, Mary."

"No, no, I didn't mean... I just..." She took a deep breath. "I say the wrong things. I see pain and disappointment everywhere and wish it weren't so. I disappoint so many." It felt as though she spoke of something else, but I didn't know what. "Sebastian says we'll be returning to Willapa soon."

"After all this time, I thought—"

"I want to stay here," she said as she grabbed at my arm. I heard a note of desperation in her voice. "But I miss our own house and having the rocking chair to myself without having to wait until Barbara is out of it." I had a matched chair to Mary's that was still in our home back in Willapa.

"Tell Sebastian you won't go back," I said.

"*Ach,* I'm not you, Emma. It's better that we go. Sebastian, well, all the people make him...nervous. And Jack's back there. Sebastian feels an...affinity to him. Family and all."

I didn't want her to leave. She was as close to a friend as I had, someone who'd been through the good times and bad. Those were treasured people not easily found. With effort, we could recover a closeness once lost.

"I brought you a birthday present," she said then, making her voice cheery. She reached into the basket. "It's one that I pieced myself. One of the good things about the Keil birthday celebrations each year is that it reminds me that your birthday is nine days later."

I untied the string and folded papers I'd reuse for my oven when I got one, one day.

"Oh, Mary, it's beautiful!"

It was a Mariner's Compass quilt, with the compass rose pieced like golden threads pouring out of a central core toward the edges.

She picked at a loose thread I couldn't see. "I knew you liked bright colors, and the compass rose looked like a sun to me, with its yellows and the sky beyond all filled with stars. I hoped it would remind you of the good things of Willapa and not the bad. I wanted to show the good direction you took for you and your family when you came here."

"I shall use it only on Sundays," I teased. "It will keep me going in the right direction."

She couldn't have known about Christian's compass words, about being sure we found that compass in our lives so we could always find our way, nor about the golden threads that call us back to our place of remembering.

"I'm so pleased you like it. I was afraid you might not take it from me, because of how hard it was to help you, and then how much I didn't."

"Mary, you did what you could. It's all any of us can do."

I marveled at my own generosity, that I had treasure enough inside of me to give away. "This came from you. It's a gracious gift for my home. My very own home. Of course I'll accept it."

"And for your birthday, Mrs. Giesy," Salome reminded me.

Mary smiled now, and I remembered that impish look. "On my birthday. Right, and smart you are," I said in Swiss, and Salome giggled. "By the way, Mary, are you wearing a hoop?" I asked.

She laughed with me then as she brushed at the tiny pleats on her bodice, as though there might be a loose thread, but there wasn't. "Don't tell," she said then. "But I used hazel brush. All those branches growing beside the Willapa were good for it. You can bend them just so." She showed me with her hands, then lifted the hem. "And Sebastian doesn't even notice that my skirts are stylish."

"Will you teach me how before you leave? Could we use blackberry branches?"

"Blackberry branches for what?" Jonathan asked, approaching.

"To cut switches for fishing," I said quickly, and Mary smiled. The secret was made all the greater in sharing it with a friend.

———

"I didn't expect you to literally build my house," I told Jonathan. Mary and Salome had left, and he and I sat, not on the beautiful quilt Mary had given me, but on the red and green wool coverlet I kept for picnic purposes. *Picnic purposes. That I have a blanket for picnics is another hopeful thought.* Mr. Ehlen worked at a peg. "Brother Keil permitted you to work out here instead of on the books today?"

"John's taken over most of the book work for the colony," Jonathan said. "So I had time." He didn't sound disappointed. "I'm still assisting in the Keil store. Keep those ledgers. It will be less pressure."

"I wasn't aware you were under pressure," I said.

"*Ja*, well, you don't know so much about everything here, Sister," he said. "John has good experience. The best man should be chosen."

My entire family was being moved to the edge of things, into the backwater of the colony. "Did you want to stop doing all the work you were doing for Keil?"

He shrugged, wiped pretzel crumbs from his very dark beard. He had thin lips revealed by his lack of mustache. Most of the older colony men wore no mustaches with their beards, a holdover custom from the old country when soldiers wore them and persecuted our ancestors. "Keil is a good manager. He needs to surround himself with the best people. I was needed for a time, and now I step aside. It's the colony way."

"Well, I need you," I said. "I wouldn't have this house going up if it weren't for you." I hugged him.

"Your Giesy name, Sister. That's what has given you a house. You should hang on to it. In these parts, it carries weight."

"Maybe. But I notice my house is being built on a site I would not have chosen. The bank is steep beside it and all covered with brush. I don't want the children going down there, but they'll want to explore. Maybe I'll have to build steps."

"It will give you new memories to live around water." He reached for a bread roll. "And we can build a fence if you like. With a gate to keep anyone from tumbling down the steps. Ida and Opal especially."

"I would like that."

"Put the goat to the side hill. She'll keep the brambles down. And there are springs. We hope eventually all the houses can receive water through wooden troughs. And you have a root cellar, don't forget. You can store cool water there and your butter. For now, you'll have more privacy to do what you want, Sister," he said. "Think of the site like that."

"What makes you think I'm going to do something that needs privacy?"

"You have a penchant for the unusual. After all," he said, standing and stretching and nodding toward the front of my house, "you got that chicken that lays blue eggs and a house with two front doors."

I moved into the house in early June. Before she left, Mary gave me the rocking chair that had come from Willapa. "I'll get its mate from Jack when we go back home," Mary said.

The boys ran up and down the stairs. Kate asked if we'd cook in the fireplace or if we'd get a stove one day, and Ida waddled through the house to the back porch where Opal was tied, out of reach so the goat wouldn't knock her over. Clara clucked on the porch rail; my bantam chickens and rooster pecked at the ground. Well, they weren't *mine*, but only in my care.

"It's all ours, then, Mama?" Christian said.

"For as long as we like," I told them. "We'll have beds one day. And I'll finish making a table from the lumber scraps. We'll slowly add furniture," I said. "My work time will go into the ledger book, and we'll be able to purchase as we need."

"The bachelors say it will take you a long time to pay for this house," Andy said, "unless you've worked out something special with Brother Keil." He added a strange twist to his words, suggesting thoughts beyond his years.

I felt my face grow warm. "I'm glad you'll be spending less time with the bachelors," I told him. "They don't always have the best information."

My father surprised me on a mid-June morning.

"Did you bring all these with you from Bethel?" I asked. Chairs and bedsteads filled the wagon bed.

"*Nein.* Your brothers and me, we made them. We brought nothing with us from Bethel we could make here. It saved on the animals."

"But this is so…unexpected. I…thank you."

He nodded. "I remembered that when you got your headaches sometimes, you liked to sit outside in the cool at night, all wrapped up in your flannel. You said the stars soothed your eyes. This big wide bench, you can leave that outside, *ja*? It'll be a good place to rest."

I ran my hands along the back of the blue bench. So smooth, and its offering, a balm. "I didn't know if you knew I'd moved into the house."

"Jonathan told us, and about his demotion."

"Does he call it that?"

"Like you, he is a buttress to Keil, doesn't think Keil can do any wrong."

"I wouldn't put me in that same barrel with my brother, at least when it comes to everything good about Keil. But I do think he has suffered with the deaths of his children. He isn't the same as he was, Papa."

"*Ja*, deaths do change people." He stared at me, then looked away. "But he's still more willing to make decisions based on economics than on faith. I suppose I should be grateful for that. He's sold land to us, by the river."

"Where the hot springs are?" My father nodded. I couldn't imagine why Keil would agree to sell land so close to Aurora, with one of the colony mills included. Maybe Keil needed cash to provide for all the new arrivals. Some had been here a year almost, but we still talked about them as "the new arrivals." Maybe it was his way of getting my father into Aurora at last.

"Are you all going to live there?" The property I knew of included a smallish log house too. There'd be bottom land for crops.

"We thought we'd live with you, Emma," my father said. "In your new house."

I was flummoxed for a few seconds, then said, "Truly? I would love that! I had no idea that you'd—" Then I saw the twinkle in his eye.

"*Nein*. I tease you," he said. He brushed the braids curled on either side of my head. It wasn't the traditional way our women wore their hair, with buns at their necks, but a style I'd seen in a *Godey's Lady's Book* that made my face looked fuller. "You have enough with four children to provide for. We'll build a house eventually." As though this moment of intimacy was as unexpected for him as for me, he pushed his hat back, set his hands on his hips, and scanned my house. "I am curious," he said, "about all your grand plans with your two front doors."

"I'd forgo them if you came to stay in my house."

He shook his head no. "We'll visit. Your mother and sisters and brothers and I, we'll stop by more now. But it's better that we stay at our own place, not one that Keil has a claim to. I worry about that for you, Emma."

"I have a written agreement, Papa. He can't move me out unless I want."

"Words on a paper are only as good as the man—or woman—who writes them." He cleared his throat, adjusted his hat again. "There was a time when I followed Brother Keil from Pennsylvania to Missouri. But Keil changed along the way, and now those of us who claim him in some part of our lives, now we each have to make up our own mind about what place he takes at our table, and when we'll sit down with him. A man has to stay loyal to his own beliefs and his God, and not to a man he thought embodied them."

"Yes, Papa."

"*Gut.* You think for yourself, Emma. That's good." My father unloaded a chair, urged me to sit in it, then continued. "For some, Keil buys a way out of the war conscription. And to some he says it will be a good thing for them to support the Union by going to war. Some he pays one thousand dollars to, so they will work at the woolen mill in Brownsville or Salem or the shops in Portland, but bring the pay back here. There is no guarantee they will even bring their money back here. It's risky. Keil doesn't ask any of the men who once advised him. He's in a powerful position, Emma."

"I have a signed agreement."

"No lawyers ever see the agreements signed. Not even yours. Do you have a copy? No? I thought as much. So if the agreement is broken, there'll be no way to enforce it. Even so, I hope for your sake that you are not wrong about Keil."

"I do worry over Jonathan being sent to fight. And David. Thank goodness William is still too young," I said.

"With the grist mill, if we need to, we'll be able to buy a replacement for David."

"So many houses need to be built," I said. "We could really use another lumber mill."

"That, and here is one thing that a Giesy and I can agree on, even if it is Helena Giesy: the church should be built soon, where we can all worship and pray, or even more will surely lose their way. Don't lose your way, Emma. Don't sit in that rocking chair of yours and forget who brought you here."

"I won't, Papa." I felt drawn to him, grateful for his presence. "Thank you for the furniture, the bench especially. And I won't be rocking in that chair much either. I'll be busy doing. That's who I am. And I'll make you proud, Papa. I will." I was suddenly certain I could.

11

The Art and Compassion

June 15, 1864. Encouraged Mr. Ehlen to make more Aurora baskets to sell and showcase at the fair. They are so tightly woven they could hold soup. How he does this with one use-less arm is surprising indeed.

July 31. Work on the church begins! They'll build a big hotel as well.

August 15. I visited Wallamet where Martin wants to go to school. Perhaps I do too one day.

The men decided that the thing to do was to build a dance hall at the state fairgrounds in Salem. Keil must have concurred. They were urged on by Henry C, of course. With his presence, the renown of the band had grown. Sometimes there were articles in the newspaper and interviews with the reed players or the brass boys, as I called them. The young boys, including Finck's son, enjoyed the music as much as anyone, though I overheard him telling Andy that the popularity of brass bands in this Oregon country surprised him. "To me it sounds like cats being thrown into a thrashing machine." I covered my mouth so as not to laugh out loud, then soberly suggested that he might find a different description, as we Aurorans loved our dogs and cats. Young Finck merely snickered. We women often commented that music was a good diversion from the boys' pranks and silliness, and much safer. Still, building a dance hall, and at some distance from Aurora proper, would be quite the undertaking.

While the men worked there, of course, the start of the church was delayed.

I supposed there were discussions with Keil about it. While we chopped onions at the hotel, Helena told us that when the band had played at French Prairie in February, it had been so popular that talk began about having a permanent structure at the fair, where the band could perform and charge a good ticket price. It would bring in needed revenue while the concerts at the Park House would be more promotion than anything.

"Will they haul lumber from here?" I wondered out loud.

"Oh, I imagine so," Helena said. "We'd want to showcase our Aurora lumber mill."

After a Sunday gathering at the Keils', we women sat together again, and talk of the dance hall returned. Scissor snips acted as background music to our chatter.

I said, "We'll need to bring food for the workmen. I'd like to help."

"Oh, my husband has that all organized," Louisa told us. "The single women can do it. You have your little ones with you and a house of your own to run now, and with that new stove, you might not know how to cook over an open flame anymore."

"How does that new stove work?" BW asked. "That must have cost a pretty penny."

"I'll pay for it," I said. "I've taken tatting to the store for sale to grow the common fund. The man's shirt I tailored should bring a good price. And the stove works quite fine. I can use it for the food we need for the dance hall workers." I sounded defensive even to my own ears.

"We'll take Kitty and Martha and the young girls with stamina to cook out there and lift a hammer as well, if they need to," Louisa said. "No need for you to disrupt your plans."

I'd been snipped short like a too-long sash.

It was true that I'd been enjoying my house. Each of the children had bedsteads now, and straw-filled mattresses with charming coverlets either my mother or sisters and I had made. The Pudding River ran within its banks, and I could barely hear its rustle above a hooting owl that serenaded outside my window at night. I had a perfect view of Mount Hood too, the snow like a white cap covering its top. My brother David had woven red and purple and yellow and green yarns on a wagon wheel, forming a round rug that lay in the center of the kitchen area. It had a compass look to it and fit well with Mary's quilt.

My mother had brought a set of dishes for me too. They'd been in one of the chest of drawers my father had made for me. My father had understood the importance of china treasures to a woman, unlike Catherine Wolfer's son. That grown boy had broken nearly every piece of Flow Blue china she had, smashing them against rocks near Laramie when he discovered how she'd "taxed" the animals with excess weight. She managed to save only one small butter plate, burying it in the cornmeal the rest of the way west. The story was a small reminder of how a son could direct his mother without interference from any other man. Remembering Andy's sometimes glowering looks at me made me fidget in my chair.

I pitched those thoughts away.

I hadn't wanted to have my ledger page get too heavy on the debit side without finding a way to make additions to the given side. So I'd made contributions. My stove wasn't a luxury. It helped me be busy, doing.

I'd found the stove advertised at Oregon City and thought it foolish not to claim one that didn't even have to be shipped in.

The children and I lived in one half of the house, using the kitchen as our gathering room and sleeping in one of the two rooms upstairs that were on either side of the stairwell. The boys had the north room, the girls had the wide hall, and I took the large room that looked out onto the trees and the distant cooking smoke rising from Aurora's houses. I'd give it up when needed and turn the boys' large room into two, taking over half for my own. But for now, I had space for the spinning wheel my mother had loaned me until they had space to set it up, and for my baskets full of yarn and fabrics. One day I hoped to have a sewing machine as I'd seen in *Godey's Lady's Book*.

I kept the downstairs parlor for guests, should any arrive.

There hadn't been many. But I knew they'd be coming; I just didn't know who or when…or if Louisa and Helena would have words with me about it. I figured going to the fairgrounds to help cook for the men would be an opportunity to discover those who needed my house but didn't know it yet.

"Maybe if one of us more seasoned went along to Salem while they built the hall, we'd be better able to plan for the fall, when the band must be there the entire time to play," I said.

"Oh, your sister, that new one, Christine, she's interested in going. She can let us know how it went," Louisa said. We were again squeezed into the Keils' house, even though I'd invited the group to use my parlor.

"Besides, I might be going," Helena said. "I can surely keep track of all the items eaten and how much we used each day."

"But they've started building the church, Helena," Louisa protested. "I thought you'd want to be here to make sure the churchmen were tended."

"Well, maybe Emma could do that," Helena said. "With her young children, she'd be able to stay nice and close to home that way, now that she has a house and isn't galloping around the country looking for land. She could feed the churchworkers."

I felt my face grow hot. "As the colony has need of me," I said, "place me wherever you wish. I'd be honored to be a part of the church building this summer. I know my father and brothers intend to help. It could be a lovely family gathering."

Being agreeable, I found, threw them off. I didn't even react to Helena's jibe about my looking for homestead property. But I was surprised when Louisa said after a time of quiet, "Well, Emma's right. The church is surely the more important structure we should tend to."

"Yes," I said. "A dance hall is just that, after all. A place for dancing feet. You love the music, Louisa. Why don't you go and be with your

husband? Brother Keil will be there, surely. There are always many con-
tacts in our capital city."

"*Nein*. I think he plans to supervise the church."

"*Ja*. I heard him say as much," Helena said. Another quiet moment
filled with the tiniest sound of needles pushing through fabric. "Then
perhaps I should stay. To help Emma, of course," she hastened to add,
when Louisa frowned, considering.

"I'll be fine tending things here," I said. "You could both go to
Salem, though travel can be so dreary." I gave an exaggerated sigh as she
moved her hip, then stretched her leg out in front of her, twirling her
ankle like the whirl on a white pine. No one said a word about her
revealing her striped stockings too.

We continued our work for a bit. "There is also voting here later
this month," Helena reminded us. "At Millers' house. We'll need to
help Martha."

Martha wasn't much younger than I, but she tended her father's
household well, and that's where the men voted. I thought I should ask
her to our quilting time, though this was Louisa's prerogative, since it
was her house.

Louisa shifted weight from her bad hip to her good one. "*Ja,* maybe
Dr. Keil will want to be here for that voting, as well as the church's
going up, so maybe he'll see how things start on the band hall and then
return," Louisa said.

"You should go, Emma," Helena said after a moment of silence.
"Louisa and I can remain here to assist with the more-demanding tasks.
They hope to finish the pharmacy, and there are several other houses
being readied." She hesitated before adding, "I've heard too that *Herr*
Keil wishes to begin building on a real hotel. He wants it three stories
or more, with a huge porch on the front for the band to play and a balcony on the rooftop where they can serenade the train. It'll be not far
from the company store and the pharmacy, the center of our growing
community."

"For stage customers?" I asked.

"The rumors about the railroad bear truth."

"You do cook up fine food," Louisa said. She apparently didn't want to talk about the railroad and her husband's new route to commerce and fame. "And maybe your boys could stay with Martin and your girls with your parents. Or maybe Kitty could watch them while you're there. Or that Christine. *Ja.* That would be a good plan."

"I'm sure the boys would enjoy time with Martin."

"You're so accommodating, Emma," Helena said. "Though I did think you'd want them with you."

"Times have changed," my mother-in-law said. "I remember when you protested mightily being separated from your sons."

My throat constricted. *If I trust the colony to leave my sons here, then I am a lax mother; if I protest others tending them, then I am shamed for not understanding the gifts others offer.*

"Whatever is best for the colony," I said.

Louisa concluded, "We older women will stay here while the young women—and you, Emma—can go help them build, if you're willing."

"I'm just happy to serve," I said. I'd check later to see if I meant it.

———

Because it was to be a dance hall, musicians who were also carpenters were selected as the best builders. Based on the number being sent to work, we women prepared hams and breads ahead and took the food with us. I hoped we'd have leftovers that we could sell to those who came by because of curiosity and the call of aroma. We'd present the best side of our colony to outsiders, the welcoming, loving side. We might have quarrels and tensions within our midst, but we had much to give away. It was the communal way: looking after one another, putting ourselves beneath the needs of others, and silencing for the outsiders those issues festering within. Like any family, we could appreciate virtues of generosity, even while irritations wedged at the edge.

Matilda Knight joined us; Christine did not. I wasn't sure whether that annoyed Helena, but when I asked Christine if she'd like to come, she declined. No one questioned her right to do so. My true sister Kitty came along, and I was grateful, since I wanted both Kate and Ida with me. Martin had agreed that Andy and Christian could remain with him during the day.

"My home is perfectly suited for you all to stay there," I told Martin, "so the boys can sleep at night in their own beds."

"It wouldn't be right, my being there when the woman of the house wasn't, don't you know," Martin protested. Color spread against his neck, nearly as red as my Running Squares block. He pushed at the straw cuffs of his shirt.

"*Ach,*" I said. "How silly to leave a house empty while others are bundling up together. I have nothing you could catch, and it would be convenient." *Andy wouldn't be listening to the gossip of the bachelors,* I thought but didn't say.

"*Ja,* well, maybe then we will."

Fortunately, Martin was not the stubborn kind.

Andy jumped up and down at the thought that he'd be remaining with Martin. "Here I thought you'd be upset that your sisters get to go," I said.

"I'm upset," Christian told me. "Who will keep Andy from punching me?"

"Martin will," I assured him. "I'll speak to him. And to you, young man." I pointed my finger at Andy. "For someone who wants to grow up to be a healing soul, you should start with your brother. Smartness mixed with unkindness makes a sour sauce." Andy lowered his eyes. I was glad to see shame on his face. "And, Christian, you don't want to become someone who tells tales on others either. Or who expects to be punched just to complain of it. Notice things. Watch. When your brother thinks you're in his way, he'll give you signs. Look for them and before he hits your arm, you take your slingshot and go outside and hit targets. Or find one of the men making harnesses and ask about their work. Offer to help Brother Ehlen with his baskets. *Do* something. Don't wait for Andy to do it *to* you."

"Yes, Mama," Christian said.

"I'm leaving you boys with Martin this one time, but if I hear there are problems, then that will never happen again, understood?"

Both boys nodded in unison.

Once I'd dreaded leaving my sons behind. Now I was content. They were content. Martin was a good friend. I allowed myself to savor hope.

———

The journey to Salem took the entire day. At the fairgrounds, we women set up our food tent in the dusk. We'd be sleeping in the wagons, but we unloaded the heavy crates we'd packed with ham and eggs and bacon and bread. I'd fixed a cooler of sorts, helped by Daniel Steinbach, an arrival from Bethel. Inside a box we'd placed straw, then set a smaller box within it. In the space between, we placed ice chunks and covered them with more straw. The butter and cream kept cool, and once we made up our dressings for greens, we'd keep the leftovers in the cooling box too. We made tables with sawhorses and boards, "planed right in Aurora Mills," as I told anyone who asked. I built up a fire while the girls found a water supply. I watched them pumping water from a hand pump, splashing it at their feet as they filled the pails.

Kitty and Matilda Knight and one of the Schwader girls came along. I felt my older age with the need to keep an eye on both my little girls and these young women too. I hoped to have more time with Matilda. I wondered why she remained in Aurora while her brothers had left. I looked forward to discovering her mysteries. Except for Matilda, the girls were too young to marry, I decided. There was plenty of time for those commitments later, if only they could grasp that. If only Kitty could. She'd been talking with misty eyes about a Bethel widower. Becoming a twenty-two-year-old stepmother to a twelve-year-old didn't seem like the wisest of decisions. But who was I to make an assessment on my sister's interests or of what troubled Matilda, if anything did? Aside from Christian, I'd certainly not done well making my choices.

Up until now, I haven't done well, but I'm doing better.

Matilda was a natural with children. She and I were the same age, but I had seniority since I was a mother. I was glad she'd had time in Willapa this past year. She used her stories from there to thread her way into Kate's life, talking about oysters and mentioning the Giesy stockade, where Kate had been born during that winter when so many of us had huddled together under that one cedar roof. "I was born where everyone could see?" Kate said. She pinched her nose. "Mama!"

At eight, Kate acted as though she knew everything there was to know, but she still lacked that self-control that would keep her from stating things better left unsaid.

Matilda laughed. "*Ja, aber* your mama had a blanket for a private place, and your papa was there to welcome you, that's the story I heard from Jacob Stauffer." John Stauffer had been a scout, but I noticed whatever Matilda said about Willapa usually included Jacob, who'd come out later. "It's a good story, Kate," Matilda continued. "To be born with family all around is a blessing."

After the men finished their meals, we cleaned up and got ready for the next meal. We barely had time to eat, and what with watching children, cooking, and serving, I felt tired indeed. Maybe I was too old to be doing these fair things, traveling from home. At the last minute Brother Keil had chosen not to come along, so at least we didn't have his directives to respond to. Eventually, we women might have time to ourselves.

I wanted to visit Durbin's livery, hoping to track down Brita. Once the brothers drew me a map, making quite a show of using what German they knew, and said it would be a long trip. "Several hours walking by foot," one said. "Almost as long riding," added the other. "But we can rent you a horse."

"I probably can't do it this time, then," I said. "But I'll keep the map."

I walked back out toward the fairgrounds, disappointed. I passed the post office and decided that I could write a letter and tell Brita we'd be coming back again for the fair, and ask if she could meet me then. I'd do that before we left.

Giving up on visiting Brita, I was free to make a detour toward Wallamet University, that place where one day my son would go to school if I could make it happen. It was a good hike from the fairgrounds, and I was glad I'd not brought the girls.

The several-story brick building rose up like a castle into the blue summer sky. It had been around for at least twenty years, based on the size of the trees growing beside it. There were classes in session. At least I could see people moving behind the windows. Martin would come here to school one day. My Andy too. I thought I should see what kind of school it really was, assess its value for Andy. I looked at the sun. I had time. I walked up the steps and went in.

My eyes adjusted to the wood-lined halls, the dark coolness a pleasant respite from my August walk. The doors on both sides were closed, but I could hear voices from beyond. A large staircase beckoned and I stepped up, my leather soles like breaths of air brushed against the oak. A door stood open. I moved toward it and watched a woman ease around the room, her long skirt swishing as she bent to comment to the female student who held a paintbrush in her hand. *A painting class!* Around her, other eyes lifted from their easels to hear what the woman said.

"You can see through the portrait that the paint is but a vehicle to bring the subject into focus in ways she might not otherwise appear. Paint captures an idea, while a daguerreotype seizes a moment." I looked toward the front of the room to see the model, a young woman wearing a shoulder-exposing gown, a velvet necklace at her throat, and her hair done up with curls and combs. My eyes moved to the student closest to me who had already completed her portrait of the model. To me, the model looked warmer on that easel than she really was sitting in the sunlight that highlighted her pale cheeks. *Paint is but a vehicle for our experience.* I thought the words, but I must have spoken them out loud, for each woman turned to me, including the instructor.

"May I help you?" she asked.

"*Nein.* No. *Ja.* I didn't mean to intrude." I started backing away. "This is a third-level course," the woman said, "for our more advanced students. We're always welcoming other artists, if you'd care to join us."

"Join? No. I was... I sketch. My son is interested in medicine. I don't live here. I'm so sorry."

She extended her hand to me the way a man does. "I'm Lucia Jordan, instructor. Perhaps you were seeking the registrar? There are always openings."

"I...*ja*. The registrar."

For a moment I put myself there in that room; I imagined my hand holding a brush, stroking the canvas with reds and blues and greens, painting the sea I remembered, the faces of my children. I sank into the images I could make that would bring me joy. I could turn my parlor into such a painting room. Like Brita, I could follow my desires; I could.

"Please, don't be shy." The instructor stood beside me, urged me through the door.

Before me was a dream I'd had for years, ripe for the plucking. I turned and ran down the steps to the sun outside. Taking a painting class would do nothing to make another's life better than my own; certainly not my children's.

———

After the first night at the fairgrounds, the smell of fresh sawdust and hammering brought out several local men who asked questions, gave the carpenters advice, and bought up our wares. They came back each day, they said, to watch the progress, but I noticed they ate more each time, and they brought others with them. By the third day, we'd gathered up a crowd, and after serving the men their dinners, I could see that we might run low on food. I'd been selling sandwiches to this ever-growing gallery, especially in the evenings, when the band quit building and played. If Keil had been along, he'd have sold tickets. As it was, we were making money with our food sales.

"Looks like we need to make some purchases," I told Kitty. "Do you want to go to the market, or do you want me to?"

"I'll go with Kitty," Matilda said. "I'd like a little break if you don't mind." Matilda had been a faithful tender of my girls, and I wanted her to have time to relax. I handed Kitty the list and told them to hurry back, for it looked like we'd have a crowd for dinner, and very likely several would stay after to listen to the music.

I wrote my letter to Brita, then decided rather than give the girls another outing the following day, I'd mail the letter myself. With the girls in hand, we walked from the fairgrounds on a dirt path, then on the boardwalk toward the post office in the back of the apothecary store. We didn't need to go as far as the shops where Matilda and Kitty would be filling their baskets. My girls trudged along, not happy to be taken from their grassy play area near the building site.

"We won't be gone long," I said. "And we might have an adventure."

"What's adventure?" Ida asked.

"It's Mama's way of making us forget that our feet hurt," Kate said. I gave Kate a warning look.

"My feet hurt?" Ida asked, looking down at her scuffed toes. I'd need to get the shoemaker to fit her for a new pair, she was growing so quickly. Her right foot looked larger than her left. I wondered if I could talk the shoemaker into making a separate shoe for each foot instead of making both from a single mold.

"That lady hurts," Ida said then. She pointed to a woman standing in the shadow of the postal/apothecary building.

A cowed-looking woman, she sank against the brick wall, her bonnet sagging at the top. Her dress was plain and the sleeves threadbare. Her small hands had knuckles red as strawberries and just as large. And she was crying silently, without even putting her hands to her face to stop the tears.

"Don't point," I told Ida as she pulled back on my hand, forcing me to stop in front of the woman.

"Mine," Ida said. She offered the woman a wrinkled white cloth, pulled from the pocket I'd sewn onto her apron.

The woman shook her head no.

"For me," Ida told her. "Take it for me."

She must have seen Ida's disappointment, for she accepted the offer.

I'd been that tearful once, that hopeless. I'd never worn threadbare clothes, but my soul had been tendering too, disintegrated and shattered as old silk from the caustic things of life. That was how this woman looked.

"Can I help you?" I asked. Then I remembered that I would as easily have answered no when someone asked if they could help, but I would accept the offer if it meant I could do something good for someone else. That was probably why the woman had taken Ida's handkerchief at the second offer.

"There's little you can do to help," she said.

"Are you waiting for someone? We're here mailing a letter, but we could wait with you if you'd like."

The woman again shook her head no. "There's no one here waiting on me. Only my children talk to me, and they're on the Clatsop Plains, far from here."

"I know where that is," I said. Something about that area, which wasn't too far from the Willapa region, rang a bell, but I couldn't recall what it was.

She lifted her head and with challenge in her voice said, "What do you know about that?"

"I used to live on the Willapa River," I said. "I remember hearing of the Clatsop people. It was a long time ago. Very wet winters." Her shoulders relaxed. "I didn't get out much."

"One finds that a common thing for women of that region." She had gray eyes that shone clear and kind now, and looked right through me when the tears had been dabbed dry.

I saw Matilda and Kitty walking along carrying their baskets of food. They waved at me from across the street. A voice nudged at my insides. "If you've nowhere to go right now," I said, "maybe you could come back and help me. We have to cook up a storm for some men building a dance hall at the fairgrounds."

"I don't dance," she said. "It's against my faith."

"I know many who share your views. We Germans love to dance, though. And the music is lovely. Surely your faith allows you to listen to the music."

"Music has seen me through my...some difficult times," she said.

"Perhaps our music will cheer you then, Miss...what did you say your name was?"

"Almira Raymond," she said. "But I don't think I'm a miss anymore, not with nine children. But I'm also no longer a...missus."

"Even though we're widowed," I said kindly, "We're still missus or, in my language, a *Frau*."

She turned away from me. "I wish I were a widow," she whispered. "It would be better than what I am."

12

Transplanting

*August. Too much happening to write often here. I'm busy
doing.*

Almira walked back with us to the dance hall. My fingers did their rubbing, announcing I was nervous. Well, I'd invited a woman I didn't
know and who had a certain challenge in her voice to spend the evening
with us. It might have been impulsive, but I saw it as an act of kindness.
She needed something, and I'd heard this inner speaking that quieted
when I extended my invitation. Compassion and food were all I had to
offer. The provision of safe harbor must come first, before one can
accept that others mean kindness. Ida's genuine offer of care must have
given her hope.

We walked past rhododendrons, plants I'd seen bloom in the
spring on my side hill near the Pudding, shadowed by tall trees. Someone in Salem had transplanted them to grow beside their porch steps,
so they looked like tamed plants, ones that had always belonged there,
rather than wild.

"Those plants give off such showy blooms in springtime," Almira
said. "I didn't realize they could be taken from the forest and would still
grow."

"It's surprising what can be transplanted," I said. I saw it as a hopeful sign that she noticed. When I was at my lowest, I couldn't pay attention to anything lovely; my mind trotted like a dog in frustrating circles.

"That could be said of more than just plants," she said. "Though
one wonders if the second soil is really ever as good for it as the first."

"It's different, I've found, but not necessarily bad." Ida held the woman's hand as we walked, and I thought Almira flinched when my daughter first touched her, but she held Ida's fingers lightly, obviously wanting to please the child. Still, her hands must hurt, the knuckles were so red.

"Your daughter reminds me of my Annie," Almira said. Her eyes watered again.

Something made me tell her that I had left Willapa under difficult circumstances. "I've transplanted myself in a new place, Mrs. Raymond. Or been transplanted, I've never been certain."

"Please. Use my Christian name, Almira. I'm not…well, I'm not married," she whispered. She wiped at the wetness pressed out of those gray eyes. She had tiny brown spots on her cheeks and at her wrists, and when she spoke she sounded like the women from cities in eastern states. "So you're alone here? With your girls?"

"We've come from Aurora, the Christian colony east of here. I'm not alone anymore. I have two sons who stayed behind and friends to help. We're here for a short time, while a few of our men build at the fairgrounds. At the colony, we all work as we can and contribute to the common good." She frowned, but I thought it might be more of a squint against the sun. "Are you familiar with Christian ways?"

"Oh yes," she said. "Quite."

She spoke it as though it was the last thing she wanted to say on that subject.

At the building site, I served her tea. She shook as she held the cup, and so I urged a biscuit on her and a slice of ham. She was very thin, wrists the width of Kate's. My older daughter had gone off with a Schwader girl to oversee the dance hall progress, but Ida stuck by Almira's side as though she'd discovered a forgotten boat and would need to keep her in tow.

"You're very kind," Almira said. "I didn't mean to impose, and I shan't trouble you beyond this lovely supper. I feel stronger now."

"It's hardly a supper," I told her. "We'll begin preparing that now, and if you're up to it, we could use the extra assistance. You can see we've quite a crowd."

"I'd be pleased to," she said. She rose, then lost her balance and drifted down the way a sheet does when unfurled onto a bed. She collapsed in a heap beside the wagon.

Matilda and Kitty ran forward to assist me help her.

"Is she sick? Who is she?"

"She's tired," I said, hoping that was true. "Let her rest."

"I found her," Ida told them. She pointed her finger in the air as though to dispute anyone's claim. "She's mine."

———

When the meal was complete, served, and consumed, the musicians revived themselves with music. We'd also brought taffy we'd pulled, with paraffin in it to keep it from melting in the August heat. The girls and Matilda and I had prepared stick candies before we left Aurora, and those we sold now for a penny, along with the taffy pieces. "We're making money, hand over stick," Kitty noted as she handed yet another young man the striped sweet. She'd fluttered her eyes at him as he'd taken the candy and turned back to the band.

It stayed light until nearly ten o'clock on this summer night, but soon the music would end and the crowd disperse. They'd have to pay to hear the band at the fair, so this was a treat for them. Perhaps it added to our food sales, since they hadn't parted with money for a ticket. The musicians improvised and joked with their audience.

I heard a startled cry behind me. Almira awoke, looked around, her left hand rubbing the knuckles of her right. "I need to go," she said. "I need to…" She looked around again, lost. She didn't seem strong enough to consider leaving. As the crowd lessened, I told her, "You're welcome to stay here with us. We sleep in the wagons. It's not too uncomfortable, as you probably noted; but in the company of so many, we're safe enough out here beneath the stars." She shook her head no. "You'd be doing me a favor," I said. "Ida will put up a fuss if you go now."

She hesitated and then said, "Perhaps, well, just for the night." She removed her bonnet for the first time. She lay down again, and Ida snuggled in next to her, as if the child had found a large doll to claim as her own. Almira was separated from her family, but it appeared that tonight she'd found safety in ours.

In the morning, the workmen put finishing touches on the dance hall door, placed the lock, and stood back to admire their work. In less than two months, we'd be back for the fair, and oh, what a grand time we'd have! I'd probably not be allowed to come back to help with provisions, though the nearly twenty dollars we'd raised in these few days would say much about the market for our German delicacies in Salem.

Almira hadn't moved all night, though I'd heard her call out twice as if in a bad dream. She still lay flat on her back, hands across her chest, casket ready should she expire in the night. Ida had wriggled and wiggled her way, so that she slept now with her head closer to Almira's knees than her face. I lifted her carefully from Almira's side. The woman breathed so shallowly that I had to look twice to see if she did. Her bodice barely lifted. The stitching on her threadbare dress was finely done.

I had one last thing to do before we headed back to Aurora. I told the men I'd be back in an hour or so. Matilda agreed to watch the girls. When I returned, Almira was awake. "I have a suggestion for you, Mrs. Raymond...I mean, Almira," I said. "At the colony we have a doctor and another man who specializes in apothecary. Your hands might improve from Arnica montana. It's this cream, but I know that sometimes mountain climbers eat the plant's roots to ease their aches or help with bruises. I'm sure we can get—"

"I don't need medicines. Discomfort is what I deserve. And I have no funds." She'd begun brushing at the thin calico and looked around as though to pick up her bag, but she had none.

"But you *can* pay. By exchanging work. It's how we do it in Aurora. We're a communal society."

"Men take many wives there," she said, throwing her shoulders back in strait-laced disapproval. "Is that how I'd be asked to pay?"

"Oh, no, no. In fact, our leader is more discouraging of marriage than not."

"That's a certainty," Matilda said. I looked at her, wondering if she'd say more, but she continued putting baskets back into the wagon.

"And certainly only one family per household is our goal, but we're short of housing. People do stay with each other, but only until they can be moved into their own homes."

"You'd have room for me?"

"We'd make room."

"I sometimes wake with nightmares. And my past... You might not be accepting of me if you knew."

"We all have secrets we'd not care to share," I said. "The book of The Acts marks our lives helping each other in wilderness places despite what we've done to end up there," I said. I told her of the Diamond Rule. "It's not up to us to condemn. I'm widowed, but I'm also separated from my second husband," I said. "Yet I'm welcomed there." I wondered if that was true, decided it was.

"I've nothing to offer," Almira said. "There's no way I can make another's life better than my own, not after what I've done."

Ida stood beside her and again reached for Almira's reddened hands. "Maybe to begin with, you could look after my children. I have two boys at home too," I said, "so while I'm cooking at the Pioneer Hotel, that would help. Ida has a leavings doll I've made her from the leftover scraps, but it's not enough some days to entertain her."

Now some could say that asking a stranger to look after the lives of the most precious suggests questionable judgment on my part, but there was something about Almira that didn't worry me. Ida had accepted her immediately. And she didn't look like the kind of woman who would have nine children without being married. She might have been divorced, but those were rare indeed in the region. Something different must have happened to Almira. She might be a strong-willed woman who was perceived as stubborn or contrary, with a husband who resented her strength. I could understand that.

"Maybe for a time. Until my strength returns. And as long as I can contribute." She paused before asking, "Will you have to ask Brother Keil's permission to have me stay at your home?"

"I don't see why. I'm only following our Diamond Rule."

Matilda interjected then, "My brother says that Brother Keil sets the tone for everything. 'He who provides the food gives the orders,' he says."

I hadn't thought of it that way—that food was the force that held families together or forced them to separate in search of it, but there was a truth to that. I'd heard stories of fathers saying to their adult children, "So long as you put your feet under my table, you'll follow my rules." That must be what they meant. My father might have said that to me if I'd moved in with them.

"She'll be taking care of my girls so that I can work at the hotel or do my seamstress work," I said. "That way she's contributing, and so am I. You arrive at a fortuitous time," I told Almira, feeling awkward talking about her with Matilda when she stood right there. "We'll be building a great deal, have more people now to feed and clothe. And your arrival helps me personally. I'll let Brother Keil know that." I wondered whether to tell Matilda the rest of it, then decided to go ahead. "I'll need to work extra now, to pay off my instruction fee anyway."

Matilda looked at me.

"I signed up to take an art course at the university," I said. "And I didn't ask Brother Keil's permission for that either."

———

I walked behind the others on the way back to Aurora. It gave me time to think. Keil would consider it frivolous and yet…as prayerful words took us through to God, why couldn't paintings take us to God's presence? Karl had told me once that there were those who said Saint Luke had not only been a physician but a painter too, an artist who painted portraits not of God, of course, but of God incarnate, God on earth: portraits of the living Christ.

I had forgotten Karl's telling me that until I stepped into that classroom the second time. Miss Jordan was teaching another class. They were painting human forms, but landscape scenes and still-life paintings formed a border around the outside edge of the classroom, a halo around the work the women painted. In the center was an iconic painting done on wood. It showed the Virgin Mary holding her Son as an infant to her face, her right hand clutching Him close while her left hand reached out as though seeking. I'd seen pictures of this before in books, but seeing it there among the other paintings brought tears to my eyes.

Paintings were ways through, the way music was, the way the parables were, the way I sometimes felt when I stitched and worked my fingers to create new fabric forms. I wanted to paint one of those icons to have in my own home, one I could sit before and calm my muddling mind into prayer. It was that hope which had propelled me to take such a drastic move as registering for the course. I hadn't paid for it yet. But I would find a way. My hope was that the agreement signed by Keil and me, permitting all of my family to be educated, would include me. I'd paint, sell the paintings, and use the money to make repayment for the course. Maybe I'd have enough left to put toward Andy's schooling too.

The beginners' course was taught for a week at a time, once a month for three months. I'd have to make arrangements for the children, trust that my work at the hotel wouldn't be missed, and get Keil to agree that this course was in service to the colony. It could be a difficult sell.

I pitched that thought away.

Maybe the pieces could help decorate the church. The craftsmen would be working on the altar. Perhaps some color would be welcomed on the church walls. Meanwhile, an iconic painting could offer comfort to those in need, like Almira. She'd become very important to me. This must have been how Christian felt when he'd brought someone into our fold. Christopher Wolff had been recruited by Christian. So had

Karl Ruge. Both men brought goodness to us all through their artistries, their intellect, and their service. I anticipated that Almira was only the first of many who would bring goodness to us all, and I was now a part of that.

"You're so brave, Emma," Matilda said as she stepped back to walk with me.

I laughed at that. "Brave? *Nein.* Foolish maybe, or a coward. I'm afraid of doing everything the same each day. I'm more afraid of dying before I've found out why I'm here than I'm scared of rubbing Brother Keil the wrong way. I'm not going to change the world, the way I once thought Christian and I might. But little things each day can make a difference. Besides, Keil ebbs and flows like the ocean. I'll catch him when the tide is out."

"Does he? He seems so...stern to me."

I'd forget at times that those newer arrivals from Bethel had been without Keil's physical presence for nearly ten years. He was almost a legend to many of them, until they faced him here. They'd gone on without him, making decisions, living their lives. It must have been difficult after all that time to find themselves somehow subservient to him, this man who wasn't any kind of god at all; a man who picked his teeth of meat, just as we all did.

"Sometimes he's willing to bestow goodness on us; sometimes he withholds. I never know which it'll be, so I may as well do what I think I ought to and hope I can convince him later if something strikes him wrong. It took me a while to get my house, but I got it. Even the stove, though I'll be some time paying for that!"

"I heard Barbara White Giesy say that was quite an extravagance."

"She would," I said. "But I'll bake good things for the colony, so I'll be giving back. And I didn't ask Keil for permission, and when it arrived he didn't tell me that I couldn't keep it. I'm sure he knew it was delivered. Sometimes we just do what we think we must."

"Well...," she said.

I waited for her to tell me more, and when she didn't I brazenly asked, "So what is it that you think he'll deny you?"

She blushed and shook her head. "Nothing," she said. "Nothing."

It was late when we arrived back at Aurora, but I didn't feel tired or restless. Stars were beginning to pop out of their dark closets, so I expected to see lamplight from my house. I didn't. I didn't think the boys would be in bed yet. It was summer and the air still warm, and playing outdoors was something they both loved to do. I set the lamp I carried on the table in the kitchen and walked to the back porch. No one was there except Opal, who bleated me her welcome. We'd built a pen for her, and she put her feet up on the railing. "Later," I told her. "I'll scratch your head later." The chickens had been put in for the night.

Both Kitty and Matilda had planned to spend the night with the Schwaders in their log home, but since it was late, I invited them both to stay with me. With Almira, they waited inside. Kitty lit the kitchen lantern so when I came back in, it was to a warm light.

"Where are the boys?" Kitty asked.

"I suppose they're still with Martin." I gathered up quilts for Almira and Matilda and Kitty and settled them in the parlor. "You're my first real guests," I said. It was too warm for a fire. That was probably why the kindling I'd placed there before we left hadn't been burned. Perhaps they'd eaten elsewhere so they didn't have to bother cleaning my dishes. "They'll be here before long."

I got the girls ready for bed and tucked them in upstairs. Ida tried to convince me to let her sleep beside Almira again, but I assured her she'd be there in the morning. She listened to me and fell fast asleep.

I came down the stairs and went through the kitchen out to the front porch, so I didn't have to bother the women sleeping inside. I sat there on my father's blue bench and waited for my sons to come home.

No need to be worried, I decided. I was adaptable. I knew that circumstances sometimes intervened to break up well-laid plans. Martin must have decided it was easier to sleep at Keils' with the boys than to prepare meals and whatnot for them in my home. I could understand that, in a way. Men didn't much like to cook a meal, and even though it would only have been mush for breakfast, something Andy could have fixed for them all, Martin was probably accustomed to a big bacon-and-egg breakfast that he'd find at the Keils'. Or for all I knew, they were fixing breakfasts for all the workmen building the church. I'd find out in the morning, I decided. I came inside, ran my fingers across the iron stove, blew out the kitchen lights, then carried my candle upstairs, well after what must have been midnight. I heard Opal bleat in the night and felt nearly as forlorn as her cry.

———

In the morning I heard the rooster crow and realized someone was already up, fixing the fire and preparing coffee for us all. When I came downstairs, Matilda smiled and admired the smooth pine floor I'd oiled myself.

"Your boys are sleeping in?" she asked.

I didn't respond. "I'll go on over to see how progress is coming on the church once the girls are awake. Want to come?"

"My brother expects me back. I can take the stage, he said."

"Oh, come with us," Kitty urged. Since her braids were neatly wrapped around her head, I knew she'd been up for a time too. "We can walk you back to the stage later."

"I wouldn't want to miss it," Matilda said.

Almira was slow to rise, and when she did, she asked to remain in the house with the girls. She commented on the stove, said it was a fine one. "It must have cost a pretty penny," she said. "More than twenty dollars."

"Twenty-five dollars. I'll be working long years for it, but it makes a fine bread."

She sighed onto the chair. "I haven't had a safe place to just sit," she said. "Not for a long time."

I wasn't sure if I should leave her here alone in the house, though I didn't know why not. I had no reason to think she'd take anything from me. She had an eye for the price of things. I hoped I wasn't being taken advantage of. And then I chided myself. I had offered her assistance and then so quickly began creating criteria I thought she should meet to receive it.

"Yes, you stay," I said. "Ida and Kate will enjoy not having to go anywhere after their long trip home."

Besides, if I did have to confront Martin about the boys or Keil about Almira, I could do that without the girls listening.

The three of us, Kitty, Matilda, and I, walked past the store. I looked in at the pharmacy, but no one was there, and the workmen had stopped building on that structure. I suspected that was how the building would go on now, moving from place to place, framing walls, then waiting for the bricks to be fired across the Pudding, then making the roof ridges, pounding the lumber to close in the walls and the rooms, putting on shingles. In between they'd work on the church, the largest structure we'd ever built from our lumber.

It was a quarter mile from the village to the Point, the place where Keil's house and the church stood. I hadn't been up this way for a while, so I didn't recognize the house going up below the creek.

"John Giesy's house," Kitty told me. "One of the finest, like Keil's." The path past it went up a steep ravine toward the fir grove. We were perspiring by the time we reached the Keil house. Kitty said she'd need to rest there. She loosened her apron at the waist and sat down on the steps. She chewed on her nail. "Go ahead. I'll catch up," she told us, as Matilda and I walked on toward the church. Men and boys congregated there, so I assumed I'd find my sons there too. Several of the men who'd been building at the fair were already at work here with their hammers. I imagined they'd gossiped about Almira Raymond, wondering who she was and why she had returned with us. Men tried to say they didn't gossip, but I remembered Christian always had more news than I did at the end of his day. As we approached, I heard Matilda gasp.

"Are you all right?"

"Yes. *Ja*. It's a surprise," she said. "The Stauffers are here."

I knew Jacob Stauffer. He was the son of John Stauffer Sr., a former scout who'd settled in Willapa. I wondered if John Sr. had moved his family here, then, but I didn't see him. Only Jacob.

"You met Jacob in Willapa?" I said.

She nodded. "We talked. Nothing more." Her neck showed reddish blotches, and her steps hurried up the hill even though it was the steepest part. "I used Mrs. Stauffer's oven. It's very good. You can regulate the heat well. O. B. Twogood sold it to them, a shop in Oregon City. We went by there when we came here. Such fine things for sale. Have you been there?" She rattled on, giving no room for answers.

"Ah," I said. "What time did you say you had to get back to the stage?"

She didn't say.

I waved my hand. "Jacob Stauffer," I shouted. "It's good to see you."

He turned to see who'd called his name and waved back to my raised hand, and then I watched his eyes move to Matilda's. He grinned from ear to ear, dropped his hammer on a pile of lumber, and walked full stride our way.

"You know Matilda Knight," I said when he reached us and removed his flat-top hat. A small dog trotted behind him.

"*Ja,* sure," he said. "We stopped at your brother's in Oregon City on the way down. He said you'd gone to Salem."

"He told you I was in Salem?"

"To help with the cooking. I worried I might miss you."

"You did? You worried you'd miss me?"

She repeated nearly everything he said, and I recognized it as that loving duplication of our hearts. Excitement welled up in her face. Jacob bent absently to pat the dog's head, but he never took his eyes off Matilda.

"I didn't know how long you'd be there. Or if you'd find work in Salem and maybe not come back here at all. Your brother said you were hoping to move out on your own perhaps, not be a burden on them, though he claimed you weren't that at all."

He removed his hat now, kept turning it over in his hands while

Matilda clasped her palms behind her. By the way she stood before him, she might have been fifteen years old instead of over thirty.

"Matilda's thinking of catching the stage back to her brother's soon. Maybe you could walk her there," I suggested.

"*Ja*, sure. Or maybe talk her out of it." He grinned.

"That would be good too," I said. I decided to add, "You can live with us, Matilda. There'll be work here. You're good with a needle. You said so yourself. Keil's opening a tailor shop for noncolonists to have work done."

"Opportunities," Jacob said.

"*Ja*," she barely whispered. "But I'd better go back and talk with my brother. See what he says."

I watched them walk side by side down the hillside. Jacob put his hand out once to catch her when Matilda slipped but chastely put his hands to his side when she was steady again. Matilda would have to work it out herself, I decided. I had to find my boys.

And find them I did, right in the middle of the building activity. Martin was there with them, of course. He'd supervised them as I knew he would have, but still it annoyed me that he hadn't stayed at the house so they'd have been there when I got home.

"The boys were good, then, Martin?"

"Very good," he said. "They're fine boys, don't you know." He didn't face me, but rather stood next to me, looking out at the construction. They'd made little progress in the few days we'd been gone, but they'd begun, and sometimes that was the hardest work of all.

"You didn't stay at my house," I said. "Didn't I tidy it up enough for you?"

"*Nein*." He cleared his throat. "Brother Keil…said otherwise."

There was no tease in Martin's voice.

"Well, I'll take them home now, then."

He stood silent next to me. I heard a crow caw in the trees. "Sister Emma, Brother Keil would have a word with you."

"We talk often."

"About the boys."

I felt my heart start to pound. "You said yourself they were good boys."

"*Ja.* That they are." He cleared his throat, and I thought his face looked pained when he turned to me and said, "It is for the best, Emma."

"What's for the best? What are you talking about?"

"Transplanting is often good. Just remember. We only want the best for all of us, to make each life better than our own."

13

Puzzle Pieces

I could see my sons in the distance, their small frames moving about like happy goats, jumping over piles of lumber, chasing friends, letting playful dogs pull at their pants. They stayed out of the close construction area, so they weren't being a nuisance. They looked fine. There had to be some reasonable explanation for why they hadn't been to see me yet and for Martin's odd hesitations and foreboding tone as he sent me off to Keil.

"I'll find Brother Keil, since you say he wants to see me. Is he back at the *gross Haus*?" Martin nodded. "Fine. I'll speak to my sons and then talk to Keil. Would you take the boys home for me after that?"

"Ah…," Martin said.

"Mama!" Christian shouted.

I waved. Christian started to run toward me, but Andy stopped him. *What's that about?* The boys waited for me to reach them as I walked farther up the hill.

"Hi, Mama," Christian said. "Did you see me jump over that pile of boards?"

I nodded, and he leaned into my skirts and I hugged him. "You look like you're having a good time, Andy," I said. He nodded but didn't speak. I motioned for him to let me hold him too, and he allowed it. I felt stiffness in his shoulders, though, and he broke the embrace first. "Martin's going to take you home in a bit. We need to catch up." I wiped at a smudge on his cheek with my thumb.

"He'll take us home to Keil's house," Andy said. It wasn't a question.

"Why would you say that? We have a home now. You have your own rooms. I know I have the quilt top stretched over your bed, but it's up with a pulley. It's out of your way. Think of it as a colorful night sky over you. We'll put it in the parlor before long. Would that be better?"

"I don't mind the quilt there, Mama," Christian said. "I like to see all the threads sticking out."

"Uncle John and Uncle Martin think we should stay with Uncle Martin now," Andy said.

A hot poker seared my heart. "Oh they do, do they? Well, we'll have a talk about that. Meanwhile, you stay right here while I go talk to Brother Keil."

Christian's face wore both confusion and fright, so I calmed myself, controlled the tremble in my voice. "It's going to be fine, Christian. Mama will be back shortly with this all straightened out. Did you have your breakfast already?"

Christian nodded his head, but Andy stared at me. What sort of thoughts had been put into his head? Not by Martin, surely. I trusted Martin.

I turned and smoothed my apron. I yanked at the pocket I'd tied at my waist. John Giesy was now deciding who should raise my sons? Would these Giesys never let me go my own way? Hadn't I given in to the ways of the colony, so my sons would be safe, so all my children would be raised well? Hadn't I done everything they'd asked of me?

I slipped on the steep path leading to Keil's house. I straightened. Kitty still sat on the steps, fanning herself. "What's the matter, Sister?" she asked. "You look as though you've seen a snake."

"Nothing," I lied. I stomped up the steps past her, opened the double doors, and immediately took the steps downstairs. That's where Keil would be. In his workroom. Plotting and planning. Maybe John Giesy was with him, and I could confront them both.

"Sister Emma," Keil greeted me with a large smile. "You've come back. I trust you had a good time at the fair?" He stood. "Though I know it wasn't quite the fair time yet, but soon, *ja*? Our new dance hall will be well received."

I reached for my pocket and nearly threw the sack of money at him, money we'd raised selling extra candies and sandwiches to the gawkers watching the dance hall go up. "Nearly twenty dollars," I said. "I realize the colony provided the goods, but my sister and I made the candies, and our labor counts for something. We women worked while there, and we were selling things. That too should count."

"*Ja.* Such things count." He picked up the bag and poured the coins out onto his workbench. He placed them into a neat pile at the edge. A few greenbacks stuck in the bag. He pulled one out, turned it over in his long, slender fingers, placed it back down. "*Gut,* Emma. You did *gut.*"

"Yes, I think I have done well. So what's this I hear about John Giesy suggesting that my sons come under the supervision of Martin? To live with him here, with you? Is that true? Why would you wish this, when I now finally have a home for them? A good home."

"Ah, Sister Emma," he sighed and sat down. He motioned for me to sit as well, but I stood. "A man's influence is essential, Emma. You know this to be so."

"I'll see that they spend time with Martin and you and my brother. Even their other uncles, John and whomever else. My father lives close by. But my sons need their mother."

"Who likes to be off doing things," Keil said. I must have looked puzzled, so he added, "Off looking for a place to homestead. Liking to travel to cotillions and dance, though she is married yet to another. Once living far away in Willapa, just to be away from here. Who gets herself an unusual chicken and a stove at colony expense."

"Those were part of my duties! Louisa and Helena suggested I go. My own mother-in-law thought it a good thing to do. I would have stayed here. I only did it for the benefit of the colony. All of it, everything I have, goes back in service."

"Looking for a homestead?"

"But I settled *here.* You built the house for me, here."

"It's clear that you are not fully committed to the colony, Emma. You've taken on the attitude of your father more than your brother, and the agreement, well, that says more than anything that you aren't truly willing to be subservient to the community. It's still you, Emma, doing what you think is best, over the good of the community. You purchase a stove, rather than add to the ledger side for things needed for your sons. You've let others look after your children…as you did these past days. You welcomed in that *Zwerg.*" I opened my mouth to defend Brita, but he held his hand up to silence me. "I said nothing about your taking in that circus person. But now I learn you've welcomed someone you lifted from the streets of Salem. We open our doors to others here, Emma, but they must share our common goals. I wonder if you really do. You're more interested in an intriguing world with strangers than in spending time with your family or raising your sons."

I never should have let the boys spend all that time with Martin. I'd thought it would be good for them, but now I could see that my willingness to be separated was interpreted as disinterest, self-centeredness, or, worse, neglect.

"I only want the best for my sons," I said. I sat down now. I shook. My arms felt weak as weeds and just as useless. "The community… You said this would be a safe place for us. And the house… It was meant to give my children a better life. To ease the burden on those staying here, in your home. So I could take care of them as a mother should."

"You tell yourself a story, Sister Emma. The house was always for your benefit, but you wrapped it in the needs of your sons. We knew it was to separate them from the colony influences. I suspected this, but John Giesy confirmed it. This is how you thought in Willapa too, *ja?* To separate is best, you might have told Christian. To separate is healthy. You told them that being independent was for the benefit of all, but it was for you. Isn't that so?"

"*Nein,*" I whispered. "I never intended to keep my sons from family. I haven't since we've been here. I let Barbara and Andreas travel with Andy. I've complied. Can't you see that? Why would you want to take their care from me?" My throat ached. I thought I'd gotten what I wanted here: safety for my children and me, protection from Jack Giesy.

Even my hope that my parents would move west had come to pass. I had my own home. But none of it was turning out as I'd planned.

"The colony will educate Andy and Christian. That's more than your own parents are able to do, *ja,* since they won't join the colony? You'll see the boys, of course. They'll have time with you. And we'll protect them from Jack's temper, and you too. In fact, Jack left because he knew Martin would be raising your sons. They are not Jack's sons, so I doubt he'll pursue interest in them, beyond what he asked for in return for leaving. Your girl, perhaps. We'll protect her from him as well, so long as you remain here. And where else would you go, Emma?"

His voice sounded far away.

"Martin's had nothing to do with this, by the bye," Keil added, "except to agree. But he will have a place for the boys as soon as the pharmacy is finished. Until then, there's still room for him and the boys to stay there. It will justify my paying the conscription fee for him as well, a side benefit so he won't have to go to war. He'll attend the university this fall too."

"Martin?"

"*Ja,* he'll take pharmacy classes, but then next year or so they will offer medical classes. He will be a big help if he is a doctor. Maybe you can look after the boys between their classes and when Martin comes back home each night."

"I can provide care but not a home to my sons?"

"There is good reason."

The clock ticked into the silence.

"The reason being that one day my son, Andy… He'll attend the university?"

"But of course, Emma. Don't you remember the agreement we both signed? I have it here." It was on top of his desk. He'd been expecting me. He read, " 'I, Emma Giesy, will agree to abide by the rules of the Aurora Colony as directed by Father Keil, *offering up what I have to give in service to the colony.*' " He emphasized the last part of the sentence. " 'In return, the colony will provide care, education, and keeping for me and my family including the building of a home designed for use by me.' See, I signed it right here," Keil said. "Didn't I agree that your children would be educated?"

Offering up what I have to give in service to the colony. It was a sentence I'd remember the rest of my days.

"I wasn't clever enough, was I?" I said, looking up at him. My throat constricted like a hangman's rope.

"Oh, Emma. You got what you wanted: a home of your own. You secured the promise of education for your sons. Even for yourself, though I can't imagine what you'd study in the university, but it was clever to include yourself. And you agreed to abide by the colony rules and to offer up what you had in service to the colony. A reasonable exchange. A colony way."

"I assumed I'd offer up my *work* and my *labor,* not my heart, not my flesh and blood, not the absence of my sons from my life." My voice broke. *I will not let him see my cry!*

He'd come around to my side of his desk. He pressed his hand against my shoulder. "Next time we may both pay a little more attention to the wording of things, *ja*? So I'm not paying for something frivolous you might want to do, while you call it 'education.'" He patted my back. "I'll see you out now," he said.

I sat for a time until I felt his hand increase pressure on my shoulders. He led me like a calf to slaughter toward the root room door. Scents of onion and potato rose to me as I walked outside. My lips were dry as dirt. Keil pulled the door shut behind me. The sunshine hit my eyes without warmth. I blinked, focused. How had this happened? What had happened?

Kitty stood as I walked up the grade toward the steps where she'd waited for me. "Ready to head up the hill and watch them work?" she said. "They'll make progress, now that our dance hall carpenters are back."

"I'm going home," I said.

"You want me to watch the boys?"

I didn't dare look toward the boys. Christian might be waiting for me, but I doubted Andy was. I couldn't bear to see the looks on either of their faces, or for them to see mine, to see me cut like a too-long hem from their lives.

"I'm sure that Martin will," I said. "No...I..."

"Emma? Are you all right?"

Keil came through the front door, stood at the top of the steps. "Good morning, ladies." He spoke in English. He carried his cane, walked between us as he came down the steps, then headed up toward the church. I watched him. In the distance, he stopped where Jacob Stauffer and Matilda had stalled on their way to the stage. Matilda stepped back, and Jacob listened to whatever it was that Keil so diligently expressed to them. Jacob said nothing back, but he tipped his hat to Matilda, then made his way back to the church construction, Keil and that little dog walking behind him.

Someone else's life had just changed in an instant.

Matilda stared after them; she turned away as we approached, biting her lip. Even in the shadow of her bonnet I could see she wept. She would have moved past us, but I stopped her. "I'm going back to my home," I said. "Something has...come up. I'll walk with you."

"All right, then," Kitty said. "But what am I supposed to do now?"

"Come with us if you wish," I said. "Or maybe Louisa has some tasks for you." Martin had turned toward me, arms at his side. "Or you can tell Martin that I'll bring the boys' things over to him later today. He needn't plan to stop by to pick them up."

"But he's standing right there, why don't—"

"Tell him! Or not," I said. "I can't say any more."

"Are you ill, Sister?" Kitty asked.

I shook my head no. Her kindness could unravel me if I let the slightest thread of warmth from her wrap around my broken soul.

"Go," I said. "I'll walk with Matilda."

Matilda walked silently beside me. I knew she was troubled, and if I'd had an ounce of compassion left in me I'd have reached out to comfort her. But I felt as though I was stuck inside a bale of thick wool and couldn't push my way out through the dingbats and twigs to get breath. I kept swallowing. I stopped. I lowered my head. I was going to be sick.

———

"Your girls are up and fed and ready to help with chores," Almira greeted us as we reached the house. Kitty had remained behind. I knew she was confused, but I couldn't explain. She'd gone off to talk with Martin or maybe the boys. I'd given her nothing to tell them; I didn't know what to say.

"Have Kate gather eggs," I said, pulling myself into the present. "And let Ida go with her. But watch out for Opal. She doesn't know her own strength. I don't want her knocking Ida over."

"Are you all right, Mrs. Giesy?" Almira asked. "I mean, Emma. You don't look well." Those gray piercing eyes.

"I need some time alone," I said. "The stagecoach should be…"

"I'm not going to take it today, if that's all right with you," Matilda said. "Your offer, for me to stay, is it still good?"

"Yes. *Ja.* There's lots of room now," I said and walked slowly up the stairs. I felt one hundred years old.

I looked about for the basket of wool I'd carded. Jonathan had built me a spinning wheel, set up on the wide hall, and I'd returned my mother's to her. This one still smelled of fresh lumber. The oils of my hands had yet to darken it. I sat now to spin that wool, grasping it too tightly at first, then loosening my grip to let it pull through my fingers. It was solid yet soft. My foot moved to the rhythm. I held the yarn in my fingertips. It was wool I'd dyed myself, red as blood from the madder root. The color didn't soothe, but the threads did. I needed something firm and familiar in my fingers, something I could hang on to that wouldn't drift away, that wouldn't be taken from me. I'd thought I couldn't be stumbled by any more surprises. I had a house, my health, good work, my girls. But none of that was enough. I'd lost my sons.

I must talk to Jonathan and see if he could intervene. My father—perhaps he'd be willing to raise my sons, or at least talk to Keil about letting me do what a mother was called to do. But these were tasks I'd do later. I was too tired now. My head began to throb.

When I came downstairs, the sun dappled through the trees, making its way toward setting. I could smell the soup that the girls must have eaten, and hopefully Almira and Matilda had as well. I didn't remember the scent rising up the stairs to me, but I hadn't been hungry. I wasn't now. I stepped out onto the porch to sit on my blue bench. Matilda was already there, her hands clasped in her lap.

"Do you know where the girls are?"

"Almira took them for a walk. I thought she came upstairs to tell you. It was quite a while ago." She had a slight lisp, so when she said "thought" it came out as "taught."

"She might have. I didn't hear it above the spinning wheel." I didn't tell her that I'd been in a trancelike place, devoid of anything but the feel of the yarn in my fingers. I sat down beside her. "You decided not to go back to your brother's right now?"

"You invited me to stay, you remember?" I didn't remember that we'd talked of it. "I can leave…" She stood up, but I reached for her hand and pulled her back down. "*Danke.* Thank you," she said. "Dr. Keil. He…he said Jacob needed to spend less time courting and more time counting his hours of work. We'd only taken a moment, and it was hardly courting. Jacob hasn't even spoken a word of interest to me except to notice I was here."

I smiled, for the first time in hours. "Oh, he's interested," I said. "Even in my stupor I could see how his eyes lit up when he saw you and how closely he stood to you, to hear your every word."

"Until Dr. Keil approached." She clucked her tongue. "I felt like a small child who'd been caught with her hand in a cookie jar. And Jacob…how humiliating to be accused of courting when he wasn't.

Ach," she said. "My brother was right. I shouldn't be here in Aurora. I should stay with them. But I thought the Stauffers might come here, since so many others from Willapa had. And I didn't want to miss him. Them, I mean."

"And so he has come," I said. "With intention to stay, since he's working on the church. I imagine he'll live with the bachelors, in that rectangular building they've put up on the Point."

"And there'll be other houses going up too," she added. "Or so he told me."

I closed my eyes and leaned my head back against the wall of my house. *My house.* That's all it was then. A house. Not a home that would hear the sounds of laughter and love and disappointment and challenge and hope poured out through the lives of my children, all together as one. It was a structure. Wood and glass and brick and an iron stove. And for it I'd given up my sons.

Perhaps Keil was right about me. My girls were off with a woman who might be a dangerous person, for all I knew. By her own admission, Almira had a "past." My judgment about people was obviously suspect, since so many of those I'd come to trust through the years weren't worthy of it. Perhaps I wasn't fit to raise my sons—or my daughters. I was a self-centered woman, a wayward daughter, a pushing wife, and not much of a friend, least of all a good mother. I wiped the tears that formed a stream from my eyes into my ears. My legs weighed heavy as anchors.

"Martin Giesy came by," Matilda said. "He wanted to talk with you."

"*Ja.* I bet he did." I opened my eyes.

She turned to look at me. "He said he'd come back later this evening, for you not to trouble yourself about bringing the boys' things. He said you'd know what he meant."

"Mama, Mama!" Ida's voice. I saw them approach and watched as Ida tried to skip, but double-stepped instead. "We made this place, in the trees, Mama. It was fun. We walked in a lab-rinse. Wasn't it called that, Mira?"

"Labyrinth," Almira said. "It's called a labyrinth."

"Lab-rinth," Ida tried again. "It looks like Path to the…to the…"

"Path Through the Wilderness? The quilt pattern?" I asked her.

"It might be best to call it a puzzle path," Almira said.

I'd heard of labyrinths, a very famous one in Chartres, France, that my uncle, the vice counselor to France, had written to us about. He'd drawn a picture shaped like a mushroom cap. It looked like a maze, made out of stones laid out on the floor of a cathedral, he'd told us. One could never get lost inside it; the only choice a person had to make was whether to enter at all. There was only one way in and one way out, and Christians came to walk there to find answers, and had been doing so for centuries. There certainly wasn't a labyrinth in Aurora.

I looked up at Almira. "It's a path I made for us in the clearing," she said. "I scraped it out with a stick, and the girls and I laid pinecones to mark the paths. Then we walked it. Or I should say they ran and jumped it! It was a joy to hear them laughing. I'd made one on the Clatsop Plains too. It was the only place I found peace, though it later got me into trouble." She looked away. "My husband discovered it and claimed it was some sort of witchcraft. He scattered all the stones that I had used to mark the trails."

Witchcraft!

"I'd forgotten the comfort that could come from walking one," she continued. She had a shine to her face that hadn't been there in the morning, or at any time since we'd met. "It reminds me that I must let go of everything and follow the path to the center of my soul and then carry what I've learned there back out to the world. Walking helps my soul wake up."

Kate plopped down on the porch and leaned against my legs. "Is Andy here?" she said. "Where are those boys?"

I took a deep breath. "They're going to be staying at the *gross Haus*," I said. "For now. Martin Giesy will look after them, and Andy's going to help him at the pharmacy, and one day he'll go to school to become a doctor."

"Can I be a doctor?" Kate asked.

"No, Kate," I said. Too quickly.

"Father Keil will let me," she pouted. "He calls me Catie. He likes me."

"You can never be sure," I said.

"There are women who become doctors," Matilda ventured.

I couldn't imagine my Kate having to make her way through medical school, with men all around making decisions that excluded her. "We'll talk about it later."

Kate said, "I'm going to school this autumn, aren't I, Mama? Karl Ruge said I could."

"Yes. You will go to school, and so will Andy and Christian. You'll see them there every day." I hesitated, then said, "But I won't."

"Why not?" Ida said.

I didn't know how to answer.

14

Walk In, Walk Out

Could I fight this? I could ask my parents to take the boys, but Keil was right: they couldn't afford to send Andy to medical school. They had children of their own, and there was Lou with her needs. Jonathan didn't have his own home either, and at least Martin would eventually have a place to stay with my sons, assuming Keil wouldn't change his mind about finishing the pharmacy. Jack was no option. None of the Giesys were. It occurred to me that Martin's reticence when he told me Jack was gone was a part of this, that Jack had exacted the promise that Martin would raise the boys and not me. Anything to harm me. Karl Ruge? He'd never consider raising my sons, and what was the point of looking for anyone else besides Martin? Martin was the best of the lot. What I needed was the way to raise them myself.

I could hire a lawyer to demand my sons remain with me but at what cost, even if I could find a lawyer to take my case? I still had the pearls. I could sell them. Surely my mother wouldn't mind if I did that for such a cause. But then where would we go? We'd be out on the street in no time, and where would that leave Andy's future or the future of any of my children? No. There was nothing I could do. If I found somewhere else to live, to take all my children with me, I'd still need a way to support them, to care for them, to educate them, to give them shelter.

That night I slept frantically, dreams of fog and mist and mazes, of being lost, seeking rescue. "It is a woman's lot," some hag inside my dreams would cackle, as I wandered through the thickening forests. "Raise them to resist, and they'll be squelched. Raise them to consent, and they'll be trampled flat like wet leaves of winter. Raise them to believe they can do…," she cackled toward my face. I woke up sweating and pulled the quilt from the bed to go sit on the blue bench outside to watch the sun come up. *Teach them to believe they can do what?*

———

"It's a terrible trial to be separated from one's children," Almira said. We sat at my table. She used a glass Andy had claimed as his favorite. "I gave birth to nine in thirteen years. My husband traveled. He was a minister who brought the gospel to the Indians and other settlers on the Plains. Then he took a job as a sub-Indian agent, and I thought he'd be home more. We lived far from the nearest settlement. But he brought…a woman with him." I looked at Almira. "He said she'd be there to help me with the children and the laundry and cooking, but instead, she helped move me out of my bed. And when he traveled, he took her with him."

I didn't know what to say.

"I bet you didn't have any more children after that," Kitty said. She'd joined us before heading to the hotel.

"Strangely, I did," Almira said. "I kept thinking I could keep him as long as I didn't turn him out. But after a time I couldn't stand the jealous feelings. I divorced him. Or tried to… You should know these details, Emma. You may not want to have me stay here, knowing this. My husband got his friends to testify and say terrible things against me. Only my oldest son and his wife came to my defense, but it was not enough. The newspaper quoted his powerful friends. It's hard to fight power."

"You got your children, though, right?" Kitty asked. "They wouldn't take children from their mother, would they?" Kitty still didn't know the details of her nephews' plight or she wouldn't have thought that.

"Legal care always goes to the father." Almira looked down at her knuckles that held the glass like claws. "Especially well-spoken men. I know it was a sin to seek divorce. He was right about that. My children are being raised by another woman, and I'm not even allowed to see them. A divorced woman and those rumors of witchcraft and all." She gave me a sad smile. "My being here might have made your plight more precarious."

"No," I said. "What happened to me, Keil had planned long before this. You needed something we had to give, and I am grateful you accepted."

I'd started sorting through the boys' things and putting them into bundles. Maybe Martin would let them come for supper sometimes. Or breakfast. Maybe I could make them special meals on their birthdays. Surely Martin would allow that. At least I wasn't banned from seeing them, the way Almira was. At least total strangers weren't going to read about my personal affairs in the Monday *Oregonian*.

As I finished sorting, Kate sang out, "Uncle Martin is here."

"Have him come into the parlor," I said. I straightened my dress and tugged loose strands of hair into the swirl of braids on either side of my head. I looked in the mirror. *Awful.* A mess. I came downstairs and entered the parlor.

I nodded toward the chair. He sat. "This isn't how I would have planned it, don't you know," Martin said. I'd offered him coffee or tea, but he'd declined. "I know how much you love those boys."

"I've bundled up their things. If I've forgotten something, you can send someone for them."

"The boys can come themselves," he said. "They're not going to keep you from seeing them, Emma."

"They? You're a part of this too, Martin."

"I tried my best, Emma. My arguments fell flat. Jack… It was the best solution, don't you know."

"No, I don't know."

"He would have hovered over your life here forever. We thought it the best and—"

"We. The 'we' that excludes me."

"But the boys will see you. It won't be like before, when you lived so far away."

"*Ja.* See, but not raise them; watch, but not influence them. Who'd want such exposure to an outrageous mother not capable of raising her own sons?"

"Emma," he said.

"Does that seem fair to you, Martin?" I still stood. "Doesn't it... frighten you that Keil can decide such things for other people? that your brother John could?"

"They mean well, Emma. They truly do. This way you're...free. To do those things that interest you. You have your house."

"My sons interest me!" My voice cracked. "My. Sons. Interest. Me." A coastal storm of grief swept across my heart. "Am I seen as so frivolous that I'd give up my sons for a house? How could you question that? How could...they?"

"As do your daughters interest you. Devote yourself to them now, Emma. You'll see Andy and Christian. You'll be a part of their lives. Let the community raise them up and educate them."

"The way the tinsmith or the turner is a part of my life?" I said. "Someone they see in passing? If there's a small need, then I might be allowed to fill it, but mostly I'm decorative, to look at from a distance?"

"More than in passing, Emma." He stood, tried to touch my shoulder, but I jerked back from him.

"Don't touch me." I stepped back. "I trusted you."

"And I kept your trust. I brought your boys to you. They've been here with you for two years, Emma. Safe. And they'll be here for many more. Just not the way you thought it would be, but when has it ever been what you thought it would be? Christian's death changed everything."

"Coming here changed everything."

"It was the path you took," he said. "A good path, made from difficult circumstances. See the good in this, Emma. There is some. You are making your sons' lives better than your own."

I turned away so he wouldn't see the anguish.

"I'll have the boys come by tomorrow. Christian's been asking for you. I told him, 'In the morning.'"

"No," I said. "I don't think I can face them."

"You've got to be stronger than they are in this. You're the adult; they're children. Your explanation will help them deal with this change."

I wanted Martin to have to face their questions. Let him bear the brunt of their confusion. If they had confusion. Andy showed no distress at all. Maybe that was what eclipsed my heart.

I stood with my back to Martin, feeling the coolness of the usually closed-off room. "Send them," I said. "If they'll come, I'll do my best to ease their distress."

Martin left then, and I stayed with my back to the door, hoping no one would come in to try to comfort me or ask me questions. I needed time to grab on to something firm. *Fabric. Wool. My God.*

"Come, Mama." I heard the door open. It was Ida's voice. "We'll show you our lab-rinse." She pulled on my hand. *Not now.*

"Mira says to call it a puzzle path," Kate said from behind her.

"I can't go with you now," I said. "I'm already walking on one."

———

"Did you know what they did to me?" I asked Karl, later in the week that seemed a month of foggy days.

"*Ja*, I heard some changes were recommended."

"Recommended? You think I had a choice?"

"We all have choice," he said. "If only about how to respond to the unpredictability of life."

"Oh, I suppose I should be asking, 'How do we see God in this?' Well, I don't." My sarcasm caused his eyebrows to lift.

"Ah, Emma," he said. "Life has not treated you well; but now you will have the opportunity to show your sons and daughters, even your sisters and brothers and your own parents, how you tithe your tragedies." His pipe, recently smoked, lay on the table, and the scent brought a comfort.

I had the girls with me. Ida played with one of the wooden toys that Martin had made for her. The sight of it no longer comforted me as it once had. "I was so blind," I said. "Why didn't I see this coming, Keil's maneuvering, John's and maybe even Helena's influence? I keep missing things," I said. "It's as though I never learn."

"Can we take the puppy to the grass?" Kate asked Karl. She held a plump black and white mongrel in her arms and had brought the dog in from outside.

"*Ja*, sure. I call him Potato using the English. Po for short," Karl told her. "Watch him so he doesn't get too close to the edge of the bridge. He doesn't know there's danger there." Ida dropped her wooden horse and followed her sister outside. I noticed then the bowl Karl had set out for the dog.

"Po keeps you company," I said.

"*Ja*, sure. One of the stage drivers dropped him off for me, thought I might be lonely and need a little companion. He guards the toll hut at night when I'm not there." He smiled. "Sister Louisa doesn't like dogs inside. You should get a dog, Emma."

"I have Opal and Clara. They're trouble enough."

"But a dog licks your face, he's so happy to see you, and curls at your feet while you work. He even acts apologetic when you step on his foot." He smiled.

"I don't have much time for sitting around with a dog curled at my feet," I said.

"They make you make time," Karl said.

I watched the girls and the dog through his open door. Yellow leaves from the alder trees drifted down, and the vine maple had turned blood red. Elderberry bushes and ferns painted the riverbanks in green. "You'll miss those stage drivers when you're back to teaching," I said.

"*Ja*, they brightened my days. I brightened theirs," he said.

"Won't you miss this, being in the classroom all the time when the school is all finished?" I turned to look at him.

"*Ja*, by goodness. Po and I have a good life right here. A nod to a sad face looking out of the stage window can change a passenger's day. They're dusty and tired and always running late. But the dog makes them grin. I ask after the drivers' families, and they like that. People

sometimes go all day long without anyone hearing them or remembering what they said the last time they came through. But"—he put his
palms out—"everything changes, Emma. Now I will teach the children
again. It's how life is, *ja*? I will cherish my time with them."

"Should I fight them, John and Keil and even Martin? Should I take
my children and disappear into the night? Would you help me again?"

"What is it that you want for your children, Emma? What do you
want for yourself?"

I'd been asking those questions ever since my conversation with
Keil. I sat down on the narrow bed Karl took his naps on. It was the
only place to sit besides the chair Karl occupied. I ran my hands over
the quilt that covered his bed, my fingers following the zigzag lines that
stitched together odd-shaped pieces of cloth. His old worn pants, a
shirt. I recognized pieces of calico in the Log Cabin quilt made from
dresses Mary Giesy stitched for her girls. Mary must have made it for
him when he'd lived with them in Willapa. She was a generous soul.

"When I was younger, I dreamed sometimes of being the first in a
footrace, with many dozens of others coming in behind me," I said. "I
imagined accolades as I crossed the finish line." I had never told anyone,
even Christian, of this dream of mine. "I had visions of people clapping
and cheering for me because I'd done something...grand. Sometimes,
I'd wake from the dream and I could still hear their cheers echoing as I
entered my day. While their voices faded, the uplift, like a hawk catching the wind and soaring toward the sun, stayed with me when I took
out the ashes, helped my mother clean the lamp globes, peeled mounds
of potatoes, changed my sisters' napkins. I thought I was called to something purposeful and important. The insignificant things I did each day
were only a prelude to the symphony that would be my life." I picked at
a piece of loose thread in the quilt's stitching. I'd bring my needle and
thread next time and restitch the seam for Karl. "Now here I am. My
sons have been taken from me. I'm separated from a husband whom I
never should have married. What I do here every day could be done
by...anyone in this communal place. There's nothing unique in it. And
the daily music of my life is a funeral dirge, nothing grand at all."

I heard the girls laughing outside and happy yips from the dog in its play. The day felt hot, and perspiration beaded above my lip.

"There's something you do that is both important and yet unfinished," Karl said. I looked to see what he referred to. His eyes turned toward the sounds made by the girls. "They need your efforts, Emma. And didn't you raise your sons to be good thinkers, independent, and kind? They don't forget that. You'll still influence that in them. You'll still see them."

"Christian, maybe. He might remember me fondly. But Andy is as lost to me as his father is."

"*Ach*, self-pity does not become you, Emma." He picked up his pipe and drew on it, then tapped it as though to light it again. Instead he said, "Christian and Andrew are alive and healthy because of your care for them. Andy wants to heal people one day, and you are a part of that dream. Christian finds joy in the outdoors and in helping others. Your girls are smart and generous. These are of your doing too. Yet you have work left to do."

"But I wanted my life to mean something," I said.

"To be ahead in the race." I nodded. Tears welled up in my eyes, and I looked away, as though to check on the girls. "Was it being in front that gave your dream its boost, or was it knowing others ran with you in a worthy race?"

I hadn't thought of those distinctions. "If I'd been the only person in the dream crossing the finish line, it wouldn't have meant as much, I guess. But weren't the others there providing the applause because I'd done something…significant? Why would they applaud over something simple and mundane like sewing a patch on a pair of pants or fixing a stew? That's all I do now."

"Is it?" he said. "Maybe the people cheering were there to inspire the dream in the first place. It could be, Emma, that what we imagine as other people doing unusual things in our dreams are really just us. Maybe you were cheering yourself on."

"You think I'm self-centered too, then, like Keil implied."

"*Nein, nein.* Take no offense here, Emma. Remember how Shakespeare tells us, 'to thine own self be true'? You are uplifted crossing the line; but you are also the one making it happen and celebrating the victory, a goal line, *Sehnsucht,* that longing that will not cease. I believe such longings are given to us by God. You don't need to depend on others to say it's so."

I couldn't help recalling that vivid dream I'd had years before where Christian and I dove under the water, and I asked if he knew where we were going, and he'd said no, he'd lost his compass. I'd awakened worried. Could it have been me, feeling adrift and lost without a compass, and not Christian at all?

Sehnsucht. That which calls us toward something we cannot ignore, to return us to relationship with God. Maybe it wasn't winning or doing something grand that mattered, but rather being in a race that filled my heart and allowed me to one day hear, "Well done," at the end. It wasn't a thought I would pitch away.

———

"Go like this, Mama," Kate said. The girls had taken me to the open place where they and Almira had formed their puzzle path. Animals had scattered the pinecones, making the narrow paths difficult to follow. "Mira says after we walk it enough, we won't need the pinecones. Our feet will be like chalk and make the pattern."

"We could bring rocks. Or branches. The wind can't sweep branches good," Ida said.

"Well," I corrected. "Wind can't sweep branches very well. I don't really have much time, girls." I'd seen Jonathan earlier in the day, but he'd avoided looking at me and kept talking to the men at the store. *I ought to go visit my father and mother, at least tell them what transpired, so they don't hear it as gossip.* I'd kept myself busy, doing. It kept me from thinking of my loss. A sniggle of memory reminded me that when I didn't grieve what I'd lost, I sometimes made poor choices. Marrying Jack was one of those.

I'd think of hopeful things. Helena had asked if I was going to the fair. If I did, I had food to prepare, things to arrange, questions to answer: Should I take the girls? Would going affirm for Keil that I was easily swayed?

But I was here now, being tugged at by my Ida. I sighed. "So tell me what I'm supposed to be doing on this trail."

"Watch," Kate said. "And smell whatever we can smell. And feel the breeze on your arms, Mama. Butterfly kisses, *ja*?" Kate walked faster and was soon on one of the switches that led her back toward us.

"Listen too, Mira says." Ida held my hands but walked in front of me to stay within the narrow borders, so my arms rested on each of her shoulders. We walked a little like Brita did, waddling from side to side, with my feet in step with hers. "What do your ears see, Mama?"

"They see…birds singing," I said. "And someone's dog is barking far away."

"That's God talking," Ida said. "Mira says God talks to us when we walk."

"If we don't talk so much," Kate chided.

I didn't think God had the voice of a barking dog, but then these days, everything was open to question.

This trip to the field was a break in the routine we'd fallen into, Kitty, Almira, Matilda, and I. We rose early and fixed a morning meal for all. Then I headed for work at the hotel and Matilda stitched on an order she'd gotten from the tailor shop. She still didn't know if she'd stay, but for now, she'd found work that satisfied.

Almira had been sleeping less. In her first days with us, she'd wake up close to the midday meal and then fall back to sleep again before dark. Now she rose earlier, heated water for the laundry, on Mondays at least; then she and Kitty would swirl the sheets and towels and underdrawers with their sticks, carrying the steaming clothes to the wringer that by then Matilda would be ready to operate. Kitty would snap the clothes, then hang them on the line to dry, well out of the reach of Opal. Then she'd leave for her time at wherever she was cooking that day—at the Keils', the construction sites, or the hotel—while

Almira watched my girls and Matilda returned to her needles and threads.

By the time I arrived back in the late afternoon, the clothes would be nearly dry, and I'd take them down, folding them into the basket. The next day, we'd heat the irons and press the sheets and towels and plain, dark dresses, each of us taking a turn with the flat iron as the day and evening waned. Sometimes we took laundry overload from the bachelors staying at the Keils'. We often brought baskets from the communal laundry house to wash and iron. I noticed that Matilda looked at the laundry marks closely, and I asked her once if she was seeking out *JS* for Jacob Stauffer. She'd blushed.

Wednesdays we baked or dried berries. Thursdays we did extra gardening, which in the fall meant putting the soil to rest, digging up potatoes with our pitchforks, burying cabbage and melons in straw. Fridays we took the rugs out to beat them and opened windows and aired out the house, cleaned the lamp globes, and mended by lamplight at night while one of us read out loud to the others. Saturdays we heated water for baths and prepared whatever we might want to eat on the following day, so we didn't have to cook or fire up the stove on Sundays—at least every other Sunday. Soon there'd be the big productions of slaughtering the hogs and rendering lard, but that would take nearly all the colony and was an almost festive time of gathering, a welcome break in everyday routines.

Today was a Sunday when Father Keil did not speak, and so the girls had insisted that I let them lead me to their "lab-rinse," as Ida called it, to "have church" instead.

"I'm slowing down, Mama," Kate told me. "If we walk too fast, we miss things."

Almira had taught her well. I kept my eyes on the ground so as not to step on Ida's heels. Leaves brisked across our path. A squirrel chattered in the trees beyond. I didn't initially see what caused Ida to stop abruptly, then break away and run.

"Andy!" she shouted. "Come on the lab-rinse with us."

He stood at the end of one of the turns. Ida skipped over the pine cones and imaginary lines and wrapped her arms around him. He hugged her back and let her lead him. "You follow me, and Mama will follow you," she told him. "We go in, and then we go out. It's fun."

I thought of hopscotch, a game we'd played as children in the dirt with squares and stones. I'd played it for hours with my sisters on Sabbath days when working wasn't allowed, grateful that quiet playing still was. This walk reminded me of that, except I didn't really have to concentrate, the way you did when standing on one foot and leaning over to pick up the pebble in hopscotch. My mind could wander.

It didn't now.

I'd encountered my son for the first time since the decision had been made for him to live with Martin. Still, there was a bit of precarious balancing going on as we moved along the path.

He walked in front of me. I followed him, keeping my hands to myself.

Ida chattered, giving him instructions for listening and watching. Kate rolled her eyes at me as I looked at her across one of the lanes where she was coming back out from the center, while we still entered in.

"Now we pray," Ida told us. We stood in a tight circle at what was apparently the end of the route to the inside. We'd go out the same way we came in. "Pray for us coming in. Pray for others going out. That's what Mira says."

"Who's Mira?" Andy asked.

"Questions later," Ida said, as she lifted her finger like a teacher correcting.

Andy's eyes met mine, and I saw in them a look of brotherly compassion but of yearning too, a look so intense I swallowed. I hoped his eyes weren't mirrors reflecting mine. "We'd best do as she says," I told him, surprised that my voice carried nothing harsh or defensive in it.

Ida was quieter on the way out, and I found I could bring to mind the names of those I loved and cared for, as my child had suggested we do: Matilda and her hopes with Jacob, Almira, Kitty, my parents. Even the foster sister, Christine. I still called her "the foster sister" instead of "my sister." Brita. I added Louisa. Helena. My children, all. I could pray for those I didn't even know, those far beyond our borders: the stage drivers Karl spoke of, soldiers on the battlefields, their families, leaders making choices. That last prayer brought me to Keil and John and Martin. I sent a prayer up for even them, amazed that I could.

At the end, I felt refreshed in a way I hadn't been when I started on this walk.

Kate waited for us at the entry point. Christian had joined her. He rushed to me and hugged my skirts at my knees. I blinked back tears.

"Wasn't that fun, Mama? Did you pray for others going out?"

"I did, Ida," I said. I still held Christian, looked at Andy then back to my daughters. "You're a good little teacher."

She beamed. "We need to eat now." She grabbed at Christian's hand, pulling him away. "That's a lot of work. We worked up an ap-tite."

I smiled. I'd heard those same phrases from Kitty when we finished the laundry.

"You'll come too, won't you, Andy?" I asked my son. He'd held back. But with my invitation, he moved up beside me, and we began to follow his brother and sisters.

"Father Keil lets John Giesy speak at the service," Andy said then. "John talks of being helpful one to another." I tried not to see John as a hypocrite, speaking of goodness to one's neighbors while he inflicted pain on his own extended family. Here I'd just prayed for him, and so quickly I was ready to condemn. I sighed.

I hadn't attended either of the two services they'd held at the Keil house since this whole thing with my sons had happened.

"It's always good to be helpful," I said.

"You didn't want Martin to take care of us, I know, Mama. But you are being helpful too," he said.

"By not fighting to keep you with me? What kind of mother does that make me?"

"We're with you," Andy said. He reached for my hand as we walked. The touch of his wet fingers to my palm made me suck in my breath. *How I love this child.* "I can help Martin now. And they will send me to school, Mama. I'll be a doctor. Like you said I could be. Martin says that can happen because you let it be so. That I should thank you for thinking so far ahead. He says you sacrificed for us, that you put aside your own wishes in order to give us this chance. That's a Christian thing to do."

"Martin tells you these things?"

"He says you took a hard thing and turned it into something better. He…admires you. He tells me I should admire you too."

I watched my feet, gripping my son's small hand while my heart took in those healing words. I slowed my pace to match Andy's. My sons didn't condemn me. They didn't expect me to fight. I could lower the standard I'd carried all my life. Nothing else that called could ever be as important as this moment in time.

———

Johanna and Lou, my sisters, leaned against their garden forks, ceasing their work as I approached. Both were tall and slender with hair the color of straw, the opposites of Christine and Kitty and me. They all lived in the small hut next to the mill my father had bought from Keil, and I imagined they used the common smokehouse or the storehouses of the colony for their staples. But we all had our own kitchen gardens too, and I could see they'd been digging potatoes. Pumpkins rose in a pyramid beside a small pit. They'd line it with straw and place the orange globes inside, covering them with leaves like a quilt, pulling them out as needed through the winter. Chickens scratched at the ground shaded by weeds they'd wisely let grow just for that purpose. Window boxes spilled what remained of large blooms.

"You can take some seeds," my sister Lou said as I eyed the flowers. "William grows them. Bigger than a fish head, some of those blooms."

"Is Papa here?" I asked.

"Working," Lou said. She wore that lopsided smile.

"In the mill?" I asked, nodding toward it.

"Delivering flour," Johanna said. "Jonathan came by to help him." She stared as though considering whether to say what she said next. "Papa's getting on in years, you know, Emma. You really should come by to see him and Mama more. They miss you."

"Do they? Mama hasn't even been at my home yet, and the path goes both ways. None of you except Kitty has sat at my table and let me serve you."

"All we need is an invitation," Johanna said.

"A family shouldn't have to wait to be invited," I told her.

"We've never been a typical family, now have we?" she said. She dropped her pitchfork then, to grab Lou's elbow before my sister lost her step. Johanna steadied her. I hadn't even seen Lou look like she would stumble; Johanna had a discerning eye. "Mama's inside," she said and returned to her work.

I entered and found my mother sewing. She patched my father's jeans, or maybe they were David's or William's. They were those hard canvas pants, what the miners used who came up from California. "These things wear forever," my mother said. "But you let a hole get started and pretty soon it's a cavern. You've got to nip things in the bud, like pruning a good grape vine."

"I wonder if I should try to fight this thing that John and Keil have set forward," I said, blurting out the thing that most crushed against my heart.

"Oh, and what would that be?" She raised her eyes to mine.

Can she really not know? No, she knows. Her eyes hold compassion. Surely it is meant for me. "They've given the boys to Martin, so he can raise them."

She winced, I thought, but said, "Martin's a good man."

Her words stung. I thought she'd be appalled and say so. "What choice do I have?" I began, as though she'd found fault with my actions. "If I insisted they stay with me, Keil would ask me to leave the house. I'd have to move back in with them or impose on the Schueles or… come here and move one of my sisters off her mat."

"There's always your husband," my mother said.

"Jack? Oh, Mama, he hurt me and the boys, he really did. I didn't make that up. And Andy, well, Andy hates him; I'm afraid of what they'd do to each other if they had to be under the same roof again."

She put her mending down. "Then you must make the best of the choices you have. I'm sorry, Emma. Sorry for the decisions you've had to make, and for some of them not working out well. But we all have to deal with such things."

"Should I talk with Papa about…moving in here?" I said. "Do you think that might dissuade Keil and let me have the boys again? We could all live right here."

"I wish we had room." She lifted her palms to the walls of the tiny house. "And if we came to live with you, it wouldn't make Keil let you have your sons back, of that I'm sure. Besides, your father wouldn't do that now. He's disillusioned with Keil and wishes your brother would see the problems the colony has as well. Your brother is devoted. I remember when your father was too."

"Jonathan hasn't even talked to me since this happened."

"I'm sure he will soon. He worries you'll force him into something. He doesn't want to distress John, who has so much on his mind."

I mocked myself. "The infamous Emma Giesy, strong as an ox, able to convince grown men to do things they otherwise wouldn't."

"You did talk Christian into staying at Willapa."

"He wanted to stay! He saw how it could help us all. It wasn't all me, Mama, despite what Louisa and Helena might tell you."

"*Ja, ja,* I know," she said. "And the Willapa people had good lives there, or they'd have left long before so many did." She watched me for a moment, then lifted her mending again. "Things change, Emma. Sometimes for the good, sometimes bad, *ja,* but always, they change. You fall in love; you grow old. Your sons live with you; they move away; they go on to school. One mends the edges of one's life to keep it from fraying. In due time, Emma. It will be better in due time."

"Christian said I was impatient."

"It is a Wagner trait," she said. Her smile was kind. "But so is doing what must be done for the good of one's family. You'll do that too, Emma."

Perhaps, as Andy said, I already had.

15

Wishful Thinking

September 15. First true guests sit in my parlor.

*September 30. Wild geese make their way across the sky. They
call to each other, they trade places, the leader tiring from
the effort of pushing aside the wind to make the others have
an easier flight. A new path is formed; all the while it looks
as though they're in the same formation, never changing, but
they are.*

The knock on the parlor door sounded almost like a dog's scratch. It
grew louder. I could hear it from the backyard where I had my chickens penned. I'd let them loose for the day and finished gathering up
their eggs, holding the blue ones aside for Ida's and Kate's lunches. I
assumed someone else would answer the door, but no one did. The
knocking grew insistent. It was an early hour for visiting.

I peeked through the window to see Louisa Keil and Helena Giesy
standing there, carrying reticules, wearing bonnets, and dressed as
though they were attending a cotillion or something almost as formal.
I retied my scarf at the back of my neck but untied my apron. It was so
early. They were granting me an honor by coming to call all dressed for
the occasion, and yet the early hour assumed almost a family right to
intrude. I took a deep breath and opened the door. I looked a fright
against their freshly laundered calico dresses.

To my smile and welcome each woman nodded, then took out a
calling card with their names printed in lovely *Fraktur* lettering that
Louisa had probably done. I had no receptacle for cards. I looked

around. Then I took down an oyster shell from its shelf; I'd cleaned it and painted a picture on the smooth side; it would have to do. I set the shell on the small table beside the bench and placed the cards there, thanking my visitors. I directed them to the bench. I'd stuffed pillows with goose feathers and quilted the covers with pieces of the children's clothes and new calico I'd purchased at the store. I motioned for them to sit down on the pillows, because the bench was so hard. They picked up the pillows, commented on the fine stitching, and then sat, with the toes of their shoes pointing straight east and looking like dark eyes peeking out from beneath their hems.

"I'll fix tea. Or coffee if you'd like."

"You have coffee?" Helena said.

"Dried peas," I corrected. Helena liked accuracy. "I throw in a few beans I've saved from each distribution."

"They weren't too expensive for a time," Helena said. "But with the war, everything is costly, don't you find?"

"I still call it coffee." I sounded like my mother's friends back in Bethel when they'd come to call.

"Oh, no need to explain, Emma," Louisa said. "We should expect that you'd have finery the rest of us only dream about."

"Finery?" I wanted to say, "At least no one took your children from you," but five of her children had died, and such words would have been a cruel reminder.

"Your own home, Emma. Before even the church is finished," Helena said.

Louisa gazed around. "Not that furbelows aren't warranted. Didn't you have them on that petticoat of yours one time?" *She knew about my ruffles?* "Frills are a good thing, especially when you make them yourself. You should put some of your paintings up. I liked your work."

"I've done so few," I told her. I longed to tell her that I'd signed up for a class, but I hadn't found a way to bring it up to Keil, to see if he'd honor that part of our agreement. In a perverse way, I didn't want to give him the satisfaction of naming yet one more thing he'd claim I'd done for myself at the expense of the colony. Wanting to take the course felt like a violation of my sons now. How could I enjoy something when the one duty of my life I hoped to succeed at, being a good mother, was now in question? Still, it struck me as a pleasantry that Louisa had noticed my bare walls and suggested that my paintings might add charm to them.

I listened for the activities of the rest of the household while I gathered the coffee things. Everyone remained quiet. They could come down the steps and into the kitchen without ever stepping into the parlor, but no one was in the kitchen yet either. The coffee boiled. I returned with it in the glass tumblers we women had made ourselves. I'd ground the edges down so they were smooth as a baby's lip. I handed the women square quilted napkins to wrap around the hot glasses.

"So you think you'll stay home from the fair this year?" Helena asked. "That's such a shame."

I'd told no one anything about my fair plans. It must be Helena's way of making a suggestion, but I didn't know which way she wanted me to go.

"I haven't decided. And I didn't think anyone would notice one way or the other."

"It's always so festive," Louisa added. "My favorite time of year. Oh, Christday is too. And Easter. And, of course, my husband's birthday."

"Someone needs to remain here to help cook," I said.

"Ah, but Christine Wagner, your new sister, has become quite a fine cook. Did we tell you she was living with us at the *gross Haus*? She seems a lovely girl and a hard worker. I'm not sure why your parents gave her up."

"She's a woman complete unto herself," I said. "Not beholden to a father, brother, husband, or son. She's on her own at twenty. My parents likely had no say in giving her up, as you put it. She can choose to live where she likes."

"She doesn't distract the men from their work, the way some young girls can," Helena said. "Does Matilda still stay with you?" She'd untied her bonnet strings and let them hang loose on either side of her neck. "Kitty's found a place here as well, we hear."

I wondered if Matilda and Kitty were subjects of the first part of her comment. "Matilda's upstairs. We have a routine. Almira rises early with me to prepare breakfasts. Matilda and Kitty help clean up, then begin other tasks before they go off to take care of colony business. Well, Kitty goes off. Matilda stays here. As has Almira, looking after the children."

"Not all the time," Helena said. I must have looked confused. "You don't leave her alone with them, do you? She really isn't supervised, Emma. Or haven't you noticed?"

"I notice Almira is helpful with my children."

"This Almira is not whom I referred to," Helena said.

"Matilda? Her work is praised from the tailor shop. She never complains but simply does what must be done. If she is sometimes off on her own, what is that to the rest of us? She is nearly thirty."

"Still, unsupervised...," Helena said.

"Weren't you unsupervised as a young girl?" I asked. "Isn't that how you met your bridge engineer, John Roebling?"

She stiffened. "We were never alone."

"Not ever?" I asked. "Even your brother and I found time to get acquainted, standing outside the door at dances during breaks from the band. No one else could hear us talking, so I'd say we must have been unsupervised too."

"That got my brother a...spirited wife," Helena said. She chuckled, but it didn't take away the sting.

"It got him a good and steady wife and three fine children, that's what it got him. Is there some reason why you decided to visit this morning, Sisters, unannounced?"

The two women looked at each other. Louisa sighed. "We don't mean to pry. But the woman staying with you. What is her name you said? Almira. She looks after the girls?"

"She does."

"Is her married name Raymond?" I nodded that it was. Louisa gasped. "You were right, Helena. She's the woman written about in the papers."

"Suppose she is. Does that matter?"

"We're…we've become aware of her presence here among us, and it's…unsettling," Helena said.

"The colony has always taken in widows and women in need," I said.

"*Ja, bitte,* it's enough that *you* live here without a husband or brother in your own home. But to have a divorced woman staying here, influencing your girls, well, we're concerned. And with single women here as well…"

"For whose welfare? Mine? My children's?" I calmed myself. I didn't want to challenge them. I wondered if Almira's presence would allow these two women to somehow bring about the removal of my daughters too.

"We mean no harm, Emma," Helena said, as though reading my mind. "It's for your safety we've come. Sometimes the perspective of others can be useful in making better decisions." She placed the quilted napkin onto her lap and smoothed it. The coffee had cooled.

"Other perspectives. *Ja,* I'm sure you're right about that," I said. "Let me introduce you to Almira. That would give you another perspective."

"Oh no," Louisa said. She spilled what was left of her coffee. I rose and got her a linen. I thought of bringing Almira in and forcing them to meet her, to see that they feared someone out of ignorance. We tend to judge more harshly from a distance.

I patted Louisa's skirt with my linen. "You'd find her a quite refined Christian woman."

"Not if she's…divorced," Helena said. "I'm not sure you'd be welcomed here if you had insisted on divorcing Jack. Our Lord was quite clear about the place of divorce. He did not like it."

I sat with the damp linen in my own lap. "Doesn't it strike you as interesting that a woman was even mentioned in Scripture in regard to divorce? I mean, women had no…power then. Why bother commenting that loving another while one was married was the only grounds that permitted a man to divorce his wife? That verse was more about how men should behave than about women. Up until then, a woman was like a…bench." I nodded my head to the bench they sat on. "A piece of property for use by her husband. Almira's divorce, from my understanding of it, resulted from her husband's bringing another woman into his bed." I hoped I wasn't sharing a secret Almira would want kept silent. "For sixteen years she endured this. In Christ's time, she would have had some status."

"That's not how the newspapers recorded it," Helena said.

"Did you read it in German?" I asked. She shook her head. "Then maybe whoever told you what was written didn't translate it well. Besides, men write the newspaper accounts, and it's likely they would give her husband's story the greater weight, over the real facts that might sympathize with a woman."

"I hadn't thought about women being property in those times," Louisa said. "How fortunate that we don't have that to deal with here in our colony, where we're all treated the same by my husband, and where divorce happens so rarely, because he is so wise about deciding who should marry or not in the first place." It was a long speech for Louisa.

"You may think we're all treated fairly, Louisa," I said. "But we are not all treated the same." I looked over at Helena. "Some of us have greater privileges than others, it's true. You suggested that about my house. I understand that some of the men receive payments to go work elsewhere in Portland, while others work here with no hope of gaining wages for their ledger pages. And some of the women are treated with more…gentleness than others, or so I've noticed."

"Well. So," Helena said. She set her coffee glass down. I thought her hand shook.

"And some wish to marry and are refused, while others are allowed to. There's nothing in Scripture to prevent marriage, as I recall, yet Brother Keil does this."

"He does what he thinks is best," Louisa defended.

"As do we all," I suggested.

"We should be going," Helena said. "We've done what we came for, to express our concern for you, Emma, with that woman being here. That was our only purpose."

"You ought to meet Almira," I countered. "She's been so good to my girls and a good friend during these past weeks without my boys with me."

"Does Matilda intend to stay with you and this…Mrs. Raymond?" Louisa asked.

"I haven't asked her. She can stay as long as she likes, as far as I'm concerned."

The two women stood. Louisa tied her bonnet strings.

"I'm sure she's awake. She made the coffee for us. Let me call her."

"*Nein, nein.* We've other tasks to tend to," Louisa said. "Another time."

"Be sure she has adequate supervision," Helena said. "We wouldn't want anything untoward to happen while these women were within your control. Such things could speak badly for you."

"Fortunately, I'm learning that I'm not in control of anything, Helena," I said. *And neither are you.*

———

It was Almira who insisted. "You told me you'd written to a friend, inviting her to meet you at the fair, remember? It's what you were doing when you found me. What if she came and you weren't there?"

Brita would understand; I was certain of that. Besides, I had no way of knowing whether she'd even gotten my letter, and she'd told me she didn't like fairs anyway.

"And there's the class. Doesn't it start soon?" Almira said. "Have you already missed a session?"

"That's a dream," I said.

She sighed. "I guess we aren't supposed to wish for things. Once I remember saying, after all that happened, that if I could just have a good night's sleep, I'd be happy. Now I have that, and I feel guilty that I have that little gift of sleep."

"Even the apostle Paul said, 'I think myself happy,' and that must mean that we're meant to be happy," I replied. "Pursuing something that matters is a part of our nature. I'm glad you're sleeping better, and now that you are, you can wish for new things. But I don't know if I wish to go to the fair. Too many reminders of when the boys were with me there."

"Walk about it," she said, a phrase I knew meant to walk that puzzle, to see what answers might come from my time there.

Instead I walked to talk with Keil. I kept my eyes alert for Andy and Christian. School was in session, but one never knew when the children would be studying botany beneath the trees. Music floated up from the grassy area near the Keil and Company Store. Henry C led the music class. Chris Wolff brought his lectures out under the trees as well, and I could see my Christian sitting there, his face scrunched in concentration. Chris read from the classics. Apparently, I walked too close, for Chris Wolff looked up at me and smiled, and when he did, my son looked up too.

"Mama!" He ran to me. "Where have you been?"

I squatted down to his level. "Working, as always," I said.

"Martin lets me help with the bottles, not just Andy," he told me proudly. "I'm working too."

"That's a good boy," I told him.

"Martin says we can come for supper soon. Can we?" I brushed his reddish hair away from his eyes. "Please? I'm sorry for whatever I did. I won't do it again."

I tried to keep from crying. Seeing them was so difficult for me, yet not finding ways to be with them was breaking Christian's heart. "Anytime you want," I said.

"*Ja,* by goodness," he said, reminding me of Karl. "I'll tell Martin and Andy we can come soon."

He hugged me quickly, ran back, and sat down. He waved at me once, then returned his eyes to his teacher.

Maybe the boys expected our family to be as my mother had said, sometimes with me, sometimes with their grandparents, sometimes with an uncle. Maybe that's all our family had ever been, this hodgepodge of people separated by our desires to serve. We were not unlike

Karl's quilt, composed of bits and pieces of discards, confusion stitched with comfort. Christian had never known his own father, and life with Jack had been anything but calm or restful. Maybe this conglomerate of people who were influencing him, keeping him warm, feeding his and Andy's bodies and spirits was superior to what they'd known when living with just me and their sisters. My girls welcomed strangers; the boys carried on as though their family home was the entire colony. Maybe I should accept that it was.

"So you want to go to the fair to cook, Sister Emma. This is why you're here?"

"In part," I told Keil. After leaving Christian at his outdoor class, I'd walked the mile up the hill and found Keil as he stood outside of the church construction. "I also wish to claim a portion of our agreement." He frowned. Several men had been hovering around him but left as I approached. He held a roll of plans, comparing what was drawn to what he saw before him. "Two bandstands around the steeple?" I said. "That'll be quite a sight from miles around. Everyone will know of the Keil church," I said.

"Aurora church," he corrected. "I didn't design the steeple to bring attention to me. I'm a humble man."

He didn't sound as though he teased, so I guessed he really did think that about himself. It surprised me sometimes, that what seemed so obvious to me about a person's demeanor could be seen as the opposite by the person. Almira was a good example. She was warm and kind and good with children, but she described herself as a sinful woman who didn't deserve happiness or joy. Keil, on the other hand, was often petulant and arrogant, indifferent to his wife and cloying to some of her friends. He made decisions that propped up certain people with thick pillows, while others suffered at the foot of the bed. Yet he saw himself as a virtuous, benevolent leader.

Perhaps that was the whole problem with me: I saw things differently. Who was I to say that Almira wasn't right in her sinful admission, or that it was me who couldn't see the goodness of Keil's colony care? People did have good days and bad days. Perhaps my judgment was as impaired, like a broken wagon tongue that ought never be allowed to pull along anything precious.

"I've come to humbly ask you to pay for an educational course that I wish to take at the university. I'd be there one week a month until the weather becomes impassable."

"Humbly?" I nodded but said nothing. "You'd be gone a week at a time? Where would you stay? You'd take your girl out of school? *Nein.* This does not seem good."

Keil had rarely indicated any concern about my girls or their education, but I saw it as a good sign that he'd give me any kind of reason rather than simply saying no.

"I have someone who would look after them."

"Ah, the Raymond woman? Do you think that's wise, Sister Emma?"

"Matilda has offered to stay as well. And Kitty. Surely you have no objection to them."

He tapped the rolled-up set of plans gently against his leg. "Matilda Knight, I'm sure, is a fine young woman. But she distracts Jacob Stauffer from his work, and he came here to be a carpenter, not to court."

"If anything, her being here makes it easier for the man to tend to his hammer and saw, knowing in the evening he might have a word or two with her," I said. "Would their marriage be so bad? Then she'd not be distracting him. And marriage seems to smother such ardor, or so I've noticed." I'd often wondered if it was the amount of saltpeter we used to preserve our meats that made separation of the sexes so easily accommodated.

"Work. That's what we're to do here, Sister Emma. Just as with you and Christian, you got little done your first year because your husband looked after a family. I didn't send him out to have his family to worry over."

"His family was on his way before you sent him out," I said.

He frowned, appeared to count months. "*Ja.* That was not known though. So, we should finish the important buildings before I approve any more marriages. That's what I told Jacob Stauffer. He understands."

"Matilda will be here for my girls while I take the class."

He gazed off toward the construction site again. Wild geese flew across us in their V formation, that sure sign of fall.

"Three weeks away is too much time. Martin is taking classes, and it is hard for him going back and forth. It would be even harder for you, Emma, a woman with children to raise."

"But the agreement—"

"Is that I will provide your education, and so I will. But I must have some say over the costs and conditions. That is only fair and reasonable, *ja*?"

"Will you limit my son's medical education as well?"

"*Ach,* Emma. Calm down now. Your son will be a doctor in due time. But you do not need to become…what is it you wanted to take a course in?"

"Painting," I said.

"Hardly practical." He lifted his hands to the sky. "As fleeting as geese."

"Great paintings soothe us," I said. "They're like music, *Herr* Keil." It had been years since I'd used that title with him. "Or fine furniture sanded to silk or a steeple that spirals into the sky. They can all help our spirits reach to higher places, to honor God. Even a luscious cake covered with whipped cream and strawberries can inspire. A painting does that too."

"Come up with another way to try to learn your painting then," he said. "A course away from here is not acceptable. Now, now"—he raised his hand to silence my next protest—"but you can go to the fair, Emma, if you wish. We have need of cooks, and you did so well with the building of the dance hall. Why not put your talents there? Of course you'd have to take the girls. It wouldn't be right to leave them alone with…the women you surround yourself with. Go along now. I'm a busy man."

Why not go? Defy Keil by leaving Matilda and Almira in charge. I could look for Brita and I'd cook. But I'd also talk to that instructor. Perhaps there were teachers who, like peddlers and those who sharpened knives, traveled from town to town. Maybe I could find one who would travel to Aurora. I may not get all I wanted, but there would always be another path to take. I just had to watch and listen to know which way to go.

16

Plots and Plans

September 30. We tended to the hogs today, all of us working together to finish before those going to the fair could leave. I heard grumbles from some of the men that Keil had once again locked himself inside his workroom and wasn't there to cheer us onward. When he's working side by side with others, the community moves steady as the river. But otherwise there is froth, and the people grumble.

Louisa and Keil, Helena, John and BW, newlyweds Frederick and Louisa Keil, and dozens of others left for the fair. The band would play and earn a tidy sum, as well as bring more renown to our community. My parents went too, taking Lou with them, according to Kitty, who stayed in much closer touch with them than I did.

I didn't go; I couldn't risk what might happen to my girls if I left them behind.

I hadn't planned on what did happen while so many were gone.

It was a Sunday, and with John and Keil at the fair, there was no church scheduled at the Keil house. Karl might have led services, or even Martin, both of whom had remained behind. Martin stopped by especially, he said, to tell me the boys would like to have more time with me. He asked if it would be all right if they spent the afternoon on Sunday. *All right?* I suspect he had studying to do and wondered if I might not work out a regular plan with him, to have the boys on Sunday afternoons so he would work. This first day had to go well. I had grand plans.

I wanted to do things I knew the boys might like, and involve the girls too. We'd roll hoops for a time. Maybe pull taffy. It was cool enough we wouldn't have to put paraffin in the sweetness to keep it from melting. I'd roast a chicken later, as I'd had enough of pork for a while.

I still had one ham left from last year—I'd wrapped it with sweet grass hay after giving the meat a good soak. We'd smoked dozens of hams, and bacon and sausage, but that one I claimed. I put a date and my initials on the bag I'd made for it. When we got ready to eat it, I wouldn't have to soak the slices to get rid of the pepper taste, because the hay sweetened it so well. Dozens hung in the smokehouse. We rendered lard by the buckets for making our pies. We'd washed, cleaned, and dried casings, then stuffed sausages for days, and I couldn't stand to look at another casing squeezed to the brim with pork and spices and chopped onion. We'd even run out of entrails, we had so many hogs to prepare, and several of us had made casings out of cloth. They were draped like thick ropes, round and round in the smokehouse, and it would be a few days before those sausages could be eaten. I guessed the good Lord made it that way, since no one cared about eating pork right after the work of slaughtering and rendering and stuffing. By the time we'd put the more disagreeable thoughts of the pork from our minds, the hams and sausages would be ready, and so would we.

That Sunday I busily prepared stick candy and my special gooseberry pie. We'd be eating chicken, or maybe a nice venison roast, if one of the Indians who made their way through the region knocked on my door. I often traded with them, giving them butter or sweet candies and, depending on the season, a ham or a sausage ring to take with them. These Indians, though tall and well fed, did not have the same pride in their eyes as the Shoalwaters who had helped us those long winters ago. Disease defined these Mollala or Calapooia people, the sicknesses reducing their numbers to mere scatterings of peoples. I'd probably not see them today anyway, as this was a season for hunting, and they traveled far from this Aurora region for that.

All through the preparations, my spirits were lifted in anticipation of my sons' visit. Kate and Ida rose earlier than normal, tramping down the stairs in their bare feet with their nightclothes still on. Almira was up and gave them their oats, putting dried berries into their bowls, and milk she'd gotten from the goat. It was going to be a grand day. We had plenty of time to enjoy even the preparations. Then the actual event we would savor.

We both turned to the light knock on the kitchen door.

"We know it isn't Louisa and Helena," I said.

"They're at the fair," Almira noted.

"And they prefer the parlor door," I said. I hadn't told her that they'd left as soon as I suggested they meet her, but I did let her know that they'd expressed concern about her being with me. I wasn't sure whether to keep such news to myself, but I decided that secrets seldom helped a person. People needed information to understand what was happening around them. I didn't want Almira to encounter Louisa and Helena on the path somewhere and not be prepared for their looks.

"Maybe Andy and Christian are here already," Kate said.

"Yea!" Ida shouted and clapped her hands as she went to the door. "Oh," she said, and let Christine Wagner in.

As always, my foster sister combed her dark hair back so tight into a bun that her eyes looked narrow inside her puffy face. She carried a basket of fresh-baked goods, and as she handed it to me, looking over the head of Ida, she said, "I know it's early and you've probably got plans. But I wondered if I could sit for a bit in your parlor."

I'd spent fewer than ten minutes with this woman, always at the hotel or at Keils' and never with so few others around. I hoped one day we'd talk. Maybe about how my parents fostered her and how she felt about that.

"Well, of course. I'll fix coffee and bring it in to you myself."

"If you please, I'd like to be there alone."

Why not go to the woods or sit in Keil's root cellar if you want to be alone?

"I guess that's all right. But won't you have breakfast with us first? We're late getting around, as you can see by my lazy girls here." I patted Kate on the top of her uncombed but still braided hair with its flyaway strands. "This is your...Aunt Christine," I told her.

"I 'member," Kate said. She hid behind me. Christine was a large woman, though she didn't use her girth to intimidate. She looked soft as dough rather than solid as a smoked ham.

Christine didn't acknowledge the girls. "I've already eaten. I need a moment to sit. Without...distractions. Then I'll be on my way." I noticed that she spoke English without a German accent.

I took her back out onto the porch, opened the living room door, and let her step in. The room looked bare in the morning light. The chair I'd painted yellow gave the only color. I really did need to find things to hang on the walls, maybe wainscot the side walls or put up short shelves for more plates. The room felt cool to me too, and I wondered if I ought to light a fire. But when I suggested that, Christine said, "Oh no. It's always so warm at the Keil house. This is just right. Thank you. I won't be any bother. Thank you. I can't thank you enough."

She moved into the room as though she walked on stepping stones across a stream: careful, full of caution, yet with purpose. She took a chair that faced the windows and porch but was on the far side of the room. She nearly sank into the pillow I'd set there.

"Are you sure I can't get you something? Water? A pretzel?" She looked so tired, her eyes sad and sunk into her round, smooth-skin face.

She shook her head. "This is all I need, right here."

"All right, then," I said and backed out. I closed the door behind me, entering through the kitchen door once again.

"These are good, Mama," Ida said. She held one of the biscuits from Christine's basket. Kitty awakened and skipped down the steps into the kitchen without encountering Christine. I smiled to myself. My house design worked well: privacy for the parlor and activity for the kitchen. I just hadn't expected my foster sister to discover the uniqueness of my design. Matilda and Almira joined us, and I told them about Christine's visit.

"Quiet. That's what I longed for when things were going so badly," Almira told me when I repeated Christine's request. Almira held one of the tin serving spoons Christian had made. "I'd try to take a walk in the afternoon, but there were always babies clinging." She swallowed. "Not that I didn't want them with me, but sometimes, for a few minutes, I needed to be alone. I wanted not to be responsible for them, for what was happening in my life. I took to walking at night. I wanted to be…still." Tears welled up in her eyes. "I've sat there, just as she is now, in your parlor, Emma, while your girls rested or played outside. You and Kitty and Matilda, gone. It's one of the greatest things you gave me by asking me to come home with you. A little peace. I know that's why I can sleep now. And I can get more done when I'm awake too."

"Every woman should have a place for herself," Matilda said. "Even when they marry."

"Especially when they marry," Almira said. "You keep that in mind, Matilda."

"I'm coming to believe that marriage isn't in my future," Matilda said. We all looked expectant, but she said nothing more.

"That makes two of us, then," Kitty said.

After the girls were dressed and we'd all finished our oats and milk, I opened the door from the stairwell to see if Christine needed anything. She wasn't there. She'd left a note, though, that read, "I'd like to come back again, but this time to stay."

———

The boys arrived before I could think further about Christine's request; and though I asked Martin to join us, he declined. It was just as well. It would be awkward with him around. Andy said he thought I'd gone to the fair. "It's nice you stayed," he added.

"I'll miss seeing Brita," I said, "but I wanted to spend time with you and for you to have time with your sisters."

"I'm glad you weren't too busy," Christian said. He ran up the stairs and found the wooden chest next to the rocking chair in the wide hall. I'd put some of his winter clothes in there, and a hoop he and Andy could roll along with a stick. I climbed the steps and watched as he surveyed his old room, now taken over by his sisters and the women who lived here. "There's a lot of girls here," he said.

I laughed. "*Ja,* there are."

He sniffed the air. "It smells like girls."

"That's the lavender," I told him. "It makes everything smell nice. All the girls doesn't mean there isn't room for you, though. You're always welcome to come and…even stay, you know." *I probably shouldn't make such suggestions; it might confuse him.* I didn't want that.

"Martin says sometime I can sleep in my old bed here. Maybe."

I felt that burn in my stomach at the idea that someone else could decide for me about my child's wishes. "Whatever Martin says," I told him. I didn't want Christian in the middle of this edgy time, but I knew my voice held some contempt, because Christian glanced up at me in the sideways look he had.

"We're going to get a dog," Kate told him, as she skipped up the stairs.

"We are?" Christian and I said in unison.

"I don't think so," I continued. "A dog won't get along with Opal or Clara. Who told you that?"

"Karl said Po needs people around. With him teaching now, the dog gets into trouble and chews things, and he'll get into the potato fields or be trampled by horses or et up by the hogs."

"That's *eaten* up by hogs," I corrected.

"We can save him, Mama."

I couldn't save anyone.

Christian said, "Martin can't have animals in the store because of all the medicines and such. A dog would be fun to have. We could come and play with it, couldn't we, Mama? Me and Andy?"

"Why, yes, you could," I said.

"And we could take the dog for a walk on our special path," Ida told him. "And we'd let you teach him, Andy, when you came here." My older son had climbed up the steps now too. "If you wanted. You too, Christian."

"A dog's a good friend to have," Andy said. "Better than a horse that wants to bite you—until he learns better." Andy smiled at me, and it was the warmest light. Christian continued chattering about the dog, and I knew I'd have to talk with Karl. But just like that, having a dog around was suddenly a brilliant idea.

Martin came to pick them up later, and they went to him with reluctance, at least I thought so. Christian chattered like a squirrel telling me some story he'd forgotten to share before. Even Andy didn't push to leave. I confess I appreciated seeing that in them. But I also knew I had to make this transition easier between Martin and me, or he might find a reason not to let them come again. "You be good and listen to Martin," I told them. "I'll see you again before you know it. Andy might need new shoes," I told Martin, who nodded.

"I'll tend to it," he said.

"Or I can."

He hesitated. "*Gut.* We'll do this together, then," Martin said.

I expelled breath I hadn't realized I'd been holding.

———

The day after the boys' visit, I went looking for Christine and found her hanging laundry on the line at the Keils'. I told her she was more than welcome to stay with us. We had room, but I was curious about why she'd made the request, and why now.

"I'd rather not say," she said. Her dark eyes looked down. Small brown spots speckled the backs of her hands, freckles that matched a few on her face. It looked like she'd tried to cover them with powder. "The Keils have been very kind to me here, and I'll continue to come to cook for them, but I want…fewer people around. Does that make me selfish?" she asked.

"I'm not the one to ask about that," I said. "People are always commenting about the things I want, saying they're to dress up myself."

"I'm better able to think when I'm alone. Time to read or maybe to mend or even listen to the birds."

"Or children laughing," I added.

She looked away.

"There are several of us living in my home, though," I reminded her. "We won't be able to assure you of that very quiet time as you had the other day."

"It'll be more time than at the Keils' and...with just women. I'll do my share. I'm not asking for charity."

"You can help, but part of why I wanted the house is for charity, to give to others what they might need and couldn't find anywhere else. It's why I have the double doors."

"It was rude of me to leave without saying good-bye."

"You proved that my design worked." I smiled. "Do you want me to tell Louisa that you're moving here?"

By the look she gave me, I thought she'd take me up on that offer, but she shook her head no. "I need to do hard things myself," she said. "It'll make me stronger."

Four days after Louisa and Helena returned from the fair, the two arrived again, complete with calling cards. "What did you say to Christine Wagner while we were gone, to make her want to leave?" Of course, Louisa held me accountable for Christine's request. Louisa told us she'd been less than amused when Christine spoke to her, then left at the end of the work day and walked to my home, with her few personal things bundled up in a tapestry bag.

"I said nothing to her, except to answer her question."

"We have a perfectly good place for her," Helena said. "She's been a fine influence among the younger girls too." She twisted then smoothed the ribbon holding her scissors at her waist.

"That won't change. She'll only be here in the evenings."

"And when she isn't working."

"I suppose it will be more difficult to assign her tasks in the evenings if she's over here," I noted.

"We didn't work her all the time," Louisa defended. "She wasn't a servant or, worse, a slave, for heaven's sake. She could have left any time she wanted."

"Apparently, she did," I said.

They sipped their tea in unison.

"I don't think your gathering up women like this is a good thing for the colony," Helena said. "Surely Dr. Keil did not intend for the house he built for you to be used as a plotting place for disruption in the colony's routine."

"A plotting place?" I laughed. "A woman has moved. There's nothing sinister in that."

"One would have thought that having your sons live elsewhere would have...tempered you, Sister Emma," Helena said.

I wouldn't dignify her words about my sons by responding to them, though I felt my face grow hot.

I stirred a spoon in my glass, biting my tongue. Oh, how I wanted to challenge these women's righteous indignation!

"I still think you should put some paintings on your wall," Louisa said. She pointed to the two open areas on either side of the brick fireplace.

"What?"

"Some color. Don't you think the walls need color, Helena?"

"Your husband thinks that paintings are frivolous," I said.

"Does he? Well, then, maybe the bare walls are best," Louisa said. She adjusted herself on the chair. Her hip must be hurting her yet again.

With a simple stitch, Louisa could be sewn into her husband's opinion. I suspected that the concerns she and Helena raised had more to do with Keil's wishes than with any real issue of theirs about Christine Wagner's moving to my home.

"I'm sure you're aware," I said, "that we have an agreement, your husband and I. That I am to use this house for the betterment of the colony, and so I am. Christine will continue to work for you and contribute. The rest of us living here do too. Matilda works for the tailor shop. Kitty works at the hotel, as do I. Almira tends to my children so I can work. You have nothing to worry about."

"Oh, we're not worried at all," Helena said. She stood and tightened her bonnet strings. "We thought that you should be."

―――――――

"What did they say?" Almira asked when I returned to the kitchen.

"*Ach,* something about my stirring up plots to disrupt." I slammed the three-legged spider onto the stove, and Kate and Ida both jumped.

"Mama," Ida said. "Be gentle."

"*Ja,* gentle." I took a deep breath.

"Because I'm here," Almira said. She sighed. "I've brought you disgrace."

"Because I'm here," Matilda countered. "*Herr* Keil wants me to go so I won't disturb Jacob's work. That's it, isn't it?"

"I'm not even interesting enough to be a suspect," Kitty said. "I can't imagine I have anything to do with it."

"It's me," Christine said. "I've put you all at risk."

"No one is at risk," I said. *Why do we women always assume we're the origin of problems?* "What could they do to us? Move me out... Take my..." I looked at the girls and at the faces of the women. "They wouldn't. No one would defend that action because they're girls." I hoped that Ida and Kate couldn't put the pieces together, understand what we talked about over the top of their heads. "John Giesy wouldn't be interested enough to get in the middle of such a scene, especially with no one coming forward saying they wanted...well, you know."

"Could they keep you from seeing your boys?" Almira whispered.

"So long as Martin has them, I don't think so. I even think I might see them more with Martin's going to school than if he weren't. We're going to work together at this. He said so."

"Still, they threatened you," Matilda said.

"Not such a big word as that. Just a little...chastening. I can live with that. I've experienced it often enough. I'm stronger now than I was." I removed the spider from the stove, the three legs balanced perfectly on the smooth surface. Keil and company couldn't make me think of myself as they saw me, just because they said it. "In fact, they've inspired me. If I'm going to be accused of plotting something, I may as well do it. They'll have a hard time convincing anyone that I've disrupted the colony with my kind of doings."

"What do you plan to do?" Kitty asked.

"For the moment, make apple dumplings and eat them ourselves, without sharing a one with the rest of the colony."

Kitty giggled. "Is that all?"

"No. But it's what I'll do at this moment. The real plotting will come later, after we have our sustenance." I smiled. A few paintings were forming in my head. I felt as invigorated as the day when the boys came to visit. Maybe even more.

17

Stories with Hopeful Endings

November 7. The girls complete their stints of morning stitching. When Kate finished hers today, she said, "I am full of enthusiasm!" Would that my life would be so.

December 1. Today Louisa tells me that they saw Brita at the fair last fall! She came by the dance hall seeking me. I feel bad now that I didn't go. But the past is past. I will write to Brita again and apologize. At least she'll know then why I wasn't there, as Louisa said they did not tell her, not wanting to be "gossips."

I had things to do. Perhaps because I felt unable to bring about all that I wanted in my own life, I looked at others' to see what I might do to advance theirs. That cleft beneath my heart, where I'd once daily tended to my boys' needs, felt empty, and I hoped that I could fill the space in part with something meaningful. I wondered if Helena and I might not share a motivation in this kind of thinking, but quickly pitched that thought away.

Finding out where Jacob Stauffer stood in relation to Matilda proved my first order of business. Was the man a serious suitor? Was he reluctant to express himself because of his concern over a woman's sensibilities? I suspected that a lot of talk about "sensibilities" was a way that those in power kept women in their place, acting as though we needed protection from the outside, cruel world. Our colony was both our family and another world. And like a wool coat, at times both warm and scratchy. We'd be more joyous if people were allowed to fall in love and hope to marry, without the consternation of achieving approval from Brother Keil.

I suppose I ought to have asked Matilda first, but I didn't want her sensibilities to overpower her. Her cautious side might choose to primly point out to me that in due time, if Jacob were truly interested, he would speak to her of marriage and then they'd secure consent from Dr. Keil. If Keil refused, they could always leave Aurora, but leaving this place had its difficulties; I was witness to that.

But I knew that life is short, and Matilda was already nearly thirty. If she was to have a marriage, which she said once she'd never expected, then there was no time to waste.

Our gathering had taken on new people: BW, my sister-in-law, and Barbara, my mother-in-law, had joined us too. I was a little edgy with their presence, never sure of their intentions. And I supposed if I'd thought about it, I would have waited to bring up the subject of Jacob and Matilda until it was just our little group. But my in-laws always made me act in ways that surprised even me.

"How does Jacob like his work detail?" I asked Matilda.

She blushed, and lowered her eyes so she didn't see the stares of BW and Barbara Giesy.

"Jacob's been peeling bark from oak trees, for the tanning factory to use," I told the women.

"It's hard work, but better than felling the trees," Matilda said.

"He seems a kind man," BW said.

"He's very gentle with children," Matilda added. We sat in my parlor on a Sunday afternoon. Christian and Ida were in the kitchen playing with jacks. I could hear their groans and cheers. Andy hadn't come, and Kate joined us with the stitching. Rain and wind had their way with the windows, but we were snug inside. It was late November, and for days the skies had been as gray as the bottom of a duck and just as soggy.

My mother-in-law had brought her piecework for a Friendship

quilt, something she'd heard about from relatives back in Pennsylvania. I'd been surprised by her request to join us, especially since this was the Sabbath and I assumed she'd think we shouldn't be working. I considered changing our routine for her and my sister-in-law, but the truth was, we weren't "working." Piecing quilts or helping one another stitch wasn't work. It was quiet, contemplative time, made all the more spiritual if the quilt we worked on would be for someone other than ourselves. I gave Barbara Malachi 3:16 and commented that we created remembrances together on our Sabbath afternoons, something Scripture permitted. If she wished to join us in doing that, she was welcome in my parlor.

Apparently those conditions were acceptable, as both women had arrived with piecework in hand. Now my mother-in-law was showing us a copy of *Godey's Lady's Book* that she'd brought with her. It described ways we could print verses on our fabric or stamp the letters of all our names. We decided on names.

"We might ask Louisa to write each one using her *Fraktur* lettering," BW said. John's wife had hair nearly as white as Barbara's, the mother-in-law we shared.

"I doubt Louisa will ever join us on a Sabbath afternoon," Kitty said.

I glanced at my in-laws, but they didn't exchange meaningful looks. They just kept stitching.

"Well, we could ask," Kitty suggested. "She might not join us on the Sabbath, but maybe on another day. We wouldn't always have to stitch at the Keil's. Your parlor is very inviting, Sister."

I didn't want a competition! "So, Jacob is good with children," I said, urging us back to the subject at hand.

"He has a droll sense of humor and sometimes teases me about a subject," Matilda said, "but I always think he's serious, so I give him reasons why he might not want to think that way, and he laughs. I know then that he just said the words to see me get all rattled. He said he likes to see the 'spark in my eyes.'"

She placed her needle into the soap square where she kept it, saying it made the needle go more easily into cloth. "He enjoys working on buildings," she continued. "He has a fine eye for finish work, where the banisters are smoothed or curlicues of wood fit into the corners. Back in Willapa, I saw some very nice chests he'd constructed in their family home."

"I suspect he doesn't get to do much finish work here," I said. "They must have two dozen buildings started and in various stages of completion, but not enough for a family to move into a finished house."

"Our men do the best they can, Emma. You mustn't be so critical."

"I just stated facts," I told BW. "No judgment intended."

"Jacob says that's discouraging, but he still likes the work. He likes to grow things too."

"I want to talk to him, then, about making some shelves for me," I told her.

"Didn't you make your own shelves in Willapa?" Barbara asked. "I heard that from Jack."

My stomach knotted at the mention of my husband. "*Ja.* Little shelves I made myself. I'm thinking of more like a...cupboard. Maybe on either side of the fireplace."

The women turned to look at the brick.

"A painting would be nice there," Kitty said. "You used to draw portraits, Emma. How come you don't do that anymore?"

"No time," I said.

"You could do that now, instead of quilting," Kitty continued. "Or hang up your painting you did of Christian, at least."

"I'm not sure I could look at his picture every day without feeling sad," I said.

"You're a married woman, Emma. You mustn't hang on to the past so," BW said.

"Your children might like seeing it," Christine pointed out.

Kate nodded agreement.

I hadn't thought of that. "I'll consider it, but I still want cupboards, and I'm going to see Jacob about them. And maybe Mr. Ehlen. He makes very nice baskets."

"And music reeds for the band's clarinet," Kitty said. "Kate told me that," she added when I raised my eyebrows, wondering where she'd gotten such news.

"I could put one of those baskets beside the hearth and fill it instead of a cupboard with dried weeds, I suppose."

"I like Mr. Ehlen," Kate said. "His arm is so interesting, how it swings like that. It's like a leash attached to him. Lorenz plays with us girls at school, along with Andy. He doesn't act all smarty the way Henry T does, because he knows Latin and Greek and his father is the music instructor. Andy knows those too, and he's not smarty."

"That's good," I said.

Kate worked on a tiny needlework of a dog's house that I'd drawn for her. I'd made the house with two front doors, like our home, and had promised her that on the back I'd paint a picture of Po, Karl's dog. I hadn't quite given in to having the dog move into our house as yet. None of the colonists let dogs sleep in their homes despite how we all indulged them with special crackers and such. When both sides of Kate's needlework and my drawing were complete, we'd put it on a leather thong and she'd wear it around her neck—something special I hoped Louisa or Helena wouldn't find too worldly. We might even make a few as Christmas gifts with other subjects: flowers or fruit.

"I think cupboards there would fit," Matilda said. "You could put a basket in the bottom shelf and still have room for china or one of your oyster shell paintings. Yes. A cupboard would be nice."

"That's what I'll do then. First thing tomorrow I'll have a talk with Brother Jacob Stauffer, and we'll see about a marriage," I said. "I mean, a cupboard."

I thought Matilda would faint, with the color that drained from her face. "Oh, you can't, Emma. You mustn't say anything at all about marriage. Father Keil won't permit it, and besides, Jacob might think I put you up to it, and what if he's horrified by my pushiness? He could leave. I might never see him again."

"Wouldn't it be better than this...waiting and wondering?" Almira said. "Sometimes not knowing is much worse than knowing and having to live with the next step. I hate not being able to take that next step."

"There's always a next step to take," I said. "Even if it's just to get your mind clear about what matters."

"Then having the courage to act on that," my Kate said. I stared at her. She stitched as though she didn't even realize what she'd said. *Are these words I often say out loud? Well, they are good ones for a child to remember.*

"I'd be mortified beyond belief if Jacob wasn't really interested in marriage; and what if he were, and then Brother Keil said no outright to him? That would be so humiliating for him. I can't imagine Jacob's defying him."

"It would be good not to defy the leadership," BW said. She would defend her John.

"He comes from sturdy Stauffer stock," I said. "He can think for himself."

"Emma, maybe you should let the Lord decide Jacob and Matilda's course. Maybe there's a reason He hasn't brought them together," BW added.

"*Ja,* his father defied Keil and stayed in Willapa. As did John," Matilda added.

"I find men sometimes need...guidance to bring what they want to the surface," I explained. "They're so...deep that they sometimes don't realize what they want or need until we women rub off the hard surface to get to that soft, all-important inside."

Silence filled the space, broken only by the sound of needle pushing through cloth.

"It's a good idea to find out where you stand," BW said finally. "But it's also true that there's a risk. She should know that."

"Anything worth having is worth a little risk," I said.

"Another one of your facts," BW noted, "not meant as judgment?"

"*Nein,* it is a judgment, one we must never forget if we're to live with abundance. No flower ever blooms unless it's willing to risk wind and rain while it reaches for sun."

————

The very next day, while the rain wept like a widow, I donned my rubber slicker and trudged up the hill to Keil's house, where I imagined Jacob would be. The men weren't doing much construction with the weather so foul, so they practiced their music and sat around working on miniatures and wooden toys. The turners continued to turn out furniture in the village shop, but at Keil's, the men told each other stories they neither believed nor remembered, apparently, because they kept repeating them through the years, laughing in the same places as though they'd just heard them. I stomped mud from my feet, slipped off my wooden shoes, and pulled up my dark stockings before entering the *gross Haus*.

It really was like a hotel, I decided. No one ever knocked at the front door. Who would hear it? Who would know to come to the door? I wondered why I'd been so intimidated by Keil's Elim, the *gross Haus* of Bethel when we lived there. I was young then, a child of seventeen. Behind Keil's Elim walls, decisions had been made about my life over which I had no control. The irony was that back then, I'd still made things happen that had changed many lives, including my husband's, including my children's. Here, despite Keil's power stripping me of the presence of my sons, it seemed Keil had less influence over men than he'd had in Bethel. Other men pushed to make decisions, and made them, when Keil attempted to slow progress by disappearing behind his workroom doors, lost in one of his moods.

Today, I didn't need to be concerned with Brother Keil first. He'd already changed my life here in Aurora. It was Jacob who mattered.

Once inside the hallway, I felt immediately steamy beneath my slicker. Christine was right. They kept the house very hot: fireplaces blazing, so many people.

It was Christine who came up the steps. "I thought I heard someone come in," she said. "Are you looking for Louisa?"

"No, Jacob Stauffer."

"Ah," she said. "I remember." A smile formed at the corners of her mouth. "Would you like me to go get him for you?" Her tone said she hoped I wouldn't. Her face looked pinched yet flushed. Probably from the work she'd been doing in the kitchen.

"I can climb those stairs as well as you," I said. "I assume he's with the bachelors?" She nodded, and I started up the three flights.

I did knock on the door at the top floor.

"Who is it?" A male voice said. A fiddle stopped playing.

"Emma Giesy," I told them. "I'd like to talk to Jacob Stauffer."

"Oh, *ja,* now you're in trouble, Jacob," I heard muffled laughter behind the door. The teasing continued, with sentences I couldn't quite make out, so I said, "I'm old enough to be his mother. Must I act like that to get you to send him out here?"

"You're not old enough to be my mother," Jacob said as he opened the door. He turned back to cast some sort of look at the men who laughed, then closed the door. He moved us into the hall, so we stood in front of the window that offered frangible light as it continued to rain. "What can I do for you, *Frau* Giesy?"

"I've some work I'd like you to do at my house," I said.

"One of the few houses finished."

"Not totally. There are things to do that I'd like you to take care of for me. I'm not sure how I could pay you. Brother Keil might not think the work I want done is…worthy of an exchange on the ledger. But perhaps I could launder your clothes or patch them—"

"*Fräulein* Knight does that for me. Sometimes." Just the mention of her name brought color to his neck.

"I'd not interfere with whatever arrangements you have with Matilda Knight," I said.

"Oh, no arrangements. No, *nein.* Nothing like that. Maybe your gooseberry pie. Now that I'd trade some work for."

"Would you now? And my…bread. I could bake you a loaf of fine crusty bread."

"Those would do," he said.

"Can you come by after your workday today?"

"*Ach.* This isn't work I do here. It's filling up time. You offer a much better way to do that. Eating gooseberry pie, I mean. And doing what I must to earn it."

"Of course, that's what you meant," I said. "Shall we head back together now?"

"*Ja.* I'll get my slicker and maybe my hammer. I may as well begin the finishing now."

Begin the finishing: wasn't that what my life was about now? It was a thought I could latch on to.

———

Later, back at my house, I came upon Christine as she finished her bath. She'd been so quiet in the kitchen, I thought she'd gone up to the bedroom. I hadn't heard her talking to the girls across the hall. Kate said she was hungry, and I had a piece of cold salmon in the icebox (something else Helena probably thought a furbelow) that would be good for her to eat, instead of the sweets my daughter craved. I moved lightly down the steps.

The door was ajar. I was certain no one was in the kitchen. But when I opened the door fully, Christine stood there unclothed, her feet in the copper tub we reserved for bathing. She stared at me, then we both looked at each other, startled.

"I'm sorry," she said.

"No, it's my intrusion."

She reached for a flannel sheet she used as a towel, and when she turned, I could see that scars like spring branches mapped her back.

———

Jacob spent several days building my cupboards in place. He'd done the work, a fine job of it too, and took extra time, I thought, to smooth the wood with beeswax. He told me I should only build them part way up the brick sides, so that one could still see the craftsmanship of Brother Yost's brickwork above it. He worked only on days when someone besides Matilda was there. "I don't want to compromise *Fräulein* Knight's reputation," he said. Almira chaperoned them, along with my girls, now that the weather kept all children out of school. Almira had them stringing dried berries and popcorn for the *Tannenbaum* we'd be trimming as Christday approached. She reported laughter between Jacob and Matilda, and quiet conversations, and long periods of silence during which she assumed Matilda tended to her tailoring and Jacob gave elbow grease to his beeswax efforts. Whenever she peeked in, she told me, "They were like two pegs in a puzzle who never got closer than their own set place."

I'd baked the promised pies and bread, and then Jacob had gone back to his other work, without a word to Matilda about their future.

I'd thought that where interest and opportunity intersected, action must follow. Surely there was interest on Jacob's part. We women had all agreed about that. And I'd provided opportunity.

We were in the kitchen when Almira said, "You have to be explicit with men. They don't see things the way we do."

Matilda said, "Maybe marriage isn't in Jacob's future. For years I never imagined it would be in mine, and I was fine. Until I met him." She blushed. "His life before he met me was probably full and well ordered, and he doesn't see any need to complicate it with a wife."

"My parents picked my husband for me," Almira said. We all looked at her. "He was tall and articulate and had a passion for Scripture, and my parents were certain that my marrying him would mean marrying up. Of course, they had no idea that he had already accepted a call to come to the mission field, a long way from Virginia. I think he saw in me a strong young girl who could survive in the wilderness, alone, more often than not. I'd be away from my family, with no one to complain to if things got difficult. Otherwise, he might have married some young, pretty thing, but I met his needs. In the beginning." She swallowed and looked away, and I wondered if she thought of the girl who was central to the divorce.

"We do meet their needs," I said. "It's part of our duty. But it's their duty to meet ours too. Once the marriage is blessed. Christian was that kind of man. It's a good thing about the Giesys. At least some of the Giesys."

"Tell the story of meeting Papa," Kate said.

"My papa story too," Ida said.

"Oh, you've heard it a dozen times," I said. I avoided looking at Kitty, hoping she wouldn't point out to Ida that Ida's father wasn't the same as Kate's. I hadn't actually made the distinction to my girls. I wasn't sure Ida even knew who Jack was in her life. "We're working on getting Matilda and Jacob together," I said. "Let's see how we can do that."

"Matilda should be like Sleeping Beauty and prick her finger with a spindle," Kate said. "Then Jacob could come wake her up."

"With a kiss," Ida said. She made a face.

"Who is Sleeping Beauty?" Almira asked.

The girls filled her in, including the bloody details. "The king had banned all the spindles, because the frog had told him his daughter would prick her finger and fall asleep. Mama says he tried to cheat fate. But some old woman didn't hear them, and she kept spinning and the princess—"

"Who was a curious sort and who loved a little risk," Kate interrupted.

"Found her," Ida finished. Ida didn't have all the details down, but I was grateful once again to Karl for securing German books for them to read, written by the Grimm brothers, even if the stories held sadness in them.

"*Sleeping Beauty* is a story of wishes fulfilled: the king and queen got the daughter they'd longed for, and even though they lost her for a hundred years, the princess was eventually rescued by her prince," Kitty said. "It's such a hopeful story." She sighed.

"Have you already kissed Jacob?" Kate asked. Her eyes grew large.

"That's a very personal question," I told her. "And not polite to ask." Matilda smiled. "I have not."

"I hope you don't have to wait a hundred years, Matilda," Kate said.

"No matter what happens," Matilda said, as she looked around at us as though memorizing each of our faces, "it doesn't mean I haven't already been rescued by love."

———

"Christine," I said. "Sit with me." I patted the bench beside me, covered with one of my quilted pillows. Everyone else had gone to bed, and she'd stepped across the stoop between the kitchen and the parlor, likely to see if the room was empty. I noticed that since I'd walked in on her, she'd kept constantly to the company of others, had taken no time to sit in the parlor alone, and was never alone with just me.

"I can come back later," she said. "I see you're reading." She nodded to the Bible I had in my lap.

"It was my husband's. Sometimes I like holding something I know he once held." A clock I'd purchased from the store ticked as it sat on Jacob Stauffer's finished shelves. "Join me," I said. An oil lamp cast shadows across the woven rug.

I wasn't sure how to broach the subject, or if I even should.

"You're wondering about the scars," she said as she sat. "You've been kind not to bring it up."

"I wouldn't have known if I hadn't interrupted your bath," I said.

"I've appreciated your not asking."

"But now I am."

She fidgeted with the chatelaine that hung from a ribbon around her neck. "Helena has a keen eye, and I knew if I stayed there, before long in the evenings we shared, she'd notice and ask questions, maybe even have me expelled." Her black eyes grew suddenly large. "You aren't going to do that, are you?"

"Because you were once beaten? No. And I don't think Helena would ask you to leave for that reason either."

"She might one day learn about something else," Christine said. She paused. "I had a child," she said. "I left it on the doorstep of a church in Shelbina, where I lived. I never returned to my father's home after that. How could I? Your mother found me, thin as a noodle, behind a boarding house I cooked at. She took me home and in an act of Christian charity so wonderfully bizarre, your parents made me one of theirs. They asked no questions. I told them I had no parents, and they fostered me."

"And here I am, asking all kinds of questions."

"But not in judgment, and I'm thankful for that. If Helena or others found out, they might be upset with you for taking me in."

"*Ach,* let them be. There's no need for you to hide yourself. You've paid a terrible price for someone's violating you."

"But that's just it. He didn't really violate me. I was a willing partner. I thought he loved me, and we'd marry one day. But he wasn't interested in marriage. And when I told him of the baby, I never heard from him again. My father, he's the one who took the whip to me when he learned of…the baby. I was big boned then too, and could conceal it for a time."

"Did your mother…?"

"She died when I was born. It was my father and me, and he never did get over her death. He blamed me for it. I made my way alone after that. Until your mother found me and took me in."

"But you decided to work for Keil and to stay there for a time."

She nodded. "Your parents' cabin is small and Johanna takes good care of Lou, and your brothers are a help to your mother. So Kitty and I decided to work elsewhere and live elsewhere, to reduce the burden on them. But there are so many people at Keils' now, with those arriving from Bethel and still so few houses built."

"The scars…from your father, then?"

"It was his way of letting me know how deeply I had sinned." She dropped her eyes, her demeanor that of a scolded dog.

"In my view, *he* performed the greater transgression. You sought to fill up an empty place with love, Christine. More than one of us has done the same and later wished we hadn't acted in quite the way we did. I have." She looked up at me, her eyes pooling with tears. "Yes, I did something that turned out poorly. I'm sure Helena will fill you in if you ask. Maybe my parents told you." She shook her head no. "I refused the help of other people, and married poorly after my husband died. Grief can be a veil against good reason. All that happened next wasn't good. In part, my sons no longer live with me because of how I managed my empty place."

"You didn't leave them on a doorstep."

"No, I didn't." *But I put them in peril.* I paused. "Did you see someone pick your baby up and take him inside?" She nodded yes. "Then you know the baby was safe. You tended him… Was it a boy?" She nodded yes. "You tended him to the very edge and then you went no further, giving him what you couldn't give him yourself just then. But you did not deserve the flogging by your father. No one ever deserves beating. Ever. There is always another way to solve a problem. Always." I took a deep breath. "And you don't need to keep covering your wounds behind your girth either. You're a lovely soul."

"I don't believe what you said, yet; but they are nice words to hear."

"One day you might." I patted her hand. It was cool to the touch, and she didn't pull it away from me. "Sometimes if we act as though a thought is true, it becomes true. We can work on it together."

18

The Hatching House

Christmas Eve. Belsnickel left treasures for the boys. My girls got another doll each that I made myself with extra clothes. I sewed them after the girls went to sleep at night so I saw the moon rise and sometimes dawn appear before I was finished. Comfort came in the stitching.

January 6. I checked on my smoked hams. Andy tells me that Henry T snuck into Keil's smokehouse and took a chunk from the biggest ham that had Brother Keil's name on it. That boy took a risk, indeed. Yet it's good to see that he's not intimidated by power. Still, I appeared appropriately appalled when Andy told me. One mustn't minimize theft, even if it appears as a prank.

The Advent season came and went. Christmas Eve arrived, and we women gave one gift each to one another at our "plotting place." The boys spent the afternoon with us, and later, after we'd walked through a melting snow to my parents' to bring them their gifts, Martin came to my home and sat with us in the parlor while we drank hot apple cider. He said the boys could spend the night if they wished to.

I didn't have the courage to ask if they wanted to, so I told him simply that they would. So they were with me on Christmas morning, and with the sounds of their laughter and even a few arguments between them and their sisters, I could pretend that all was as it should be. I thought of the verse in Hosea about lifting the yoke from our jaws, and God bending down to feed us. I felt fed.

The day went too quickly, and then I knew Martin would be coming for them, so I told the boys to get ready. "Are we going home?" Christian asked.

I thought of Martin's presence as their home now and realized that home for me is where those we love reside. "Yes," I said. I brushed his straight hair out of his eyes. "You're going home."

I walked over to Karl Ruge's hut a few days later. Since the weather kept the school closed from December until spring, he'd gone back to his toll bridge booth. Po bounded up to me as I knocked. I squatted down. "Doesn't your papa let you stay inside in this cold weather?" I asked. An old rug twisted where the dog had been sleeping out of the rain and snow beneath the dripping eaves. Karl opened the door. "Poor little thing. He'll freeze out here."

"He's too warm inside. Down, Po," Karl said as the dog trotted in behind me, a big black spot wagging back and forth on his otherwise white tail. He lay down by the stove as though it belonged to him. I saw a torn-up basket still able to hold kindling, and a once perfectly good shoe, all chewed up.

"Too warm," I said as I bent to scratch the dog's ears. "That's a story."

Karl grinned. "He'd have you believe he's neglected, but he isn't. You can see that. To what do I owe the pleasure of this visit?"

"It's Epiphany. Twelfth Day. And I have one last present to give, to you. I've woven a runner for your table," I said.

"*Ach,* you're not supposed to tell me," he said. He untied the string and rolled it out. "Such bright colors. Purple, red, green. *Ja,* by goodness, this is really good. *Danke.* I have for you a little something too."

He handed me a huge package, so large I had to set it down on the table. I unwrapped the paper, which I'd save for checking my stove heat. Inside the package lay several folds of fabric. Calicos and woolens, cotton blends with wool. All bright colors. Double pinks and cinnamon pinks, chocolate browns, purples known as fugitive dyes that would fade into browns. They were all store-bought material, machine printed, from back East from the looks of them. There must have been fifteen different pieces in all, perhaps five yards of each. One with tiny red stars I recognized as a fabric featured in a dress in *Godey's Lady's Book*. Another was a royal Prussian blue dotted with pink flowers throughout.

"These are…beautiful. I… The girls will love these for dresses."

"*Ja,* maybe for you too." He looked away.

"Oh, look, Karl. This one is one of those 'changeable fabrics.' See, where the light reflects differently against the warp and weft?" It was a rust color but had flecks of gold or yellow. I held it up to the window light, so he could see the shifts in it. "It feels like wool and silk." He nodded. "It must have been terribly expensive, Karl. You shouldn't have." I truly meant it.

"I notice on the ledger sheets that mostly cloth and needles and thread are what you buy, Emma."

"And stoves and chickens and iceboxes." I laughed. "The whole world knows what we do here with those ledger sheets, *ja?*" I wondered if everyone knew that he'd ordered these for me.

"I don't pry," he said. "I happened to see the ledger one time. I looked for my page for the shoemaker to draw my foot onto. I needed new boots. Joe Knight helped me order your cloth from a Portland store."

He was such a good friend. So faithful, so thoughtful in what he offered and gave up, asking nothing in return. "I thank you. And thank Joe Knight too."

Karl busied himself making tea. Always when I spent time with Karl like this, I thought of Christian and our time together. Karl had known me through all my phases. The years with Christian and Karl at Willapa had been good years, and Karl's presence after Christian's death still remained the cornerstone of how we Christian colonists should act to make another's life better than our own. Maybe if I hadn't rushed into the marriage with Jack… I pitched that thought away. "Speaking of Joe Knight, his sister Matilda is much enamored with Jacob Stauffer. You know this?"

"So I hear. And he likewise," Karl said.

"*Ja?* This is *gut.* But why hasn't he asked to marry her? They'd be happy together, don't you think?" I folded the material back up and rewrapped it, keeping my tea set safely to the side. The steam of it smelled of spices.

"He has no way to build a house for her. They'd be far down on the list. And Wilhelm has given his usual remarks that marriage takes one away from the true mission of our work here."

"He didn't think his son Frederick's work would be diminished by *his* marriage," I said. I couldn't keep the sarcasm from my voice.

"It is Wilhelm's way, Emma," he said. "You know this."

Karl's loyalty to Keil was much like my brother Jonathan's. It was a puzzle to me, one I might never solve but, like the labyrinth, might have to walk around.

"What if he and Matilda lived with me until they could get a home built by the colony? Might he ask to marry her, then?"

Karl shrugged. "He might, if he would accept your kindness. Some people are reluctant to accept the goodwill of others, *ja?*"

I felt my face grow warm. "But then we'd have the problem of the ceremony itself. Keil wouldn't officiate."

The dog now sprawled at my feet, and Karl nearly tripped over him. "*Ach,* this dog. You need to take him, Emma. The girls would love him, and he could stay inside all the time, then."

"What if I did take him?" I said. "And in exchange, you officiate at their marriage. Don't you have such credentials?"

"*Ja.* But I would not defy Wilhelm in his own place," he said.

"No. You wouldn't want to do that." I drank my tea. "But what if you officiated at their marriage *away* from here? In Oregon City, let's say. Or even in Portland. Would you consider doing that?"

"In exchange for your taking the dog? *Ja.* This could be arranged."

"Well then. All that's left is for Jacob to ask for Matilda's hand in marriage. Do you want me to push that along? Or will you?"

"I'll talk to him today," he said. "If it means this Po will be one more Epiphany gift I give to you."

———

February 20, 1865, was festive. It felt like spring with warm, balmy air swirling dried grasses as fresh green pushed them away. Green spears of daffodil shot up through the pungent earth. Within a month, they'd give us blooms.

I brought the girls with me, Kate insisting that I let her ride the *Kartoffel* horse that Andy had told her about. "He won't bite anymore, Andy says, and if he does try, I should carry a hot potato with me."

"Andy told you this?" She nodded. "He's a big horse."

"I can do it, Mama." The horses were kept in a long Pennsylvania-style barn, one of the few in the region. Most of the Oregon farmers allowed their stock to graze in the wetness, as it was seldom very cold. But we Germans liked to bring them inside, give them a dry, warm place to know they were appreciated. We saddled the *Kartoffel* horse, and Kate rode beside us in my father's wagon, twisting up the road north from Aurora. We'd placed twists of white bunting on the harness and another on the wagon side to announce that we rode to something joyous.

It had been a while since I'd been to Oregon City. We didn't go as far as those thundering falls but turned off instead onto a wagon road that led through a stand of oak. I'd decided against asking for Andy and Christian to attend, fearing Keil might object. I was pretty certain Martin wouldn't be there, because Keil had not sanctioned the marriage.

But when I saw John and BW's wagon parked by the Knights' home, north of Aurora on Baker Prairie, I wished I had asked for the boys. I said it out loud to my sister.

"BW came because she was a part of the plan," Kitty said. "She wouldn't have missed the results of your house hatching."

"Hatching at my house? That sounds ominous," I said.

Kitty laughed. "Well, isn't that what you do there? I mean, we all do it."

"I guess I hadn't thought of it as hatching, which sounds sinister to me, as though it wasn't natural."

"But hatching is natural, Emma. Look at your chickens. If they didn't hatch, we wouldn't have chicken soup eventually. Or a wedding cake."

"Still, I like to think I was a part of something Providential."

"Wouldn't we all?" Kitty said. "Sorting what's ours and what isn't, there's the challenge. If you remember, you were always kindling your own—"

"I remember," I said.

I was as proud as if Matilda were my own daughter. Fortunately my chickens were laying, since the cake I agreed to provide required fifteen big eggs. Most of them were blue. I used saleratus to add the rise, but with butter and flour and seeded raisins and ground mace and nearly a pint of molasses, and of course, ground cinnamon and cloves to improve everyone's digestion, I ended up with four rounds. Layered between each, I spread a buttery frosting. I cut a small piece of the cloth Karl gave me to make a tiny quilt that I constructed a little frame for. It might have fit in a doll's house, and I told Matilda she could give it to her first girl to play with one day, but it gave a splash of color to the cake top, and it matched Matilda's finely tailored dress.

I'd asked Matilda to go through the material that Karl had given me to choose a fabric for her wedding dress. She picked a printed plaid in greens and reds, the perfect festive colors. The entire Sunday afternoon crowd stitched on that dress. Maybe I should say we hatched it.

It wouldn't have taken much to bring a larger smile to Matilda's face, but on her wedding day, Kitty wove fresh holly in Matilda's hair, and she looked as young as Christine.

"I know I owe this to you," she said as we stood in her parents' bedroom. "Jacob never would have asked me to marry him if you hadn't arranged for Karl to officiate."

"It wasn't me," I said. "Oh, I might have pushed it along, but happiness is from God, and this is too, I'm sure of it."

"A place to live too, though. You've given us that."

"Passing along a gift I was given and hoping to make your lives better than my own. It's the Diamond Rule, remember? Besides, with three other women, two young girls, and one dog he'll share space with, I suspect Jacob will make some noise about moving up on that list for a house. Or maybe even start one of his own before long. But I am pleased to be able to make my home yours. And I thank you for accepting the offer. As Karl once told me, 'You give to others when you let them give to you.' "

Several of the Schuele family attended. Both Almira and Christine said they'd stay home and look after the dog. Of course, all the Knights were there, and the Stauffers arrived from Willapa. They talked of moving to Aurora later since Jacob was planning to remain.

The surprise was that Chris Wolff officiated instead of Karl.

"He was a Lutheran minister in Marietta, Ohio, before he joined with Keil," Karl told me. "And he kept many of the Lutheran tenets while he led the faithful back in Bethel. It's a good thing to do for Jacob and Matilda."

"Doctor Wolff had no problem doing this?" I asked.

"He has never found celibacy to be a critical feature of the Christian faith," Karl said. "He may have had words with Wilhelm over it, but I doubt it. He believes securely in communal ways, in sharing our wealth with one another so no one is in need. He was in charge of marriages and funerals back in Bethel. Besides, the marriage is here on Baker Prairie. What business is it of Keil's, then?"

I raised an eyebrow at Karl's last comment, for it was the testiest thing I'd ever heard him say of Keil.

We had a grand day, and while I was a little weepy remembering the joy of my own wedding day long ago, I didn't stay back there in my mind. Instead, I brought Christian into my present thoughts, reminding him that it wouldn't be long before our sons and daughter would be speaking such marriage vows. On the way home, we tied Kate's horse to the back of the wagon, and Kate rode with us, falling asleep in my lap. I brushed at her hair. *I'll have you in my home for a few more years,* I thought. My mother and sisters rode with us, and I decided we all needed festive days like this, to mix memory with promise. How sad it was that we didn't have more weddings to attend.

It wasn't hatching, I decided, as I carried Kate and then my Ida into the house and handed them into Almira's arms. What we'd done in getting Matilda and Jacob married was to be servants. Chris Wolff saw this marriage as a good thing or he wouldn't have officiated, and Karl had made it happen (so I now had the dog). These were good people, and surely a marriage between them could bring nothing but praise and joy to the faithful. Yes, things could go wrong and often did, but having a partner to walk with through them was a gift indeed.

———

We gave the newly married the south room, the one over the parlor, and Kitty, Christine, and Almira assumed one end of the other upstairs bedroom, with the girls sharing a bed at the other end with me. It took some adjusting. There was now a dog to accommodate as well, and we had our moments. One day, Opal followed Kate, Ida, and Po into the house and jumped up onto the kitchen table, dropping what looked like raisins but weren't. That day we made new rules of who managed the door when animals were about. I asked Jacob if he might convert our back kitchen door into one that could be open at the top and remain closed at the bottom, so we could get fresh air in while keeping animals out. Opal could plop her hooves and head up to look in, but I doubted she'd make the leap over the door to the inside. He said he could, and did.

I always attended the twice-monthly service at the Keil house, in part because I knew that the boys would be there, sitting across the room from me on the men's side. An ache always preceded my seeing their heads come through the door, but it eased as I listened to the music, and my spirits would lift if I caught Christian's eye and he smiled and waved at me, or if Andy nodded to me before I nodded first.

On the off Sundays, the boys came to my home and played with their sisters and the other children who might have come with their mothers that day.

Kitty attended the Keil church with me, but the others often didn't. It wasn't a requirement that people attend the worship at the Keils', at least not a requirement in order to remain living at my house. I should not have been surprised, then, when at a Sunday afternoon gathering in my parlor—on an off Sunday when Keil did not preach—Louisa and Helena arrived too.

I could hardly turn them away, but their presence interrupted the spontaneity of our gathering, as had also happened the day that Barbara and BW had attended. Any change in a routine causes some readjustment. Hadn't we had less spontaneity the first few times that Christine had joined us? And Martha Miller came sometimes too, a quiet, kind girl. Our little grouping felt safe; Louisa and Helena's presence menaced that safety a bit.

"We thought we should have more time with you," Helena said. "We see so little of you, Emma."

"I see you every other Sunday," I said.

"Such interesting things that affect the colony have arisen from your home, Sister Emma." She'd frowned when we first brought out Barbara's Friendship quilt, but when we explained that it would be a gift given away charitably, "as our Lord once healed on the Sabbath," Helena nodded and lifted her needle from her own chatelaine.

"Not all that much happens when we meet here," I sighed. "My boys don't live here anymore, but then you knew that before I did. Little occurs in Aurora without everyone's soon knowing. So there are no secrets, not really."

"*Ja,* but they do well with Martin, don't you think?"

"They wouldn't be there if I didn't think it was a good place for them," I said.

"Well, of course they wouldn't be," Louisa said. "It's a nice arrangement that works out well for everyone. My husband wouldn't have approved it otherwise."

Approved it? He engineered it. These were thoughts I chose not to say. Louisa continued. "Both Martin and, one day, Andy will make fine doctors, and the colony needs that. It's good you understand that, Emma. My boy August has trained himself well in herbs and all too. But he's back there in Bethel. I don't get to see him." She took a deep breath.

I didn't point out that August was a grown man she was missing, while I had young sons who didn't live with me.

"Besides," Helena said, "we wanted to see those cabinets Jacob Stauffer made. I was also hoping you'd returned to your painting, Emma. It was such a comfort to you when you first arrived in Aurora."

"It was my voice then," I said, "when I didn't have one. Now I do feel heard more, even if I don't get my way."

"*Ja,* submission means not always getting our own way," Helena said.

I wasn't ready to say I was submissive, but her definition was one I'd consider.

"Andy will be scientifically trained when he goes to school," Kitty said. "Not that herbs are not healing, but August didn't really have 'the touch.' Remember, we lived in Bethel after you came west. August, well, I don't mean to be critical."

"He didn't? He followed his father everywhere, held the horses for him when he had to tend to an ill person." Louisa sounded defensive.

"Maybe he held horses well," Kitty said.

I wondered what might have gone on back in Bethel, where August Keil had been sent and in the process escaped the smallpox deaths of his brothers and sisters. My parents, too, had found disruption in the arrival of August. But they'd found more dissension with Andrew Giesy, from what I'd gleaned in their conversations.

"Andy will make a good doctor, Emma," Helena said. "He's from our Giesy line. And isn't it nice that the colony will pay?"

The colony pays, but there is always a price.

"And how long do you plan to remain with us, Mistress Raymond?" Helena asked then.

Almira had been quietly stitching, not saying a word, so a question directed to her startled us all. She stared at Helena, who continued, "I mean no disrespect. I'm only making conversation. It must get crowded here. And you've added another."

Christine had a frightened-deer look on her face.

"Jacob Stauffer's been an easy addition," I said. "He puts the dog out at night if need be and has built shelves in the bedroom. They're up above us even now," I said and pointed to the room over the parlor.

"You let the dog stay in the house?" Helena said.

"How heavenly," Louisa said, looking upward to where Jacob and Matilda's footsteps could be heard above us.

"It may not be," Kitty said. "They have the girls up there across the hall, and one of the shelves in their room is storage for Kate's and Ida's stockings and leavings dolls. They rarely get any time alone with the girls' knocking on their door."

"They'll stay as long as they need to," I said. "Almira can remain as long as she likes too. You're of help to all of us here"—I turned to acknowledge that she sat in the room with us—"and when the girls are in school, you intend to add your hands to the work at the tannery, isn't that right?"

"If they'll have me with these knuckles," Almira said. "Though they're doing much better with that salve you gave me, Emma. Otherwise I'll find other work."

"Well, it's good that you and Christine and the new Stauffers have a place to live, with so many other worthy people waiting on houses. You didn't have to wait for long, Emma. Maybe the Stauffers won't have to either," Helena said.

"How fortunate I am, then, to be able to give rooms in this one so generously provided by the colony."

"How fortunate you are."

Everyone smiled sweetly. Almira rose to bring in tea. Kitty looked bewildered, and Christine exhaled. The afternoon proceeded civilly, and I discovered that a jibe gracefully acknowledged frames a picture of success.

———

Spring arrived with a blush of warm air that moved the scented blossoms from their limbs. In March, Mr. Lincoln was reinaugurated in Washington DC, and we hoped his reelection would bring the war to a close. New beginnings occurred for everyone, and we prayed we wouldn't have to worry over any more of our Oregon boys going off to fight.

The bustle of spring planting, of cleaning and sweeping mud from our rugs and doorsteps kept each of us occupied. With so many women living under one roof, the rhythm of our bodies could be seen by the string of washed rags stained by our blood hanging side by side on the line, almost exactly the same days of each month. Jacob took all of this in stride, and we often heard him and Matilda laughing behind their closed door. They didn't seem to mind staying on with us, but they made themselves scarce when the women gathered for those Sabbath afternoons, sharing laughter and pleasantries and speaking prayers for the war's end.

Sometimes Matilda still joined in the stitching. She worked on a "lifelong project," as she called it. The quilt cover she stitched was composed of blocks of yellow diamonds with vibrant dark blue centers sewn onto a backing of angry ocean blue. She'd made a bright red border around them all and called it her Sunflower quilt. The boldness, repetition, and form were things I'd never seen before. It wasn't pieced of leftover material either. Jacob wasn't earning enough money outside the colony to purchase so much fabric of single colors like that. Perhaps her father bought the cloth.

Matilda wanted to quilt it herself too. She placed fifteen stitches per inch, tiny as dots. The quilted pattern stitched into the dark blue formed an intriguing shape. When I looked closely, I could see it was a sand dollar, reminiscent of life along Willapa Bay. The patterns, material choice, and her unique quilting style all spoke of her independence, her history, her love of beauty and life. We women found our voices in our textiles.

I was in my thirties now, feeling the need to do something significant with my life, a lifelong project of my own. I knew a great many women who had died before they turned forty, not of accidents but of what was wearing out. I said as much to what I now called our house church. Helena and Louisa were there that day, but it was a Saturday, so mending was allowed, not just stitching on a quilt for someone else.

"Where do you learn such things?" Helena asked Matilda. "I'll be fifty this December, and I don't worry about doing something grand with my life. Living is enough."

"But it is scriptural, isn't it, Helena? To seek and pursue?" I asked.

"A deeper faith, yes. But not some wild adventure. Heaven knows what that might entail with you, Emma."

We all laughed, and Helena looked startled, as though she hadn't expected to say anything funny.

"It probably does look like I've done more than my share of unusual things. And, now that you say it, those actions have improved my faith. I hated water and river crossings, and I ended up twice living by a river. When we try something we think we can't do, we have to trust more in someone larger than ourselves. More in one another too. Approaching the end of what might be my final decade spurs me on."

"Having children is adventurous," Louisa said. "That should be enough to give a woman pause and deepen her faith. Don't you agree, Almira?"

Almira nodded agreement. "But it's also tedious and can drain a woman's faith. 'Is this all I'm meant to do?' I asked myself that at times, with a broom in my hand."

"Tedious?" This from Matilda, who looked up from her work.

"Washing, mending, sewing, cooking. I know it's important work, but I have this other part of me, as though I had two doors: one open to service and one open to my heart," Almira said. "Tedium gets in the way of both!"

"Those second doors don't get pushed open very often," I said. "I miss adventure. I miss...affection. A son's hug, for example."

Louisa added, "Instead of a son breaking his mother's dishes on the trail before her very eyes. Poor Catherine Wolfer." We all shook our heads in sympathy.

"Though just learning something new, like how to stitch a different quilt block, helps," I said. "Or considering those Greek nouns that Brother Wolff talks about in the evening class. Who knew that 'hearth' was a word that gave birth to the English word 'focus'? That gives what we women do in our kitchens at the fire a certain weight, doesn't it? Warmth and passion for a life."

"Affection only gets a girl into trouble," Helena pronounced. "She has to make decisions she wishes she didn't have to make."

I kept my eyes from seeking Christine's, but Kitty said, "You can only say that if you've been romanced. I haven't, so I guess I'd like to know that for myself. That would be a door I'd like opened. A real adventure."

"Without getting into trouble," Louisa warned, her scissors raised toward Kitty.

"What kind of adventure did you have in mind, Emma?" This from Almira.

"I remember you climbed to the top of the mill in Willapa, for the view. Or so I heard," Helena said.

"This summer, I think we should…climb something higher. Mount Hood." That just came to me, like my thoughts used to, when saying them out loud was the first time I heard them myself.

"Climb Mount Hood?" Christine shriveled into the bench pillow she sat on. Her skirts billowed out around her. "The height…"

"You're so daring, Emma," Martha Miller noted. "I wish I had an ounce of that in me."

"We'd have to find out about it," I said. "Talk to someone who has done it. Maybe not go all the way to the top. We don't want to be foolish."

"I should hope not. It's eleven thousand feet high," Helena said. "It's not feasible for a woman to do."

"It would be formidable," Almira said. She looked at her hands.

"I'm not sure I could hang on to…whatever it is people must hang on to, to keep themselves safe."

"One of us might die there," Martha said.

"If it's Emma, we'll put on her headstone, 'I didn't plan for this,'" Kitty said, and I nudged her with my elbow but smiled.

"Planning is half the fun of it. Few people have climbed that mountain, or so Karl told me. No woman that I know of," I said. "Imagine the view from there!"

"Imagine the snow," Kitty said.

"It's a good three days' ride to the base, and then it would take a day or more to climb it. You'd have to bring food," Helena said. "You'd have to have animals and people to look after them while you went on this whim. You know nothing of mountain climbing. I'm Swiss, Emma. I know about mountains." Helena was adamant. "It would be a foolish, foolish thing for you to do. You have children to think of. *Ach!* Don't spur these younger women to go along with such nonsense. Louisa is right. Being a mother, or for that matter being a woman, is adventure enough."

She took the heat from my pan. "It was an idea," I said. "Something we could all work on together that had some passion in it. Something…invigorating."

"Well, think of another," Helena said. She tugged on her scissors ribbon.

"The men have their band they get to go around the country and play with. The girls' chorus doesn't even get to sing away from Aurora," Kitty complained. She brightened. "Maybe we should push for a joined boys' and girls' chorus."

"Talk to Chris Wolff before you engage in something like that," Louisa said.

"Yes, he might broach the subject with Brother Keil, so you won't need to," Almira said.

"That could be dangerous," Louisa said.

I laughed, and she looked startled but then smiled.

"But at least not life threatening, Sister Louisa," I said.

The afternoon faded with grace. A family gathering, that's what it was. Family, a word that Chris Wolff said came from the Latin *famulus,* meaning "servant." We were sisters, serving one another, serving our families.

Then an interruption as we stitched. "You didn't even knock," Martha Miller said to Mr. Ehlen's rush through the door. She rarely challenged anyone, let alone an elder like Mr. Ehlen.

"Mr. Lincoln's been assassinated," he said, his loose arm flinging wildly as he turned to catch each of our eyes. "Friday last, at Ford Theatre. Telegraph just came through."

A universal gasp stilled the room. We sat with hands across our mouths to keep from screaming.

"Tragic," Almira said at last. "How very, very tragic."

"I'm going home," Louisa said. She gathered up her things, followed by Helena.

Kate waved good-bye at her and asked, "What's wrong, Mama? Who was Mr. Lincoln?"

"He was our president," I told Kate. "And someone took his life."

"What did they do with it?" Ida asked. I pulled her to me.

"Like Papa?" Kate said.

"Like Papa, yes," I said. I felt tears begin, for the senselessness of such a loss, for the uncertainty flooding in that assassin's wake.

"We will lower the flag to half staff," Mr. Ehlen said. Matilda and Jacob stood at the stairwell, having descended at the sound of Mr. Ehlen's voice. "And *Herr* Keil wishes us to gather at his house. The band will play. We will pray, *ja?*"

"I'll tell others," Mr. Ehlen said, swinging that useless arm as he headed out. "At times like this we need to gather close."

The rest of us stayed for a time, bowed our heads in silence, each lost to our thoughts, speaking our prayers. I could hear Kitty crying softly; others too. Then Kate began a prayer for the president's family, for us, for "all people including the man who is making everyone cry." I wished now, more than ever, that the church were finished, but it wasn't. Not yet. So many distractions. I prayed at that moment for my children, that their lives would be full and long. I prayed for Jacob and Matilda, that their marriage would be rich and blessed with children. I prayed Kate's prayer and for myself, that I'd be found worthy as I worked to do the everyday things that kept a family whole, that I'd listen to that voice. I prayed I'd have the courage to let myself be led.

19

Two Doors

That fall of 1865, Captain John Vogt brought in eleven wagons, all pulled by big Missouri mules. Nearly one hundred additional Bethelites increased our population and the demands on our resources. They'd left Missouri shortly after the president's assassination, uncertain about what would happen now in this divided country. The co-conspirators had been tried and hanged in July while the Bethelites traveled west, but their deaths didn't mean that grief was now relieved. I wondered what these latest Bethelites thought when they arrived and found themselves not in a thriving village but bunked down with other families still awaiting housing.

Sometimes the wait for houses here in Keil's town gave me a kind of warped satisfaction. After all, it was for lack of housing in Willapa that first winter that Keil had separated the colony. He couldn't believe we had so few homes prepared for the arrival of two hundred fifty people. Yet there'd been people living in Aurora now for ten years, and out of the nearly six hundred people who now claimed Aurora as their home, only half had single homes to live in. I never said that out loud to anyone, but I felt some vindication when I heard the mumblings of both newcomers and old-timers about what they found once they left Bethel. Aurora was not yet anyone's *Heimat*, that special place of belonging, that I could see.

The apothecary shop, or pharmacy, was nearly complete though, and Martin moved into it with my sons about the time the colony band and many others headed for the state fair that fall. Martin didn't play in the band, but he was busy with his studies, and I asked if the boys might travel with us. I was pleasantly surprised when he said they could. The bile in my stomach had begun to lessen each time I asked for permission to have time with my own sons. We were doing this together, after all, not because I was a failure as a mother, but because it was the best for my sons. Karl would remind me that I had given my heart to my sons, and I did what I did in love for them. "Such love will be rewarded," he said. It was a belief I held on to.

I took the girls with me to the fair that year and convinced my sister Christine that she should come as well. "You can help cook, but you can also enjoy yourself. You work so hard and such long hours, I worry over you," I told her.

"Penance," she'd said and smiled, making her round face open up in warmth like the sun.

"Nonsense. It's time you did what young women do, enjoy themselves."

We began planning yet again for the fair, as much an announcement of seasonal change as the vine maple turning red. Almira sounded enthusiastic at first but then decided she wouldn't join us. She worried about old memories in Salem, she said. While I assured her that time scrubs away much of the edge of sharp memories, she didn't believe it. She'd become quiet of late, and sleeping more, as when she'd first come to stay with us. She didn't seem interested in talking about why. "I'll stay with Po," she said. "Keep him from chewing Opal's ears into shredded meat." She scratched the dog's head. "That's all right, isn't it? That I stay here alone in your home, without you here?"

"Matilda and Jacob are here, and besides, it is your home too. You contribute to the colony," I said.

"I've never officially joined."

"I'm not sure how one 'officially joins,' " I said.

Kitty expressed readiness to pack up for the fair, but she'd been asked to remain behind, to help cook for the bachelors and newcomers at the Keil house. So Christine and my children and Jonathan filled the Wagner wagon. I looked forward to seeing Brita and having time with my children, but I wondered if I was doing Almira a disservice by leaving her behind.

The band was a huge success at the fair. This second year of the new hall crystallized their prominence. There were stories that the governor would invite them to play for a holiday ball, or that they'd be invited to do a tour by someone named Ben Holladay, who was interested in railroad expansion. I suspected our Keil had been having words with him.

I confess to a bit of nostalgia as I walked around the exhibits in the Homemaking and Household Arts tents. There was that Nancy Thornton's name again, signed right on her paintings. She gave art lessons in Oregon City, or once had. The address on her exhibitor's card attached to the landscape read Salem. If it was too far to travel for a class at the university, it would be too far to travel for a private class too. I'd never even taken myself off that Wallamet class list, so even if I did find a way to join, they might not trust that I'd follow through in the future. I didn't trust me either.

Looking into the paintings was a gift I gave myself. A scene of an Indian encampment near a shoreline brought back good memories of a day when Christian and Andy and Kate and I had camped at the Bay. I stopped before a portrait of a woman spinning. She wore a dark green dress, no apron, as though the work she did was for another purpose than just everyday tedium. Window light illuminated her concentrated face. Her hands had large knuckles not unlike Almira's. She was beautiful. The painting was beautiful in its simplicity. I felt my eyes tear up that such a humble subject could make me feel prayerful in the midst of a festive fair.

"You paint like that, Mama," Kate said. I softly brushed at her hair, took in her words as a compliment.

Andy lagged behind as we walked through the exhibits, and at one point he asked if he could go to the horse barns instead.

"Looking at art is good for a future medical person," I told him.

"Why?"

I wasn't sure how to answer. Keil didn't seem to appreciate art; I didn't know if Martin did. "Because healing is knowledge and science wrapped up in experience and heart," I said. "Art helps us reach deeper into the heart, and we experience things we otherwise never could. It tells us something about people, about what they draw on to help a physician heal them. A doctor and patient must work together. There's artistry in that."

He grunted, but I thought he paid more attention to the artists' works.

Most of those exhibiting were women. Louisa had entered her *Fraktur* lettering. I respected the time she'd taken to make the letterings, but even more I admired her willingness to exhibit them and have them judged each year. They'd gotten only a white ribbon, but somehow just seeing them made Louisa stand higher in my eyes. At least she had entered her work. It was an art. Some might call it frivolous, but I could see the careful strokes of her brush, and she must have mixed her own paints. Perhaps she even cut and smoothed the boards she painted on. I suspected that her work took as much time and careful attention as making a sampler, and there were plenty of those on display. Perhaps the work comforted her in her losses. I thought I'd ask her. It might be the reason she urged me to keep painting, a gift she wanted to give me.

Near the exit, a painting of two doors caught my eye. One was a lavish portal with gold-embossed curlicues and what looked like emerald stones inlaid. A rich woman's door. The other was equally intriguing for its spare and splendid nature. No embossing, just fine-grained wood painted white, promising the calm of simplicity behind it. I stood there a long time. The artist couldn't know that I would see it and go to my own inner world of doorways to open, yet she'd conducted my experience, the way Henry C conducted listening experiences for his audiences of the Aurora Band. Music, stories, art, even our quilts and samplers were all products that Keil might deem less important than the compounding of medicines for healing. But like those medicines, the artists' imaginations emerged from the backwaters of their spirits into the stream that the viewer brought to that place, and there they merged. Two experiences. One for the artist and one for the viewer. Both of us receiving something quite grand.

I remembered what Almira had said in our discussion at the house church on the day of Mr. Lincoln's death. We'd talked about two doors: one for service and one for seeking deeper meaning for ourselves as women. We felt completed taking care of others, our children and families, even members of the larger communal family. And yet the demands of others sometimes pushed aside our own need to be creative in more personal ways. Perhaps that was why the quilting time offered so much. It let us open both doors at once. Even Almira, who didn't quilt, found ways to open both doors. She looked after others but was revived when she walked her "lab-rinse" path.

I continued meandering through the exhibit hall, answering questions raised by my children. But I couldn't keep the idea of the blend of richness and simplicity from my thoughts. Simple contentment followed our house church gatherings where we read Scripture, talked with one another of its meaning while we had our hands on fabric. But I always felt as rich as a queen then too. Joy could so easily disappear from our efforts, be as temporary as an aroma. A woman had to nurture what was behind both doors to truly feel whole. And only she can decide which door to devote time to.

It was a thought I'd share with Almira when I returned.

———

Music lightened our steps at this first fair after the end of the war. Christine enjoyed the dancing, once Kitty and I pushed her to it. "I had partners waiting," she said. Her round face glowed with perspiration, her cheeks as pink as watermelon. "One said he didn't think so large a woman could be so light upon her feet. Should I take that as a compliment? Or not?" She laughed.

"We women take good words wherever we can get them," I said. "When I saw Adam Knight after not seeing him for years, he told me, 'You weather well, Sister Emma.' He compared me to a good leather saddle, but I decided to not take offense where none was intended."

"I haven't danced since we came to Aurora," she said. "And not much before that either. It's been lovely. Thank you for making me come."

"You've earned your dancing shoes," I said. "We'd best get back to preparing the sausages. When the horse races finish, we'll have a crowd of hungry people making their demands."

"Like at the *gross Haus*," she said and laughed.

It was good to see her out with young people and for her to realize that her smile and willingness to move to music brought her young men interested in dancing with her. Several came by to talk later, and I heard a giggle from her that was new to me. She was a woman noticed, and it brought both high color and delight to her being.

Andy and Christian were accustomed to a regular routine, I could tell. Christian especially whined when the evening meal dragged on because we were serving others from the tent. "He goes to bed early," Andy told me. Andy spent most of his time in the science exhibits or walking the barns, talking to the men who cared for the animals. He said they had lots of ideas for mending broken limbs or sore muscles, ideas he thought Martin might find interesting. Jonathan was off talking business somewhere, and some others from the colony were selling food too, though most brought enough only for themselves. Several had something exhibited or were related to the musicians. Despite that, we were heavily outnumbered, we German Americans, and I became conscious of my still-stumbling English when people from outside our colony talked with me.

That night I bundled down with my children. The stars, like silver candles on black silk, formed a canopy overhead. I heard Christine's laughter in the distance. She had not yet joined us in the wagon. And while the cool evening air threatened to bring me a headache, I talked it away. "I will think myself happy," I said and thought it fortunate that Christine was doing the same.

In the morning I looked for Christine in the quilts beside me. I hadn't been awake when she joined us. She wasn't there, and I assumed she'd gotten up early to begin fixing bacon and eggs for the many hungry customers. I needed to remind her that she didn't always have to be the first one up. Jonathan still slept, as did the boys. I sat up, stretched, and looked around. I didn't smell bacon cooking. The fairgrounds were as still as a cemetery. I couldn't see Christine anywhere.

Discomfort accompanied me to the wash tent where I carried my bucket. I splashed water on my face, considering what to do. Christine was a grown woman, an adult. She could certainly take care of herself. If I were Christine, I'd resent intrusion and the assumption that something might be amiss.

Still, she was my sister. When she rushed into the wash tent with her hair pulled loose from its usual swirl of braids around her head, I said nothing except, "Good morning," and put aside that niggling of anxiety that rose there when she answered, "*Ja,* the very best."

Later that day I told the children, "Let's see if we can find Brita." She hadn't appeared anywhere at the fair. Andy and Christian walked with their sisters and me to the livery where we'd last seen her. The Durbin brothers said they hadn't heard from her. I wondered if she'd perhaps left the area completely. Maybe she'd gone to the gold fields near Canyon City, east of here, to make her fortune. I issued yet another letter to general delivery. Andy expressed equal disappointment when we couldn't locate Charles or Pearl or Stanley.

"They moved away," Christian said as we walked back.

"We're the ones who moved, silly," Andy said.

"As it happens, you're both right," I told them. "They moved to Salem, and you boys moved to Martin's. Changes like that happen all the time. But they'll find us in Aurora if they need to."

"You moved too, Mama. To that house. Where you wash the clothes and feed the dog and pick up eggs."

That house. He doesn't call it a home. "That house," I said. "That's right. There are people who have a fine roof over their heads at my home too."

"You're a two-door, Mama," Christian said. "That's what Henry says."

"And what do you suppose he means by my being 'two-door'?" The band instructor's son had quite a lip for quips.

"One for all your friends to come in, and one for your boys to go out."

The words stung.

"There'll always be a place for you there," I said. "Your going out is only from the house, not from my heart."

"But we're the only boys who don't live with our mother," he said.

"*Ja*, well, that's not your fault," I said. "You've done nothing wrong."

"Then why can't we come home to that house?" Christian asked.

I suppose it was time I told a story they might be able to live with. I chose my words. I could give him a door with longing behind it, or one that moved him toward satisfaction, a way to be a good steward of his disappointments. "When your papa died, your uncles thought it best that one of them should stand in for him, take his place to be your papa, to look after you. I didn't think we needed anyone until later, and then I chose one of Papa's cousins instead. Jack."

"Oh, Jack."

"My choice wasn't so good, *ja*, even though I meant the best. Sometimes one's best isn't. So we came here, but still your uncles and others thought it best that you boys live with a man to guide you. When we stayed at Keils', there were lots of men to guide. Then I got that house and they chose Martin, and he's a good man and I agreed. You'll go on to school when you're older. And someday you might be the uncle who helps your sister's children or someone else's child. It's a way of family passing goodness on. Does that make sense?"

"*Ja*. I wish Martin made cinnamon rolls like yours. Then I wouldn't miss that house so much."

"I'll bring them to you," I said, holding him close. "It's the least I can do."

———

In the spring of 1866, Brother Keil announced that several young men would be asked to preach in his stead. He said this at a Sabbath service and gave names. Several were newer arrivals, men who'd come the previous year. John Giesy shifted in his seat with the announcement, but I thought Chris Wolff, Dr. Wolff as many called him, looked pleased. Karl Ruge did too.

The winter months following the fair had been filled with "consternation," as my brother called it. He claimed people were distressed with Keil because he devoted as many resources to the hotel building as to the church, and because few houses had been constructed in the six months since the last group from Bethel had arrived.

Jonathan was a great defender of Keil, telling me, as he ate bacon and eggs at my house, that Keil had authorized the building of Jonathan's house at the north edge of the village. Jonathan complained that people could do more for themselves and not put so much pressure on Dr. Keil to do it for them. "People would rather use their tongues to complain," he told me, "than their hands to take action. The apostle Paul said all parts of our bodies must work together, each in their own unique way, but some of these colonists would prefer to push us all into one single way of doing something."

"Keil did set it up like that," I said. "He wanted to make all the decisions, so he does have to live with the consequences."

"For good reasons, he made these decisions!" Jonathan's face grew red. He'd put on much weight of late, and now he started to gasp.

I got him a glass of water and didn't pursue the subject further. But obviously, others had been expressing their opinions that we needed more leaders, that we needed to expand the work. Those conversations might have been heard by Brother Keil, as he'd announced the change soon after the new arrivals.

At our house church gathering that afternoon, neither Louisa nor Helena attended. The rest of the regulars were there, except for Jacob, who had begun work on a log home. The entire Stauffer family, including Jacob and Matilda, would move into this log home before long. On this house church day, Jacob had ridden out to check on progress.

We opened our gatherings with a reading. Matilda chose a verse of Scripture, and I'd suggested that we talk about where we saw God in such a verse. We'd had such conversations before, and even when

Louisa or Helena came, they didn't seem offended by our exploring how mere women might see God in Scripture. After all, we weren't arguing doctrine, just speaking of our lives. Then one day Martha added that we ought to talk about how we saw God *within* our lives, not only in the verse. That had caused some to shift uneasily beneath their hoops. Kitty rose to get us all more tea. Almira coughed until she had to leave. But then I said what I thought. The verse happened to be about the tax collector Zacchaeus.

I said, "To me, the verse says that even the most ostracized person on the edge could find a place within the love of God. I've seen that for myself, when I felt I needed to leave Willapa. And the verse says, too, that I had the choice to accept the love and healing salve that were offered, but then I needed to do something with it, act outwardly to show that I had been truly changed. For me, that's been the hardest part."

The room had grown quiet. No one else said anything until Almira asked, "But don't you think being brought into something good when one has been at the edge, doesn't that mean one will not make decisions that put one back out at the edge again? I mean, once having chosen to receive, if we make a mistake, it must be because we weren't really healed…right?"

Martha expressed her view. Matilda too. Christine stayed silent. She was with us that day. Since the fair, she'd often been absent on these afternoons. I didn't ask where she'd gone. But it was Kitty who offered comfort.

"That scripture describes grace, Almira. It says we get to start over. We get to be restored. In between, we offer that same grace to others, and that's a way to show that we've been changed. But it doesn't mean we won't have to start again. We have a way back, so we don't have to stay at the outside."

"We start over and over, like in the puzzle path," Kate said. I smiled at her. *She is growing in wisdom, my daughter.*

"I guess it has its one way in and one way out, and we have to keep moving. So yes, maybe that's so, Kate," Kitty said. Kate beamed.

———

On the following Sabbath, our Scripture verse was from First Timothy, the second chapter, in which all were asked to pray for all men, but especially kings and those in authority, so that there might be peace, and the word of God could be more easily spread.

"It means that when people are at war," BW said, "that it's difficult to spread the love of God to others. Others see only the warring side, and with people of faith fighting on both sides, how can others know the true story?"

"I think it means we have to submit to those in authority. And pray for them," Almira said.

"I didn't see anything about submission," Matilda said. "Jacob and I don't think of our marriage as his having 'authority' over me, nor my trying to get it over him. We're together on things. Most of the time. We talk things out until we are. I think that's what it means."

We stitched for a time in silence, then Matilda spoke again. "I wish we'd have our own house, instead of having his whole family and brothers and sisters live there, but none of them are married. Jacob's the first. It's the charitable thing to do, all live together."

"Who will have authority with all those women living there?" Kitty said. "Have you thought about that?"

"We'll all pray for you," Martha said, "with that many women in one house."

"I'll need it," she said, and we laughed.

"What did you think of Brother Keil's announcement last week?" I asked. "I wonder if this scripture says anything about that?"

"I found it very strange," Kitty said.

Christine said nothing.

Almira, who rarely went with us, had attended that morning. "Are the sermons tiring him? Maybe that's why he's asked others to preach for him. I know my husband worked very hard on his messages each week, to make them faithful to Scripture."

"Too bad your husband didn't *live* faithful to Scripture," Kitty said.

I saw Almira flinch. It might be all right to criticize a family member ourselves, but hearing anyone else do it could be wounding, indeed.

"It wasn't all him," Almira defended. "That girl. And I suppose me. I never did stand up to him the way that girl did. He liked her obstinacy. He never struck her. Anyway, he worked on his sermons. They tired him. That's all I was saying."

"It's a surprise that Keil would allow anyone besides John or Karl to preach. It sounded like even Dr. Wolff might preach sometime," Martha said. She had a chipped tooth that made some of her words sing.

"Maybe some of the younger men will be groomed as new leaders," Kitty said. Her crooked pinky finger stuck out as she spoke with her hand in the air. "Maybe they'll need wives."

"I like listening to Chris Wolff," I said. "He reads Shakespeare and Cicero and classic books that I hope he's introducing our children to in school."

"They're pushing for articles of agreement," Christine said. Her voice was so soft, I had to ask her to repeat what she'd said. Sometimes the loom I'd had Jacob set up in the parlor made a lot of noise. I'd been weaving a blue-dyed yarn made from boiling galls, the pockets of insects that formed on the stems of ragweed. It wasn't Prussian blue, but it was pretty. And we'd give the rug away to Matilda and Jacob when they moved into their house, so we all felt we weren't really working on the Sabbath, we were serving.

"Agreeing about what?" I asked.

She shrugged. "That's all I know for certain. There are snippets of conversations that I hear over the dinner talk. They're more open on the work sites, in complaining about who has gotten what property or how quickly something has occurred. The younger men seem impatient. The hotel will be finished before the church, from the looks of it. Some are excited about the railroad being courted, and others, well, they think it will mean the downfall of our community. The younger men, they want new life. A 'western life,' they call it, where they're free to be independent."

"But they fear risking the wrath of Keil or of doing something on their own and failing," Matilda said. I looked at her. "Jacob tells me. That's why he's building our log home. We'd never get a lumber home. You're very fortunate, Emma."

"Yes, I am," I said. "What would the articles of agreement say? About how money is distributed, or who gets the land? About marriages or not?"

"All of that. And that he'll have a council, a group who will advise him about issues, and he agrees to listen to them. More men in authority, maybe. So decisions can get made, even when Keil is in one of his low moods."

"Goodness. Papa might rejoin if that happens," Kitty said. "Back in Bethel, Andrew Giesy didn't listen. That's what Papa said, anyway. Who knew who was really in authority? Keil was out here, but his son was back there claiming he carried his father's staff. And Andrew made decisions. Many of you were at Willapa... It was very confusing."

"And I suspect not very many new people found a path to our Christian way either, with all that uncertainty," I said.

"Just like here," Kitty said. "Except for Almira, there hasn't been an outsider who has joined us for years. And lots of former members have left. Like the Knights."

"They're still close by," Matilda defended. "They'd help if we needed them. They're helping build our log home."

"They're going to put into writing what we colonists believe," Christine said.

"It's always easier to say, 'Come join me,' when you can say what you truly believe," Almira said.

"*Ja,*" I said. "Kitty's right. It's pretty hard to win souls when everyone is feuding or moving around in different directions. So maybe this is what this scripture is really about."

That and the need to make certain we open our doors wide and that what's on the other side shines light into darkness.

20

Dedication

The colony principles were issued that summer. They emphasized again that all we possessed was to be placed within a common fund, that we'd labor for one another. They spoke of the value of marriage, that the family was to be honored as led by God, and they covered decision making and promised homes for each family. Of course, it affirmed again that Keil was our leader. Our house church women talked about the new principles, expressing surprise that naming Keil as the "president and autocrat" didn't appear until number ten. Even the importance of plain living as number eleven was further down than I'd thought it would be.

We were stuck on number ten, though, as along with naming Keil as leader, it suggested that a vote might take place if big changes were proposed, to indicate "general consent of the community." It was probably too much to imagine such a vote would include women, but one could hope.

"Someone has thought these out carefully," Matilda observed.

Jacob's sister, Sarah, had joined us that day, and she added, "I heard that years and years ago, Chris Wolff and Karl Ruge, maybe Henry Finck, were together in Germany, and they presented a list of principles like this to the Prussian leaders. Then they had to flee, because the prince thought it was a challenge to his authority."

"This could look like that," I said, "if you were a crowned prince."

"At least he put God and parents first," Almira said. "And the family. Family. It's so important. Children…" Her voice trailed off, and she got up shortly after that and went upstairs.

"I like number seven myself," Kitty said. "Maybe if I do find someone to marry, Keil won't tell us we can't. The carpenters are strong and sturdy. I rather like taking dinner baskets out to them. I might find a good man out there."

"Number nine says 'the children' and doesn't exclude girls from the school. Thank goodness for Karl in that!" Matilda said.

"I wonder who the advisors are," Sarah said.

"One thing's for certain, they won't be women," Kitty said.

"At least not up front," I added. "We women might never be official advisors, in authority, but that doesn't mean we don't have persuasion with the men in our lives."

"You haven't talked Papa into having us all live together, though," Kitty reminded me.

"Persuasion takes patience," I said. It was a belief I just realized I held.

The new rules said nothing about widows specifically. And Kitty liked that marriage was supported. She read, "The family is strictly maintained; people marry, raise, and train children." I wondered if it might be an opening for me, to bring my children back into my own personal fold. What might "strictly maintained" really mean? I'd have to ask Karl. He always had insights.

———

That fall, I didn't hear so much grumbling from the workers, so we assumed the advisors now had a voice in the affairs of the colony, at least in the men's affairs, and that our prayers for "all that are in authority" were being answered. The church building stood nearly finished. We learned from Henry C that bells for the belfry had been ordered from Ohio. The hotel's three floors, with windows in the attic, had finishers working into dusk. Ben Holladay, the railroad man, attended a number of our concerts in the Park House, a newly built structure that was nestled in the trees not far from Keil's house. Many new trails had been created through the forest area near the Park House, a building that either Keil (or the advisors) had ordered built for the band's performances. Mr. Holladay and Dr. Keil "took many walks on the paths," Louisa told us. Mr. Holladay was a visionary, as she called him, who would help the colony continue to grow into the outside world. She'd say that because her husband did. Still, I noticed that the band building was finished before the church was.

It bothered me, too, that we weren't recruiting any longer, as Christian had done in the old days, using the light of faith and the comfort of communal efforts to bring people into our fold. Instead, our production lured people in: our fine leather goods, our medicinal wines, our turned furniture and textiles. It wasn't the same to me. People bought our products, but they weren't drawn to our ways of looking after one another and tending to the less fortunate. Our colony grew mostly through the arrivals of those from Willapa or Bethel, rather than through new, invigorated blood. I guessed that like any group, we wanted people to join us, but then we resisted the changes they brought with them. Even our house church changed with each new addition. Change was in the nature of the people who gathered together, whatever the original purpose. Trying to keep a group the same proved a futile effort. But when my mind began muddling over perceived injustices and uncertainties, I tried, as Karl had advised, to find God in the changes and walked my puzzle path of thinking right back to God's power to influence everything, when we allowed it.

The shoemaker and saddler had picked up so many new accounts that they ran short of materials. Whenever Keil or one of his advisors learned of a stand of oak needing to be cleared, our men would be volunteered to do the clearing, so they could take the bark from the trees, so important to the fine tanning that we did. Ashes from the burned bark were blended with water to remove the hair from the deer and cow hides.

This was work Almira found she could do: stuffing the hides into the trough, punching them down with a stick, then waiting three days and currying the hair off. It wasn't "careful work" as she called it, so her hands, large knuckles and all, could keep up. Since she'd been going out to work on tanning, Almira acted happier. She didn't as often leave us, to go upstairs alone to read or outside to walk. Sometimes she even joined us at the Park House for a concert.

Our house church had to change its meeting times, since the band played in the park so often on Sunday afternoons. I wondered whether it was anything deliberate on Keil's part, this taking away from our Sabbath meetings. Maybe he'd changed the Sunday band times in order to keep our house church women from sharing our complaints with one another. He also announced that from now on, the Sabbath celebrations would begin on Saturday at noon. All work would stop then. We'd have music and eat together. Worship would begin on Sunday morning with yet more music and a meal on Sunday afternoon.

Maybe he thought there was power in our women's meetings, power needing curtailment. It was an idea that hadn't occurred to me before.

We women adapted and began meeting midweek.

I almost felt sorry for the men, who lacked this place of comfort to work and talk. We'd try new recipes out on one another, to see who could make the best Scatter Soup with the thinnest dumpling batter carrying the greatest taste. I loved watching how the ribbon of flour and eggs formed odd shapes as they were swirled into the hot soup. "It must be your Clara's blue eggs that give yours that fine flavor," Matilda told me, smacking her lips in a most unladylike manner after she'd scooped up the soft-cooked forms.

"*Nein*, it's her meat broth," Louisa told her. "What do you put in that, Emma?"

"I'll never tell," I said. We almost never told our cooking secrets. My mother made a meatloaf dish with a rare flavor, and she had always hoarded that recipe and probably would until her dying day.

While we stitched, we shared our burdens and prayed for one another, and in between, we sang rounds, a venture begun by Kitty. I have to say I found it refreshing to hear those repeating loops of women's voices, singing psalms and sometimes tunes Kitty said came from Shakespeare's time that children sang around the Maypole. The second group began while the first went on to higher tones. It was like a dance of voices, and I could join in, the lilt of others' voices carrying mine along, even though I sang out of tune.

"Henry C said that to lose one's temper means to be out of tempo in a song," Helena said when we finished a round. "I find that quite comforting."

"You've never lost your temper, ever," Louisa told her. "Have you?"

"I've had my moments," Helena confessed.

No one lifted an eye from the quilt spread before us at this surprising admission.

"Isn't it nice to know, then, that you're simply out of balance?" Kitty offered. "That makes you a lot more like the rest of us."

"I have to say that being called unbalanced has never seemed so…embracing," Helena told her.

Nothing subversive occurred at our house church, just piecing and patching. Acceptance of the way things were fell more easily on my shoulders when we gathered as we did. The distance from my parents, the loss of my sons, the uncertainties for my daughters' lives, even the fate of a world where war once raged became weights carried with me by my friends. Maybe Keil's decisions weren't meant to demean us women; rather he and the advisors simply didn't take our interests into account. We'd long ago taught them that they didn't have to; we knew so well how to adapt.

Louisa would say the men "had the economy" on their minds, so they didn't consider a woman's needs. But I remembered one day when Kate came home and told me she'd learned something in Greek. "Oikos," she said. "It means 'household.'"

"That's nice," I told her, and continued to beat at the rug hanging over the line.

"But, Mama, it means two things, like our two doors. It means… econ…economy too. Dr. Wolff says that in the household, we look after one another and share, and that should be the basis of our lives. He says we shouldn't try to get too big or try to do too much without helping one another. We should all live like it's our house, and in the kitchen, where the cooking stove is, that's where the econ…"

"Economy," I finished for her.

"That's where everything is. In the kitchen. We get fed, and we give to others and make our weavings and trade them, but we see one another every day. That's our *oikos*," she said. "The Greek is easier to say."

She was right. We women had the greatest place to be: at the hearth, the center of it all. The men had their own pressures, and a part of me almost felt regret for them.

From my upstairs window, I could see one of their big pressures: the hotel, looming tall and large. The stage stopped there, but to justify such a huge building we'd need many more customers. We'd need the railroad to bring them. But even there, it was the kitchen *oikos* that mattered. Food sustained us. Without many outside people purchasing our food, the building would be like a boil on the back of the colony, instead of a precious pearl worn to embellish the colony's bodice.

Our colony was defined by colony principles that in truth were established more for the men than for us women. We women had our own principles, I decided. We continued on as we had: tending our families, sprinkling the mundane with occasional song, interrupting our trials with a bit of laughter, and welcoming the acceptance of friends. Keil's rule had never changed that. A woman's *oikos* threaded its way through the ages to this century, in this place. A place I now called home.

Matilda and Jacob prepared to move into their family home during the fall of 1866. They announced they'd be moving soon and that Matilda was with child.

"I guess my house was private enough," I teased, and Matilda's face burned red. How I'd miss them! Yet again, another change.

At one of our house church gatherings, Matilda told us that Martin, who was attending her instead of a midwife, had heard two heartbeats through his stethoscope. Louisa said well, of course: hers and the baby's, any midwife would know that. But Matilda said he'd heard two very fast beating hearts in addition to her own, and they must belong to two infants.

"Twins!"

"Will they have two biblical cords?" Ida asked. We'd looked at each other and laughed.

The prospect of twins set us all to spinning and knitting, and we agreed how good it was that Matilda would have sisters-in-law living with her, and wasn't it interesting the way things worked out sometimes, the very thing you thought you didn't want turned out to be something you didn't know you'd need. She'd have good help with two children being born at once. She was older to be having a first child—children—so being attended by someone with medical training was a gift as well.

Many of us at the house church had taken turns sitting at the loom through the rainy months, and now we rolled out the rug woven with braids of color: purple and blue and a pink hue. I'd quilted a Nine Patch pillow top, and Kitty and Christine had begun two cradle quilts for Matilda's twins. They chose an Old Maid pattern that Matilda chuckled at. My own mother joined our gatherings now since I'd made a special effort to invite her. She brought Johanna and Lou with her. My mother pointed out that we could mark the place for stitches on the quilt top with soap. It made the needles go through easier and would wash out. All of us stitched the quilt pieces that Matilda had created during her first year of marriage, a new quilt she'd worked on since completing her Sunflower quilt. She backed this new covering as she had the other, using strips of flannel or whatever she had, including pieces her mother had brought from Pennsylvania and a striped piece from Bethel.

A quilt, I decided, allowed us some control in an often-powerless world. We could put pieces together in the way we wished, with no one grumbling much about how we did it. Even the mistakes could be fixed with little thinking, unlike in life sometimes. Quilting was better with the presence of older women like my mother to dribble little bits of wisdom into the room as we worked.

"I'll remember this time of family," Matilda said, "each time I look at this quilt."

Matilda didn't think she'd be able to join us very often after her move so far out from the village, but after the babies came, she thought she could. They were expected in the spring of 1867, and she promised she'd bring them along to meet us all just as soon as she could.

"For me to play with?" Ida asked.

"*Ja.* So you can check on their biblical cords," Matilda told her.

We kept Matilda from lifting a thing, while Jacob and his friends carried the furniture he'd built for them down from my home, placed the bed and dresser in the wagon, and drove south a few miles to what we now called Stauffer Farm.

Despite the rain and mud and our own loss at having them go, we made the move memorable. Jacob had planted apple trees near the split-rail fence and maple trees to line the rutted road. The log house boasted two stories and offered a beautiful view of the prairie land surrounding it. I suspected that from the second floor window, you could almost see the steeple of the church that rose one hundred fourteen feet into the Oregon sky. Facing east, I wondered if on a clear, clear day one might see the snowy cap of Mount Hood, the way I could from my home. A clothesline stood ready to catch the wind and the quilts Matilda would air there.

Stauffer Farm was what I'd always imagined Christian and I would have one day. Yes, we'd had a small cabin on the Willapa, but that was only to have been the beginning. I found myself wistful, watching Matilda and Jacob begin their new lives. It was never easy for me to say good-bye to routine. I took a deep breath and walked up the steps. Being hopeful for them scrubbed the dust of change off of me.

———

"Maybe we should move back into their room, now that they've gone," Kitty said. "We could have more privacy that way." We were in our usual stitching place, starting a new project of some table runners. It was just the four of us plus my girls.

"I've gotten used to having everyone in the same room," Almira said. "My husband and I had a small cabin, and the children all slept within breathing space of one another. This has sort of reminded me of that. It's comforting."

"You really miss them, don't you, Almira?" Kitty asked.

Almira lowered those gray eyes. "More of late. I wonder if I did the right thing in leaving him. Them." No one interrupted. Then she said, "I've thought perhaps I should ask him to take me back."

We cast questioning looks at one another, not sure what to say.

"What would be different?" Christine asked then. "Don't go doing the same thing and expecting a different result. That makes a person crazy. Trust me. I know."

"I'm wiser, that would be different. What do you think, Emma?" Almira asked.

She walked on slippery rocks, as far as I was concerned. Our situations were too similar, and yet I knew she felt she'd failed her faith by securing a divorce. That was one reason I hadn't sought a divorce from Jack, that and not wanting to bring yet one more issue of disgrace for my family to deal with or for wagging tongues to talk about. No one divorced quietly in these western places.

"You could forgive him," I said. "Because to not do that will only hold you hostage. But I'm not sure you should forget what he did, or try again unless there's evidence you both have changed. You're welcome here for as long as you like."

"He's still living with the girl, well, she's a woman now, isn't she?" Kitty asked. "He hasn't realized how much he hurt you, or showed that he wants it any different. You'd be going back into the same situation."

"I don't know if he hasn't. I haven't seen him now for years. But it wouldn't be the same. I'm different, even if he isn't,"

"Don't you want tenderness from him now, though?" Kitty asked. "If you don't get it, you'll wish you had, and be upset all over again."

"Your older children...?" Christine said.

"They say nothing's different." She sighed. "I miss them all so much." Her voice caught. Across the room from her, Christine's lip quivered too, and so did Kitty's. Soon we'd all be crying. I imagined that Almira cried for the lost joys and for the separation from her children, as much as from missing her husband. But one didn't know, not really. When she cried, we just cried with her and for our own losses as well.

"Don't decide now," Christine said. She patted Almira's hand. "It's winter, and the rains weigh you down, and everything smells musty and damp, and even old ways look better in memory. None of us makes the best decisions then. Although I don't always make the best decisions when the sun's out shining either." She wiped at her eyes, gave a wry smile to me.

"I don't want this to be all there is to my life," Almira whispered. "Not that I'm not grateful to you all. I am. But—"

"You want to feel useful," I offered. She nodded. "To your family. I do understand."

———

We decided to keep Matilda and Jacob's room open, use it as a dressing room but make it easier to invite others in to stay. We'd keep our bedroom constellation, so we could hear our sleeping breaths come out like stars in the quiet of the night.

It was while Christine and I were dressing together before going to Keil's church one morning that I noticed that she did not need a hoop beneath her skirt. As she turned, her body formed the flow while the cloth settled over a woman who was very much with child.

———

Helena appeared at our house church gatherings after the church building was finished but before it was dedicated. Word was that the dedication would wait for the bells to arrive. We wouldn't worship in the building until then. Louisa Keil, the senior, did not come with her that day. The group always changed a bit when they attended; it was much more difficult to talk about them when they were present! I wondered if I added more to a conversation when I was absent than when I was present. I pitched that thought away.

Helena asked if any of us had been inside the new church, and I expected a chastisement when no one said they had.

"We await the dedication," Christine said. She held a pile of fabric lumped over her stomach.

I'd peeked through the women's door while the church was being built. Yes, I had suggested to my brother that they didn't need separate doors for men and women, that we were together all week long; why did we have to be separate at church? But he said it wasn't his decision to talk about doors. Someone else had already decided.

"The sounds inside are splendid," Helena said. "A speaking voice makes one think they are in those limestone caves back in Missouri, where a single note resonates, filling it full. You'll hear a whisper at the back of the sanctuary all the way to the front."

"So we'd best not be chattering during services," Kitty said.

"Not what I meant," Helena said. "I meant that it's going to make all voices sound as though they sang in a heavenly choir."

"That choir ought to have both male and female voices," Kitty said.

"I'm sure they'll let the girls' choir perform, as well as the men's," Almira said. "So long as they remain separate."

"But imagine both men and women singing…together," Kitty said. Her persistence surprised us all.

Helena straightened her shoulders, and Matilda, who had joined us this day, said, "Let's sing one of our rounds. You haven't been here for those, have you, Helena?"

"Yes, I have," Helena responded, but Kitty started us out anyway, by dividing the room into threes, telling us the song, and then leading the first group. We didn't even need to watch each other; we could just sing. Kitty had the finest soprano voice.

"That was lovely," Helena said when we finished. She'd stopped working while we sang, folding her hands over her scissors in her lap.

"A community of voice," I said. "Covering up the individual flaws, *ja?*"

"Kitty," Helena said, "it might be a better dedication chorus if we joined our voices *with* the men's. Since the bells have not arrived, we'd have time to practice."

I stared at her. Was this the Helena I knew, who thought we women should all remember our places, live only for Brother Keil's directives? And she'd made a suggestion that Louisa would probably object to if she'd been present. "Helena," I said, "I can't believe you said that."

"*Ach.* What could be a more beautiful statement of dedication of our worship house than to express it in music of men *and* women, girls *and* boys?"

"Do you think *Herr* Keil would allow that?" Kitty asked. "I've always wanted to sing in a mixed chorus. And not just to have time with the men," she defended herself, as though anyone had challenged.

"Ask the advisors," I said. "See if they might really advise."

"This is a possibility," Helena said. She turned to me then. "But maybe you'd do the asking, Emma?"

"I can't carry a tune in a candlestick holder," I said. "Kitty would be more convincing."

"*Ja,* but you carry a tune with your words." Both Kitty and Helena spoke at the same time. They laughed while the rest of the group agreed, "*Ach, ja!*"

"You think I could influence *Herr* Keil in this way? I don't know."

"You have much more persuasion than you might think, Emma," Helena said.

"*Ja?* Just not about what really matters."

While I considered when would be the perfect time to ask Keil about the music, I also wondered about the best time to speak to Christine. One evening, she and I were upstairs in what had been Matilda and Jacob's room, changing from our modest hoop skirts into the straight lines of our nightdresses. Almira and Kitty chattered with the girls in the room beyond the hall. I tied the soft ribbon at my neckline and checked the stitching on the patch I'd had to sew on after Po jumped up in greeting, tearing a corner piece with his sharp claws. I stared at it much too long, looking for words. I knew I couldn't wait much longer.

"Christine," I said, not asking, but thinking out loud, "you're expecting a big change soon, aren't you?"

I heard her intake of breath.

Her shoulders sank. "I'm not sure what to do," she said. "I'm nearly four months along."

"I'm sure no one else has noticed," I said. "I wouldn't have except, well, we share a changing room here."

"One advantage of being a big-boned girl, as my father used to say. My real father, not yours." Her eyes watered. "I'll leave, Emma. I don't want to put you into any difficulty with having an unwed mother staying with you. I didn't know how to tell you. My becoming...this way...while I stayed under your roof could bring criticism to you." She sat on the rocking chair now, at the edge of the seat. It didn't rock or soothe.

"You remain as long as you like," I said. "Don't even think about my reputation. I've done enough things to it myself." Her lips loosened into a sad smile. "What have you thought about doing for yourself?"

"Going to Portland, where no one knows me. I'll have the baby and place it in a basket. I'll leave it on the doorstep of someone kind. There are many kind people in the world. I'm sure I can find one of them. I thought at one of the churches. That's what I did last time."

She's been through this before. I forgot that.

"Dare I ask about the father?"

"I'd rather not say."

"From the fair," I said.

"Oh no." She looked up at me. "That gentleman was a gentleman. We only talked and danced. I know you thought I wasn't well behaved, but I was."

Had I judged her with my eyes?

"No, it was, well, someone closer." Her face turned beet red. "I suppose I didn't resist his advances as I should have. I thought being at your house would help. I could be alone, away from temptation in the evenings after my chores were complete. Being my size, I didn't expect any man to pay attention to me. I hoped none would after what happened, well, before. Then you invited me to the fair, and I found it was pleasant and I didn't have to be afraid. But I didn't know how to sort out a friend from someone... Before long, things just happened." She looked up at me. "But that's no excuse. It's not his fault. He was only being playful, he said. I knew from the beginning." She sighed. "But I was hopeful that he might really care for me."

"I've told myself similar stories with sad endings," I said. I pulled a small stool up to her and sat, taking her hands in mine. "Does the man know there were consequences to his...playfulness?"

She shook her head no. "But he isn't a candidate for marriage." I waited for her to continue, but she didn't.

"You deserve better anyway," I told her. "I wonder if there isn't some other path for you to take, besides leaving your baby on a doorstep and having to find a new life somewhere far away."

"It's for the best," she said, "my plan. The loss of this baby will be just penance for what I did, twice now. I don't deserve anything but punishment, for not learning from the first mistake."

"*Ach,* Christine, the size of our infractions doesn't matter, at least I don't think it does. Little acts can be as devastating as big ones." I thought of my little indiscretions that had resulted in the colony removing my sons from me; at least I still believed my actions were the primary reasons. "'Take us the foxes, the little foxes, that spoil the vines' is a scripture right in the middle of one of the Bible's great love stories. We can have wonderful romances, but then small things can spoil it. I've made my own big mistakes, but it's the little ones that have caught me in the end. God is somewhere in this, Christine. In the big and small of it. We have to let ourselves be found."

"If that's so, I wish God would show Himself," she said.

"That's just what we'll ask for, then."

We sat quietly for a time. I could hear the sound of her breath coming in and out steadily. The other women made noises in the next room, muffled as a child's sleepy chuckle. I heard Po bark once in play. I knew, in these wilderness places, that's where we'd find grace, but it was still so hard to accept it. I ached for Christine, sent my arrow prayers. I stood up and found her a handkerchief in the hanky drawer of the cabinet. She wiped at her eyes and sighed.

"Sometimes I'd like to go to sleep and then wake up and have this all be over with. Be a sleeping beauty who never gets kissed again into wakefulness." She smiled a bit.

"No prince is going to come along and wake us up, I agree with you about that," I said. "I tried to make a man into a prince who wasn't. At least you haven't done that. I fell asleep all by myself, and unlike that Grimms' tale, I was the only one who could decide to wake up. That's when I accepted Karl's help and came here. You're my sister, Christine." I took her in my arms. "The good news is once we do wake up, we find out we're really not alone."

21

Sweet Scents

Together, a few days later, Helena, Kitty, and I made our way to Henry C. Finck, to see whether he'd consider conducting a joined choir of both boys and girls, men and women at the dedication. We chose him first in our plan of action. I considered the consequences if we failed at this. Keil would have another black mark to put against my name. He could use this to move me from the house or, worse, take my girls from me so they wouldn't be exposed to such a "contrary woman." But Helena's part in this gave me hope. And working with her and my sister made the risk worthwhile.

"But of course," Henry C. Finck said, exuberant. "It's good Wilhelm has approved such a novelty."

Helena and I looked at each other. I wondered if her need to be precise and correct in all things would force her to explain that we had yet to talk to Brother Keil.

"Well, he hasn't exactly—," Kitty began.

"Yes, yes," Helena interrupted. She explained rapidly that she thought it was a splendid idea. "Wouldn't it sing great praises to our Lord, who had to wait so many years for this church to be finished?"

Henry C narrowed his eyes. "Wilhelm hasn't approved such a thing, has he? He's not that…inspired in his thinking these days." I swallowed. "But I am," he went on cheerfully. "So we'll rehearse, and if Wilhelm complains, we'll explain that boys and girls singing together are no worldlier than having the railroad come to our hotel. He certainly wants that to happen."

"We'll get full approval before we do this," Helena told him. "We'd not put you in a compromising situation. You can be certain of that."

The three of us giggled like schoolgirls as we walked from there to Karl Ruge, basking in our first success. I didn't even go over the details of what had just transpired, for fear Helena might have second thoughts about a sin of omission. At Karl's house, I led with our request as though Wilhelm had already approved.

"Karl," I said, "Professor Finck tells us that having a mixed boys and girls' choir sing at the dedication would be a glorious thing."

"I've heard nothing about it," he said.

"But there's nothing scriptural to preclude it, is there? Surely Wilhelm would note such a thing, *ja*?" I said. "Or John Giesy would."

"*Ja*, well, I see no problem. It might put the dedication back if we need long rehearsals, though. Wilhelm would like to proceed quickly now."

"Henry didn't seem to think there'd be any delay," I said. "We'll be ready when the bells are." I bent down to scratch Po's head. He had trotted along with us, as much mine as my children's now, to visit his old master.

"I bet he's spoiled by the girls, but then every dog in the village is spoiled by someone."

"The dogs see us as we are and never complain about it," I said. "Who could be a better friend than that?"

He put tobacco in his long pipe, then grinned at me, and we chatted a bit longer about the weather and wondering when the bells would arrive. Then we marched off to Chris Wolff.

"Dr. Wolff," Helena said. "Is there anything scriptural to preclude having both boys and girls sing together in the church? Say for a dedication?"

"Or even elsewhere," I added. Helena frowned, and I realized I might have overstepped my bounds, pushing into a field before we'd gotten the gate open.

"Handel's *Messiah* is composed for orchestra and the voices of men and women. Why would Wilhelm question the scriptural nature of it? Or is it you women who are worried over such a thing?" We looked demure. "Well, nothing to worry. It would be a lovely thing for our dedication, to go with our bells. I'm sure Henry has something properly arranged, *ja*?"

"He's probably working on it right now," Kitty said.

From there we took our list of support to Wilhelm.

"Do you think we should talk with Louisa first?" I asked as we walked up the hill.

Helena shook her head. "I don't want to involve her, for if we fail in winning Wilhelm's support, she would have to bear the brunt of his refusal. He might forbid her to come to…your gatherings. She wouldn't want that," Helena said. "She enjoys coming to your home, Emma."

"Does she?"

"We all do. Well, every now and then."

I took that compliment in.

It had been some time since I'd seen Keil's workroom next to the root cellar. The earthy smells would always remind me of nursing Ida, seeing Brita for the first time, the day I faced off with Jack. Here, too, I'd learned that Keil had arranged my sons' lives away from mine.

"To what do I owe this visit of three lovely *Fräulein*?" Keil asked as he waved us in.

Kitty said, "Emma's not a *Fräulein*, she's—"

"The question has arisen as to the appropriateness of having both men and women sing for the dedication," Helena cut her off briskly.

"What? Of course both choirs can sing," Keil said. "The human voice is a gift from God and one that must be given back. First the boys will sing, then the girls."

"*Ja*, my thoughts exactly," Helena said. "But Karl and Chris Wolff and Henry Finck seem to think it would be quite a feather in your cap if we blended the choirs for the first time. Not unlike the great German composers combining voice with instruments, men and women, together."

"Only if you approve, of course," I said.

"Or maybe you already approved it, and that's the reason they're so enthusiastic," Kitty said. *My sister has possibilities.*

He paused, frowned. "I might have approved it…*ja*. I think something was said a while back." He pulled at the gray strand of beard below his chin. "You women needn't worry yourselves over it. It is for a worshipful event. We men will take care of the theology of things. Men and women can sing together, *ja*. Sometimes you women are so simple in your thinking."

Kitty opened her mouth to speak, but I squeezed her arm with my fingers. She looked at me while Helena nodded sagely. We said our good-byes and stepped outside the root room. The sweet scents of earth and a warm March breeze greeted us.

"Why didn't you correct him?" Kitty said. "His thinking we women are such simpletons of thought."

"Sometimes it's good just to be happy, rather than being right," I said.

"Let's sing a round to celebrate," Kitty said as we started down the hill.

"There's only the three of us," I said.

"You can do it, Emma," Kitty said.

"She can do most anything," Helena agreed, but she put her hands over her ears when I sang my part, because as always, it was quite out of tune with the other voices.

The bells at last arrived. One large bell and two companions of graduated size had been shipped out of Ohio from the Buckeye Bell Foundry, by ship down the Ohio to New Orleans, then around Cape Horn, up the Pacific coast to the Columbia, up the river to the Willamette, to a landing area not far from Butteville. Then a new road had to be scoured out all the way from the river to Aurora, because the terrible weight of the bells would have ruined the existing road. Jonathan and my father and brothers joined the workers laying down boards for the wagon to skid across. My father acted familiar with the landing site, suggesting the best way to bring the vehicle up the bank's grade, talking to Wilhelm and John as though they were old friends, pointing, directing.

The children made an adventure of it, and all other colony work stopped as the wagon with four ox teams slowly made its way from the Willamette toward the Point, where the church stood with its empty belfry, awaiting those bells.

Several of us rode out in regular wagons, bringing food for the trip that took two days. The work group and those who served them rested midday. Now, returning to the effort, the labor took on a festive air, with singing and laughter and shouts of direction and joy when the wagon skidded forward. There were several pauses for ham slabs, water, and rolls.

"It's an everyday feast," Kate said as we served.

"An everyday feast. Yes. As each day should be," I told her, then sent her off to give Christian and Andy special cinnamon rolls. I'd seen them in the distance with a group of boys and made sure there were enough for all of them, even that quipping Finck boy.

It would be quite an event, lifting the heavy bells into the belfry, but it was a reassurance to us all that they'd actually arrived. At last there'd be the dedication. Helena giggled like a schoolgirl, skipping along beside the flat wagon pulling the heavy bells.

"They're so perfect," she kept saying.

Extra teams were added to bring the heavy load up the hill past the *gross Haus*. That night, the bells were left covered in the wagon, while the men planned the next day's work. They talked of using pulleys and teams of horses and boys who were willing to ride up with the bells to help set them in place.

Andy volunteered.

"It's dangerous," I told him.

He shrugged his shoulders. "It's not as if I'm going to stand on my head on it," he said.

The next day we watched with held breath as the huge bells were lifted into the belfry, a slow pull using a team of horses, thick ropes, and dexterous young men who guided the hooks into the specially built rafter. In the end, no one had to ride up on the bells, which were cradled in a web of stout ropes. I was grateful for that. When the men reached the opening to the belfry to receive the largest bell first, several pulled it toward the iron hooks. A cheer rose up as the clanger rang out. After lifting the second and third into the belfry, they set them on the floor, no time left to hang them until the following day.

People slapped one another on the back, and the men cheered the food we served them, as though we feasted at a cotillion. Even my family participated. My brothers came back from Oregon City to help. My mother brought *Aepfel Raist*, a toasted bread and apple pudding I remembered from my childhood. Geraniums bloomed a flashing red in a bucket on the table. My brother William grew them. How he got such huge flowers was a mystery.

"It's nice, isn't it, Mama? William's flowers are so large! I wonder how he does that." I sighed. "It's just so nice to have everyone happy together, like when we were in Bethel."

She didn't say anything at first. "I didn't think you were ever happy back there, with Christian gone so often. Isn't that why you left us to come west?"

"I was happy. I wanted to be happier," I said. "To go where my husband went."

"And did you get what you wanted?"

I looked at her. My mother had rarely offered to be reflective with me. She sounded like I'd abandoned them by leaving with Christian. Maybe she'd expected that she'd have a daughter close by, to help with the raising of my younger brothers and sisters. I hadn't thought of that before.

"Not everything. The boys...but I've made the best of what's happened. It took me a while, but I think my choices have been better. At least they've been mine, Mama."

"They haven't always turned out well."

"Things happen, whether I make plans for them or not," I said, "but I decide how to react. That's always mine to choose."

"You weren't raised to think with such...self-centeredness."

It was the most she'd said to me of how she felt about anything in years. I wished I didn't have to disagree with her. "Not self-centered,

Mama," I said gently. "Maybe in the beginning, *ja*, I stumbled and fell, but I let others help me up. I walked my way back from that dark time." I paused. "Maybe it is selfish to want a good life, a meaningful life formed of a simple one. You're one of the kindest, most generous women I know. You took in Christine. You tend my sisters. You've brought many babies into the world as a midwife. You've done those things for others, but didn't they bring you happiness too? That doesn't make you self-centered. It makes you...loving. I'd like to think I've honored how you raised me. I'm truly sad if you think I haven't."

She picked up the bowl that had once held her pudding. It was empty now. She stared at it, then said, "I might have spoken out of turn, Daughter. You'll have to forgive me."

She walked away before I could think of anything more to say.

———

After everyone had gone home but the sun still hugged the horizon, I asked Kitty if she'd like to take a walk with me.

"To the labyrinth?"

I shook my head no. "To the church."

"We'll be there all day tomorrow with the bells getting set," she said.

"There's something I want to do there," I told her. Christine agreed to watch the girls as we made the quarter-mile trek, across the village and up the ravine toward the church. The sunset burned vibrant orange, and the trees formed perfect scissor cuts, like *Scherenschnitte* against the sky. Po trotted along beside us, sniffing at the history that had passed that way hours before.

As we walked by John Giesy's home, Kitty said, "I never noticed before, but John and Barbara's house has two front doors, like yours."

"My house was built first, so he copied me," I joked.

"Isn't copying a way of saying they like what they see?"

We carried our lanterns high—we'd need them later—and hiked up our skirts, tucking them into our apron bands so we could take longer strides. Once outside the church, we stopped to catch our breath. Crickets chirped now and swallows swooped, already finding a place in the belfry to claim as theirs. I thought a bat might have dipped from out of the firs and swirled back, waiting for the moon. The windows were framed in a Gothic look, with arches that flowed away from the point in graceful ways. I didn't know who had designed the window frames, but they looked artful. That pleased me, to see our little colony weaving art into useful things.

"So what is it you want to do?" Kitty asked. "Now that we're here."

"We're going up into the belfry," I said.

"What?"

"Think of the view."

"I'm not going up there. I don't like heights."

"You won't be alone," I said. "We'll do it together, for the adventure of it. Don't you sometimes want to do something just because you can?"

"Not really."

"I do. There's so little in my life I can really make happen, and this is something I can. Come on." We went inside, but Kitty refused to climb the stairs into the belfry. So I wrapped twine around my skirts at the ankles and climbed up by myself.

The flight up reminded me of the mill in Willapa, how I looked out over the landscape to see a whole new world that awaited me. I'd made a mess of that world not long after, but I'd come through it. I was here. Safe. My children were safe. They had futures. Even my parents had joined me, and our relationship held promise of change.

As I caught my breath, I ran my hands over the medium bell sitting on the belfry floor. The bell came up to my chest. Fortunately, it stood next to the smallest bell. I set the lantern down, took off my shoes, and used the smaller bell to climb up onto the medium bell. The metal felt cool, the top slick with condensation from the cooler evening, but my stocking feet eventually took hold. Careful not to bump my head on the bell already hung, I bent over and put my hands flat against the metal. I pushed myself up like a caterpillar unrolling and lifted my feet skyward. It had been years since I'd done such a thing! Then I looked out through the open portals into the sun-settling night.

"What are you doing up there?" Kitty shouted up. "Let's go."

Blood rushed to my head, and my skirts slid up my legs against the twine, but I could see the sunset reflect against the smaller bell. "Just a little longer," I whispered more for me than for Kitty. Out through the window openings, the world was upside-down and bathed in a kind of smoky grace, a quiet confusion that had its own order, just not what one expected. I'd done this sort of thing as a child, stood on my hands upside down to see the world a new way. It was who I was, I decided, always looking at things from a different angle, standing on a precarious edge. The view was new and unique.

I looked down at my hand. The crooked fingers would always be a reminder of Jack. But they'd remind me, too, of my strength, my ability to take necessary next steps for my family. Maybe I wouldn't bring a dozen people to the faith the way Christian had; maybe I wouldn't tend a large family as my mother did; maybe I'd never be as faithful as Helena and Louisa, but I was who I was; I would leave a legacy of everyday devotion both to my family and to the delights of life, including standing upside down on a bell.

I let my feet come down, then slid to stand upright. I panted. My arms were still strong, but they quivered from the exertion. I looked out through the openings. The landscape wrapped around me. Beauty from mountains to rivers. Fir-lined paths leading to prairie flowers spread like petals at a wedding on the grass. This was a place of belonging. Christian had never been a part of this, and yet he was. I'd brought him here through his children, through my growing, changing faith. I didn't have to go back to where he was or to what had been; I'd taken him here, just as I could keep finding myself here, in this place.

"Get down here," Kitty shouted up at me.

I looked for a moment at the smallest bell, holding the lantern high above it, and laughed.

"What are you laughing about up there?" Kitty said.

"Come up and see," I shouted down.

A pause, then, "Oh, all right."

It took her a while. "Don't tell anyone we were even up here," she said, panting. She held the sides of the room as though it would fall apart if she let go. "Now, what's so funny?"

"There are cherubs carved into the bell. At least the smallest bell. See?"

She peered. It was growing dark. "Well, that's fitting," Kitty said. "For a church bell. What's funny about that?"

"They're naked cherubs," I told her.

She looked aghast. "I wonder if Keil noticed!"

On our walk back in the dark, I told her I'd stood on my hands on the bell. Kitty asked, "What made you do that?"

I swung my sister's hand. "Something Andy said when I tried to caution him about the dangers of riding up on that bell. He said, 'I'm not standing on my head on it,' and I thought of how often I get upset or worried over things better left to Providence to manage. Everything isn't dangerous, but I make it so sometimes. In my mind."

I could stop fighting to get my sons back and fight instead to ensure they had all that they needed, that my daughters had what they deserved to live good lives. In the meantime, I'd enjoy time with them all as I could. "Instead, I could enjoy life," I told her. "Kick up my heels on a bell, nice and safe."

"And only a little strange."

———

The men finished hanging all three bells. Helena said that the light of the Holy Spirit had visited those bells in the night; she'd seen a light coming from the belfry. She called it a miracle, though others told her it must have been the moonlight reflecting against them. They tolled the bells then, one after the other, mellow, rich tones that reached across the valley and would in time be the hallmark of our village, announcing the need for firemen, ringing in celebrations, and mourning a colonist's death.

A spring storm threatened throughout dedication day but never materialized. It seemed a fitting sign, since so often I worried and agonized over things that never came to pass and could lose the joy of what was before me while I lamented "what might be later."

The bells rang out, calling everyone together. The Aurora Band played, standing on the platform that circled the top of the steeple. The Pie and Beer Band warmed up at the lower balcony, and sometimes the bands played back and forth to each other, as though across a mountain valley. Inside the church, large pillars rose up on both the men's and women's sides. We'd made one inroad this day with our blended chorus.

The oldest women sat toward the front and at the center, with the rest of us graduated on either side of them, as though we were those smaller companion bells. Barbara Giesy had the front row. Helena settled between Giesy nieces. My mother sat in the row with me and my girls. Midway up the center aisle stood a large wood stove, with a steel drum to help spread the heat in the winter. Behind it and a little higher rose the altar. It wasn't ornately carved as I'd expected. Instead it reminded me of a swan's neck, graceful as the turned pillars. Two lovely candelabra held oil laps, and the wooden benches were as smooth as a baby's bottom.

"What do you call these?" Ida whispered as she patted the bench. "A bench?"

"Kitty calls them stinks," she said. "I told her that was wrong."

"Oh, pews," I said. "That's another name for them. Not stinks, but pews."

The pillars in the center had been turned by Jacob Miller, and they were elegantly spare, much like the other crafts of the colony. Today Oregon grape leaves had been pasted around the pillars, giving them a festive air. And from the tables set along the back, we could smell the food that we'd be consuming when the service was complete.

I looked to my sons, sitting on the other side of the church with Martin. I really didn't know what they thought of this church building, or what they thought of the spiritual life that would go on within it or outside of it. I'd done my best to introduce them to experiences of faith, but my own journey had been so garbled at times—and still was—that I found few ways to even talk about it with them. I saw things differently; but I kept seeking, questioning; and that seemed an important part of one's faith journey. It couldn't be wise to become so certain of how God worked in the world that we stopped seeing evidence of divine surprise.

That was probably heretical thinking—frivolous. Perhaps that was why Keil and Martin and John thought I wasn't competent enough to raise my sons. They might think that the spiritual life of girls wasn't nearly so worrisome and that I could muddle my way through guiding them. But Martin said the separation was more for the benefit of the colony and my sons than for a punishment of me. I'd hang on to that.

Then the girls and boys rose and stood together. Even Ida at five years shuffled forward, turned to face us. She opened her mouth wide as an apple to sing, proclaiming the "wonders God had done." For today, that was really all that mattered.

Andy and Christian stood in the back rows, Andy already so tall. John and BW's girls stood in the row before them. A dozen others filled out the choir. Then the combined chorus raised their voices to sing that great German hymn of tradition, "Dear Christians, One and All Rejoice," the first verse perfect for this day:

And with united heart and voice
And holy rapture singing,
Proclaim the wonders God hath done...

I patted Christine's hand and leaned forward to catch Helena's eye. She winked. At least I think she winked. She might have been blinking back tears.

———

We learned later in the week that yet another group from Bethel had headed out for Oregon. Seventy-five more were to arrive in the fall of

1867, in a mule-team train led by yet another old friend and former scout. Land deeds were being given over to some of the earlier arrivals, so they now had property in their own names. I think Keil did this because the younger men urged the advisors to do so and they'd listened. It was rumored that those coming from Bethel had lost the guiding purpose to make another's life better than their own. They wanted to be like others in the West, independent, earning something to leave to their children when they died. In many ways, I saw Aurora becoming less of a colony and more of a village, no longer distinguished by its expression of faith, just one with a common treasury. I was surprised that I felt sad.

One spring afternoon, my girls and I unrolled a blanket at the Park House while the Aurora Band played. Then Kitty walked with the girls through the forest nearby, and my parents and younger sisters joined me on the blanket. I hoped they'd start coming to the church now so I'd see them more often. I'd asked them specifically to eat with us that day.

"I hear you're thinking of climbing Mount Hood," my father said.

"*Ach,* who told you that?"

"It would be a silly waste of time," my mother said. "I thought you'd outgrown some of those things."

"It was just an idea." *I wonder where they heard of it?* "We were looking for things to invigorate our days."

"Raising children isn't enough?" my mother asked.

"They stimulate in a different way," I said. Andy would be fourteen this fall, and he already stood taller than I. Martin said Andy knew all the ins and outs of running the pharmacy when Martin was away at school. He expected to finish up before long and had promised me again that Andy would be sent off to Wallamet University once he turned eighteen. Wasn't that the greatest work of a mother, to help her children achieve what they could?

"Andy will be tall like his father," my sister Johanna said. She looked out to where Andy was warming up his clarinet. Johanna had weepy eyes, maybe from the spring blossoms, for she constantly wiped at them.

"He's a nice young man," my father said. "I see him at the pharmacy at times, and he's always very polite to his uncles when they come in. Christian's quite the storyteller. Both fine boys."

I couldn't help myself from smiling.

"And my girls?"

"They're fine too, Emma."

"Don't you miss the boys?" my mother asked.

"Of course I do." I always felt a pang of guilt whenever anyone mentioned that my sons weren't raised by me. With my parents, it was worse. "But they are well tended by Martin." I was too tired to fight it again, and maybe not be able to give them the life that they obviously have had there, the good life. "Andy will study medicine."

"*Ja,* we hear that Henry Finck's son will go to that Harvard school when he's old enough. He might be the first from Oregon to attend," Johanna said.

"The boys have learned Latin and Greek and had excellent teachers," I added to my sister's comment. "The girls, too, are receiving such instruction. At least the promising students are." Ida had begun classes, and Kate hadn't said anything about Latin as yet. "I wouldn't have been able to offer that to them as a widow—as a woman alone—if I hadn't come back here. And I've tried to do my best to give back all that's been provided."

My father patted my shoulder. "I heard about your house church," he said. "Will you stop that now that there is at last a real church?"

I fidgeted on the blanket, smoothed a wrinkle or two with my palm, gaining time for my answer.

"Keil still only plans to meet every other Sunday, and some of us do remember the fourth commandment to honor the Sabbath and keep it holy."

"They say it's as important as the fifth," my mother said.

Again I felt that twang of guilt. "Have I not honored you?" I asked. "I offered my home to you, but you didn't want to move in with me. Or live in a house that Keil provided? Was that it?"

"We understood the offer," my mother said. "We just miss seeing you. You rarely come by."

"Ja," my sister Lou said, "it can be pretty invigorating when I have one of my fits." She smiled, and I thought how hard it must be for her, for all of them. I did have a very blessed life. Maybe I stayed away from seeing them because I couldn't give to them in the way Johanna and my brothers did. Maybe I anticipated parental barbs and didn't feel strong enough to hear them without having the words sting me like wasps.

"We miss Christine too," my mother said. "She used to come by every day on her way back from the Keil house to yours, but she hasn't of late. I don't see her here today, either. Kitty keeps us filled in on you, Emma, you and your gaggle of women."

"I bet she does."

"What's this strange path you have the girls walking? Some kind of witchcraft or voodoo?" This from my father.

I laughed. "If Kitty told you that, you'd better question the other tales she tells you. It could be a quilt design, you know, Mama, like that one you made that looks like a carpenter's square, with a path in between going toward the center. Or Walk Through the Wilderness."

"Someone said it was like a labyrinth," Johanna said.

"Your very own brother is the one who told us about labyrinths," I told my father. "They're ancient ways of praying, that's all. They put feet to our thoughts and our words. I find it very soothing."

"First you want invigorating, then something to calm you. You have two sides to your wishes, don't you, Emma?" Johanna said.

"We all do," I said.

"She has two doors to her house," Lou said. "Why not two doors to her heart?"

I looked at her. She was right. There were many doubles in my life: two husbands, two boys, two girls. Twice I'd allowed others to raise my sons. I could be morose and sad and wallow in my headaches, or I could behave in ways that gave encouragement and hope, too. I could be pushy and prophetic.

"Maybe two doors means you need twice the opportunity to get something right," my mother said.

"Or when I get discouraged, there's always more than one way out." I was surprised to see my mother nod in agreement at that.

———

Someone knocked on the kitchen front door while the moon was still up. I grabbed my robe, looked out the window to see if I could recognize a wagon, but saw only a lone horse hitched to the front rail. I raced down the steps, throwing a knit shawl over my nightdress, and opened the door to Andy.

"Martin sent me. He's gone on ahead. Matilda's babies are coming early, and Jacob says she's having a hard time of it."

"I'll get dressed and come with you."

"No, he said to pray for them, for him too, to get the women together to do that."

"I'll gather the women, but as soon as I'm dressed, I'll come out there. Have you told Louisa and Helena, those at the Keils'?" He nodded. "Good. Go then. Let your grandmother know. She's a good midwife. I'll see you there."

I awoke the others, and they talked softly as they moved to the room that had been Matilda and Jacob's. "Maybe praying for them in here will make the prayers more powerful," Kitty said. I told her I didn't think it worked that way, but that wherever they gathered would be fine. "You're not going out there without us, are you?" Kitty added.

Maybe I didn't have the right to tell them they should stay home or to go. "I'm going," I said as I dressed. Then I remembered the girls. "But if you'd stay with the girls…"

"I will," Almira said. "I wouldn't want anyone thinking that my presence there brought about bad spirits."

"I can't believe they would, but thank you," I said.

Christine said she'd remain behind too. "Matilda will have her family there," she said.

Kitty's shoulders sagged. "You go, Emma. Martin sent Andy to tell you about it and for us to pray. We'll do that. You ride careful."

At the barns, the stableman was already up. He'd saddled the *Kartoffel* horse for Andy and gotten Martin off in his carriage. Now he saddled a big roan that murmured to me as I touched my head to his nostrils and sighed. I pulled up the hem of my skirt and tucked it into my apron, then stepped onto a stump and swung my leg over the saddle. I pressed my knees, and the horse took off at a fast but comfortable canter.

As I rode, I sent up prayers that Matilda would be all right, that her children would arrive healthy and alive. Many babies came early and lived. My mother had told of keeping a tiny infant, in a box no bigger than for knives, behind the stove where the water usually heated. That baby would die of old age, she'd said on his first birthday. And she was right.

But there were so many that didn't. Matilda and Jacob had had a late start on their happiness, and in my mind, these babies were to help them catch up with joy. *Please let them be all right.*

By the time I tied the reins to the rail in front of Stauffer Farm, the sun poked its head over the treetops. I heard the buzz of bees already at the apple blossoms. The morning breeze brushed cool against my sweaty face. I saw Andy's horse tied beside Martin's buggy, tail switching. I recognized Jacob's father, a former scout, standing on the porch, a pipe in his hand. John nodded to me. "Emma," he said. "It's good you've come."

"*Ja*, I will do what I can to—"

Jacob burst through the door then and stumbled toward the porch rail post. He clung to it as though if he let go, he would sink like a rock into swirling water.

"Jacob?" I touched his shoulder.

He turned to me. His eyes were like caverns deep in his head. I knew what lay behind the door he'd just exited.

22

Sweeping in Front of the Door

April 10. Maybe the 11th, 1867. Whatever days, they run together. Matilda Stauffer gave birth early to her twins, and then she died. One twin survives, though like a tiny stitch in Matilda's sunflower quilt, so fragile, so easily she could yet be snipped away. The twin girl was buried in her mother's grave. Jacob's sisters, Sarah and Rosana, care for the baby they named Matilda, for her mother. One day she'll have the quilt her mother made, but it will never comfort as would a mother's love.

"But we prayed," Christine said, "all of us did, that they would be all right. How can that not have happened? Didn't we do it right?"

Her lament set us all on edge as we gathered at the house church. It had been two weeks since Matilda's death, and I'd made several trips out to Stauffer Farm. Opal was tethered at the post there, giving milk for the baby. I came to comfort those grieving Matilda and her infant, but also to soothe my own sadness. I carried another worry too, hidden like a small child, hoping no one would notice the broken milk pitcher. I didn't want Jacob to become an angry man, to blame himself for moving toward a marriage that instead of giving him joy now left him empty. Jacob hadn't talked to me, and his sisters said he spoke to no one, just sat in the room and stared. He didn't seem able to look at the baby much either when they brought the infant to him.

"We did what we could do," Almira said. "It isn't ours to decide such things as life or death. The things in between, yes, those belong to us. Doing something worthwhile. Giving back to others. That we can control, but not life or death."

"Amen to that," Louisa said. Since the dedication of the church, Louisa had been a regular at our house church. Once or twice she even asked an opinion about how to talk to her daughter-in-law about the way she kneaded bread dough, or what we thought of a new *Fraktur* design she'd made. Today she continued, "I know something about death. My son Willie died, and I could do nothing for him. I prayed for them all. The same with my girls and Elias."

"Gloriunda, Aurora, Louisa," I said, not sure why I wanted to hear the girls' names spoken out loud.

"All such good girls," Louisa nodded. "And I prayed that they'd live, or that I might die instead."

"Your prayers weren't answered," Christine said.

"So we go on. Don't we? It is what makes us human, to live and endure the deaths of those we love. Maybe if we're young enough, we try again to have children. Maybe if we lose a husband, we try again to marry, *ja*, Emma? That doesn't always work so well, *nein*, but we try to find, if not a reason, a comfort in what happens. We find God in it, eventually."

"Why pray, then?" Christine asked in her tentative voice. "If we can't make things happen through our prayers, then why bother?"

"Our faith overcomes death," Almira said. "That is our hope. At least that's how I see it."

It occurred to me in that moment that this was a way we found Providence within the trials, within these expressions of grief and wonder, of uncertainty and hope. We meandered on our faith paths, not only through the Scripture readings and our leaders' interpretations, but through hearing of how others lived through tragedy and trial. I'd once thought it took great courage to live isolated and alone, but living with one another took more. Our reward was hearing words that rang a bell within our souls. We'd be encouraged by the toll.

"I think prayer is how God moves us, more than how we get God to move," I said. "It's as with any friend or husband or wife: you talk, you share, you don't always understand, but you are there and you feel them there, and somehow you can live inside the loose threads of life because of that. Prayer, for me, is like a basket filled with love from which one draws courage for the next step forward."

"That's a lovely thought, Emma," Helena said. She stared at me. I couldn't read her expression.

"Is it?" I hadn't known I knew that until I'd said it.

"Though I'm not sure how scriptural," she added.

"It sounds scriptural," Louisa said. "I'm sure Scripture promises we'll be fed and filled up. In Hosea there's a verse like that."

"In Malachi, it says people who fear the Lord hearken together, and that our prayers are heard. They create a scroll of remembrances."

"What's 'hearken' mean, anyway?" Kate asked.

"To listen attentively with one's heart. The verse gives support to the times we gather here, on our own, without one of the advisors to guide us in spiritual discussions." I expected Helena to protest, but she didn't.

A spring rain surprised us and patted against the windowpanes. Matilda's death, and her baby's, had left us subdued as we sewed. We'd brought Matilda's Sunflower quilt back with us and were reinforcing the hex wheel pattern, as though doing so would make the quilt stronger and last longer for her surviving child.

"When I knew the rest of you were praying, I guess it did help some," Christine said. "I didn't feel so alone."

"It's what I like about all of us living here together," Kitty said.

"We don't all live here," Martha Miller pointed out.

"I know that," Kitty defended. "But we all live in this place together, this Aurora, and that has the same…I don't know, comfort, I guess. People know one another and care about one another, even if there are skirmishes now and then. There always are in families."

"I've wondered if I should have…meddled," I said. "Getting them married and all." I'm not sure why I confessed such a thing. But saying it out loud gave relief. I took in a deep breath. Perhaps my wayward ways could be curtailed by confession now and then.

"My husband has good reasons not to permit marriages," Louisa said. She held her needle up in the air, making her point. "There is pain within those vows. You ought to remember that, Emma."

"Yet if we avoid making a commitment to someone else, hoping to avoid pain, that doesn't work, either," Almira said. "Separation is just another sort of pain."

"I suppose there are wounds outside of marriage too," Louisa said. "But listening to my husband when he refuses permission to marry can prevent a good share of such discomfort."

"Who's to say that I might not have had even more pain in my life if I hadn't married Christian? We had more than five years together, and they were good years."

"Apparently not enough to last a lifetime," Louisa said. "You married again."

"Even the apostle Paul said it was better to marry than to burn," Kitty said. She pooched her lower lip out the way Kate sometimes did. "You'd think God would send someone my way, so I wouldn't burn up."

"I remember reading Goethe, our old German poet," Martha said. " 'Love and desire are the spirit's wings to great deeds.' " I didn't know she read the classics. "You made a way for Jacob and Matilda. I suspect that for a time, they soared."

"Thank you for that, Martha." My words came out as a whisper.

"We all pushed it along," Kitty said. "And Matilda was happy for it. You helped give her that happiness. And baby Matilda's life testifies to their love. And who knows? Jacob may marry again one day since the first time was a joy for him." She looked up at the rain coming against the window. "Maybe I'll bake a special torte for him. I'll take it out there myself, and I'll just hearken to him."

"Goethe also said that 'a useless life is an early death,' " Martha continued. "Matilda's life was far from useless."

We talked more about who was to say whether Matilda's few short years of happiness with Jacob were enough to outweigh her youthful death. My girls listened intently, their eyes moving back and forth between the speakers, but staying silent as though they understood the importance of this discussion. Po yawned in the corner near the fireplace, got up, turned around three times, and plopped back down.

Christine said, "She had a loving husband, months of knowing she would give birth to twins. She had a family caring for her. She had a beautiful home. She had us. She gave away gifts to friends. She laughed often. She quilted with such truth and beauty. And she had her faith. One of her babies survived and is being loved by many. I'm not sure there is more to a full life than that, even if she'd lived to be one hundred."

We all nodded, hearkening together.

———

Private conversations were difficult to have at my home.

"Christine," I said when she'd returned from work at the Keil house. She pulled her straw hat off, set it on the table beside the door. "I wonder if you'd care to take a walk with me." I was tired from working at the new hotel myself and then coming home to help Almira with the wash. Kitty and Christine had said they'd do the ironing tomorrow. It had grown hot in the dip where our village settled, but at least near the river we had a breeze in the evening, and often it pushed away the mosquitoes and other insects too. Mount Hood loomed white and lustrous in the distance. Christine put her hat back on, and I locked my arm in hers as we walked down the steps side by side. "Have I done something wrong?" she said.

"No. But it's nearly your time and—"

"You're wondering what will happen," she said. We'd found the path, but it was now unmarked, except for our own worn footsteps from the season before. The pine cones and branches the girls lined the paths with had been brushed away by winds and animals, including Po.

We walked around the path in silence for a while, following the footsteps of others. Po sniffed at twigs and lifted his head from time to time to assure himself that we stayed close.

I'd told Christine that praying for ourselves as we walked toward the center and praying for others on the way out was a good practice. It's what I did now, hearing only the crunch of our feet on the pebbles and last year's leaves. Crows called to us. When we made it back out, I could smell the cooking fires from homes near my house. Bacon and bean and sausage scents drifted in the air.

"So let's discuss this plan. You're going to leave us and go to Portland?" She nodded. "I wonder when you thought to do that, or how you planned to get there."

She shrugged her now broad shoulders, picked up a long stem of grass, and chewed on it. My father often did that as he thought. "I'll catch a ride with someone. Maybe take the stage?" She sounded tentative.

"Before the baby arrives or after?"

"Oh, before."

"So you have somewhere to stay, to deliver the baby once you reach Portland?"

"No. But I can find someone, someplace. I did last time."

"Christine, I want to say this kindly, but I believe you're in this situation because you really didn't think things through the last time. And now you're avoiding thinking of things again."

"I'm not avoiding it, exactly," she said.

"Planning ahead does remind us of times when we didn't do it before," I said. "I know about that. But remember those little foxes that can spoil the fruit? Well, putting off important things can spoil the vineyard too."

Christine raised her voice. "Matilda and Jacob planned a life, and see what happened? Maybe we're meant to float along and let fate take us where it will, like a leaf in the stream."

"Christine, waiting for things to occur—"

"He didn't overcome me. I was willing," she blurted out. "That's what I feel so terrible about. It means I'll probably do it again. And maybe again, because I don't know how to judge what's genuine affection or not. I don't know how to say no to something I should."

"You said he wasn't the marrying kind. What made you say that?" I hoped her answer wouldn't be, *"Because he's already married."*

"He likes his ale, and he goes to Portland at times, and he says he plays cards there. He isn't a musician. He doesn't have anything to really fill his time after he works, except to be flirtatious, to find willing girls, I guess. A man serious about finding a wife wouldn't do that. Jacob Stauffer never did those things. What Matilda said about him, why she liked him, that's what I'd like in a husband one day too, though after this, who would ever marry me?"

"Any number of good men might marry you. But you might never find a husband, Christine, and it would have not a thing to do with your worthiness for one. A lot of women don't marry and not only because they're a part of a colony where the leader frowns on weddings. After wars, when so many men die, there often aren't enough men available to marry every willing woman. Some women prefer alone time and not having to ask permission or explain." These were good things I found about not living with Jack, especially that not-seeking-permission part.

"I'll meet someone in Portland," she said. "Or maybe I'll curl up after the baby comes and…" She shrugged.

"You've been walking on a path that takes you to the same place, all the while telling yourself you aren't there. When you can trust yourself to act in your best interest, Christine, then you'll have a full life, even if you never marry."

"Are we supposed to think so much about ourselves? Isn't that self-centered? Our mother often mentioned that."

"Scripture says to love our neighbor as ourselves. We can best care for others if we truly care about ourselves. A healthy person has more to give than one who thinks of curling up and…disappearing."

"What do you think I should do?" she said.

"I'm not sure, but leaving it to chance isn't wise. Sometimes we have to lean on friends and trust them for the next step."

"I worry about Almira," Christine said after we'd walked in silence. I assumed that Christine had had enough of "planning" for one day.

"You know the German poet Martha mentioned, Goethe?" She nodded her head. "He also wrote that when we sweep in front of our own doors, then the whole world will be clean. Don't you worry about Almira. You have just one door to worry about, but how well you sweep in front of it will help the rest of this world get tended to as well."

I stopped at the pharmacy to talk to Martin about Christian celebrating his birthday with us at the end of the month. The only birthdays the colony really celebrated were the Keils', in March. Most of us didn't make any fuss over our children's birthdays or our own, but even after Christian turned nine, I still wanted a little celebration for him. And I wanted something more for my headaches too. The headaches had increased after Matilda's death, and my own cycle of living made a change in flow. I knew I couldn't be with child but wondered whether I wasn't too young for such bodily changes so early. Or maybe they weren't early. Maybe this was the sign that my own body was slowing down. What would be left for me to do, once my girls were raised? Would I find a life as Helena had, at times strident and other times serene, just being in service? Whatever might have passed between Helena and Wilhelm Keil had apparently ceased, for I saw no evidence of special treatment or even the distant looks of longing that I'd once thought I'd seen. Maybe my skills of observation were fading along with my body, my flow being replaced by headaches, pinched eyes, and an occasional cough.

Andy was there. His back was to me, and he concentrated so intensely on his work that I startled him when I spoke from across the counter. He dropped the mortar he'd been holding. I apologized; he cleaned up what had been spilled and then asked how he could help me. *I'm merely a customer to him. Where is that tenderness I thought we were finding?*

"I need to speak to Martin, about headache medicine," I said. "I wanted to ask him, too, if he had anything for weeping eyes. Your aunt Johanna has that trouble."

"Martin sent a poultice to her," he said.

"Did he? Well, that was thoughtful. Did she come by?"

"Often. But I noticed it, too, when I visit."

"Well, that's good, then." We stood awkwardly, my head throbbing, and a strange ache settled in my heart. "I never see the family unless I go there," I said. "They never visit me. I run into them at the Park House sometimes. Well, it's good she gets out, then."

"He has powders for Aunt Lou too. Aunt Louisa, I mean. She prefers to be called Louisa, did you know that?" I hadn't. "I'll tell him you were here."

I almost raised the question of his coming to our home for my little party for Christian, but another customer walked in, nodded to me, and asked Andy if he had something for an aching tooth.

"A hops pack works well," I said.

Andy frowned. I'd intruded. This was his place, not mine.

"It'll have to be pulled," Andy told him, as he looked in the man's mouth. "Martin told you that before."

The man looked sheepish but nodded his head. "*Ja*, I dread that. When should I come back, then, Andrew? May as well get it over with. I can't go seranatin' with a bad tooth, now, can I?"

My son set up an appointment for him, and I saw in the interaction a strong young man, capable of garnering confidence from his elders, though he had few years and much yet to learn. But it saddened me that he didn't smile at the man whose tooth hurt him so; it saddened me that he was growing older and would soon have no need for a mother's influence, even from a distance. And I grieved a bit that he didn't call me Mother when he said good-bye.

I found Christian at the Ehlen house. Mr. Ehlen and his daughters cooked good meals, Christian told me. He looked torn when I asked him if he'd like to come to dinner, a late birthday celebration at the end of the month. "We was going to go up into the mountains and do some fishing," he said. I let his grammar error go, and he continued, "It'll be a good time of year, won't it, Mr. Ehlen?" The older man nodded. "Can we do it some other time, Mama?"

"Of course," I said. "You can all come, Mr. Ehlen, if you'd like." Everyone nodded agreement, but they didn't offer up a date.

I walked back slowly toward my house. Keil or the committee had ordered signs made for the streets, and one day we'd have addresses like when we lived in Bethel. But for now if anyone came looking for another, they'd simply knock on any door and be directed.

I wasn't ready to go home yet. My head hurt, but the sun felt good on my face, so I kept walking. My boys had their own lives. Soon my girls, too, would find pursuits with friends. They'd marry and be gone, and how would I fill my time, then? Stitch clothes. Put up preserves. Cook and bake. Karl said there were women hoping to change laws, so they could vote and keep their own earnings. Maybe my persuasive talents could be applied to such work. Making a meaningful life as a single woman was a challenge for more people than Christine or Kitty or Almira. It was my challenge too, even though I wasn't a single woman.

I walked past the Park House. The late afternoon shadows were like ripples of changing light across the green. It reminded me of the material Karl had purchased for me, the one that changed colors as you lifted it to the sunlight. I walked the paths for a time, then came through the trees to stand before the church. It was open and I went inside. Christine sat there. I didn't make a sound, but I wondered if perhaps the answer to her need was with me.

———

"There's something I want to tell you all," Christine began.

The four of us remained in the parlor: Kitty, Almira, Christine, and me. I'd not spoken to her that day in the church. Instead I'd gone back through the paths at the Park House and spent that evening with my aching head out beneath the stars, wrapped in my Running Squares quilt. The longer I stayed there, the better I felt about telling Christine that I'd take her child and raise it as my own. It would be my renewal.

I knew about babies. What could anyone do to me if I suddenly appeared with a child in my arms? No one would ever have to know where the child came from, and I could simply say that I was acting on the Diamond Rule, making another's life better than my own.

So when Christine spoke, I thought she would tell the others of her dilemma, and I could offer my solution.

"Almira is going to take my baby," Christine said instead.

"What baby?" Kitty asked.

"The one I'm going to have sometime soon. It's a very long story," she said, silencing questions already forming on Kitty's tongue. "She's made plans to return to the Clatsop Plains to be closer to her children. I'll go with her."

"You have?" I turned to Almira.

She looked back serenely.

"But won't people wonder where you got this child?" Kitty asked. "Won't they say despicable things about you, Almira, arriving as a divorced woman, with a baby?"

"They might," Almira said. "But I'm stronger now because of my time here. And this baby needs a good home that I can provide with my son and his wife. They've invited me to return to them, since I finally wrote and told them where I'd been. It will be a good thing for me to do, to care for their children and for this one."

"I'll have the baby there, Emma. At Almira's children's home. No one here will need to know, if everything goes all right."

"Your first child, it could be difficult," Kitty said. "Mama was a midwife for first-time mothers, and she said it was always a surprise what might happen."

"Don't you think it's a good idea, Emma?" Christine asked me directly now. "I planned it out, just like you said I should. I worked out the details with Almira."

"Yes. Of course. I thought you'd…stay here. Have the baby here. I'll be sorry to see you and Almira both leave."

"There'll be someone else to take my place," Almira said. "I couldn't be moving on if you hadn't rescued me."

"Wagners do that," Kitty said. She looked at Christine. "But you don't even look like you'll soon have a baby."

"You don't have to see to believe."

"Is the father someone we know?" Kitty asked.

"It's better if I don't say. Almira will be the baby's mother, and she can make up whatever story she wants."

"Well, I am flummoxed," Kitty said. She put the yardage she'd been stitching in a heap on her lap. "So much going on, and I didn't even know it. You knew, Emma?"

"I knew that Christine worked out a problem. I didn't know that she'd found so…agreeable a solution."

"It's just the beginning," Christine said. "I've been thinking of what you said, Emma. I've thought of sweeping in front of my own door and keeping it clean."

"You don't have your own door," Kitty said.

"Little foxes can spoil the wine. That's what you said. But if small things can bring spoilage, then perhaps minor changes made each day can bring goodness to the wine too."

"I thought you were talking about doors," Kitty said.

"I'll make day-by-day changes in my own life, so I won't complicate another infant's life in the way I have now tangled up…other lives."

Christine spoke further about the baby, Almira's move, and her travel plans when that time came. She'd be gone for a time; she'd have to be. Almira's departure would leave a gap in my days, as Christian's and Matilda's deaths had. As my sons' leaving had. Christine was right: little things done daily could bring good changes. I'd been thinking of a bigger investment in change, having Christine's baby to raise, but that was not to be. I sat listening to their words, thinking of brooms and making sweeps in front of my door. I had two doors to tend to. Family stood behind each.

23

Let Us Get Together

Running Squares. A piece from my own quilt made in honor of Christian.

Blue fabric. My mother made a dress for me as a child using this material. She said the Germans discovered indigo blue, and we should be proud of our heritage. My mother brought it with her. I'm glad I have the fabric swatch at least, a fine reminder of the gift. It's not enough to wrap my string of pearls in, though. Just a swatch.

Calico with blue flowers and yellow centers. Matilda's baby clothes. The swatch makes me think of Matilda's quilt with the vibrant sun colors. With leftover material I made a sleeping dress for Christine's baby. Maybe I should call it Almira's baby in case someone should ever see this fabric diary.

Christine planned to leave with Almira within the week. We talked of how we'd explain her absence and Almira's too. "I'm mostly concerned about our parents," Christine said. "They'll be so disappointed in me if they know the truth, if they learn of what I've done. I'm not sure they'd forgive me."

Knowing my family, there might be strain. I was living evidence that something could strain and there could still be stretch in the tension. Christine's leaving could trouble my parents, unless we created some story that would make it understandable to them and even to the Keil household. She wouldn't be working there anymore.

Then there was the father. I couldn't help but wonder who he was, and I found myself picturing any number of men who'd find Christine's company acceptable. But for all I knew, the father didn't even live in the colony now. The bachelors came and went. I hoped that her earlier plan to travel toward Portland hadn't been based on some string of interest in him she still clutched.

Kitty had a few pennies saved from her potato harvest last fall. Christine, too, had resources from her savings from before she came to Aurora. We sewed a wardrobe for the baby, but in an effort to keep the secret, put the cloth aside whenever Louisa or Helena or BW or my own mother attended our house church. We considered offering ourselves to area farms to help with spring plantings for pay to accumulate the last that we'd need. But then Almira's children sent money for the stage and fare for the ship that would take them on the Columbia River to the Clatsop Plains.

"I had peacefulness about the final fare the last time I walked the puzzle path," Almira said. "I knew what we needed would be provided." She purchased the tickets to take them north. She was going back stronger and with a purpose, to raise another child well.

The day of their departure, my daughters were at school. I thought of letting them come with us to say good-bye, but they'd said those words the night before, and I didn't want them to miss any of their studies.

I held Almira in my arms, then stepped back to take her hands in mine. I felt the stiffness of her knuckles. Martin's creams had helped her, but not as much as I had hoped. "You have a safe journey now. Write when you can. Be sure to tell us about Christine. Maybe send a telegram and say *'Strudel'* for a girl and *'Kartoffel'* for a boy." She nodded, hugged Kitty. I gave Almira a traveling desk that I'd built, using the same lumber that I'd had to make the curlicue addition to the porch supports. The inside was lined with the fabric that we'd pieced together to back Matilda's Sunflower quilt. "Small pieces of fabric to help remind you of your time here," I told her.

"It's been good time, Emma," Almira said. "I've watched how you dealt with your sadness over your sons by finding ways to give to others. Your generosity to me, I can never repay you. I'll remember the Diamond Rule. You are the sparkle in that rule." I started to protest, but she silenced me with her finger to my lips. Her finger felt warm and tender. "I know. The rule grows from your beliefs. But still, you live the rule. I see it. I'll remember."

For Christine, I'd sewn a wrapper from the yardage Karl had given me. I put tucks across the bodice and made it look somewhat opulent, with special stitches and a few tiny beads I'd put on the ledger book account at the Keil and Company Store. Those who might notice these two women would decide the larger of the two had gotten that way by overeating, indulging in life's riches, rather than harboring a child beneath the folds.

"You'll visit our parents?" Christine asked as we loaded her bag onto the stage. "Tell them I'm helping Almira. They'll understand that, won't they?"

"It's the perfect story," I said. "And not a lie either. In a few months' time you can return and no one will be the wiser."

"Helena won't like that explanation, I suppose," Christine said. "Or Louisa either."

"Let me worry about them," I said. "You get to the Clatsop Plains before that baby arrives." The last I whispered, so that the other riders on the stage couldn't hear, and neither could the driver.

"You've been a good sister to me, Emma," Almira told me. "I was a washbucket of nerves when I met you, not worth the soap it took to clean me up."

"You were never so worthless." I laughed.

"Yes I was. I slept and took and didn't give much back at all for months."

"I had room and resources, thanks to the colony."

"Thanks to your faithfulness too," she said. "I could restore my own." She straightened her hat; a flourish of Clara's blue feathers clutched the top and side of her head, making her look stylish and festive. Her skin glowed pink with the flush of a new adventure. If her husband saw her like this, vibrant and alive, he might well wish her back in his life, if not his bed.

"You be careful now," I said. "Don't do anything rash when you see him."

She blushed. "What makes you think I'll see him?"

"Oh, they always show up. I've never understood why people think a divorce will separate one from a difficult relationship; it just changes the circumstances under which those conflicts appear."

Almira grimaced, and I realized my thoughtlessness. "I didn't mean… I shouldn't have said that, Almira. I'm sorry. I know you didn't want to take that route. I only meant that men—"

"I know what you meant," she said. "It's a sign of my grit that I can hear that and not wither away with the words. Especially because what you say is right. He is the father of my children, and I loved him many years. That's the truth. And so is how that truth could be shattered, and everything I'd once loved vanish." Christian came immediately into my head…followed by Jack. There'd be another encounter with Jack, I was sure of that. "When I do see my husband," Almira continued, "I'll remember that I don't have to endure any of the humiliation he might bring. I can look for the small, good things that time might have allowed into our changed lives. And if there are none, then he can't humiliate me unless I allow it. And I won't."

Christine let out a rush of air, and I turned to her. "Are you all right?"

"I just need to get off my feet," she said. "They've swollen to the size of spittoons. If I don't sit down soon, I'll have to make another trip to the privy."

Almira stepped up into the stage, then turned to take Christine's hand. I pushed from behind. She truly had become a very large woman. She settled onto the smooth seat with a heavy hushed sound of the material swishing on leather. The scent of lavender rose up from the sachet pouch Christine wore. Almira squeezed in beside her. There were three passengers crowded together on the opposite side. Christine stared at them. She looked back at me with a grimace of someone who'd watched a snake crawl across her foot and was too frightened to shout. "It'll be all right," I told her. "It will."

"Let us go a May-ing, let us go a May-ing, one and all a joyous time," Kitty began. She sang the round from behind me. Christine laughed then and let out a long sigh. Almira patted her hand. No one sang the second stanza.

I hoped the jolting of the stage wouldn't create an adventure for those passengers or, worse, cause complications for Christine. At least Almira had birthed babies in her life—nine in thirteen years—so she'd know what to do. Christine was in good hands, and so was Almira. Kitty and I stepped back.

The driver closed the stage door. He pulled himself up onto the seat, lifted the lines of reins for the six-horse team, clicked his tongue at the animals, and off they went.

I might never see Almira again, but she was a part of who I'd become. Christine was family, fostered into the Wagner clan, and I was certain she'd return; but Almira was family too. Family had enlarged to include those I'd served. I added it to my gratitude list as the stage rattled across the bridge, taking them to their new lives.

———

Summer came on fluffy white clouds whose shadows played hide-and-seek with the fields. There were the usual changes in the months that followed. Keil agreed to a few more marriages but prevented others, and no one seemed to know why. He moved his workroom to the top floor of the *gross Haus,* sending the bachelors to bunk more closely together on the far side. In his workroom, he composed music along with several other colony men. A demand for traveling trunks increased, and furniture and workshops were built to accommodate the interest. We women painted them our colony blue, the color of the summer sky. The turners formed spool beds on a lathe, and people as far away as Seattle and San Francisco heard of our work and placed orders. Jacob Miller's turned work on the church attracted attention each time we entered, and there was talk of building another Keil house for Frederick and Louisa, with Jacob doing the railings and the pillars.

After Almira and Christine left, I took it upon myself to visit my parents daily. At first it was to tell them that Christine had traveled with Almira, that she wanted to see more of the territory and so had gone along.

"I'm surprised the Keils would let her go like that," my mother said. Jonathan was having breakfast there, and I realized that though he lived in a small house on his own, he must spend a fair amount of time with our parents. He had dirt under his fingernails, so he'd also been farming, a task added to his ledger keeping.

"She's an adult," my father noted. "Guess he can't tell adults much what to do. Unless they let him." I took that to be a swipe at my allowing Martin to raise my sons, but I didn't say so.

"Now, Father," Jonathan chastised. "Keil's mellowed. You ought to give the man another chance, truly."

"I don't despise the man at all," my father said. "I like being in charge of my own destiny. But this place has become more an economic community than a religious one. Saddens me."

"Me too," I said. "There are many in need of the Lord's love expressed through communal ways. Ways that Christian believed in, and you."

My father grunted his pleasure.

"I hope Christine comes back soon," my sister Louisa said. "She always brought candies from the Keils' house."

"I happen to have some peppermint sticks," I said. "Would you like one?"

She did, and that became my opening each time I stopped. It was a small act that brightened their day and mine too. Sometimes Kate and Ida were with me, and once Andy delivered a cone of medicine to my youngest brother, William, while I was there. With all the people around, I hoped no one would notice my awkwardness in my son's presence. He was old beyond his years, my son, and chattered easily with my father about world affairs and local politics. He tipped his cap at me when he left and said, "Mother."

I don't know why the gesture brought tears to my eyes, but it did. Maybe with more time, we'd find a path, or perhaps form a new one, one like Almira's puzzle path, which required no decisions about right or wrong ways, just the courage to enter in.

Helena and Louisa weren't quite so forgiving of Christine's departure. I invited them to the house church especially, offering dry plate cakes. They had to be served hot to stay crisp. While they brushed sugar from their faces, I told them that Almira had left and Christine had gone along to assist for a time.

"Who told her she could leave without letting anyone know?" Helena said. Then, more kindly she added, "She has a lovely voice, and I thought she added much to the choir."

"She told me," I said. "And it was time for Almira to go back. She felt that she should take care of old things, and Christine agreed to help her."

Louisa harrumphed. "Christine ate enough for two while she was here those last months. Honestly, she blew up like a mushroom. Took more than her share at the grain distribution. That's what my dear Wilhelm said, though I don't know how he'd know for certain. He didn't attend the distributions."

"She baked for the colony," Martha Miller said. She'd joined us, and though she didn't know the details, she had a conciliatory way about her. She was neutral. Probably why the elections were always held at her father's home. "So it might not have been that she ate it all."

"Maybe her time away will help her put things into better proportions," I said.

"Just as well that Almira's gone," Helena said. "I never liked those paths she had. It's like something from the druids, walking in certain ways through the woods like that." She shivered.

"It's simply a way of praying," I said. "Didn't you pray as you walked across the plains?"

"We came around the Horn," Helena corrected.

"*Ach, ja.* I forgot. But didn't you walk about the ship and pray? I find it restful. Almira and the girls do too, to walk those paths."

"Prayers aren't supposed to be restful," Helena said. "They're supposed to humble us and make us think about the errors of our ways."

" 'I think myself happy.' The apostle Paul wrote that. Surely one result of a prayer ought to be happiness and hope. Isn't hope the whole message of our faith?"

Helena whisked her hand at me as she said, "*Ach,* sometimes I don't know where you get your ideas from, Emma. No wonder Wilhelm didn't want the boys exposed so much to your thinking."

After all this time, her words still stung.

I took a deep breath, offered her another cake. "Fortunately I had early years with them, and isn't there another scripture that says if you raise your children up in the ways that they shall go, when they are older they will not depart from them?"

"*Ja,* it may be too late."

"Or just enough time," I said.

I could hope.

Christian arrived at our door one morning a few days after. "I'm running errands for the telegraph," he told me proudly. I invited him in for breakfast. The girls were both up and dressed and welcomed him like a lost relative. Well, I suppose in a way, that's what he was. He scooped up the cornmeal pancakes, added molasses and dried berries, and said, " 'Member when I ground the corn for you, Mama?" I said that I did, and any time he wanted to come back and do that, he sure could. He beamed. "Do you still keep the water bucket cool in the root cellar?" he asked but didn't wait for my answer. "This water tastes better than at Martin's and Brother Keil's houses. Oh, here's the telegram," he said, pulling it from his shirt. He patted Po, whose tail pounded on the floor beneath the table.

"I have a telegram? And you just now gave it to me?"

"I was hungry," he defended.

I read it. "It's from Almira," I said. "Remember her?" Christian still scratched at Po's head, shook the dog's ears, and nodded yes that he did. "I remember Opal too," he said. "Is she tied up out there?"

"She's in a pen," Kate said. "We lent her out until Jacob got his own goat. But she has to stay tied now, or she'd come right inside here and eat everything on the table, dirty knees and all. She came upstairs once."

"In my room?" Christian asked.

"Po chased her out. He grabs at her ears," Kate said. "And we have to watch him with Clara too."

"She stayed with us," Ida said, bringing us back to the telegram. "Almira did. She's family, *ja*, Mama?"

I nodded, then read to myself.

"What's it say, Mama?" Kate asked.

"It's about food," Christian said.

"You read it?" Kate said. "That's not nice, is it, Mama?"

"It's nice that Christian can read, but you ought not to read other people's private words," I told him.

"Not many words to worry over," Christian said.

"That's not really your place to decide," I said. "Kate's correct. If you want to keep your job as a telegraph man, you'll have to keep the words they give you very private."

"*Strudel* and *Kartoffel*. That's all I remember, Mama. I won't say it to anyone else, except when I want to eat it." He grinned.

———

In August, Barbara Giesy, my mother-in-law and widow of Andreas, passed away. She was old by the standards of so many women. She would have reached seventy-four in December. It spoke to the good care she'd had all her life, despite the hard work she was asked to perform. In her later years, Helena had tended her, as had her daughter-in-law BW. Andy acted as a pallbearer, and the band played the funeral dirge that Keil had composed for his Willie those many years before.

The large bell began the funeral procession from John's house, and then the next size bell, and then the smallest, the tolling going on until the casket reached the church. The bells pealed again when we headed toward the cemetery where she would be buried. I decided that day, as I stood off to the edge of the gravestones, that when I died I wanted to be buried here too, but not near the Giesy plot. Somewhere off to the side. Somewhere at the edge. Maybe with my daughters' families. That's where I belonged.

Fall brought harvest and news that some of our "boys," who had been staked by Keil and headed to the gold fields near Canyon City, had made good of it. They came back for the winter to report. Few had found gold, but they'd tried their hand at storekeeping and cobbling shoes. They noted a market for hops and encouraged us to plant more land in that crop, assured that we could sell it to supplement their "meager fare," as they described it. I remembered that we'd sold oysters to the California gold market years ago and thought those men ate well. None of our colony boys looked as if they'd had to skip a meal. Most just said they were tired and cold and didn't want to spend another winter in the Blue Mountains, surrounded by miners with nothing better to do than drink and fight and lament their lost loves while they waited for spring. They were happy to be home in Aurora.

The Oregon State Fair had come around in October, as it always did. The band rehearsed its pieces, seranatin' us (as some called it) well into the night. We had more horses to enter in the races, and our cattle looked sleek and prime. I thought it might be due to our huge barns made to care for the animals and keep them out of the weather.

Most of the colony found a reason to attend the fair that year.

I decided to enter something I'd made after Matilda died. Using scraps of fabric, I pieced the odd shapes and sizes, with stark angles and curved edges, onto a fabric backing. But instead of quilting it as I'd always done, I made tiny replicas of some of the shapes and stuffed them with bits of wool so they rose up off the fabric. I hand-tacked the patches and used a small buttonhole stitch over the raw edges. I'd seen a woman working on a quilt like this when Christian and the scouts and I had ridden across the west those years before. The quiltmaker had hailed from Virginia, and she called what she did appliqué.

Mine, when I finished, I framed. It was more a picture than a quilt that could bring comfort or warmth, though I hoped it brought rest for one's eyes. I gave it depth with the stuffed pieces. I wanted people to touch it, to feel the give within the appliqué, to know that it was made of sturdy, discarded stuff but could still be purposeful.

I'd made a landscape scene, bucolic some might say, composed of blue sky and clouds hovering over a log home. A river skirted the edge, and trees soared above the white painted fence circling the yard. Four children, a goat, a sheep, and one dog lounged about. The house had two doors, and I made them with cloth flaps so that the doors could actually be opened if one took the time. Behind one door a tiny candle glowed, an effort of creation that had kept me up well into the night. Behind the other, against a dark wall, a bowl of apples, made with French knots of embroidery thread, graced a table. It had taken me many hours, and I'd shared my efforts with my girls. Both had a fine hand with the needle, and I thought back at how I would otherwise have filled my time if my boys had been daily in my life. Maybe I never would have found quiet encouragement within fabric. My entry hung in the Household Arts exhibit tent.

The girls slept by our wagon now. Po snored at my feet, his long, skinny tail flapping the floor any time I said his name. This wasn't the life Christian and I had planned, but it was a good life. I'd woven meaning into the loose threads that had taken me from Bethel to Willapa and now to Aurora. It dawned on me that I'd found my *Heimat* at last in Aurora.

I'd urged my parents to attend the fair and bring Louisa too. Johanna didn't think I understood how much work it would be, but I offered to stay with them, to bring my girls, and even cook up enough for all of us. That way we could enjoy ourselves, or they could, while I fixed meals over the open fire. I rather liked the informality of fair cooking, where no one complained about the extra dirt that might make its way into their potatoes, the way they did at home if they found a dog or goat hair in the mix.

They agreed to go. Jonathan drove a wagon and so did my father, though neither Christian nor Andy was allowed to accompany us— Martin had his classes, and Andrew covered the store. I wasn't sure why Christian had been kept back. Some things just happened. We had all the rest of our family there—the girls, Kitty, and my younger brothers, who didn't stay with us but who at least took their meals with us. They bunked at the horse barns, and I suspected they made wagers on the outcomes of the races.

Christine, too, was absent, but it wasn't upsetting. There was an ebb and flow to this family; sometimes it supported and sometimes it tore at the edges, as our colony could.

We ate and walked and listened and took in the smells of the fair and the fall. A cluster of people slowed our meandering through the Household Arts exhibit, and it took a few minutes before I realized that a crowd was standing in front of my entry. My mother peered around a woman and took a long look. She said she thought the little doors a clever stitching.

"A scene with cloth," my mother said. "But small enough to hang on a wall, and those pieces that rise up. How interesting." She leaned in, touched the puffy clouds, and ran her hand over the texture of the fibers. "Appliqué," she read. Then she saw my name on the ticket. She gasped. "I had no idea you did such work, Emma. That's my daughter's work," she told anyone around her. I beamed. "Will you show me how?"

"We can begin today if you want," I said.

"*Nein.* We will have that be a winter project. You bring the girls, and we'll sit around the fire. Maybe Christine will be back by then, and you can teach us all."

There were tucks in our relationship that might never be smoothed out, but that didn't have to mean we could not go on sewing up new memories, stitching otherwise-frayed hems. I could imagine myself sitting with them, talking, my showing them a stitch and their telling me of their day. Papa might smoke out on the porch. I'd bring Po along, so he could walk me and the girls home at the end of the evening. Maybe they'd ask us to spend the night, which we'd decline because of the tiny space, but it would feel right to have been invited. The home art, as my piece was called in the fair, would be a good place for our experiences and imagination to intersect. We'd create an artifact that might take on a life of its own.

We walked out into the sunlight, and I squinted, nearly stumbling over a shovel leaned against the side of the exhibit barn.

"Are you all right?" A small, callused hand reached out for mine. "I didn't mean to leave the shovel aleaning there. I hope you didn't get hurt?"

I recognized the voice and smiled as I looked into the eyes of Brita. "I daydreamed," I said. "It wasn't your fault at all."

24

To Provide For

October 6. Received my second ribbon at the fair. I appliquéd but a small portion. Instead, I used red thread to outline every piece of fabric regardless of its color or texture. It reminded me of the veins I see in the back of my mother's hands, only I have made the color red instead of blue. My mother said it looked confused, but I didn't mind. It looked organized to me.

Brita's eyes were pinched, and dirt filled in lines around them that I hadn't remembered.

"Where are the boys?" I looked around.

"They are finding work, staying with farmers who can feed them and give them a warm bed at night. I never could make it once we left the livery."

"I'm sorry. Why didn't you go back to the Durbin brothers or come to Aurora?" I asked. "We'd have made room for you. Did you never get my letters?"

"I wanted to do it myself," she said.

I remembered my own difficulty in reaching for hands that could keep me from falling. "You can come now," I told her. "You'd be welcome."

She shook her head. "I work here, at the fair."

"But you always said you would never go back to the carnival."

She bristled, straightened her back. "I'm not in the circus. I pick up things. I guess they thought I was so close to the ground, my back wouldn't hurt with the reaching and bending. It's good work. I tidy things up."

"Well, of course it's good work. Tidying is what we women do, and usually no one even notices unless we don't." She smiled, her shoulders relaxed. "Would you consider coming later? The fair doesn't last but four or five days. Then what? I have a home. You could bring your boys."

I saw it all in a flash: There'd be the sounds of boys in my house again. We'd find reason to laugh in the midst of our work. "The girls will love seeing Pearl again too," I said.

Her eyes filled with tears. "I'd best return to my station. It was good to see you again, Emma. Tell your boys and those girls hello for me." She looked away.

"Where is Pearl?" The boys were old enough to have been farmed out to hopefully kind couples, but Pearl was a young one. "You never said."

"She didn't make it," she said. A sob broke from her throat. "It was a silly plan, my ahomesteading. Pearl got ill. We were far from the town. She died before I could get her to a doctor." Her grief caught in her throat. "We can't always do everything we set our hearts on, can we? I risked it all, and in the end I had to give up."

Her words bored like an ocean drill into the oyster of my heart. So much of what I'd hoped for hadn't come about either, no matter how much I longed for it, prayed for it. Yet my life was full. All of my children lived. My sons stayed healthy and would go on to school one day; my girls skipped with activity, were being educated with the warmth of family to surround them, and they, too, would pursue their *Sehnsucht,* their dreams and desires. I didn't get to see my boys daily or influence them as I might like, but I still saw them. I wished they'd choose to see me more often, but my own parents felt the same way about me. One could never seem to satisfy that longing for a visit by a child, except to live with them. Or live so close that it felt as though one did. But families then had to suffer the irritations of familiarity rather than the agonies of perceived neglect. There was no perfect solution.

Brita and I moved out of the way so others could walk around us. I touched her shoulder. "I'm so sorry, Brita. Losing a child…" I remembered when Christian died, how my time with his mother after that had been when I'd felt the closest to her. She'd lost a child; I'd lost my husband. But they still weighed unequally; losing a child weighed more.

"My heart has a slice right through it," she said, drawing her wide palm like a sword across her small chest. "I don't know what'll ever be a-mending it. She might have lived if I'd been less stubborn. I thought I could keep her fever down. I couldn't. I don't think the boys will ever forgive me, either. But then, I'll never forgive myself."

"Oh, Brita, we all do things we later regret. It's another thing you and I have in common with everyone else who admits it. But Pearl would want you to forgive yourself. I just know it."

I'd done so many things that I regretted. But I'd also taken steps to change through the years, to cherish what I had, to nurture hope, and to use new brush strokes to bring vibrancy to the painting of my life. I wanted that for my friend too.

"Brita. Get the boys back and come stay with us. If only for a time. We could feed you…not out of pity, but because we can, and you could give back, get restored until you know what you want to do next, truly."

She shook her head. "It would only be a temporary fix," she said. "Like putting a tack where a nail is needed."

"What's wrong with that?"

"It's a coward's way out."

"Oh, Brita, how can you say that? You once lived in a cave; you didn't plan to live there forever, did you?"

In the distance I could hear the band playing. At the end of the piece came applause. If we'd been sitting there watching and listening, we'd have heard the musicians talk briefly to one another, the movement of music papers, and then they'd clear the spit valves on their horns, that little whistle of sound that Henry C, the conductor, said wasn't really spit but pure water formed from their breath as it condensed on the metal. The band began again. My sisters and parents had moved on to stand outside the dance hall door, leaving us alone.

"I never planned a long time in the cave or to stay at Aurora, but I did think the homestead would be forever," she said. She poked at the ground with her picking-up stick. "I thought my purpose was to save those boys, build a home for them and Pearl, and have a place no one could ever take away from us."

"Maybe it never was to be the house," I said. She frowned, looking up at me. "Your purpose. Maybe it was to be with them, wherever that was, however that might be. Maybe that was the goal, and where you did that, or the adjustments you had to make, the kind of shelter you provided, standing tall for them…as tall as you could, maybe that's all that really matters in the end. For any of us."

"Maybe," she said. "But I failed there, too, then."

"It's only one step. You can take the next one. I'll walk with you."

I couldn't convince her, any more than my relatives and friends could have convinced me those dark days in Willapa. But what I'd said to her, what I'd thought out loud before I even knew it, that was what I planned to piece and stitch and frame one day to remind myself: "It's not the house but the shelter." That's what truly mattered.

———

Christine returned in November. I hardly recognized her. She was thinner than when she'd first come to Aurora, long before she'd danced at the fair with an interested man. But it was more than her physical change that I noticed: she had an air about her, a spirit of anticipation that drew others to her. She said she'd waited to return until after the fair, not wanting to see any old friends just yet. "I'm learning to live inside this new person," she said. "Sometimes I can bend over to stoke the fire and stand back up without even leaning on a staff. I can move without making waves."

"You were always light on your feet," Kitty said.

"I eat and work the same," she said. "But I feel filled up now. The time with Almira was good. We walked new paths, ones she made at her son's house. Maybe it was the walking," she said. "But I did plenty of that here too." She shrugged her shoulders, seemed to accept the change in her life without absolute explanation.

"You look...different," Kitty said. "Happier."

"I am that. I remembered things you said, Emma, about being worthy, from the inside out. That's the door I've opened."

When we were alone, she told me about the delivery of her twins and her sadness when she said good-bye to them and returned here. "But Almira is good to them. And her children are good to her, the older boy and his wife. I didn't meet Almira's husband, but I don't think she's even thinking of returning to him. She said she'd find happiness every morning when she looked in the eyes of those children. I named one Emma," Christine said, "and the other one Karl."

"Not..."

"Not for his father, no, no. *Nein.* For Karl Ruge. The teacher. He was always so kind to me. When my son grows up, I want him to be like Karl. And my daughter, well, Almira's daughter, I'm hoping she'll be generous, like you."

"*Ach,* no," I said and waved my hand in dismissal.

"You ought to let a compliment come your way now and then," Christine said.

Twice now I'd been described as generous, and that thought surprised. My sister Johanna, through her love for my parents and brothers and sisters, stood much higher on the ladder of compassion than I did.

"When you take a compliment in, you do your children a favor," Christine continued. "Almira said letting her children watch their father demean her was one of the worst things she did to them. She didn't realize that until she'd had time here to heal. She's going to let me be a part of the children's lives. I'll be like an aunt to them. It will be best for us all."

"You've exchanged wisdom for your weight," I said. She grinned.

———

At the harvest dances, Christine had her share of beaus inviting her to *Schottische* or to do the webfoot quickstep. She appeared to enjoy herself, but she told me one day, as we kneaded dough together preparing for the Christmas celebrations of December, that she didn't think she'd ever marry. I cajoled her, telling her she was yet young and any number of things could happen to her that she didn't now think possible. But she said she couldn't tell any potential husband about her three babies, and she couldn't imagine beginning a marriage without telling someone she loved the whole truth. It was a sacrifice she thought made sense.

"I'm sure there are useful things for me to do. And I can be happy knowing I've done good work, apart from caring for a husband or children."

"Jacob Stauffer said something like that a few weeks back," I said. I sprinkled flour onto the table and folded the dough over yet again. "He said he'd done good work in providing for Matilda, giving her a good home and happiness for however short a time. I was so glad to see him thinking that way."

"He'll marry again sometime," Christine said. She patted her dough into shape, then placed it in the tin and sprinkled salt across the top. "Maybe Martha Miller."

"Are you matchmaking?" I said. "I thought that was my job." She laughed. "You may be a little late anyway," I said. "Jacob told me that Christina Wolfer had brought him a chocolate cake with that coconut on it. His eyes lit up as he described it. She served it on that blue plate her mother rescued on the trail."

"I hope her brother doesn't find out his mother still has that butter plate," Christine said.

"Food is the elixir for grief," I said. "That's something we know, *ja?*"

"But it's not all that fills us up."

I echoed Karl and made her laugh when I said, "*Ja,* by goodness, that's right."

I washed the girls' hair on Saturday before the Christmas gathering began. I wondered if this schedule of limited worship was Keil's way of being sure we didn't get caught up in ritual. If he'd done it to halt our house church, that hadn't worked. We still met, and we worshiped as we worked. And on the off Sundays, when the church was empty, I often went there in the mornings myself and would find Helena there, sometimes Karl Ruge, or others of the colony worshiping. *Maybe that's Keil's intention after all, that we worship on our own without a named leader.* Certainly no one was really being groomed to replace him, except for the advisors. But I'd never known a church to be run by a group without a named leader.

Despite the kindling in the kitchen stove, the room felt damp and cool with all of us having our hair washed. We heated the water in big copper pots on the stove, had the girls lean over another blue washtub, and poured the water over their hair first. We collected the wastewater and would reuse it for the next head of hair. Kitty scrubbed with our soap; Christine rinsed, keeping fresh water heated. I dried Ida's hair, rubbing her curly strands between the flannel towels before continuing the routine with Kate, who was young woman enough she could do it on her own. But I liked the ritual as much as she seemed to. After all of us had wet hair and were hoping it would dry before it froze and broke off, someone rubbed our heads as dry as they could, and we'd begin running the comb through our tangles, making the best of the some-times tearful pulls against our scalps. Kitty introduced another round to sing that acted as distraction.

I did like this time together. I inhaled the aroma of the soap and hair rinse, which didn't really seem to help with tangles all that much but did make our hair smell grand. I liked knowing that simple water and soap would make another feel good, and that my children and sis-ters had clean and mended clothes to put on later. It comforted me knowing we had wood enough for the winter, stacked up beside the wash house, and that both Po and Opal were happy inside it during cold nights like tonight. *Ja,* I'd brought Clara into a cage at night so she could be safe inside too. Our flock of colony chickens had their roost house to stay warm in. We women had boots to wear and gloves with sheep's wool lining and knitted hats to go over our wet hair. We'd be lucky if the long strands dried by morning, tucked inside braids. Still, it was a satisfying time. Kitty's music made it almost a time of worship.

We'd all go to the dance at the Park House later that evening. Some children would swirl with their fathers; women would chatter and talk, the older ones bringing their stitching to sit on the side, the younger ones eyeing the bachelors with hopefulness in their hearts. There were still so few marriages. People from the Shaker community in the East had visited us last summer, and they felt celibacy had great merit. But after they left, I heard one of the advisors say he was glad to see they'd gone. "They never laughed or smiled and were plain as white cows. A few frills never hurt anyone."

The Pie and Beer Band was frills. They might play that night (being paid in pie and beer), or sometimes the Aurora Band if they weren't engaged for money by a noncolonist group somewhere else. Both Ida and Kate loved to attend the dances. Often they'd see their brothers there, which was always the highlight for me too.

I'd been unable to convince Brita to return with us, but she agreed to give me her address and promised to write back. I wondered if there was something yet I could do to bring her boys to her.

On a dance night, back when Jacob and Matilda still lived with us, Jacob would make sure we all had our gloves on and knitted mufflers at our necks and heads before stepping out into the night. The sound of a man's voice could soothe, and I missed that. A once happily married woman never forgot the pleasure of hearing a man's voice say her name. She never forgot the pleasure of a lover's touch to her lips either, but that was something I could do little about. I'd have to content myself with having my brothers come to dinner more often, to hear their voices and feel the brush of beard on my cheeks.

We five females made our way through the light-falling snow the quarter mile or so, up toward the Keils' and then through the trees to the Park House. We reminded one another to carry our lanterns high. My hair still felt wet as we walked, and I wondered what would happen if I cut it short so it could dry overnight in the winter. That would raise some eyebrows. It probably wasn't worth the upset it would cause, though I noticed any number of girls and women now wore their hair straight back, or with braids at the sides and not just parted down the center. There'd been clicking of tongues when I'd first changed my hairstyle to pin my braids in circles above my ears. As a young wife, I'd found it amusing to introduce such an insignificant onion into the colony stew.

Christine got asked to dance almost as soon as we came through the door. My parents had come that evening, and as I greeted them, I saw that Louisa and Johanna were there too. While I feared it might happen, Louisa never had one quaking episode. Like Christine, she was asked to dance and did so, despite Johanna's frown when her sister took the gentleman's hand and began gliding around the floor. I looked around for Andrew and Christian. Both boys were standing with others, the Ehlen children and a Will boy. I watched my older son move over toward Rosina Stauffer, who had Jacob and Matilda's baby in her arms. He peered into the blanket, looked up at the baby's aunt, and said something that made her laugh. He'd been there for the delivery. He'd had to witness death and life within the same scene at such an early age. It was part of a doctor's life, I supposed, and Andrew had come to it early. His interest in medicine would stick. Martin had nurtured it well.

I took a cup of hot cider. Martin Giesy talked quietly with Martha Miller. Did I see something pass between them? No one had asked me to dance, and that suited me fine. I was one of the ineligible women who wasn't interested in romantic love and assumed I never would be again. I'd had my one great love. Family and friendship warmed me now. Karl might say it was *philos* love, the word the Greeks used to describe friendship and sisterhood. Once, I felt isolated even in the midst of a crowd, but not now. Perhaps taking in this kind of love was necessary to work our way through that bewilderment of living, the uncertainties of seeking through murky water. One needed time to mend and stitch together a life that gathered friendships and that other kind of Greek love, *agape,* a selfless love where one gives without expecting anything in return. A spiritual love. A mother's love.

"Would you care to dance?" It was my father.

"It's a *Schottische,*" I said. "We need three."

"I've already cornered Andy," my father said, motioning for my older son to join us. *He still calls him as a child, 'Andy' instead of 'Andrew.' Maybe a mother can call him that but still let him grow into a young man too.* I took a deep breath. "And Christian's been commandeered by his sisters. Ida's been dogging him all evening, so we Wagners will take the floor together."

We wove our way through the hops and skips and arm circles while the band played the slow waltz tune. It had been years since I'd danced with my father...maybe at my wedding. Yes, we might have danced on that day. I smiled. And here was Andy on my other arm. He grinned. My mother and sisters clapped their hands in rhythm, and then William had our mother on one arm and Johanna on the other.

What I needed was a way to continue the dance of my life, to take small steps that would keep me light on my feet and moving forward into meaning. Maybe whatever new spirit Christine had returned with I could discover without having to go through more misery to find it. I could still offer my home to the homeless. I could weave and make quilts, make peppermint candies and sell them, form shelves out of scrap wood. My appliqués held promise. I cooked and served at the hotel. I could wash my girls' hair, scent it with the finest herbs I could find, and give them and my mother and sisters time and the benefit of my experience, such as it was.

My father and Andy swung me around. I sensed there was something more to do in my life, a new kind of yearning. I didn't know what it was. For this evening at least, I'd live with that not knowing, trusting that like most emotions, it would not last forever.

———

Christmas celebrations came and went. I always thought of Jack at those times, wondering if he'd travel to Aurora. He hadn't. The girls at least had stopped asking if he'd be coming. Kate remembered him vaguely. When I saw the boys, neither mentioned their stepfather. I had a kind of settledness about Jack that took little from me now.

The new year arrived to firecrackers, and in March, the Keil birthday celebrations took our time. I turned my almanac to a new year of my life and read with interest in the *Oregonian* that a woman, Fannie Case, planned to climb Mount Hood. The summer moved to its usual rhythm, and in August, Karl told me there was another article that said Fannie Case had done it, had climbed Mount Hood.

"She's a music teacher," Karl told me. "Climbing that big mountain." He shook his head in amazement. We stood outside the schoolhouse. "I wonder what made her want to do that?"

"The adventure of it," I said. "Being in front."

"*Ja*. I know some women who like being first," he said with teasing in his voice.

"Now that I think of it, I bet there were Indian women who climbed it before she did," I suggested. "We always forget about their firsts. I'll ask the woman who brings us huckleberries and salmon to find out what the real story is."

"You were the first woman to come west for our colony," Karl said.

"*Ja,* no matter what happens, I will always have that."

———

On Christmas morning 1868, it came to me, my new *Sehnsucht.* I suspect it was the aroma of baked bread and the goose dressing and the pies I'd had in the oven since well before sunrise. Or it might have been Kate's words, interrupting my humming as I worked.

"Mama." Kate put her arms around me while I bent to the oven.

She was nearly thirteen and already as tall as I. "I will always remember you best in the kitchen."

"Will you? Why's that?"

"Because food mends everything, before I even know I need a stitch to tie me up."

I laughed. "Food and sewing. You've put those together in a funny way." I turned to hold her to me, brushed the hair from her braid, tucking the loose strands back in. Her nightdress smelled of lavender, a scent I'd put into the soap. Her body was changing into a young woman's.

"Not sewing, Mama. Doing what Andy's going to do. Mending people. That's what you do too."

"Do I?"

She nodded. "Almira's hands were better when she left because of that cream you gave to her."

"Uncle Martin mixed that up for her," I said.

"But you asked him to do it. And Aunt Christine looked so different when she came back. Her eyes sparkle more. You did that for her, didn't you, Mama? I saw you had a present for her when she left. It had magic in it. Foooood," she said lengthening the middle of the word as though it was a song.

"It wasn't food, though."

"No? But food is best." She grinned and motioned by lifting her eyebrows toward a cinnamon cake cooling on the table. "People who cook are good menders," she said. "And people who clean are good workers. We need both, right, Mama? I'm a cleaner."

That much was true. When she was younger, she'd lose things; but since we'd been here in Aurora, she was the tidier of my two. Her eyes lifted to the cinnamon cake.

"*Ja, ja.* You can have a slice, but just one. We save it for the gathering. We're going to your *Oma* and *Opa's* today. We need enough for Auntie Louisa and Johanna and William and Jonathan—"

"They're not aunties! Not William and Jonathan," Ida said, coming into the room.

"No, they aren't. I meant we must save enough for everyone to have a taste."

"So they'll come back for more?"

"*Ja,*" I said. "Satisfaction is only for a time. People always want more."

I hugged her to me, gathered Ida up too. It was human nature to always want more. But it was also part of who we were, to desire being filled up, to be satisfied. People did that in different ways. I felt full when I walked the paths in prayer, when I painted, or when I cut those strips of fabric and formed them into shapes. Music filled me. Dancing gave me delight. But I felt most satisfied when I could listen to the stories people told me while I fed them, stories of their everyday but also of their hopes and dreams of someday. Even if I couldn't fix what it was they wished for—I thought of Brita—I could always listen and I could serve sprinkling words of hope, like cinnamon, to bring out the flavor.

That was my yearning, I decided, that seasoning I needed. And I thought I knew now what to do to achieve the sweetness that is promised in the proverb about desire. I just had to get Keil to agree.

25

Restored to a Former State

December 31. Today we prepared to celebrate the new year. My young Christian brought a goose for me to stuff. Mr. Ehlen took him to the river, and they brought the large fowl back through the heavier-than-usual snowfall. Imported turkeys sell for thirty dollars each in Portland, so he might have made good money selling rather than giving the bird away. I invited him and his brother to eat with us on the first of the new year, but they chose to eat with the Ehlens, and I could understand why. Teaching a boy to hunt was nothing I could do, and neither could Martin. So Mr. Ehlen filled that order with aplomb. Kate said she wished to visit her brothers and so headed there after our meal. But it might be more her interest in a certain Ehlen boy, Lorenz, that drew her early from our table.

At the house church gathering in January 1869, I posed my idea. "What if the colony built a restaurant at the fairgrounds?" I suggested. "We have a dance hall, and that earns a fair penny. We have a hotel here that people love to come to, to eat our food, and the stage always stops for a meal. Why not build a place where people can sit and eat and enjoy a little rest while they're at the fair?"

"Build another building? *Ach*," Helena said. "Already people write back to Bethel that they're hardly in Aurora, they're off doing band performances or building somewhere else. The crops need tending. We are farmers first here, and have always been. It worries me how we get so extended and distracted from our purposes."

"How do you know people are writing letters of complaint?" Louisa asked her.

"Andrew, my brother back in Bethel, tells me. He says the Bauer boys are not happy here. He notes a number of confusions about land issues, both in Bethel and Aurora, and people don't like that kind of bewilderment. This is a religious colony. That should be our foundation. Not all these other money ventures."

Louisa's face looked blotchy and red. "The things my husband proposes help us pay for things we need here, so we can give to one another, Helena. I know you meant no criticism, but these ventures, as you call them, help us keep this a Christian community, able to meet the needs of so many. It helps pay for things like…church bells, among other things," she said. "We couldn't make a trade for those. We had to have cash."

"*Ja, ja.* So you say."

It sounded to me as though they'd had this conversation before.

"What would you serve there, Emma?" BW asked. "Everything we serve at the hotel?"

"Party foods," I said. " 'Restaurant' is a French word that means to 'restore to a former state.' We'd return people to a satisfied state. It means providing food for someone too, of course. But people come to the fair and want to be restored, to find something to distract them from their troubles or give them a way to walk through them in the weeks ahead."

"The way art can restore," Kate said.

"Or how our stitching restores us," Martha Miller said.

They were moving from the fair. I brought them back. "Sore feet, late evenings, talking to strangers and friends at length can get their rhythms out of step when they're at the fair. They don't eat as well as they might, so they end up not feeling well and going home early. Maybe not even buying tickets for the concerts or other events. If we gave them a place to sit and served them sumptuous food, they'd be rested. Make them feel special. Food is love, and love is food," I said, as cheerfully as I could. "We can show them that love, and they'll remember where they received it and maybe come to the hotel for more after the fair is over."

"Maybe even join the colony." Louisa sighed.

"That seems presumptuous," Helena said. "I doubt food would bring about conversions."

"But who's to say that feeding people isn't of the highest spiritual work a person can do?" I said it out loud, something I hadn't realized I believed. "It's what women have done since…the Garden of Eden."

"Let's not discuss what happened as a result of that," Helena chided.

"We could have a Fourth of July event with special food we'd serve on that holiday. Or do a Thanksgiving Day at the fair," Kitty said. "Or maybe a German American day with all German foods, nothing else."

"Why not a May Day event in October with a Maypole and everything as we do here?" Kitty said. "We could have a chorus singing while we served."

"That might compete with the band performances," Louisa said. "We wouldn't want that."

"But music while we work, people would love hearing that," I said. "We could roast one of our beef in a large pit, bring our dried fruit, make dishes with all our own produce, and tell people they could purchase such things at the hotel. Not everyone who comes to the fair has even heard of Aurora. This way, they would."

"Several of us would have to stay there the entire time and work," Louisa cautioned. "They've extended the fair time now to more than four days. It wouldn't be much of a respite for the women." She sighed. "I've always enjoyed the fair, making things to exhibit and all. There'd be scant time for that if we had a restaurant to run."

"We could still go to the dances," Christine said. "We could spell each other."

"*Ja*, you like dancing, don't you?" Louisa said. She smiled at Christine as though she were her daughter. "Aurora did too."

"We could display our quilts," Kitty offered. "And tell people about our tailor shop. And our wines."

"For medicinal purposes only," Louisa added, raising a needle to the air.

"Is beer medicinal?" Ida asked. No one answered.

"It might be fun," Martha said. "Your girls could help serve, right, Emma? They'd meet interesting people. Practice their English. And I'd prefer to be doing something other than wandering around looking at exhibits." That last word sang out through a chipped front tooth.

"We might just rival the band," I said, "with people knowing us for how we feed our friends."

"This must not be a competition, Emma," Louisa said.

"Emma doesn't know how to do things any differently than that," Helena said. "Not that competition is a bad thing, you understand. But always being first. It can be troublesome."

They still didn't understand me. I didn't want to be first; I wanted to be remembered for something worthwhile, for something even adventurous at times. Christian had understood me and never tried to take the wild from me. He knew it wasn't meant to be disruptive or arrogant. It was to take in life and savor it fully.

"Everyone should either ring the bells or stand upside down on them," I said and grinned at Kitty. Louisa looked up, confused. "Besides, 'Small cheer and great welcome makes a merry feast.' That's from Shakespeare," I said, hoping to redirect the subject yet again.

" 'Fools make feasts and wise men eat them.' That's what Benjamin Franklin wrote in his almanac," Helena noted.

"I'm willing to be a fool on behalf of the colony and let the wise men eat our dishes. Wise women too. We'll give them a great welcome when they enter our building," I said.

"Don't you think a tent would be sufficient?" Helena said.

"No. A building. As permanent as the dance hall. People could as easily remember Aurora for a fine platter of roasted meat or a delicate cake frosted with cream or even ice cream as they remember Aurora for the band's songs. Our biggest challenge will be finding enough ice on a hot October day. A structure says, 'We're here to stay,' while a tent, well, it can be taken down and forgotten."

"Ice cream makes my mouth water," Kitty said.

"Which is exactly what we want for fairgoers. But we don't want to sell them food only. We want to serve them. To be hospitable, provide what people need without making them feel…well, like they're needy at all. We'll help them rest and take in the benefits of a lovely meal and the music, so they will be filled up. We'll offer our best manners."

Christine stood up to declaim, " 'Being set at the table, scratch not thyself, and take thou heed as much as thou canst not to spit, cough and blow at thy nose; but if it be needful, do it dexterously, without much noise, turning thy face sidelong.' " She giggled and sat down.

"Wherever did you hear that?" Helena asked.

"In an old book about manners and such that Almira read to me."

"She truly was a woman of suspicious experiences," Helena noted. She stuck herself with her needle, moaned a little, then sucked at the puncture.

"Just like Emma used to be," Louisa said. "And she's turned out quite well, I'd say, with our influence."

I didn't wait to let Louisa's goodwill gather moss. "So should we approach the advisors or Brother Keil or—"

"I'll approach Wilhelm," Louisa said. "And let him know that we have a way to bring more people to our hotel. This is for a good cause, Helena. And all it requires is an investment of lumber and effort."

"I might even ask my father if he'll donate some of the boards," I said.

"*Gut.* That would be *gut,* Emma. The more people we involve in this, the better. But let me smooth the way with my husband first."

"*Ja,* you'll need to grease this well," Helena said.

"And while you're talking to him, Helena and Kitty and I will do our rounds with the advisors," I said. "We combined the male and female chorus that way."

"That was Wilhelm's idea, I thought," Louisa said.

"*Ja*. It was, but we women know how to grease things," Helena said. "After all that time in the kitchen, it's something we know how to do."

———

I tried not to get my hopes up too high. Wilhelm could still be unpredictable. BW hadn't disagreed with any of our discussion, so if Wilhelm did, there was always another door we could go through to John or the advisory council. A mixed chorus required little investment; a building did. So far, buildings had been built only at Wilhelm's behest.

I wondered about Louisa's ability to make her case with Keil. But she was his partner, at least as much as Keil would let her be. She had entertained Ben Holladay, the railroad mogul, so she must support the plan for the hotel to become a train stop one day. And her words had silenced Helena on the matter and given support to the restaurant idea. But this idea came from a woman, and that could make it suspect in Keil's mind. We'd just have to wait and see.

When we gathered next around the quilt frame—we were completing one for Elizabeth, John and BW's daughter, to put into her dowry (we'd be stitching one for my Kate next)—Louisa brought good news. Wilhelm loved the idea of a restaurant at the fairgrounds. He knew the ropes he had to pull to get permission to build, and he'd try to keep the colony as the only business offering full meals there. He had an idea of design, or so he told Louisa, but we all knew what it would be: a rectangle with a fireplace at one end and perhaps a good cooking stove, if we insisted. It would be furnished with rectangular tables with benches, so people could sit with friends but also might slide down to make room for strangers. We'd paint everything blue, all the benches and the tables.

Keil's only reservation, according to Louisa, was that we women would have to spend our entire time at the fair working. "He didn't think that was, well, fair. He wants meals to be available at all hours, but that means constant duty for us."

"He didn't think our working all the time was equitable?" Kitty asked. "But we work here all the time. Why would he care about our doing so in Salem?"

"Maybe he didn't want others to think poorly of our men," Martha said, "letting us cook at all hours like that. Maybe he wants some men to cook?"

"Most men don't cook a thing," Christine said. "Maybe when they're out hunting, but we're always packing things up for the bachelors to take, so they don't have to do much about feeding themselves."

"Fairgoers wouldn't expect to see men cooking. They wouldn't trust it," Helena said.

"The great chefs of the world are all men," I said. "My uncle in France writes of exquisite dishes, and once he even asked my father to send him a barrel of buffalo tongues he planned to prepare."

"Did Papa do that?" Kitty asked.

"I don't think so. It wouldn't be an easy order to fill. We won't have it on our menu since we won't have a fancy chef to prepare it," I said and laughed.

"Well, you see. Men can cook, if they get the recognition for it," Louisa said.

"It's the everyday preparation that they shy away from, the things we have to do constantly, deciding the night before what we'll have to eat for the next day, based on what we know is in the larder. Men don't have to think that far ahead. I bet those French chefs have women underlings to do their dicing and chopping and shopping the markets for them," Christine chimed in.

I thought of Kate's comment about everyday feasts and how it was fine women's work.

"My Wilhelm has been meeting with Ben Holladay. He took over the contract for the railroad development last year, and..." Louisa hesitated, perhaps because she wasn't sure whether we knew of this transaction, but everyone already did. It was the talk of the colony. "My husband sold him a strip of land, right through the middle of Aurora, to bring the rail line south."

"How ironic," Helena said. She continued to stitch as she talked. "We leave Bethel because the railroad comes so close it might contaminate our young people, and now we'll have the railroad in our own backyard."

"We don't have that many young people to contaminate," Kitty said, "because we don't have many weddings."

I saw Martha cover a smile behind a cough.

"Wilhelm only wants the best for us," Louisa defended. "Mr. Holladay has invited the colony band to go on tour. He'll send them up to the Puget Sound area, where you were married to Jack Giesy, Emma. Wasn't it up there somewhere?" I nodded as she continued, glad Ida wasn't here. "Then they'll cross the country on the train, and he'll pay them five hundred dollars for their concerts and pay all their expenses while they're gone."

"No one's going to pay for replacing their work here, though," Helena said.

"I wish I could go on an excursion like that," Kitty said, her voice dreamy.

"Not even the Pie and Beer Band will be going," Louisa said. "The tour will bring in money for many things the colony needs, things we can't trade for, and it will publicize the railroad and our hotel. And there's no reason why we can't announce as they tour that we'll have our restaurant at the fair. Despite the fact that Mr. Holladay is paying them good money, my Wilhelm is willing to allow this, to build a building that will be the first restaurant at the Oregon State Fair. As you suggested, Emma."

"You didn't tell him it was my idea, did you?"

She blushed. "*Nein.* I let him think it was mine."

There was a time when I'd have been annoyed by Louisa's admission, but this time I thought she'd done the wisest thing.

It was the talk of Aurora as spring grew near. The colony men were selected to build, and the material was hauled in large wagons over the road to Salem. Meanwhile, the contingent of musicians went off on their tour, and those of us left behind assumed additional responsibilities. We planted seed potatoes, including those I'd kept in my basement, far away from Opal. I'd heard that several goats over by Needy had eaten raw potatoes, and all had died. So had some pigs.

"Potatoes have got to be cooked if they're to be fed to animals," my mother told me when I visited and reported the Needy livestock deaths. She had a number of what Americans called old wives' tales about things related to food. She was frequently right. I vowed to listen to her more.

My father had donated money for lumber for the restaurant building, and in return, Wilhelm said he'd put a sign up saying, "Contributed in part by Wagner and Heirs."

"I like it that you didn't tell Keil to say 'Wagner and Sons,'" I told my father. I still stopped by their small home nearly every day, if only for a moment. It surprised me how much we had to talk about when I saw my family often, instead of the occasional crossing of paths near the park. I could ask about my sisters' samplers or about the tree they'd planted that didn't seem to want to grow. It was a lesson to me, that the frequency of interactions might carry as much weight as their length. Despite my discomfort in seeing my sons at Martin's, it was what I needed to do with them too, to make my presence known regularly so they wouldn't forget who I was. Perhaps it was already too late, but I'd at least see if more regular contact tied us together with a stronger thread.

"Well, I have more than one son and more than one daughter, and whatever is left after I die will go to all of you."

"To your daughters too?" I asked.

"And your mother, of course," my father continued. "If it's in the will that way, the law can't take it from you." A puff of smoke lifted up from his corncob pipe, and I coughed.

I cleared my throat. "But most would say, 'and Sons,' rather than include their daughters as heirs. Thank you, Papa."

"I've disagreed with the lot of you at one time or another," he said. "But you're still all my heirs."

I coughed again and felt the closeness of the bodies in the room, the clutter and lack of places to take in a deep, filling-up breath. Kate's tidying up our house took on new importance as I reflected on how well organized our space was. Clearly, we had room for them all.

"Have you given any more thought to perhaps moving into my house?" I asked. "I could spell Johanna and Mother too. We'd all be there as one family, and there's more room there than here. I'm a good cook."

"Bragging doesn't become you," my mother said. "Humility, Emma. Remember. Not so self-centered."

"It isn't bragging to state a simple truth," I said. "I do cook well. And you sew well. And Johanna takes care of Louisa well, and she's a fine dancer. William raises fine crops of flowers. I wish my geraniums had such blooms. And so it goes. We don't have to discount our talents, do we? That isn't humility."

"I can tell you William's flower secrets," my mother said.

"Humility is knowing where your talents come from," Johanna said.

"And I do," I told my sister. "I may have had some crossed paths a while back. I may even have gone astray for a time, but I do know where my strength comes from, my imagination, even my—"

"Wildness?" my mother said. She grinned, though.

"High spirit," I corrected. I also knew that it was part of who I was, to take a few steps back before I could go forward; that I hadn't always honored the pearls of wisdom that had come into my life, nor known how to accept them. "Our talents are gifts. I didn't think anyone would want to receive mine, but now I know that demeans the One who gave them to me. It takes the meaning right out of them."

Johanna said, "Though that wasn't what we were talking about."

"You had invited us to come live with you. Again," my mother said.

"But we'll decline again," my father told me.

"I like how we're all mushed in together in this house. It's…cozy," my mother said.

"Not that we don't appreciate the offer," my father continued. "But your house is still owned by the colony, and that means at any time, well, changes could be made."

"Change comes anyway," I said.

"I'll stick with Martin's way," my father said. I must have looked confused. "He's been paying for that apothecary shop himself. Out of what he's earned, helping people who weren't colonists but who needed care."

"Martin owns the building?"

"He does. And I suspect it's because he didn't want to be surprised by anything that Wilhelm might decide. He intends to have his practice there, and I'm sure he didn't want Wilhelm intruding."

"He never said…"

"What happened to you made a change in Martin's life, in more ways than having two boys around to raise. Help raise," he added. My face must have asked for that distinction. "He's done well by your sons, but I think he wishes you were more in their lives, even though he knows it must be hard for you to see them there with him. He wanted that education, but somehow he got caught up in your life with your boys too."

I hadn't thought that Martin might have felt like a pawn of sorts, who'd had to decide, like me, whether to argue with the powers that were or make the best of it, hoping I would make the best of it too.

And I had.

It wasn't the best arrangement for raising a family: brothers and sisters separated, the boys not living with their mother. But it was better than when they'd lived with Jack, and it was probably better than our trying to homestead, the way Brita had, and bearing the consequences.

"I didn't think Martin felt I neglected the boys," I said.

"Oh, not neglect so much," my father said. "He knows it must be painful to come by and then have to leave them behind. He understands. But they miss you. They do."

"I should make a greater effort," I said.

"Parents push beyond what is comfortable for themselves, in order to provide for their children. It's what's required," my father said.

"*Ja,* and my sons are a part of the Wagner and Heirs, and I don't want them to forget that either."

———

I'd thought Wilhelm would go along on the band tour, since he'd composed several of their pieces, but Henry C conducted while Wilhelm supervised the building of the restaurant. The band members would have many stories to share when they returned, which was supposed to happen in September, so they'd have a few weeks to rest up before their scheduled return to the fair.

I'd decided to put my newfound plan for more frequent visits to my sons into practice, so one day in late September, I made my way to the apothecary. Po trotted along behind Ida and me. Kate was at the Ehlens', helping the girls, she'd told me. Po rubbed his nose at the back of my knees.

I hoped to see Martin as well and ask him about his owning his own building. I could always use that as the reason I was there, if my sons appeared standoffish. I had to overcome those distances to stay in their lives, though I could see how disappearing could be easier than facing the uncertainty of what each new encounter might bring. I took a deep breath. I was doing a good thing, a mothering thing.

I had Ida in hand. We found Andy playing the clarinet.

"Are you rehearsing for the Pie and Beer Band?" He shook his head, with the instrument mouthpiece clamped between his teeth. "Well, maybe next year," I said.

He didn't say anything, didn't release the instrument.

"Play something," Ida said.

He ran a scale. His eyes smiled at her, but he still didn't say anything to her. She told him it sounded nice, and he played a tune that might have accompanied a round. Silence filled the room when he stopped.

I couldn't stand that silence. It was like a bell that clanged 'poor mothering,' ringing to the village. "Is Martin here?" He shook his head again. "Can *you* talk with me?"

He took the mouthpiece out of his mouth, ran his hand through his blunt-cut hair. He was getting too old to have such a boy's cut. "If you want to have me cut your hair sometime, I will," I said. "Into a man's cut. You're a young man now. Both you and Christian."

He lowered his head. "Martin cuts it. He said his mother used to cut his, so he does it pretty much the same way for us. Sometimes Martha Miller comes by, and she cuts it too. It's all right."

"Martha? Oh, well, that's nice. But I can cut hair for all three of you. Would you like me to do yours now? I'll go home and get my scissors."

"Nope," he said. He used the word the way Lorenz Ehlen did, popping the *p*. "But you can come back tonight. Martin will be here then, and so will Christian. I really need to practice now."

"I'd like to sit and listen if that's all right. Ida won't be a bother. And look, Po is already asleep at your feet."

"It makes me nervous for people to listen," he said. He bent to pat the dog's head.

"But when you perform, you let people watch you," I said. "You're quite talented, I can tell."

"Goethe says that our talents are 'formed in stillness; a character in the world's torrent.'"

I brushed the hair from his eyes. He didn't flinch away.

"I've had plenty of torrent," he said. "Besides, I like my time alone. As you do, Mama."

"Of course," I told him. "We'll give you what you're used to, then." I picked up offense, where perhaps none was intended, but I couldn't stop it. I still had so much to learn. I took Ida's hand, whistled to the dog, and left, carrying offense with me.

I wasn't sure what had annoyed me so. Maybe the mention of Martha's cutting his hair, but I didn't know why it should. Maybe there'd always be this space between my son and me in the musical score of our lives. Maybe harmonious chords would never follow, no matter how I set myself to make it happen.

26

A Swept Porch

While I was outside checking on my chickens, Andy came out through the back door, breathing hard. "You need to come," he said. "It's *Opa*. Something's wrong with him. Martin's out helping someone else." He caught his breath, and I grabbed my shawl. "I'll let Kate know to stay and look after her sister."

Andy and I fast-walked down the main street, passed by the hotel, and nearly ran down the grassy slope to the mill site where my parents lived. In the distance the sulfur steam rose off the hot springs on the property, giving the site an eerie look in the afternoon dusk. Andy said Jonathan had come for Martin, then ridden on, while Andy headed to my house. "He said to get you. He'd try to find Dr. Keil if he couldn't locate Martin."

"They're still at the fair, building," I said. "Have you seen your *Opa* yet?"

He shook his head that he hadn't. "But Jonathan says he wanders in the room. He doesn't talk. His eyes look like he sees far in the distance but can't focus when you say his name."

"Not at all like *Opa*, is it?" I said. *He's too young to be dying.*

"Will he drink tea?" I asked my mother when we came through the door. I didn't need but a cursory look at my father to know that something was very wrong. Jonathan had given a good description, though he'd left out that haunted look of confusion that framed my father's face. His skin felt strange to the touch too, clammy but not feverish.

"I don't know," she said. "I don't know." She clasped her hands together. My mother had midwifed and helped mend any number of people and was always a calm presence. But things changed when the person needing mending was someone you loved.

I gave directions to my sisters to heat water for tea. To Andy I said, "See if there are sunflower seeds anywhere around. Grind them up and we'll try to get him to take them."

My father looked disgusted when I asked him questions and brushed his hands at me as though I intruded. William, my youngest brother, stood off to the side, chewing on his cuticle. "Go out to the hot spring," I directed. "Bring in a bucket of the sulfur water." He dashed out without questioning me, grateful, apparently, to have something to do.

"What'll you do with that water?" Andy asked. "It smells terrible."

"It will help purify the blood," I said. "That's what he needs. Mama, do you have potatoes here, raw?" She nodded, so I set her and Johanna to peeling several. William returned, and I told him to bring in the apple press. "Leave a good half inch of potato on the peels," I said. "Get a carrot; do you have raw carrots?" With the peels in a pile, I told them to squeeze them in the apple press and then pour boiling water over them. "As soon as it's cooled enough, we'll try to get him to drink it."

Raw potatoes could kill a goat, but their juice, I knew, could help clear the mind of a bewildered person. My mother had told me that once, long ago. She'd just forgotten it in her distress.

"You'd think I'd remember that," she said as she watched.

"Our minds don't always think too clearly when there's a catastrophe looming. Not that this is," I added quickly, to her widening eyes.

Andy coaxed my father into drinking both the sulfur water and then the potato juice. He resisted the sunflower seeds, but when Andy ground them with the pestle and put the paste onto his grandfather's lip, he licked it.

"What'll I do now?" my mother asked, as she patted his hand. My father had sat down at last. He looked from left to right, a wild animal fear in his eyes.

"Do what you're doing, Mama," I said. "Talk softly. About everyday things."

"He picked up an armful of wood to bring in for the fire. We don't even need a fire yet at night, though he's always so cold. The fire nearly sweats us out of here in an evening, even when a cooling breeze shows up. I couldn't talk him out of it. So he went out. William said he'd do it, but you know your father. He had to do it himself. You must get that independent streak from him, Emma," my mother said.

I opened my mouth to speak but thought better of it.

"And then he dropped them on the floor, just let the kindling roll out there. I said to him, 'Mr. Wagner, what are you doing?' and he looked at me like I was some sort of idiot. That's when I saw his face. But he wouldn't settle down, he kept moving about, stumbling over the kindling until we got it picked up."

Martin arrived with Jonathan then. The trained physician knelt in front of my father, and I saw in him the kind man who had once sent me healing herbs to help my ailing son, the compassionate man who had brought my sons to me before he took them as his own to raise. No, before he *accepted* them as his own to raise.

"The side of his face," Martin said. "Did you notice?" I had. Andy nodded. "I think he's had a kind of stroke," he said, as much to Andy as to me. "The left side seems affected."

"He drank some of the sulfur water, in the tea. And the potato and carrot juice," I said. Martin nodded agreement. "Andy got him to take the sunflower-seed paste."

"That was good, the potato juice. It will help the body take in the sulfur. And the mineral water's a good idea too. What made you think of that?"

"I don't know," I said. "I smelled it as we made our way here, and I was saying, 'Help him help him help him,' and then I thought maybe the water would be a healing thing."

"You'll have to cut back on that rich food you feed him, Mrs. Wagner. And maybe we'll hide his pipe too, so you can all get a good breath in," Martin said. He told Jonathan to be in charge of hiding the pipe. "You might hide your own as well," Martin said. "You could be next, making your heart work that hard."

"Why doesn't he talk?" Louisa said. "It looks like he wants to. He moves his mouth like a fish."

No words came out.

"We'll hope his speech comes back. I see it happening at times. But he may not get the use of his arm back," Martin said. "I don't know. We'll have to wait and see. In a few days, we might try lifting that arm. We'll need to keep it moving, so it doesn't atrophy...shrink from lack of use," he explained to Louisa's frown.

He listened to my father's heart, and then he told Andy that he'd mix up some powders and have him bring it back for my father. "I don't think he's in pain, so no laudanum. That's really all we can do for now," he said. "Except if you can get him to drink a little of the sulfur water every day, that might be good. Might help a few others around here too. It never occurred to me. Quite inventive, Emma. But then you always did see things in unique ways, though some of us failed to appreciate it."

I stayed with my parents that evening and waited for Andy to return with the powders. Johanna left us long enough to tell my girls where I was and that I'd spend the night. Before she left she said she'd stay the night with them. I thanked her for letting me be here to tend this tail of my family. Christian, we learned, was staying at the Ehlens'.

The room felt warm with so many people in it, and I wondered why my father had even thought he should build a fire. Perhaps he'd been growing ill for a time, and tonight's load of wood had been the kindling that had set his heart aflame.

I tucked my mother into their bed, assured her I'd stay awake to be with my father should he need anything in the night. He'd fallen asleep in his chair. The breaths of my brothers and sisters eased into the room as they drifted off to sleep. They slept peacefully, and I thought that it was something I could do, give rest to them by simply being there to sit beside the hearth.

Andy came back with the powders Martin sent, and he asked me if I thought my father would die.

"Some day," I said. "But I'm not sure about now. He's breathing easier; I can feel his pulse, and it's steady though weak."

Andy accepted what I said and then sat with his knees open, his hands clasped between them. He didn't look up at me when he spoke. "I'm glad you were home. I guess I should have gone to find Dr. Keil, but I thought you would want to know about *Opa*." I assured him that he'd done the right thing, especially since Jonathan was finding Martin and Keil was off in Salem.

"The sulfur," he said. "What does it do?"

"I'm not sure. But that water is full of minerals. People soak in such hot waters back East. Even the Indians do, I'm told, so it has to be healing."

"That was good, though, thinking of that."

"Thank you," I said. "One day you'll be in school and learning about all kinds of new treatments for people. But you'll bring things from your experiences too, and those can be just as helpful."

"I do want to go to medical school, Mama," he said.

"I know that. And you will. We'll all make sure that can happen. You found the sunflower seeds and got him to eat them. So thank you for that."

"We both did good, then," he said.

I decided not to correct his grammar. I put my arm around him instead and breathed gratitude when he leaned into my chest.

———

In the days that followed, I let my mother know what I was planning. I knew they wouldn't move in with me, but they'd need help now, and I could give it. Our father wasn't going to be able to operate the mill, that was clear.

"Papa could sell the mill property," Jonathan told me. "It would be enough for him to buy land somewhere else, with a house on it. Maybe down by the Willamette. He likes that place, though he's never gotten the owner to agree to sell."

"I looked at property across the Pudding River in Clackamas County," I told him. "When Andy and I were out homestead hunting those years. They might sell. It has a larger house on it now. We could plant the fields. Everyone could work at that together."

"You'd leave your house? Your two-door house?"

"I would. For them. I'd still work for the colony, but Papa's going to need a different way to do things. Will you help me do this? Handle the land sale for him and make the purchase?"

"*Ja.* It's a good idea, Emma."

"If there's not enough with the sale of Papa's land, I have a string of pearls. Mama gave them to me. If we need them…"

"Let's wait and see."

———

It had happened quickly, as life does. John Giesy bought my father's property. My brother David Jr. returned from Oregon City to help my parents move. He wore a long beard, grown since I'd last seen him months before. I worried some that making such a huge change might delay my father's recovery, but I could tell almost at once that he liked the landscape.

"It's not the river place Jonathan said you liked, Papa, but maybe later we can sell this one and go there. For now, the boys will keep busy planting fields, and Mama will have a good garden, and before long, I'll bring the girls and we'll move in with you. I'll be home each night to see that you're all well. When school starts, the girls will come with me to Aurora each day, so it'll work out. It will."

His vacant eyes brightened, I thought, but I couldn't be sure.

———

Helena said that Christine did a fine job cooking for the workers at the fair, but she was constantly fending off young men. "That's not anything you'd have to worry over, Emma," Helena added. She chuckled and gave a snort to her laughter.

"*Ja,* we senior women know when we've passed our prime."

Helena nodded and patted my arm, still too engaged with her joke to speak.

We were at my house. Baskets filled with fabric and the many things I planned to move sat like stepping stones around the walls.

"You were serious when you said you'd restore things at home. But what about us?" Christine said. "Will the colony let us continue to live here? This was your house, Emma. Everyone knew that."

"I'll talk with Jonathan," I told her. Then in deference to Louisa's being with us, I added, "He can confer with Brother Keil. I thought I'd covered all the pies, but I guess not."

"But if we can't stay here, where will we meet for our house church?" Kitty asked.

"We can go back to our house," Louisa said. "Though there's been something pleasant about getting out and about. Well, I'm getting older. Maybe staying at home would be just as easy."

"You can come to my house," Martha Miller said. "Mine and Martin's." She cleared her throat. "We're getting married in September."

———

When Christine and I were alone again, churning butter at the new hotel, I told her how the house had felt so empty with everyone gone at the fair. The girls found friends to be with, and I'd been the only one rattling around in the house until Andy's fateful knock on the door telling me of our father's illness.

"I thought maybe you'd use the time to paint while we were gone, not move away."

"I walked the path. And visited my sons. And took the girls on a picnic. They were troubled I hadn't gone along to help cook so they could go too."

"The burdens of life fall unfairly," Christine said, and she laughed.

I told her I'd sat out under the stars with the girls; we'd checked the hams hanging in the smokehouse. I'd showed them how to make a special knot on the sampler I'd drawn for them, and Kate made

progress on hers, stitching in bright colors, "Not a house, but shelter."
"I'll sign it 'Catie Giesy,'" she said, a twinkle in her eyes. "That's what
Lorenz Ehlen calls me."

I'd gone through my fabrics, hoping Christine would choose what
she'd like for a quilt.

"Maybe a Friendship quilt," she said. "But I don't need one for a
dowry to attract a future husband."

"Apparently Martha didn't either."

"Kitty might. She so wants to get married."

"It may not happen for her. Sometimes it doesn't, and it's better
than making a bad marriage, just to say you could," I said.

"Are you...saddened by Martin's marriage?"

"Why would I be sad? I'm still married," I said.

"I know. But I guess I always thought that you and Martin, well,
he's been such a part of the boys' lives."

"And continues to be. It might actually be better for them, having
a woman around all the time. Even if it isn't me."

"We share that in a way, don't we? Giving up our children for their
benefit."

"I still need to have a conversation with Martin about it." He was
caught up in this web too, as I was. But we had our own parts in the
stretching of it.

"I've decided to return to the Keils' to live," Christine said. "It'll be
easier staying there than coming in from so far out in Clackamas where
you'll be. I don't like riding horses much, and you'll need to from there.
But Kitty told me she'll move in with you all, if that's agreeable."

"Of course. Jonathan said he could convince Keil to let you both
stay at the house, though."

"It wouldn't be the same without you. That house was what we
needed for a time. But now we don't. Someone else can move into it
and be happy there. The way we were."

"I guess that's the way I felt about it too. I'll miss it...but it was just
a house." *I can't believe I said that.* "So tell me about Kitty, when you
were building at the fair. Did she have a good time?"

Christine told me that our sister was witty and warm as she spoke to fairgoers. Despite not being invited to dance when the band practiced at night, she smiled, tapped time to the music, and chatted with young children who'd been brought along to listen.

"At least she has her choir to keep her occupied," I said. "And she's good with little ones, so it's nice that they had someone to talk with while their parents danced."

We churned awhile more, and then she asked, "Will you ever... divorce and remarry?"

"I've no plans to," I said. "Where would I find a husband who could put up with me?" She laughed with me. "No, I have my sons. I have my daughters. I have my goat and chicken and dog, and I have you all! I have Providence to guide me. What more could I want?"

"I'm glad you're not disappointed about being left behind," Christine said. She stayed silent for a time, and then she told me why it was good I hadn't come along, a reason that had nothing to do with my father and mother's needing me. "This man stopped by," she said. "It was late. He was loud and boisterous and asked for you. Wanted his wife to serve him. I didn't know who he was, but Louisa did, and she tried to calm him. Kitty acted rattled. Has she ever met your husband before?"

I dipped my head yes. "But Kitty holds a fantasy about Jack Giesy. He was someone she thought she fancied, when he was back in Bethel. She hadn't seen him since he'd come west. And I didn't think she believed me about the reason I left him years before. Unfortunately, he still is my husband."

"It was good that you weren't there," Christine repeated.

"If I go next fall, at least I'll know to expect him," I said. The thought didn't frighten me, as it might have once, or keep me from doing what I'd decided.

"Oh, and that little *Zwerg,* your friend Brita asked for you," Christine said.

"How was she?"

"*Gut.* She had her boys with her. She said she'd come to see us here one day soon, but she had work she did now 'year around,' as she put it. I was to tell you that you were right, things always did change, and she could look for the people who'd be around to help. She had, and they did."

"I wish she'd come here," I said. "We have plenty of room. Or we did. I won't be able to be so free with my invitations now, will I? I'll have others to negotiate with."

"That's a family. It ebbs and flows," Christine said. "Maybe next year we'll have more people out from Bethel or new immigrants, people who might need a place of rest for a time. Confederate soldiers heading west, freed slaves. Widows and orphans. They might all show up at your doorstep. It's pretty certain that the railroad is coming through, isn't it? That'll bring visitors."

But I hadn't wanted to just have visitors. I'd wanted my home to be a place to offer an everyday feast, as Kate put it, for those needing mending, as I'd needed it once. That would change now too.

" 'The help of God is closer than the door,' " Christine said. "Brita said that."

"She's apparently swept well in front of her own."

27

Stitching Pieces of a Family

On October 4, 1870, the wood-powered steam engine roared into Aurora with its passenger cars and stopped in front of the hotel. The men had laid a wooden bridge across the track for easier walking, so while the Aurora Band played a welcoming tune, women from the outside lifted the hems of their long skirts and managed their hoops to climb the hotel steps and look back. They waved at the welcoming Aurora crowd.

I stood on the hotel porch, ready to slip back inside and finish serving that first train car full of guests. We had fifteen minutes to deliver this meal and somehow not let the guests feel rushed, while the train hissed and heaved outside the door, waiting for their return. Hospitality had its challenges.

But we accomplished it! Potato salad with warm vinegar, roasted beef, sliced hams cured with sugar, and a large fish that one of the surviving Calapooias had caught that morning were served beside greens plucked from the gardens behind the hotel. Nuts and dried fruits, plumped up with spring water, and mounds of whipped cream that Kitty and others had beat up minutes before the train's arrival, provided the finishing touches to our gastronomical scene. Flowers from my brother's garden made bright bouquets for the table. While we cooked, we sang—those who could carry a tune—and then we sent them satisfied, we hoped, on their way.

We cheered ourselves along with guests who weren't being carted away to Portland by train. Those guests who'd come by buggy or ridden in could be more leisurely in their eating. Back in the kitchen, Kitty began a round, and the rest of us joined in as we scoured pans and opened the back door to let out some of the oven heat.

"Did I tell you," Kitty said at the end of the song, "that the Indian who brought the fish in this morning asked if his girls could take singing lessons here?"

"From Henry C?" I asked.

"From me." Her face turned the softest shade of pink. "He heard me singing. I guess he's heard me before, and he said his daughters wished that they could sing like the White Bird."

"You'll have something to look forward to this winter," I told her.

"Do you think I should ask permission from Brother Keil or maybe Henry C?"

"You're using a talent of yours." I thought again of Goethe, with talent formed in stillness and character in storm. Kitty had had her share of storms too. Not being married when you wished you were was a storm. It might not compare to the loss of children, but it was character-building just the same. Yet she had talents to offer and did. I looped my arm in hers and put my head to her temple. "You're making someone else's life better than your own. Who could argue with that?"

"*Ja.* That's what I'll tell them if they ask."

The fair that year was the biggest ever, and I was called to cook. It was the first of a new decade. Men on stilt legs ambled around as I imagined giraffes must walk, shouting about demonstrations, markets, or products to buy. The horse barns boasted a record number of equines, and the races promised to be close. The Household Arts exhibit was twice as large as before, with dozens of samplers and quilts on display, flowering plants, and preserves lining the shelves like perfect children dressed in pinks and blues. Dr. Keil had his wine there; Mr. Ehlen's tightly woven baskets stood out, and he had several clarinet reeds for sale. Some were purchased by visitors from New York, who said they were of the finest.

Christian had made a basket to enter in the fair. He grabbed my hand to show me as soon as Martin and Martha and the boys arrived.

"It's been a while since you've been to this fair, hasn't it?" I asked him after we'd admired his fine work. We made our way along the grass-beaten paths back to the restaurant. It was after the band's performance, and most of the restaurant patrons had eaten and left. Martin drank his coffee, and Martha sat with her hands clasped in her lap. Her hat shadowed her face in the lantern light. Po lay on the floor by the door, being good by staying outside but not running off whenever another dog sniffed by.

"We came one time when Brita was here," Christian said. "Remember, Andy? We rolled rings and had a kite." My older son nodded, as he swirled a spoon into a coffee drink he'd added sweet cream to. His brother was twelve and could be annoying, I was sure, but Andy treated him with respect. "I like the fair."

"I do too," I told Christian. "Thank you for bringing them along." I nodded to Martin and Martha.

"It's our pleasure," Martin said.

"You know, you could invite them yourself, anytime you want, Emma. And come visit them more often too." Martha still had that sweet, youngish voice of women her age.

"It's an awkward thing, isn't it?" I said, deciding not to step over the discomfort. "I did talk with Brother Keil, and he says the current arrangement is working well, with the boys on track like a steam engine to go on to the university one day. That's what I've always wanted for them. Medical school for you," I said as I turned to Andy. He didn't look at me. "With us living a distance from the colony now, it isn't always easy to work out times to come by."

Kate, Ida, the Ehlen boy, and several others huddled together, walking near the dance hall. They stopped chattering when they saw us sitting in the restaurant with the door wide open. "It's time you settled down," I said. They groaned, their pleasant plans so rudely interrupted. "Lorenz, I thank you for escorting my daughters safely here," I told him.

He clicked his heels and said, "I'm heading to the bachelor tents right now, Mrs. Giesy." Then, along with several other young men who had been with the mixed young people's group, he did.

"You could come visit us anytime," I continued to Andy, telling Martin too. "I would love to have you waking up every day at your grandparent's home, to fix your breakfast, to…cut your hair. But I know that staying where you are, you're of help to people."

"The same way you are," Christian said. "That's what Martha says."

Martha blushed, and I felt my own face grow warm with the compliment.

"I'm helping *Opa* and *Oma, ja.* Maybe Johanna too, so she's not the only one who can look after your aunt Louisa. And I believe I'm helping both of you, because you'll be able to go on to school. And your sisters are getting a good education. The hotel will make money; the money can go to pay your tuition; I work at the hotel; it all comes around. Like that. We're all busy doing."

"Andy is good help to me," Martin said. He patted Martha's hand. It must be difficult for her to take on the raising of boys.

"And you too, Martha, are certainly helping make another's life better than your own. I'm grateful to you," I added.

"Are you? I assumed, well, that you'd be upset. It's why I didn't say anything about our getting married any earlier than I did. I didn't want to have to explain why I wasn't coming to the house church anymore."

"But then you offered your home," I said.

"And you've rarely come."

"I'll make a point of it. Next Sunday."

"Good. We'll see what we see," Martha said. It was a phrase I remembered from my friend Sarah Woodard, back in Willapa.

"Let things flow as they will. *Ja.*"

We heard the scrapes and thumps of the band putting their instruments away in wooden cases. The hawkers at the carnival sites had settled down. Even the dogs had stopped barking.

"I'd like to live with Mama and *Opa* and *Oma*," Christian said then. He looked at me. My eyes must have shown great surprise. "Uncle Martin?"

Andy stared at his brother, his thoughts, as usual, well hidden.

"I don't know," Martin said. "Maybe you could. You'd have your *Opa*'s influence, and things have changed here with Keil. Emma, you no longer occupy the house… He might feel that having one of your boys live with you and your parents is warranted." Martin looked at me. "Would you like me to speak with Wilhelm, Emma?"

"*Ja,*" I said, when I got my voice back. "I'll accept all the help I can get."

———

A few days later at the end of the fair, we were packing up when Almira came by. She had the children with her, which gave Christine delight. Almira's eyes sparkled as she accepted a child from Almira's daughter-in-law. Christine and Almira shared a one-arm embrace. We welcomed Almira and her daughter-in-law to rest on one of the blue benches we'd brought with us. Kate got the women jugs of water, and we sat for a moment, catching up.

It was then that Jack Giesy sauntered through the grounds. Almira gasped when he stared at us from a distance. My own heart had started to pound. "Do you know that man?" I asked.

She shook her head no. "He looks so much like my former husband," Almira said. "Those brooding eyes, that clenched jaw." She shook her head again. "I'm relieved it isn't him."

"I know him," I said. "That *is* my husband."

He'd aged since I'd seen him last. As he moved closer I saw the lines that drained what had once been a handsome face. He looked worn as old shoe leather. Thinning hair robbed him of some of his height, though when he stood in front of me, I still looked up at him and felt myself step back from the force of him.

He put his hands down on the table in front of us and pushed his chest toward me, his face close. And while my heart pounded, I didn't feel the terror that had once caused me to cower or run. I knew I wasn't alone.

"Is there something I can do for you?" I asked.

"Serve me," he said.

"I'm sorry, but we've closed down for the season."

Po had stood up at the sound of Jack's gruffness, but now he lay back down, and that encouraged me. I had friends and more, an attitude refreshed.

"Aren't you the hospitable one?" He sneered the words, then sat. He leaned back and tossed coins at me. "Brother Keil would object to your turning away good cash," he said. "Figure something out to feed a man. You're good at figuring." A coin spun on the table, the only sound besides my own shortened breathing. "How much hospitality will this coin buy me?"

"More than you deserve," I said. "If you weren't the father of one of my children, I wouldn't give you a cup of water. But then I'd give a poor dog even that."

A dark cloud of disgust shadowed his face, and I knew I'd gone too far. *I still have much to learn.*

Quick as a snake strike, Jack grabbed at my wrist. "You'd compare a Giesy to a dog?"

I pulled back as Ida interrupted. "There's a sausage left, Mama," she said. She came from behind me and handed it to me. "Would the man like it?" *I hope Ida didn't hear me say what I did about his being the father of one of my children!* I wondered if Jack would recognize his daughter. He was in one of his dark moods that could sometimes leave as quickly as a squall passing over the Willapa firs. I prayed that would happen now, but it didn't. Instead, he took the sausage, tossed it on the ground. Po grabbed it and ran off.

Jack swung his arm to signal to someone. "Bastian! Mary! Come see your rel-a-tive Emma—my dear wife." He dragged the words to remind me of my status.

I hadn't seen Mary and Sebastian Giesy since the day they left Aurora after bringing me the rocker that matched Jack's. And leaving me that Compass quilt. *Compass. I know the direction I'm going now.* I hadn't known they were even at the fair. Mary had probably kept Jack away, hoping to spare me of this.

"Look what I've found here," Jack shouted.

"Let's go, Jack," Sebastian said. He stood nearly as tall as Jack, and he held Jack's arm, attempting to turn him from the small crowd growing around us. "No need to make a fuss."

"Make a fuss? The way you make fusses?" Jack said. He pushed at Sebastian.

"Sebastian, let's go," Mary pleaded.

"Women should be seen and not heard," Jack shouted at her, choosing to confront a woman's pleas as opposed to Sebastian's. Jack swayed. *He must have been drinking.*

Mary pulled on Sebastian's suit coat. "Let's just go. Please."

It all happened so fast! Sebastian pushed her out of the way, not in protection but with the familiarity of force, and Mary stumbled, her hooped skirts catching on the side of the table. Her straw hat was askew, and the reticule she carried at her wrist had tightened with obvious pain above her glove. I caught her before she fell, and she gave me a look. I saw in her eyes understanding mixed with my own former fears.

It has happened to her. I'd never known. We'd kept the secrets all those years ago in Willapa, and in so doing I'd disintegrated, the way caustic chemicals tender the finest cloth.

"Mary," I whispered as I held her arm, untwisted her purse. "I didn't know. We could have helped each—"

"Feed me, Wife!" Jack shouted over Sebastian's shoulder as he was being pushed away.

Andy intervened then.

"Jack, we'll get you something to eat," he said. "Won't we, Mama?" His voice was calm and assured. He didn't try to touch Jack, and while my son was nearly as tall as his stepfather, he stood sideways to him, nothing to intimidate, a young man using his wisdom as strength.

Jack shook off Sebastian's arm. He straightened. "About time someone maybe could pay attention to what I need," Jack said to the crowd.

My son was right: Feed the man what he asked for. Don't challenge him straight on. Let him save face and move on.

"I'll help you," Mary said. She moved with me to the wagon.

Beyond earshot I said to her, "You don't need to put up with—"

"No, no, Emma. It's all right. I'll be all right. It's only happened once. Really. Jack urged Sebastian on one time. But Jack will settle down. I was afraid this would happen. It's why I didn't want Sebastian to come by the restaurant. I thought Jack might recognize Ida or be angry if he saw you happy. Boshie wouldn't have pushed at me except that he knew I'd been right to try to keep Jack away."

"My fears have always been for Andy," I said. "That he and Jack would—"

"He did good, Emma. You did good to take him away years ago, give him tools to deal with such men. He's a good man, a good Giesy, your son. So is my Sebastian. My husband doesn't..." Her eyes dropped to the bread she cut. The knife shook in her hands. "I'm safe there; truly, I am."

"If you ever aren't, don't do what I did. Ask for help before it's too late. You have a place to call home. In Aurora."

We served the cold potato salad and big slices of bread with Aurora pear butter to my husband. He ate in haste while he and Andy spoke of the weather and crops as though they'd often talked of such men things. Then he succumbed to Sebastian's encouragement, and the three of them left. Mary turned back to me and mouthed the words, *I'll remember.*" I prayed that she would.

"That's my father, isn't it?" Ida asked. "I knew he was your husband, Mama. I just didn't know that he... You said he was the father of one of your children. It has to be me."

"He is," I said. "And there was a time when he wasn't as he is now. His behavior is no reflection on you, Ida."

"Why didn't you tell me?"

"I didn't know how. I didn't know how to say that I'd made such a mistake once. All I knew and know is that you're the best thing that ever happened between us. A gift I didn't deserve."

"Will you tell me about him?"

"As you wish," I said. I held her to me. I'd have to face those times, but I could be hopeful now about the stories of strength I could tell. "You had many fathers who cared for you in Aurora, Ida. Just remember that. And a sister and brothers, too, who showed great love for you." I rocked her in my arms and looked at Andy.

"You did well, Andy," I said. "So well." I wanted to take my son in my arms and hug him, but I didn't want to risk his rejection, and my arms were full. "I'm so proud of you. Jack's a sad man, but he's no threat to us now. I almost challenged him into something unnecessary, bringing out his worst traits. You brought out his best, helping him calm down and go away again in calm."

Andy nodded. I thought he might have moved just a little closer to me. I released Ida, holding her with one arm, then put the other around Andy's shoulder and patted the striped shirt he wore. He let me.

"There are always safe ways through the wilderness, *ja*? I kissed Ida's head, leaned into Andy. "Your mother just needs to keep learning the paths."

28

Life Exhibits

March 26, 1871. Yet another year passes. My hair is graying
just as Po's is, at the edges. Karl brought by my annual
almanac. "And step by step, along the path of life, there's
nothing true but Heaven," Goethe wrote. Like the old friends
we are, Karl and I sat and talked of promising students he
had, my son being one. He smoked his pipe while I stitched.
My older son will be eighteen this year; Kate, Catie, my beau-
tiful older daughter, has turned sixteen. My two youngest fill
me with delight. The dreams I had to raise my family are
coming true, though not as I had planned.

At Easter, we gathered together to etch eggs. My Clara, the Araucana
chicken, laid three blue ones and one olive green egg, whose colors made
the perfect backdrop for our etchings. I loved making these sculpture
paintings, and while no one outside our family would probably be interested in them, I did consider entering them at the fair this coming
fall. That's what I was thinking about, more than "the plan," which my
brothers and sisters and mother hadn't mentioned for some weeks,
knowing plans take time to implement. I carried a basket of eggs from
the chicken coop to my parents' house. In Aurora, I knew that the
apple trees were in bloom at Henry C's orchard; the millrace water
rushed pleasantly. Building continued but things were calm there, the
pause before spring squalls blew through.

At my parents' home, I saw progress too. My father was talking
again, though with a slight slur to his speech. His mind was good, and

when we failed to understand him quickly enough, he'd write his thoughts down. He directed my brothers in their work, using his one arm mostly.

We sat at my parents' blue table, each of us lost to our thoughts as we etched. Jonathan had found a buyer for my pearls. I kept back the one small one from Willapa Bay that Christian had given me, but the remainder had been a gift from my mother. She'd agreed to the sale; even though it was now my gift to give away, I wanted her approval. With the cash, we'd add the rooms we needed to the house, pay off the property, and buy seed for our crops. One day my father would deed all to Wagner and Heirs. That was what he wanted.

Oak and fir trees clustered at the edge of the property, and some land had already been cleared and planted in crops. We'd harnessed the spring, so fresh water welcomed, and much of that early demanding work had already been done. We'd made a puzzle path beneath the trees, a place for quiet thought.

We'd carried on from someone else's broken dream, turning it into our own hope. For frosting on the cake, it had a fine view of Mount Hood to the east. We'd all left the Aurora Colony, all except Andy and Christine and Jonathan; yet we were still connected. Even Kitty had decided to come back home to live.

My sisters and I worked at fixing and serving, continuing our commitments to the colony. At our new home, my father sat in the rocking chair that matched Mary's, and when my brothers weren't clearing ground or getting ready to plant crops, they built fences for the chickens.

"Always farmers," my father said. "Stay that way."

Kitty and Christine and I would still work at Aurora, especially now with the railroad bringing in hundreds of guests. We still made our way as a group every other Sunday to the church. We walked past my old two-door house. Someone else lived there now. I didn't miss it, not really. I only missed seeing my son.

———

The fair in the fall of 1871 outdid the previous year's. New performances and a larger carnival brought people out from their simple homesteads and small villages, as well as from cities far away. Some fairgoers still packed their own baskets of food, but many more made their way to our place of restorative meals. I cooked the entire time and found it always brought me joy.

Jack Giesy showed up again. At first I felt that same rush of fear and outrage, but then I remembered Andy's ways with him, and I did the same, not provoking. He could only have power over me if I allowed it. Jack asked for food. I served him. He ate. And when he saw that I still had friends to stand beside me, he left. I was never sure what Jack wanted besides power. I gave him none over me or my children. I rested in the confidence of my community, my family, my God.

Andy had begun classes at Wallamet. Henry T. Finck, that wise-mouthed boy, headed off to Harvard. Both boys had been well prepared by their good teachers Chris Wolff, Henry C, and Karl Ruge. I stopped by to see Andy in his classroom, since I was there at the fair. He turned a shade of radish when he saw me, and I waved, then slipped quickly away. No young man wants his mother hovering while he follows his desire. Even I knew that.

Kate walked hand in hand with Lorenz Ehlen when they thought no one was looking. I could see the two of them marrying one day. I wouldn't allow Keil to interfere, should he consider it. That year, I also saw Brita! She brought me laughter and reminded me that I could bring hope to myself, as well as to those I love.

One welcome change was that Johanna joined the festivities that year without Louisa. Kitty and Christine had remained behind and agreed to help our mother look after her. Johanna surprised us all by participating in the first art classes that Nancy E. Thornton had ever offered at the fair. My sister was quite gifted, but she'd had little time to paint. Now that Kitty and I lived at home and could help, she would.

Ida entered an apple pie and earned a ribbon. Next year she said she'd make a quilt to enter—if I'd help her.

Oh, and I made a drawing of my two youngest children, transferred it to cloth, cut fabric pieces out, and appliquéd them. It did not win a single prize, except in my heart when Christian said, "It's different, Mama. I like especially those bright colored pieces along the edge. They're from a quilt you made me, aren't they? Can I take it with me when I leave your home to go to school? So I'll always have pieces of my family with me?"

Of course I agreed. What more could any mother wish for? What more could any woman want?

I visited Wilhelm Keil one day in the spring of 1872. It was a journey I needed to make. I rode through the landscape of colored leaves and crisp air. Even though we no longer had a house in Aurora proper, I knew now I'd never live far from here. Willapa had been my test; Aurora, my new beginning.

Keil looked tired that morning. He wore one of his finely tailored suits, but crumbs from his breakfast biscuit dribbled on his vest. An old pair of slippers covered his feet, and he shuffled them as he made his way to the workroom door, answering my knock. I was a bit winded by climbing up all those stairs, breathless, but not because I feared the man as I had back in Bethel as a young wife begging to convince him, but simply short of breath, as a woman growing older.

"Ah, *Frau* Giesy," he said. "It's been a long time."

"I've been busy at the hotel."

"*Ja.* Louisa keeps me informed, from your little house church gatherings at Martin's." He shook his head. "It offered something inconsequential for you women." He waved his hand as though brushing at flies. "And no harm that we men could see. Otherwise I'd have put a stop to it."

He'd gone from considering our meeting at Martin's house to a previous time, when it was my house church that he must have struggled with, if only for a time.

A part of me wanted to point out to him how many good things had come from our little house church: a safe harbor for abused women, new lives for a young girl's twins and their mother, the beauty of a mixed chorus, a place to grieve the death of a friend and her child, countless quilts and coverlets and baby clothes, not to mention ideas for a restaurant at a fair. In that little house church, lives were comforted and shaped in ways none of us would ever know. But trying to inform him would have distracted me from my mission.

The windows were open, and a breeze moved some of the papers lying on his workroom desk. He turned to the rustle and set down a wide-bottomed bottle to keep them from fluttering. Silently I handed him my gift, my special pork fruitcake, knowing he'd like the salt and lard mixed with fruit. Like Karl, he had aged, and he might welcome those intense tastes that rose from fermenting fruit in flour.

"*Danke*, Emma. Your parents are well?"

I nodded agreement.

"Honoring the mother and father, *ja*, this is *gut*, Emma. But you did not need to move to do this. You could have had them move in with you. Right into your two-front-door house."

"They wanted a place to call their own. Just as Martin has. And others that you've deeded a house to. I didn't think you'd deed my house to me."

This wasn't something I'd intended to bring up, but I thought, *Why not ask?*

"You're right. I would not. If anything, it would need to go to Jack Giesy. You are still married to him."

"This is something I'm likely never to forget," I said. "But what you could do, that would help my family, is deed that house to Jonathan. I'm sure he'd make room for guests, if the hotel overflows. He'd use it for the good of Aurora."

"Jonathan wants to live in your house?"

"I haven't asked him. But it would be good for him to have that assurance. He's worked hard for you through these years."

He took a fork full of the cake, poked into one of the cherry preserves. "*Ja*. This could be arranged," he said at last.

He'll deed it to a man but not a woman. Some things will never change.

"What matters now," I continued, "is that you will honor our original agreement. That's why I've come to see you." He frowned a bit, and I thought he might have actually forgotten it. "That you would educate me and my family in return for my using the house for the good of the colony. Does that still stand?"

"Should it?"

"What more could I do for the colony than what I have?" I said. "I came west with my husband for it; I gave my sons to it, to be raised by someone within the colony who is not their father. Andy lives now with others even though I have room for him in my home, in my life. He'll be a doctor here one day. I've made the colony my second family. I've worked and done what I could to live the Diamond Rule. If you keep your word, you will truly be making my sons' and daughters' lives better than your own. I can die an old woman, knowing I, too, did something to make others' lives better than my own."

"It will be a long time before you are an old woman, Emma Giesy," Keil said. He had a glint in his eye, which I ignored. I waited in silence. He sighed. "A long time before you'll die too, I suspect. Like me, a streak of ornery keeps our blood flowing." He lifted my chin with his fingers, stared into my eyes. "I saw what Chris saw in you, and I thought he should tame you. He never did. You might have been easier to manage if he had." His smile held a tint of sadness. "But you might also then still be there in Willapa with Jack on your hands. You might not have endured. Instead, you are here and you have brought…interest. *Ja.* Fascinating interest to our colony." He sat down stiffly.

I stepped back a pace, reflecting. I understood now some of Keil's own ways in our long struggle. I had more power than I'd thought.

"You have suffered, Sister Emma. I know this too."

I had suffered. Some of it of my own doing; some of the torrent that I hoped built character, deepened my faith. "*Ja,* but suffering is a part of living. Karl Ruge reminds me of the many kindnesses I've received in my life. He quotes a German master who wrote, 'One who suffers for love suffers not and his suffering is fruitful in God's sight.' "

"*Ja*, that is Meister Eckhart. In that, I believe he was right."

He folded his hands on his desk top and sighed. "Ah, Emma, Emma. You did suffer for the love of your sons, but you have been fruitful from it. *Ja*, of course we will do our best to educate your sons, all the way through. Like his father, Christian serves and adds much to Brother Ehlen's life when he visits. Andy shows a singular talent for medicine, for tending others instead of forcing them to certain things."

"Beyond talent, I believe he is a compassionate man," I said. "Maybe his suffering has helped him become that."

"He's been a good match for Martin's work, *ja*? He does well in school?"

"People will choose a hopeful approach to life, if they're allowed," I said, "rather than being pushed into it or, worse, scorned into it."

He stepped over that. "Your girls, too, may go on to school. That's happening more now. Girls going." He picked up his pipe and tapped the tobacco from it, drew on it to make a little whistle sound.

"If they don't marry, they can contribute in other ways, *ja*? We women have our plans."

He didn't seem to notice my slight to his history of marriage restrictions.

"You and your plans. Those fancy chickens," Keil said. "You want to do something more with those, I suppose, on your new farm."

"*Ja*. Chickens and sheep. We Germans are farmers at heart." I sat down.

"Your father's place always had the best flowers," he said.

I laughed. "*Ja*. My mother finally told me how that happens. William carries out the thunder bucket every morning and dilutes it with spring water, then feeds the plants with it."

Keil laughed at that. "I'll start doing the same," he said.

The breeze moved across my face, cooling me. I sat amazed at my calm when once this man had frightened me so. Here we sat talking almost like equals. After all was said and done, in Aurora, I'd found my *Heimat*, what we Germans called the home of our hearts where we put down roots and were free to be as we were created to be. "There is this art class," I continued. "That one I wanted to take years ago. I would sign up again. I'd like you to pay for it."

He raised an eyebrow. "It's always something with you, Emma."

"I'm learning there is always a new desire. It is who we are, we Germans. All of us have dreams, or should have. You did long ago."

He nodded. "I dreamed of a second Eden," he said. "Here in Aurora. Other societies, back East, they dreamed it too, but ours is still here, *ja*? We did something right." He had a faraway look in his eyes.

"Have more cake. Eat your fill," I urged. He took another bite, then laid the fork on the edge of the snow white plate.

"An art class. Taught by a woman, I suppose." I nodded. He lifted his fork, took another bite, then used the fork to point at me. "Well, this I approve," he said. "We colonists are known for our craftsmanship. You're entitled to improve such…talents. Women do have them, or so my dear wife keeps reminding me. I saw that Sunflower quilt *Frau* Stauffer made before she died. An engineering marvel." High praise coming from Keil, and too bad that Matilda didn't live to hear it. "I'd prefer a man be your teacher," Keil continued. "You need strong reins, *ja*? There is a boy in Bethel with such skills. Perhaps I'll ask him to come west. He could teach you—"

"I'll not wait that long," I said.

"*Ja*. Well, better an art class than climbing some mountain."

I smiled. "Oh, I'd never do anything so dangerous as that. At least not before I turn fifty."

"You could get hurt risking such things," he said.

"*Ja*. I could suffer," I said. "But I'd find my way through it, I'm hopeful of that."

He held up his empty plate like a small boy, seeking more. "This is very *gut*, Emma. Excellent taste. A bit of sweet and sour. Just right. I will tell Louisa. You could stay for supper at the *gross Haus*, share with her the recipe? You could serve as you did of old, when you first came and huddled outside the door there with your children and that little *Zwerg*."

"I do have good experience in cooking and serving," I said.

I took the empty plate from him, stood. "But tonight I have my family to go home to," I said. "Thank you for permitting the class." He brushed his hand to the air, dismissively, as though his permission and payment were nothing. Or perhaps he was telling me I hadn't even needed to ask. I pitched that thought away. We'd come a long way, Brother Keil and I. Both of us, still changing.

"I'll bring the recipe when I come next time," I told him. My ruffled petticoat swirled against my legs as I turned to leave.

"*Danke. Danke.*"

"I can only hope it will appease your hunger," I said. "As I'm hoping that the art class will satisfy mine."

"That will be good, Emma. You are a good woman, a good servant."

I blushed with his compliment but knew I didn't need it. I nodded good-bye, then went out through the root room door, whistling a tune as I left, already reworking that recipe.

Author's Notes
and Acknowledgments

It's difficult for me to leave Emma. In part, I am reluctant because so many have made her journey come alive for me, including many readers. The Aurora Colony Historical Society opened its archives, and the board, staff, and volunteers gave of their time and stories to bring this woman, her community, and her journey to life. For this reason I've dedicated this final book in the Change and Cherish Historical Series to them.

Many have assisted me, but special appreciation goes to curator Patrick Harris, executive director John Holley, and staff members Janus Childs, Pam Weninger, and Elizabeth Corley. Board members Norm Bauer, Gail Robinson, Jim Kopp, and Annette James continued to offer wise counsel and encouragement throughout the series. Volunteers Irene Westwood and Roberta Hutton opened doors to history that would otherwise have been closed, and I'm grateful beyond words. Each of these people gave of themselves in the way the colonists did, helping make someone else's life better than their own—in this instance, mine.

I am indebted to direct descendants of Emma: David and Patricia Wagner (Emma's great-nephew through William's line), Mike and Ariana Truman (Emma's great-grandson through Catie Ehlen's line), and Louise Hankeson (Emma's great-granddaughter through Christian's line), all of Portland, Oregon, who shared their homes, letters, photographs, fiber arts, musical instruments, and even recipes handed down from Emma and her daughter. Members of the Jerry Giesy families (descendants of Emma's first husband's brothers) provided treasured looks at calling cards and opportunities to explore the lives of the descendants who have peopled my life for the past three years. I'm deeply grateful to them all, especially for their willingness to share

family stories, including the ones related to Christian's death and
Emma's spirited life, and for allowing me to speculate to fill in historical gaps.

Erhard and Elfi Gross again offered advice and suggestions related
to the German language used by Emma and others, though any errors
in usage are mine. Their years operating a bed-and-breakfast in Astoria,
Oregon, helped inform me about the wonderful German cuisine that I
hope reflected well on Emma's own efforts in this book. Most of the
recipes mentioned came from either the *Aurora Colony Heritage Recipes*
cookbook or from the 1915 *Kenilworth Presbyterian Cook Book* that
included recipes from Emma and her daughter. Author and quilter
Mary Bywater Cross introduced me to Emma through her book *Quilts
of the Oregon Trail*. How could I ever thank her enough for that?

Retta and Steven Braun, owners of the historic Frederick Keil
House, allowed us to visit, to photograph, and to get a feel for the root
cellar and the flow of life in the early *gross Haus* built close to the colony
church, neither of which still stands. Frederick did indeed marry
Emma's niece, Louisa Giesy, and they lived in the house, which is said
to have the same floor plan as the *gross Haus*. I'm grateful for the
Brauns' hospitality and their continued efforts to maintain this piece of
Aurora history. Suzie Wolfer, a colony descendant, loaned me period
books on herbal healing that both Keil and Martin Giesy might have
used, and shared tea and stories with me. Descendants of many of these
families—Keil and Wolfer, Will and Stauffer and Steinbach in Aurora
and Portland, Oregon; in Ohio and Pennsylvania; and Lucille Bower
back in Bethel, Missouri—shared photographs and stories that brought
insights into the telling of this community.

In previous books in the series, I included a suggested list of reading material related to communal societies and the Aurora Colony
specifically. For this last book, I relied heavily on Eugene Edmund
Snyder's book *Aurora, Their Last Utopia: Oregon's Christian Commune
1856–1883;* as well as drawings done by Clark Moor Will, a descendant of a colony member, and his remembrances; those published by
the Aurora Historical Society; and those included in the Marion

County Historical Society newsletters. In step with the incredible memory of Patrick Harris and the volunteers, colony archives, and descendant records and stories, I did my best to stay true to the historical record. I did, however, diverge for some story elements, and I want to convey those detours now.

From the record, we know that Emma returned to the colony in 1861, and from a divorce petition she filed thirty years later, in 1891, we learn of the circumstances under which she left Willapa and returned to Aurora. We know she didn't initially have her sons with her, but it is not clear why. From a letter Emma wrote to her parents in 1862 from the Aurora Colony (reproduced nearly verbatim in the text), we learn that she did have all four of her children with her by then since she comments on that. Her father has a ledger page in November 1862, telling us when they arrived; but there are few entries after that date, for either her parents or for Emma herself. It is noteworthy that Emma is the only woman with a colony ledger page in her own name. After 1862, most items for her sons are listed under Martin Giesy's name, so something happened that meant Emma's sons were no longer with her. This is verified by later census records. Did she have her own funds and thus didn't need to use the colony communal supplies? Did Jack provide resources? There's no evidence of either. Yet a house was built for Emma sometime around 1864–65. It still stands. Did she leave the colony in the interim? Did her parents live with her in that house? Did she go with them, if in fact they left? If she had a house, why were her sons with Martin still living in the *gross Haus*? Was she banished for some reason? These are all speculative questions, and I have tried to answer them while staying true to Emma and the rest of the historical record. These questions became threads for the fabric of fiction.

There were tensions between her family back in Bethel and Andrew Giesy the manager and August Keil, Keil's son who was sent there to encourage dispersing of property so the Bethelites would come west. But letters suggest that the Bethelites were quite happy where they were, and the more primitive conditions in Aurora forestalled the migration. The difficulties between Emma's parents and the Giesys of

Bethel appear to be related to personal property ownership, and this would indeed have created conflict in what was to be a largely communal society. Whether this was the source of tension between Emma and her parents is speculative. But when Emma's father died in 1873, he did have an estate to leave to "Wagner and Heirs," and it was a portion of this estate that in Emma's 1891 divorce petition she claimed as money used to purchase her property that was hers and hers alone. She was apparently hoping to prevent Jack Giesy from making a claim against her property, telling us that he continued as a force in her life, one I believe she managed well over time.

A newspaper account in the 1870s suggests that Emma lived with her parents near Aurora at least for a time. Following her father's death, Emma and her mother and siblings "officially joined the Aurora Colony," according to colony records. Up until then, Emma had apparently kept herself at the edge, separate, even though she lived and worked there, perhaps as a final statement that the Willapa group was indeed its own entity, much as Bethel was.

Jonathan Wagner helped negotiate the purchase of property along the Willamette River in 1874 for his mother and siblings. The property acquired belonged to George Law Curry and his wife, Chloe Boone. Curry was Oregon's territorial governor from 1854 to 1859. The property remained in the Wagner family until becoming the development of Charbonneau, which is how it is known today. David Wagner did own a grist mill in Aurora, and the flour sacks were stenciled with "Wagner and Heirs," just as Emma had noted.

After her father's death, Emma took her inheritance—something unique for a woman to even have in that period—and bought property. Two years later she sold it, doubling her money. She later loaned money to her son Andrew, who did indeed go on to become a physician, though his original schooling was provided by the colony. In census records he is recorded as a helper at the pharmacy. He continued to live with Martin Giesy and Martha Miller after their marriage until he left for school.

Andrew graduated from Willamette University in 1876 and did

postgraduate work at Jefferson Medical College in Philadelphia, earning his MD degree in 1882. He returned to serve as a colony physician for three years. Andrew was named assistant physician at the Oregon State Hospital in Salem in 1885. In 1886, he married Ida Harriet Church. They had one son. Andy eventually opened a private practice in Portland, in the new specialty of obstetrics and gynecology. It appears likely that the loan to him was for the additional training, so Emma did continue a relationship with her son.

Christian married Louisa Ehlen, and his sister Catherine (Kate/Catie) married Lorenz Ehlen, thus blending these two families. The Ehlens were known for their basket making, weaving, reed making, farming, and carpentry skills. In later life, Emma lived for a time with her son's family and still later with her daughter's family in Portland, Oregon. Census records also show her living for a time with Ida's family, the Beckes. Emma stayed connected to her children. On May 17, 1916, Emma died. She had lived with Catie for some years and was a member of the Kenilworth Presbyterian Church in Portland at the time of her death. Incidentally, Catie did change how she spelled her name, as evidenced by a sampler contained in the colony's collection of artifacts.

Emma did make one visit back to Willapa after she left there in 1861. She was well into her eighties at the time and was described as being alert and knowledgeable. She visited Christian's grave and recalled fondly her journey across the continent with the scouts in 1853. She said little else about her time in Willapa.

Ida, the daughter of Jack and Emma, married Henry Becke, a farmer, and the families all remained within the Northwest for many years after the dissolution of the colony. Ida and her daughters were known for their quilting, a continuing family tradition. Some of these quilts, as well as a sewing machine said to belong to Emma and likely used by Ida, are often on display in the colony during the colony quilt show held each fall.

A house, with two front doors, was built for Emma. We know of such a house from a photograph with the notation that it was built by Jonathan Wagner "for his widowed aunt and her three children." We know where it was located in Aurora proper, and it probably had a view of Mount Hood. The notation errs in that it was not Jonathan's aunt but his *sister,* Emma, for whom the house was built. We believe she had only her daughters with her, but she may have had Christian as well, at least for a time, which would account for the "three" children mentioned. The house built for Emma became the home of John and Elizabeth Kraus, the daughter of John and Barbara (BW) Giesy, and in the 1970s the house was given as a gift by the Kraus family to the Colony Historical Society. It was moved from its original site on Liberty and Third to its current site next to the ox barn on Second Street and is known today as Kraus House.

Whether Emma used the house to welcome others like herself, who lived at the edge, is also not historically certain, but I wanted to convey the essence of care and community that the Aurorans were known for through the years. Serving and restoring through music and good food were hallmarks of the colony, and through such work I believe Emma found peace and meaning. Stories relate that no one in need was turned away, and I felt that Emma might well have been at the center, living the art of hospitality and spiritual understanding within a family setting, and in so doing demonstrating how profoundly an ordinary life can touch the lives of others.

Almira Raymond was an actual historical woman who endured the trials mentioned, and she might well have known Emma, or Emma might have known about her, given the notoriety of her divorce. We also don't know whether Emma and the others found comfort in walking paths, but reports from the Rapp Society of Pennsylvania, of which her parents were a part, describe several such labyrinth paths, and it was likely Emma would have enjoyed their replication and perhaps used them as a way to keep her from falling back from hope.

Whether or not Emma found that the gift of music soothed her soul is unknown. But the old German proverb, "Music washes the soul of the dirt of daily living," is a sampler included in the Bethel Colony Museum in Bethel, Missouri. Emma might well have heard this proverb spoken and taken its message into her heart. We do know that workers in the colony—as did many workers of old—sang as part of their everyday experiences in the potato and bean fields or while bathing their children at home. We also know that the Aurorans, including Emma, were deeply attached to the landscape, seeking *Heimat*, that special homeland where roots could grow deep. They likely found solace at the Park House nestled beneath the trees, where paths meandered and people picnicked as the band played.

Christine was fostered by the Wagner family. Her name appears on a special accounting of residents of Phillipsburg, listing those in the David Wagner home. The translation, *1833 Residents of Phillipsburg (Now Monaca), Pennsylvania,* was compiled by Dr. Eileen Aiken English in 2004 (Skeeter Hill Press). Many colonists did adopt or foster children as a way of expanding their population. That's all we know of Christine; the rest of her journey is purely fictional. None of Emma's sisters married; only her youngest brother, William, did. Emma did move with her family in 1870 to a property not far from Aurora, though she remained connected to the colony.

I also detoured in my storytelling regarding the marriage of Matilda and Jacob Stauffer, placing it just outside of Aurora, rather than in Willapa where it likely took place. Whether they lived in the house with Emma as portrayed is unlikely. What happened to Matilda and her babies is documented, as is her incredible creativity with needle and thread. Quilts of hers have been handed down, and her descendants have graciously permitted them to be displayed during quilt exhibits of the colony. Jacob Stauffer did build a two-story log home outside of Aurora in 1865, which today belongs to the Aurora Colony Historical Society. I wanted to explore Keil's restrictive marriage policy and the way it was sometimes thwarted by marriages performed away from the colony, and so I used Matilda and Jacob to do that. (One factual story concerns a couple who dated each other for thirty years, marrying only after Keil died. That way, when the colony assets were divided, the man received his portion and the single woman received a portion that amounted to half of what the man received. A married couple only received the man's portion; a wife's contribution to the colony effort was not counted.)

We don't know the actual date of Matilda and Jacob's marriage, but we do know the dates of their children's births. Jacob Stauffer later married Christina Wolfer, the sister who watched her brother break all those dishes along the trail. The rescued butter dish was handed down through the family along with the story. In 2007, the dish was given to the Aurora Colony Museum by a descendant, where the story continues to be told.

Every year, thousands of school children learn about early colony life by spending a morning at the Stauffer Farmstead. They cut fir branches to make candle holders, dip into wax to make their own candles, piece together swatches for quilt blocks, knead biscuits and watch them being baked in the old cast-iron stove. Children also make cedar shakes and write their names on them, recording their journeys into the past while taking some of that past with them when they leave. The shakes were originally used to side the smokehouse and other colony structures. Making primitive crafts that children can hold in their hands may be the finest way of bringing history alive in this technological age.

Life did seem to revolve around the Oregon State Fair, which was usually held in October after harvest. The colony's dance hall and the first restaurant at the state fairgrounds brought them wide renown. Many items are listed in the *Oregonian* records as being exhibited by the Aurora families, though Dr. Keil's are the most prominent. The Aurora Band toured at the expense of railroad magnate Ben Holladay. The band was known throughout the region, performing at Butteville, Oregon, as they first performed in the 1850s, and at the colony's elaborate three-story hotel, especially when the train brought in its first travelers in October 1870. The Pie and Beer Band played second fiddle, so to speak, to the Aurora Band. After a remarkable discovery in 2005 of original compositions of music, the historical society has begun the work of restoring and performing this music, including introducing it to schoolchildren. Already two public concerts of the works have been performed. Many of the instruments were handmade and of unusual designs. The Ehlen family, which Emma's daughter and son married into, was known for their skill at making reeds for wind instruments.

The colonists were also known far and wide for their food, served at the fair and at the hotel. Though the hotel was but thirty minutes by train from Portland and the end of the line, for years the train stopped in Aurora for meals "served within 15 minutes." Many other patrons took leisurely Sunday rides to the colony to participate in the restoration promised by fine German cuisine.

Most of the growth of the colony occurred through arrivals of Bethelites and the Willapa residents coming south to Oregon. By 1867, nearly all of the Willapa Giesys related to Emma had come to Aurora, except for Jacob/Jack Giesy and Sebastian and Mary. Interestingly, other Giesys came to Willapa from Ohio after the Civil War. The Giesy clan continued to look after the stockade that Christian and the scouts built in 1855–56, until it crumbled with age. They also tend the cemetery where both Willie Keil and Christian Giesy, among others, are buried. Willie Keil's burial site is marked by Washington State highway maps. Joni Blake graciously assisted in early readings of this series.

The pharmacy, the Keil and Company Store, and the colony church were some of the later buildings to be erected by the colonists in Aurora. The church was dismantled in 1911, and the lumber used elsewhere. The pews, however, found a home in the Aurora Presbyterian Church, which stands across from the ox barn, and some of the hand-turned pillars became part of the museum's changing exhibits. Several original colony buildings are identified by markers for visitors taking a walking tour of Aurora today.

Changes in the economy of Aurora and the eroding of communal life are well documented. Keil may have wanted his people to be self-reliant and to find spiritual strength through their work and their arts, or perhaps he wanted to stand out from neighboring religious practices and thus did not preach except twice a month. The record shows he did stop preaching for a time and that the deaths of his children caused an enormous change in his demeanor. With the arrival of Christopher Wolff, colony youngsters gained a more consistent school experience. After that, younger men were invited to preach, and perhaps these same young men became the advisors when the agreements (included at the end of this section) were developed. Henry C. Finck was the music instructor, and his son Henry T was the first Oregonian to matriculate to Harvard. Karl Ruge continued to live at the *gross Haus,* tend the bridge as toll keeper, and teach.

Descendants report innuendos about inappropriate relationships between Keil and some of the women, and with certain families in the colony. I did attempt to incorporate some of that uncertainty, which can occur in communal groups where there is but one recognized leader and where that leader fails to prepare anyone else to take his place. Sexual innuendo is about power and its use. I hoped to convey the misuse of Keil's power through a variety of means, without denying or minimizing the genuine commitment of the colonists to demonstrate the Diamond Rule by making others' lives better than their own, as they believed they were called to do by Christ's words. They were loyal Unionists during the War Between the States. They were communal in the sense of carrying out their Christian beliefs from the book of Acts, that each should give to a common fund and draw whatever was needed from it. They hoped to demonstrate the power of Christian love, operating within the larger world, by living compassionately and with joy, working well with one another and with their neighbors. A further discussion of these issues and others affecting the communal nature of Aurora can be found in Dr. James Kopp's book *Eden Within Eden: Oregon's Utopian Heritage,* to be published in 2008.

Wilhelm Keil died suddenly on December 30, 1877. By then, many colony properties had already been placed into individual hands, but much remained deeded in only Wilhelm Keil's name in Aurora and in Bethel, in the name of his holding company. His family might have claimed it all, in both Bethel and Aurora, but Louisa and her surviving sons did not. Louisa died in 1879, and negotiations continued uninterrupted to dissolve both colonies and to distribute the monies in an equitable manner. Willapa was not included in any of these negotiations, so we can assume that it was indeed a separate colony, as Emma had always hoped; or that by the time of Keil's death, nearly all of the former Bethelites who had stayed at Willapa had found their way to Aurora and were thus a part of that final distribution. While there were some disagreements during the years of negotiations, the colony was successfully dissolved in January 1883 with no lawsuits. A Bethel Colony Heritage Society continues in Bethel, Missouri, with a fall celebration each year to commemorate the colonists' lives there.

The Keils are buried, along with Helena Giesy and other selected colonists, in a small cemetery not far from where the church stood in Aurora. The headstones of Wilhelm, Louisa, and Willie, their oldest son, who died as they were leaving Bethel to come west and who was brought across the continent to be buried in Washington Territory, have the motif of weeping willows; the other Keil headstones do not. Emma is buried in the Aurora Community Cemetery, not with the Giesy family, but at the edge of the Ehlen family plot.

The community of Aurora continues to be on the National Historic Register, and some of the original buildings are maintained as a part of the museum, where visitors can see a rotation of exhibits centered on various families, a range of colony artifacts, the herb garden, and the annual October quilt show. Many communities claim connection to this colony: those from Bethel, Willapa, and Aurora proper; surrounding communities where names like Knight are prominent; and descendants of those who interacted with the colonists, purchasing their tin lanterns and medicines, trading pottery for tailored clothing, attending events at the Park House or the fair, worshiping at the colony church, whether they were colonists or not. Should you visit this historical village where six hundred live today, you'll find antiques stores in old colony buildings, pleasant walkways lined with flowers, and much of the same gentle hospitality that made it the most successful communal society in the west. Your visit will likely make you a storyteller too, just as it did for me. In 2009, the National Communal Society will meet in the Aurora area to correspond to Oregon's one hundred fiftieth anniversary of statehood and to continue to explore stories of this remarkable group of German Americans in the west.

Many other helpers, from the editorial and production team at WaterBrook Multnomah Publishing Group to my neighbors not far from Starvation Lane, contributed greatly to this story and gave aid and comfort in remarkable ways. There are too many to name them all. Carol, Judy, Susan, Blair, Laura, Nancy, Gabby, Kay, Sandy, Dudley, Erin, and of course, Jerry, must be mentioned for their constancy in my life. Thank you.

Because of my own visits in researching the life of Emma Wagner Giesy, I have new stories to tell. Some will be included in a nonfiction book that will celebrate the quilts and crafts of the colony, especially their fiber arts, music, food, basket making, and furniture. *Aurora: An American Experience in Quilt and Craft* will be released by WaterBrook Multnomah Publishing Group in the fall of 2008 and will feature Emma's quilts and many of the eighty quilts made by colonists during the colony period.

For further information contact www.auroracolony.com, Aurora Colony Historical Society, P.O. Box 202, Aurora, OR 97002, (503) 678-5754. Thank you for helping me keep stories of remarkable historical women and their families alive. I hope you're inspired to record your own family stories and the rich legacies they left behind.

Jane Kirkpatrick

READERS GUIDE

1. Emma writes, "I questioned whether expectation was a virtue one could nurture, or if once lost, would never sprout again." Can hope be learned? Can we change how we feel, or must we depend on others to behave in ways that bring us nurture? Did Emma find a way to nurture expectation over anxiety?

2. The Jan Richardson quote in the front of this book speaks of community rhythms. What rhythms did Emma discover in Aurora? How did grief and loss interfere with her acceptance of those rhythms?

3. In your own communities (book groups, professional associations, faith communities, etc.) have you ever felt at the edge? What was that like? What strengths did you gain from being in "the backwaters"? What were the trials? How did the women in Emma's house church, and Brita, represent people at the edge?

4. Most novels begin with a character having a desire. What did Emma desire? Did she achieve it? How did the author show Emma's desires changing? How do our desires change as we enter new communities or face new trials or opportunities?

5. What roles did landscape, relationships, faith, and work play in the telling of Emma's journey? Can you identify how these four threads are woven into the fabric of your own life? Do they bring you strength or threaten to bring tendering to the experiences of your life, causing disintegration from exposure to caustic material, rather than nurturing?

6. Did Emma work hard enough to bring unity to her family? Did she rely on her own strengths, rather than trying to "see God" in the situation, as Karl advised her often? Were there steps she didn't take that she could have used to bring her family together? What surprised you, if anything, about her decision to allow her sons to remain with Martin?

7. What outside factors began to change the communal aspect of the Aurora Colony? Did Emma's activities contribute to that change in any way? What role did the deaths of the Keil children play in how the colony changed?

8. Communal societies are marked by tension between individual needs and community desires. While most of us don't live in communal societies, how do we experience those same kinds of tensions? How do conflicts get resolved without the presence of a communal leader to dictate what will happen for the good of the community?

9. What role did quilting, painting, singing, even making glasses provide in Emma's journey to find meaning? What role do the arts and crafts play in our lives? Are they undervalued as sources of mending in our lives? How might their status be enhanced? Or should they be?

10. What impact did the absence of a church building have on Aurora's development and in the lives of Emma, Louisa, Helena, Matilda, and the other colonists? Why do you think Keil waited so long to build the house of worship? And why did he limit services to twice a month? How does a person of faith continue to grow spiritually when a religious leader restricts curiosity and exploration of faith issues?

11. Where did the house church women draw their strength from? What do you think the verse from Malachi, presented at the beginning of this book, has to say about hearkening together and creating books of remembrances? How do you experience that happening in your life? How could you?

12. If you speculated about future relationships between Emma and her children, how might you characterize them? What about her relationship with her siblings and her parents? Are there times when tensions with immediate family cannot be resolved? What hinge can keep us together, agreeing to disagree, perhaps, while remaining engaged? What hinders those resolutions in families today?

13. Are women the brooms of the world, as artist Alison Saar observed in the initial story quote? How do ordinary women find meaning within everyday life? How does the Goethe observation (page 300) that Emma makes about sweeping in front of our porches relate to this artist's quote?

14. What *restored* (as in the French for "restaurant") Emma? What restores you? Can you teach and share those skills, experiences, behaviors, and actions with those you love? What support would you need in order to find that restoration in your life?

THE AURORA COLONY ARTICLES
OF AGREEMENT—1867

1. All government should be parental, to imitate the parental government of God.
2. Societies should be formed on the model of the family.
3. All interests and all property are kept absolutely in common.
4. Members labor faithfully for the general welfare and support.
5. The means of living is drawn from the general treasury.
6. Neither religion nor the harmony of nature teaches community in nothing further than property and labor.
7. The family is strictly maintained; people marry, raise, and train children.
8. Each family has its own house, or separate apartments, in one of the large buildings.
9. The children of the community are sent to school, open year round.
10. Dr. Keil is president and autocrat. He has selected advisors to assist in the management of affairs. When vitally important changes or experiment is contemplated, nothing is done without the general consent of the community.
11. Plain living and rigid economy are inculcated as duties from each to the whole: Labor regularly and waste nothing. Each workshop has a foreman. The fittest comes to the front. Men shall not be confined to one kind of labor. If brick masons are needed and the shoemaker is not busy, the shoemaker makes brick.

GLOSSARY OF GERMAN AND CHINOOK WORDS

German

aber	but
ach!	oh no!
Ach, jammer!	an expression of frustration
auf Wiedersehen, or informally, *tschuess*	good-bye
Belsnickel	a traditional Christmas persona bringing gifts
Peltz Nickel	a punishing companion of *Belsnickel*
bitte	please
Christkind	Christ child
Dreck	dirt or excrement
Dummkopf	dummy or stupid
Elend	misery
Fraktur	unique printing designs; a German calligraphy
Frau	Mrs.
Fräulein	Miss
gross Haus	grand house
gut	good
Hasenpfeffer	rabbit or hare
Heimat	more than a house, a place of belonging

Herr	Mr.
Hinterviertel	seat or a person's backside
ja	yes, pronounced "ya"
Junge	boy
Kartoffel	potato
Kind	child
Kinder	children
Komm und is	Come and dine
Liebchen	darling or sweetheart
nein	no
nicht jetzt	not now
Oma	grandmother
Opa	grandfather
Scatter Soup	made with a slim batter similar to Chinese egg drop
Schellenbaum	A bell-like instrument known in English as the Turkish Crescent. Popular in the eight-eenth and early nine-teenth centuries, the large instrument combined music with a symbol of authority or standard of allegiance
Scherenschnitte	German folk art; cutout paper pieces are glued together to create objects such as trees, flowers, animals, or decorative elements for certificates
Schottische	a dance with three
Sehnsucht	a yearning or longing (of the human spirit) for something of meaning
Spätzel	egg noodles

Tannenbaum	a tree, especially at Christmastime
Ve	we
verdammt	damn
Volk	folks
Zwerg	dwarf

Chinook/Chehalis

cum'tux	understand, as in, "Do you understand?"
ho-ey-ho-ey	exchange or trade
klose	good
muck-a-muck	eat
Nch'I-Wana	Columbia River
omtz	give
tolo	boy

Thank you for reading this series. If you care to leave a comment—and I would love to hear from you—go to www.jkbooks.com, www.face book.com/theauthorjanekirkpatrick, www.twitter.com/janekirkpatrick, or www.pinterest.com/janekirkpatrick. You may also sign up for my monthly *Story Sparks* newsletter at www.jkbooks.com. If my schedule allows, I often meet with book groups by phone or Skype to discuss my books. I'd love to hear how you've made room in your lives for these stories.

    Warmly,

    Jane Kirkpatrick

Discover the Kinship & Courage series
by Jane Kirkpatrick

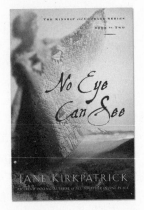

Mazy left home to head West with her husband. But when
tragedy strikes, an extraordinary community of women
is formed—one that conquers the land and their fears.

The Tender Ties series
Based on a true story

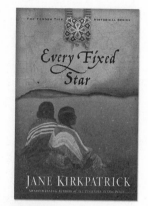

During the volatile fur-trapping era of the early
1800s, in a land occupied and torn by foreign powers,
a mother seeks to weave her family and her past into
a fabric that will not tear.

Read an excerpt from these books and more
at WaterBrookMultnomah.com!

Portraits of the Heart series

Named to Library Journal's
Best Books of 2009 and was a
Christy finalist, 2010

Based on Jane's grandmother's life as a turn of the
century photographer in Winona, Minnesota. This
coming of age story captures the interplay between
temptation and faith that marks a woman's pursuit
of her dreams. Includes historical photos from the
collection of Jessie Ann Gaebele.

Read an excerpt from these books and more
at WaterBrookMultnomah.com!

Journey through the
Dream Catcher series

The Dream Catcher series includes four frontier
stories based on actual historical couples who had
a dream and how their faith and families enabled
them to succeed.

Read an excerpt from these books and more
at WaterBrookMultnomah.com!

Bold Lives Honored Through Story

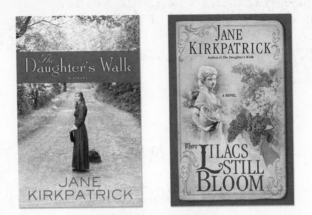

Get lost in these individual titles about courage,
generosity, and independence, based on
the lives of real women.

Read excerpts from these books and more
at WaterBrookMultnomah.com!